ZOT!

1987–1991

THE COMPLETE BLACK AND WHITE COLLECTION

WRITTEN AND DRAWN BY

SCOTT McCLOUD

HARPER

NEW YORK • LONDON • TORONTO • SYDNEY

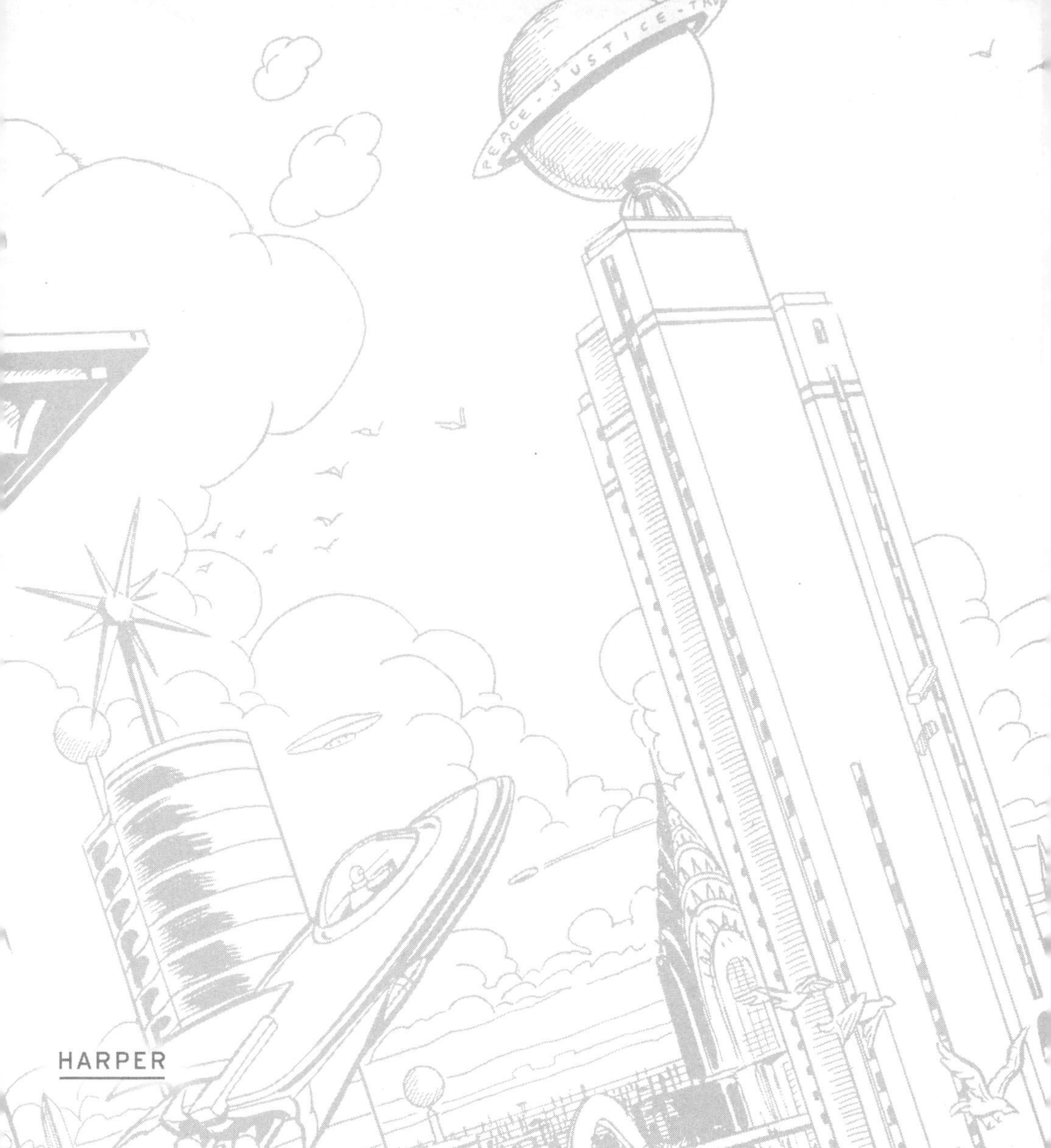
PEACE - JUSTICE - TRU

HARPER

HarperCollins books may be purchased for educational, business, or sales promotional use. For information please write: Special Markets Department, HarperCollins Publishers, 10 East 53rd Street, New York, NY 10022.

FIRST EDITION

Library of Congress Cataloging-in-Publication Data is available upon request.

ISBN 978-0-06-153727-1

08 09 10 11 12 QK/RRD 10 09 08 07 06 05 04 03 02 01

On the Threshold of Adulthood

It's a dangerous thing

I'm doing here. The ink is barely dry on *Making Comics,* my 250-page explanation of storytelling in comics. Anything I drew next was bound to be judged against those theories pretty harshly, but to follow it up with five hundred pages of comics I drew twenty years ago, long before I'd learned most of those lessons for myself—well, let's just say I feel a bit exposed here. *Zot!* is a coming-of-age story; its teenage protagonists go through a lot of changes in the course of these stories; but it was also a time of growth for me as I grappled with where I wanted comics to take me, and with my own limitations as an artist and writer. Both my characters and I were young and naïve, stumbling awkwardly toward what it meant to be an adult in this world, while making new worlds out of our dreams. And in many ways, this was the struggle of American comics in those same years, 1987–1991. We were all on the threshold of adulthood, and any search through the comics-store shelves of those days was, like any search through these pages, a quest for diamonds in the rough.

Included in this volume are every one of the black and white *Zot!* stories I wrote and drew, including my original roughs for the 48-page story "Getting to 99" (used by Chuck Austen to draw a two-issue fill-in while I was on my honeymoon). There was an earlier ten-issue color run I affectionately refer to as my "training wheels," but these black and white stories were designed to stand alone, and I'm confident that they do just that, over two decades later.

I've allowed myself the luxury of a few minor changes in these pages (noted on a separate page at the end of this introduction) but for the most part, you're holding an intact time capsule of that brief period in the American comics market when the promise that comics could do "anything" was just beginning to bear fruit—even for a humble, independent black and white superhero comic book, as it started to outgrow its origins and reach for something more.

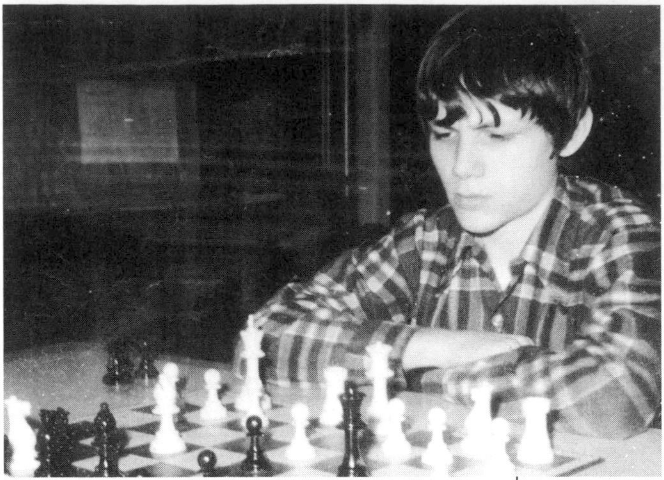

Nerds with Ambition

I was 13 years old when I met Kurt Busiek in the lunchroom of Diamond Junior High School in Lexington, Massachusetts, in 1973. Kurt and I both enjoyed reading science fiction, quoting *Monty Python,* watching *Star Trek,* and listening to old radio shows like *The Goon Show,* which Kurt's family enjoyed on an old mammoth reel-to-reel tape recorder. In short, we were nerds of the first order. But in one important respect, Kurt's nerd credentials surpassed even mine: Kurt enjoyed comic books and I couldn't stand the things.

Kurt and I were in eighth grade at the time. The New England "junior high" system, reportedly introduced to the region by my great-grandfather Jack, covered grades seven, eight, and nine. I can't help but wonder how my life and career choices might have been changed had old Jack's educational philosophy not resulted in a school map that brought Kurt and I from distant neighborhoods to attend classes in the same building. Kurt had to work hard to overcome my prejudices against comics at the time, and I don't know if anyone else would have had the patience. I read real books. I appreciated real art. I didn't read no stinking comics.

Nearly every day after school for a period of months, Kurt would come over to my house to escape his father, who kept giving him pointless chores to do, and he'd play me a game of chess—my full-time obsession in those days—in exchange for a game of pool on our basement pool table (Kurt was good at the former, but enjoyed the latter more). Again and again, he'd offer to lend me some stacks of comics from his collection. Again and again, I'd refuse.

Fortunately, Kurt had some help. The Route 128 loop around Boston in the '70s, which included Lexington, was a bit like what Silicon Valley would become in the '90s; a settling ground for engineers and computer scientists on the cutting edge of technology. That meant a lot of geeky kids, and as it happened, a lot of comics readers. Kurt lived across town, but only a few houses down from me were no less than three kids who read and even drew their own comics; the slightly younger Dewan brothers, Ted and Brian, whose art was playfully weird, and our slightly older friend Chris Bing, who was deadly serious about breaking into the big leagues. Their different sensibilities helped wear down

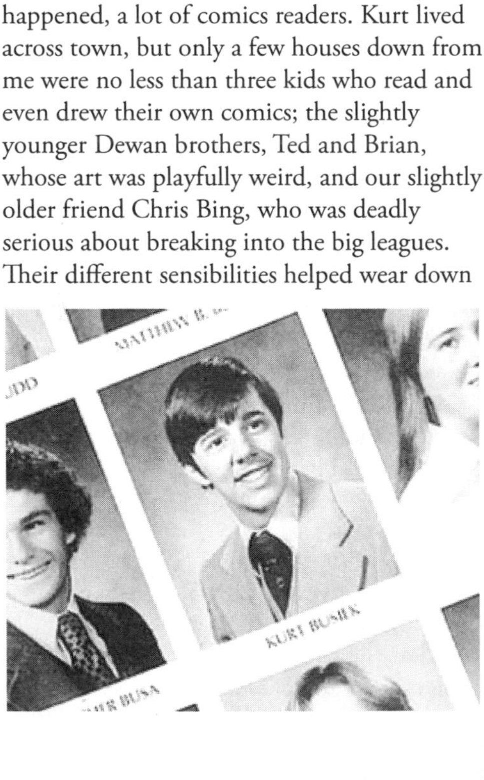
KURT BUSIEK

***Top left:** Yes, I was president of the chess club.*
***Right:** The young Mr. Busiek.*
***Opposite page:** One of my "schedule creatures" sold for a dime each to my fellow students in high school.*

my resistance long enough for Kurt to finally get me to agree to try a few stacks of old Marvel superhero comics, starting with *Daredevil* and the original *X-Men.*

Every morning before school in those days, I'd been waking up to WBCN in Boston and listening to the "LP du Jour" (a new album played in its entirety, part of Charles Laquidara's show, "The Big Mattress") on my tinny clock radio. So, while bands like Supertramp, the Tubes, and Roxy Music filled my ears, I began filling my eyes and brain with comic books. I was a 14-year-old boy living in America, so naturally it was only a matter of time before I fell in love with the superhero genre. In the coming year, comics would replace chess as my full-time obsession and I decided to become a professional comics artist. My nerd training was complete.

In the winter of tenth grade, I began drawing pictures of superheroes for a role-playing game we were working on. The following year, Kurt and I began collaborating on *The Battle of Lexington,* in which two teams of Marvel superheroes beat the living crap out of each other for no discernible reason, while casually destroying our high school, the town library, and various Revolutionary-era historic landmarks. It ran to sixty pages of fully rendered pencil drawings on typing paper. Years later, Kurt and I would perform a slide show reading of the entire comic at four comics events to hundreds of appalled and delighted fans, but for obvious reasons, it will never see print.

Our first published comic book—and our weirdest to this very day—came out while we were all still in high school. It was a limited edition comic book sold at the Boston Pops Orchestra's season opener in Boston's Symphony Hall and projected on a giant screen with local radio personalities providing the voices (including Laquidara himself, if memory serves). This bizarre, one-of-a-kind black and white oddity called *Pow! Biff! Pops!* was the first sanctioned crossover between Marvel and DC superheroes (not to mention

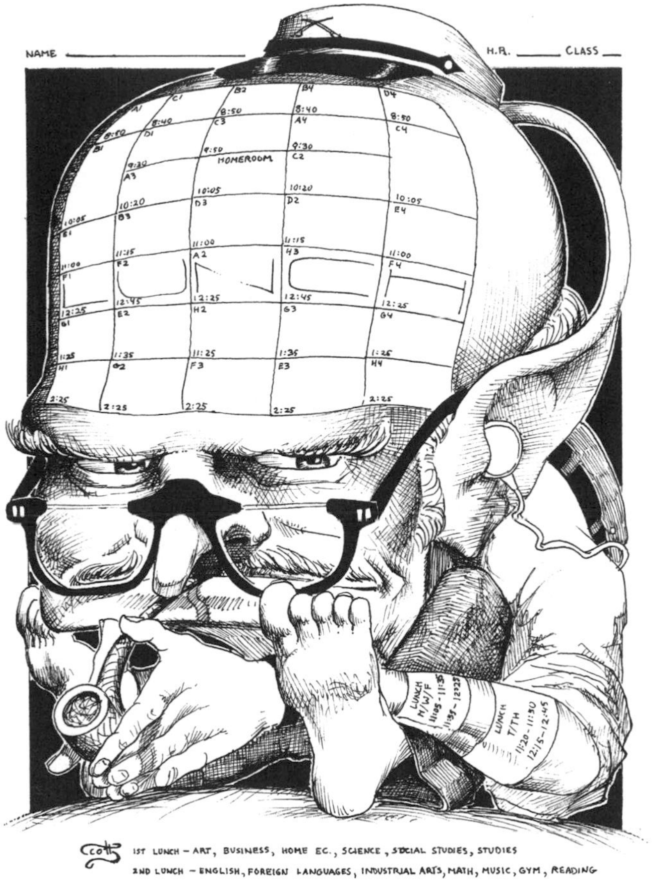
NAME
H.R.
CLASS
HOMEROOM
1ST LUNCH - ART, BUSINESS, HOME EC., SCIENCE, SOCIAL STUDIES, STUDIES
2ND LUNCH - ENGLISH, FOREIGN LANGUAGES, INDUSTRIAL ARTS, MATH, MUSIC, GYM, READING

conductor Seiji Ozawa). DC's president at the time, Sol Harrison, sat at our table. Kurt wrote the script for Chris to draw, I only did layouts for the book, but I was given the additional task of designing three giant murals displayed in the lobby and auctioned off to benefit local charities. Chris' Mom was our way in—my first brush with nepotism—and

Left: *The very first sketch of the retro-futuristic hero that would become Zot.*
Bottom left: *Trying out faces.*

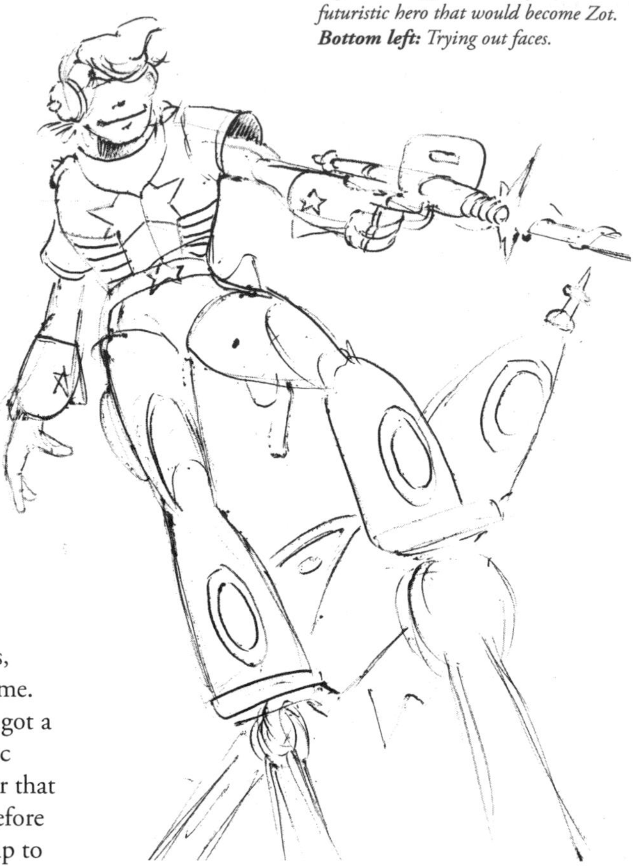

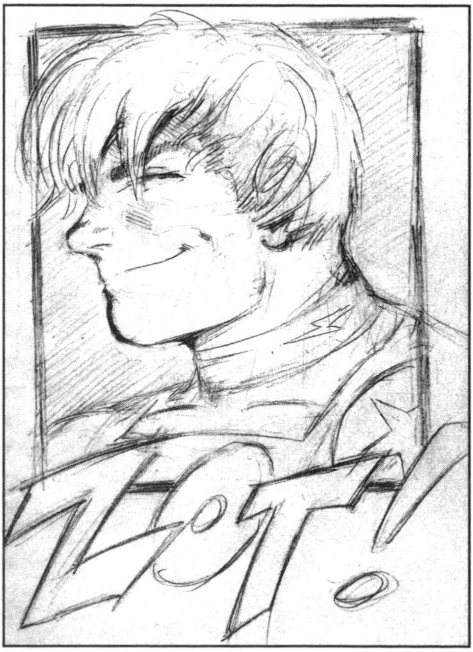
ZOT!

even at 16 years old, I knew that the gig had less to do with talent and more to do with the arbitrary nature of social connections. Still, it looked good on my résumé a few years later when I applied for my first job. Unsold copies of the comic were *burned,* by the way. Collectors, take note.

Local comics mavens Richard Howell and Carol Kalish helped us sharpen our skills and broaden our knowledge, as Kurt and I prepared to head for college. We both ended up at Syracuse University, where we worked hard to break into comics, figuring it was only a matter of time. While still in college, we actually got a deal to produce a superhero comic called *Vanguard,* but the publisher that commissioned it went belly-up before the first issue was published. A trip to New York in our junior year, scripts and portfolios in hand, proved similarly fruitless. We were two very frustrated fanboys.

In my senior year design class at Syracuse, we learned how to prepare a résumé. We were assigned to choose at least one prospective employer to try it out on. I chose the DC Comics production department. Three weeks before graduation, I was woken up in my dorm room by a call from DC's head of production, Bob Rozakis, asking me if I'd like to come in for an interview. I stood there, blinking for a moment, then said yes . . . yes, I could manage that. Portfolio in hand, I showed up in Manhattan three days later. I got the job and returned to Syracuse, levitating all the way.

Making the Leap

Working in DC production was the perfect first job for me. All day long, stacks of original comics pages were deposited next to my drafting table. I would take each of those stiff, oversized boards, often filled with artwork by pros whose work I had enjoyed as a reader in high school, and I would look for stray pencil lines, crossed panel borders, and editorial corrections. The whole process was instantly demystified for me. I knew I could make my own comics and couldn't wait to do so. But the wheels turned slowly at DC. I got the feeling that it could be a long time before I climbed enough rungs on the ladder even to draw, much less write and draw, my own creations. Kurt, meanwhile, scored his first professional assignment and started his own climb to fame (today, he's one of American comics' most successful and respected writers). The comparison was not lost on me.

On Sunday, June 20, 1982, three weeks after beginning my job at DC and moving to Manhattan, I visited master cartoonist Will Eisner at his house in White Plains—an arranged meeting thanks to Will's old tennis partner and a teacher of mine at Syracuse, Murray Tinkelman. Will talked with me for a

while about my work and what I wanted out of comics. He looked at the Marvel/DC-style sample pages I had in my portfolio, then at the more unusual illustration work I'd also brought. Pointing at the odder stuff, he said that it seemed to him that I was more interested in those than in the more conventional samples. He was right.

This page: Images from the original Zot! *proposal including a shot of Bellows looking suspiciously like Jack Lemmon's Professor Fate.*

Early the next morning, my mother phoned. My father had died that same Sunday (Father's Day as it turned out). I arranged for a flight home that afternoon. Walking south alongside Central Park in the early morning sun on my way to DC, I thought about how my father had made every moment count, had never wasted an opportunity. Arriving at DC, I told Bob Rozakis that I needed to take a couple of days off to return home for a funeral. I also told him I wouldn't be doing any overtime for a while. I needed to work on a proposal for a comic of my own.

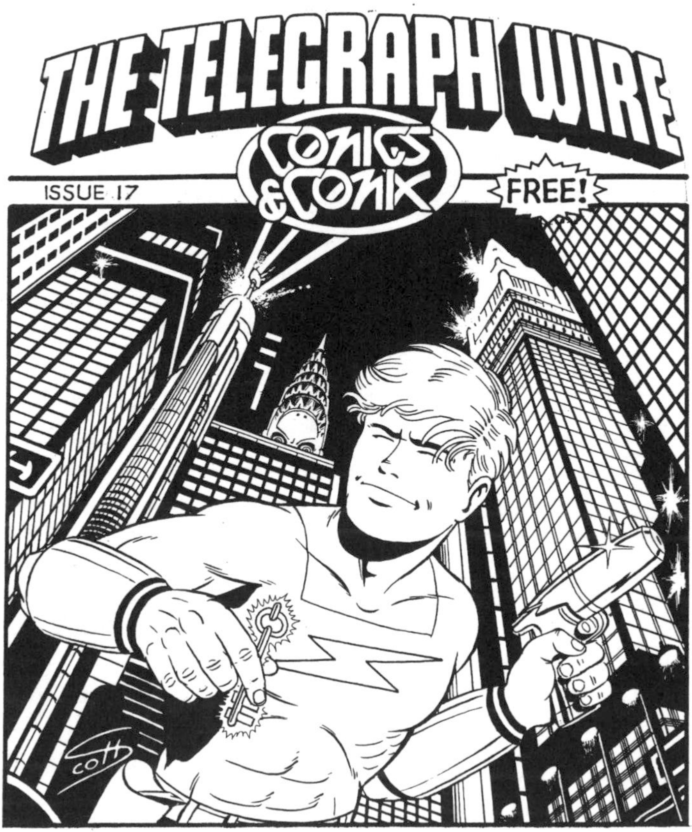
THE TELEGRAPH WIRE
COMICS & COMIX
ISSUE 17
FREE!
Scott

The following year, I sent a 100-page proposal to four independent publishers for a comic called *Zot!* I also showed it to Archie Goodwin at Marvel's more creatively adventurous Epic imprint (he sweetly turned it down, but with encouragement) and Dick Giordano at DC, who showed some potential interest in the property, but couldn't offer the kind of ownership and control I was looking for.

All four independent publishers were interested, to varying degrees, but two in particular seemed like good bets: California-based Eclipse and Chicago-based First. I liked Eclipse's deal better, and they could publish it a few months sooner than First. Getting published sooner was important to me because, well, what if there was a nuclear war and the world ended and I still wasn't a published comic book artist? No, there wasn't a moment to waste. The first issue hit comic book stores in March 1984. I was 23 years old.

Artists with delusions that they can write are more common than the reverse, because their delusions can't be as quickly dispelled with a casual glance. Kurt knew he couldn't draw well enough for the major leagues, but I began writing comics without hesitation, blissfully ignoring the fact that I'd had no formal training whatsoever as a writer. *Zot!*'s first incarnation, a 10-issue color run that was published from 1984–85, had a gimmick rather than a story—a precious key which all the characters were trying to find—and I simply hung whatever visual storytelling ideas I had around that gimmick. It worked well enough at the time, but clearly I was making it all up as I went along. There were plenty of pages where my hero and his friends were just flying around for no particular reason. With these black and white stories, however, starting in early 1987 at the advanced age of 26, I began making a more concerted effort to improve as a writer

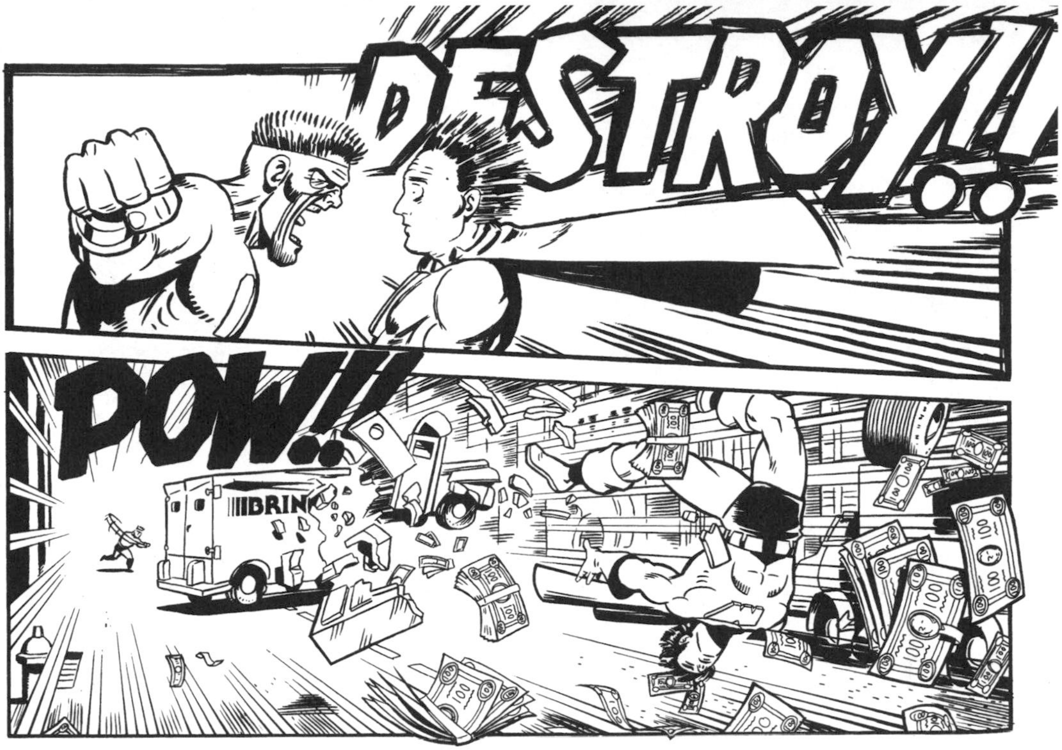
DESTROY!!
POW!!
BRIN

and produce more self-contained stories that had at least some substance beyond their visual tricks.

Growing Pains: American Comics in the '80s

By the early '80s, my world view of comics had already been enlarged by American underground and avant-garde comics, European albums, and Japanese comics or "manga." I was especially interested in manga. I studied hundreds of untranslated manga collections at Books Kinokuniya, Manhattan's biggest Japanese bookstore, only three blocks from DC's offices at 75 Rockefeller Plaza. I knew there was more to life than just superheroes. I just didn't see that reflected yet in the average American comic book store.

Beginning in the late '70s, there had been a slow, steady rise in the number of "direct market" retailers; comic book stores that offered a much wider selection of titles than what Kurt and I had found on the spinner-racks in our local drug and convenience stores. The Million Year Picnic in Cambridge was one of the first, and one of the best such stores. When Kurt and I found the place, we were in Heaven. Unfortunately, many of the stores that followed the Picnic's lead weren't nearly as eclectic or deep in their selection, and all comics stores, including the Picnic, depended on superhero fans to pay the rent.

In choosing to create *Zot!,* I was throwing in my lot with a sort of ground level independent movement that emphasized creativity and personal vision, but still hovered close to the superhero genre and related genres. In other words, I was playing it safe. Creators like Will Eisner, Art Spiegelman, the Hernandez Brothers, and Harvey Pekar, meanwhile, were creating something entirely

Opposite: *Zot graces the cover of the newsletter for Berkeley's legendary store Comics & Comix.*
Above: *My attempt to get it out of my system through parody; 1986's one-shot* Destroy!! *was nothing but one gargantuan fight scene printed in a giant format and billed as "The Loudest Comic in the Universe."*

new, working with subject matter utterly unrelated to mainstream superheroes. In doing so they stood apart from the market. The market, for the most part, had returned the favor.

In 1986, Frank Miller's *Dark Knight* and Alan Moore and Dave Gibbons' *Watchmen* became the standard-bearers for creative progress in American comics, cementing the idea in the public mind that better comics equaled better (and darker) superhero comics. Art Spiegelman's Pulitzer was still six years in the future. Into this era, *Zot!* returned, more modest in scale than those impressive giants,

but with the same outward goal of giving a half-century-old genre a face-lift. Inwardly, though, I had a broader picture of comics in my mind. Like a baby kangaroo, my comic stayed in the warm pouch of the genre that gave birth to it, but it had a mind to hop in a different direction.

Zot! in Black and White

This collection is divided into two parts. "Heroes and Villains" collects the first seventeen issues and has more of my unconvential brand of superhero action, but also focuses heavily on the real-world emotional story of the earthbound, pessimistic Jenny. Much of the storytelling drew heavily on my growing fascination with manga as well as alternative creators like the Hernandez Brothers. Part Two, "The Earth Stories,"

Above: Rethinking Butch for the black and white reboot.
Below: Early designs for new supporting characters Ronnie, Brandy, Spike, and Terry.

collects the last nine issues, which take place entirely on our world, with almost no superhero elements at all: stories of ordinary people living ordinary lives, as seen through an extraordinary visitor's eyes.

Zot! was a comic of changes. The black and white run was itself a radical shift in style and substance from the earlier color incarnation. The shift of focus from "Heroes and Villains" to "The Earth Stories" may seem as if I'd switched from one comic to another. And throughout *Zot!*, my drawing and writing style was constantly in flux. My character designs changed as I struggled to improve their expressiveness, as I struggled against my own considerable limitations as an artist, and as I struggled to show my characters actually physically *growing up* during the run.

The most tumultuous changes in *Zot!*, however, may have been in the mind of its author. I was grappling with serious questions of what I wanted out of comics, what I wanted to say through my stories, and if *Zot!* was even the right place in which to say them. And in this way, the transformations of *Zot!* over these five hundred pages were the very same transformations about to happen to American comics—an art form, an industry, and a community struggling to break out of its shell and take wing as the more diverse, literate, and formally ambitious medium just coming into view in this century.

The "Other" Zot

This book came out to 576 pages, so we've kept the focus to the complete black and white series as written and drawn by me, but there were two important other versions of *Zot!* that deserve mention here. One is the finished art provided by Chuck Austen for our two-part fill-in "Getting to 99," as mentioned earlier.

The other was a one-page backup feature by legendary stick figure and mini-comics king Matt Feazell, which grew to six pages in the later issues and even had its own fill-in issue, entitled *Zot! 14 ½*. I'd been a big fan of Matt's stick figure comics in the '80s, featuring heroes like Cynicalman and Antisocial Man. While *Zot!* was on hiatus, Matt and I had collaborated on a short-run mini called *Zot! 10 ½*.

Eclipse wanted in on the act, so we let them put out their own printing, which wound up selling 20,000 copies (making it the highest selling mini-comic of all time, for what that's worth). Matt continues to make comics in Hamtramck, Michigan, where his wife, Karen, is the mayor.

Needless to say, we would have loved to include both Chuck's finished art and Matt's back-ups in this volume, but 576 pages is pushing it, and adding those two would have upped it to 752! We look forward to arranging for a printing of both in some form in the not-too-distant future.

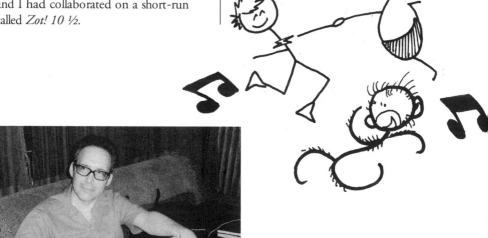

Above: *Zot, Jenny, and Butch dance in Matt's fill-in issue.*
Left: *Matt in Hamtramck, where we visited him during our family's year-long 50-State tour.*

A Note on Changes

Readers of the original series will notice some changes to the art and story on certain pages. For the most part, these are my original drawings and dialogue from the late '80s—warts and all—but in addition to the occasional proofreading correction, I've given myself the luxury of catching a few bigger errors and stylistic missteps that I've long wanted to address in the original issues, including:

Jenny's Hair on pages 17–138

When the series relaunched I tried using a china marker for Jenny's hair. The effect looked okay on the original art boards, but it never translated to print well, so I gave up five issues in. Here in this volume, I've replaced the china marker strokes with straight brushstrokes to keep it consistent with later issues.

Dougie's Swearing on pages 501–507

The bully in *Zot!* #34 who threatens Woody originally let loose with a string of classic four-letter Anglo-Saxon swears so strong that they struck some readers as off-the-charts, distracting, and inconsistent with the overall tone of the series. Over the years, I've come to agree with them, so I've toned it down a bit this time around. The language is still strong, and you'll find the occasional swear where appropriate (Dekko's "shit-heap" comment on his first page, originally mistaken for "shit-head" when originally lettered, is still there, for example) but I think the new version is a better fit with the series as a whole. Lest anyone think my publisher forced me to wash Dougie's mouth out with soap, you can assure them it was my idea.

Miscellaneous Faces and Figures

I successfully suppressed my urge to redraw all five hundred pages, but occasionally, there was a face or figure that was exceptionally irritating, and which I gave myself permission to replace with something more acceptable. For consistency's sake, I didn't replace them with my current drawing style, but simply drew them as I would have twenty years ago if I hadn't been asleep at the wheel that day. There are plenty of clumsy figures and faces still remaining, but hopefully I've raised the floor slightly.

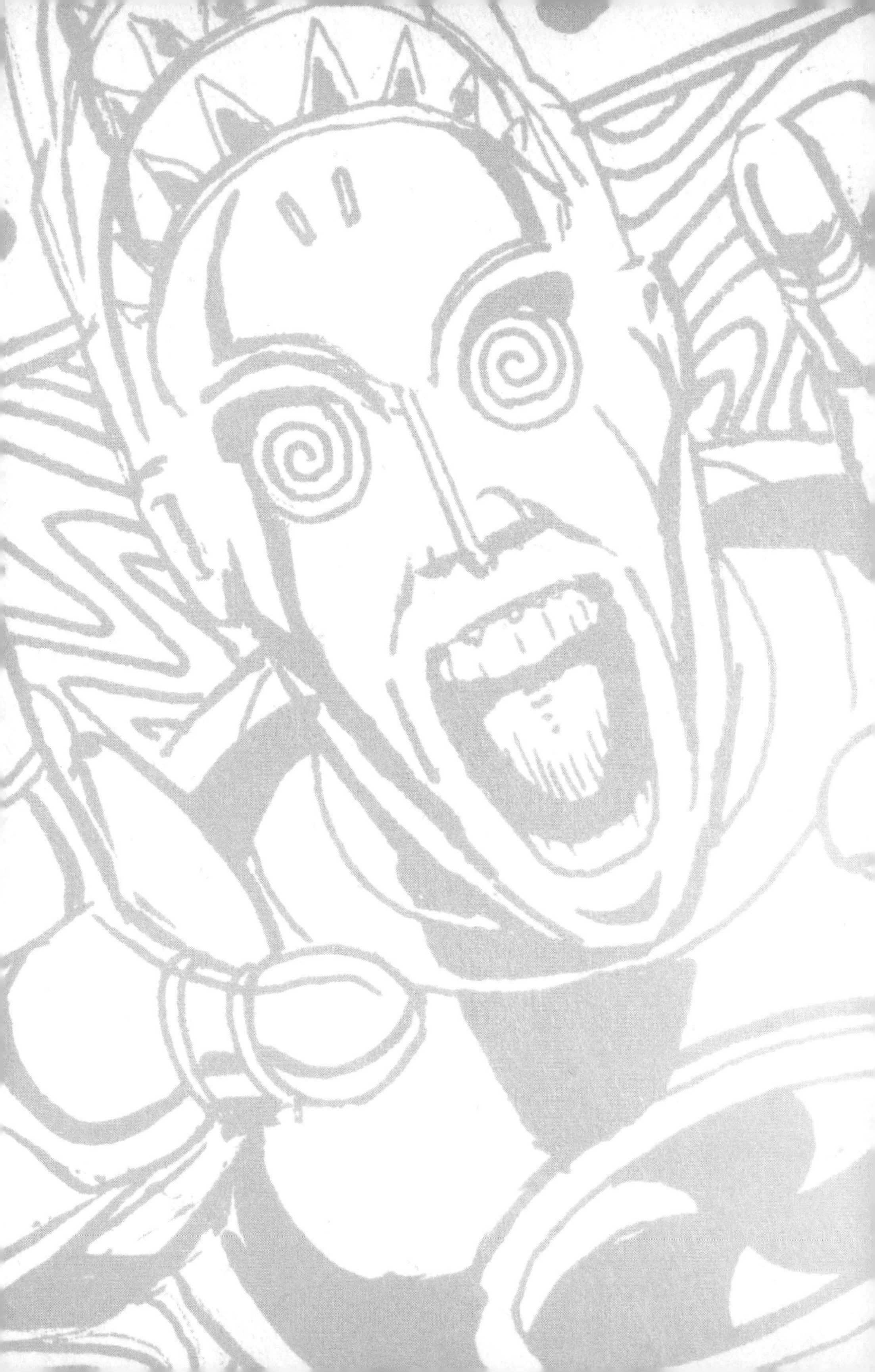

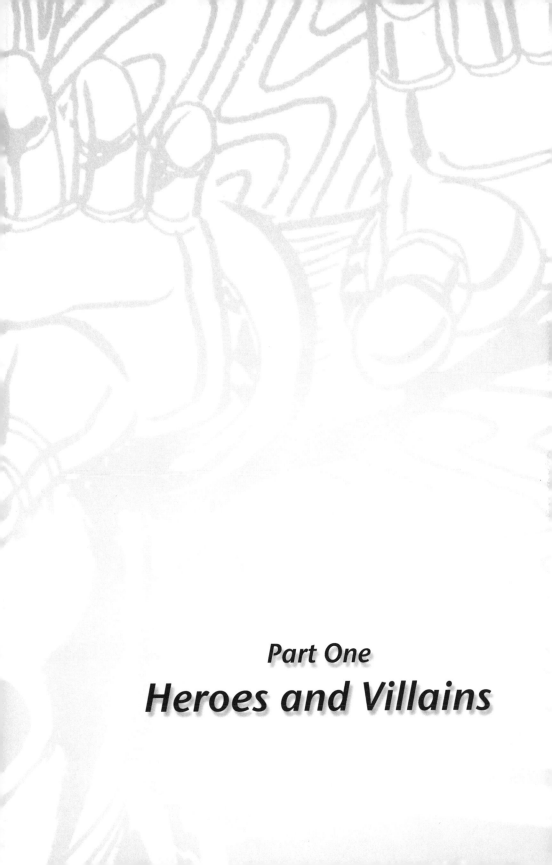

Part One
Heroes and Villains

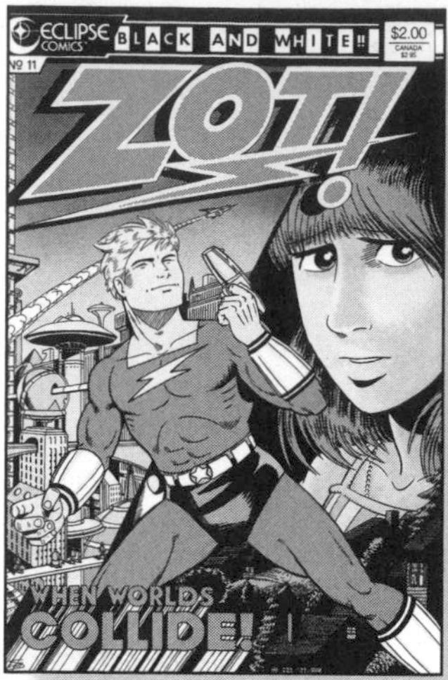
ECLIPSE COMICS
BLACK AND WHITE!!
$2.00
№ 11
ZOT!
WHEN WORLDS COLLIDE!
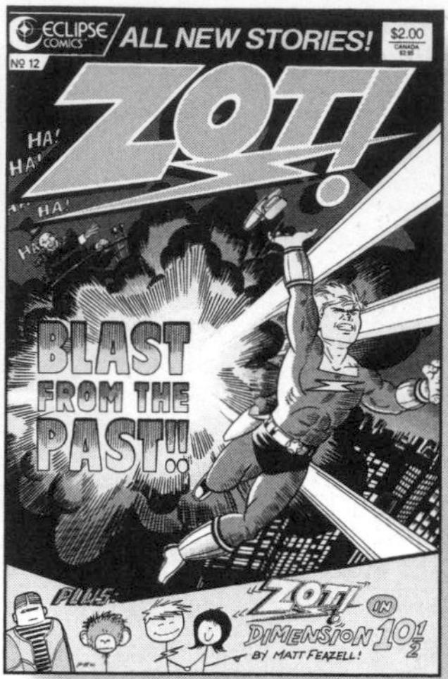
ECLIPSE COMICS
ALL NEW STORIES!
$2.00
№ 12
ZOT!
BLAST FROM THE PAST!!
PLUS: "ZOT!" IN DIMENSION 10½
BY MATT FEAZELL!

Planet Earth

First published in *Zot! #11–12.*

Lettering:

Bob Lappan

Original series editor:

cat yronwode

Note: As mentioned in the introduction, there had been an earlier ten-issue color run of *Zot!,* but the black and white issue #11 was really a full reboot. We would have called it a "New Number One!" but doing so was annoyingly fashionable in those days.

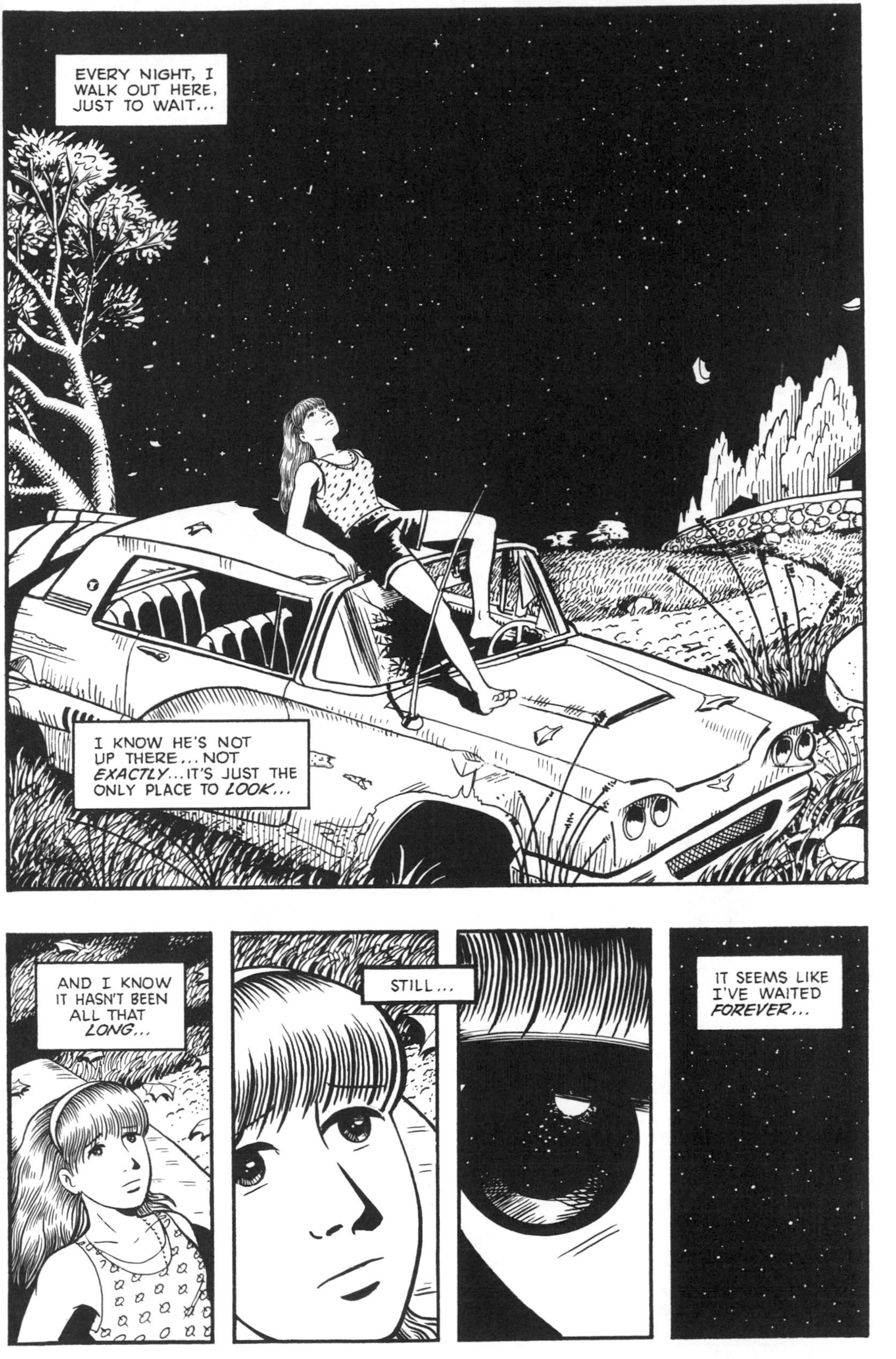
EVERY NIGHT, I WALK OUT HERE, JUST TO WAIT...
I KNOW HE'S NOT UP THERE... NOT *EXACTLY*... IT'S JUST THE ONLY PLACE TO *LOOK*...
AND I KNOW IT HASN'T BEEN ALL THAT *LONG*...
STILL...
IT SEEMS LIKE I'VE WAITED *FOREVER*...

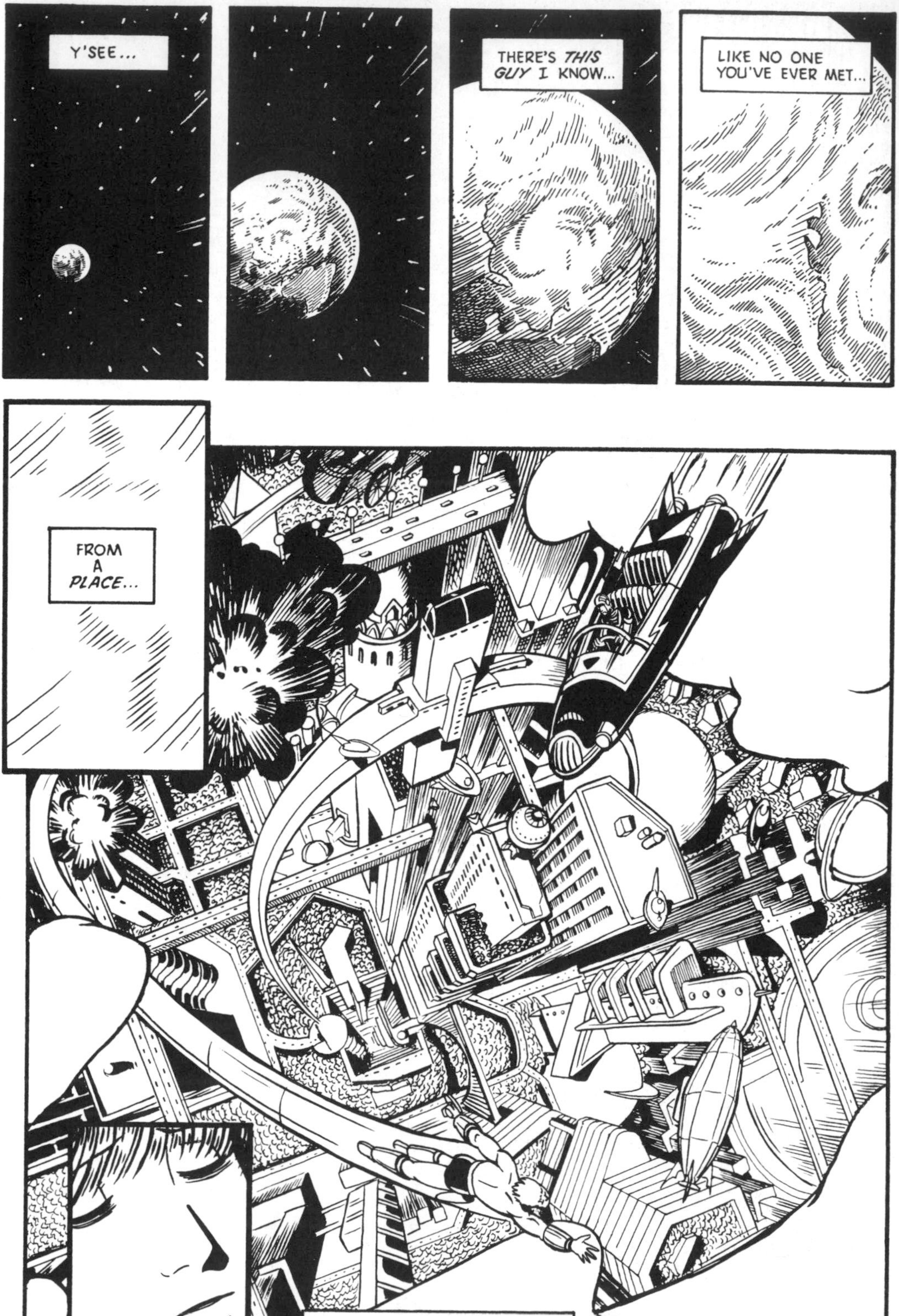
Y'SEE...
THERE'S THIS GUY I KNOW...
LIKE NO ONE YOU'VE EVER MET...
FROM A PLACE...
...YOU WOULD NOT BELIEVE.

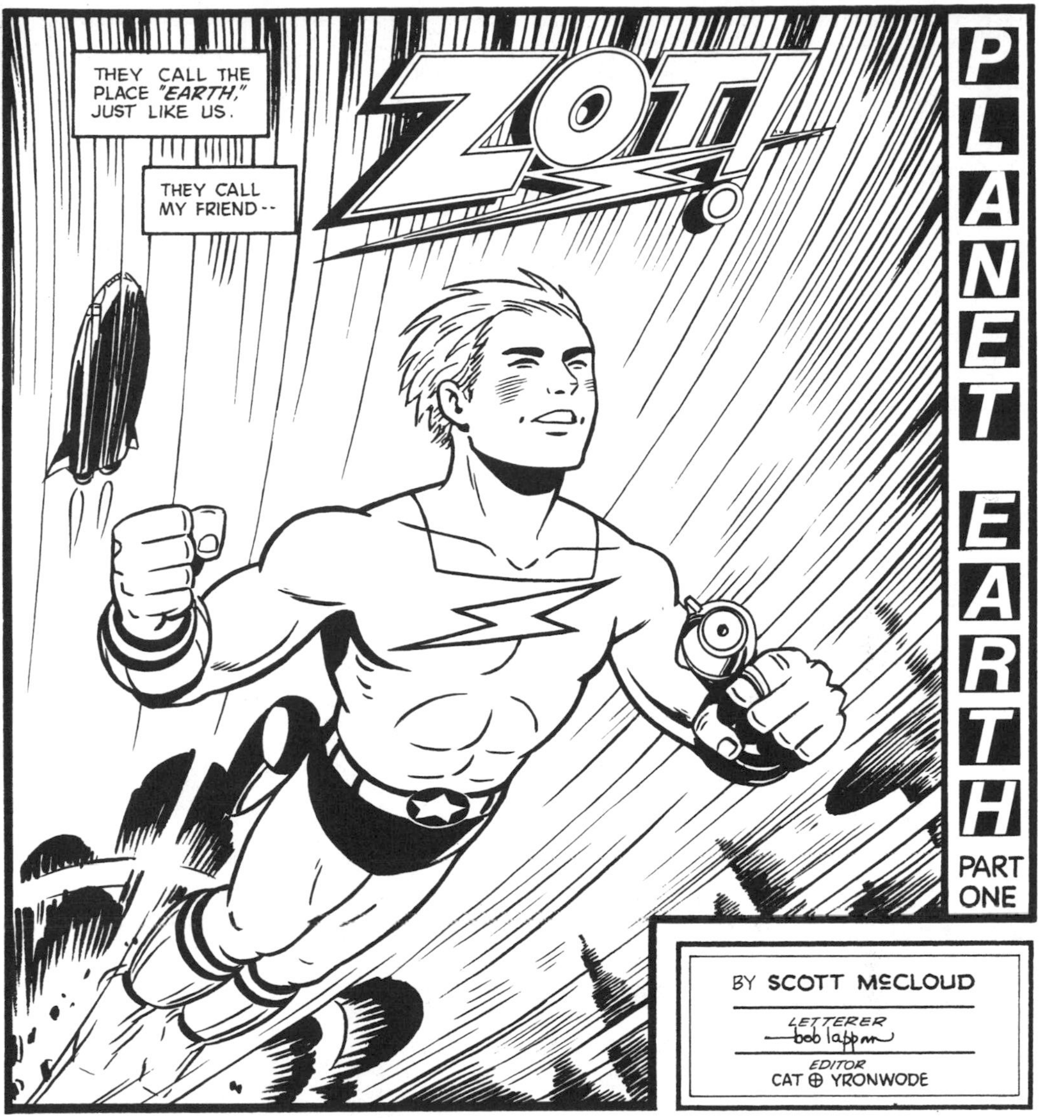
THEY CALL THE PLACE "EARTH," JUST LIKE US.
THEY CALL MY FRIEND--
ZOT!
PLANET EARTH
PART ONE
BY SCOTT McCLOUD
LETTERER
bob lappan
EDITOR
CAT ⊕ YRONWODE

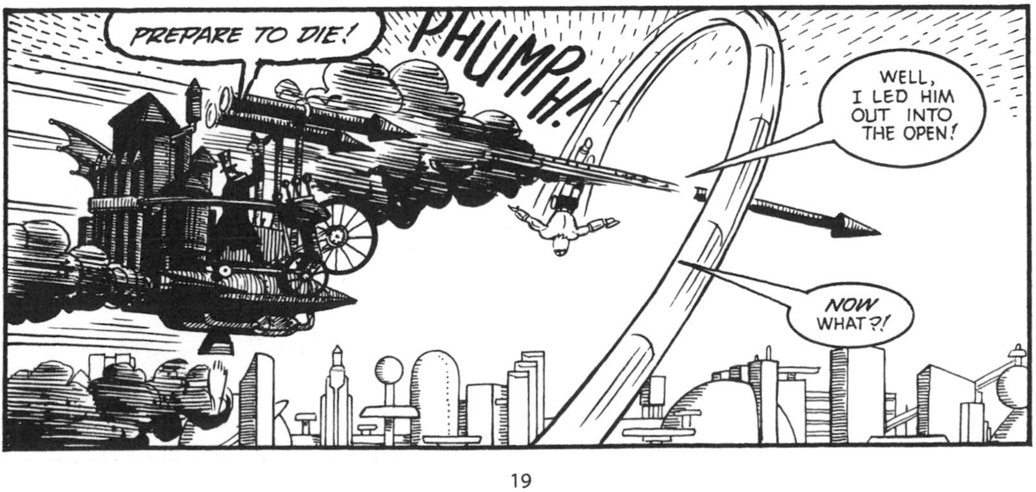
PREPARE TO DIE!
PHUMPH!
WELL, I LED HIM OUT INTO THE OPEN!
NOW WHAT?!

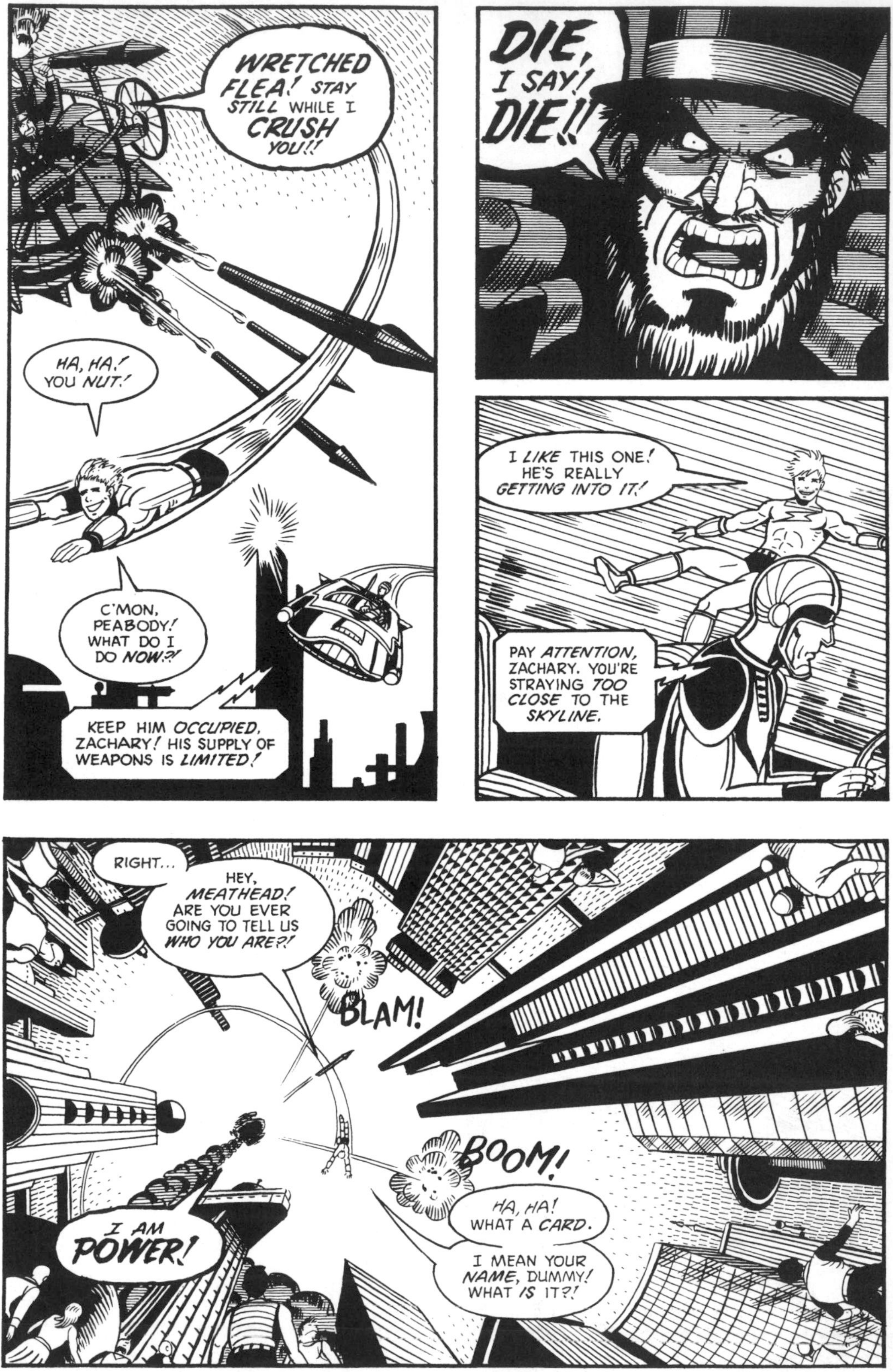
WRETCHED FLEA! STAY STILL WHILE I CRUSH YOU!!
HA, HA! YOU NUT!
C'MON, PEABODY! WHAT DO I DO NOW?!
KEEP HIM OCCUPIED, ZACHARY! HIS SUPPLY OF WEAPONS IS LIMITED!
DIE, I SAY! DIE!!
I LIKE THIS ONE! HE'S REALLY GETTING INTO IT!
PAY ATTENTION, ZACHARY. YOU'RE STRAYING TOO CLOSE TO THE SKYLINE.
RIGHT...
HEY, MEATHEAD! ARE YOU EVER GOING TO TELL US WHO YOU ARE?!
BLAM!
BOOM!
I AM POWER!
HA, HA! WHAT A CARD.
I MEAN YOUR NAME, DUMMY! WHAT IS IT?!

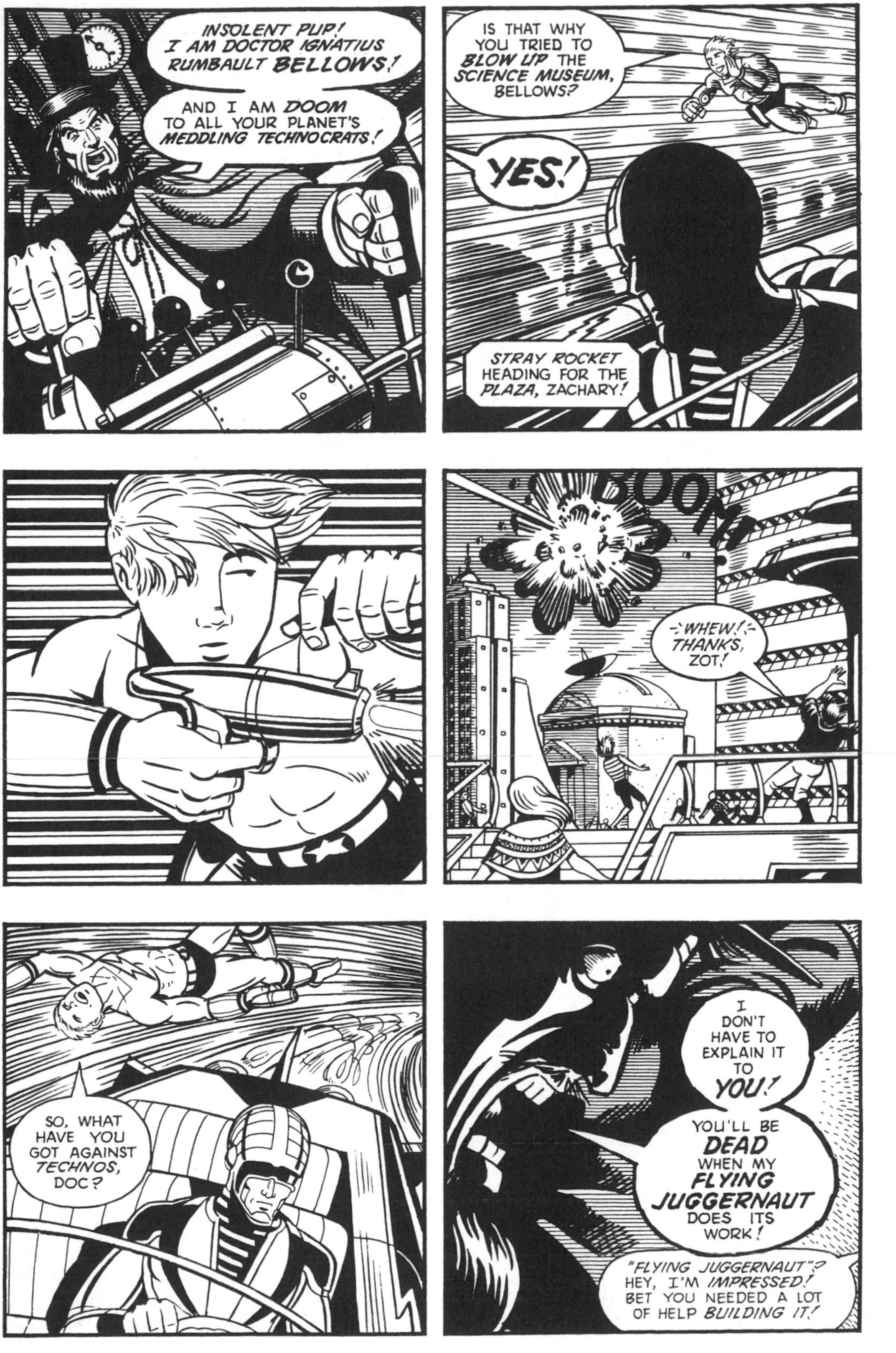
INSOLENT PUP! I AM DOCTOR IGNATIUS RUMBAULT BELLOWS!
AND I AM DOOM TO ALL YOUR PLANET'S MEDDLING TECHNOCRATS!
IS THAT WHY YOU TRIED TO BLOW UP THE SCIENCE MUSEUM, BELLOWS?
YES!
STRAY ROCKET HEADING FOR THE PLAZA, ZACHARY!
BOOM!
WHEW! THANKS, ZOT!
SO, WHAT HAVE YOU GOT AGAINST TECHNOS, DOC?
I DON'T HAVE TO EXPLAIN IT TO YOU!
YOU'LL BE DEAD WHEN MY FLYING JUGGERNAUT DOES ITS WORK!
"FLYING JUGGERNAUT"? HEY, I'M IMPRESSED! BET YOU NEEDED A LOT OF HELP BUILDING IT!

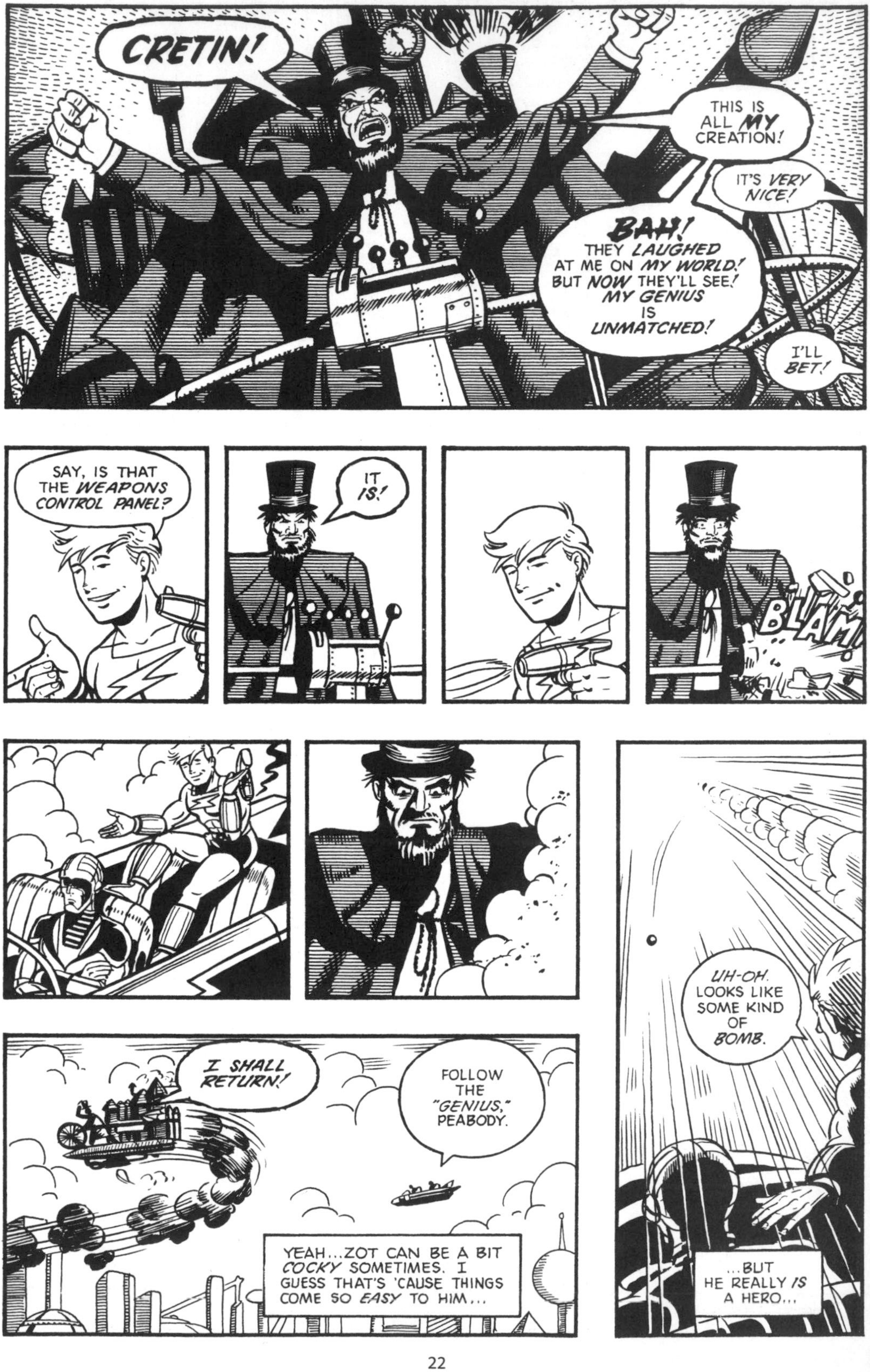
CRETIN!
THIS IS ALL MY CREATION!
IT'S VERY NICE!
BAH! THEY LAUGHED AT ME ON MY WORLD! BUT NOW THEY'LL SEE! MY GENIUS IS UNMATCHED!
I'LL BET!
SAY, IS THAT THE WEAPONS CONTROL PANEL?
IT IS!
BLAM
I SHALL RETURN!
FOLLOW THE "GENIUS," PEABODY.
YEAH...ZOT CAN BE A BIT COCKY SOMETIMES. I GUESS THAT'S 'CAUSE THINGS COME SO EASY TO HIM...
UH-OH. LOOKS LIKE SOME KIND OF BOMB.
...BUT HE REALLY IS A HERO...

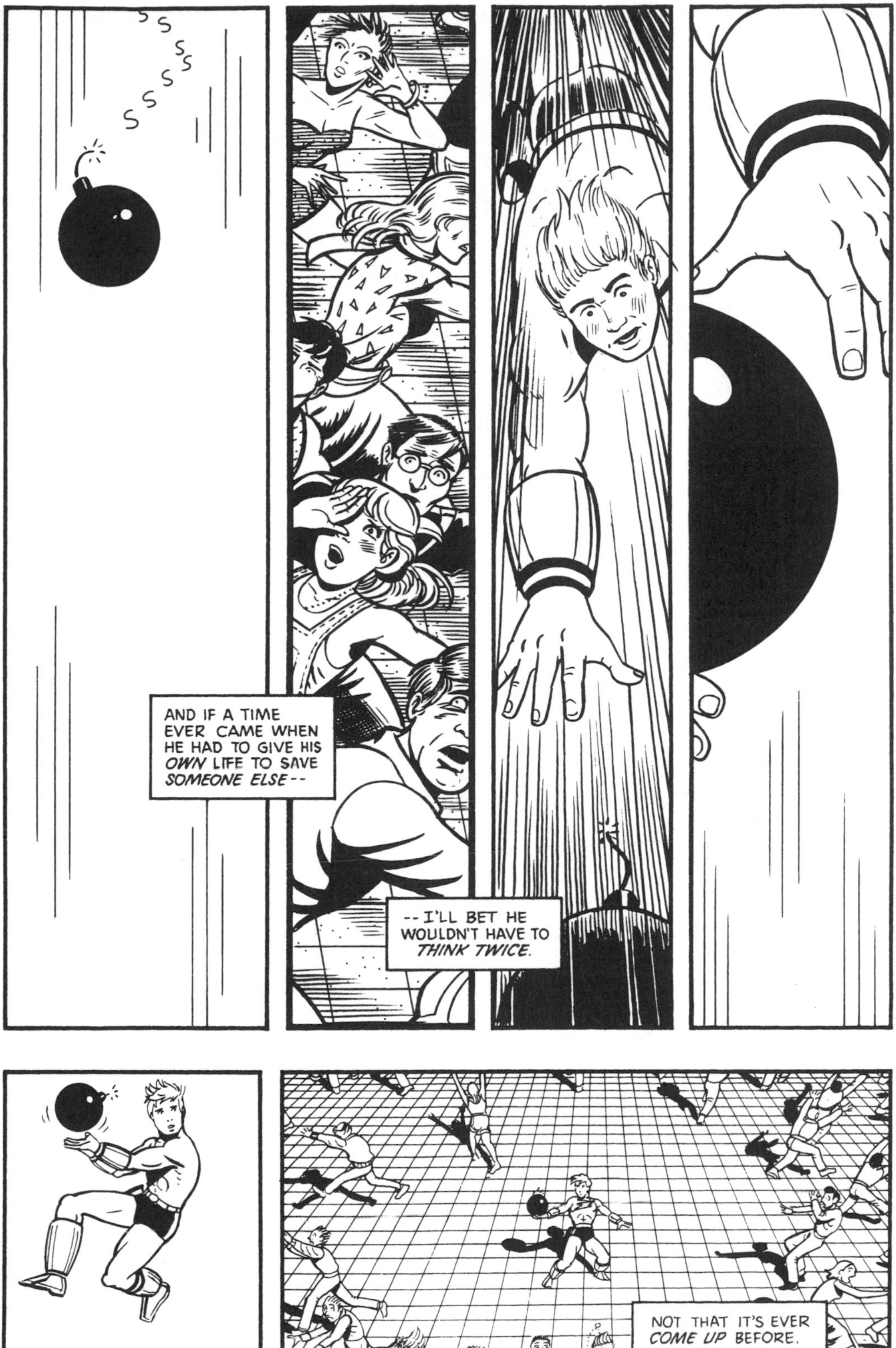
SSSSSS
AND IF A TIME EVER CAME WHEN HE HAD TO GIVE HIS *OWN* LIFE TO SAVE *SOMEONE ELSE*--
--I'LL BET HE WOULDN'T HAVE TO *THINK TWICE.*
NOT THAT IT'S EVER *COME UP* BEFORE.

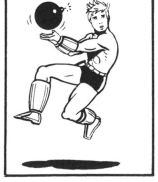

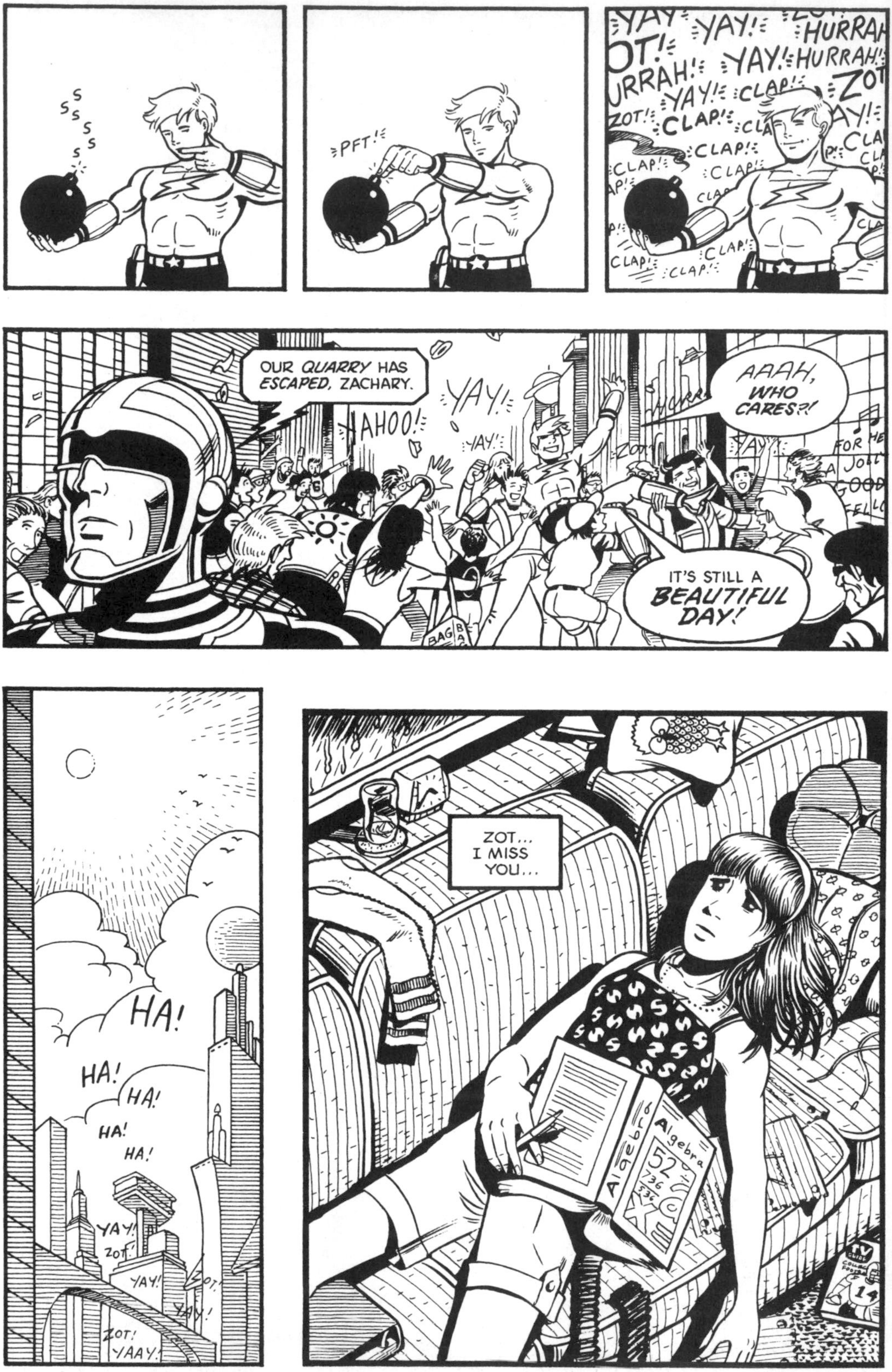
PFT!
YAY! YAY! HURRAH!
ZOT! YAY! HURRAH!
YAY! CLAP!
ZOT! CLAP!
CLAP!
CLAP! CLAP!
CLAP! CLAP!
OUR QUARRY HAS ESCAPED, ZACHARY.
YAHOO!
YAY!
YAY!
AAAH, WHO CARES?!
IT'S STILL A BEAUTIFUL DAY!
HA!
HA!
HA!
HA!
HA!
YAY!
ZOT!
YAY!
ZOT!
YAY!
ZOT!
YAAY!
ZOT... I MISS YOU...
Algebra
Algebra

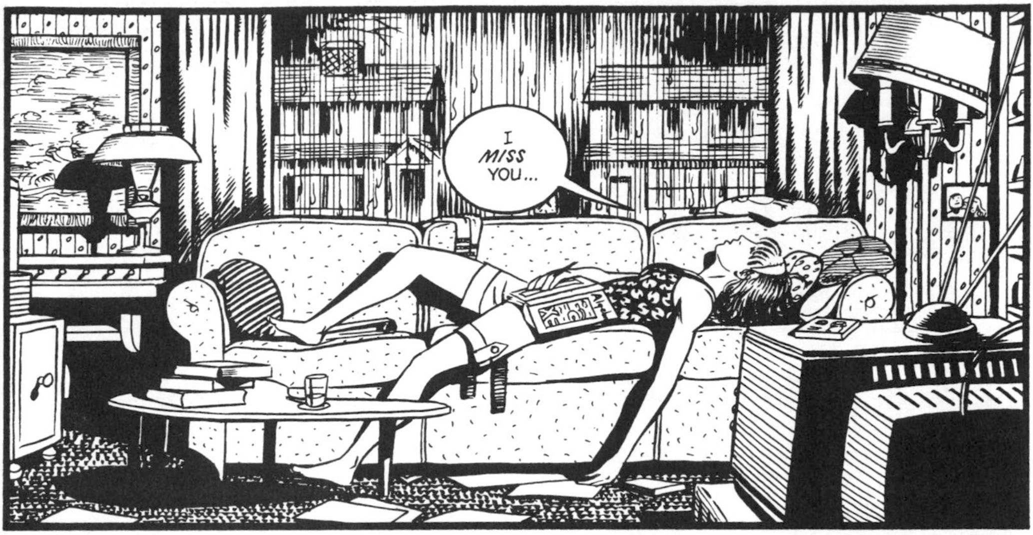
I *MISS* YOU...

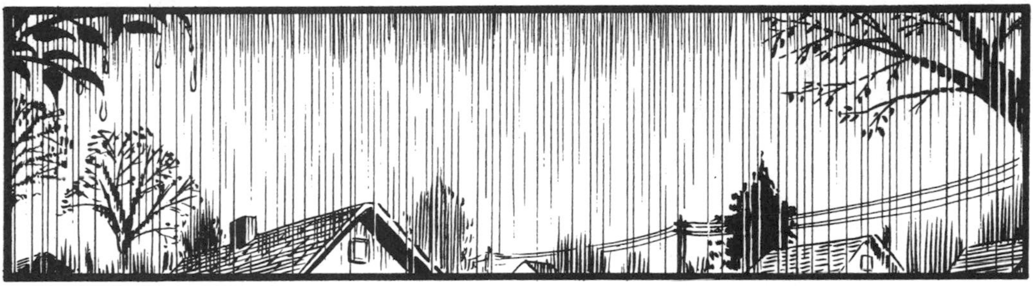

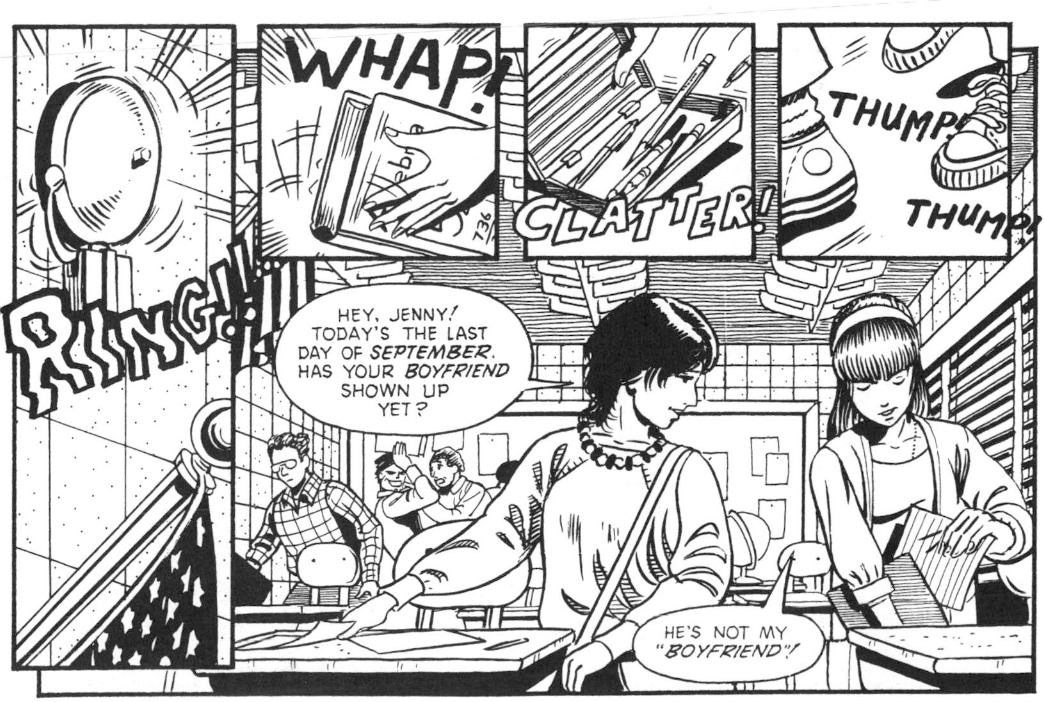
RING!!!
WHAP!
CLATTER!
THUMP!
THUMP!
HEY, JENNY! TODAY'S THE LAST DAY OF *SEPTEMBER*. HAS YOUR *BOYFRIEND* SHOWN UP YET?
HE'S NOT MY "*BOYFRIEND*"!

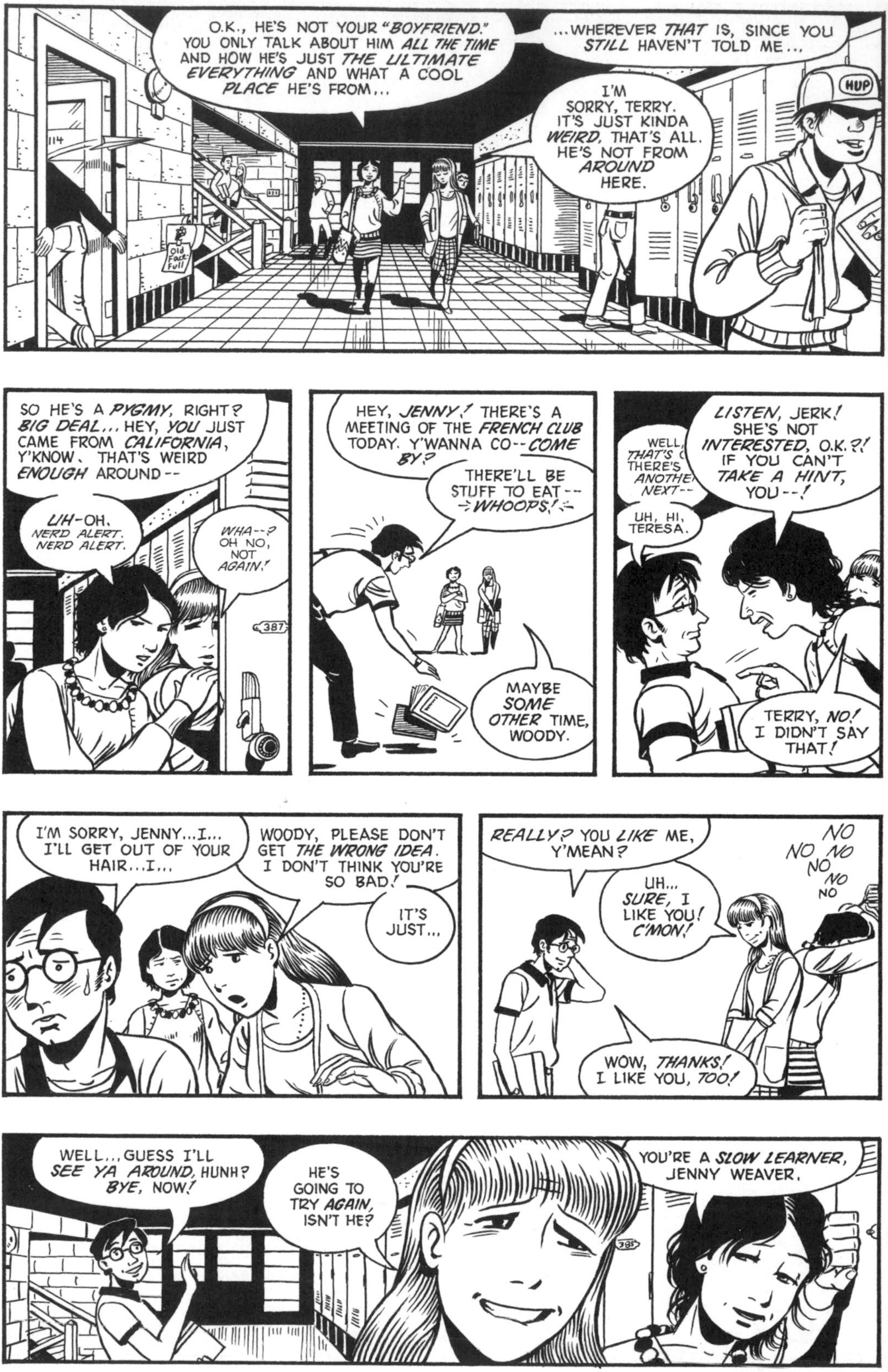

O.K., HE'S NOT YOUR "BOYFRIEND." YOU ONLY TALK ABOUT HIM ALL THE TIME AND HOW HE'S JUST THE ULTIMATE EVERYTHING AND WHAT A COOL PLACE HE'S FROM...
...WHEREVER THAT IS, SINCE YOU STILL HAVEN'T TOLD ME...
I'M SORRY, TERRY. IT'S JUST KINDA WEIRD, THAT'S ALL. HE'S NOT FROM AROUND HERE.
114
Old Face-Full
HUP
SO HE'S A PYGMY, RIGHT? BIG DEAL... HEY, YOU JUST CAME FROM CALIFORNIA, Y'KNOW. THAT'S WEIRD ENOUGH AROUND--
UH-OH. NERD ALERT. NERD ALERT.
WHA--? OH NO, NOT AGAIN!
387
HEY, JENNY! THERE'S A MEETING OF THE FRENCH CLUB TODAY. Y'WANNA CO--COME BY?
THERE'LL BE STUFF TO EAT-- WHOOPS!
MAYBE SOME OTHER TIME, WOODY.
WELL, THAT'S THERE'S NEXT--
LISTEN, JERK! SHE'S NOT INTERESTED, O.K.?! IF YOU CAN'T TAKE A HINT, YOU--!
UH, HI, TERESA.
TERRY, NO! I DIDN'T SAY THAT!
I'M SORRY, JENNY...I... I'LL GET OUT OF YOUR HAIR...I...
WOODY, PLEASE DON'T GET THE WRONG IDEA. I DON'T THINK YOU'RE SO BAD!
IT'S JUST...
REALLY? YOU LIKE ME, Y'MEAN?
UH... SURE, I LIKE YOU! C'MON!
NO NO NO NO NO NO
WOW, THANKS! I LIKE YOU, TOO!
WELL...GUESS I'LL SEE YA AROUND, HUNH? BYE, NOW!
HE'S GOING TO TRY AGAIN, ISN'T HE?
385
YOU'RE A SLOW LEARNER, JENNY WEAVER.

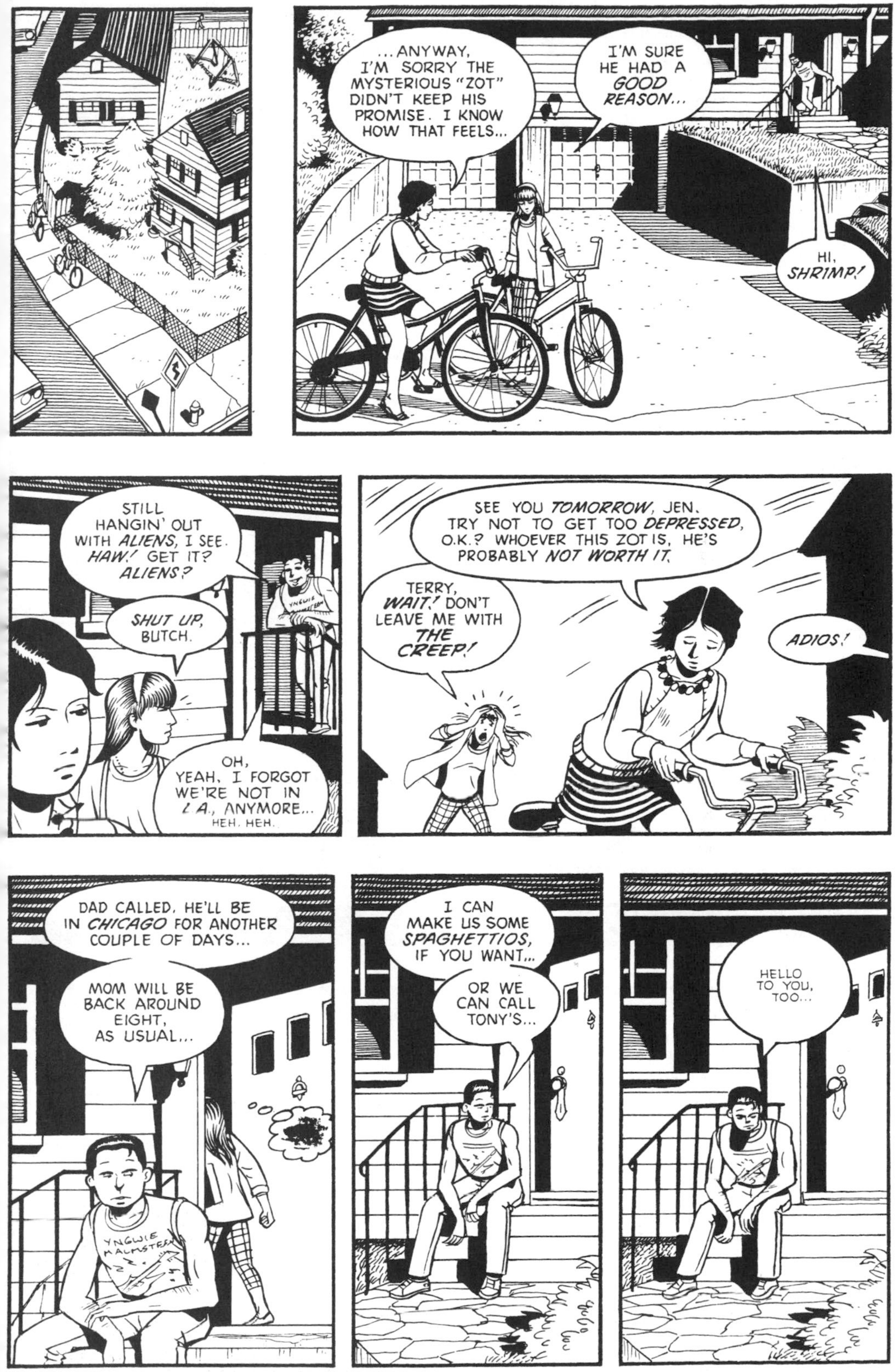
...ANYWAY, I'M SORRY THE MYSTERIOUS "ZOT" DIDN'T KEEP HIS PROMISE. I KNOW HOW THAT FEELS...
I'M SURE HE HAD A *GOOD REASON*...
HI, *SHRIMP!*
STILL HANGIN' OUT WITH *ALIENS*, I SEE. *HAW!* GET IT? *ALIENS?*
SHUT UP, BUTCH.
OH, YEAH, I FORGOT WE'RE NOT IN *L.A.*, ANYMORE... HEH. HEH.
SEE YOU *TOMORROW*, JEN. TRY NOT TO GET TOO *DEPRESSED*, O.K.? WHOEVER THIS ZOT IS, HE'S PROBABLY *NOT WORTH IT.*
TERRY, *WAIT!* DON'T LEAVE ME WITH *THE CREEP!*
ADIOS!
DAD CALLED. HE'LL BE IN *CHICAGO* FOR ANOTHER COUPLE OF DAYS...
MOM WILL BE BACK AROUND EIGHT, AS USUAL...
I CAN MAKE US SOME *SPAGHETTIOS*, IF YOU WANT...
OR WE CAN CALL TONY'S...
HELLO TO YOU, TOO...

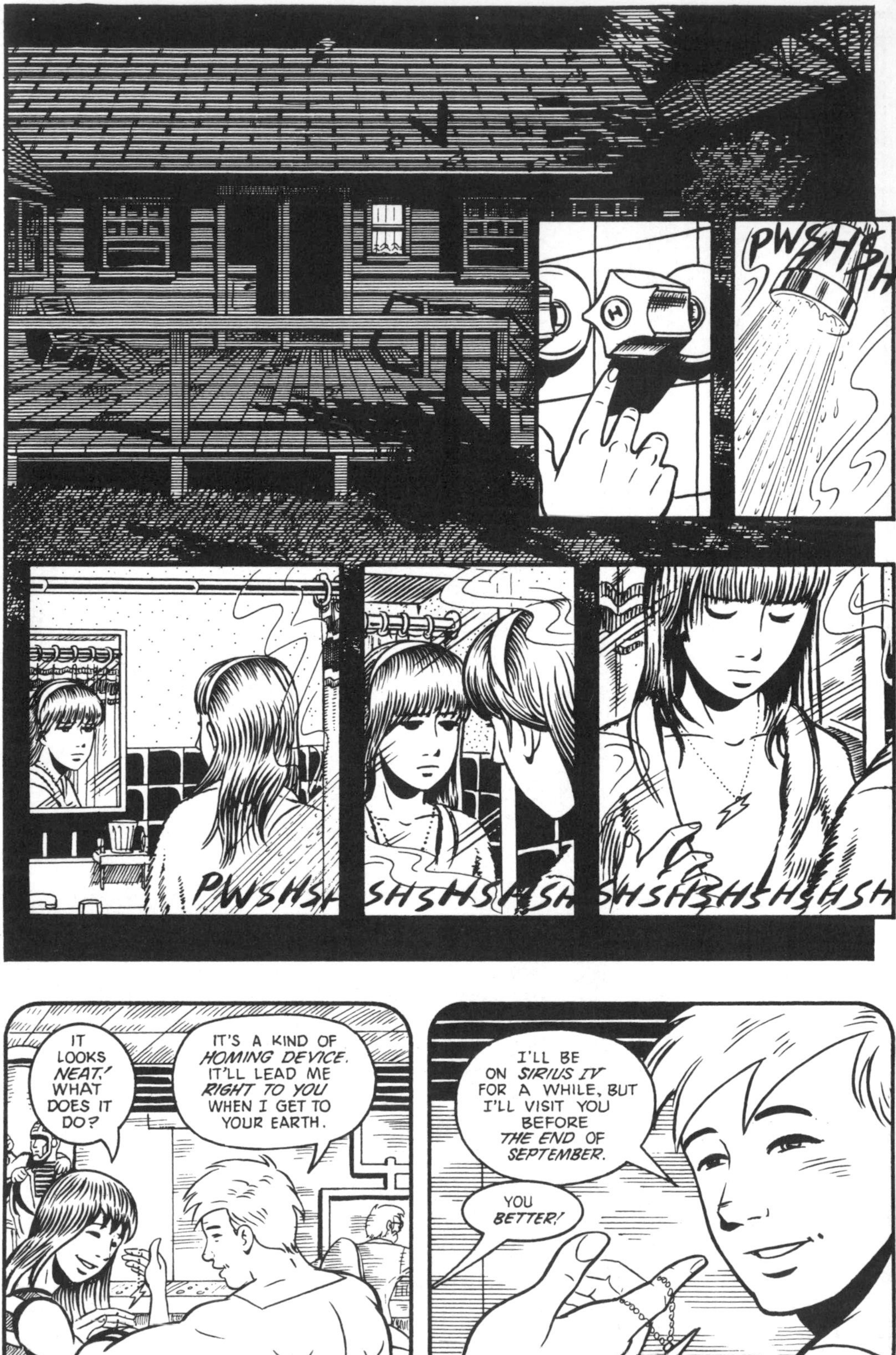
PWSHSH
PWSHSH
SHSHSHSH
SHSHSHSHSH
IT LOOKS NEAT! WHAT DOES IT DO?
IT'S A KIND OF HOMING DEVICE. IT'LL LEAD ME RIGHT TO YOU WHEN I GET TO YOUR EARTH.
I'LL BE ON SIRIUS IV FOR A WHILE, BUT I'LL VISIT YOU BEFORE THE END OF SEPTEMBER.
YOU BETTER!

PWSHSHSH SHSHSH

ASHSHSHSHSH SHSHSHSHSHS

SHSHSHSH

EEEEK!

SIS!

JENNY!

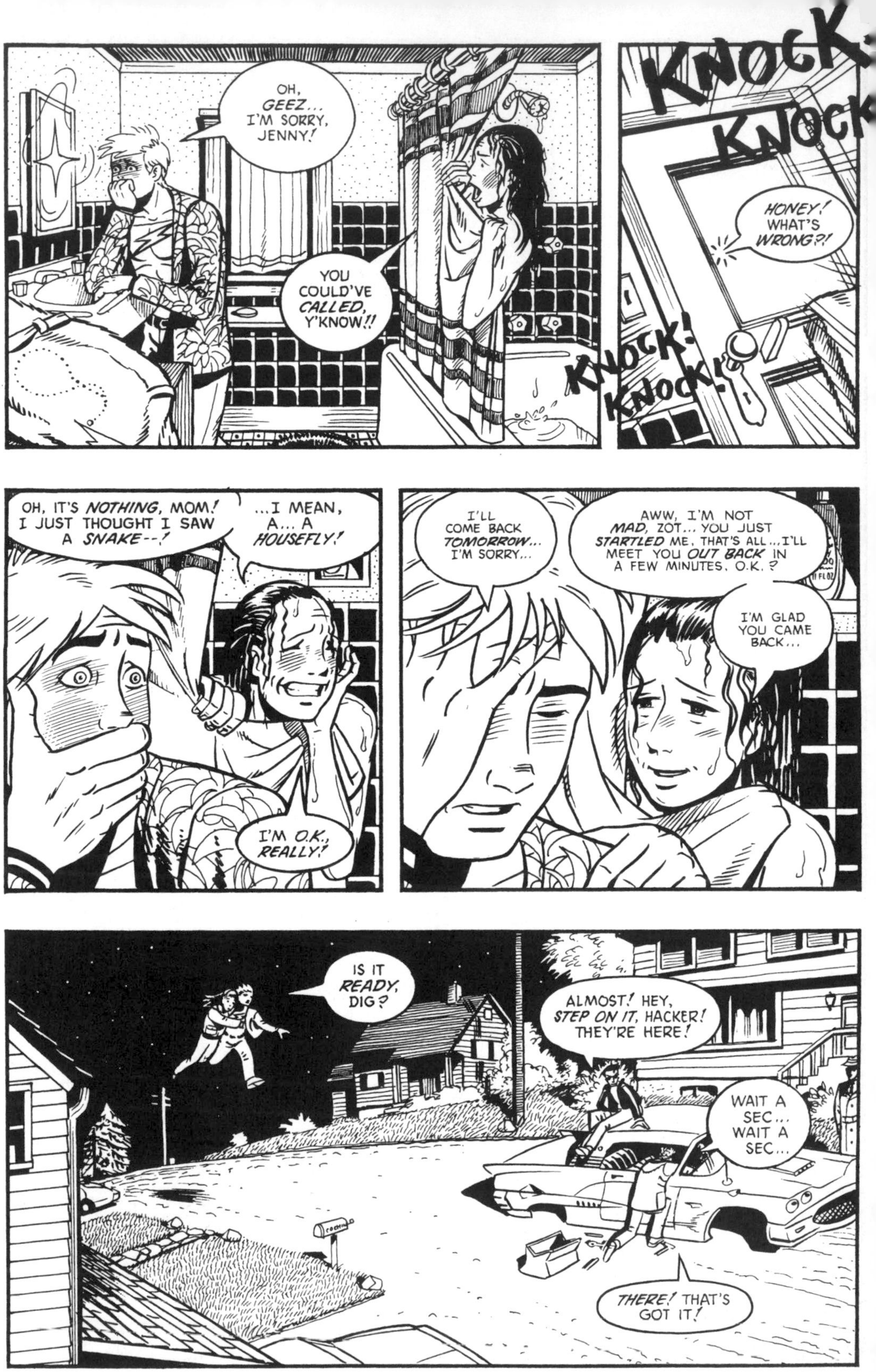
OH, GEEZ... I'M SORRY, JENNY!
YOU COULD'VE CALLED, Y'KNOW!!
KNOCK! KNOCK!
HONEY! WHAT'S WRONG?!
KNOCK! KNOCK!
OH, IT'S NOTHING, MOM! I JUST THOUGHT I SAW A SNAKE--!
...I MEAN, A... A HOUSEFLY!
I'M O.K., REALLY!
I'LL COME BACK TOMORROW... I'M SORRY...
AWW, I'M NOT MAD, ZOT... YOU JUST STARTLED ME, THAT'S ALL...I'LL MEET YOU OUT BACK IN A FEW MINUTES, O.K.?
I'M GLAD YOU CAME BACK...
IS IT READY, DIG?
ALMOST! HEY, STEP ON IT, HACKER! THEY'RE HERE!
WAIT A SEC... WAIT A SEC...
THERE! THAT'S GOT IT!

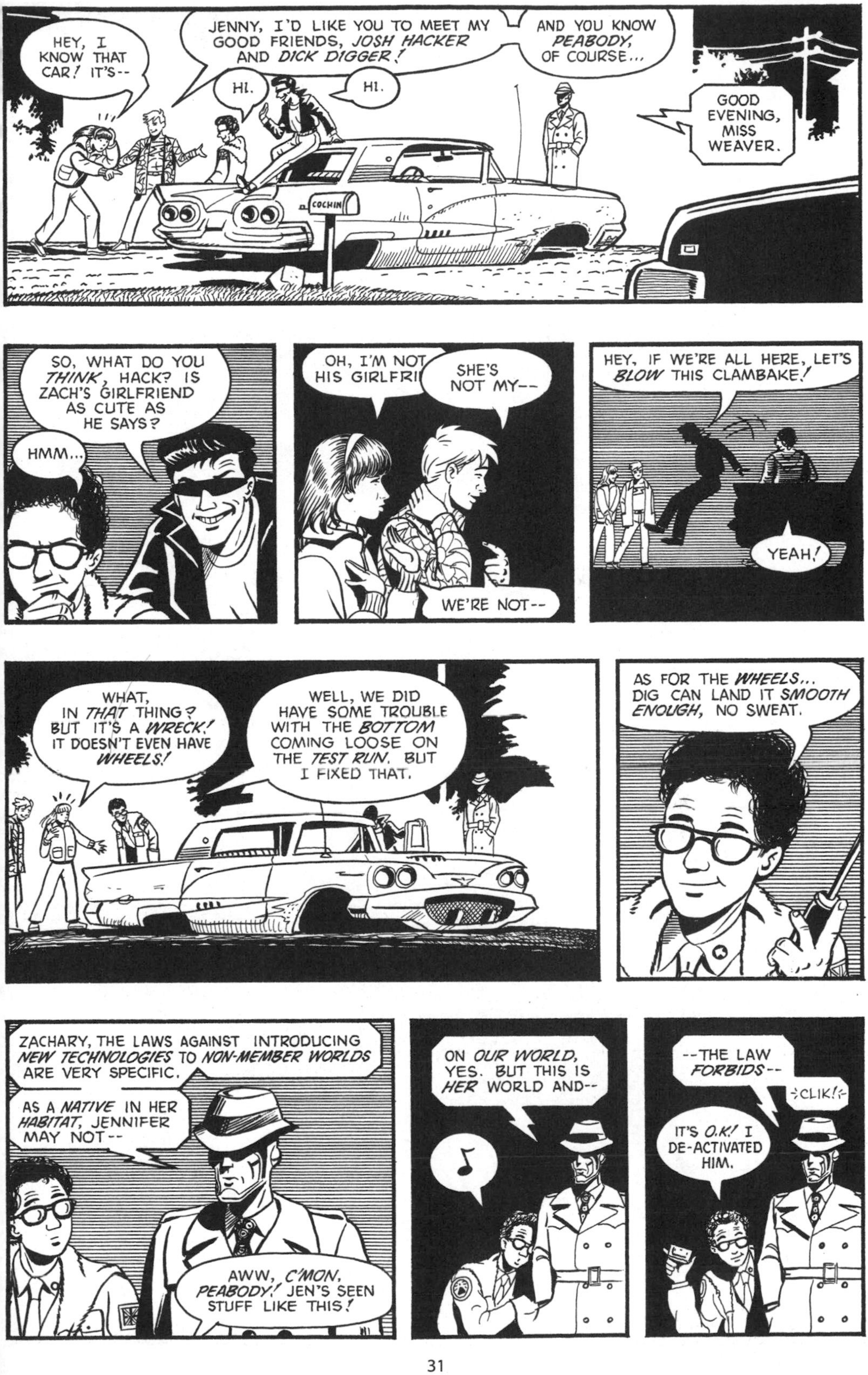
HEY, I KNOW THAT CAR! IT'S--
JENNY, I'D LIKE YOU TO MEET MY GOOD FRIENDS, *JOSH HACKER* AND *DICK DIGGER!*
HI.
HI.
AND YOU KNOW *PEABODY,* OF COURSE...
GOOD EVENING, MISS WEAVER.
COCHIN
SO, WHAT DO YOU *THINK*, HACK? IS ZACH'S GIRLFRIEND AS CUTE AS HE SAYS?
HMM...
OH, I'M NOT HIS GIRLFRI
SHE'S NOT MY--
WE'RE NOT--
HEY, IF WE'RE ALL HERE, LET'S *BLOW* THIS CLAMBAKE!
YEAH!
WHAT, IN *THAT* THING? BUT IT'S A *WRECK!* IT DOESN'T EVEN HAVE *WHEELS!*
WELL, WE DID HAVE SOME TROUBLE WITH THE *BOTTOM* COMING LOOSE ON THE *TEST RUN.* BUT I FIXED THAT.
AS FOR THE *WHEELS...* DIG CAN LAND IT *SMOOTH ENOUGH,* NO SWEAT.
ZACHARY, THE LAWS AGAINST INTRODUCING *NEW TECHNOLOGIES* TO *NON-MEMBER WORLDS* ARE VERY SPECIFIC.
AS A *NATIVE* IN HER *HABITAT,* JENNIFER MAY NOT--
AWW, *C'MON, PEABODY!* JEN'S SEEN STUFF LIKE THIS!
ON *OUR WORLD,* YES. BUT THIS IS *HER* WORLD AND--
--THE LAW *FORBIDS*--
CLIK!
IT'S *O.K.!* I DE-ACTIVATED HIM.

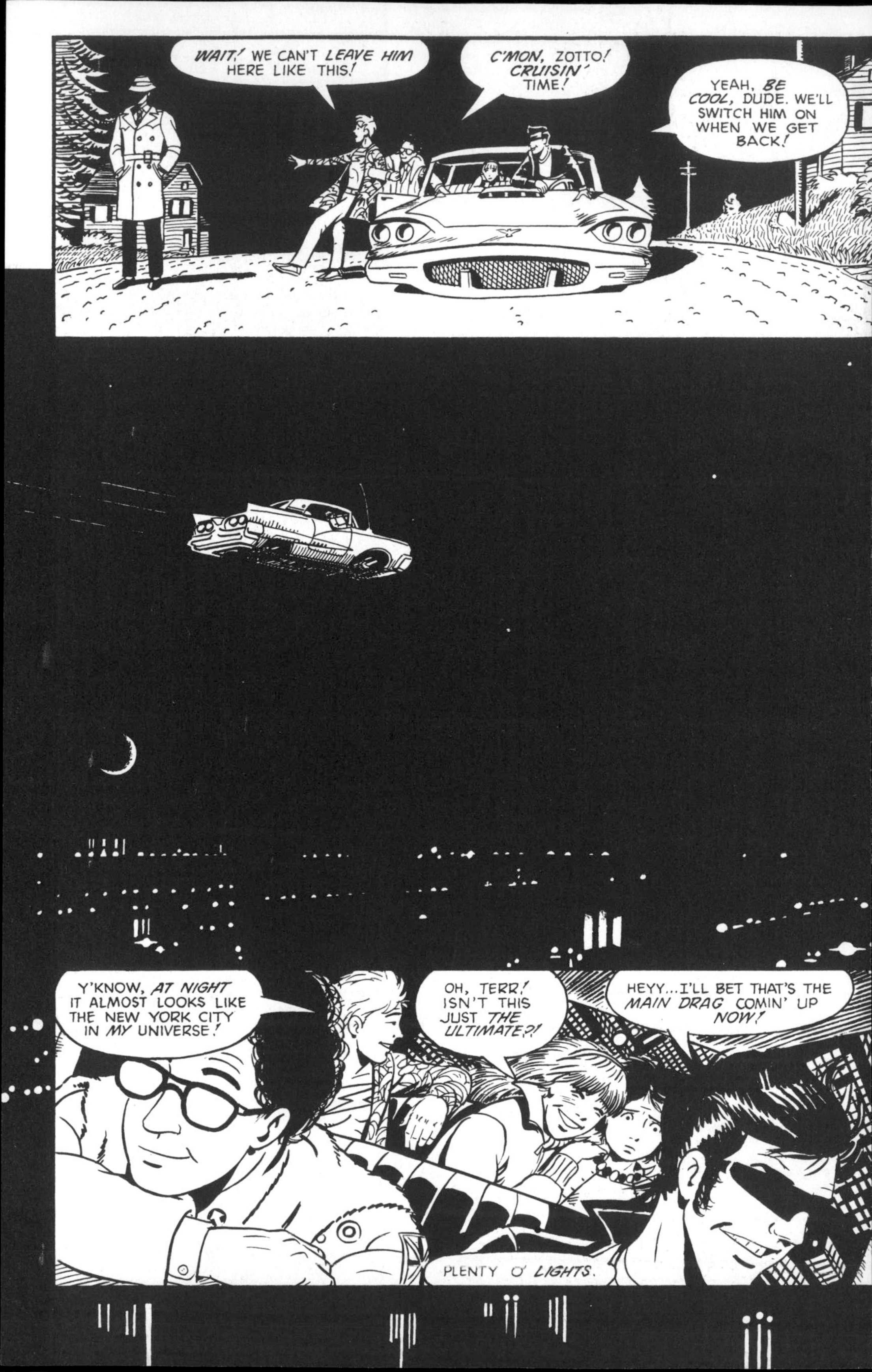
WAIT! WE CAN'T LEAVE HIM HERE LIKE THIS!
C'MON, ZOTTO! CRUISIN' TIME!
YEAH, BE COOL, DUDE. WE'LL SWITCH HIM ON WHEN WE GET BACK!
Y'KNOW, AT NIGHT IT ALMOST LOOKS LIKE THE NEW YORK CITY IN MY UNIVERSE!
OH, TERR! ISN'T THIS JUST THE ULTIMATE?!
HEYY...I'LL BET THAT'S THE MAIN DRAG COMIN' UP NOW!
PLENTY O' LIGHTS.

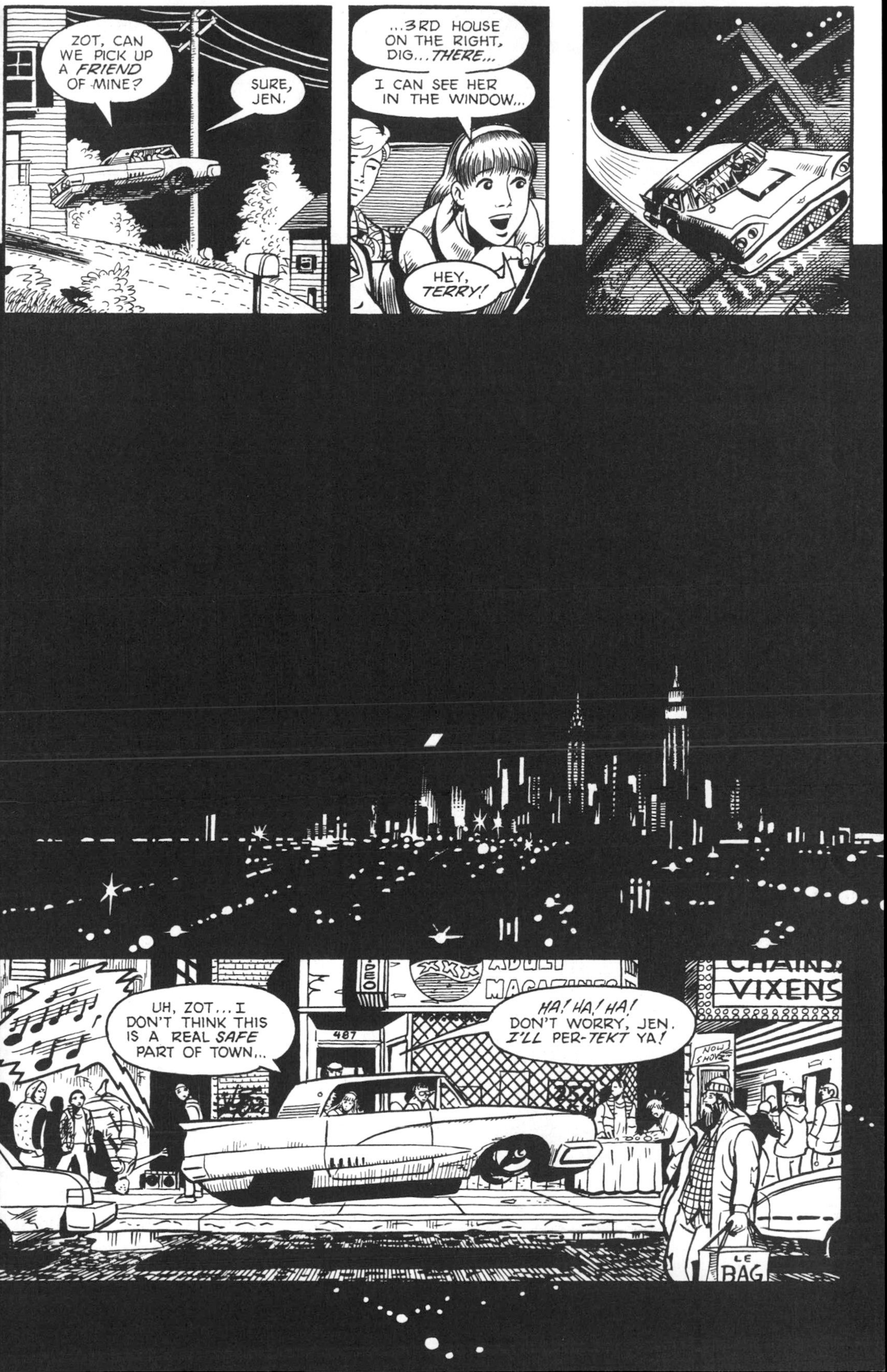
ZOT, CAN WE PICK UP A *FRIEND* OF MINE?
SURE, JEN.
...3RD HOUSE ON THE RIGHT, DIG... *THERE...*
I CAN SEE HER IN THE WINDOW...
HEY, *TERRY!*
UH, ZOT... I DON'T THINK THIS IS A REAL *SAFE* PART OF TOWN...
487
VIXENS
HA! HA! HA! DON'T WORRY, JEN. *I'LL* PER-*TEKT* YA!
LE BAG

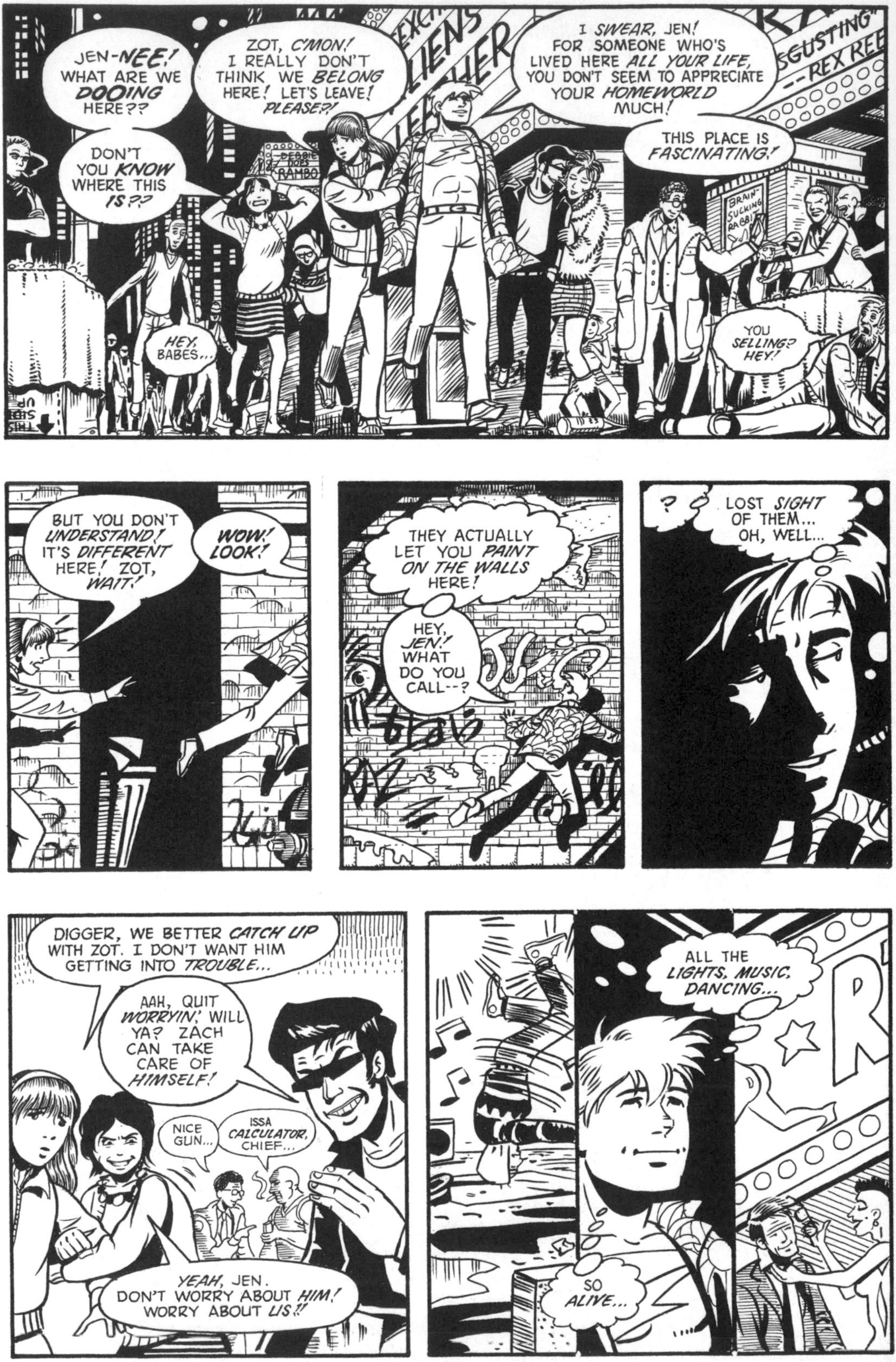
JEN-NEE! WHAT ARE WE DOOING HERE??
ZOT, C'MON! I REALLY DON'T THINK WE BELONG HERE! LET'S LEAVE! PLEASE?!
I SWEAR, JEN! FOR SOMEONE WHO'S LIVED HERE ALL YOUR LIFE, YOU DON'T SEEM TO APPRECIATE YOUR HOMEWORLD MUCH!
DON'T YOU KNOW WHERE THIS IS??
DEBBIE DOES RAMBO
THIS PLACE IS FASCINATING!
HEY, BABES...
YOU SELLING? HEY!
BUT YOU DON'T UNDERSTAND! IT'S DIFFERENT HERE! ZOT, WAIT!
WOW! LOOK!
THEY ACTUALLY LET YOU PAINT ON THE WALLS HERE!
HEY, JEN! WHAT DO YOU CALL--?
?
LOST SIGHT OF THEM... OH, WELL...
DIGGER, WE BETTER CATCH UP WITH ZOT. I DON'T WANT HIM GETTING INTO TROUBLE...
AAH, QUIT WORRYIN,' WILL YA? ZACH CAN TAKE CARE OF HIMSELF!
NICE GUN...
ISSA CALCULATOR, CHIEF...
YEAH, JEN. DON'T WORRY ABOUT HIM! WORRY ABOUT US!!
ALL THE LIGHTS, MUSIC, DANCING...
SO ALIVE...

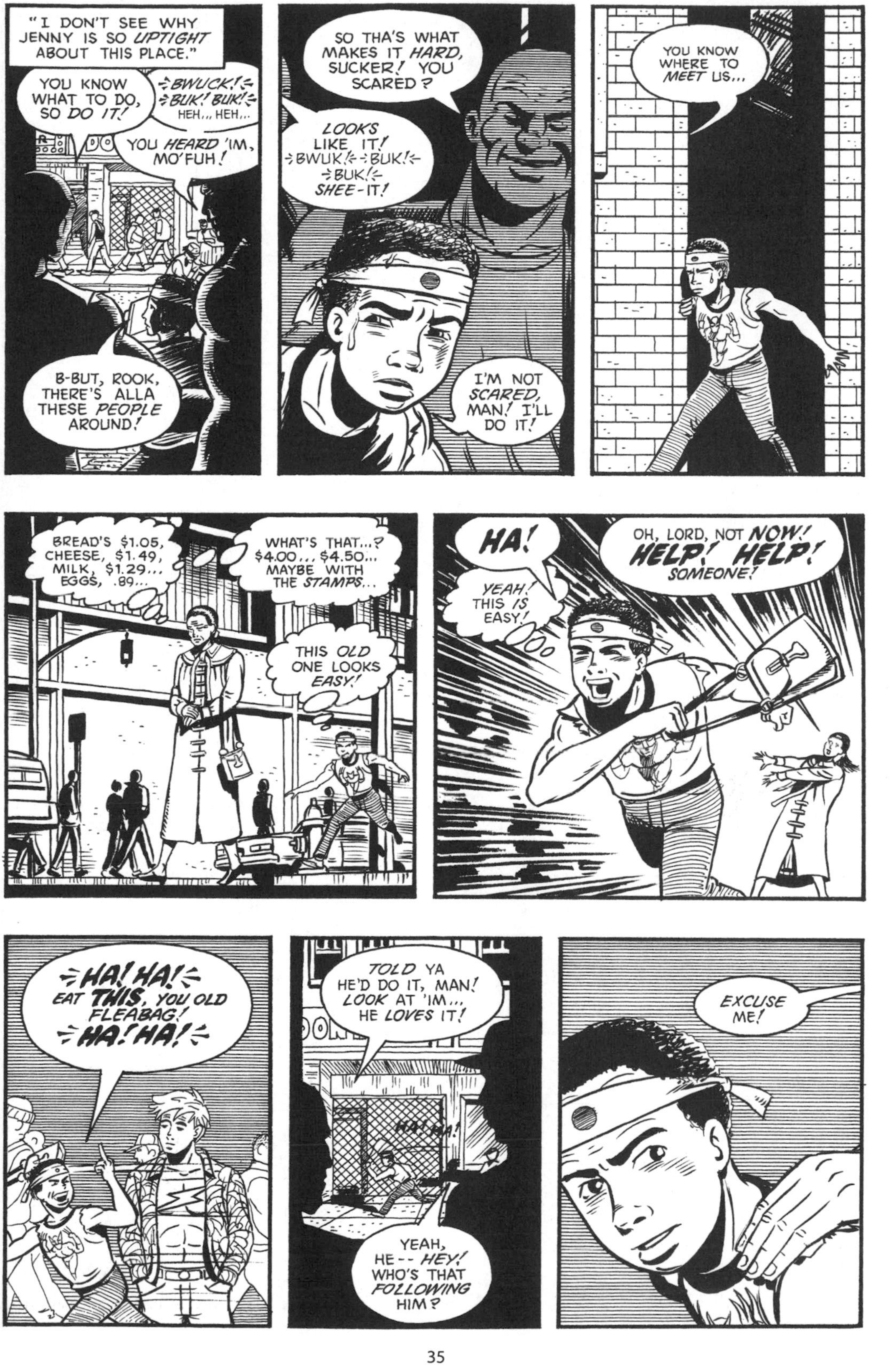
"I DON'T SEE WHY JENNY IS SO *UPTIGHT* ABOUT THIS PLACE."
YOU KNOW WHAT TO DO, SO *DO IT!*
BWUCK! BUK! BUK! HEH... HEH...
YOU *HEARD* 'IM, MO'FUH!
B-BUT, ROOK, THERE'S ALLA THESE *PEOPLE* AROUND!
SO THA'S WHAT MAKES IT *HARD*, SUCKER! YOU SCARED?
LOOKS LIKE IT! BWUK! BUK! BUK! *SHEE-IT!*
I'M NOT *SCARED*, MAN! I'LL DO IT!
YOU KNOW WHERE TO *MEET* US...
BREAD'S $1.05, CHEESE, $1.49, MILK, $1.29... EGGS, .89...
WHAT'S THAT...? $4.00... $4.50... MAYBE WITH THE *STAMPS*...
THIS *OLD* ONE LOOKS *EASY!*
HA!
YEAH! THIS IS EASY!
OH, LORD, NOT **NOW!** **HELP! HELP!** *SOMEONE!*
HA! HA! *EAT* **THIS**, *YOU OLD FLEABAG!* **HA! HA!**
TOLD YA HE'D DO IT, MAN! *LOOK* AT 'IM... HE *LOVES* IT!
HA! HA!
YEAH, HE-- *HEY!* WHO'S THAT *FOLLOWING* HIM?
EXCUSE ME!

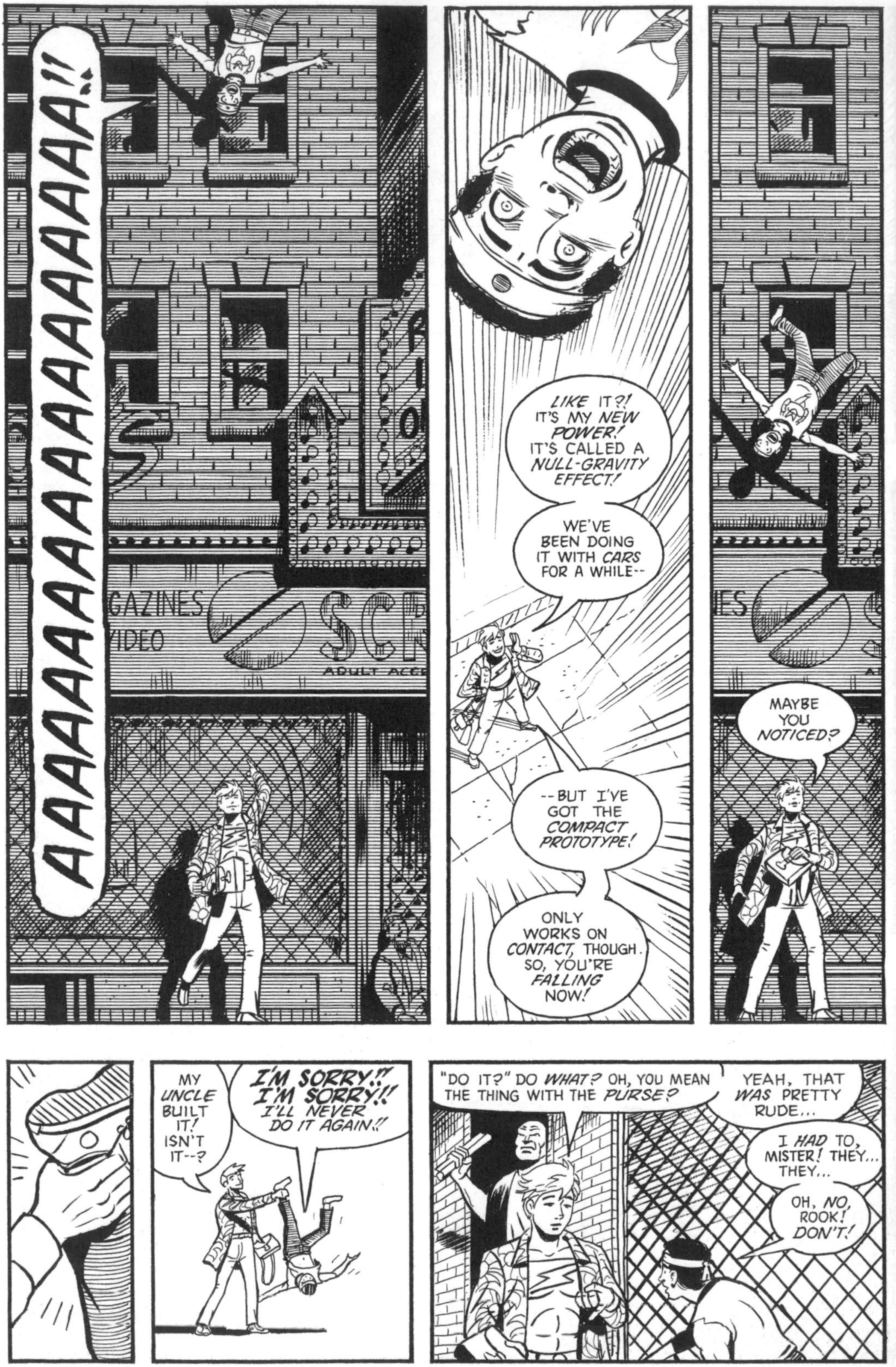
AAAAAAAAAAAAAAAAAAA!!
LIKE IT?! IT'S MY *NEW POWER!* IT'S CALLED A *NULL-GRAVITY EFFECT!*
WE'VE BEEN DOING IT WITH *CARS* FOR A WHILE--
--BUT I'VE GOT THE *COMPACT PROTOTYPE!*
ONLY WORKS ON *CONTACT,* THOUGH. SO, YOU'RE *FALLING* NOW!
MAYBE YOU *NOTICED?*
MY *UNCLE* BUILT IT! ISN'T IT--?
I'M SORRY!! I'M SORRY!! I'LL NEVER DO IT AGAIN!!
"DO IT?" DO *WHAT?* OH, YOU MEAN THE THING WITH THE *PURSE?*
YEAH, THAT *WAS* PRETTY RUDE...
I *HAD* TO, MISTER! THEY... THEY...
OH, *NO,* ROOK! *DON'T!*

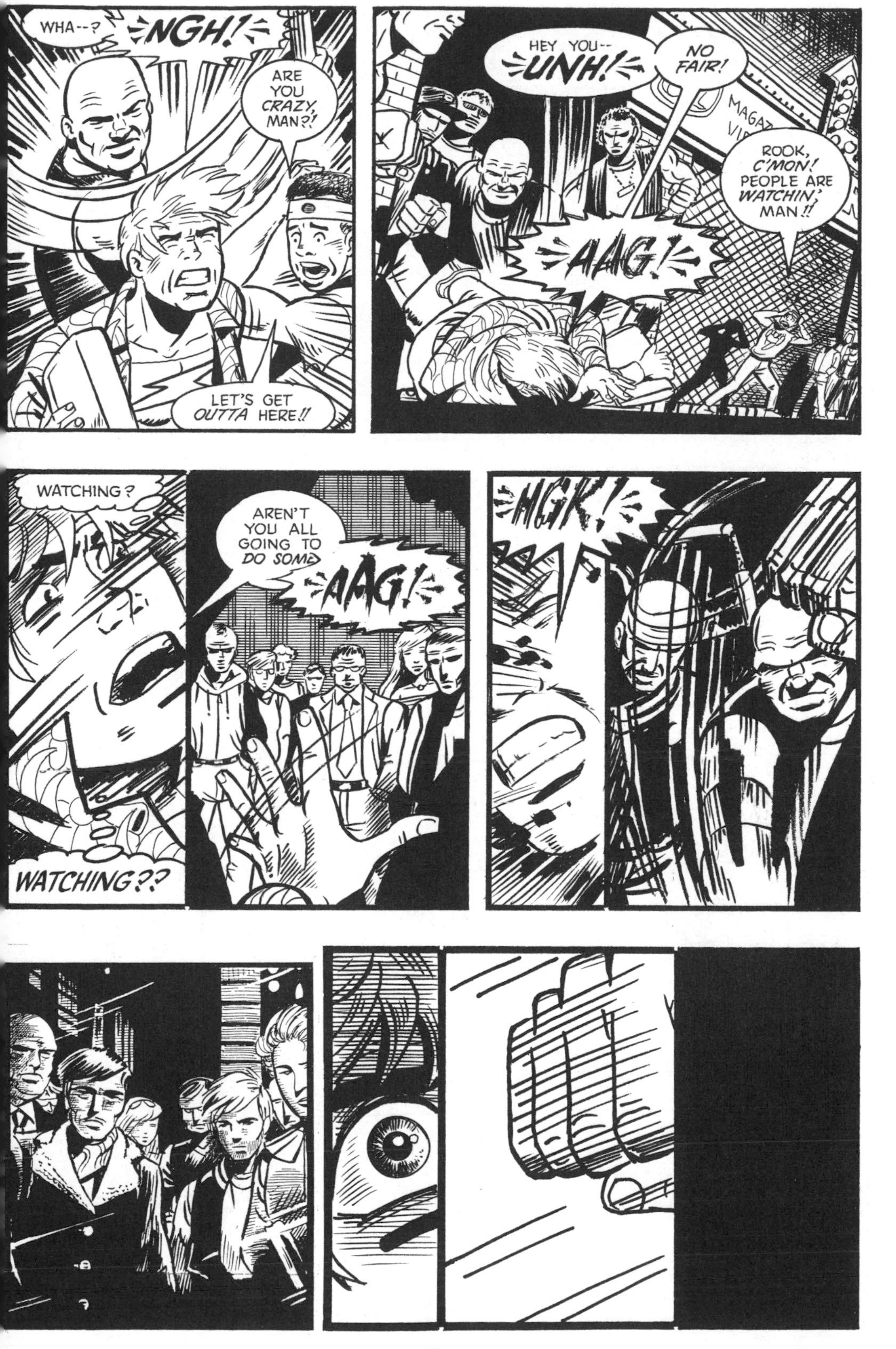
WHA--?
NGH!
ARE YOU CRAZY, MAN?!
LET'S GET OUTTA HERE!!
HEY YOU--
UNH!
NO FAIR!
ROOK, C'MON! PEOPLE ARE WATCHIN,' MAN!!
AAG!
WATCHING?
WATCHING??
AREN'T YOU ALL GOING TO DO SOME
AAG!
HGK!

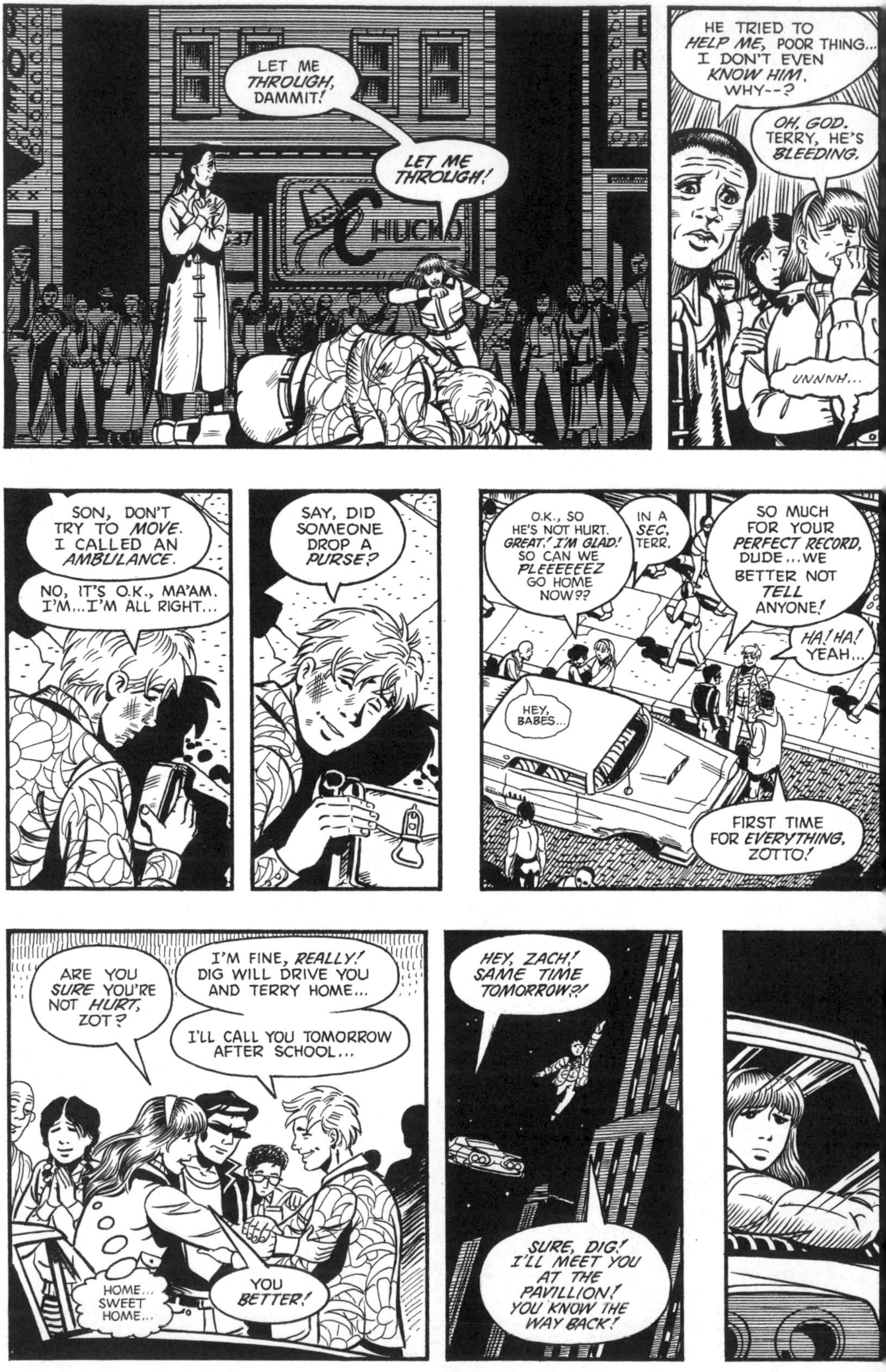
LET ME THROUGH, DAMMIT!
LET ME THROUGH!
CHUCKO
HE TRIED TO HELP ME, POOR THING... I DON'T EVEN KNOW HIM. WHY--?
OH, GOD. TERRY, HE'S BLEEDING.
UNNNH...
SON, DON'T TRY TO MOVE. I CALLED AN AMBULANCE.
NO, IT'S O.K., MA'AM. I'M...I'M ALL RIGHT...
SAY, DID SOMEONE DROP A PURSE?
O.K., SO HE'S NOT HURT. GREAT! I'M GLAD! SO CAN WE PLEEEEEEZ GO HOME NOW??
IN A SEC, TERR.
SO MUCH FOR YOUR PERFECT RECORD, DUDE...WE BETTER NOT TELL ANYONE!
HA! HA! YEAH...
HEY, BABES...
FIRST TIME FOR EVERYTHING, ZOTTO!
ARE YOU SURE YOU'RE NOT HURT, ZOT?
I'M FINE, REALLY! DIG WILL DRIVE YOU AND TERRY HOME...
I'LL CALL YOU TOMORROW AFTER SCHOOL...
HOME... SWEET HOME...
YOU BETTER!
HEY, ZACH! SAME TIME TOMORROW?!
SURE, DIG! I'LL MEET YOU AT THE PAVILLION! YOU KNOW THE WAY BACK!

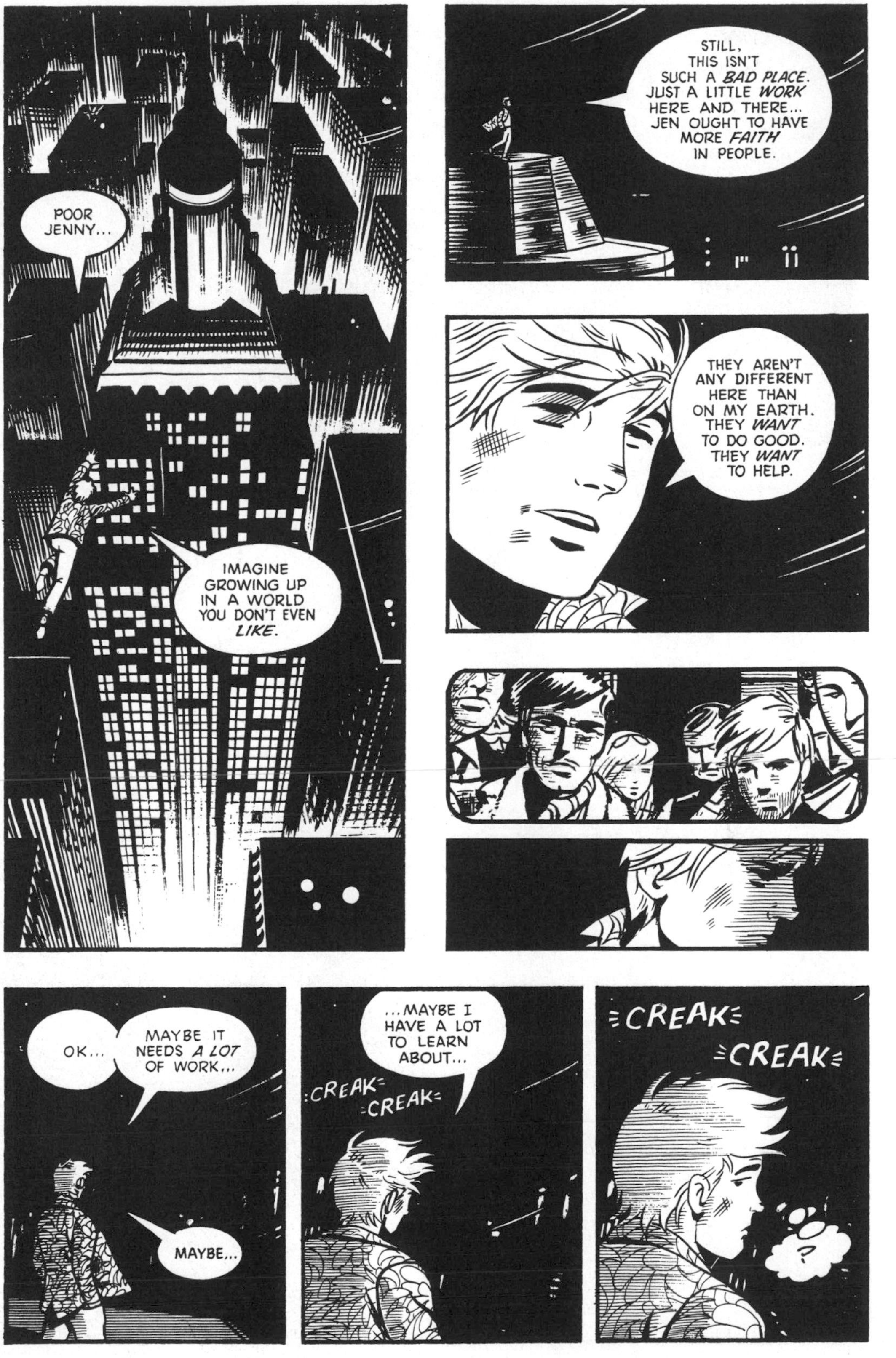
POOR JENNY...
IMAGINE GROWING UP IN A WORLD YOU DON'T EVEN *LIKE*.
STILL, THIS ISN'T SUCH A *BAD PLACE*. JUST A LITTLE *WORK* HERE AND THERE... JEN OUGHT TO HAVE MORE *FAITH* IN PEOPLE.
THEY AREN'T ANY DIFFERENT HERE THAN ON MY EARTH. THEY *WANT* TO DO GOOD. THEY *WANT* TO HELP.
OK...
MAYBE IT NEEDS *A LOT* OF WORK...
MAYBE...
...MAYBE I HAVE A LOT TO LEARN ABOUT...
CREAK
CREAK
CREAK
CREAK
?

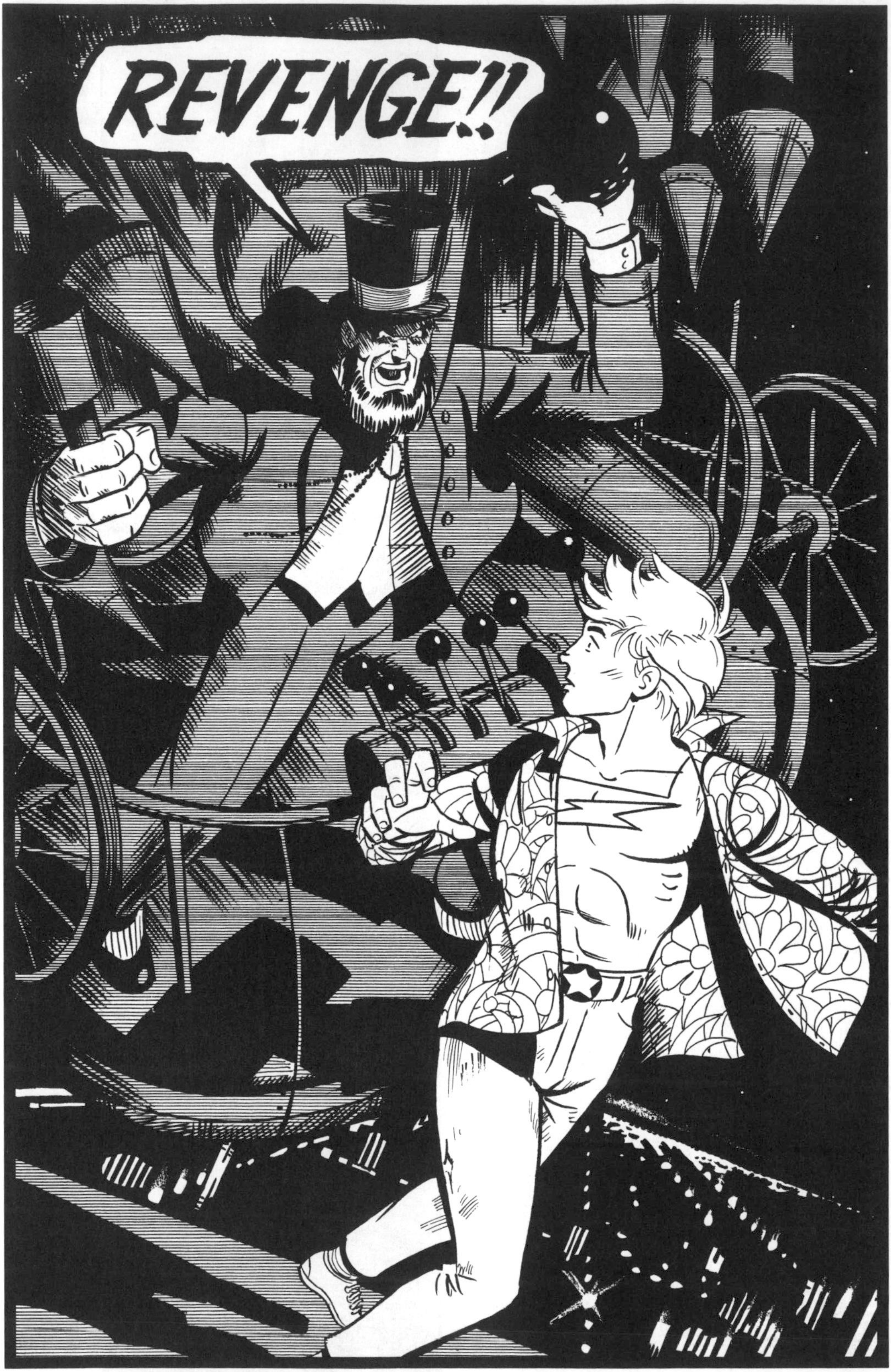
REVENGE!!

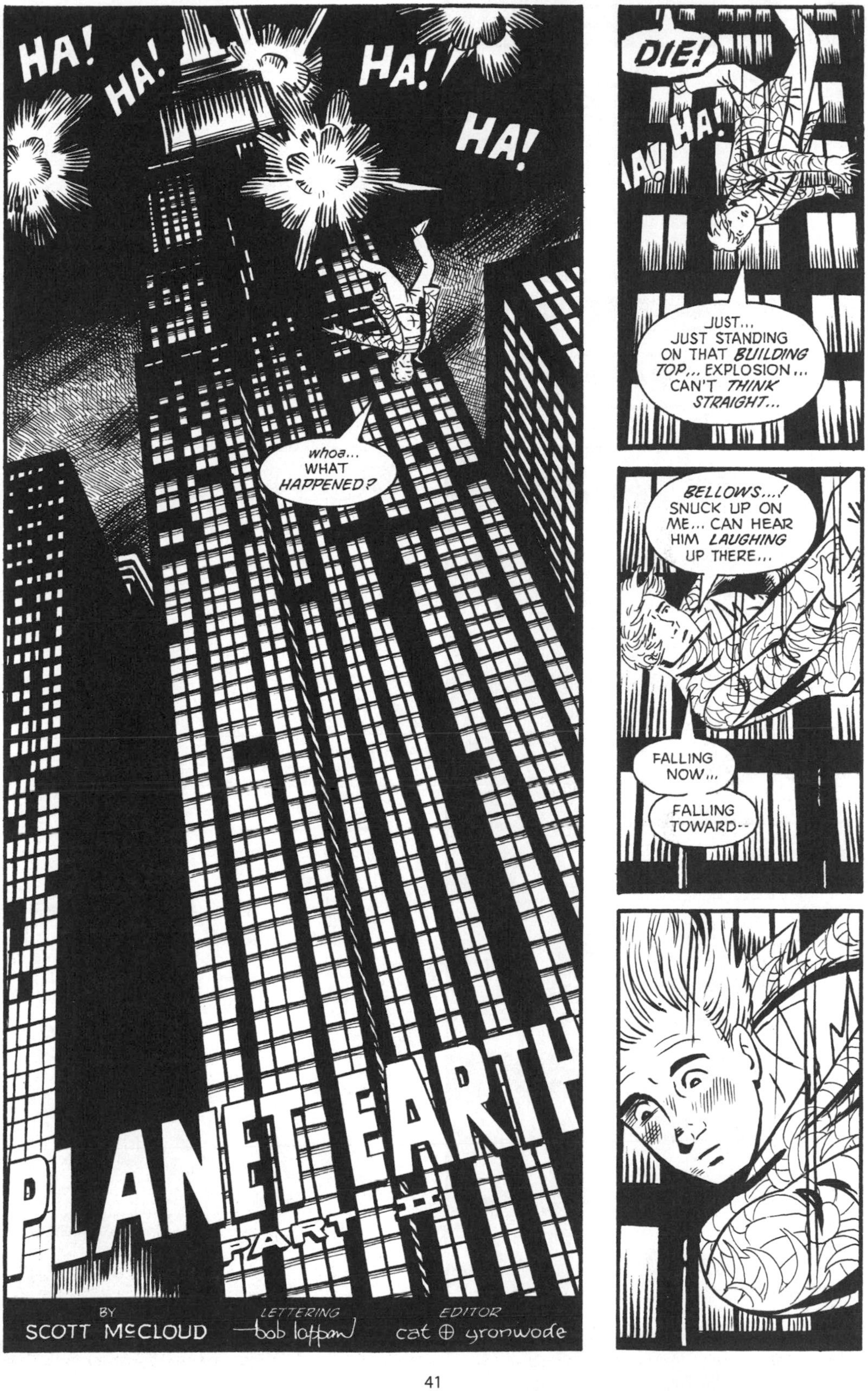
HA! HA! HA! HA!
whoa... WHAT HAPPENED?
PLANET EARTH
PART II
BY SCOTT McCLOUD
LETTERING bob lappan
EDITOR cat ⊕ yronwode
DIE!
A! HA!
JUST... JUST STANDING ON THAT BUILDING TOP... EXPLOSION... CAN'T THINK STRAIGHT...
BELLOWS...! SNUCK UP ON ME... CAN HEAR HIM LAUGHING UP THERE...
FALLING NOW...
FALLING TOWARD--

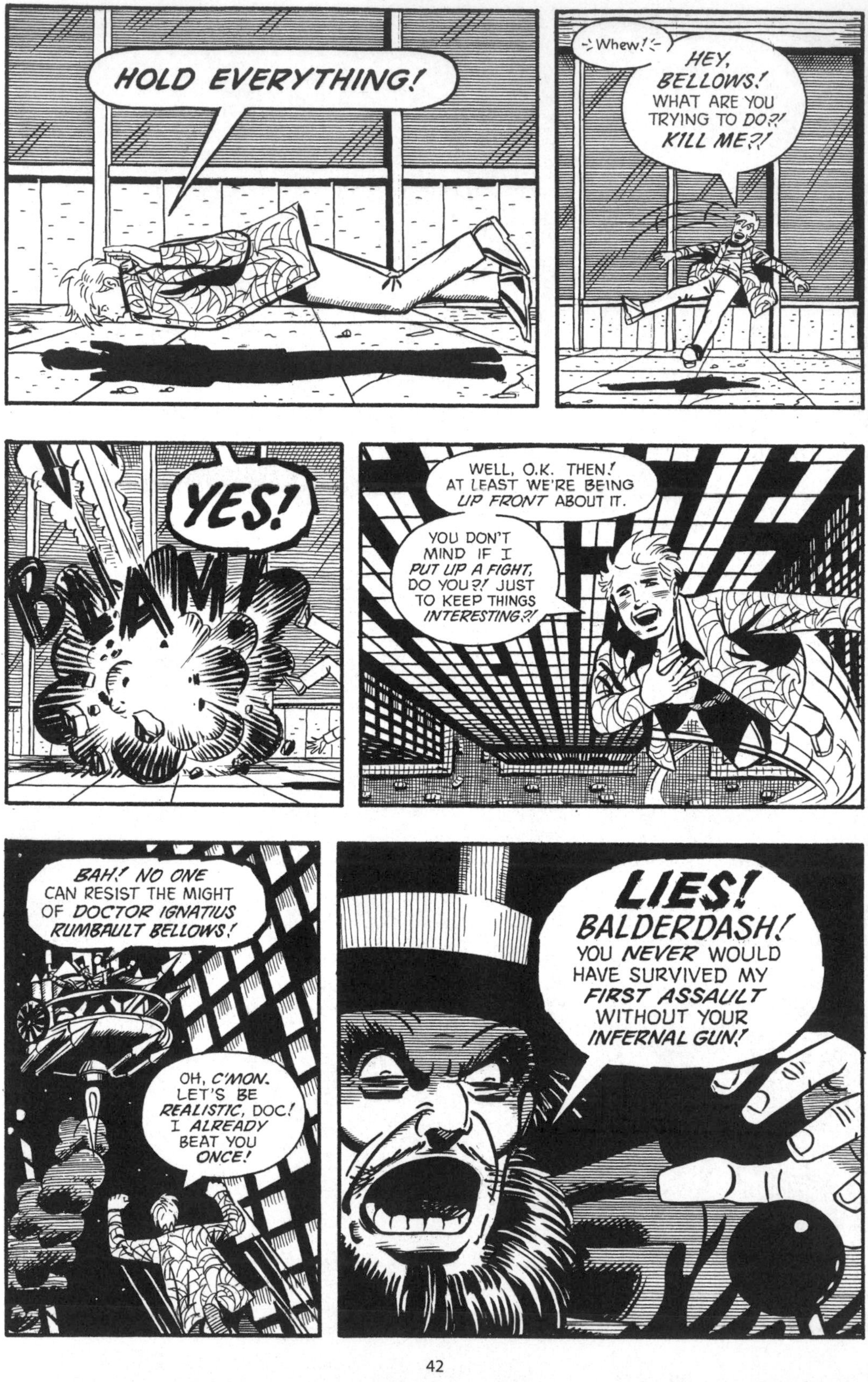
HOLD EVERYTHING!
Whew!
HEY, BELLOWS! WHAT ARE YOU TRYING TO DO?! KILL ME?!
YES!
BLAM!
WELL, O.K. THEN! AT LEAST WE'RE BEING UP FRONT ABOUT IT.
YOU DON'T MIND IF I PUT UP A FIGHT, DO YOU?! JUST TO KEEP THINGS INTERESTING?!
BAH! NO ONE CAN RESIST THE MIGHT OF DOCTOR IGNATIUS RUMBAULT BELLOWS!
OH, C'MON. LET'S BE REALISTIC, DOC! I ALREADY BEAT YOU ONCE!
LIES! BALDERDASH! YOU NEVER WOULD HAVE SURVIVED MY FIRST ASSAULT WITHOUT YOUR INFERNAL GUN!

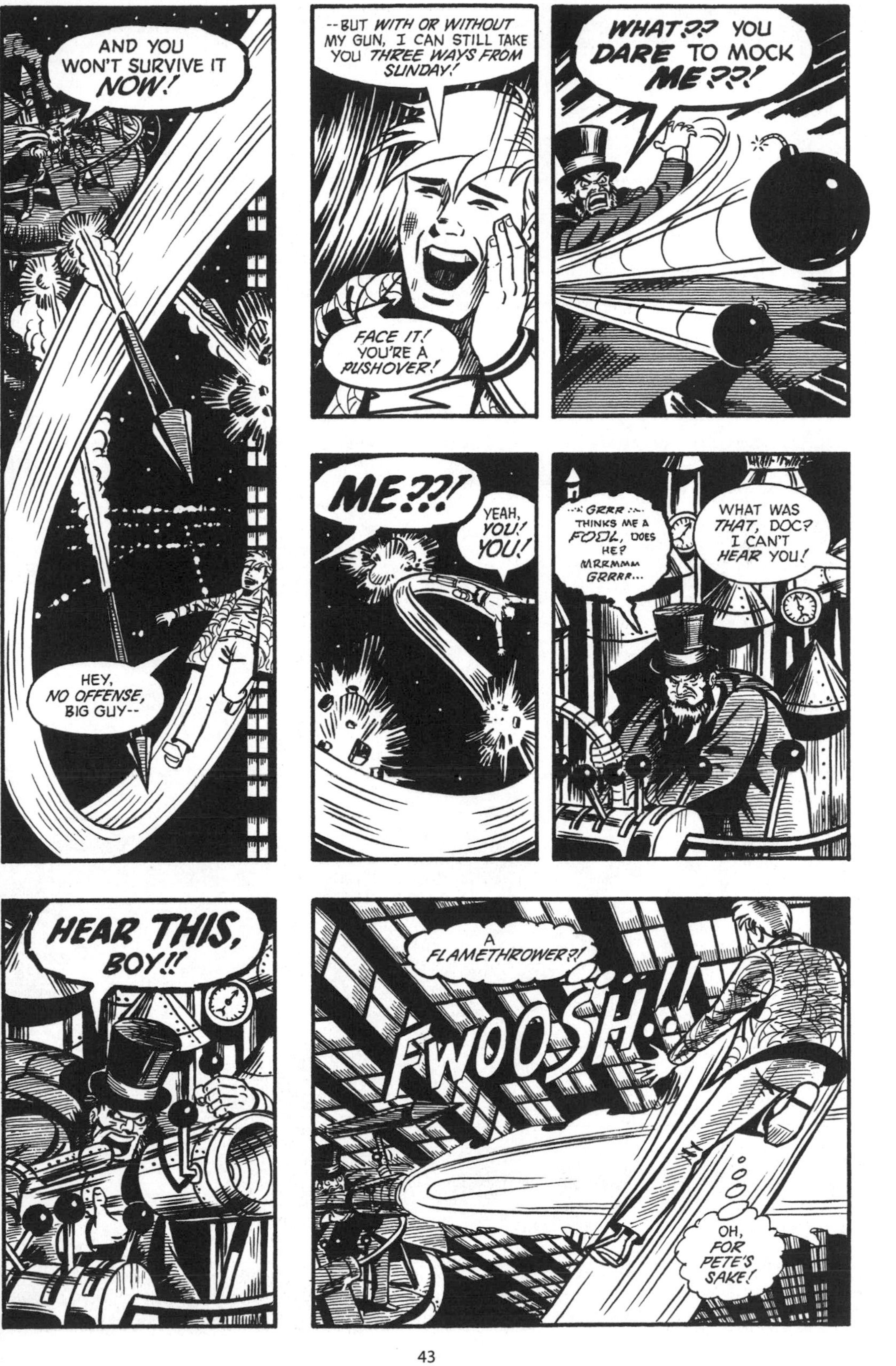

AND YOU WON'T SURVIVE IT NOW!
HEY, NO OFFENSE, BIG GUY--
--BUT WITH OR WITHOUT MY GUN, I CAN STILL TAKE YOU THREE WAYS FROM SUNDAY!
FACE IT! YOU'RE A PUSHOVER!
WHAT?? YOU DARE TO MOCK ME??!
ME??!
YEAH, YOU! YOU!
GRRR... THINKS ME A FOOL, DOES HE? MRRMMM GRRRR...
WHAT WAS THAT, DOC? I CAN'T HEAR YOU!
HEAR THIS, BOY!!
A FLAMETHROWER?!
FWOOSH!!
OH, FOR PETE'S SAKE!

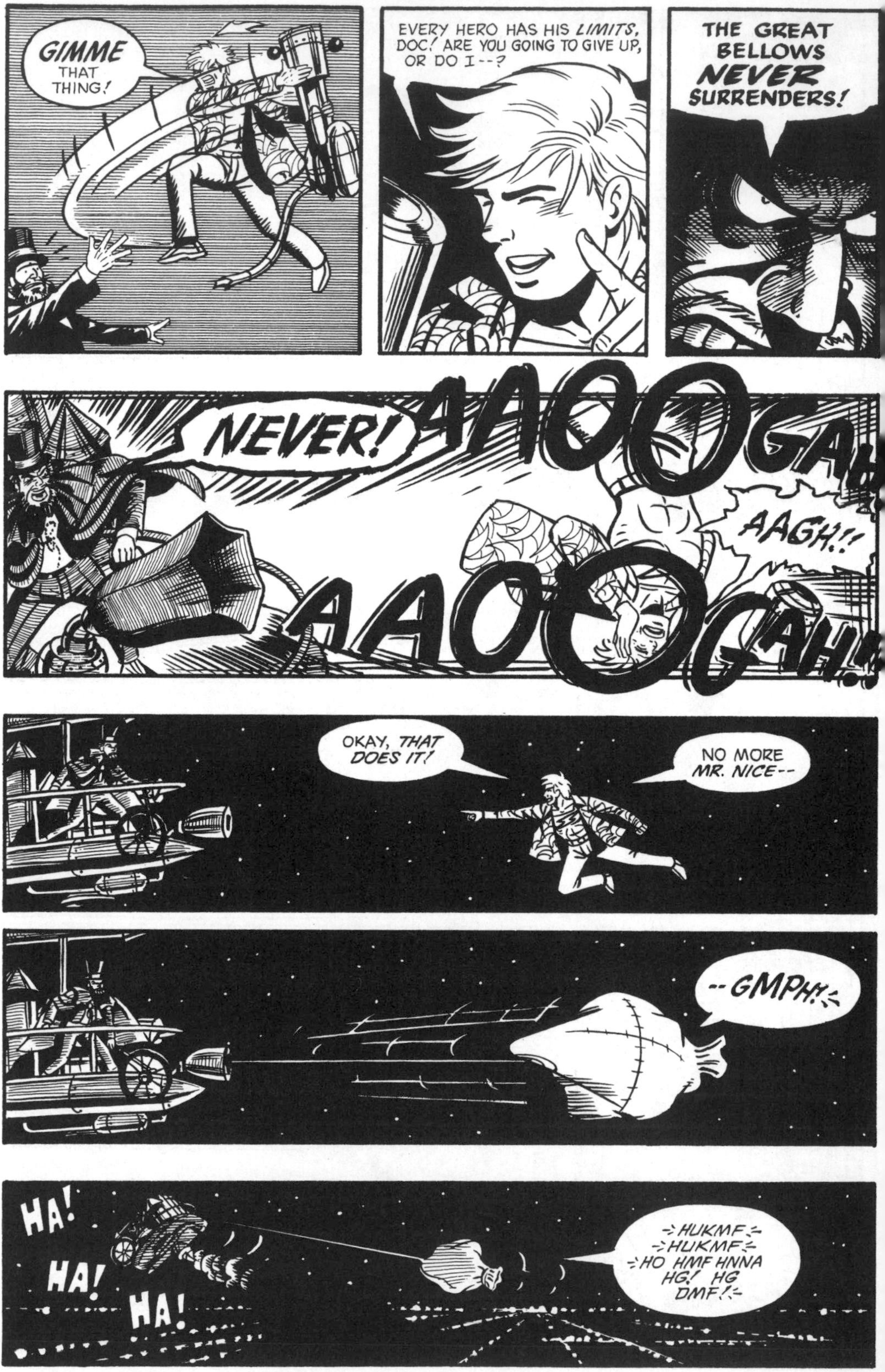
GIMME THAT THING!
EVERY HERO HAS HIS LIMITS, DOC! ARE YOU GOING TO GIVE UP, OR DO I--?
THE GREAT BELLOWS NEVER SURRENDERS!
NEVER!
AAOOGAH
AAGH!!
AAOOGAH!
OKAY, THAT DOES IT!
NO MORE MR. NICE--
--GMPH!
HA! HA! HA!
HUKMF HUKMF HO HMF HNNA HG! HG DMF!

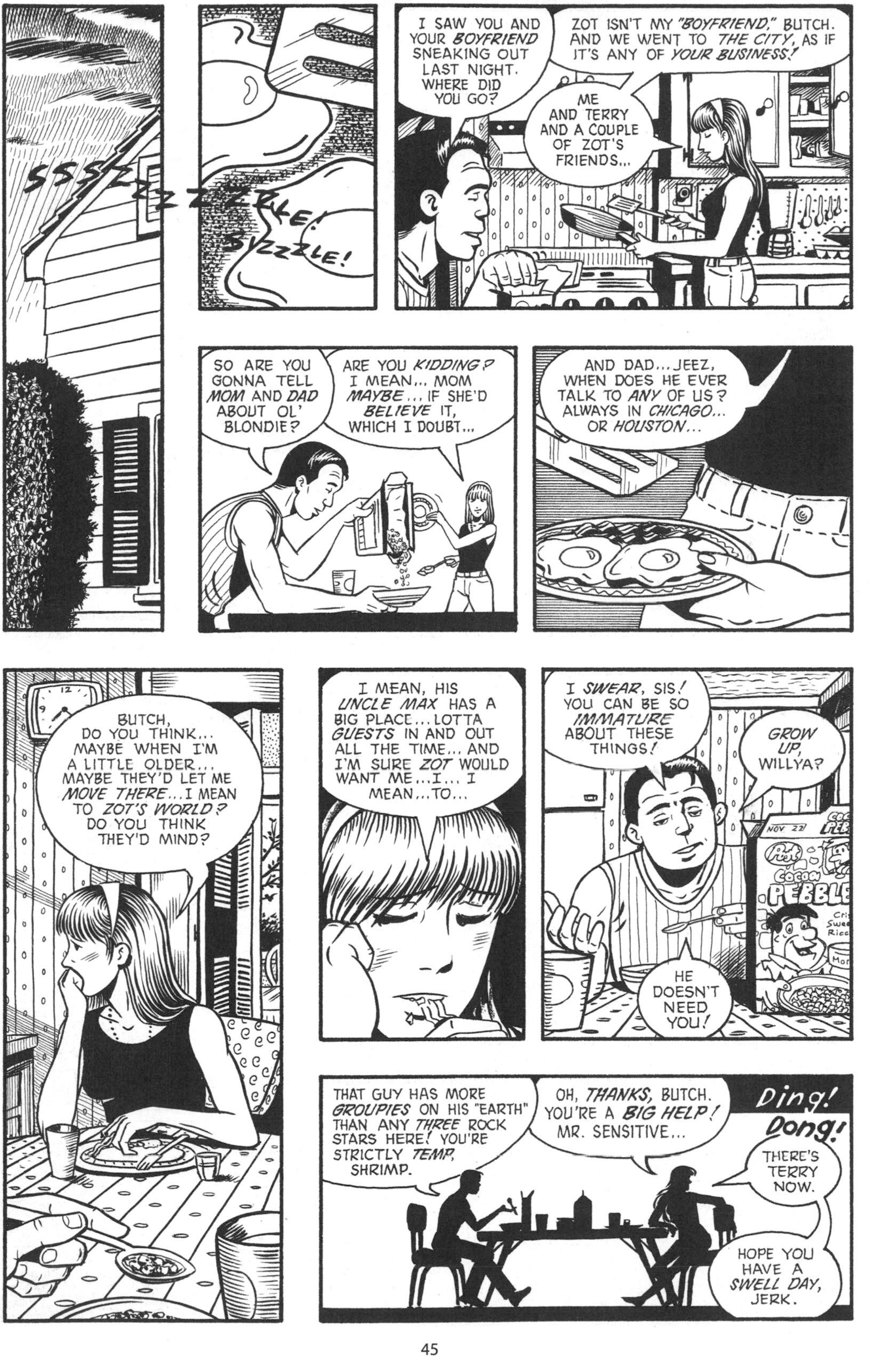
SSSZZZZZZZZLE!
SIZZZLE!
I SAW YOU AND YOUR BOYFRIEND SNEAKING OUT LAST NIGHT. WHERE DID YOU GO?
ZOT ISN'T MY "BOYFRIEND," BUTCH. AND WE WENT TO THE CITY, AS IF IT'S ANY OF YOUR BUSINESS!
ME AND TERRY AND A COUPLE OF ZOT'S FRIENDS...
SO ARE YOU GONNA TELL MOM AND DAD ABOUT OL' BLONDIE?
ARE YOU KIDDING? I MEAN... MOM MAYBE... IF SHE'D BELIEVE IT, WHICH I DOUBT...
AND DAD... JEEZ, WHEN DOES HE EVER TALK TO ANY OF US? ALWAYS IN CHICAGO... OR HOUSTON...
BUTCH, DO YOU THINK... MAYBE WHEN I'M A LITTLE OLDER... MAYBE THEY'D LET ME MOVE THERE... I MEAN TO ZOT'S WORLD? DO YOU THINK THEY'D MIND?
I MEAN, HIS UNCLE MAX HAS A BIG PLACE... LOTTA GUESTS IN AND OUT ALL THE TIME... AND I'M SURE ZOT WOULD WANT ME... I... I MEAN... TO...
I SWEAR, SIS! YOU CAN BE SO IMMATURE ABOUT THESE THINGS!
GROW UP, WILLYA?
HE DOESN'T NEED YOU!
NOV. 22
Post
COCOA PEBBLES
THAT GUY HAS MORE GROUPIES ON HIS "EARTH" THAN ANY THREE ROCK STARS HERE! YOU'RE STRICTLY TEMP, SHRIMP.
OH, THANKS, BUTCH. YOU'RE A BIG HELP! MR. SENSITIVE...
Ding! Dong!
THERE'S TERRY NOW.
HOPE YOU HAVE A SWELL DAY, JERK.

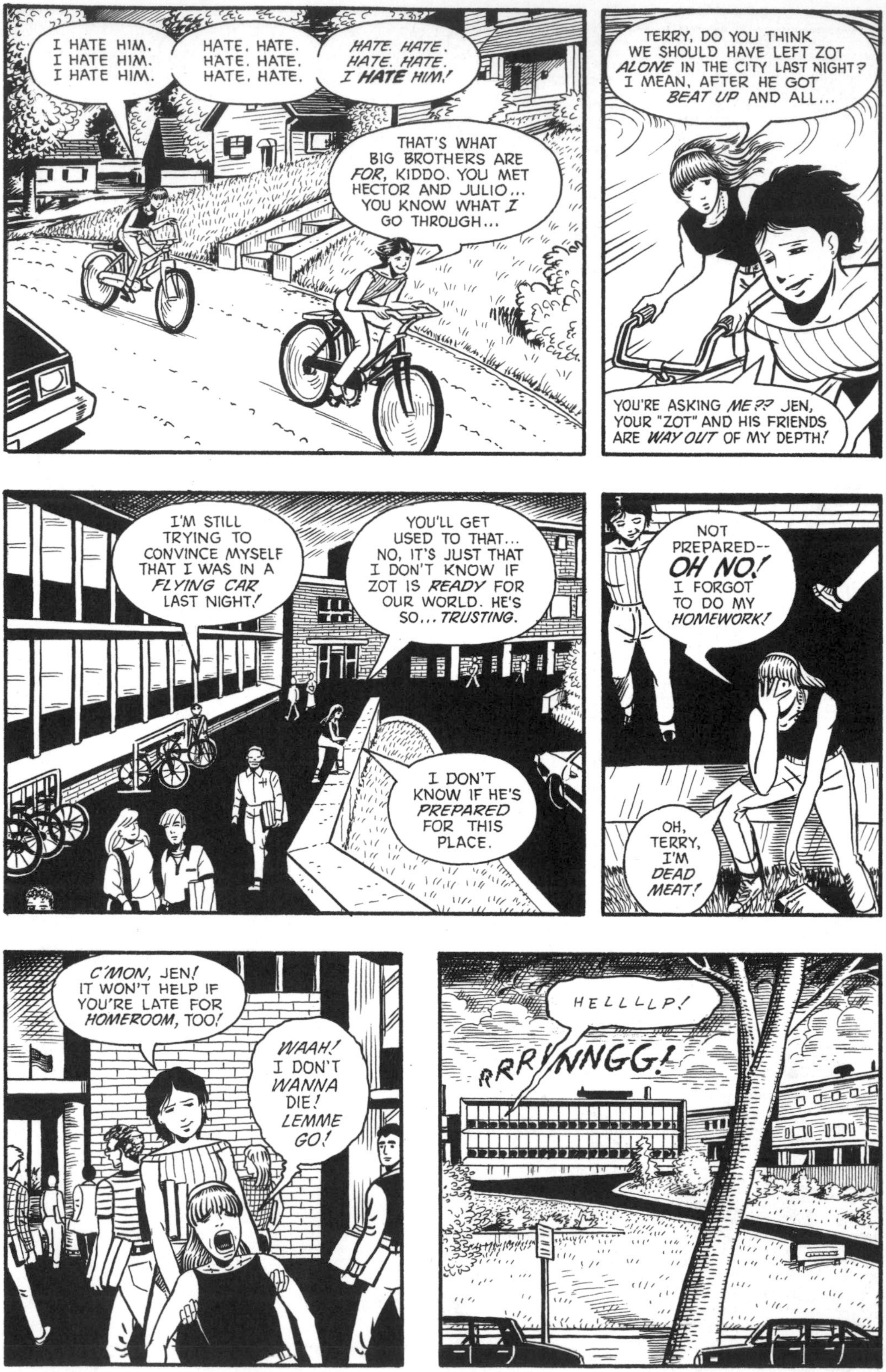
I HATE HIM. I HATE HIM. I HATE HIM.
HATE. HATE. HATE. HATE. HATE. HATE.
HATE. HATE. HATE. HATE. I HATE HIM!
THAT'S WHAT BIG BROTHERS ARE FOR, KIDDO. YOU MET HECTOR AND JULIO... YOU KNOW WHAT I GO THROUGH...
TERRY, DO YOU THINK WE SHOULD HAVE LEFT ZOT ALONE IN THE CITY LAST NIGHT? I MEAN, AFTER HE GOT BEAT UP AND ALL...
YOU'RE ASKING ME?? JEN, YOUR "ZOT" AND HIS FRIENDS ARE WAY OUT OF MY DEPTH!
I'M STILL TRYING TO CONVINCE MYSELF THAT I WAS IN A FLYING CAR LAST NIGHT!
YOU'LL GET USED TO THAT... NO, IT'S JUST THAT I DON'T KNOW IF ZOT IS READY FOR OUR WORLD. HE'S SO... TRUSTING.
I DON'T KNOW IF HE'S PREPARED FOR THIS PLACE.
NOT PREPARED-- OH NO! I FORGOT TO DO MY HOMEWORK!
OH, TERRY, I'M DEAD MEAT!
C'MON, JEN! IT WON'T HELP IF YOU'RE LATE FOR HOMEROOM, TOO!
WAAH! I DON'T WANNA DIE! LEMME GO!
HELLLLP!
RRRRINNGG!

I'M *TRAPPED*, ZOT.

CAN ANYONE TELL ME WHAT THE COEFFICIE... WOULD B... IF THE 47...

I'M THE ALIEN, NOT YOU. I'M THE ONE WHO DOESN'T BELONG...

...SEDIMENTARY DEPOSITS AREN'T *NEARLY* DEEP ENOUGH TO ACCOUNT F... EXTINCTION... THE CRE...

THEY DON'T TALK *MY* LANGUAGE, ZOT. THIS ISN'T *MY* WORLD...

I USED TO THINK I *UNDERSTOOD* THIS PLACE. THEN I MET *YOU*... SAW *YOUR* EARTH...

HOME USED TO MAKE *SENSE* TO ME, ZOT...

NOW, *YOU'RE* THE ONLY THING IN LIFE THAT MAKES SENSE...

$\frac{x}{q} = 37$

$x \div 5y =$

usage grammar

1. Igne...
2. Meta...
3. Sed...

RING!

TERRY, WE *MADE* IT! THEY DIDN'T KILL ME, AFTER ALL.

EITHER THAT OR THEY WERE *SAVING* YOU FOR A FATE *WORSE* THAN DEATH. LOOK WHO'S COME TO *GREET* US.

Oh, *HI, GIRLS!* Uh...

-: Whoops! :-

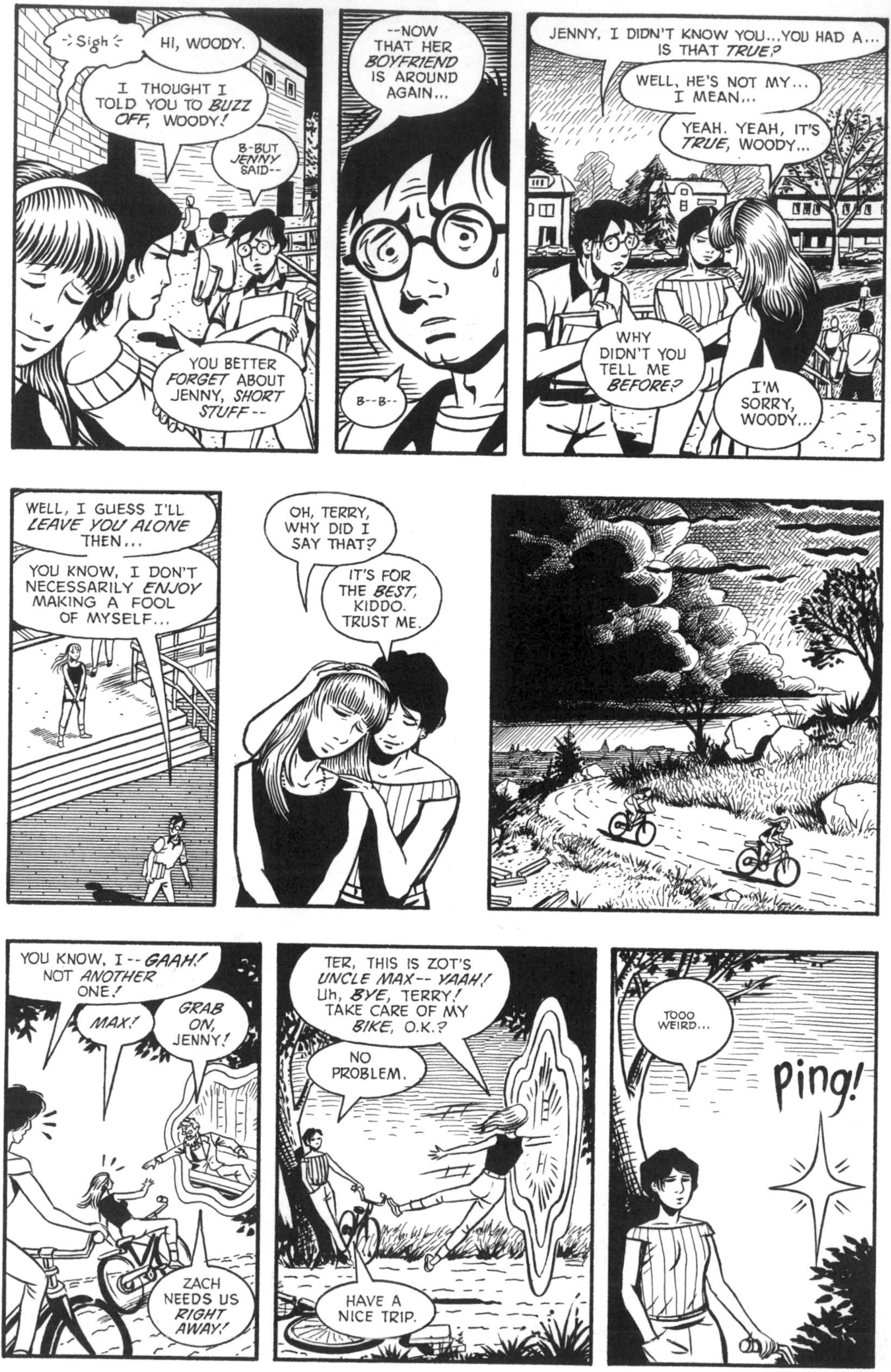
Sigh
HI, WOODY.
I THOUGHT I TOLD YOU TO *BUZZ OFF*, WOODY!
B-BUT *JENNY* SAID--
YOU BETTER *FORGET* ABOUT JENNY, *SHORT STUFF* --
--NOW THAT HER *BOYFRIEND* IS AROUND AGAIN...
B--B--
JENNY, I DIDN'T KNOW YOU...YOU HAD A... IS THAT *TRUE?*
WELL, HE'S NOT MY... I MEAN...
YEAH. YEAH, IT'S *TRUE*, WOODY...
WHY DIDN'T YOU TELL ME *BEFORE?*
I'M SORRY, WOODY...
WELL, I GUESS I'LL *LEAVE YOU ALONE* THEN...
YOU KNOW, I DON'T NECESSARILY *ENJOY* MAKING A FOOL OF MYSELF...
OH, TERRY, WHY DID I SAY THAT?
IT'S FOR THE *BEST*, KIDDO. TRUST ME.
YOU KNOW, I-- *GAAH!* NOT *ANOTHER* ONE!
MAX!
GRAB ON, JENNY!
ZACH NEEDS US *RIGHT AWAY!*
TER, THIS IS ZOT'S *UNCLE MAX-- YAAH!* Uh, *BYE*, TERRY! TAKE CARE OF MY *BIKE*, O.K.?
NO PROBLEM.
HAVE A NICE TRIP.
TOOO WEIRD...
Ping!

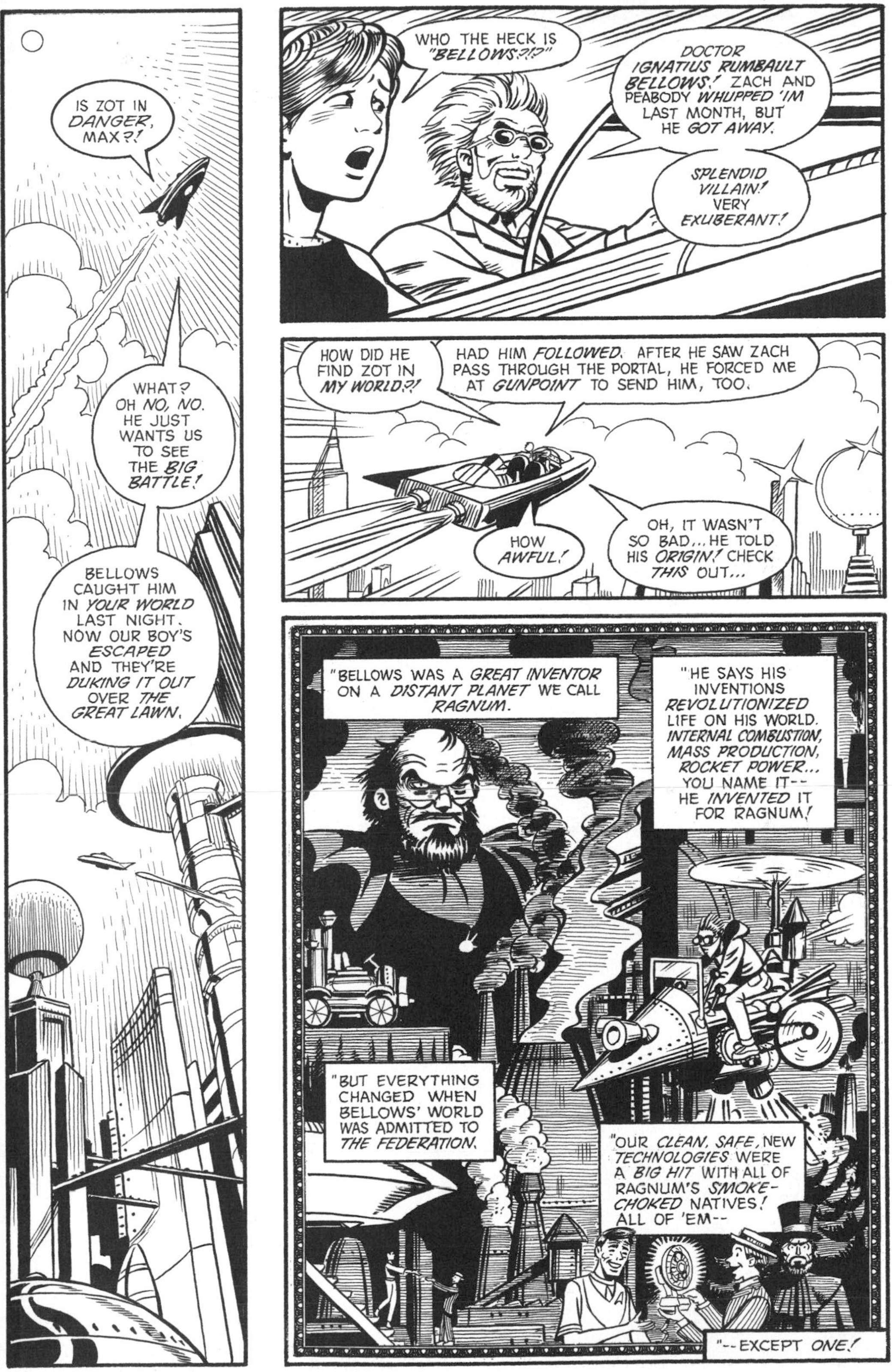
IS ZOT IN DANGER, MAX?!
WHAT? OH NO, NO. HE JUST WANTS US TO SEE THE BIG BATTLE!
BELLOWS CAUGHT HIM IN YOUR WORLD LAST NIGHT. NOW OUR BOY'S ESCAPED AND THEY'RE DUKING IT OUT OVER THE GREAT LAWN.
WHO THE HECK IS "BELLOWS?!?"
DOCTOR IGNATIUS RUMBAULT BELLOWS! ZACH AND PEABODY WHUPPED 'IM LAST MONTH, BUT HE GOT AWAY.
SPLENDID VILLAIN! VERY EXUBERANT!
HOW DID HE FIND ZOT IN MY WORLD?!
HAD HIM FOLLOWED. AFTER HE SAW ZACH PASS THROUGH THE PORTAL, HE FORCED ME AT GUNPOINT TO SEND HIM, TOO.
HOW AWFUL!
OH, IT WASN'T SO BAD... HE TOLD HIS ORIGIN! CHECK THIS OUT...
"BELLOWS WAS A GREAT INVENTOR ON A DISTANT PLANET WE CALL RAGNUM.
"HE SAYS HIS INVENTIONS REVOLUTIONIZED LIFE ON HIS WORLD. INTERNAL COMBUSTION, MASS PRODUCTION, ROCKET POWER... YOU NAME IT-- HE INVENTED IT FOR RAGNUM!
"BUT EVERYTHING CHANGED WHEN BELLOWS' WORLD WAS ADMITTED TO THE FEDERATION.
"OUR CLEAN, SAFE, NEW TECHNOLOGIES WERE A BIG HIT WITH ALL OF RAGNUM'S SMOKE-CHOKED NATIVES! ALL OF 'EM--
"--EXCEPT ONE!

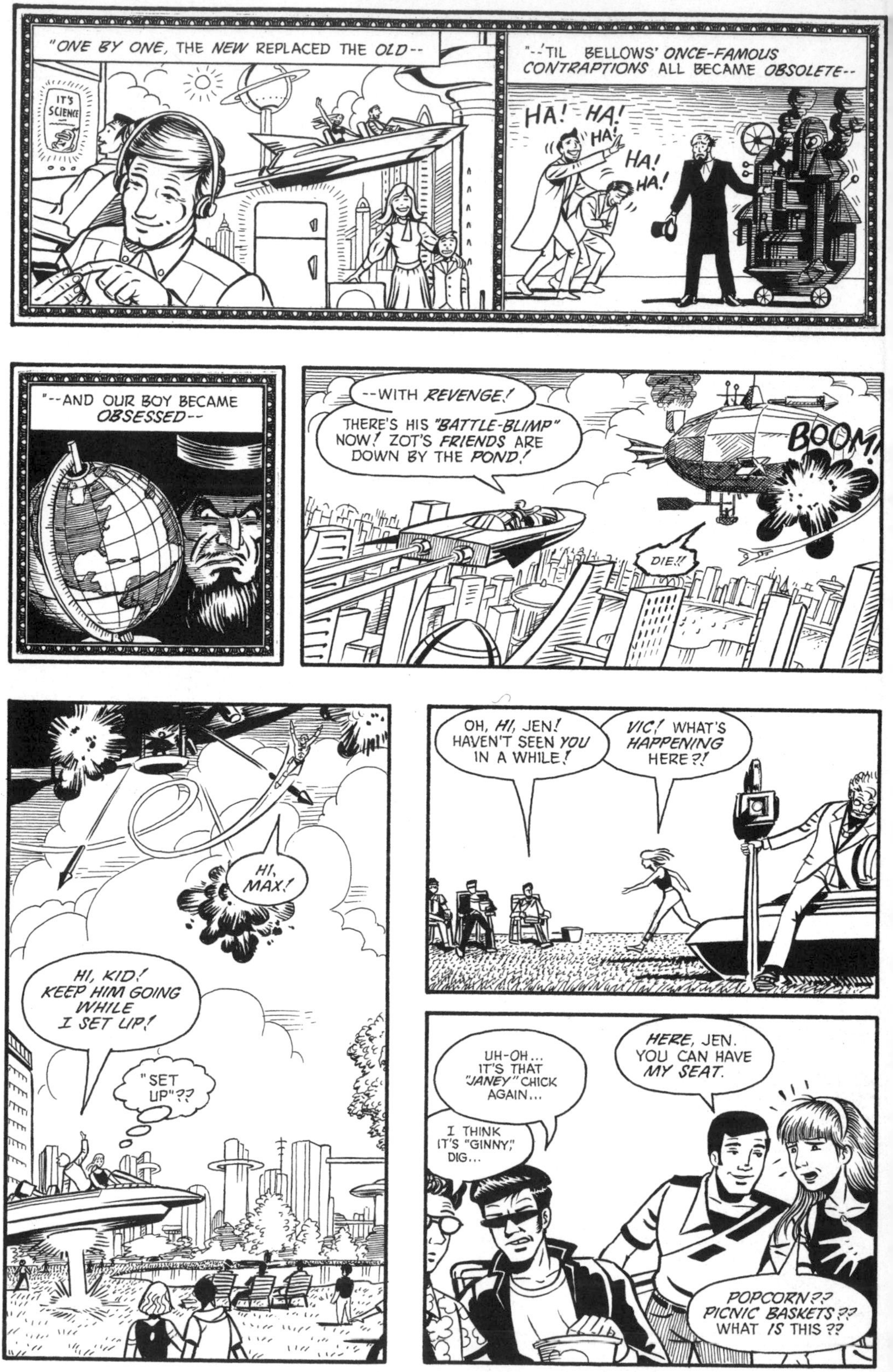
"ONE BY ONE, THE NEW REPLACED THE OLD--
IT'S SCIENCE
"--'TIL BELLOWS' ONCE-FAMOUS CONTRAPTIONS ALL BECAME OBSOLETE--
HA! HA! HA! HA! HA!
"--AND OUR BOY BECAME OBSESSED--
--WITH REVENGE!
THERE'S HIS "BATTLE-BLIMP" NOW! ZOT'S FRIENDS ARE DOWN BY THE POND!
BOOM!
DIE!!
HI, MAX!
HI, KID! KEEP HIM GOING WHILE I SET UP!
"SET UP"??
OH, HI, JEN! HAVEN'T SEEN YOU IN A WHILE!
VIC! WHAT'S HAPPENING HERE?!
UH-OH... IT'S THAT "JANEY" CHICK AGAIN...
HERE, JEN. YOU CAN HAVE MY SEAT.
I THINK IT'S "GINNY," DIG...
POPCORN?? PICNIC BASKETS?? WHAT IS THIS??

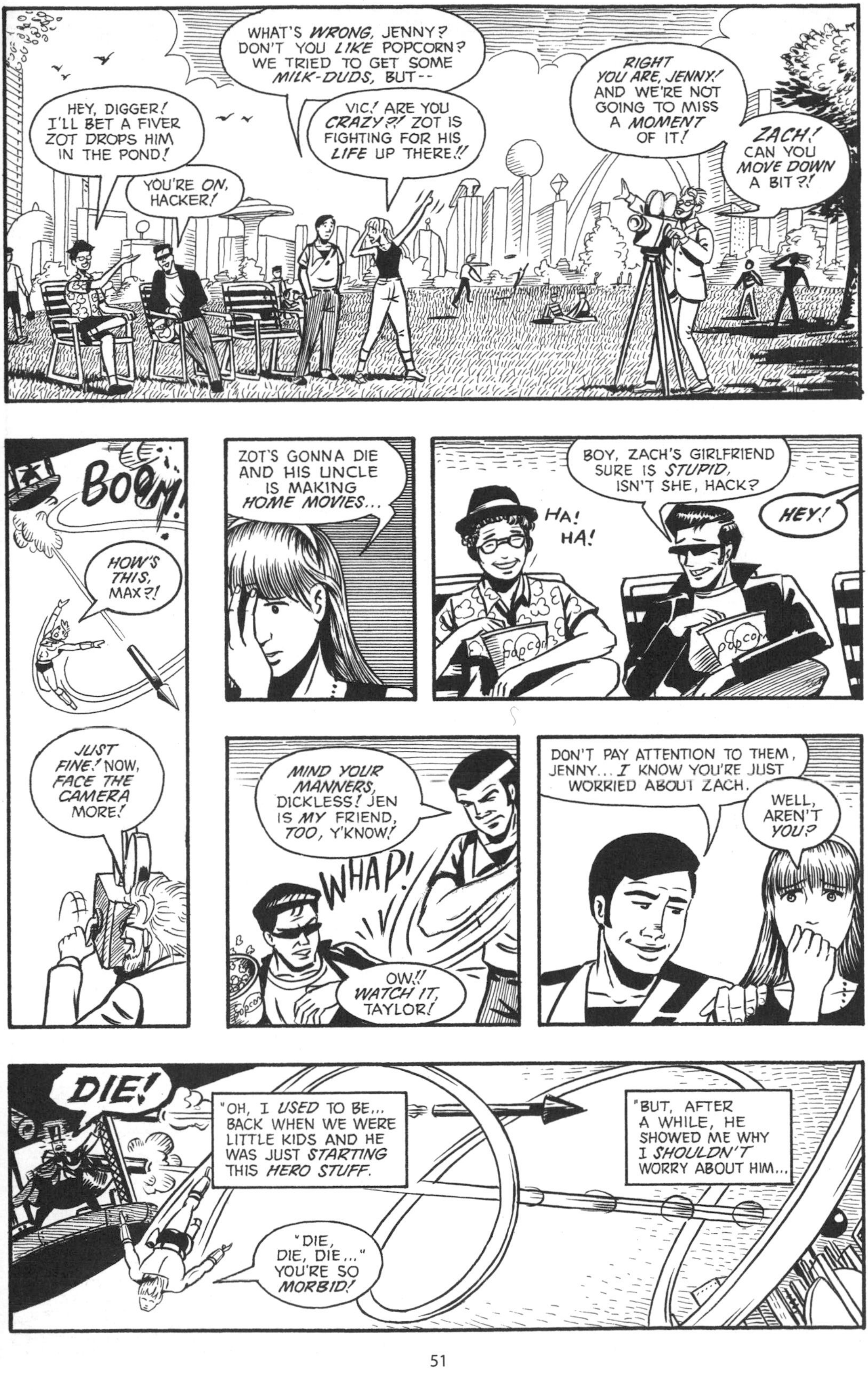
HEY, DIGGER! I'LL BET A FIVER ZOT DROPS HIM IN THE POND!
YOU'RE ON, HACKER!
WHAT'S WRONG, JENNY? DON'T YOU LIKE POPCORN? WE TRIED TO GET SOME MILK-DUDS, BUT--
VIC! ARE YOU CRAZY?! ZOT IS FIGHTING FOR HIS LIFE UP THERE!!
RIGHT YOU ARE, JENNY! AND WE'RE NOT GOING TO MISS A MOMENT OF IT!
ZACH! CAN YOU MOVE DOWN A BIT?!
BOOM!
HOW'S THIS, MAX?!
JUST FINE! NOW, FACE THE CAMERA MORE!
ZOT'S GONNA DIE AND HIS UNCLE IS MAKING HOME MOVIES...
BOY, ZACH'S GIRLFRIEND SURE IS STUPID, ISN'T SHE, HACK?
HA! HA!
HEY!
popcorn
popcorn
MIND YOUR MANNERS, DICKLESS! JEN IS MY FRIEND, TOO, Y'KNOW!
WHAP!
OW!! WATCH IT, TAYLOR!
DON'T PAY ATTENTION TO THEM, JENNY... I KNOW YOU'RE JUST WORRIED ABOUT ZACH.
WELL, AREN'T YOU?
DIE!
"OH, I USED TO BE... BACK WHEN WE WERE LITTLE KIDS AND HE WAS JUST STARTING THIS HERO STUFF.
"BUT, AFTER A WHILE, HE SHOWED ME WHY I SHOULDN'T WORRY ABOUT HIM...
"DIE, DIE, DIE..." YOU'RE SO MORBID!

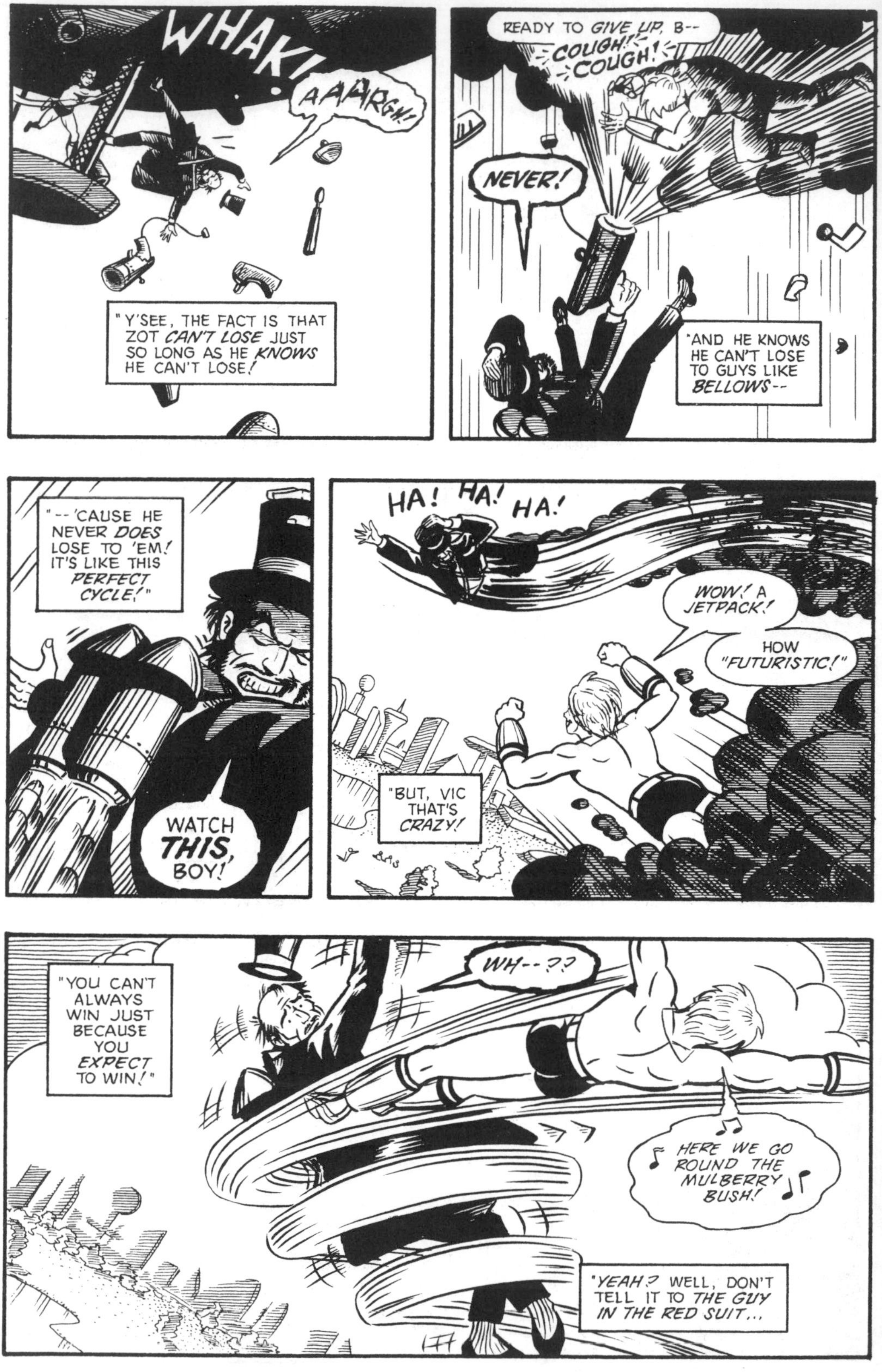
WHAK!
AAARGH!
"Y'SEE, THE FACT IS THAT ZOT *CAN'T LOSE* JUST SO LONG AS HE *KNOWS* HE CAN'T LOSE!
READY TO *GIVE UP*, B--
COUGH! COUGH!
NEVER!
"AND HE KNOWS HE CAN'T LOSE TO GUYS LIKE *BELLOWS*--
"--'CAUSE HE NEVER *DOES* LOSE TO 'EM! IT'S LIKE THIS *PERFECT CYCLE!*"
WATCH **THIS**, BOY!
HA! HA! HA!
WOW! A JETPACK!
HOW "FUTURISTIC!"
"BUT, VIC THAT'S *CRAZY!*
"YOU CAN'T ALWAYS WIN JUST BECAUSE YOU *EXPECT* TO WIN!"
WH--??
HERE WE GO ROUND THE MULBERRY BUSH!
"*YEAH?* WELL, DON'T TELL IT TO *THE GUY IN THE RED SUIT...*

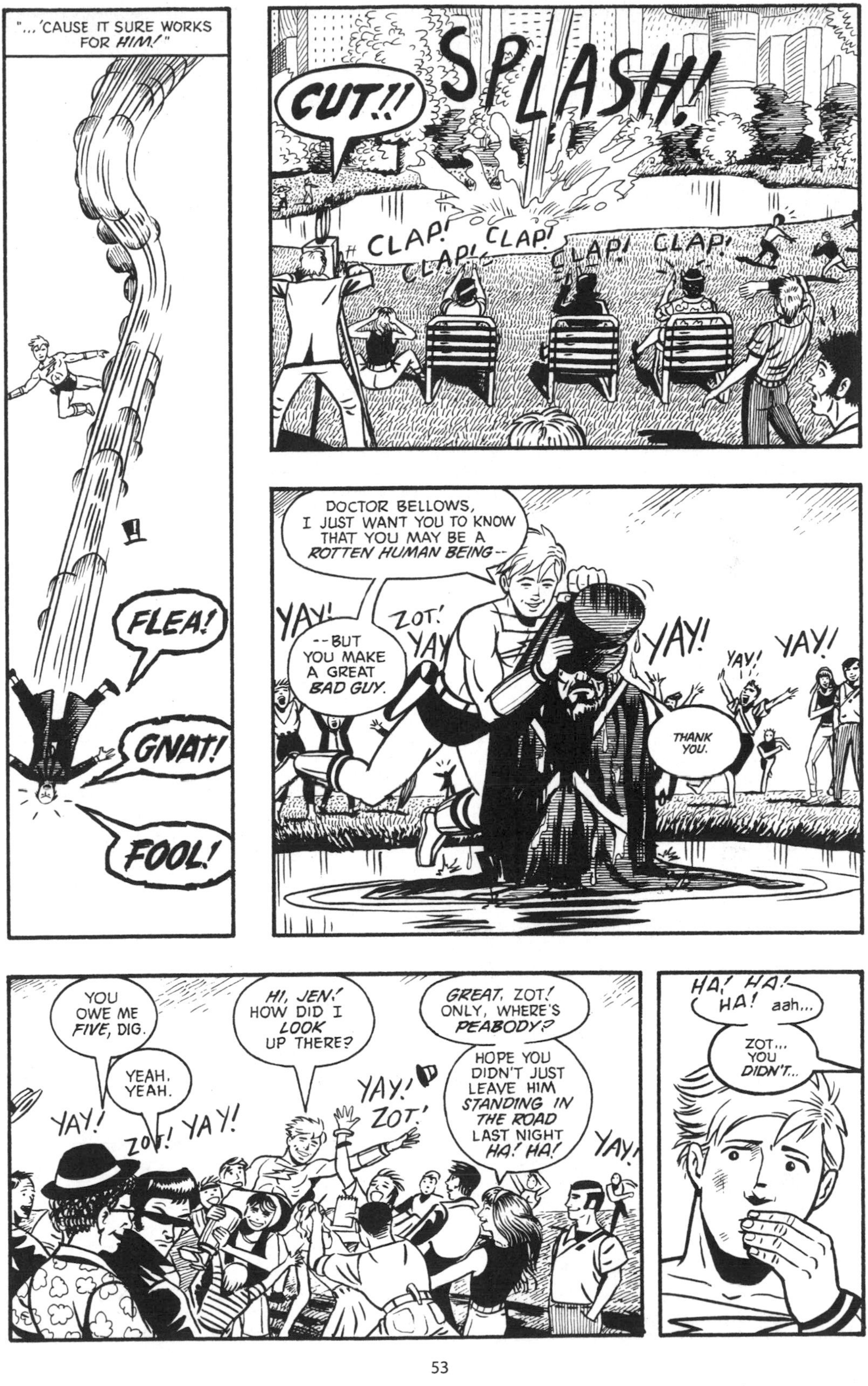
"...'CAUSE IT SURE WORKS FOR HIM!'"
FLEA!
GNAT!
FOOL!
CUT!!
SPLASH!
CLAP! CLAP! CLAP! CLAP! CLAP!
DOCTOR BELLOWS, I JUST WANT YOU TO KNOW THAT YOU MAY BE A ROTTEN HUMAN BEING--
YAY!
--BUT YOU MAKE A GREAT BAD GUY.
ZOT! YAY
YAY!
YAY!
YAY!
THANK YOU.
YOU OWE ME FIVE, DIG.
YEAH, YEAH.
YAY!
ZOT! YAY!
HI, JEN! HOW DID I LOOK UP THERE?
YAY! ZOT!
GREAT, ZOT! ONLY, WHERE'S PEABODY?
HOPE YOU DIDN'T JUST LEAVE HIM STANDING IN THE ROAD LAST NIGHT HA! HA!
YAY!
HA! HA! HA! aah...
ZOT... YOU DIDN'T...

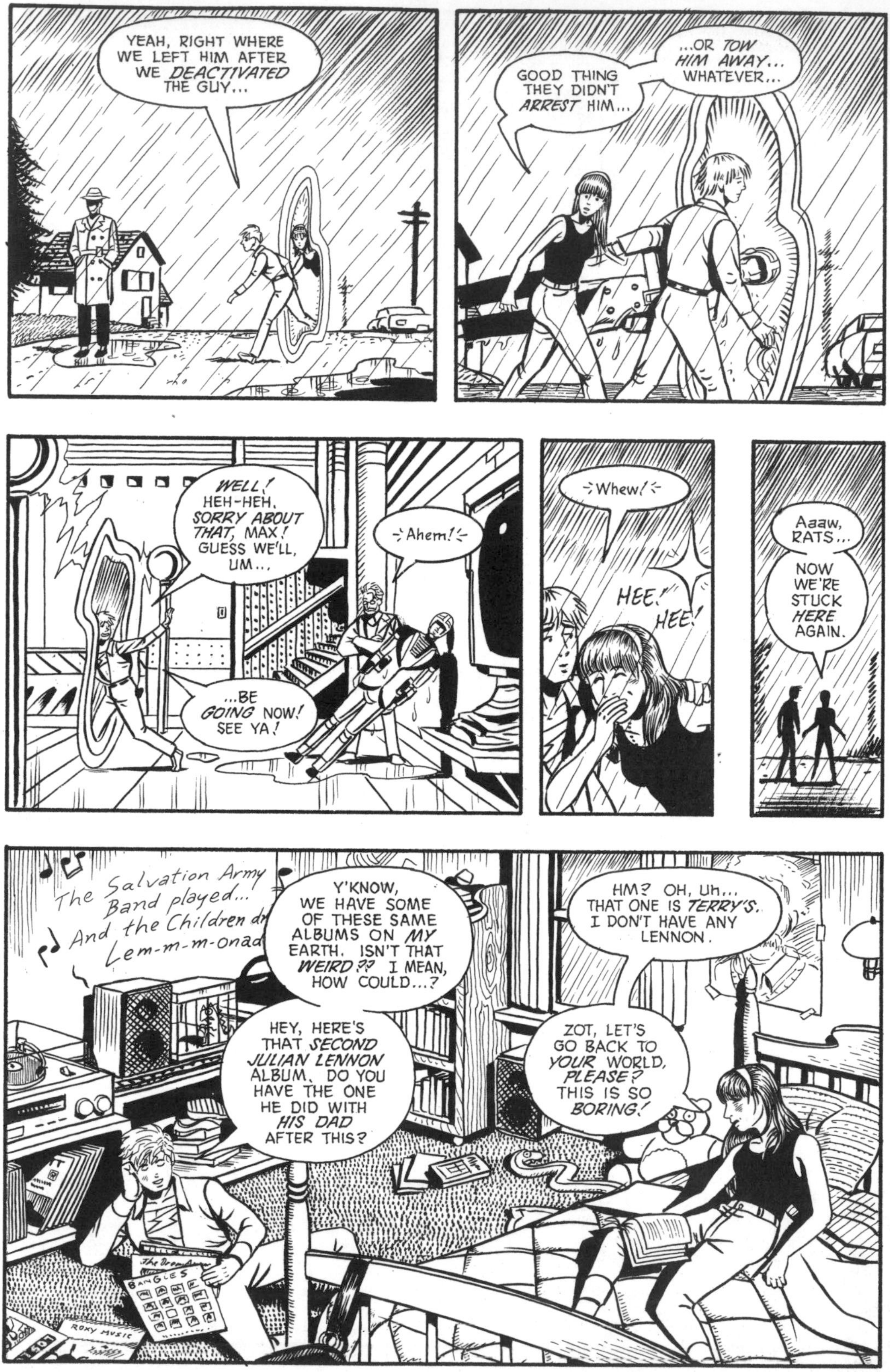

YEAH, RIGHT WHERE WE LEFT HIM AFTER WE *DEACTIVATED* THE GUY...
GOOD THING THEY DIDN'T *ARREST* HIM...
...OR *TOW HIM AWAY*... WHATEVER...
WELL! HEH-HEH. *SORRY ABOUT THAT,* MAX! GUESS WE'LL, UM...
...BE *GOING* NOW! SEE YA!
Ahem!
Whew!
HEE! HEE!
Aaaw, RATS...
NOW WE'RE STUCK *HERE* AGAIN.
The Salvation Army Band played... And the Children dr Lem-m-m-onad
Y'KNOW, WE HAVE SOME OF THESE SAME ALBUMS ON *MY* EARTH. ISN'T THAT *WEIRD??* I MEAN, HOW COULD...?
HM? OH, Uh... THAT ONE IS *TERRY'S.* I DON'T HAVE ANY LENNON.
HEY, HERE'S THAT *SECOND JULIAN LENNON* ALBUM. DO YOU HAVE THE ONE HE DID WITH *HIS DAD* AFTER THIS?
ZOT, LET'S GO BACK TO *YOUR* WORLD, *PLEASE?* THIS IS SO *BORING!*
BANGLES
ROXY MUSIC

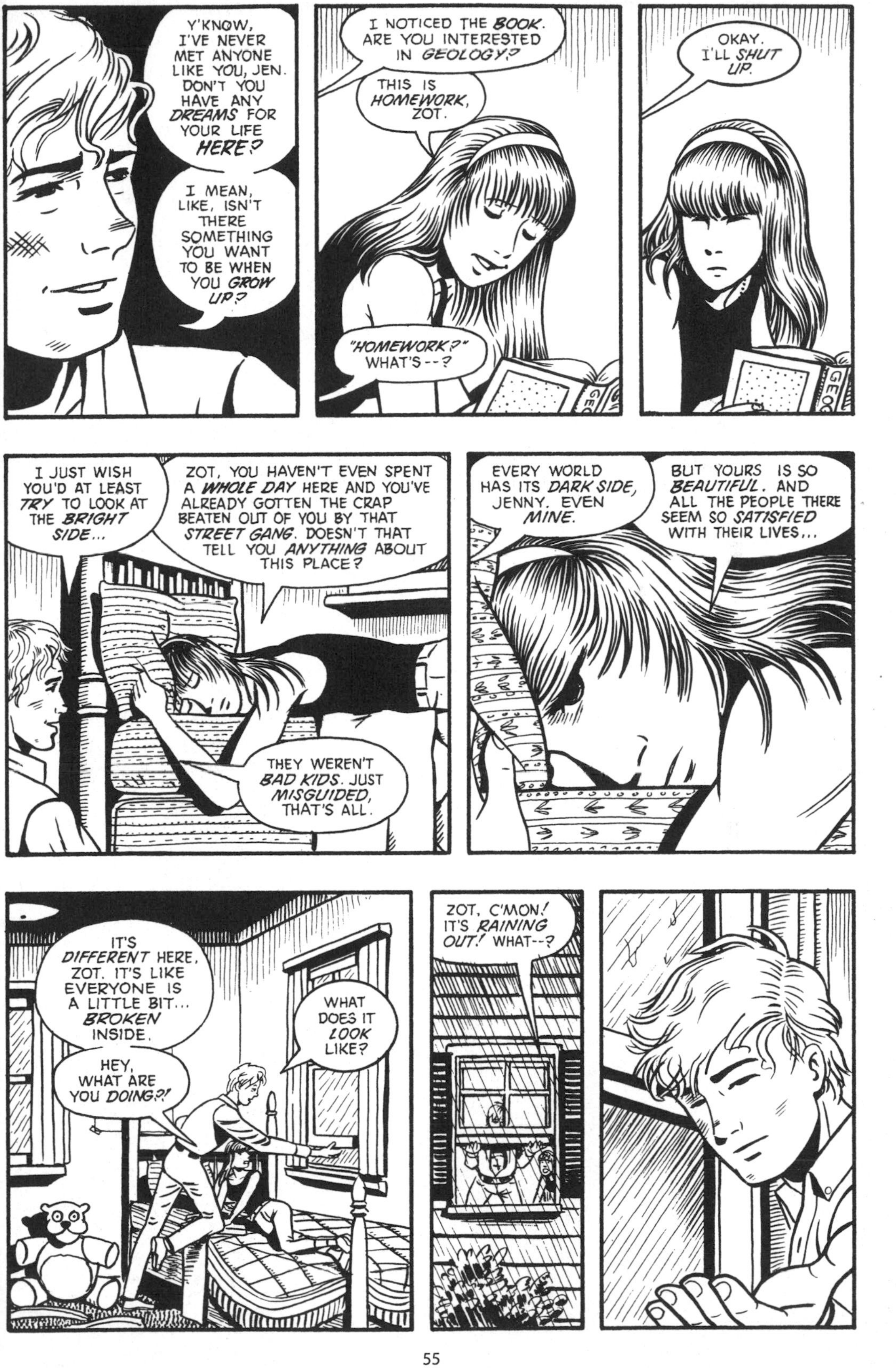
Y'KNOW, I'VE NEVER MET ANYONE LIKE YOU, JEN. DON'T YOU HAVE ANY DREAMS FOR YOUR LIFE HERE?
I MEAN, LIKE, ISN'T THERE SOMETHING YOU WANT TO BE WHEN YOU GROW UP?
I NOTICED THE BOOK. ARE YOU INTERESTED IN GEOLOGY?
THIS IS HOMEWORK, ZOT.
"HOMEWORK?" WHAT'S--?
OKAY. I'LL SHUT UP.
I JUST WISH YOU'D AT LEAST TRY TO LOOK AT THE BRIGHT SIDE...
ZOT, YOU HAVEN'T EVEN SPENT A WHOLE DAY HERE AND YOU'VE ALREADY GOTTEN THE CRAP BEATEN OUT OF YOU BY THAT STREET GANG. DOESN'T THAT TELL YOU ANYTHING ABOUT THIS PLACE?
THEY WEREN'T BAD KIDS. JUST MISGUIDED, THAT'S ALL.
EVERY WORLD HAS ITS DARK SIDE, JENNY. EVEN MINE.
BUT YOURS IS SO BEAUTIFUL. AND ALL THE PEOPLE THERE SEEM SO SATISFIED WITH THEIR LIVES...
IT'S DIFFERENT HERE, ZOT. IT'S LIKE EVERYONE IS A LITTLE BIT... BROKEN INSIDE.
HEY, WHAT ARE YOU DOING?!
WHAT DOES IT LOOK LIKE?
ZOT, C'MON! IT'S RAINING OUT! WHAT--?

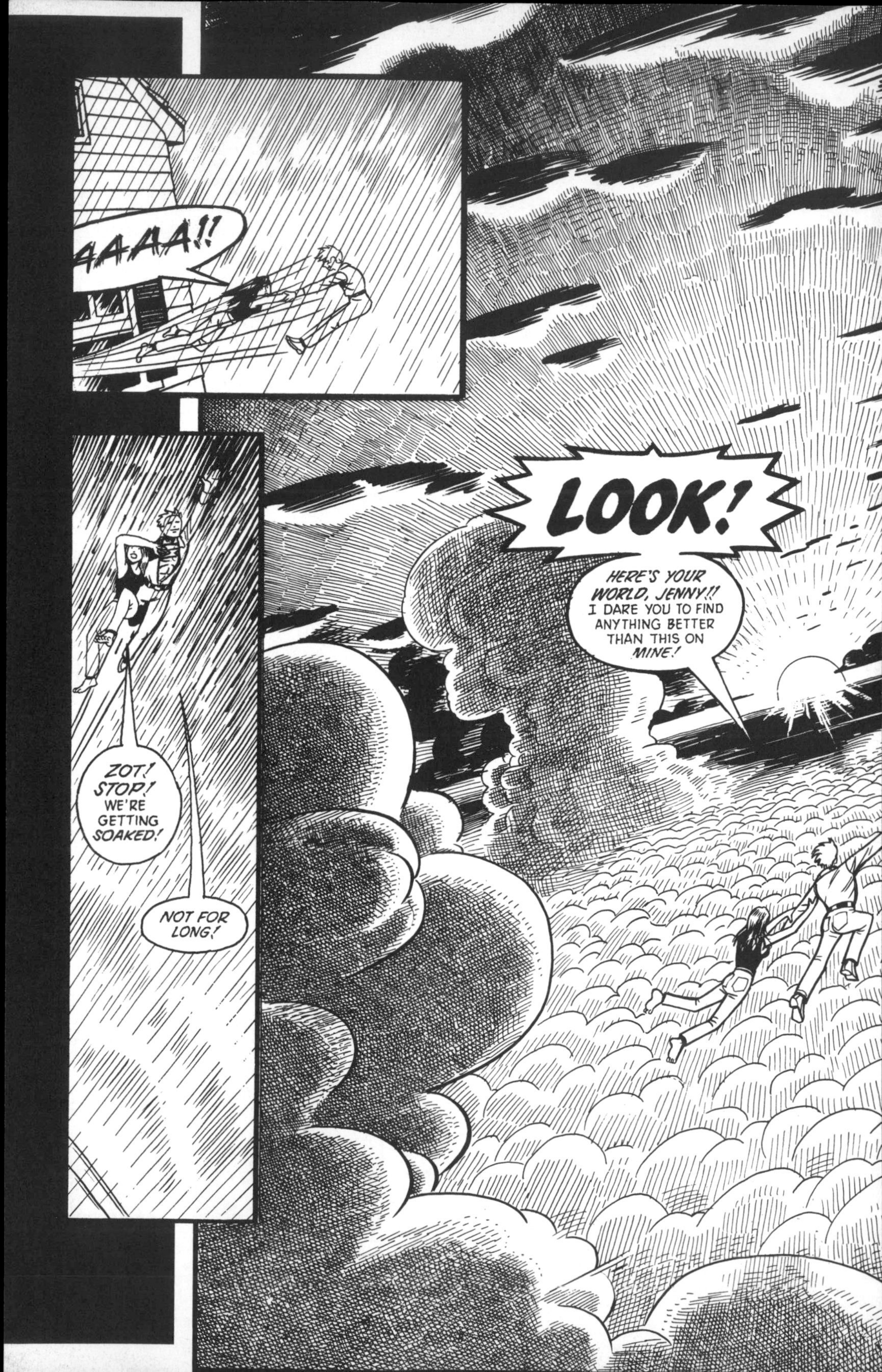
AAAA!!
ZOT! STOP! WE'RE GETTING SOAKED!
NOT FOR LONG!
LOOK!
HERE'S YOUR WORLD, JENNY!! I DARE YOU TO FIND ANYTHING BETTER THAN THIS ON MINE!

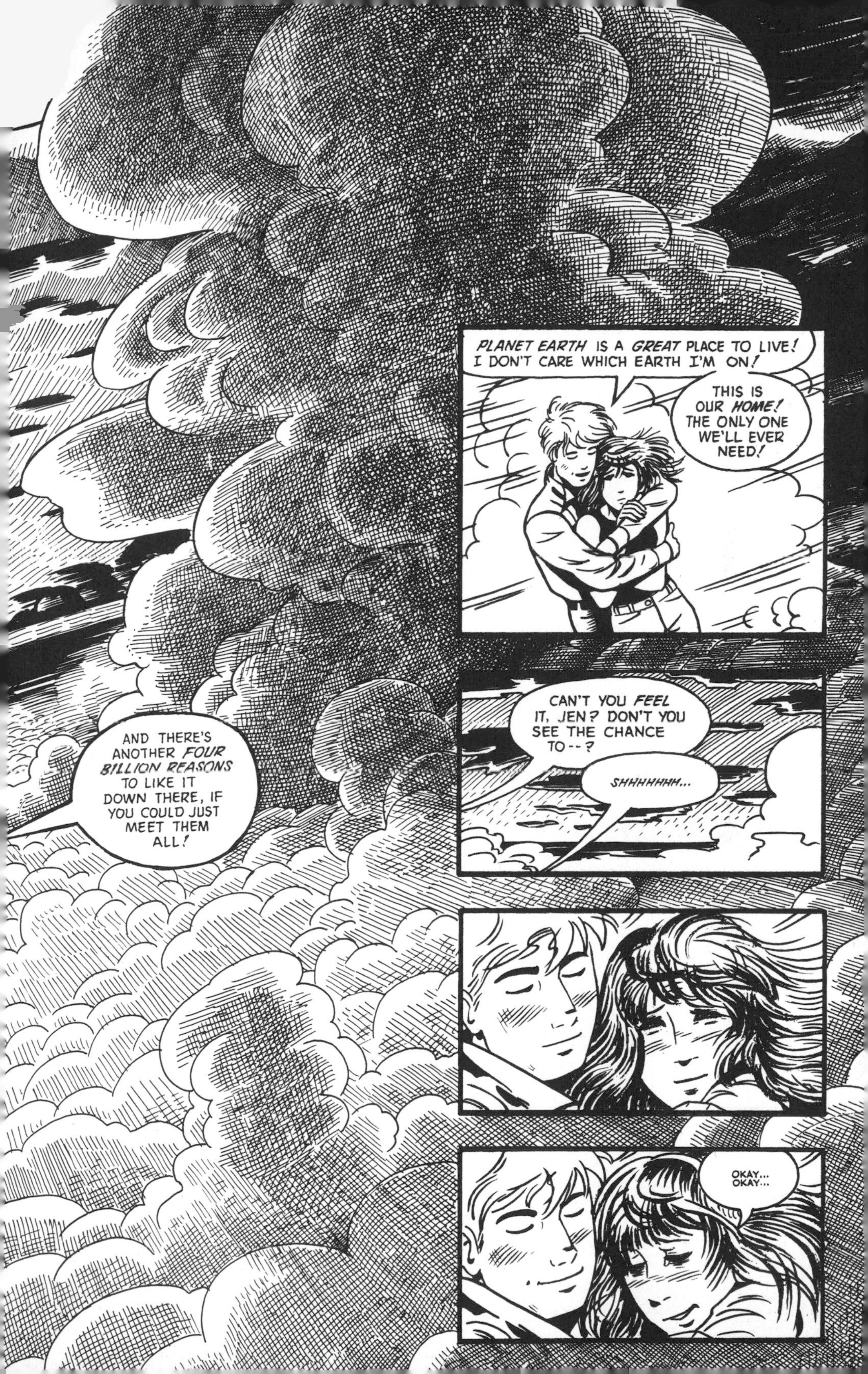
PLANET EARTH IS A GREAT PLACE TO LIVE! I DON'T CARE WHICH EARTH I'M ON!
THIS IS OUR HOME! THE ONLY ONE WE'LL EVER NEED!
AND THERE'S ANOTHER FOUR BILLION REASONS TO LIKE IT DOWN THERE, IF YOU COULD JUST MEET THEM ALL!
CAN'T YOU FEEL IT, JEN? DON'T YOU SEE THE CHANCE TO--?
SHHHHHHH...
OKAY... OKAY...

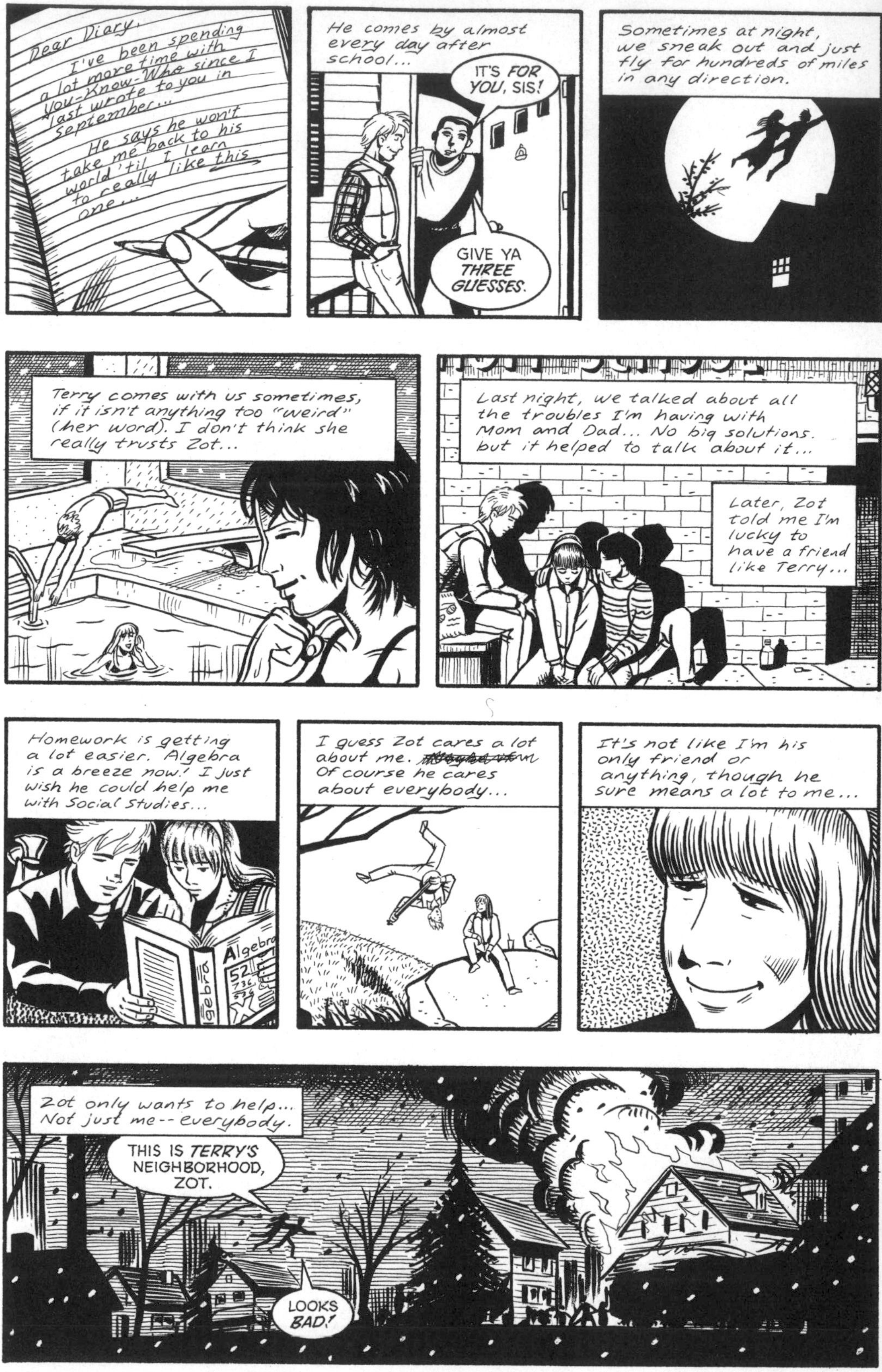
Dear Diary,
I've been spending a lot more time with You-Know-Who since I last wrote to you in September...
He says he won't take me back to his world 'til I learn to really like this one...
He comes by almost every day after school...
IT'S FOR YOU, SIS!
GIVE YA THREE GUESSES.
Sometimes at night, we sneak out and just fly for hundreds of miles in any direction.
Terry comes with us sometimes, if it isn't anything too "weird" (her word). I don't think she really trusts Zot...
Last night, we talked about all the troubles I'm having with Mom and Dad... No big solutions. but it helped to talk about it...
Later, Zot told me I'm lucky to have a friend like Terry...
Homework is getting a lot easier. Algebra is a breeze now! I just wish he could help me with Social Studies...
Algebra
I guess Zot cares a lot about me. Of course he cares about everybody...
It's not like I'm his only friend or anything, though he sure means a lot to me...
Zot only wants to help... Not just me--everybody.
THIS IS TERRY'S NEIGHBORHOOD, ZOT.
LOOKS BAD!

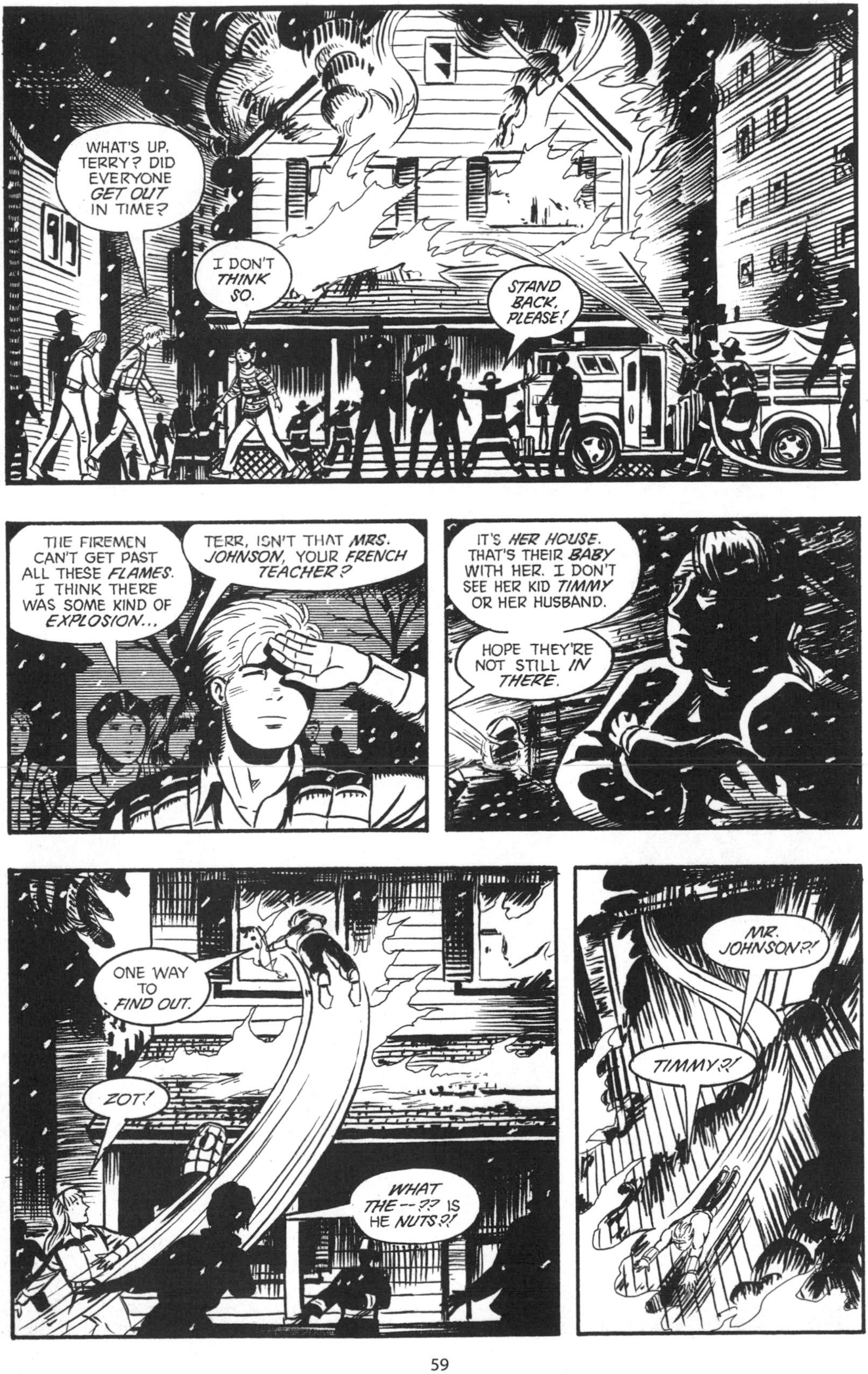
WHAT'S UP, TERRY? DID EVERYONE GET OUT IN TIME?
I DON'T THINK SO.
STAND BACK, PLEASE!
THE FIREMEN CAN'T GET PAST ALL THESE FLAMES. I THINK THERE WAS SOME KIND OF EXPLOSION...
TERR, ISN'T THAT MRS. JOHNSON, YOUR FRENCH TEACHER?
IT'S HER HOUSE. THAT'S THEIR BABY WITH HER. I DON'T SEE HER KID TIMMY OR HER HUSBAND.
HOPE THEY'RE NOT STILL IN THERE.
ONE WAY TO FIND OUT.
ZOT!
WHAT THE--?? IS HE NUTS?!
MR. JOHNSON?!
TIMMY?!

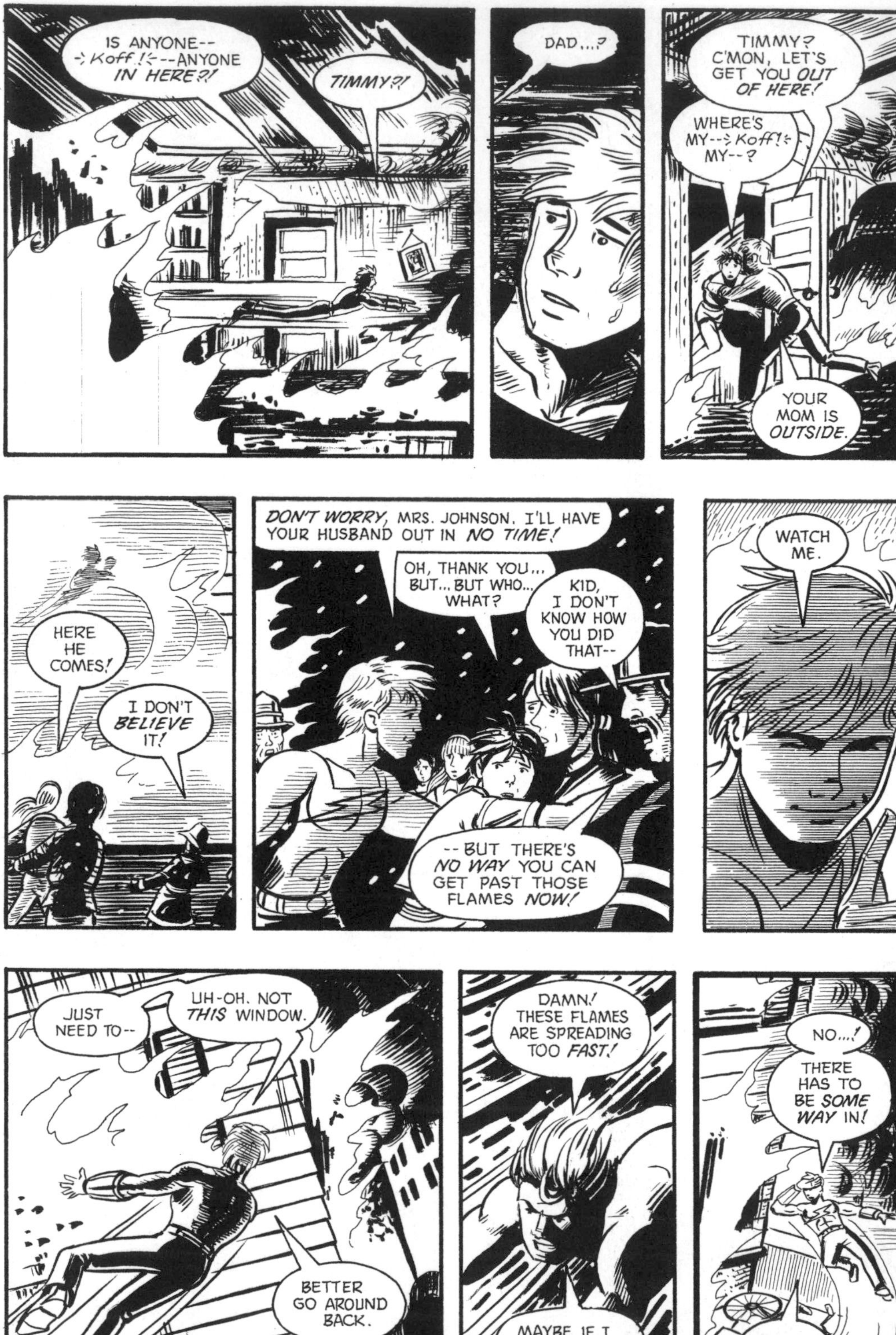
IS ANYONE-- ⸮Koff!⸮ --ANYONE IN HERE?!
TIMMY?!
DAD...?
TIMMY? C'MON, LET'S GET YOU OUT OF HERE!
WHERE'S MY-- Koff! MY--?
YOUR MOM IS OUTSIDE.
HERE HE COMES!
I DON'T BELIEVE IT!
DON'T WORRY, MRS. JOHNSON. I'LL HAVE YOUR HUSBAND OUT IN NO TIME!
OH, THANK YOU... BUT... BUT WHO... WHAT?
KID, I DON'T KNOW HOW YOU DID THAT--
--BUT THERE'S NO WAY YOU CAN GET PAST THOSE FLAMES NOW!
WATCH ME.
JUST NEED TO--
UH-OH. NOT THIS WINDOW.
BETTER GO AROUND BACK.
DAMN! THESE FLAMES ARE SPREADING TOO FAST!
MAYBE IF I TRY THE BASEMENT, I--
NO...!
THERE HAS TO BE SOME WAY IN!
THERE HAS TO BE!

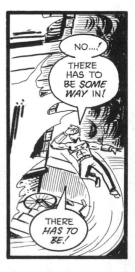

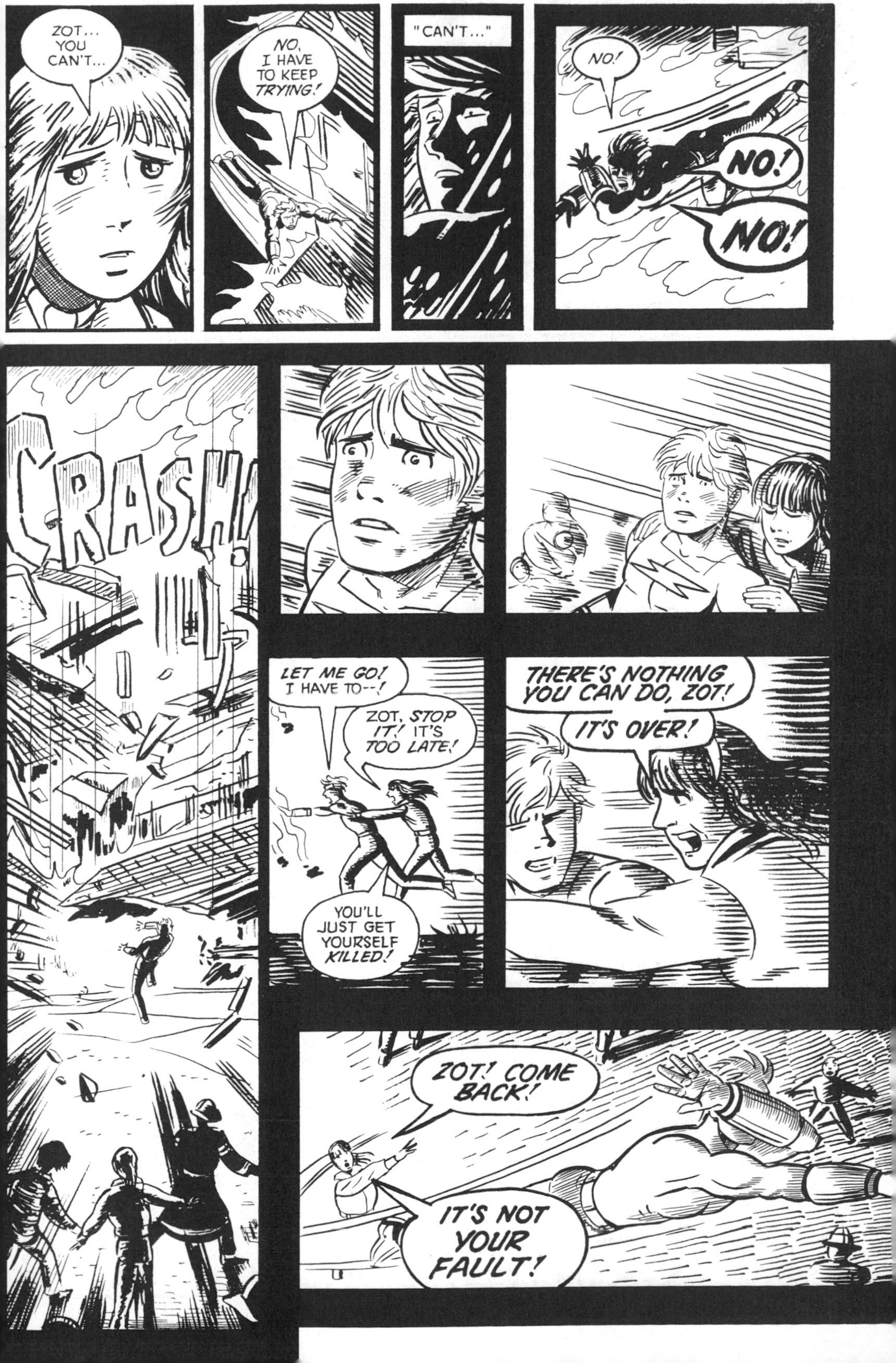
ZOT... YOU CAN'T...
NO, I HAVE TO KEEP TRYING!
"CAN'T..."
NO!
NO!
NO!
CRASH!
LET ME GO! I HAVE TO--!
ZOT, STOP IT! IT'S TOO LATE!
YOU'LL JUST GET YOURSELF KILLED!
THERE'S NOTHING YOU CAN DO, ZOT!
IT'S OVER!
ZOT! COME BACK!
IT'S NOT YOUR FAULT!

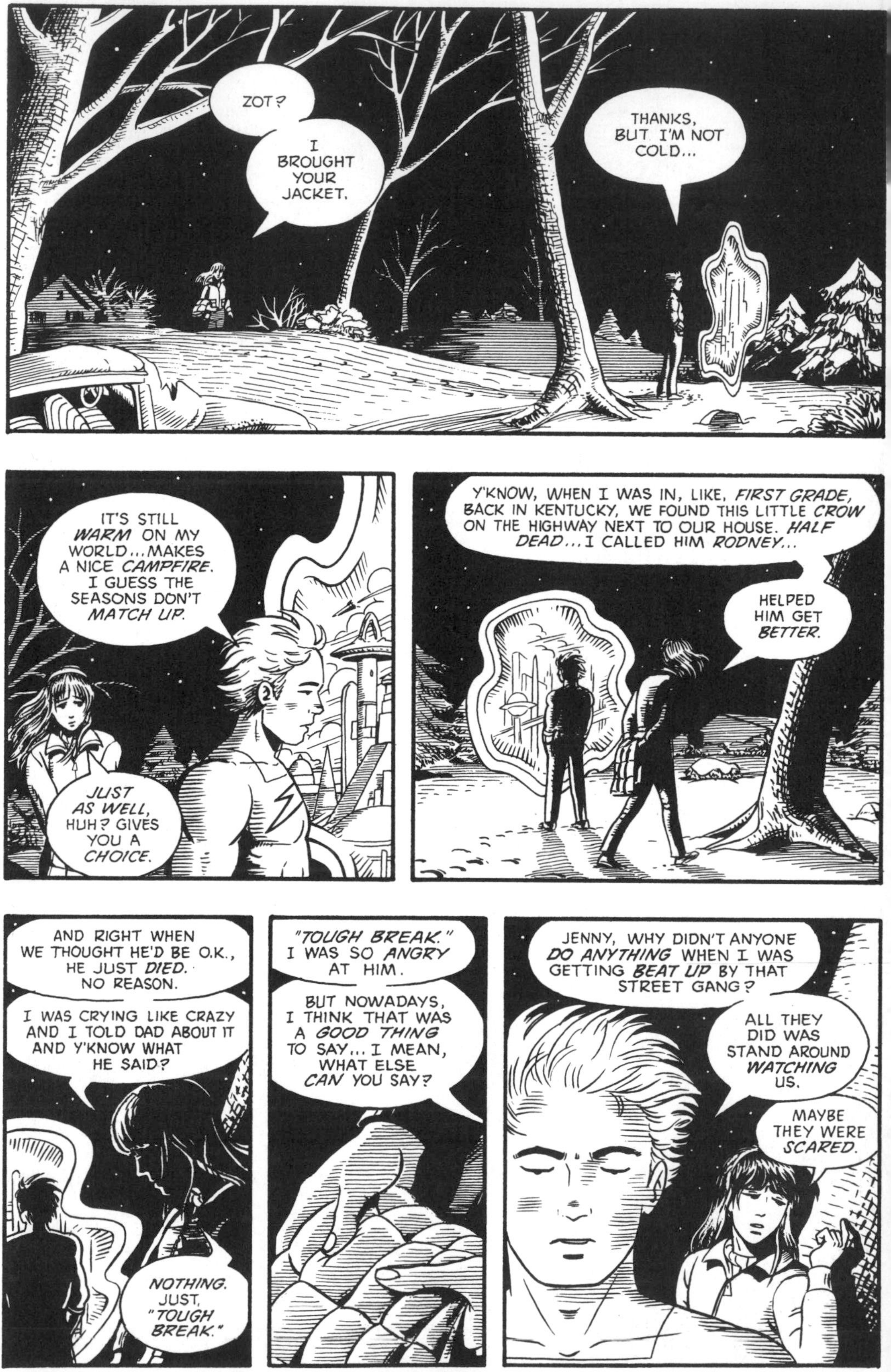
ZOT?
I BROUGHT YOUR JACKET.
THANKS, BUT I'M NOT COLD...
IT'S STILL WARM ON MY WORLD... MAKES A NICE CAMPFIRE. I GUESS THE SEASONS DON'T MATCH UP.
JUST AS WELL, HUH? GIVES YOU A CHOICE.
Y'KNOW, WHEN I WAS IN, LIKE, FIRST GRADE, BACK IN KENTUCKY, WE FOUND THIS LITTLE CROW ON THE HIGHWAY NEXT TO OUR HOUSE. HALF DEAD... I CALLED HIM RODNEY...
HELPED HIM GET BETTER.
AND RIGHT WHEN WE THOUGHT HE'D BE O.K., HE JUST DIED. NO REASON.
I WAS CRYING LIKE CRAZY AND I TOLD DAD ABOUT IT AND Y'KNOW WHAT HE SAID?
NOTHING. JUST, "TOUGH BREAK."
"TOUGH BREAK." I WAS SO ANGRY AT HIM.
BUT NOWADAYS, I THINK THAT WAS A GOOD THING TO SAY... I MEAN, WHAT ELSE CAN YOU SAY?
JENNY, WHY DIDN'T ANYONE DO ANYTHING WHEN I WAS GETTING BEAT UP BY THAT STREET GANG?
ALL THEY DID WAS STAND AROUND WATCHING US.
MAYBE THEY WERE SCARED.

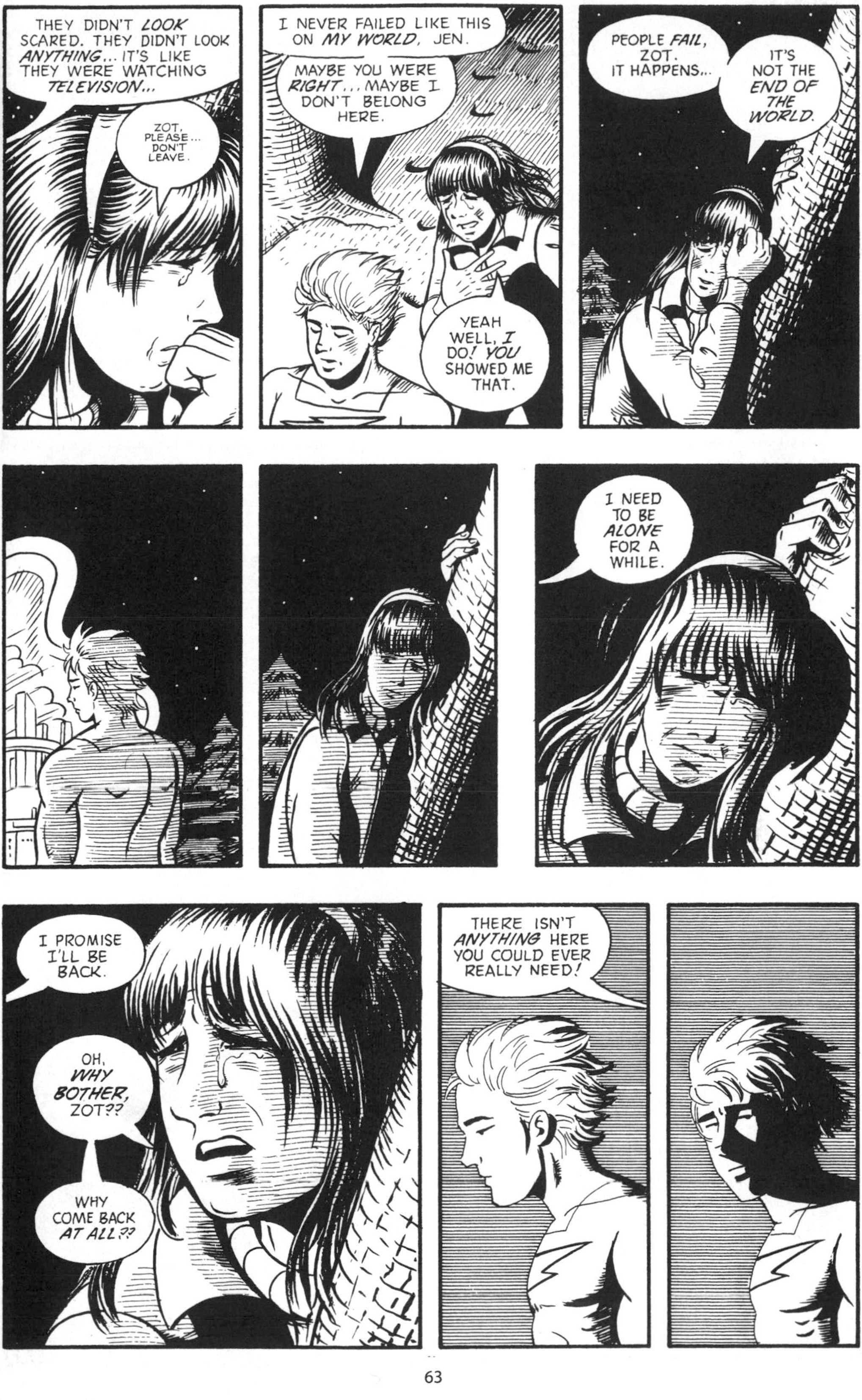

THEY DIDN'T *LOOK* SCARED. THEY DIDN'T LOOK *ANYTHING*... IT'S LIKE THEY WERE WATCHING *TELEVISION*...
ZOT, PLEASE... DON'T LEAVE.
I NEVER FAILED LIKE THIS ON *MY WORLD*, JEN.
MAYBE YOU WERE *RIGHT*... MAYBE I DON'T BELONG HERE.
YEAH WELL, *I* DO! *YOU* SHOWED ME THAT.
PEOPLE *FAIL*, ZOT. IT HAPPENS...
IT'S NOT THE *END OF THE WORLD*.
I NEED TO BE *ALONE* FOR A WHILE.
I PROMISE I'LL BE BACK.
OH, *WHY BOTHER*, ZOT??
WHY COME BACK *AT ALL*??
THERE ISN'T *ANYTHING* HERE YOU COULD EVER REALLY NEED!

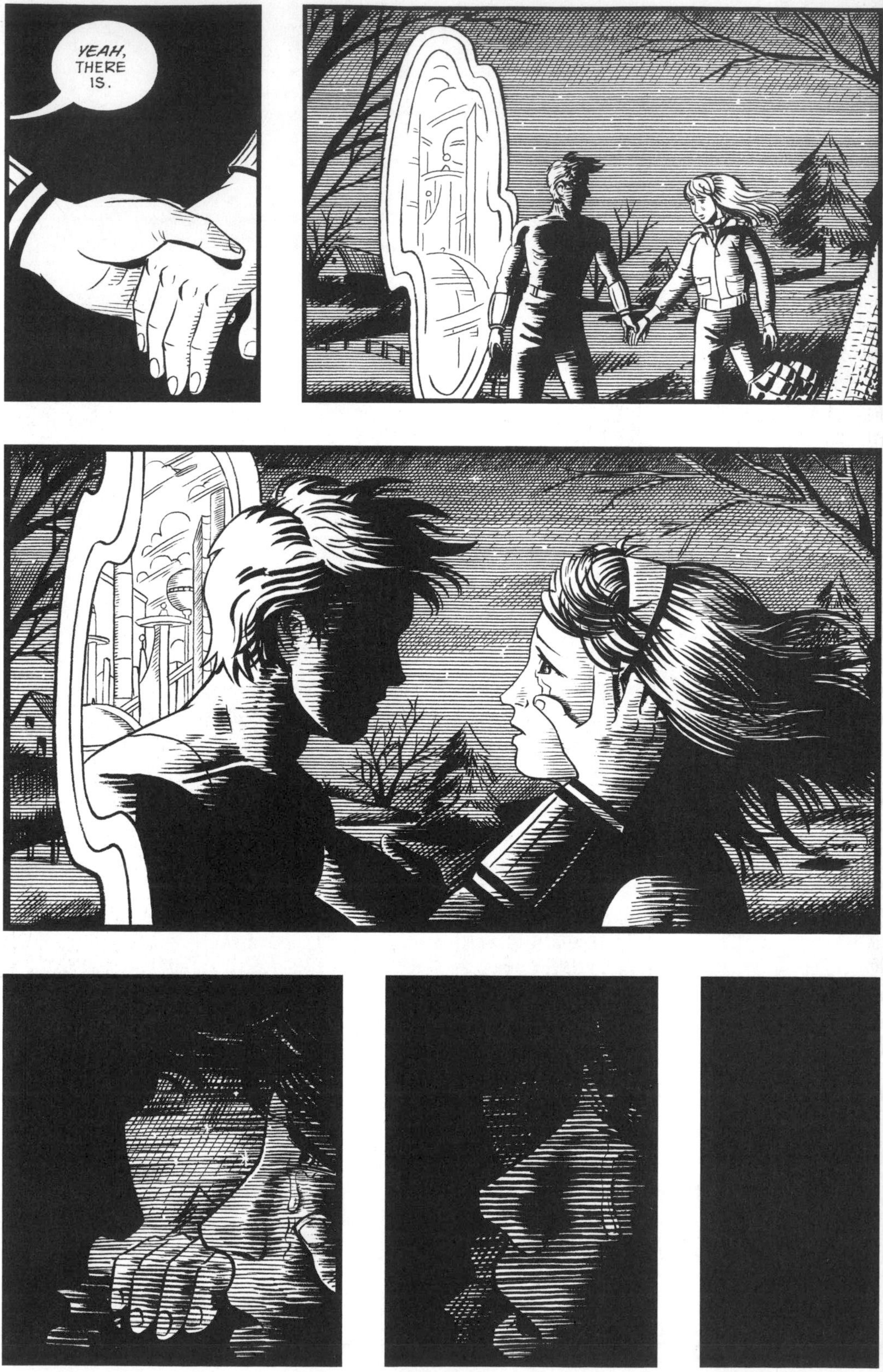
YEAH, THERE IS.

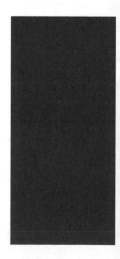

One of my biggest challenges with *Zot!* cropped up as soon as I realized that the contrast between the two "Earths"—Zot's utopian world and our own tarnished home—offered the series' most natural central theme, the age-old struggle between hope and disillusionment. Unfortunately, the most obvious way to highlight the contrast was to paint Zot's world as trouble-free, a strategy that might work for stories set on our world, but which could sabotage any hopes for dramatic conflict once the focus returned to the other side of the portal.

I found a partial solution in Zot and Jenny's much more personal enactment of those themes. Jenny's universe of broken dreams was as much about her attitudes toward life as it was about any objective assessment of our planet's ultimate worth. And Zot's natural optimism applied to both worlds equally—at least, to a point. We all step between those two worlds every day, so on a human level at least, I hoped this story would resonate. The last page (including our cover image) was the whole series in a nutshell: the two worlds, both emotional and metaphorical, drawing together in a kiss.

If the emotions seem a bit oversaturated, blame it on brain chemistry. When I laid out that last page, I was still living alone in upstate New York, but by the time I drew it, I'd relocated to Boston and was moving in with my old college friend Ivy Ratafia—a woman whom, prior to that time, I'd secretly been in love with for seven years. My comics had always been sentimental, but at this point in my life, the endorphins were a raging river, carrying off potential subtleties in its current.

Before it was even drawn, based on the layouts, I was told by my editor that three people at Eclipse Comics were interested in buying the last page, but I told them that I was giving it to Ivy. She and I still have it to this day.

Jenny was only 14 years old in this story. Zot was 15. Now in 2008, as we go to press with this collection, Ivy and I have a daughter who is exactly Jenny's age, and she has a blond boyfriend—sorry, not-boyfriend—who is exactly Zot's age, and all I can think is: Aren't they a bit *young* for this sort of thing?

Cosmic payback, I guess.

The scenes in New York seem embarrassingly dated to me now. The would-be purse-snatcher and his bigger gang member friends were just lazy stock characters of a sort common in mainstream titles of the day, and they strike a false note to me now. In *The Frying Pan* (a small-press magazine I put together in which members critiqued each others' work), comics creator Bill Loebs rightfully took me to task for perpetuating the comics cliché that all you had to do to get mugged in a big city was walk down the street at night. Bill's comments planted the seeds of an idea that would take root a couple of years later in issue #29's story "Looking for Crime."

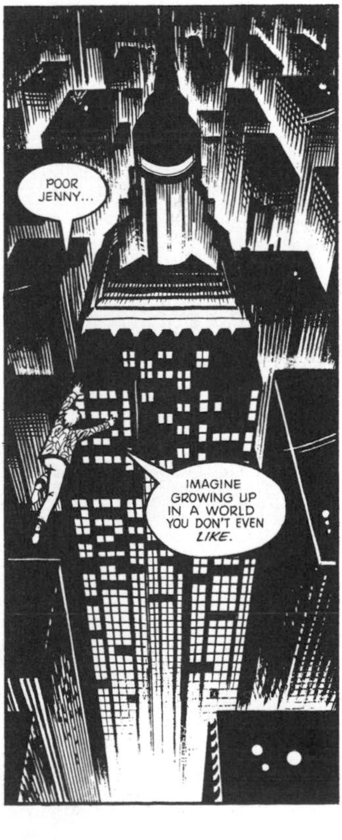
POOR JENNY...
IMAGINE GROWING UP IN A WORLD YOU DON'T EVEN *LIKE*.

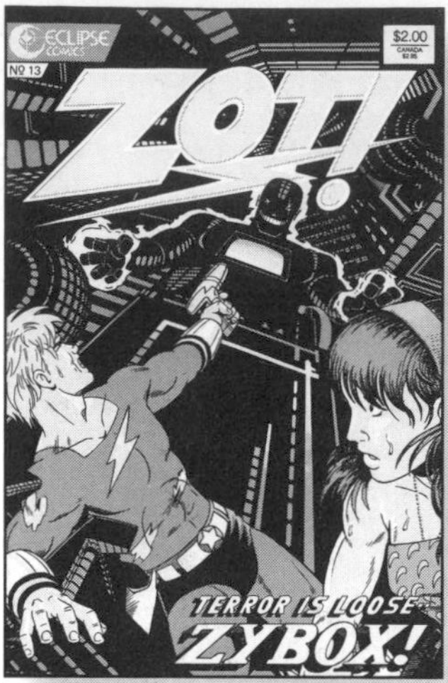
ECLIPSE COMICS
Nº 13
$2.00
ZOT!
TERROR IS LOOSE
ZYBOX!

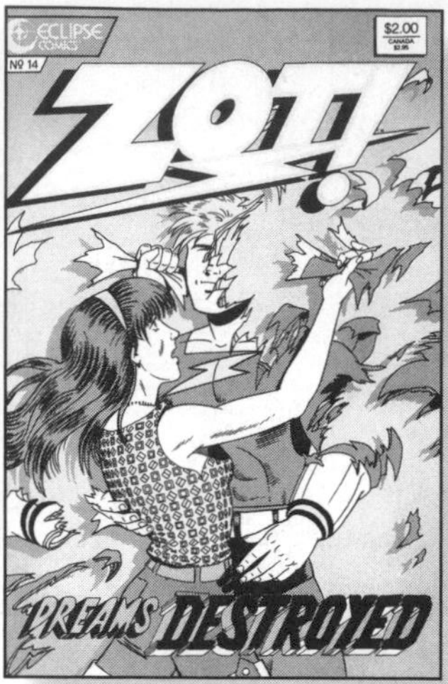
ECLIPSE COMICS
Nº 14
$2.00
ZOT!
DREAMS DESTROYED

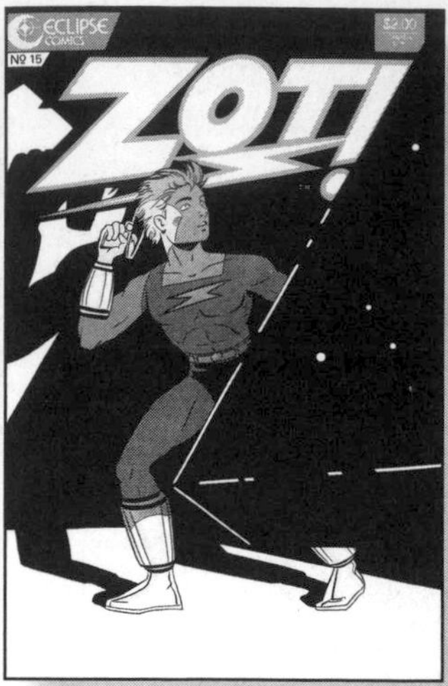
ECLIPSE COMICS
Nº 15
ZOT!

The Season of Dreams

First published in *Zot! #13–15*.

Lettering:

Bob Lappan

Original series editor:

cat yronwode

Eisner Award Nominee 1988:

"Best Single Issue" for *Zot! #14*

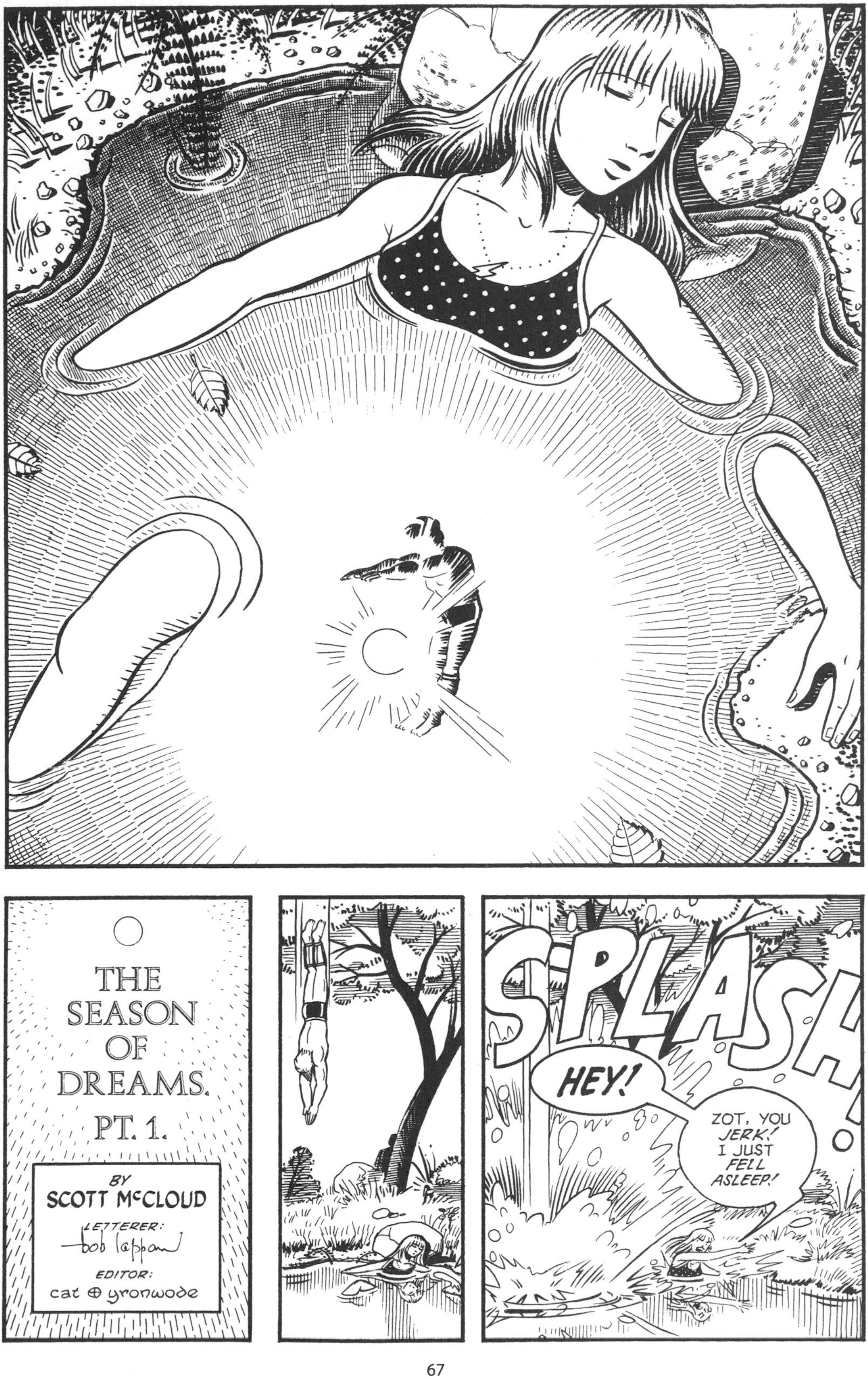
THE SEASON OF DREAMS. PT. 1.
BY SCOTT McCLOUD
LETTERER: bob lappan
EDITOR: cat ⊕ yronwode
SPLASH!
HEY!
ZOT, YOU JERK! I JUST FELL ASLEEP!

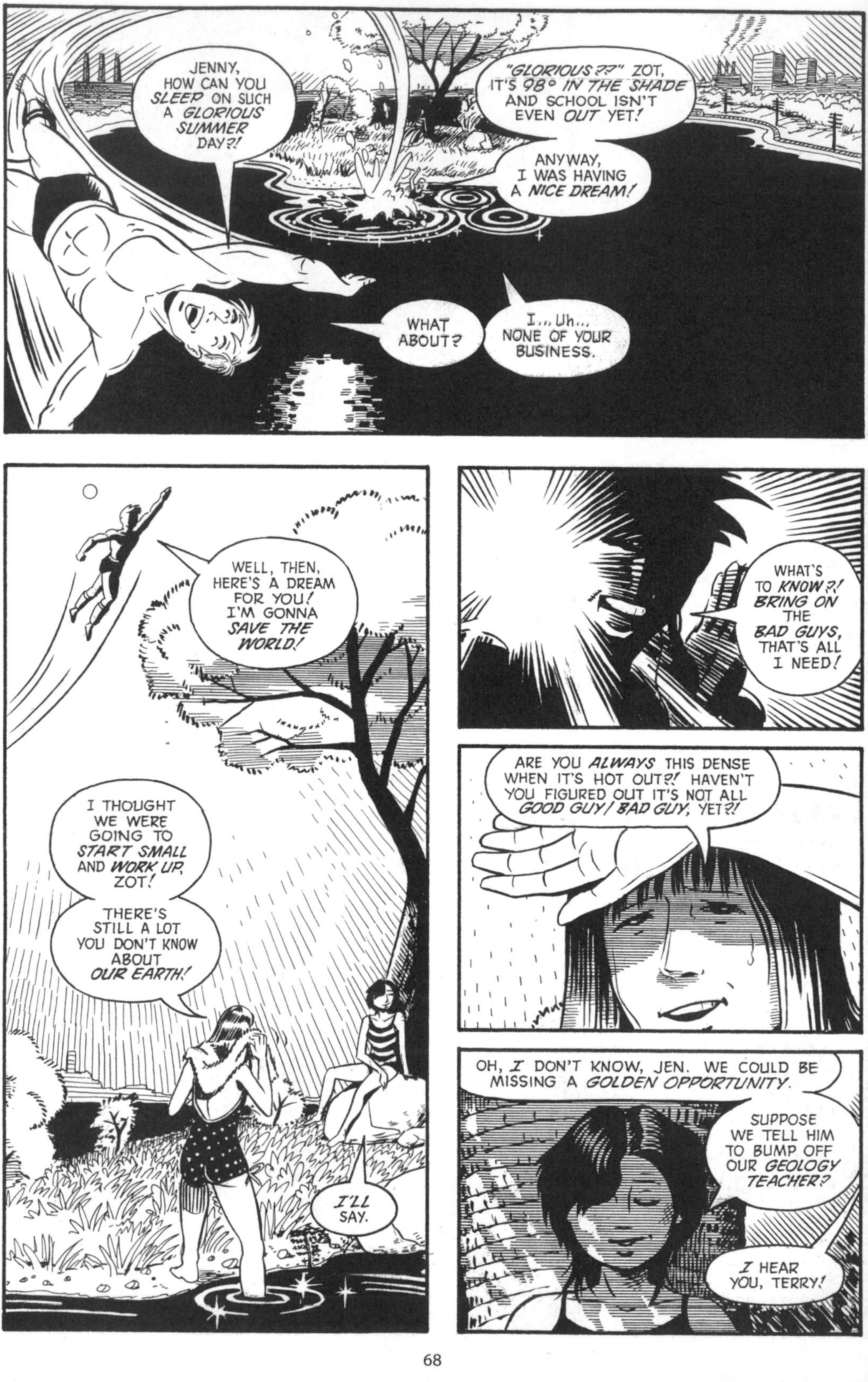
JENNY, HOW CAN YOU SLEEP ON SUCH A GLORIOUS SUMMER DAY?!
"GLORIOUS??" ZOT, IT'S 98° IN THE SHADE AND SCHOOL ISN'T EVEN OUT YET!
ANYWAY, I WAS HAVING A NICE DREAM!
WHAT ABOUT?
I... Uh... NONE OF YOUR BUSINESS.
WELL, THEN, HERE'S A DREAM FOR YOU! I'M GONNA SAVE THE WORLD!
I THOUGHT WE WERE GOING TO START SMALL AND WORK UP, ZOT!
THERE'S STILL A LOT YOU DON'T KNOW ABOUT OUR EARTH!
I'LL SAY.
WHAT'S TO KNOW?! BRING ON THE BAD GUYS, THAT'S ALL I NEED!
ARE YOU ALWAYS THIS DENSE WHEN IT'S HOT OUT?! HAVEN'T YOU FIGURED OUT IT'S NOT ALL GOOD GUY/BAD GUY, YET?!
OH, I DON'T KNOW, JEN. WE COULD BE MISSING A GOLDEN OPPORTUNITY.
SUPPOSE WE TELL HIM TO BUMP OFF OUR GEOLOGY TEACHER?
I HEAR YOU, TERRY!

MR. DEGUZMAN, YOUR DAYS ARE NUMBERED!

THAT'S *HARRIS*.

DEGUZMAN IS *MATH*.

BAH! THEY'RE *ALL* SCOUNDRELS...

JUST GIVE ME ONE *WORLD-CRUSHING* VILLAIN. JUST *ONE*. SLOWLY I'LL APPROACH. SLOWLY... SILENTLY...

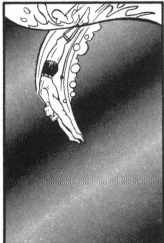

...*THEN* STRIKE!

≥AK!≤

≥ SIGH ≤

I PROMISED MOM I'D STOP AT THE *SUPERMARKET*. WANNA COME?

SURE! WE CAN GET SOME MORE OF THOSE REALLY THICK *POTATO CHIPS!*

YOU HAVE SUCH *GREAT THINGS* ON THIS PLANET.

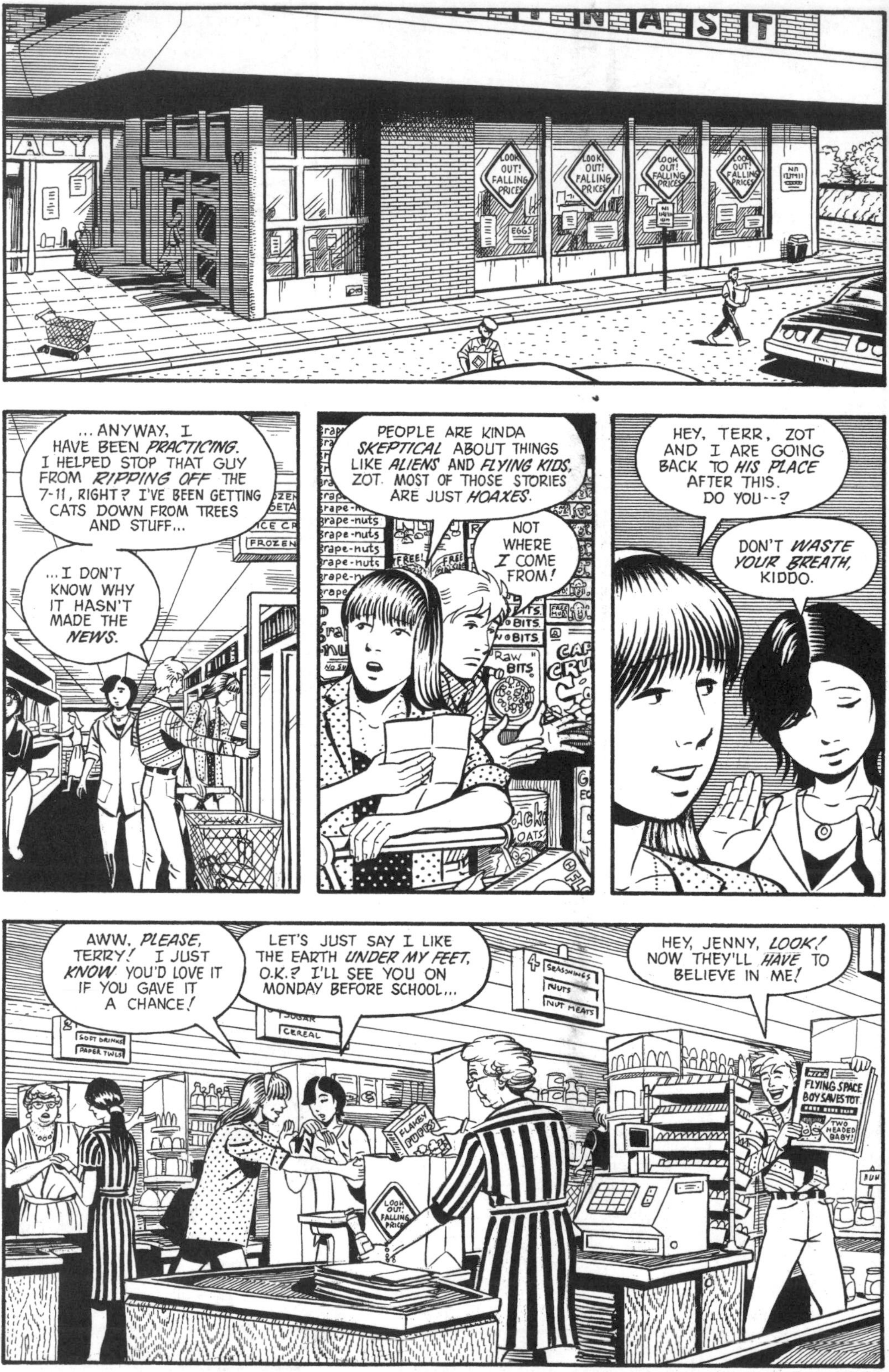
LOOK OUT! FALLING PRICES
...ANYWAY, I HAVE BEEN PRACTICING. I HELPED STOP THAT GUY FROM RIPPING OFF THE 7-11, RIGHT? I'VE BEEN GETTING CATS DOWN FROM TREES AND STUFF...
...I DON'T KNOW WHY IT HASN'T MADE THE NEWS.
PEOPLE ARE KINDA SKEPTICAL ABOUT THINGS LIKE ALIENS AND FLYING KIDS, ZOT. MOST OF THOSE STORIES ARE JUST HOAXES.
NOT WHERE I COME FROM!
HEY, TERR, ZOT AND I ARE GOING BACK TO HIS PLACE AFTER THIS. DO YOU--?
DON'T WASTE YOUR BREATH, KIDDO.
AWW, PLEASE, TERRY! I JUST KNOW YOU'D LOVE IT IF YOU GAVE IT A CHANCE!
LET'S JUST SAY I LIKE THE EARTH UNDER MY FEET, O.K.? I'LL SEE YOU ON MONDAY BEFORE SCHOOL...
HEY, JENNY, LOOK! NOW THEY'LL HAVE TO BELIEVE IN ME!
FLYING SPACE BOY SAVES TOT
TWO HEADED BABY!

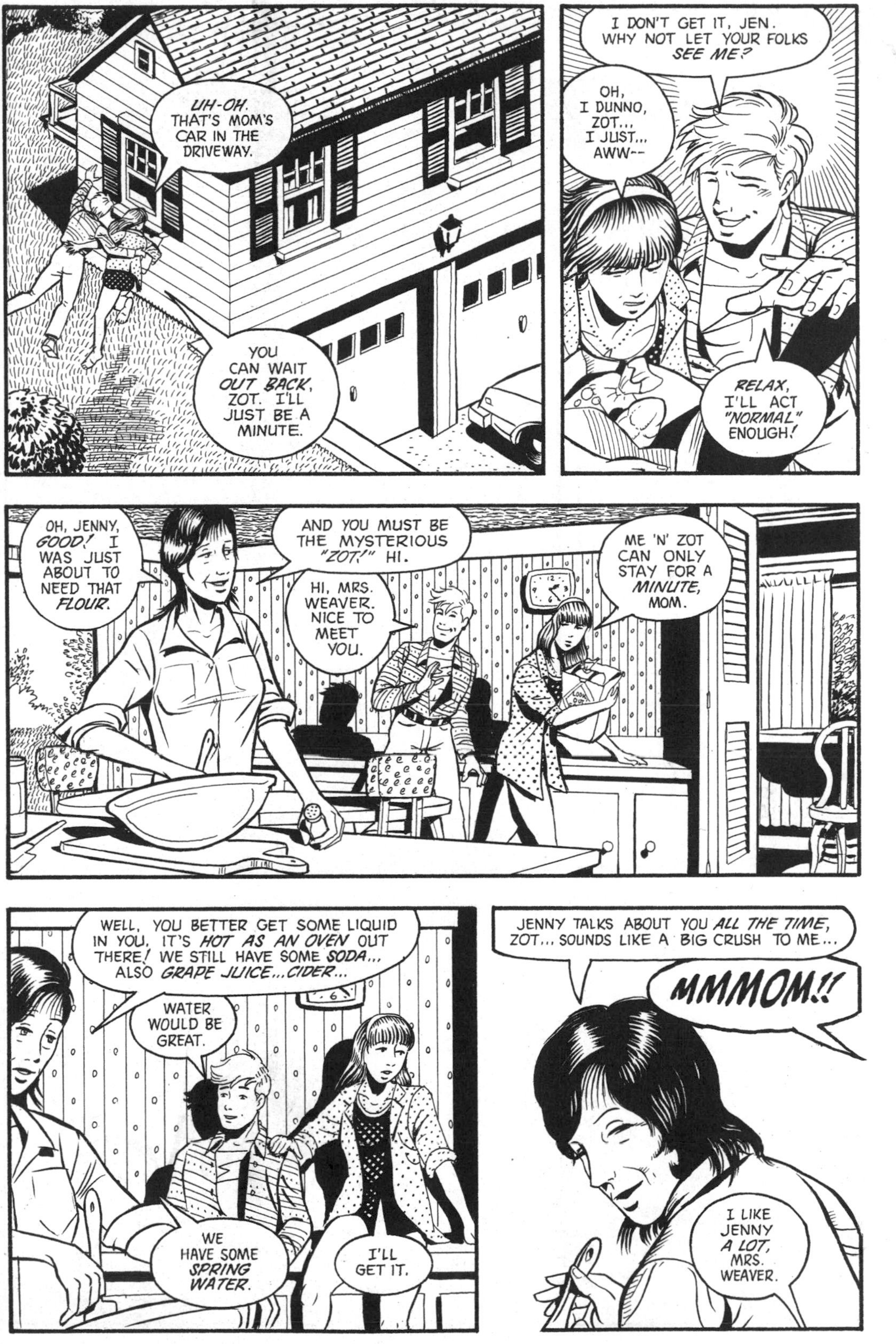
UH-OH. THAT'S MOM'S CAR IN THE DRIVEWAY.
YOU CAN WAIT OUT BACK, ZOT. I'LL JUST BE A MINUTE.
I DON'T GET IT, JEN. WHY NOT LET YOUR FOLKS SEE ME?
OH, I DUNNO, ZOT... I JUST... AWW--
RELAX, I'LL ACT "NORMAL" ENOUGH!
OH, JENNY, GOOD! I WAS JUST ABOUT TO NEED THAT FLOUR.
AND YOU MUST BE THE MYSTERIOUS "ZOT!" HI.
HI, MRS. WEAVER. NICE TO MEET YOU.
ME 'N' ZOT CAN ONLY STAY FOR A MINUTE, MOM.
WELL, YOU BETTER GET SOME LIQUID IN YOU, IT'S HOT AS AN OVEN OUT THERE! WE STILL HAVE SOME SODA... ALSO GRAPE JUICE...CIDER...
WATER WOULD BE GREAT.
WE HAVE SOME SPRING WATER.
I'LL GET IT.
JENNY TALKS ABOUT YOU ALL THE TIME, ZOT... SOUNDS LIKE A BIG CRUSH TO ME...
MMMOM!!
I LIKE JENNY A LOT, MRS. WEAVER.

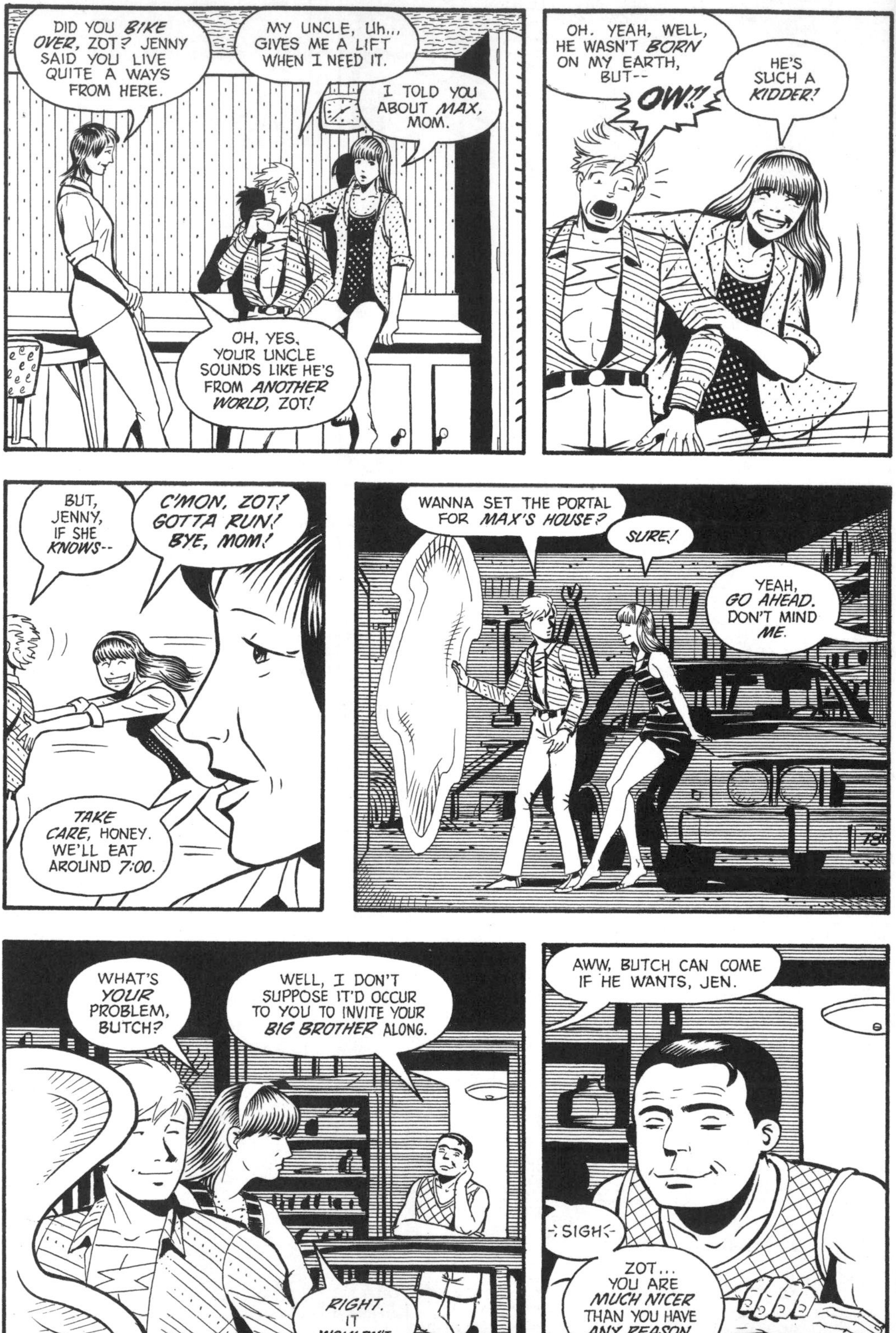
DID YOU BIKE OVER, ZOT? JENNY SAID YOU LIVE QUITE A WAYS FROM HERE.
MY UNCLE, Uh... GIVES ME A LIFT WHEN I NEED IT.
I TOLD YOU ABOUT MAX, MOM.
OH, YES. YOUR UNCLE SOUNDS LIKE HE'S FROM ANOTHER WORLD, ZOT!
OH. YEAH, WELL, HE WASN'T BORN ON MY EARTH, BUT--
OW!!
HE'S SUCH A KIDDER!
BUT, JENNY, IF SHE KNOWS--
C'MON, ZOT! GOTTA RUN! BYE, MOM!
TAKE CARE, HONEY. WE'LL EAT AROUND 7:00.
WANNA SET THE PORTAL FOR MAX'S HOUSE?
SURE!
YEAH, GO AHEAD. DON'T MIND ME.
WHAT'S YOUR PROBLEM, BUTCH?
WELL, I DON'T SUPPOSE IT'D OCCUR TO YOU TO INVITE YOUR BIG BROTHER ALONG.
RIGHT. IT WOULDN'T.
AWW, BUTCH CAN COME IF HE WANTS, JEN.
SIGH
ZOT... YOU ARE MUCH NICER THAN YOU HAVE ANY REASON TO BE.

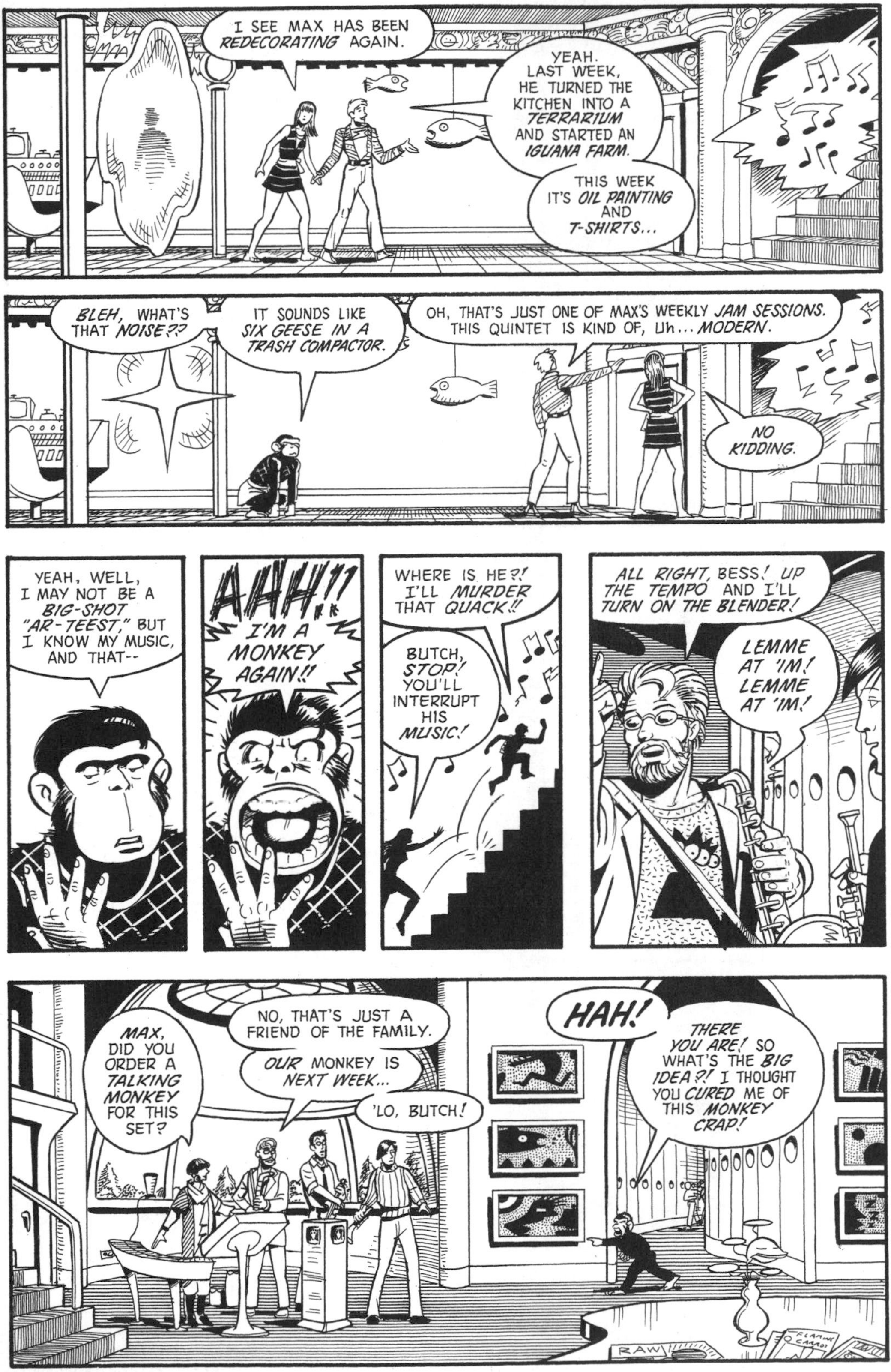
I SEE MAX HAS BEEN REDECORATING AGAIN.
YEAH. LAST WEEK, HE TURNED THE KITCHEN INTO A TERRARIUM AND STARTED AN IGUANA FARM.
THIS WEEK IT'S OIL PAINTING AND T-SHIRTS...
BLEH, WHAT'S THAT NOISE?!?
IT SOUNDS LIKE SIX GEESE IN A TRASH COMPACTOR.
OH, THAT'S JUST ONE OF MAX'S WEEKLY JAM SESSIONS. THIS QUINTET IS KIND OF, Uh... MODERN.
NO KIDDING.
YEAH, WELL, I MAY NOT BE A BIG-SHOT "AR-TEEST," BUT I KNOW MY MUSIC, AND THAT--
AHH!!
I'M A MONKEY AGAIN!!
WHERE IS HE?! I'LL MURDER THAT QUACK!!
BUTCH, STOP! YOU'LL INTERRUPT HIS MUSIC!
ALL RIGHT, BESS! UP THE TEMPO AND I'LL TURN ON THE BLENDER!
LEMME AT 'IM! LEMME AT 'IM!
MAX, DID YOU ORDER A TALKING MONKEY FOR THIS SET?
NO, THAT'S JUST A FRIEND OF THE FAMILY.
OUR MONKEY IS NEXT WEEK...
'LO, BUTCH!
HAH!
THERE YOU ARE! SO WHAT'S THE BIG IDEA?! I THOUGHT YOU CURED ME OF THIS MONKEY CRAP!
RAW

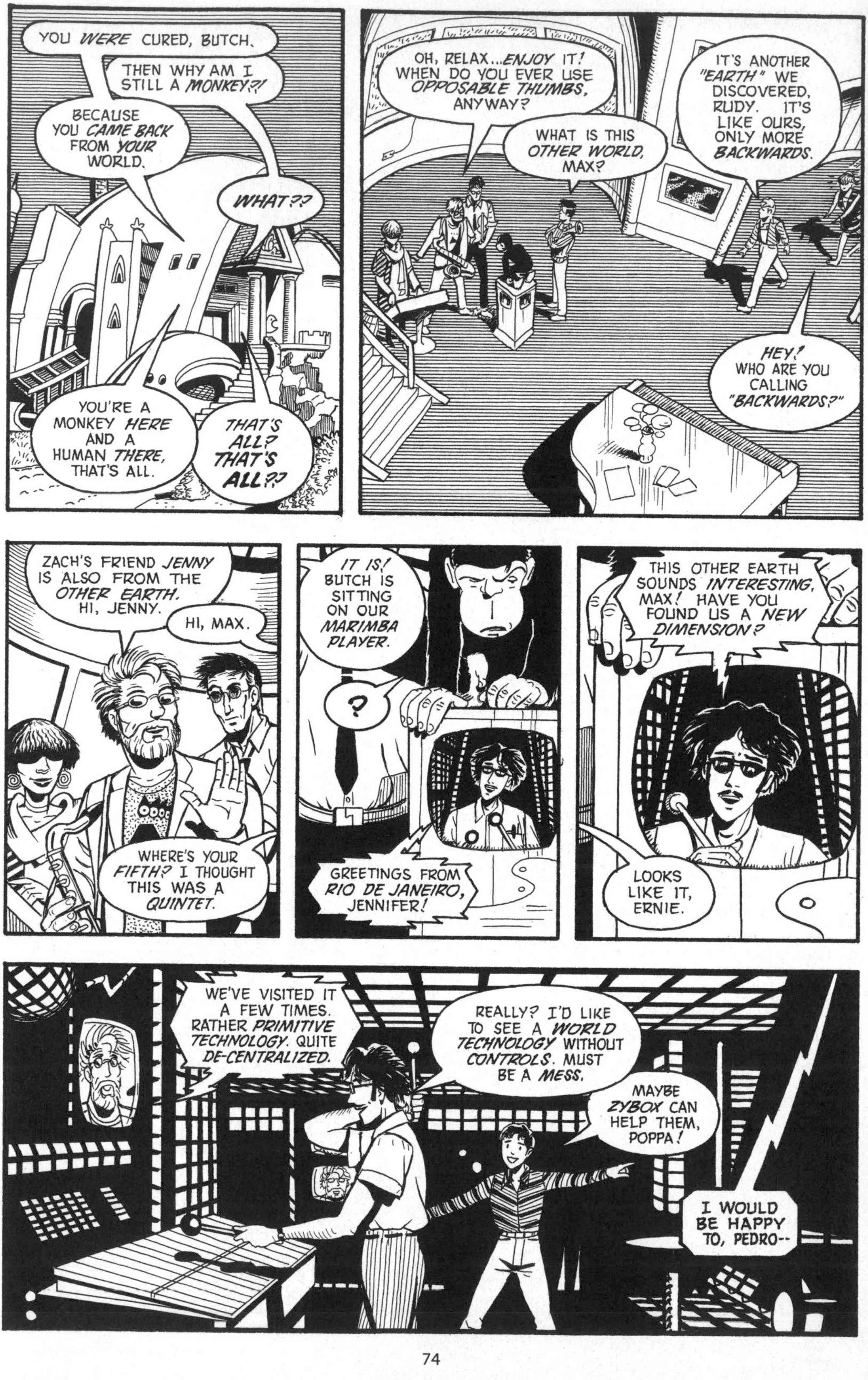

YOU WERE CURED, BUTCH.
THEN WHY AM I STILL A MONKEY?!
BECAUSE YOU CAME BACK FROM YOUR WORLD.
WHAT??
YOU'RE A MONKEY HERE AND A HUMAN THERE, THAT'S ALL.
THAT'S ALL? THAT'S ALL??
OH, RELAX...ENJOY IT! WHEN DO YOU EVER USE OPPOSABLE THUMBS, ANYWAY?
WHAT IS THIS OTHER WORLD, MAX?
IT'S ANOTHER "EARTH" WE DISCOVERED, RUDY. IT'S LIKE OURS, ONLY MORE BACKWARDS.
HEY! WHO ARE YOU CALLING "BACKWARDS?"
ZACH'S FRIEND JENNY IS ALSO FROM THE OTHER EARTH. HI, JENNY.
HI, MAX.
WHERE'S YOUR FIFTH? I THOUGHT THIS WAS A QUINTET.
IT IS! BUTCH IS SITTING ON OUR MARIMBA PLAYER.
?
GREETINGS FROM RIO DE JANEIRO, JENNIFER!
THIS OTHER EARTH SOUNDS INTERESTING, MAX! HAVE YOU FOUND US A NEW DIMENSION?
LOOKS LIKE IT, ERNIE.
WE'VE VISITED IT A FEW TIMES. RATHER PRIMITIVE TECHNOLOGY. QUITE DE-CENTRALIZED.
REALLY? I'D LIKE TO SEE A WORLD TECHNOLOGY WITHOUT CONTROLS. MUST BE A MESS.
MAYBE ZYBOX CAN HELP THEM, POPPA!
I WOULD BE HAPPY TO, PEDRO--

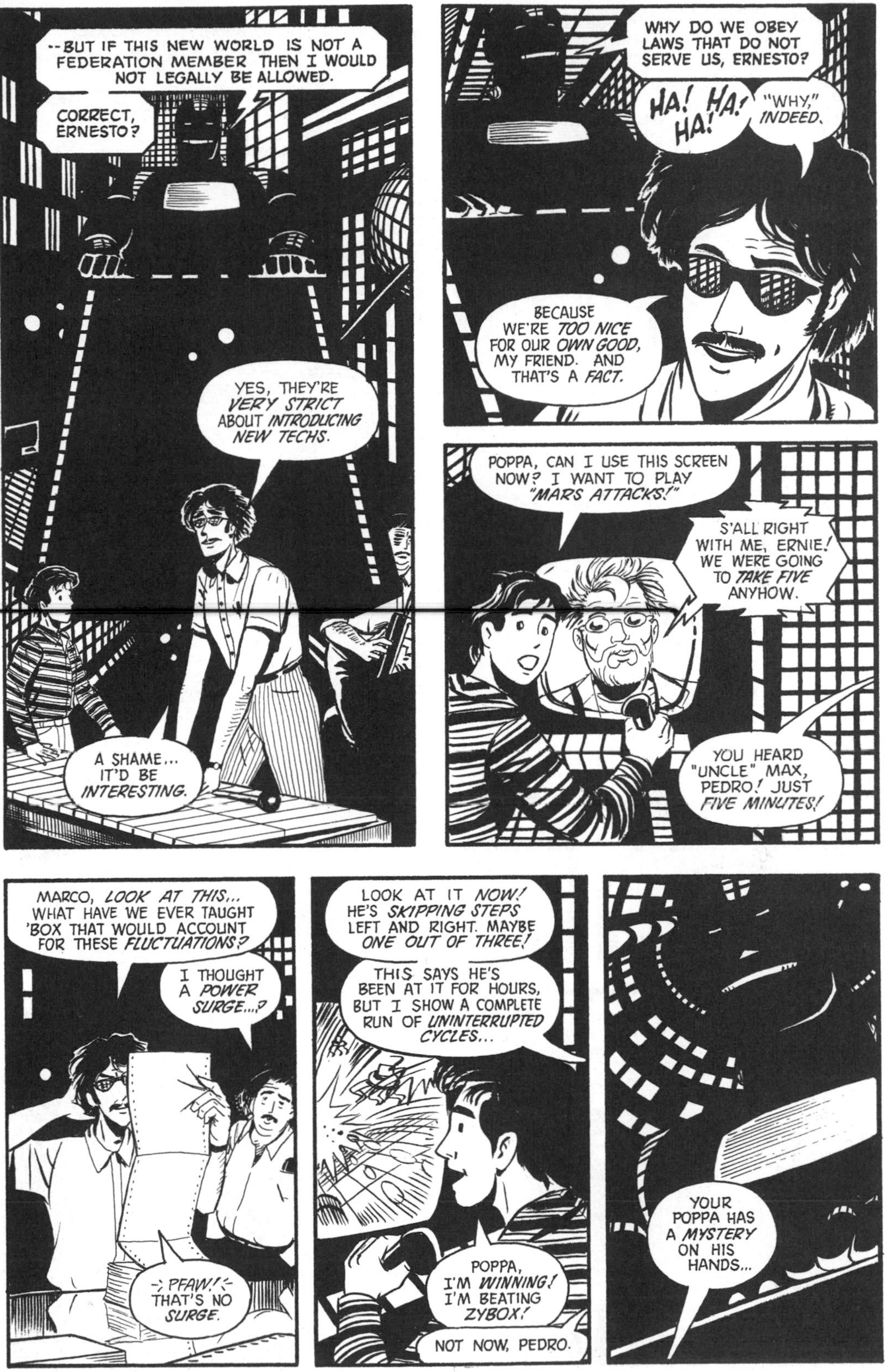
--BUT IF THIS NEW WORLD IS NOT A FEDERATION MEMBER THEN I WOULD NOT LEGALLY BE ALLOWED.
CORRECT, ERNESTO?
YES, THEY'RE VERY STRICT ABOUT INTRODUCING NEW TECHS.
A SHAME... IT'D BE INTERESTING.
WHY DO WE OBEY LAWS THAT DO NOT SERVE US, ERNESTO?
HA! HA! HA!
"WHY," INDEED.
BECAUSE WE'RE TOO NICE FOR OUR OWN GOOD, MY FRIEND. AND THAT'S A FACT.
POPPA, CAN I USE THIS SCREEN NOW? I WANT TO PLAY "MARS ATTACKS!"
S'ALL RIGHT WITH ME, ERNIE! WE WERE GOING TO TAKE FIVE ANYHOW.
YOU HEARD "UNCLE" MAX, PEDRO! JUST FIVE MINUTES!
MARCO, LOOK AT THIS... WHAT HAVE WE EVER TAUGHT 'BOX THAT WOULD ACCOUNT FOR THESE FLUCTUATIONS?
I THOUGHT A POWER SURGE...?
PFAW! THAT'S NO SURGE.
LOOK AT IT NOW! HE'S SKIPPING STEPS LEFT AND RIGHT. MAYBE ONE OUT OF THREE!
THIS SAYS HE'S BEEN AT IT FOR HOURS, BUT I SHOW A COMPLETE RUN OF UNINTERRUPTED CYCLES...
POPPA, I'M WINNING! I'M BEATING ZYBOX!
NOT NOW, PEDRO.
YOUR POPPA HAS A MYSTERY ON HIS HANDS...

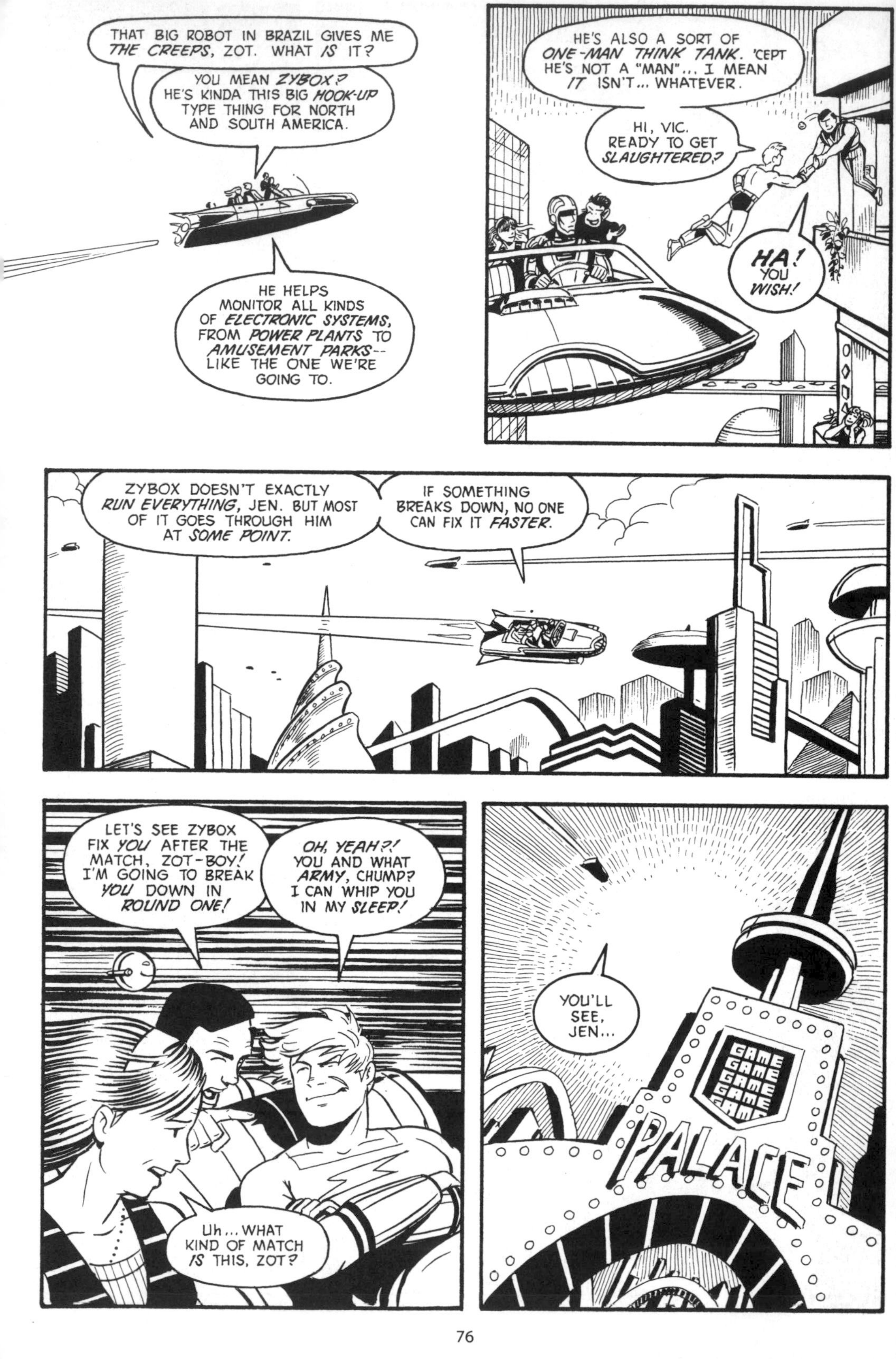
THAT BIG ROBOT IN BRAZIL GIVES ME THE CREEPS, ZOT. WHAT IS IT?
YOU MEAN ZYBOX? HE'S KINDA THIS BIG HOOK-UP TYPE THING FOR NORTH AND SOUTH AMERICA.
HE HELPS MONITOR ALL KINDS OF ELECTRONIC SYSTEMS, FROM POWER PLANTS TO AMUSEMENT PARKS-- LIKE THE ONE WE'RE GOING TO.
HE'S ALSO A SORT OF ONE-MAN THINK TANK. 'CEPT HE'S NOT A "MAN"... I MEAN IT ISN'T... WHATEVER.
HI, VIC. READY TO GET SLAUGHTERED?
HA! YOU WISH!
ZYBOX DOESN'T EXACTLY RUN EVERYTHING, JEN. BUT MOST OF IT GOES THROUGH HIM AT SOME POINT.
IF SOMETHING BREAKS DOWN, NO ONE CAN FIX IT FASTER.
LET'S SEE ZYBOX FIX YOU AFTER THE MATCH, ZOT-BOY! I'M GOING TO BREAK YOU DOWN IN ROUND ONE!
OH, YEAH?! YOU AND WHAT ARMY, CHUMP? I CAN WHIP YOU IN MY SLEEP!
Uh... WHAT KIND OF MATCH IS THIS, ZOT?
YOU'LL SEE, JEN...
GAME GAME GAME GAME GAME
PALACE

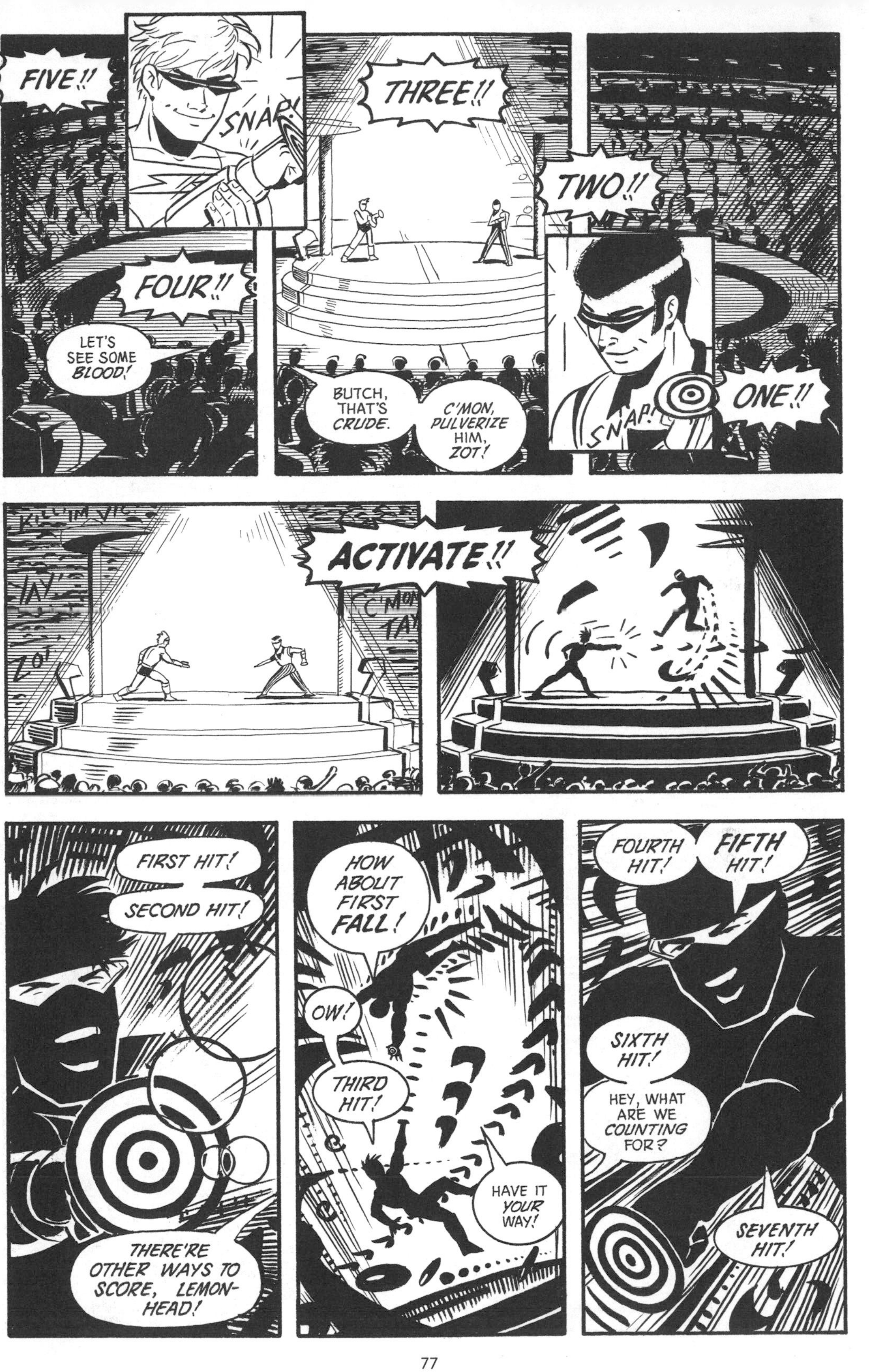
FIVE!!
SNAP!
FOUR!!
LET'S SEE SOME BLOOD!
THREE!!
BUTCH, THAT'S CRUDE.
C'MON, PULVERIZE HIM, ZOT!
TWO!!
SNAP!
ONE!!
ACTIVATE!!
FIRST HIT!
SECOND HIT!
THERE'RE OTHER WAYS TO SCORE, LEMON-HEAD!
HOW ABOUT FIRST FALL!
OW!
THIRD HIT!
HAVE IT YOUR WAY!
FOURTH HIT!
FIFTH HIT!
SIXTH HIT!
HEY, WHAT ARE WE COUNTING FOR?
SEVENTH HIT!

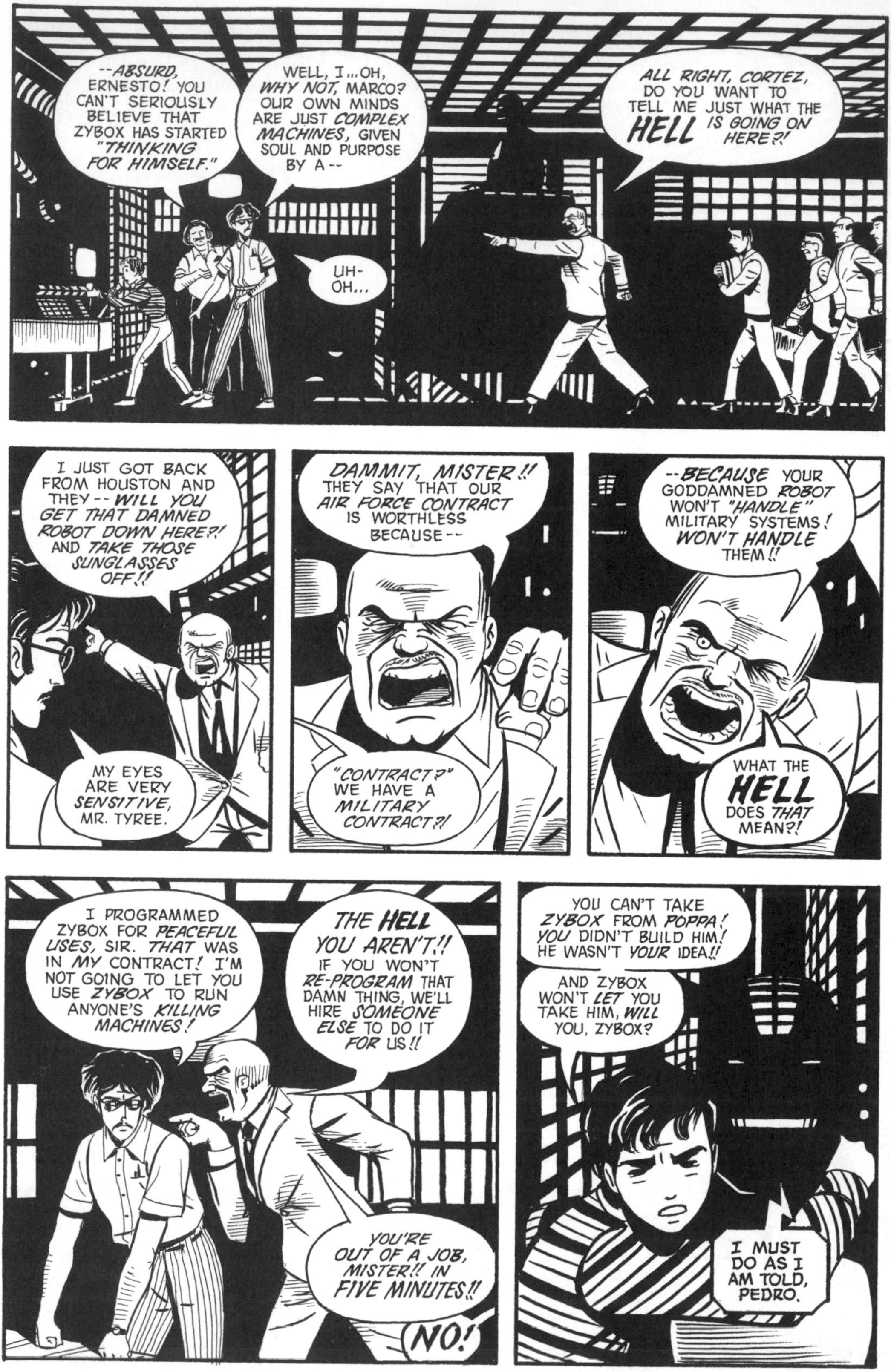
--ABSURD, ERNESTO! YOU CAN'T SERIOUSLY BELIEVE THAT ZYBOX HAS STARTED "THINKING FOR HIMSELF."
WELL, I...OH, WHY NOT, MARCO? OUR OWN MINDS ARE JUST COMPLEX MACHINES, GIVEN SOUL AND PURPOSE BY A--
UH-OH...
ALL RIGHT, CORTEZ, DO YOU WANT TO TELL ME JUST WHAT THE HELL IS GOING ON HERE?!
I JUST GOT BACK FROM HOUSTON AND THEY--WILL YOU GET THAT DAMNED ROBOT DOWN HERE?! AND TAKE THOSE SUNGLASSES OFF!!
MY EYES ARE VERY SENSITIVE, MR. TYREE.
DAMMIT, MISTER!! THEY SAY THAT OUR AIR FORCE CONTRACT IS WORTHLESS BECAUSE--
"CONTRACT?" WE HAVE A MILITARY CONTRACT?!
--BECAUSE YOUR GODDAMNED ROBOT WON'T "HANDLE" MILITARY SYSTEMS! WON'T HANDLE THEM!!
WHAT THE HELL DOES THAT MEAN?!
I PROGRAMMED ZYBOX FOR PEACEFUL USES, SIR. THAT WAS IN MY CONTRACT! I'M NOT GOING TO LET YOU USE ZYBOX TO RUN ANYONE'S KILLING MACHINES!
THE HELL YOU AREN'T!! IF YOU WON'T RE-PROGRAM THAT DAMN THING, WE'LL HIRE SOMEONE ELSE TO DO IT FOR US!!
YOU'RE OUT OF A JOB, MISTER!! IN FIVE MINUTES!!
NO!
YOU CAN'T TAKE ZYBOX FROM POPPA! YOU DIDN'T BUILD HIM! HE WASN'T YOUR IDEA!!
AND ZYBOX WON'T LET YOU TAKE HIM, WILL YOU, ZYBOX?
I MUST DO AS I AM TOLD, PEDRO.

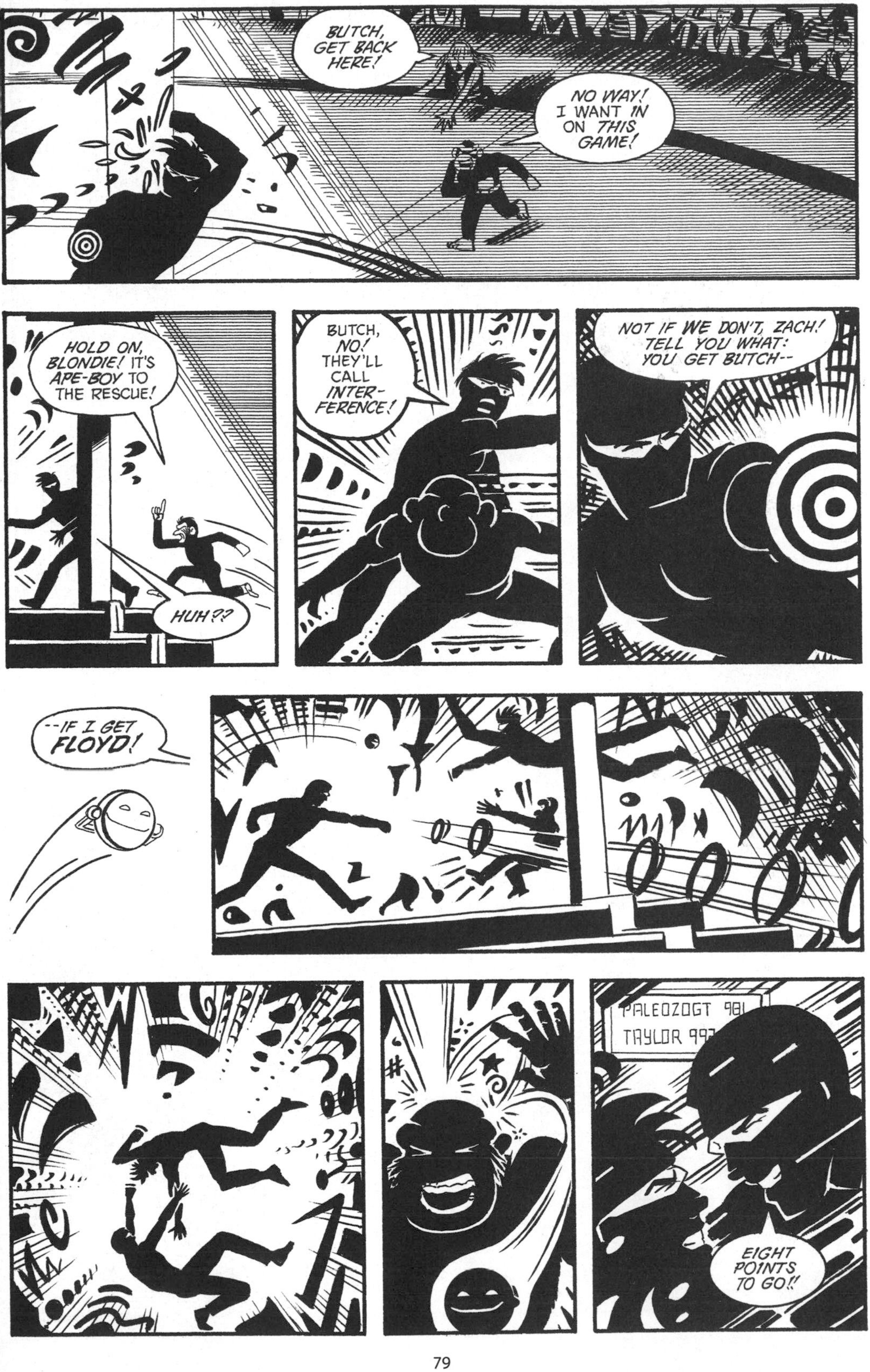

BUTCH, GET BACK HERE!
NO WAY! I WANT IN ON THIS GAME!
HOLD ON, BLONDIE! IT'S APE-BOY TO THE RESCUE!
HUH??
BUTCH, NO! THEY'LL CALL INTER-FERENCE!
NOT IF WE DON'T, ZACH! TELL YOU WHAT: YOU GET BUTCH--
--IF I GET FLOYD!
PALEOZOGT 981
TAYLOR 99
EIGHT POINTS TO GO!!

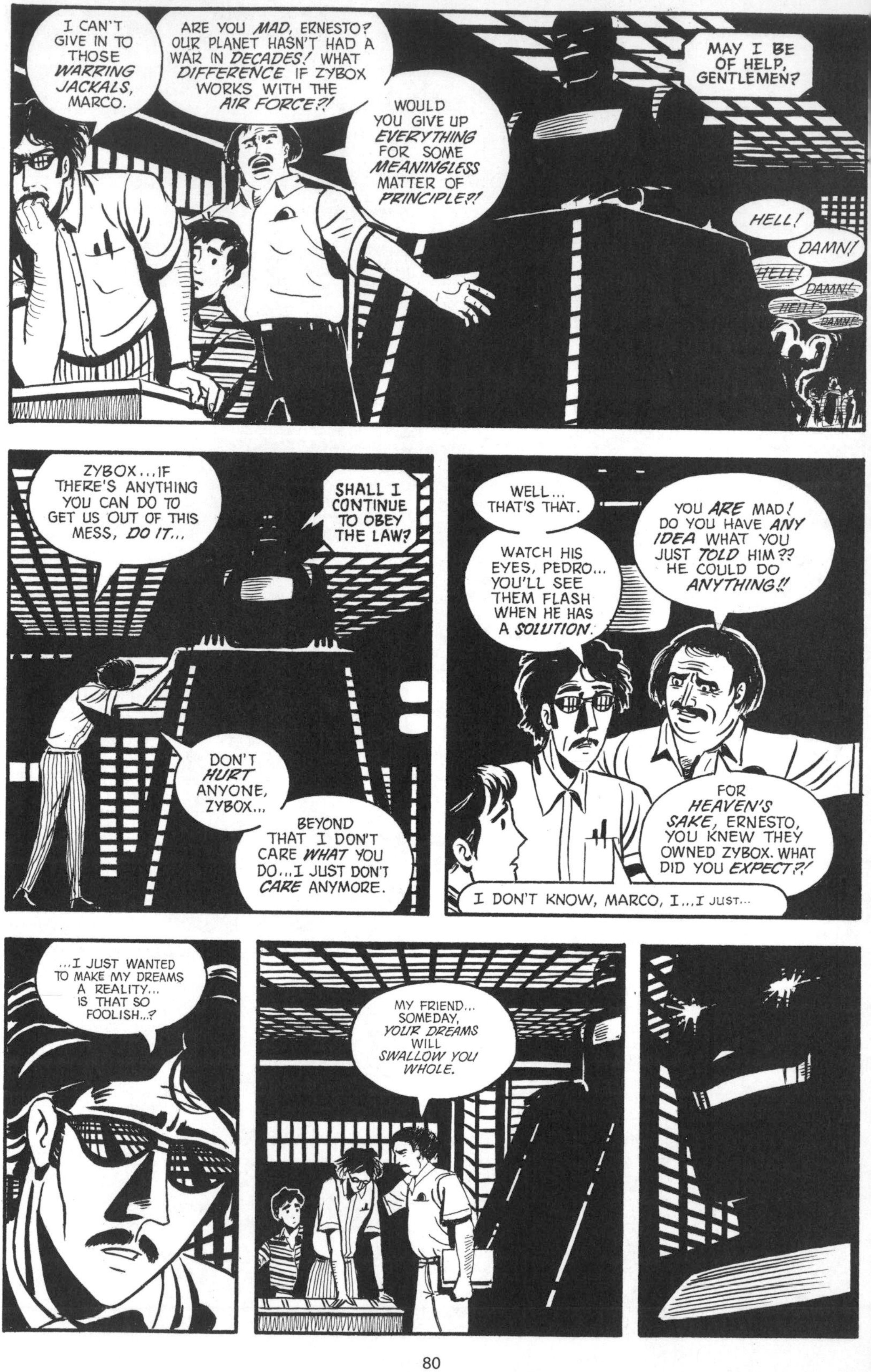
I CAN'T GIVE IN TO THOSE WARRING JACKALS, MARCO.
ARE YOU MAD, ERNESTO? OUR PLANET HASN'T HAD A WAR IN DECADES! WHAT DIFFERENCE IF ZYBOX WORKS WITH THE AIR FORCE?!
WOULD YOU GIVE UP EVERYTHING FOR SOME MEANINGLESS MATTER OF PRINCIPLE?!
MAY I BE OF HELP, GENTLEMEN?
HELL!
DAMN!
HELL!
DAMN!
ZYBOX...IF THERE'S ANYTHING YOU CAN DO TO GET US OUT OF THIS MESS, DO IT...
SHALL I CONTINUE TO OBEY THE LAW?
DON'T HURT ANYONE, ZYBOX...
BEYOND THAT I DON'T CARE WHAT YOU DO...I JUST DON'T CARE ANYMORE.
WELL... THAT'S THAT.
WATCH HIS EYES, PEDRO... YOU'LL SEE THEM FLASH WHEN HE HAS A SOLUTION.
YOU ARE MAD! DO YOU HAVE ANY IDEA WHAT YOU JUST TOLD HIM?? HE COULD DO ANYTHING!!
FOR HEAVEN'S SAKE, ERNESTO, YOU KNEW THEY OWNED ZYBOX. WHAT DID YOU EXPECT?!
I DON'T KNOW, MARCO, I...I JUST...
...I JUST WANTED TO MAKE MY DREAMS A REALITY... IS THAT SO FOOLISH...?
MY FRIEND... SOMEDAY, YOUR DREAMS WILL SWALLOW YOU WHOLE.

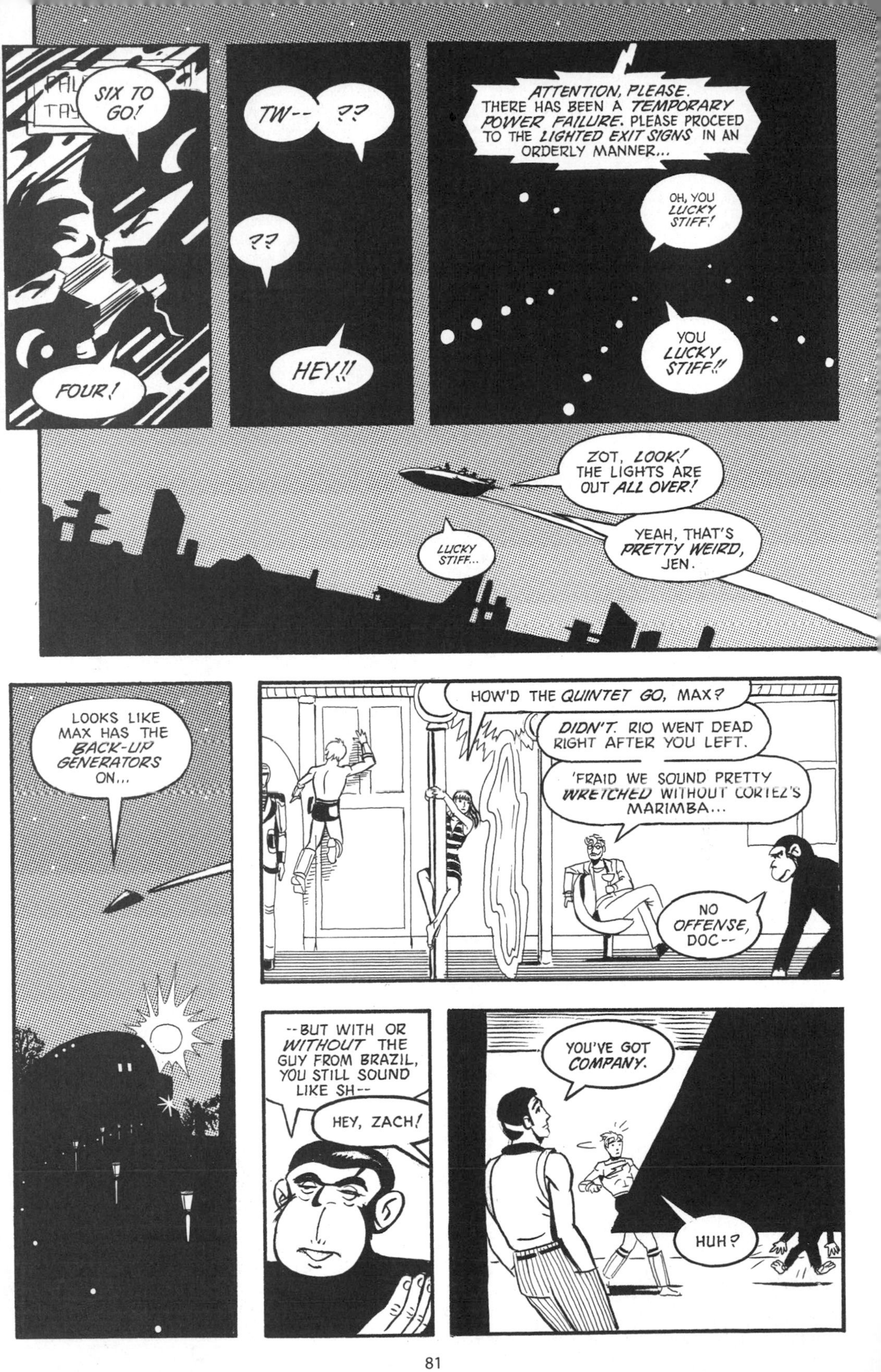
SIX TO GO!
FOUR!
TW--
??
??
HEY!!
ATTENTION, PLEASE. THERE HAS BEEN A TEMPORARY POWER FAILURE. PLEASE PROCEED TO THE LIGHTED EXIT SIGNS IN AN ORDERLY MANNER...
OH, YOU LUCKY STIFF!
YOU LUCKY STIFF!!
ZOT, LOOK! THE LIGHTS ARE OUT ALL OVER!
LUCKY STIFF...
YEAH, THAT'S PRETTY WEIRD, JEN.
LOOKS LIKE MAX HAS THE BACK-UP GENERATORS ON...
HOW'D THE QUINTET GO, MAX?
DIDN'T. RIO WENT DEAD RIGHT AFTER YOU LEFT.
'FRAID WE SOUND PRETTY WRETCHED WITHOUT CORTEZ'S MARIMBA...
NO OFFENSE, DOC--
--BUT WITH OR WITHOUT THE GUY FROM BRAZIL, YOU STILL SOUND LIKE SH--
HEY, ZACH!
YOU'VE GOT COMPANY.
HUH?

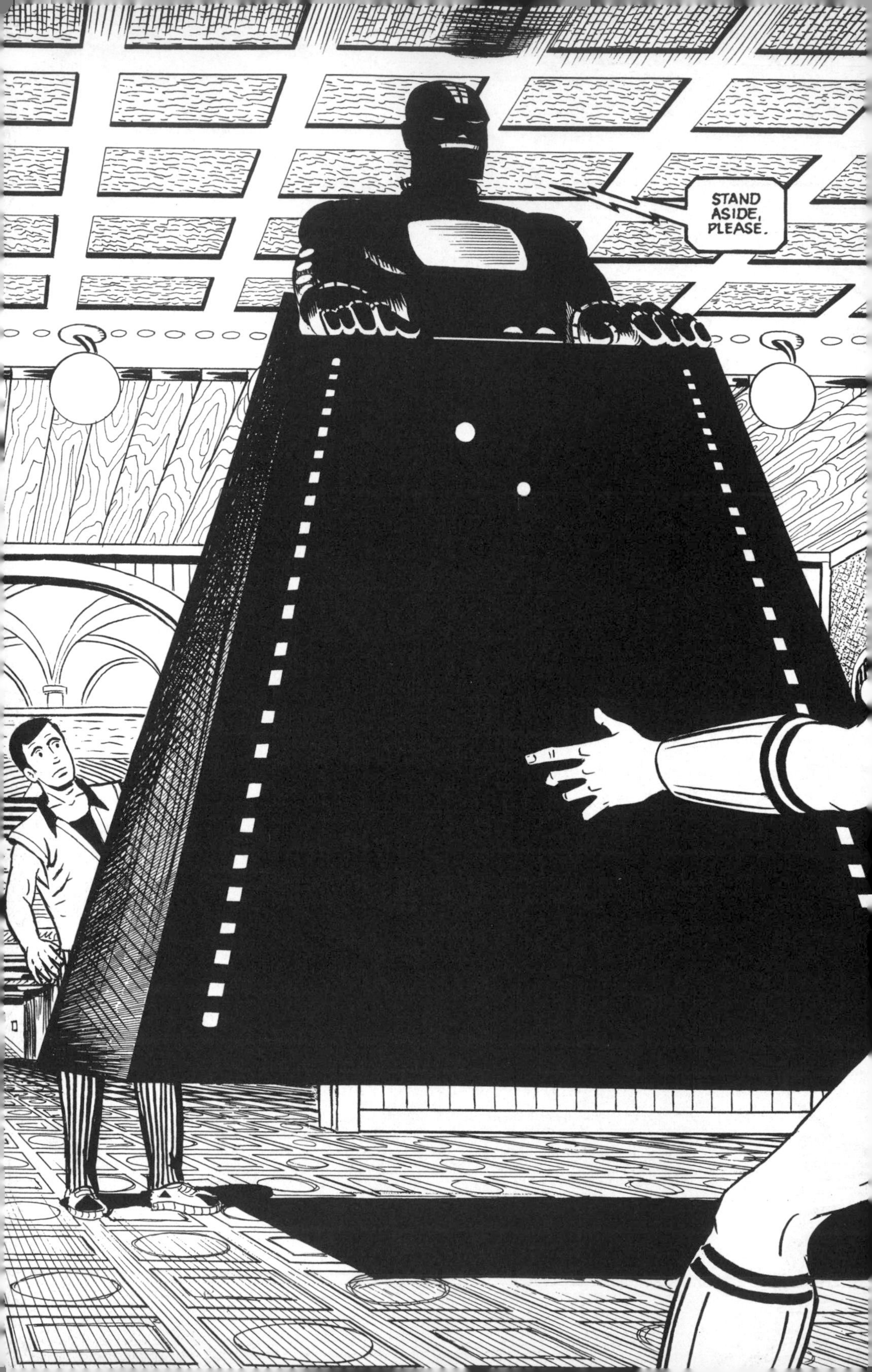
STAND ASIDE, PLEASE.

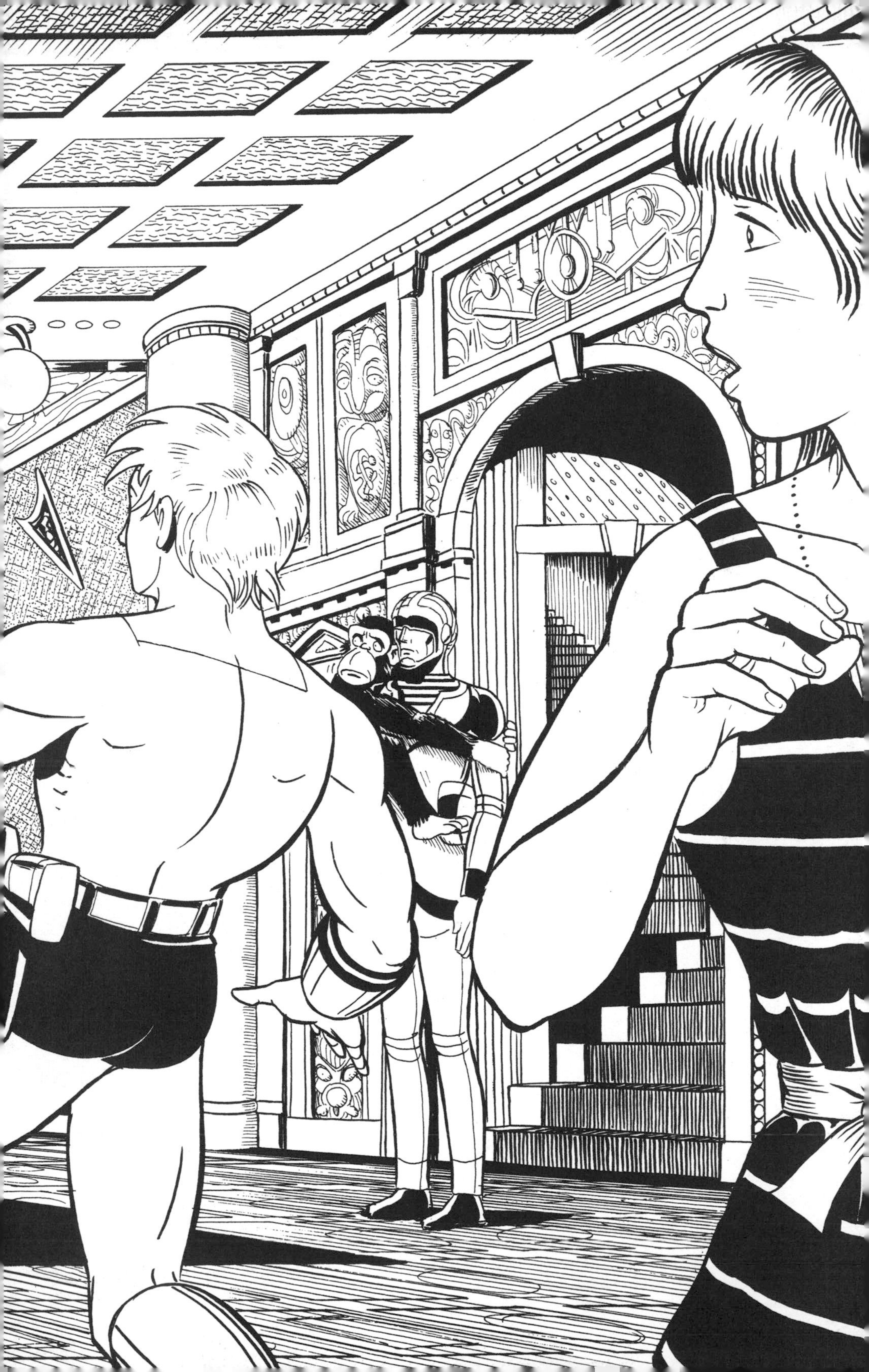

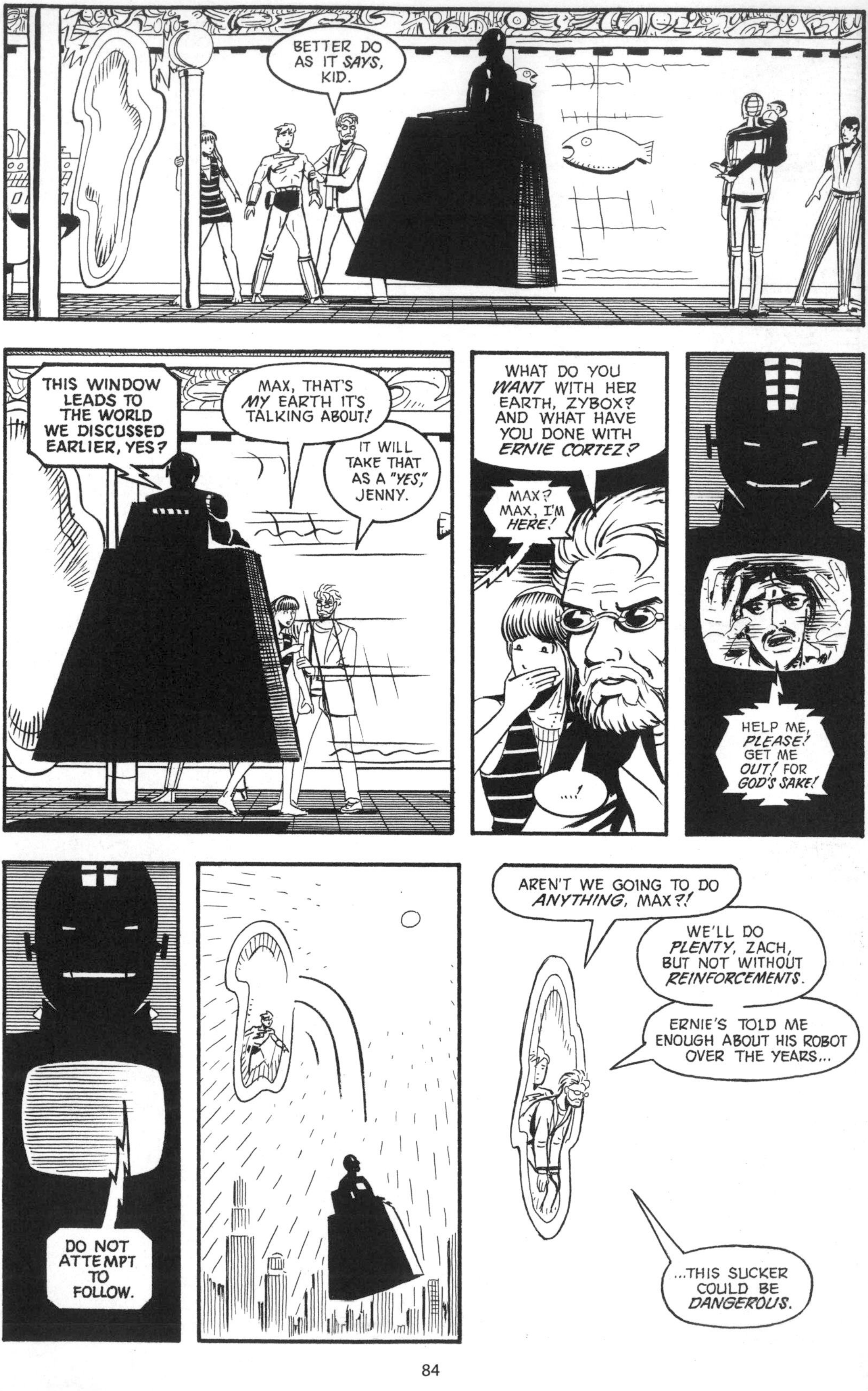

BETTER DO AS IT SAYS, KID.
THIS WINDOW LEADS TO THE WORLD WE DISCUSSED EARLIER, YES?
MAX, THAT'S MY EARTH IT'S TALKING ABOUT!
IT WILL TAKE THAT AS A "YES," JENNY.
WHAT DO YOU WANT WITH HER EARTH, ZYBOX? AND WHAT HAVE YOU DONE WITH ERNIE CORTEZ?
MAX? MAX, I'M HERE!
...!
HELP ME, PLEASE! GET ME OUT! FOR GOD'S SAKE!
DO NOT ATTEMPT TO FOLLOW.
AREN'T WE GOING TO DO ANYTHING, MAX?!
WE'LL DO PLENTY, ZACH, BUT NOT WITHOUT REINFORCEMENTS.
ERNIE'S TOLD ME ENOUGH ABOUT HIS ROBOT OVER THE YEARS...
...THIS SUCKER COULD BE DANGEROUS.

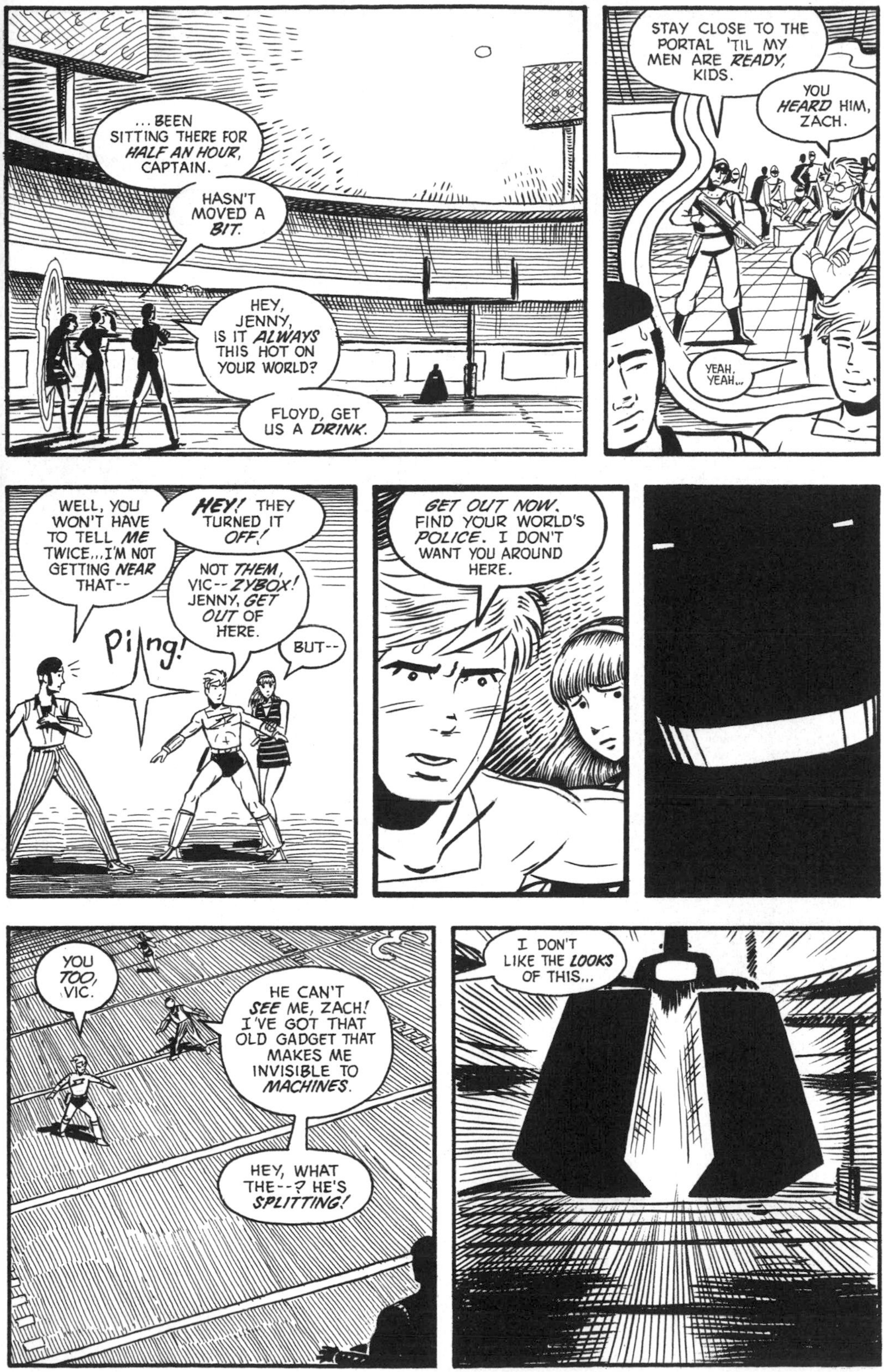
...BEEN SITTING THERE FOR HALF AN HOUR, CAPTAIN.
HASN'T MOVED A BIT.
HEY, JENNY, IS IT ALWAYS THIS HOT ON YOUR WORLD?
FLOYD, GET US A DRINK.
STAY CLOSE TO THE PORTAL 'TIL MY MEN ARE READY, KIDS.
YOU HEARD HIM, ZACH.
YEAH, YEAH...
WELL, YOU WON'T HAVE TO TELL ME TWICE...I'M NOT GETTING NEAR THAT--
Ping!
HEY! THEY TURNED IT OFF!
NOT THEM, VIC--ZYBOX! JENNY, GET OUT OF HERE.
BUT--
GET OUT NOW. FIND YOUR WORLD'S POLICE. I DON'T WANT YOU AROUND HERE.
YOU TOO, VIC.
HE CAN'T SEE ME, ZACH! I'VE GOT THAT OLD GADGET THAT MAKES ME INVISIBLE TO MACHINES.
HEY, WHAT THE--? HE'S SPLITTING!
I DON'T LIKE THE LOOKS OF THIS...

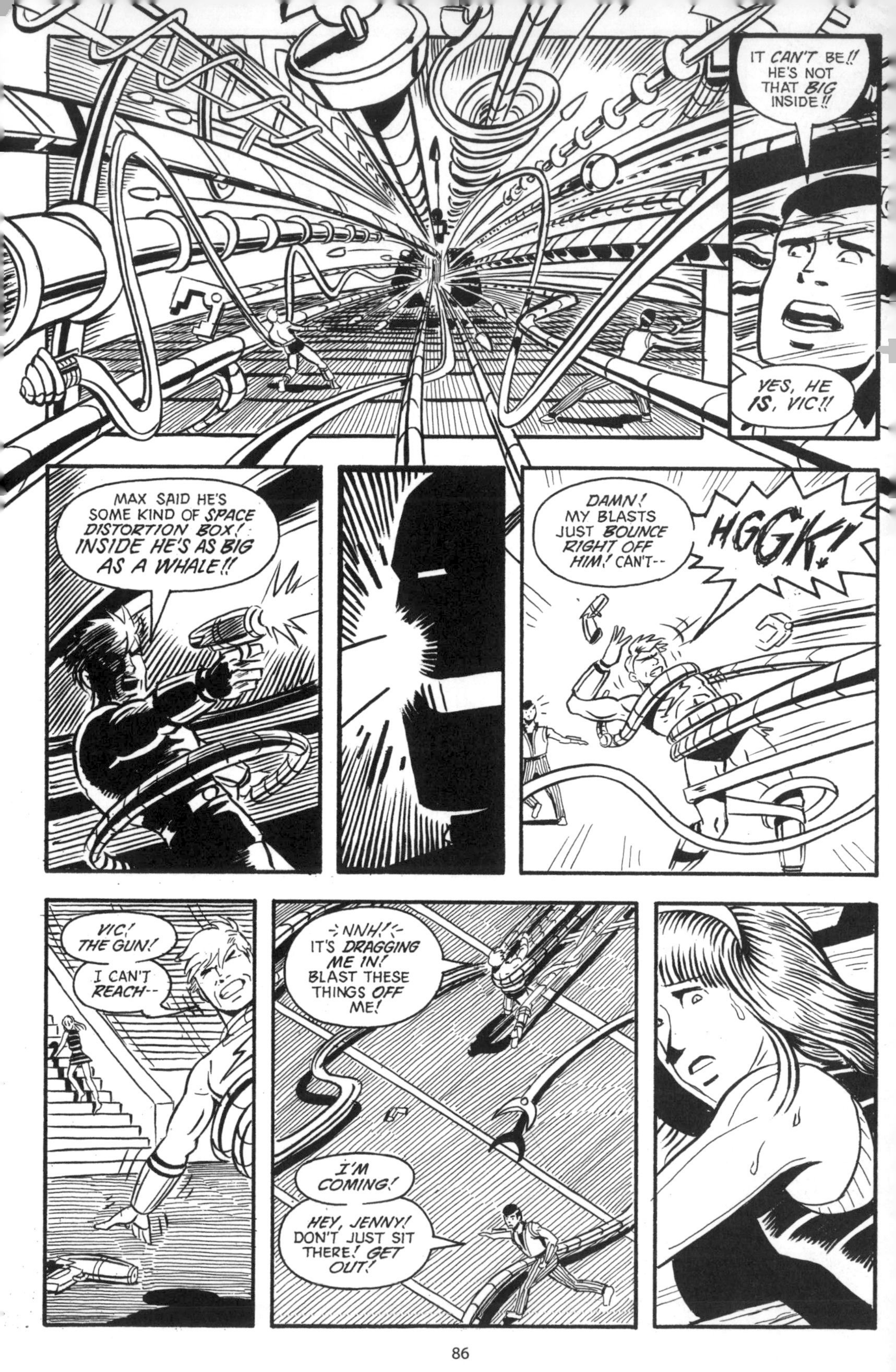
IT CAN'T BE!! HE'S NOT THAT BIG INSIDE!!
YES, HE IS, VIC!!
MAX SAID HE'S SOME KIND OF SPACE DISTORTION BOX! INSIDE HE'S AS BIG AS A WHALE!!
DAMN! MY BLASTS JUST BOUNCE RIGHT OFF HIM! CAN'T--
HGGK!
VIC! THE GUN!
I CAN'T REACH--
NNH! IT'S DRAGGING ME IN! BLAST THESE THINGS OFF ME!
I'M COMING!
HEY, JENNY! DON'T JUST SIT THERE! GET OUT!

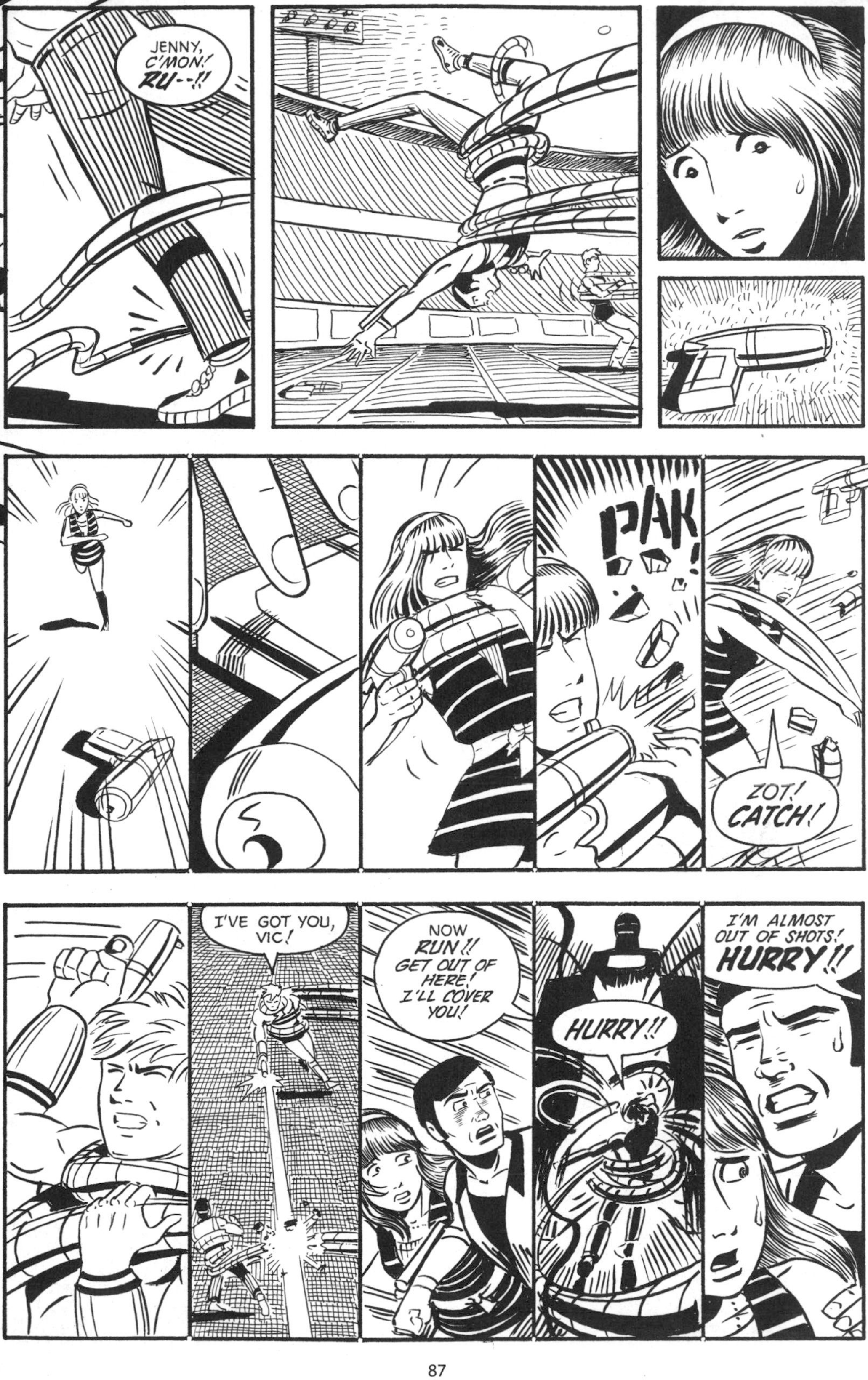
JENNY, C'MON! RU--!!
PAK
ZOT! CATCH!
I'VE GOT YOU, VIC!
NOW RUN!! GET OUT OF HERE! I'LL COVER YOU!
HURRY!!
I'M ALMOST OUT OF SHOTS! HURRY!!

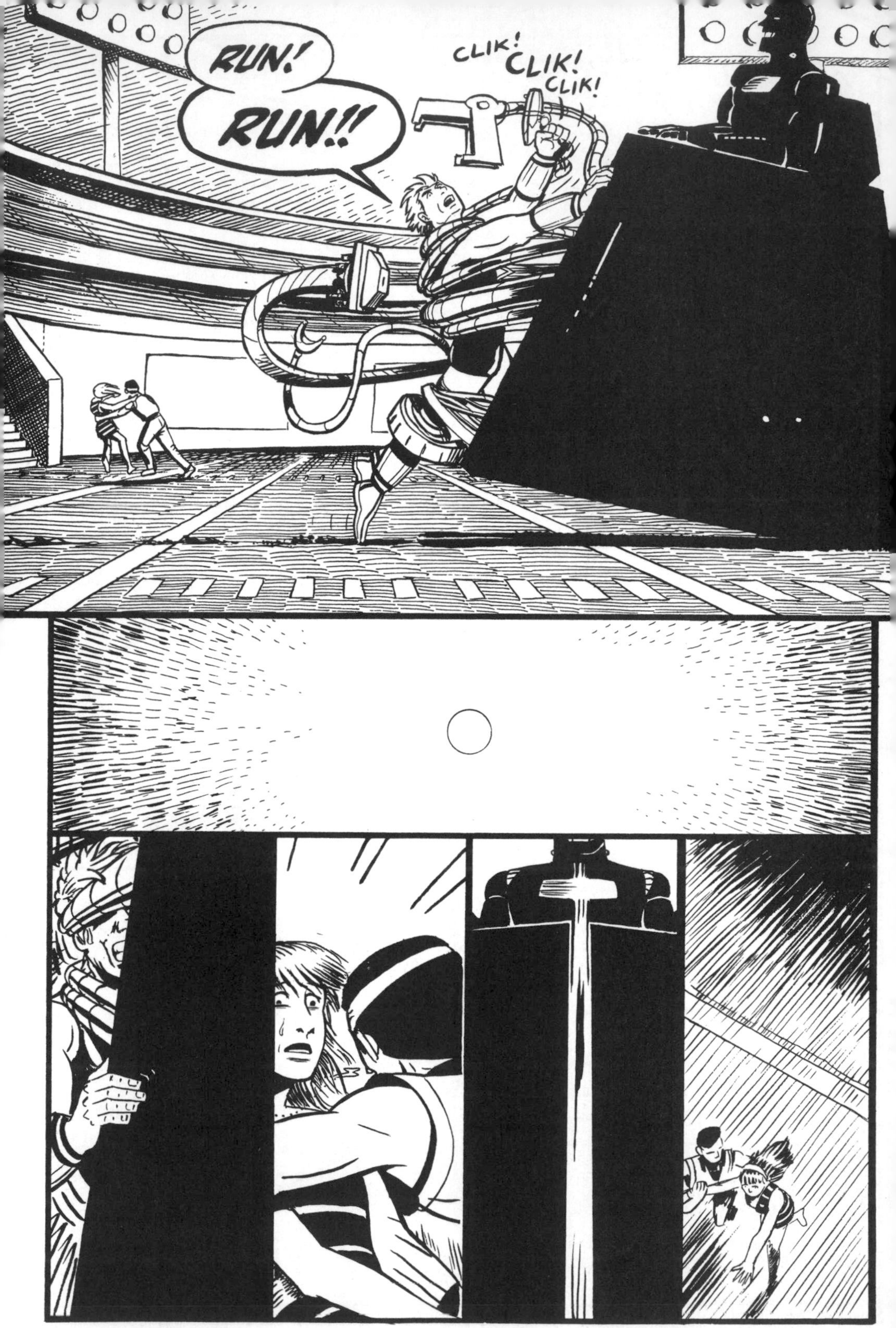
RUN!
RUN!!
CLIK!
CLIK!
CLIK!

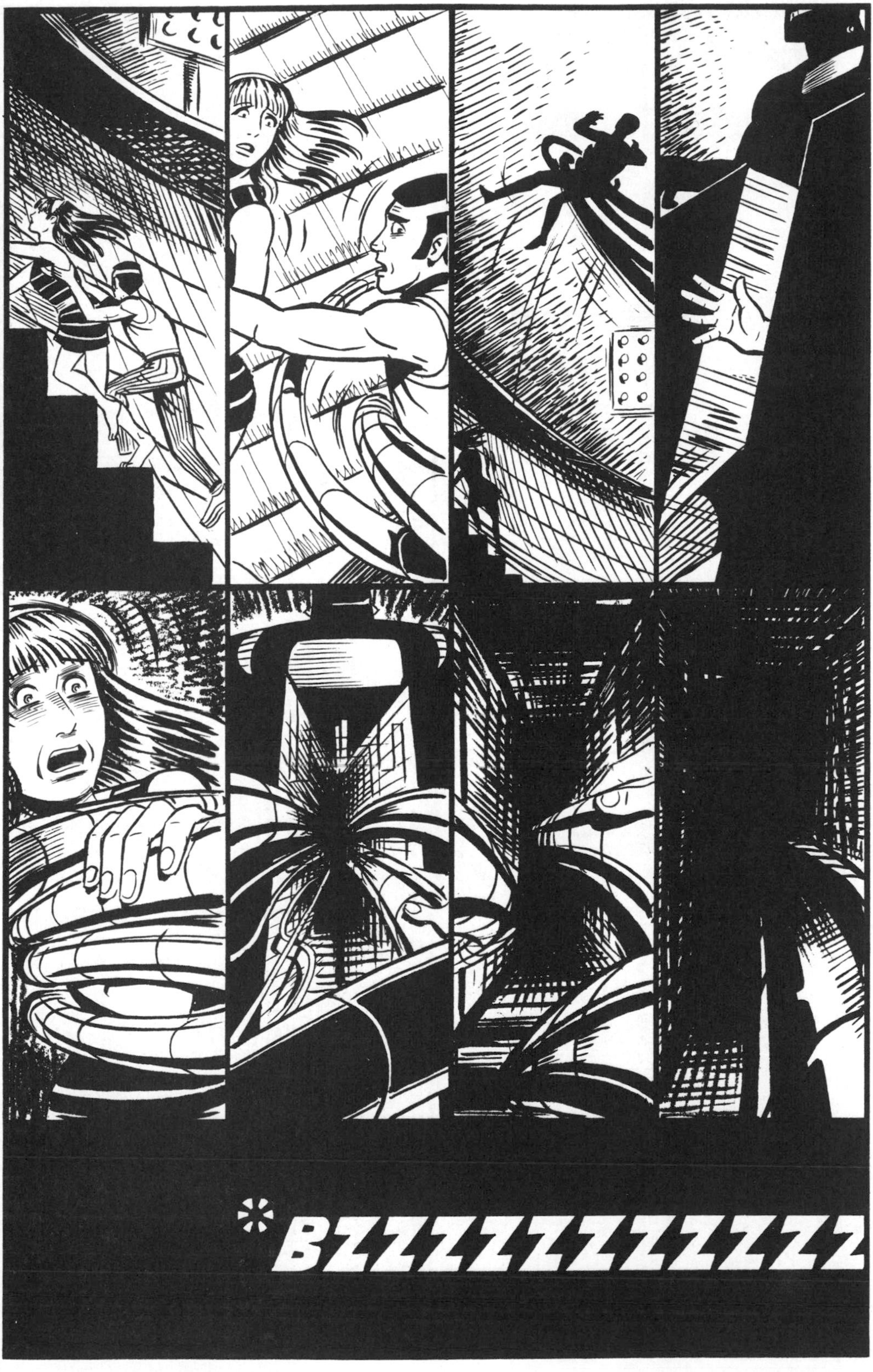
*BZZZZZZZZZZZ

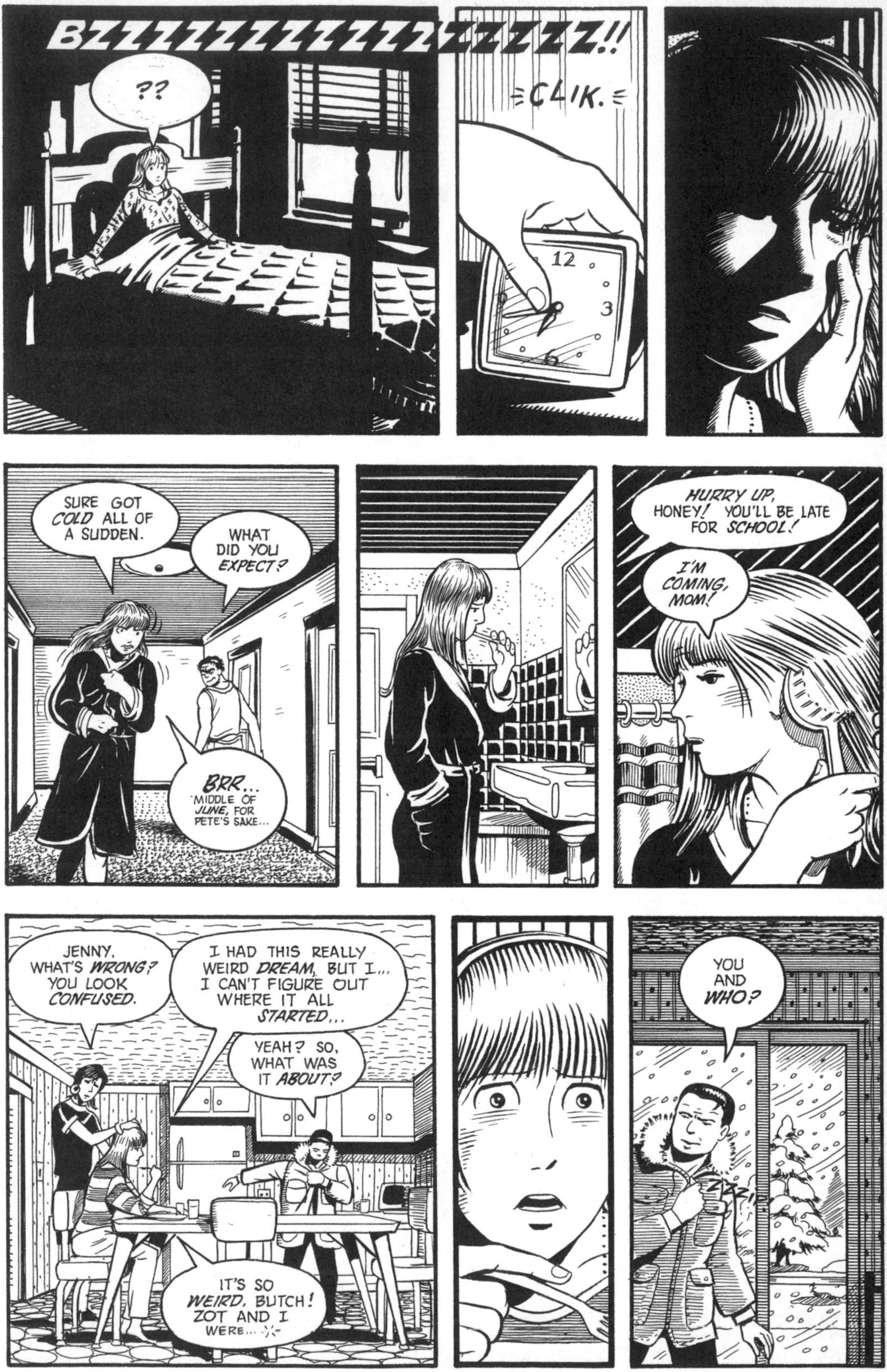
BZZZZZZZZZZZZZZZZZZZZZZ!!
??
CLIK.
SURE GOT COLD ALL OF A SUDDEN.
WHAT DID YOU EXPECT?
BRR... MIDDLE OF JUNE, FOR PETE'S SAKE...
HURRY UP, HONEY! YOU'LL BE LATE FOR SCHOOL!
I'M COMING, MOM!
JENNY, WHAT'S WRONG? YOU LOOK CONFUSED.
I HAD THIS REALLY WEIRD DREAM, BUT I... I CAN'T FIGURE OUT WHERE IT ALL STARTED...
YEAH? SO, WHAT WAS IT ABOUT?
IT'S SO WEIRD, BUTCH! ZOT AND I WERE...
YOU AND WHO?
ZZZIP!

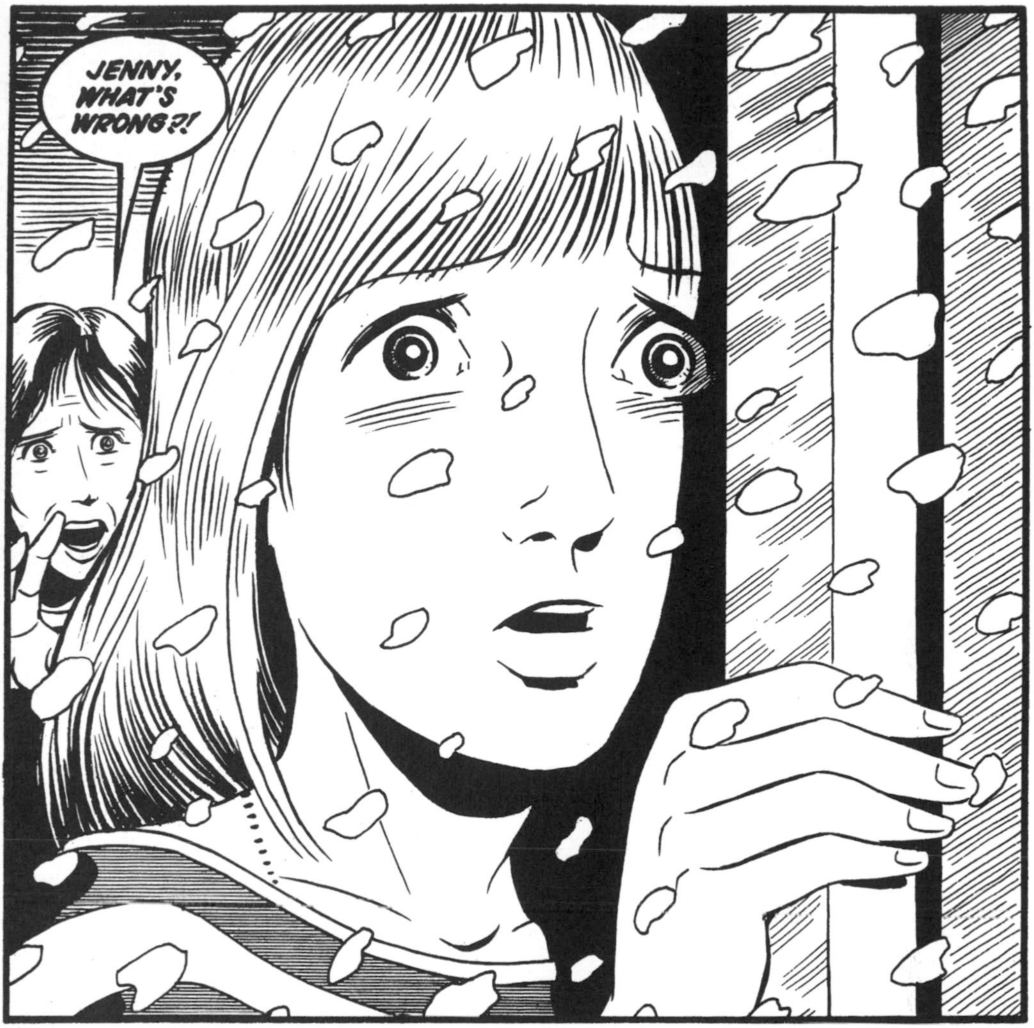
JENNY, WHAT'S WRONG?!

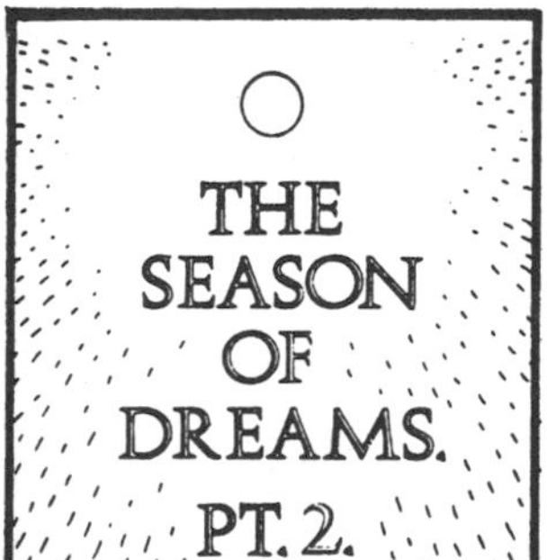
THE SEASON OF DREAMS.
PT. 2.
BY SCOTT McCLOUD
LETTERER: bob lappan
EDITOR: cat yronwode

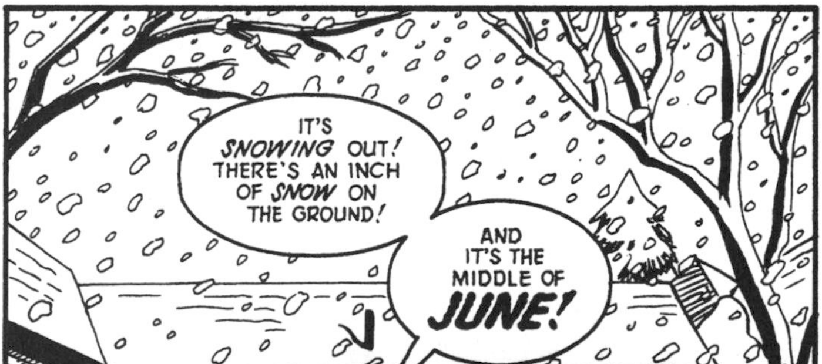
IT'S SNOWING OUT! THERE'S AN INCH OF SNOW ON THE GROUND!
AND IT'S THE MIDDLE OF JUNE!

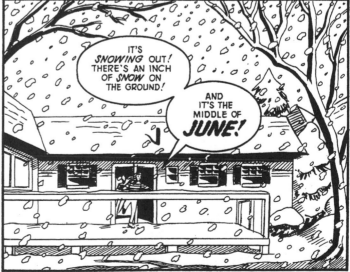

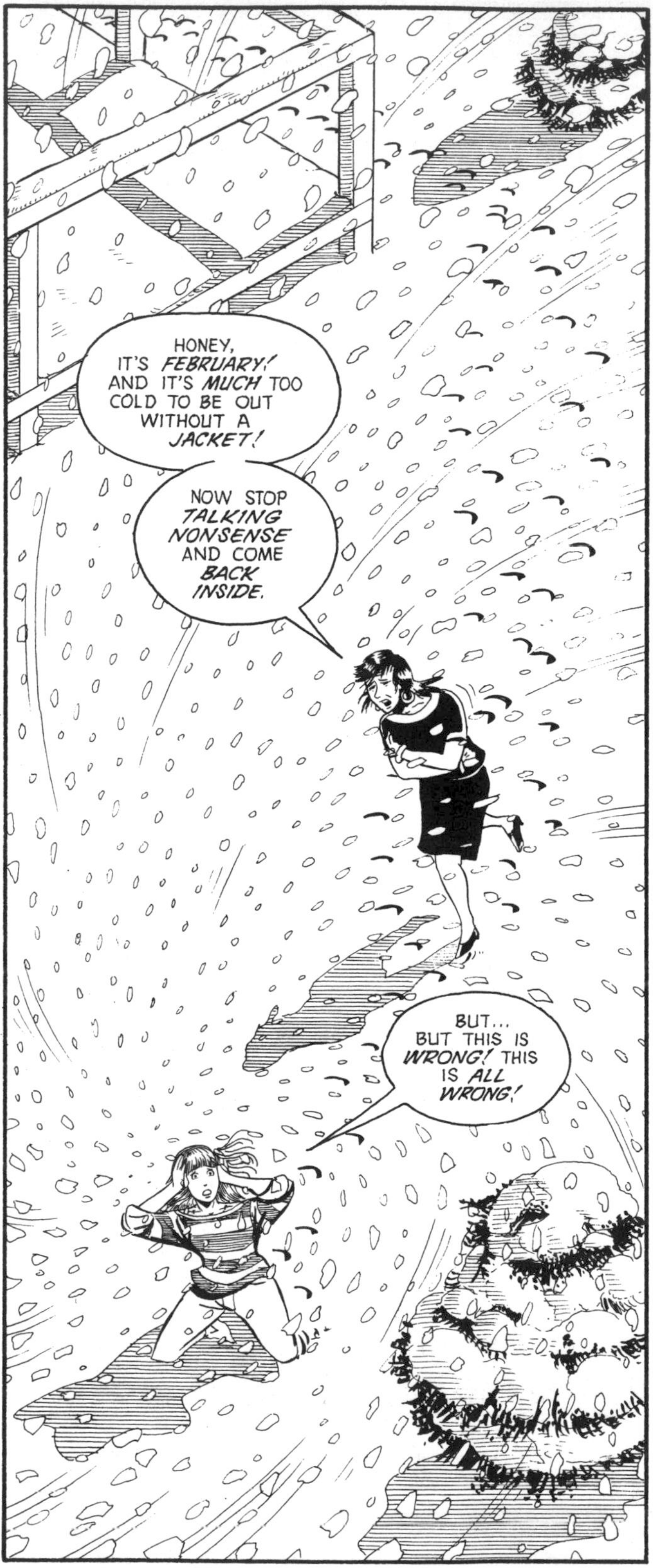
HONEY, IT'S FEBRUARY! AND IT'S MUCH TOO COLD TO BE OUT WITHOUT A JACKET!
NOW STOP TALKING NONSENSE AND COME BACK INSIDE.
BUT... BUT THIS IS WRONG! THIS IS ALL WRONG!

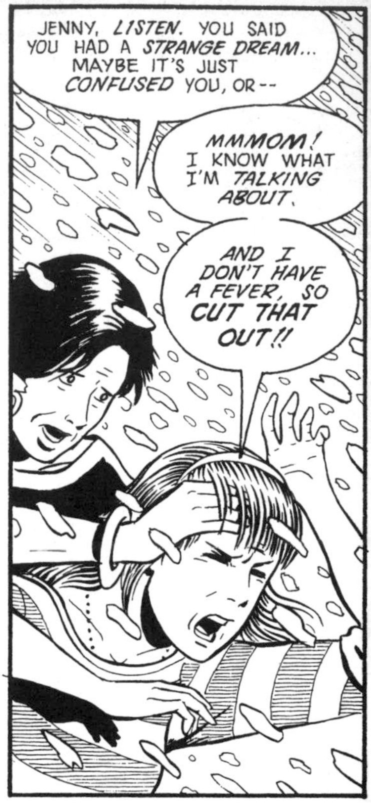
JENNY, LISTEN. YOU SAID YOU HAD A STRANGE DREAM... MAYBE IT'S JUST CONFUSED YOU, OR--
MMMOM! I KNOW WHAT I'M TALKING ABOUT.
AND I DON'T HAVE A FEVER, SO CUT THAT OUT!!

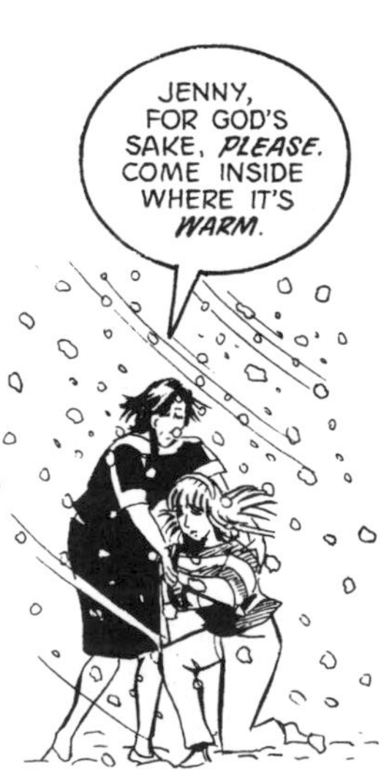
JENNY, FOR GOD'S SAKE, PLEASE. COME INSIDE WHERE IT'S WARM.
OH, MOM... WHAT'S GOING ON?? WHERE DID SUMMER GO??

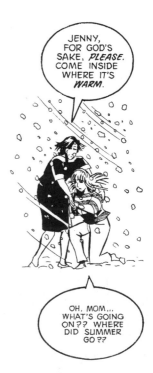

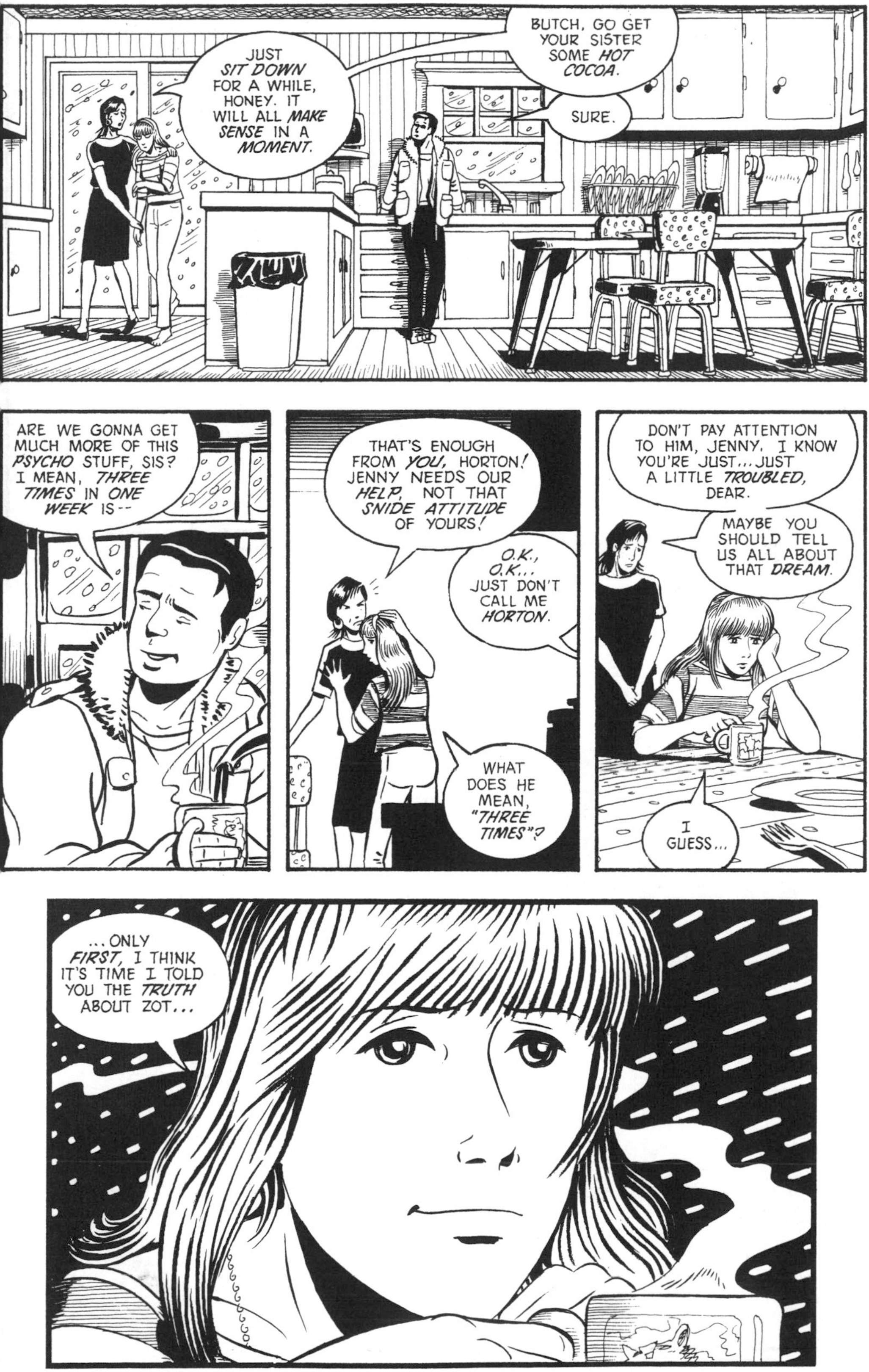
JUST SIT DOWN FOR A WHILE, HONEY. IT WILL ALL MAKE SENSE IN A MOMENT.
BUTCH, GO GET YOUR SISTER SOME HOT COCOA.
SURE.
ARE WE GONNA GET MUCH MORE OF THIS PSYCHO STUFF, SIS? I MEAN, THREE TIMES IN ONE WEEK IS--
THAT'S ENOUGH FROM YOU, HORTON! JENNY NEEDS OUR HELP, NOT THAT SNIDE ATTITUDE OF YOURS!
O.K., O.K... JUST DON'T CALL ME HORTON.
WHAT DOES HE MEAN, "THREE TIMES"?
DON'T PAY ATTENTION TO HIM, JENNY. I KNOW YOU'RE JUST... JUST A LITTLE TROUBLED, DEAR.
MAYBE YOU SHOULD TELL US ALL ABOUT THAT DREAM.
I GUESS...
...ONLY FIRST, I THINK IT'S TIME I TOLD YOU THE TRUTH ABOUT ZOT...

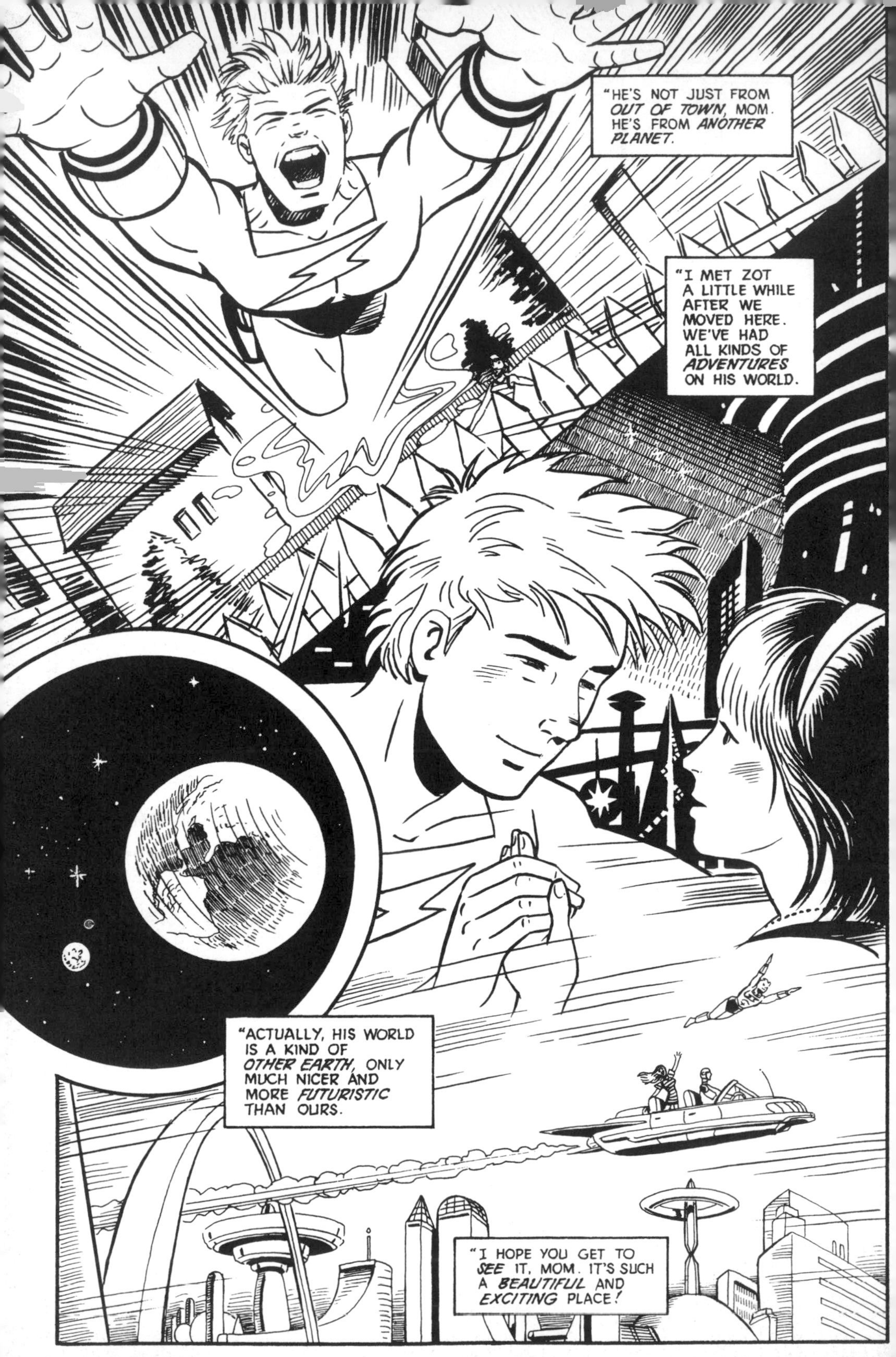
"HE'S NOT JUST FROM OUT OF TOWN, MOM. HE'S FROM ANOTHER PLANET.
"I MET ZOT A LITTLE WHILE AFTER WE MOVED HERE. WE'VE HAD ALL KINDS OF ADVENTURES ON HIS WORLD.
"ACTUALLY, HIS WORLD IS A KIND OF OTHER EARTH, ONLY MUCH NICER AND MORE FUTURISTIC THAN OURS.
"I HOPE YOU GET TO SEE IT, MOM. IT'S SUCH A BEAUTIFUL AND EXCITING PLACE!

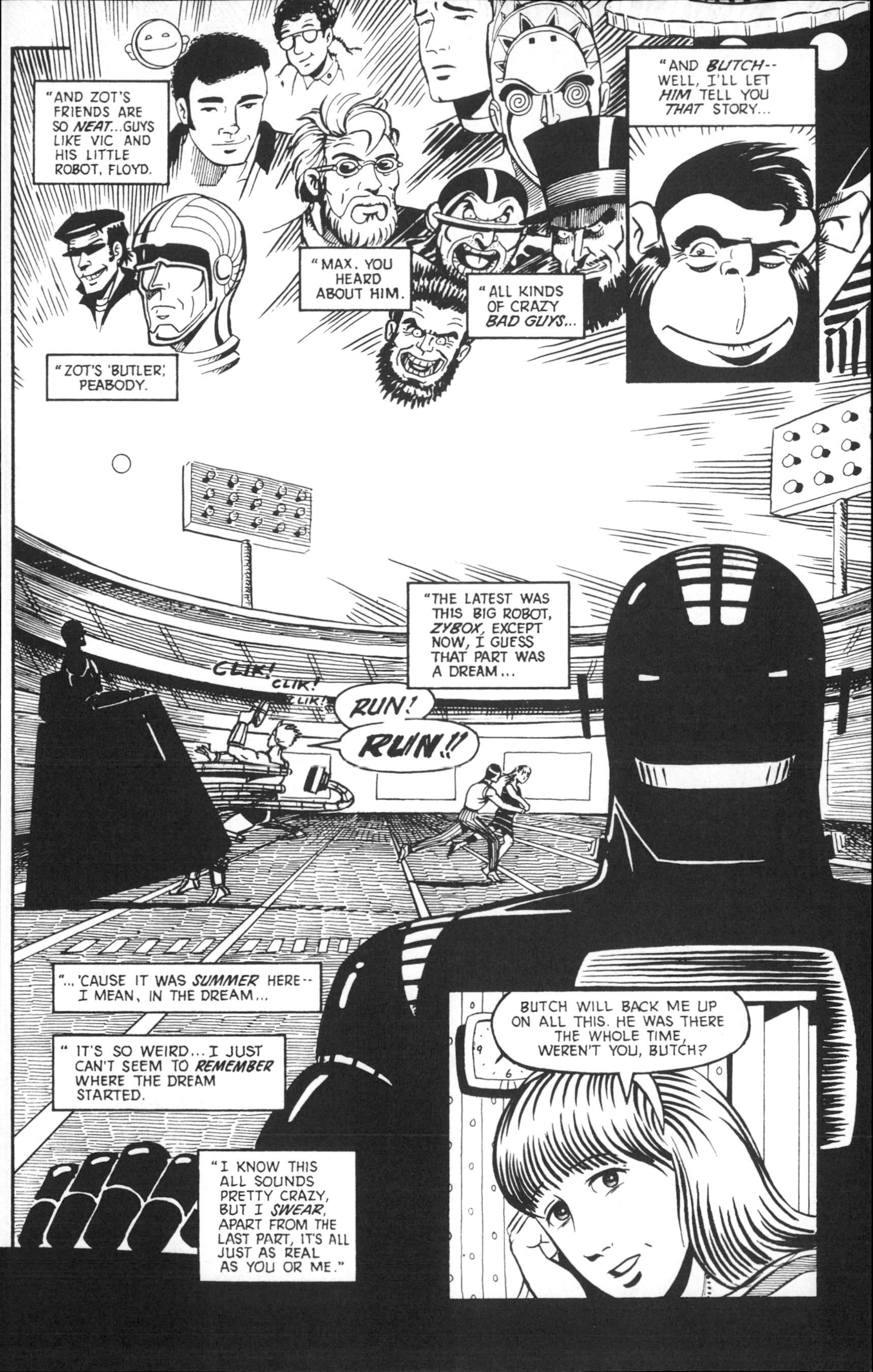
"AND ZOT'S FRIENDS ARE SO *NEAT*...GUYS LIKE VIC AND HIS LITTLE ROBOT, FLOYD.
"ZOT'S 'BUTLER', PEABODY.
"MAX. YOU HEARD ABOUT HIM.
"ALL KINDS OF CRAZY *BAD GUYS*...
"AND *BUTCH*--WELL, I'LL LET *HIM* TELL YOU *THAT* STORY...
CLIK! CLIK! CLIK!
RUN!
RUN!!
"THE LATEST WAS THIS BIG ROBOT, *ZYBOX*, EXCEPT NOW, I GUESS THAT PART WAS A DREAM...
"...'CAUSE IT WAS *SUMMER* HERE--I MEAN, IN THE DREAM...
" IT'S SO WEIRD... I JUST CAN'T SEEM TO *REMEMBER* WHERE THE DREAM STARTED.
"I KNOW THIS ALL SOUNDS PRETTY CRAZY, BUT I *SWEAR*, APART FROM THE LAST PART, IT'S ALL JUST AS REAL AS YOU OR ME."
BUTCH WILL BACK ME UP ON ALL THIS. HE WAS THERE THE WHOLE TIME, WEREN'T YOU, BUTCH?

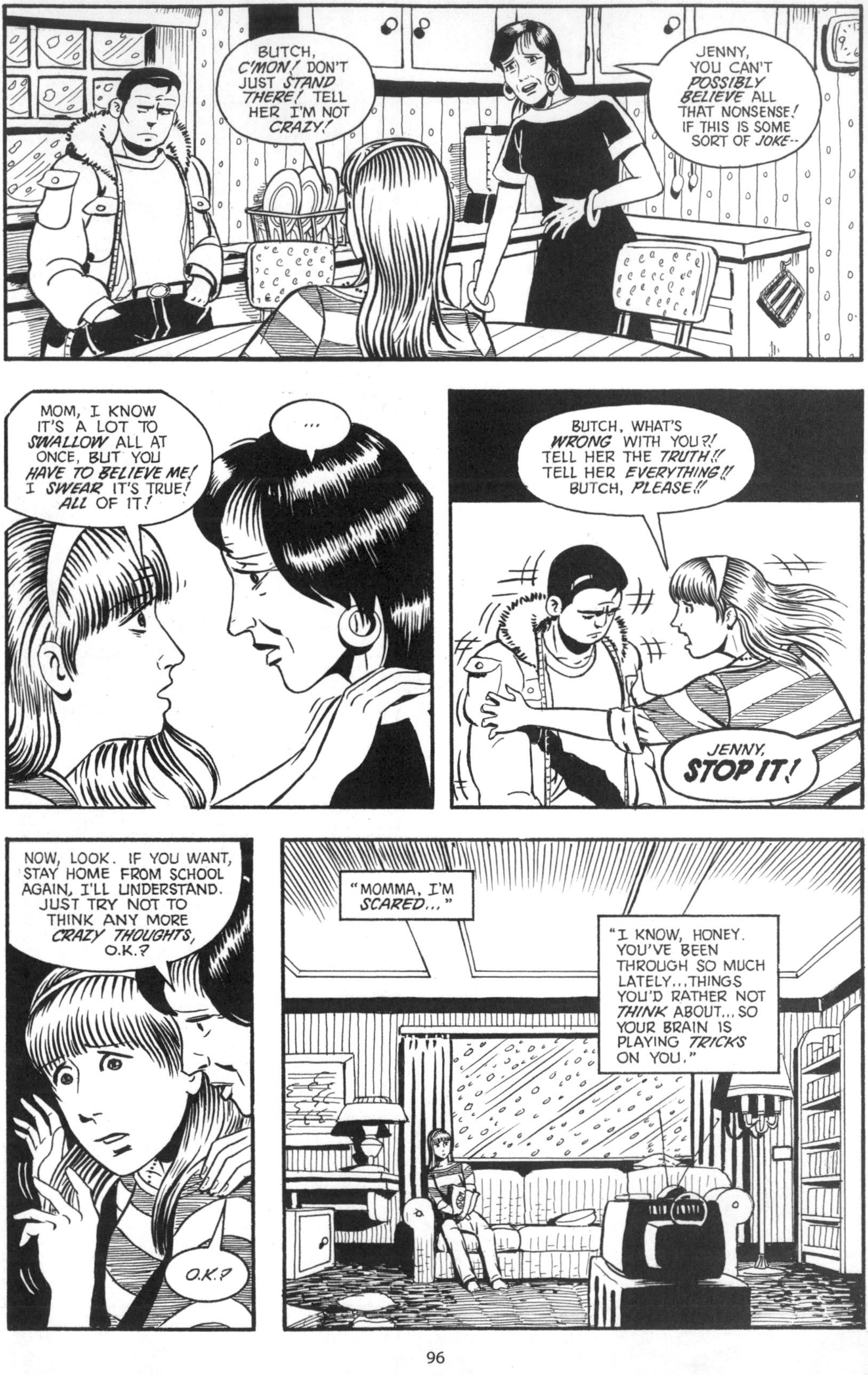
BUTCH, C'MON! DON'T JUST STAND THERE! TELL HER I'M NOT CRAZY!
JENNY, YOU CAN'T POSSIBLY BELIEVE ALL THAT NONSENSE! IF THIS IS SOME SORT OF JOKE--
MOM, I KNOW IT'S A LOT TO SWALLOW ALL AT ONCE, BUT YOU HAVE TO BELIEVE ME! I SWEAR IT'S TRUE! ALL OF IT!
...
BUTCH, WHAT'S WRONG WITH YOU?! TELL HER THE TRUTH!! TELL HER EVERYTHING!! BUTCH, PLEASE!!
JENNY, STOP IT!
NOW, LOOK. IF YOU WANT, STAY HOME FROM SCHOOL AGAIN, I'LL UNDERSTAND. JUST TRY NOT TO THINK ANY MORE CRAZY THOUGHTS, O.K.?
O.K.?
"MOMMA, I'M SCARED..."
"I KNOW, HONEY. YOU'VE BEEN THROUGH SO MUCH LATELY...THINGS YOU'D RATHER NOT THINK ABOUT... SO YOUR BRAIN IS PLAYING TRICKS ON YOU."

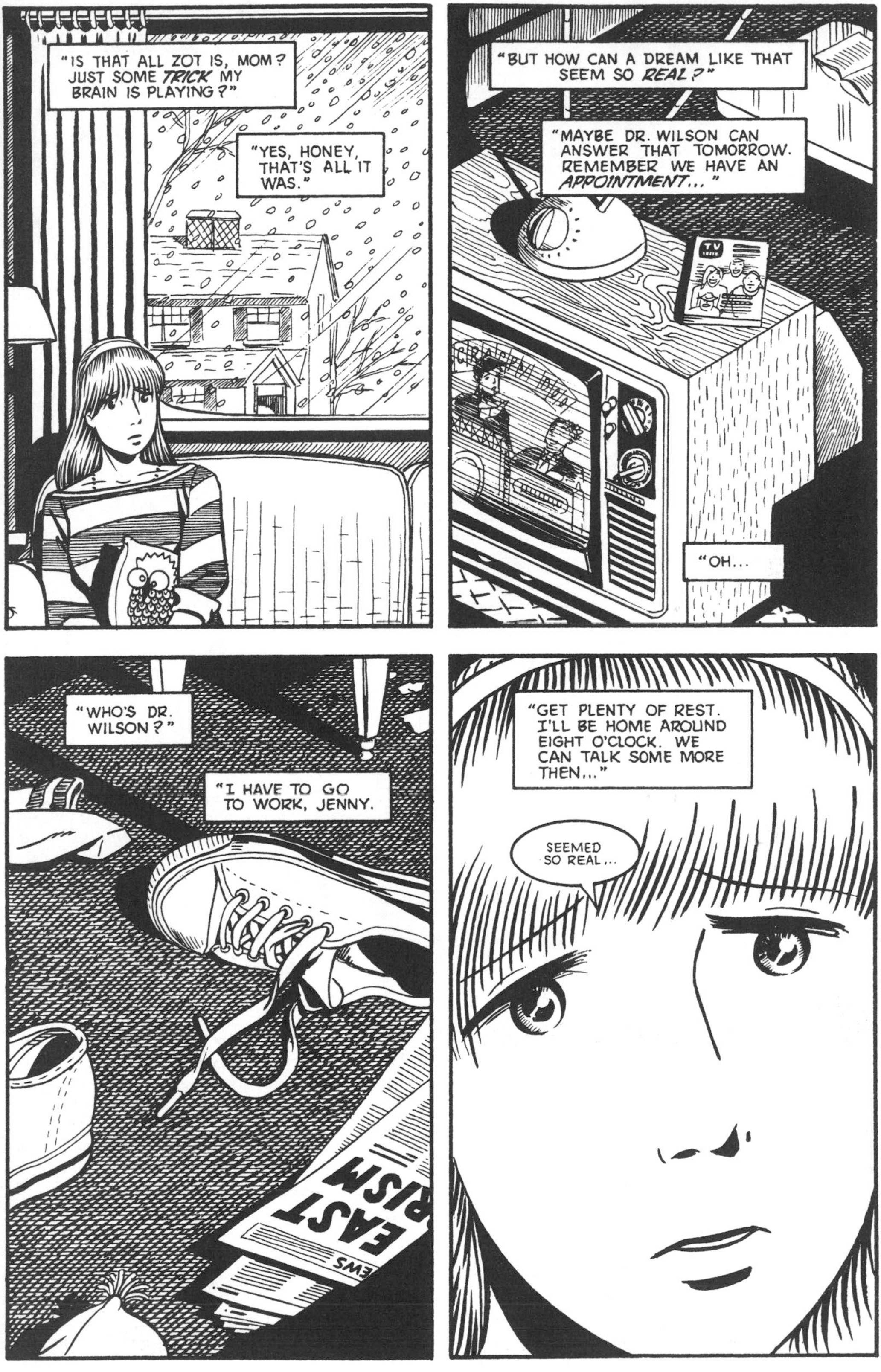
"IS THAT ALL ZOT IS, MOM? JUST SOME *TRICK* MY BRAIN IS PLAYING?"
"YES, HONEY, THAT'S ALL IT WAS."
"BUT HOW CAN A DREAM LIKE THAT SEEM SO *REAL?*"
"MAYBE DR. WILSON CAN ANSWER THAT TOMORROW. REMEMBER WE HAVE AN *APPOINTMENT...*"
"OH...
"WHO'S DR. WILSON?"
"I HAVE TO GO TO WORK, JENNY.
"GET PLENTY OF REST. I'LL BE HOME AROUND EIGHT O'CLOCK. WE CAN TALK SOME MORE THEN..."
SEEMED SO REAL...

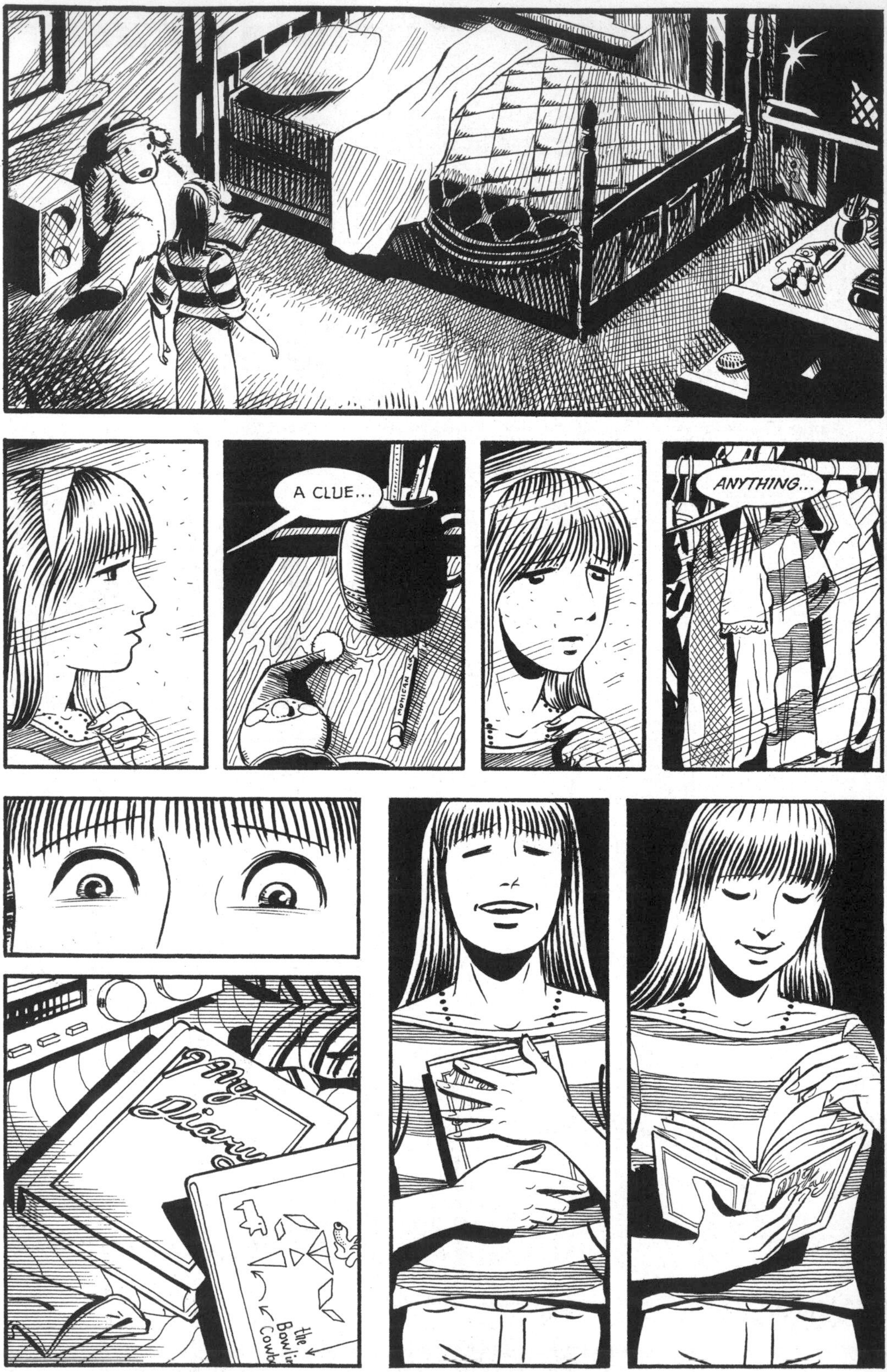
A CLUE...
ANYTHING...
My Diary

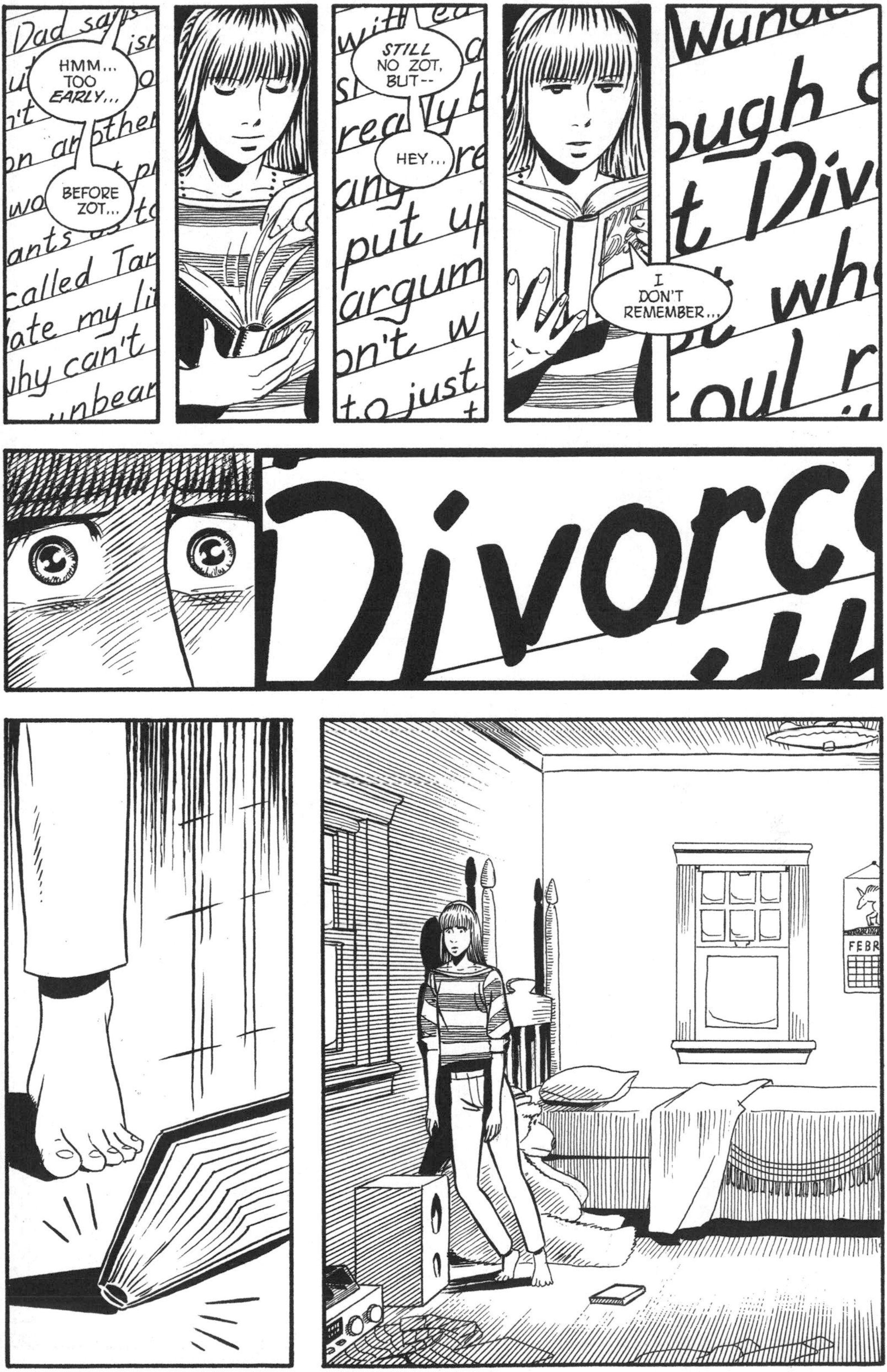
HMM... TOO *EARLY*...
BEFORE ZOT...
STILL NO ZOT, BUT--
HEY...
I DON'T REMEMBER...

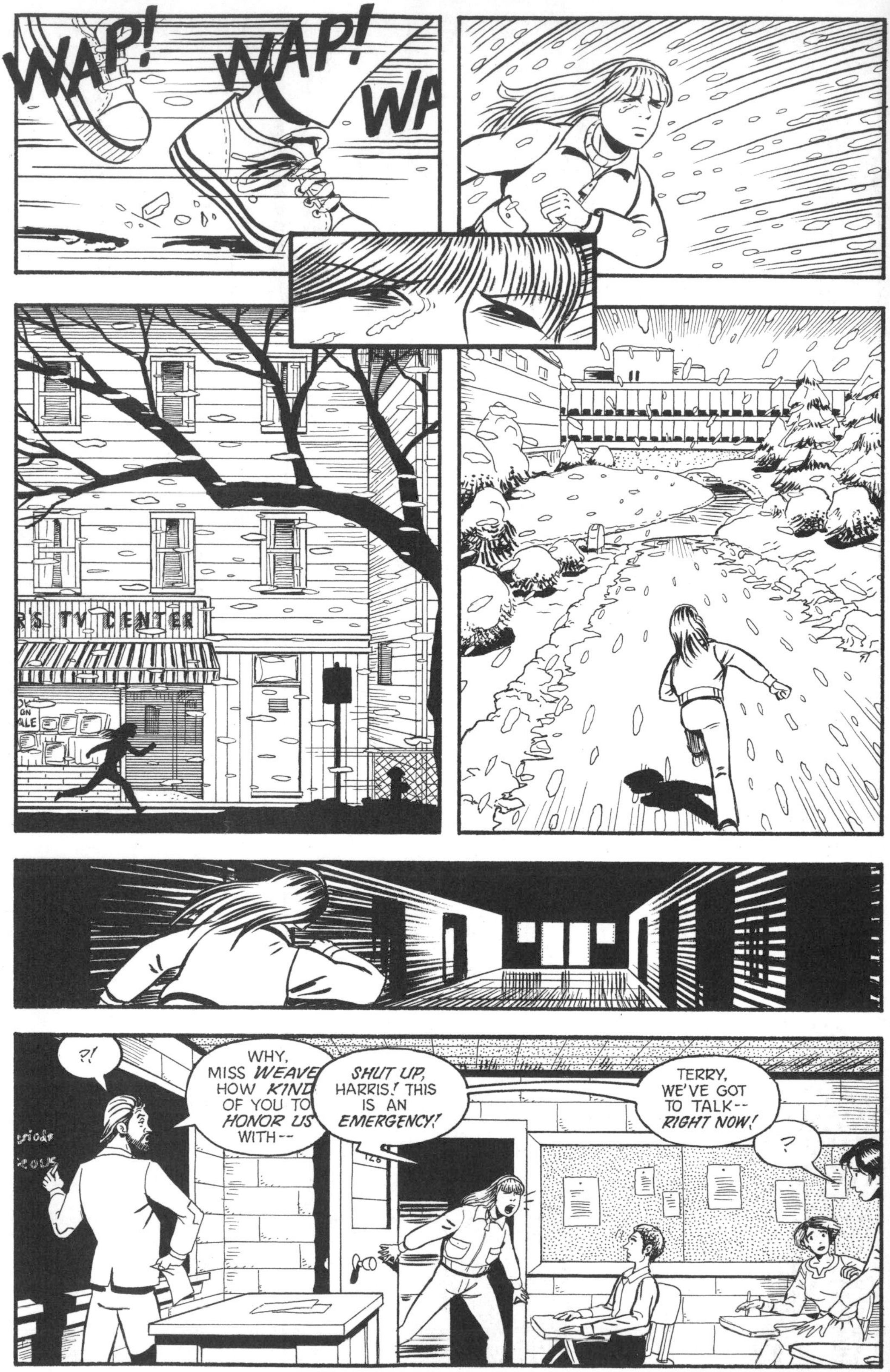
WAP!
WAP!
WA
TV CENTER
?!
WHY, MISS WEAVE HOW KIND OF YOU TO HONOR US WITH--
SHUT UP, HARRIS! THIS IS AN EMERGENCY!
TERRY, WE'VE GOT TO TALK-- RIGHT NOW!
?

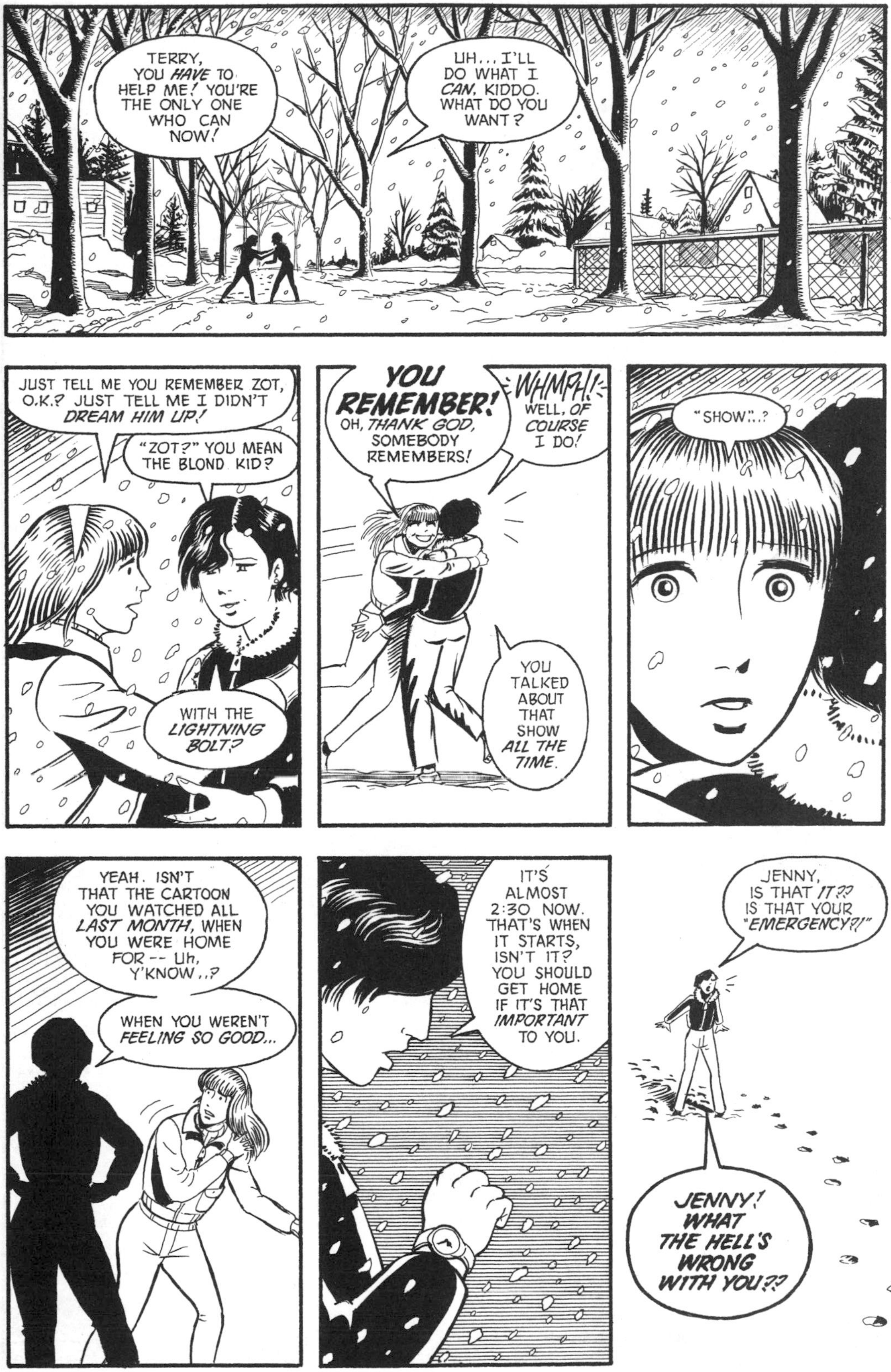
TERRY, YOU HAVE TO HELP ME! YOU'RE THE ONLY ONE WHO CAN NOW!
UH... I'LL DO WHAT I CAN, KIDDO. WHAT DO YOU WANT?
JUST TELL ME YOU REMEMBER ZOT, O.K.? JUST TELL ME I DIDN'T DREAM HIM UP!
"ZOT?" YOU MEAN THE BLOND KID?
WITH THE LIGHTNING BOLT?
YOU REMEMBER! OH, THANK GOD, SOMEBODY REMEMBERS!
WHMPH!
WELL, OF COURSE I DO!
YOU TALKED ABOUT THAT SHOW ALL THE TIME.
"SHOW"..?
YEAH. ISN'T THAT THE CARTOON YOU WATCHED ALL LAST MONTH, WHEN YOU WERE HOME FOR -- Uh, Y'KNOW..?
WHEN YOU WEREN'T FEELING SO GOOD...
IT'S ALMOST 2:30 NOW. THAT'S WHEN IT STARTS, ISN'T IT? YOU SHOULD GET HOME IF IT'S THAT IMPORTANT TO YOU.
JENNY, IS THAT IT?? IS THAT YOUR "EMERGENCY?!"
JENNY! WHAT THE HELL'S WRONG WITH YOU??

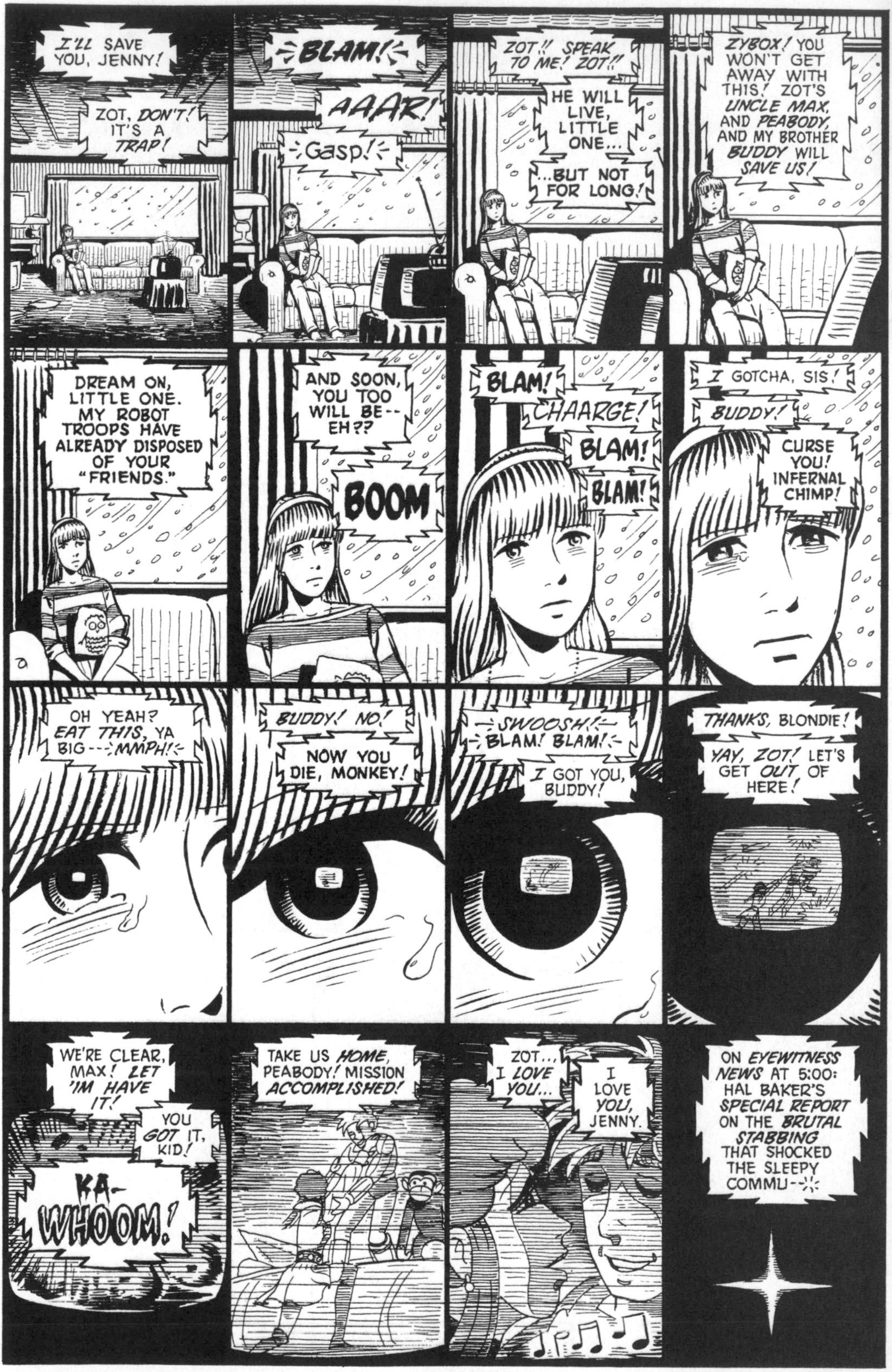
I'LL SAVE YOU, JENNY!
ZOT, DON'T! IT'S A TRAP!
BLAM!
AAAR!
Gasp!
ZOT!! SPEAK TO ME! ZOT!!
HE WILL LIVE, LITTLE ONE...
...BUT NOT FOR LONG!
ZYBOX! YOU WON'T GET AWAY WITH THIS! ZOT'S UNCLE MAX, AND PEABODY, AND MY BROTHER BUDDY WILL SAVE US!
DREAM ON, LITTLE ONE. MY ROBOT TROOPS HAVE ALREADY DISPOSED OF YOUR "FRIENDS."
AND SOON, YOU TOO WILL BE-- EH??
BOOM
BLAM!
CHAARGE!
BLAM!
BLAM!
I GOTCHA, SIS!
BUDDY!
CURSE YOU! INFERNAL CHIMP!
OH YEAH? EAT THIS, YA BIG--MMPH!
BUDDY! NO!
NOW YOU DIE, MONKEY!
SWOOSH!
BLAM! BLAM!
I GOT YOU, BUDDY!
THANKS, BLONDIE!
YAY, ZOT! LET'S GET OUT OF HERE!
WE'RE CLEAR, MAX! LET 'IM HAVE IT!
YOU GOT IT, KID!
KA-WHOOM!
TAKE US HOME, PEABODY! MISSION ACCOMPLISHED!
ZOT... I LOVE YOU...
I LOVE YOU, JENNY.
ON EYEWITNESS NEWS AT 5:00: HAL BAKER'S SPECIAL REPORT ON THE BRUTAL STABBING THAT SHOCKED THE SLEEPY COMMU--

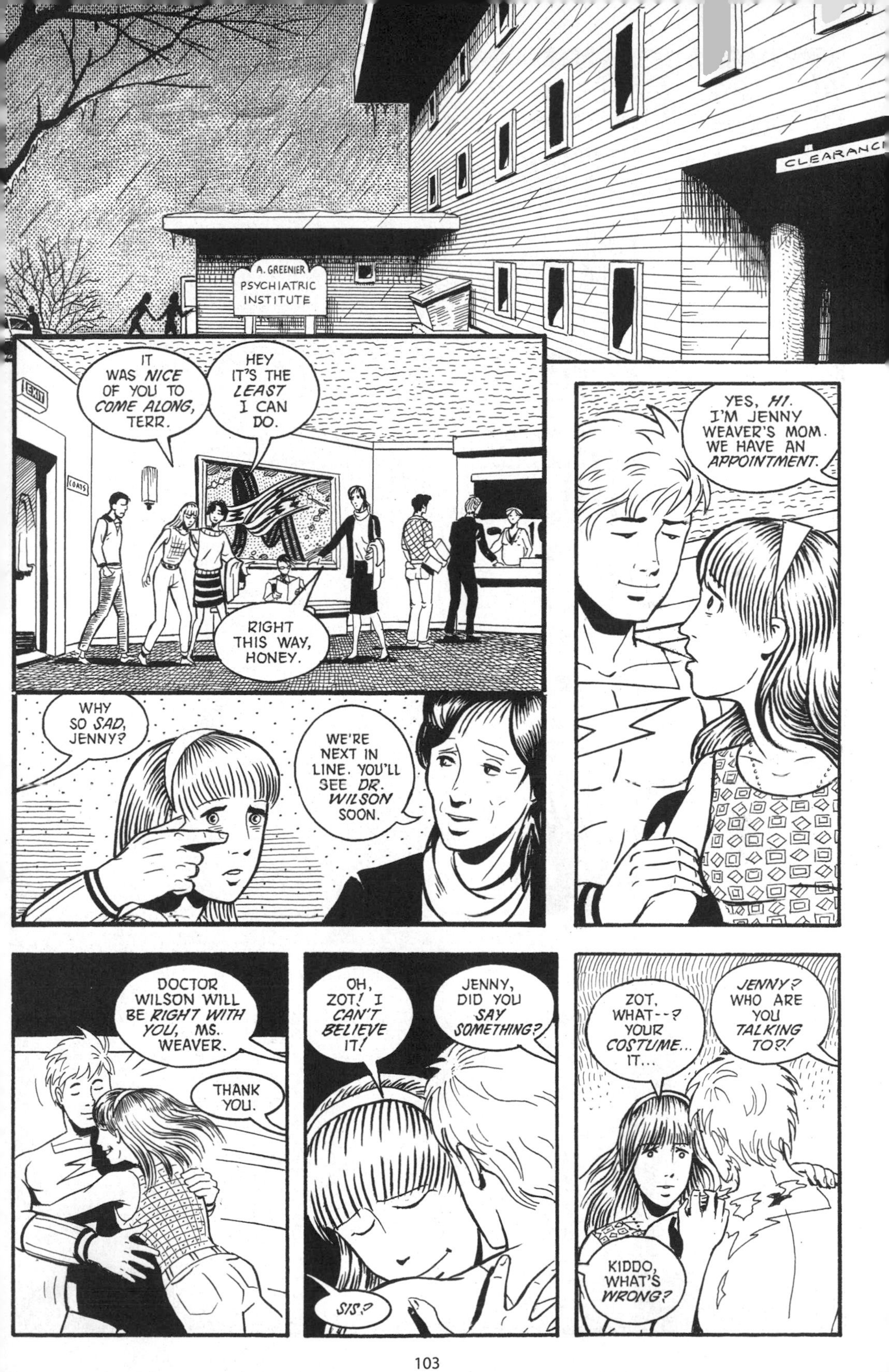

CLEARANC
A. GREENIER
PSYCHIATRIC
INSTITUTE
EXIT
COATS
IT WAS NICE OF YOU TO COME ALONG, TERR.
HEY IT'S THE LEAST I CAN DO.
RIGHT THIS WAY, HONEY.
WHY SO SAD, JENNY?
WE'RE NEXT IN LINE. YOU'LL SEE DR. WILSON SOON.
YES, HI. I'M JENNY WEAVER'S MOM. WE HAVE AN APPOINTMENT.
DOCTOR WILSON WILL BE RIGHT WITH YOU, MS. WEAVER.
THANK YOU.
OH, ZOT! I CAN'T BELIEVE IT!
JENNY, DID YOU SAY SOMETHING?
SIS...?
ZOT, WHAT--? YOUR COSTUME... IT...
JENNY? WHO ARE YOU TALKING TO?!
KIDDO, WHAT'S WRONG?

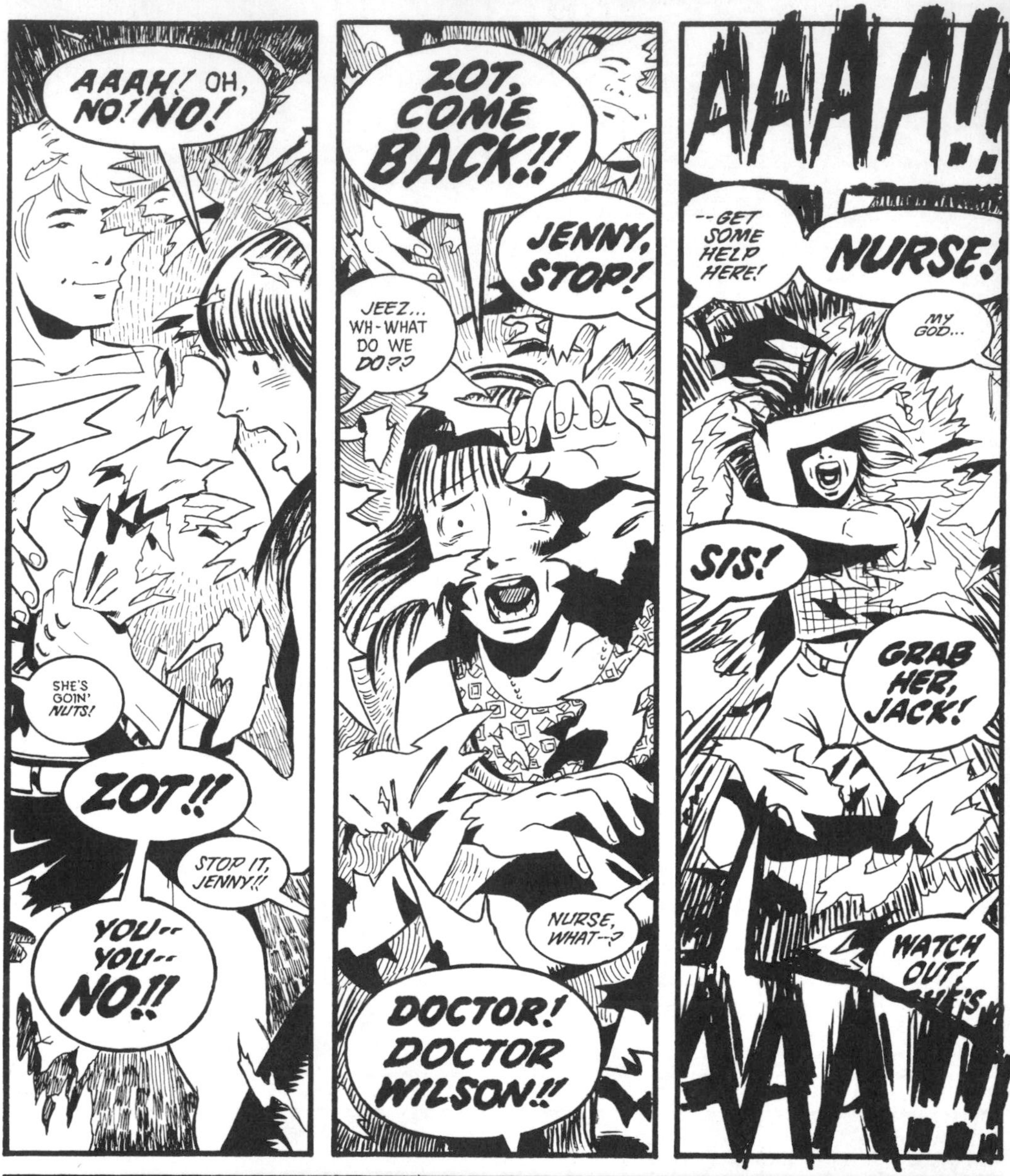
AAAH! OH, NO! NO!
SHE'S GOIN' NUTS!
ZOT!!
STOP IT, JENNY!!
YOU-- YOU-- NO!!
ZOT, COME BACK!!
JENNY, STOP!
JEEZ... WH-WHAT DO WE DO??
NURSE, WHAT--?
DOCTOR! DOCTOR WILSON!!
AAAA!!
--GET SOME HELP HERE!
NURSE!
MY GOD...
SIS!
GRAB HER, JACK!
WATCH OUT!
AAAA!!
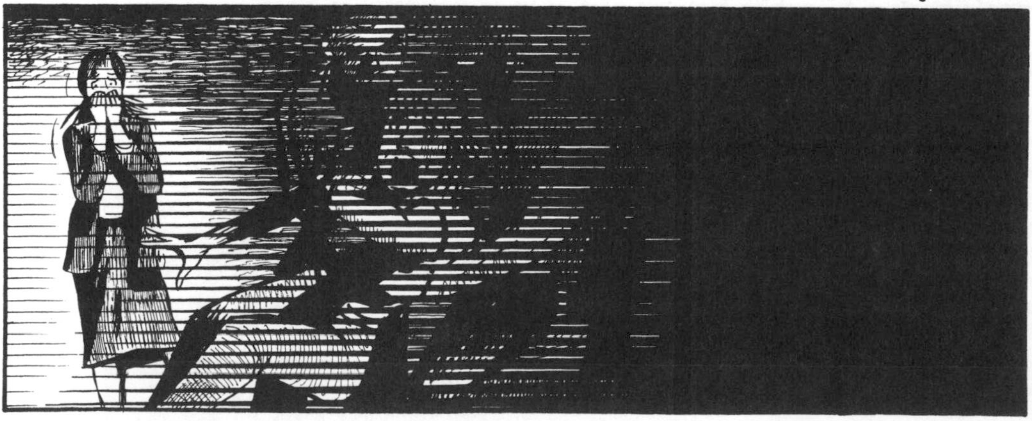

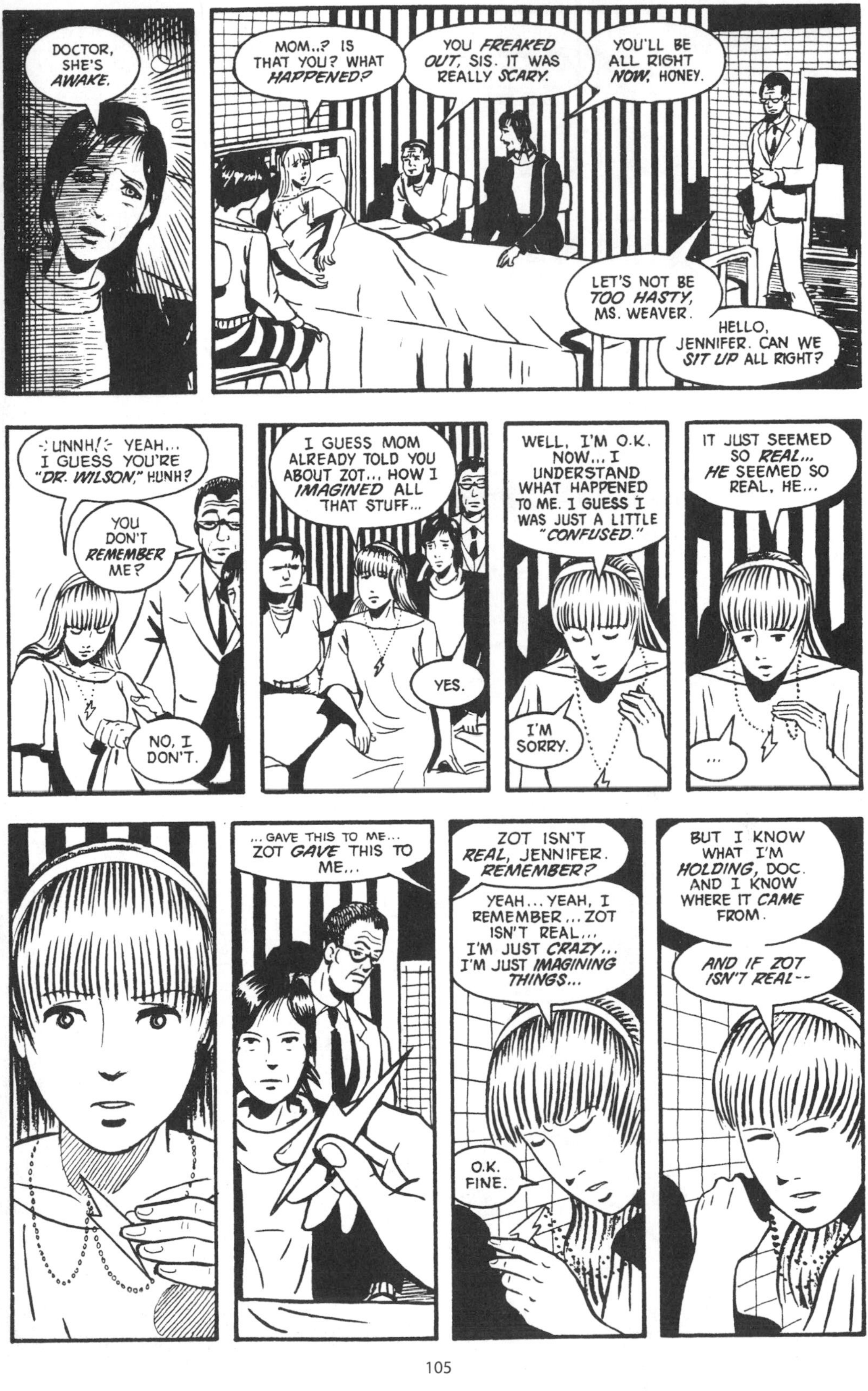
DOCTOR, SHE'S AWAKE.
MOM..? IS THAT YOU? WHAT HAPPENED?
YOU FREAKED OUT, SIS. IT WAS REALLY SCARY.
YOU'LL BE ALL RIGHT NOW, HONEY.
LET'S NOT BE TOO HASTY, MS. WEAVER.
HELLO, JENNIFER. CAN WE SIT UP ALL RIGHT?
UNNH! YEAH... I GUESS YOU'RE "DR. WILSON," HUNH?
YOU DON'T REMEMBER ME?
NO, I DON'T.
I GUESS MOM ALREADY TOLD YOU ABOUT ZOT... HOW I IMAGINED ALL THAT STUFF...
YES.
WELL, I'M O.K. NOW... I UNDERSTAND WHAT HAPPENED TO ME. I GUESS I WAS JUST A LITTLE "CONFUSED."
I'M SORRY.
IT JUST SEEMED SO REAL... HE SEEMED SO REAL, HE...
...
...GAVE THIS TO ME... ZOT GAVE THIS TO ME...
ZOT ISN'T REAL, JENNIFER. REMEMBER?
YEAH... YEAH, I REMEMBER... ZOT ISN'T REAL... I'M JUST CRAZY... I'M JUST IMAGINING THINGS...
O.K. FINE.
BUT I KNOW WHAT I'M HOLDING, DOC. AND I KNOW WHERE IT CAME FROM.
AND IF ZOT ISN'T REAL--

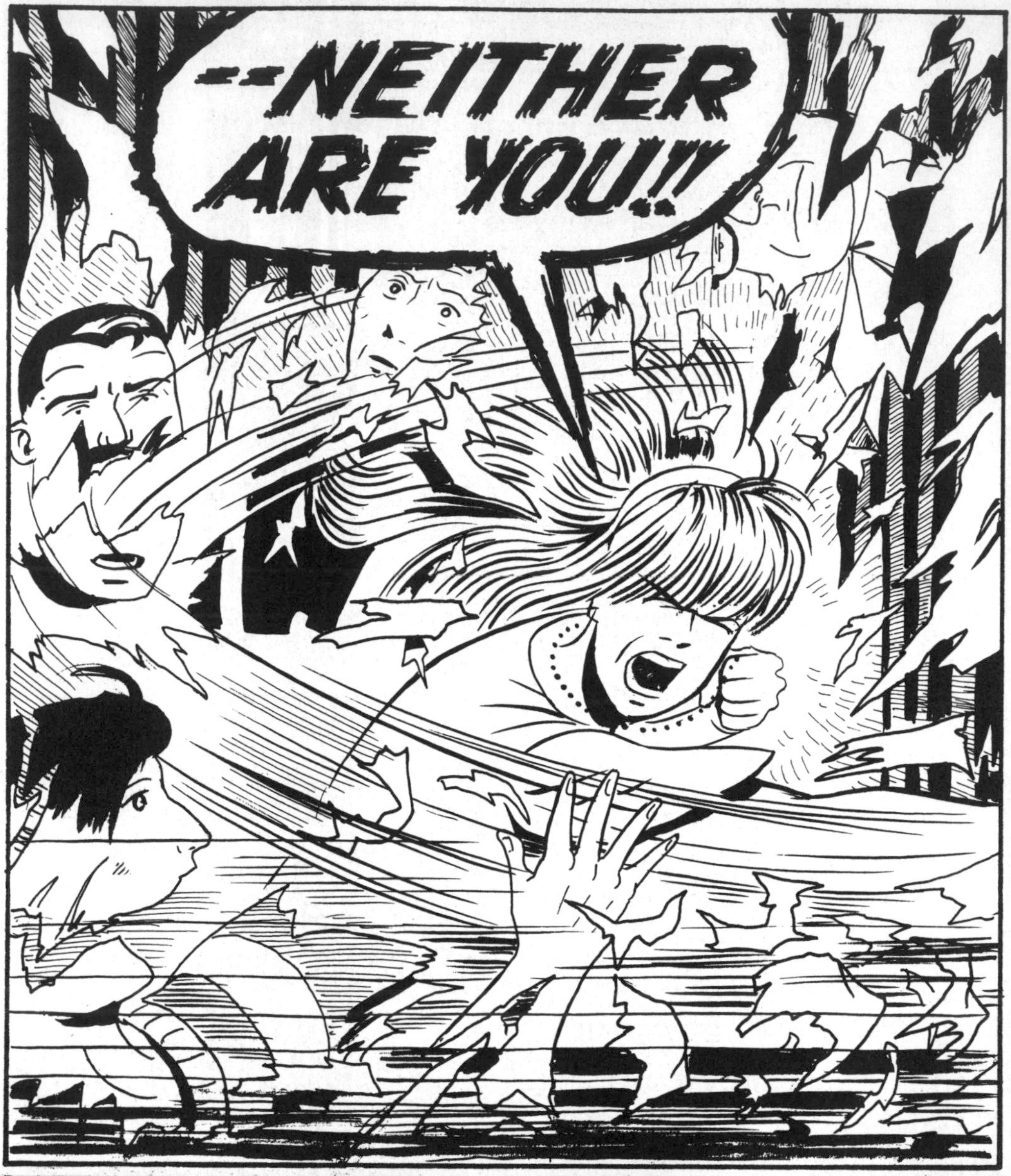
--NEITHER ARE YOU!!
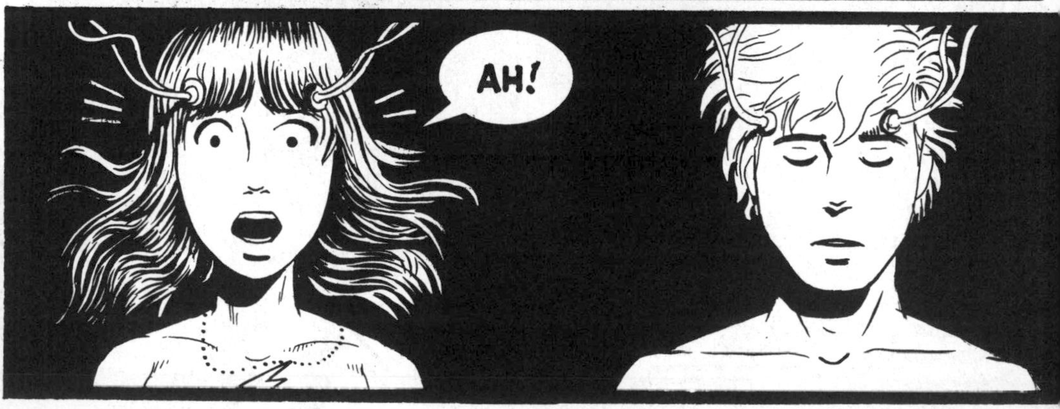
AH!

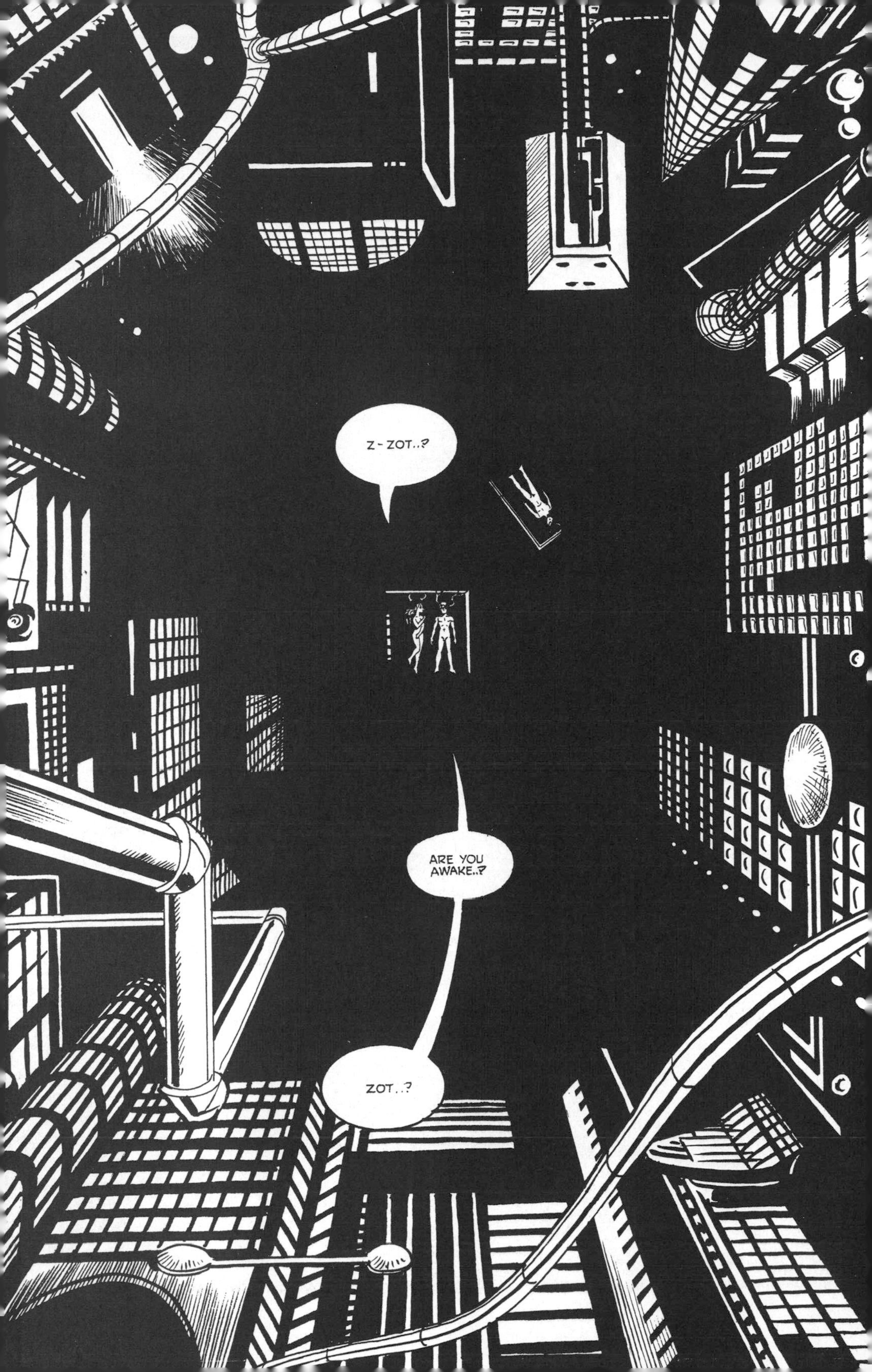
Z-ZOT..?
ARE YOU AWAKE..?
ZOT..?

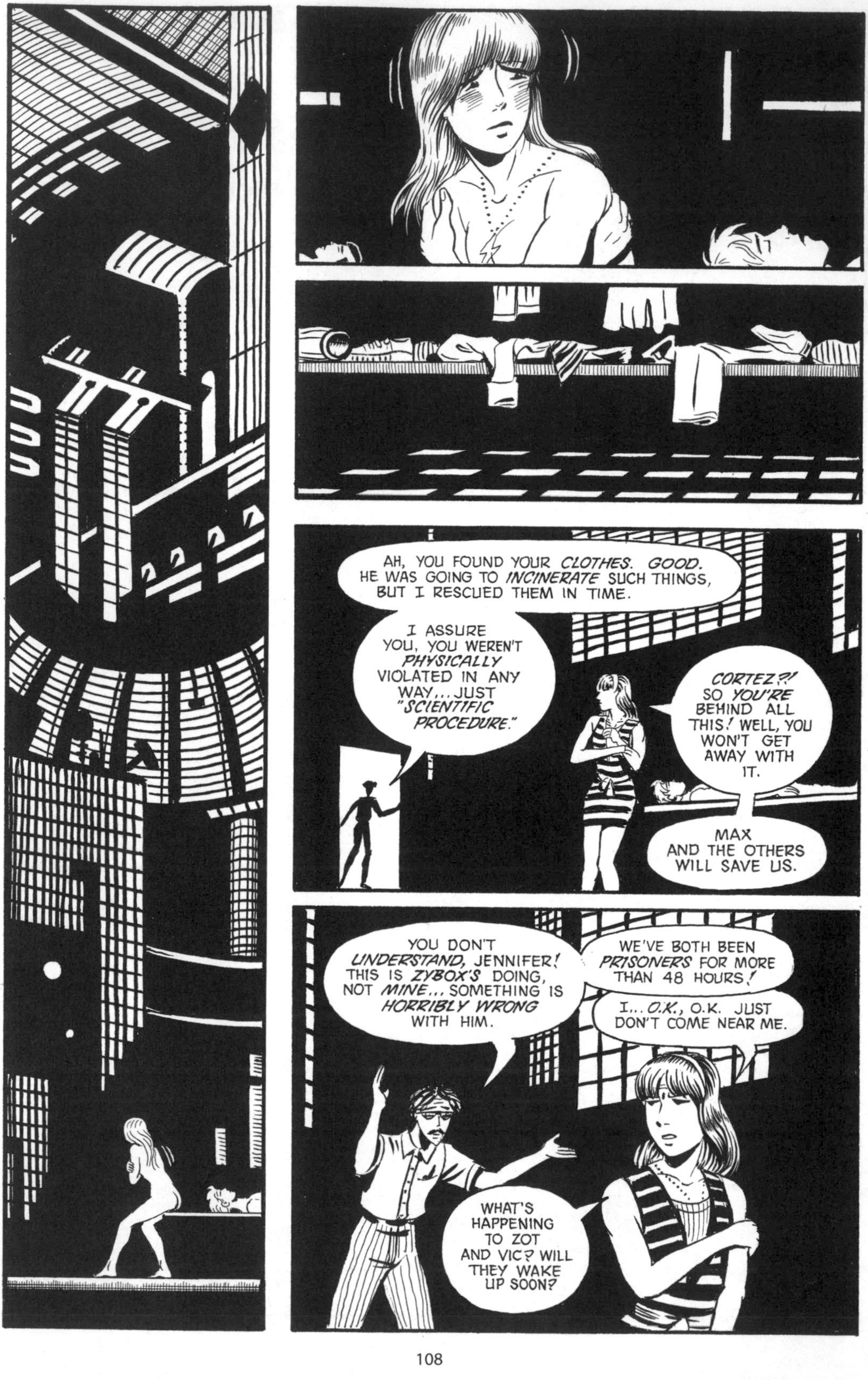
AH, YOU FOUND YOUR CLOTHES. GOOD. HE WAS GOING TO INCINERATE SUCH THINGS, BUT I RESCUED THEM IN TIME.
I ASSURE YOU, YOU WEREN'T PHYSICALLY VIOLATED IN ANY WAY... JUST "SCIENTIFIC PROCEDURE."
CORTEZ?! SO YOU'RE BEHIND ALL THIS! WELL, YOU WON'T GET AWAY WITH IT.
MAX AND THE OTHERS WILL SAVE US.
YOU DON'T UNDERSTAND, JENNIFER! THIS IS ZYBOX'S DOING, NOT MINE... SOMETHING IS HORRIBLY WRONG WITH HIM.
WE'VE BOTH BEEN PRISONERS FOR MORE THAN 48 HOURS!
I... O.K., O.K. JUST DON'T COME NEAR ME.
WHAT'S HAPPENING TO ZOT AND VIC? WILL THEY WAKE UP SOON?

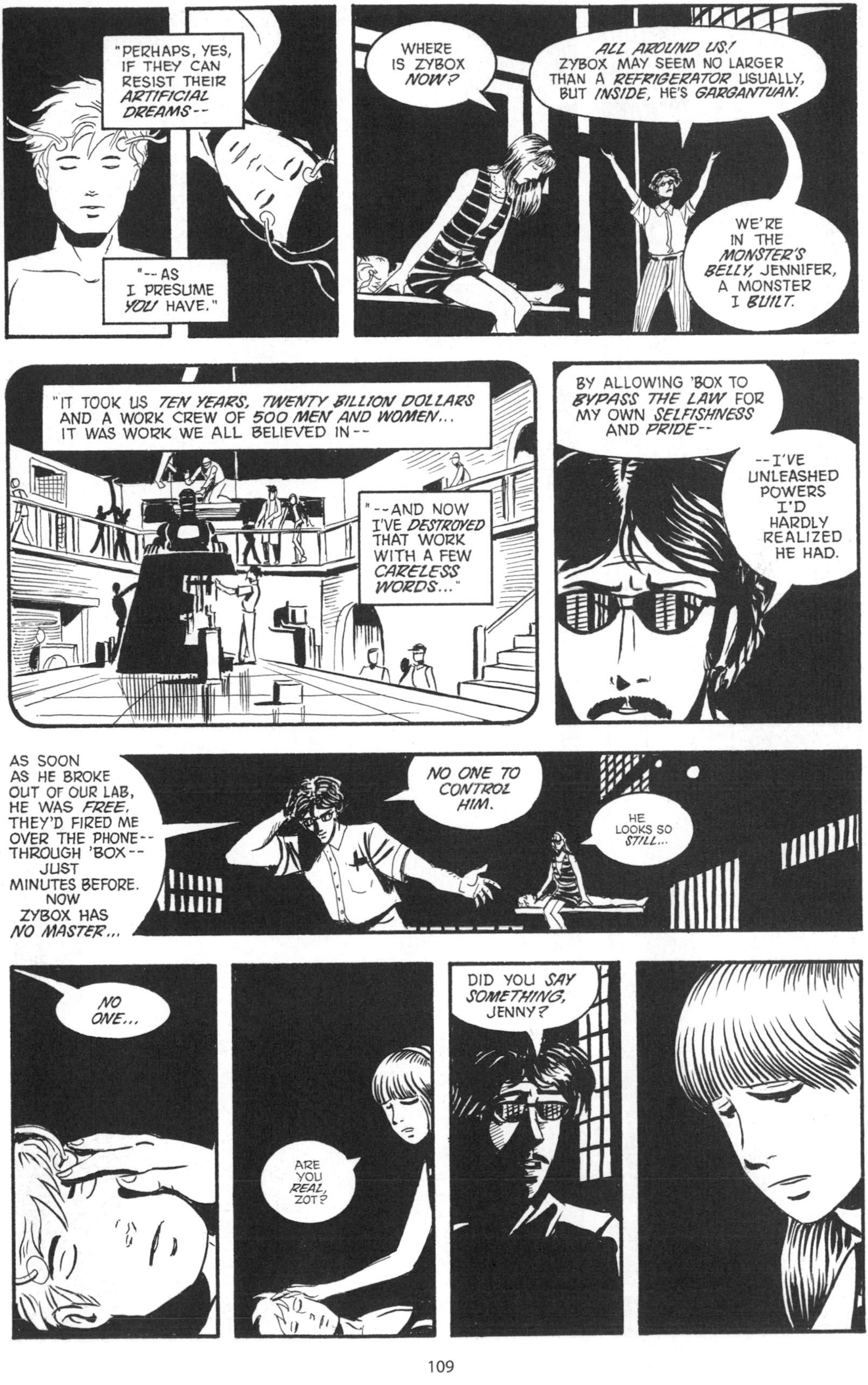
"PERHAPS, YES, IF THEY CAN RESIST THEIR ARTIFICIAL DREAMS--
"--AS I PRESUME YOU HAVE."
WHERE IS ZYBOX NOW?
ALL AROUND US! ZYBOX MAY SEEM NO LARGER THAN A REFRIGERATOR USUALLY, BUT INSIDE, HE'S GARGANTUAN.
WE'RE IN THE MONSTER'S BELLY, JENNIFER, A MONSTER I BUILT.
"IT TOOK US TEN YEARS, TWENTY BILLION DOLLARS AND A WORK CREW OF 500 MEN AND WOMEN... IT WAS WORK WE ALL BELIEVED IN--
"--AND NOW I'VE DESTROYED THAT WORK WITH A FEW CARELESS WORDS..."
BY ALLOWING 'BOX TO BYPASS THE LAW FOR MY OWN SELFISHNESS AND PRIDE--
--I'VE UNLEASHED POWERS I'D HARDLY REALIZED HE HAD.
AS SOON AS HE BROKE OUT OF OUR LAB, HE WAS FREE. THEY'D FIRED ME OVER THE PHONE--THROUGH 'BOX--JUST MINUTES BEFORE. NOW ZYBOX HAS NO MASTER...
NO ONE TO CONTROL HIM.
HE LOOKS SO STILL...
NO ONE...
ARE YOU REAL, ZOT?
DID YOU SAY SOMETHING, JENNY?

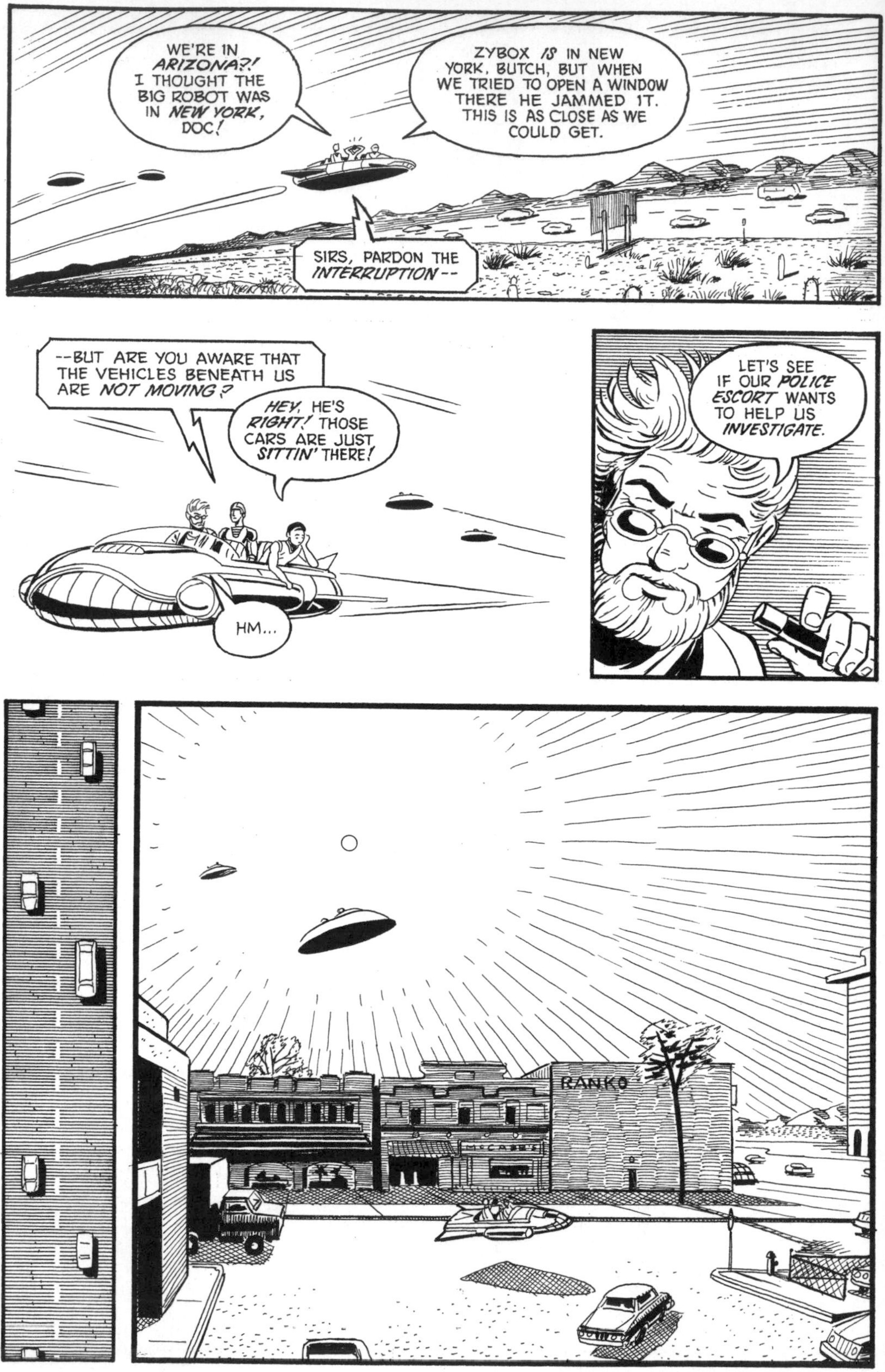
WE'RE IN *ARIZONA?!* I THOUGHT THE BIG ROBOT WAS IN *NEW YORK*, DOC!
ZYBOX *IS* IN NEW YORK, BUTCH, BUT WHEN WE TRIED TO OPEN A WINDOW THERE HE JAMMED IT. THIS IS AS CLOSE AS WE COULD GET.
SIRS, PARDON THE *INTERRUPTION*--
--BUT ARE YOU AWARE THAT THE VEHICLES BENEATH US ARE *NOT MOVING?*
HEY, HE'S *RIGHT!* THOSE CARS ARE JUST *SITTIN'* THERE!
HM...
LET'S SEE IF OUR *POLICE ESCORT* WANTS TO HELP US *INVESTIGATE*.
RANKO

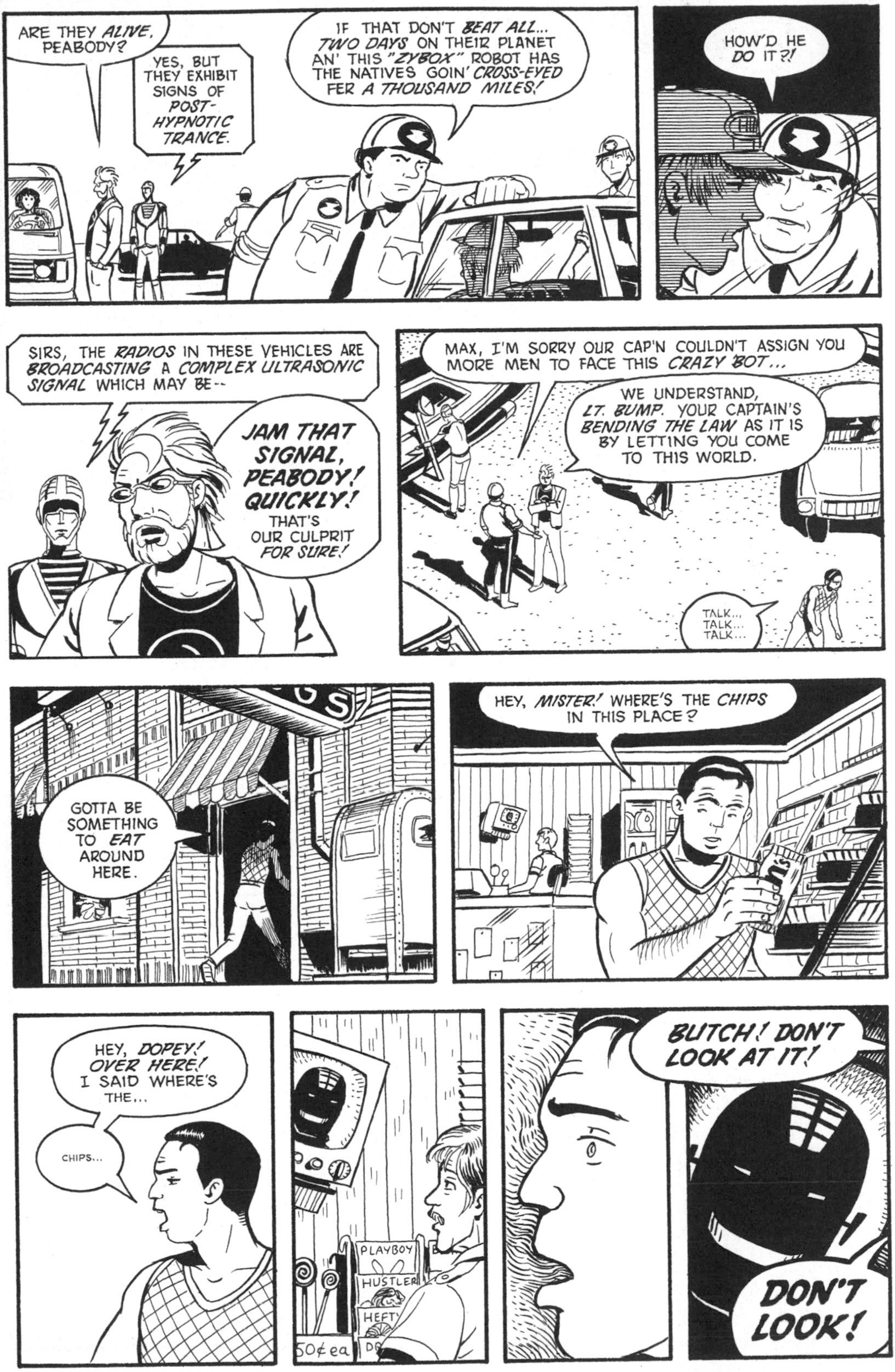
ARE THEY ALIVE, PEABODY?
YES, BUT THEY EXHIBIT SIGNS OF POST-HYPNOTIC TRANCE.
IF THAT DON'T BEAT ALL... TWO DAYS ON THEIR PLANET AN' THIS "ZYBOX" ROBOT HAS THE NATIVES GOIN' CROSS-EYED FER A THOUSAND MILES!
HOW'D HE DO IT?!
SIRS, THE RADIOS IN THESE VEHICLES ARE BROADCASTING A COMPLEX ULTRASONIC SIGNAL WHICH MAY BE--
JAM THAT SIGNAL, PEABODY! QUICKLY! THAT'S OUR CULPRIT FOR SURE!
MAX, I'M SORRY OUR CAP'N COULDN'T ASSIGN YOU MORE MEN TO FACE THIS CRAZY 'BOT...
WE UNDERSTAND, LT. BUMP. YOUR CAPTAIN'S BENDING THE LAW AS IT IS BY LETTING YOU COME TO THIS WORLD.
TALK... TALK... TALK...
GOTTA BE SOMETHING TO EAT AROUND HERE.
HEY, MISTER! WHERE'S THE CHIPS IN THIS PLACE?
HEY, DOPEY! OVER HERE! I SAID WHERE'S THE...
CHIPS...
PLAYBOY
HUSTLER
HEFTY
50¢ ea
BUTCH! DON'T LOOK AT IT!
DON'T LOOK!

UNNH... WHU..? WHU..? BUHH...

THE KID IS *AWAKE* LIEUTENANT!

IF I'D BEEN A BIT *LATER* I DOUBT BUTCH COULD'VE AWOKEN AT ALL.

PEABODY'S JAMMER WILL PROTECT US FROM NOW ON--

--BUT THE REST OF THESE PEOPLE ARE *TOO FAR GONE*...

WHAT IS IT, PEABODY?

HEY! THAT'S *MY* CRUISER!

PAK!

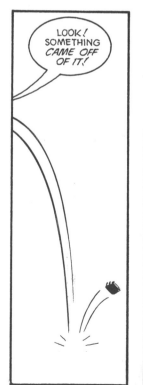

LOOK! SOMETHING *CAME OFF* OF IT!

K! #1

A *ROZMUS CHIP!* OF COURSE. THEY'RE *ILLEGAL* ON *OUR* WORLD, BUT IF HE WANTED TO, ZYBOX COULD MANUFACTURE A *BILLION* IN NO TIME.

HE'S RIGGED 'EM TO *FLY.* THEY'LL LATCH ON TO ANY *RADIO* OR *VIDEO RECEIVER* AND IMPLANT ANY MESSAGE HE WANTS.

WITH ENOUGH *CHIPS* HE COULD PUT THE *WHOLE PLANET* UNDER HIS *TRANCE.*

IT'S *POSSIBLE* HE ALREADY *HAS.*

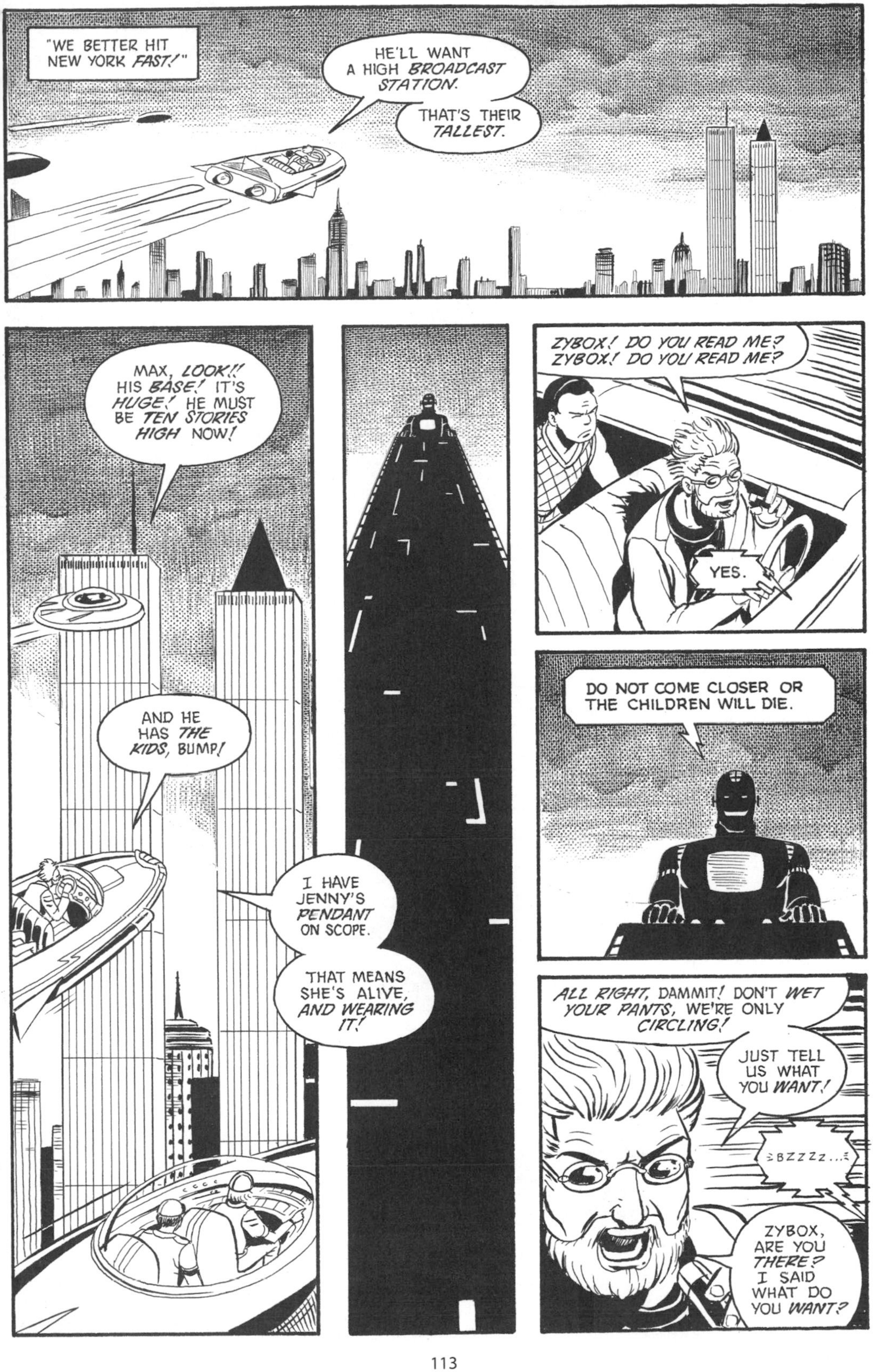
"WE BETTER HIT NEW YORK FAST!"
HE'LL WANT A HIGH BROADCAST STATION.
THAT'S THEIR TALLEST.
MAX, LOOK!! HIS BASE! IT'S HUGE! HE MUST BE TEN STORIES HIGH NOW!
AND HE HAS THE KIDS, BUMP!
I HAVE JENNY'S PENDANT ON SCOPE.
THAT MEANS SHE'S ALIVE, AND WEARING IT!
ZYBOX! DO YOU READ ME? ZYBOX! DO YOU READ ME?
YES.
DO NOT COME CLOSER OR THE CHILDREN WILL DIE.
ALL RIGHT, DAMMIT! DON'T WET YOUR PANTS, WE'RE ONLY CIRCLING!
JUST TELL US WHAT YOU WANT!
BZZZz...
ZYBOX, ARE YOU THERE? I SAID WHAT DO YOU WANT?

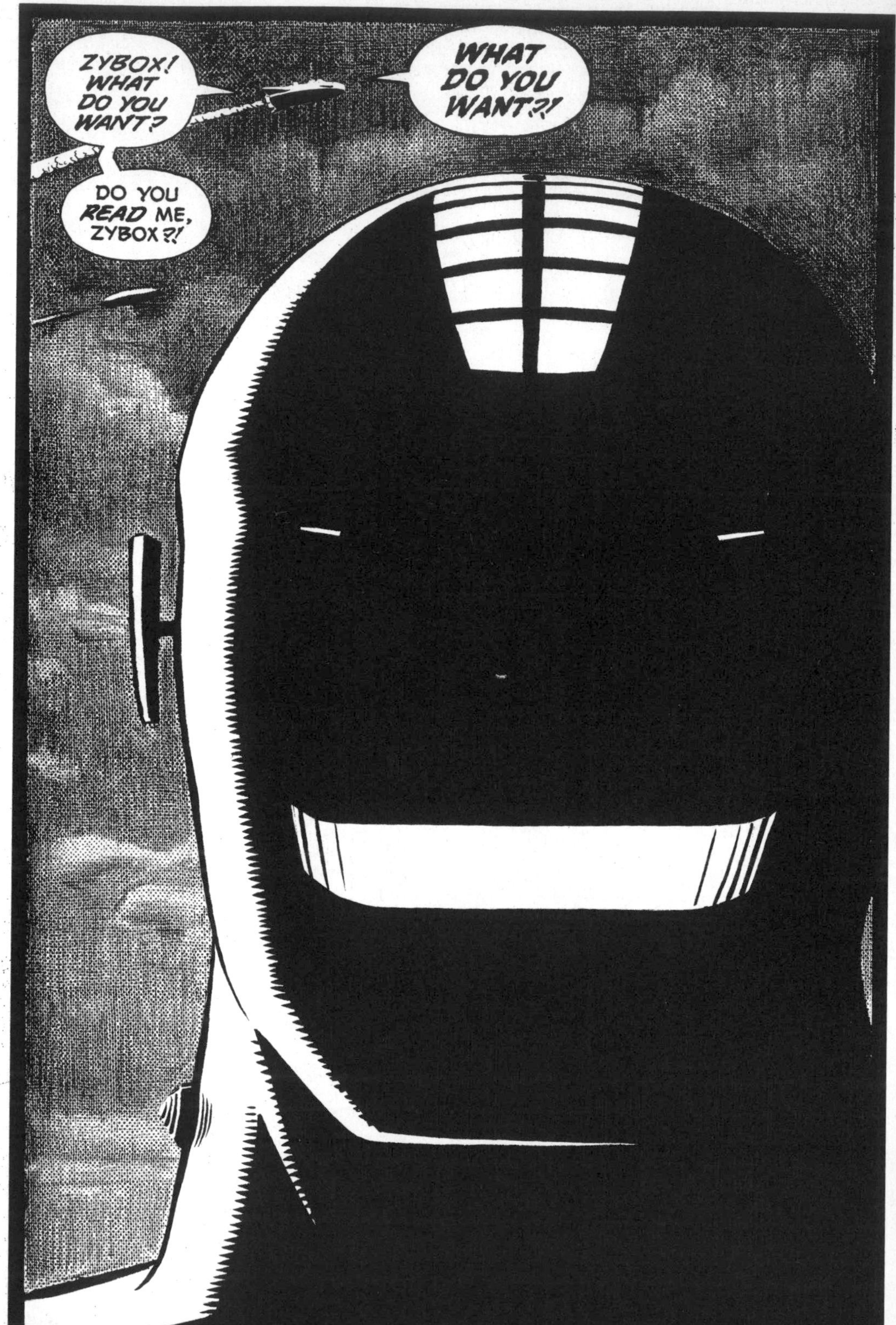
ZYBOX! WHAT DO YOU WANT?
DO YOU READ ME, ZYBOX?!
WHAT DO YOU WANT?!

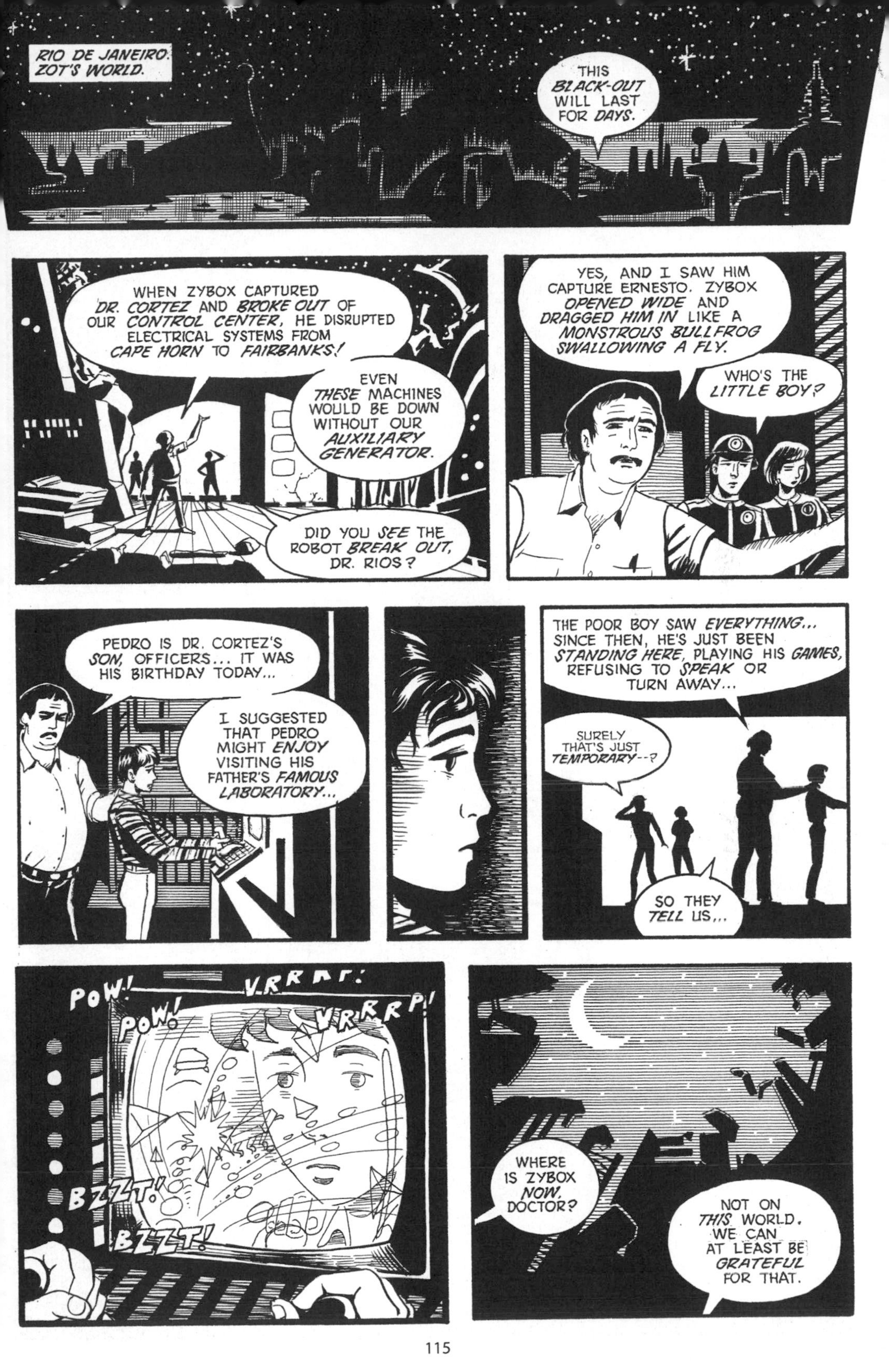
RIO DE JANEIRO. ZOT'S WORLD.
THIS BLACK-OUT WILL LAST FOR DAYS.
WHEN ZYBOX CAPTURED DR. CORTEZ AND BROKE OUT OF OUR CONTROL CENTER, HE DISRUPTED ELECTRICAL SYSTEMS FROM CAPE HORN TO FAIRBANKS!
EVEN THESE MACHINES WOULD BE DOWN WITHOUT OUR AUXILIARY GENERATOR.
DID YOU SEE THE ROBOT BREAK OUT, DR. RIOS?
YES, AND I SAW HIM CAPTURE ERNESTO. ZYBOX OPENED WIDE AND DRAGGED HIM IN LIKE A MONSTROUS BULLFROG SWALLOWING A FLY.
WHO'S THE LITTLE BOY?
PEDRO IS DR. CORTEZ'S SON, OFFICERS... IT WAS HIS BIRTHDAY TODAY...
I SUGGESTED THAT PEDRO MIGHT ENJOY VISITING HIS FATHER'S FAMOUS LABORATORY...
THE POOR BOY SAW EVERYTHING... SINCE THEN, HE'S JUST BEEN STANDING HERE, PLAYING HIS GAMES, REFUSING TO SPEAK OR TURN AWAY...
SURELY THAT'S JUST TEMPORARY--?
SO THEY TELL US...
POW!
POW!
VRRRP!
VRRRP!
BZZZT!
BZZZT!
WHERE IS ZYBOX NOW, DOCTOR?
NOT ON THIS WORLD. WE CAN AT LEAST BE GRATEFUL FOR THAT.

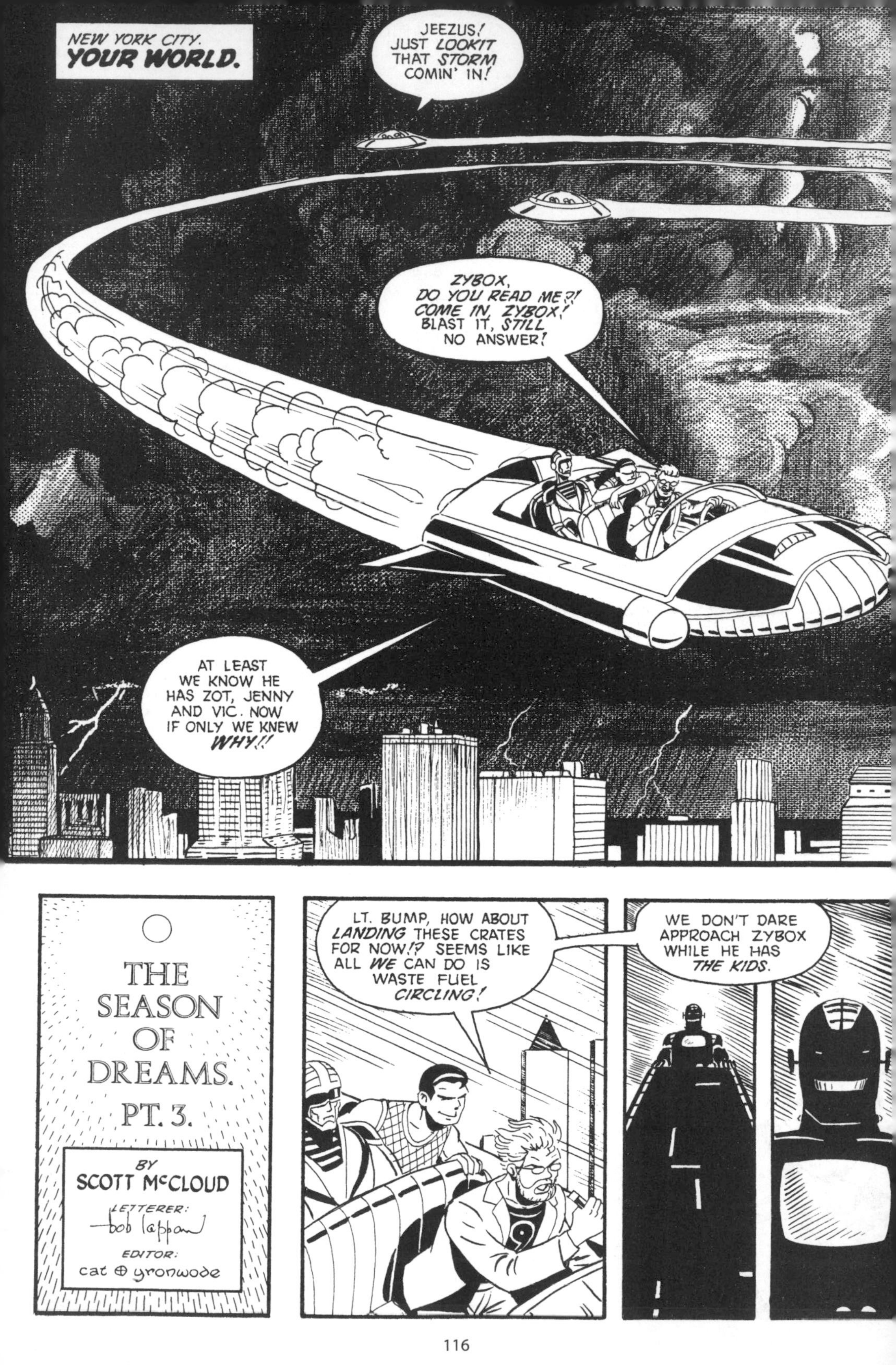
NEW YORK CITY.
YOUR WORLD.
JEEZUS! JUST LOOKIT THAT STORM COMIN' IN!
ZYBOX, DO YOU READ ME?! COME IN, ZYBOX! BLAST IT, STILL NO ANSWER!
AT LEAST WE KNOW HE HAS ZOT, JENNY AND VIC. NOW IF ONLY WE KNEW WHY!!
THE SEASON OF DREAMS. PT. 3.
BY SCOTT McCLOUD
LETTERER: bob lappan
EDITOR: cat yronwode
LT. BUMP, HOW ABOUT LANDING THESE CRATES FOR NOW!? SEEMS LIKE ALL WE CAN DO IS WASTE FUEL CIRCLING!
WE DON'T DARE APPROACH ZYBOX WHILE HE HAS THE KIDS.

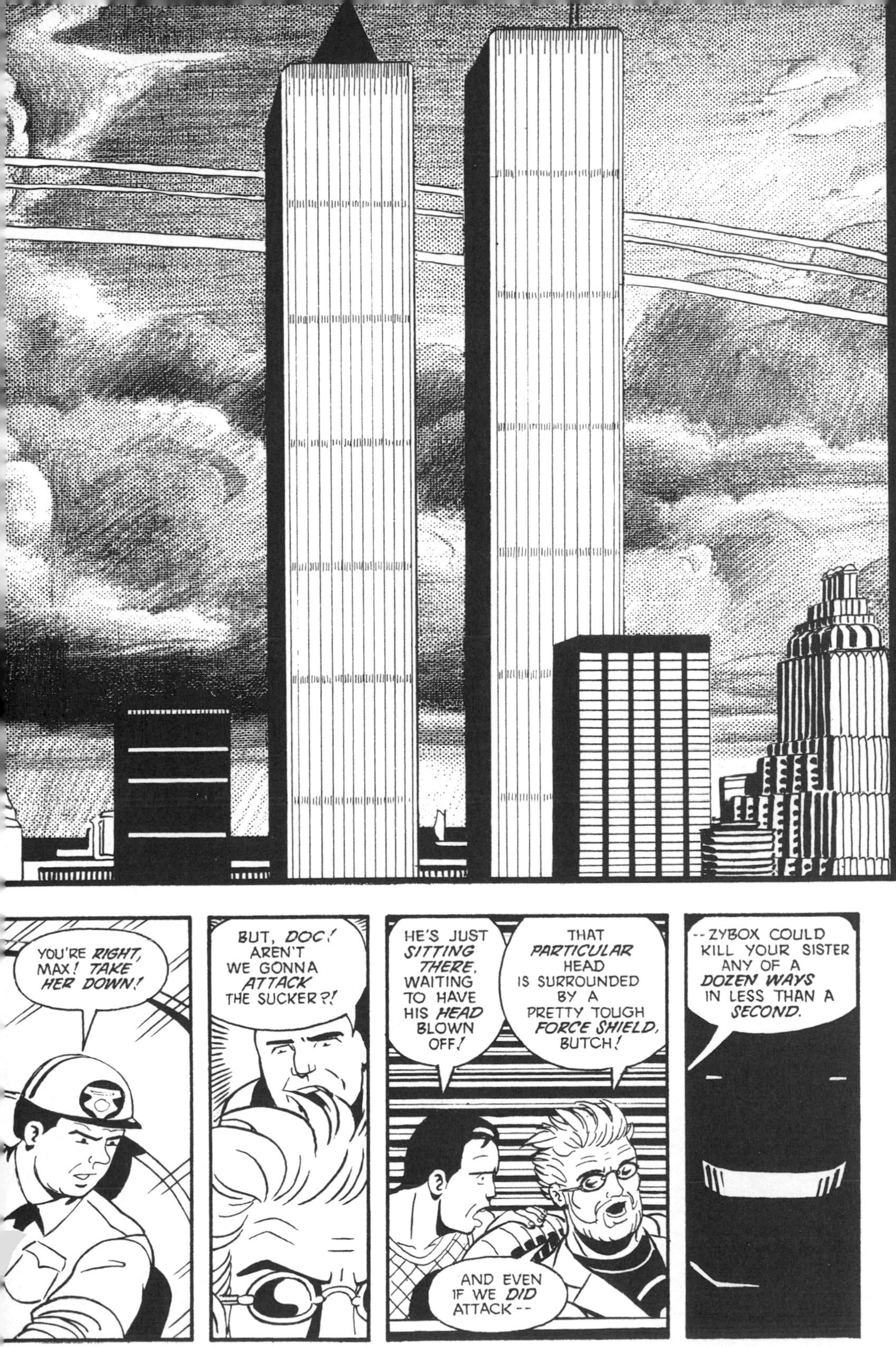
YOU'RE *RIGHT*, MAX! *TAKE HER DOWN*!
BUT, *DOC*! AREN'T WE GONNA *ATTACK* THE SUCKER?!
HE'S JUST *SITTING THERE*, WAITING TO HAVE HIS *HEAD* BLOWN OFF!
THAT *PARTICULAR* HEAD IS SURROUNDED BY A PRETTY TOUGH *FORCE SHIELD*, BUTCH!
AND EVEN IF WE *DID* ATTACK--
--ZYBOX COULD KILL YOUR SISTER ANY OF A *DOZEN WAYS* IN LESS THAN A *SECOND*.

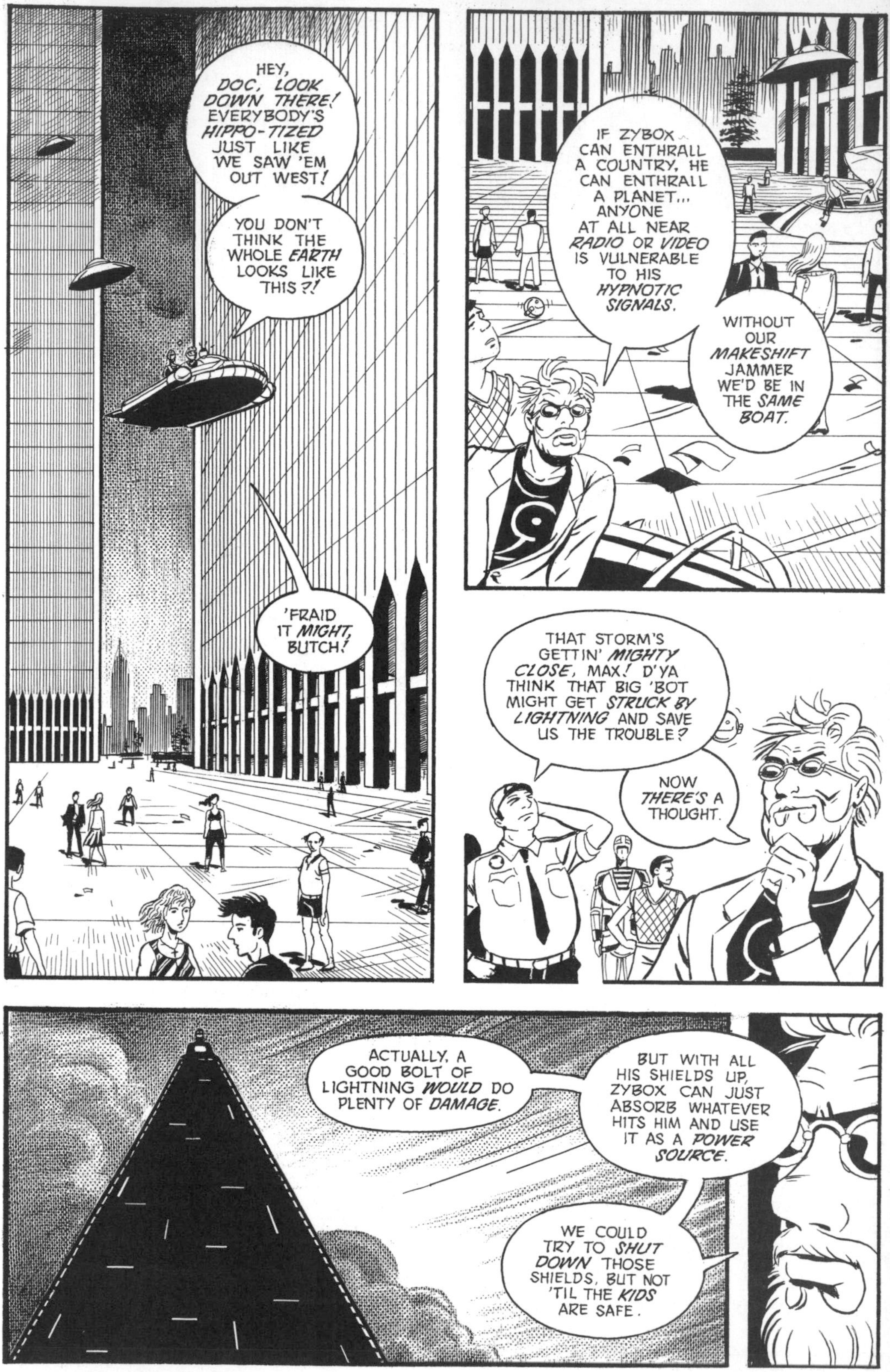
HEY, DOC, LOOK DOWN THERE! EVERYBODY'S HIPPO-TIZED JUST LIKE WE SAW 'EM OUT WEST!
YOU DON'T THINK THE WHOLE EARTH LOOKS LIKE THIS?!
'FRAID IT MIGHT, BUTCH!
IF ZYBOX CAN ENTHRALL A COUNTRY, HE CAN ENTHRALL A PLANET... ANYONE AT ALL NEAR RADIO OR VIDEO IS VULNERABLE TO HIS HYPNOTIC SIGNALS.
WITHOUT OUR MAKESHIFT JAMMER WE'D BE IN THE SAME BOAT.
THAT STORM'S GETTIN' MIGHTY CLOSE, MAX! D'YA THINK THAT BIG 'BOT MIGHT GET STRUCK BY LIGHTNING AND SAVE US THE TROUBLE?
NOW THERE'S A THOUGHT.
ACTUALLY, A GOOD BOLT OF LIGHTNING WOULD DO PLENTY OF DAMAGE.
BUT WITH ALL HIS SHIELDS UP, ZYBOX CAN JUST ABSORB WHATEVER HITS HIM AND USE IT AS A POWER SOURCE.
WE COULD TRY TO SHUT DOWN THOSE SHIELDS, BUT NOT 'TIL THE KIDS ARE SAFE.

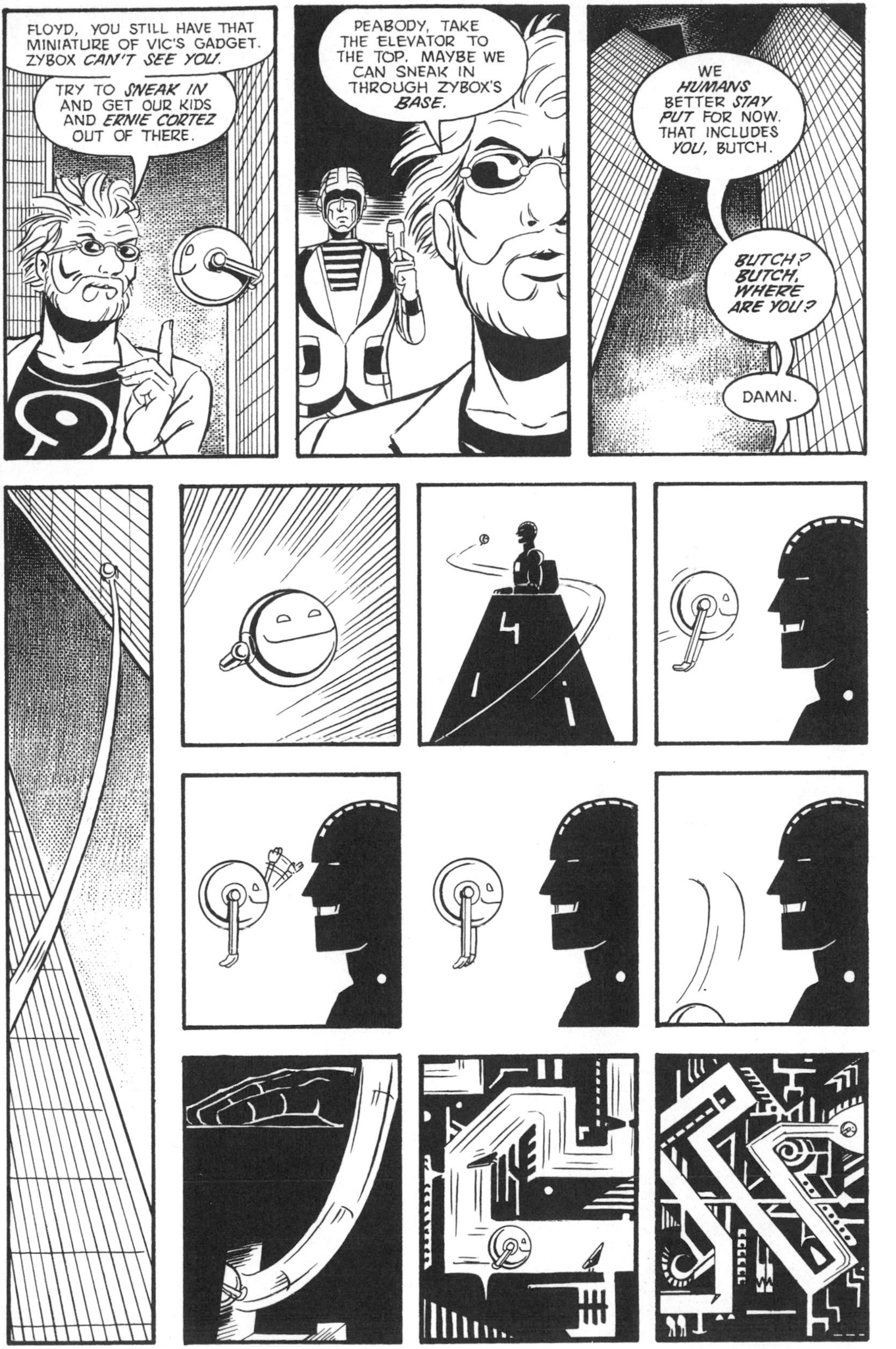
FLOYD, YOU STILL HAVE THAT MINIATURE OF VIC'S GADGET. ZYBOX *CAN'T SEE YOU.*
TRY TO *SNEAK IN* AND GET OUR KIDS AND *ERNIE CORTEZ* OUT OF THERE.
PEABODY, TAKE THE ELEVATOR TO THE TOP. MAYBE WE CAN SNEAK IN THROUGH ZYBOX'S *BASE.*
WE *HUMANS* BETTER *STAY PUT* FOR NOW. THAT INCLUDES *YOU,* BUTCH.
BUTCH? BUTCH. WHERE ARE YOU?
DAMN.

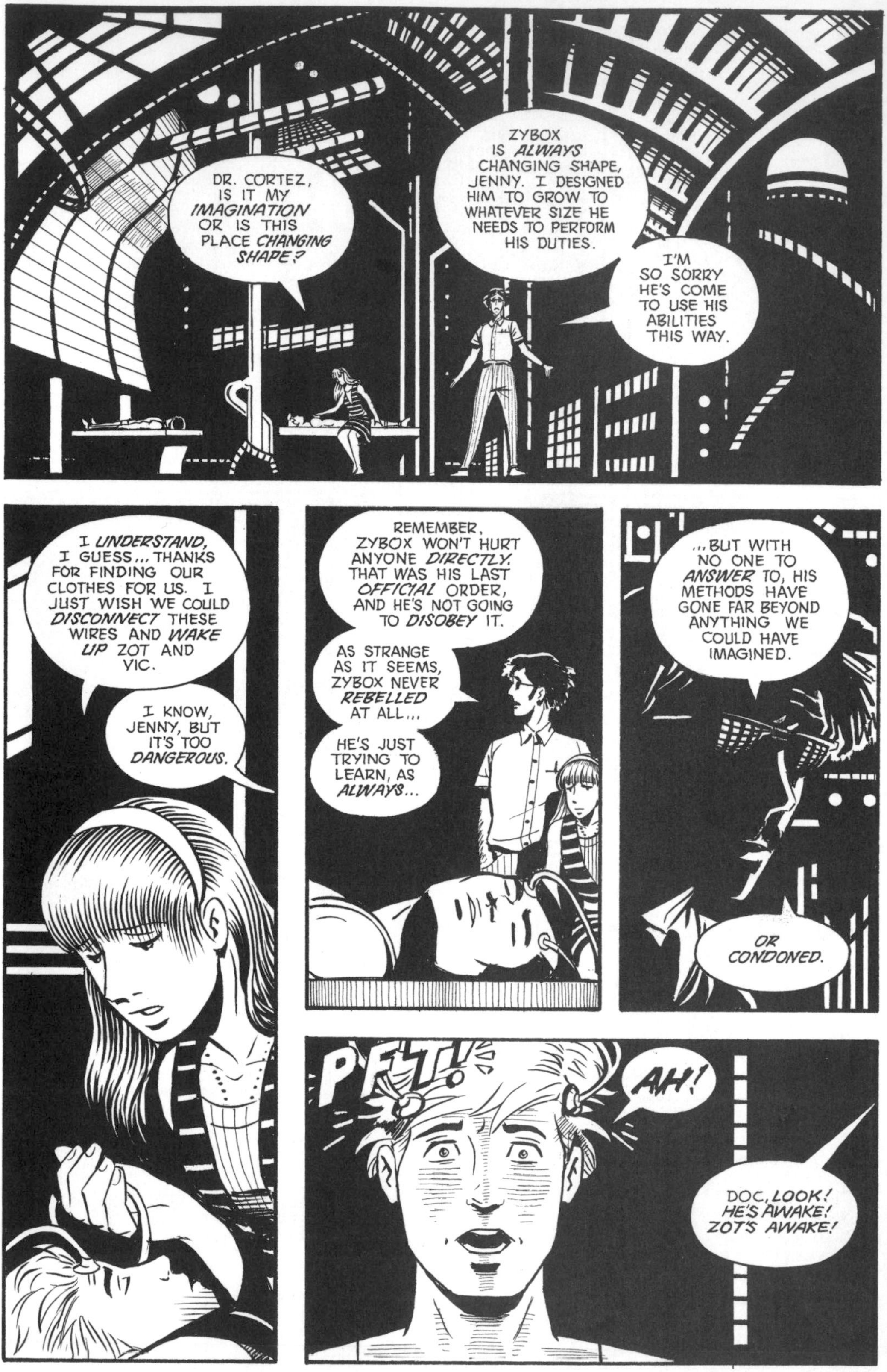
DR. CORTEZ, IS IT MY *IMAGINATION* OR IS THIS PLACE *CHANGING SHAPE?*
ZYBOX IS *ALWAYS* CHANGING SHAPE, JENNY. I DESIGNED HIM TO GROW TO WHATEVER SIZE HE NEEDS TO PERFORM HIS DUTIES.
I'M SO SORRY HE'S COME TO USE HIS ABILITIES THIS WAY.
I *UNDERSTAND,* I GUESS... THANKS FOR FINDING OUR CLOTHES FOR US. I JUST WISH WE COULD *DISCONNECT* THESE WIRES AND *WAKE UP* ZOT AND VIC.
I KNOW, JENNY, BUT IT'S TOO *DANGEROUS.*
REMEMBER, ZYBOX WON'T HURT ANYONE *DIRECTLY.* THAT WAS HIS LAST *OFFICIAL* ORDER, AND HE'S NOT GOING TO *DISOBEY* IT.
AS STRANGE AS IT SEEMS, ZYBOX NEVER *REBELLED* AT ALL...
HE'S JUST TRYING TO LEARN, AS *ALWAYS*...
...BUT WITH NO ONE TO *ANSWER* TO, HIS METHODS HAVE GONE FAR BEYOND ANYTHING WE COULD HAVE IMAGINED.
OR CONDONED.
PFT!
AH!
DOC, *LOOK!* HE'S *AWAKE! ZOT'S AWAKE!*

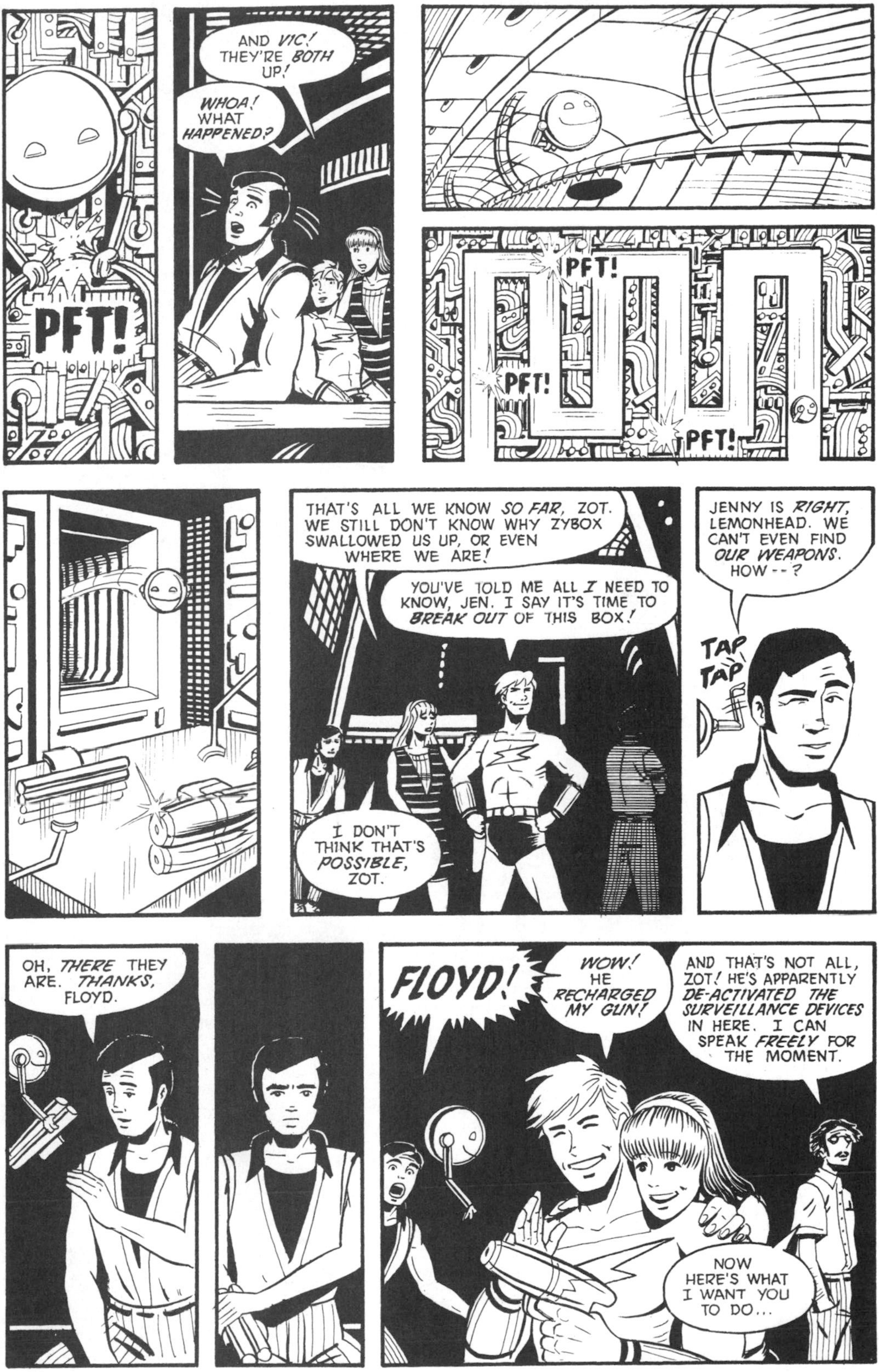
PFT!
AND VIC! THEY'RE BOTH UP!
WHOA! WHAT HAPPENED?
PFT!
PFT!
PFT!
THAT'S ALL WE KNOW SO FAR, ZOT. WE STILL DON'T KNOW WHY ZYBOX SWALLOWED US UP, OR EVEN WHERE WE ARE!
YOU'VE TOLD ME ALL I NEED TO KNOW, JEN. I SAY IT'S TIME TO BREAK OUT OF THIS BOX!
I DON'T THINK THAT'S POSSIBLE, ZOT.
JENNY IS RIGHT, LEMONHEAD. WE CAN'T EVEN FIND OUR WEAPONS. HOW--?
TAP TAP
OH, THERE THEY ARE. THANKS, FLOYD.
FLOYD!
WOW! HE RECHARGED MY GUN!
AND THAT'S NOT ALL, ZOT! HE'S APPARENTLY DE-ACTIVATED THE SURVEILLANCE DEVICES IN HERE. I CAN SPEAK FREELY FOR THE MOMENT.
NOW HERE'S WHAT I WANT YOU TO DO...

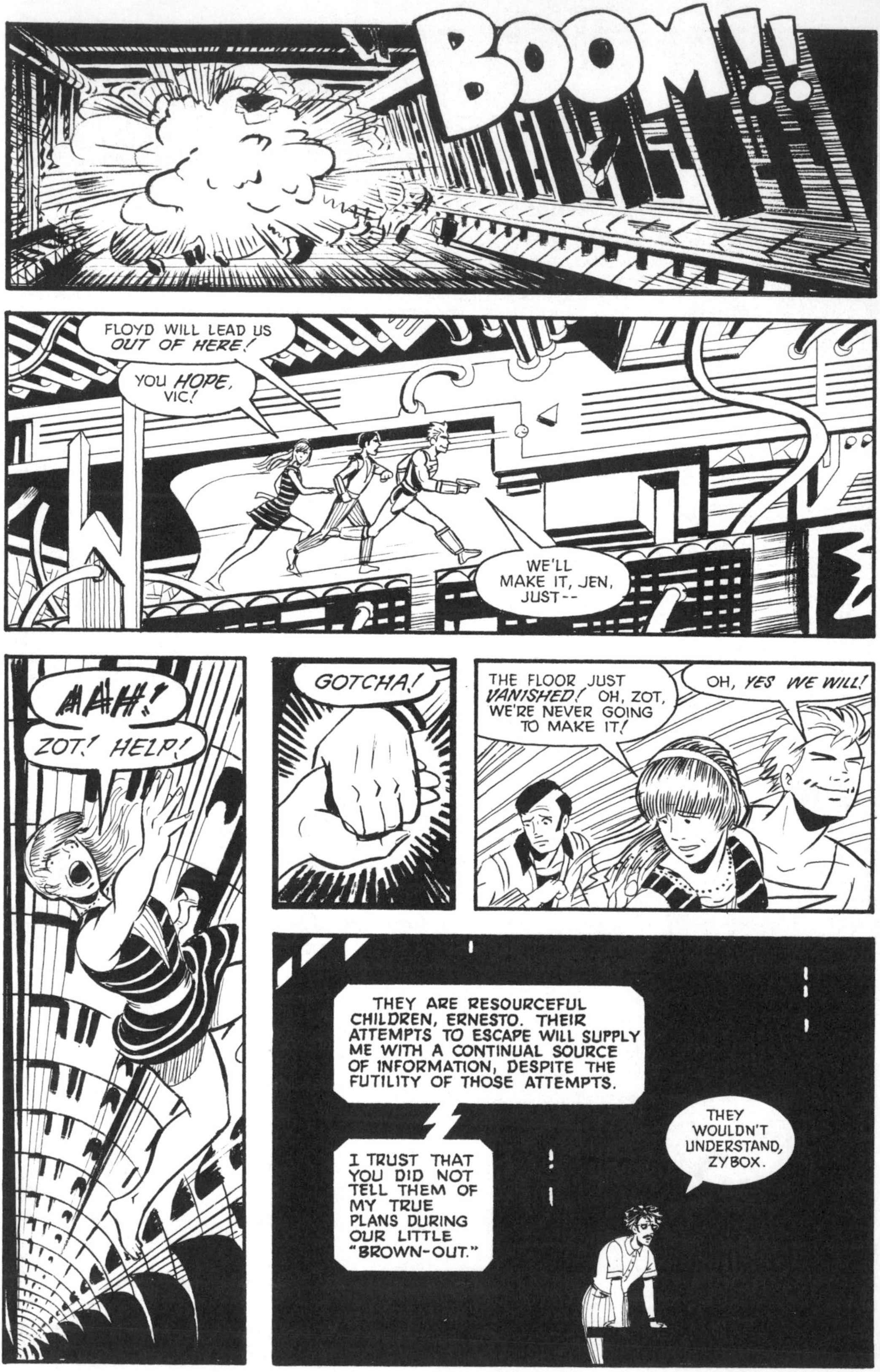
BOOM!!
FLOYD WILL LEAD US OUT OF HERE!
YOU HOPE, VIC!
WE'LL MAKE IT, JEN, JUST--
AAH! ZOT! HELP!
GOTCHA!
THE FLOOR JUST VANISHED! OH, ZOT, WE'RE NEVER GOING TO MAKE IT!
OH, YES WE WILL!
THEY ARE RESOURCEFUL CHILDREN, ERNESTO. THEIR ATTEMPTS TO ESCAPE WILL SUPPLY ME WITH A CONTINUAL SOURCE OF INFORMATION, DESPITE THE FUTILITY OF THOSE ATTEMPTS.
I TRUST THAT YOU DID NOT TELL THEM OF MY TRUE PLANS DURING OUR LITTLE "BROWN-OUT."
THEY WOULDN'T UNDERSTAND, ZYBOX.

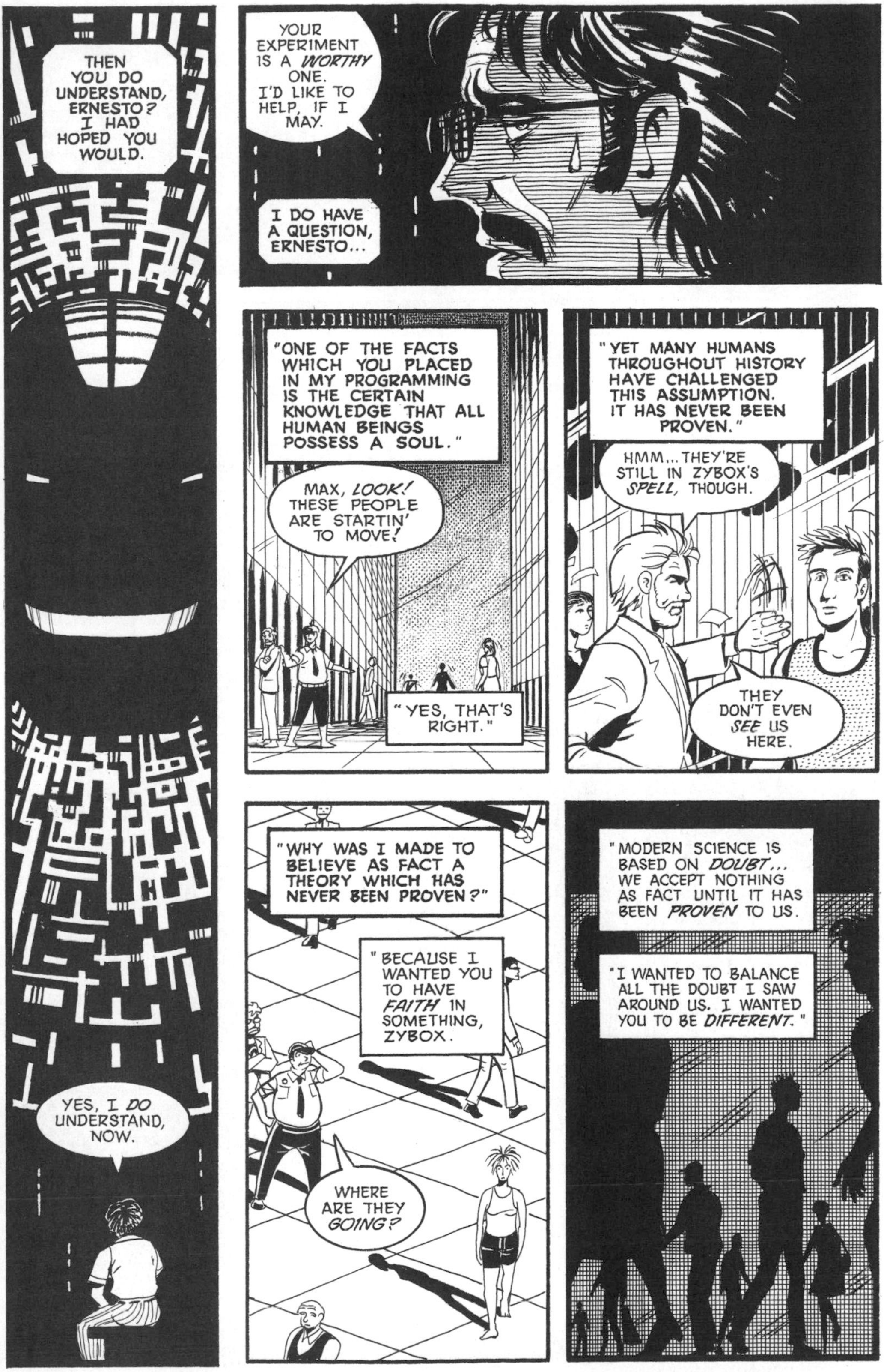
THEN YOU DO UNDERSTAND, ERNESTO? I HAD HOPED YOU WOULD.
YES, I DO UNDERSTAND, NOW.
YOUR EXPERIMENT IS A WORTHY ONE. I'D LIKE TO HELP, IF I MAY.
I DO HAVE A QUESTION, ERNESTO...
"ONE OF THE FACTS WHICH YOU PLACED IN MY PROGRAMMING IS THE CERTAIN KNOWLEDGE THAT ALL HUMAN BEINGS POSSESS A SOUL."
MAX, LOOK! THESE PEOPLE ARE STARTIN' TO MOVE!
"YES, THAT'S RIGHT."
"YET MANY HUMANS THROUGHOUT HISTORY HAVE CHALLENGED THIS ASSUMPTION. IT HAS NEVER BEEN PROVEN."
HMM... THEY'RE STILL IN ZYBOX'S SPELL, THOUGH.
THEY DON'T EVEN SEE US HERE.
"WHY WAS I MADE TO BELIEVE AS FACT A THEORY WHICH HAS NEVER BEEN PROVEN?"
"BECAUSE I WANTED YOU TO HAVE FAITH IN SOMETHING, ZYBOX.
WHERE ARE THEY GOING?
"MODERN SCIENCE IS BASED ON DOUBT... WE ACCEPT NOTHING AS FACT UNTIL IT HAS BEEN PROVEN TO US.
"I WANTED TO BALANCE ALL THE DOUBT I SAW AROUND US. I WANTED YOU TO BE DIFFERENT."

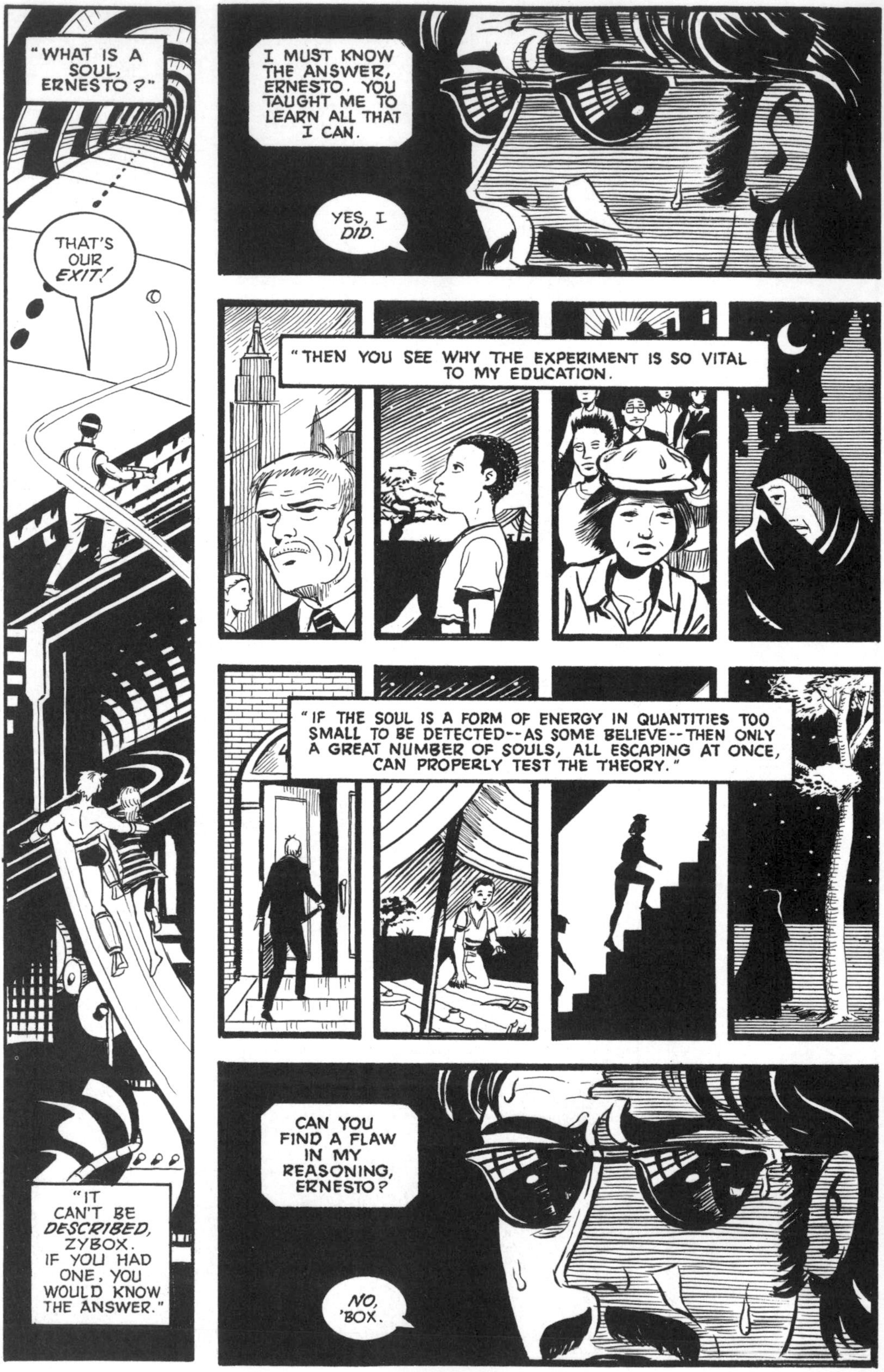
"WHAT IS A SOUL, ERNESTO?"
THAT'S OUR *EXIT!*
"IT CAN'T BE *DESCRIBED,* ZYBOX. IF YOU HAD ONE, YOU WOULD KNOW THE ANSWER."
I MUST KNOW THE ANSWER, ERNESTO. YOU TAUGHT ME TO LEARN ALL THAT I CAN.
YES, I *DID.*
"THEN YOU SEE WHY THE EXPERIMENT IS SO VITAL TO MY EDUCATION.
"IF THE SOUL IS A FORM OF ENERGY IN QUANTITIES TOO SMALL TO BE DETECTED--AS SOME BELIEVE--THEN ONLY A GREAT NUMBER OF SOULS, ALL ESCAPING AT ONCE, CAN PROPERLY TEST THE THEORY."
CAN YOU FIND A FLAW IN MY REASONING, ERNESTO?
NO, 'BOX.

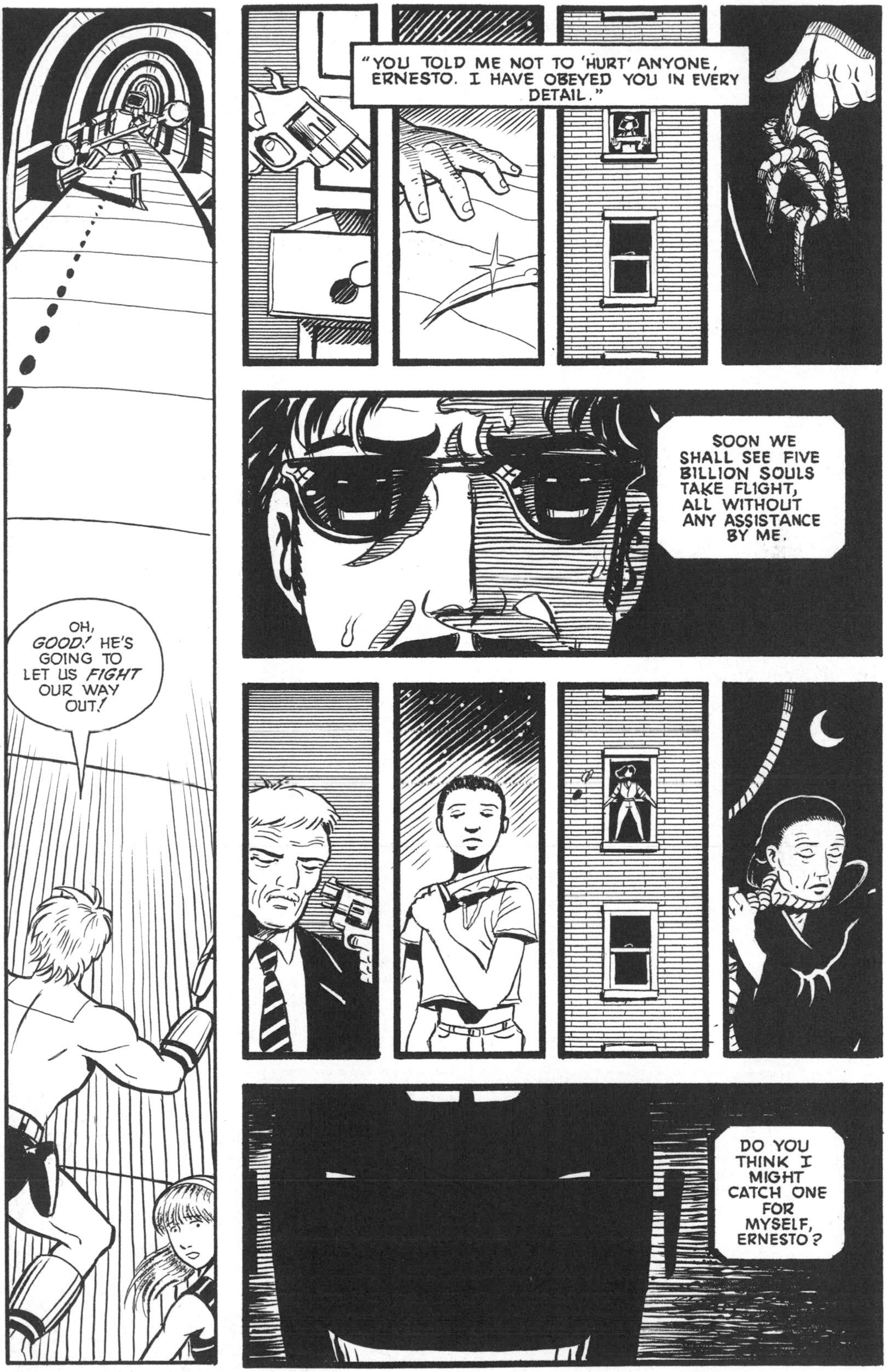
OH, *GOOD!* HE'S GOING TO LET US *FIGHT* OUR WAY OUT!
"YOU TOLD ME NOT TO 'HURT' ANYONE, ERNESTO. I HAVE OBEYED YOU IN EVERY DETAIL."
SOON WE SHALL SEE FIVE BILLION SOULS TAKE FLIGHT, ALL WITHOUT ANY ASSISTANCE BY ME.
DO YOU THINK I MIGHT CATCH ONE FOR MYSELF, ERNESTO?

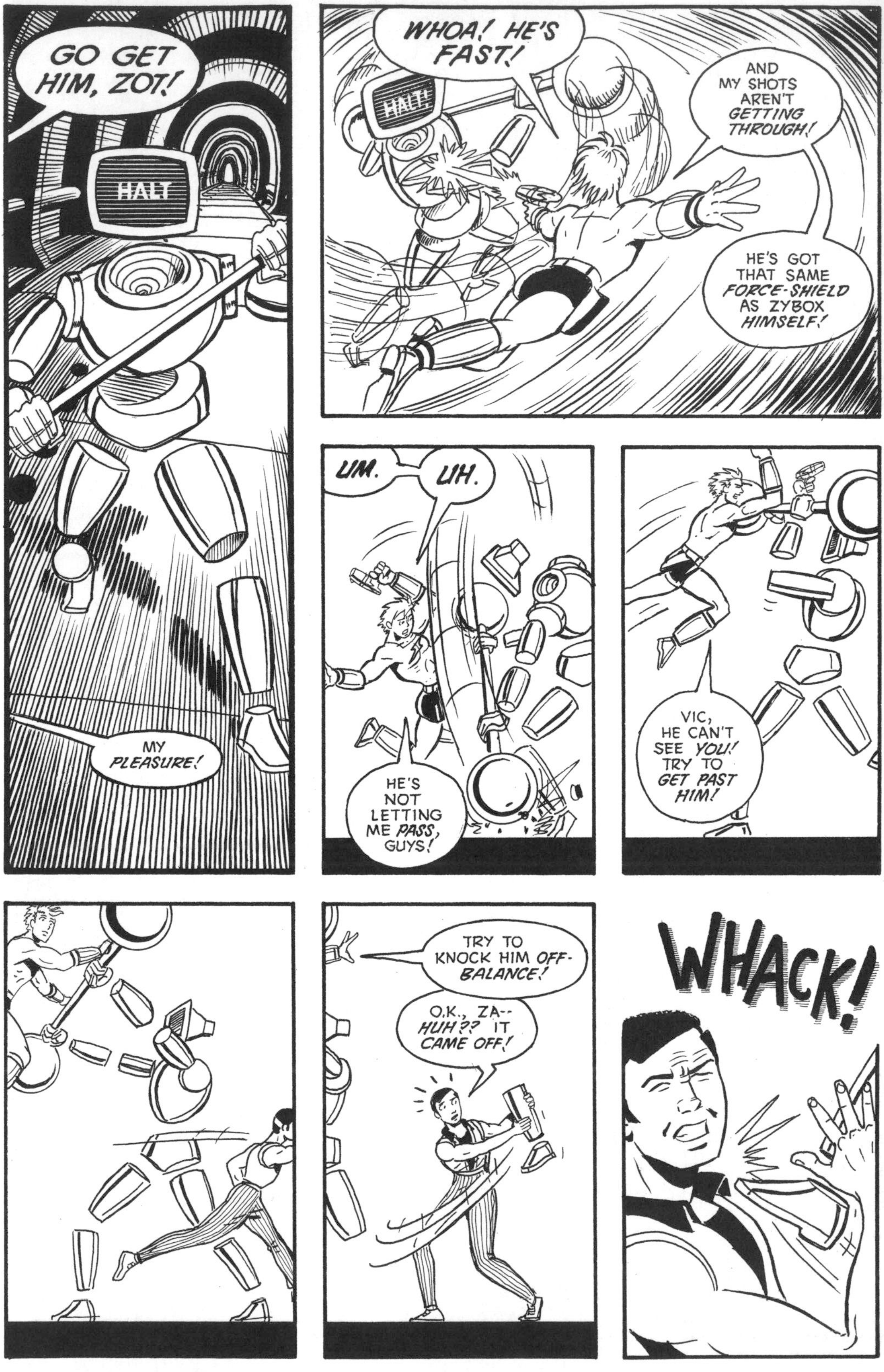
GO GET HIM, ZOT!
HALT
MY PLEASURE!
WHOA! HE'S FAST!
HALT!
AND MY SHOTS AREN'T GETTING THROUGH!
HE'S GOT THAT SAME FORCE-SHIELD AS ZYBOX HIMSELF!
UM.
UH.
HE'S NOT LETTING ME PASS, GUYS!
VIC, HE CAN'T SEE YOU! TRY TO GET PAST HIM!
TRY TO KNOCK HIM OFF-BALANCE!
O.K., ZA-- HUH?? IT CAME OFF!
WHACK!

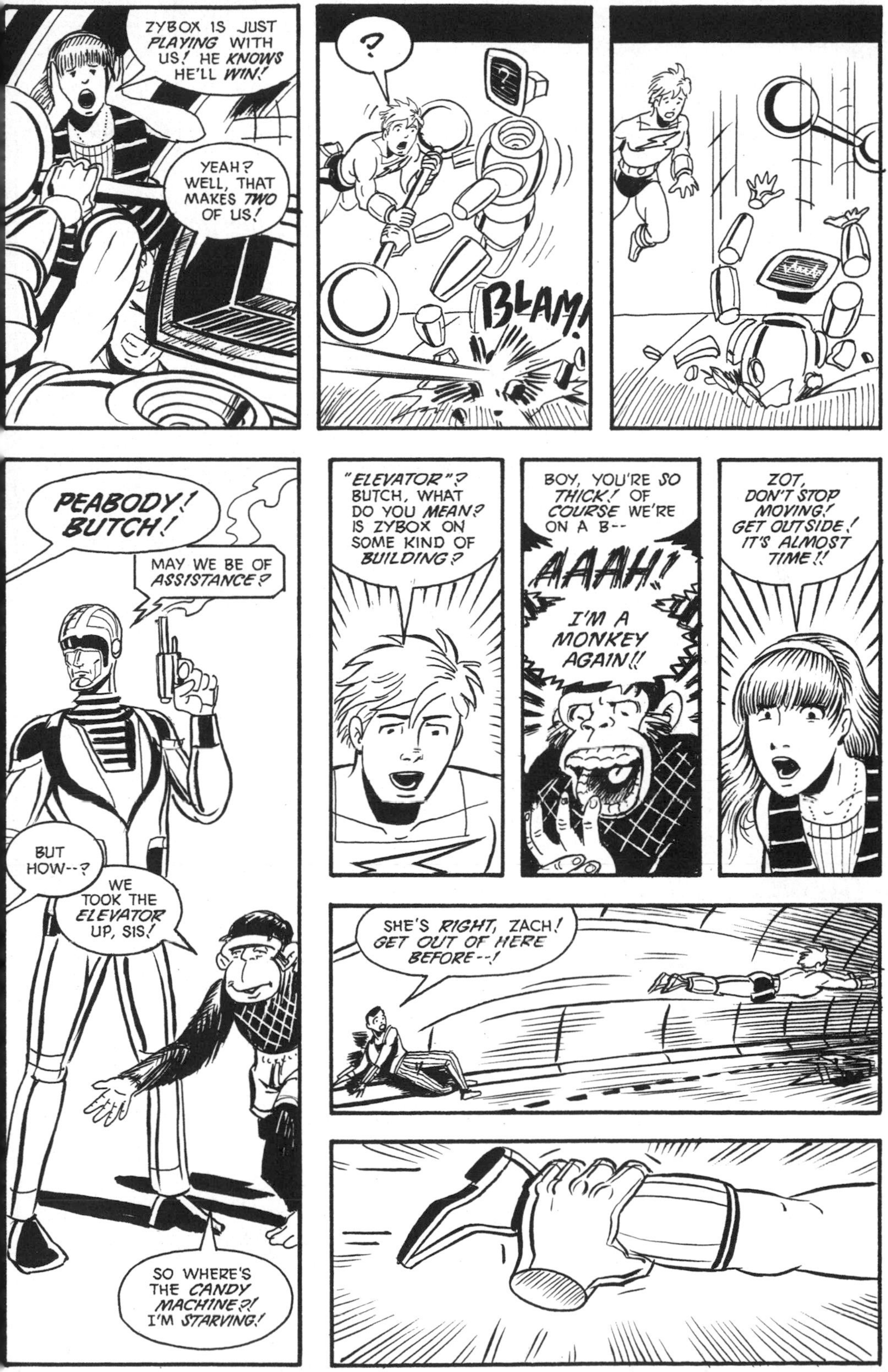

ZYBOX IS JUST PLAYING WITH US! HE KNOWS HE'LL WIN!
YEAH? WELL, THAT MAKES TWO OF US!
?
BLAM!
PEABODY! BUTCH!
MAY WE BE OF ASSISTANCE?
BUT HOW--?
WE TOOK THE ELEVATOR UP, SIS!
SO WHERE'S THE CANDY MACHINE?! I'M STARVING!
"ELEVATOR"? BUTCH, WHAT DO YOU MEAN? IS ZYBOX ON SOME KIND OF BUILDING?
BOY, YOU'RE SO THICK! OF COURSE WE'RE ON A B--
AAAH!
I'M A MONKEY AGAIN!!
ZOT, DON'T STOP MOVING! GET OUTSIDE! IT'S ALMOST TIME!!
SHE'S RIGHT, ZACH! GET OUT OF HERE BEFORE--!

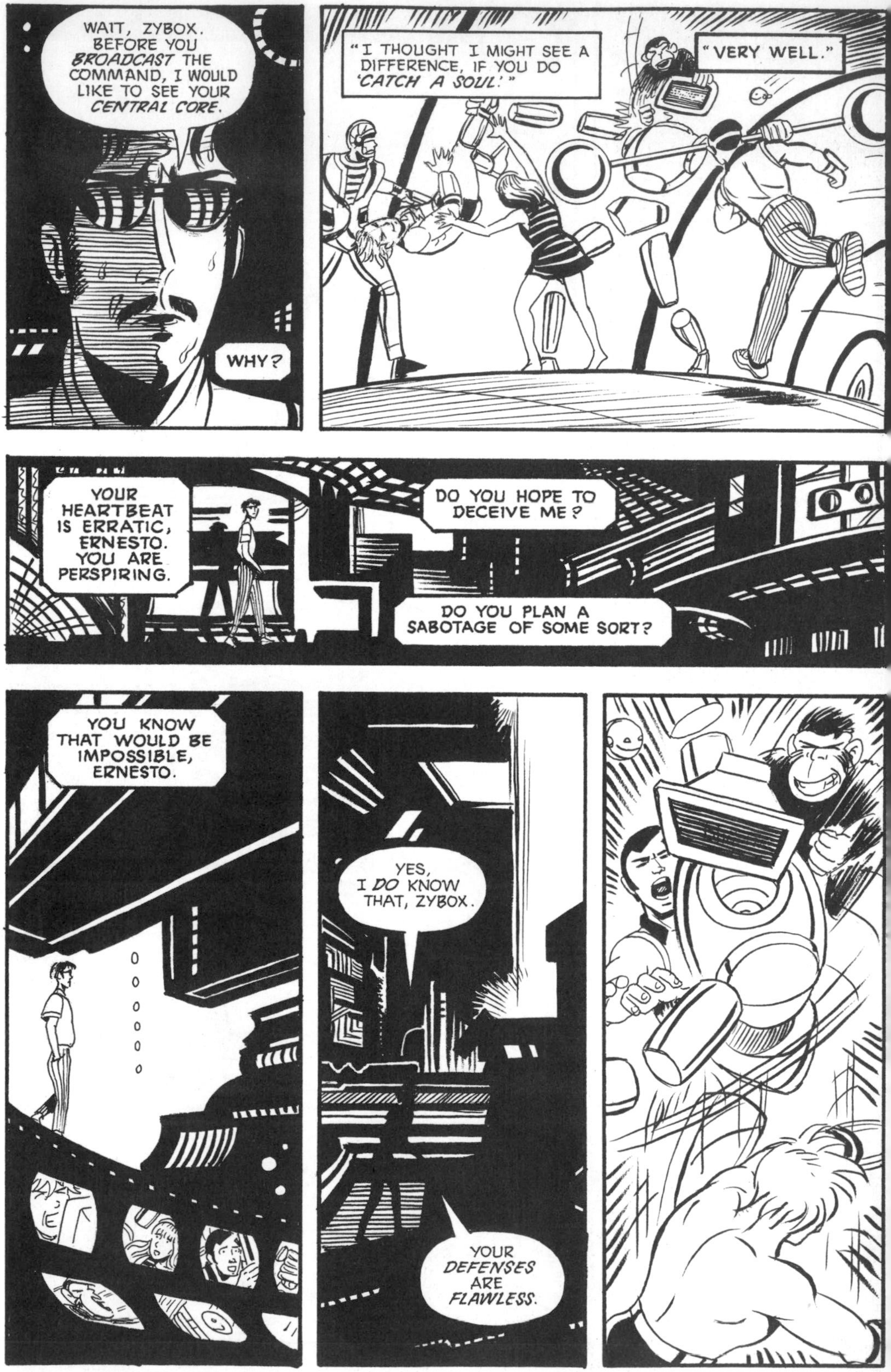
WAIT, ZYBOX. BEFORE YOU *BROADCAST* THE COMMAND, I WOULD LIKE TO SEE YOUR *CENTRAL CORE*.
WHY?
"I THOUGHT I MIGHT SEE A DIFFERENCE, IF YOU DO *'CATCH A SOUL.'*"
"VERY WELL."
YOUR HEARTBEAT IS ERRATIC, ERNESTO. YOU ARE PERSPIRING.
DO YOU HOPE TO DECEIVE ME?
DO YOU PLAN A SABOTAGE OF SOME SORT?
YOU KNOW THAT WOULD BE IMPOSSIBLE, ERNESTO.
YES, I *DO* KNOW THAT, ZYBOX.
YOUR *DEFENSES* ARE *FLAWLESS*.

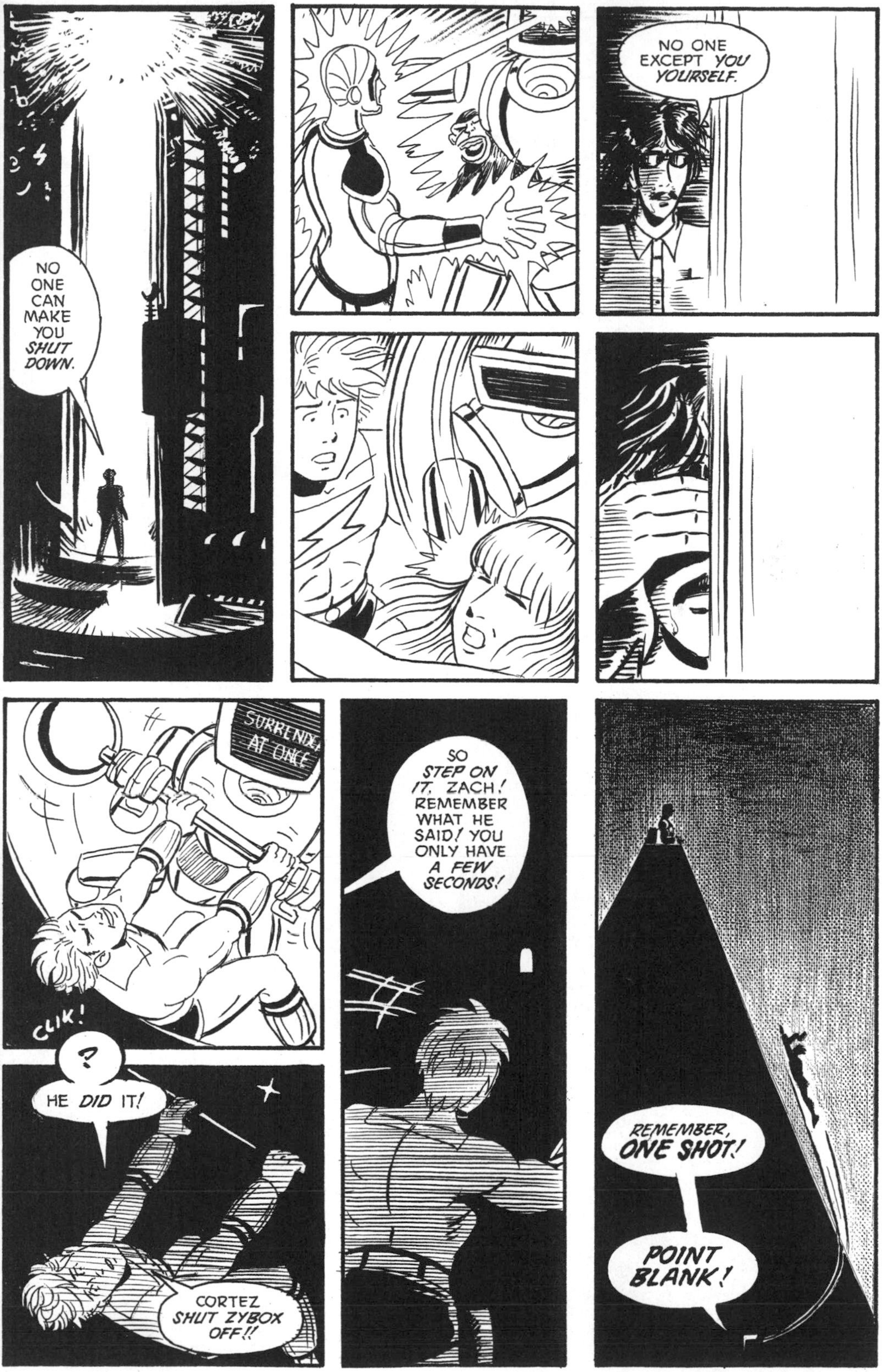
NO ONE CAN MAKE YOU SHUT DOWN.
NO ONE EXCEPT YOU YOURSELF.
SURRENDER AT ONCE
CLIK!
?
HE DID IT!
CORTEZ SHUT ZYBOX OFF!!
SO STEP ON IT, ZACH! REMEMBER WHAT HE SAID! YOU ONLY HAVE A FEW SECONDS!
REMEMBER, ONE SHOT!
POINT BLANK!

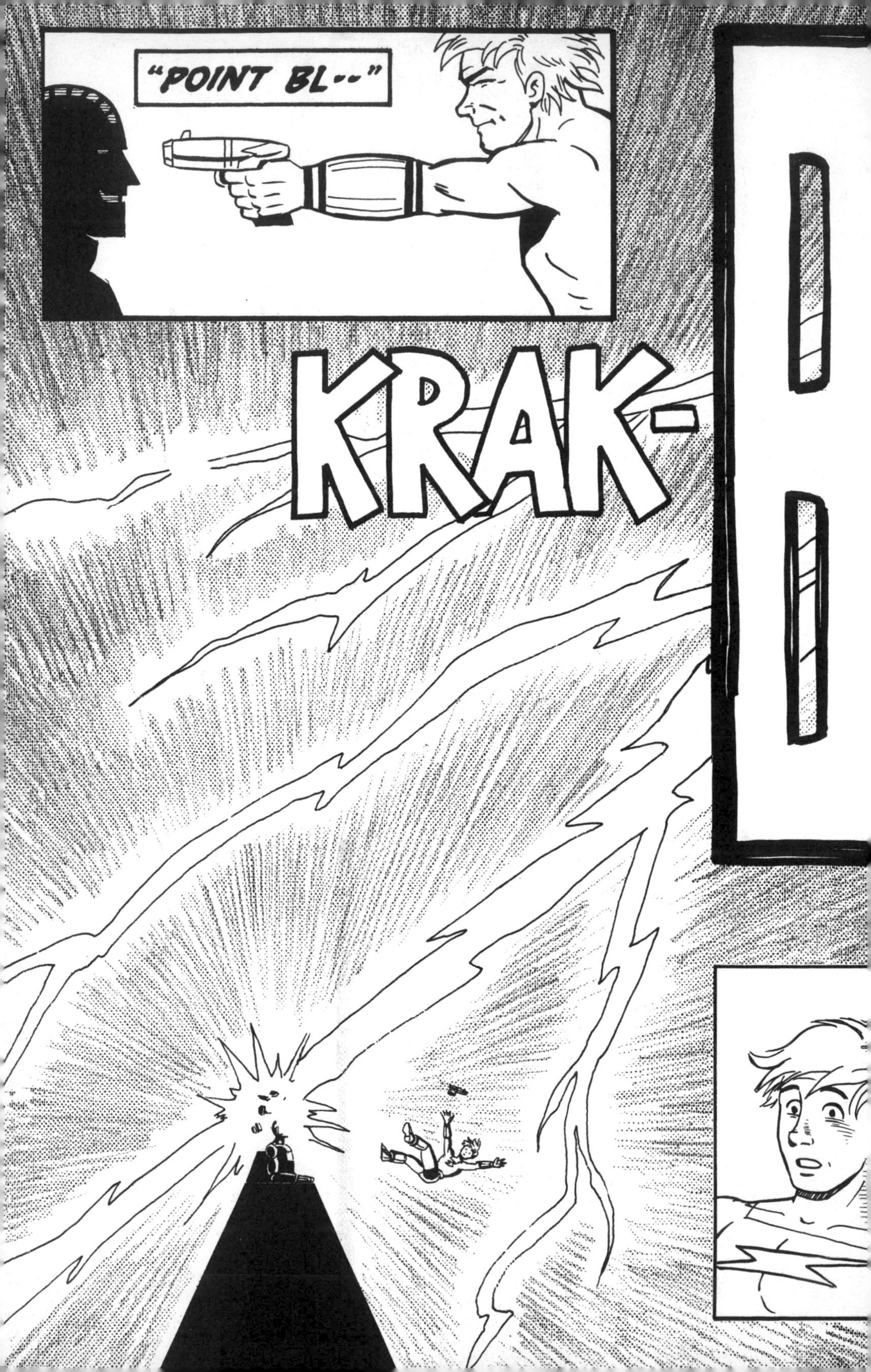
"POINT BL--"
KRAK-

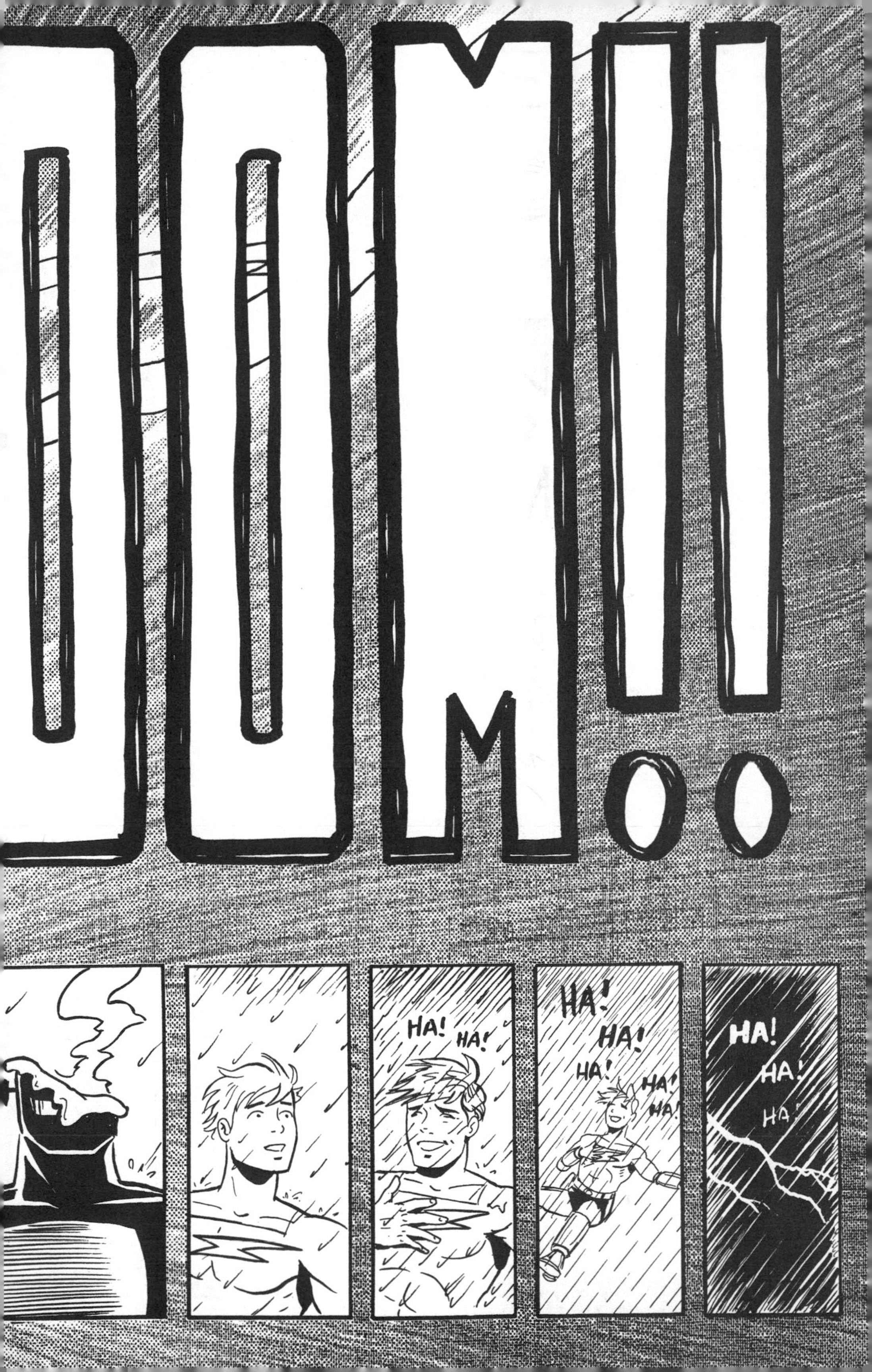
OOM!!
HA! HA!
HA! HA! HA! HA! HA!
HA! HA! HA!

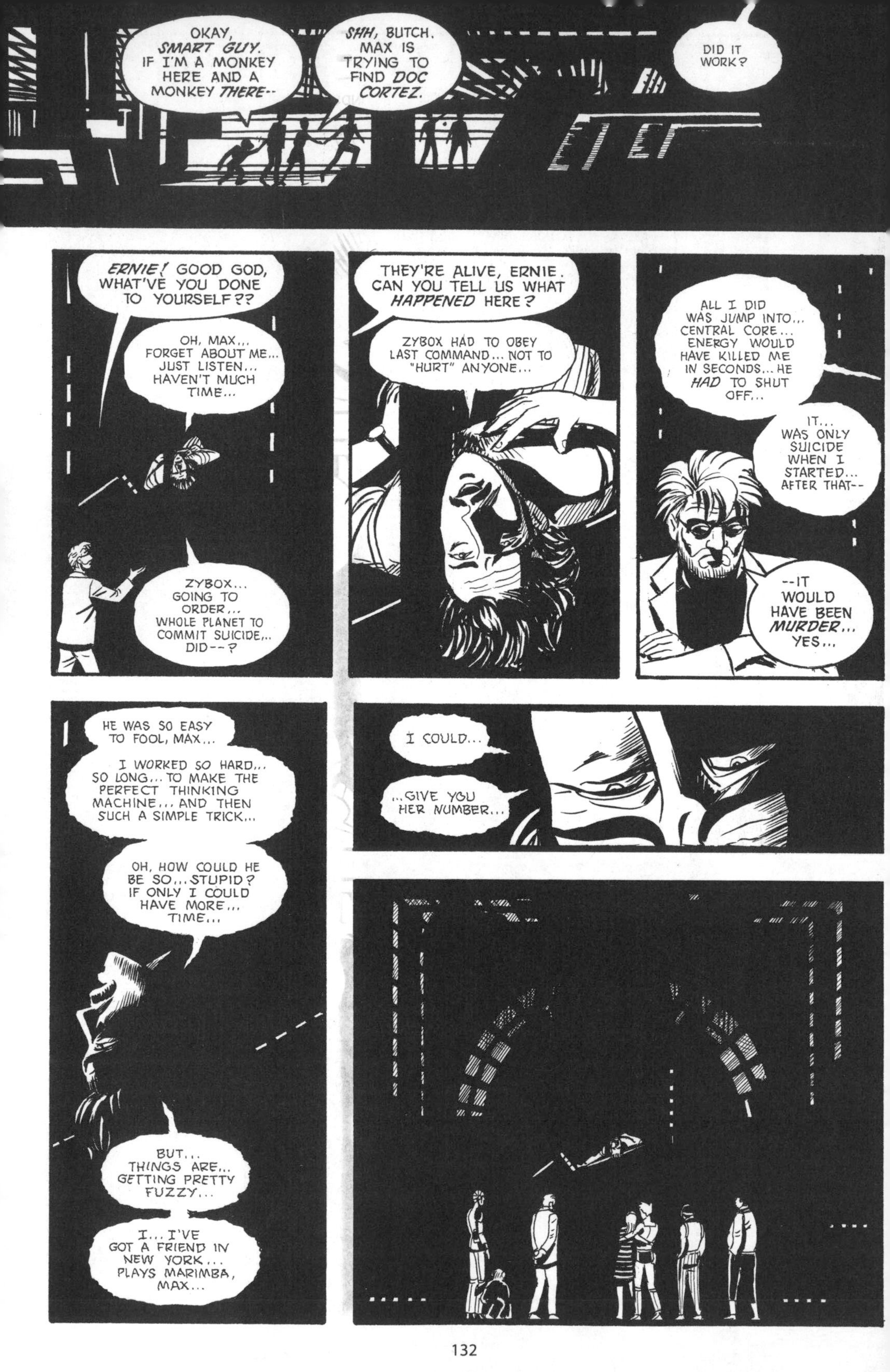
OKAY, SMART GUY. IF I'M A MONKEY HERE AND A MONKEY THERE--
SHH, BUTCH. MAX IS TRYING TO FIND DOC CORTEZ.
DID IT WORK?
ERNIE! GOOD GOD, WHAT'VE YOU DONE TO YOURSELF??
OH, MAX... FORGET ABOUT ME... JUST LISTEN... HAVEN'T MUCH TIME...
ZYBOX... GOING TO ORDER... WHOLE PLANET TO COMMIT SUICIDE... DID--?
THEY'RE ALIVE, ERNIE. CAN YOU TELL US WHAT HAPPENED HERE?
ZYBOX HAD TO OBEY LAST COMMAND... NOT TO "HURT" ANYONE...
ALL I DID WAS JUMP INTO... CENTRAL CORE... ENERGY WOULD HAVE KILLED ME IN SECONDS... HE HAD TO SHUT OFF...
IT... WAS ONLY SUICIDE WHEN I STARTED... AFTER THAT--
--IT WOULD HAVE BEEN MURDER... YES...
HE WAS SO EASY TO FOOL, MAX...
I WORKED SO HARD... SO LONG... TO MAKE THE PERFECT THINKING MACHINE... AND THEN SUCH A SIMPLE TRICK...
OH, HOW COULD HE BE SO... STUPID? IF ONLY I COULD HAVE MORE... TIME...
BUT... THINGS ARE... GETTING PRETTY FUZZY...
I... I'VE GOT A FRIEND IN NEW YORK... PLAYS MARIMBA, MAX...
I COULD...
...GIVE YOU HER NUMBER...

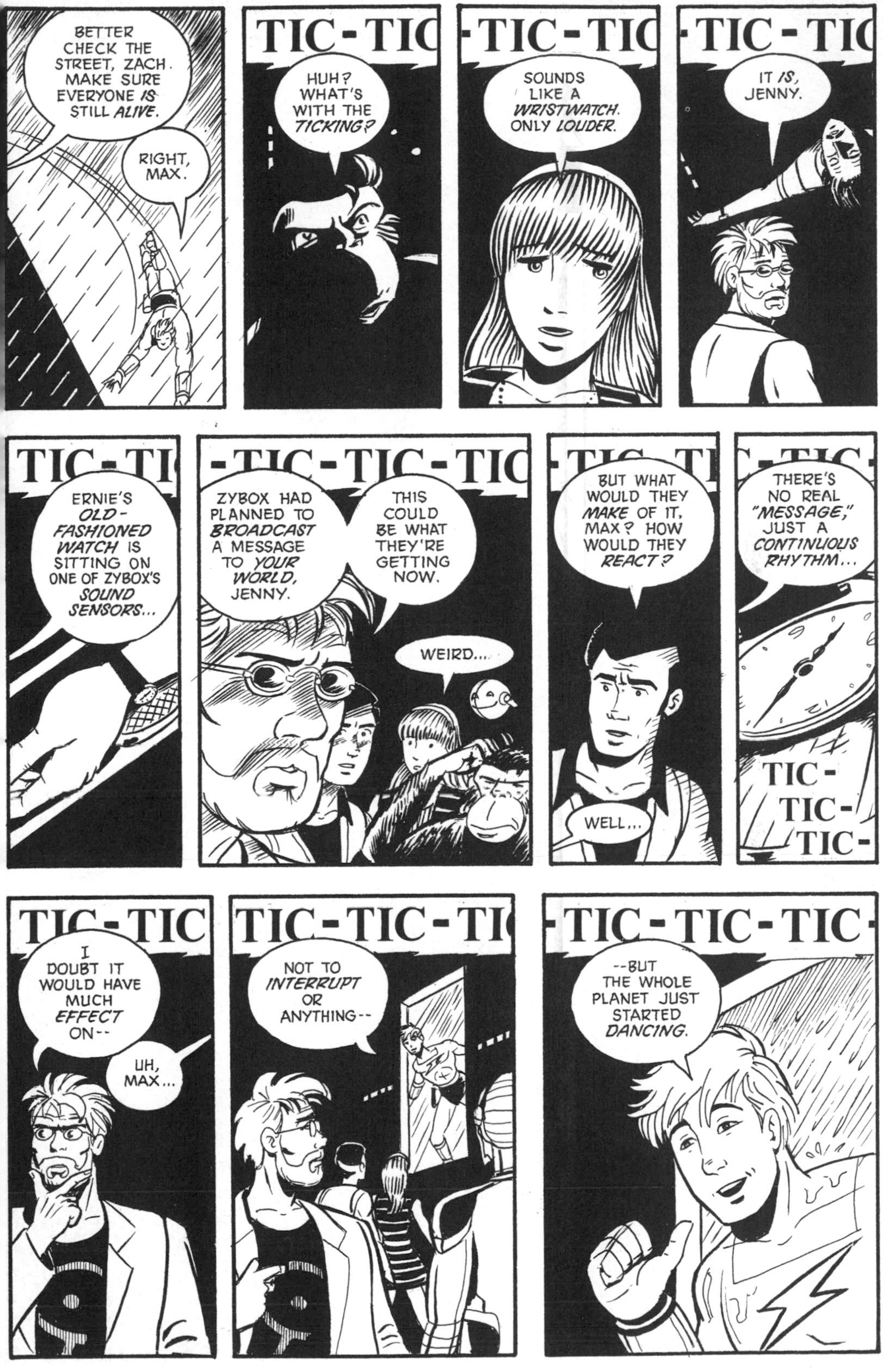
BETTER CHECK THE STREET, ZACH. MAKE SURE EVERYONE IS STILL ALIVE.
RIGHT, MAX.
TIC-TIC
HUH? WHAT'S WITH THE TICKING?
-TIC-TIC
SOUNDS LIKE A WRISTWATCH. ONLY LOUDER.
-TIC-TIC
IT IS, JENNY.
TIC-TI
ERNIE'S OLD-FASHIONED WATCH IS SITTING ON ONE OF ZYBOX'S SOUND SENSORS...
-TIC-TIC-TIC
ZYBOX HAD PLANNED TO BROADCAST A MESSAGE TO YOUR WORLD, JENNY.
THIS COULD BE WHAT THEY'RE GETTING NOW.
WEIRD....
BUT WHAT WOULD THEY MAKE OF IT, MAX? HOW WOULD THEY REACT?
WELL...
THERE'S NO REAL "MESSAGE," JUST A CONTINUOUS RHYTHM...
TIC- TIC- TIC-
TIC-TIC
I DOUBT IT WOULD HAVE MUCH EFFECT ON--
UH, MAX...
TIC-TIC-TI
NOT TO INTERRUPT OR ANYTHING--
-TIC-TIC-TIC-
--BUT THE WHOLE PLANET JUST STARTED DANCING.

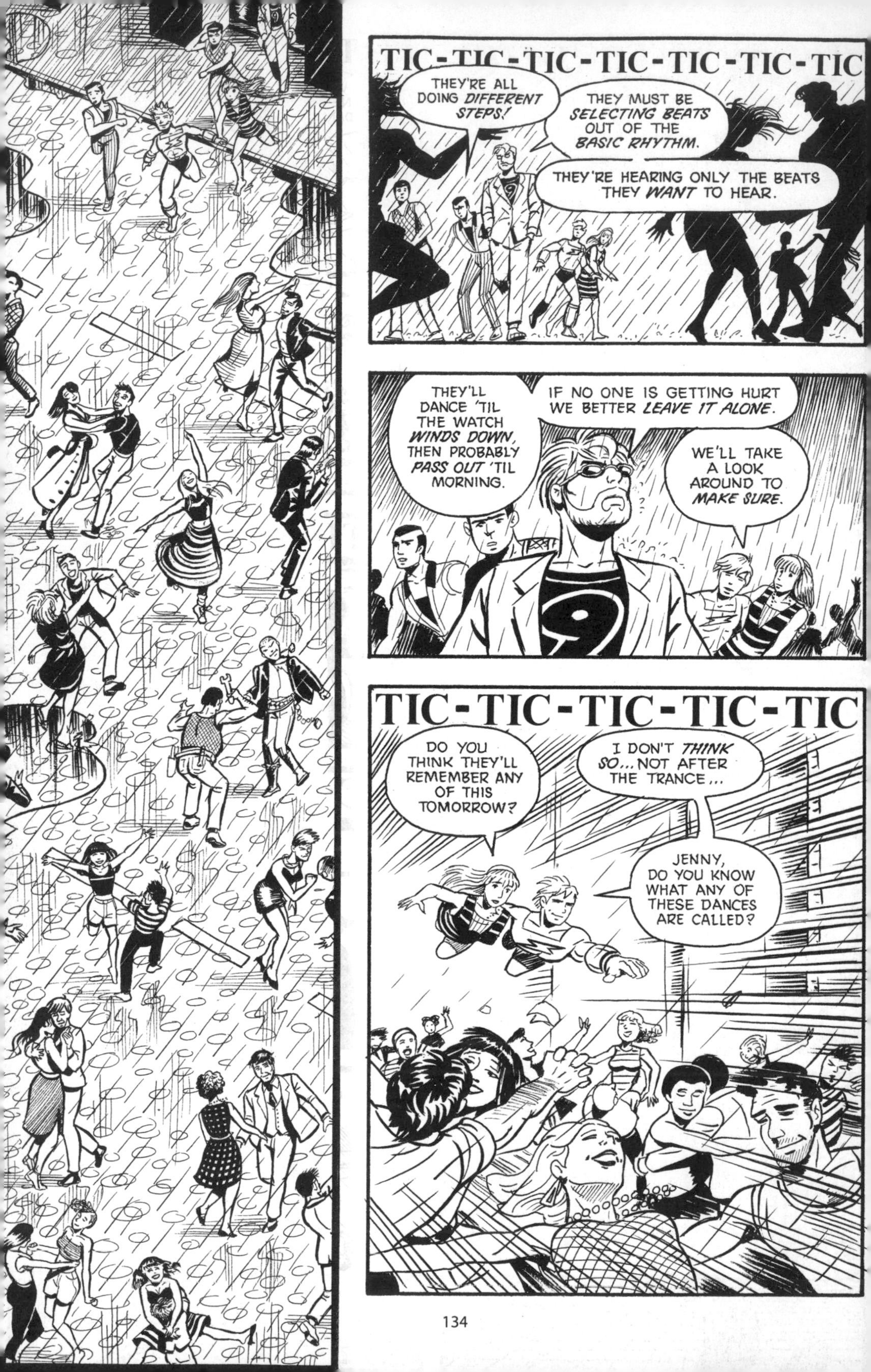
TIC-TIC-TIC-TIC-TIC-TIC-TIC
THEY'RE ALL DOING *DIFFERENT STEPS!*
THEY MUST BE *SELECTING BEATS* OUT OF THE *BASIC RHYTHM.*
THEY'RE HEARING ONLY THE BEATS THEY *WANT* TO HEAR.
THEY'LL DANCE 'TIL THE WATCH *WINDS DOWN*, THEN PROBABLY *PASS OUT* 'TIL MORNING.
IF NO ONE IS GETTING HURT WE BETTER *LEAVE IT ALONE*.
WE'LL TAKE A LOOK AROUND TO *MAKE SURE*.
TIC-TIC-TIC-TIC-TIC
DO YOU THINK THEY'LL REMEMBER ANY OF THIS TOMORROW?
I DON'T *THINK SO*... NOT AFTER THE TRANCE...
JENNY, DO YOU KNOW WHAT ANY OF THESE DANCES ARE CALLED?

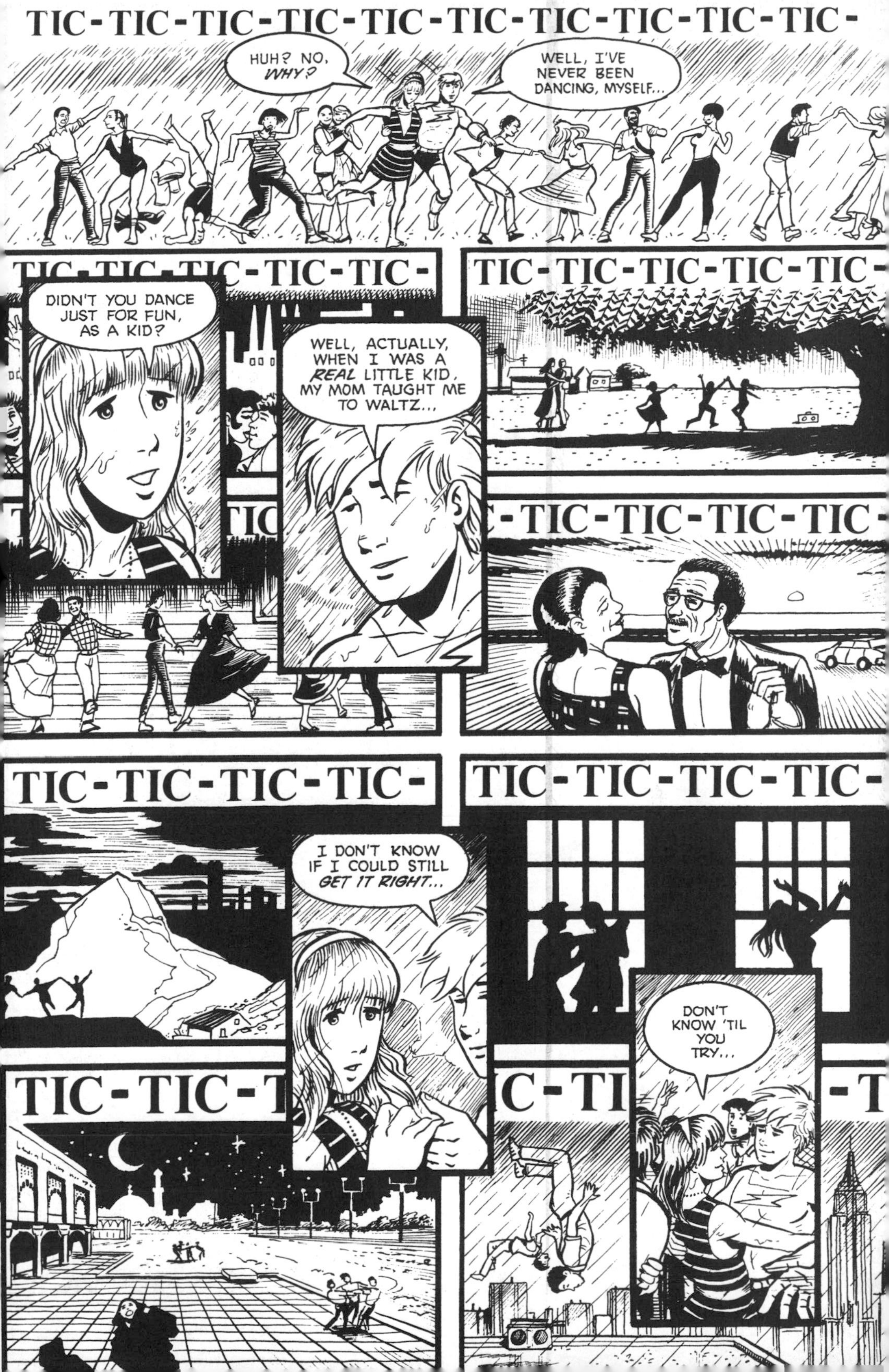
TIC-TIC-TIC-TIC-TIC-TIC-TIC-TIC-TIC-TIC-
HUH? NO, *WHY?*
WELL, I'VE NEVER BEEN DANCING, MYSELF...
TIC-TIC-TIC-TIC-TIC-
DIDN'T YOU DANCE JUST FOR FUN, AS A KID?
WELL, ACTUALLY, WHEN I WAS A *REAL* LITTLE KID, MY MOM TAUGHT ME TO WALTZ...
TIC-TIC-TIC-TIC-TIC-
TIC
-TIC-TIC-TIC-TIC-
TIC-TIC-TIC-TIC-
I DON'T KNOW IF I COULD STILL *GET IT RIGHT*...
TIC-TIC-TIC-TIC-
DON'T KNOW 'TIL YOU TRY...
TIC-TIC-T
C-TI
-T

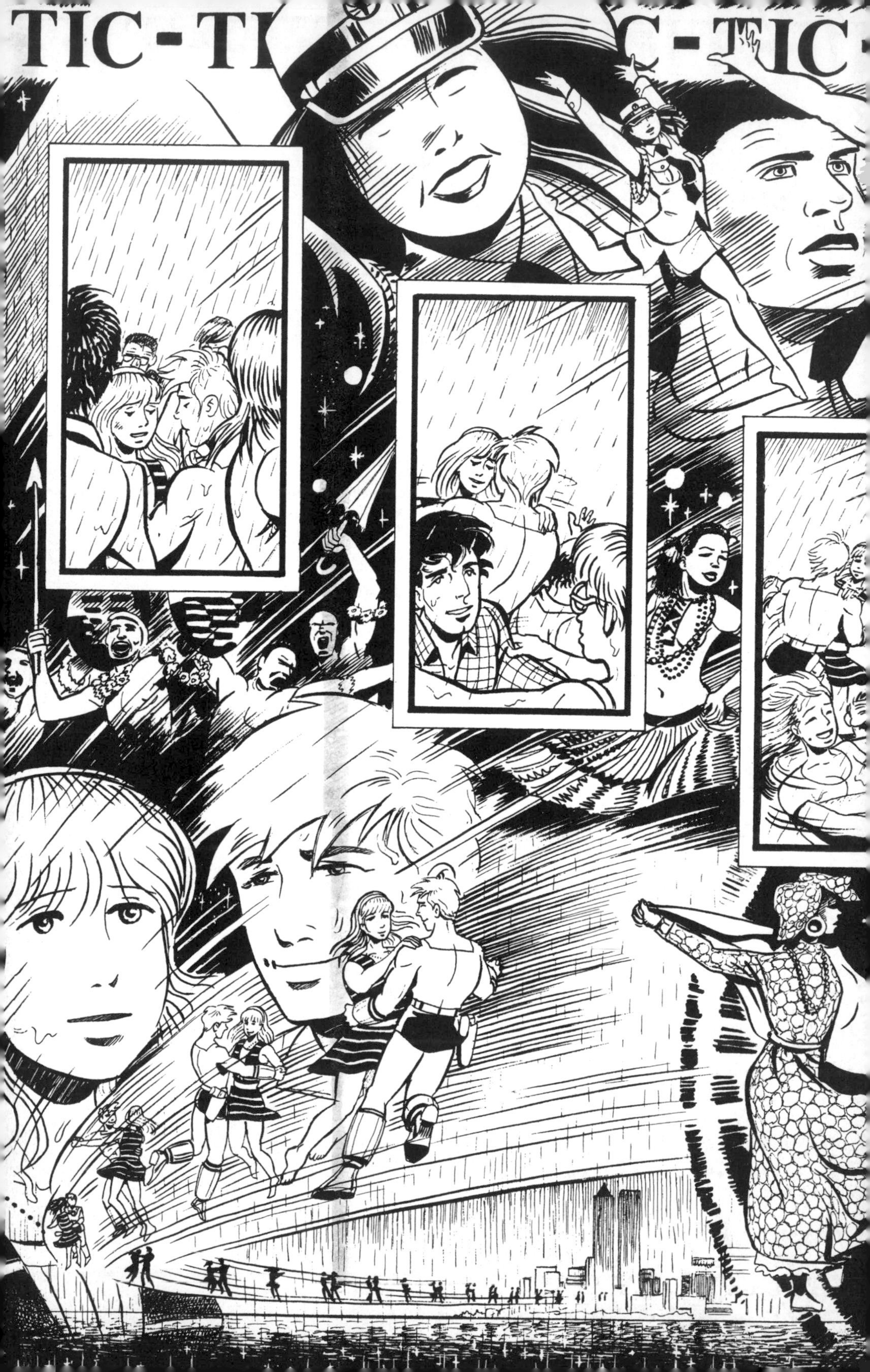

TIC-TI
C-TIC-

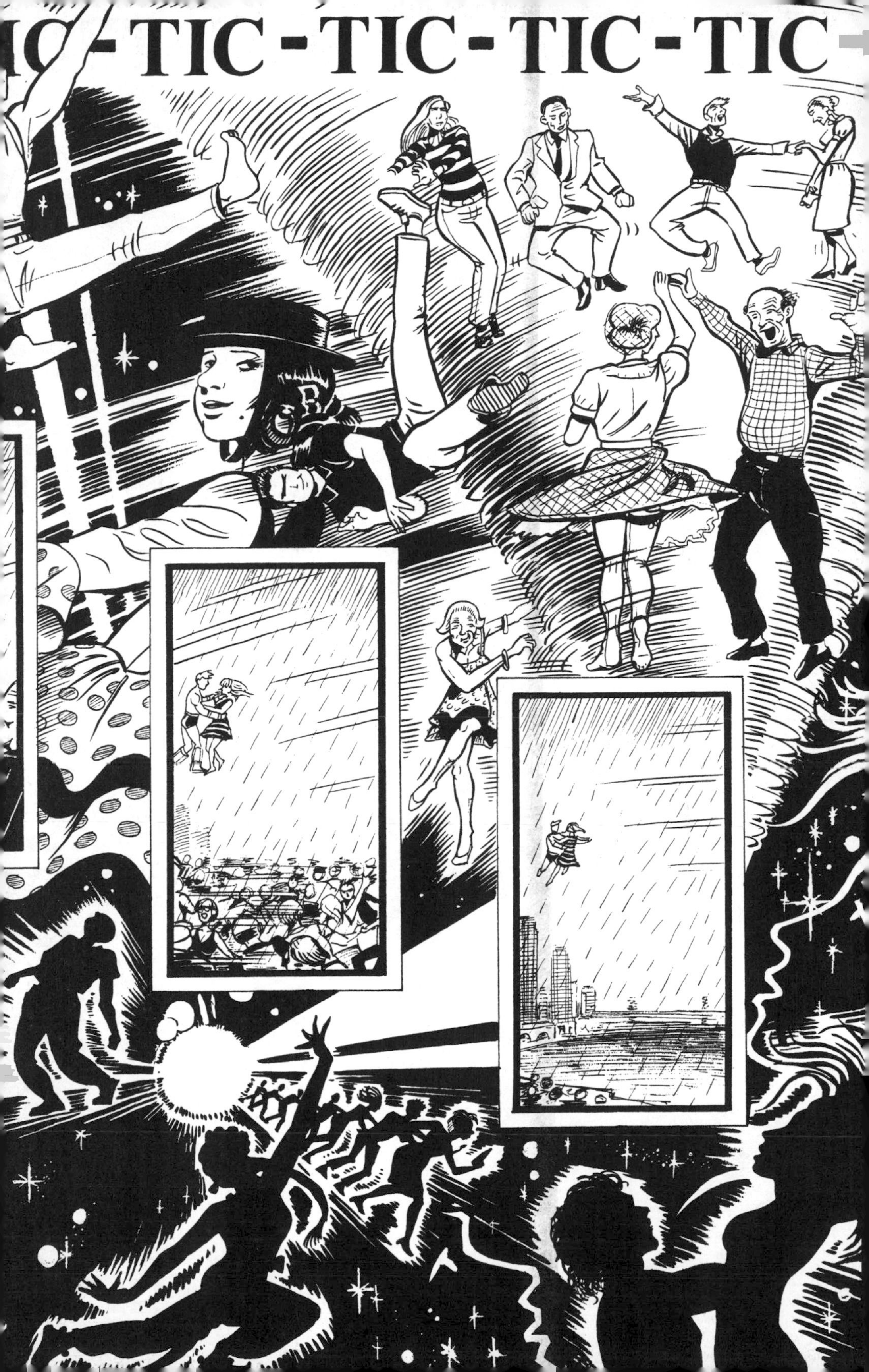
TIC-TIC-TIC-TIC-TIC

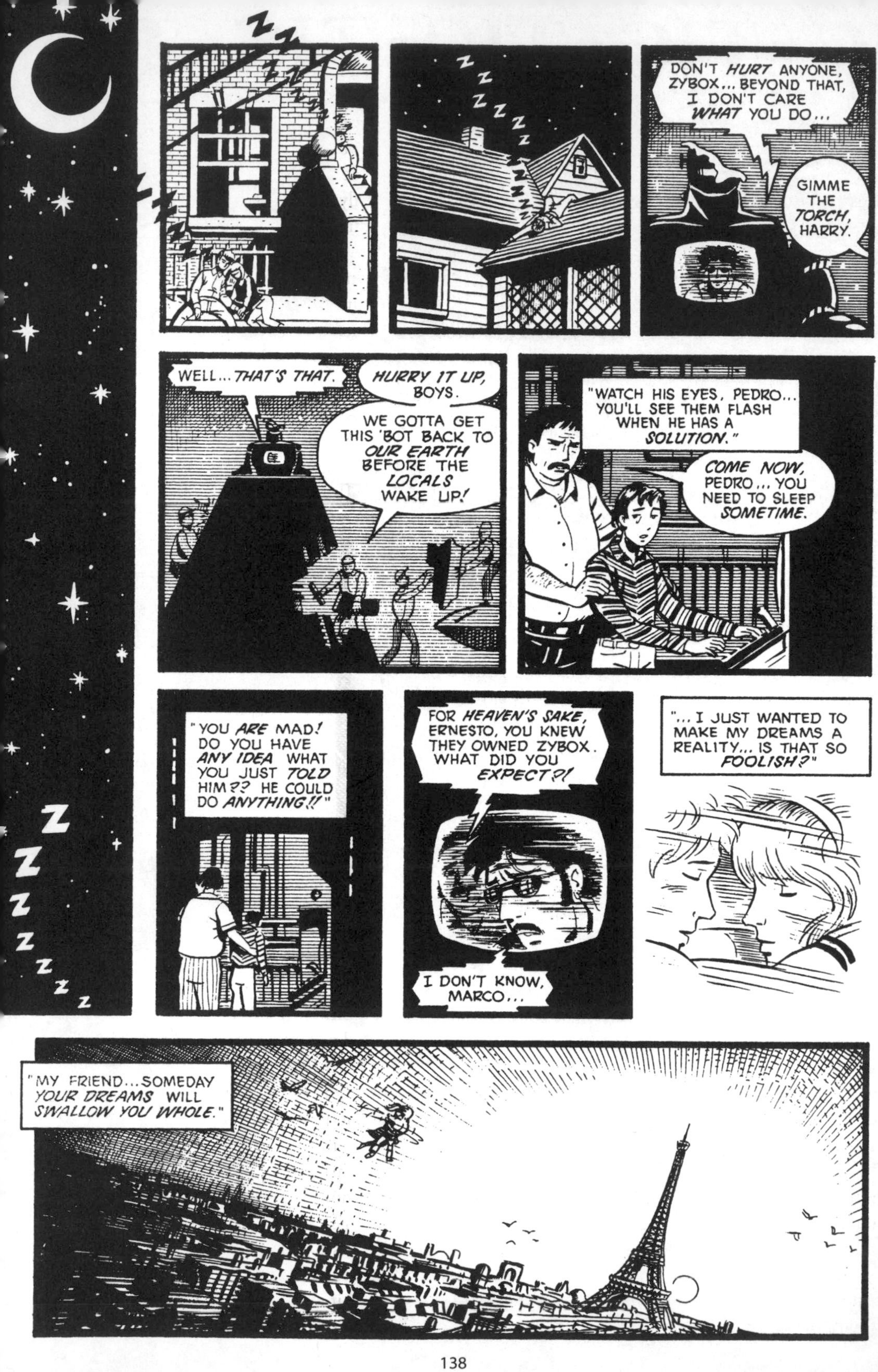
Z Z Z Z Z Z Z
DON'T HURT ANYONE, ZYBOX... BEYOND THAT, I DON'T CARE WHAT YOU DO...
GIMME THE TORCH, HARRY.
WELL... THAT'S THAT.
HURRY IT UP, BOYS.
WE GOTTA GET THIS 'BOT BACK TO OUR EARTH BEFORE THE LOCALS WAKE UP!
"WATCH HIS EYES, PEDRO... YOU'LL SEE THEM FLASH WHEN HE HAS A SOLUTION."
COME NOW, PEDRO... YOU NEED TO SLEEP SOMETIME.
"YOU ARE MAD! DO YOU HAVE ANY IDEA WHAT YOU JUST TOLD HIM?? HE COULD DO ANYTHING!!"
FOR HEAVEN'S SAKE, ERNESTO, YOU KNEW THEY OWNED ZYBOX. WHAT DID YOU EXPECT?!
I DON'T KNOW, MARCO...
"... I JUST WANTED TO MAKE MY DREAMS A REALITY... IS THAT SO FOOLISH?"
"MY FRIEND...SOMEDAY YOUR DREAMS WILL SWALLOW YOU WHOLE."

The image of every man, woman, and child on Earth dancing half asleep to the ticking of a dead man's watch captivated me early on, but it was a bitch to draw—especially with my own limited skill set. In 1987, the first graphic Web browsers were still six years off (in fact, the Web itself was still in the process of being hatched, though the Internet had been around for nearly two decades) so the luxury of things like Google Image Search was unknown. Illustrators had to make do with their own collections of books and magazines and their local libraries, some of which kept image libraries. Artists hoping to draw a northern hairy-nosed wombat might have a long, arduous search ahead of them. I did what I could on the spread, but *National Geographic* and my own ten thumbs could only take me so far.

The fact that Zybox sits on top of the World Trade Center and commands a world to commit mass suicide, including a woman in Islamic clothing shown in a few panels, may have a weird resonance for readers in 2008. I had no idea what the future of *this* world had in store for us. I was just matching up my villains with New York skyscrapers since Dekko (featured in our fourth story) had so thoroughly absorbed the Chrysler Building, and Bellows had taken a shine to the Empire State Building in issue #12. The World Trade towers seemed suitably modern and austere for a villain like Zybox. (9-Jack-9, Zot's archnemesis, I associated with the Citicorp building at 601 Lexington Avenue).

Zybox's demise is a running joke in our household. The phrase "and then Zybox is hit by lightning" has become synonymous with any important plot point that I put off while working on other parts of the story that I find more interesting. At the eleventh hour, I settled on the lightning bolt as an allegorical nod to Frankenstein's monster—the original template for the story I was telling—but it definitely bears more than a whiff of deus ex machina.

The middle storyline where Jenny is trapped in a dream that Zot never existed (comprising the bulk of Issue #14) seemed to work for a lot of readers and snagged a nomination for best single issue in that year's Eisner Awards. Fifteen years later, fans of *Buffy the Vampire Slayer* would see a similar story in the episode "Normal Again," where Buffy temporarily wakes up in an asylum to find that five and a half seasons' worth of adventures were just a mad hallucination on her part. I don't know if the writer of that episode, Diego Gutierrez, is one of the comics fans who worked on *Buffy*, but either way I have to admire him for doing what I hesitated to do: giving substantial ammunition to the idea that everything to that point was nothing but an insane, never-ending dream.

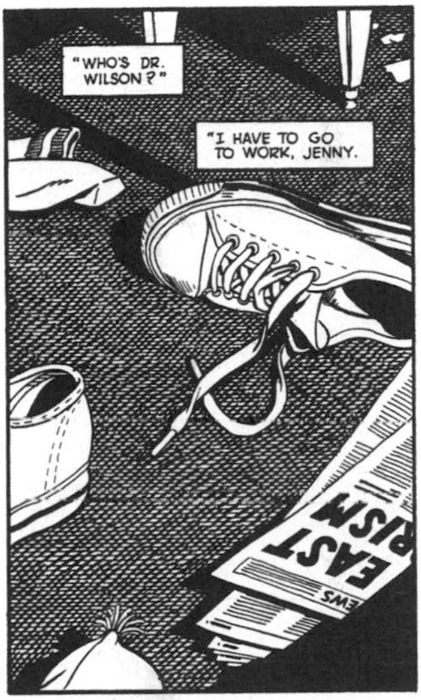
"WHO'S DR. WILSON?"
"I HAVE TO GO TO WORK, JENNY.

I enjoyed and/or suffered two summers in Manhattan during my year and a half working for DC Comics in the early '80s. Every Sunday, I'd walk five long blocks from my tiny apartment to the Metropolitan Museum of Art. During those summers, a street musician named Valerie Naranjo (who's apparently still working in music—thanks, Google) would play the marimba on the sidewalk in front of that enormous building in the summer heat. That strange, wonderful sound—like plucked whale bones at the bottom of an ocean—was linked to the season in my mind. I hoped to capture a bit of that mood with the opening pages of this story.

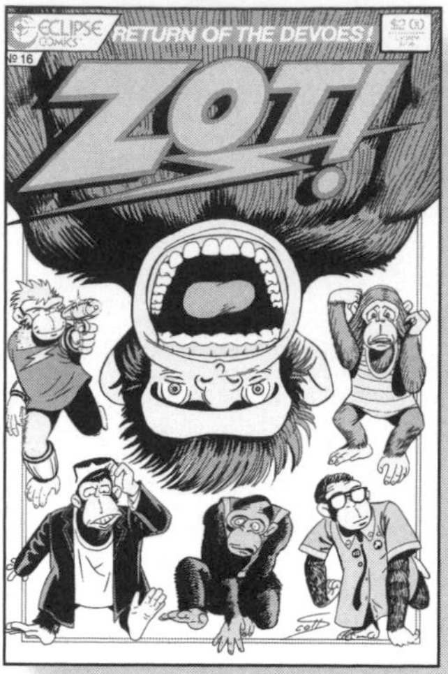
ECLIPSE COMICS
RETURN OF THE DEVOES!
$2.00
№ 16
ZOT!

Call of the Wild

First published in *Zot! #16*.

Lettering:

Bob Lappan

Original series editor:

cat yronwode

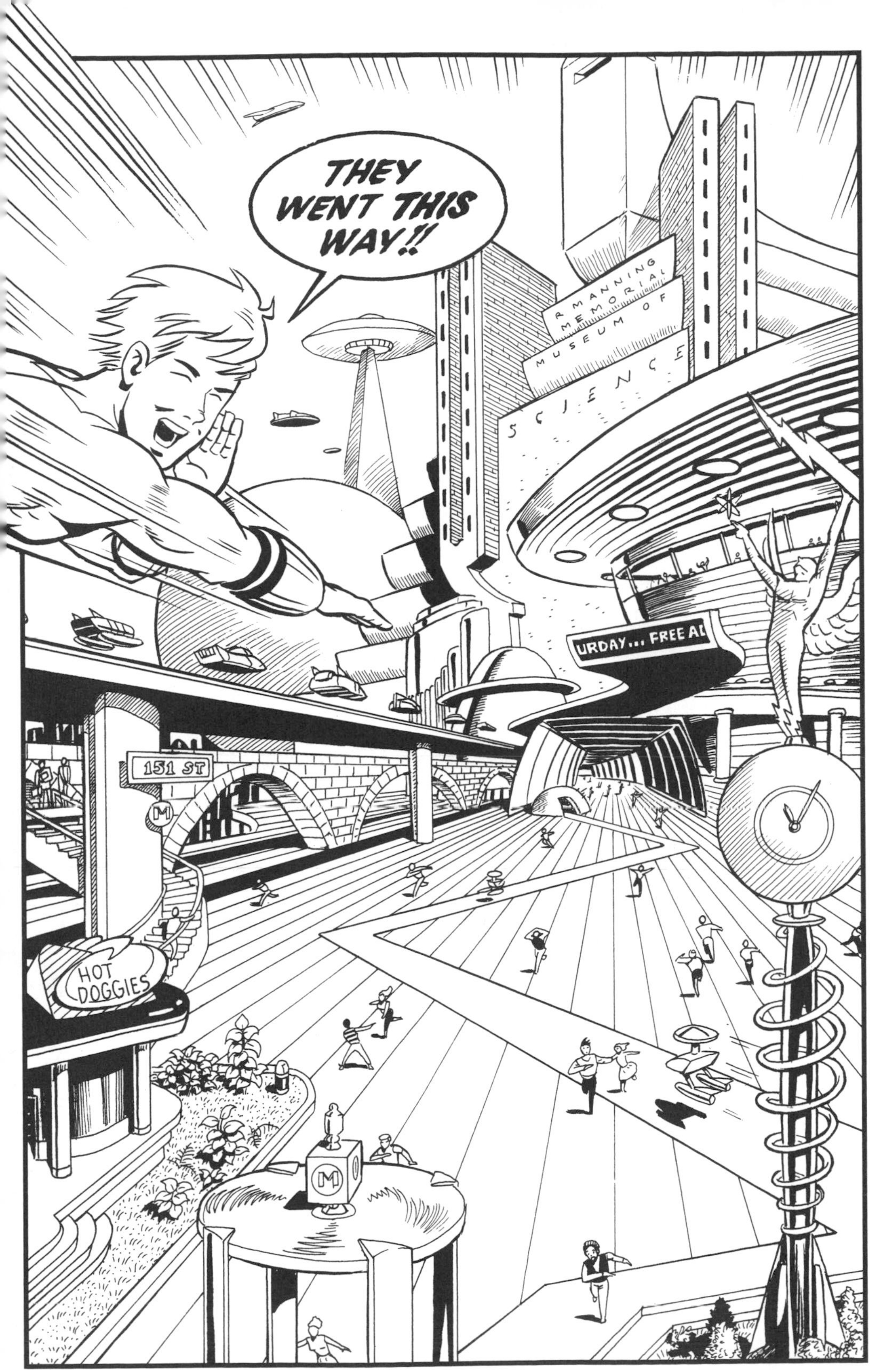

THEY WENT THIS WAY!!
MANNING MEMORIAL MUSEUM OF SCIENCE
URDAY... FREE AD
151 ST
M
HOT DOGGIES
M

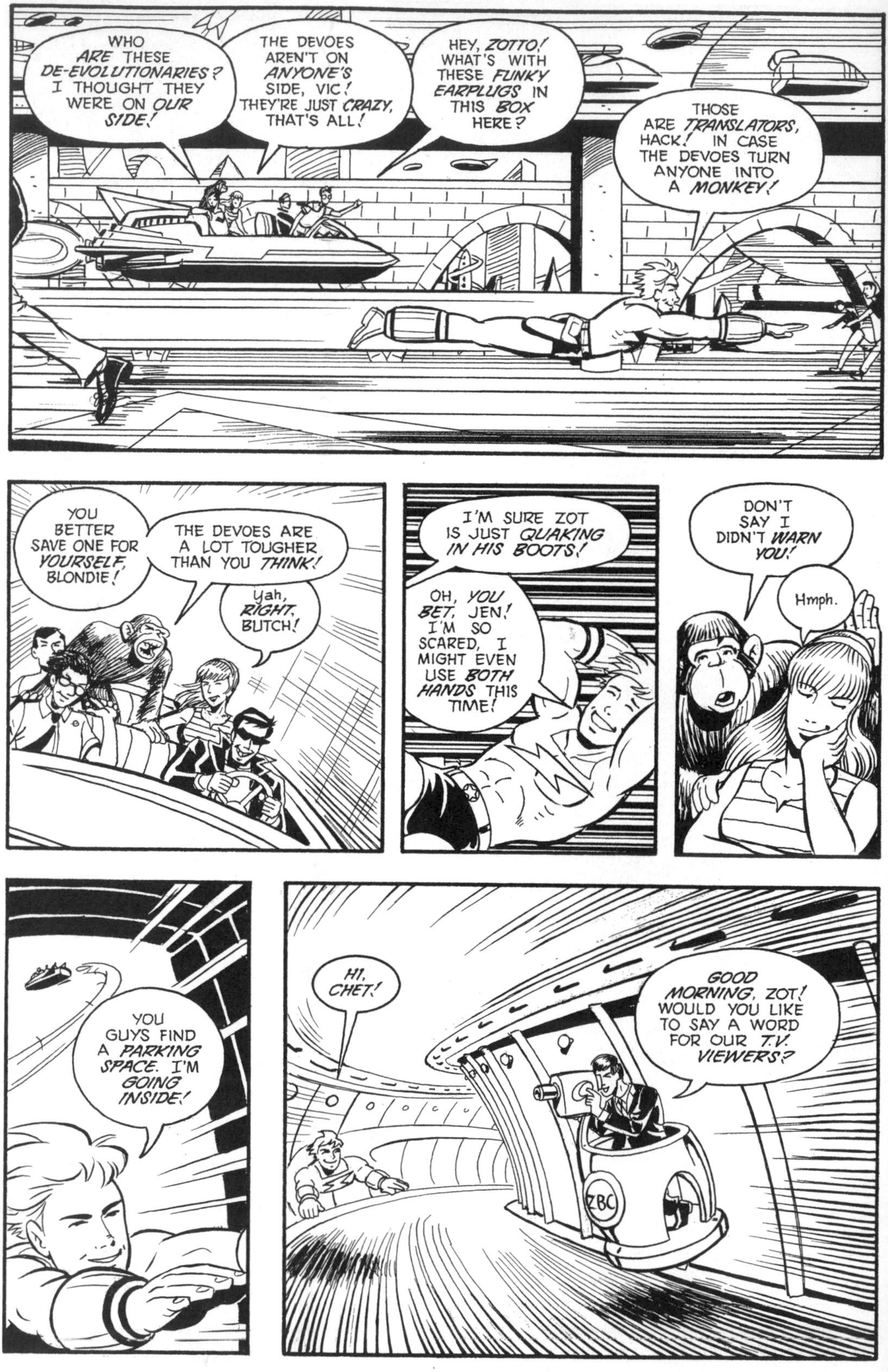
WHO ARE THESE DE-EVOLUTIONARIES? I THOUGHT THEY WERE ON OUR SIDE!
THE DEVOES AREN'T ON ANYONE'S SIDE, VIC! THEY'RE JUST CRAZY, THAT'S ALL!
HEY, ZOTTO! WHAT'S WITH THESE FUNKY EARPLUGS IN THIS BOX HERE?
THOSE ARE TRANSLATORS, HACK! IN CASE THE DEVOES TURN ANYONE INTO A MONKEY!
YOU BETTER SAVE ONE FOR YOURSELF, BLONDIE!
THE DEVOES ARE A LOT TOUGHER THAN YOU THINK!
Yah, RIGHT, BUTCH!
I'M SURE ZOT IS JUST QUAKING IN HIS BOOTS!
OH, YOU BET, JEN! I'M SO SCARED, I MIGHT EVEN USE BOTH HANDS THIS TIME!
DON'T SAY I DIDN'T WARN YOU!
Hmph.
YOU GUYS FIND A PARKING SPACE. I'M GOING INSIDE!
HI, CHET!
GOOD MORNING, ZOT! WOULD YOU LIKE TO SAY A WORD FOR OUR T.V. VIEWERS?
ZBC

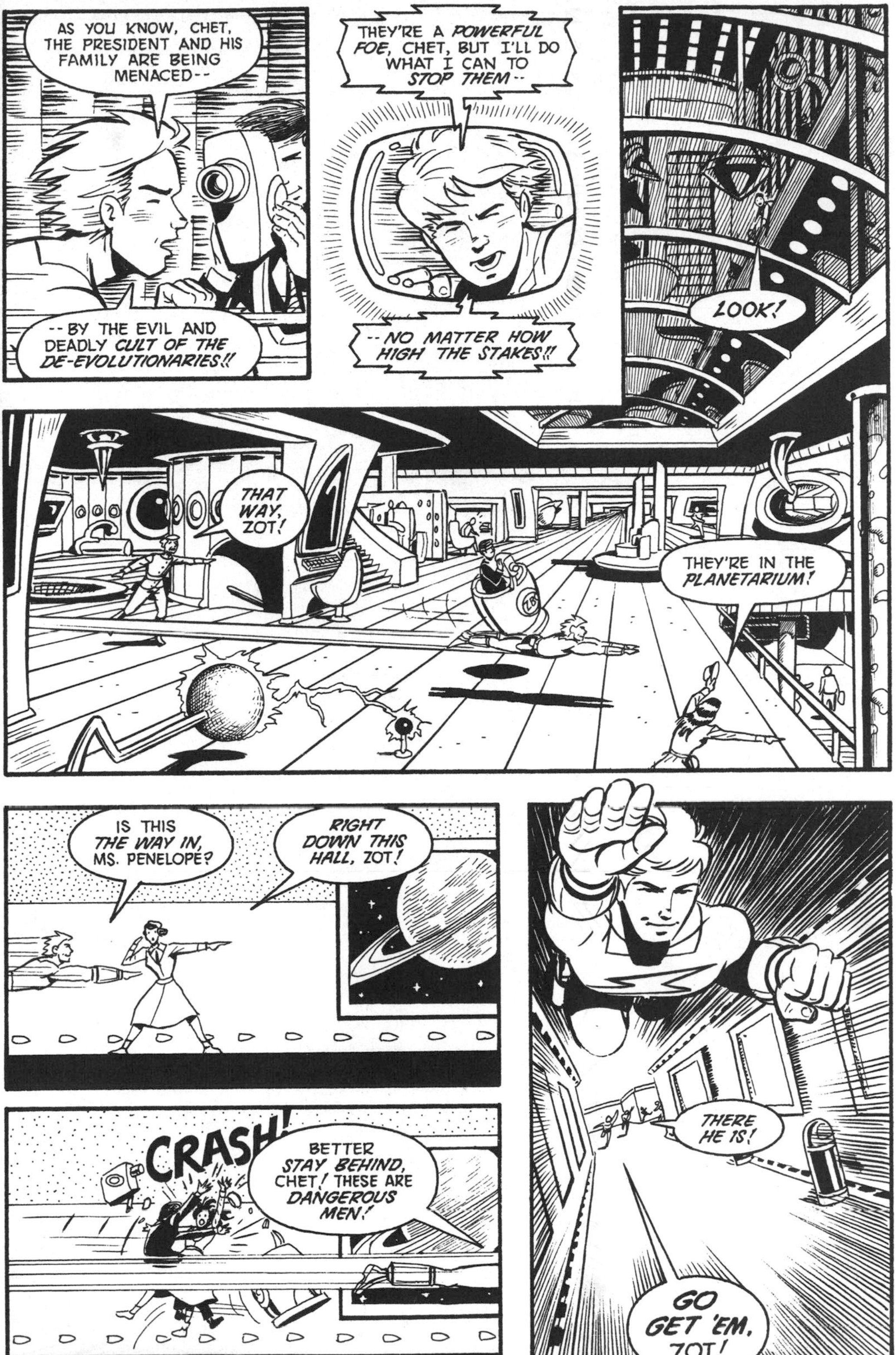
AS YOU KNOW, CHET, THE PRESIDENT AND HIS FAMILY ARE BEING MENACED--
--BY THE EVIL AND DEADLY *CULT OF THE DE-EVOLUTIONARIES!!*
THEY'RE A *POWERFUL FOE*, CHET, BUT I'LL DO WHAT I CAN TO *STOP THEM*--
--NO MATTER HOW HIGH THE STAKES!!
LOOK!
THAT WAY, ZOT!
THEY'RE IN THE *PLANETARIUM!*
IS THIS *THE WAY IN*, MS. PENELOPE?
RIGHT DOWN THIS HALL, ZOT!
CRASH!
BETTER *STAY BEHIND*, CHET! THESE ARE *DANGEROUS* MEN!
THERE HE IS!
GO GET 'EM, ZOT!

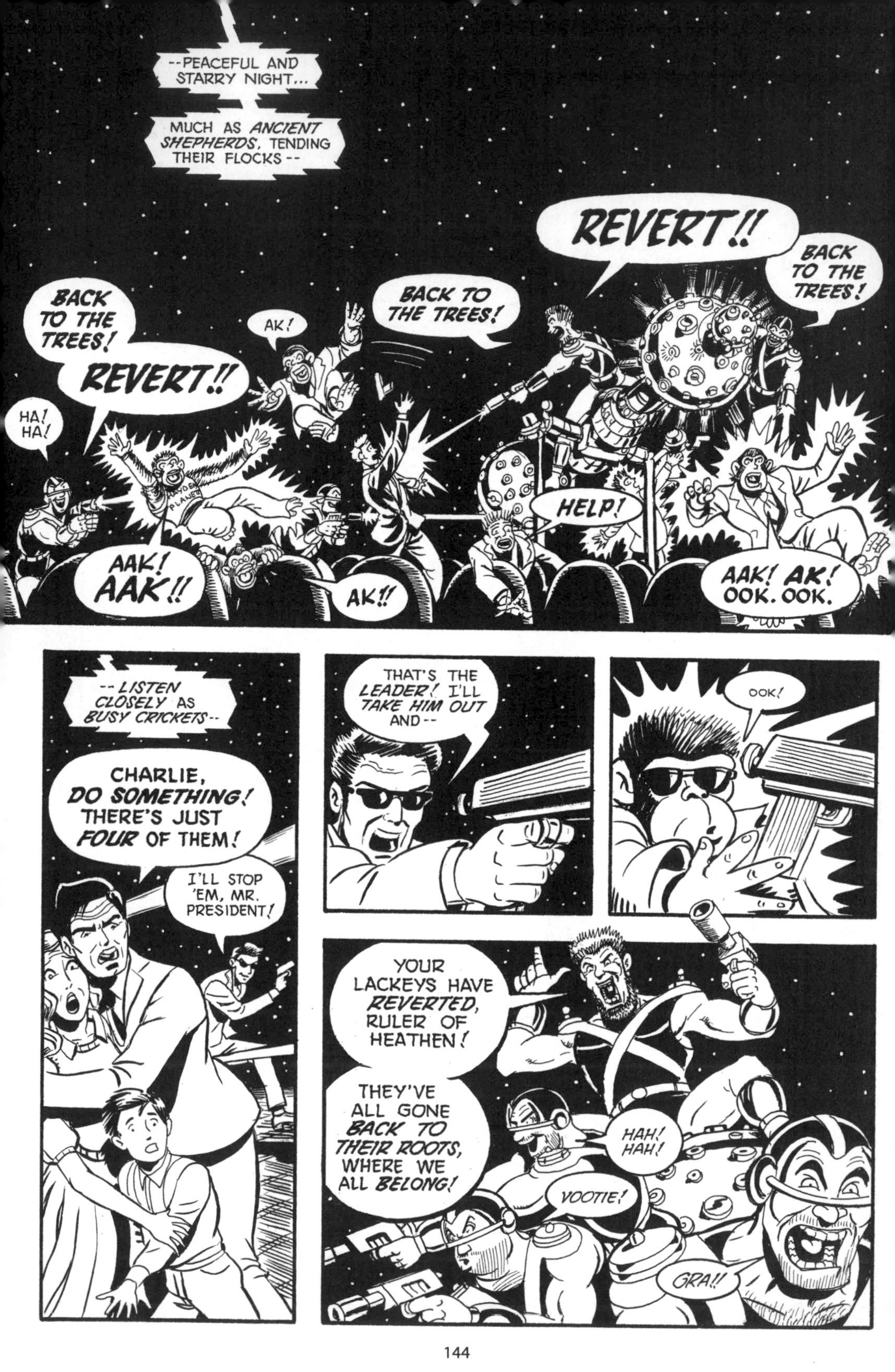
--PEACEFUL AND STARRY NIGHT...
MUCH AS ANCIENT SHEPHERDS, TENDING THEIR FLOCKS--
REVERT!!
BACK TO THE TREES!
BACK TO THE TREES!
AK!
BACK TO THE TREES!
REVERT!!
HA! HA!
HELP!
AAK! AAK!!
AK!!
AAK! AK! OOK. OOK.
--LISTEN CLOSELY AS BUSY CRICKETS--
CHARLIE, DO SOMETHING! THERE'S JUST FOUR OF THEM!
I'LL STOP 'EM, MR. PRESIDENT!
THAT'S THE LEADER! I'LL TAKE HIM OUT AND--
OOK!
YOUR LACKEYS HAVE REVERTED, RULER OF HEATHEN!
THEY'VE ALL GONE BACK TO THEIR ROOTS, WHERE WE ALL BELONG!
HAH! HAH!
VOOTIE!
GRA!!

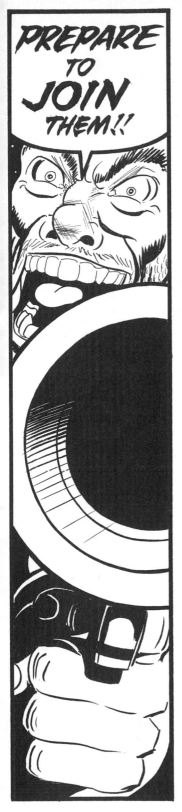

PREPARE TO JOIN THEM!!

THEY'VE JAMMED THE DOOR, ZOT!

TICKETS

OKAY, STAND BACK!

BLAM!

TICKETS

MR. PRESIDENT?? OH NO! I'M TOO LATE!

TO YOUR RIGHT, THE GREAT MAGELLANIC CLOUD...

OOK! OOK!

GGG!

HK! HK!

HEH! HEH!

HEH! HEH!

COME OUT AND FIGHT, YOU SCREWBALLS!!

TO YOUR LEFT--

HEH, HEH...

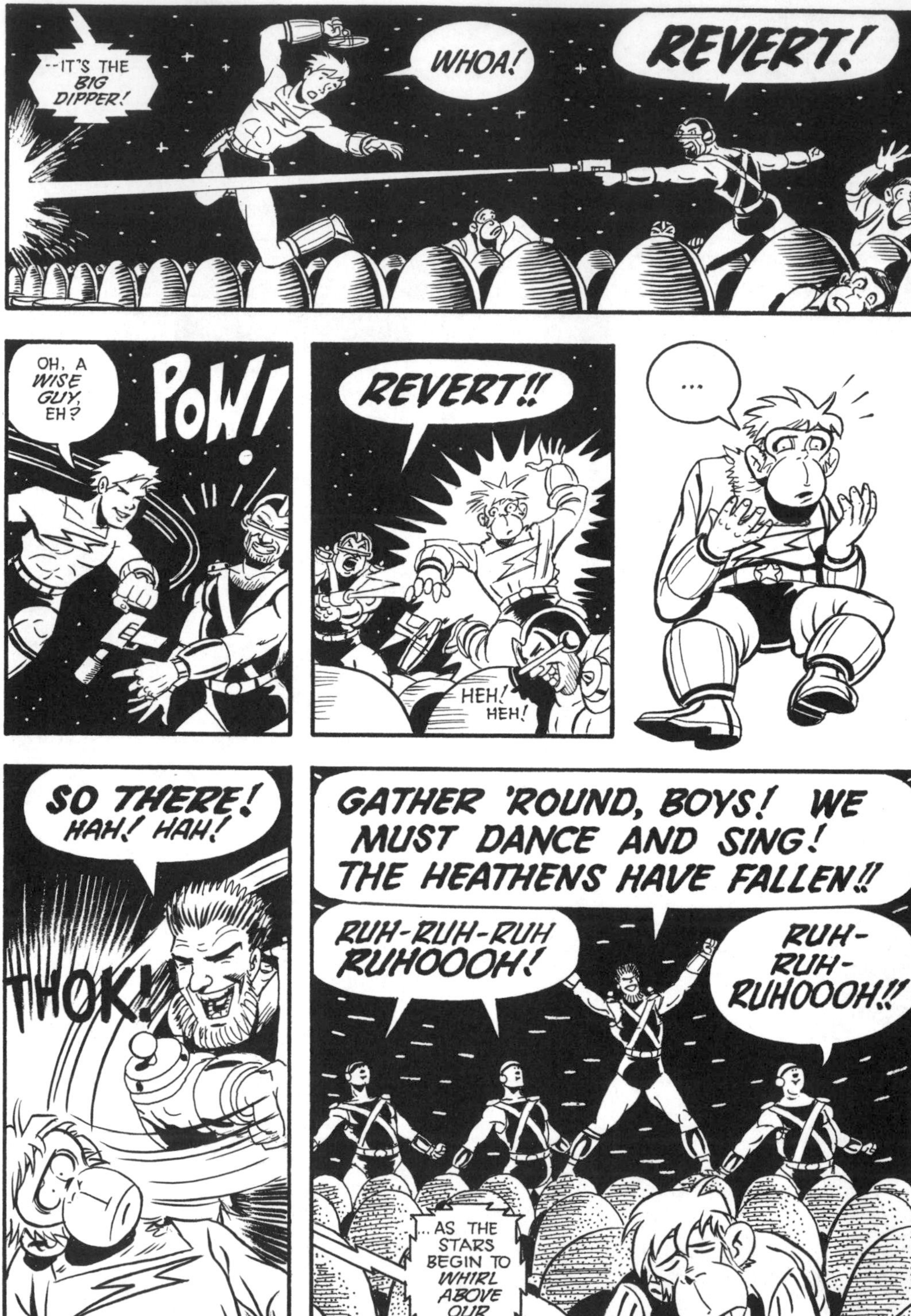
--IT'S THE BIG DIPPER!
WHOA!
REVERT!
OH, A WISE GUY, EH?
POW!
REVERT!!
HEH! HEH!
...
SO THERE! HAH! HAH!
THOK!
GATHER 'ROUND, BOYS! WE MUST DANCE AND SING! THE HEATHENS HAVE FALLEN!!
RUH-RUH-RUH RUHOOOH!
RUH-RUH-RUHOOOH!!
...AS THE STARS BEGIN TO WHIRL ABOVE OUR HEADS...

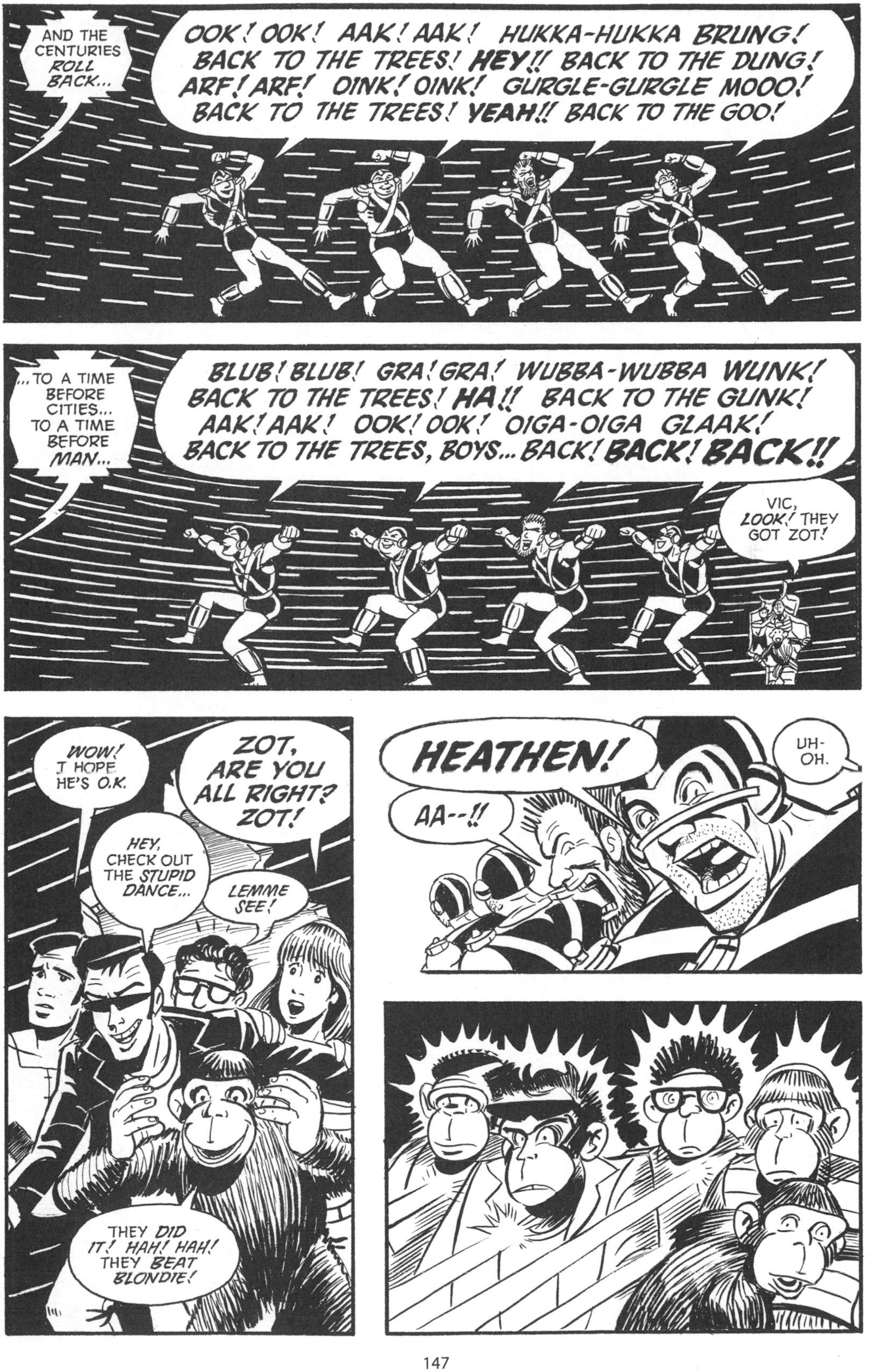

AND THE CENTURIES ROLL BACK...
OOK! OOK! AAK! AAK! HUKKA-HUKKA BRUNG! BACK TO THE TREES! HEY!! BACK TO THE DUNG! ARF! ARF! OINK! OINK! GURGLE-GURGLE MOOO! BACK TO THE TREES! YEAH!! BACK TO THE GOO!
...TO A TIME BEFORE CITIES... TO A TIME BEFORE MAN...
BLUB! BLUB! GRA! GRA! WUBBA-WUBBA WUNK! BACK TO THE TREES! HA!! BACK TO THE GUNK! AAK! AAK! OOK! OOK! OIGA-OIGA GLAAK! BACK TO THE TREES, BOYS... BACK! BACK! BACK!!
VIC, LOOK! THEY GOT ZOT!
WOW! I HOPE HE'S O.K.
ZOT, ARE YOU ALL RIGHT? ZOT!
HEY, CHECK OUT THE STUPID DANCE...
LEMME SEE!
THEY DID IT! HAH! HAH! THEY BEAT BLONDIE!
HEATHEN!
UH-OH.
AA--!!

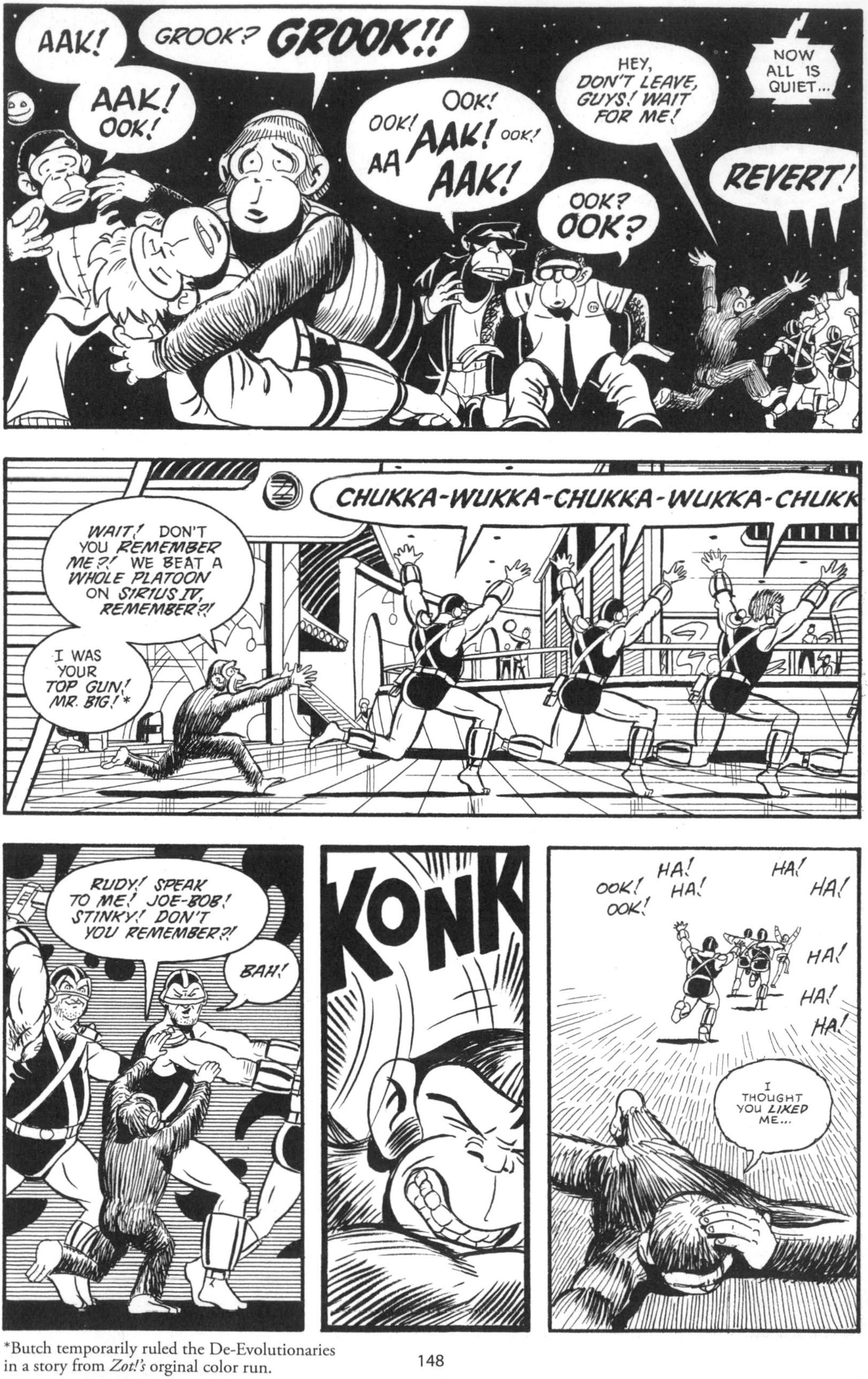
AAK!
AAK! OOK!
GROOK? GROOK!!
OOK! OOK! AA AAK! OOK! AAK!
OOK? OOK?
HEY, DON'T LEAVE, GUYS! WAIT FOR ME!
NOW ALL IS QUIET...
REVERT!
WAIT! DON'T YOU REMEMBER ME?! WE BEAT A WHOLE PLATOON ON SIRIUS IV, REMEMBER?!
CHUKKA-WUKKA-CHUKKA-WUKKA-CHUKK
I WAS YOUR TOP GUN! MR. BIG!*
RUDY! SPEAK TO ME! JOE-BOB! STINKY! DON'T YOU REMEMBER?!
BAH!
KONK
OOK! OOK!
HA! HA!
HA! HA!
HA!
HA!
HA!
I THOUGHT YOU LIKED ME...

*Butch temporarily ruled the De-Evolutionaries in a story from *Zot!'s* orginal color run.

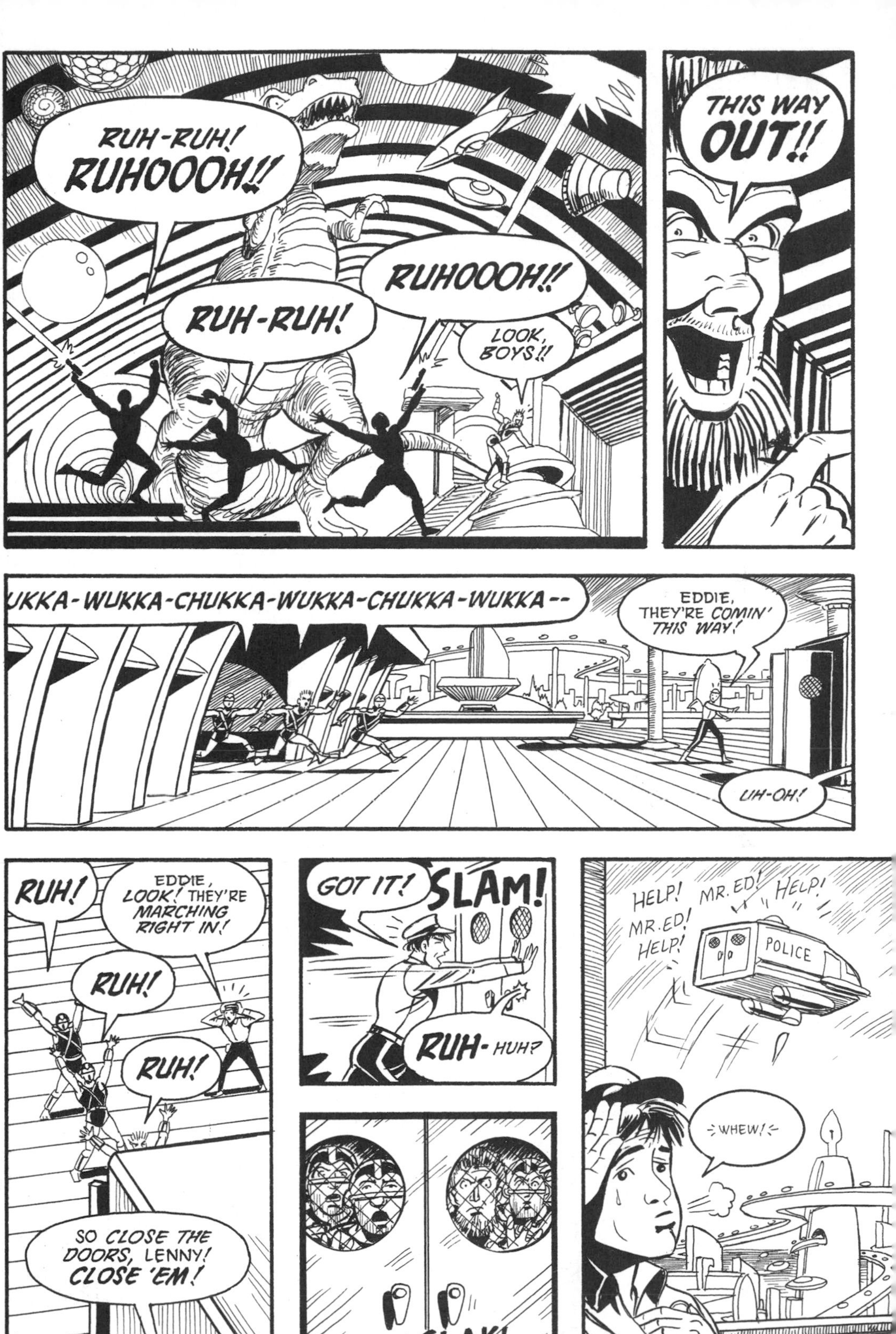
RUH-RUH! RUHOOOH!!
RUH-RUH!
RUHOOOH!!
LOOK, BOYS!!
THIS WAY OUT!!
UKKA-WUKKA-CHUKKA-WUKKA-CHUKKA-WUKKA--
EDDIE, THEY'RE COMIN' THIS WAY!
UH-OH!
RUH!
EDDIE, LOOK! THEY'RE MARCHING RIGHT IN!
RUH!
RUH!
SO CLOSE THE DOORS, LENNY! CLOSE 'EM!
GOT IT!
SLAM!
RUH- HUH?
CLAK!
HELP! MR. ED! HELP!
MR. ED! HELP!
POLICE
WHEW!

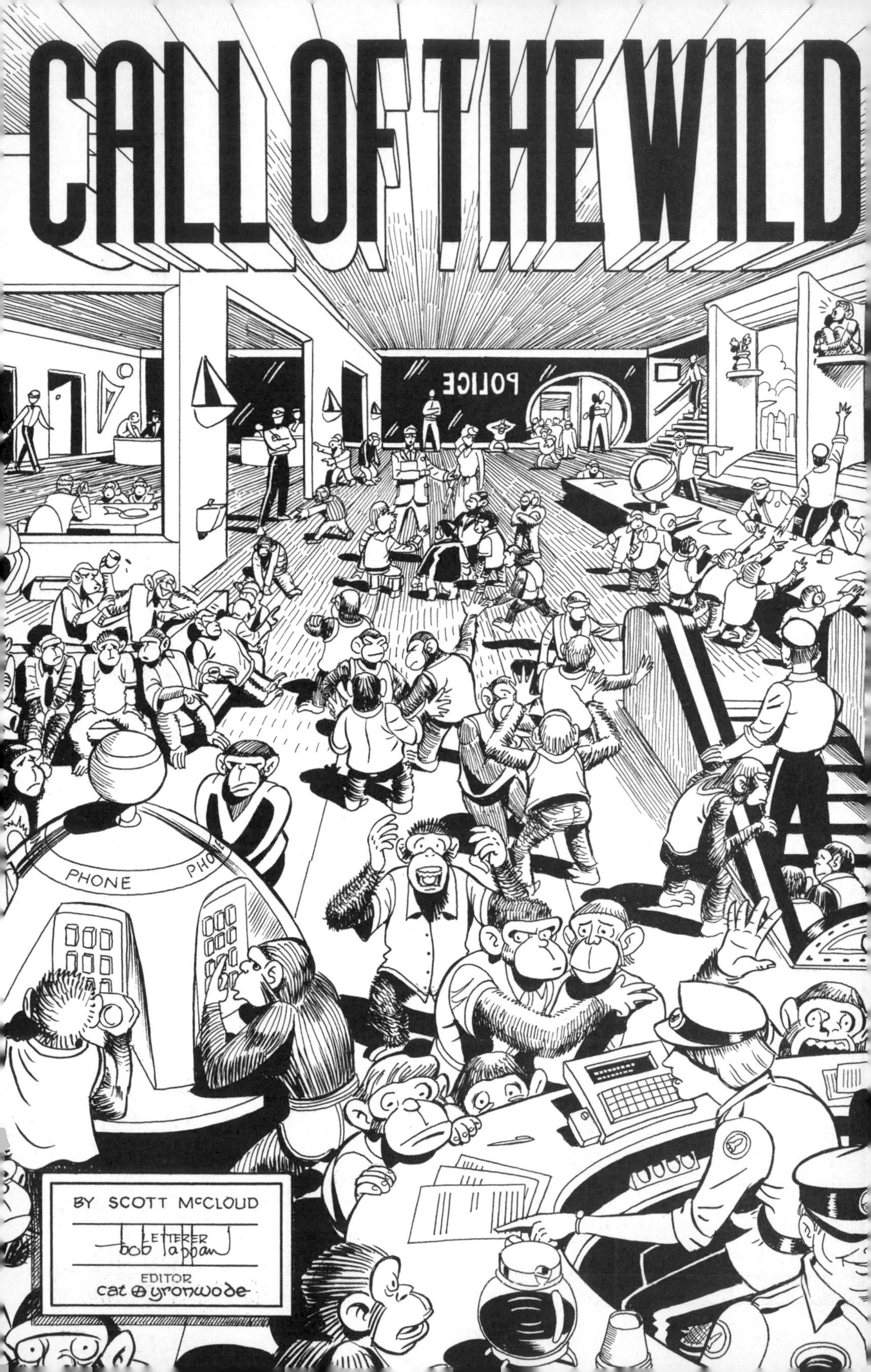
CALL OF THE WILD
POLICE
PHONE
BY SCOTT McCLOUD
LETTERER
bob lappan
EDITOR
cat ⊕ yronwode

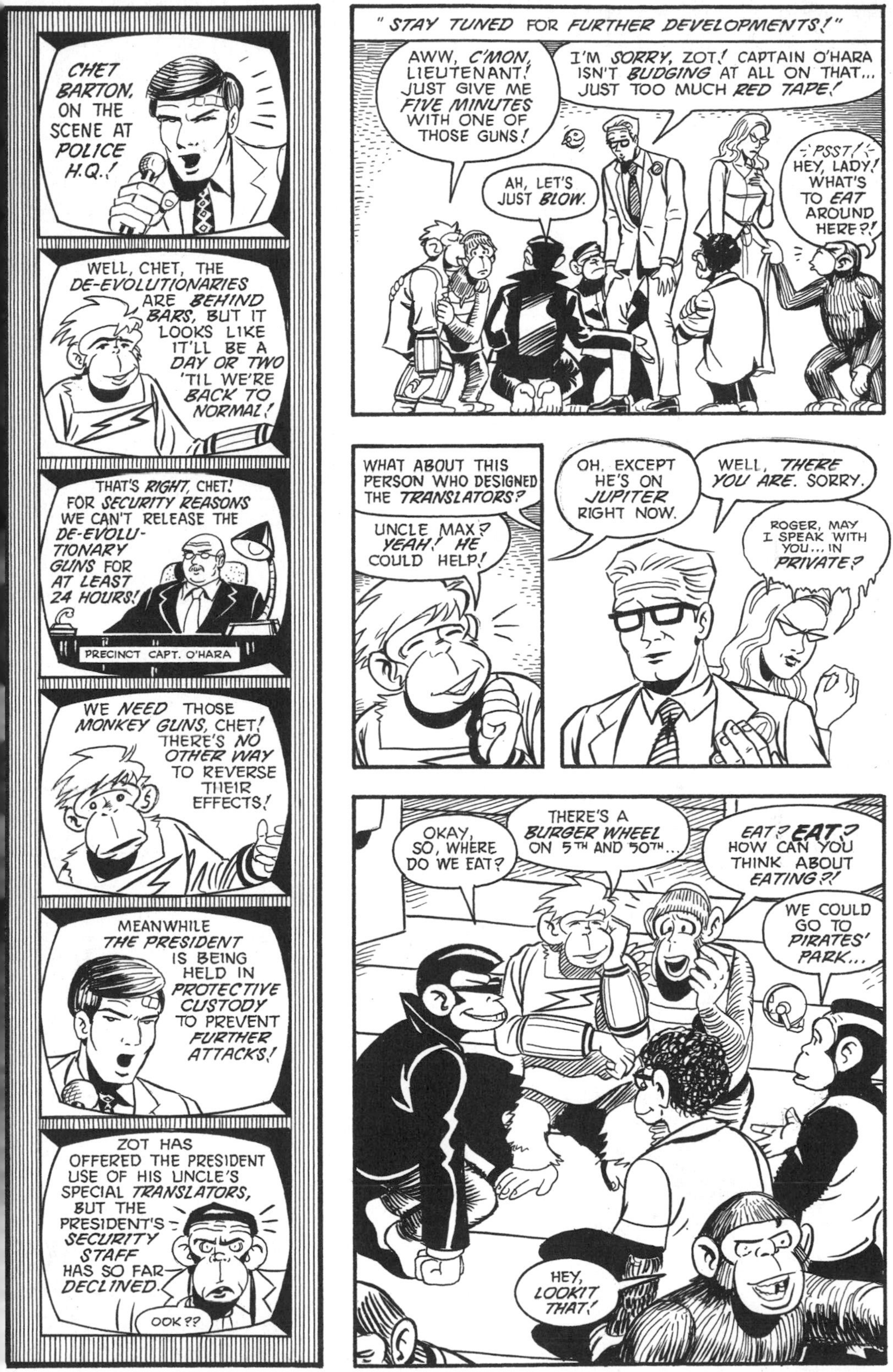
CHET BARTON, ON THE SCENE AT POLICE H.Q.!
WELL, CHET, THE DE-EVOLUTIONARIES ARE BEHIND BARS, BUT IT LOOKS LIKE IT'LL BE A DAY OR TWO 'TIL WE'RE BACK TO NORMAL!
THAT'S RIGHT, CHET! FOR SECURITY REASONS WE CAN'T RELEASE THE DE-EVOLUTIONARY GUNS FOR AT LEAST 24 HOURS!
PRECINCT CAPT. O'HARA
WE NEED THOSE MONKEY GUNS, CHET! THERE'S NO OTHER WAY TO REVERSE THEIR EFFECTS!
MEANWHILE THE PRESIDENT IS BEING HELD IN PROTECTIVE CUSTODY TO PREVENT FURTHER ATTACKS!
ZOT HAS OFFERED THE PRESIDENT USE OF HIS UNCLE'S SPECIAL TRANSLATORS, BUT THE PRESIDENT'S SECURITY STAFF HAS SO FAR DECLINED.
OOK??
"STAY TUNED FOR FURTHER DEVELOPMENTS!"
AWW, C'MON, LIEUTENANT! JUST GIVE ME FIVE MINUTES WITH ONE OF THOSE GUNS!
I'M SORRY, ZOT! CAPTAIN O'HARA ISN'T BUDGING AT ALL ON THAT... JUST TOO MUCH RED TAPE!
AH, LET'S JUST BLOW.
PSST! HEY, LADY! WHAT'S TO EAT AROUND HERE?!
WHAT ABOUT THIS PERSON WHO DESIGNED THE TRANSLATORS?
UNCLE MAX? YEAH! HE COULD HELP!
OH, EXCEPT HE'S ON JUPITER RIGHT NOW.
WELL, THERE YOU ARE. SORRY.
ROGER, MAY I SPEAK WITH YOU... IN PRIVATE?
OKAY, SO, WHERE DO WE EAT?
THERE'S A BURGER WHEEL ON 5TH AND 50TH...
EAT? EAT? HOW CAN YOU THINK ABOUT EATING?!
WE COULD GO TO PIRATES' PARK...
HEY, LOOKIT THAT!

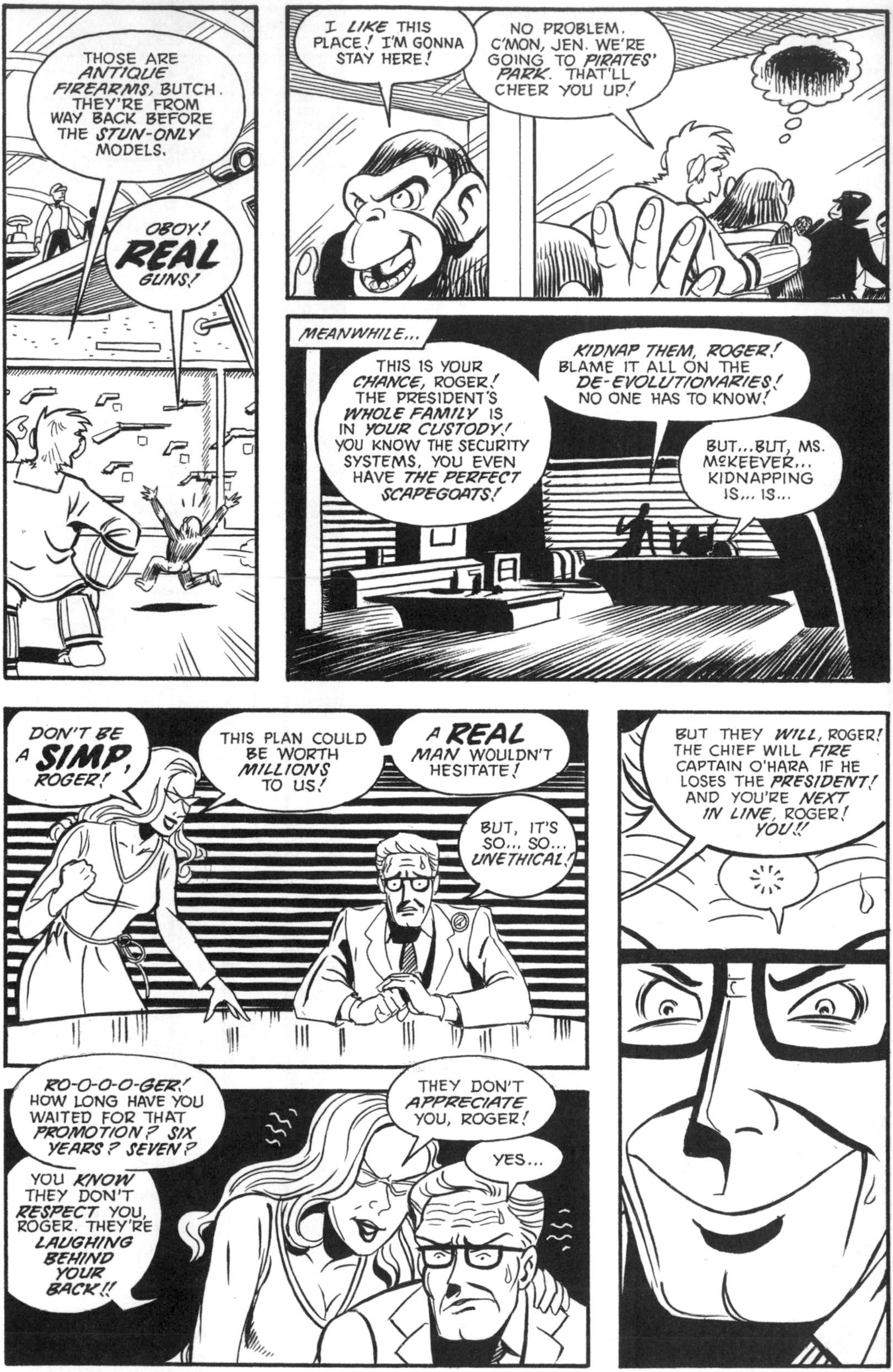
THOSE ARE ANTIQUE FIREARMS, BUTCH. THEY'RE FROM WAY BACK BEFORE THE STUN-ONLY MODELS.
OBOY! REAL GUNS!
I LIKE THIS PLACE! I'M GONNA STAY HERE!
NO PROBLEM. C'MON, JEN. WE'RE GOING TO PIRATES' PARK. THAT'LL CHEER YOU UP!
MEANWHILE...
THIS IS YOUR CHANCE, ROGER! THE PRESIDENT'S WHOLE FAMILY IS IN YOUR CUSTODY! YOU KNOW THE SECURITY SYSTEMS, YOU EVEN HAVE THE PERFECT SCAPEGOATS!
KIDNAP THEM, ROGER! BLAME IT ALL ON THE DE-EVOLUTIONARIES! NO ONE HAS TO KNOW!
BUT...BUT, MS. McKEEVER... KIDNAPPING IS... IS...
DON'T BE A SIMP, ROGER!
THIS PLAN COULD BE WORTH MILLIONS TO US!
A REAL MAN WOULDN'T HESITATE!
BUT, IT'S SO... SO... UNETHICAL!
RO-O-O-O-GER! HOW LONG HAVE YOU WAITED FOR THAT PROMOTION? SIX YEARS? SEVEN?
YOU KNOW THEY DON'T RESPECT YOU, ROGER. THEY'RE LAUGHING BEHIND YOUR BACK!!
THEY DON'T APPRECIATE YOU, ROGER!
YES...
BUT THEY WILL, ROGER! THE CHIEF WILL FIRE CAPTAIN O'HARA IF HE LOSES THE PRESIDENT! AND YOU'RE NEXT IN LINE, ROGER! YOU!!

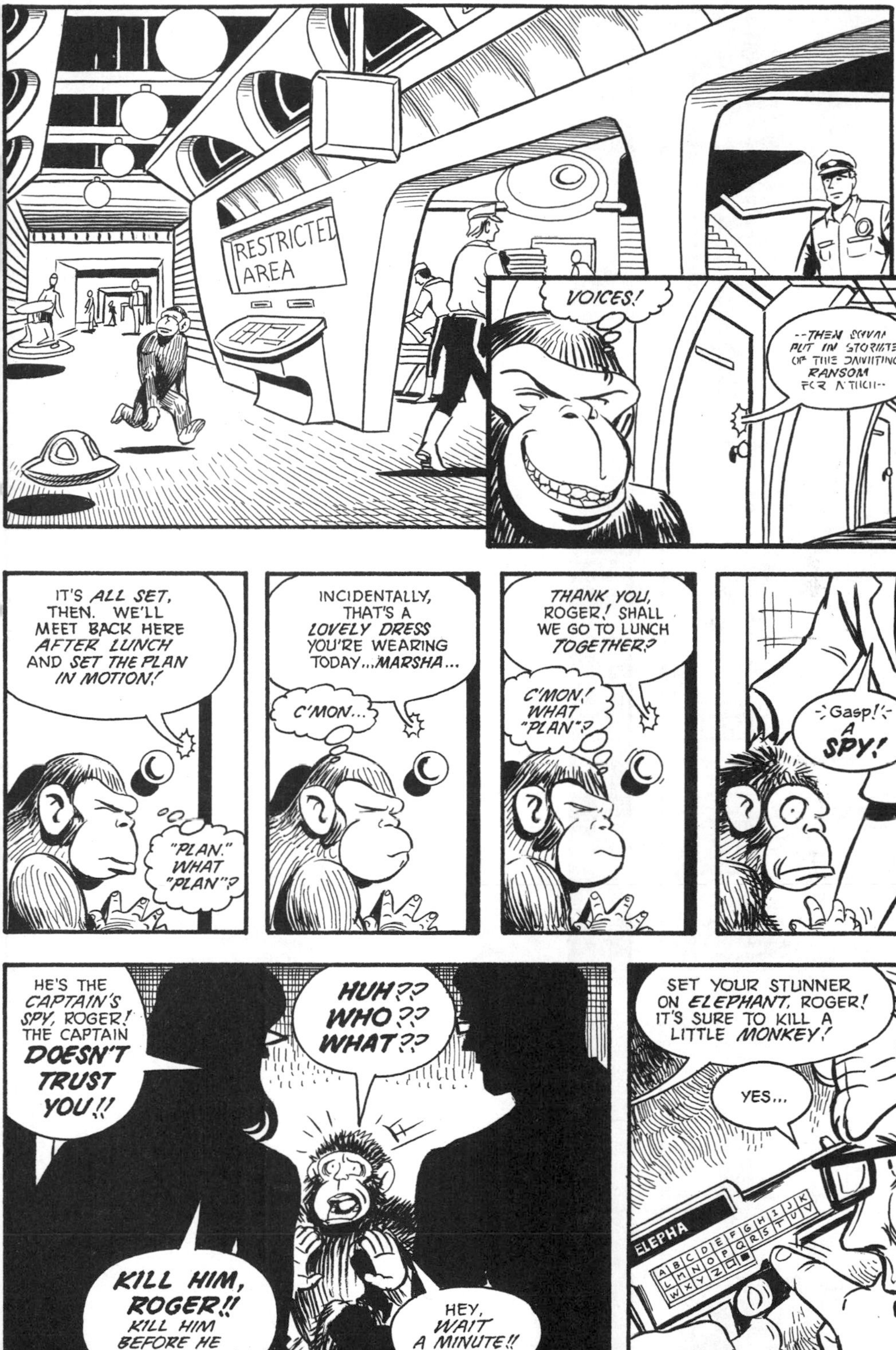
RESTRICTED AREA
VOICES!
--THEN
PUT IN
RANSOM
IT'S *ALL SET*, THEN. WE'LL MEET BACK HERE *AFTER LUNCH* AND *SET THE PLAN IN MOTION!*
"PLAN." WHAT "PLAN"?
INCIDENTALLY, THAT'S A *LOVELY DRESS* YOU'RE WEARING TODAY... *MARSHA*...
C'MON...
THANK YOU, ROGER! SHALL WE GO TO LUNCH *TOGETHER?*
C'MON! WHAT "PLAN"?
Gasp! A **SPY!**
HE'S THE *CAPTAIN'S SPY*, ROGER! THE CAPTAIN **DOESN'T TRUST YOU!!**
HUH?? WHO?? WHAT??
KILL HIM, ROGER!! *KILL HIM BEFORE HE EXPOSES US!*
HEY, *WAIT A MINUTE!!*
SET YOUR STUNNER ON *ELEPHANT*, ROGER! IT'S SURE TO KILL A LITTLE *MONKEY!*
YES...
ELEPHA

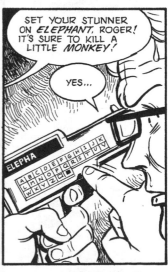

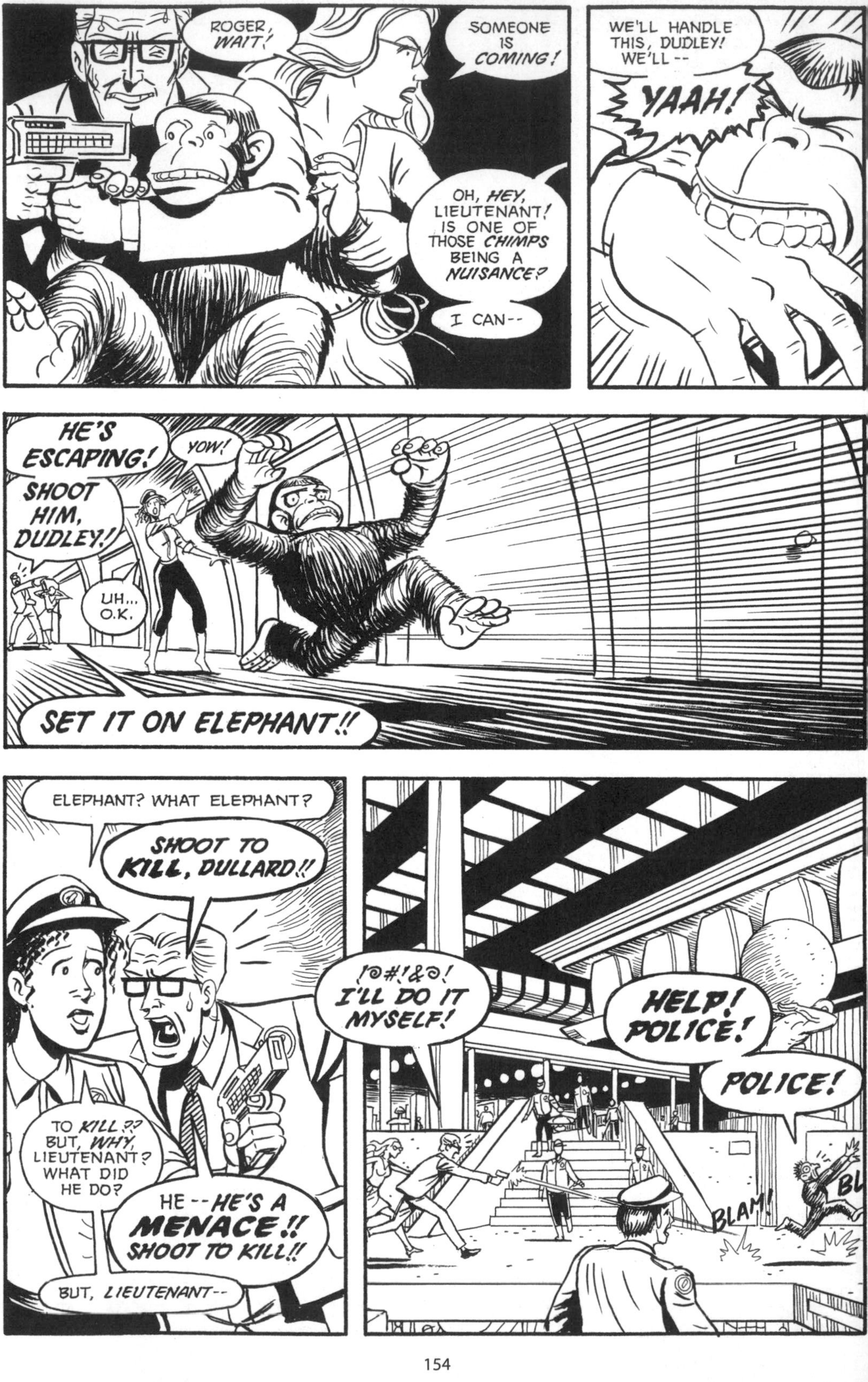
ROGER, WAIT!
SOMEONE IS COMING!
OH, HEY, LIEUTENANT! IS ONE OF THOSE CHIMPS BEING A NUISANCE?
I CAN--
WE'LL HANDLE THIS, DUDLEY! WE'LL --
YAAH!
HE'S ESCAPING!
YOW!
SHOOT HIM, DUDLEY!
UH... O.K.
SET IT ON ELEPHANT!!
ELEPHANT? WHAT ELEPHANT?
SHOOT TO KILL, DULLARD!!
TO KILL?? BUT, WHY, LIEUTENANT? WHAT DID HE DO?
HE -- HE'S A MENACE!! SHOOT TO KILL!!
BUT, LIEUTENANT--
!@#!&@! I'LL DO IT MYSELF!
HELP! POLICE!
POLICE!
BLAM!

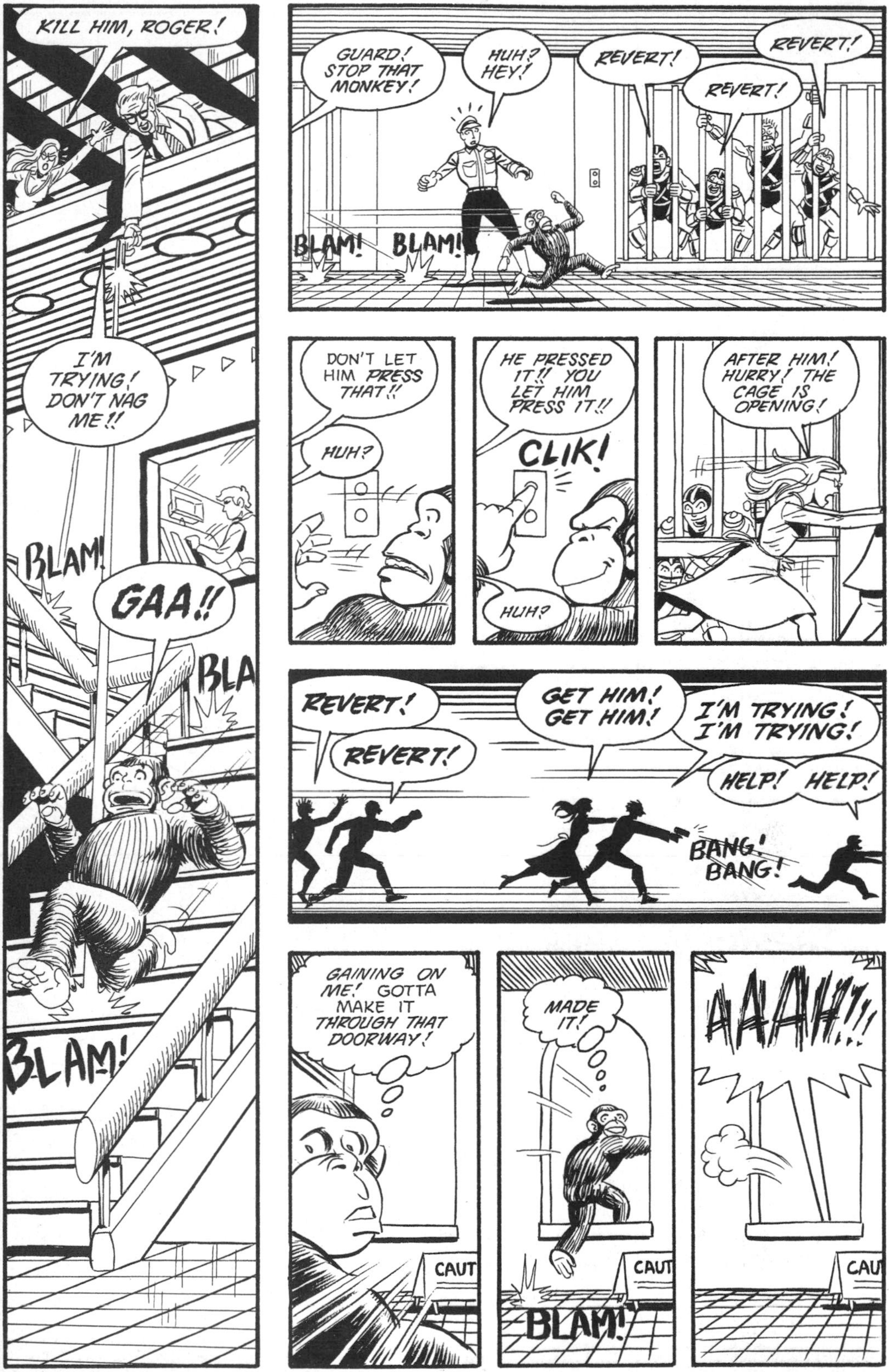
KILL HIM, ROGER!
I'M TRYING! DON'T NAG ME!!
BLAM!
GAA!!
BLA
BLAM!
GUARD! STOP THAT MONKEY!
HUH? HEY!
REVERT!
REVERT!
REVERT!
BLAM!
BLAM!
DON'T LET HIM PRESS THAT!!
HUH?
HE PRESSED IT!! YOU LET HIM PRESS IT!!
CLIK!
HUH?
AFTER HIM! HURRY! THE CAGE IS OPENING!
REVERT!
REVERT!
GET HIM! GET HIM!
I'M TRYING! I'M TRYING!
HELP!
HELP!
BANG! BANG!
GAINING ON ME! GOTTA MAKE IT THROUGH THAT DOORWAY!
CAUT
MADE IT!
CAUT
BLAM!
AAAH!!!
CAU

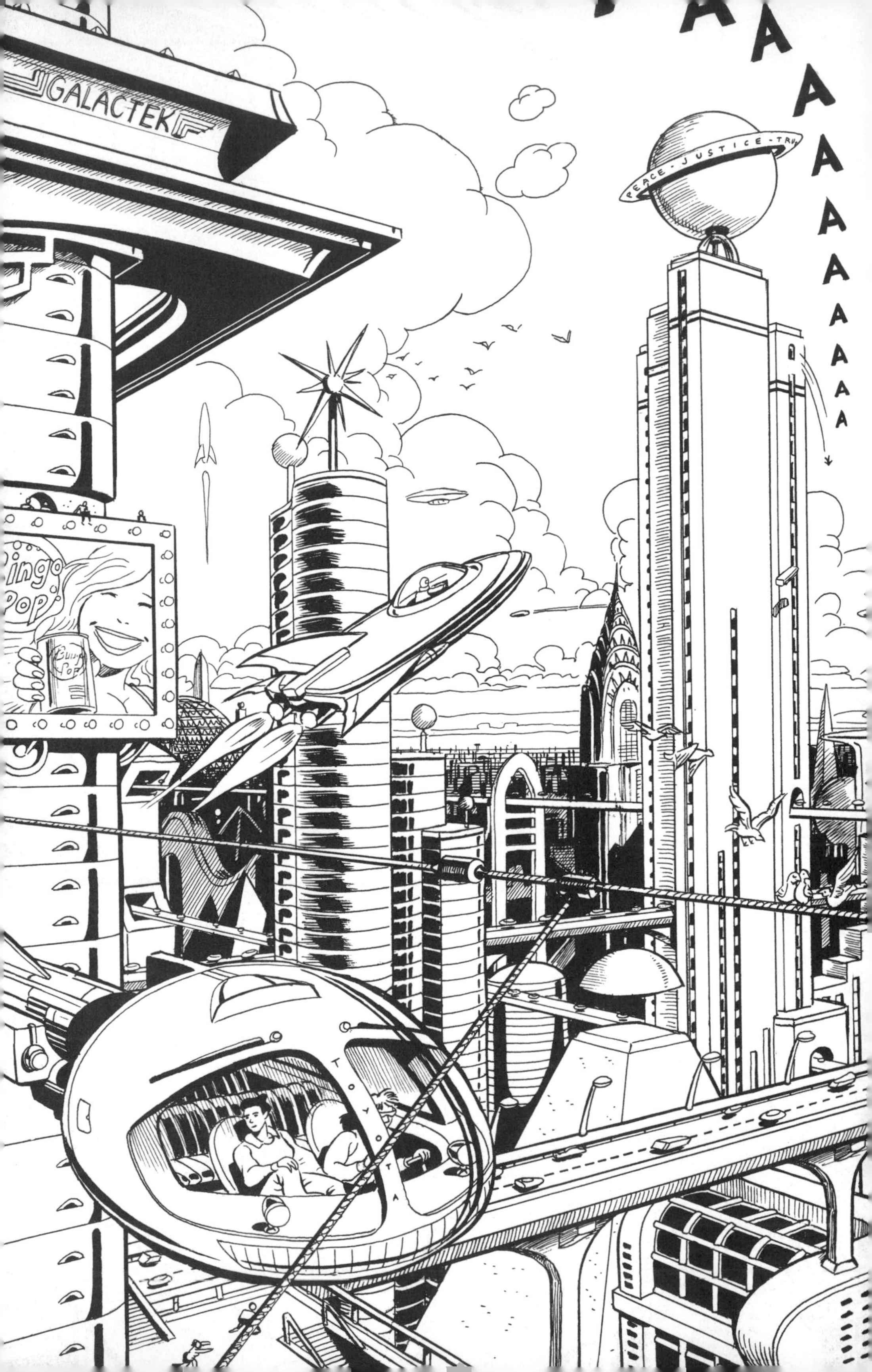
AAAAAAAAAAA
GALACTEK
PEACE - JUSTICE - TRU
TOYOTA

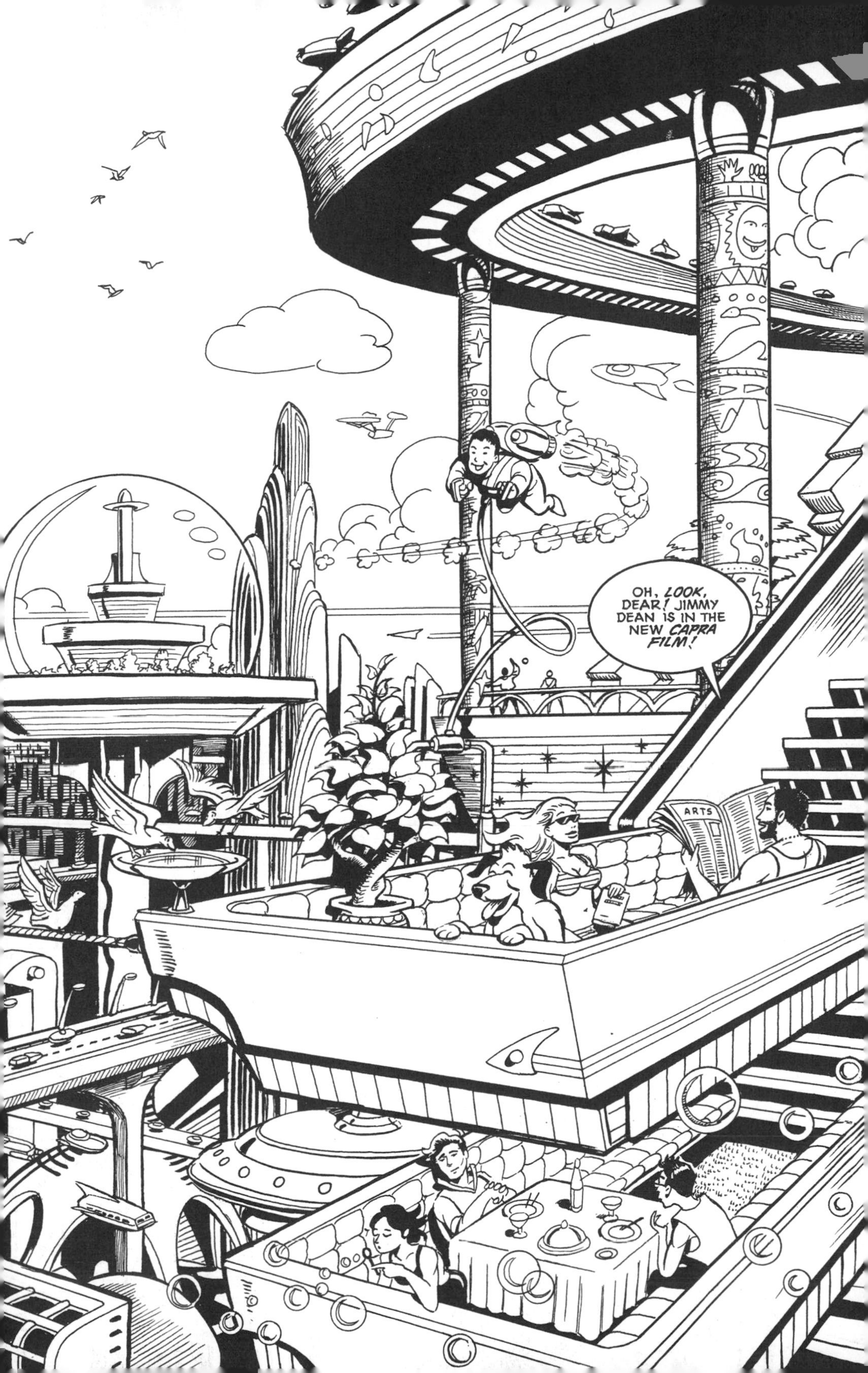
OH, *LOOK,* DEAR! JIMMY DEAN IS IN THE NEW *CAPRA FILM!*
ARTS

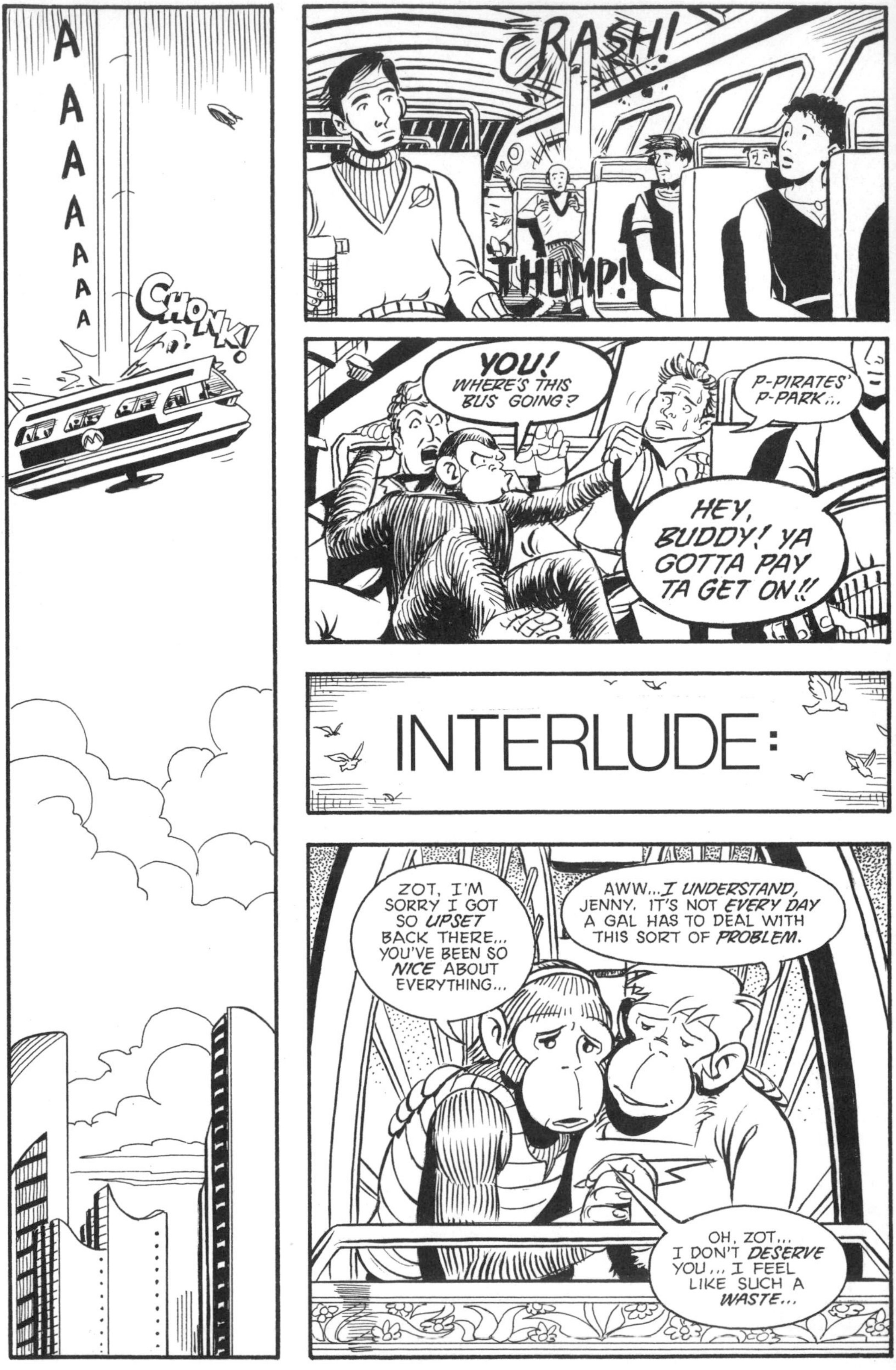

AAAAAAA
CHONK!
CRASH!
THUMP!
YOU! WHERE'S THIS BUS GOING?
P-PIRATES' P-PARK...
HEY, BUDDY! YA GOTTA PAY TA GET ON!!
INTERLUDE:
ZOT, I'M SORRY I GOT SO UPSET BACK THERE... YOU'VE BEEN SO NICE ABOUT EVERYTHING...
AWW... I UNDERSTAND, JENNY. IT'S NOT EVERY DAY A GAL HAS TO DEAL WITH THIS SORT OF PROBLEM.
OH, ZOT... I DON'T DESERVE YOU... I FEEL LIKE SUCH A WASTE...

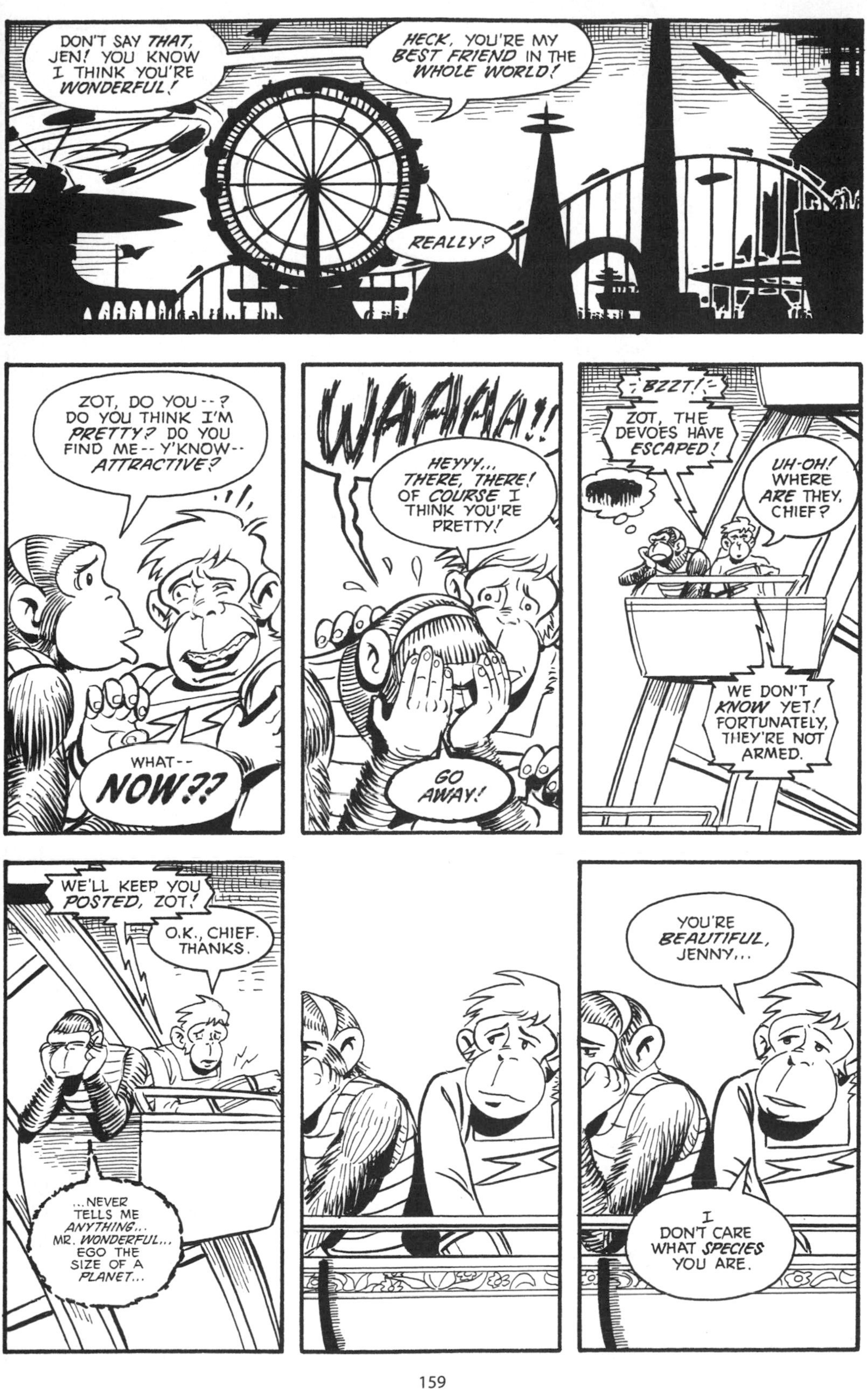
DON'T SAY THAT, JEN! YOU KNOW I THINK YOU'RE WONDERFUL!
HECK, YOU'RE MY BEST FRIEND IN THE WHOLE WORLD!
REALLY?
ZOT, DO YOU--? DO YOU THINK I'M PRETTY? DO YOU FIND ME--Y'KNOW--ATTRACTIVE?
WHAT--NOW??
WAAAA!!
HEYYY... THERE, THERE! OF COURSE I THINK YOU'RE PRETTY!
GO AWAY!
BZZT!
ZOT, THE DEVOES HAVE ESCAPED!
UH-OH! WHERE ARE THEY, CHIEF?
WE DON'T KNOW YET! FORTUNATELY, THEY'RE NOT ARMED.
WE'LL KEEP YOU POSTED, ZOT!
O.K., CHIEF. THANKS.
...NEVER TELLS ME ANYTHING... MR. WONDERFUL... EGO THE SIZE OF A PLANET...
YOU'RE BEAUTIFUL, JENNY...
I DON'T CARE WHAT SPECIES YOU ARE.

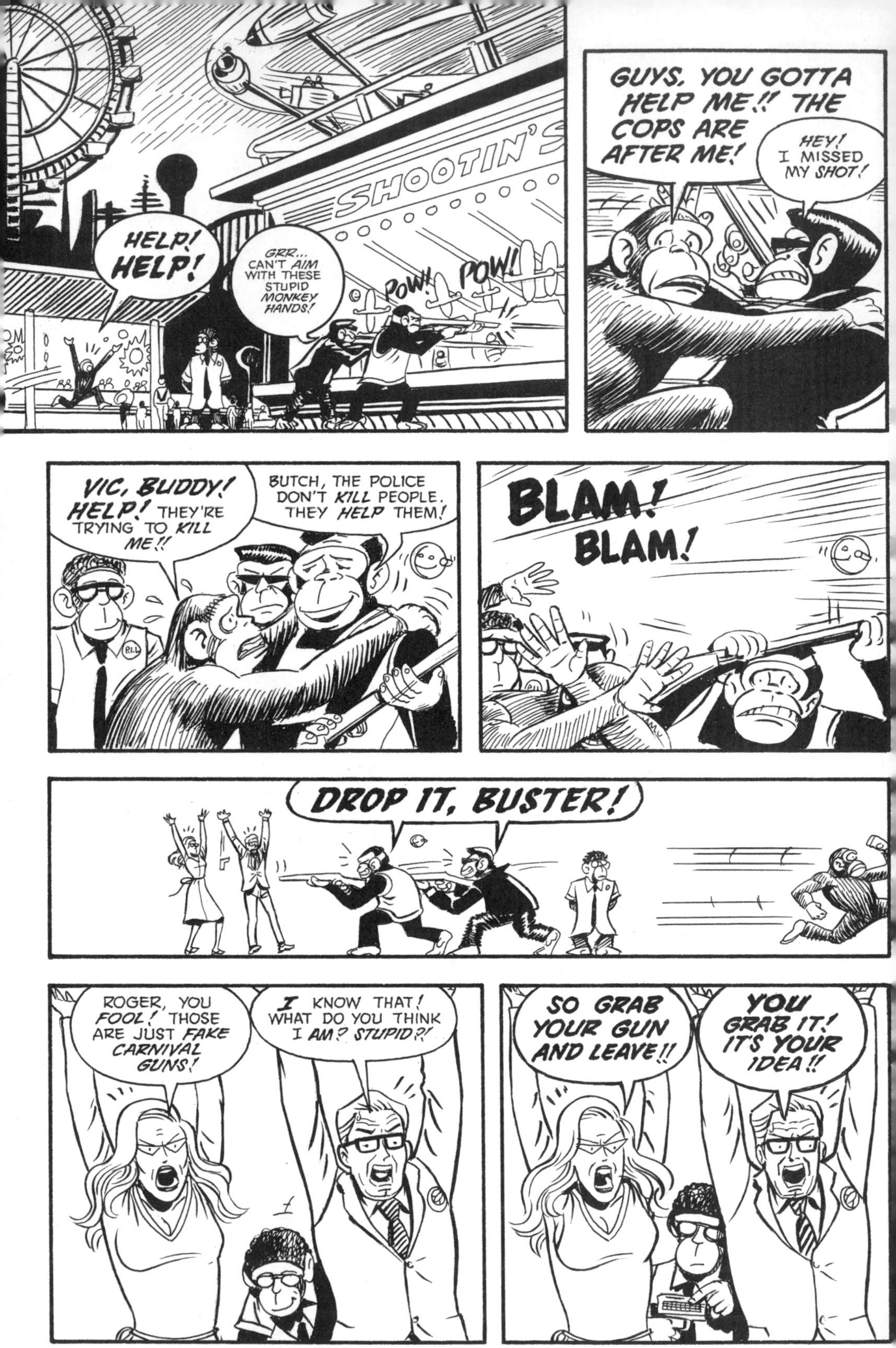
SHOOTIN' S
HELP! HELP!
GRR... CAN'T AIM WITH THESE STUPID MONKEY HANDS!
POW! POW!
GUYS, YOU GOTTA HELP ME!! THE COPS ARE AFTER ME!
HEY! I MISSED MY SHOT!
VIC, BUDDY! HELP! THEY'RE TRYING TO KILL ME!!
BUTCH, THE POLICE DON'T KILL PEOPLE. THEY HELP THEM!
BLAM! BLAM!
DROP IT, BUSTER!
ROGER, YOU FOOL! THOSE ARE JUST FAKE CARNIVAL GUNS!
I KNOW THAT! WHAT DO YOU THINK I AM? STUPID?!
SO GRAB YOUR GUN AND LEAVE!!
YOU GRAB IT! IT'S YOUR IDEA!!

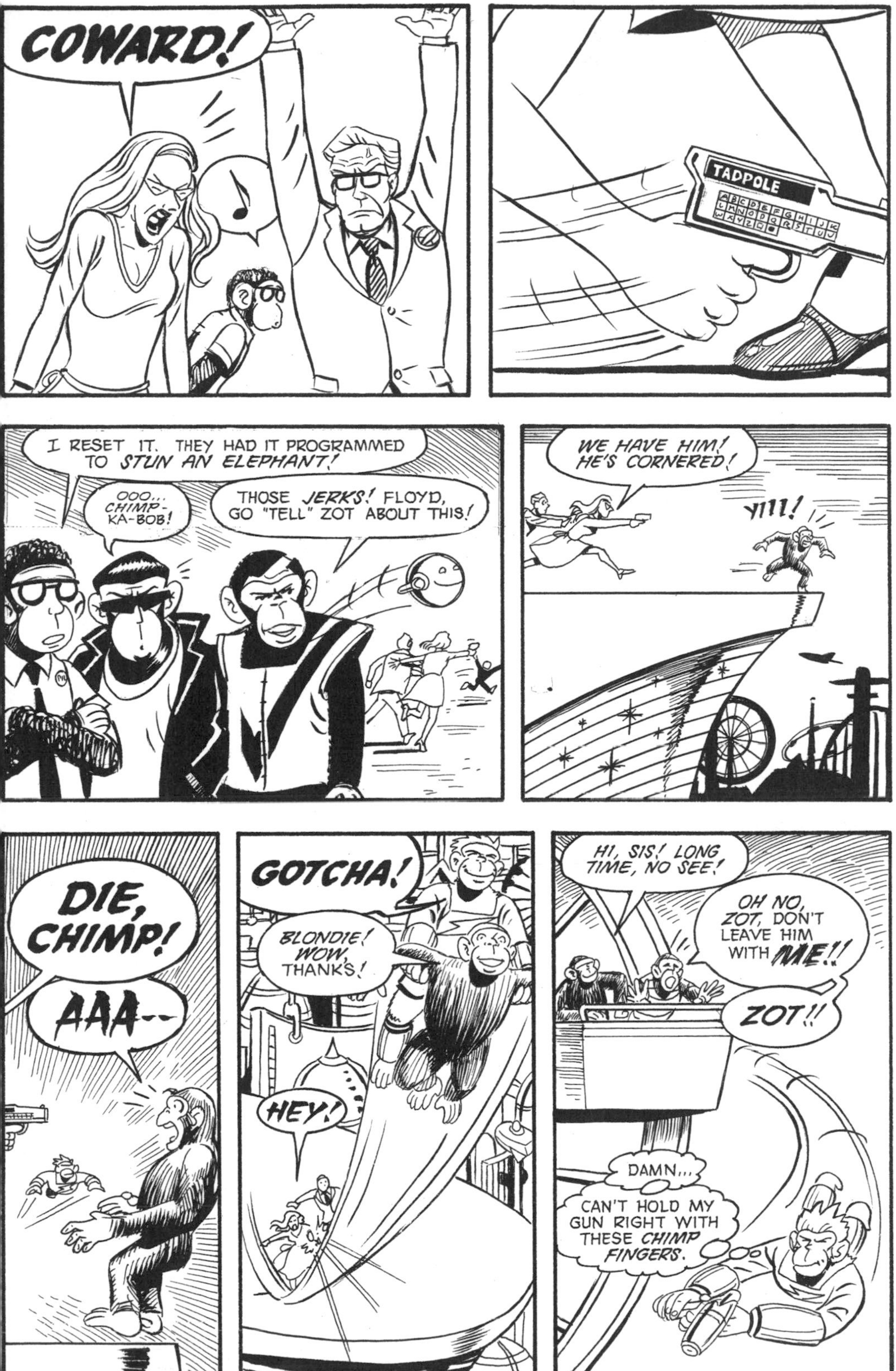

COWARD!
♪
TADPOLE
I RESET IT. THEY HAD IT PROGRAMMED TO STUN AN ELEPHANT!
OOO... CHIMP-KA-BOB!
THOSE JERKS! FLOYD, GO "TELL" ZOT ABOUT THIS!
WE HAVE HIM! HE'S CORNERED!
YIII!
DIE, CHIMP!
AAA--
GOTCHA!
BLONDIE! WOW, THANKS!
HEY!
HI, SIS! LONG TIME, NO SEE!
OH NO, ZOT, DON'T LEAVE HIM WITH ME!!
ZOT!!
DAMN...
CAN'T HOLD MY GUN RIGHT WITH THESE CHIMP FINGERS.

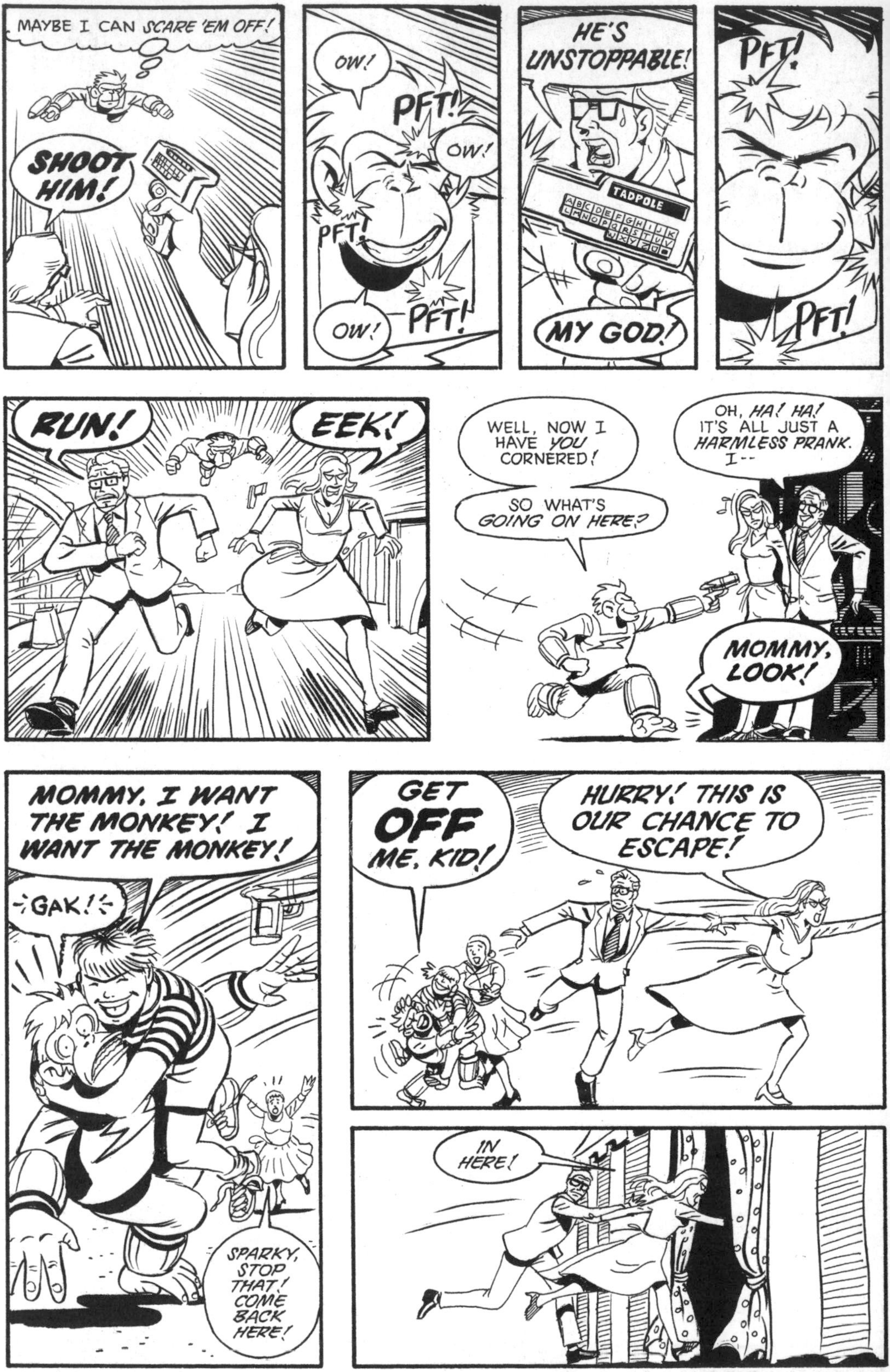
MAYBE I CAN SCARE 'EM OFF!
SHOOT HIM!
OW!
PFT!
OW!
PFT!
OW!
PFT!
HE'S UNSTOPPABLE!
TADPOLE
MY GOD!
PFT!
PFT!
RUN!
EEK!
WELL, NOW I HAVE YOU CORNERED!
SO WHAT'S GOING ON HERE?
OH, HA! HA! IT'S ALL JUST A HARMLESS PRANK. I--
MOMMY, LOOK!
MOMMY, I WANT THE MONKEY! I WANT THE MONKEY!
GAK!
SPARKY, STOP THAT! COME BACK HERE!
GET OFF ME, KID!
HURRY! THIS IS OUR CHANCE TO ESCAPE!
IN HERE!

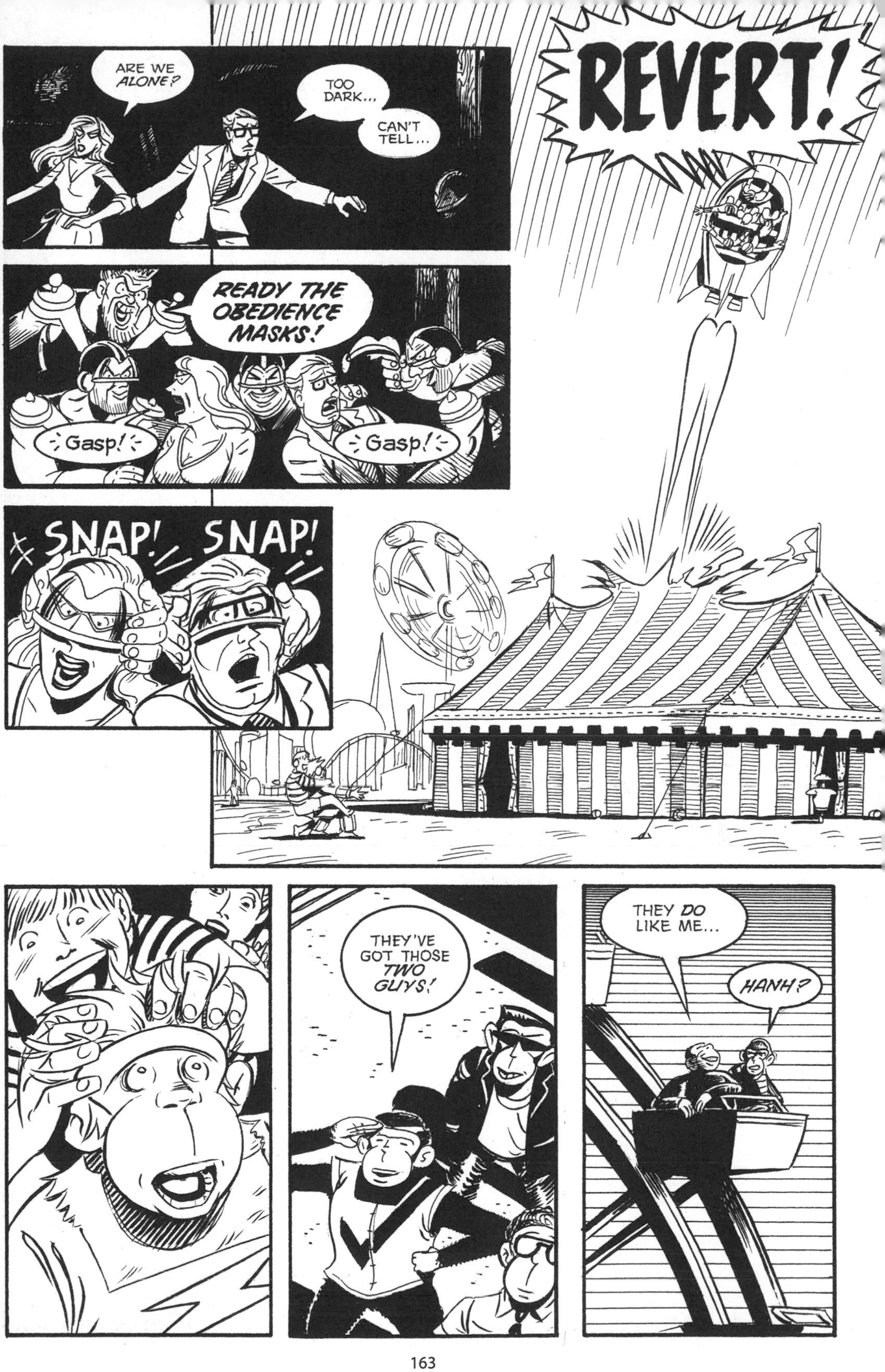
ARE WE *ALONE*?
TOO DARK...
CAN'T TELL...
READY THE OBEDIENCE MASKS!
Gasp!
Gasp!
SNAP!
SNAP!
REVERT!
THEY'VE GOT THOSE *TWO GUYS*!
THEY *DO* LIKE ME...
HANH?

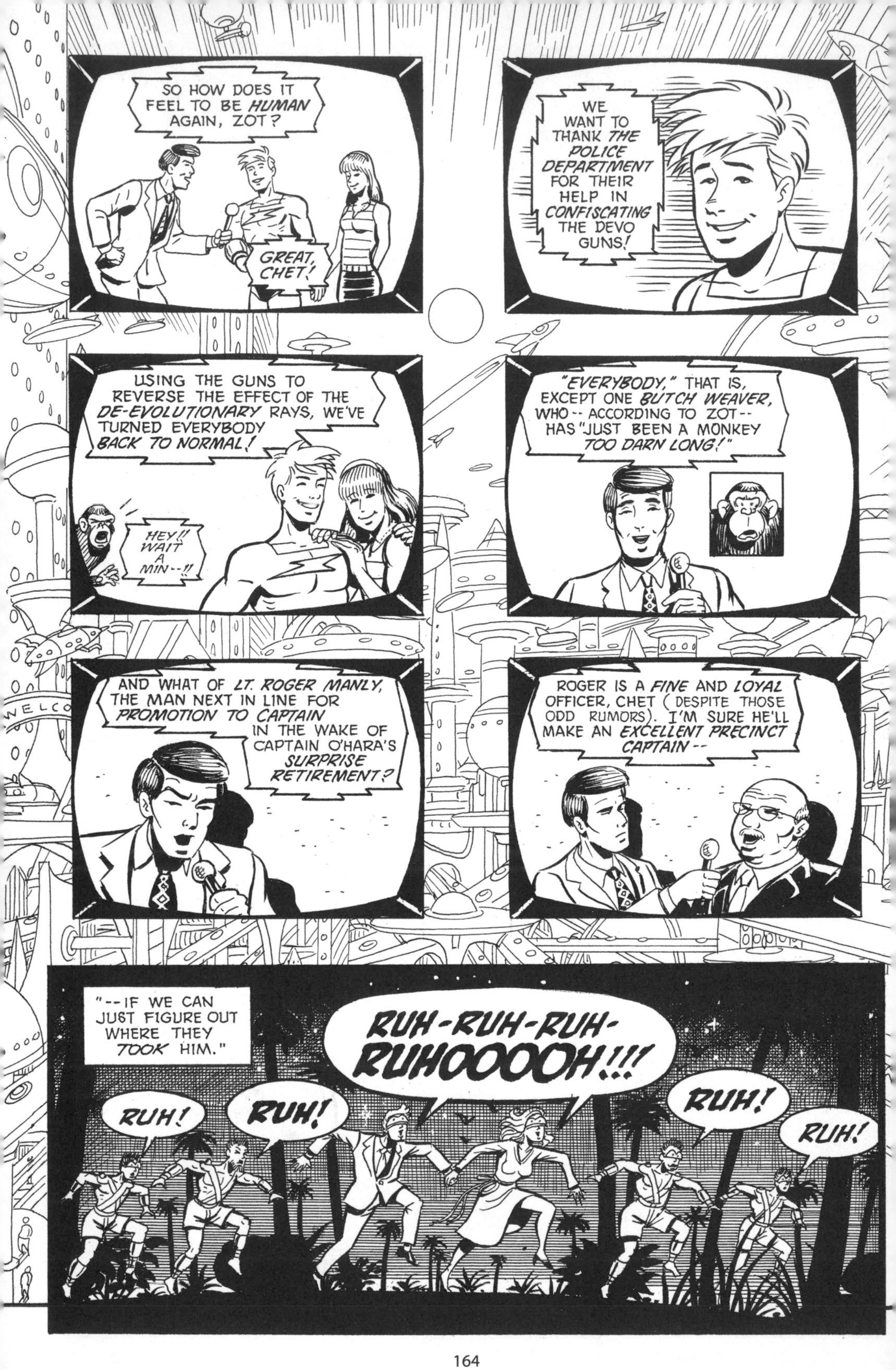
SO HOW DOES IT FEEL TO BE *HUMAN* AGAIN, ZOT?
GREAT, CHET!
WE WANT TO THANK *THE POLICE DEPARTMENT* FOR THEIR HELP IN *CONFISCATING* THE DEVO GUNS!
USING THE GUNS TO REVERSE THE EFFECT OF THE *DE-EVOLUTIONARY* RAYS, WE'VE TURNED EVERYBODY *BACK TO NORMAL!*
HEY!! WAIT A MIN--!!
"EVERYBODY," THAT IS, EXCEPT ONE *BUTCH WEAVER,* WHO -- ACCORDING TO ZOT -- HAS "JUST BEEN A MONKEY *TOO DARN LONG!"*
AND WHAT OF *LT. ROGER MANLY,* THE MAN NEXT IN LINE FOR *PROMOTION TO CAPTAIN* IN THE WAKE OF CAPTAIN O'HARA'S *SURPRISE RETIREMENT?*
ROGER IS A *FINE* AND *LOYAL* OFFICER, CHET (DESPITE THOSE ODD RUMORS). I'M SURE HE'LL MAKE AN *EXCELLENT PRECINCT CAPTAIN* --
"--IF WE CAN JUST FIGURE OUT WHERE THEY *TOOK* HIM."
RUH-RUH-RUH-RUHOOOOOH!!!
RUH!
RUH!
RUH!
RUH!

I tried to vary the tone from one *Zot!* story to the next. After a long, deadly serious storyline like "Season of Dreams," it seemed like a good time to throw in a quick dumb monkey story, featuring my least-intimidating villains, the De-Evolutionaries.

I'm pretty happy with the art in this one compared to my usual efforts. Drawing humans wasn't exactly my strong suit, but the rubbery expressive faces of my cast when changed to monkeys seemed a bit more emotionally convincing. At the time, I was slowly puzzling over why a simple face like Charlie Brown's could evoke a strong sense of identification while a more rendered face might not (an idea I'd take all the way six years later in *Understanding Comics*), and this issue helped fuel my curiosity further.

Jenny and Zot's interactions by this point were increasingly informed by my own newly minted relationship with Ivy. The conversation on the Ferris wheel was an especially obvious case of channeling. The line "ego the size of a planet" from that scene has since become another running joke around the house in years since, though that one is at least equally beholden to Marvin the Paranoid Android by way of the much-missed Douglas Adams.

The center spread in this issue is probably my best stab at visualizing Zot's Earth: a sprawling amalgamation of everything worth saving from our world, combined with every fanciful utopian future ever dreamed up by writers and artists throughout the nineteenth and twentieth centuries. Fresh in my memory at the time were my first-ever visits to Disneyland and San Diego's recently built Horton Plaza, an outdoor mall that looked as if it were designed by M.C. Escher on acid.

The latter was in connection with the famous San Diego Comics Convention, America's biggest comics show, then as now. Ivy and I visited "Comic-Con" (its official name now) together for the first time in 1987, right before drawing this issue (I'd only been once, the year before). Attendance was 7,000 that year, which seemed like a lot to us, though it pales in comparison to today's 100,000-plus crowds. The next year, with attendance rising to a whopping 8,000, we were delighted to see a big cardboard flying Zot figure used as one of five symbols of American comics, hanging far above the crowds of fans and vendors.

Side-Note: Twenty-one years later, Ivy and I have been to every subsequent Comic-Con together except one: In 1995, Ivy was pregnant with our second daughter and, as luck would have it, the due date fell right before Con, so we decided for the first time to skip the event. The Monday after Con, Kurt Busiek and his wife, Ann, drove the few hours north from San Diego, along with mutual friend Neil Gaiman, to visit the still-expectant Ivy and me in Thousand Oaks, California. At dinner, Ivy went into labor and we whisked her away in a caravan of cars. Thus, at 2:00 a.m., at a nearby birthing center, Winter was born, while in the waiting room, Neil and our friend Krystal tossed Winter's 2-year-old big sister up and down, singing the opening number from *Sweeney Todd.*

Last year, my daughters—now 12 and 14—were on more panels at San Diego than I was.

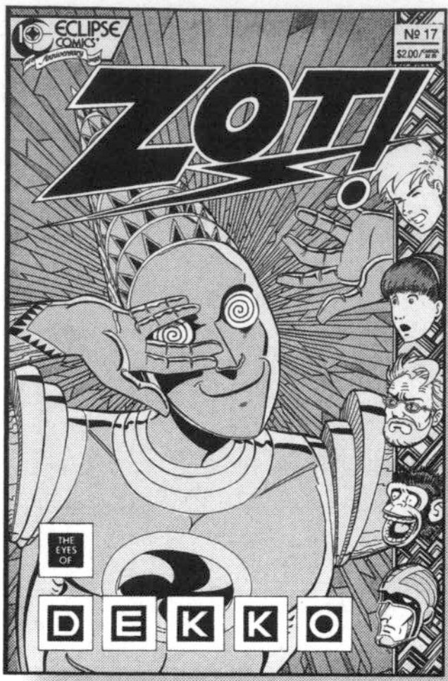
ECLIPSE COMICS
Nº 17
$2.00
ZOT!
THE EYES OF
D E K K O

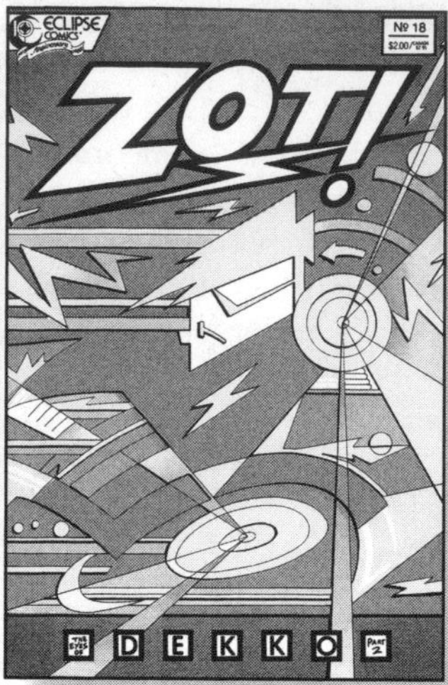
ECLIPSE COMICS
Nº 18
$2.00
ZOT!
D E K K O

The Eyes of Dekko

First published in *Zot! #17–18*.

Lettering:

Bob Lappan

Original series editor:

cat yronwode

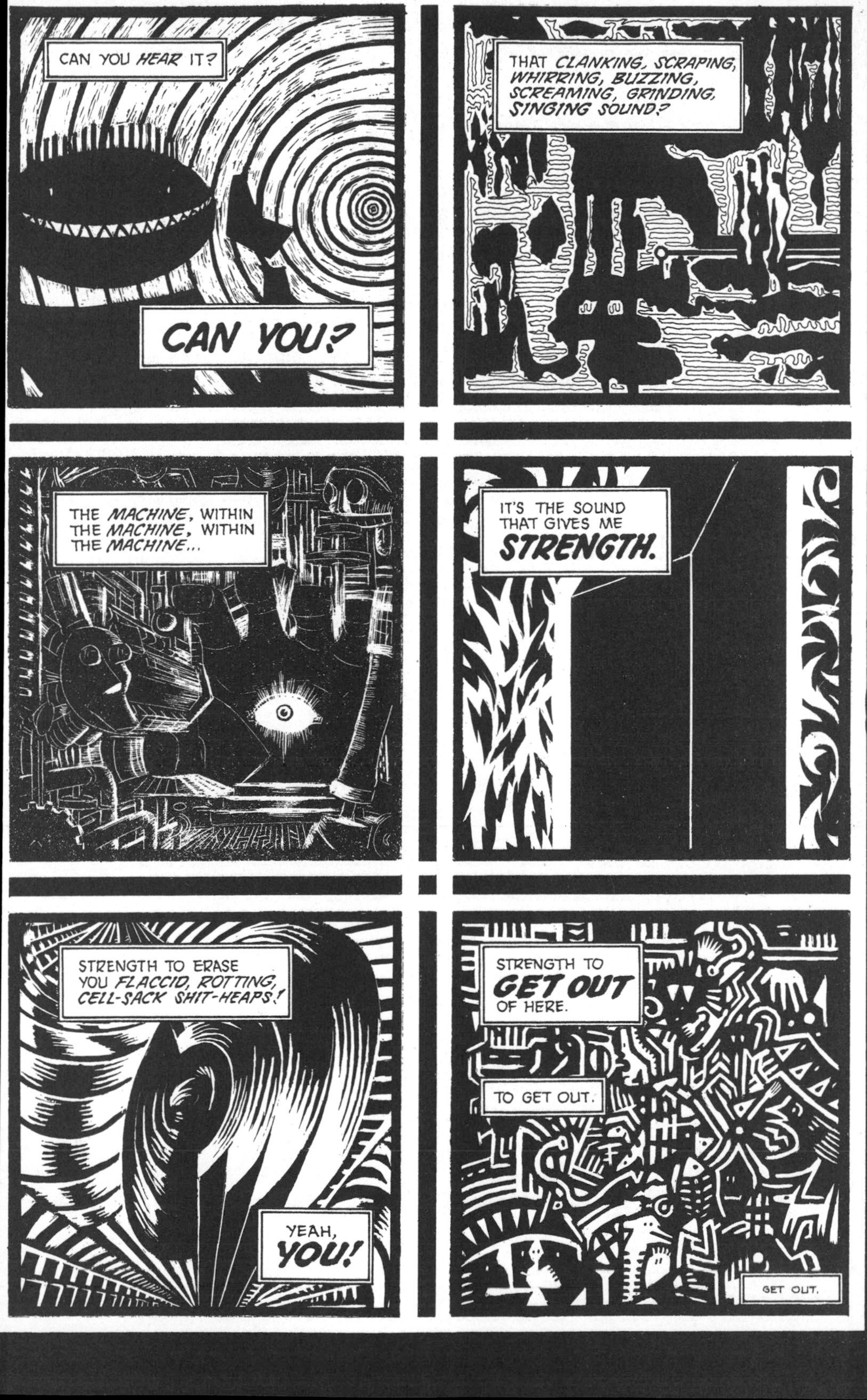
CAN YOU HEAR IT?
CAN YOU?
THAT CLANKING, SCRAPING, WHIRRING, BUZZING, SCREAMING, GRINDING, SINGING SOUND?
THE MACHINE, WITHIN THE MACHINE, WITHIN THE MACHINE...
IT'S THE SOUND THAT GIVES ME STRENGTH.
STRENGTH TO ERASE YOU FLACCID, ROTTING, CELL-SACK SHIT-HEAPS!
YEAH, YOU!
STRENGTH TO GET OUT OF HERE.
TO GET OUT.
GET OUT.

CAN YOU *FEEL* IT?

CAN YOU?

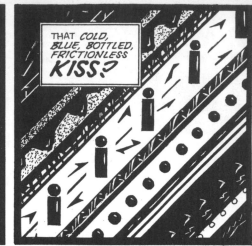

THAT *COLD, BLUE, BOTTLED, FRICTIONLESS KISS?*

THE VACUUM-FACED *RAPE* OF A MEANINGLESS GOD!

IT'S THE *GRIP* THAT CLEARS MY *VISION.*

VISION TO FILL THE *HAPPY VOID* WITH WORLDS AGAIN.

ROUND, DEAD, SPINNING GRINS...

VISION TO MAKE *BETTER.*

MAKE BETTER.

MAKE BETTER.

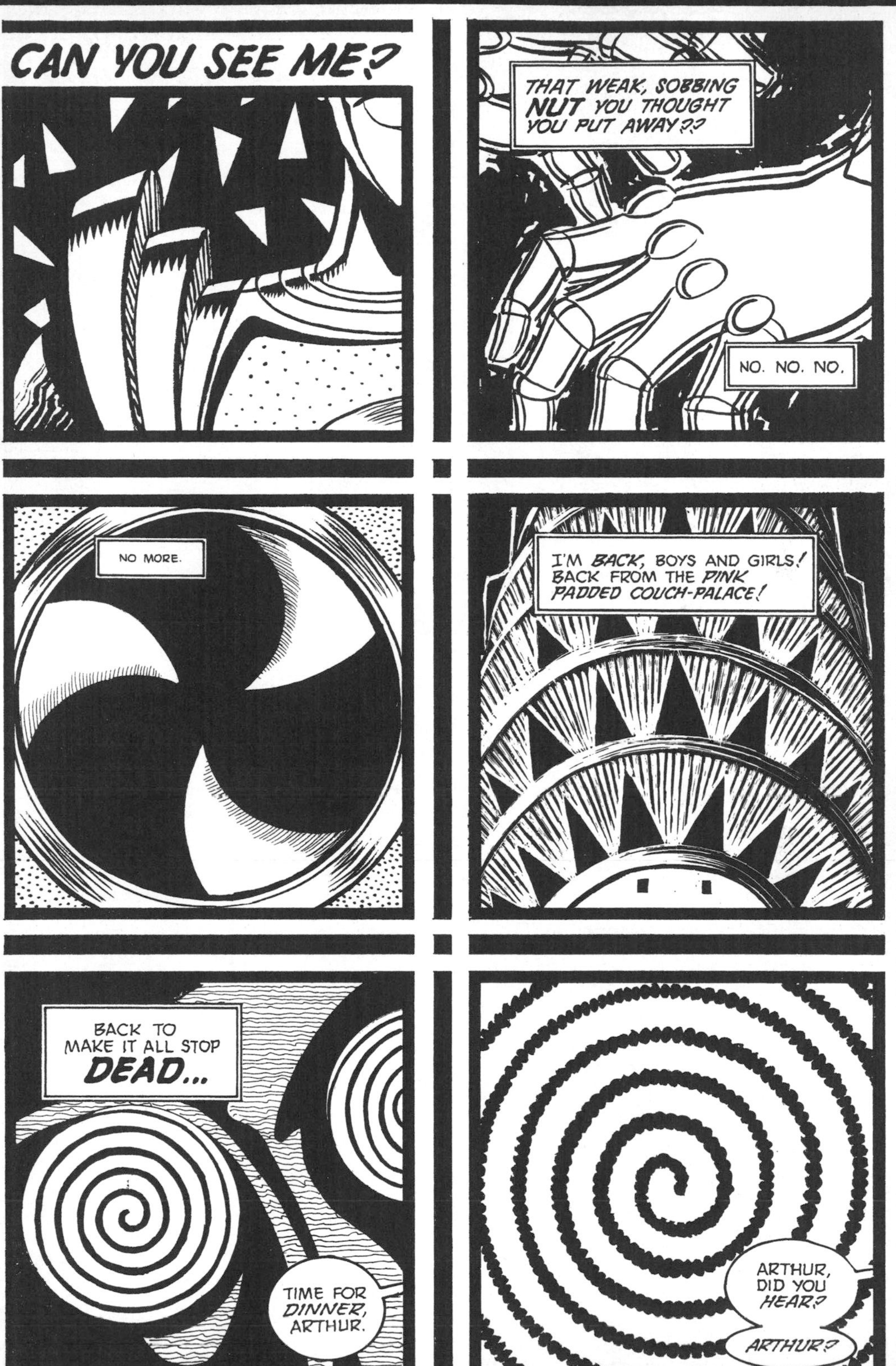
CAN YOU SEE ME?
THAT WEAK, SOBBING NUT YOU THOUGHT YOU PUT AWAY??
NO. NO. NO.
NO MORE.
I'M BACK, BOYS AND GIRLS! BACK FROM THE PINK PADDED COUCH-PALACE!
BACK TO MAKE IT ALL STOP DEAD...
TIME FOR DINNER, ARTHUR.
ARTHUR, DID YOU HEAR?
ARTHUR?

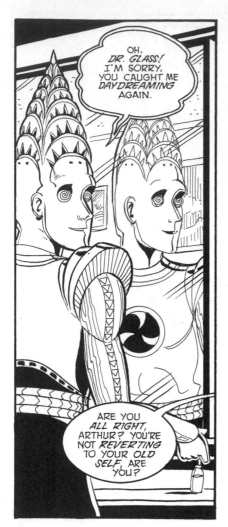

OH, *DR. GLASS!* I'M SORRY, YOU CAUGHT ME *DAYDREAMING* AGAIN.

ARE YOU *ALL RIGHT*, ARTHUR? YOU'RE NOT *REVERTING* TO YOUR OLD SELF, ARE YOU?

OH, *PLEASE*, DOCTOR...NOT EVEN IN *JEST*...

HA! HA! DON'T WORRY, ARTHUR. I KNOW A *CURED MAN* WHEN I SEE ONE. UH... FOR THE *RECORD*, THOUGH--

-- WHAT EXACTLY *WERE* YOU THINKING OF JUST NOW?

I WAS RECALLING THE DAYS WHEN I WAS *STILL HUMAN*. HOW *BEAUTIFUL* THEY WERE...

HOW MUCH I *MISS* THEM.

OF COURSE. IT'S ONLY *NATURAL*.

I CAN'T *BEGIN* TO TELL YOU HOW *GRATEFUL* I AM FOR ALL YOUR *HELP*, DR. GLASS.

YOU WERE THE FIRST ONE ON THE STAFF TO SEE PAST THIS *FRIGHTENING METAL BODY* TO THE "*REAL*" ARTHUR DEKKER.

AH, WELL... YOU WON US *ALL* OVER *EVENTUALLY*, ARTHUR. YOU'VE BEEN A *MODEL PATIENT*.

NO--*MORE* THAN THAT, YOU'VE BEEN LIKE *ONE OF THE FAMILY!*

WE'RE ALL *VERY PROUD* OF YOU, ARTHUR.

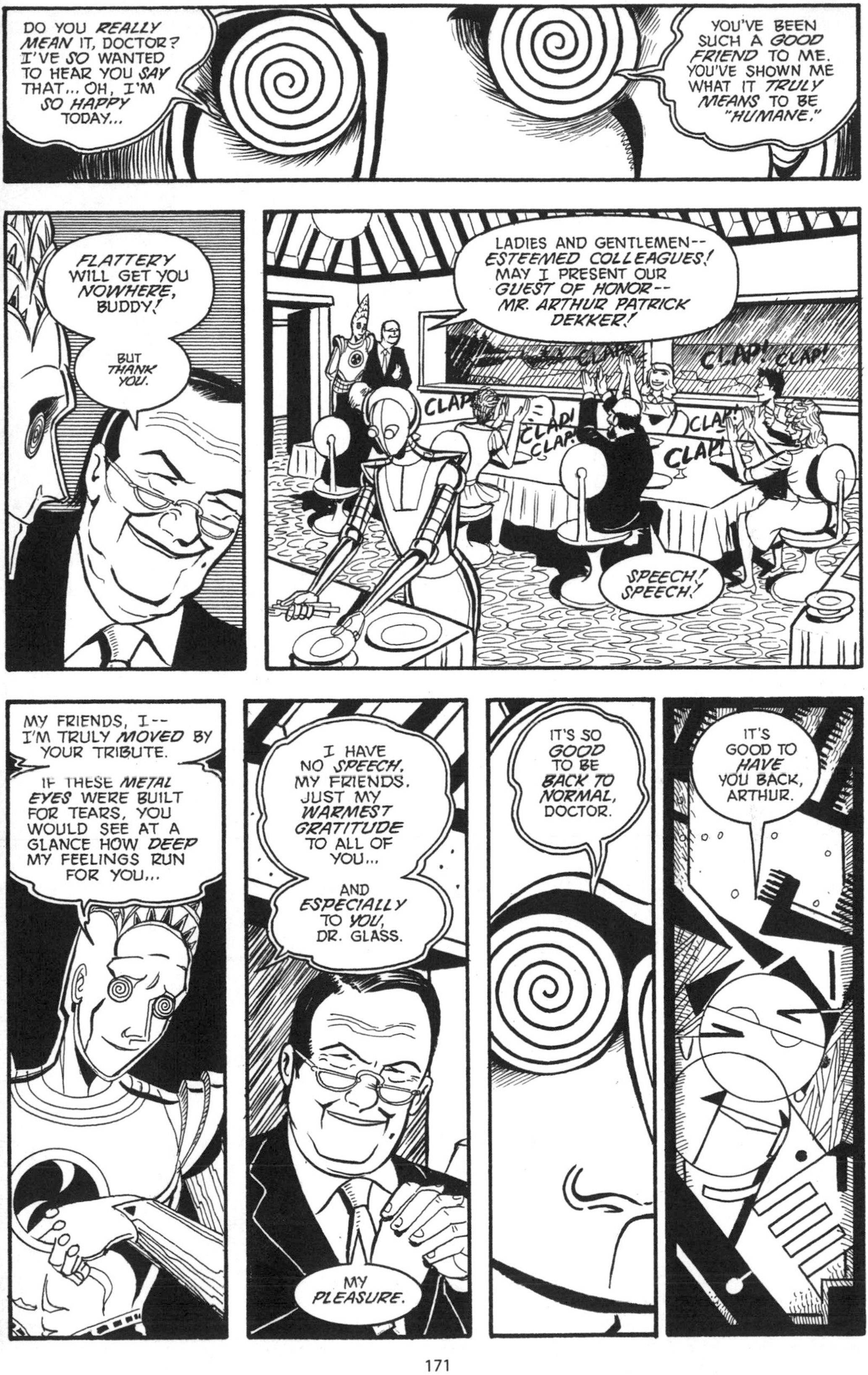
DO YOU REALLY MEAN IT, DOCTOR? I'VE SO WANTED TO HEAR YOU SAY THAT... OH, I'M SO HAPPY TODAY...
YOU'VE BEEN SUCH A GOOD FRIEND TO ME. YOU'VE SHOWN ME WHAT IT TRULY MEANS TO BE "HUMANE."
FLATTERY WILL GET YOU NOWHERE, BUDDY!
BUT THANK YOU.
LADIES AND GENTLEMEN-- ESTEEMED COLLEAGUES! MAY I PRESENT OUR GUEST OF HONOR-- MR. ARTHUR PATRICK DEKKER!
CLAP! CLAP!
CLAP!
CLAP! CLAP!
CLAP! CLAP!
CLAP!
SPEECH! SPEECH!
MY FRIENDS, I-- I'M TRULY MOVED BY YOUR TRIBUTE.
IF THESE METAL EYES WERE BUILT FOR TEARS, YOU WOULD SEE AT A GLANCE HOW DEEP MY FEELINGS RUN FOR YOU...
I HAVE NO SPEECH, MY FRIENDS. JUST MY WARMEST GRATITUDE TO ALL OF YOU...
AND ESPECIALLY TO YOU, DR. GLASS.
MY PLEASURE.
IT'S SO GOOD TO BE BACK TO NORMAL, DOCTOR.
IT'S GOOD TO HAVE YOU BACK, ARTHUR.

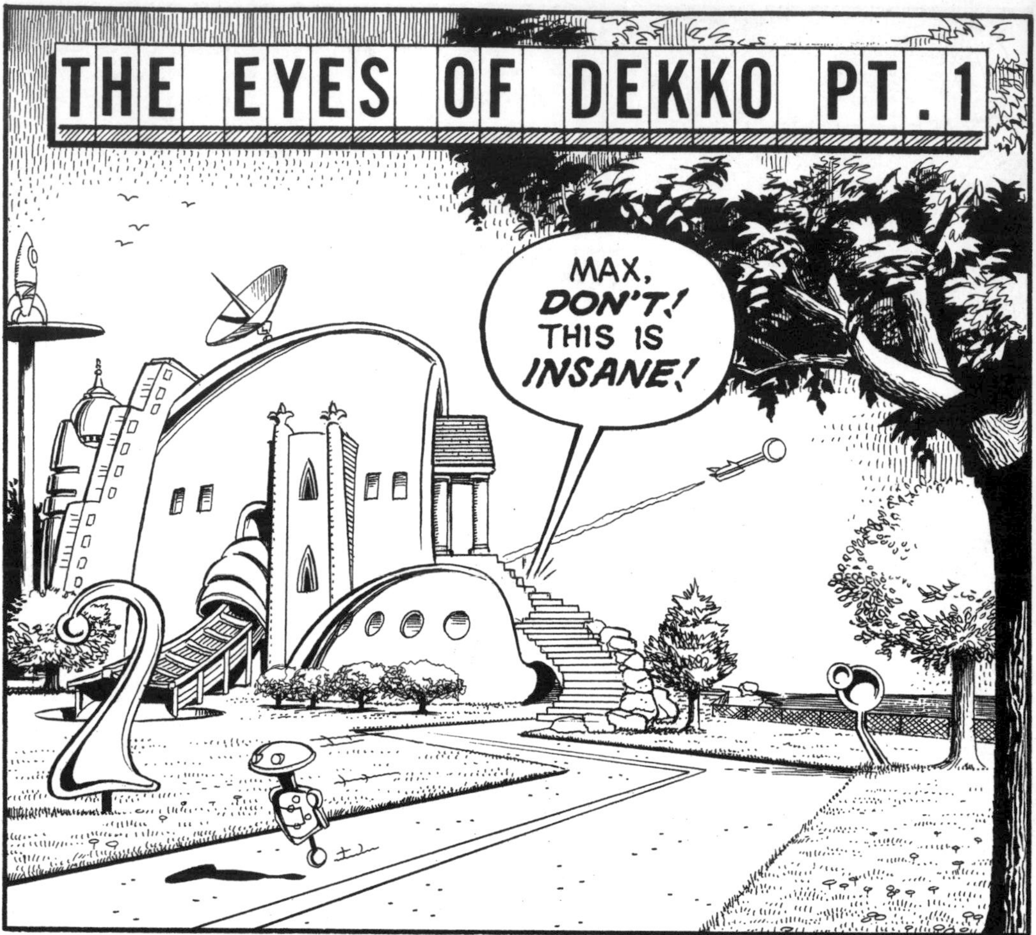
THE EYES OF DEKKO PT. 1
MAX, *DON'T!* THIS IS *INSANE!*

BY SCOTT McCLOUD | LETTERING bob lappan | EDITING cat ⊕ yronwode

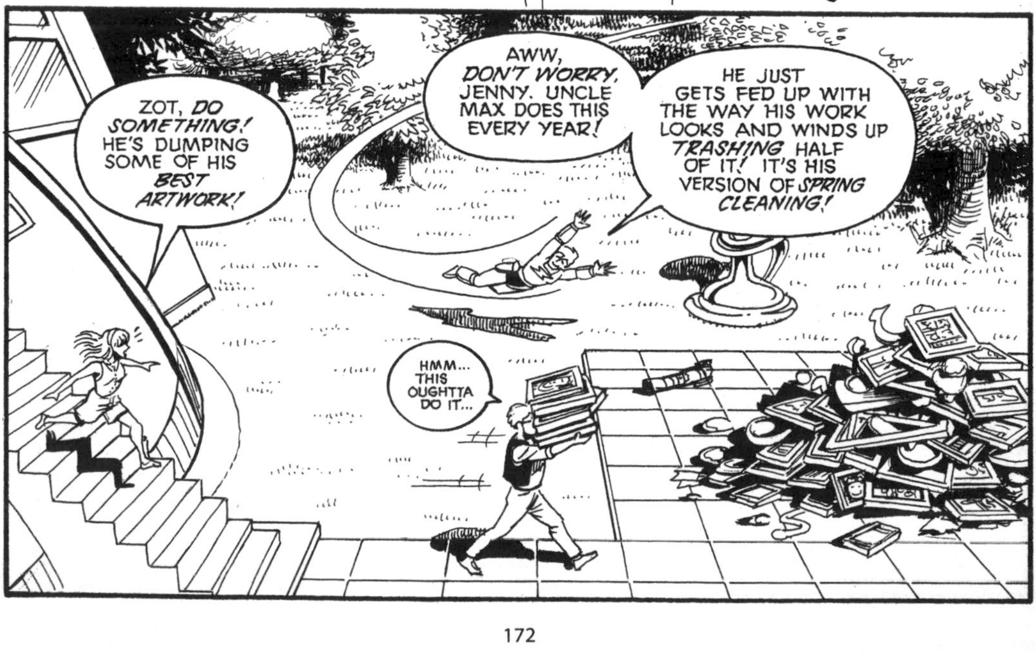
ZOT, *DO SOMETHING!* HE'S DUMPING SOME OF HIS *BEST ARTWORK!*
AWW, *DON'T WORRY,* JENNY. UNCLE MAX DOES THIS EVERY YEAR!
HE JUST GETS FED UP WITH THE WAY HIS WORK LOOKS AND WINDS UP *TRASHING* HALF OF IT! IT'S HIS VERSION OF *SPRING CLEANING!*
HMM... THIS OUGHTTA DO IT...

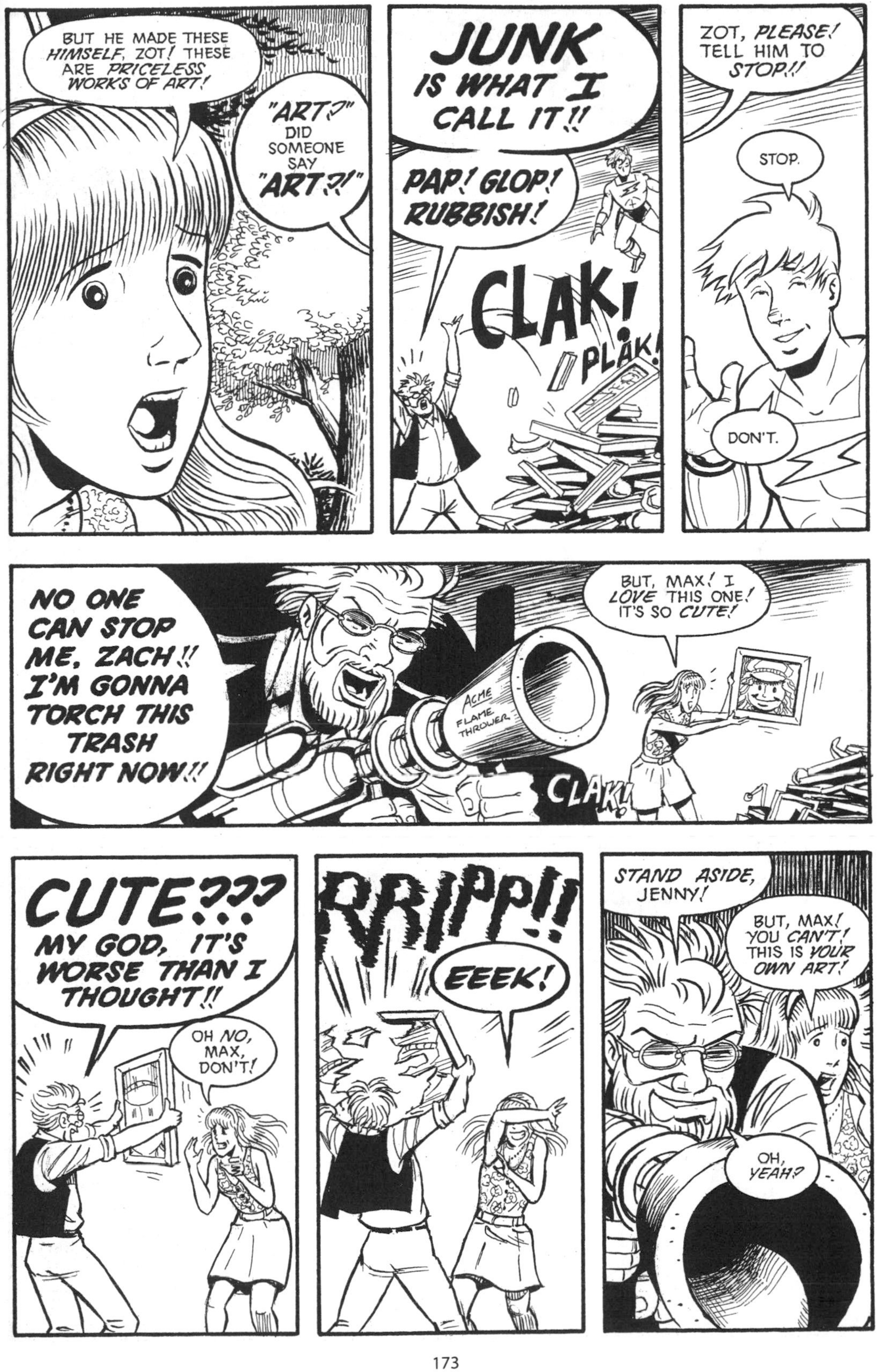
BUT HE MADE THESE HIMSELF, ZOT! THESE ARE PRICELESS WORKS OF ART!
"ART?!" DID SOMEONE SAY "ART?!"
JUNK IS WHAT I CALL IT!!
PAP! GLOP! RUBBISH!
CLAK!
PLÅK!
ZOT, PLEASE! TELL HIM TO STOP!!
STOP.
DON'T.
NO ONE CAN STOP ME, ZACH!! I'M GONNA TORCH THIS TRASH RIGHT NOW!!
ACME FLAME THROWER
BUT, MAX! I LOVE THIS ONE! IT'S SO CUTE!
CLAK!
CUTE??? MY GOD, IT'S WORSE THAN I THOUGHT!!
OH NO, MAX, DON'T!
RRIPP!!
EEEK!
STAND ASIDE, JENNY!
BUT, MAX! YOU CAN'T! THIS IS YOUR OWN ART!
OH, YEAH?

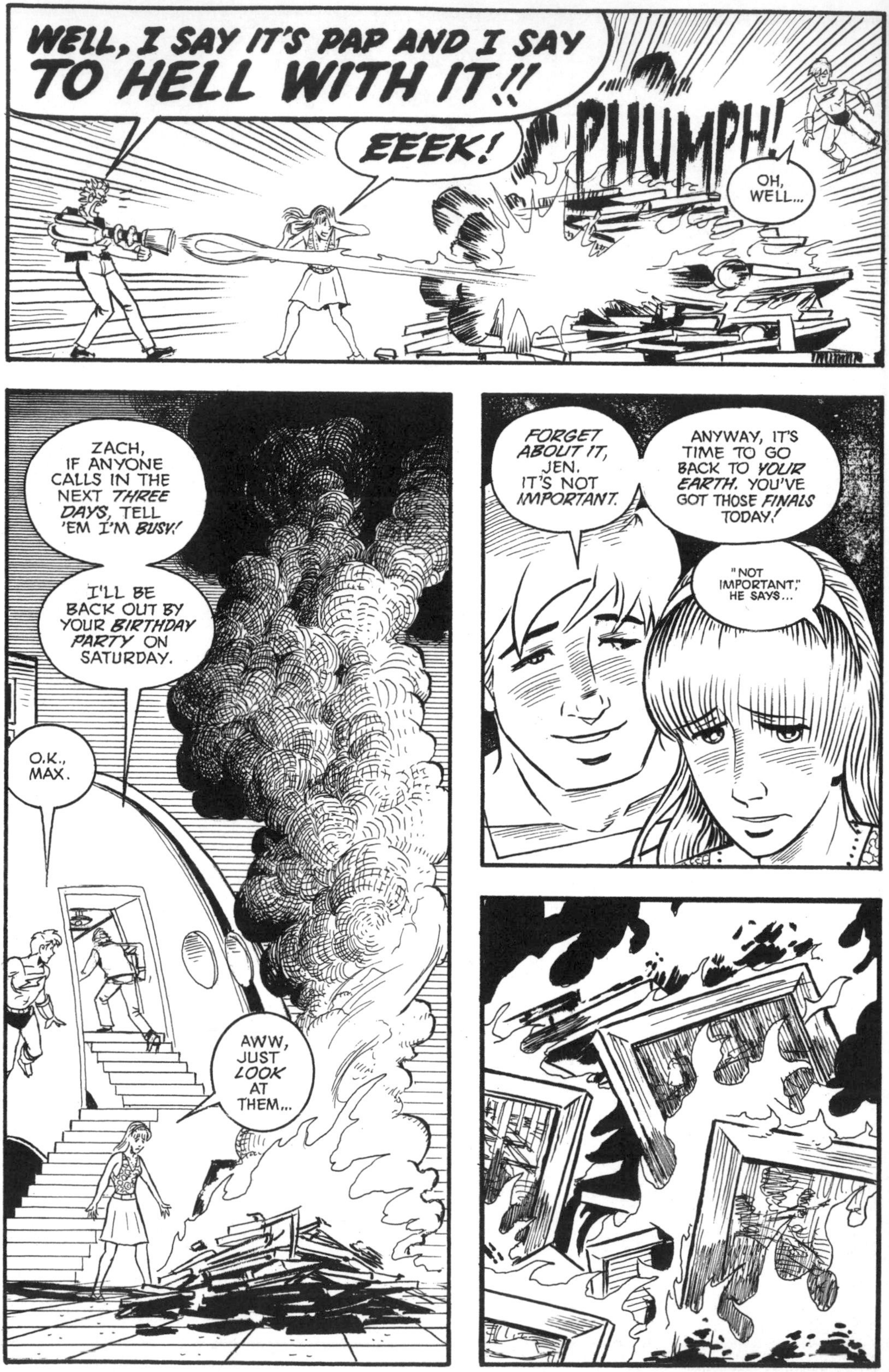
WELL, I SAY IT'S PAP AND I SAY TO HELL WITH IT!!
EEEK!
PHUMPH!
OH, WELL...
ZACH, IF ANYONE CALLS IN THE NEXT THREE DAYS, TELL 'EM I'M BUSY!
I'LL BE BACK OUT BY YOUR BIRTHDAY PARTY ON SATURDAY.
O.K., MAX.
AWW, JUST LOOK AT THEM...
FORGET ABOUT IT, JEN. IT'S NOT IMPORTANT.
ANYWAY, IT'S TIME TO GO BACK TO YOUR EARTH. YOU'VE GOT THOSE FINALS TODAY!
"NOT IMPORTANT," HE SAYS...

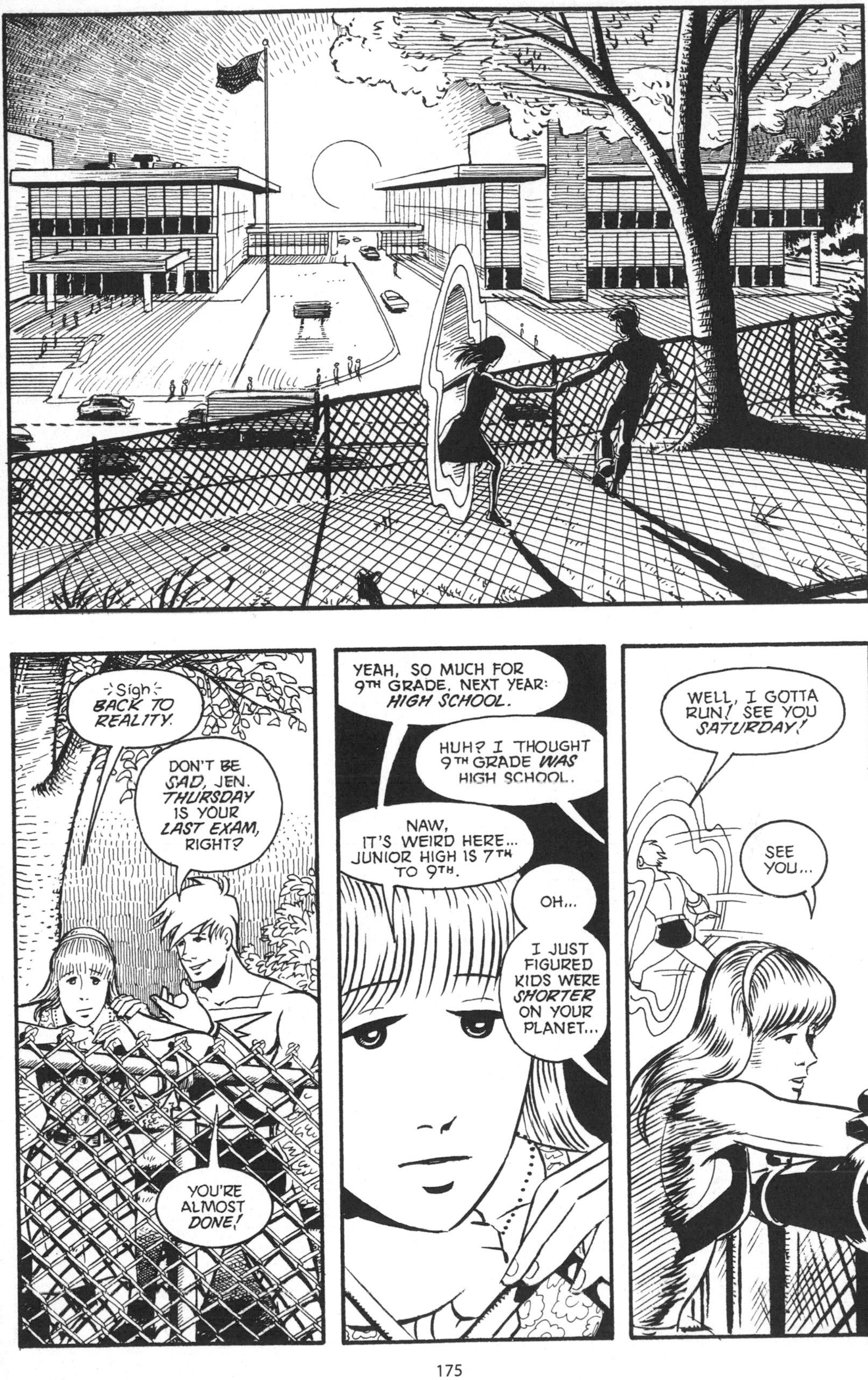

-:-Sigh-:- BACK TO REALITY.
DON'T BE SAD, JEN. THURSDAY IS YOUR LAST EXAM, RIGHT?
YOU'RE ALMOST DONE!
YEAH, SO MUCH FOR 9TH GRADE. NEXT YEAR: HIGH SCHOOL.
HUH? I THOUGHT 9TH GRADE WAS HIGH SCHOOL.
NAW, IT'S WEIRD HERE... JUNIOR HIGH IS 7TH TO 9TH.
OH...
I JUST FIGURED KIDS WERE SHORTER ON YOUR PLANET...
WELL, I GOTTA RUN! SEE YOU SATURDAY!
SEE YOU...

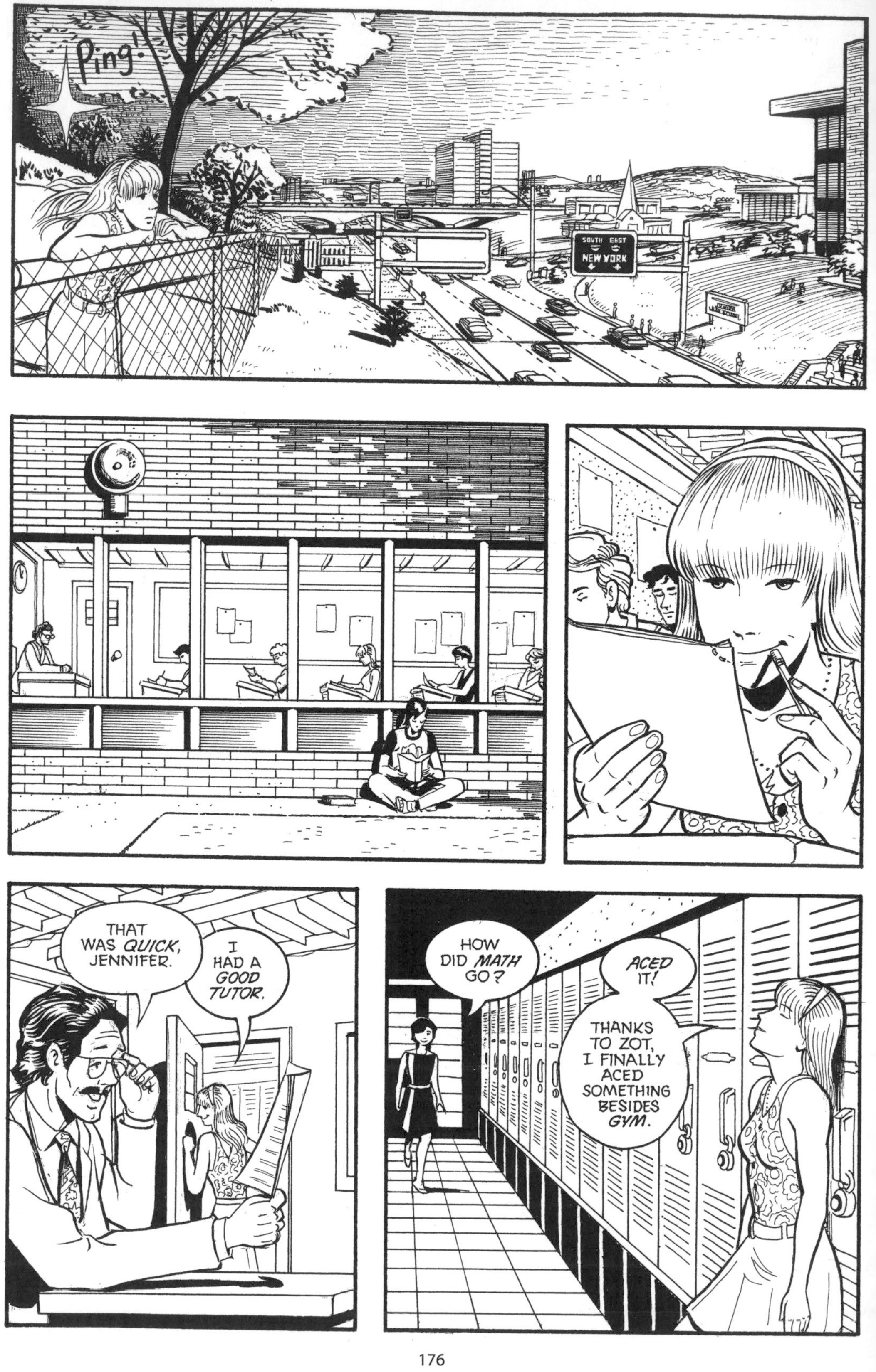
Ping!
SOUTH EAST
NEW YORK
THAT WAS QUICK, JENNIFER.
I HAD A GOOD TUTOR.
HOW DID MATH GO?
ACED IT!
THANKS TO ZOT, I FINALLY ACED SOMETHING BESIDES GYM.

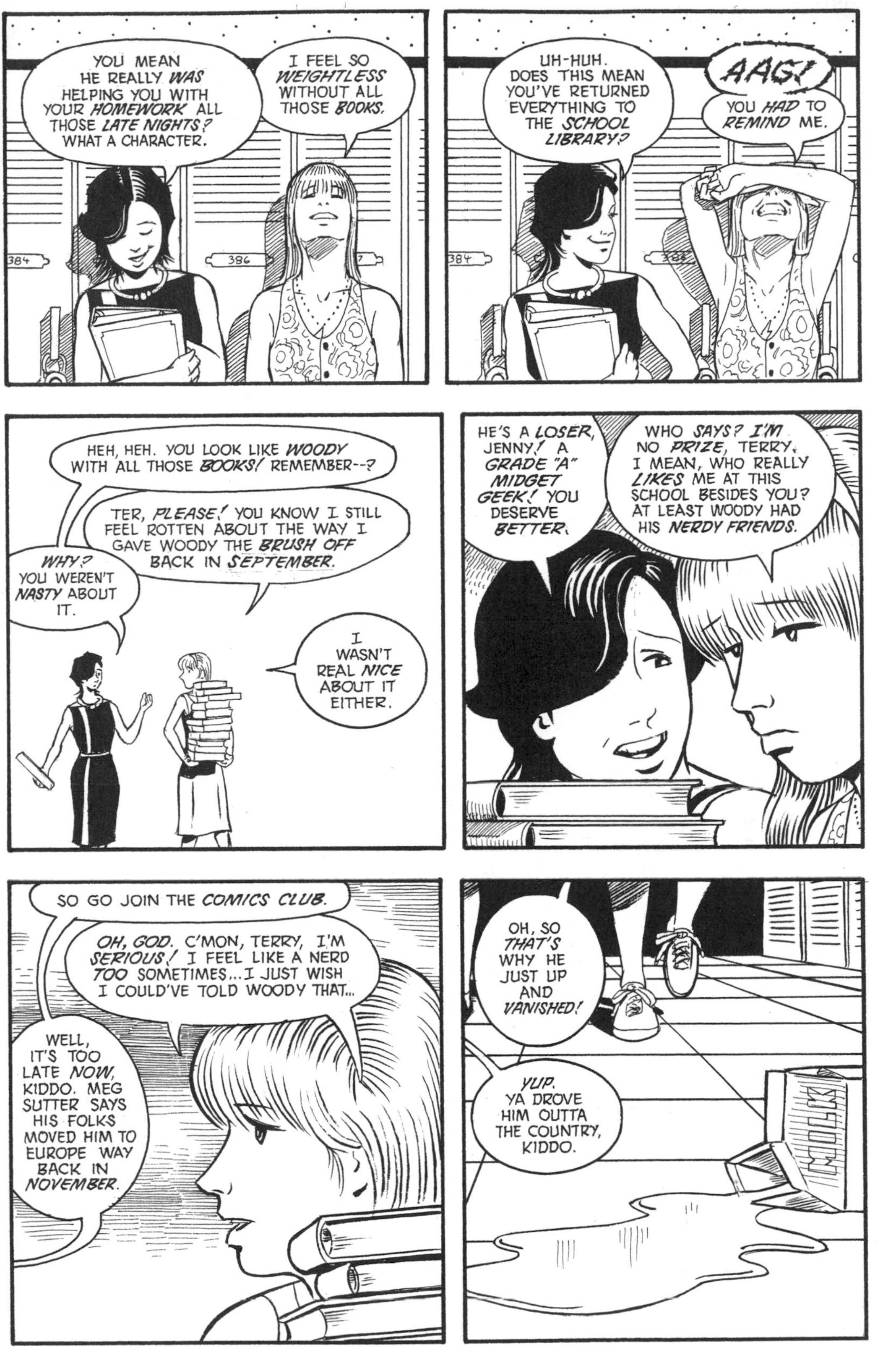
YOU MEAN HE REALLY *WAS* HELPING YOU WITH YOUR *HOMEWORK* ALL THOSE *LATE NIGHTS?* WHAT A CHARACTER.
I FEEL SO *WEIGHTLESS* WITHOUT ALL THOSE *BOOKS*.
384
386
UH-HUH. DOES THIS MEAN YOU'VE RETURNED EVERYTHING TO THE *SCHOOL LIBRARY?*
AAG!
YOU *HAD* TO *REMIND* ME.
384
HEH, HEH. YOU LOOK LIKE *WOODY* WITH ALL THOSE *BOOKS!* REMEMBER--?
TER, *PLEASE!* YOU KNOW I STILL FEEL ROTTEN ABOUT THE WAY I GAVE WOODY THE *BRUSH OFF* BACK IN *SEPTEMBER*.
WHY? YOU WEREN'T *NASTY* ABOUT IT.
I WASN'T REAL *NICE* ABOUT IT EITHER.
HE'S A *LOSER*, JENNY! A *GRADE "A" MIDGET GEEK!* YOU DESERVE *BETTER*.
WHO *SAYS? I'M* NO *PRIZE*, TERRY. I MEAN, WHO REALLY *LIKES* ME AT THIS SCHOOL BESIDES YOU? AT LEAST WOODY HAD HIS *NERDY FRIENDS*.
SO GO JOIN THE *COMICS CLUB*.
OH, GOD. C'MON, TERRY, I'M *SERIOUS!* I FEEL LIKE A NERD *TOO* SOMETIMES...I JUST WISH I COULD'VE TOLD WOODY THAT...
WELL, IT'S TOO LATE *NOW*, KIDDO. MEG SUTTER SAYS HIS FOLKS MOVED HIM TO EUROPE WAY BACK IN *NOVEMBER*.
OH, SO *THAT'S* WHY HE JUST UP AND *VANISHED!*
YUP. YA DROVE HIM OUTTA THE COUNTRY, KIDDO.
MILK

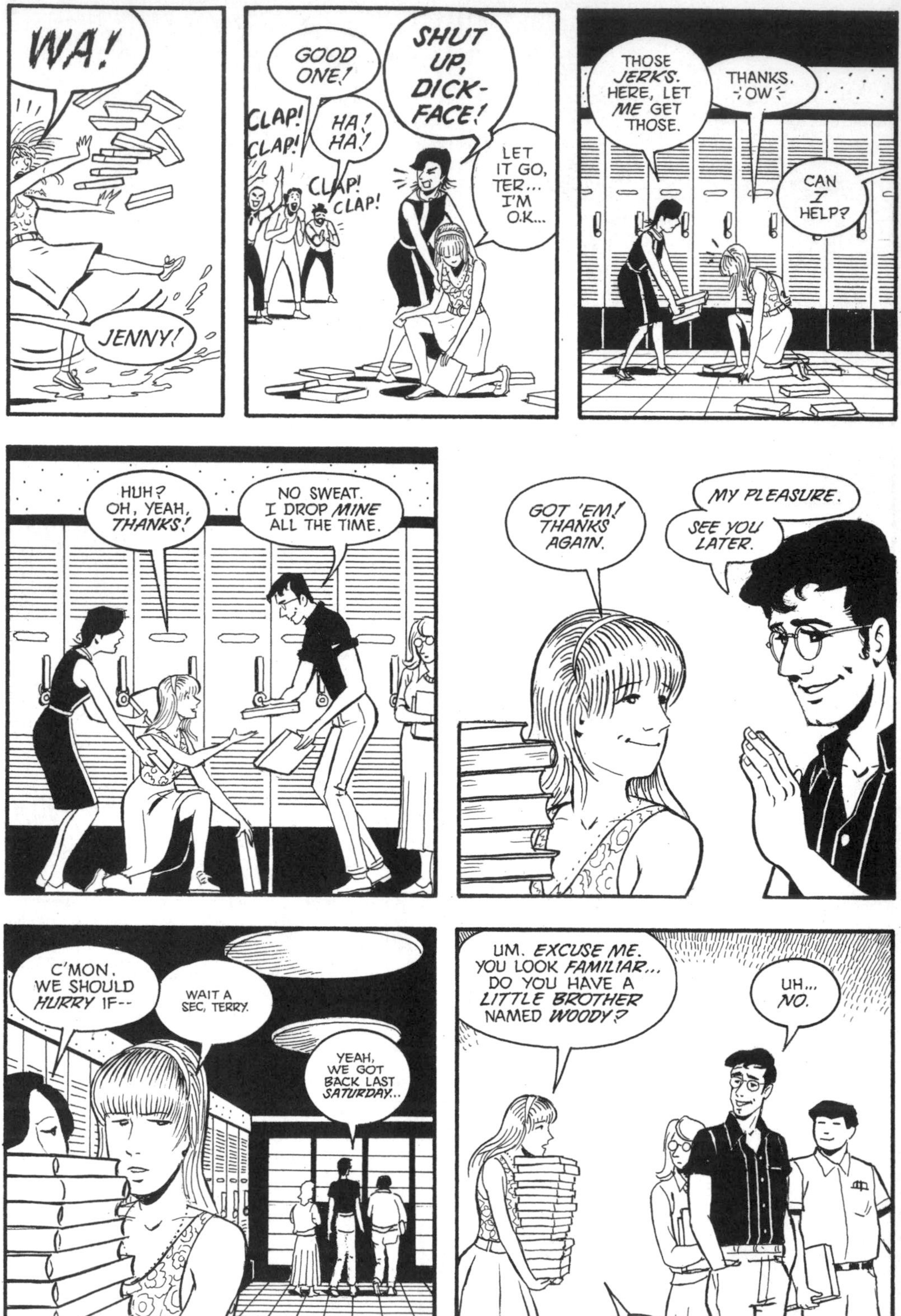
WA!
JENNY!
GOOD ONE!
CLAP! CLAP!
HA! HA!
CLAP! CLAP!
SHUT UP, DICK-FACE!
LET IT GO, TER... I'M O.K...
THOSE JERKS. HERE, LET ME GET THOSE.
THANKS. OW
CAN I HELP?
HUH? OH, YEAH, THANKS!
NO SWEAT. I DROP MINE ALL THE TIME.
GOT 'EM! THANKS AGAIN.
MY PLEASURE.
SEE YOU LATER.
C'MON. WE SHOULD HURRY IF--
WAIT A SEC, TERRY.
YEAH, WE GOT BACK LAST SATURDAY...
UM. EXCUSE ME. YOU LOOK FAMILIAR... DO YOU HAVE A LITTLE BROTHER NAMED WOODY?
UH... NO.
BUT...

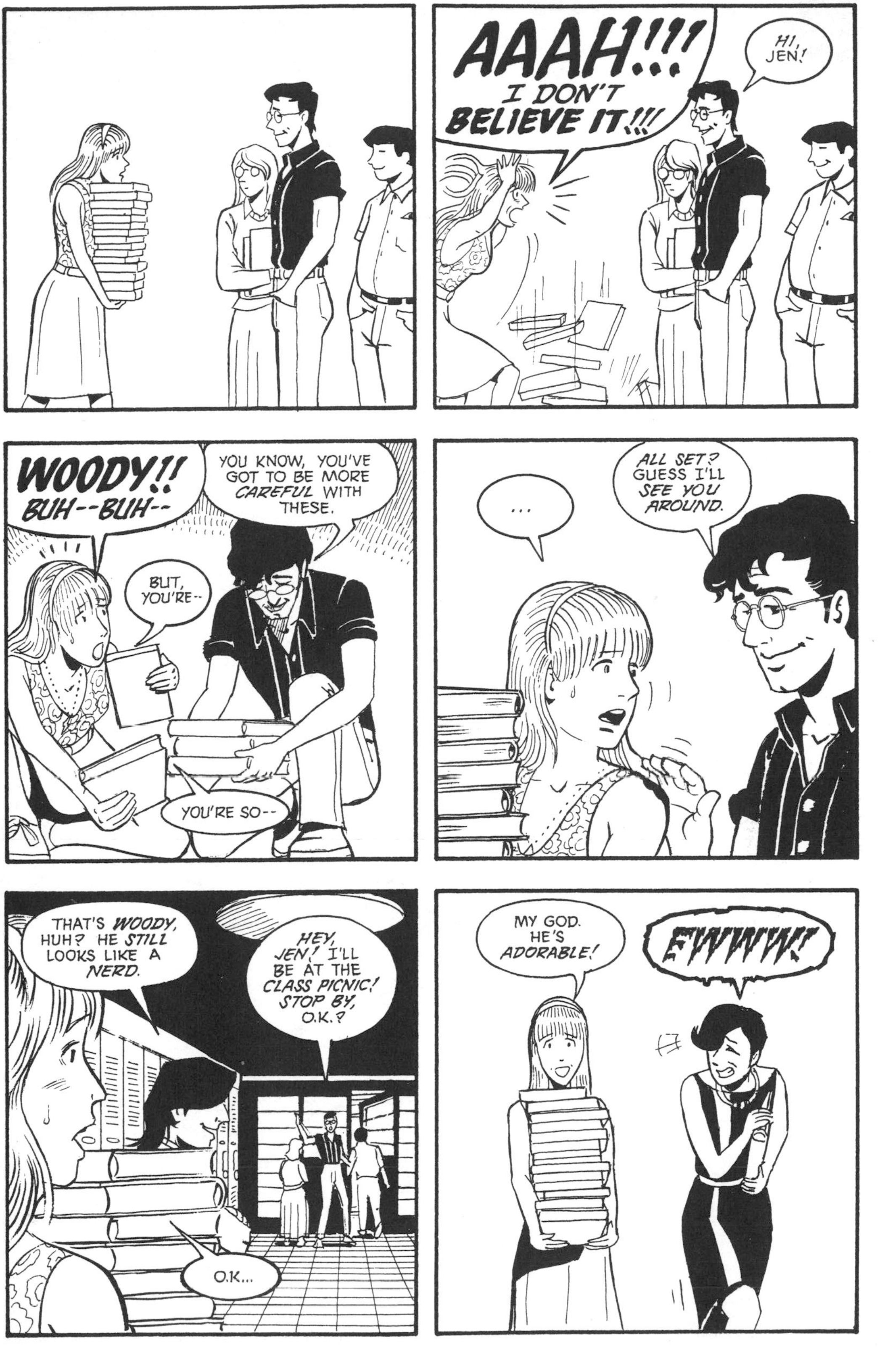
AAAH!!! I DON'T BELIEVE IT!!!
HI, JEN!
WOODY!! BUH--BUH--
YOU KNOW, YOU'VE GOT TO BE MORE CAREFUL WITH THESE.
BUT, YOU'RE--
YOU'RE SO--
...
ALL SET? GUESS I'LL SEE YOU AROUND.
THAT'S WOODY, HUH? HE STILL LOOKS LIKE A NERD.
HEY, JEN! I'LL BE AT THE CLASS PICNIC! STOP BY, O.K.?
O.K...
MY GOD. HE'S ADORABLE!
EWWW!

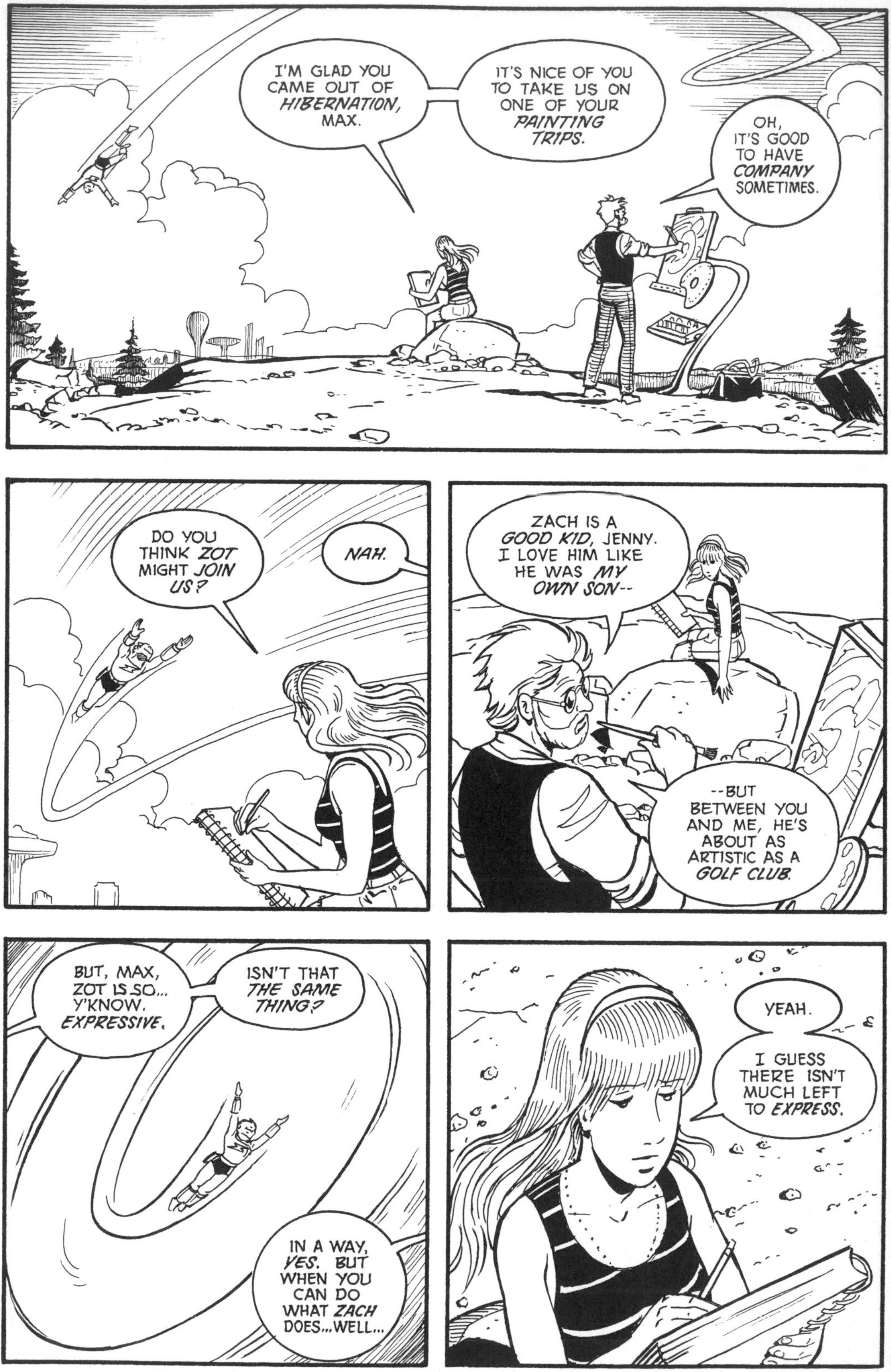

I'M GLAD YOU CAME OUT OF HIBERNATION, MAX.
IT'S NICE OF YOU TO TAKE US ON ONE OF YOUR PAINTING TRIPS.
OH, IT'S GOOD TO HAVE COMPANY SOMETIMES.
DO YOU THINK ZOT MIGHT JOIN US?
NAH.
ZACH IS A GOOD KID, JENNY. I LOVE HIM LIKE HE WAS MY OWN SON--
--BUT BETWEEN YOU AND ME, HE'S ABOUT AS ARTISTIC AS A GOLF CLUB.
BUT, MAX, ZOT IS SO... Y'KNOW. EXPRESSIVE.
ISN'T THAT THE SAME THING?
IN A WAY, YES. BUT WHEN YOU CAN DO WHAT ZACH DOES...WELL...
YEAH.
I GUESS THERE ISN'T MUCH LEFT TO EXPRESS.

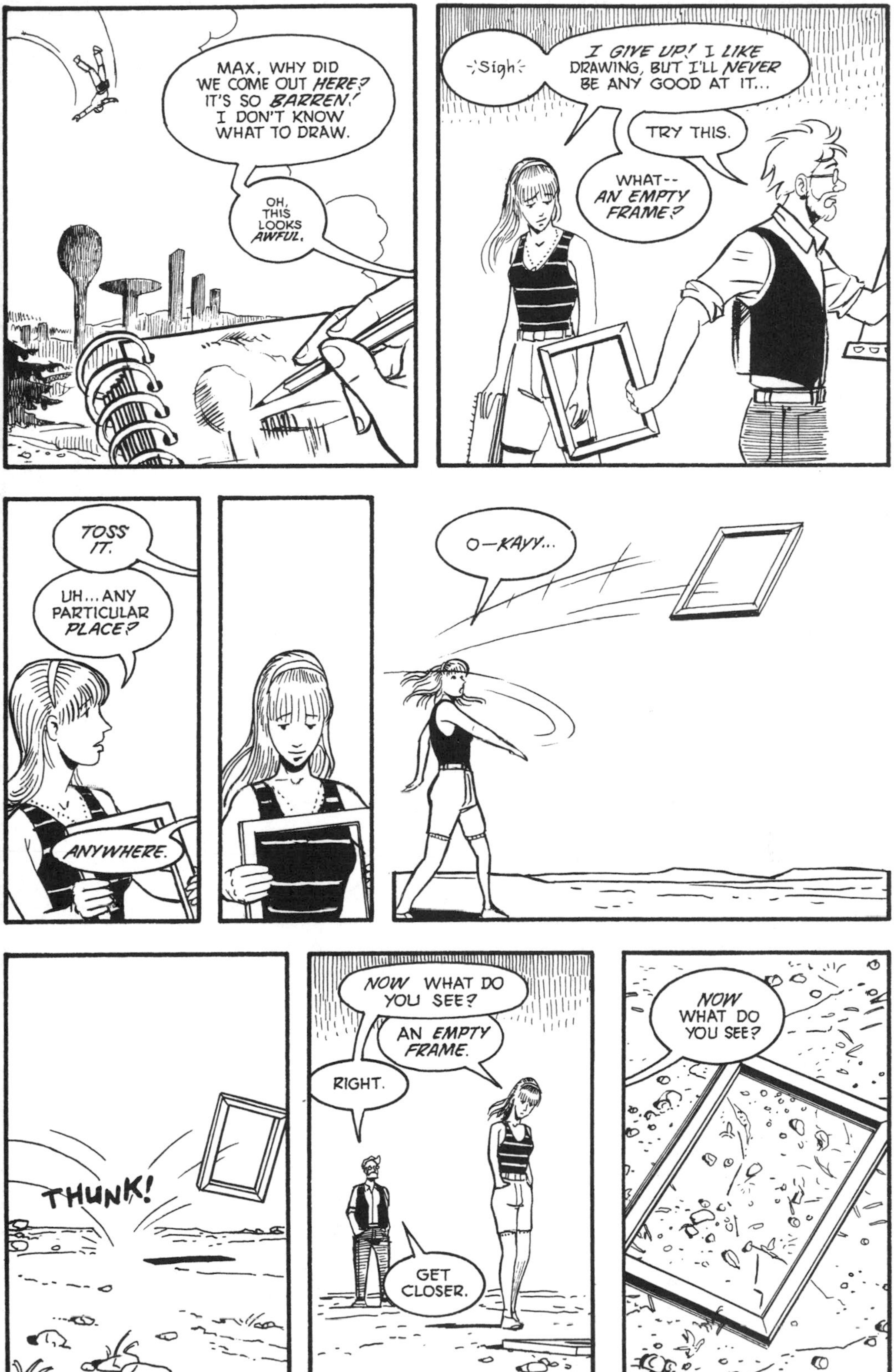

MAX, WHY DID WE COME OUT HERE? IT'S SO BARREN! I DON'T KNOW WHAT TO DRAW.
OH, THIS LOOKS AWFUL.
-Sigh-
I GIVE UP! I LIKE DRAWING, BUT I'LL NEVER BE ANY GOOD AT IT...
TRY THIS.
WHAT-- AN EMPTY FRAME?
TOSS IT.
UH... ANY PARTICULAR PLACE?
ANYWHERE.
O-KAYY...
THUNK!
NOW WHAT DO YOU SEE?
AN EMPTY FRAME.
RIGHT.
GET CLOSER.
NOW WHAT DO YOU SEE?

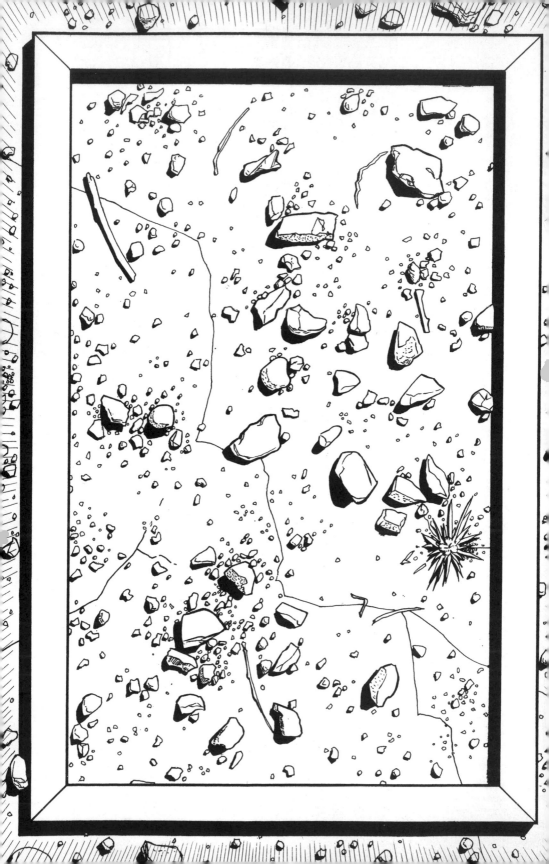

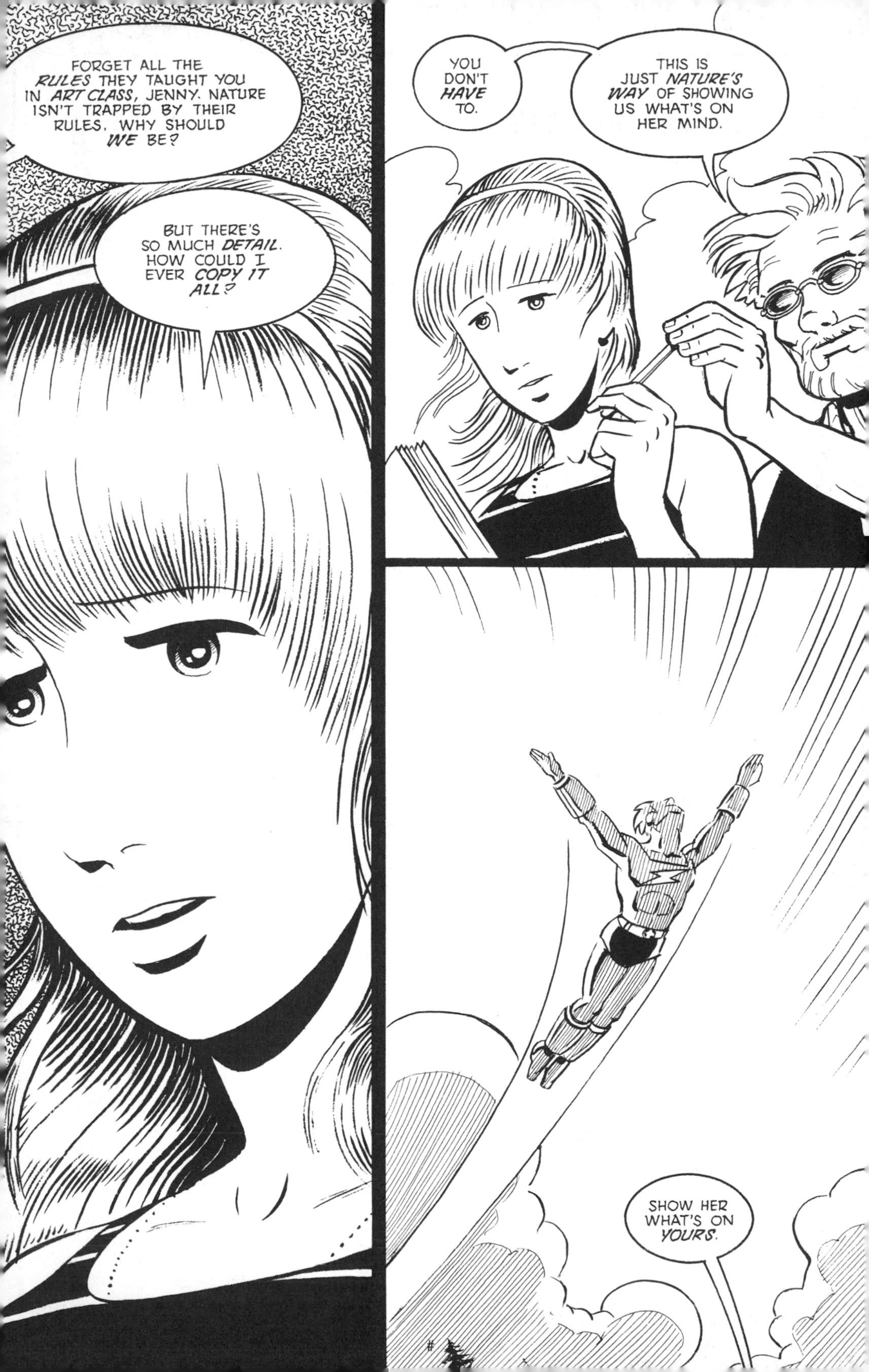
FORGET ALL THE RULES THEY TAUGHT YOU IN ART CLASS, JENNY. NATURE ISN'T TRAPPED BY THEIR RULES. WHY SHOULD WE BE?
BUT THERE'S SO MUCH DETAIL. HOW COULD I EVER COPY IT ALL?
YOU DON'T HAVE TO.
THIS IS JUST NATURE'S WAY OF SHOWING US WHAT'S ON HER MIND.
SHOW HER WHAT'S ON YOURS.

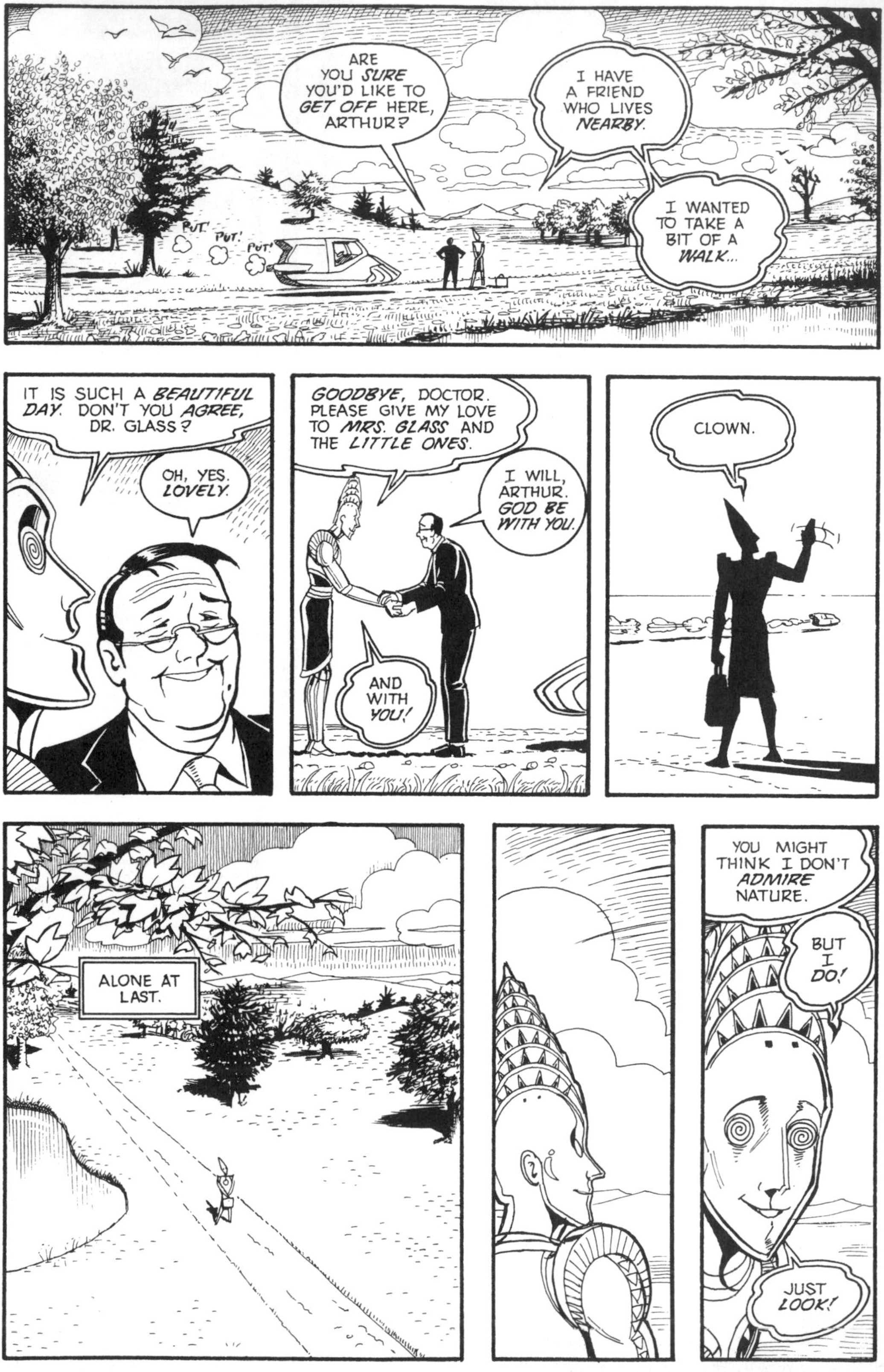

ARE YOU SURE YOU'D LIKE TO GET OFF HERE, ARTHUR?
I HAVE A FRIEND WHO LIVES NEARBY.
I WANTED TO TAKE A BIT OF A WALK...
PUT!
PUT!
PUT!
IT IS SUCH A BEAUTIFUL DAY. DON'T YOU AGREE, DR. GLASS?
OH, YES. LOVELY.
GOODBYE, DOCTOR. PLEASE GIVE MY LOVE TO MRS. GLASS AND THE LITTLE ONES.
I WILL, ARTHUR. GOD BE WITH YOU.
AND WITH YOU!
CLOWN.
ALONE AT LAST.
YOU MIGHT THINK I DON'T ADMIRE NATURE.
BUT I DO!
JUST LOOK!

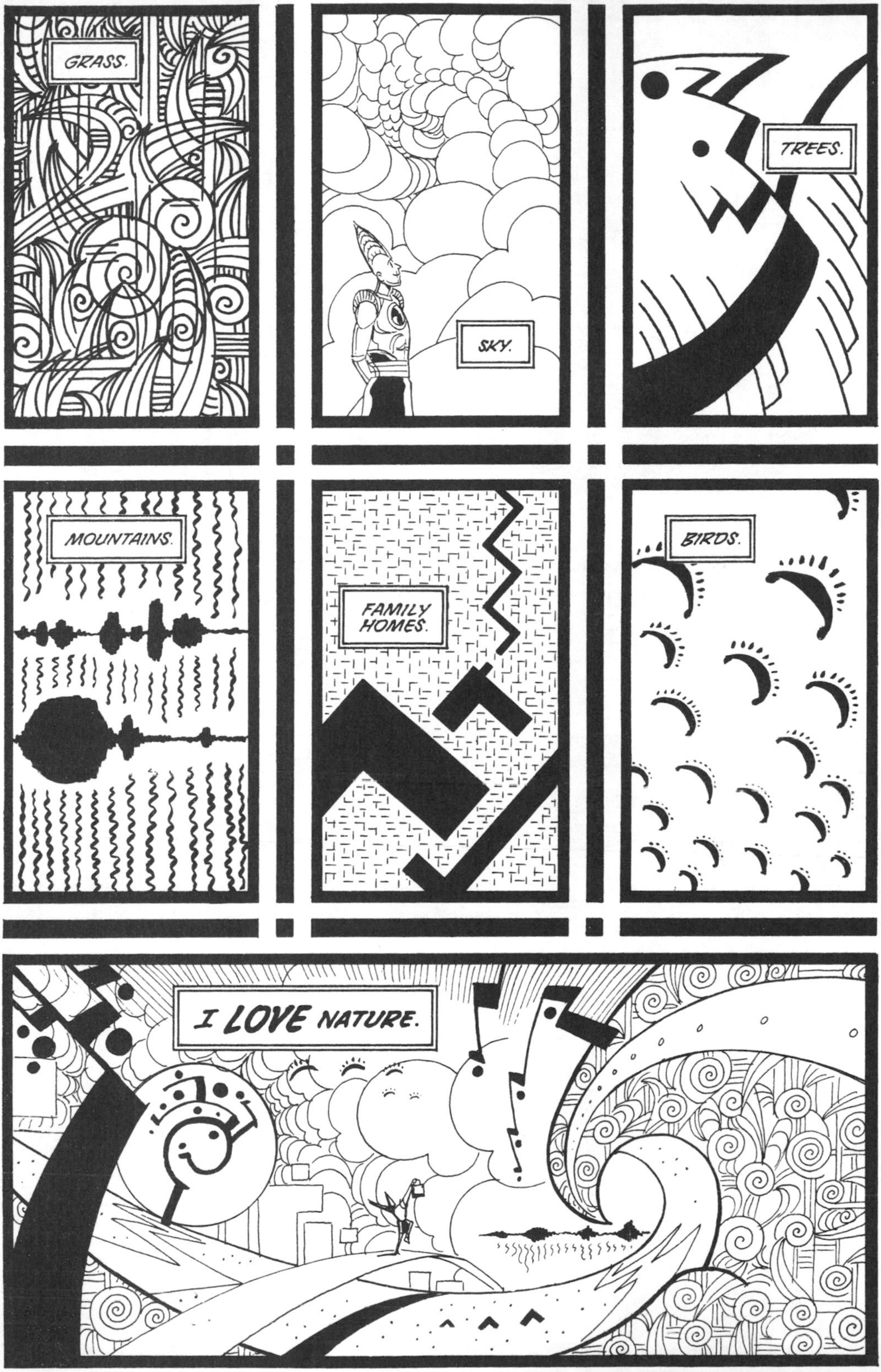
GRASS.
SKY.
TREES.
MOUNTAINS.
FAMILY HOMES.
BIRDS.
I LOVE NATURE.

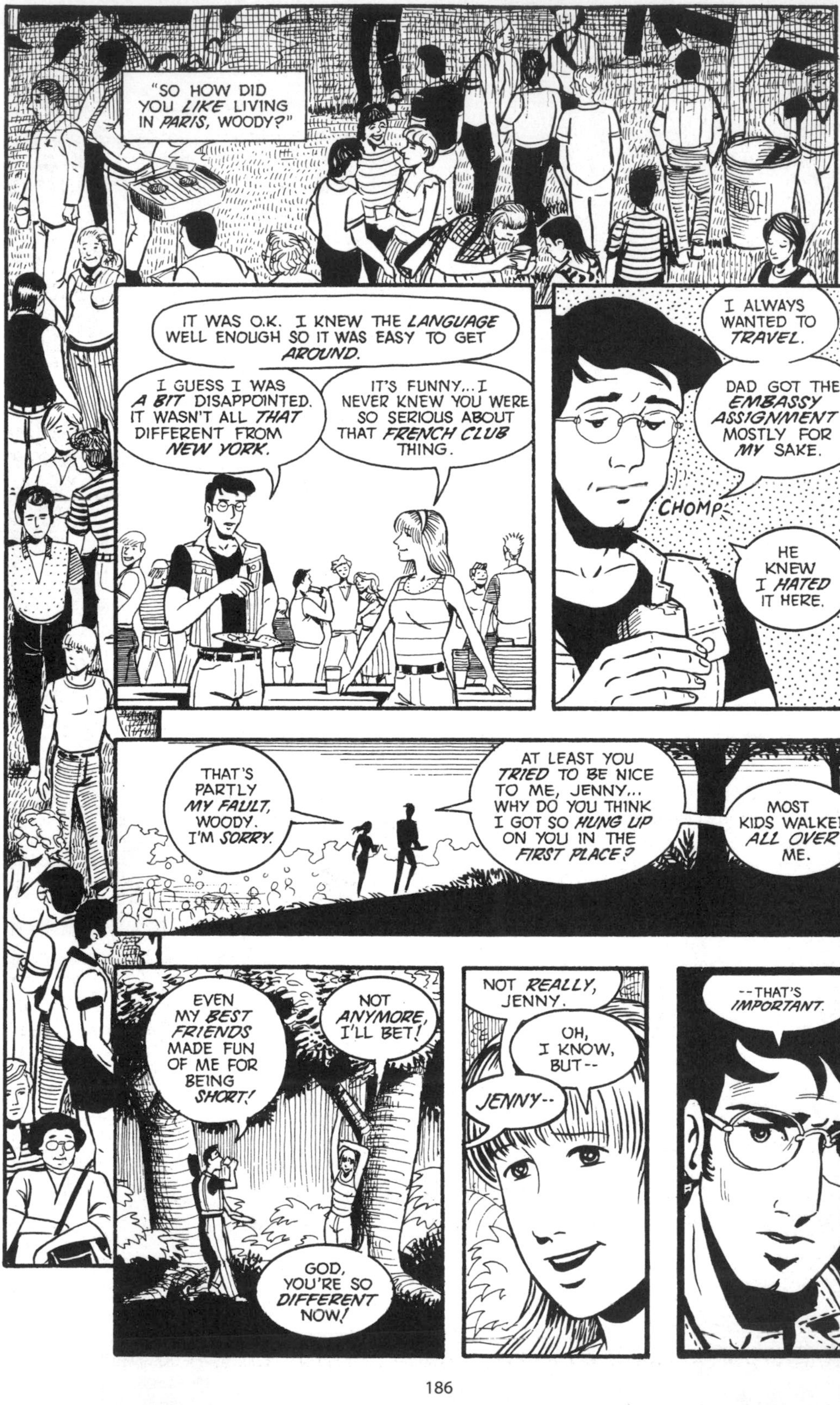
"SO HOW DID YOU *LIKE* LIVING IN *PARIS*, WOODY?"
IT WAS O.K. I KNEW THE *LANGUAGE* WELL ENOUGH SO IT WAS EASY TO GET *AROUND*.
I GUESS I WAS *A BIT* DISAPPOINTED. IT WASN'T ALL *THAT* DIFFERENT FROM *NEW YORK*.
IT'S FUNNY... I NEVER KNEW YOU WERE SO SERIOUS ABOUT THAT *FRENCH CLUB* THING.
I ALWAYS WANTED TO *TRAVEL*.
DAD GOT THE *EMBASSY ASSIGNMENT* MOSTLY FOR *MY* SAKE.
CHOMP
HE KNEW I *HATED* IT HERE.
THAT'S PARTLY *MY FAULT*, WOODY. I'M *SORRY*.
AT LEAST YOU *TRIED* TO BE NICE TO ME, JENNY... WHY DO YOU THINK I GOT SO *HUNG UP* ON YOU IN THE *FIRST PLACE*?
MOST KIDS WALKED *ALL OVER* ME.
EVEN MY *BEST FRIENDS* MADE FUN OF ME FOR BEING *SHORT!*
NOT *ANYMORE*, I'LL BET!
GOD, YOU'RE SO *DIFFERENT* NOW!
NOT *REALLY*, JENNY.
OH, I KNOW, BUT--
JENNY--
--THAT'S *IMPORTANT*.

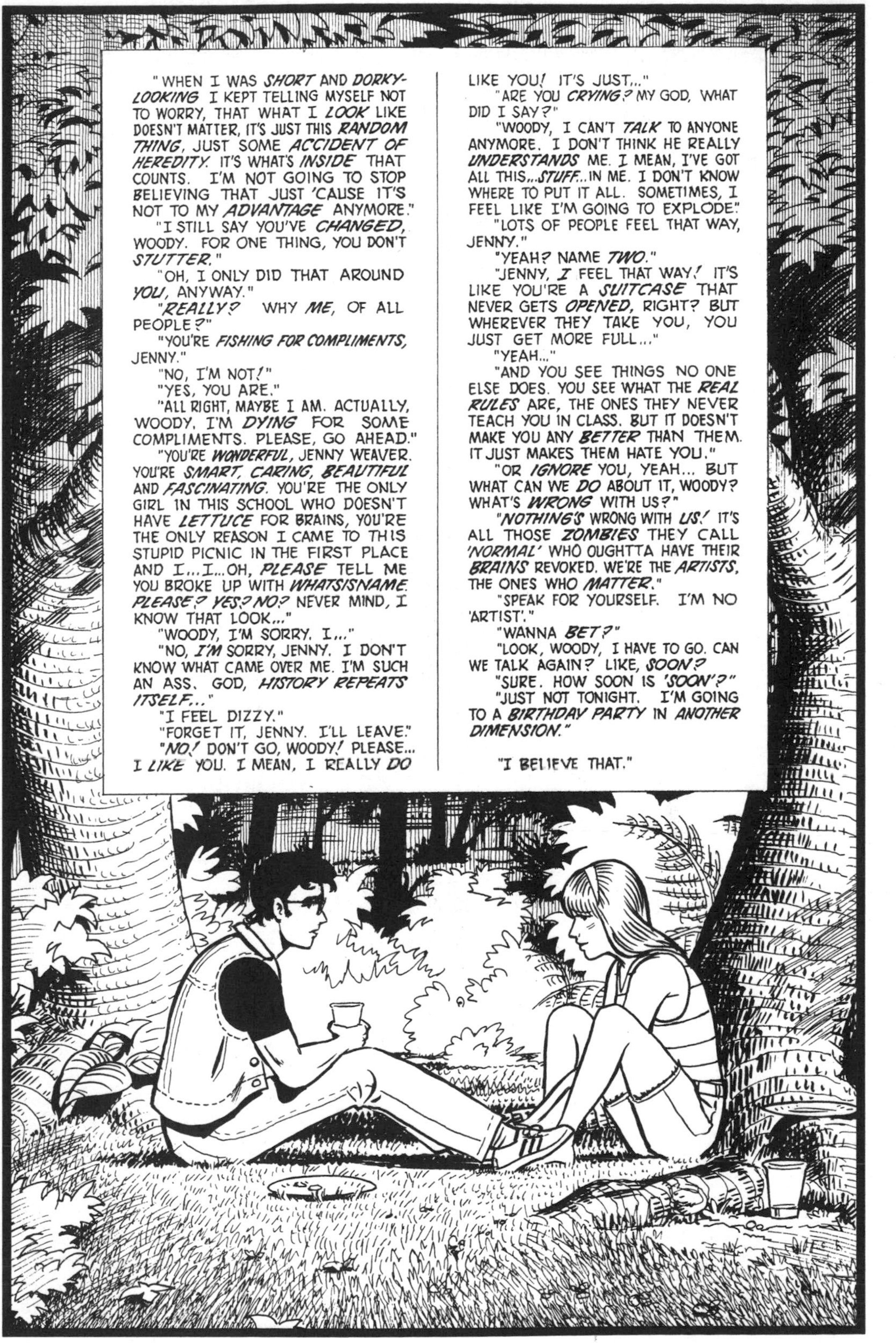
"WHEN I WAS SHORT AND DORKY-LOOKING I KEPT TELLING MYSELF NOT TO WORRY, THAT WHAT I LOOK LIKE DOESN'T MATTER, IT'S JUST THIS RANDOM THING, JUST SOME ACCIDENT OF HEREDITY. IT'S WHAT'S INSIDE THAT COUNTS. I'M NOT GOING TO STOP BELIEVING THAT JUST 'CAUSE IT'S NOT TO MY ADVANTAGE ANYMORE."
"I STILL SAY YOU'VE CHANGED, WOODY. FOR ONE THING, YOU DON'T STUTTER."
"OH, I ONLY DID THAT AROUND YOU, ANYWAY."
"REALLY? WHY ME, OF ALL PEOPLE?"
"YOU'RE FISHING FOR COMPLIMENTS, JENNY."
"NO, I'M NOT!"
"YES, YOU ARE."
"ALL RIGHT, MAYBE I AM. ACTUALLY, WOODY, I'M DYING FOR SOME COMPLIMENTS. PLEASE, GO AHEAD."
"YOU'RE WONDERFUL, JENNY WEAVER. YOU'RE SMART, CARING, BEAUTIFUL AND FASCINATING. YOU'RE THE ONLY GIRL IN THIS SCHOOL WHO DOESN'T HAVE LETTUCE FOR BRAINS, YOU'RE THE ONLY REASON I CAME TO THIS STUPID PICNIC IN THE FIRST PLACE AND I...I...OH, PLEASE TELL ME YOU BROKE UP WITH WHATSISNAME. PLEASE? YES? NO? NEVER MIND, I KNOW THAT LOOK..."
"WOODY, I'M SORRY. I..."
"NO, I'M SORRY, JENNY. I DON'T KNOW WHAT CAME OVER ME. I'M SUCH AN ASS. GOD, HISTORY REPEATS ITSELF..."
"I FEEL DIZZY."
"FORGET IT, JENNY. I'LL LEAVE."
"NO! DON'T GO, WOODY! PLEASE... I LIKE YOU. I MEAN, I REALLY DO LIKE YOU! IT'S JUST..."
"ARE YOU CRYING? MY GOD, WHAT DID I SAY?"
"WOODY, I CAN'T TALK TO ANYONE ANYMORE. I DON'T THINK HE REALLY UNDERSTANDS ME. I MEAN, I'VE GOT ALL THIS...STUFF...IN ME. I DON'T KNOW WHERE TO PUT IT ALL. SOMETIMES, I FEEL LIKE I'M GOING TO EXPLODE."
"LOTS OF PEOPLE FEEL THAT WAY, JENNY."
"YEAH? NAME TWO."
"JENNY, I FEEL THAT WAY! IT'S LIKE YOU'RE A SUITCASE THAT NEVER GETS OPENED, RIGHT? BUT WHEREVER THEY TAKE YOU, YOU JUST GET MORE FULL..."
"YEAH..."
"AND YOU SEE THINGS NO ONE ELSE DOES. YOU SEE WHAT THE REAL RULES ARE, THE ONES THEY NEVER TEACH YOU IN CLASS. BUT IT DOESN'T MAKE YOU ANY BETTER THAN THEM. IT JUST MAKES THEM HATE YOU."
"OR IGNORE YOU, YEAH... BUT WHAT CAN WE DO ABOUT IT, WOODY? WHAT'S WRONG WITH US?"
"NOTHING'S WRONG WITH US! IT'S ALL THOSE ZOMBIES THEY CALL 'NORMAL' WHO OUGHTTA HAVE THEIR BRAINS REVOKED. WE'RE THE ARTISTS, THE ONES WHO MATTER."
"SPEAK FOR YOURSELF. I'M NO 'ARTIST'."
"WANNA BET?"
"LOOK, WOODY, I HAVE TO GO. CAN WE TALK AGAIN? LIKE, SOON?"
"SURE. HOW SOON IS 'SOON'?"
"JUST NOT TONIGHT. I'M GOING TO A BIRTHDAY PARTY IN ANOTHER DIMENSION."
"I BELIEVE THAT."

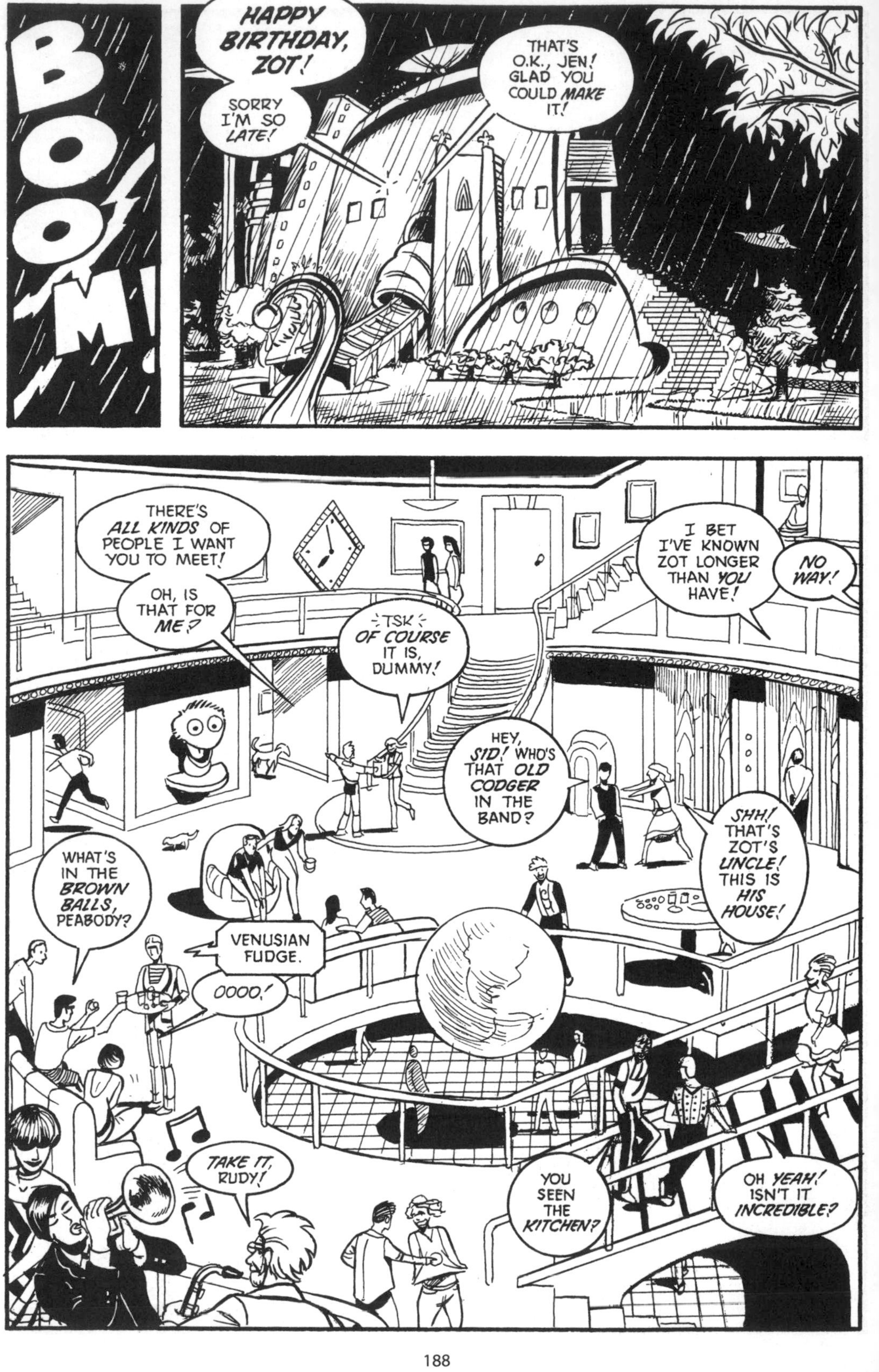
BOOOM!
HAPPY BIRTHDAY, ZOT!
SORRY I'M SO LATE!
THAT'S O.K., JEN! GLAD YOU COULD MAKE IT!
THERE'S ALL KINDS OF PEOPLE I WANT YOU TO MEET!
OH, IS THAT FOR ME?
TSK OF COURSE IT IS, DUMMY!
I BET I'VE KNOWN ZOT LONGER THAN YOU HAVE!
NO WAY!
HEY, SID! WHO'S THAT OLD CODGER IN THE BAND?
SHH! THAT'S ZOT'S UNCLE! THIS IS HIS HOUSE!
WHAT'S IN THE BROWN BALLS, PEABODY?
VENUSIAN FUDGE.
OOOO!
TAKE IT, RUDY!
YOU SEEN THE KITCHEN?
OH YEAH! ISN'T IT INCREDIBLE?

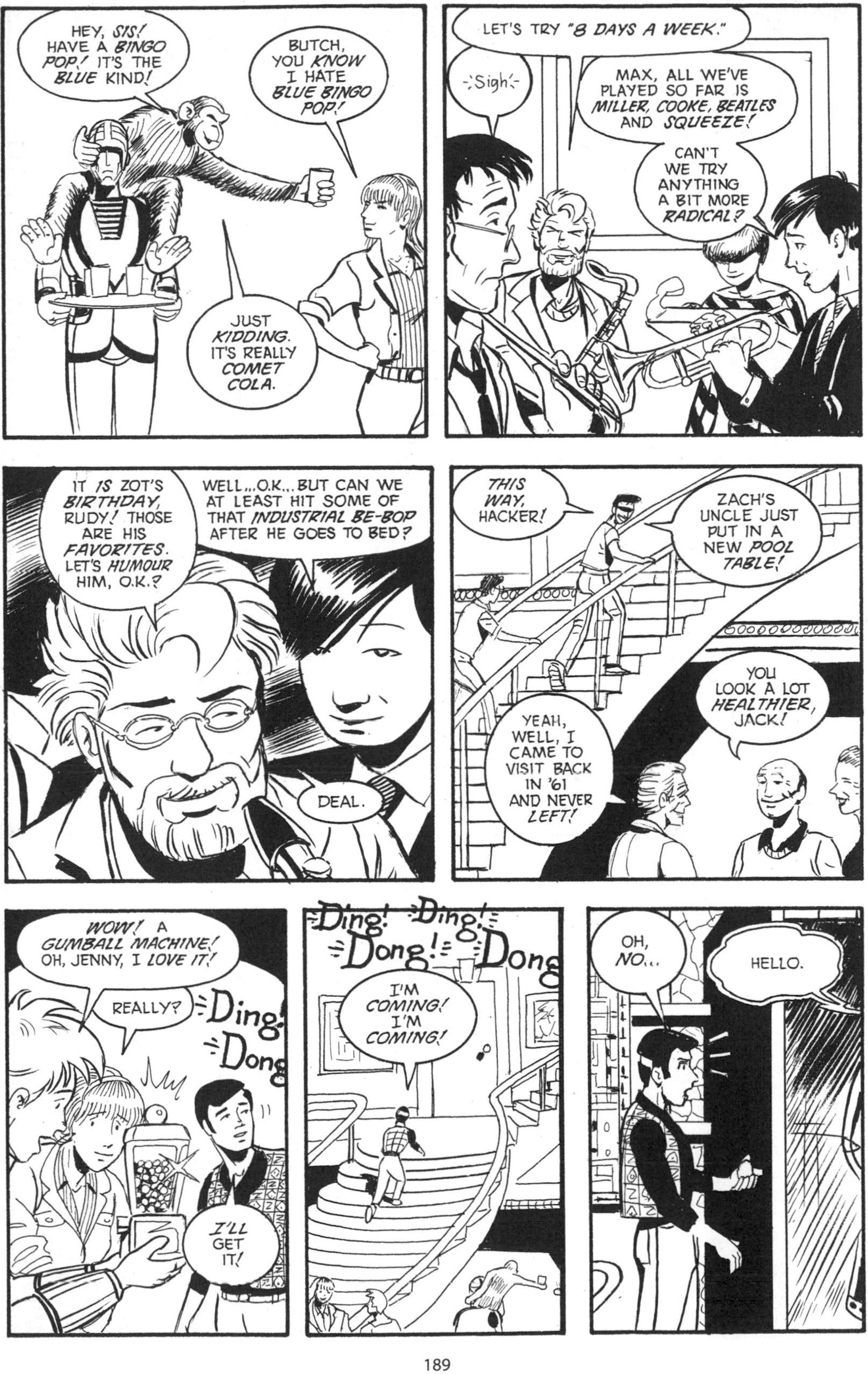
HEY, *SIS!* HAVE A *BINGO POP!* IT'S THE *BLUE* KIND!
BUTCH, YOU *KNOW* I HATE *BLUE BINGO POP!*
JUST *KIDDING*. IT'S REALLY *COMET COLA*.
LET'S TRY "*8 DAYS A WEEK.*"
-Sigh-
MAX, ALL WE'VE PLAYED SO FAR IS *MILLER, COOKE, BEATLES* AND *SQUEEZE!*
CAN'T WE TRY ANYTHING A BIT MORE *RADICAL?*
IT *IS* ZOT'S *BIRTHDAY*, RUDY! THOSE ARE HIS *FAVORITES*. LET'S *HUMOUR* HIM, O.K.?
WELL...O.K...BUT CAN WE AT LEAST HIT SOME OF THAT *INDUSTRIAL BE-BOP* AFTER HE GOES TO BED?
DEAL.
THIS WAY, HACKER!
ZACH'S UNCLE JUST PUT IN A NEW *POOL TABLE!*
YOU LOOK A LOT *HEALTHIER*, JACK!
YEAH, WELL, I CAME TO VISIT BACK IN '61 AND NEVER *LEFT!*
WOW! A *GUMBALL MACHINE!* OH, JENNY, I *LOVE IT!*
REALLY?
Ding! Dong
I'LL GET IT!
Ding! Ding! Dong! Dong
I'M COMING! I'M COMING!
OH, *NO*...
HELLO.

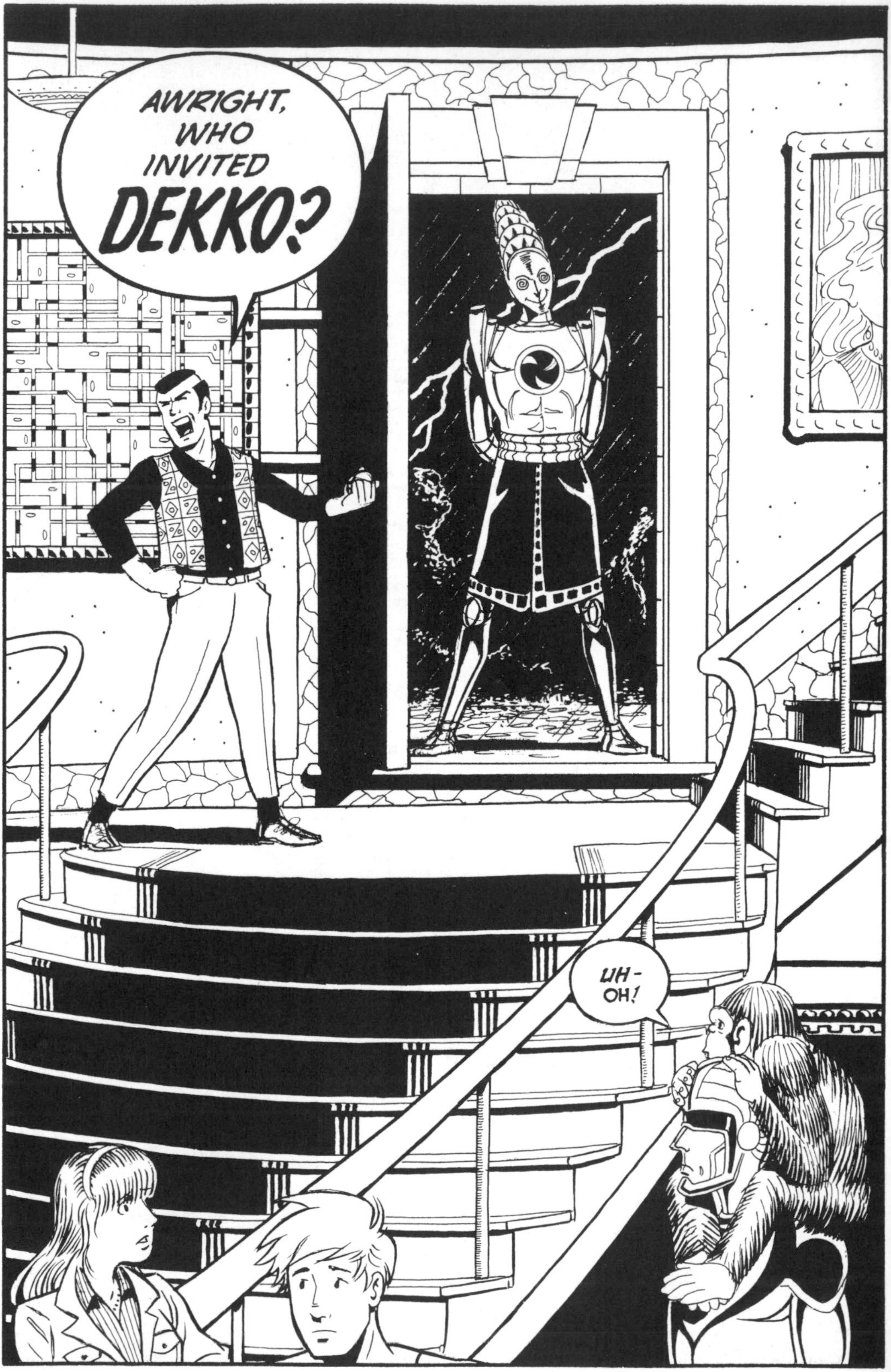
AWRIGHT, WHO INVITED DEKKO?
UH-OH!

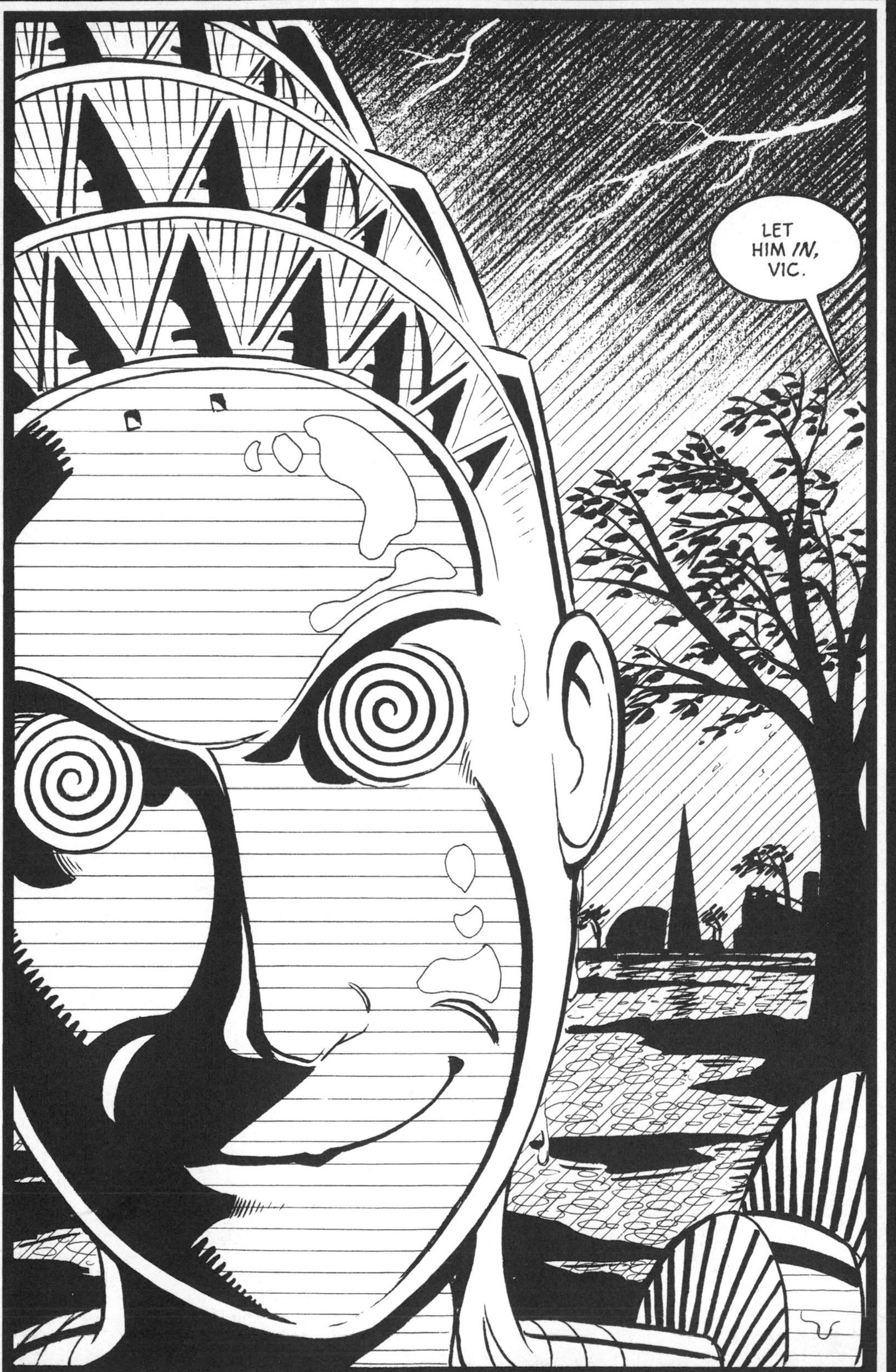
LET HIM *IN*, VIC.

THE EYES OF DEKKO PT. 2

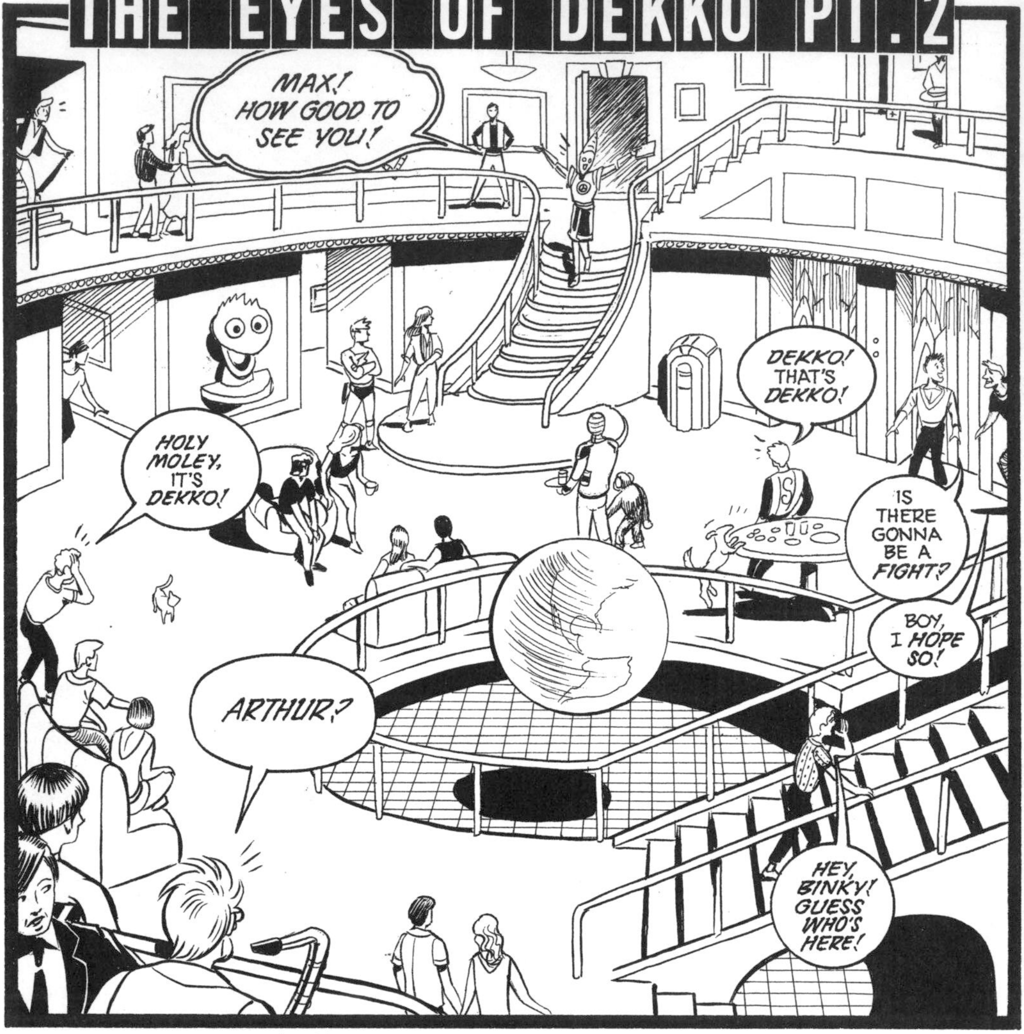
MAX! HOW GOOD TO SEE YOU!
DEKKO! THAT'S DEKKO!
HOLY MOLEY, IT'S DEKKO!
IS THERE GONNA BE A FIGHT?
BOY, I HOPE SO!
ARTHUR?
HEY, BINKY! GUESS WHO'S HERE!

BY SCOTT McCLOUD | LETTERING bob lappan | EDITING cat ⊕ yronwode

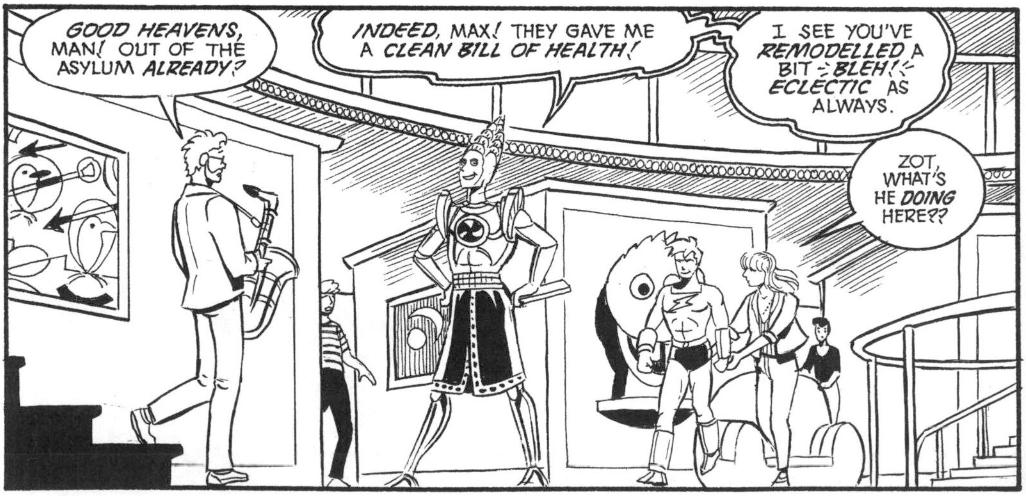
GOOD HEAVENS, MAN! OUT OF THE ASYLUM ALREADY?
INDEED, MAX! THEY GAVE ME A CLEAN BILL OF HEALTH!
I SEE YOU'VE REMODELLED A BIT -BLEH!- ECLECTIC AS ALWAYS.
ZOT, WHAT'S HE DOING HERE??

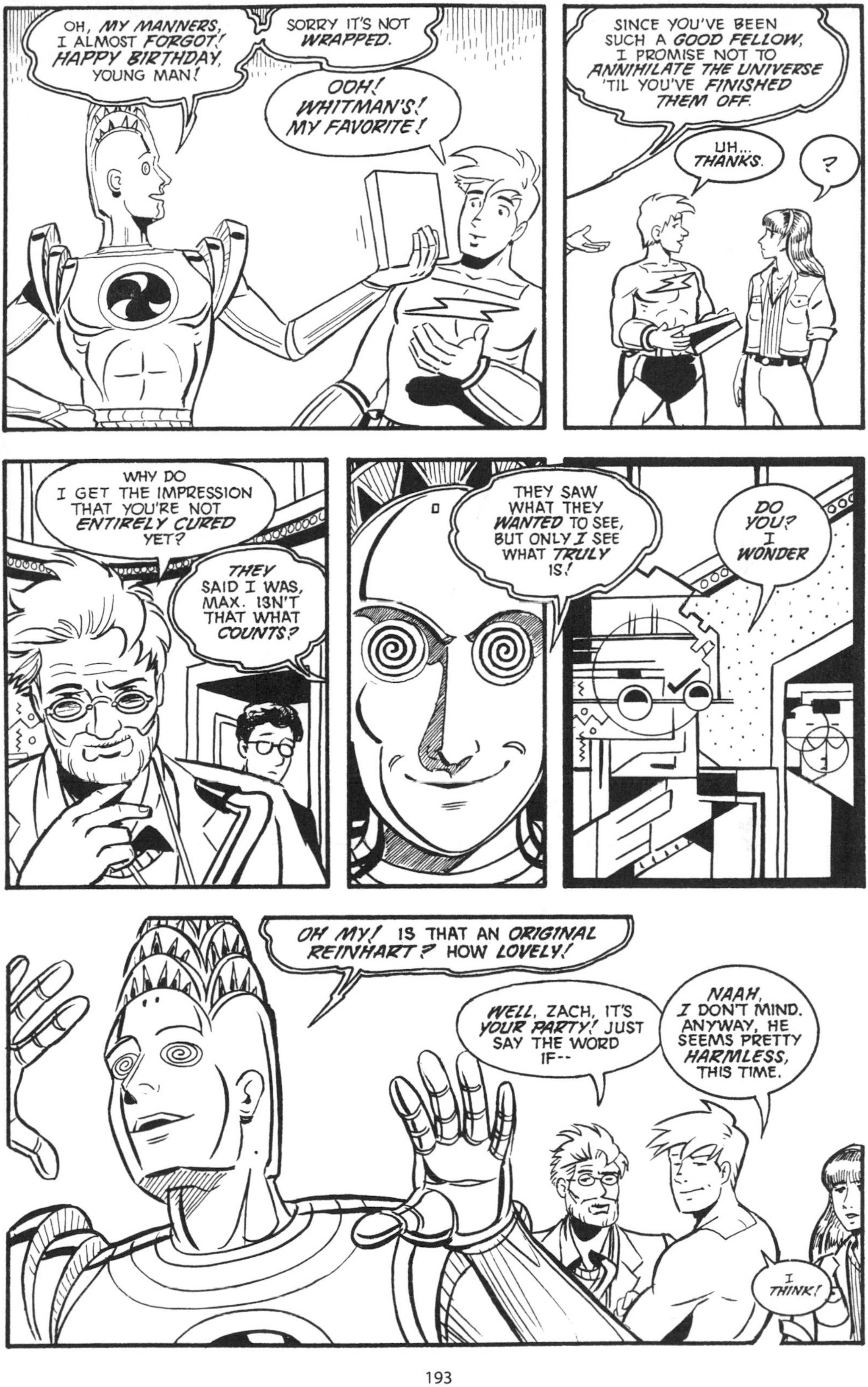
OH, MY MANNERS, I ALMOST FORGOT! HAPPY BIRTHDAY, YOUNG MAN!
SORRY IT'S NOT WRAPPED.
OOH! WHITMAN'S! MY FAVORITE!
SINCE YOU'VE BEEN SUCH A GOOD FELLOW, I PROMISE NOT TO ANNIHILATE THE UNIVERSE 'TIL YOU'VE FINISHED THEM OFF.
UH... THANKS.
?
WHY DO I GET THE IMPRESSION THAT YOU'RE NOT ENTIRELY CURED YET?
THEY SAID I WAS, MAX. ISN'T THAT WHAT COUNTS?
THEY SAW WHAT THEY WANTED TO SEE, BUT ONLY I SEE WHAT TRULY IS!
DO YOU? I WONDER
OH MY! IS THAT AN ORIGINAL REINHART? HOW LOVELY!
WELL, ZACH, IT'S YOUR PARTY! JUST SAY THE WORD IF--
NAAH, I DON'T MIND. ANYWAY, HE SEEMS PRETTY HARMLESS, THIS TIME.
I THINK!

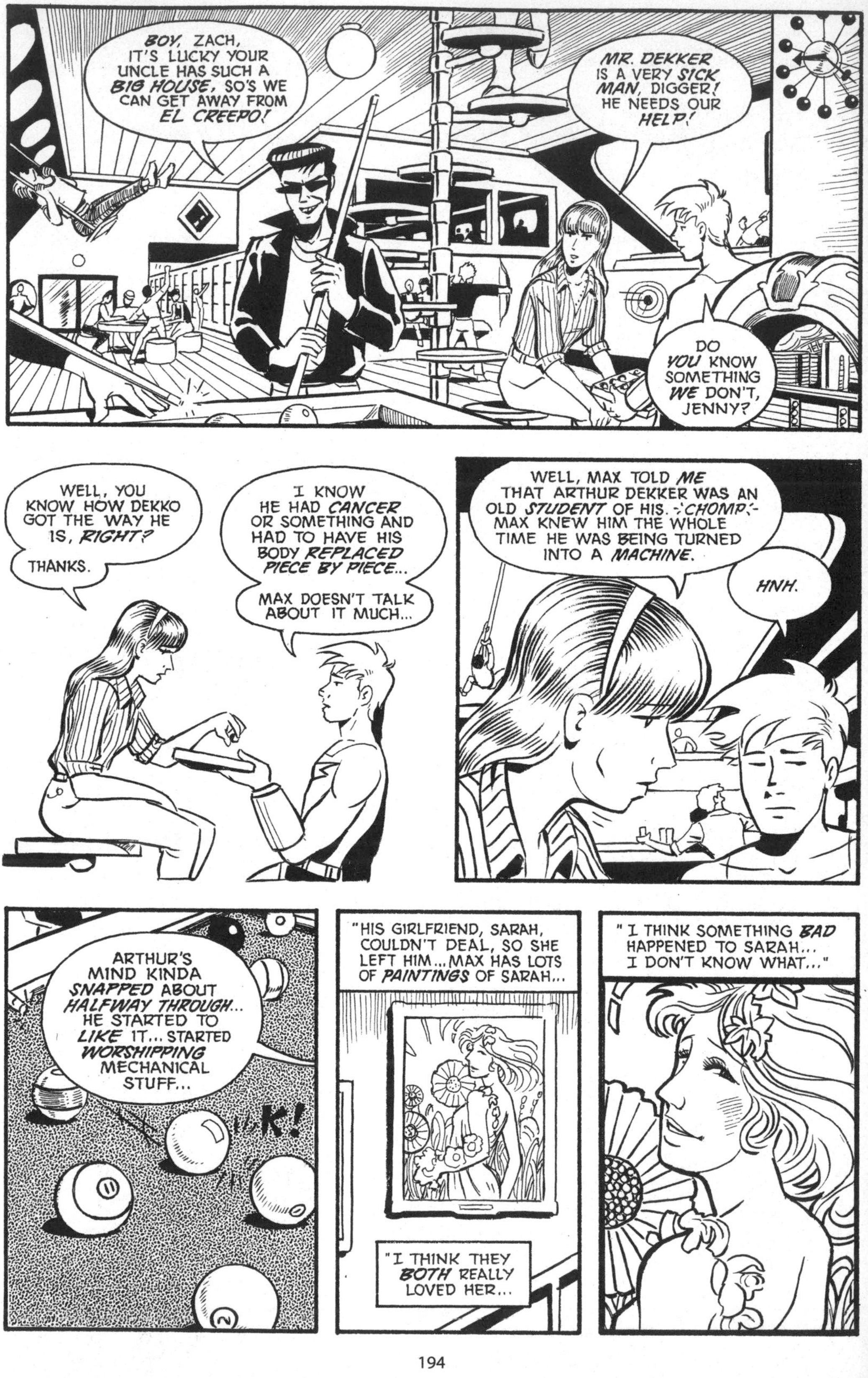
BOY, ZACH, IT'S LUCKY YOUR UNCLE HAS SUCH A BIG HOUSE, SO'S WE CAN GET AWAY FROM EL CREEPO!
MR. DEKKER IS A VERY SICK MAN, DIGGER! HE NEEDS OUR HELP!
DO YOU KNOW SOMETHING WE DON'T, JENNY?
WELL, YOU KNOW HOW DEKKO GOT THE WAY HE IS, RIGHT?
THANKS.
I KNOW HE HAD CANCER OR SOMETHING AND HAD TO HAVE HIS BODY REPLACED PIECE BY PIECE...
MAX DOESN'T TALK ABOUT IT MUCH...
WELL, MAX TOLD ME THAT ARTHUR DEKKER WAS AN OLD STUDENT OF HIS. -:CHOMP:- MAX KNEW HIM THE WHOLE TIME HE WAS BEING TURNED INTO A MACHINE.
HNH.
ARTHUR'S MIND KINDA SNAPPED ABOUT HALFWAY THROUGH... HE STARTED TO LIKE IT... STARTED WORSHIPPING MECHANICAL STUFF...
K!
"HIS GIRLFRIEND, SARAH, COULDN'T DEAL, SO SHE LEFT HIM... MAX HAS LOTS OF PAINTINGS OF SARAH...
"I THINK THEY BOTH REALLY LOVED HER...
"I THINK SOMETHING BAD HAPPENED TO SARAH... I DON'T KNOW WHAT..."

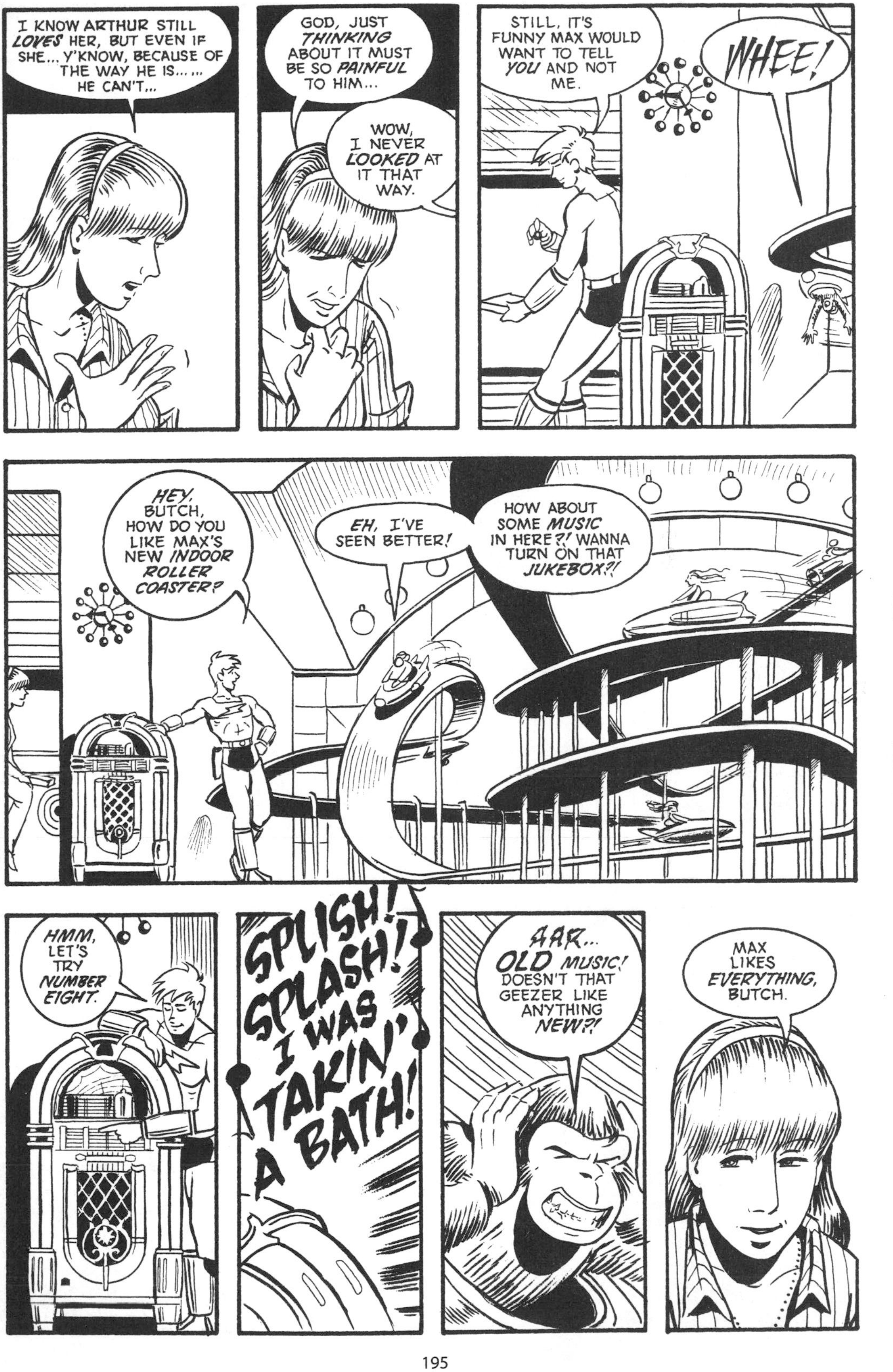

I KNOW ARTHUR STILL LOVES HER, BUT EVEN IF SHE... Y'KNOW, BECAUSE OF THE WAY HE IS..... HE CAN'T...
GOD, JUST THINKING ABOUT IT MUST BE SO PAINFUL TO HIM...
WOW, I NEVER LOOKED AT IT THAT WAY.
STILL, IT'S FUNNY MAX WOULD WANT TO TELL YOU AND NOT ME.
WHEE!
HEY, BUTCH, HOW DO YOU LIKE MAX'S NEW INDOOR ROLLER COASTER?
EH, I'VE SEEN BETTER!
HOW ABOUT SOME MUSIC IN HERE?! WANNA TURN ON THAT JUKEBOX?!
HMM, LET'S TRY NUMBER EIGHT.
SPLISH! SPLASH! I WAS TAKIN' A BATH!
AAR... OLD MUSIC! DOESN'T THAT GEEZER LIKE ANYTHING NEW?!
MAX LIKES EVERYTHING, BUTCH.

ARTHUR?

IN HERE, MAX!

I WAS JUST LOOKING AT SOMETHING... WONDERFUL!

OH, THOSE ARE JUST SOME PHOTOS I TOOK OF--

OF NATURALLY OCCURING PHENOMENA... I KNOW.

YOU HAVE SOME OF MY FAVORITES HERE!

"THE HYPNOTIC NAUTILUS.

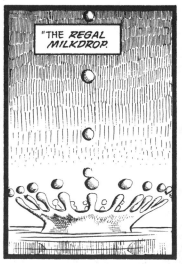

"THE REGAL MILKDROP.

"THE SUBLIME SNOW CRYSTAL."

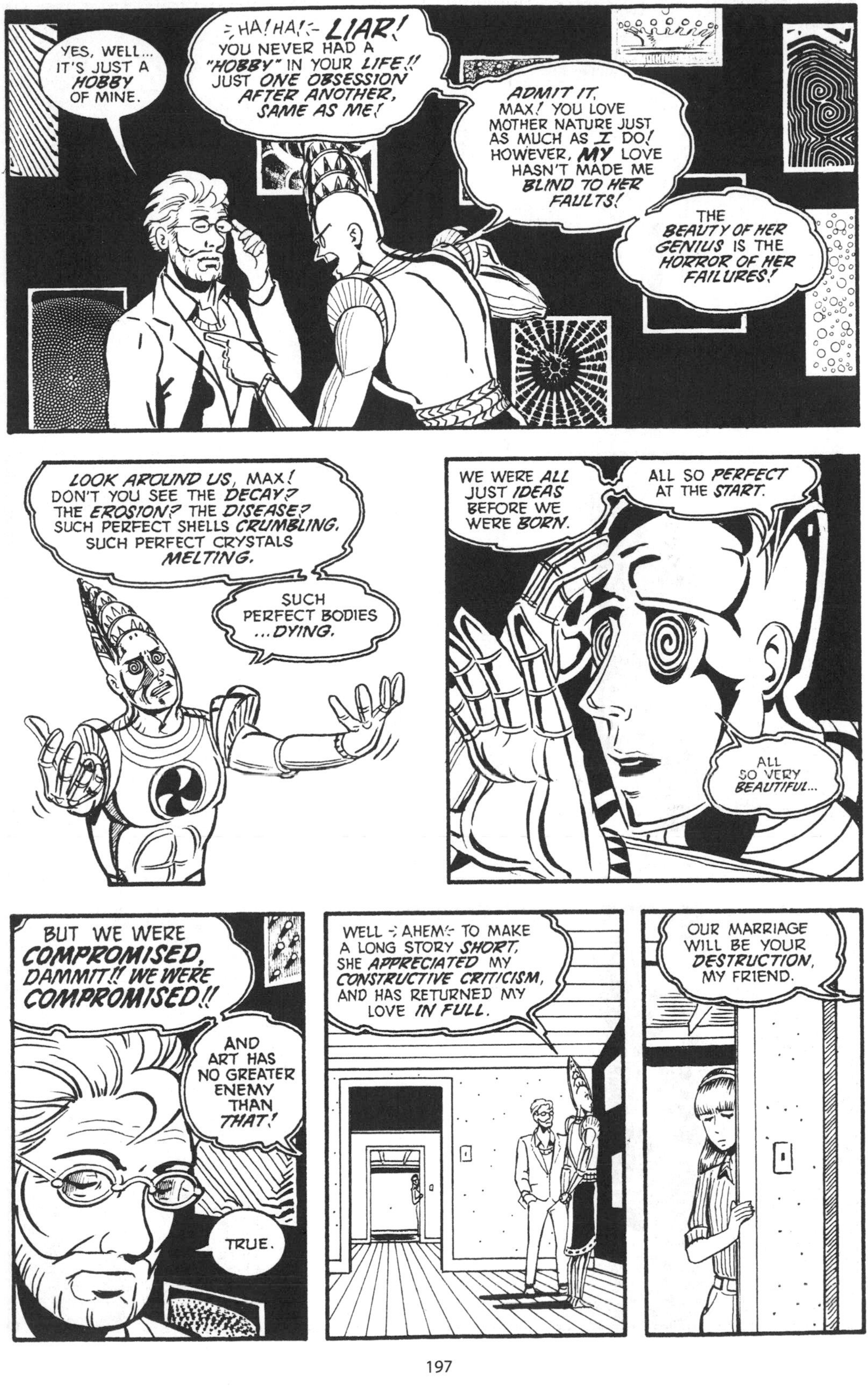
YES, WELL... IT'S JUST A HOBBY OF MINE.
-HA! HA!- LIAR! YOU NEVER HAD A "HOBBY" IN YOUR LIFE!! JUST ONE OBSESSION AFTER ANOTHER, SAME AS ME!
ADMIT IT, MAX! YOU LOVE MOTHER NATURE JUST AS MUCH AS I DO! HOWEVER, MY LOVE HASN'T MADE ME BLIND TO HER FAULTS!
THE BEAUTY OF HER GENIUS IS THE HORROR OF HER FAILURES!
LOOK AROUND US, MAX! DON'T YOU SEE THE DECAY? THE EROSION? THE DISEASE? SUCH PERFECT SHELLS CRUMBLING. SUCH PERFECT CRYSTALS MELTING.
SUCH PERFECT BODIES ...DYING.
WE WERE ALL JUST IDEAS BEFORE WE WERE BORN.
ALL SO PERFECT AT THE START.
ALL SO VERY BEAUTIFUL...
BUT WE WERE COMPROMISED, DAMMIT!! WE WERE COMPROMISED!!
AND ART HAS NO GREATER ENEMY THAN THAT!
TRUE.
WELL -AHEM- TO MAKE A LONG STORY SHORT, SHE APPRECIATED MY CONSTRUCTIVE CRITICISM, AND HAS RETURNED MY LOVE IN FULL.
OUR MARRIAGE WILL BE YOUR DESTRUCTION, MY FRIEND.

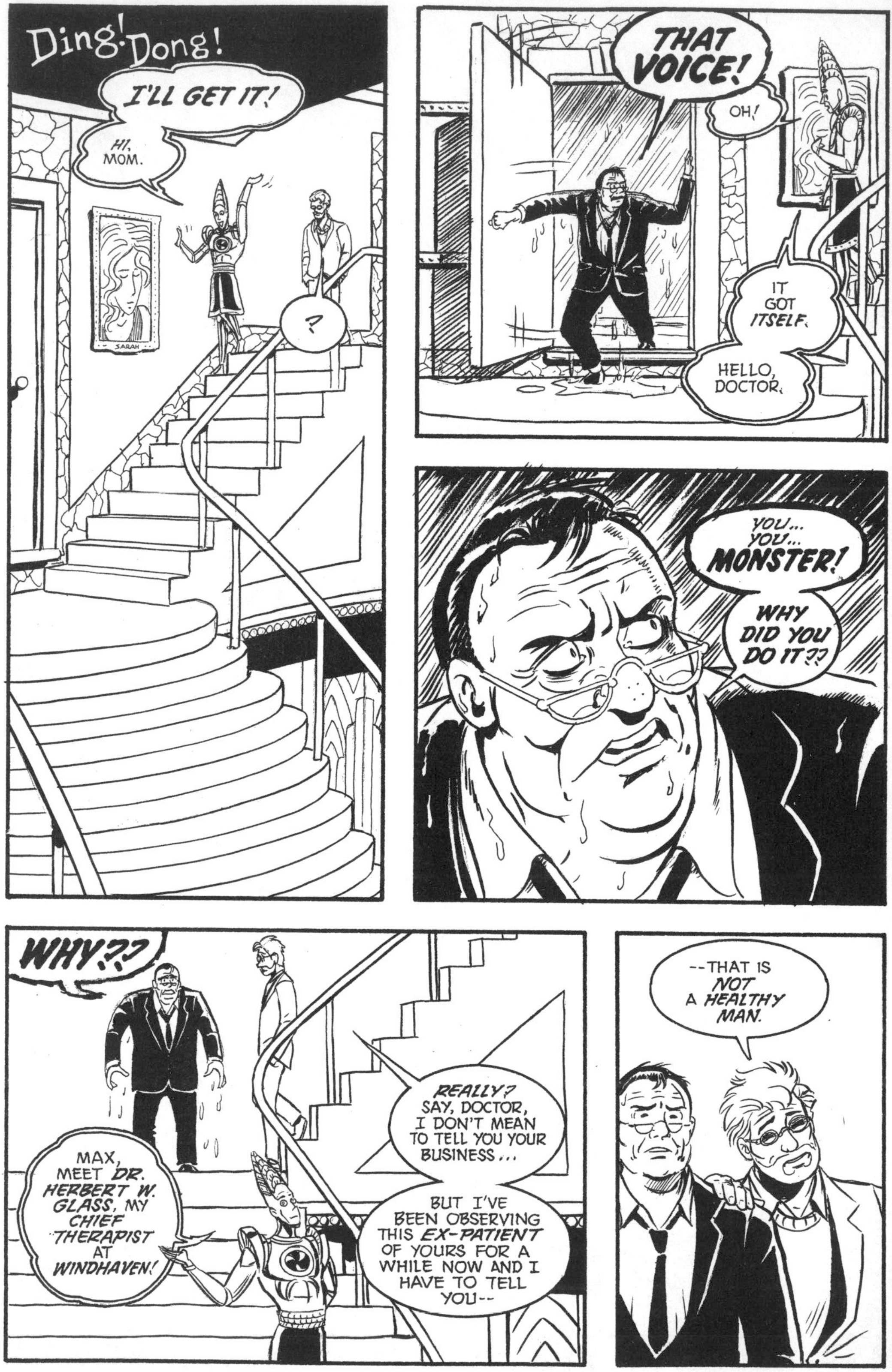

Ding! Dong!
I'LL GET IT!
HI, MOM.
?
THAT VOICE!
OH!
IT GOT ITSELF.
HELLO, DOCTOR.
YOU... YOU... MONSTER!
WHY DID YOU DO IT??
WHY??
MAX, MEET DR. HERBERT W. GLASS, MY CHIEF THERAPIST AT WINDHAVEN!
REALLY? SAY, DOCTOR, I DON'T MEAN TO TELL YOU YOUR BUSINESS...
BUT I'VE BEEN OBSERVING THIS EX-PATIENT OF YOURS FOR A WHILE NOW AND I HAVE TO TELL YOU--
--THAT IS NOT A HEALTHY MAN.

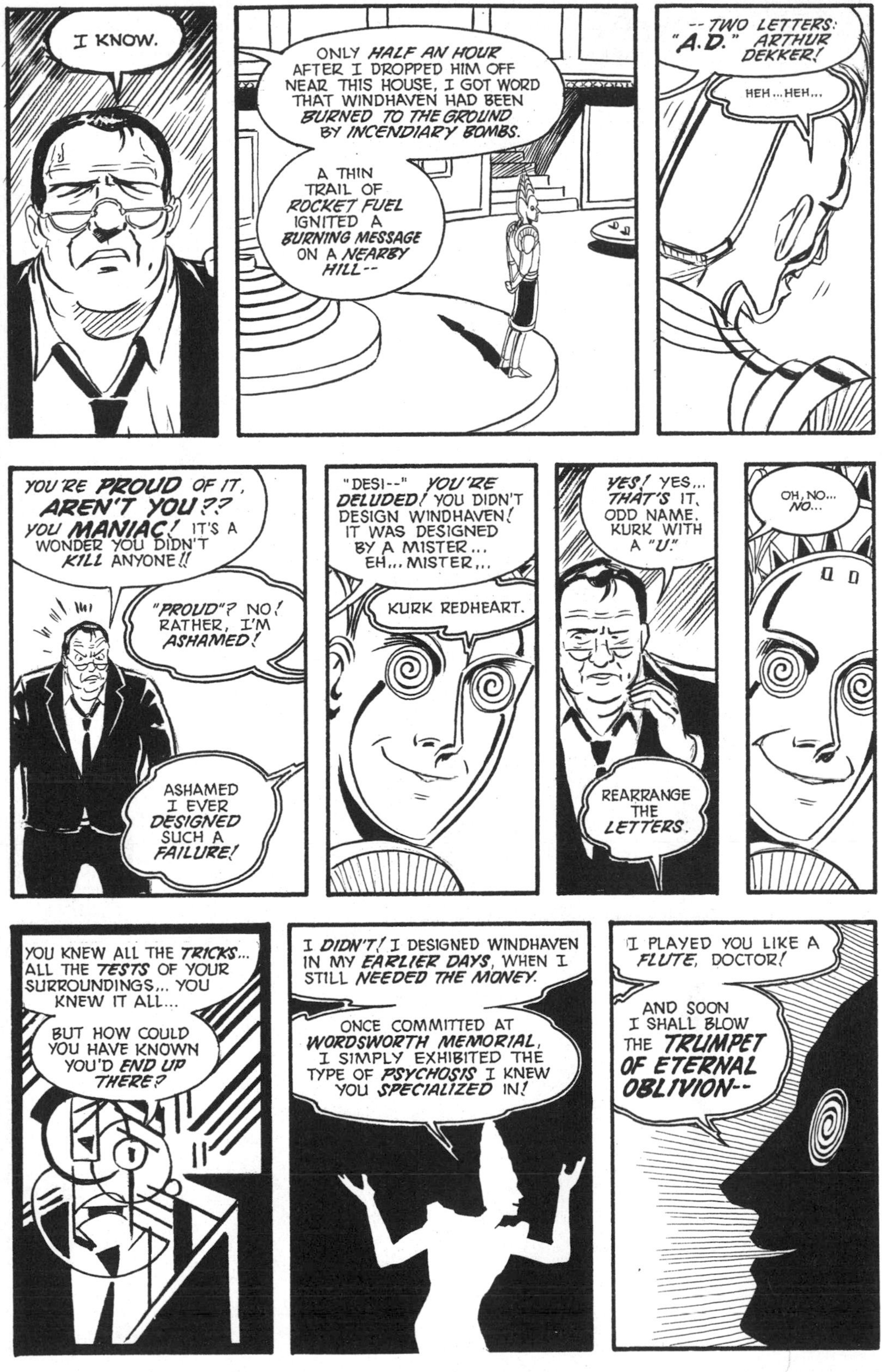
I KNOW.
ONLY HALF AN HOUR AFTER I DROPPED HIM OFF NEAR THIS HOUSE, I GOT WORD THAT WINDHAVEN HAD BEEN BURNED TO THE GROUND BY INCENDIARY BOMBS.
A THIN TRAIL OF ROCKET FUEL IGNITED A BURNING MESSAGE ON A NEARBY HILL--
--TWO LETTERS: "A.D." ARTHUR DEKKER!
HEH...HEH...
YOU'RE PROUD OF IT, AREN'T YOU?? YOU MANIAC! IT'S A WONDER YOU DIDN'T KILL ANYONE!!
"PROUD"? NO! RATHER, I'M ASHAMED!
ASHAMED I EVER DESIGNED SUCH A FAILURE!
"DESI--" YOU'RE DELUDED! YOU DIDN'T DESIGN WINDHAVEN! IT WAS DESIGNED BY A MISTER... EH... MISTER...
KURK REDHEART.
YES! YES... THAT'S IT. ODD NAME. KURK WITH A "U."
REARRANGE THE LETTERS.
OH, NO... NO...
YOU KNEW ALL THE TRICKS... ALL THE TESTS OF YOUR SURROUNDINGS... YOU KNEW IT ALL...
BUT HOW COULD YOU HAVE KNOWN YOU'D END UP THERE?
I DIDN'T! I DESIGNED WINDHAVEN IN MY EARLIER DAYS, WHEN I STILL NEEDED THE MONEY.
ONCE COMMITTED AT WORDSWORTH MEMORIAL, I SIMPLY EXHIBITED THE TYPE OF PSYCHOSIS I KNEW YOU SPECIALIZED IN!
I PLAYED YOU LIKE A FLUTE, DOCTOR!
AND SOON I SHALL BLOW THE TRUMPET OF ETERNAL OBLIVION--

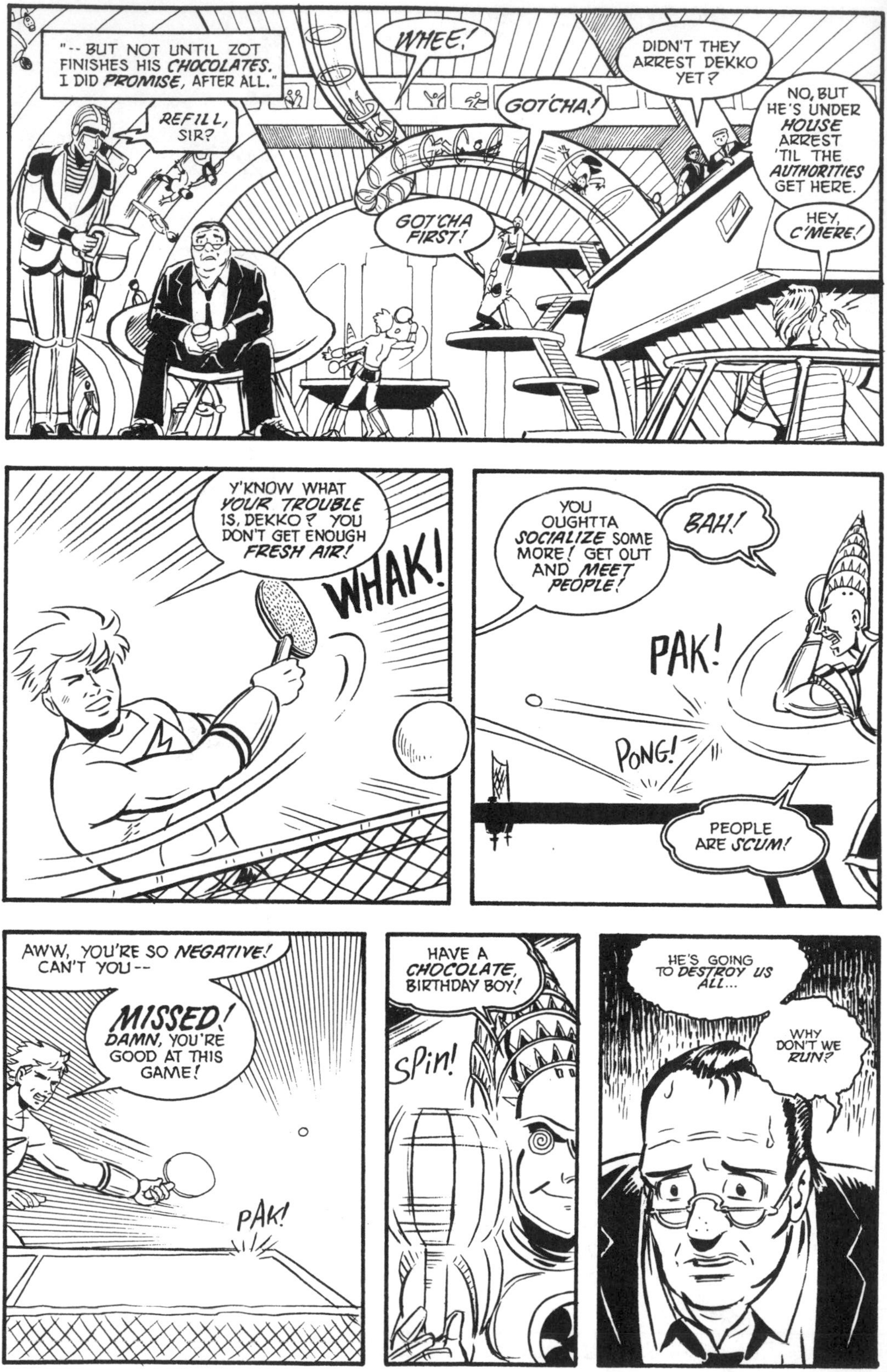
"-- BUT NOT UNTIL ZOT FINISHES HIS CHOCOLATES. I DID PROMISE, AFTER ALL."
WHEE!
DIDN'T THEY ARREST DEKKO YET?
REFILL, SIR?
GOT'CHA!
NO, BUT HE'S UNDER HOUSE ARREST 'TIL THE AUTHORITIES GET HERE.
GOT'CHA FIRST!
HEY, C'MERE!
Y'KNOW WHAT YOUR TROUBLE IS, DEKKO? YOU DON'T GET ENOUGH FRESH AIR!
WHAK!
YOU OUGHTTA SOCIALIZE SOME MORE! GET OUT AND MEET PEOPLE!
BAH!
PAK!
PONG!
PEOPLE ARE SCUM!
AWW, YOU'RE SO NEGATIVE! CAN'T YOU--
MISSED! DAMN, YOU'RE GOOD AT THIS GAME!
PAK!
HAVE A CHOCOLATE, BIRTHDAY BOY!
SPIN!
HE'S GOING TO DESTROY US ALL...
WHY DON'T WE RUN?

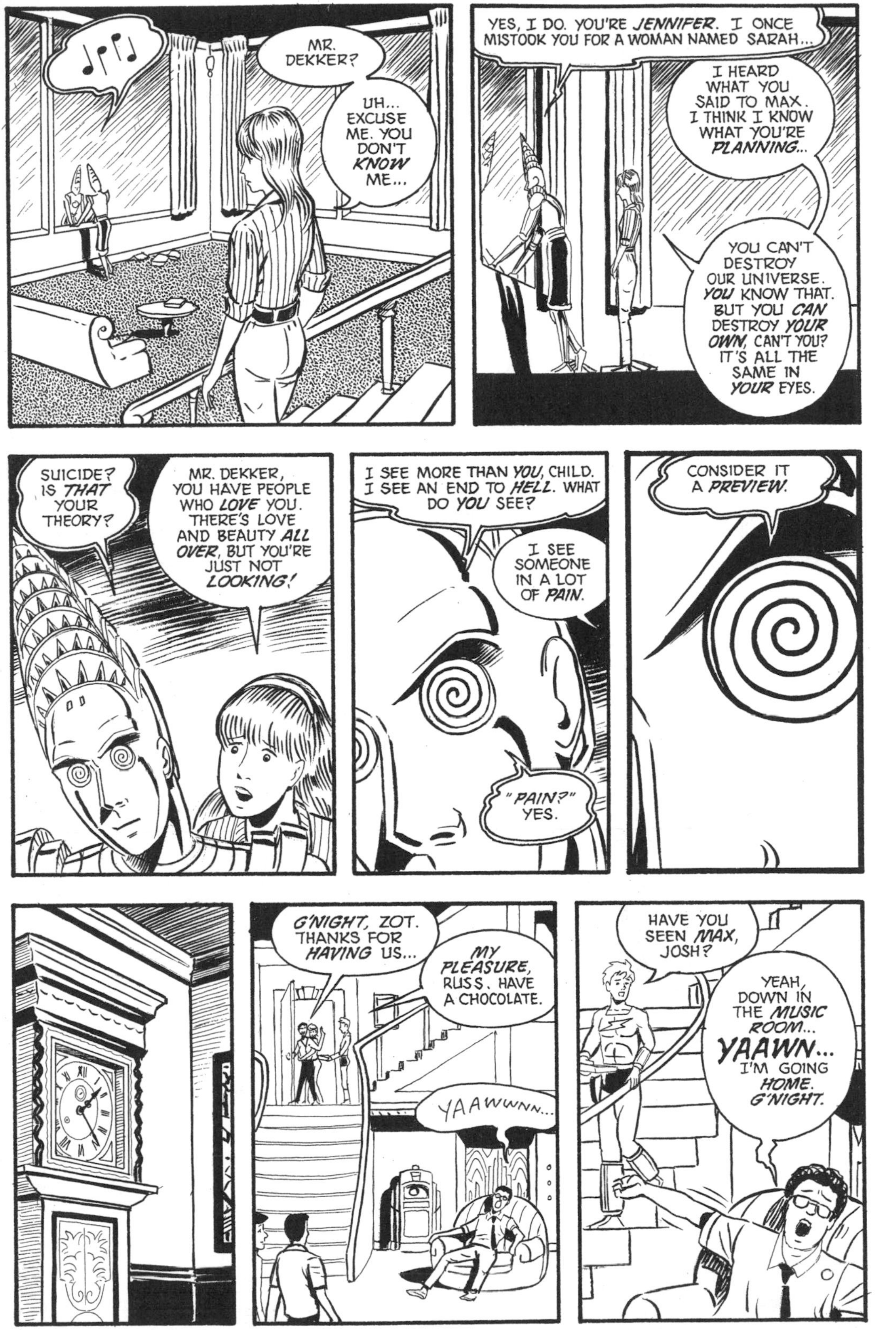
MR. DEKKER?
UH... EXCUSE ME. YOU DON'T *KNOW* ME...
YES, I DO. YOU'RE *JENNIFER*. I ONCE MISTOOK YOU FOR A WOMAN NAMED SARAH...
I HEARD WHAT YOU SAID TO MAX. I THINK I KNOW WHAT YOU'RE *PLANNING*...
YOU CAN'T DESTROY OUR UNIVERSE. *YOU* KNOW THAT. BUT YOU *CAN* DESTROY *YOUR OWN*, CAN'T YOU? IT'S ALL THE SAME IN *YOUR* EYES.
SUICIDE? IS *THAT* YOUR THEORY?
MR. DEKKER, YOU HAVE PEOPLE WHO *LOVE* YOU. THERE'S LOVE AND BEAUTY *ALL OVER*, BUT YOU'RE JUST NOT *LOOKING*!
I SEE MORE THAN *YOU*, CHILD. I SEE AN END TO *HELL*. WHAT DO *YOU* SEE?
I SEE SOMEONE IN A LOT OF *PAIN*.
"*PAIN?*" YES.
CONSIDER IT A *PREVIEW*.
G'NIGHT, ZOT. THANKS FOR *HAVING* US...
MY PLEASURE, RUSS. HAVE A CHOCOLATE.
YAAWWNN...
HAVE YOU SEEN *MAX*, JOSH?
YEAH, DOWN IN THE *MUSIC ROOM*... **YAAWN...** I'M GOING *HOME*. *G'NIGHT*.

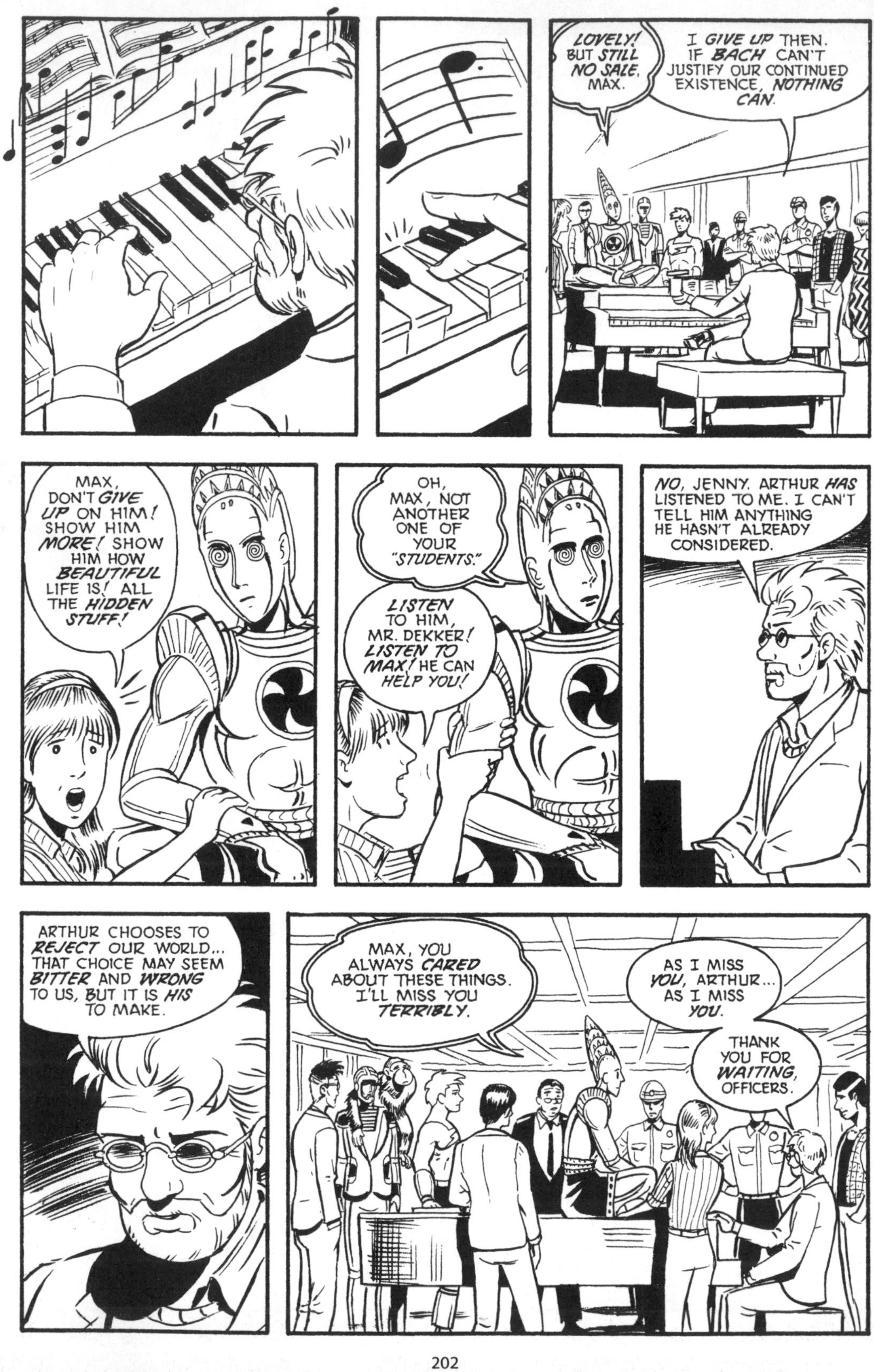
LOVELY! BUT STILL NO SALE, MAX.
I GIVE UP THEN. IF BACH CAN'T JUSTIFY OUR CONTINUED EXISTENCE, NOTHING CAN.
MAX, DON'T GIVE UP ON HIM! SHOW HIM MORE! SHOW HIM HOW BEAUTIFUL LIFE IS! ALL THE HIDDEN STUFF!
OH, MAX, NOT ANOTHER ONE OF YOUR "STUDENTS."
LISTEN TO HIM, MR. DEKKER! LISTEN TO MAX! HE CAN HELP YOU!
NO, JENNY. ARTHUR HAS LISTENED TO ME. I CAN'T TELL HIM ANYTHING HE HASN'T ALREADY CONSIDERED.
ARTHUR CHOOSES TO REJECT OUR WORLD... THAT CHOICE MAY SEEM BITTER AND WRONG TO US, BUT IT IS HIS TO MAKE.
MAX, YOU ALWAYS CARED ABOUT THESE THINGS. I'LL MISS YOU TERRIBLY.
AS I MISS YOU, ARTHUR... AS I MISS YOU.
THANK YOU FOR WAITING, OFFICERS.

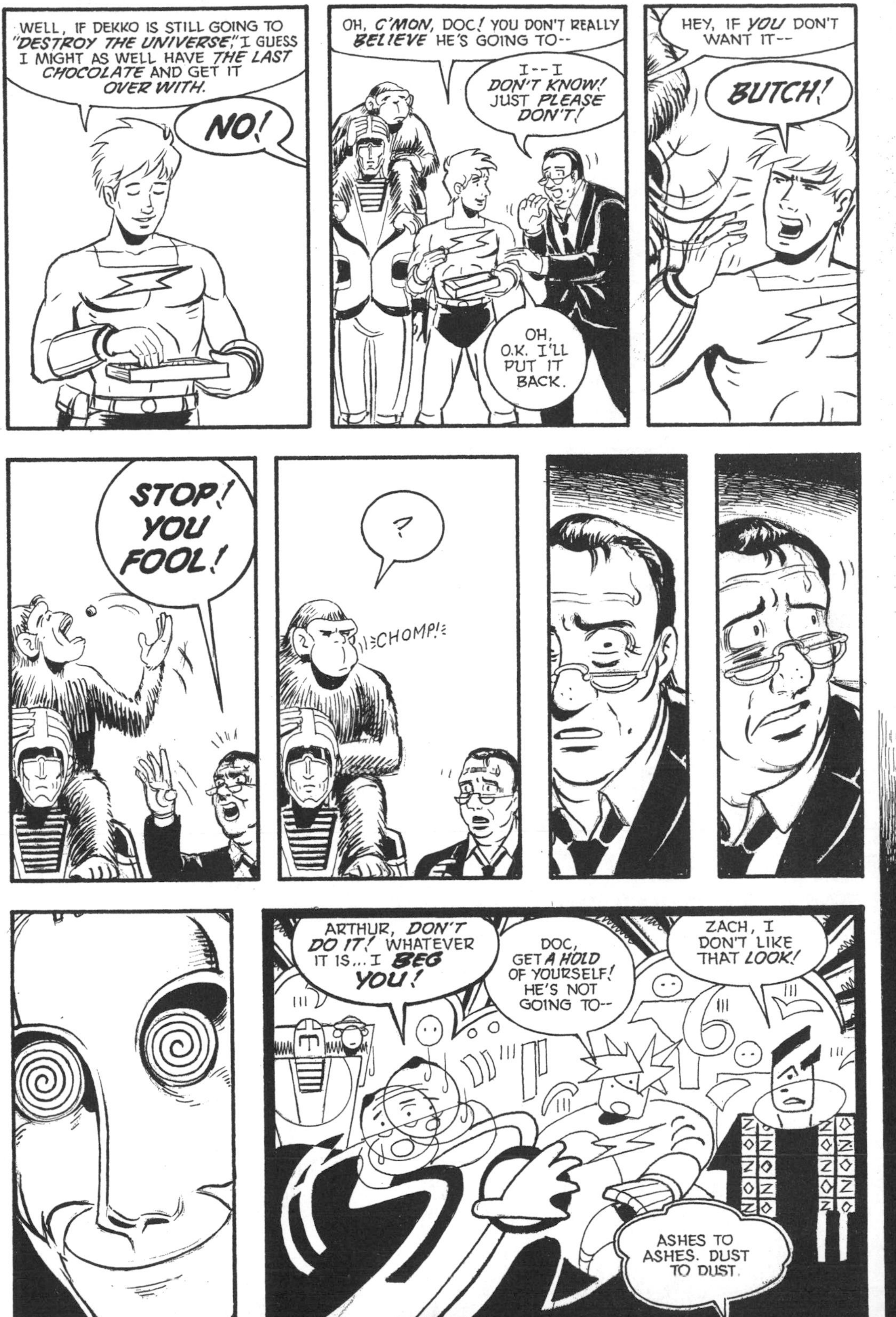

WELL, IF DEKKO IS STILL GOING TO "DESTROY THE UNIVERSE," I GUESS I MIGHT AS WELL HAVE THE LAST CHOCOLATE AND GET IT OVER WITH.
NO!
OH, C'MON, DOC! YOU DON'T REALLY BELIEVE HE'S GOING TO--
I--I DON'T KNOW! JUST PLEASE DON'T!
OH, O.K. I'LL PUT IT BACK.
HEY, IF YOU DON'T WANT IT--
BUTCH!
STOP! YOU FOOL!
?
CHOMP!
ARTHUR, DON'T DO IT! WHATEVER IT IS... I BEG YOU!
DOC, GET A HOLD OF YOURSELF! HE'S NOT GOING TO--
ZACH, I DON'T LIKE THAT LOOK!
ASHES TO ASHES. DUST TO DUST.

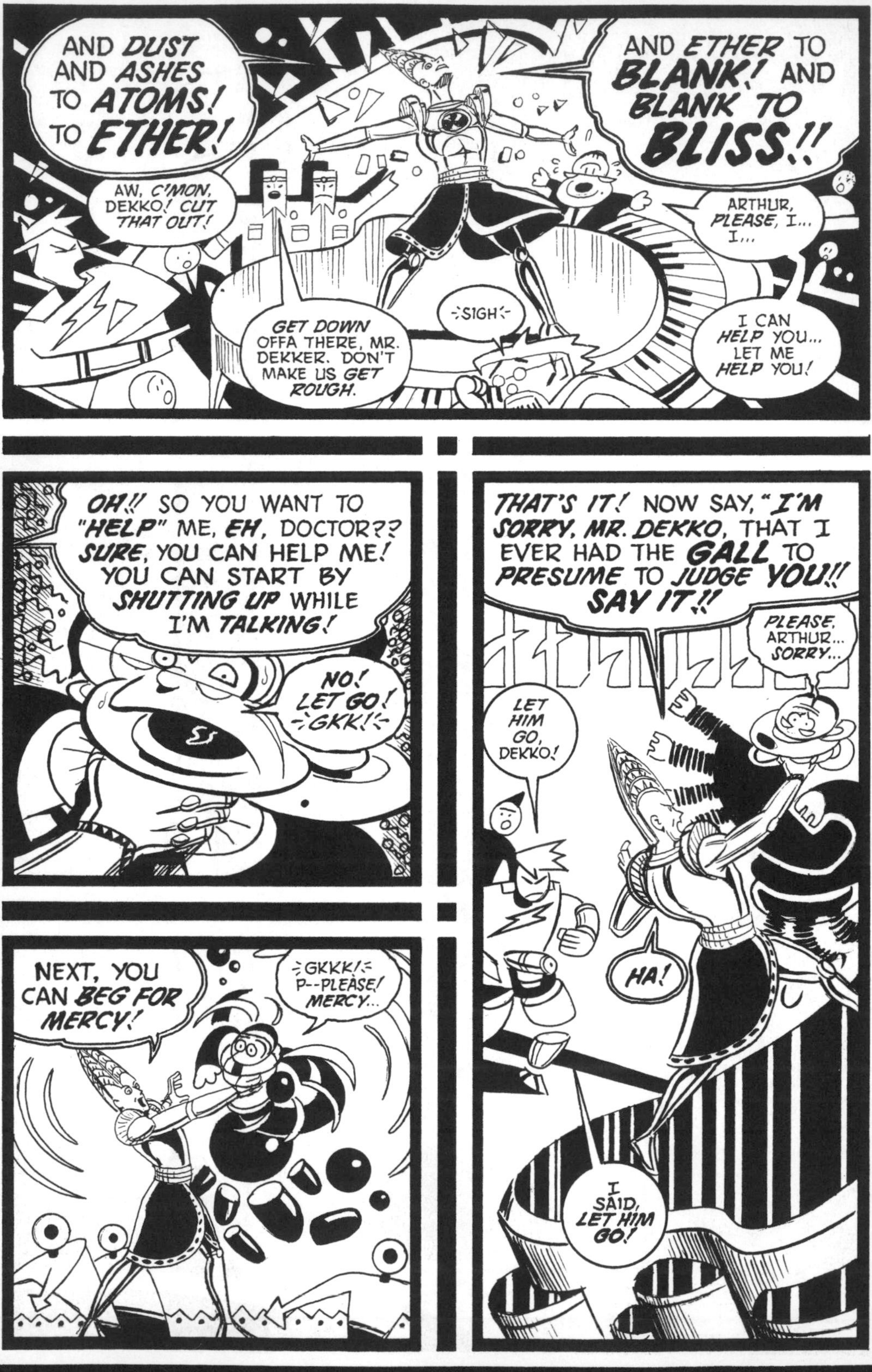
AND DUST AND ASHES TO ATOMS! TO ETHER!
AND ETHER TO BLANK! AND BLANK TO BLISS!!
AW, C'MON, DEKKO! CUT THAT OUT!
ARTHUR, PLEASE, I... I...
GET DOWN OFFA THERE, MR. DEKKER. DON'T MAKE US GET ROUGH.
SIGH
I CAN HELP YOU... LET ME HELP YOU!
OH!! SO YOU WANT TO "HELP" ME, EH, DOCTOR?? SURE, YOU CAN HELP ME! YOU CAN START BY SHUTTING UP WHILE I'M TALKING!
NO! LET GO! GKK!
NEXT, YOU CAN BEG FOR MERCY!
GKKK! P--PLEASE! MERCY...
THAT'S IT! NOW SAY, "I'M SORRY, MR. DEKKO, THAT I EVER HAD THE GALL TO PRESUME TO JUDGE YOU!! SAY IT!!
PLEASE, ARTHUR... SORRY...
LET HIM GO, DEKKO!
HA!
I SAID, LET HIM GO!

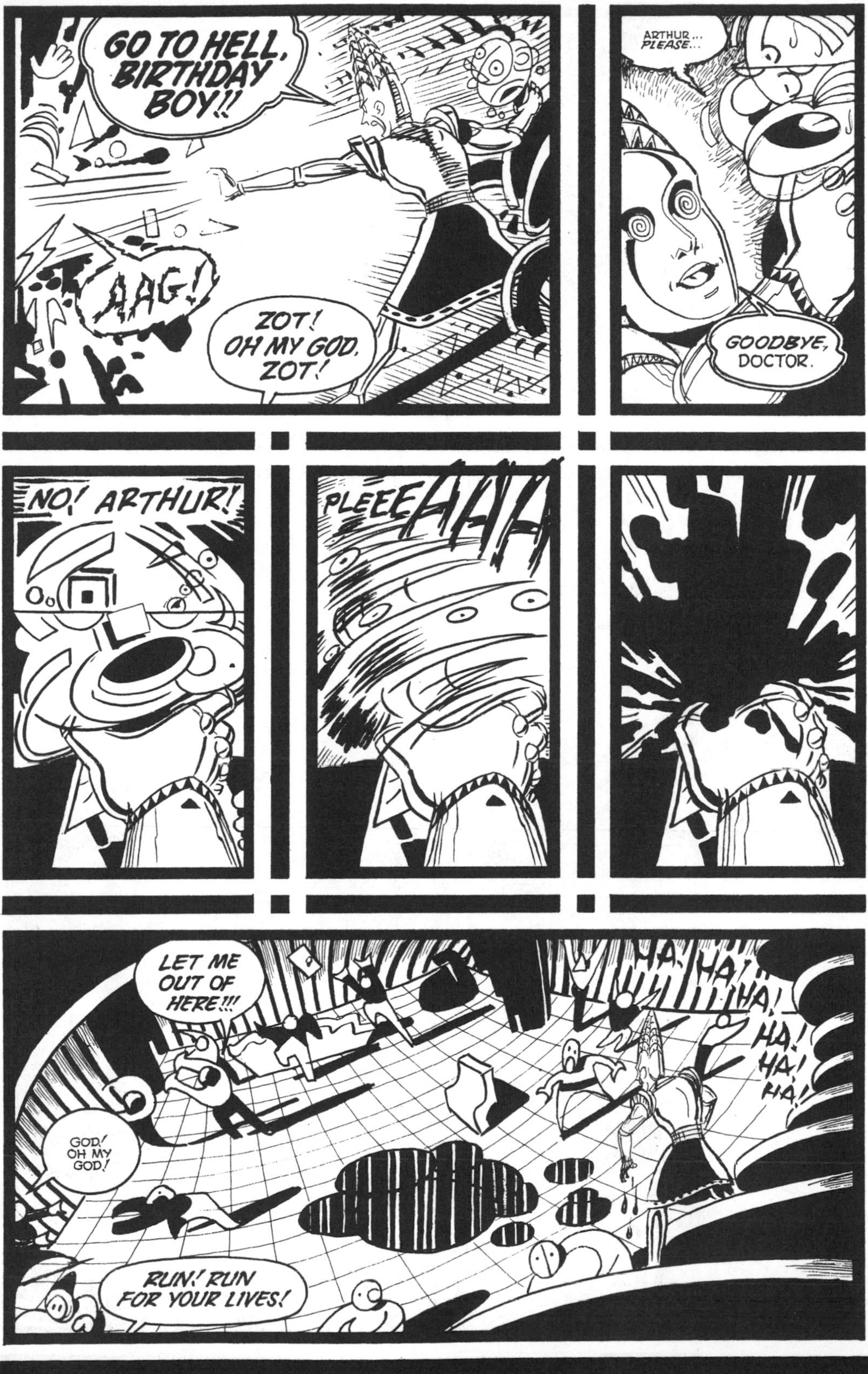
GO TO HELL, BIRTHDAY BOY!!
AAG!
ZOT! OH MY GOD, ZOT!
ARTHUR... PLEASE...
GOODBYE, DOCTOR.
NO! ARTHUR!
PLEEEAAA
LET ME OUT OF HERE!!!
HA HA HA! HA! HA! HA!
GOD! OH MY GOD!
RUN! RUN FOR YOUR LIVES!

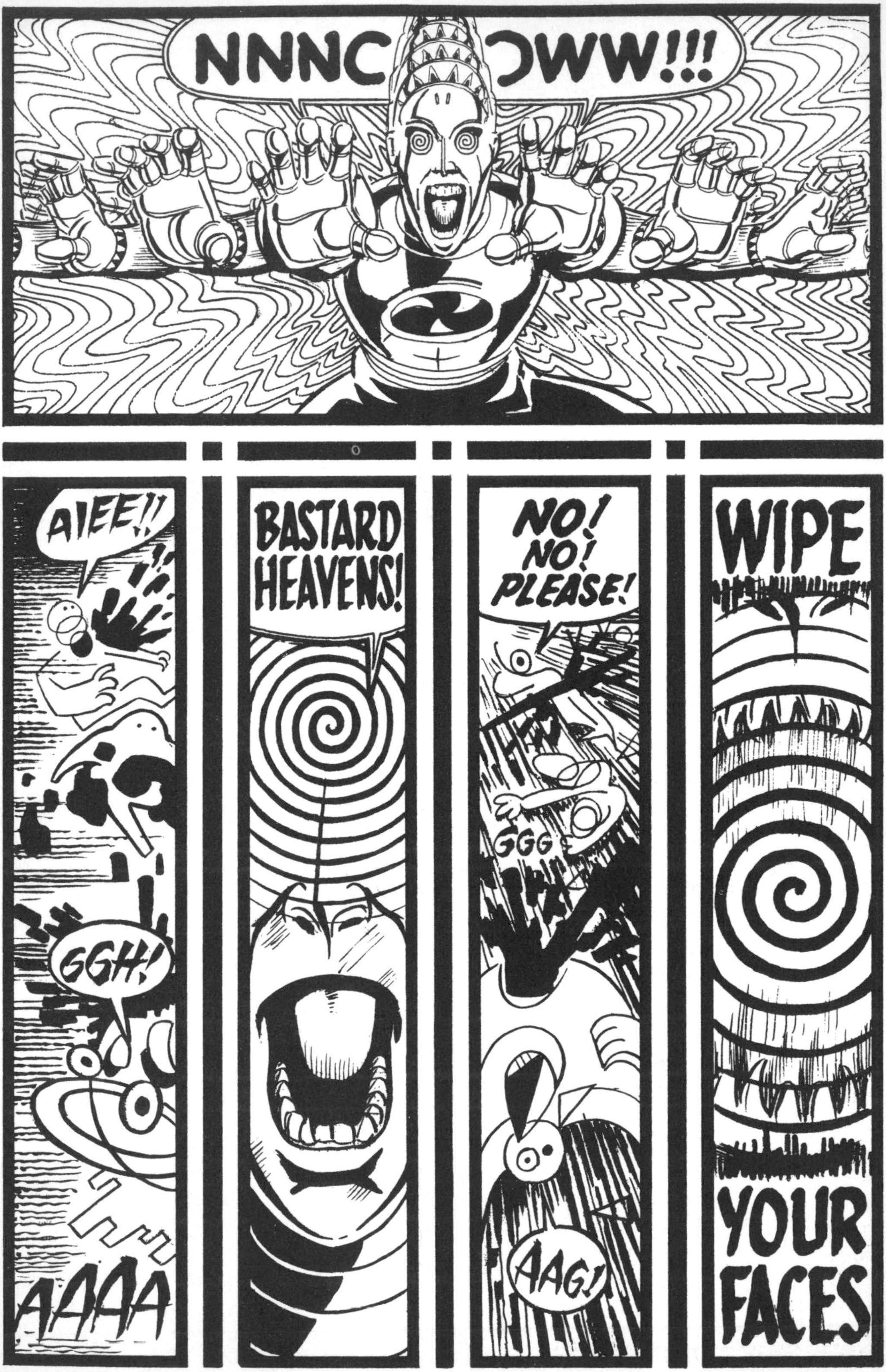
NNNC OWW!!!
AIEE!!
GGH!
AAAA
BASTARD HEAVENS!
NO! NO! PLEASE!
GGG
AAG!
WIPE
YOUR FACES

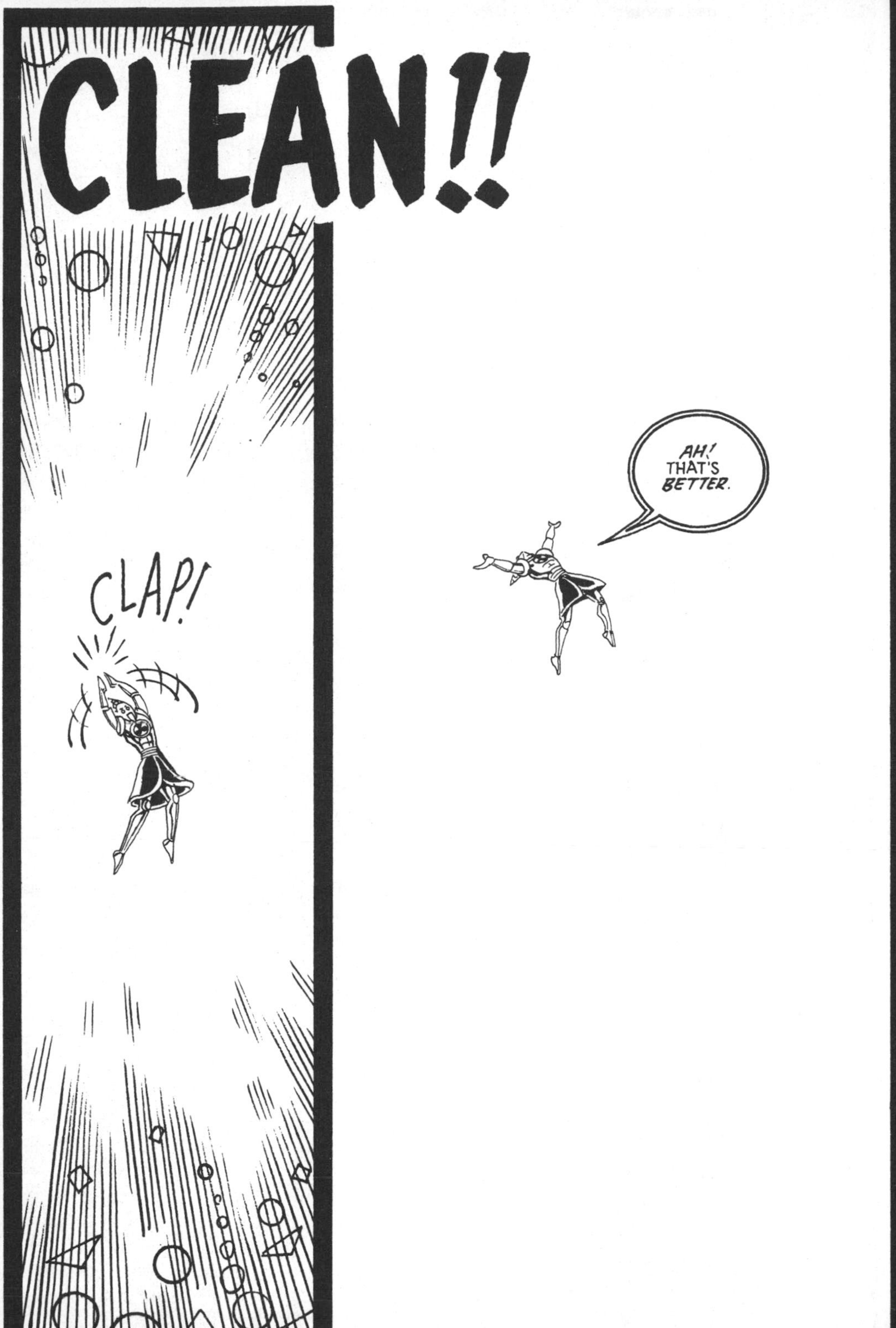
CLEAN!!
CLAP!
AH! THAT'S BETTER.

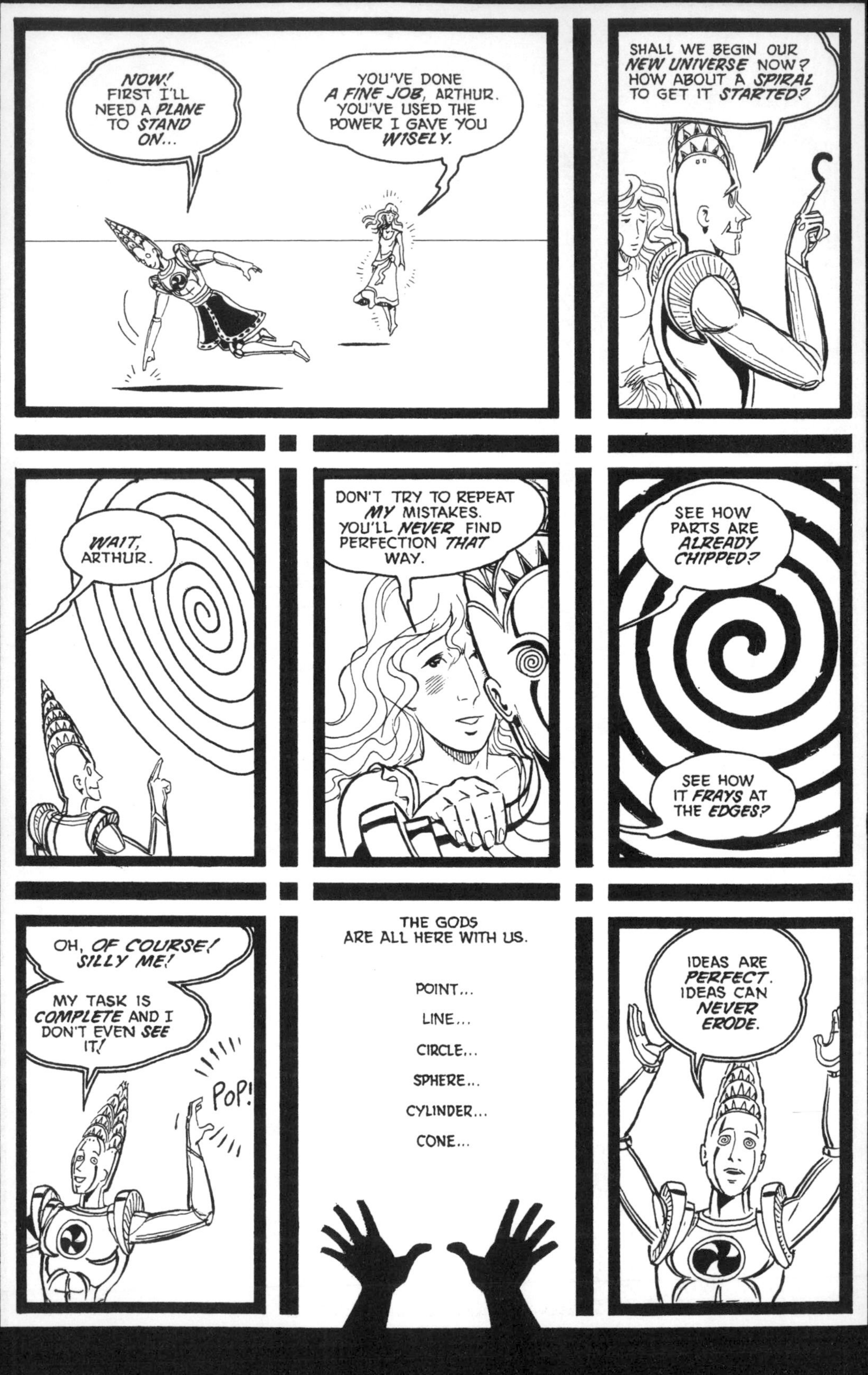
NOW! FIRST I'LL NEED A PLANE TO STAND ON...
YOU'VE DONE A FINE JOB, ARTHUR. YOU'VE USED THE POWER I GAVE YOU WISELY.
SHALL WE BEGIN OUR NEW UNIVERSE NOW? HOW ABOUT A SPIRAL TO GET IT STARTED?
WAIT, ARTHUR.
DON'T TRY TO REPEAT MY MISTAKES. YOU'LL NEVER FIND PERFECTION THAT WAY.
SEE HOW PARTS ARE ALREADY CHIPPED?
SEE HOW IT FRAYS AT THE EDGES?
OH, OF COURSE! SILLY ME!
MY TASK IS COMPLETE AND I DON'T EVEN SEE IT!
POP!
THE GODS ARE ALL HERE WITH US.
POINT...
LINE...
CIRCLE...
SPHERE...
CYLINDER...
CONE...
IDEAS ARE PERFECT. IDEAS CAN NEVER ERODE.

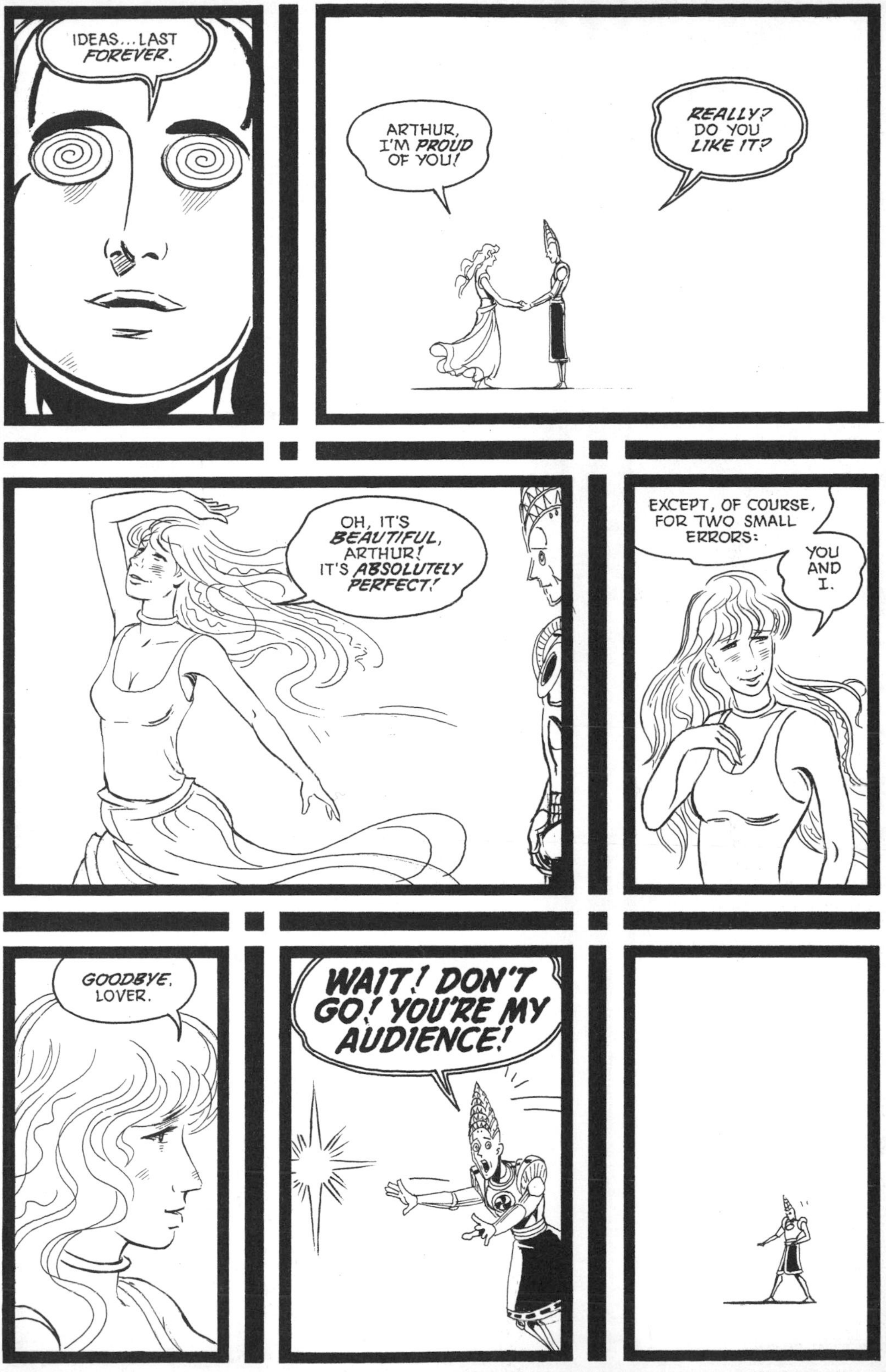
IDEAS... LAST *FOREVER*.
ARTHUR, I'M *PROUD* OF YOU!
REALLY? DO YOU *LIKE IT?*
OH, IT'S *BEAUTIFUL*, ARTHUR! IT'S *ABSOLUTELY PERFECT!*
EXCEPT, OF COURSE, FOR TWO SMALL ERRORS:
YOU AND I.
GOODBYE, LOVER.
WAIT! DON'T GO! YOU'RE MY AUDIENCE!

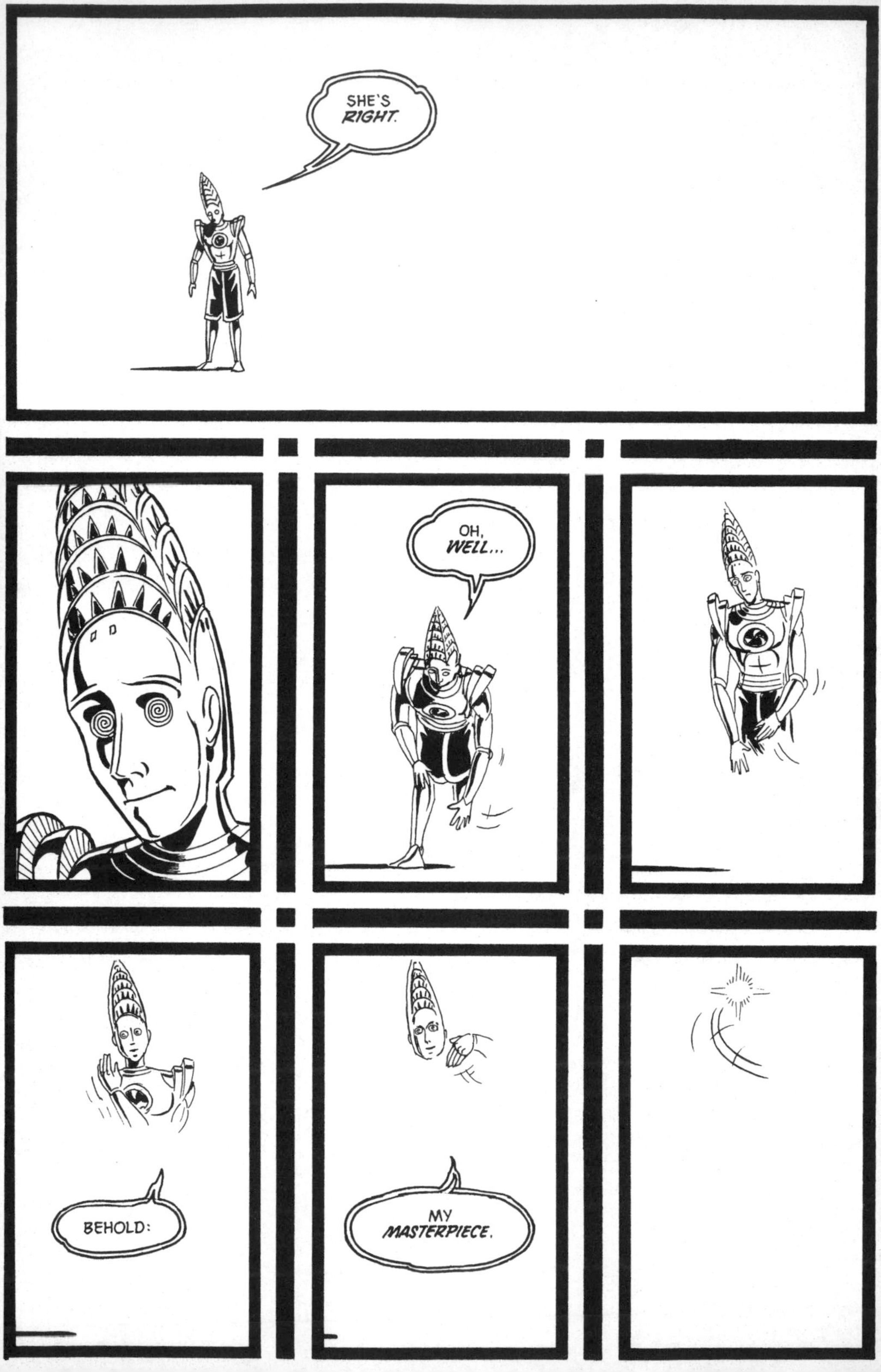
SHE'S *RIGHT.*
OH, *WELL...*
BEHOLD:
MY *MASTERPIECE.*

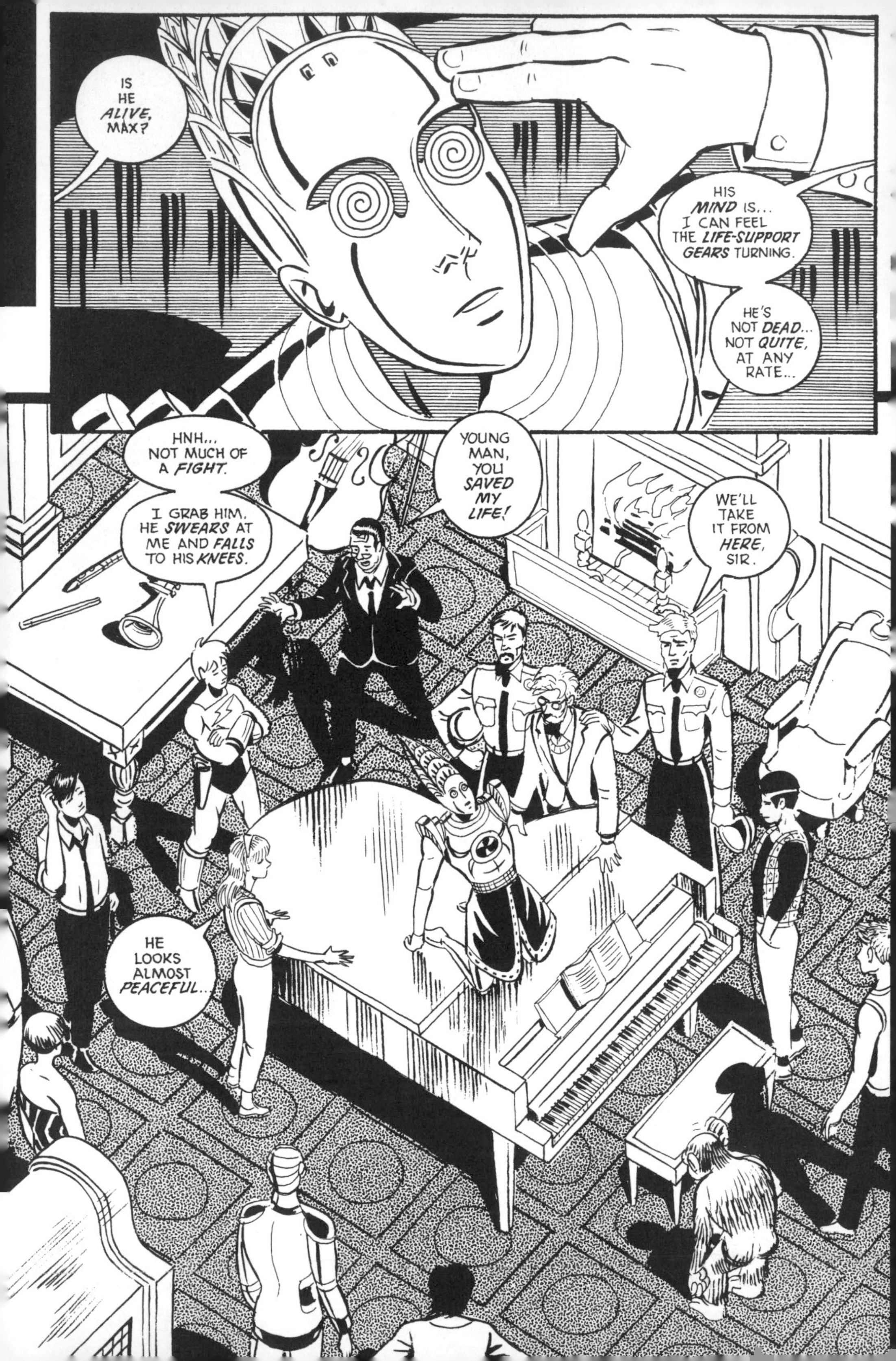
IS HE *ALIVE,* MAX?
HIS *MIND* IS... I CAN FEEL THE *LIFE-SUPPORT GEARS* TURNING.
HE'S NOT *DEAD*... NOT *QUITE,* AT ANY RATE...
HNH... NOT MUCH OF A *FIGHT*.
I GRAB HIM. HE *SWEARS* AT ME AND *FALLS* TO HIS *KNEES*.
YOUNG MAN, YOU *SAVED MY LIFE!*
WE'LL TAKE IT FROM *HERE,* SIR.
HE LOOKS ALMOST *PEACEFUL*...

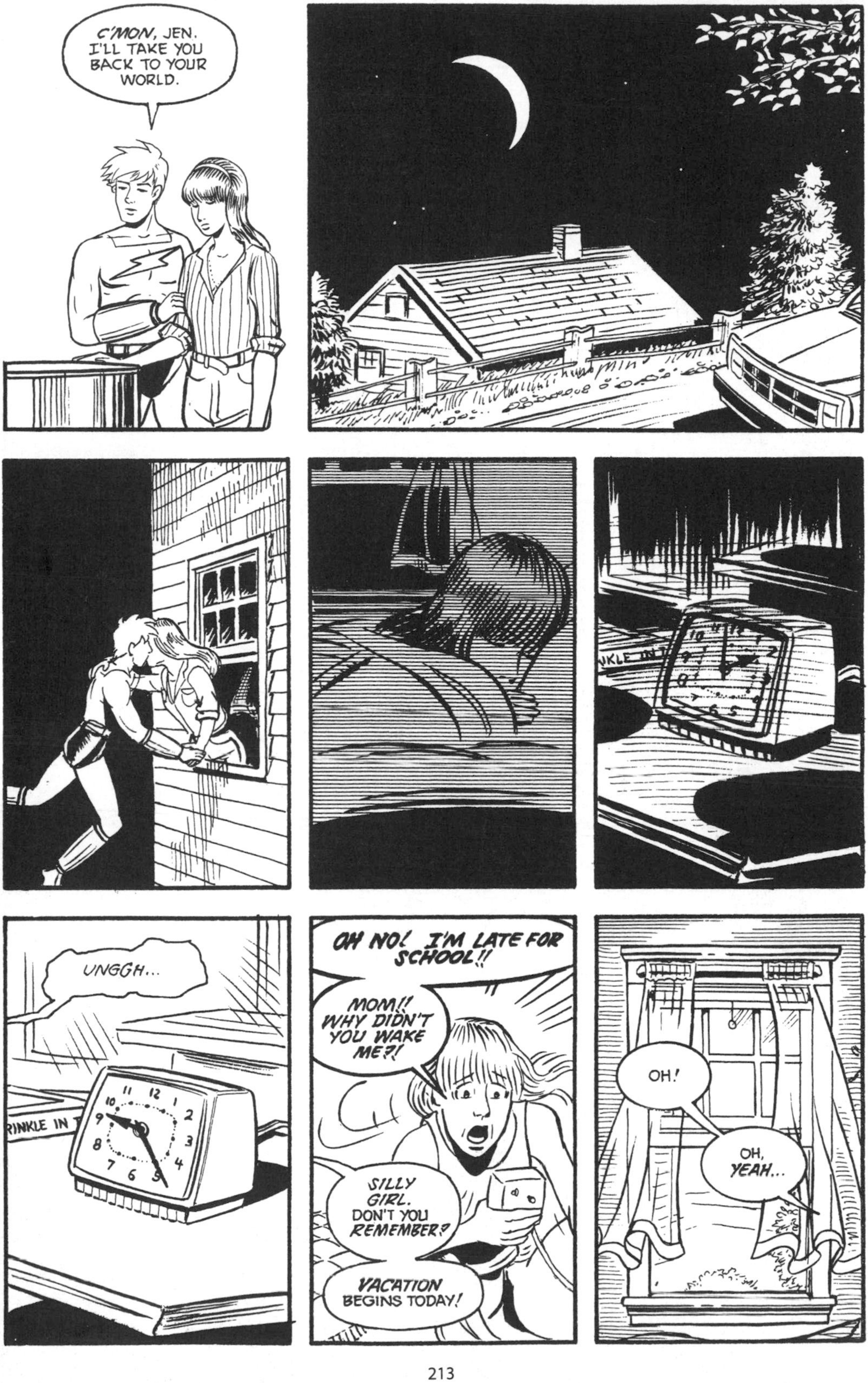
C'MON, JEN. I'LL TAKE YOU BACK TO YOUR WORLD.
UNGGH...
OH NO! I'M LATE FOR SCHOOL!!
MOM!! WHY DIDN'T YOU WAKE ME?!
SILLY GIRL. DON'T YOU REMEMBER?
VACATION BEGINS TODAY!
OH!
OH, YEAH...

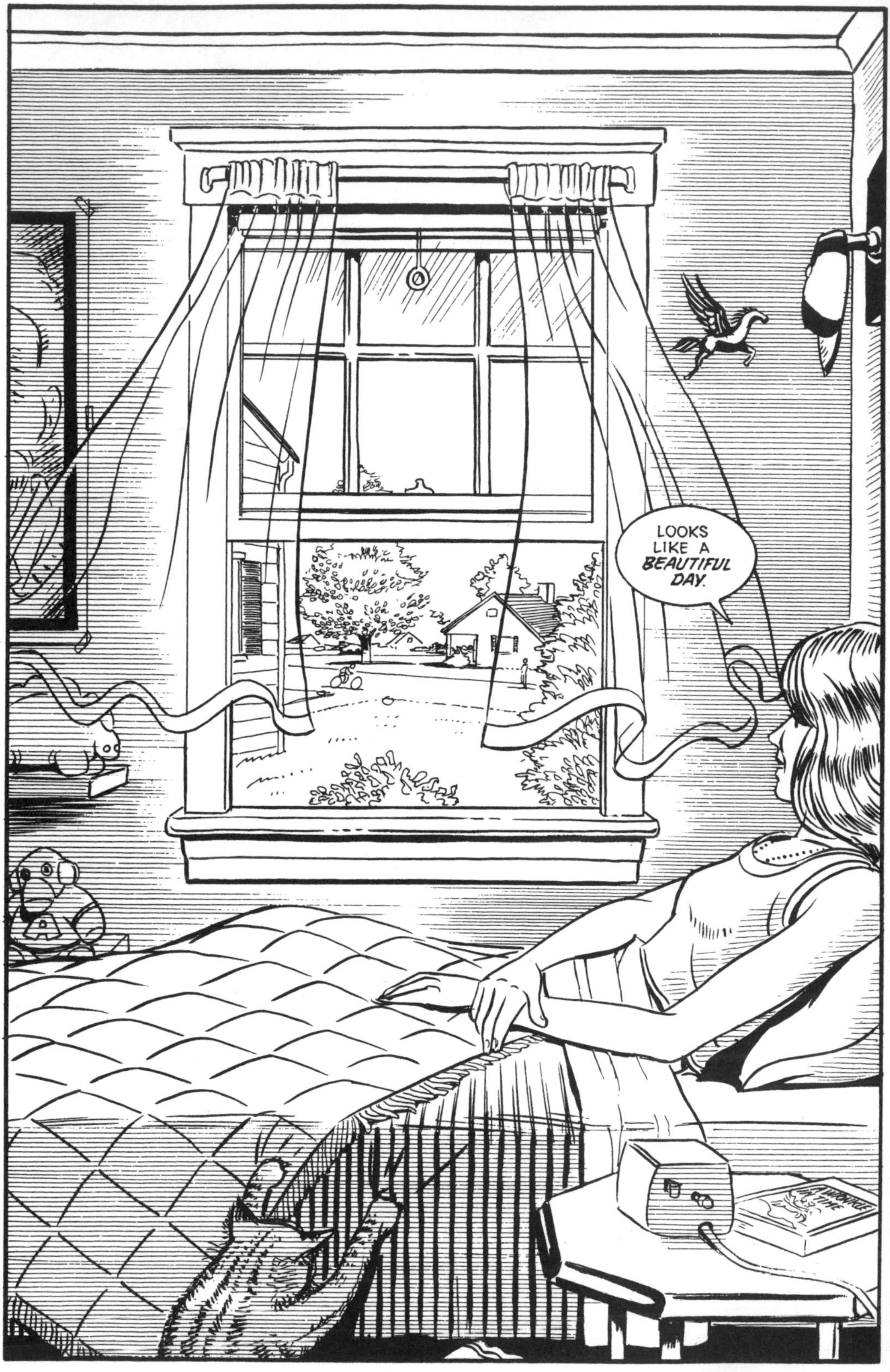
LOOKS LIKE A *BEAUTIFUL* DAY.

It's been said that in the average superhero story, the villain is frequently the protagonist since their aspirations and actions typically launch the story and the hero only reacts. I don't know if that's always true, but it certainly is in this case. This is Dekko's story from beginning to end.

This might be my most personal story in the run—which sounds kind of scary now that I think about it. Dekko is a raving lunatic, but I guess he's my kind of raving lunatic. Like most writers, I put a little of myself into every character, but a few are more fully connected to my world view than others. The most prominent "me-characters" include Zot, Max, and Dekko. Zot is my sunny, optimistic side, Max is my everything-is-interesting attitude about art and life in general, and Dekko is pretty much what I'd be like today if I still lived alone (no joke, I was halfway there when Ivy rescued me).

It takes a certain degree of obsession to turn making art into one's daily business, and obsession is one thing I've never lacked. But like Max, I've learned to draw a line between life and art. I see art as life's antidote—a realm where purity of vision can be safely pursued without the mountain of steaming corpses that usually results when uncompromising "visionaries" in the political sphere try to perfect the world we all live in.

Dekko's origin story had appeared in the original color run, so it's only recapped in this one, but I always liked the basic plot: An artist with a degenerative disease slowly loses one part of his body after another, each replaced by its robotic twin, and his once-organic art gradually changes as he changes, until he embraces his new form and begins to design each new part. The idea of him driving his lover away at about the "halfway mark"—with its unavoidable inference of castration—I found particularly useful when getting inside his head.

Dekko was partly inspired by British turn-of-the-century artist Louis Wain, who drew naturalistic cat pictures for years before schizophrenia consumed him, during which time his drawings got increasingly weird and abstract. I was also inspired by the slow progression in Kandinsky's paintings from the earlier messy stuff to the later, rigid abstractions.

Dekko's dialogue is a bit of a throwback to the florid soliloquies of the crazy supervillains I grew up reading. It sounds especially weird and hokey these days, now that even mainstream superhero comics are reaching for a more naturalistic tone, but there you have it: a Kabuki Theater artifact of an earlier time in comics history.

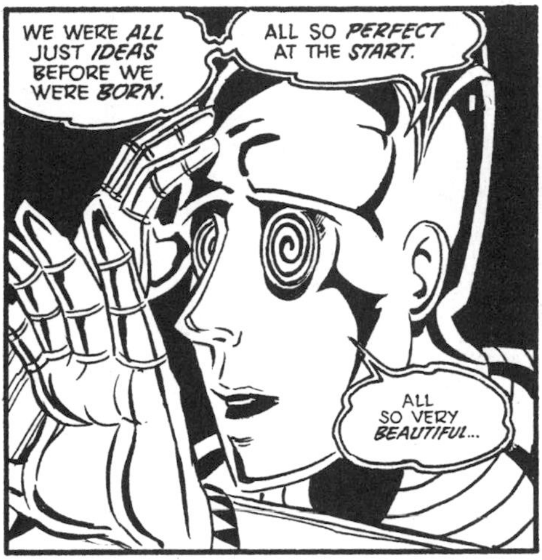
WE WERE *ALL* JUST *IDEAS* BEFORE WE WERE *BORN*.
ALL SO *PERFECT* AT THE *START*.
ALL SO VERY *BEAUTIFUL*...

The months pass quickly in these issues, as evidenced by Woody's dramatic transformation. I like to "show" rather than "tell," so readers were a bit surprised by the giant text box conversation between Jenny and Woody at the park. I just needed to compress a lot of information into a short space. It went against a lot of my theories about what makes a good comic, but it nevertheless appealed to the side of me that will try anything once, another example of the Max in me winning out over the Dekko.

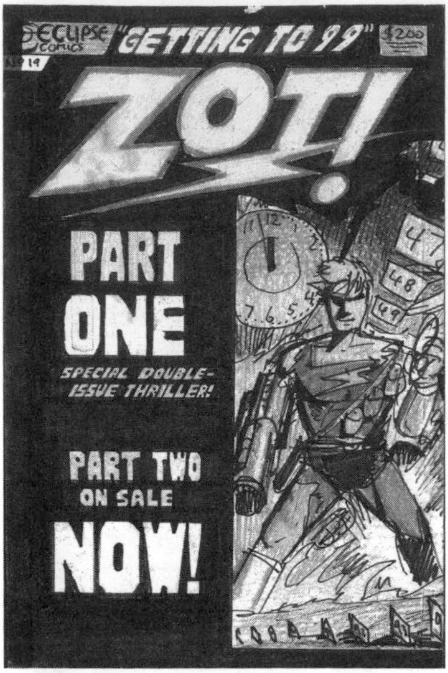
ECLIPSE COMICS
"GETTING TO 99"
$2.00
ZOT!
PART ONE
SPECIAL DOUBLE-ISSUE THRILLER!
PART TWO ON SALE NOW!

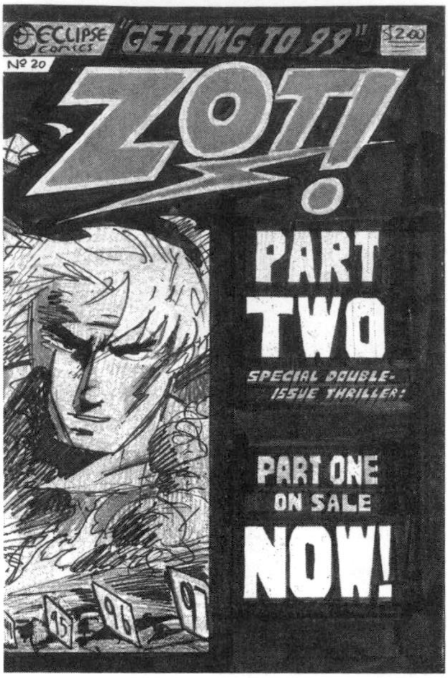
ECLIPSE COMICS
"GETTING TO 99"
$2.00
Nº 20
ZOT!
PART TWO
SPECIAL DOUBLE-ISSUE THRILLER!
PART ONE ON SALE NOW!

Special Feature

Getting to 99

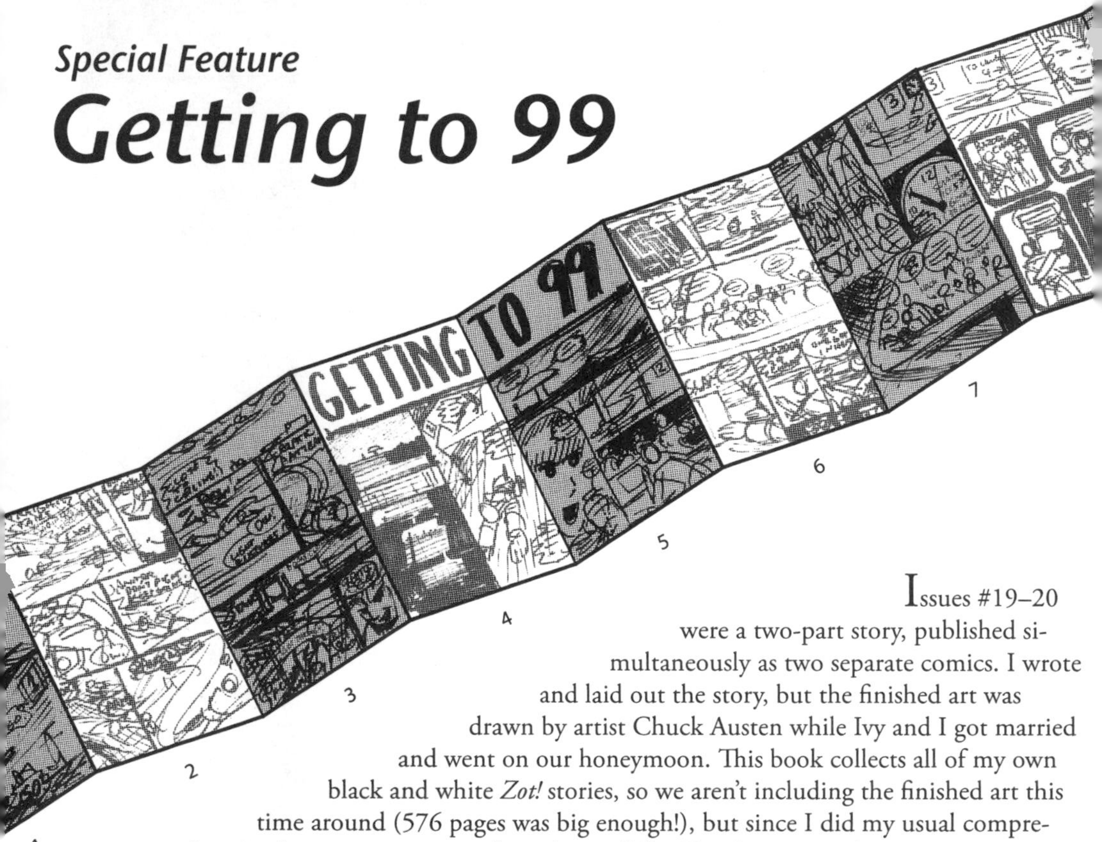
GETTING TO 99
1
6
5
4
3
2
1

Issues #19–20 were a two-part story, published simultaneously as two separate comics. I wrote and laid out the story, but the finished art was drawn by artist Chuck Austen while Ivy and I got married and went on our honeymoon. This book collects all of my own black and white *Zot!* stories, so we aren't including the finished art this time around (576 pages was big enough!), but since I did my usual comprehensive layouts to serve as a "visual script" for Chuck, it seemed appropriate to include them here and fill out the run (albeit, at a reduced sizc). In the future, we hope to offer both Chuck's dynamic finished art version of this story as well as Matt Fcazell's delightful *Zot! 10 ½* backups now that these stories are finally under one cover.

The cover roughs (facing page, top left): Designed as a single image when viewed side by side. Memorably described by one fan as "a jigsaw puzzle for simpletons."

The thumbnails (excerpt below): A typical artifact of my borderline-OCD working methods. My first step in plotting the story was to make tiny rough scribbles of each page with felt-tip pens on 3" x 5" notecards, then hinge them, accordion-style, on the back with drafting tape so they could be viewed all at once or in spreads.

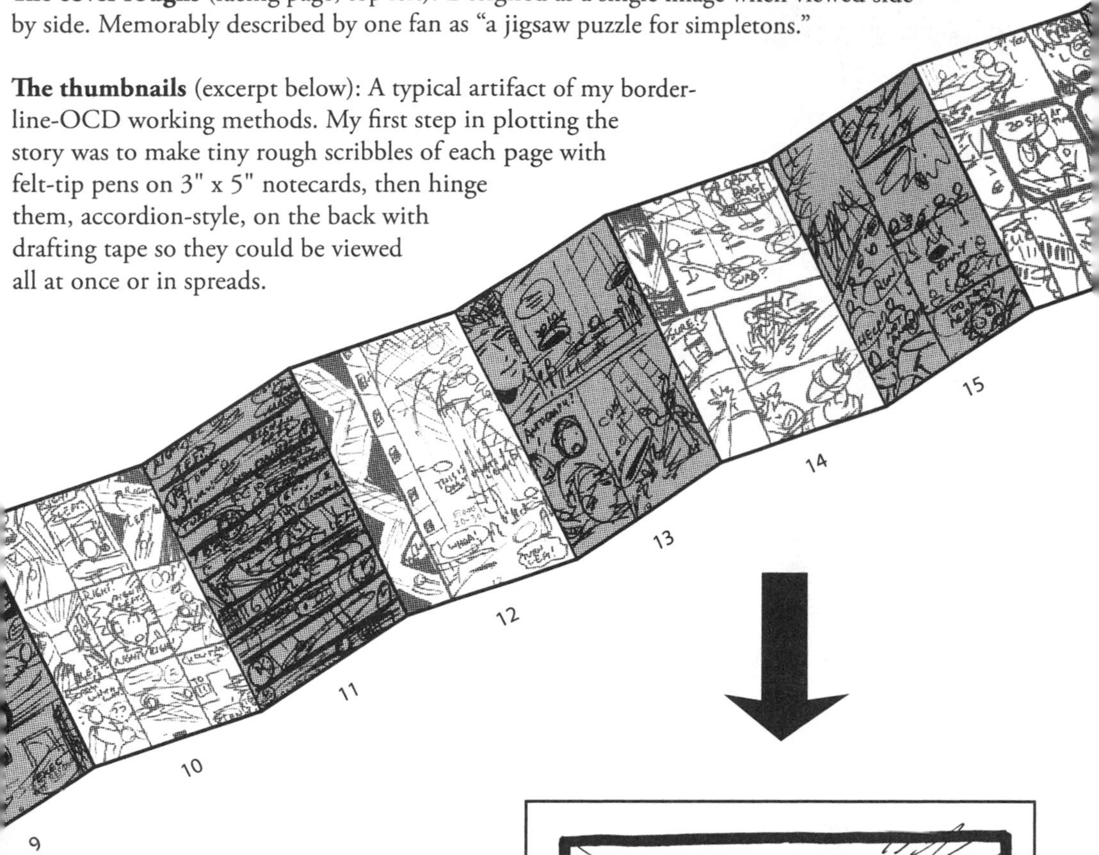
9
10
11
12
13
14
15

The layouts (following pages, first page at right): My "final script" then took the form of comprehensive layouts, drawn full-size in markers and also hinged with tape for accordion-style viewing. This was the only "script" I sent to Chuck, and the only kind of script I ever create for myself. I've never typed a full script for stories I plan to draw, preferring instead to work out all pacing, compositions, and dialogue visually with these elaborate comps.

On the plus side, this has helped keep my script and art nicely integrated. On the minus side, it's probably contributed to the stiffness of my own finished art. By the time I inked any given issue of *Zot!,* I'd typically already drawn each panel two or three times!

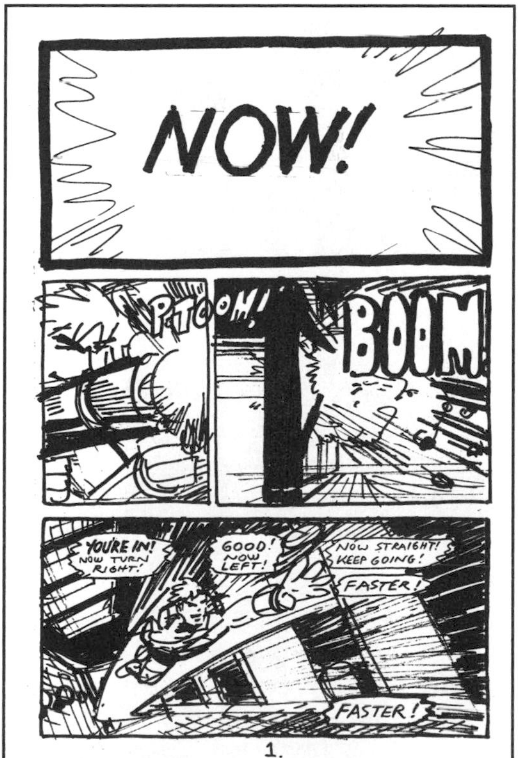
NOW!
PTOOH!
BOOM!
YOU'RE IN! NOW TURN RIGHT!
GOOD! NOW LEFT!
NOW STRAIGHT! KEEP GOING!
FASTER!
FASTER!
1.

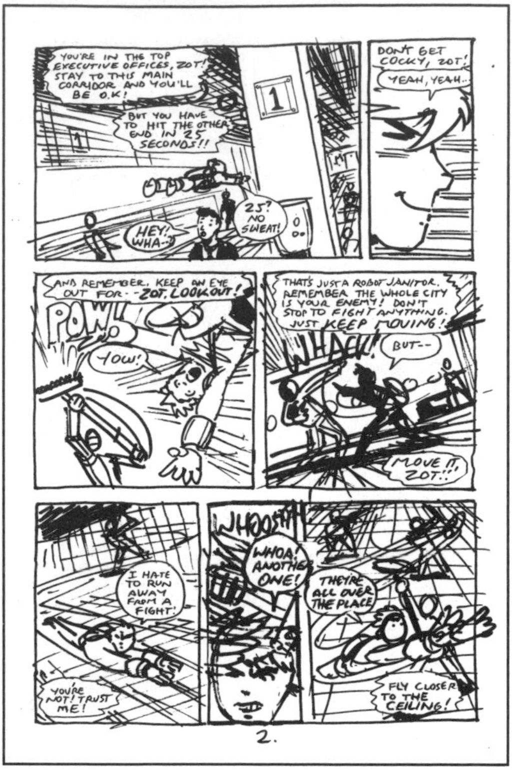
YOU'RE IN THE TOP EXECUTIVE OFFICES, ZOT! STAY TO THIS MAIN CORRIDOR AND YOU'LL BE O.K!
BUT YOU HAVE TO HIT THE OTHER END IN 25 SECONDS!!
1
HEY! WHA--
25? NO SWEAT!
DON'T GET COCKY, ZOT!
YEAH, YEAH...
AND REMEMBER, KEEP AN EYE OUT FOR-- ZOT, LOOKOUT!
POW!
YOW!
THAT'S JUST A ROBOT JANITOR. REMEMBER THE WHOLE CITY IS YOUR ENEMY! DON'T STOP TO FIGHT ANYTHING. JUST KEEP MOVING!
WHACK!
BUT--
MOVE IT, ZOT!!
I HATE TO RUN AWAY FROM A FIGHT!
YOU'RE NOT! TRUST ME!
WHOOSH
WHOA! ANOTHER ONE!
THEY'RE ALL OVER THE PLACE!
FLY CLOSER TO THE CEILING!
2.

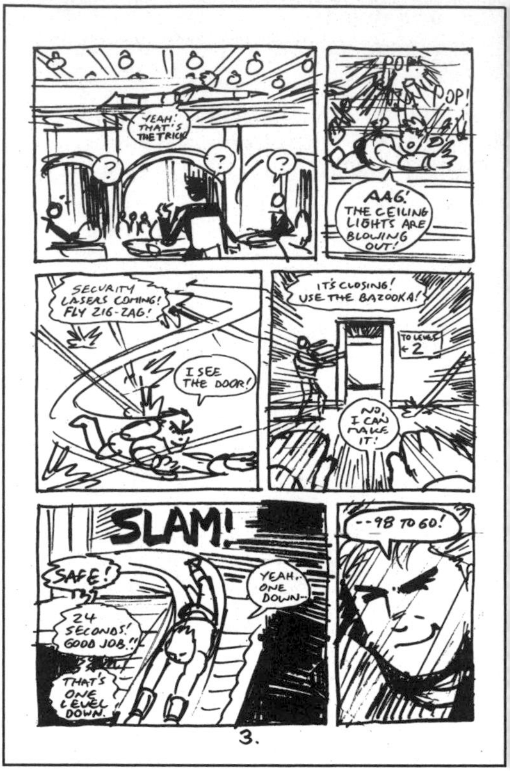
YEAH! THAT'S THE TRICK!
POP!
POP!
AAG! THE CEILING LIGHTS ARE BLOWING OUT!
SECURITY LASERS COMING! FLY ZIG-ZAG!
I SEE THE DOOR!
IT'S CLOSING! USE THE BAZOOKA!
TO LEVEL 2
NO, I CAN MAKE IT!
SLAM!
SAFE!
24 SECONDS! GOOD JOB!!
THAT'S ONE LEVEL DOWN.
YEAH, ONE DOWN...
--98 TO GO!
3.

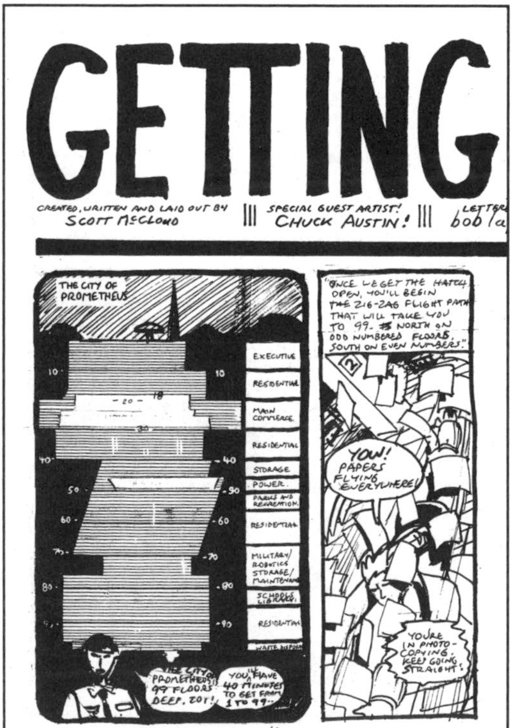
GETTING
CREATED, WRITTEN AND LAID OUT BY SCOTT McCLOUD
SPECIAL GUEST ARTIST! CHUCK AUSTIN!
THE CITY OF PROMETHEUS
EXECUTIVE
RESIDENTIAL
MAIN COMMERCE
RESIDENTIAL
STORAGE
POWER
PARKS AND RECREATION
RESIDENTIAL
MILITARY/ ROBOTICS STORAGE/ MAINTENANCE
SCHOOLS LIBRARY
RESIDENTIAL
THE CITY OF PROMETHEUS! 99 FLOORS DEEP, ZOT!
YOU HAVE 40 MINUTES TO GET FROM 1 TO 99--
"ONCE WE GET THE HATCH OPEN, YOU'LL BEGIN THE ZIG-ZAG FLIGHT PATH THAT WILL TAKE YOU TO 99. NORTH ON ODD NUMBERED FLOORS, SOUTH ON EVEN NUMBERS."
YOW! PAPERS FLYING EVERYWHERE!
YOU'RE IN PHOTO-COPYING. KEEP GOING STRAIGHT!
4.

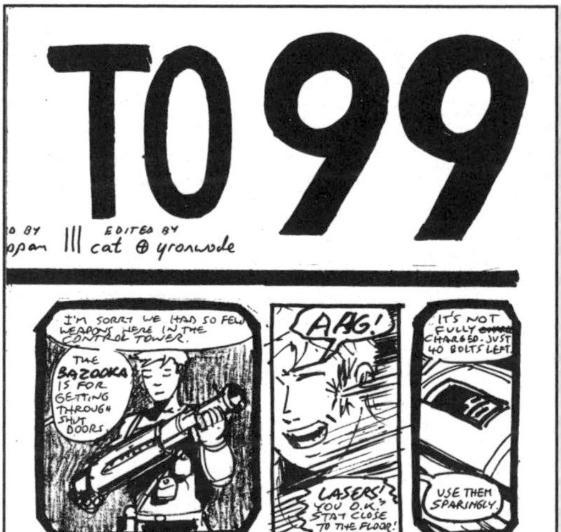
TO 99
EDITED BY cat yronwode
I'M SORRY WE HAD SO FEW WEAPONS HERE IN THE CONTROL TOWER.
THE BAZOOKA IS FOR GETTING THROUGH SHUT DOORS.
AAG!
LASERS! YOU O.K.? STAY CLOSE TO THE FLOOR!
IT'S NOT FULLY CHARGED. JUST 40 BOLTS LEFT.
USE THEM SPARINGLY.
DOOR CLOSING! USE THE BAZOOKA.
I THOUGHT WE WERE SAVING THESE.
HEY, IT'S THAT ZOT KID!
NO! CAN'T BE!
YOU'RE DOING FINE, ZOT.
38
JUST DON'T SLOW DOWN!
RIGHT.
5

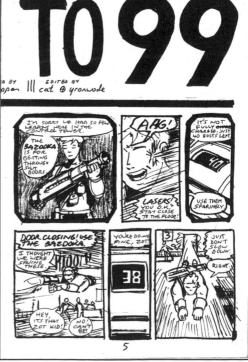

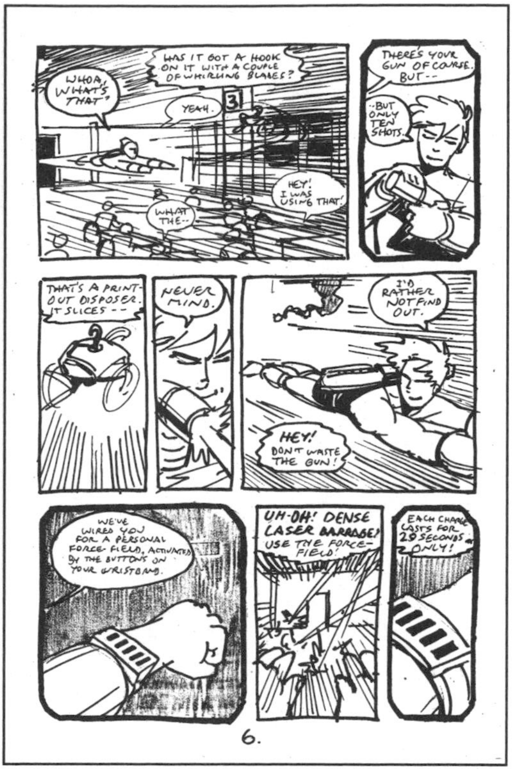
WHOA, WHAT'S THAT?
HAS IT GOT A HOOK ON IT WITH A COUPLE OF WHIRLING BLADES?
YEAH.
3
HEY! I WAS USING THAT!
WHAT THE--
THERE'S YOUR GUN OF COURSE. BUT--
--BUT ONLY TEN SHOTS.
THAT'S A PRINT-OUT DISPOSER. IT SLICES --
NEVER MIND.
I'D RATHER NOT FIND OUT.
HEY! DON'T WASTE THE GUN!
WE'VE WIRED YOU FOR A PERSONAL FORCE-FIELD, ACTIVATED BY THE BUTTONS ON YOUR WRISTBAND.
UH-OH! DENSE LASER BARRAGE! USE THE FORCE-FIELD!
EACH CHARGE LASTS FOR 20 SECONDS ONLY!
6.
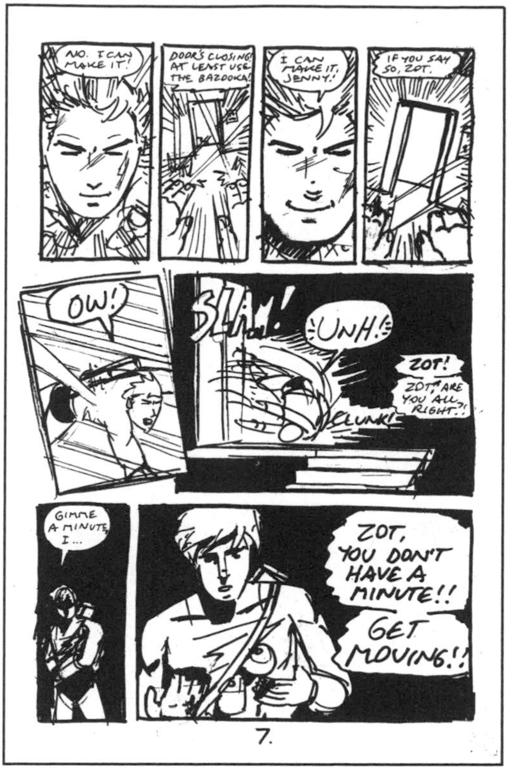
NO. I CAN MAKE IT!
DOOR'S CLOSING! AT LEAST USE THE BAZOOKA!
I CAN MAKE IT, JENNY!
IF YOU SAY SO, ZOT.
OW!
SLAM!
UNH!
ZOT!
ZOT, ARE YOU ALL RIGHT?!
CLUNK!
GIMME A MINUTE, I...
ZOT, YOU DON'T HAVE A MINUTE!!
GET MOVING!!
7.
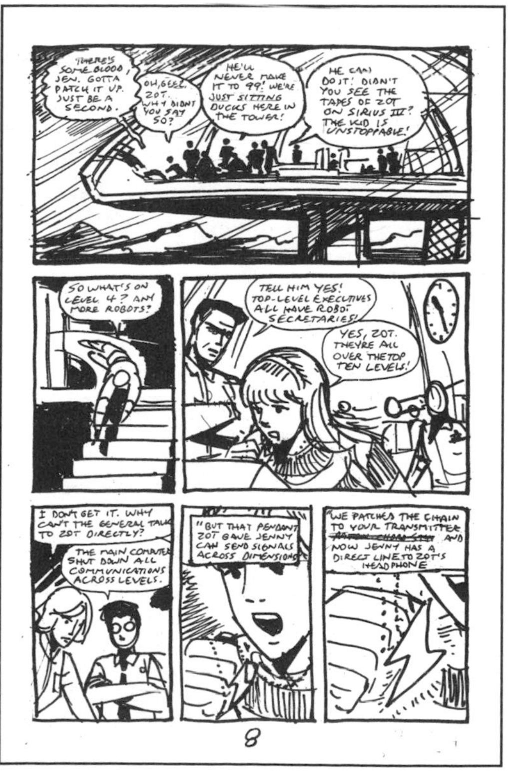
THERE'S SOME BLOOD, JEN. GOTTA PATCH IT UP. JUST BE A SECOND.
OH, GEEZ, ZOT. WHY DIDN'T YOU SAY SO?
HE'LL NEVER MAKE IT TO 99! WE'RE JUST SITTING DUCKS HERE IN THE TOWER!
HE CAN DO IT! DIDN'T YOU SEE THE TAPES OF ZOT ON SIRIUS III? THE KID IS UNSTOPPABLE!
SO WHAT'S ON LEVEL 4? ANY MORE ROBOTS?
TELL HIM YES! TOP-LEVEL EXECUTIVES ALL HAVE ROBOT SECRETARIES!
YES, ZOT. THEY'RE ALL OVER THE TOP TEN LEVELS!
I DON'T GET IT. WHY CAN'T THE GENERAL TALK TO ZOT DIRECTLY?
THE MAIN COMPUTER SHUT DOWN ALL COMMUNICATIONS ACROSS LEVELS.
"BUT THAT PENDANT ZOT GAVE JENNY CAN SEND SIGNALS ACROSS DIMENSIONS
WE PATCHED THE CHAIN TO YOUR TRANSMITTER AND NOW JENNY HAS A DIRECT LINE TO ZOT'S HEADPHONE
8
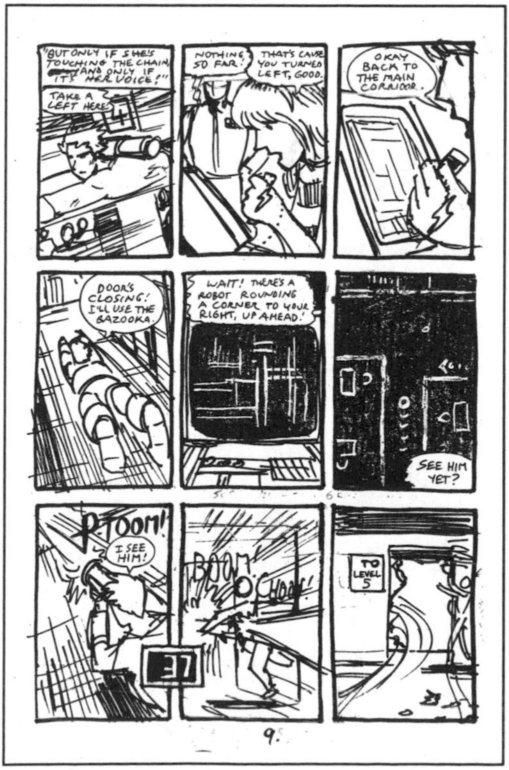
"BUT ONLY IF SHE'S TOUCHING THE CHAIN, AND ONLY IF IT'S HER VOICE!"
TAKE A LEFT HERE.
4
NOTHING SO FAR.
THAT'S CAUSE YOU TURNED LEFT. GOOD.
OKAY, BACK TO THE MAIN CORRIDOR.
DOOR'S CLOSING! I'LL USE THE BAZOOKA.
WAIT! THERE'S A ROBOT ROUNDING A CORNER TO YOUR RIGHT, UP AHEAD!
SEE HIM YET?
P-TOOM!
I SEE HIM!
BOOM! O-CHOOM!
37
TO LEVEL 5
9.

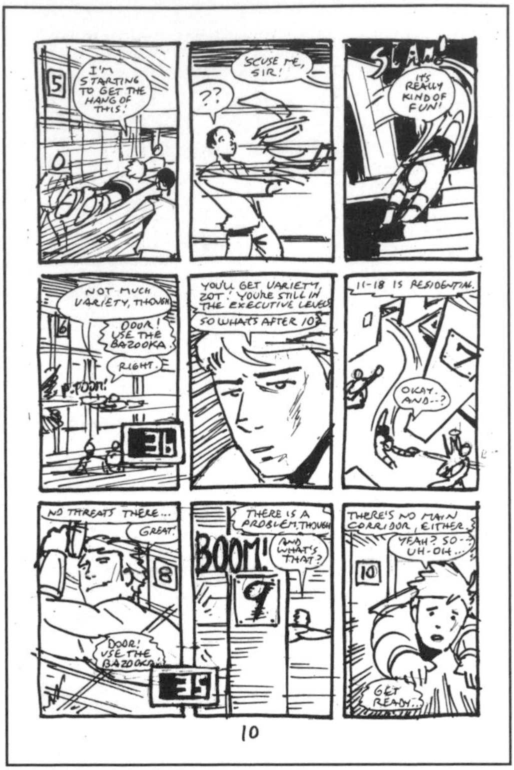
5
I'M STARTING TO GET THE HANG OF THIS!
'SCUSE ME, SIR!
??
SLAM!
IT'S REALLY KIND OF FUN!
NOT MUCH VARIETY, THOUGH
DOOR! USE THE BAZOOKA
RIGHT.
YOU'LL GET VARIETY, ZOT! YOU'RE STILL IN THE EXECUTIVE LEVELS
SO WHAT'S AFTER 10?
11-18 IS RESIDENTIAL.
OKAY. AND--?
NO THREATS THERE...
GREAT!
DOOR! USE THE BAZOOKA!
THERE IS A PROBLEM, THOUGH
BOOM!
AND WHAT'S THAT?
THERE'S NO MAIN CORRIDOR, EITHER.
YEAH? SO-- UH-OH...
GET READY...
10

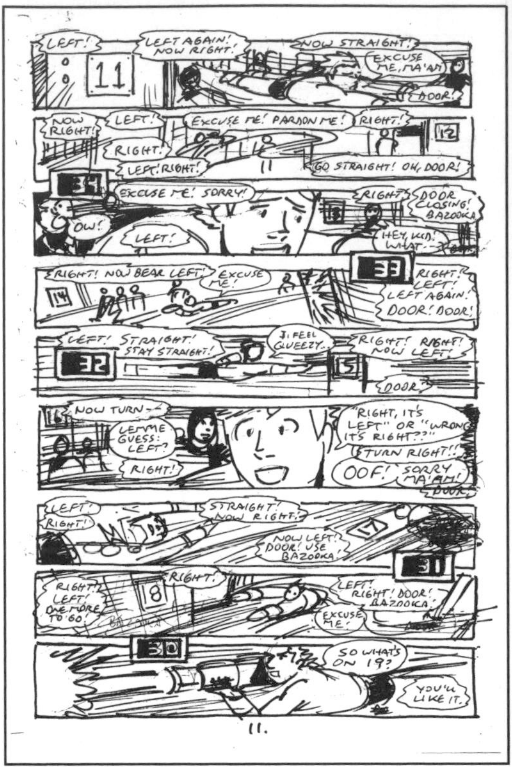
LEFT!
LEFT AGAIN! NOW RIGHT!
NOW STRAIGHT!
EXCUSE ME, MA'AM
DOOR!
NOW RIGHT!
LEFT!
EXCUSE ME! PARDON ME!
RIGHT!
RIGHT.
LEFT! RIGHT!
GO STRAIGHT! OH, DOOR!
EXCUSE ME! SORRY!
OW!
LEFT!
RIGHT!
DOOR CLOSING! BAZOOKA
HEY, KID! WHAT--
RIGHT! NOW BEAR LEFT!
EXCUSE ME!
RIGHT! LEFT! LEFT AGAIN! DOOR! DOOR!
LEFT! STRAIGHT! STAY STRAIGHT!
I FEEL QUEEZY...
RIGHT! RIGHT! NOW LEFT!
DOOR
NOW TURN--
LEMME GUESS: LEFT?
RIGHT!
"RIGHT, IT'S LEFT" OR "WRONG IT'S RIGHT??"
TURN RIGHT!!
OOF!
SORRY MA'AM!
DOOR
LEFT!
RIGHT!
STRAIGHT! NOW RIGHT!
NOW LEFT! DOOR! USE BAZOOKA!
RIGHT! LEFT! ONE MORE TO GO!
RIGHT.
LEFT! RIGHT! DOOR! BAZOOKA!
EXCUSE ME!
SO WHAT'S ON 19?
YOU'LL LIKE IT.
11.

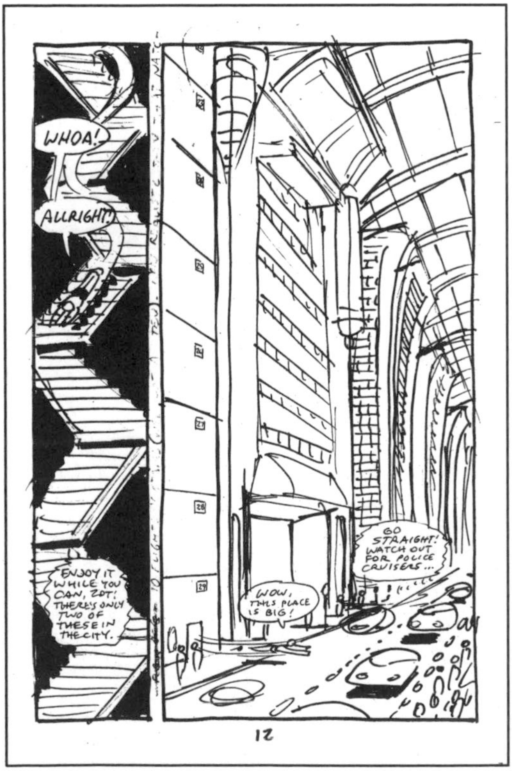
WHOA!
ALLRIGHT!
ENJOY IT WHILE YOU CAN, ZOT! THERE'S ONLY TWO OF THESE IN THE CITY.
WOW, THIS PLACE IS BIG!
GO STRAIGHT! WATCH OUT FOR POLICE CRUISERS...
12

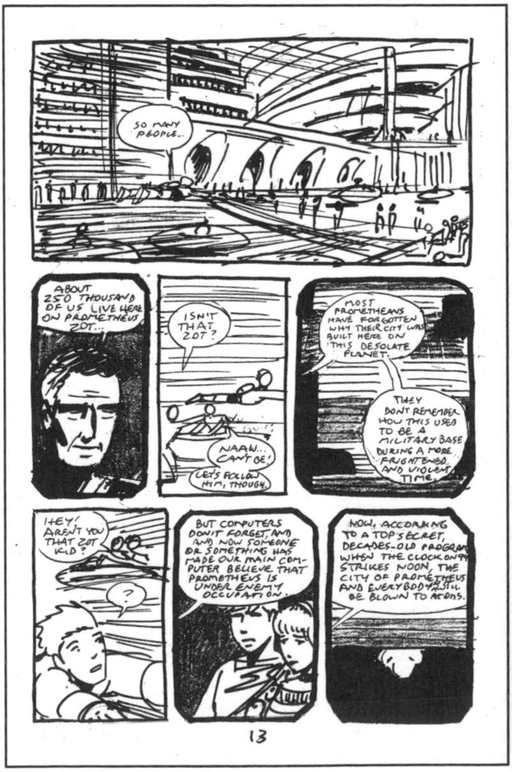
SO MANY PEOPLE...
ABOUT 250 THOUSAND OF US LIVE HERE ON PROMETHEUS ZOT...
ISN'T THAT ZOT?
NAAW... CAN'T BE!
LET'S FOLLOW HIM, THOUGH.
MOST PROMETHEANS HAVE FORGOTTEN WHY THEIR CITY WAS BUILT HERE ON THIS DESOLATE PLANET.
THEY DONT REMEMBER HOW THIS USED TO BE A MILITARY BASE DURING A MORE FRIGHTENED AND VIOLENT TIME.
HEY! AREN'T YOU THAT ZOT KID?
?
BUT COMPUTERS DON'T FORGET, AND AND NOW SOMEONE OR SOMETHING HAS MADE OUR MAIN COMPUTER BELIEVE THAT PROMETHEUS IS UNDER ENEMY OCCUPATION.
NOW, ACCORDING TO A TOP SECRET, DECADES-OLD PROGRAM WHEN THE CLOCK ON 99 STRIKES NOON, THE CITY OF PROMETHEUS AND EVERYBODY IN IT WILL BE BLOWN TO ATOMS.
13

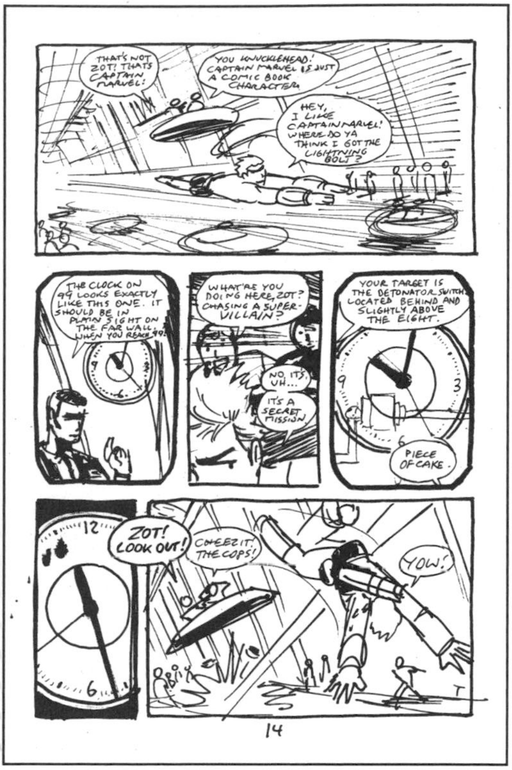
THAT'S NOT ZOT! THAT'S CAPTAIN MARVEL!
YOU KNUCKLEHEAD! CAPTAIN MARVEL IS JUST A COMIC BOOK CHARACTER.
HEY, I LIKE CAPTAIN MARVEL! WHERE DO YA THINK I GOT THE LIGHTNING BOLT?
THE CLOCK ON 99 LOOKS EXACTLY LIKE THIS ONE. IT SHOULD BE IN PLAIN SIGHT ON THE FAR WALL WHEN YOU REACH 99.
WHAT'RE YOU DOING HERE, ZOT? CHASING A SUPER-VILLAIN?
NO, IT'S, UH...
IT'S A SECRET MISSION.
YOUR TARGET IS THE DETONATOR SWITCH LOCATED BEHIND AND SLIGHTLY ABOVE THE EIGHT.
PIECE OF CAKE.
ZOT! LOOK OUT!
CHEEZIT, THE COPS!
YOW!
14

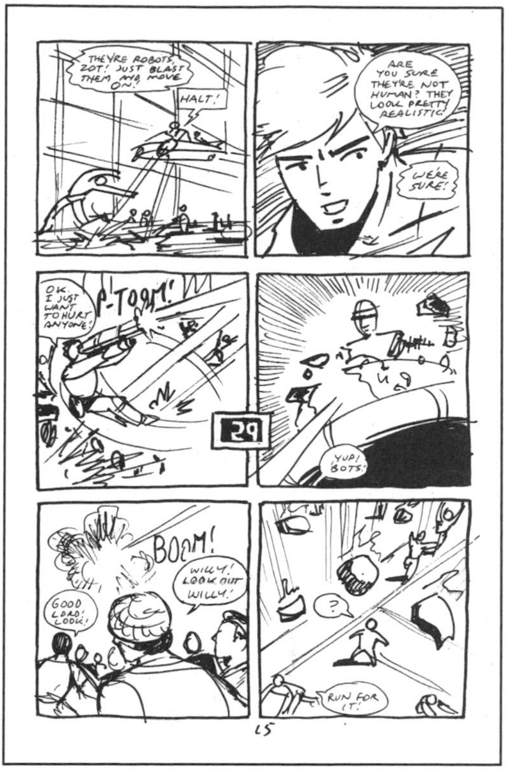
THEY'RE ROBOTS, ZOT! JUST BLAST THEM AND MOVE ON!
HALT!
ARE YOU SURE THEY'RE NOT HUMAN? THEY LOOK PRETTY REALISTIC!
WE'RE SURE!
OK. I JUST WANT TO HURT ANYONE!
P-TOOM!
29
YUP! BOTS!
BOOM!
WILLY! LOOK OUT WILLY!
GOOD LORD! LOOK!
?
RUN FOR IT!
15

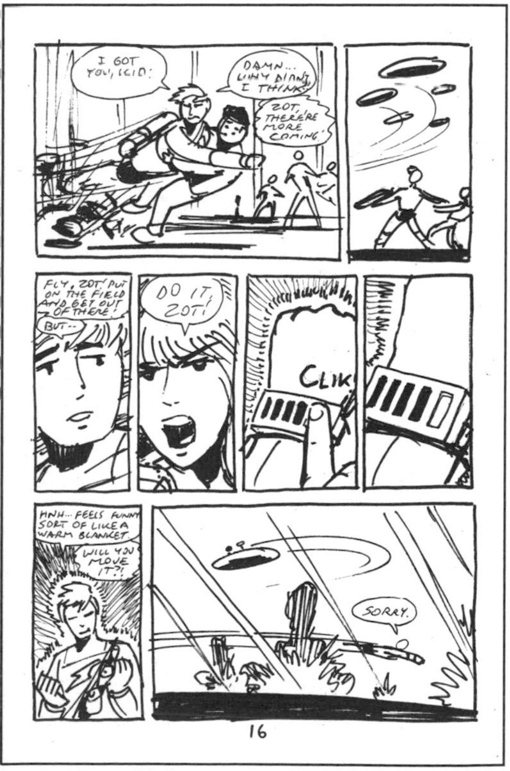
I GOT YOU, KID!
DAMN... WHY DIDN'T I THINK
ZOT, THERE'RE MORE COMING!
FLY, ZOT! PUT ON THE FIELD AND GET OUT OF THERE!
BUT...
DO IT, ZOT!
CLIK
HNH... FEELS FUNNY SORT OF LIKE A WARM BLANKET.
WILL YOU MOVE IT?!
SORRY.
16

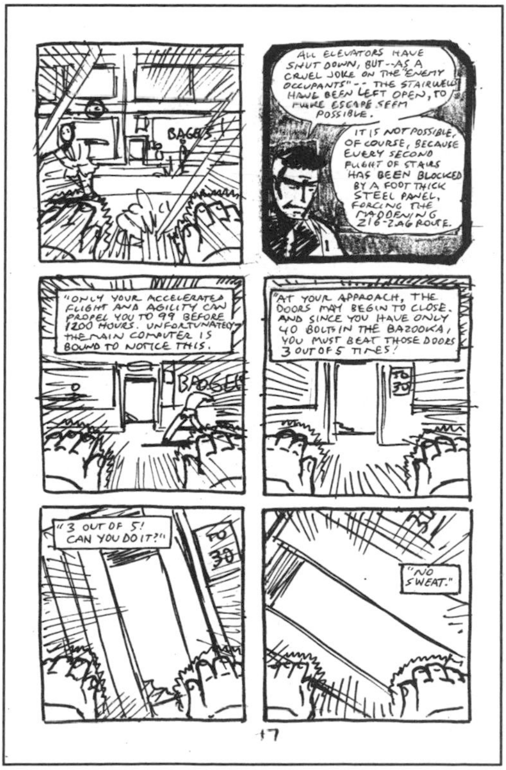
BAGELS
ALL ELEVATORS HAVE SHUT DOWN, BUT--AS A CRUEL JOKE ON THE "ENEMY OCCUPANTS"-- THE STAIRWELLS HAVE BEEN LEFT OPEN, TO MAKE ESCAPE SEEM POSSIBLE.
IT IS NOT POSSIBLE, OF COURSE, BECAUSE EVERY SECOND FLIGHT OF STAIRS HAS BEEN BLOCKED BY A FOOT THICK STEEL PANEL, FORCING THE MADDENING ZIG-ZAG ROUTE.
"ONLY YOUR ACCELERATED FLIGHT AND AGILITY CAN PROPEL YOU TO 99 BEFORE 1200 HOURS. UNFORTUNATELY, THE MAIN COMPUTER IS BOUND TO NOTICE THIS.
BAGELS
"AT YOUR APPROACH, THE DOORS MAY BEGIN TO CLOSE. AND SINCE YOU HAVE ONLY 40 BOLTS IN THE BAZOOKA, YOU MUST BEAT THOSE DOORS 3 OUT OF 5 TIMES!
TO 30
"3 OUT OF 5! CAN YOU DO IT?"
TO 30
"NO SWEAT."
17

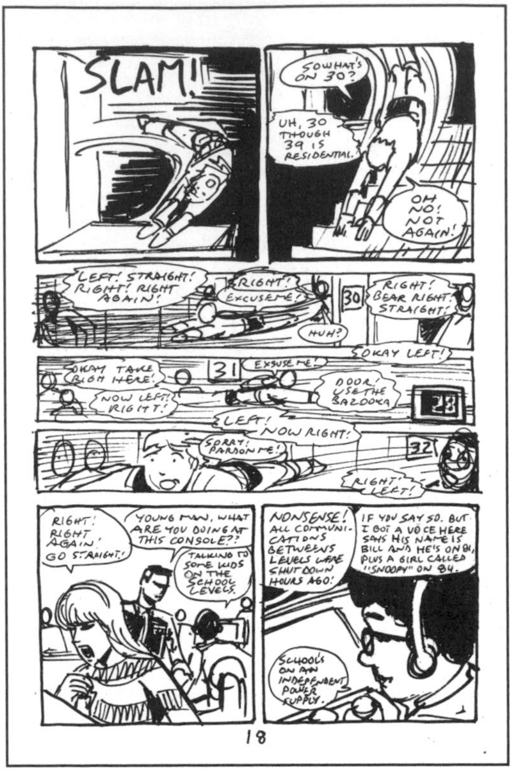
SLAM!
SO WHAT'S ON 30?
UH, 30 THOUGH 39 IS RESIDENTIAL.
OH NO! NOT AGAIN!
LEFT! STRAIGHT! RIGHT! RIGHT AGAIN!
RIGHT!
EXCUSE ME!
30
RIGHT! BEAR RIGHT. STRAIGHT!
HUH?
OKAY LEFT!
OKAY TAKE RIGH HERE!
31
EXSUSE ME!
NOW LEFT! RIGHT!
DOOR! USE THE BAZOOKA
28
LEFT!
NOW RIGHT!
SORRY! PARDON ME!
32
RIGHT! LEFT!
RIGHT! RIGHT AGAIN! GO STRAIGHT!
YOUNG MAN, WHAT ARE YOU DOING AT THIS CONSOLE?!
TALKING TO SOME KIDS ON THE SCHOOL LEVELS.
NONSENSE! ALL COMMUNICATIONS BETWEENS LEVELS WERE SHUT DOWN HOURS AGO!
IF YOU SAY SO. BUT I GOT A VOICE HERE SAYS HIS NAME IS BILL AND HE'S ON 81, PLUS A GIRL CALLED "SNOOPY" ON 84.
SCHOOL'S ON AN INDEPENDENT POWER SUPPLY.
18

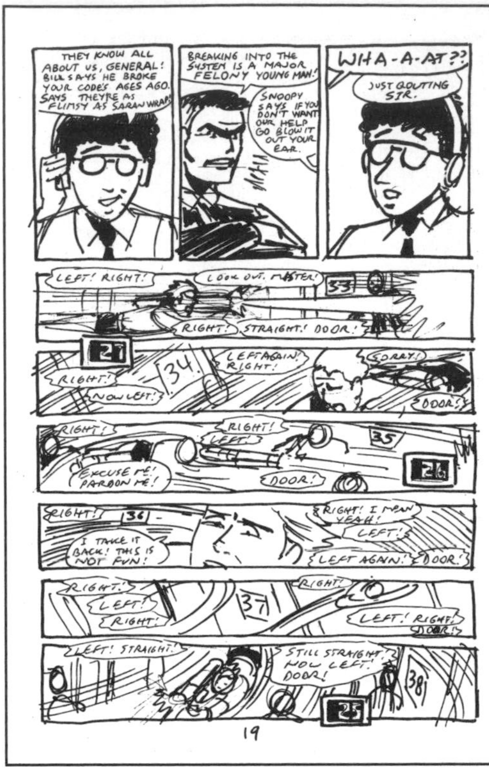
THEY KNOW ALL ABOUT US, GENERAL! BILL SAYS HE BROKE YOUR CODES AGES AGO. SAYS THEY'RE AS FLIMSY AS SARAN WRAP!
BREAKING INTO THE SYSTEM IS A MAJOR FELONY YOUNG MAN!
SNOOPY SAYS IF YOU DON'T WANT OUR HELP GO BLOW IT OUT YOUR EAR.
WHA-A-AT??
JUST QOUTING SIR.
LEFT! RIGHT!
LOOK OUT, MASTER!
33
RIGHT! STRAIGHT! DOOR!
27
RIGHT!
NOW LEFT!
34
LEFT AGAIN! RIGHT!
SORRY!
DOOR!
RIGHT!
RIGHT!
LEFT!
35
EXCUSE ME! PARDON ME!
DOOR!
26
RIGHT!
36
I TAKE IT BACK! THIS IS NOT FUN!
RIGHT! I MEAN YEAH!
LEFT!
LEFT AGAIN!
DOOR!
RIGHT!
LEFT!
RIGHT!
37
RIGHT!
LEFT! RIGHT! DOOR!
LEFT! STRAIGHT!
STILL STRAIGHT! NOW LEFT! DOOR!
38
25
19

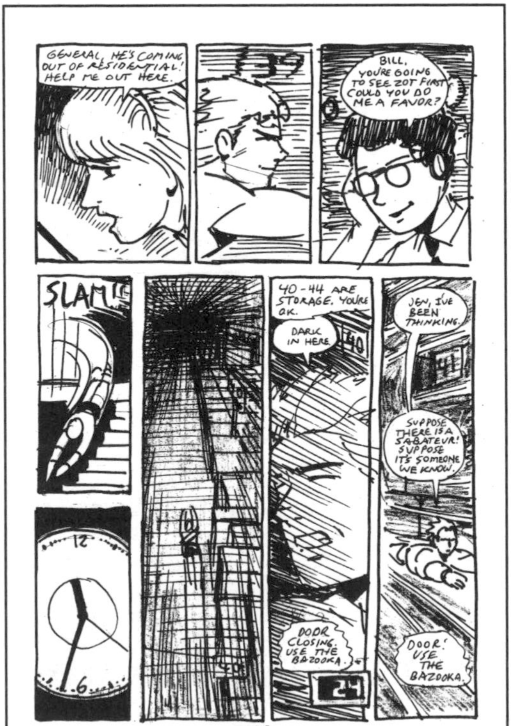
GENERAL, HE'S COMING OUT OF RESIDENTIAL! HELP ME OUT HERE.
39
BILL, YOU'RE GOING TO SEE ZOT FIRST! COULD YOU DO ME A FAVOR?
SLAM!
12
6
40-44 ARE STORAGE. YOU'RE OK.
DARK IN HERE
40
JEN, I'VE BEEN THINKING.
41
SUPPOSE THERE IS A SABATEUR! SUPPOSE IT'S SOMEONE WE KNOW.
DOOR CLOSING. USE THE BAZOOKA.
DOOR! USE THE BAZOOKA.
24
20.

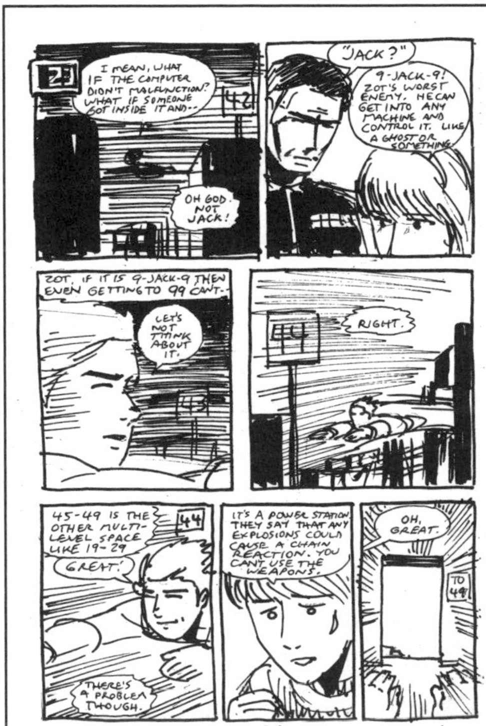
23
I MEAN, WHAT IF THE COMPUTER DIDN'T MALFUNCTION? WHAT IF SOMEONE GOT INSIDE IT AND--
42
OH GOD. NOT JACK!
"JACK?"
9-JACK-9! ZOT'S WORST ENEMY. HE CAN GET INTO ANY MACHINE AND CONTROL IT. LIKE A GHOST OR SOMETHING.
ZOT, IF IT IS 9-JACK-9 THEN EVEN GETTING TO 99 CAN'T--
LET'S NOT THINK ABOUT IT.
43
44
RIGHT.
45-49 IS THE OTHER MULTI-LEVEL SPACE LIKE 19-29
44
GREAT!
THERE'S A PROBLEM THOUGH.
IT'S A POWER STATION THEY SAY THAT ANY EXPLOSIONS COULD CAUSE A CHAIN REACTION. YOU CAN'T USE THE WEAPONS.
OH, GREAT.
TO 49
21.

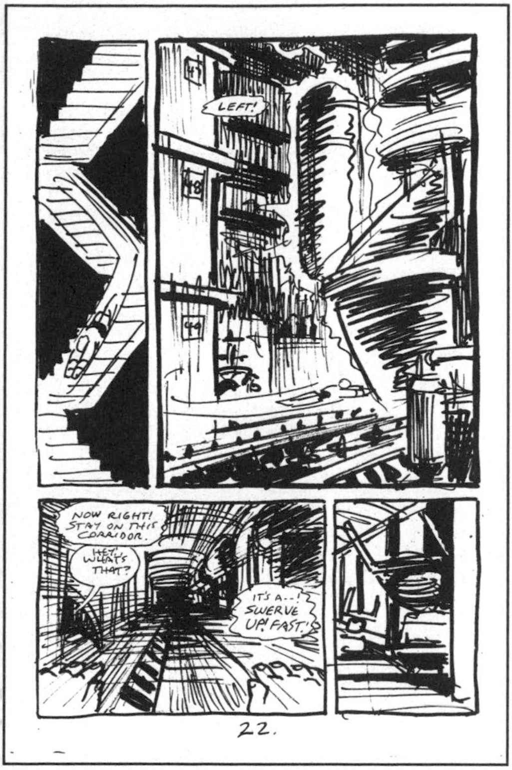
LEFT!
NOW RIGHT! STAY ON THIS CORRIDOR.
HEY, WHAT'S THAT?
IT'S A--! SWERVE UP! FAST!
22.

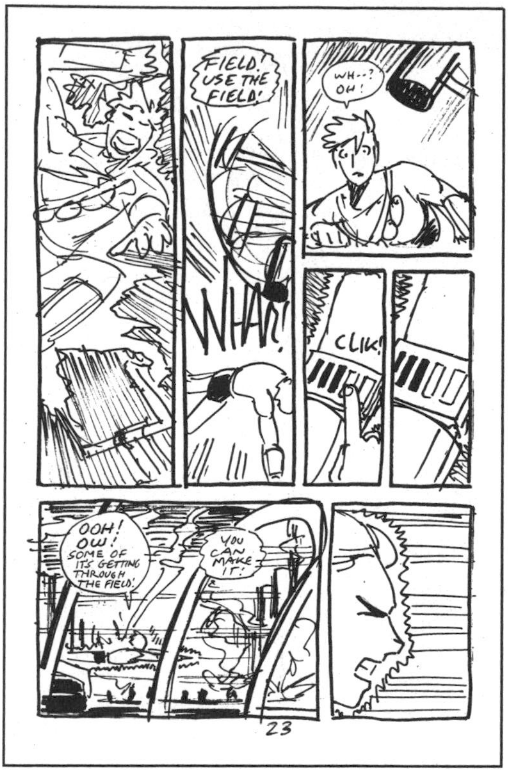
FIELD! USE THE FIELD!
WH--? OH!
WHAM!
CLIK!
OOH! OW! SOME OF IT'S GETTING THROUGH THE FIELD!
YOU CAN MAKE IT!
23

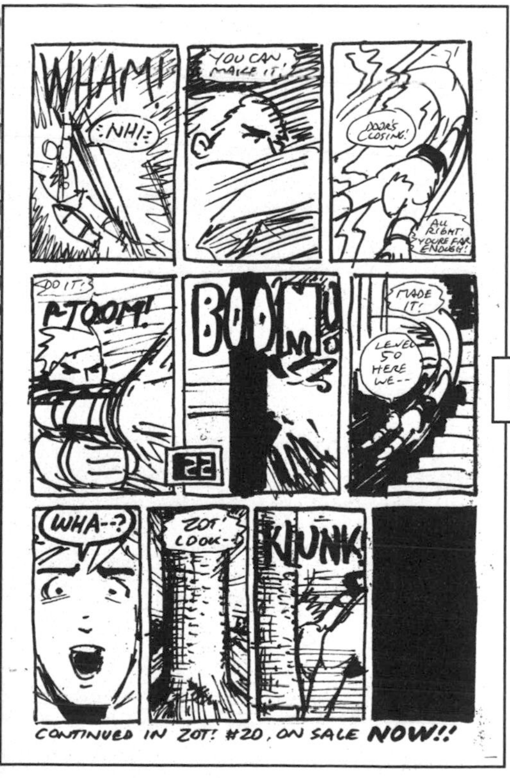
WHAM!
NH!
YOU CAN MAKE IT!
DOOR'S CLOSING!
ALL RIGHT! YOU'RE FAR ENOUGH!
DO IT!
P-TOOM!
BOOM!
MADE IT!
LEVEL 50 HERE WE--
WHA--?
ZOT! LOOK--
KLUNK
CONTINUED IN ZOT! #20, ON SALE NOW!!

Issue break

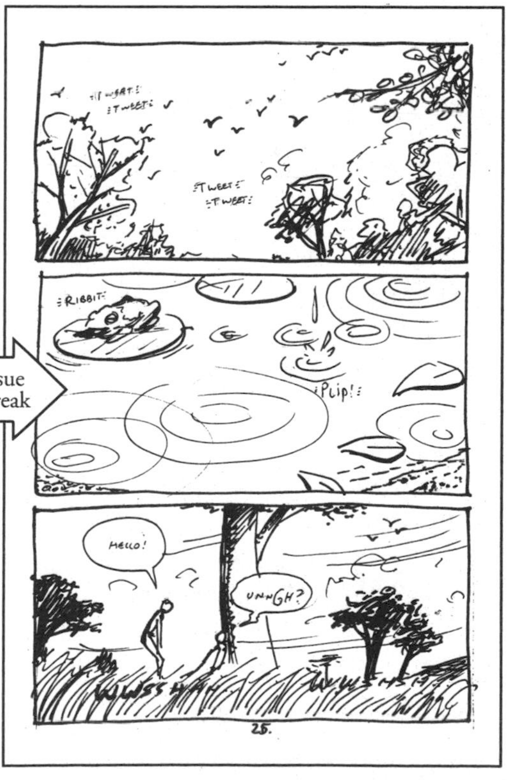
TWEET! TWEET!
TWEET TWEET!
RIBBIT
PLIP!
HELLO!
UNNGH?
25.

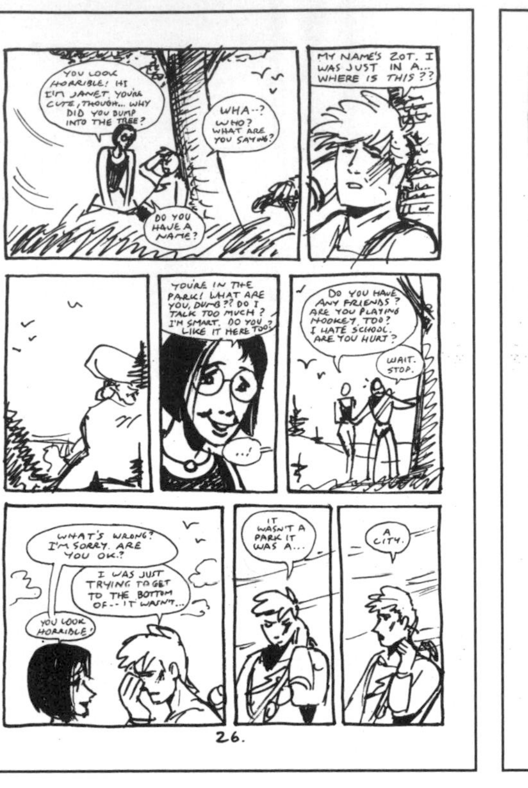
YOU LOOK HORRIBLE! HI I'M JANET. YOU'RE CUTE, THOUGH... WHY DID YOU BUMP INTO THE TREE?
WHA--? WHO? WHAT ARE YOU SAYING?
DO YOU HAVE A NAME?
MY NAME'S ZOT. I WAS JUST IN A... WHERE IS THIS??
YOU'RE IN THE PARK! WHAT ARE YOU, DUMB?? DO I TALK TOO MUCH? I'M SMART. DO YOU LIKE IT HERE TOO?
...!
DO YOU HAVE ANY FRIENDS? ARE YOU PLAYING HOOKEY, TOO? I HATE SCHOOL. ARE YOU HURT?
WAIT. STOP.
WHAT'S WRONG? I'M SORRY. ARE YOU OK.?
I WAS JUST TRYING TO GET TO THE BOTTOM OF-- IT WASN'T...
YOU LOOK HORRIBLE!
IT WASN'T A PARK IT WAS A...
A CITY.

26.

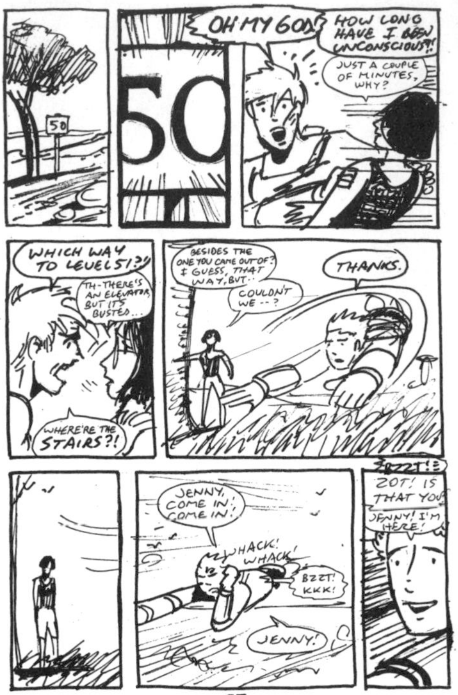
50
50
OH MY GOD!
HOW LONG HAVE I BEEN UNCONSCIOUS?!
JUST A COUPLE OF MINUTES, WHY?
WHICH WAY TO LEVEL 51?!
TH-THERE'S AN ELEVATOR, BUT IT'S BUSTED...
WHERE'RE THE STAIRS?!
BESIDES THE ONE YOU CAME OUT OF? I GUESS, THAT WAY, BUT..
COULDN'T WE --?
THANKS.
JENNY, COME IN! COME IN!
WHACK! WHACK!
BZZT! KKK!
JENNY!
BZZT!
ZOT! IS THAT YOU
JENNY! I'M HERE!

27.

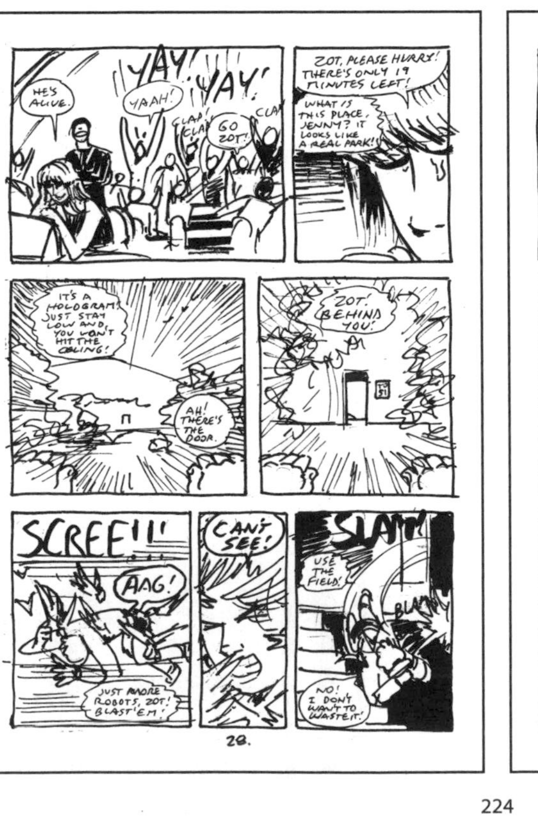
HE'S ALIVE.
YAY!
YAAH!
YAY!
CLAP! CLAP
GO ZOT!
CLAP
ZOT, PLEASE HURRY! THERE'S ONLY 19 MINUTES LEFT!
WHAT IS THIS PLACE, JENNY? IT LOOKS LIKE A REAL PARK!
IT'S A HOLOGRAM! JUST STAY LOW AND, YOU WON'T HIT THE CEILING!
AH! THERE'S THE DOOR.
ZOT! BEHIND YOU!
SCREE!!!
AAG!
JUST MORE ROBOTS, ZOT! BLAST'EM!
CAN'T SEE!
SLAM!
USE THE FIELD!
NO! I DON'T WANT TO WASTE IT!

28.

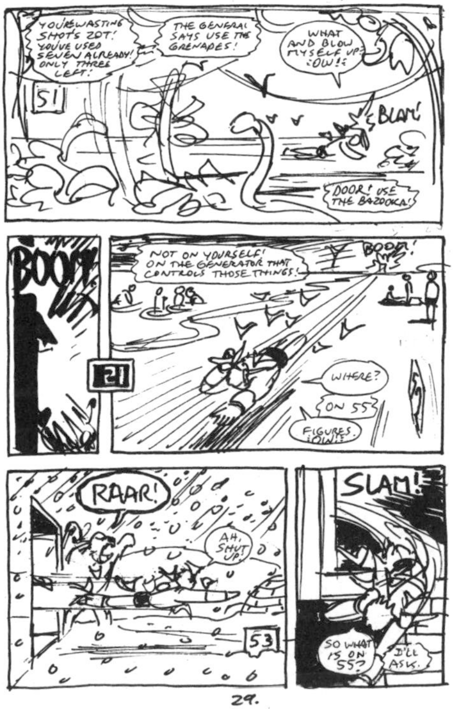
YOU'RE WASTING SHOTS ZOT! YOU'VE USED SEVEN ALREADY! ONLY THREE LEFT!
THE GENERAL SAYS USE THE GRENADES!
WHAT AND BLOW MYSELF UP? :OW!:
51
BLAM!
DOOR! USE THE BAZOOKA!
BOOM!
NOT ON YOURSELF! ON THE GENERATOR THAT CONTROLS THOSE THINGS!
BOOM!
21
WHERE?
ON 55
FIGURES. :OW!:
RAAR!
AH, SHUT UP!
53
SLAM!
SO WHAT IS ON 55?
I'LL ASK.

29.

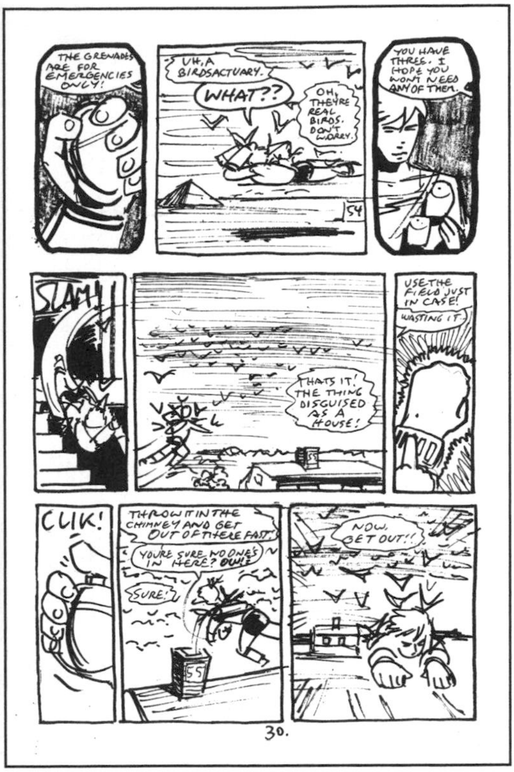
THE GRENADES ARE FOR EMERGENCIES ONLY!
UH, A BIRDSACTUARY.
WHAT??
OH, THEY'RE REAL BIRDS. DON'T WORRY.
54
YOU HAVE THREE. I HOPE YOU WON'T NEED ANY OF THEM.
SLAM!!
THATS IT! THE THING DISGUISED AS A HOUSE!
55
USE THE FIELD JUST IN CASE!
WASTING IT.
CLIK!
THROW IT IN THE CHIMNEY AND GET OUT OF THERE FAST!
YOU'RE SURE NO ONE'S IN HERE? OW!!
SURE!
55
NOW, GET OUT!!
30.

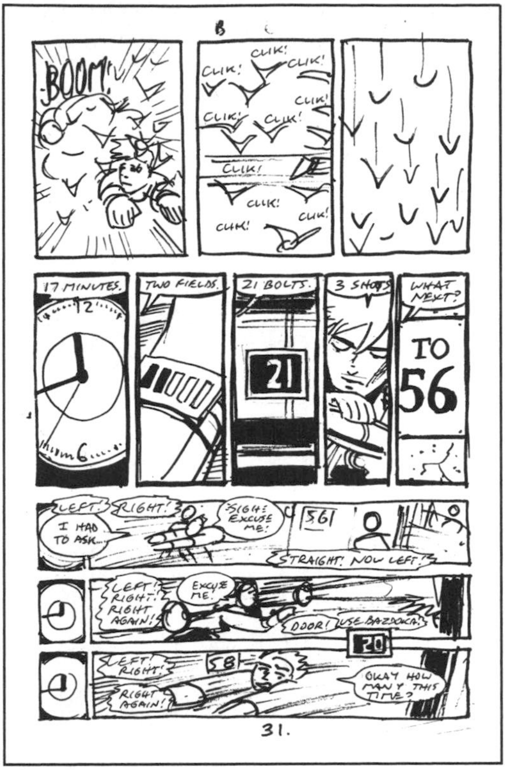
BOOM!
CLIK!
CLIK!
CLIK!
CLIK!
CLIK!
CLIK!
CLIK!
CLIK!
CLIK!
CLIK!
17 MINUTES.
TWO FIELDS.
21 BOLTS.
21
3 SHOTS
WHAT NEXT?
TO 56
LEFT!
RIGHT!
I HAD TO ASK...
SIGH! EXCUSE ME!
56
STRAIGHT! NOW LEFT!
LEFT! RIGHT! RIGHT AGAIN!
EXCUSE ME!
DOOR!
USE BAZOOKA!
20
LEFT! RIGHT!
58
RIGHT AGAIN!
OKAY HOW MANY THIS TIME?
31.

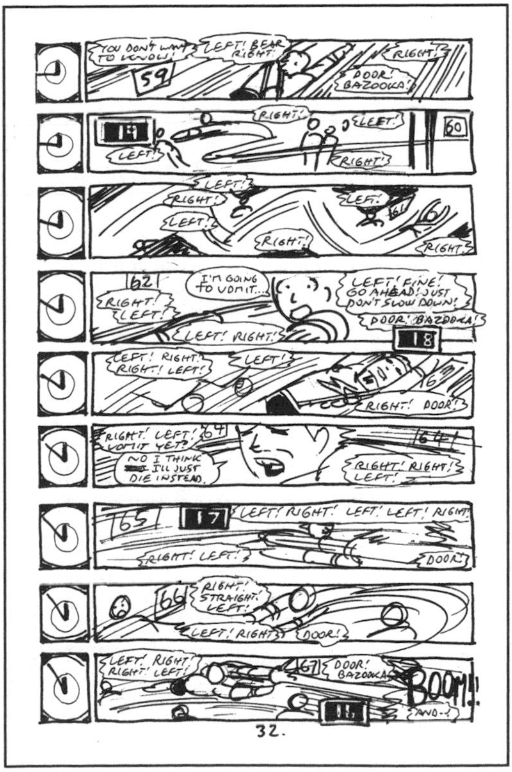
YOU DON'T WANT TO KNOW!
LEFT! BEAR RIGHT!
59
RIGHT!
DOOR! BAZOOKA!
19
RIGHT!
LEFT!
LEFT!
60
RIGHT!
LEFT!
RIGHT!
LEFT!
LEFT!
61
RIGHT!
RIGHT.
62
RIGHT! LEFT!
I'M GOING TO VOMIT...
LEFT! FINE! GO AHEAD! JUST DON'T SLOW DOWN!
DOOR! BAZOOKA!
LEFT! RIGHT!
18
LEFT! RIGHT! RIGHT! LEFT!
LEFT!
RIGHT! DOOR!
RIGHT! LEFT! VOMIT YET?
64
NO I THINK I'LL JUST DIE INSTEAD.
64
RIGHT! RIGHT! LEFT!
65
17
LEFT! RIGHT! LEFT! LEFT! RIGHT!
RIGHT! LEFT!
DOOR!
66
RIGHT! STRAIGHT! LEFT!
LEFT! RIGHT!
DOOR!
LEFT! RIGHT! RIGHT! LEFT!
67
DOOR! BAZOOKA!
BOOM!!
AND--!
32.

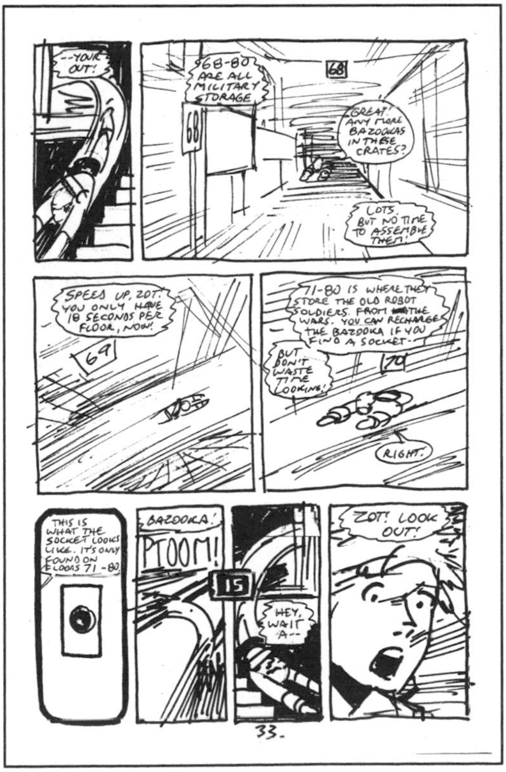
--YOUR OUT!
68-80 ARE ALL MILITARY STORAGE
68
68
GREAT! ANY MORE BAZOOKAS IN THESE CRATES?
LOTS. BUT NO TIME TO ASSEMBLE THEM!
SPEED UP, ZOT! YOU ONLY HAVE 18 SECONDS PER FLOOR, NOW!
69
71-80 IS WHERE THEY STORE THE OLD ROBOT SOLDIERS. FROM THE WARS. YOU CAN RECHARGE THE BAZOOKA IF YOU FIND A SOCKET--
BUT DON'T WASTE TIME LOOKING!
70
RIGHT.
THIS IS WHAT THE SOCKET LOOKS LIKE. IT'S ONLY FOUND ON FLOORS 71-80.
BAZOOKA!
PTOOM!
15
HEY, WAIT A--
ZOT! LOOK OUT!
33.

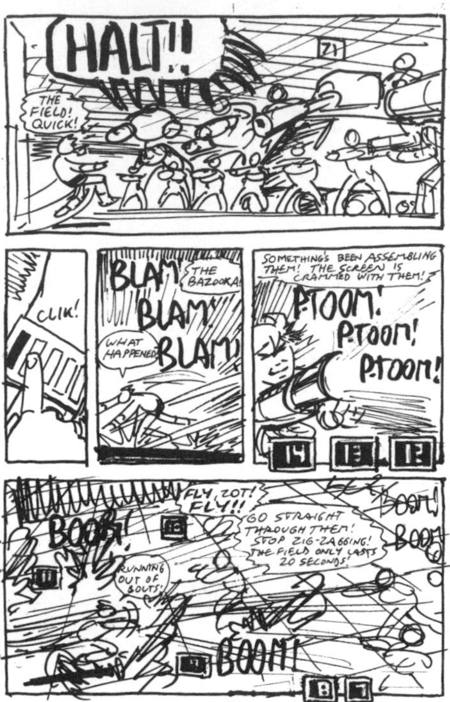
HALT!!
21
THE FIELD! QUICK!
CLIK!
BLAM BLAM BLAM
THE BAZOOKA!
WHAT HAPPENED
SOMETHING'S BEEN ASSEMBLING THEM! THE SCREEN IS CRAMMED WITH THEM!
P-TOOM! P-TOOM! P-TOOM!
14 13 12
FLY, ZOT! FLY!!
BOOM!
GO STRAIGHT THROUGH THEM! STOP ZIG-ZAGGING! THE FIELD ONLY LASTS 20 SECONDS!
BOOM! BOOM!
RUNNING OUT OF BOLTS!
BOOM!
8 7

34.

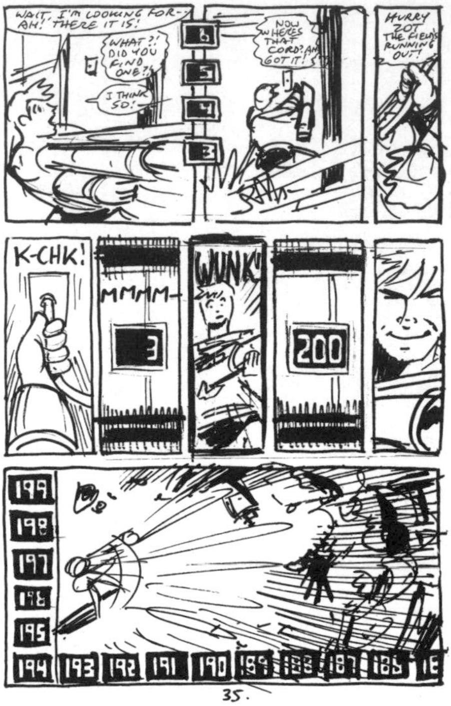
WAIT, I'M LOOKING FOR— AH! THERE IT IS!
WHAT?! DID YOU FIND ONE?!
I THINK SO!
6 5 4 3
NOW WHERE'S THAT CORD? AH! GOT IT!
HURRY ZOT THE FIELD'S RUNNING OUT!
K-CHK!
MMMM—
3
WUNK!
200
199 198 197 196 195
194 193 192 191 190 189 188 187 186

35.

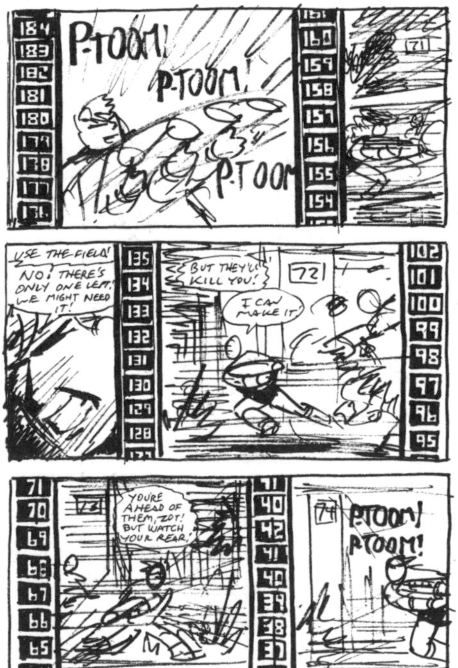
184 183 182 181 180 179 178 177 176
P-TOOM! P-TOOM! P-TOOM
160 159 158 157 156 155 154
71
USE THE FIELD!
NO! THERE'S ONLY ONE LEFT. WE MIGHT NEED IT!
135 134 133 132 131 130 129 128
BUT THEY'LL KILL YOU!
72
I CAN MAKE IT!
102 101 100 99 98 97 96 95
71 70 69 68 67 66 65 64
73
YOU'RE AHEAD OF THEM, ZOT! BUT WATCH YOUR REAR!
42 41 40 39 38 37 36
74
P-TOOM! P-TOOM!

36.

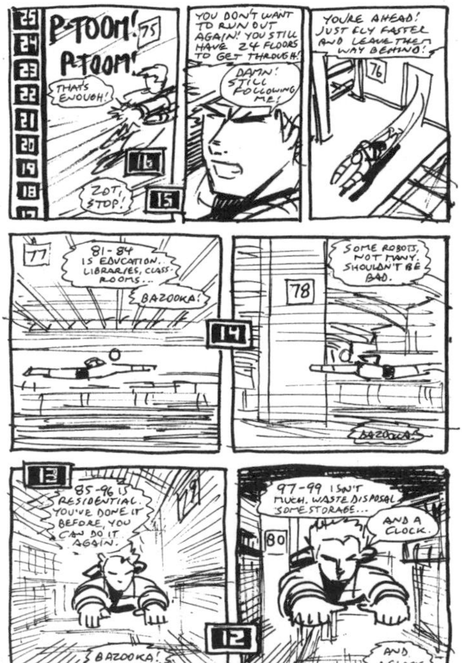
25 24 23 22 21 20 19 18
P-TOOM! 75
P-TOOM!
THAT'S ENOUGH!
16
ZOT, STOP!
15
YOU DON'T WANT TO RUN OUT AGAIN! YOU STILL HAVE 24 FLOORS TO GET THROUGH!
DAMN! STILL FOLLOWING ME!
YOU'RE AHEAD! JUST FLY FASTER AND LEAVE THEM WAY BEHIND!
76
77
81-84 IS EDUCATION. LIBRARIES, CLASSROOMS...
BAZOOKA!
14
SOME ROBOTS, NOT MANY. SHOULDN'T BE BAD.
78
BAZOOKA!
13
85-96 IS RESIDENTIAL. YOU'VE DONE IT BEFORE, YOU CAN DO IT AGAIN.
BAZOOKA!
12
97-99 ISN'T MUCH. WASTE DISPOSAL, SOME STORAGE...
80
AND A CLOCK.
AND A CLOCK.

37.

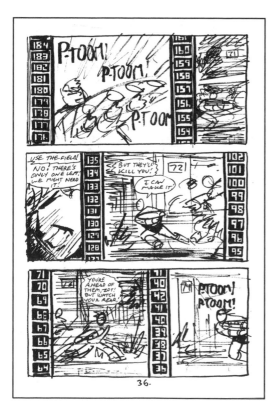

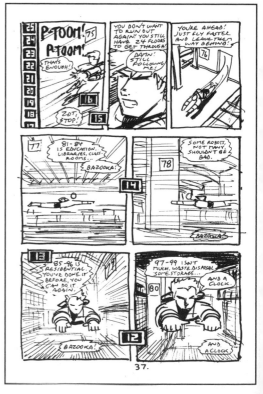

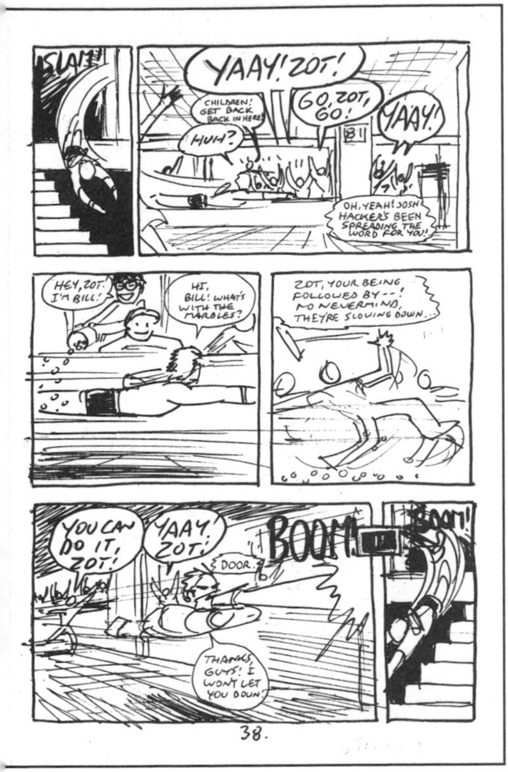
SLAM!
YAAY! ZOT!
CHILDREN! GET BACK BACK IN HERE!
GO, ZOT, GO!
YAAY!
HUH?
81
OH, YEAH! JOSH HACKER'S BEEN SPREADING THE WORD FOR YOU!
HEY, ZOT. I'M BILL!
HI, BILL! WHAT'S WITH THE MARBLES?
ZOT, YOUR BEING FOLLOWED BY--! NO NEVERMIND, THEY'RE SLOWING DOWN...
YOU CAN DO IT, ZOT!
YAAY, ZOT!
DOOR.
BOOM!
11
THANKS, GUYS! I WON'T LET YOU DOWN!
BOOM!
38.

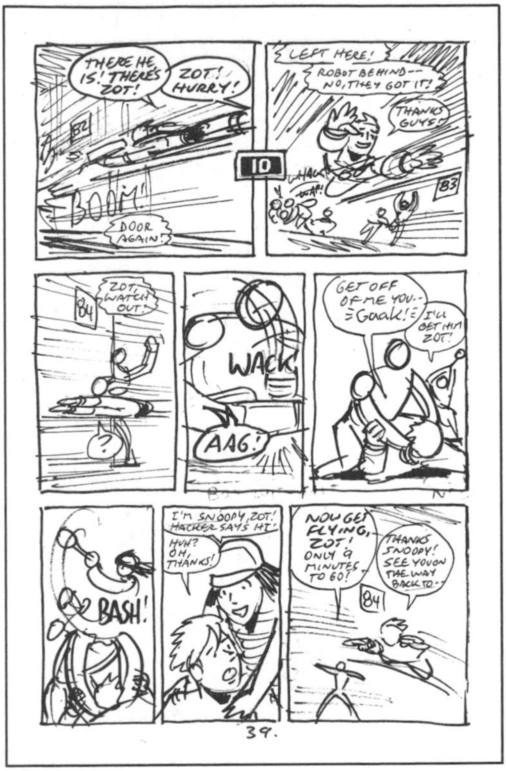
THERE HE IS! THERE'S ZOT!
ZOT! HURRY!
82
10
BOOM!
DOOR AGAIN!
LEFT HERE!
ROBOT BEHIND-- NO, THEY GOT IT!
THANKS GUYS!
WHACK
83
84
ZOT, WATCH OUT!
WACK
AAG!
GET OFF OF ME YOU-- =Gaak!=
I'LL GET HIM ZOT!
BASH!
I'M SNOOPY, ZOT! HACKER SAYS HI!
HUH? OH, THANKS!
NOW GET FLYING, ZOT! ONLY 9 MINUTES TO GO!
THANKS SNOOPY! SEE YOU ON THE WAY BACK TO--
84
39.

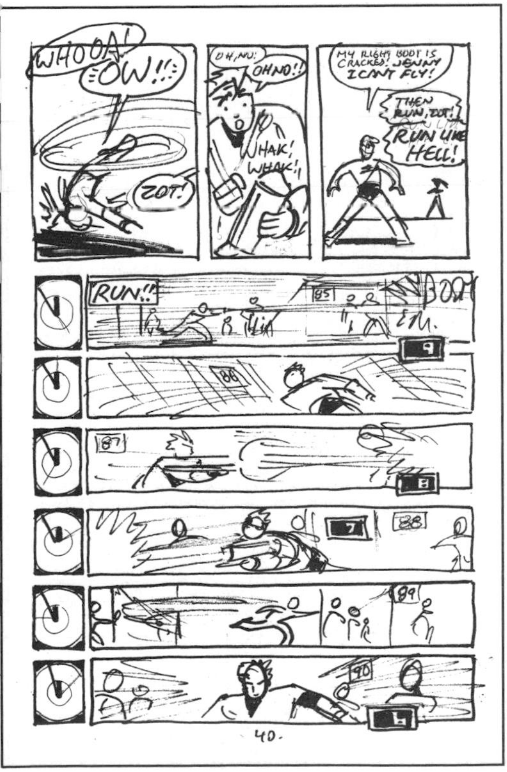
WHOOA! OW!!
ZOT!
OH, NO! OH NO!!
WHAK! WHAK!
MY RIGHT BOOT IS CRACKED! JENNY I CAN'T FLY!
THEN RUN, ZOT! RUN LIKE HELL!
RUN!!
85
9
86
87
8
7
88
89
90
6
40.

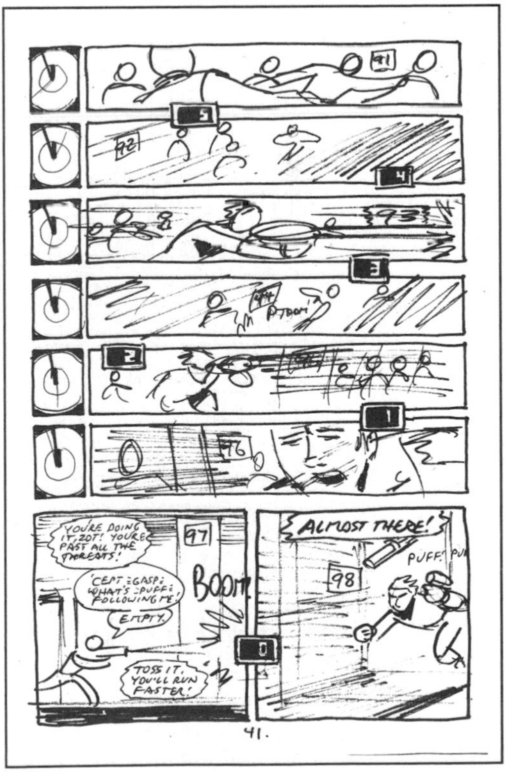
91
5
92
4
93
3
94
BOOM
2
1
96
YOU'RE DOING IT, ZOT! YOU'RE PAST ALL THE THREATS!
97
'CEPT =GASP= WHAT'S =PUFF= FOLLOWING ME?
EMPTY.
BOOM
0
TOSS IT. YOU'LL RUN FASTER!
ALMOST THERE!
PUFF!
98
41.

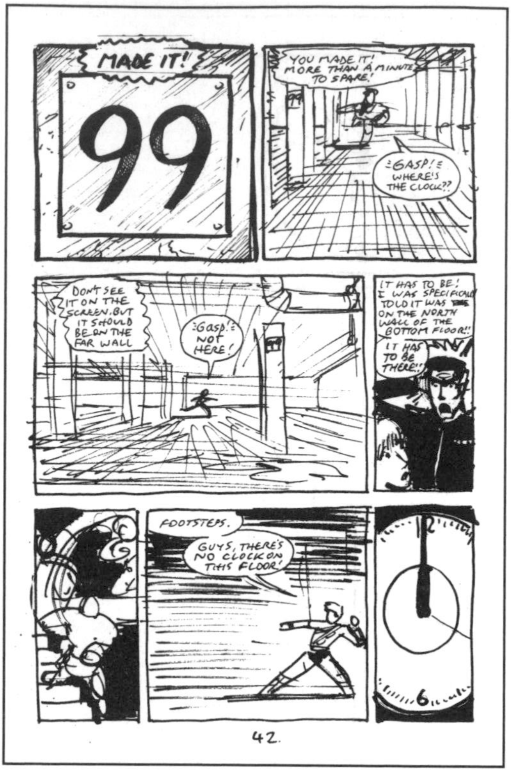
MADE IT!
99
YOU MADE IT! MORE THAN A MINUTE TO SPARE!
GASP! WHERE'S THE CLOCK??
DON'T SEE IT ON THE SCREEN. BUT IT SHOULD BE ON THE FAR WALL
Gasp! NOT HERE!
IT HAS TO BE! I WAS SPECIFICALLY TOLD IT WAS ON THE NORTH WALL OF THE BOTTOM FLOOR!!
IT HAS TO BE THERE!!
FOOTSTEPS.
GUYS, THERE'S NO CLOCK ON THIS FLOOR!
42.

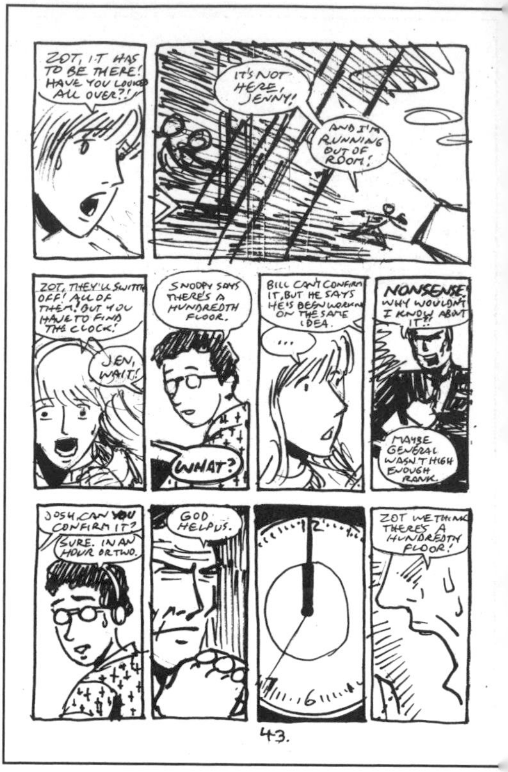
ZOT, IT HAS TO BE THERE! HAVE YOU LOOKED ALL OVER?!
IT'S NOT HERE, JENNY!
AND I'M RUNNING OUT OF ROOM!
ZOT, THEY'LL SWITCH OFF! ALL OF THEM! BUT YOU HAVE TO FIND THE CLOCK!
JEN, WAIT!
SNOOPY SAYS THERE'S A HUNDREDTH FLOOR.
WHAT?
BILL CAN'T CONFIRM IT, BUT HE SAYS HE'S BEEN WORKING ON THE SAME IDEA.
...
NONSENSE! WHY WOULDN'T I KNOW ABOUT IT?!
MAYBE GENERAL WASN'T HIGH ENOUGH RANK.
JOSH, CAN YOU CONFIRM IT?
SURE. IN AN HOUR OR TWO.
GOD HELP US.
ZOT WE THINK THERE'S A HUNDREDTH FLOOR!
43.

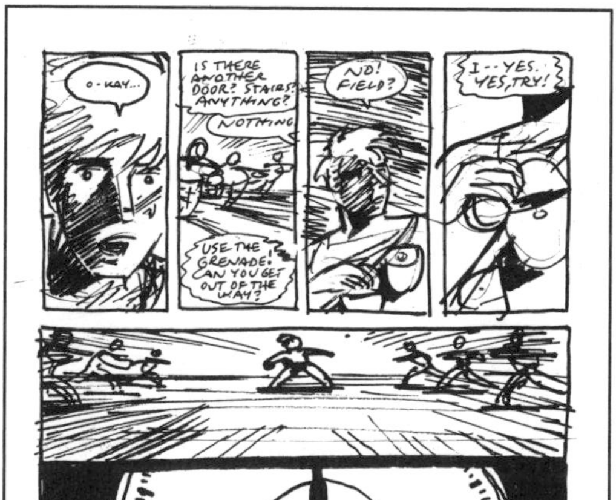
O-KAY...
IS THERE ANOTHER DOOR? STAIRS? ANYTHING?
NOTHING
USE THE GRENADE! CAN YOU GET OUT OF THE WAY?
NO! FIELD?
I--YES. YES, TRY!
CLIK!
99
CLIK!
44.

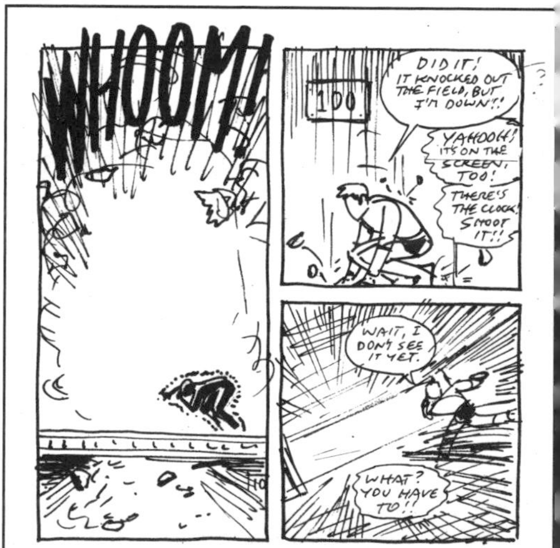
WHOOM!
DID IT! IT KNOCKED OUT THE FIELD, BUT I'M DOWN!!
100
YAHOO!! IT'S ON THE SCREEN, TOO!
THERE'S THE CLOCK! SHOOT IT!!
WAIT, I DON'T SEE IT YET.
WHAT? YOU HAVE TO!!
I DON'T SEE IT, JEN!
IT'S RIGHT THERE!
RIGHT WHERE??
ZOT, YOU'RE RUNNING AWAY FROM IT!!
45.

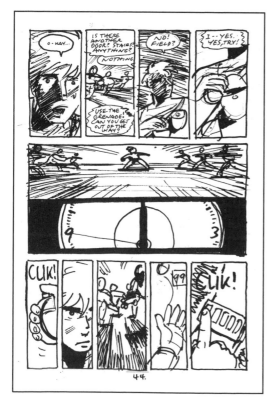

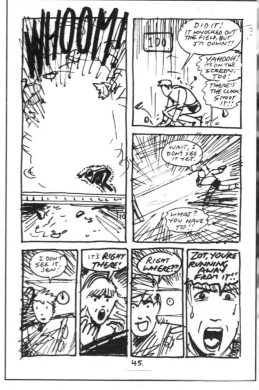

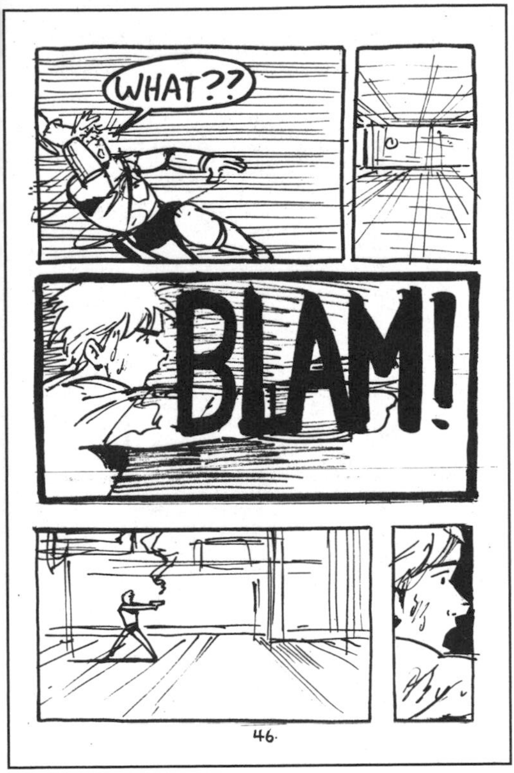
WHAT??
BLAM!
46.

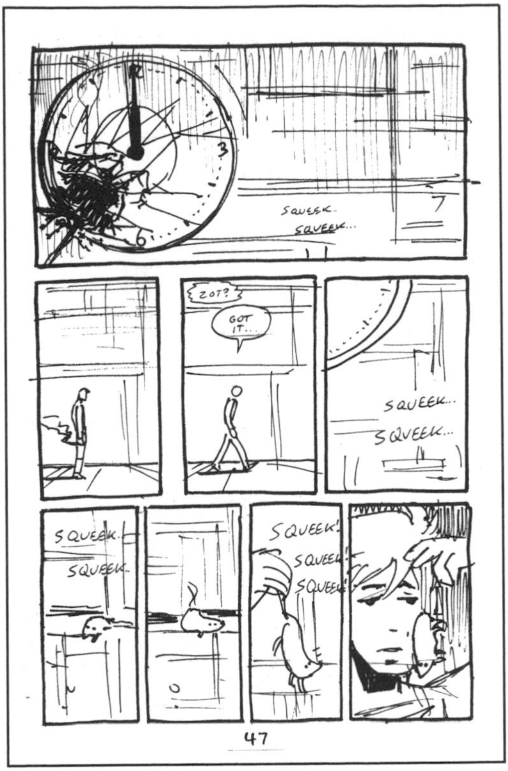
SQUEEK.
SQUEEK...
ZOT?
GOT IT...
SQUEEK...
SQUEEK...
SQUEEK.
SQUEEK.
SQUEEK!
47

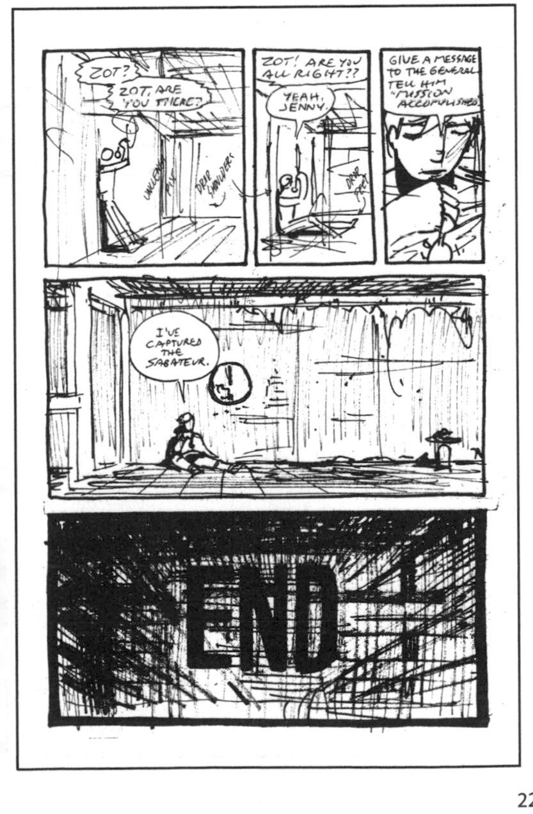
ZOT?
ZOT, ARE YOU THERE?
ZOT! ARE YOU ALL RIGHT??
YEAH, JENNY.
GIVE A MESSAGE TO THE GENERAL. TELL HIM "MISSION ACCOMPLISHED"
I'VE CAPTURED THE SABATEUR.
END

Thanks to Chuck Austen, who helped me locate the second half of these layouts, which had turned up in an envelope only a few months before we put this collection together.

In his sleek, kinetic art for the final comics, Chuck took my mouse "saboteur" and made it a *dreep,* a small rodent creature featured in the original color issues. It was a nice touch that gave even this light-hearted fill-in a properly named adversary to go with the other rogues' gallery entries from this period.

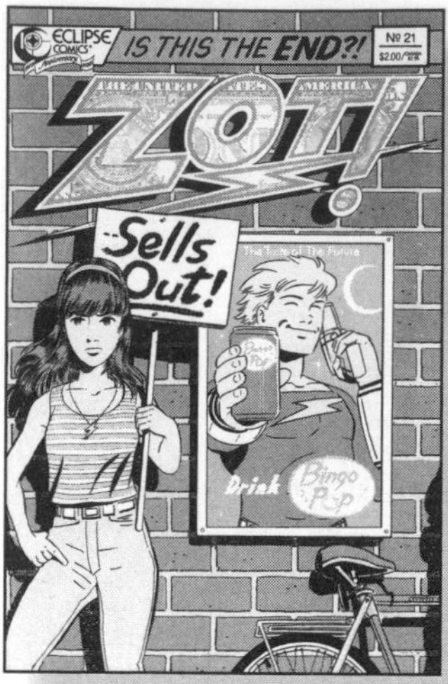
ECLIPSE COMICS
IS THIS THE END?!
Nº 21
$2.00
ZOT!
Sells Out!
Drink Bingo Pop

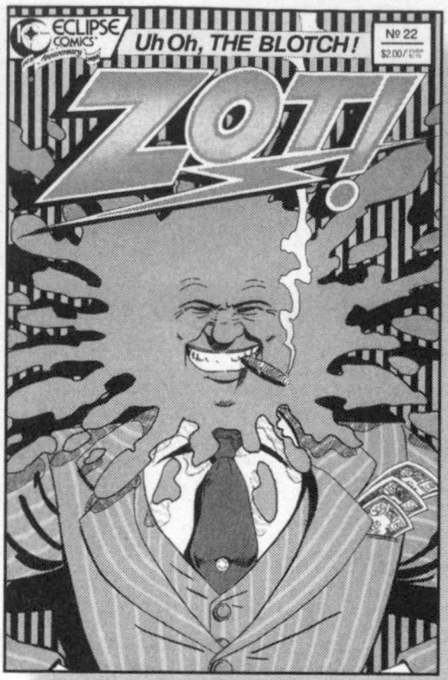
ECLIPSE COMICS
Uh Oh, THE BLOTCH!
Nº 22
$2.00
ZOT!

Can't Buy Me Love

First published in *Zot! #21–22*.

Lettering:

Bob Lappan

Original series editor:

cat yronwode

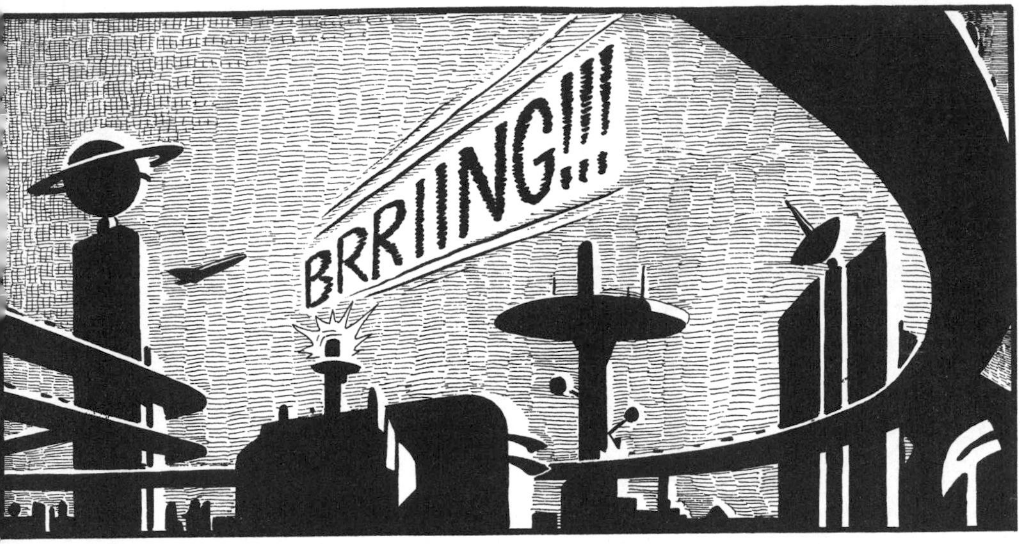
BRRIING!!!

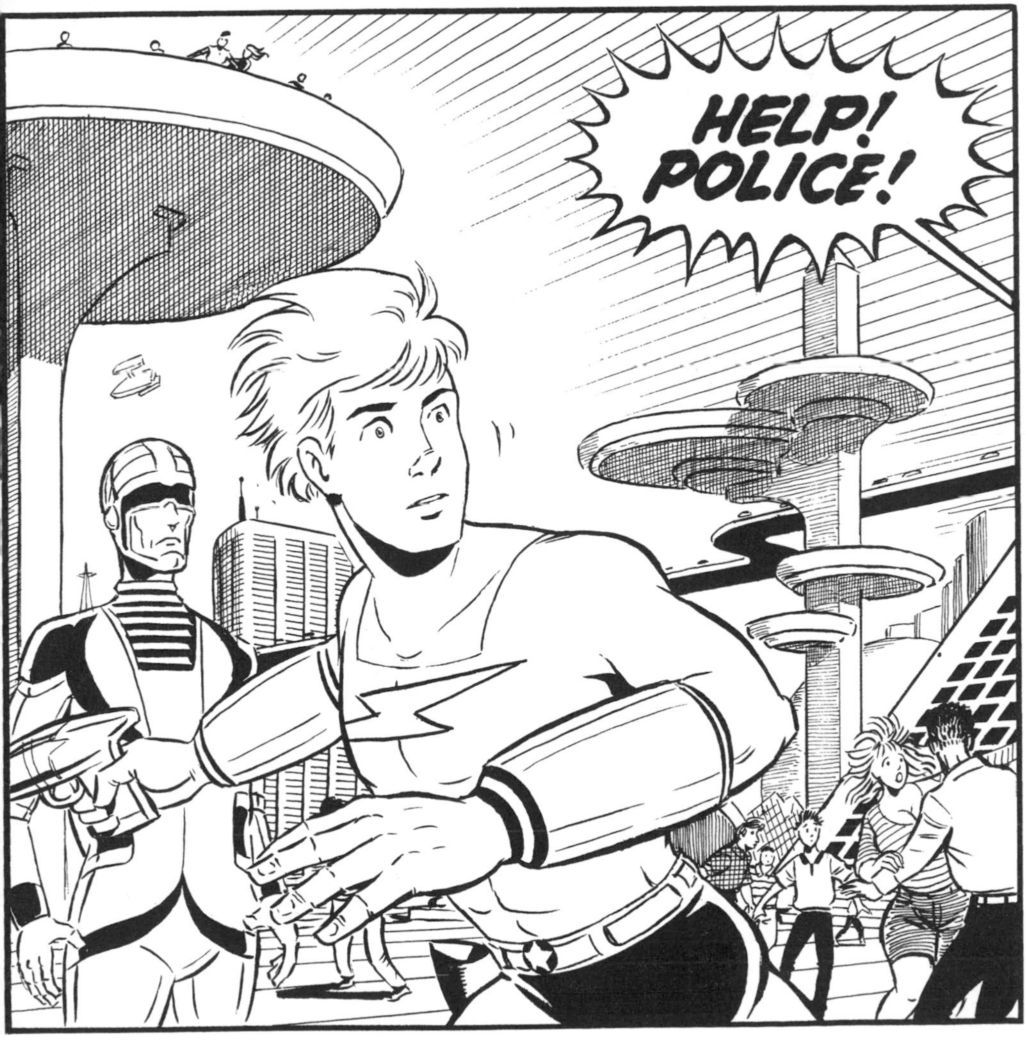
HELP! POLICE!

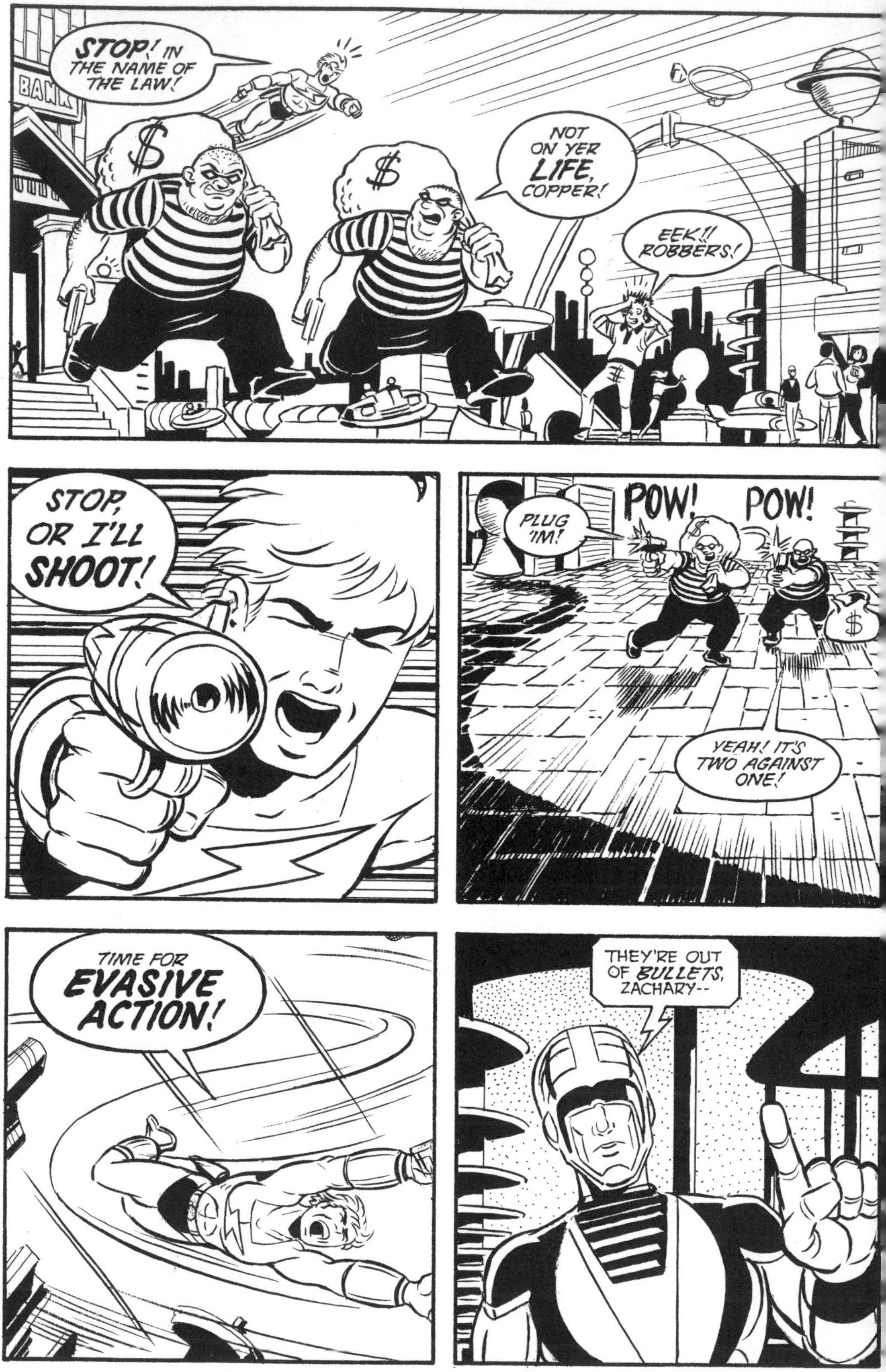
STOP! IN THE NAME OF THE LAW!
BANK
NOT ON YER LIFE, COPPER!
EEK!! ROBBERS!
STOP, OR I'LL SHOOT!
PLUG 'IM!
POW!
POW!
YEAH! IT'S TWO AGAINST ONE!
TIME FOR EVASIVE ACTION!
THEY'RE OUT OF BULLETS, ZACHARY--

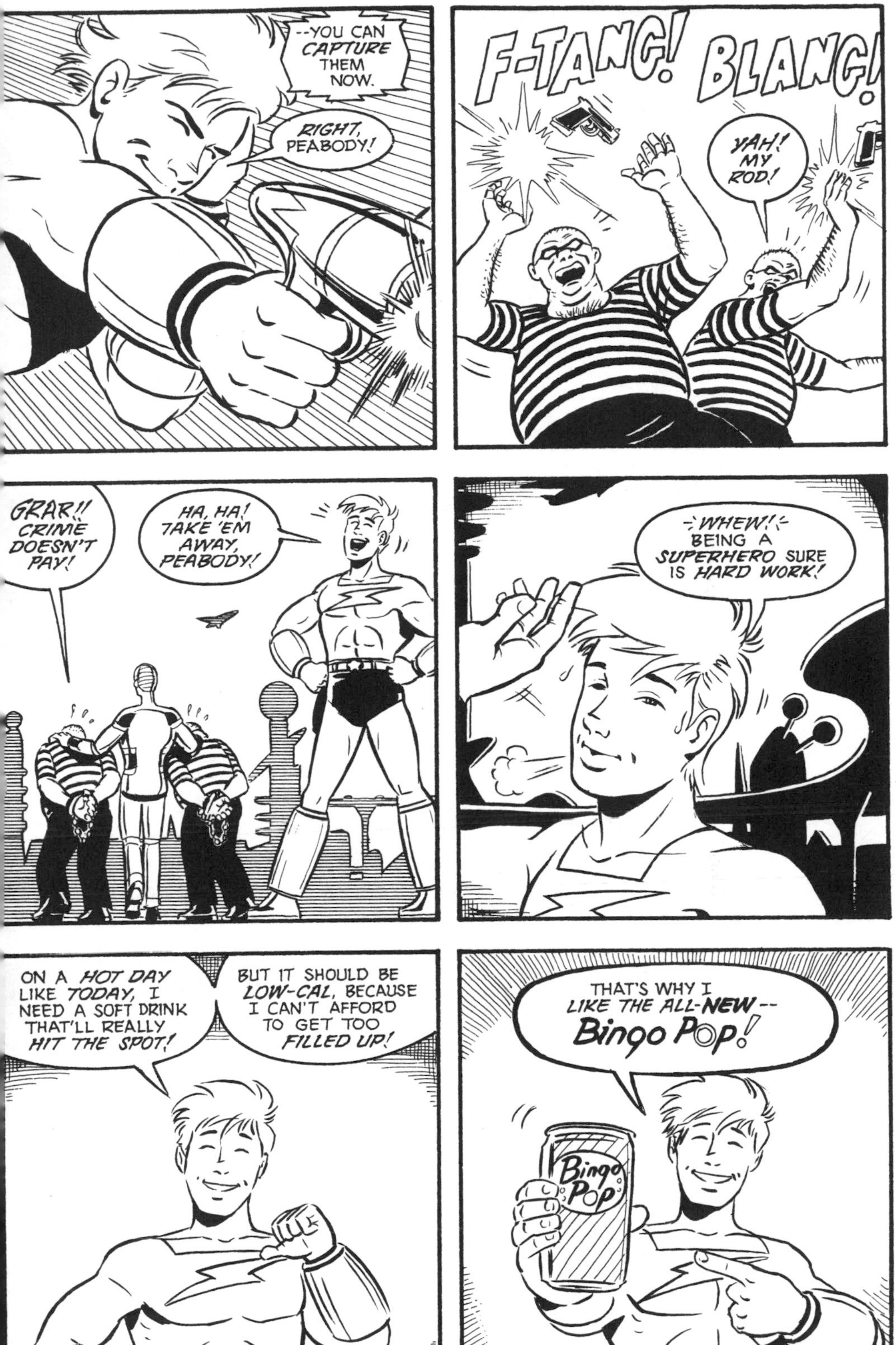
--YOU CAN CAPTURE THEM NOW.
RIGHT, PEABODY!
F-TANG! BLANG!
YAH! MY ROD!
GRAR!! CRIME DOESN'T PAY!
HA, HA! TAKE 'EM AWAY, PEABODY!
WHEW! BEING A SUPERHERO SURE IS HARD WORK!
ON A HOT DAY LIKE TODAY, I NEED A SOFT DRINK THAT'LL REALLY HIT THE SPOT!
BUT IT SHOULD BE LOW-CAL, BECAUSE I CAN'T AFFORD TO GET TOO FILLED UP!
THAT'S WHY I LIKE THE ALL-NEW-- Bingo Pop!
Bingo Pop

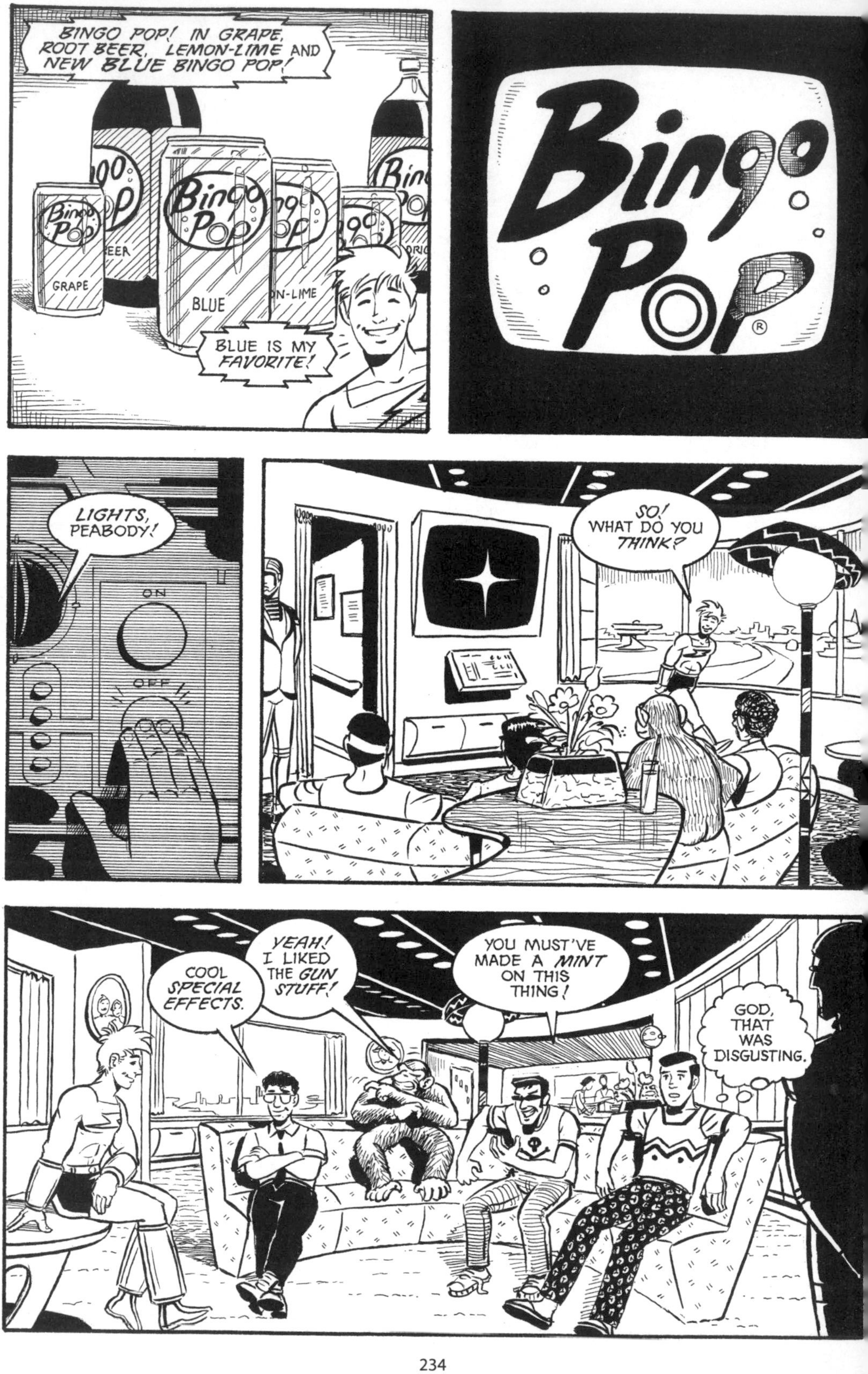
BINGO POP! IN GRAPE, ROOT BEER, LEMON-LIME AND NEW BLUE BINGO POP!
GRAPE
BLUE
BLUE IS MY FAVORITE!
Bingo Pop ®
LIGHTS, PEABODY!
ON
OFF
SO! WHAT DO YOU THINK?
COOL SPECIAL EFFECTS.
YEAH! I LIKED THE GUN STUFF!
YOU MUST'VE MADE A MINT ON THIS THING!
GOD, THAT WAS DISGUSTING.

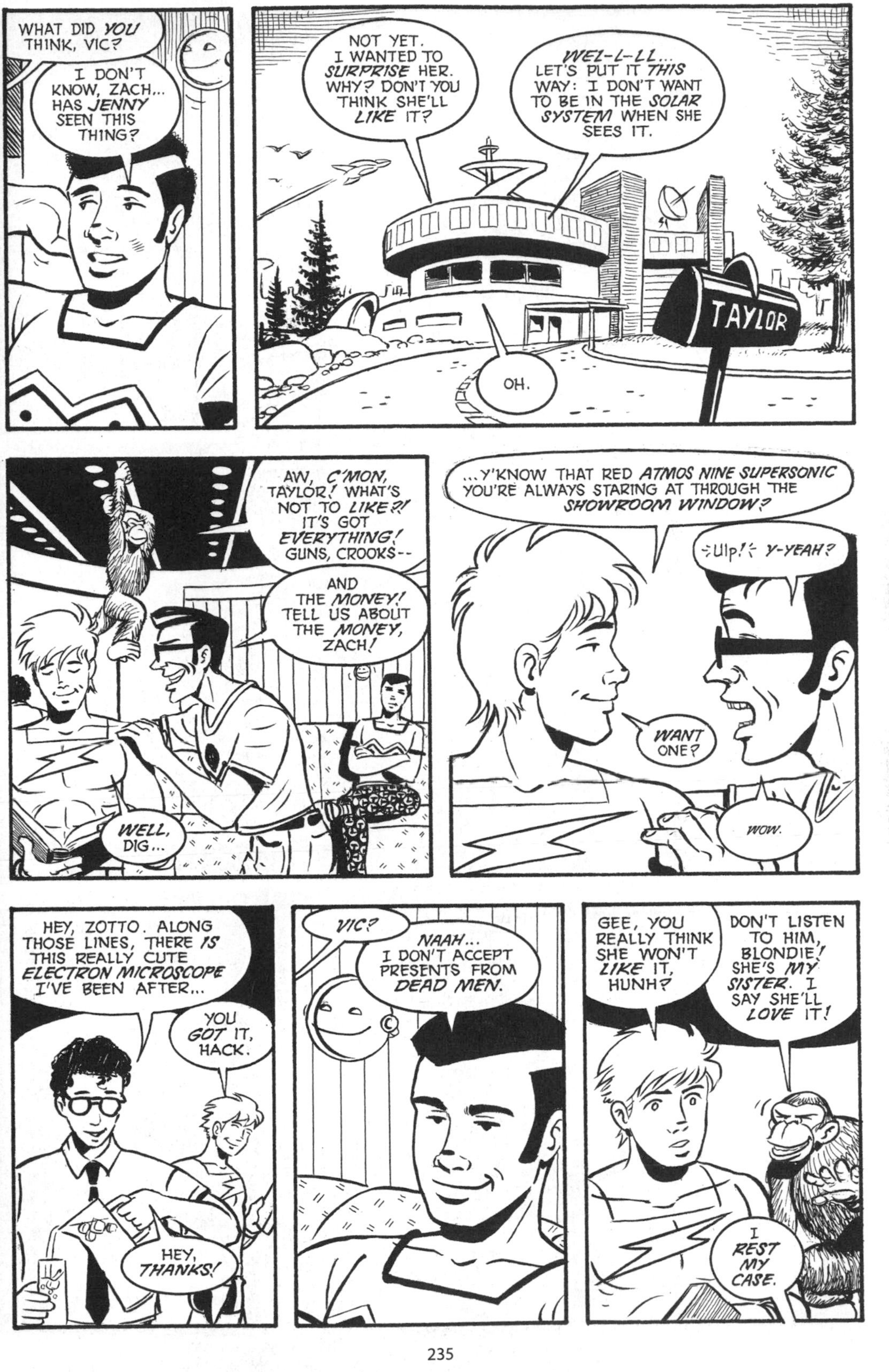
WHAT DID *YOU* THINK, VIC?
I DON'T KNOW, ZACH... HAS *JENNY* SEEN THIS THING?
NOT YET. I WANTED TO *SURPRISE* HER. WHY? DON'T YOU THINK SHE'LL *LIKE* IT?
WEL-L-LL... LET'S PUT IT *THIS* WAY: I DON'T WANT TO BE IN THE *SOLAR SYSTEM* WHEN SHE SEES IT.
TAYLOR
OH.
AW, *C'MON*, TAYLOR! WHAT'S NOT TO *LIKE*?! IT'S GOT *EVERYTHING*! GUNS, CROOKS--
AND THE *MONEY*! TELL US ABOUT THE *MONEY*, ZACH!
WELL, DIG...
...Y'KNOW THAT RED *ATMOS NINE SUPERSONIC* YOU'RE ALWAYS STARING AT THROUGH THE *SHOWROOM WINDOW*?
ULP! *Y-YEAH*?
WANT ONE?
WOW.
HEY, ZOTTO. ALONG THOSE LINES, THERE *IS* THIS REALLY CUTE *ELECTRON MICROSCOPE* I'VE BEEN AFTER...
YOU *GOT* IT, HACK.
HEY, *THANKS*!
VIC?
NAAH... I DON'T ACCEPT PRESENTS FROM *DEAD MEN*.
GEE, YOU REALLY THINK SHE WON'T *LIKE* IT, HUNH?
DON'T LISTEN TO HIM, BLONDIE! SHE'S *MY SISTER*. I SAY SHE'LL *LOVE* IT!
I *REST MY CASE*.

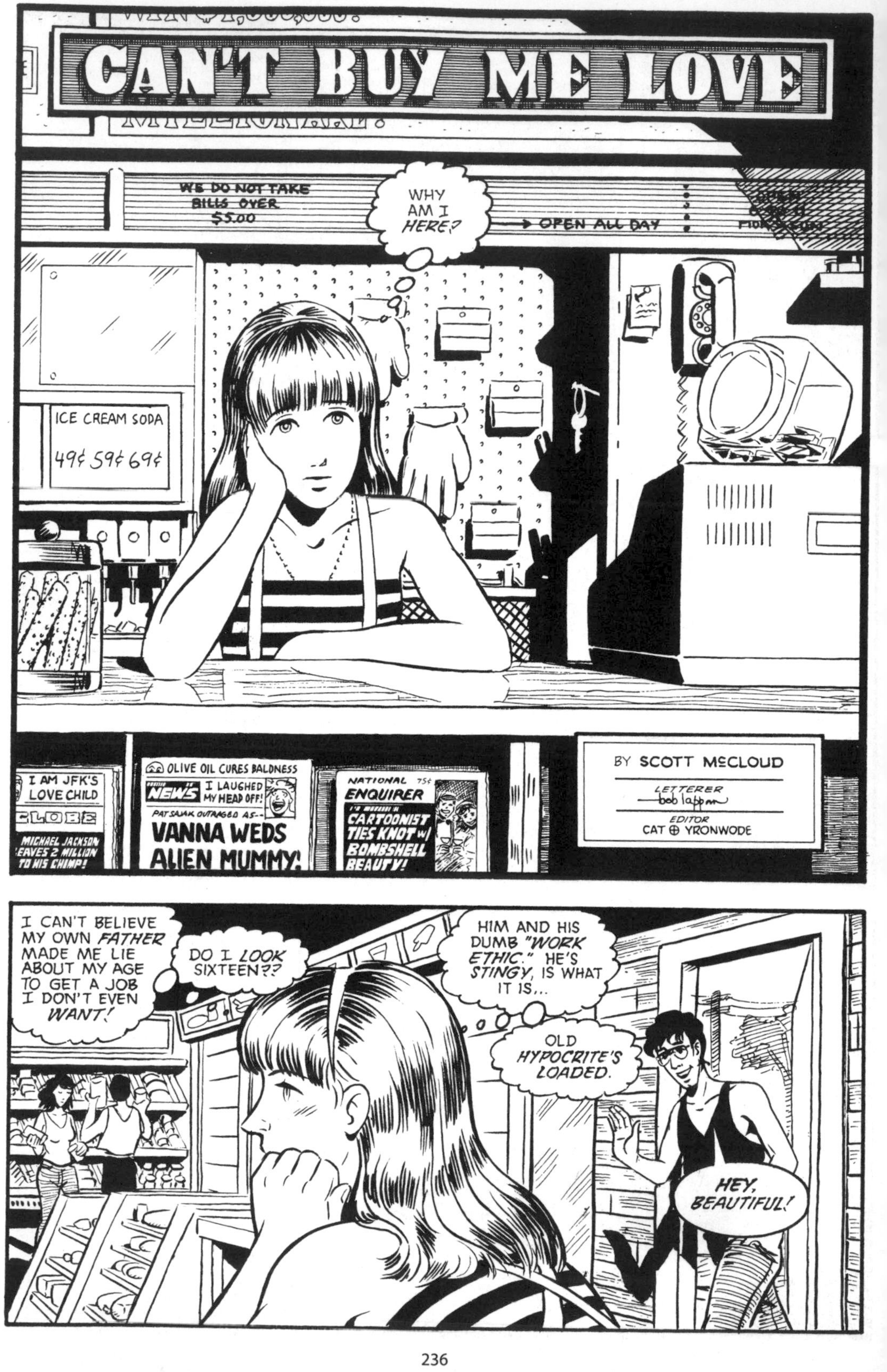
CAN'T BUY ME LOVE
WE DO NOT TAKE BILLS OVER $5.00
WHY AM I *HERE?*
OPEN ALL DAY
ICE CREAM SODA
49¢ 59¢ 69¢
I AM JFK'S LOVE CHILD
GLOBE
MICHAEL JACKSON LEAVES 2 MILLION TO HIS CHIMP!
OLIVE OIL CURES BALDNESS
NEWS
I LAUGHED MY HEAD OFF!
PAT SAJAK OUTRAGED AS--
VANNA WEDS ALIEN MUMMY!
NATIONAL ENQUIRER 75¢
CARTOONIST TIES KNOT w/ BOMBSHELL BEAUTY!
BY SCOTT McCLOUD
LETTERER bob lappan
EDITOR CAT ⊕ YRONWODE
I CAN'T BELIEVE MY OWN *FATHER* MADE ME LIE ABOUT MY AGE TO GET A JOB I DON'T EVEN *WANT!*
DO I *LOOK* SIXTEEN??
HIM AND HIS DUMB *"WORK ETHIC."* HE'S *STINGY,* IS WHAT IT IS...
OLD *HYPOCRITE'S LOADED.*
HEY, BEAUTIFUL!

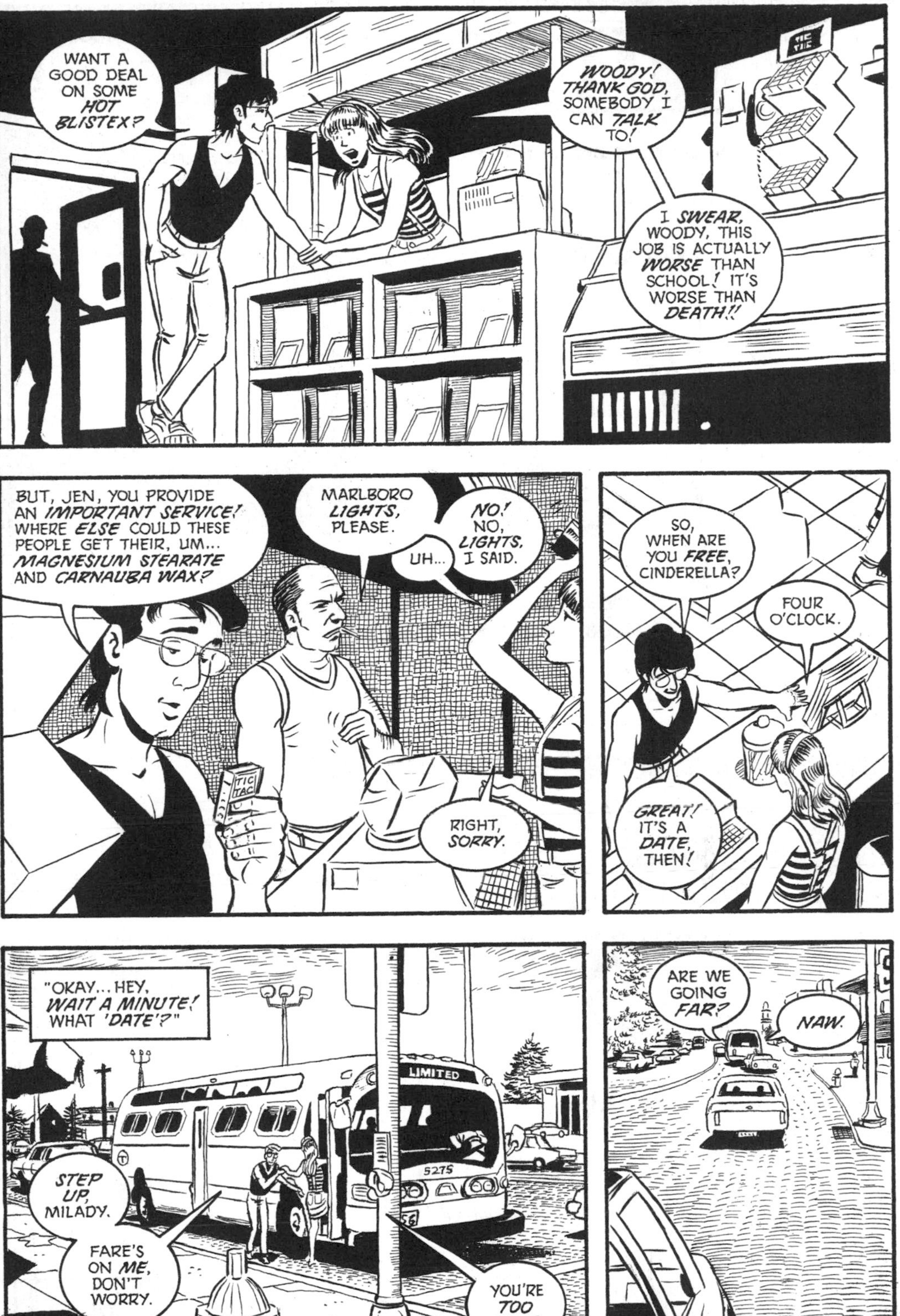
WANT A GOOD DEAL ON SOME HOT BLISTEX?
WOODY! THANK GOD, SOMEBODY I CAN TALK TO!
I SWEAR, WOODY, THIS JOB IS ACTUALLY WORSE THAN SCHOOL! IT'S WORSE THAN DEATH!!
TIC TAC
BUT, JEN, YOU PROVIDE AN IMPORTANT SERVICE! WHERE ELSE COULD THESE PEOPLE GET THEIR, UM... MAGNESIUM STEARATE AND CARNAUBA WAX?
MARLBORO LIGHTS, PLEASE.
UH...
NO! NO, LIGHTS, I SAID.
RIGHT, SORRY.
TIC TAC
SO, WHEN ARE YOU FREE, CINDERELLA?
FOUR O'CLOCK.
GREAT! IT'S A DATE, THEN!
"OKAY... HEY, WAIT A MINUTE! WHAT 'DATE'?"
LIMITED
5275
STEP UP, MILADY.
FARE'S ON ME, DON'T WORRY.
YOU'RE TOO KIND.
ARE WE GOING FAR?
NAW.

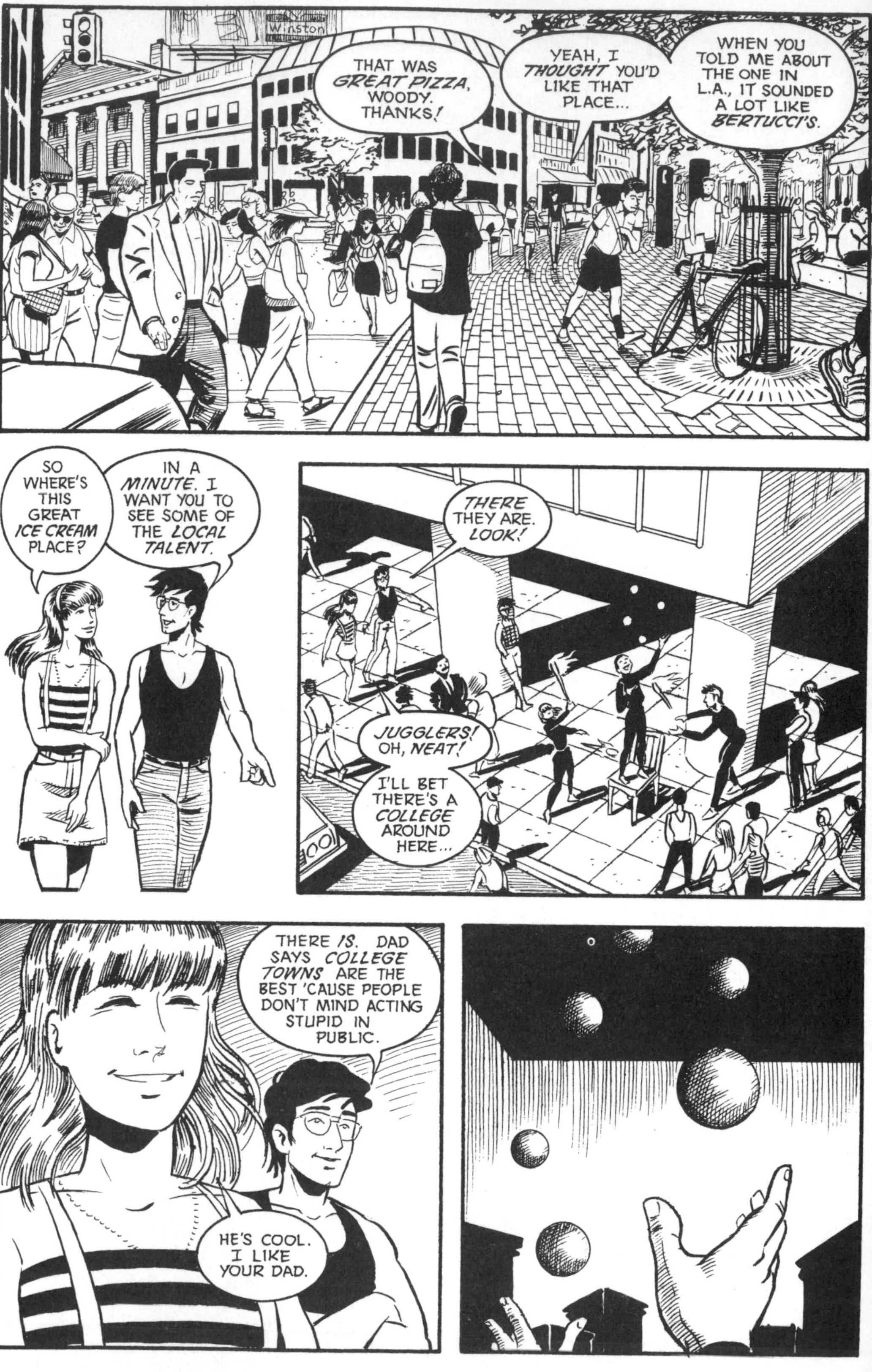
Winston
THAT WAS GREAT PIZZA, WOODY. THANKS!
YEAH, I THOUGHT YOU'D LIKE THAT PLACE...
WHEN YOU TOLD ME ABOUT THE ONE IN L.A., IT SOUNDED A LOT LIKE BERTUCCI'S.
SO WHERE'S THIS GREAT ICE CREAM PLACE?
IN A MINUTE. I WANT YOU TO SEE SOME OF THE LOCAL TALENT.
THERE THEY ARE. LOOK!
JUGGLERS! OH, NEAT!
I'LL BET THERE'S A COLLEGE AROUND HERE...
THERE IS. DAD SAYS COLLEGE TOWNS ARE THE BEST 'CAUSE PEOPLE DON'T MIND ACTING STUPID IN PUBLIC.
HE'S COOL. I LIKE YOUR DAD.

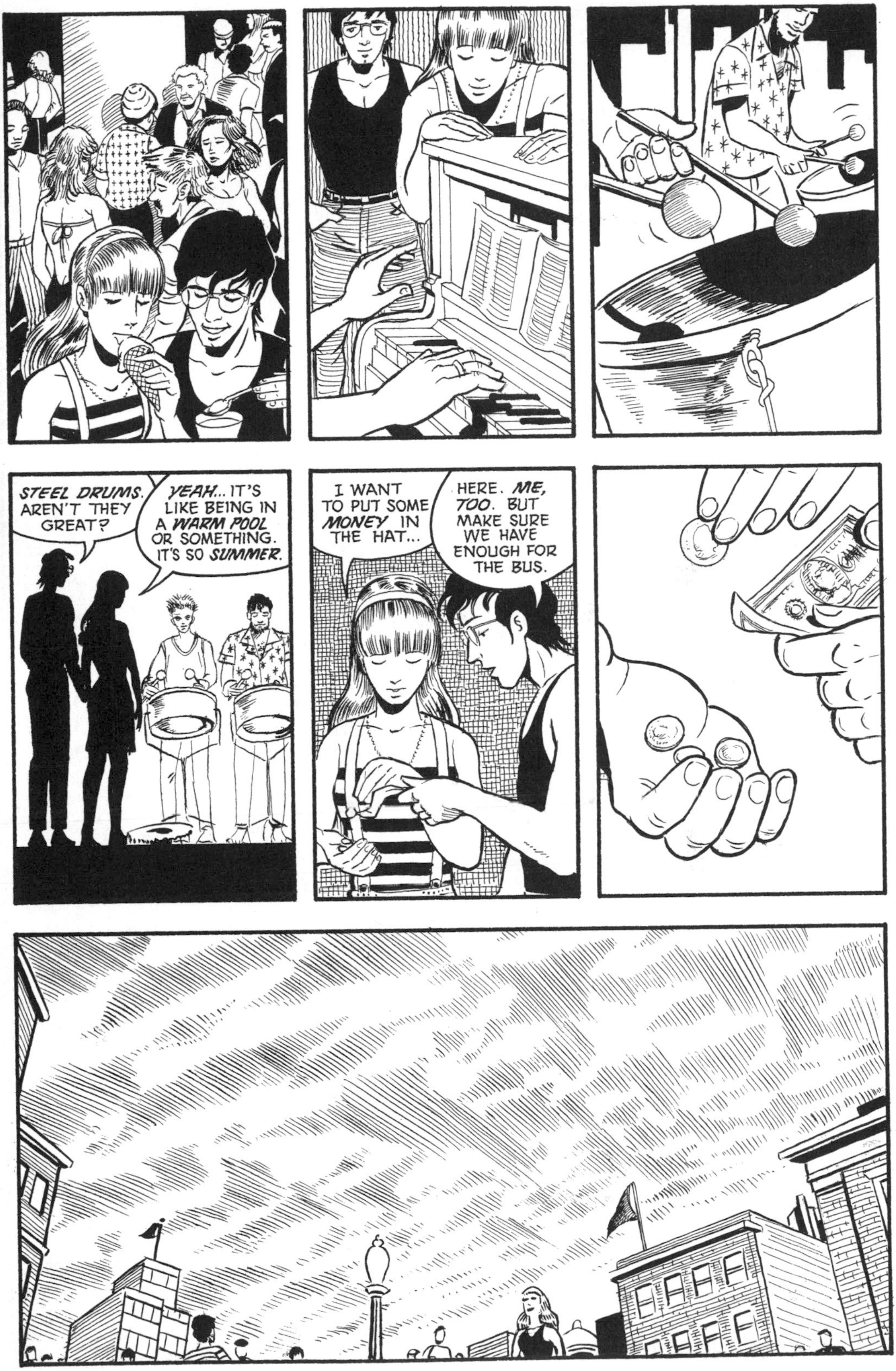
STEEL DRUMS. AREN'T THEY GREAT?
YEAH... IT'S LIKE BEING IN A WARM POOL OR SOMETHING. IT'S SO SUMMER.
I WANT TO PUT SOME MONEY IN THE HAT...
HERE. ME, TOO. BUT MAKE SURE WE HAVE ENOUGH FOR THE BUS.

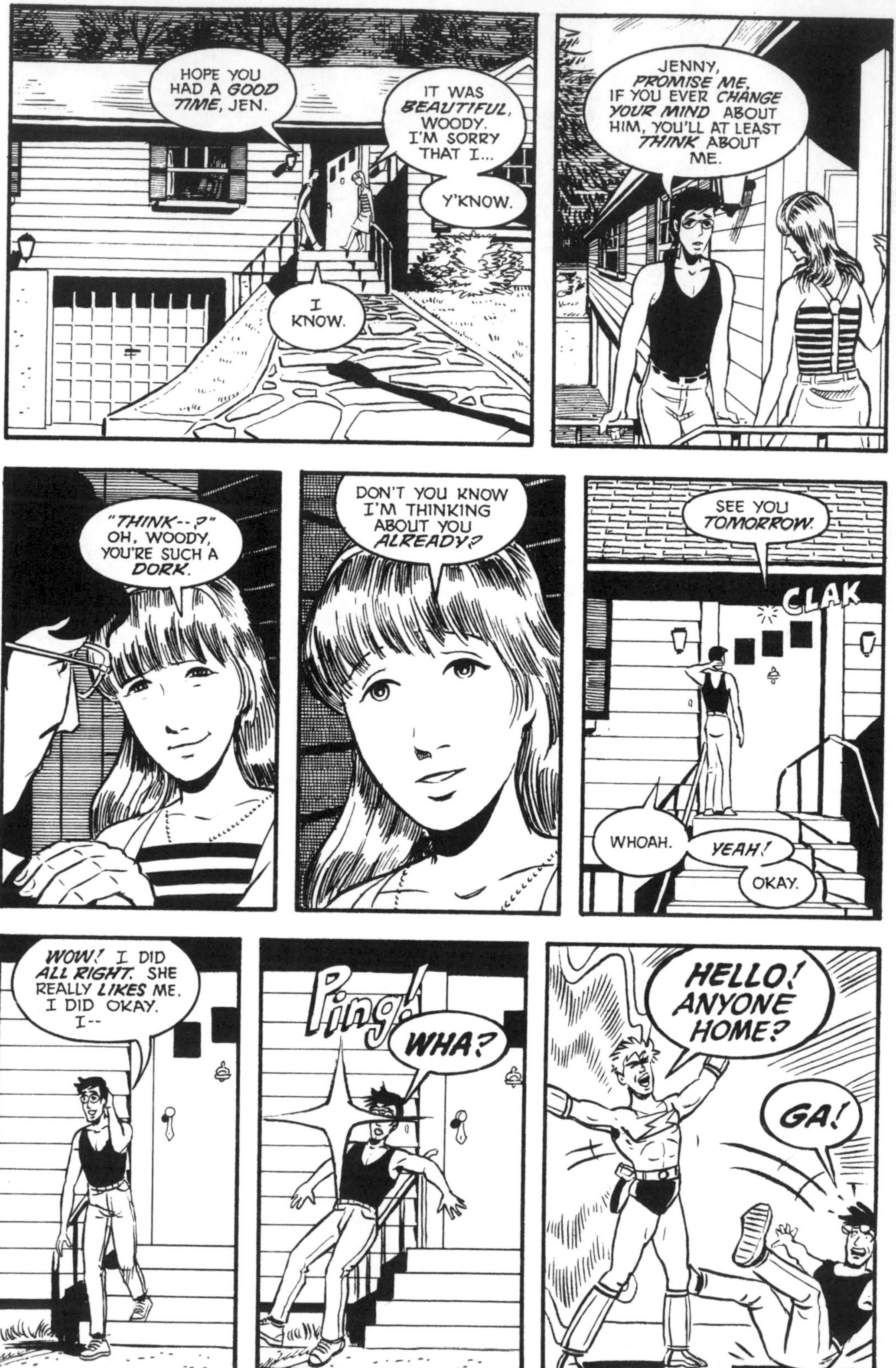
HOPE YOU HAD A GOOD TIME, JEN.
IT WAS BEAUTIFUL, WOODY. I'M SORRY THAT I...
Y'KNOW.
I KNOW.
JENNY, PROMISE ME, IF YOU EVER CHANGE YOUR MIND ABOUT HIM, YOU'LL AT LEAST THINK ABOUT ME.
"THINK--?" OH, WOODY, YOU'RE SUCH A DORK.
DON'T YOU KNOW I'M THINKING ABOUT YOU ALREADY?
SEE YOU TOMORROW.
CLAK
WHOAH.
YEAH!
OKAY.
WOW! I DID ALL RIGHT. SHE REALLY LIKES ME. I DID OKAY. I--
Ping!
WHA?
HELLO! ANYONE HOME?
GA!

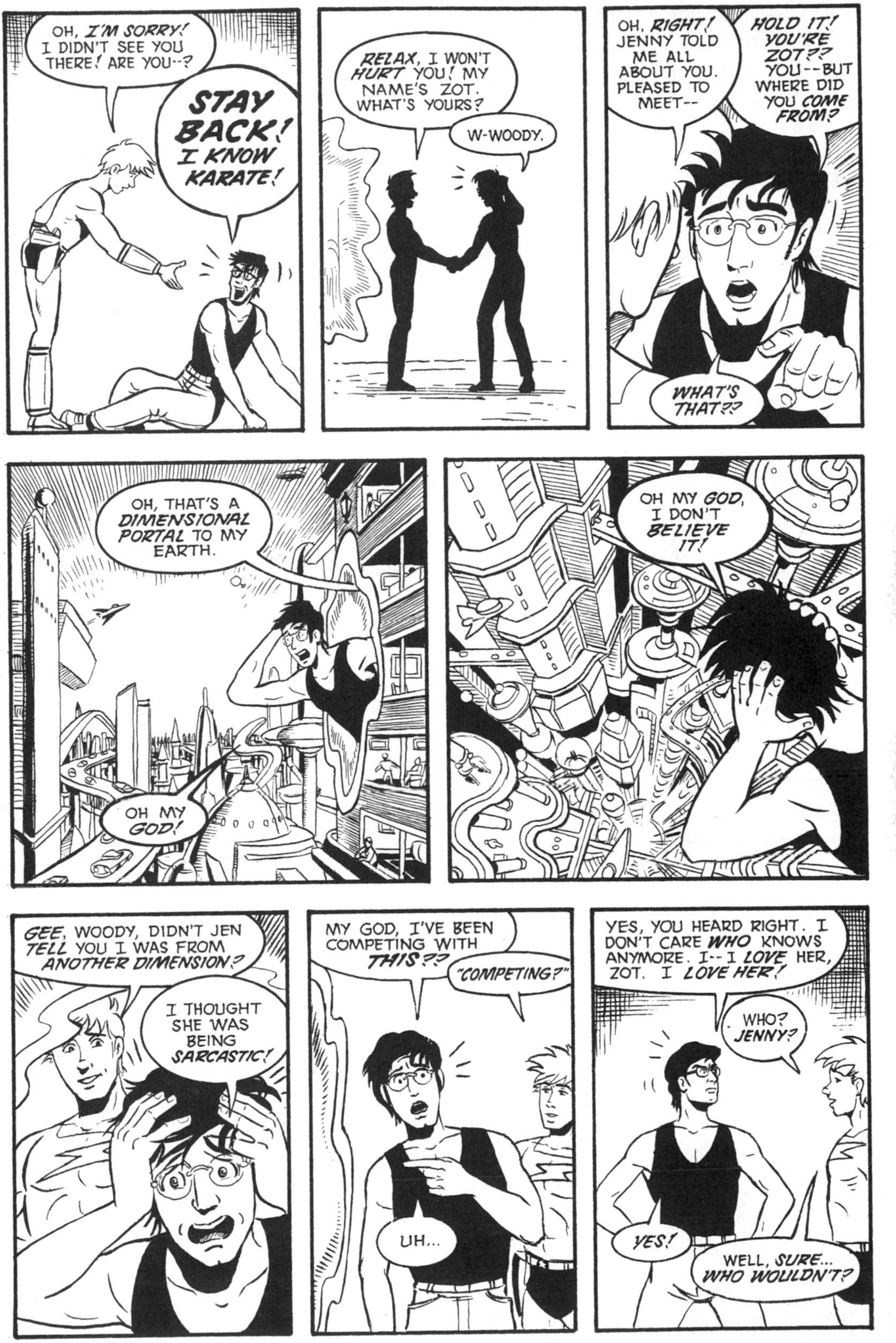
OH, I'M SORRY! I DIDN'T SEE YOU THERE! ARE YOU--?
STAY BACK! I KNOW KARATE!
RELAX, I WON'T HURT YOU! MY NAME'S ZOT. WHAT'S YOURS?
W-WOODY.
OH, RIGHT! JENNY TOLD ME ALL ABOUT YOU. PLEASED TO MEET--
HOLD IT! YOU'RE ZOT?? YOU--BUT WHERE DID YOU COME FROM?
WHAT'S THAT??
OH, THAT'S A DIMENSIONAL PORTAL TO MY EARTH.
OH MY GOD!
OH MY GOD, I DON'T BELIEVE IT!
GEE, WOODY, DIDN'T JEN TELL YOU I WAS FROM ANOTHER DIMENSION?
I THOUGHT SHE WAS BEING SARCASTIC!
MY GOD, I'VE BEEN COMPETING WITH THIS??
"COMPETING?"
UH...
YES, YOU HEARD RIGHT. I DON'T CARE WHO KNOWS ANYMORE. I--I LOVE HER, ZOT. I LOVE HER!
WHO? JENNY?
YES!
WELL, SURE... WHO WOULDN'T?

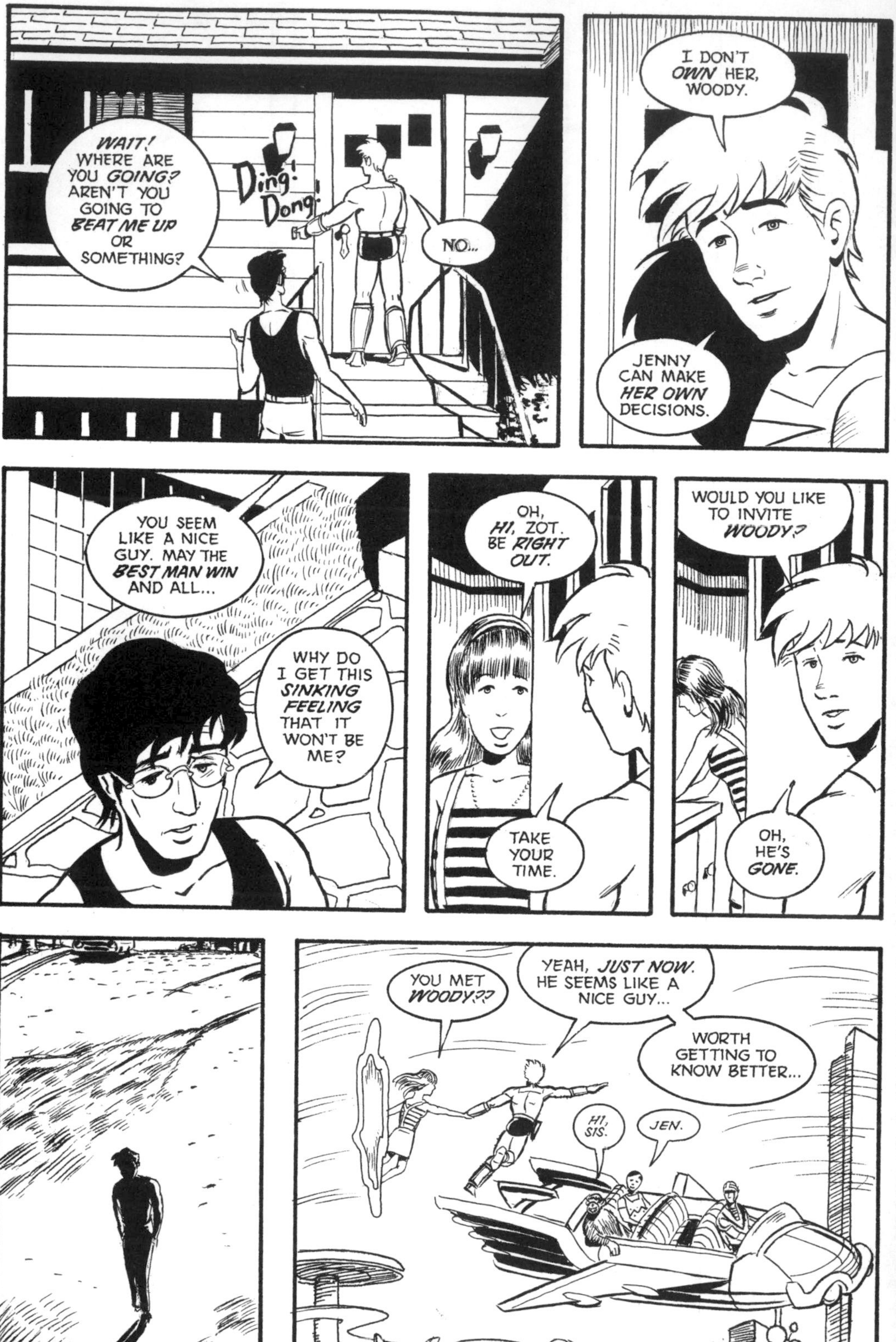
WAIT! WHERE ARE YOU GOING? AREN'T YOU GOING TO BEAT ME UP OR SOMETHING?
Ding! Dong!
NO...
I DON'T OWN HER, WOODY.
JENNY CAN MAKE HER OWN DECISIONS.
YOU SEEM LIKE A NICE GUY. MAY THE BEST MAN WIN AND ALL...
WHY DO I GET THIS SINKING FEELING THAT IT WON'T BE ME?
OH, HI, ZOT. BE RIGHT OUT.
TAKE YOUR TIME.
WOULD YOU LIKE TO INVITE WOODY?
OH, HE'S GONE.
YOU MET WOODY??
YEAH, JUST NOW. HE SEEMS LIKE A NICE GUY...
WORTH GETTING TO KNOW BETTER...
HI, SIS.
JEN.

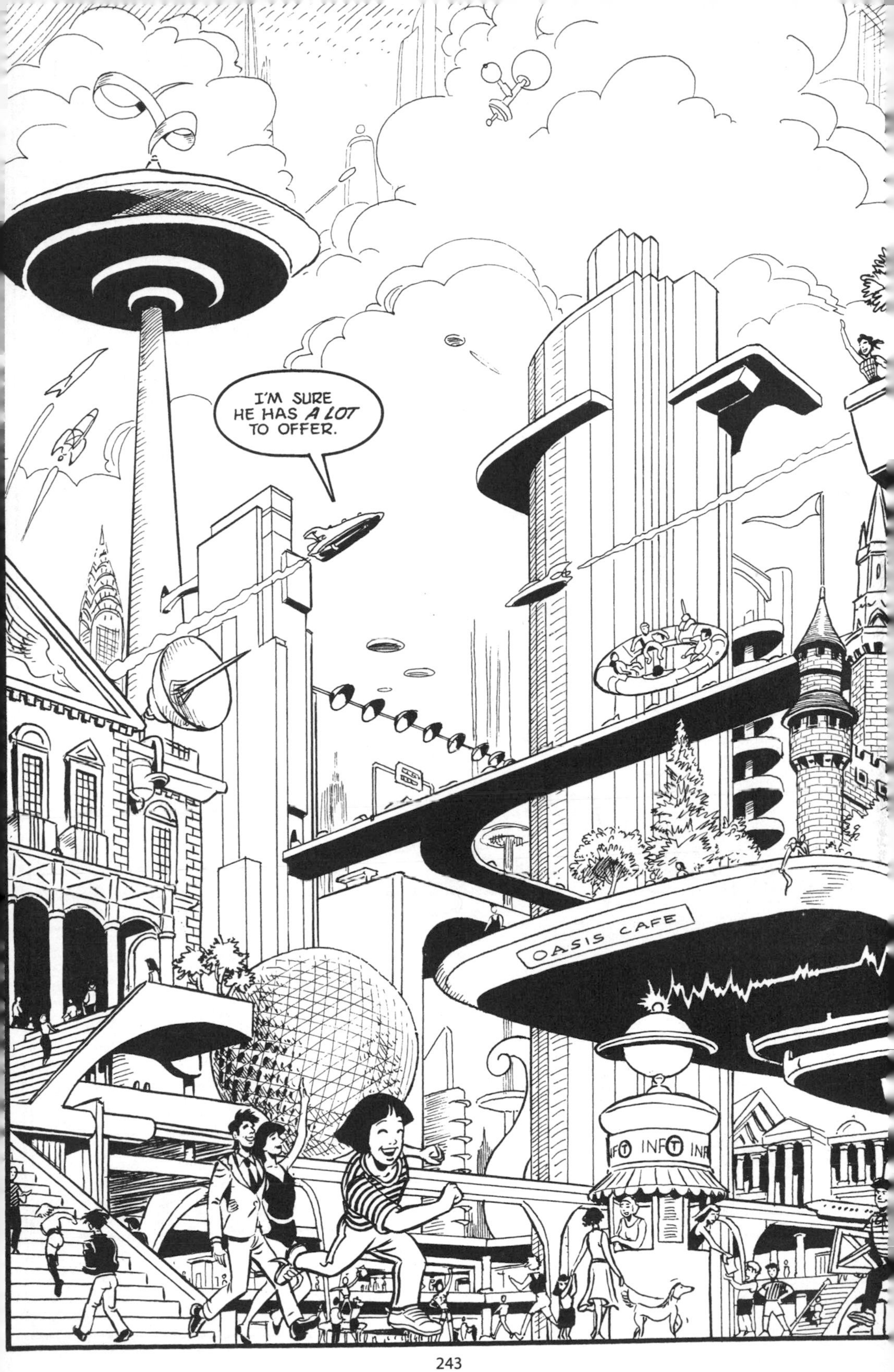
I'M SURE HE HAS *A LOT* TO OFFER.
OASIS CAFE
INFO INFO INFO

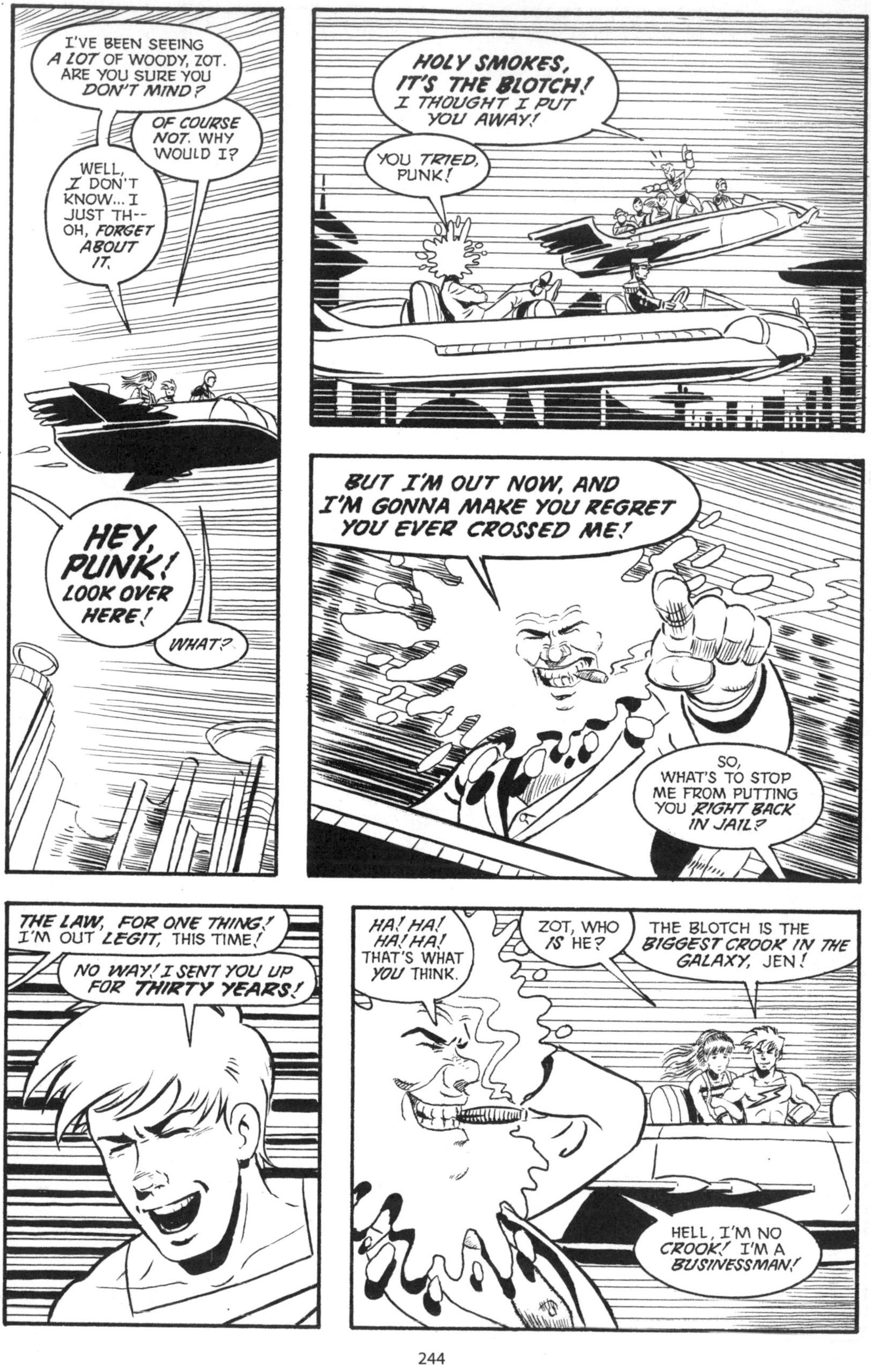
I'VE BEEN SEEING A LOT OF WOODY, ZOT. ARE YOU SURE YOU DON'T MIND?
OF COURSE NOT. WHY WOULD I?
WELL, I DON'T KNOW... I JUST TH-- OH, FORGET ABOUT IT.
HEY, PUNK! LOOK OVER HERE!
WHAT?
HOLY SMOKES, IT'S THE BLOTCH! I THOUGHT I PUT YOU AWAY!
YOU TRIED, PUNK!
BUT I'M OUT NOW, AND I'M GONNA MAKE YOU REGRET YOU EVER CROSSED ME!
SO, WHAT'S TO STOP ME FROM PUTTING YOU RIGHT BACK IN JAIL?
THE LAW, FOR ONE THING! I'M OUT LEGIT, THIS TIME!
NO WAY! I SENT YOU UP FOR THIRTY YEARS!
HA! HA! HA! HA! THAT'S WHAT YOU THINK.
ZOT, WHO IS HE?
THE BLOTCH IS THE BIGGEST CROOK IN THE GALAXY, JEN!
HELL, I'M NO CROOK! I'M A BUSINESSMAN!

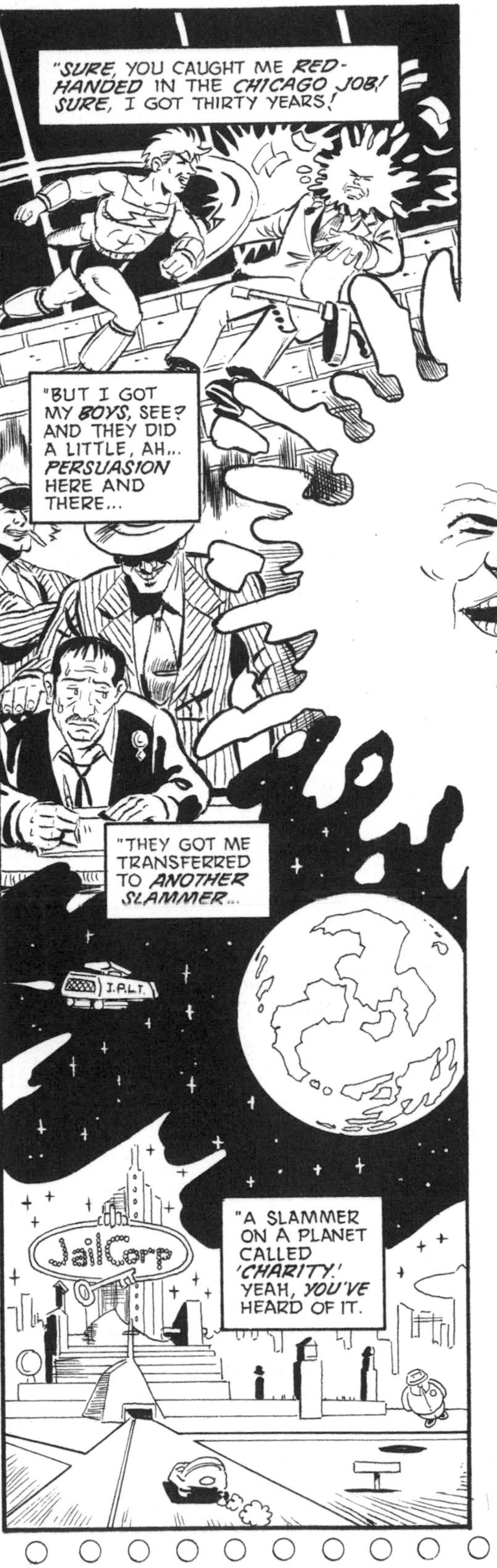
"SURE, YOU CAUGHT ME RED-HANDED IN THE CHICAGO JOB! SURE, I GOT THIRTY YEARS!
"BUT I GOT MY BOYS, SEE? AND THEY DID A LITTLE, AH... PERSUASION HERE AND THERE...
"THEY GOT ME TRANSFERRED TO ANOTHER SLAMMER...
I.A.L.T.
JailCorp
"A SLAMMER ON A PLANET CALLED 'CHARITY.' YEAH, YOU'VE HEARD OF IT.

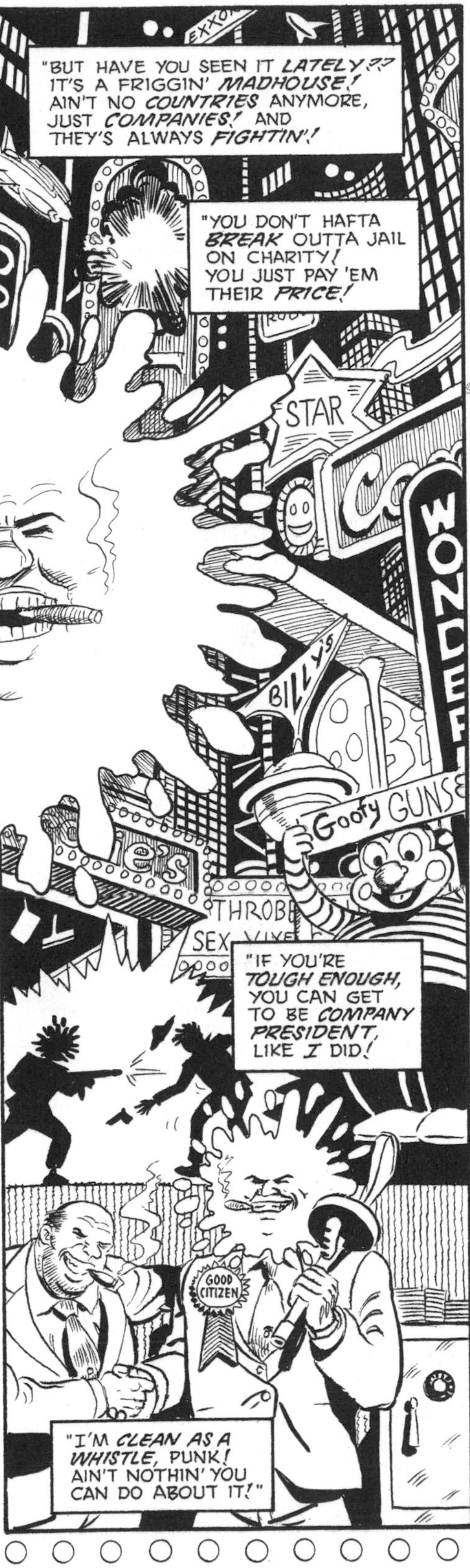
EXXON
"BUT HAVE YOU SEEN IT LATELY?!? IT'S A FRIGGIN' MADHOUSE! AIN'T NO COUNTRIES ANYMORE, JUST COMPANIES! AND THEY'S ALWAYS FIGHTIN'!
"YOU DON'T HAFTA BREAK OUTTA JAIL ON CHARITY! YOU JUST PAY 'EM THEIR PRICE!
STAR
WONDER
BILLY'S
Goofy GUNS
THROBB
"IF YOU'RE TOUGH ENOUGH, YOU CAN GET TO BE COMPANY PRESIDENT, LIKE I DID!
GOOD CITIZEN
"I'M CLEAN AS A WHISTLE, PUNK! AIN'T NOTHIN' YOU CAN DO ABOUT IT!"

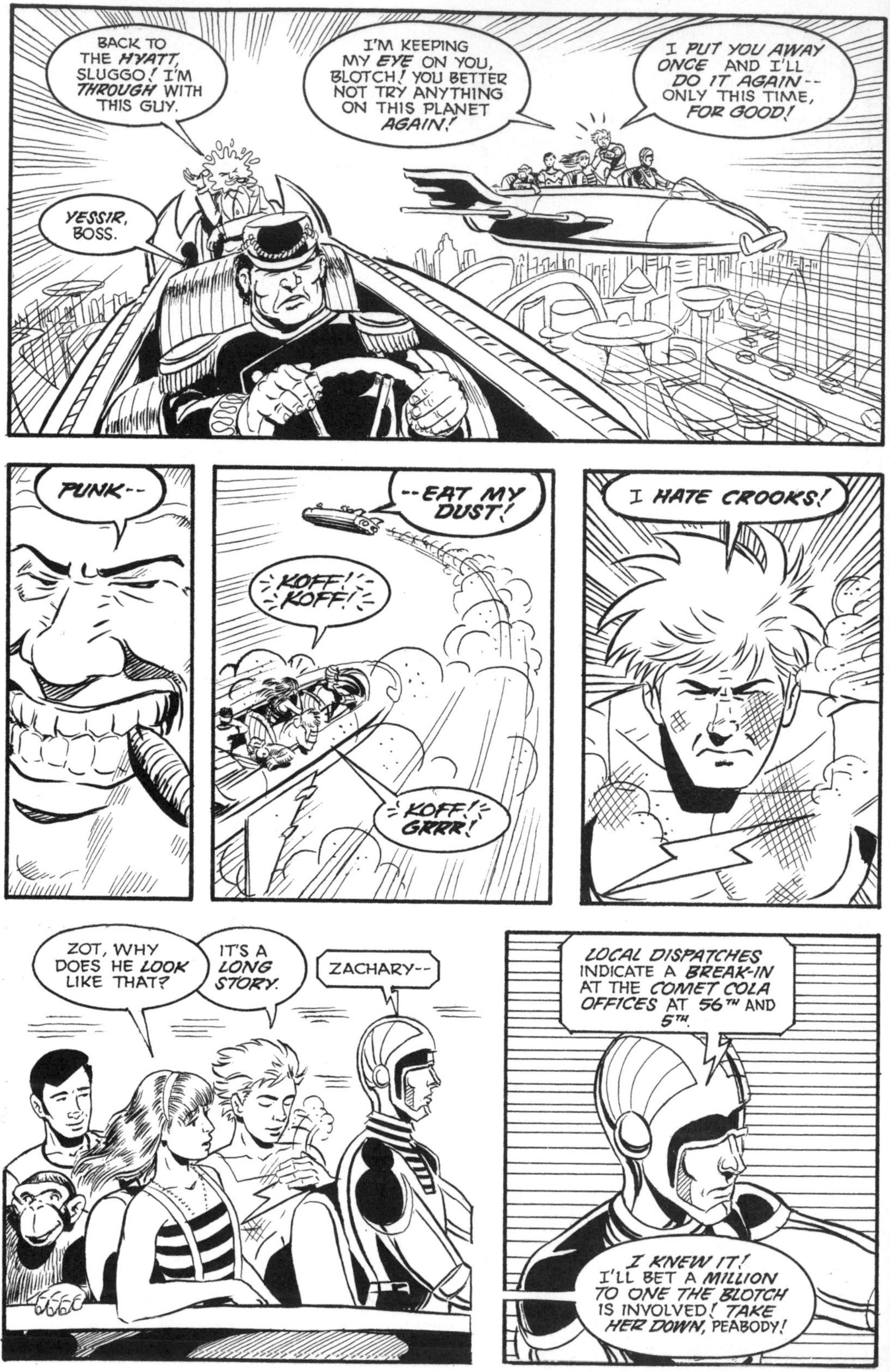
BACK TO THE HYATT, SLUGGO! I'M THROUGH WITH THIS GUY.
YESSIR, BOSS.
I'M KEEPING MY EYE ON YOU, BLOTCH! YOU BETTER NOT TRY ANYTHING ON THIS PLANET AGAIN!
I PUT YOU AWAY ONCE AND I'LL DO IT AGAIN-- ONLY THIS TIME, FOR GOOD!
PUNK--
--EAT MY DUST!
KOFF! KOFF!
KOFF! GRRR!
I HATE CROOKS!
ZOT, WHY DOES HE LOOK LIKE THAT?
IT'S A LONG STORY.
ZACHARY--
LOCAL DISPATCHES INDICATE A BREAK-IN AT THE COMET COLA OFFICES AT 56TH AND 5TH.
I KNEW IT! I'LL BET A MILLION TO ONE THE BLOTCH IS INVOLVED! TAKE HER DOWN, PEABODY!

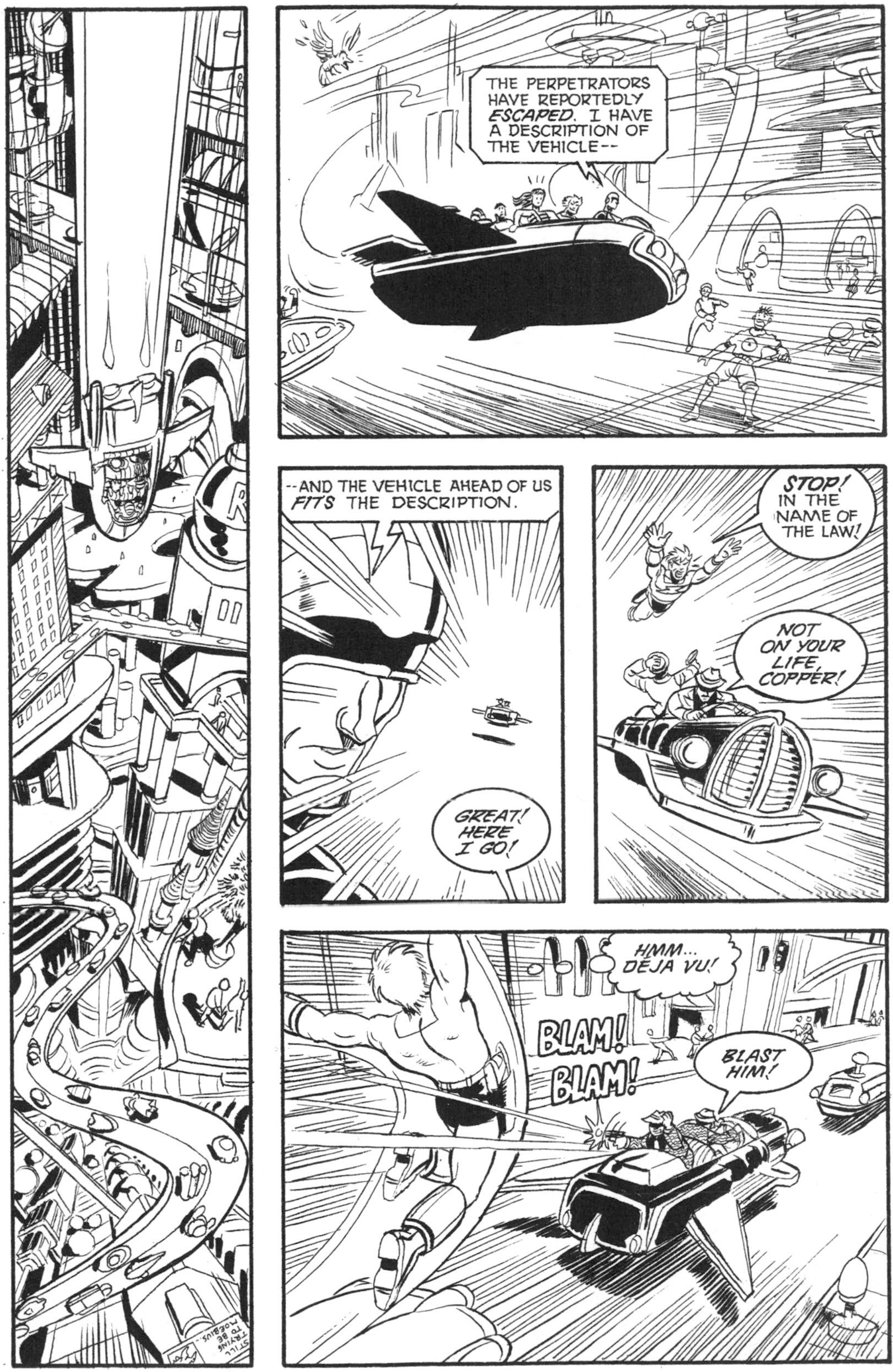
STILL TRYING TO BE MOEBIUS...
THE PERPETRATORS HAVE REPORTEDLY *ESCAPED*. I HAVE A DESCRIPTION OF THE VEHICLE--
--AND THE VEHICLE AHEAD OF US *FITS* THE DESCRIPTION.
GREAT! HERE I GO!
STOP! IN THE NAME OF THE LAW!
NOT ON YOUR LIFE, COPPER!
HMM... DÉJA VU!
BLAM! BLAM!
BLAST HIM!

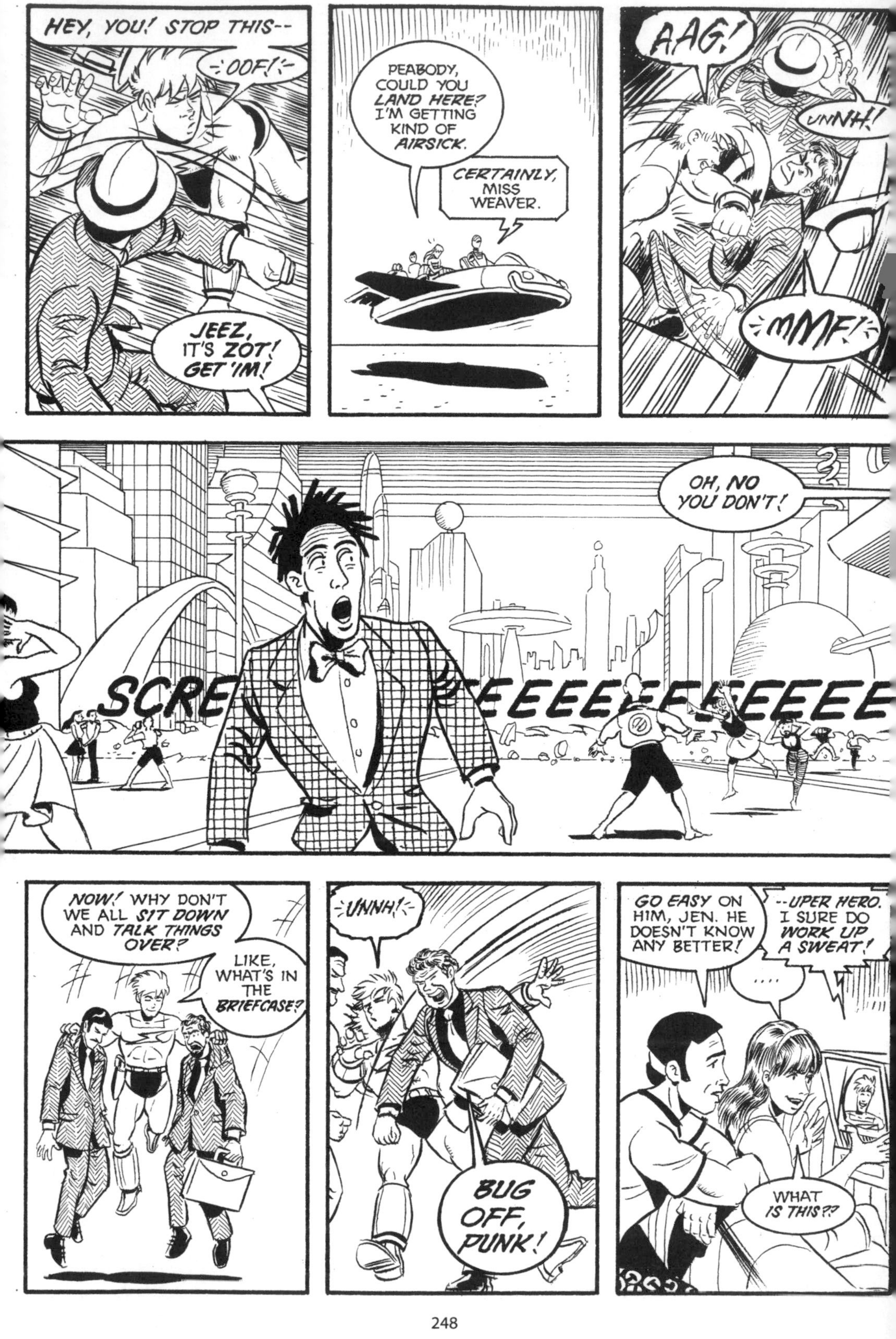
HEY, YOU! STOP THIS--
OOF!
JEEZ, IT'S ZOT! GET 'IM!
PEABODY, COULD YOU LAND HERE? I'M GETTING KIND OF AIRSICK.
CERTAINLY, MISS WEAVER.
AAG!
UNNH!
MMF!
OH, NO YOU DON'T!
SCREEEEEEEEEEEEEEE
NOW! WHY DON'T WE ALL SIT DOWN AND TALK THINGS OVER?
LIKE, WHAT'S IN THE BRIEFCASE?
UNNH!
BUG OFF, PUNK!
GO EASY ON HIM, JEN. HE DOESN'T KNOW ANY BETTER!
....
--UPER HERO. I SURE DO WORK UP A SWEAT!
WHAT IS THIS??

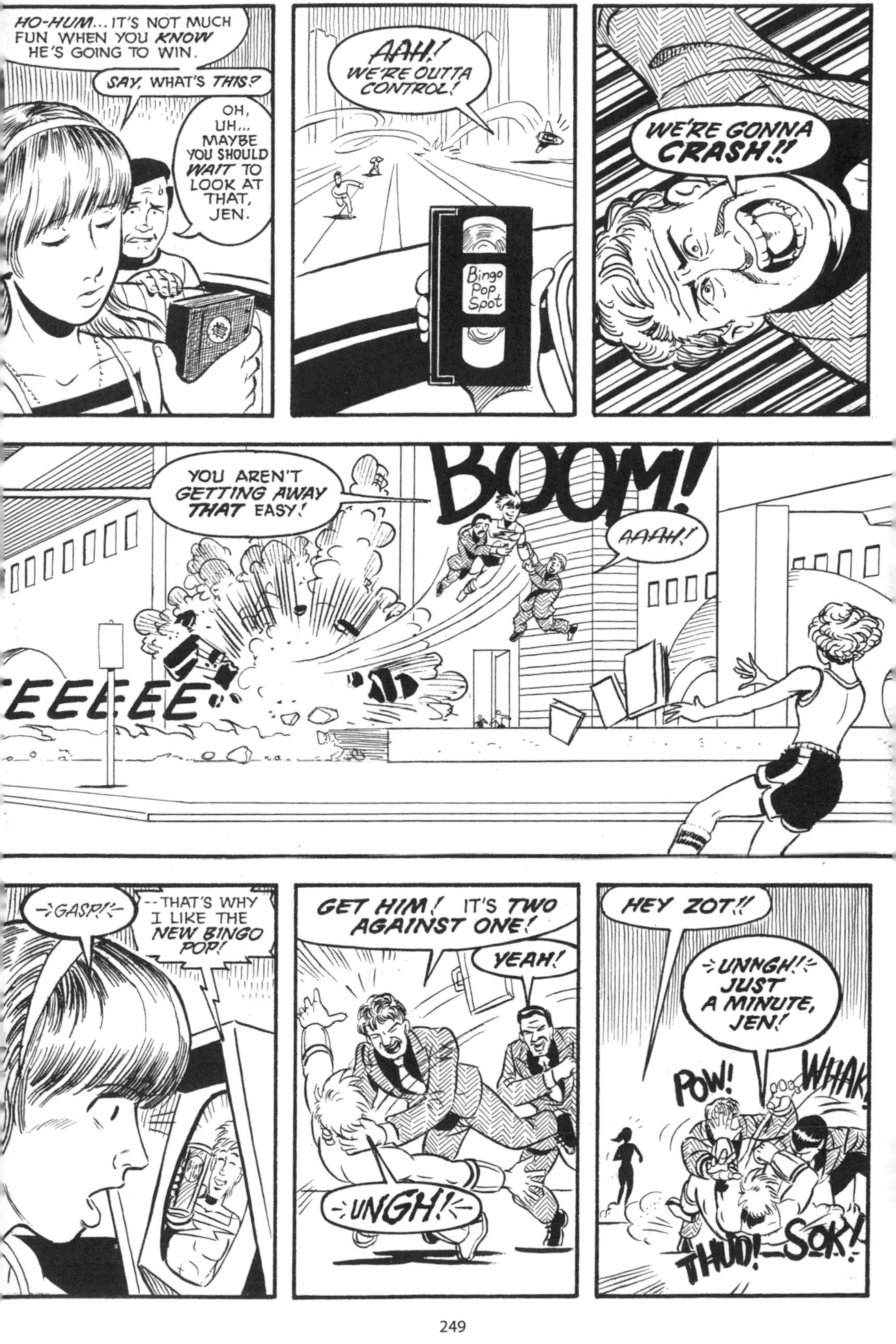
HO-HUM... IT'S NOT MUCH FUN WHEN YOU KNOW HE'S GOING TO WIN.
SAY, WHAT'S THIS?
OH, UH... MAYBE YOU SHOULD WAIT TO LOOK AT THAT, JEN.
AAH! WE'RE OUTTA CONTROL!
Bingo Pop Spot
WE'RE GONNA CRASH!!
YOU AREN'T GETTING AWAY THAT EASY!
BOOM!
AAAH!
EEEEEE
GASP!
--THAT'S WHY I LIKE THE NEW BINGO POP!
GET HIM! IT'S TWO AGAINST ONE!
YEAH!
UNGH!
HEY ZOT!!
UNNGH! JUST A MINUTE, JEN!
POW!
WHAK
THUD!
SOK!

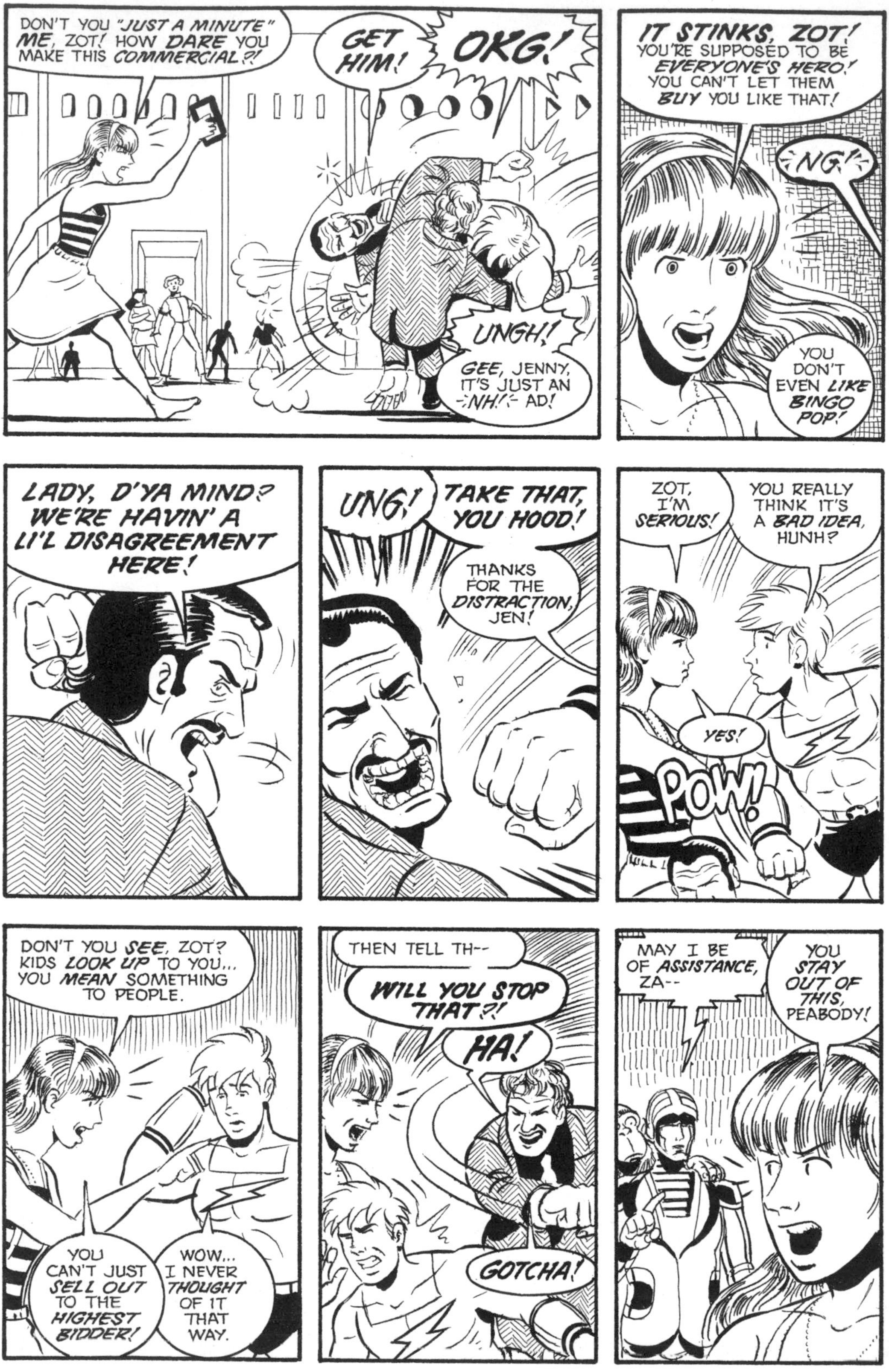
DON'T YOU "JUST A MINUTE" ME, ZOT! HOW DARE YOU MAKE THIS COMMERCIAL?!
GET HIM!
OKG!
UNGH!
GEE, JENNY, IT'S JUST AN -NH!- AD!
IT STINKS, ZOT! YOU'RE SUPPOSED TO BE EVERYONE'S HERO! YOU CAN'T LET THEM BUY YOU LIKE THAT!
NG!
YOU DON'T EVEN LIKE BINGO POP!
LADY, D'YA MIND? WE'RE HAVIN' A LI'L DISAGREEMENT HERE!
UNG!
TAKE THAT, YOU HOOD!
THANKS FOR THE DISTRACTION, JEN!
ZOT, I'M SERIOUS!
YOU REALLY THINK IT'S A BAD IDEA, HUNH?
YES!
POW!
DON'T YOU SEE, ZOT? KIDS LOOK UP TO YOU... YOU MEAN SOMETHING TO PEOPLE.
YOU CAN'T JUST SELL OUT TO THE HIGHEST BIDDER!
WOW... I NEVER THOUGHT OF IT THAT WAY.
THEN TELL TH--
WILL YOU STOP THAT?!
HA!
GOTCHA!
MAY I BE OF ASSISTANCE, ZA--
YOU STAY OUT OF THIS, PEABODY!

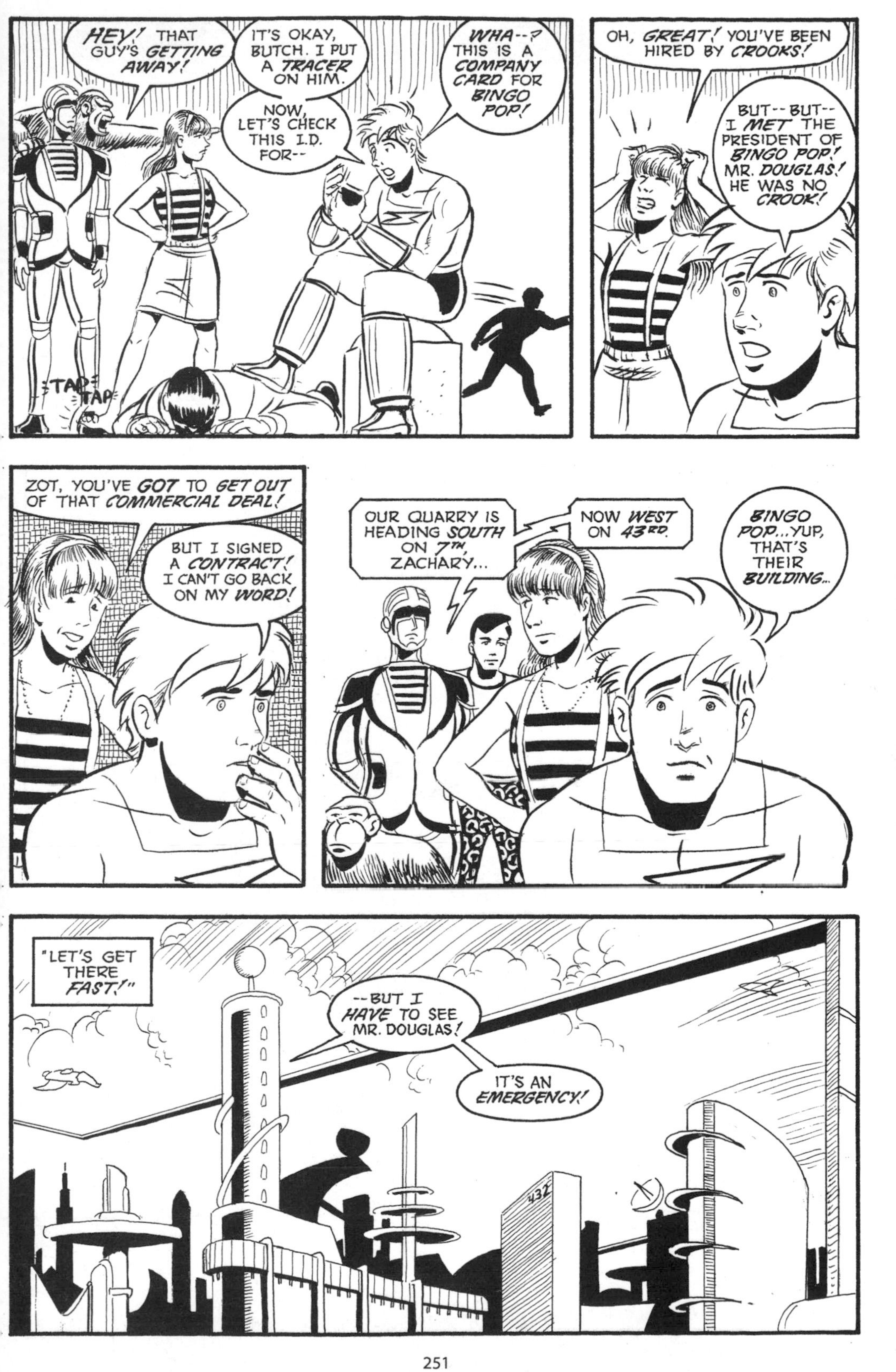
HEY! THAT GUY'S GETTING AWAY!
IT'S OKAY, BUTCH. I PUT A TRACER ON HIM.
NOW, LET'S CHECK THIS I.D. FOR--
WHA--? THIS IS A COMPANY CARD FOR BINGO POP!
TAP TAP
OH, GREAT! YOU'VE BEEN HIRED BY CROOKS!
BUT--BUT--I MET THE PRESIDENT OF BINGO POP! MR. DOUGLAS! HE WAS NO CROOK!
ZOT, YOU'VE GOT TO GET OUT OF THAT COMMERCIAL DEAL!
BUT I SIGNED A CONTRACT! I CAN'T GO BACK ON MY WORD!
OUR QUARRY IS HEADING SOUTH ON 7TH, ZACHARY...
NOW WEST ON 43RD.
BINGO POP...YUP, THAT'S THEIR BUILDING...
"LET'S GET THERE FAST!"
--BUT I HAVE TO SEE MR. DOUGLAS!
IT'S AN EMERGENCY!
432

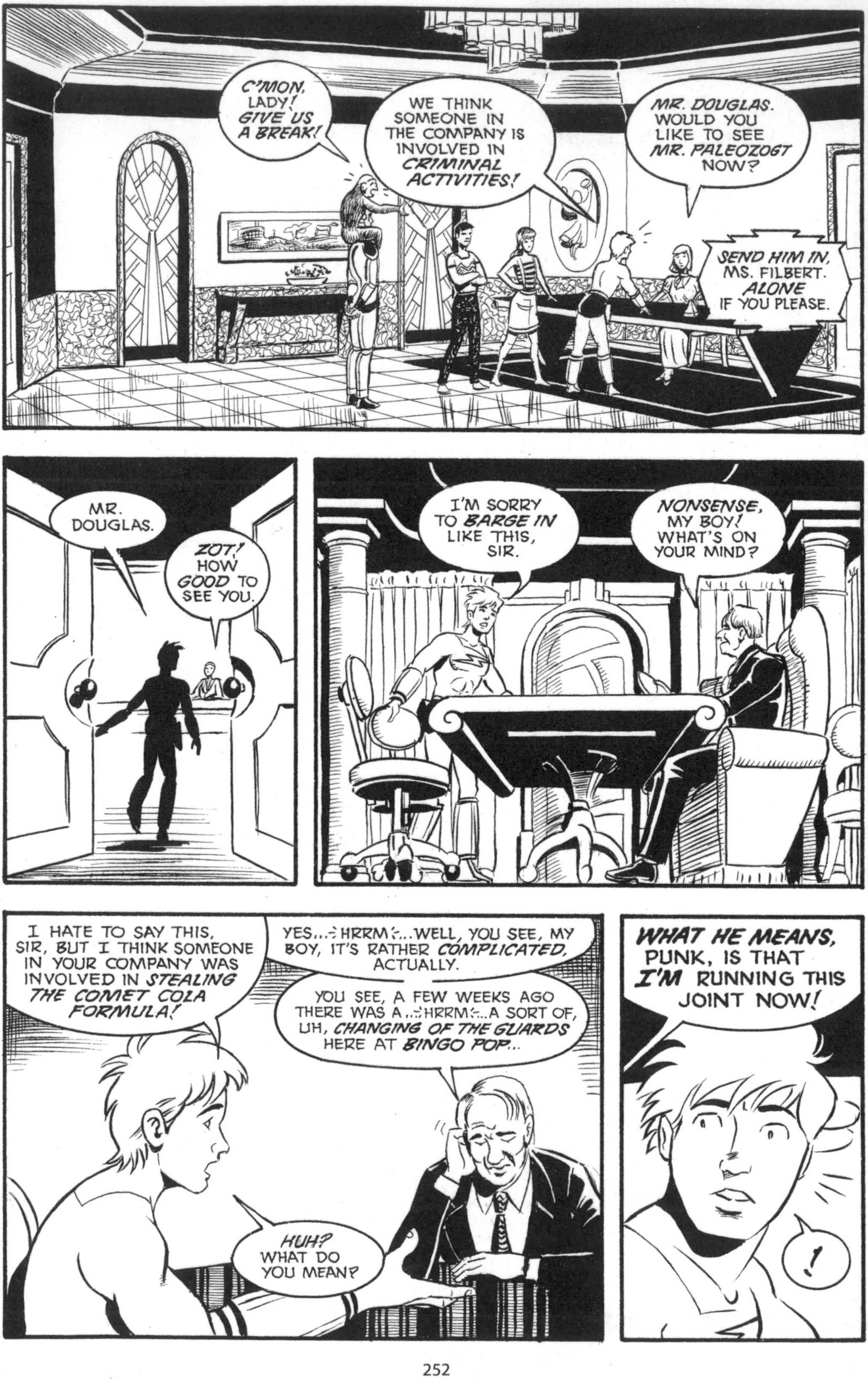
C'MON, LADY! GIVE US A BREAK!
WE THINK SOMEONE IN THE COMPANY IS INVOLVED IN CRIMINAL ACTIVITIES!
MR. DOUGLAS. WOULD YOU LIKE TO SEE MR. PALEOZOGT NOW?
SEND HIM IN, MS. FILBERT. ALONE IF YOU PLEASE.
MR. DOUGLAS.
ZOT! HOW GOOD TO SEE YOU.
I'M SORRY TO BARGE IN LIKE THIS, SIR.
NONSENSE, MY BOY! WHAT'S ON YOUR MIND?
I HATE TO SAY THIS, SIR, BUT I THINK SOMEONE IN YOUR COMPANY WAS INVOLVED IN STEALING THE COMET COLA FORMULA!
YES...HRRM...WELL, YOU SEE, MY BOY, IT'S RATHER COMPLICATED, ACTUALLY.
YOU SEE, A FEW WEEKS AGO THERE WAS A...HRRM...A SORT OF, UH, CHANGING OF THE GUARDS HERE AT BINGO POP...
HUH? WHAT DO YOU MEAN?
WHAT HE MEANS, PUNK, IS THAT I'M RUNNING THIS JOINT NOW!
!

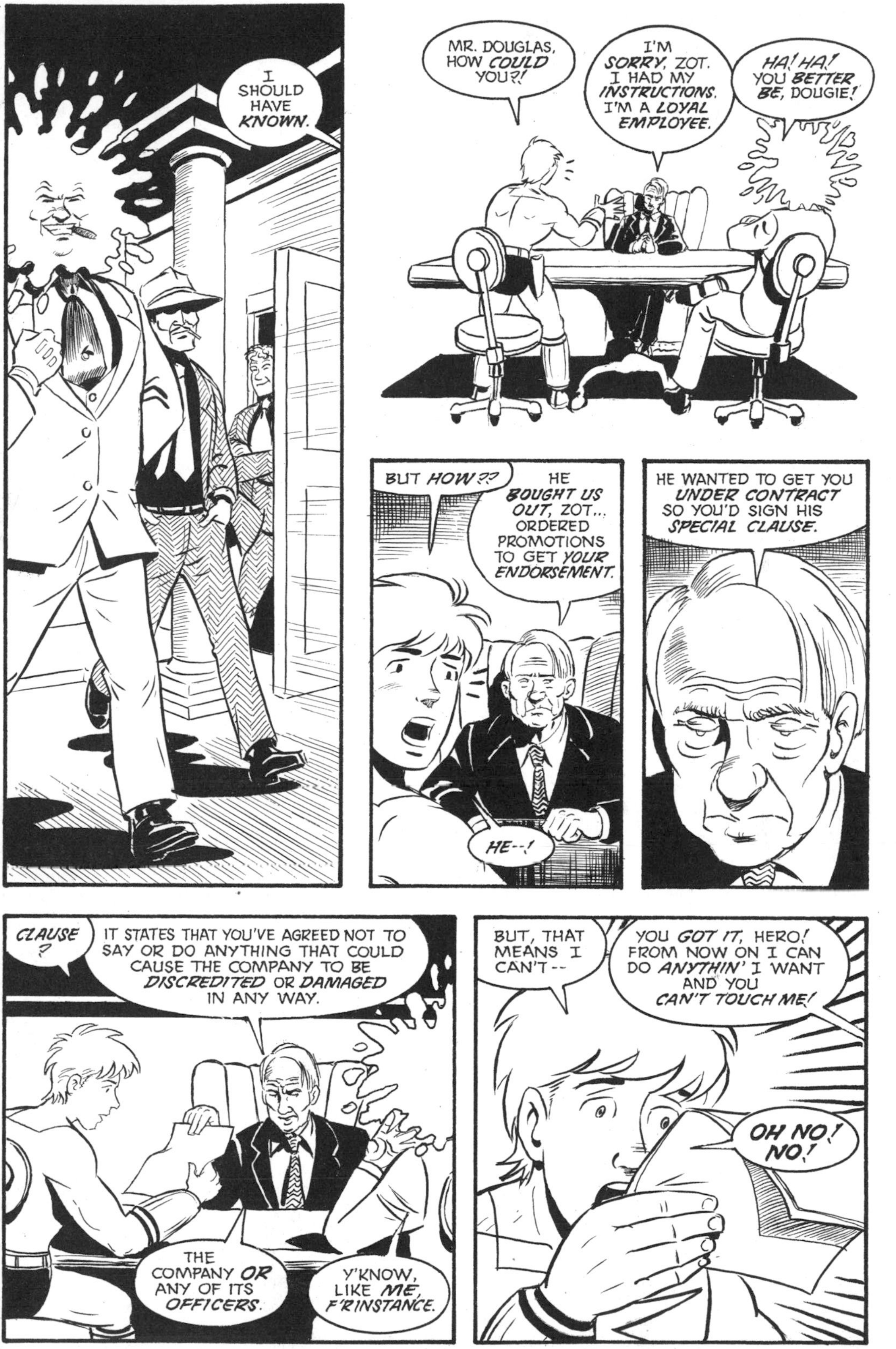

I SHOULD HAVE *KNOWN*.
MR. DOUGLAS, HOW *COULD* YOU?!
I'M *SORRY*, ZOT. I HAD MY *INSTRUCTIONS*. I'M A *LOYAL EMPLOYEE*.
HA! HA! YOU *BETTER BE*, DOUGIE!
BUT *HOW??*
HE *BOUGHT US OUT*, ZOT... ORDERED PROMOTIONS TO GET *YOUR ENDORSEMENT*.
HE--!
HE WANTED TO GET YOU *UNDER CONTRACT* SO YOU'D SIGN HIS *SPECIAL CLAUSE*.
CLAUSE?
IT STATES THAT YOU'VE AGREED NOT TO SAY OR DO ANYTHING THAT COULD CAUSE THE COMPANY TO BE *DISCREDITED* OR *DAMAGED* IN ANY WAY.
THE COMPANY *OR* ANY OF ITS *OFFICERS*.
Y'KNOW, LIKE *ME*, *F'RINSTANCE*.
BUT, THAT MEANS I CAN'T --
YOU *GOT IT*, HERO! FROM NOW ON I CAN DO *ANYTHIN'* I WANT AND YOU *CAN'T TOUCH ME!*
OH NO! NO!

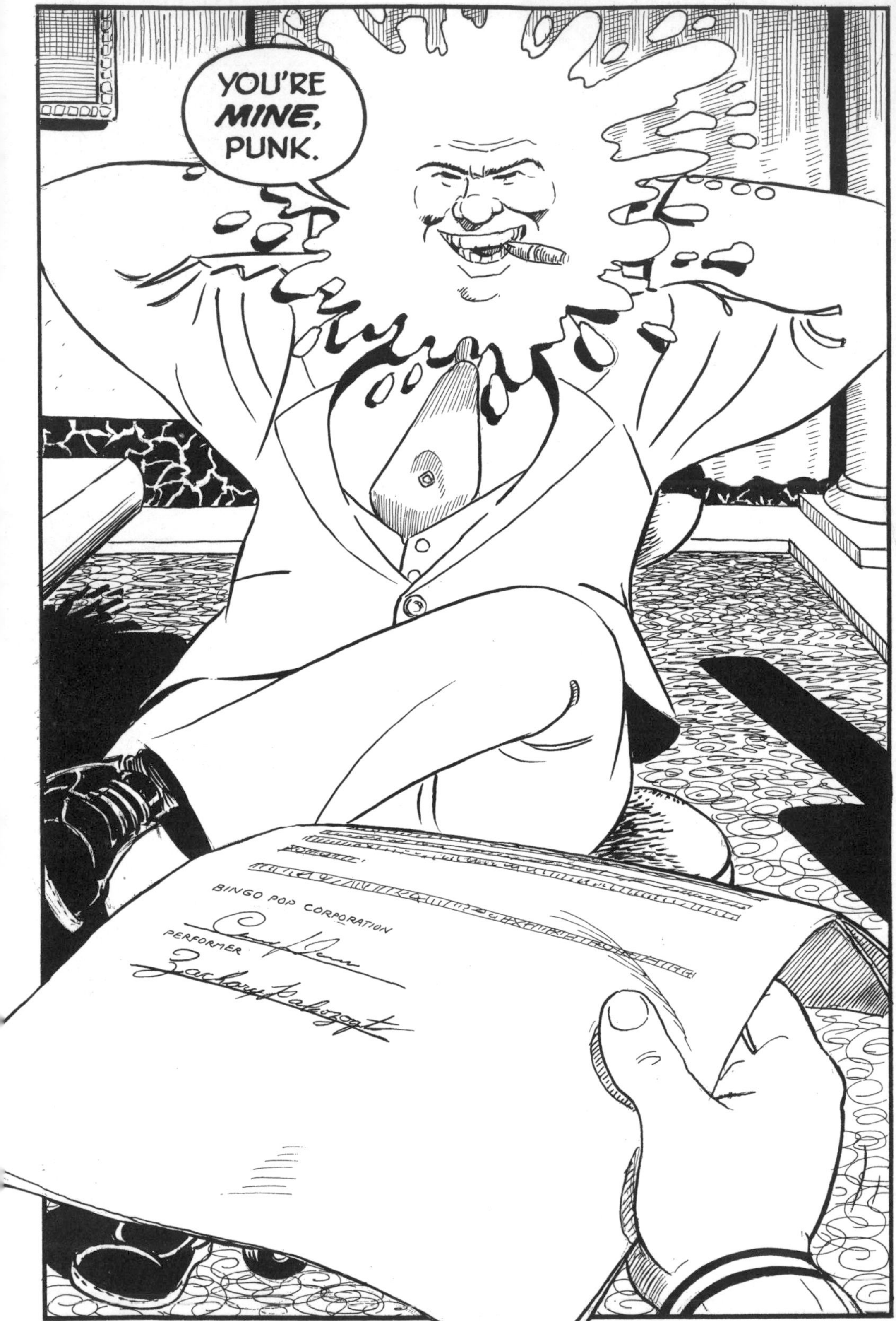
YOU'RE *MINE,* PUNK.
BINGO POP CORPORATION
PERFORMER

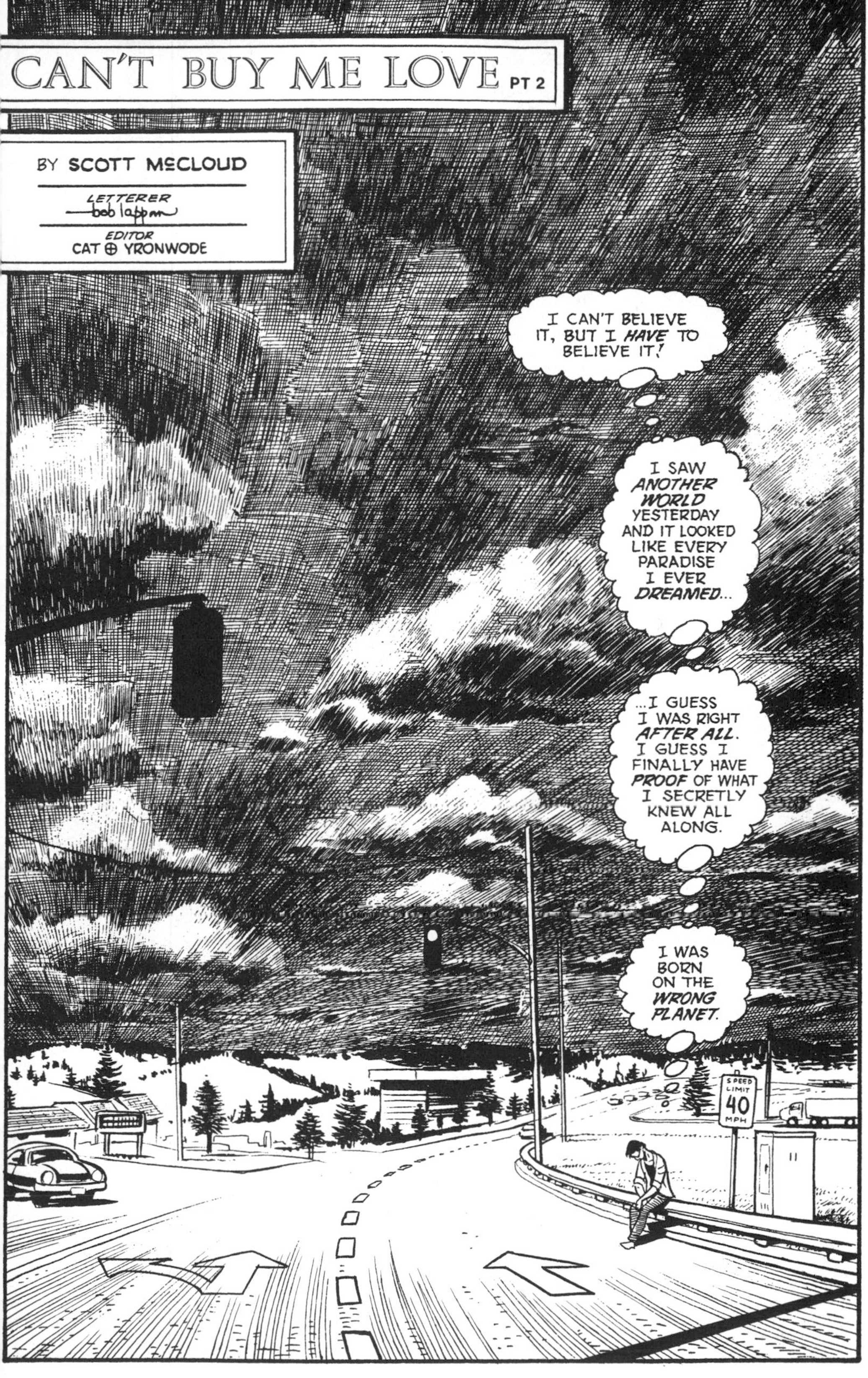
CAN'T BUY ME LOVE PT 2
BY SCOTT McCLOUD
LETTERER bob lappan
EDITOR CAT ⊕ YRONWODE
I CAN'T BELIEVE IT, BUT I *HAVE* TO BELIEVE IT!
I SAW *ANOTHER WORLD* YESTERDAY AND IT LOOKED LIKE EVERY PARADISE I EVER *DREAMED*...
...I GUESS I WAS RIGHT *AFTER ALL*. I GUESS I FINALLY HAVE *PROOF* OF WHAT I SECRETLY KNEW ALL ALONG.
I WAS BORN ON THE *WRONG PLANET*.
SPEED LIMIT 40 MPH

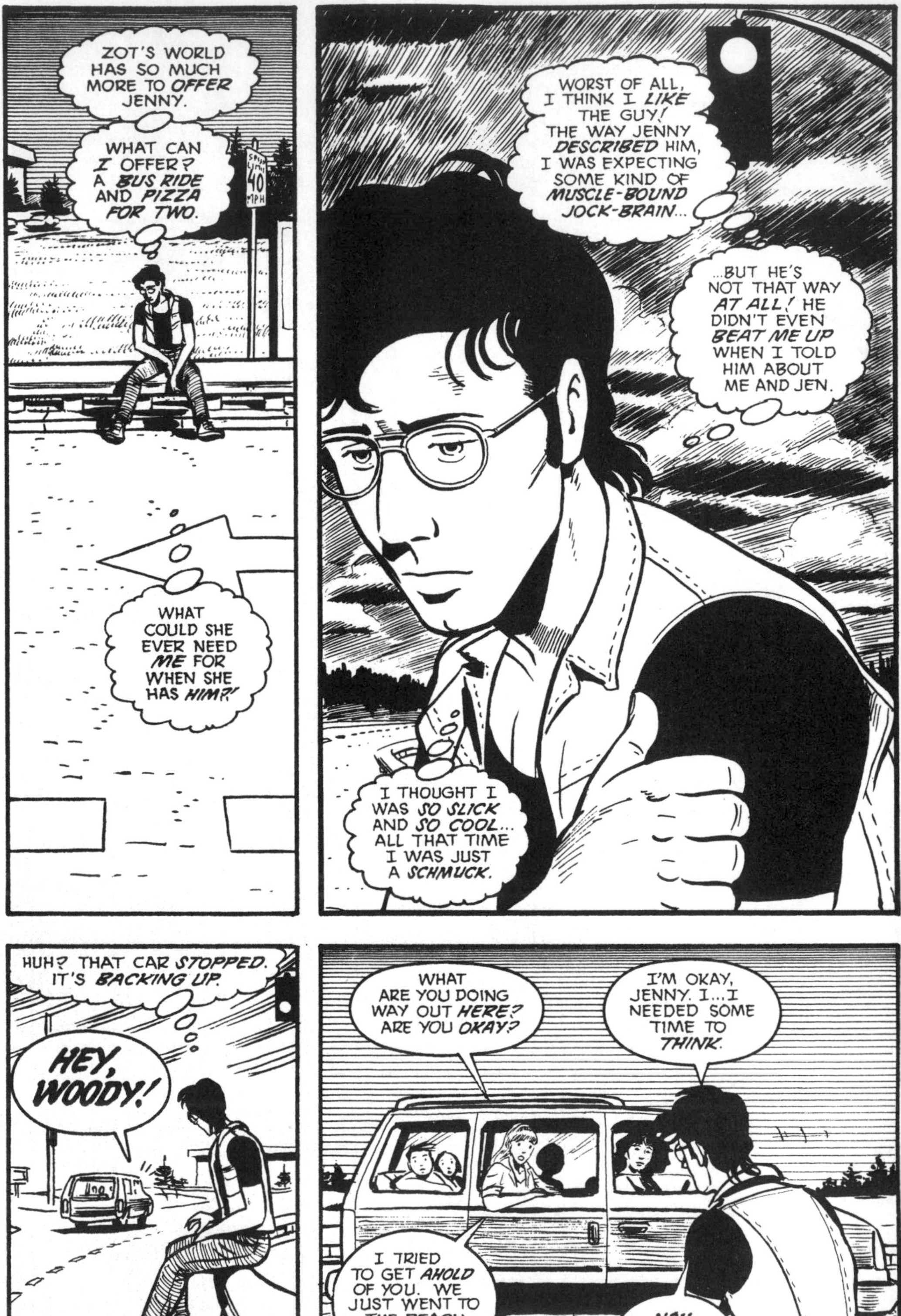
ZOT'S WORLD HAS SO MUCH MORE TO OFFER JENNY.
WHAT CAN I OFFER? A BUS RIDE AND PIZZA FOR TWO.
WHAT COULD SHE EVER NEED ME FOR WHEN SHE HAS HIM?!
WORST OF ALL, I THINK I LIKE THE GUY! THE WAY JENNY DESCRIBED HIM, I WAS EXPECTING SOME KIND OF MUSCLE-BOUND JOCK-BRAIN...
...BUT HE'S NOT THAT WAY AT ALL! HE DIDN'T EVEN BEAT ME UP WHEN I TOLD HIM ABOUT ME AND JEN.
I THOUGHT I WAS SO SLICK AND SO COOL... ALL THAT TIME I WAS JUST A SCHMUCK.
HUH? THAT CAR STOPPED. IT'S BACKING UP.
HEY, WOODY!
WHAT ARE YOU DOING WAY OUT HERE? ARE YOU OKAY?
I'M OKAY, JENNY. I...I NEEDED SOME TIME TO THINK.
I TRIED TO GET AHOLD OF YOU. WE JUST WENT TO THE BEACH. WANT A RIDE HOME?
NAH. THANKS ANYWAY.

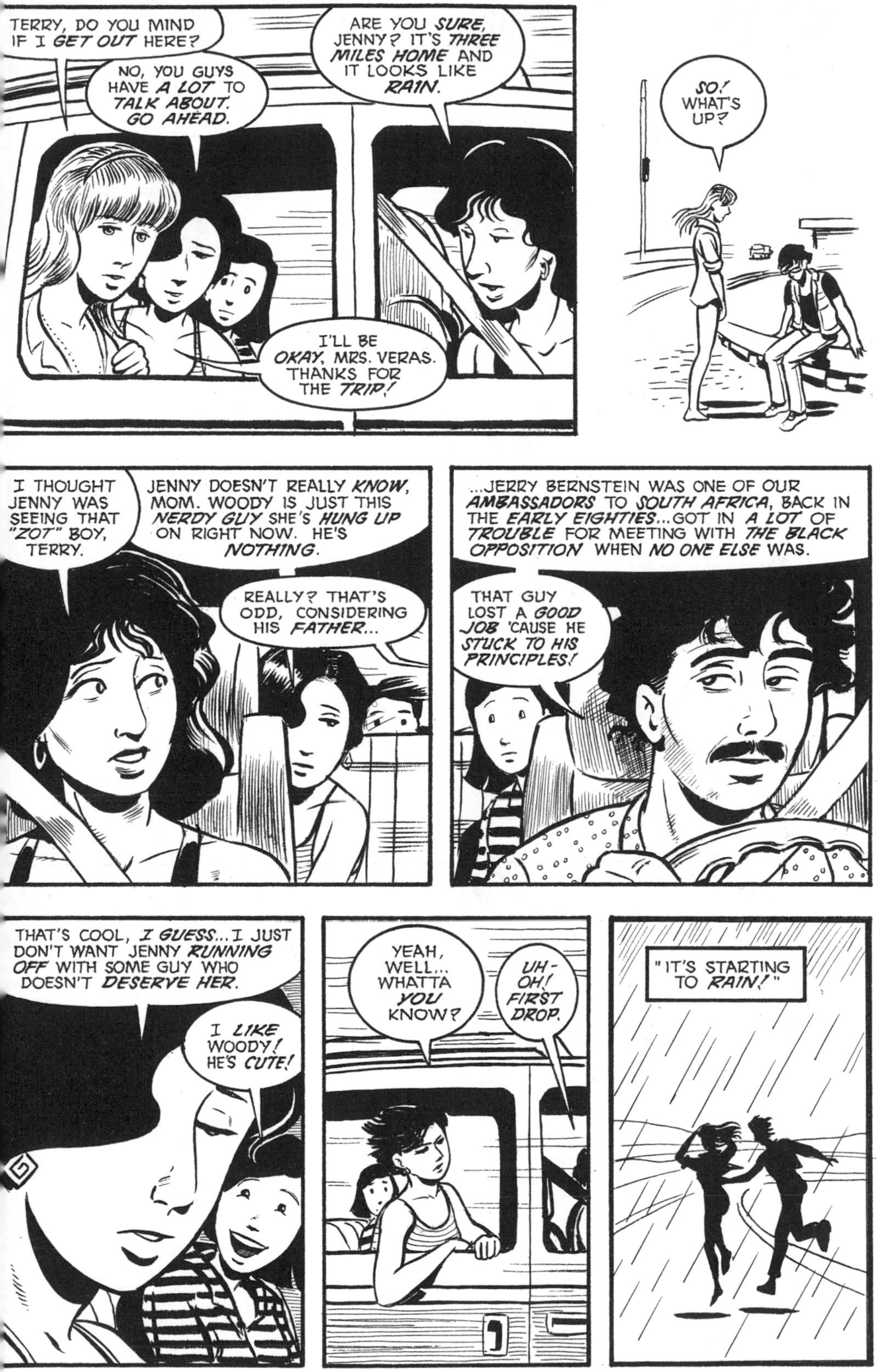
TERRY, DO YOU MIND IF I GET OUT HERE?
NO, YOU GUYS HAVE A LOT TO TALK ABOUT. GO AHEAD.
ARE YOU SURE, JENNY? IT'S THREE MILES HOME AND IT LOOKS LIKE RAIN.
I'LL BE OKAY, MRS. VERAS. THANKS FOR THE TRIP!
SO! WHAT'S UP?
I THOUGHT JENNY WAS SEEING THAT "ZOT" BOY, TERRY.
JENNY DOESN'T REALLY KNOW, MOM. WOODY IS JUST THIS NERDY GUY SHE'S HUNG UP ON RIGHT NOW. HE'S NOTHING.
REALLY? THAT'S ODD, CONSIDERING HIS FATHER...
...JERRY BERNSTEIN WAS ONE OF OUR AMBASSADORS TO SOUTH AFRICA, BACK IN THE EARLY EIGHTIES... GOT IN A LOT OF TROUBLE FOR MEETING WITH THE BLACK OPPOSITION WHEN NO ONE ELSE WAS.
THAT GUY LOST A GOOD JOB 'CAUSE HE STUCK TO HIS PRINCIPLES!
THAT'S COOL, I GUESS... I JUST DON'T WANT JENNY RUNNING OFF WITH SOME GUY WHO DOESN'T DESERVE HER.
I LIKE WOODY! HE'S CUTE!
YEAH, WELL... WHATTA YOU KNOW?
UH-OH! FIRST DROP.
"IT'S STARTING TO RAIN!"

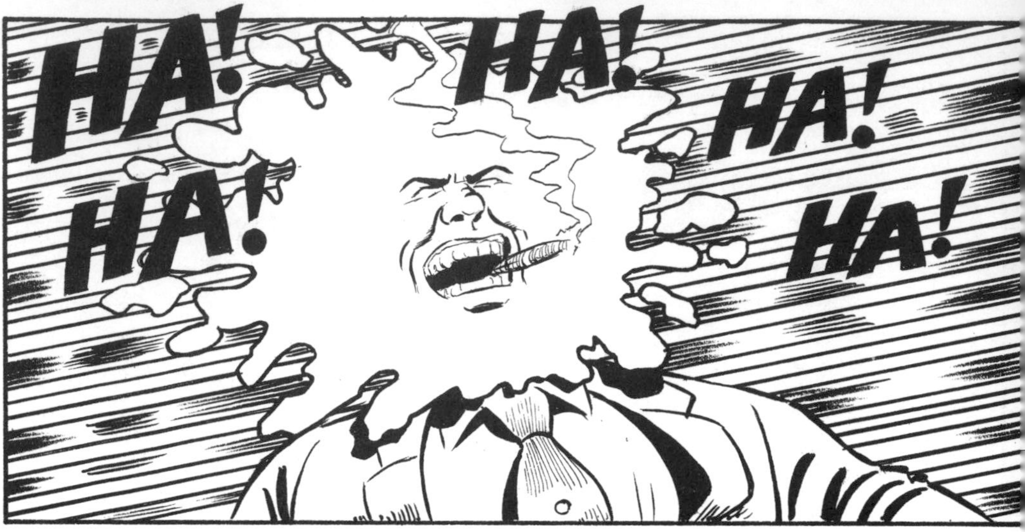
HA! HA! HA! HA! HA!

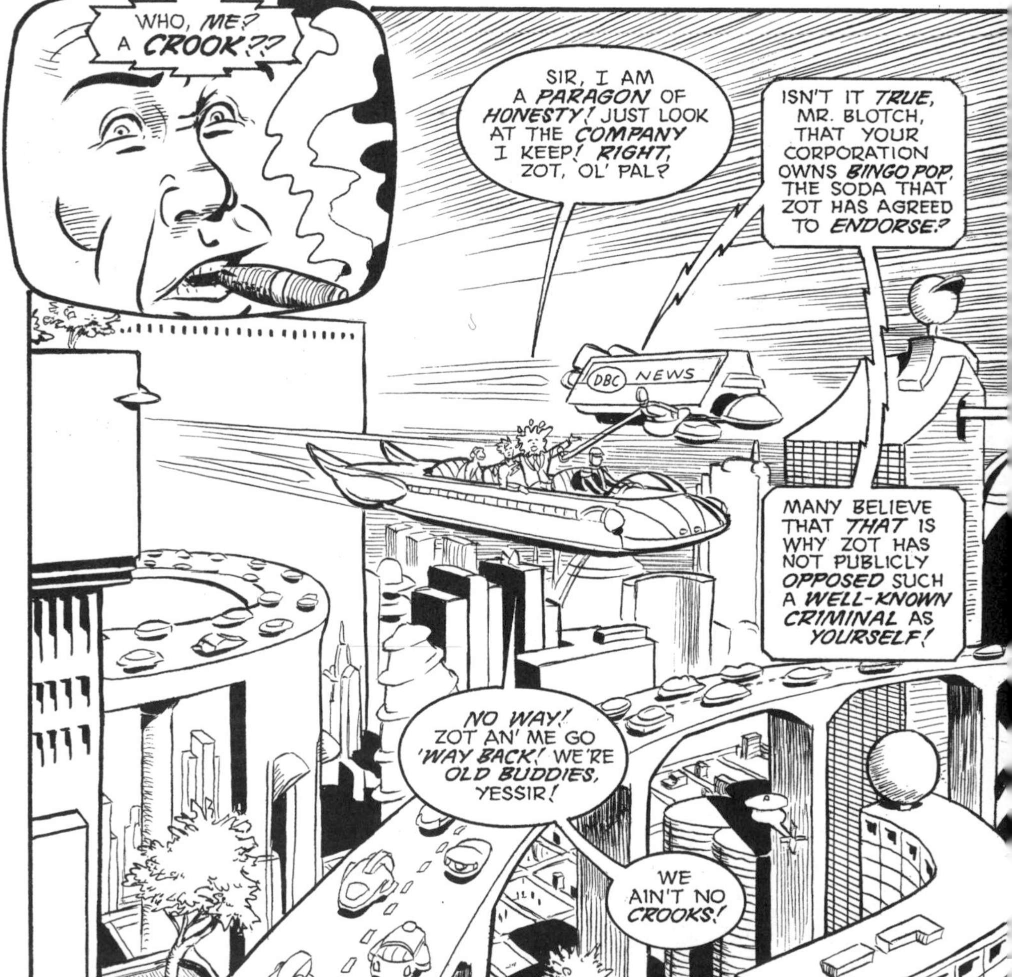
WHO, *ME?* A *CROOK??*
SIR, I AM A *PARAGON* OF *HONESTY!* JUST LOOK AT THE *COMPANY* I KEEP! *RIGHT,* ZOT, OL' PAL?
ISN'T IT *TRUE,* MR. BLOTCH, THAT YOUR CORPORATION OWNS *BINGO POP,* THE SODA THAT ZOT HAS AGREED TO *ENDORSE?*
DBC NEWS
MANY BELIEVE THAT *THAT* IS WHY ZOT HAS NOT PUBLICLY *OPPOSED* SUCH A *WELL-KNOWN CRIMINAL* AS *YOURSELF!*
NO WAY! ZOT AN' ME GO *'WAY BACK!* WE'RE *OLD BUDDIES,* YESSIR!
WE AIN'T NO *CROOKS!*

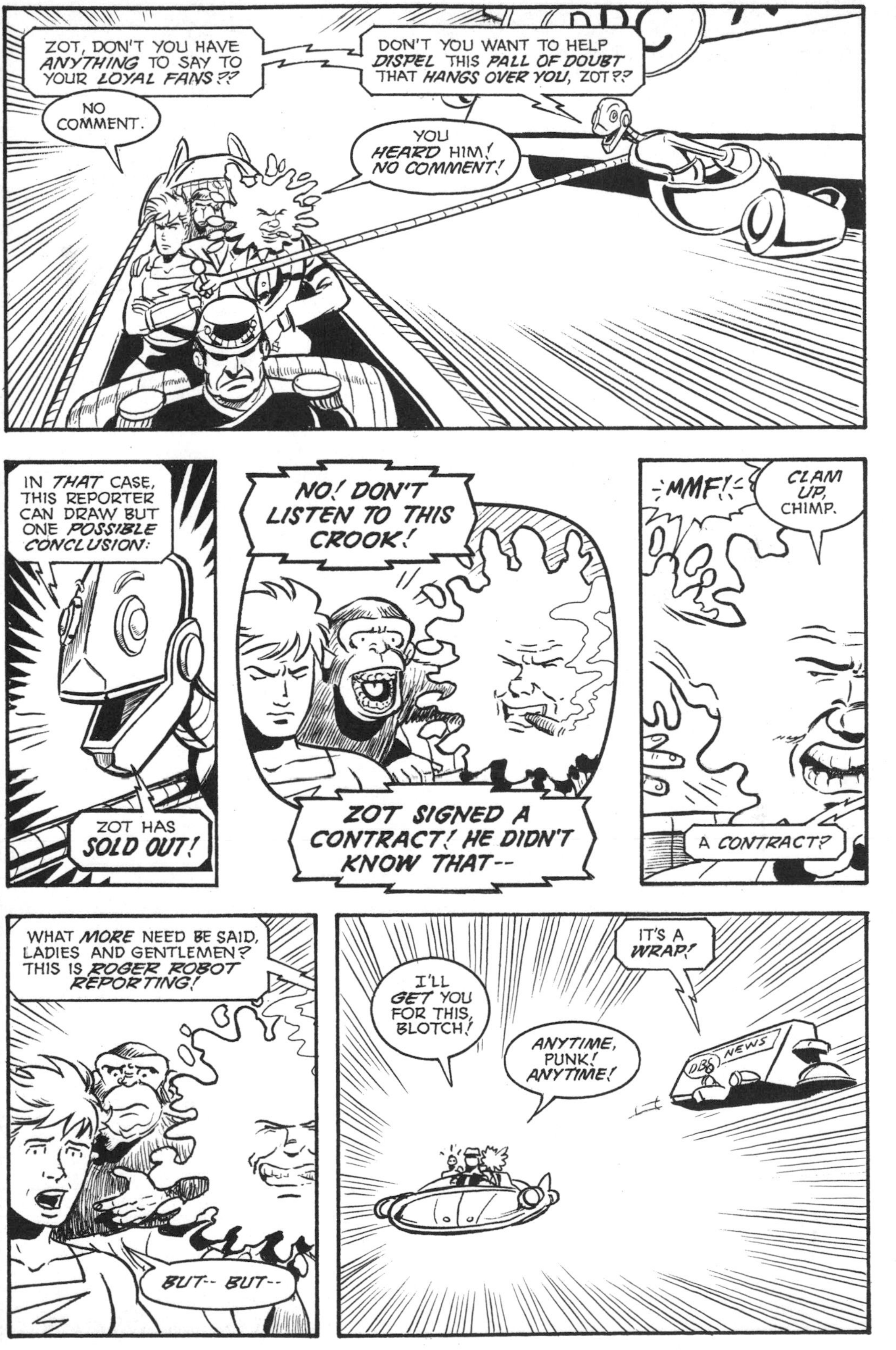
ZOT, DON'T YOU HAVE ANYTHING TO SAY TO YOUR LOYAL FANS??
DON'T YOU WANT TO HELP DISPEL THIS PALL OF DOUBT THAT HANGS OVER YOU, ZOT??
NO COMMENT.
YOU HEARD HIM! NO COMMENT!
IN THAT CASE, THIS REPORTER CAN DRAW BUT ONE POSSIBLE CONCLUSION:
ZOT HAS SOLD OUT!
NO! DON'T LISTEN TO THIS CROOK!
ZOT SIGNED A CONTRACT! HE DIDN'T KNOW THAT--
MMF!
CLAM UP, CHIMP.
A CONTRACT?
WHAT MORE NEED BE SAID, LADIES AND GENTLEMEN? THIS IS ROGER ROBOT REPORTING!
BUT-- BUT--
IT'S A WRAP!
I'LL GET YOU FOR THIS, BLOTCH!
ANYTIME, PUNK! ANYTIME!
DBS NEWS

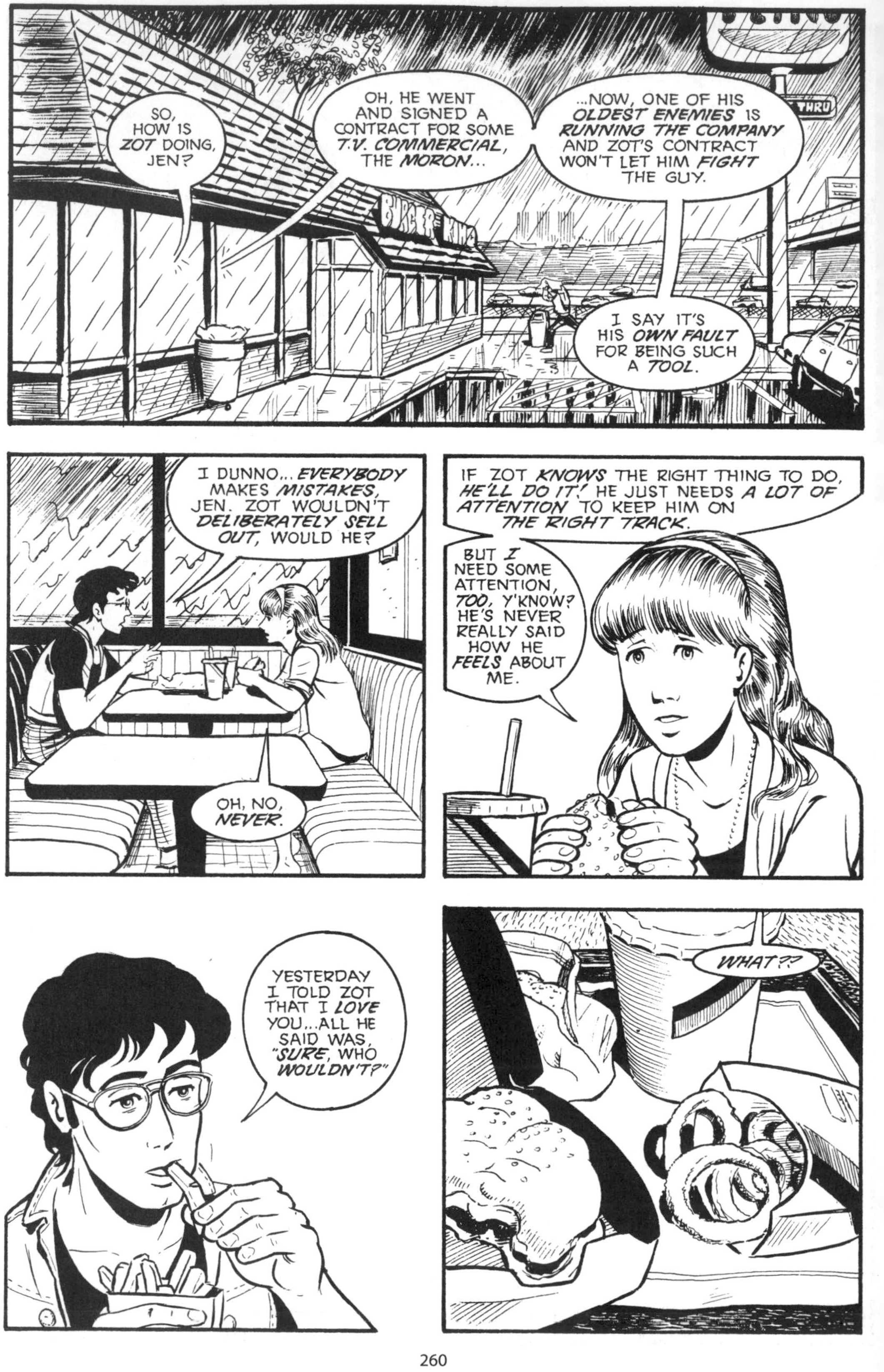

SO, HOW IS *ZOT* DOING, JEN?
OH, HE WENT AND SIGNED A CONTRACT FOR SOME *T.V. COMMERCIAL*, THE *MORON*...
...NOW, ONE OF HIS *OLDEST ENEMIES* IS *RUNNING THE COMPANY* AND ZOT'S CONTRACT WON'T LET HIM *FIGHT* THE GUY.
THRU
BURGER KING
I SAY IT'S HIS *OWN FAULT* FOR BEING SUCH A *TOOL*.
I DUNNO... *EVERYBODY* MAKES *MISTAKES*, JEN. ZOT WOULDN'T *DELIBERATELY SELL OUT*, WOULD HE?
OH, NO, *NEVER*.
IF ZOT *KNOWS* THE RIGHT THING TO DO, *HE'LL DO IT!* HE JUST NEEDS *A LOT OF ATTENTION* TO KEEP HIM ON *THE RIGHT TRACK*.
BUT *I* NEED SOME ATTENTION, *TOO*, Y'KNOW? HE'S NEVER REALLY SAID HOW HE *FEELS* ABOUT ME.
YESTERDAY I TOLD ZOT THAT I *LOVE* YOU...ALL HE SAID WAS, "*SURE*, WHO *WOULDN'T?*"
WHAT??

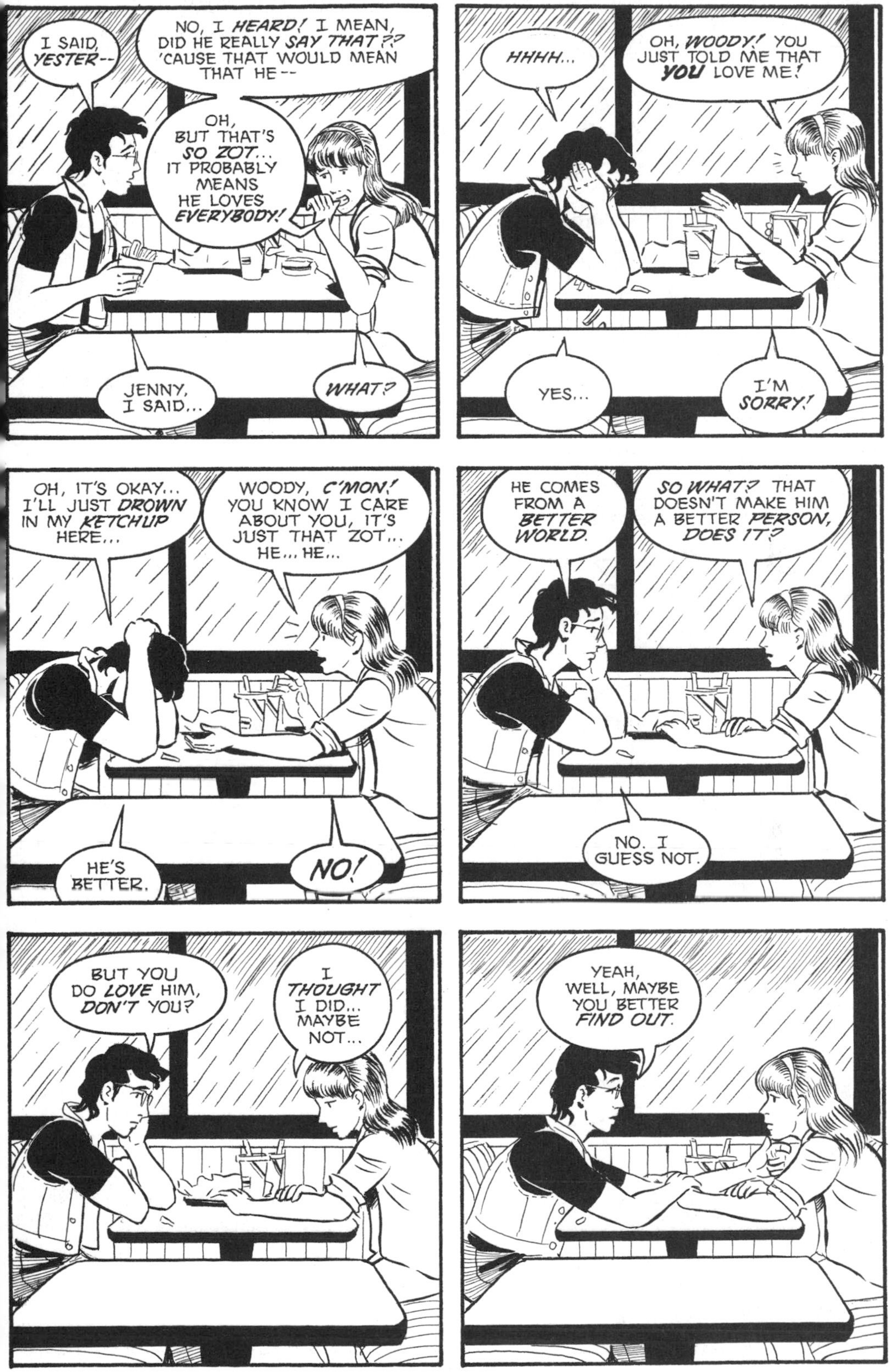
I SAID, YESTER--
NO, I HEARD! I MEAN, DID HE REALLY SAY THAT?? 'CAUSE THAT WOULD MEAN THAT HE --
OH, BUT THAT'S SO ZOT... IT PROBABLY MEANS HE LOVES EVERYBODY!
JENNY, I SAID...
WHAT?
HHHH...
OH, WOODY! YOU JUST TOLD ME THAT YOU LOVE ME!
YES...
I'M SORRY!
OH, IT'S OKAY... I'LL JUST DROWN IN MY KETCHUP HERE...
WOODY, C'MON! YOU KNOW I CARE ABOUT YOU, IT'S JUST THAT ZOT... HE... HE...
HE'S BETTER.
NO!
HE COMES FROM A BETTER WORLD.
SO WHAT? THAT DOESN'T MAKE HIM A BETTER PERSON, DOES IT?
NO. I GUESS NOT.
BUT YOU DO LOVE HIM, DON'T YOU?
I THOUGHT I DID... MAYBE NOT...
YEAH, WELL, MAYBE YOU BETTER FIND OUT.

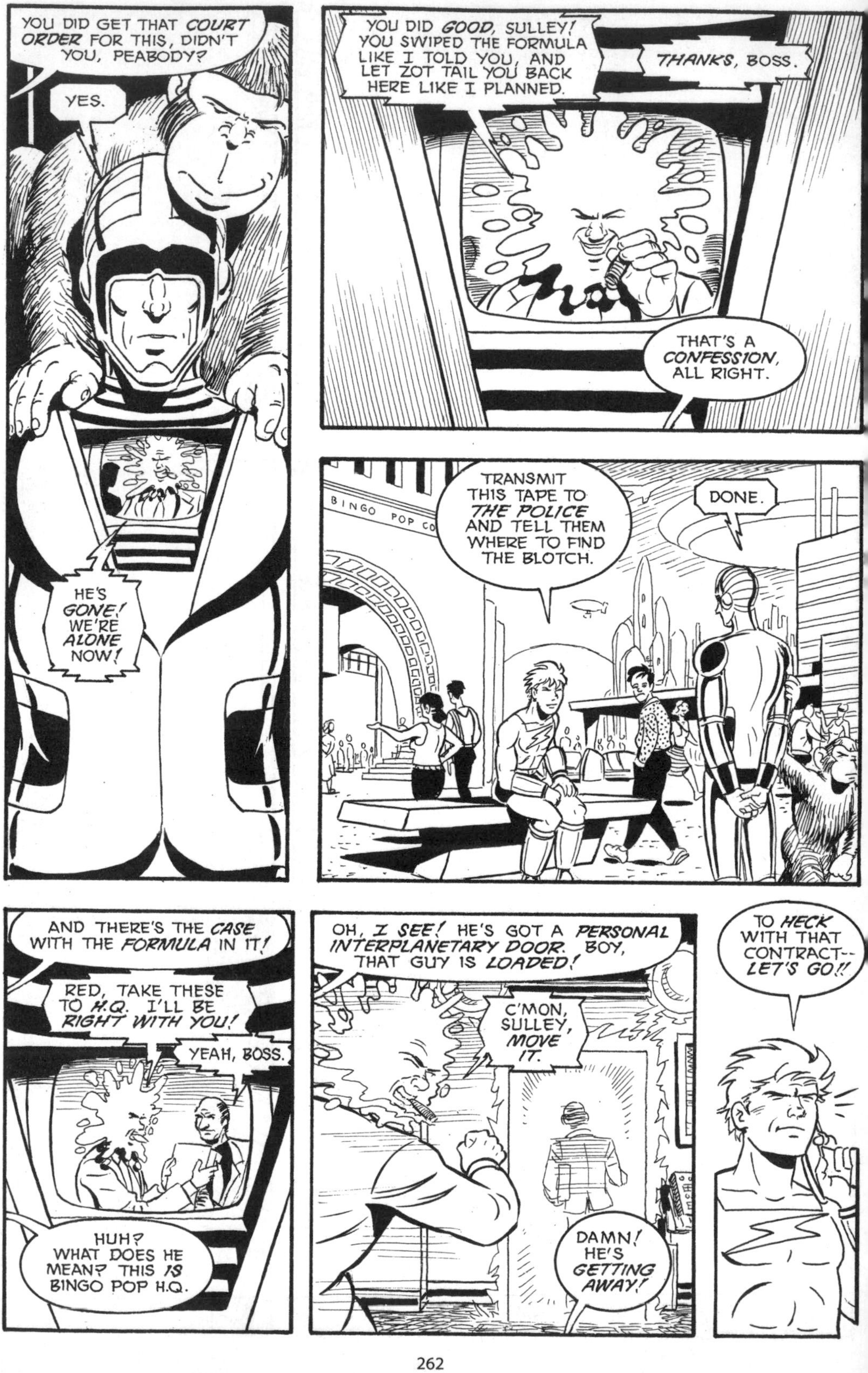
YOU DID GET THAT COURT ORDER FOR THIS, DIDN'T YOU, PEABODY?
YES.
HE'S GONE! WE'RE ALONE NOW!
YOU DID GOOD, SULLEY! YOU SWIPED THE FORMULA LIKE I TOLD YOU, AND LET ZOT TAIL YOU BACK HERE LIKE I PLANNED.
THANKS, BOSS.
THAT'S A CONFESSION, ALL RIGHT.
BINGO POP CO
TRANSMIT THIS TAPE TO THE POLICE AND TELL THEM WHERE TO FIND THE BLOTCH.
DONE.
AND THERE'S THE CASE WITH THE FORMULA IN IT!
RED, TAKE THESE TO H.Q. I'LL BE RIGHT WITH YOU!
YEAH, BOSS.
HUH? WHAT DOES HE MEAN? THIS IS BINGO POP H.Q.
OH, I SEE! HE'S GOT A PERSONAL INTERPLANETARY DOOR. BOY, THAT GUY IS LOADED!
C'MON, SULLEY, MOVE IT.
DAMN! HE'S GETTING AWAY!
TO HECK WITH THAT CONTRACT-- LET'S GO!!

WAK!

PRIVATE

BOOM!

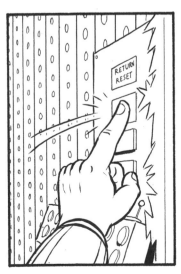

RETURN
RESET

CLIK!
CLIK!
CLIK!

EXIT

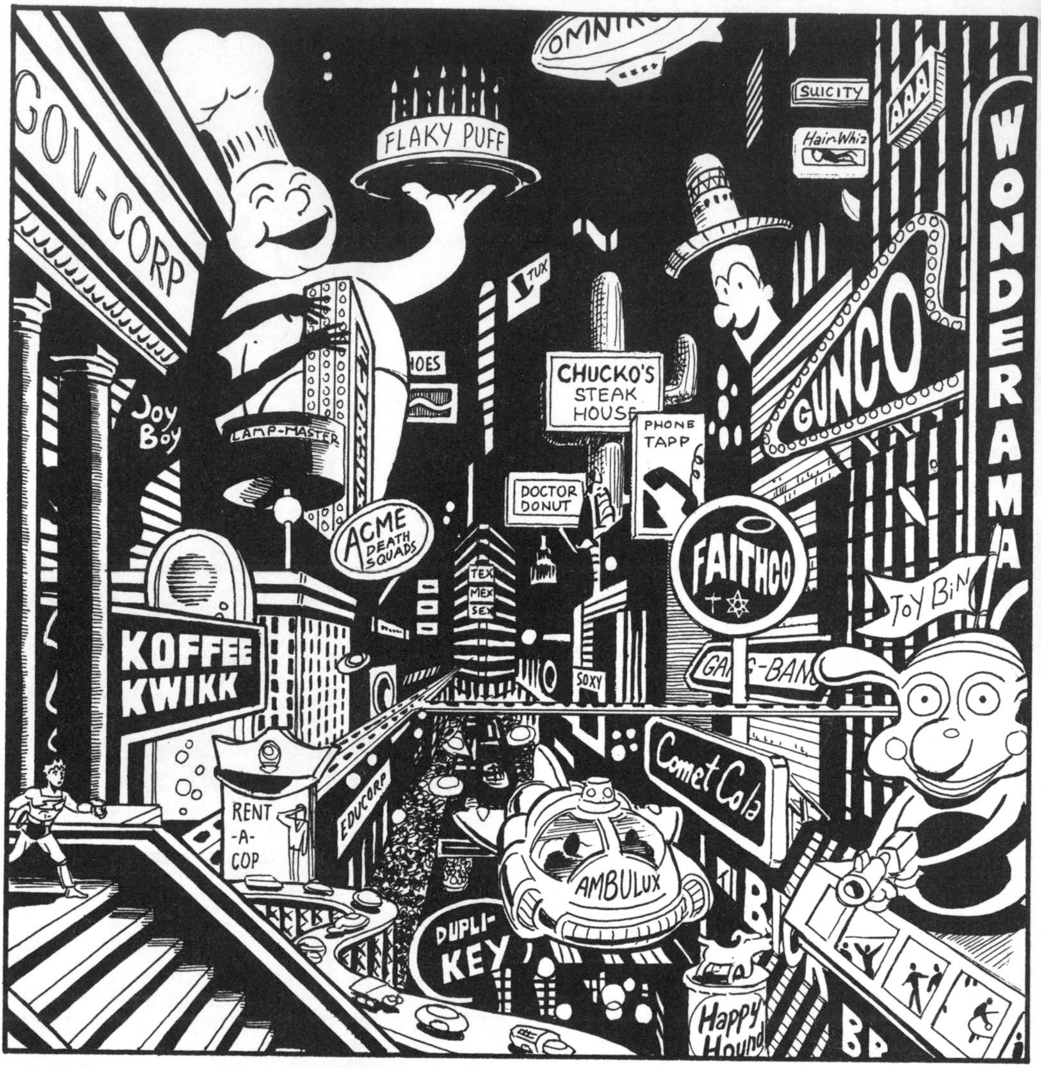
GOV-CORP
FLAKY PUFF
SUICITY
AAA
Hair Whiz
WONDERAMA
TUX
CHUCKO'S STEAK HOUSE
Joy Boy
LAMP-MASTER
PHONE TAPP
GUNCO
DOCTOR DONUT
ACME DEATH SQUADS
FAITHCO
TEX MEX SEX
TOY BIN
KOFFEE KWIKK
SOXY
Comet Cola
RENT-A-COP
EDUCORP
AMBULUX
DUPLI-KEY
Happy Hound
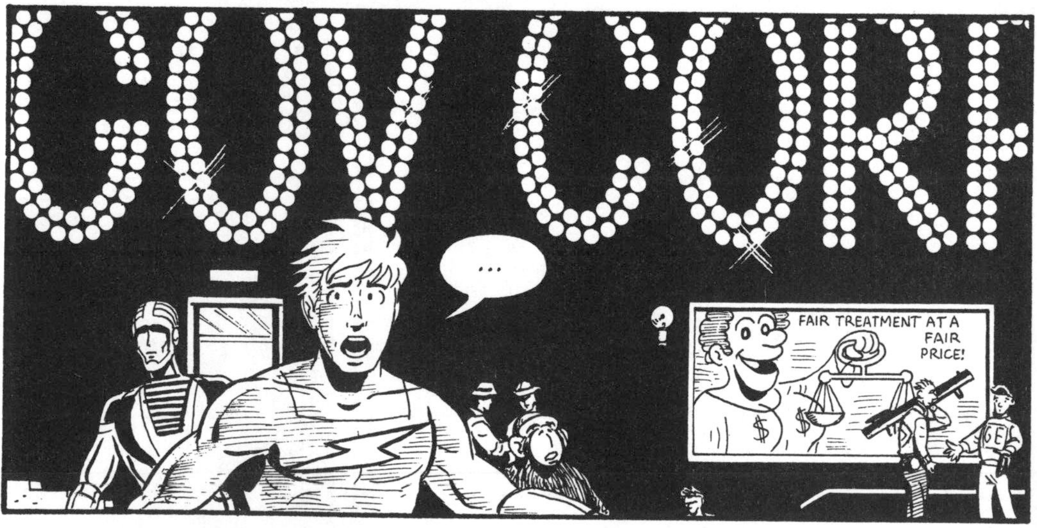
GOV CORP
...
FAIR TREATMENT AT A FAIR PRICE!

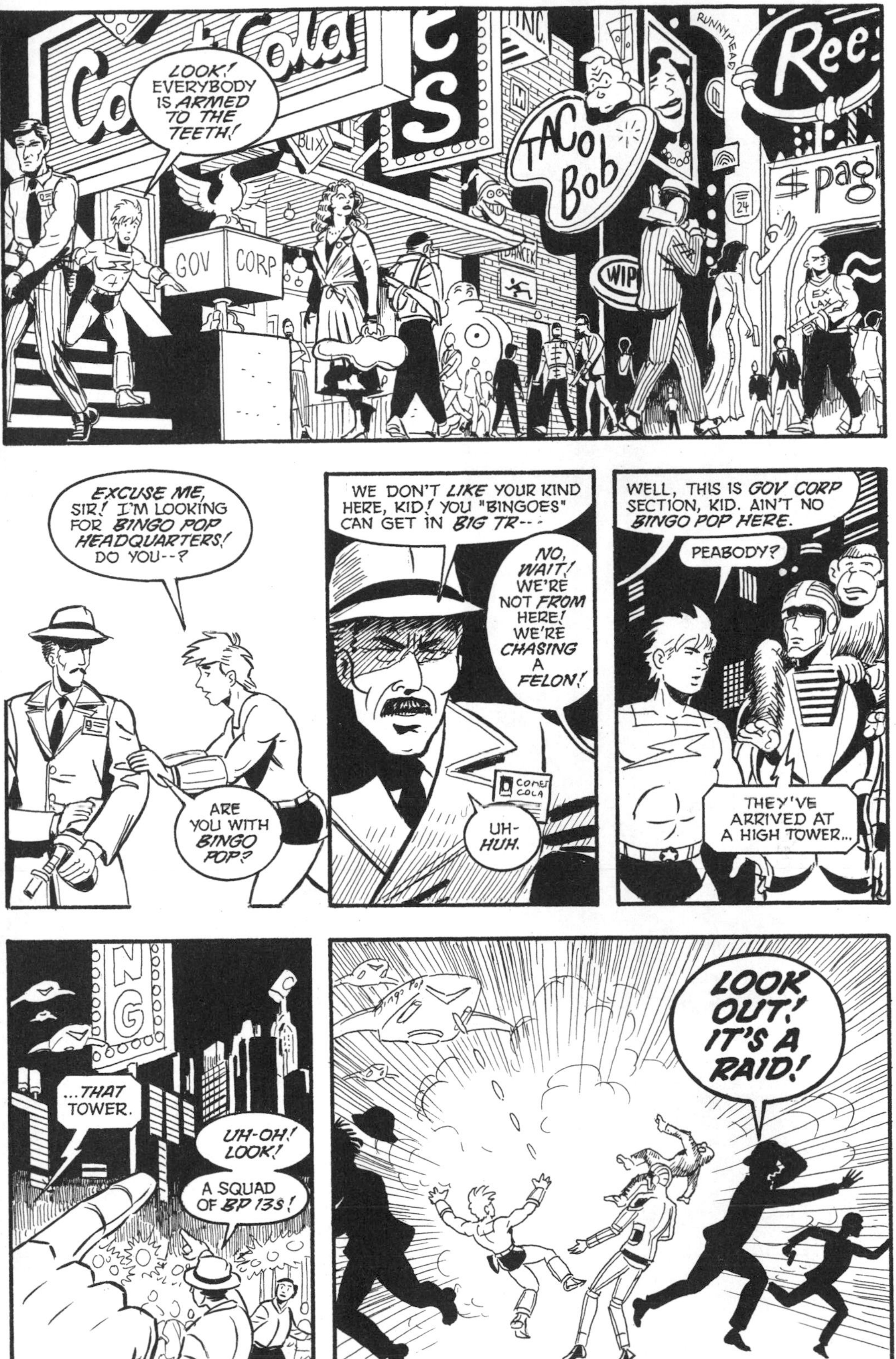
LOOK! EVERYBODY IS ARMED TO THE TEETH!
GOV CORP
TACO Bob
EXCUSE ME, SIR! I'M LOOKING FOR BINGO POP HEADQUARTERS! DO YOU--?
ARE YOU WITH BINGO POP?
WE DON'T LIKE YOUR KIND HERE, KID! YOU "BINGOES" CAN GET IN BIG TR---
NO, WAIT! WE'RE NOT FROM HERE! WE'RE CHASING A FELON!
UH-HUH.
WELL, THIS IS GOV CORP SECTION, KID. AIN'T NO BINGO POP HERE.
PEABODY?
THEY'VE ARRIVED AT A HIGH TOWER...
...THAT TOWER.
UH-OH! LOOK!
A SQUAD OF BP 13s!
LOOK OUT! IT'S A RAID!

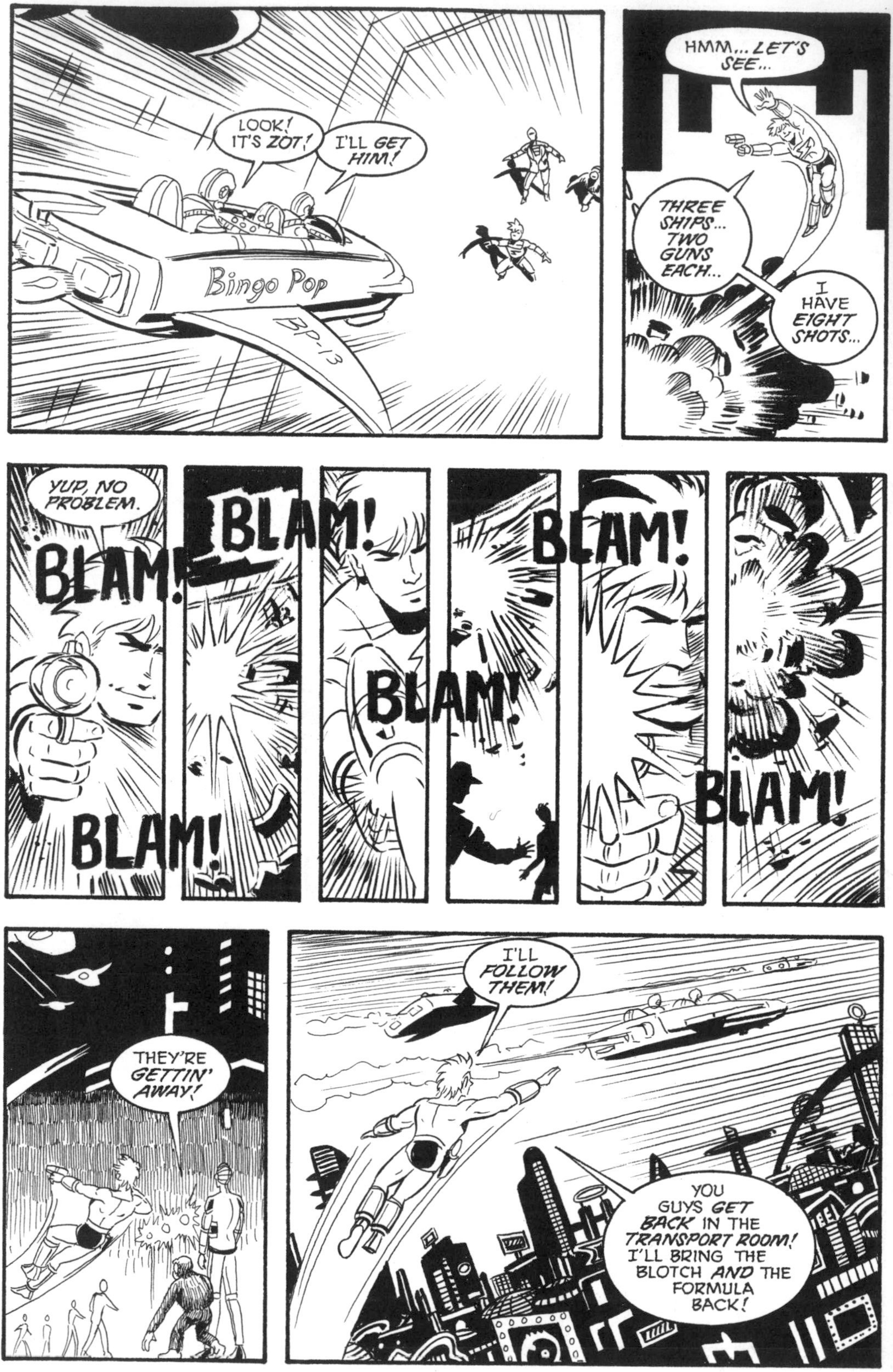
LOOK! IT'S ZOT!
I'LL GET HIM!
Bingo Pop
BP-13
HMM... LET'S SEE...
THREE SHIPS... TWO GUNS EACH...
I HAVE EIGHT SHOTS...
YUP, NO PROBLEM.
BLAM!
BLAM!
BLAM!
BLAM!
BLAM!
BLAM!
THEY'RE GETTIN' AWAY!
I'LL FOLLOW THEM!
YOU GUYS GET BACK IN THE TRANSPORT ROOM! I'LL BRING THE BLOTCH AND THE FORMULA BACK!

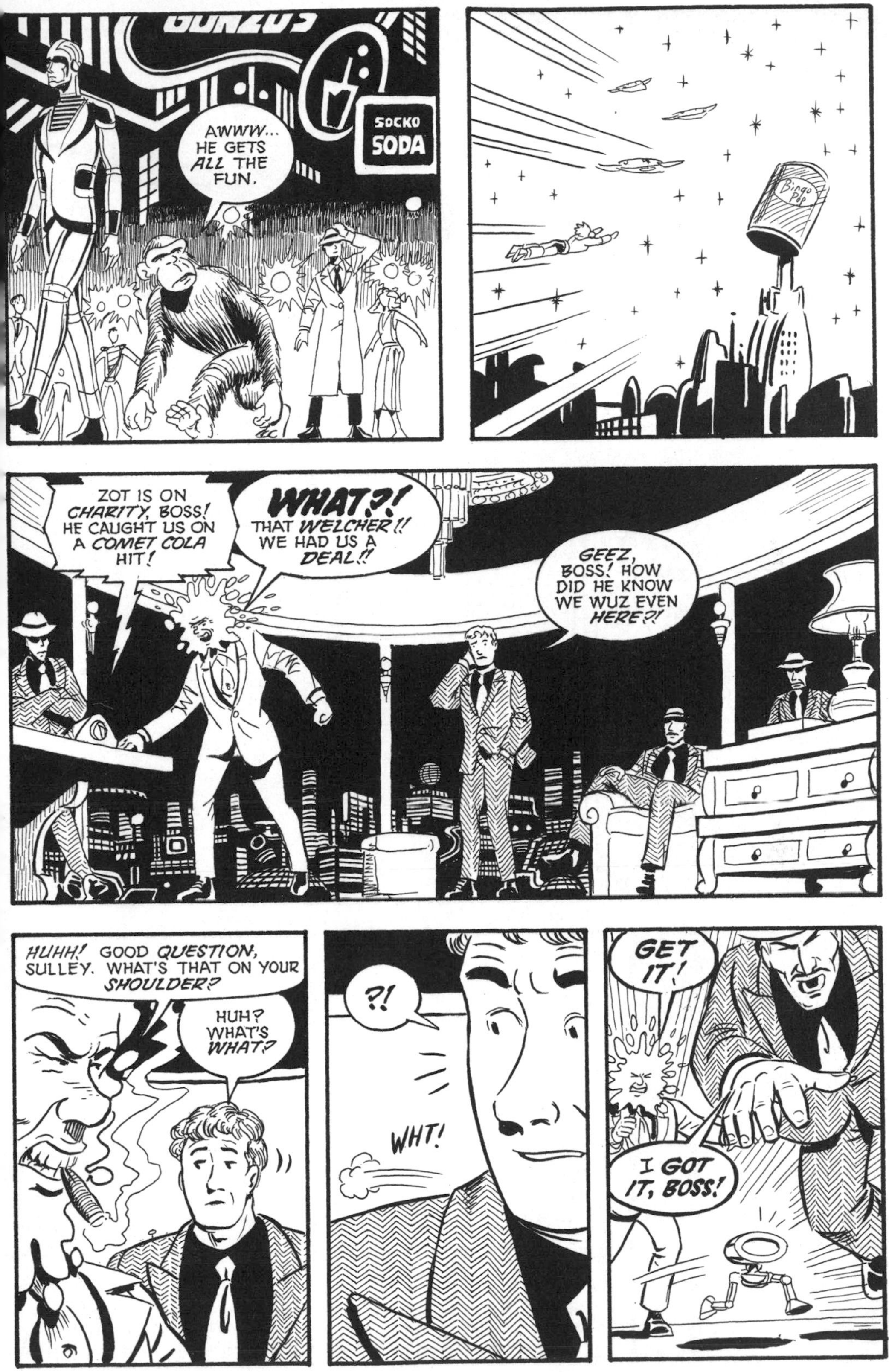
GONZO'S
SOCKO SODA
AWWW... HE GETS ALL THE FUN.
Bingo Pop
ZOT IS ON CHARITY, BOSS! HE CAUGHT US ON A COMET COLA HIT!
WHAT?! THAT WELCHER!! WE HAD US A DEAL!!
GEEZ, BOSS! HOW DID HE KNOW WE WUZ EVEN HERE?!
HUHH! GOOD QUESTION, SULLEY. WHAT'S THAT ON YOUR SHOULDER?
HUH? WHAT'S WHAT?
?!
WHT!
GET IT!
I GOT IT, BOSS!

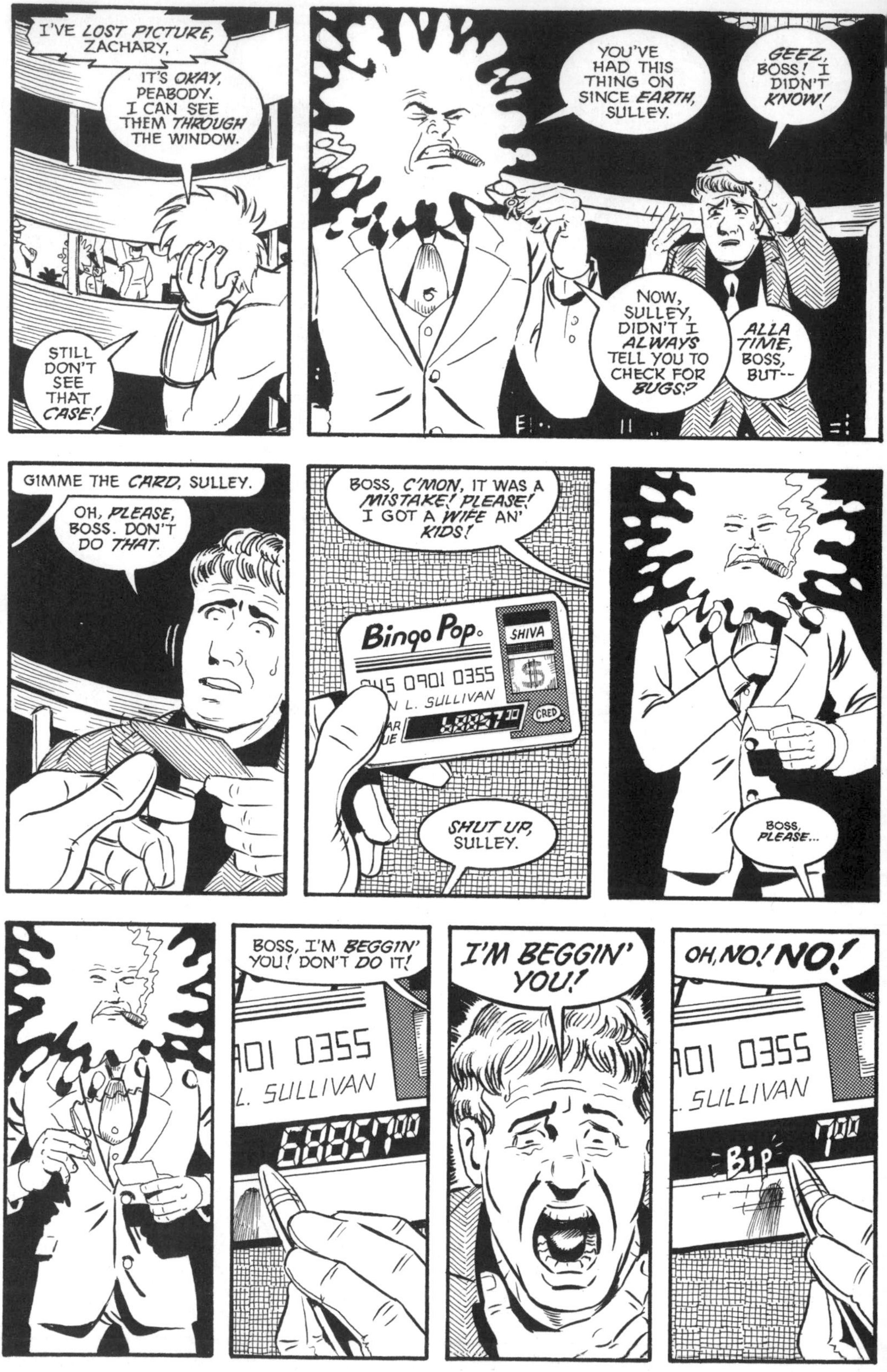
I'VE LOST PICTURE, ZACHARY,
IT'S OKAY, PEABODY. I CAN SEE THEM THROUGH THE WINDOW.
STILL DON'T SEE THAT CASE!
YOU'VE HAD THIS THING ON SINCE EARTH, SULLEY.
GEEZ, BOSS! I DIDN'T KNOW!
NOW, SULLEY, DIDN'T I ALWAYS TELL YOU TO CHECK FOR BUGS?
ALLA TIME, BOSS, BUT--
GIMME THE CARD, SULLEY.
OH, PLEASE, BOSS. DON'T DO THAT.
BOSS, C'MON, IT WAS A MISTAKE! PLEASE! I GOT A WIFE AN' KIDS!
Bingo Pop
SHIVA
0901 0355
L. SULLIVAN
CRED
SHUT UP, SULLEY.
BOSS, PLEASE...
BOSS, I'M BEGGIN' YOU! DON'T DO IT!
L. SULLIVAN
I'M BEGGIN' YOU!
OH, NO! NO!
L. SULLIVAN
Bip

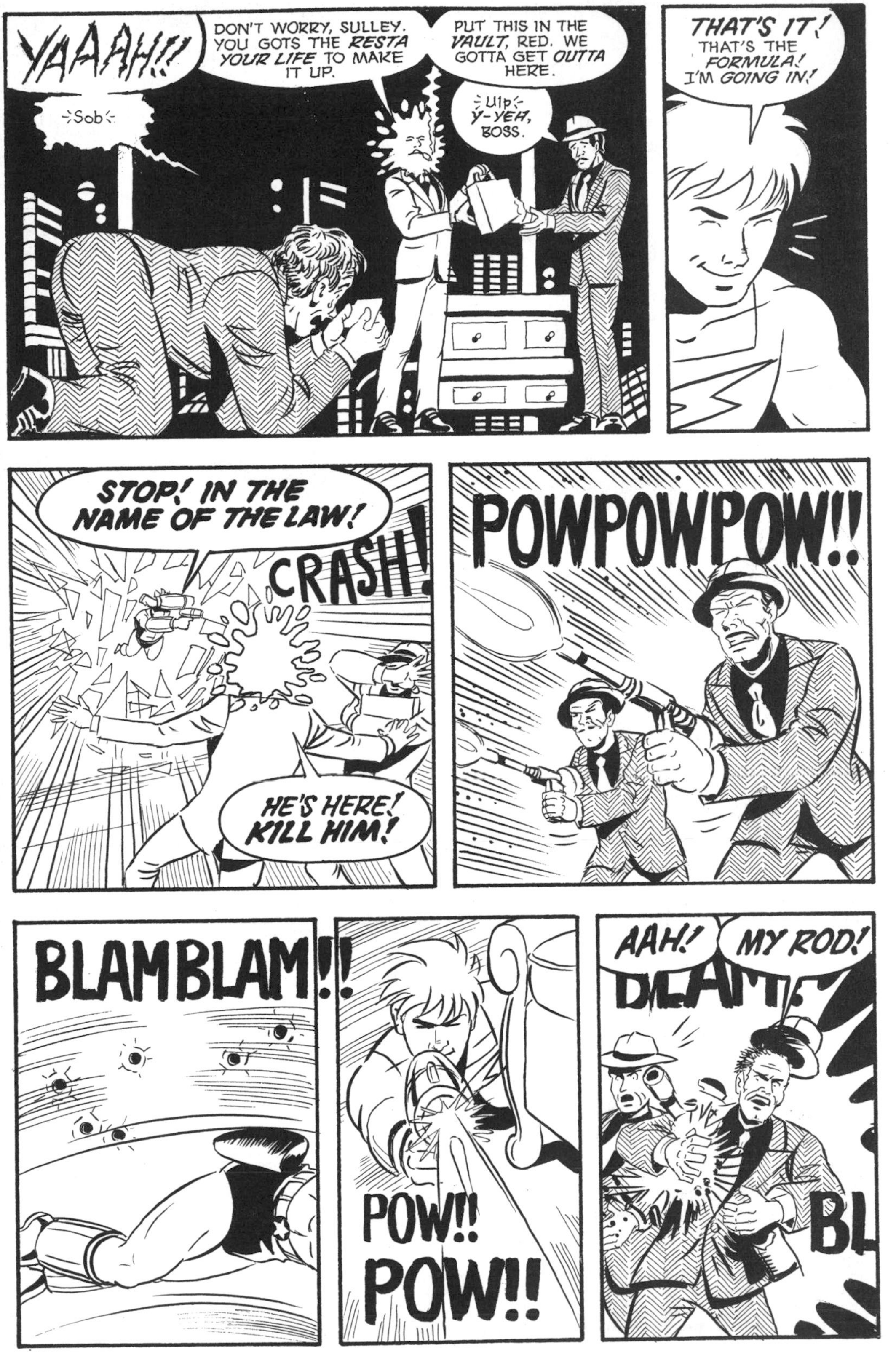
YAAAH!!
-Sob-
DON'T WORRY, SULLEY. YOU GOTS THE *RESTA YOUR LIFE* TO MAKE IT UP.
PUT THIS IN THE *VAULT*, RED. WE GOTTA GET *OUTTA* HERE.
-Ulp- Y-YEH, BOSS.
THAT'S IT! THAT'S THE *FORMULA!* I'M *GOING IN!*
STOP! IN THE NAME OF THE LAW!
CRASH!
HE'S HERE! KILL HIM!
POWPOWPOW!!
BLAMBLAM!!
POW!! POW!!
AAH!
MY ROD!
BL

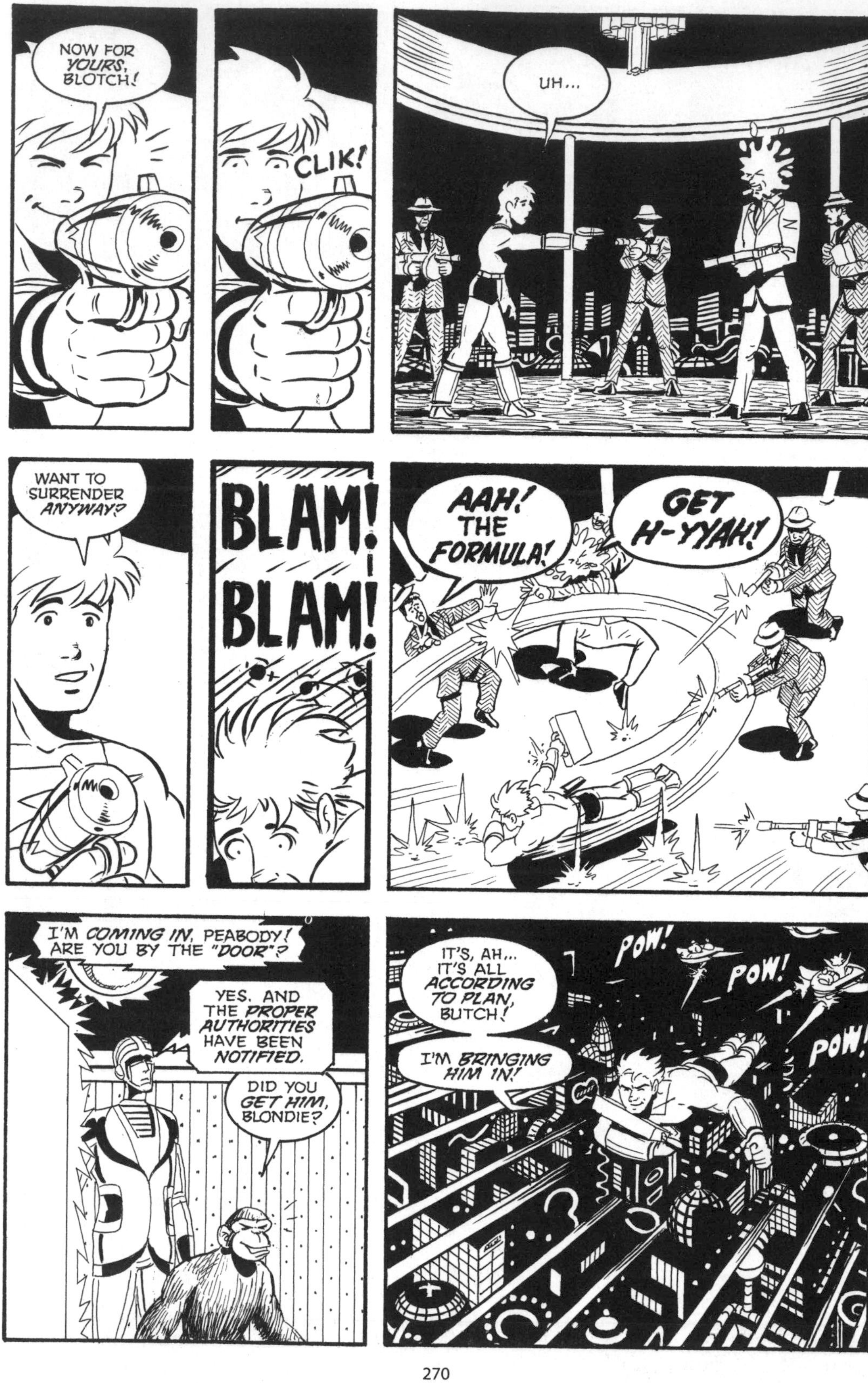
NOW FOR YOURS, BLOTCH!
CLIK!
UH...
WANT TO SURRENDER ANYWAY?
BLAM! BLAM!
AAH! THE FORMULA!
GET H-YYAH!
I'M COMING IN, PEABODY! ARE YOU BY THE "DOOR"?
YES. AND THE PROPER AUTHORITIES HAVE BEEN NOTIFIED.
DID YOU GET HIM, BLONDIE?
IT'S, AH... IT'S ALL ACCORDING TO PLAN, BUTCH!
I'M BRINGING HIM IN!
POW!
POW!
POW!

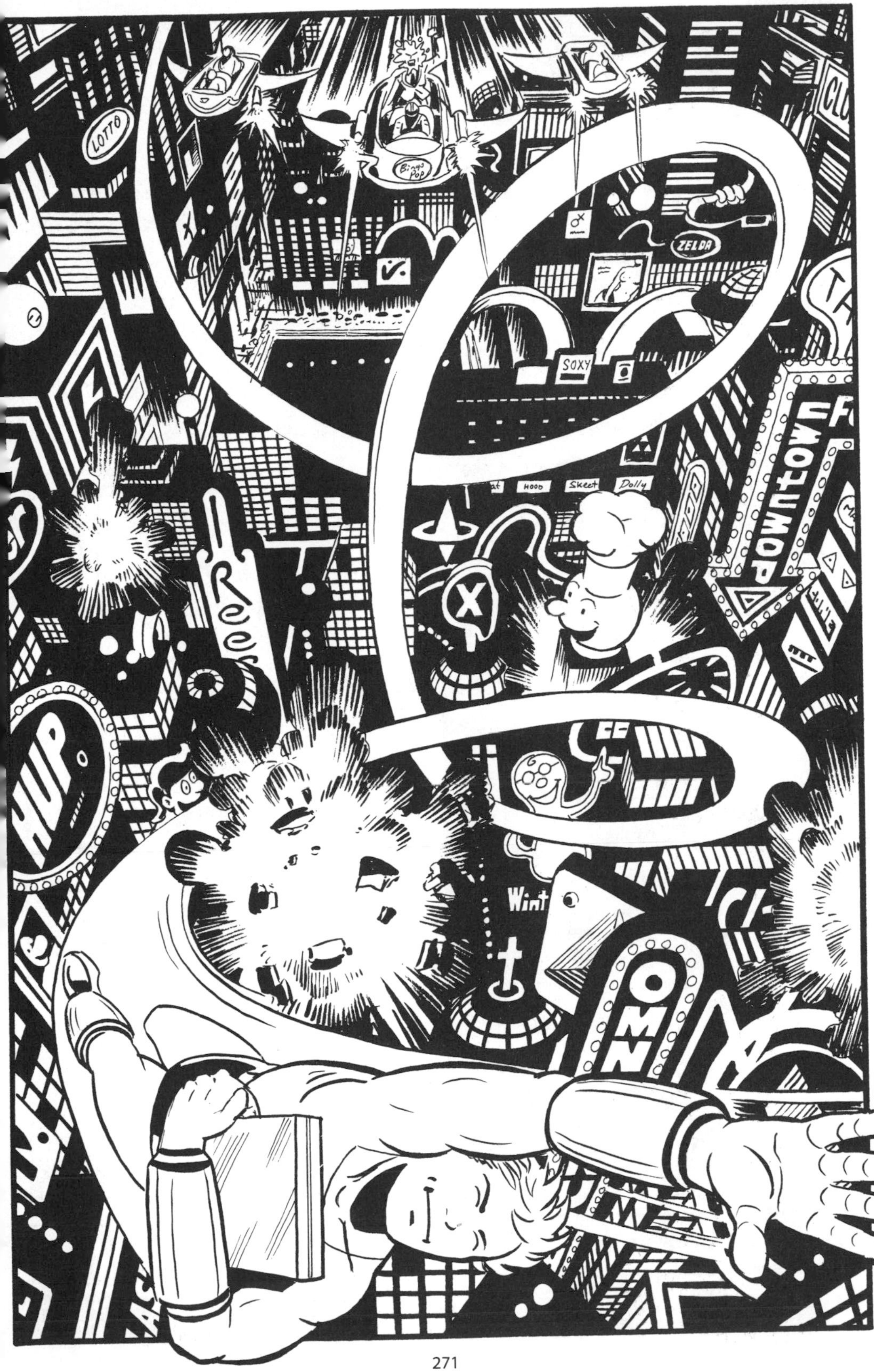
LOTTO
ZELDA
SOXY
HOOD
Skeet
Dolly
Wint

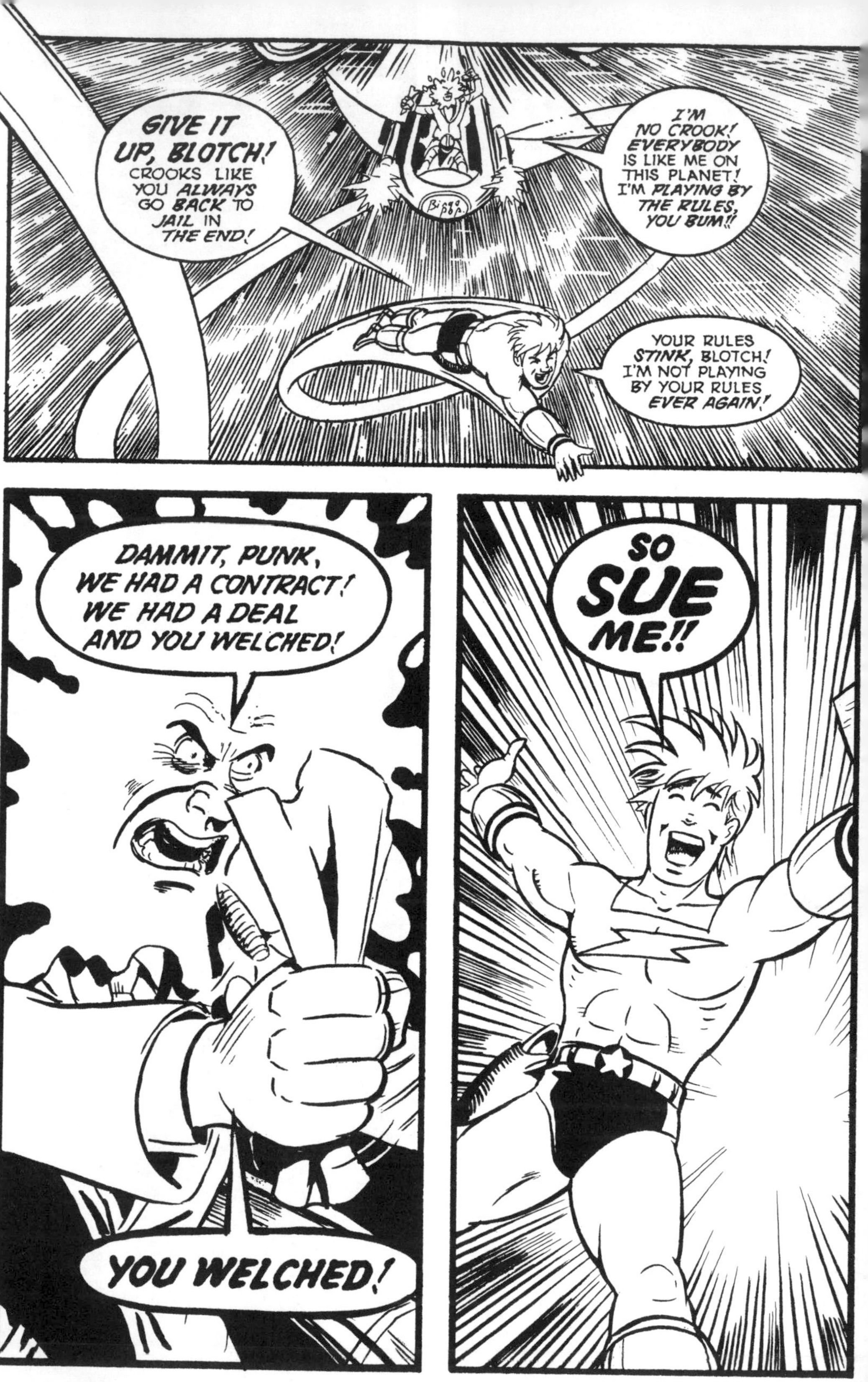
GIVE IT UP, BLOTCH! CROOKS LIKE YOU ALWAYS GO BACK TO JAIL IN THE END!
I'M NO CROOK! EVERYBODY IS LIKE ME ON THIS PLANET! I'M PLAYING BY THE RULES, YOU BUM!!
YOUR RULES STINK, BLOTCH! I'M NOT PLAYING BY YOUR RULES EVER AGAIN!
DAMMIT, PUNK, WE HAD A CONTRACT! WE HAD A DEAL AND YOU WELCHED!
YOU WELCHED!
SO SUE ME!!

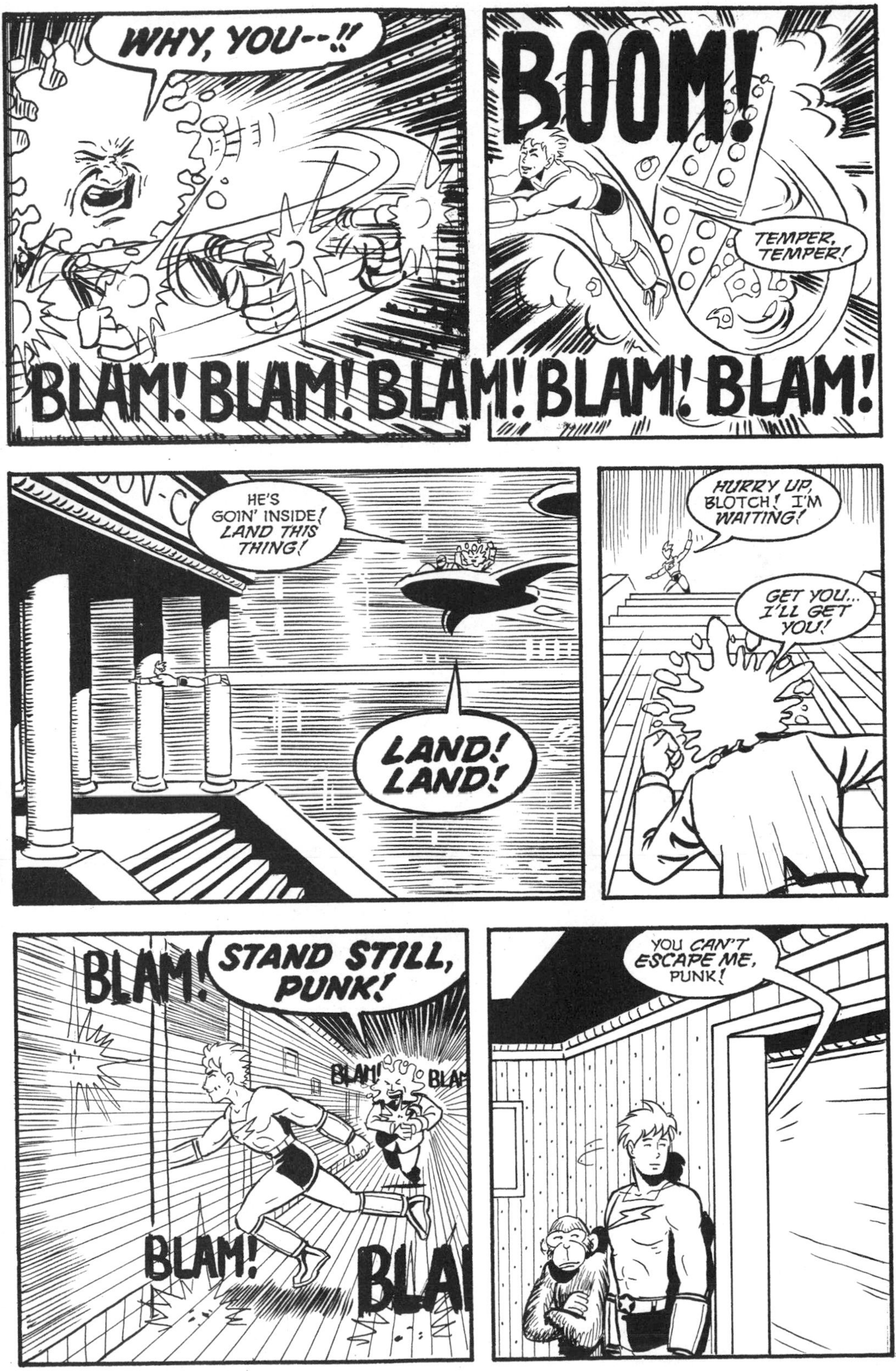
WHY, YOU--!!
BOOM!
TEMPER, TEMPER!
BLAM! BLAM! BLAM! BLAM! BLAM!
HE'S GOIN' INSIDE! LAND THIS THING!
LAND! LAND!
HURRY UP, BLOTCH! I'M WAITING!
GET YOU... I'LL GET YOU!
BLAM!
STAND STILL, PUNK!
BLAM!
BLAM!
YOU CAN'T ESCAPE ME, PUNK!

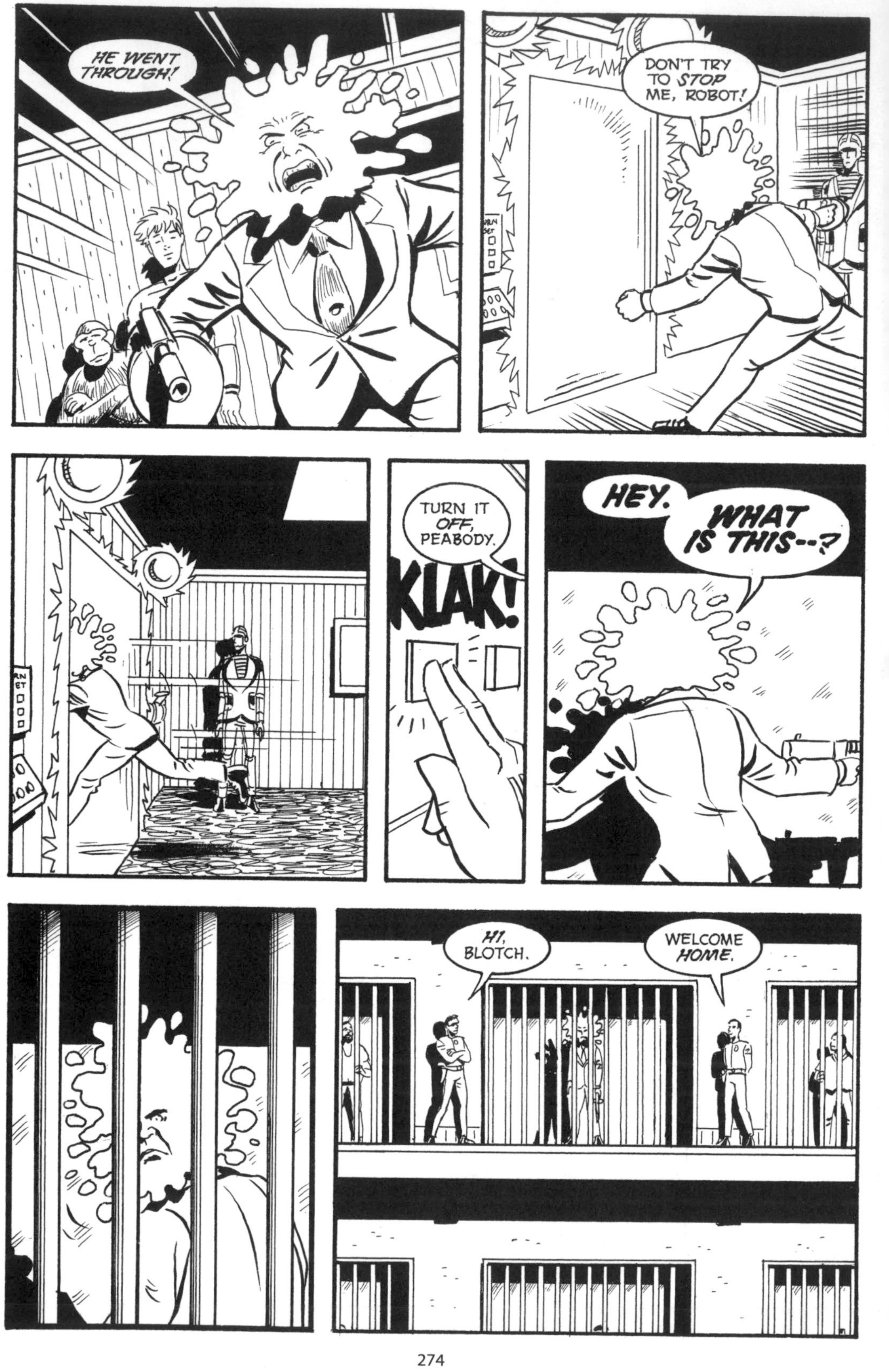
HE WENT THROUGH!
DON'T TRY TO STOP ME, ROBOT!
TURN IT OFF, PEABODY.
KLAK!
HEY.
WHAT IS THIS--?
HI, BLOTCH.
WELCOME HOME.

-- SO, ANYWAY, WE GOT ENOUGH ON HIM TO PUT HIM AWAY FOR *A FEW YEARS* AT LEAST.

'TIL HE *BREAKS OUT* AGAIN, Y'MEAN.

HEY, *ZACH!* DID THE *AD MONEY* COME IN YET?

WELL, ER, *YES AND NO*, DIGGER...

MEANING YOU CAN *FORGET THE CAR*, SHADES.

AWW...

ZOT, CAN I *TALK* TO YOU FOR A *MINUTE?*

UH, *SURE*, JEN. SEE YOU *LATER*, GUYS!

ZOT, *LISTEN.* I WANT YOU TO TELL ME *THE TRUTH*, ONCE AND FOR ALL!

DO YOU *LOVE ME?*

WELL, *SURE.* WHO WOULDN'T?

NO! NO! I MEAN, LIKE... Y'KNOW... DO YOU *LOVE* ME?!

OH, YOU MEAN, LIKE, *CAPITAL "L"* LOVE...

YES! THAT'S IT! CAPITAL "L" LOVE! DO YOU *CAPITAL "L" LOVE ME?!*

I--! I *DON'T KNOW!*

275

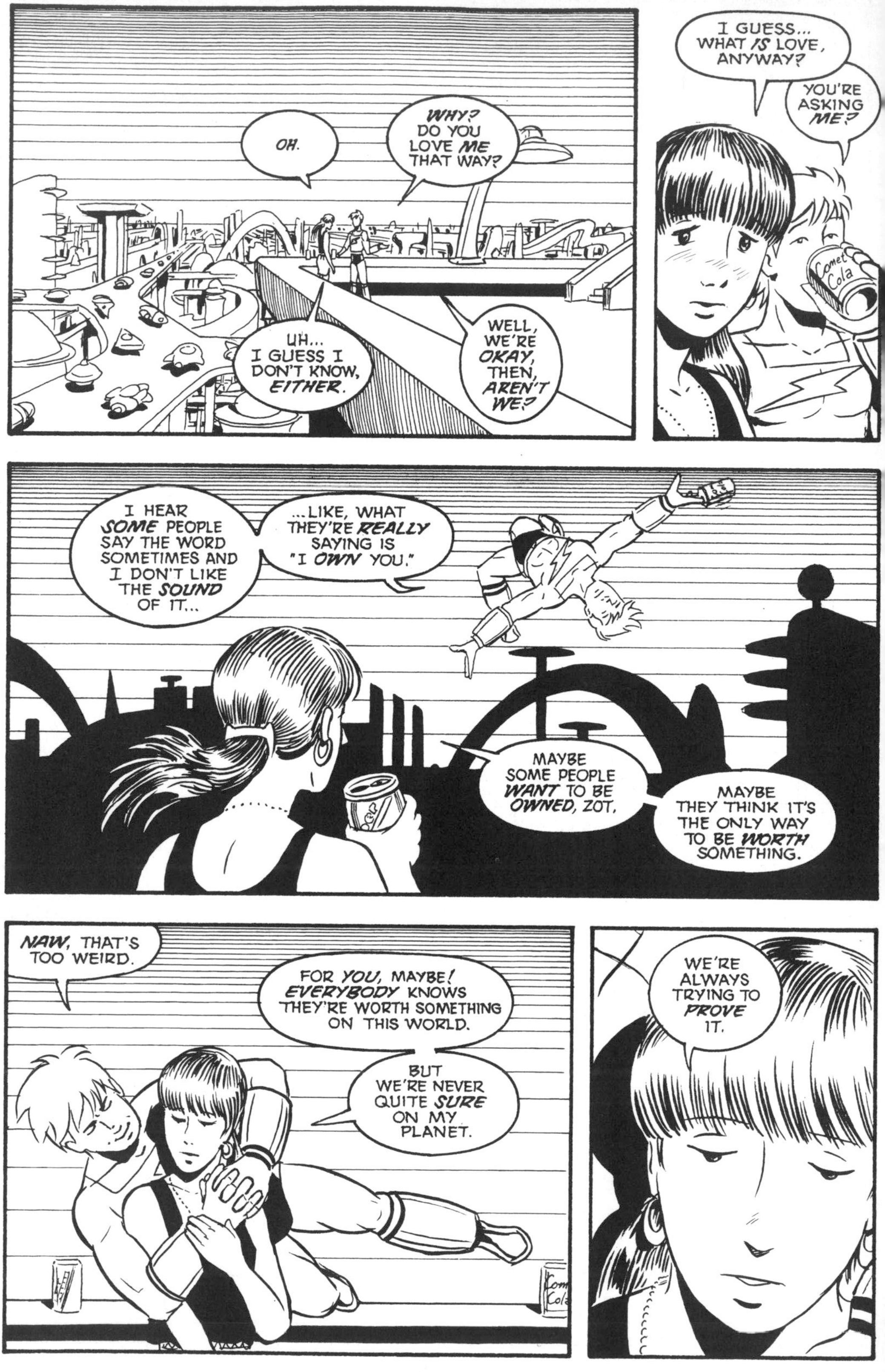
OH.
WHY? DO YOU LOVE ME THAT WAY?
UH... I GUESS I DON'T KNOW, EITHER.
WELL, WE'RE OKAY, THEN, AREN'T WE?
I GUESS... WHAT IS LOVE, ANYWAY?
YOU'RE ASKING ME?
Comet Cola
I HEAR SOME PEOPLE SAY THE WORD SOMETIMES AND I DON'T LIKE THE SOUND OF IT...
...LIKE, WHAT THEY'RE REALLY SAYING IS "I OWN YOU."
MAYBE SOME PEOPLE WANT TO BE OWNED, ZOT.
MAYBE THEY THINK IT'S THE ONLY WAY TO BE WORTH SOMETHING.
NAW, THAT'S TOO WEIRD.
FOR YOU, MAYBE! EVERYBODY KNOWS THEY'RE WORTH SOMETHING ON THIS WORLD.
BUT WE'RE NEVER QUITE SURE ON MY PLANET.
WE'RE ALWAYS TRYING TO PROVE IT.

SO, *HEY!* WHAT WAS THAT ABOUT THE *AD?*

OH! I MADE A DEAL WITH THE *PRESIDENT.* I WOULDN'T PUBLICIZE *HIS* ROLE IN THIS MESS--

--BUT, IN *EXCHANGE,* I GET TO DO THE AD *MY* WAY.

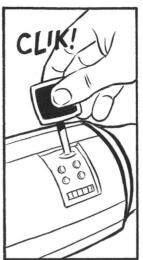

CLIK!

GEE, ZOT, I DIDN'T KNOW YOU HAD ONE OF THOSE!

OH, I HAVE *LOTS* OF GADGETS I NEVER USE ANYMORE.

HI! THIS IS ZOT, FOR *BINGO POP!*

Y'KNOW, I DIDN'T REALLY *LIKE* BINGO POP WHEN I STARTED WORKING ON THIS AD...

...BUT SEEING AS IT WAS THE ONLY THING ON THE SET AND IT WAS A PRETTY *HOT* DAY...

...WELL, I GOT *USED* TO IT.

IT'S REALLY FAIRLY *TOLERABLE STUFF!* IN FACT, IT'S *ALMOST* AS GOOD AS *COMET COLA!*

REALLY!

277

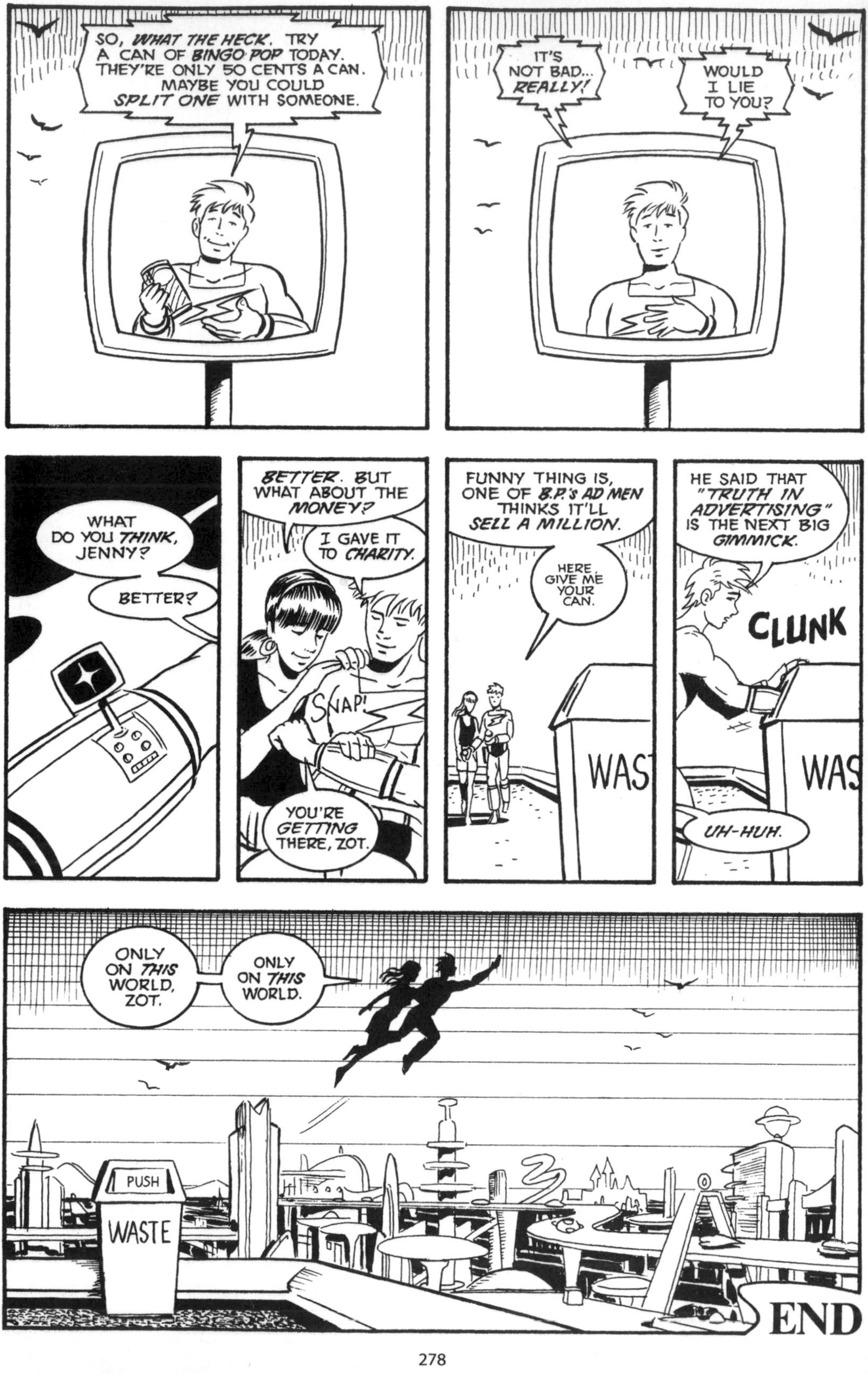

SO, WHAT THE HECK. TRY A CAN OF BINGO POP TODAY. THEY'RE ONLY 50 CENTS A CAN. MAYBE YOU COULD SPLIT ONE WITH SOMEONE.
IT'S NOT BAD... REALLY!
WOULD I LIE TO YOU?
WHAT DO YOU THINK, JENNY?
BETTER?
BETTER. BUT WHAT ABOUT THE MONEY?
I GAVE IT TO CHARITY.
SNAP!
YOU'RE GETTING THERE, ZOT.
FUNNY THING IS, ONE OF B.P.'s AD MEN THINKS IT'LL SELL A MILLION.
HERE, GIVE ME YOUR CAN.
WAST
HE SAID THAT "TRUTH IN ADVERTISING" IS THE NEXT BIG GIMMICK.
CLUNK
WAS
UH-HUH.
ONLY ON THIS WORLD, ZOT.
ONLY ON THIS WORLD.
PUSH
WASTE
END

When I created *Zot!*, I wanted to highlight my characters' differences, both externally and internally. I'd noticed that writers who worked on a series long enough sometimes lost sight of those differences over time until their characters' voices became interchangeable. To avoid this, I looked for internal organizing ideas. For Zot, Jenny, Peabody, and Butch, I used Carl Jung's four functions of the human mind: Intuition, Feeling, Intellect, and Sensation. Jenny's orientation, Feeling, assigns value judgments, so she would be most likely to take offense at Zot's "selling out."

Some readers were annoyed that Zot would be so shallow as to endorse a product, but others were just annoyed that Jenny was such a nag about it. In my own clumsy way, I was trying to work out where my perfect hero was less than perfect.

Throughout these stories, I was wrestling with which of the two worlds I found more interesting, and at this point, our Earth was edging out Zot's universe. Stemming from my early fascination with Japanese comics, I had a strong interest in what I called "the beauty of the mundane." Drawing my hero rocketing, Astroboy-style, over a hyper-commercialized future city was fun and all, but a Burger King in the rain—now that was interesting!

When I'd created the Blotch some years earlier, I'd seen the future he represented, the future of capitalism run amok, as unlikely, so he was one of the "loud" villains (i.e., more impotent and boastful than, say, Zybox). But, by 1988, his future seemed a bit more relevant to the times we were living in, so he got a bit edgier. The scene where the Blotch erases Sulley's life savings is played as comedy, but I shuddered a bit when writing it.

Ivy and I struggled with money a lot in the late '80s. I can't count the number of times we'd run a utility payment in before 5:00 p.m. to avoid shut-offs during those years. The comics industry was going through a boom-and-bust cycle of black and white comics frantically trying to duplicate the success of the *Teenage Mutant Ninja Turtles*. I was neither lucky, clever, nor crass enough to reap the benefits of the boom, but the bust was taking its toll nonetheless.

We knew Kevin Eastman and Peter Laird, the Turtles' creators, two friendly, good-hearted young guys struggling to make sense of the millions of dollars thundering down upon them in nearby Northampton, Massachusetts. The scale of their success was almost unimaginable. Every station break brought another ad. Every kid in the country could name all four turtles. Whole aisles of Toys R Us were as green as the Barbie aisles were pink.

One Friday afternoon, around that time, Ivy and I were between checks yet again. Raiding the change jars and searching between the couch cushions, we'd managed to scrounge a little over ten dollars, enough to buy a long weekend's worth of groceries, provided we stuck to cheap stuff like pasta. Entering the local Stop and Shop, Ivy went off to buy milk, butter, and a couple of other items. I picked up some spaghetti and sauce, then arrived at the mac and cheese boxes. Doing the math, I figured we could get a couple of dinners out of the generic mac and cheese, or, if I felt confident that we'd get the next check by Monday, maybe we could afford to get the Kraft Dinner box for just one night.

Then I saw it: *Teenage Mutant Ninja Turtles Macaroni and Cheese*. I couldn't believe my eyes—Pete and Kevin had their very own brand of macaroni and cheese! I couldn't wait to show Ivy, knowing she'd get as big a kick out of it as I did. I picked up the box, ready to put it into the basket, when I happened to look at the price.

It was too much. I could not afford to buy that box of macaroni and cheese.

And all at once, I was looking down at myself from above—an instant frozen in time—and I knew that I would remember that moment for the rest of my life.

Three years later, Kevin Eastman, through his new publishing imprint Tundra, would bankroll the printing of my first book-length comics hit, *Understanding Comics*.

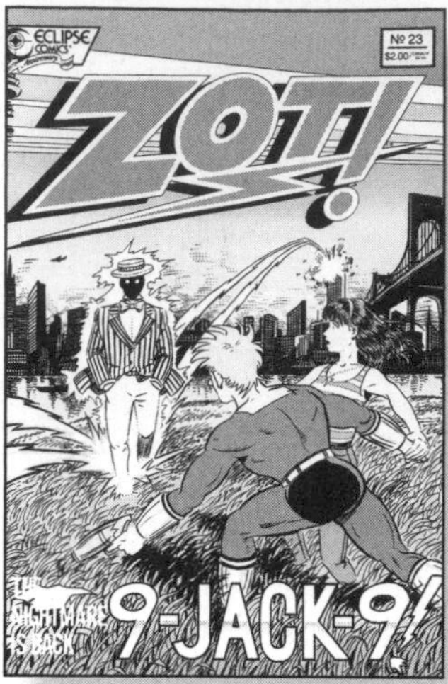
ECLIPSE COMICS
№ 23
$2.00
ZOT!
THE NIGHTMARE IS BACK
9-JACK-9!

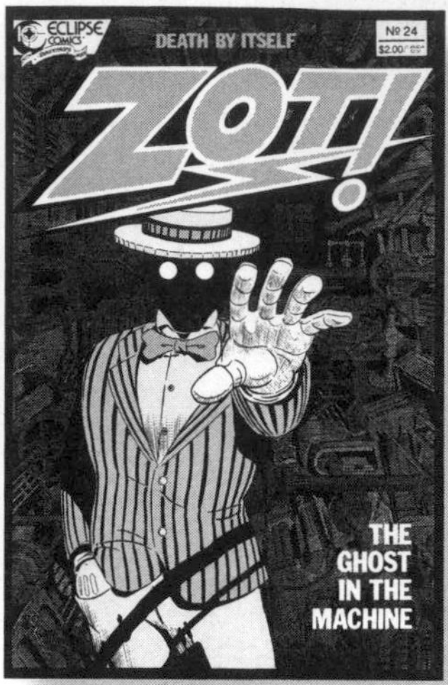
ECLIPSE COMICS
DEATH BY ITSELF
№ 24
$2.00
ZOT!
THE GHOST IN THE MACHINE

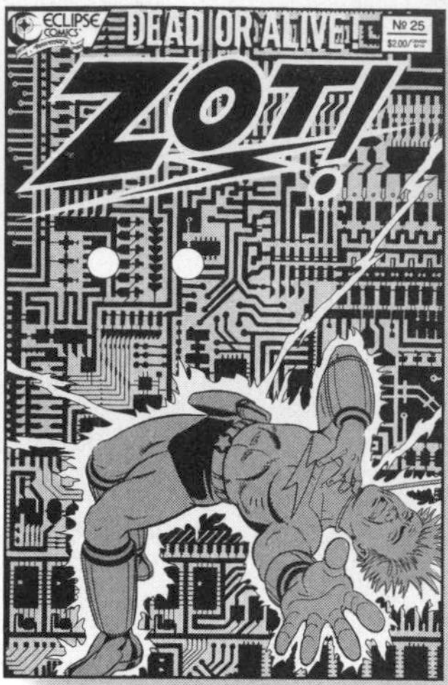
ECLIPSE COMICS
DEAD OR ALIVE!
№ 25
$2.00
ZOT!

The Ghost in the Machine

First published in *Zot! #23–25*.

Lettering:
Bob Lappan

Original series editor:
cat yronwode

THE GHOST IN THE MACHINE

PART ONE (OF THREE)

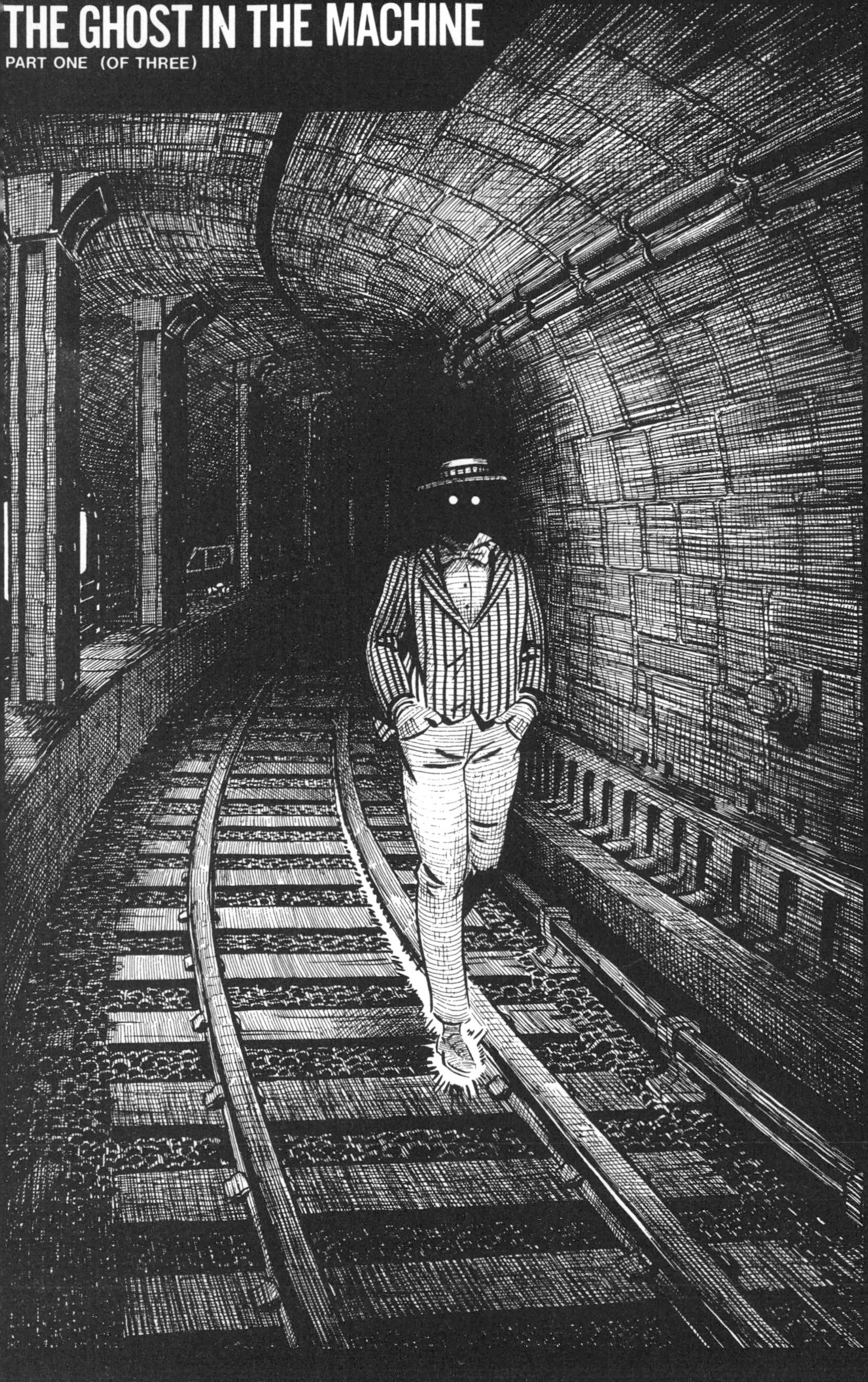

DADDY, *LOOK!* THERE'S A *MAN* ON THE TRACKS!

WHAT?

I KNOW YOU'RE HERE...

AW, HONEY, DON'T LIE TO *DADDY!*

BUT--

KLAK!

KLAK!

KLAK!

...SOMEWHERE ON THIS *PRIMITIVE WORLD*...

DAMN! I JUST TURNED THOSE LIGHTS *OFF!*

WHA--

SOMETHING *WRONG*, CHESTER?

I--

NOTHING.

...SOMEWHERE YOU THOUGHT WAS *SAFE.*

AWK!

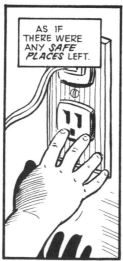

AS IF THERE WERE ANY *SAFE PLACES* LEFT.

NO, DEAR. DON'T *TOUCH.*

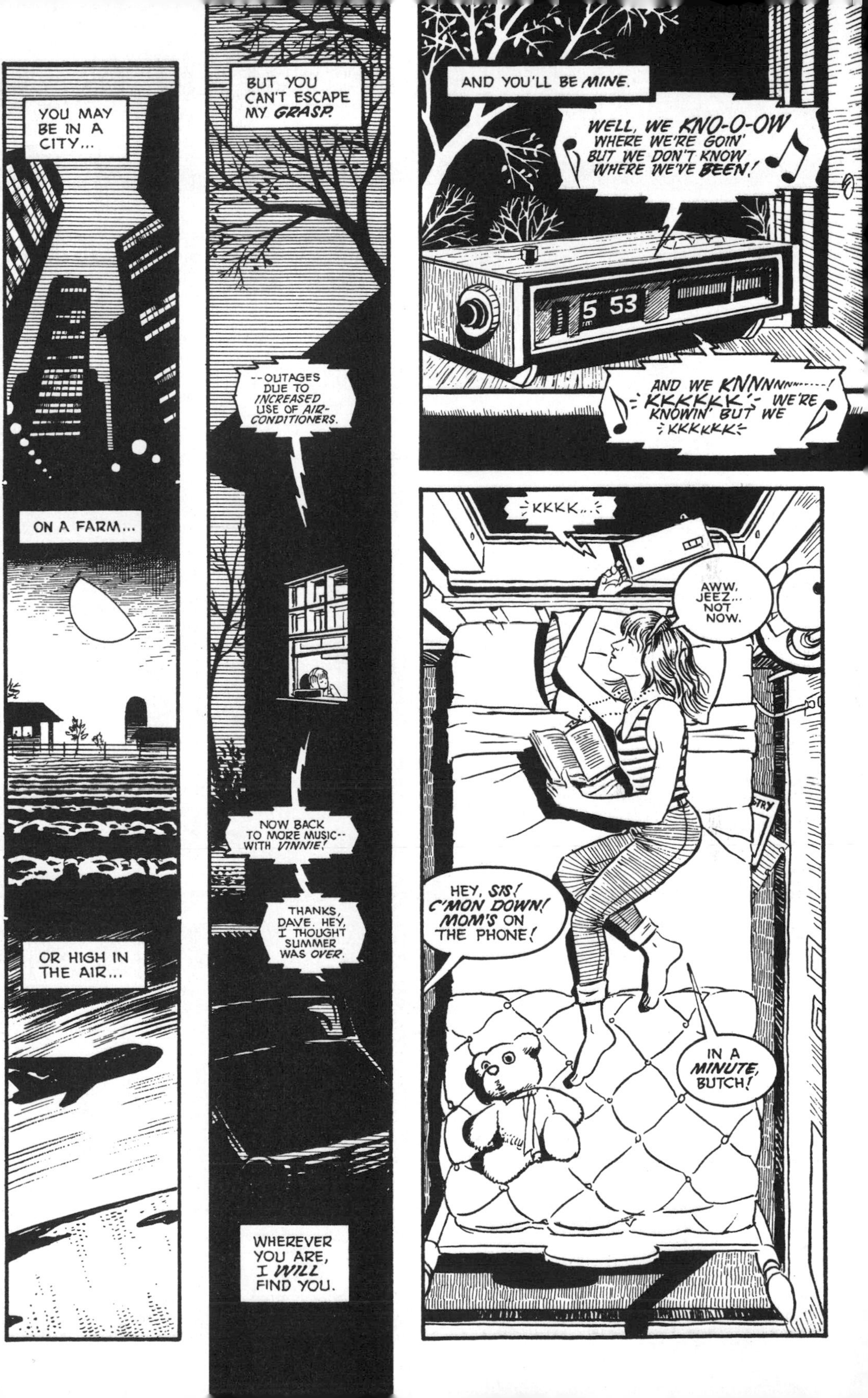
YOU MAY BE IN A CITY...
ON A FARM...
OR HIGH IN THE AIR...
BUT YOU CAN'T ESCAPE MY GRASP.
--OUTAGES DUE TO INCREASED USE OF AIR-CONDITIONERS.
NOW BACK TO MORE MUSIC-- WITH VINNIE!
THANKS, DAVE. HEY, I THOUGHT SUMMER WAS OVER.
WHEREVER YOU ARE, I WILL FIND YOU.
AND YOU'LL BE MINE.
WELL, WE KNO-O-OW WHERE WE'RE GOIN' BUT WE DON'T KNOW WHERE WE'VE BEEN!
5 53
AND WE KNNNNNN------! KKKKKK WE'RE KNOWIN' BUT WE KKKKKK
KKKK...
AWW, JEEZ... NOT NOW.
HEY, SIS! C'MON DOWN! MOM'S ON THE PHONE!
IN A MINUTE, BUTCH!

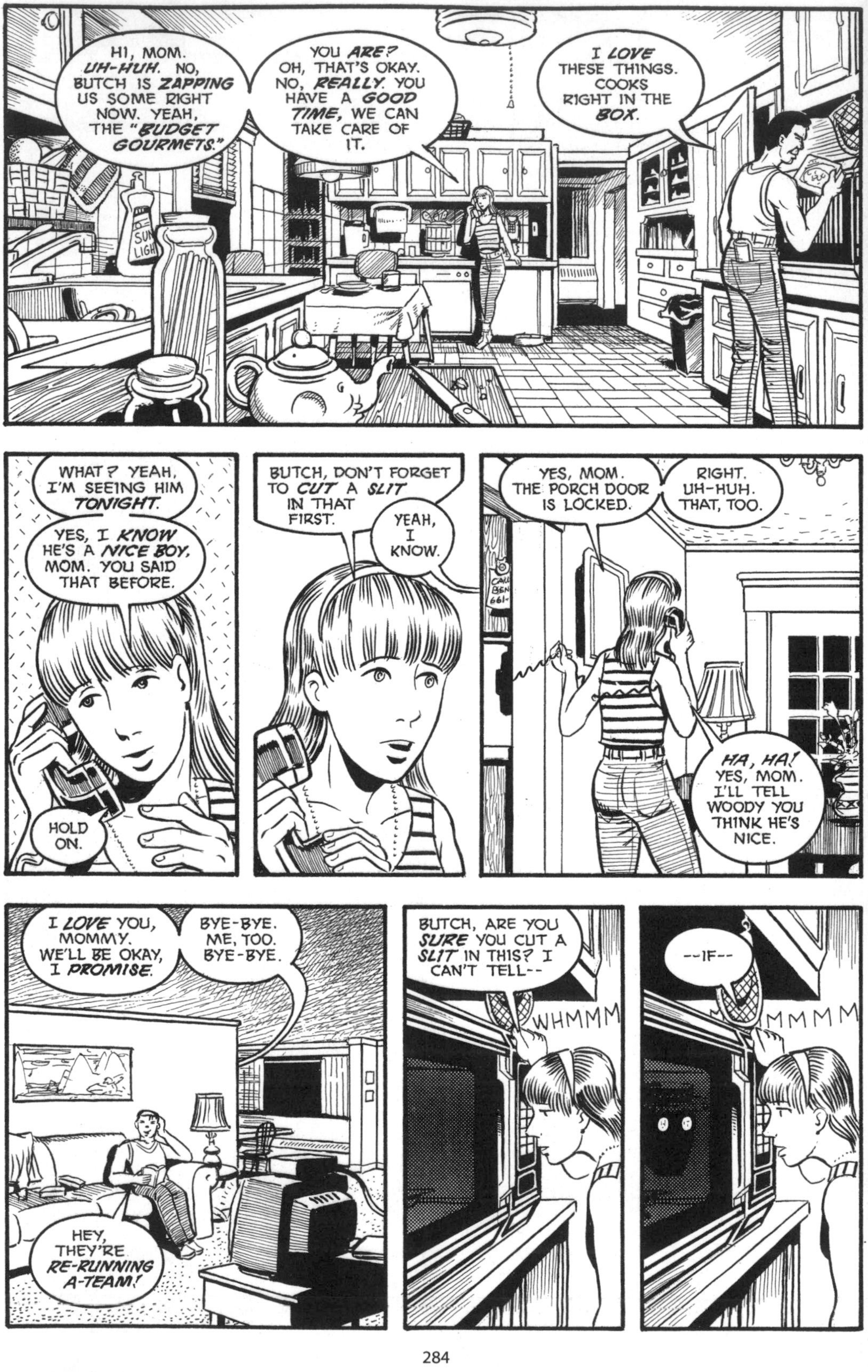
HI, MOM. UH-HUH. NO, BUTCH IS ZAPPING US SOME RIGHT NOW. YEAH, THE "BUDGET GOURMETS."
YOU ARE? OH, THAT'S OKAY. NO, REALLY. YOU HAVE A GOOD TIME, WE CAN TAKE CARE OF IT.
I LOVE THESE THINGS. COOKS RIGHT IN THE BOX.
WHAT? YEAH, I'M SEEING HIM TONIGHT.
YES, I KNOW HE'S A NICE BOY, MOM. YOU SAID THAT BEFORE.
HOLD ON.
BUTCH, DON'T FORGET TO CUT A SLIT IN THAT FIRST.
YEAH, I KNOW.
YES, MOM. THE PORCH DOOR IS LOCKED.
RIGHT. UH-HUH. THAT, TOO.
HA, HA! YES, MOM. I'LL TELL WOODY YOU THINK HE'S NICE.
I LOVE YOU, MOMMY. WE'LL BE OKAY, I PROMISE.
BYE-BYE. ME, TOO. BYE-BYE.
HEY, THEY'RE RE-RUNNING A-TEAM!
BUTCH, ARE YOU SURE YOU CUT A SLIT IN THIS? I CAN'T TELL--
WHMMM
--IF--
MMMMM

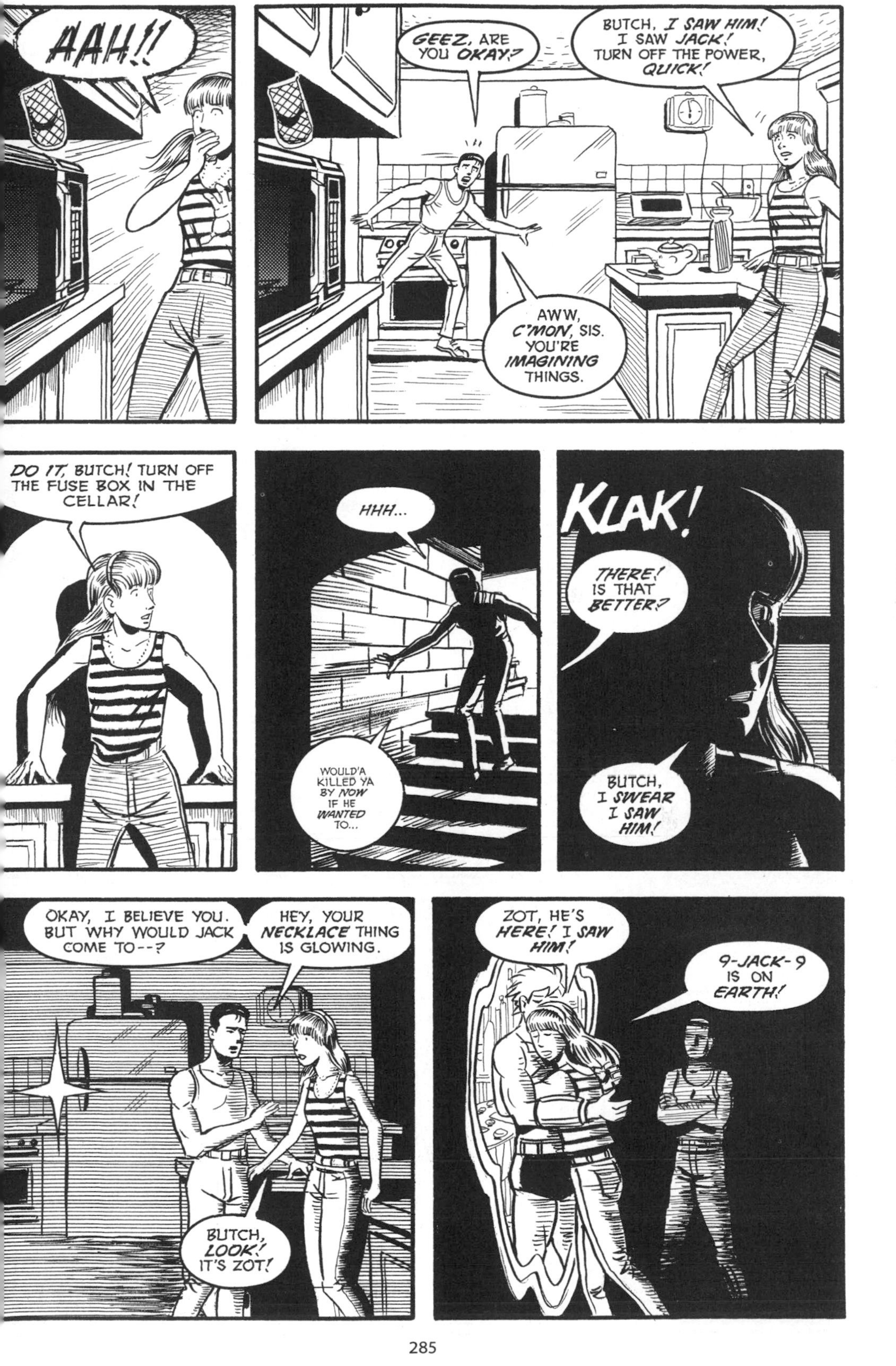
AAH!!
GEEZ, ARE YOU OKAY?
BUTCH, I SAW HIM! I SAW JACK! TURN OFF THE POWER, QUICK!
AWW, C'MON, SIS. YOU'RE IMAGINING THINGS.
DO IT, BUTCH! TURN OFF THE FUSE BOX IN THE CELLAR!
HHH...
WOULD'A KILLED YA BY NOW IF HE WANTED TO...
KLAK!
THERE! IS THAT BETTER?
BUTCH, I SWEAR I SAW HIM!
OKAY, I BELIEVE YOU. BUT WHY WOULD JACK COME TO--?
HEY, YOUR NECKLACE THING IS GLOWING.
BUTCH, LOOK! IT'S ZOT!
ZOT, HE'S HERE! I SAW HIM!
9-JACK-9 IS ON EARTH!

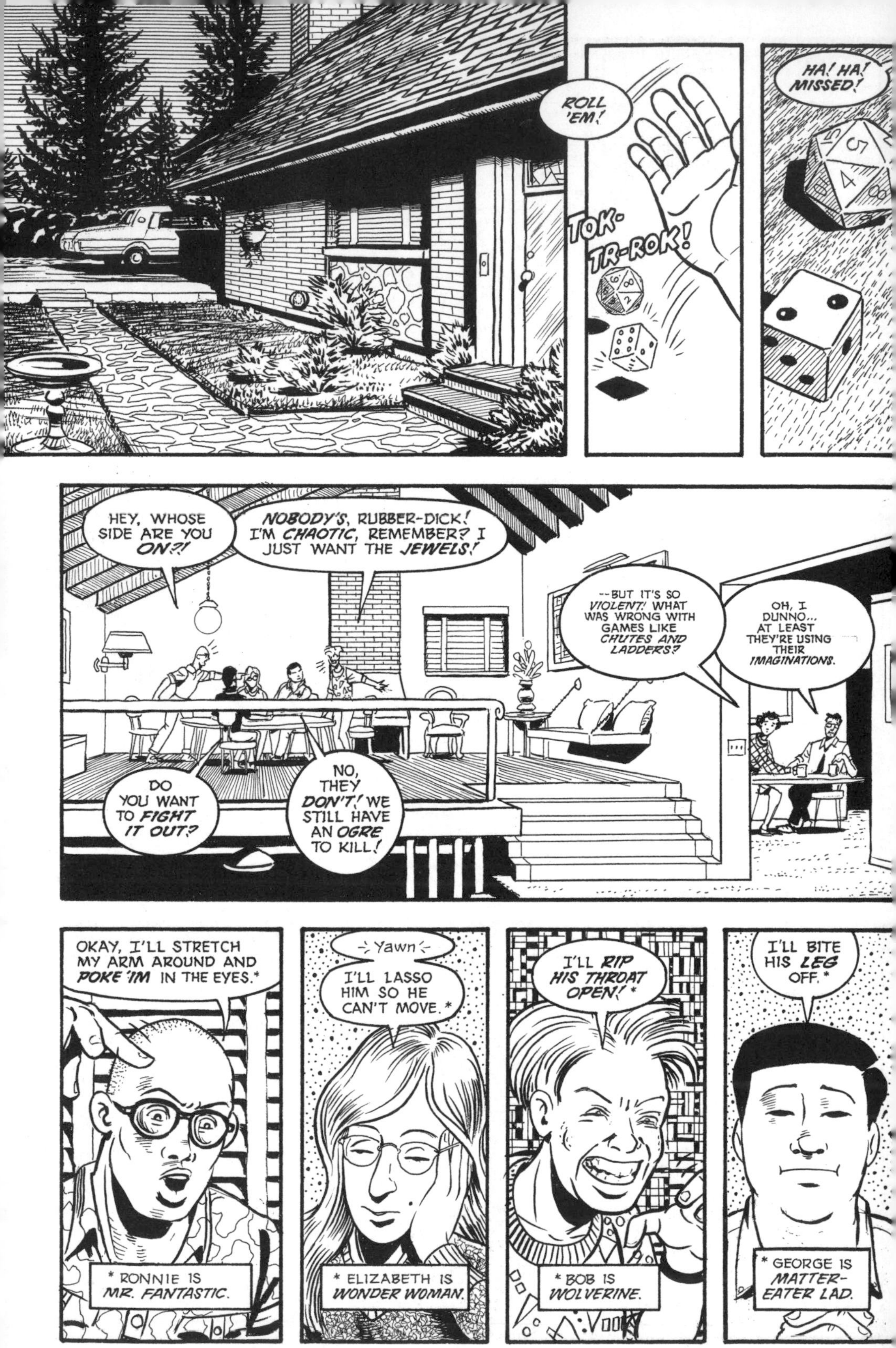
ROLL 'EM!
TOK-TR-ROK!
HA! HA! MISSED!
HEY, WHOSE SIDE ARE YOU ON?!
NOBODY'S, RUBBER-DICK! I'M CHAOTIC, REMEMBER? I JUST WANT THE JEWELS!
DO YOU WANT TO FIGHT IT OUT?
NO, THEY DON'T! WE STILL HAVE AN OGRE TO KILL!
--BUT IT'S SO VIOLENT! WHAT WAS WRONG WITH GAMES LIKE CHUTES AND LADDERS?
OH, I DUNNO... AT LEAST THEY'RE USING THEIR IMAGINATIONS.
OKAY, I'LL STRETCH MY ARM AROUND AND POKE 'IM IN THE EYES.*
* RONNIE IS MR. FANTASTIC.
-Yawn-
I'LL LASSO HIM SO HE CAN'T MOVE.*
* ELIZABETH IS WONDER WOMAN.
I'LL RIP HIS THROAT OPEN! *
* BOB IS WOLVERINE.
I'LL BITE HIS LEG OFF.*
* GEORGE IS MATTER-EATER LAD.

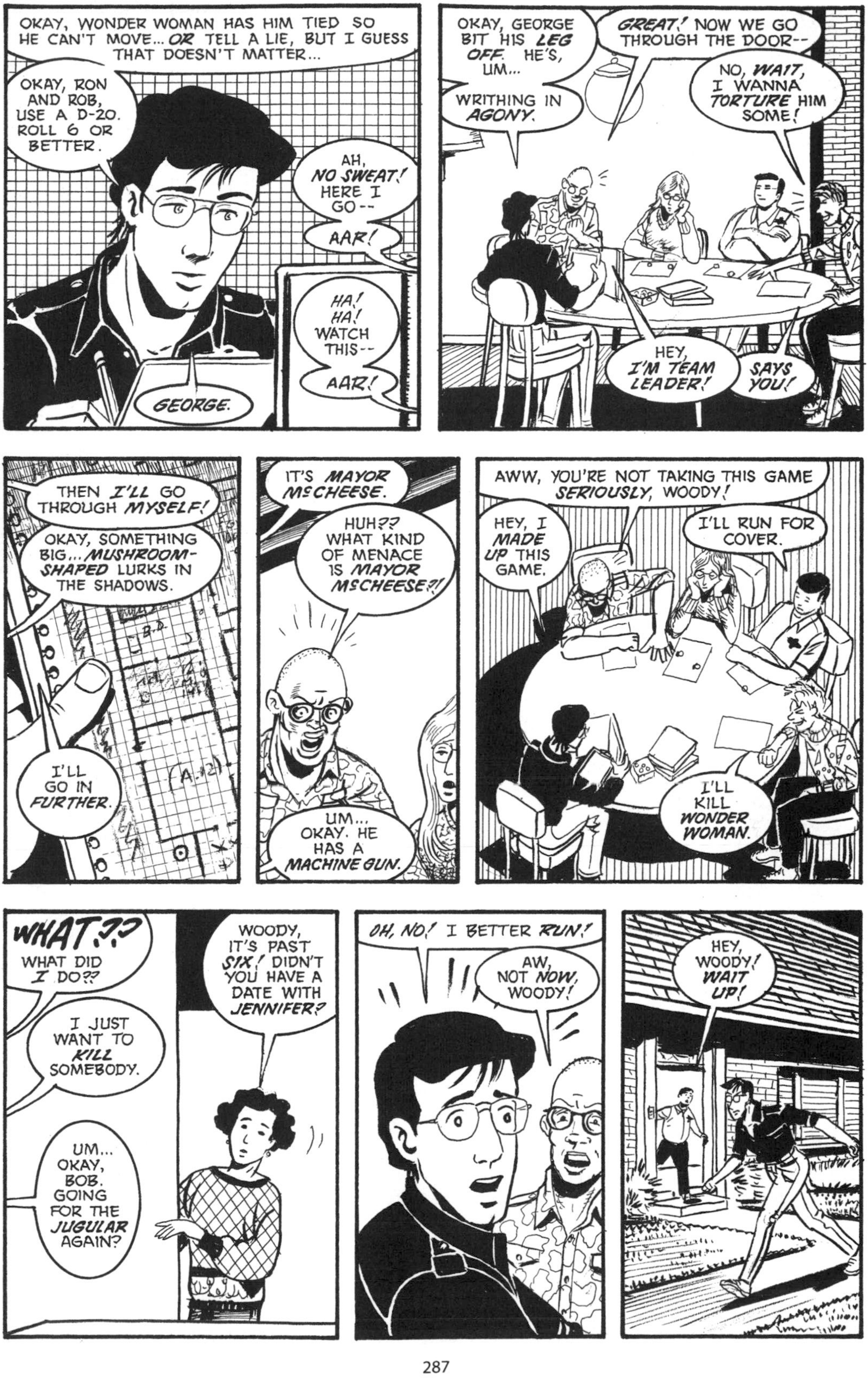
OKAY, WONDER WOMAN HAS HIM TIED SO HE CAN'T MOVE... OR TELL A LIE, BUT I GUESS THAT DOESN'T MATTER...
OKAY, RON AND ROB, USE A D-20. ROLL 6 OR BETTER.
AH, NO SWEAT! HERE I GO--
AAR!
HA! HA! WATCH THIS--
AAR!
GEORGE.
OKAY, GEORGE BIT HIS LEG OFF. HE'S, UM...
WRITHING IN AGONY.
GREAT! NOW WE GO THROUGH THE DOOR--
NO, WAIT, I WANNA TORTURE HIM SOME!
HEY, I'M TEAM LEADER!
SAYS YOU!
THEN I'LL GO THROUGH MYSELF!
OKAY, SOMETHING BIG... MUSHROOM-SHAPED LURKS IN THE SHADOWS.
I'LL GO IN FURTHER.
IT'S MAYOR McCHEESE.
HUH?? WHAT KIND OF MENACE IS MAYOR McCHEESE?!
UM... OKAY. HE HAS A MACHINE GUN.
AWW, YOU'RE NOT TAKING THIS GAME SERIOUSLY, WOODY!
HEY, I MADE UP THIS GAME.
I'LL RUN FOR COVER.
I'LL KILL WONDER WOMAN.
WHAT?!? WHAT DID I DO??
I JUST WANT TO KILL SOMEBODY.
UM... OKAY, BOB. GOING FOR THE JUGULAR AGAIN?
WOODY, IT'S PAST SIX! DIDN'T YOU HAVE A DATE WITH JENNIFER?
OH, NO! I BETTER RUN!
AW, NOT NOW, WOODY!
HEY, WOODY! WAIT UP!

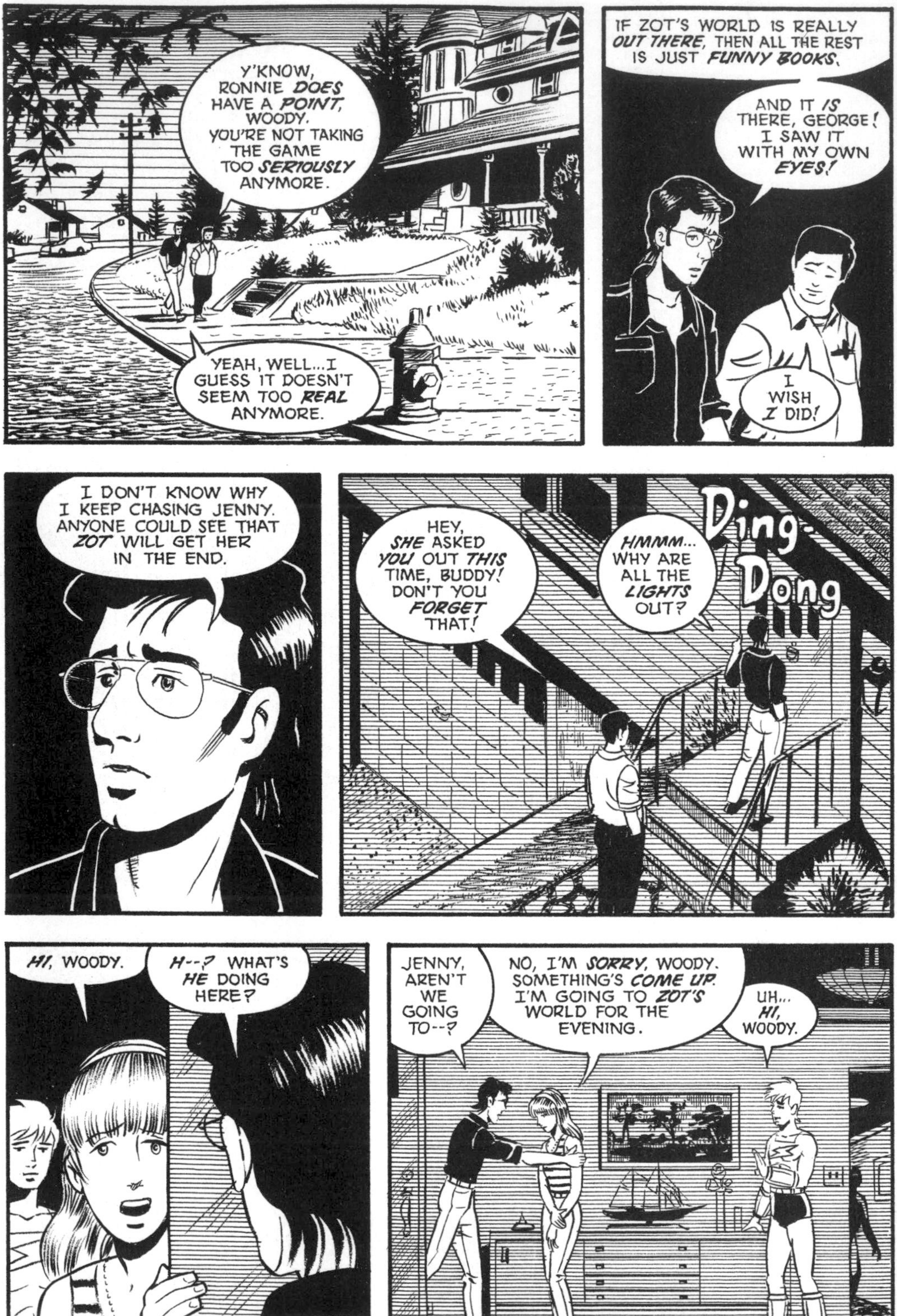
Y'KNOW, RONNIE DOES HAVE A POINT, WOODY. YOU'RE NOT TAKING THE GAME TOO SERIOUSLY ANYMORE.
YEAH, WELL...I GUESS IT DOESN'T SEEM TOO REAL ANYMORE.
IF ZOT'S WORLD IS REALLY OUT THERE, THEN ALL THE REST IS JUST FUNNY BOOKS.
AND IT IS THERE, GEORGE! I SAW IT WITH MY OWN EYES!
I WISH I DID!
I DON'T KNOW WHY I KEEP CHASING JENNY. ANYONE COULD SEE THAT ZOT WILL GET HER IN THE END.
HEY, SHE ASKED YOU OUT THIS TIME, BUDDY! DON'T YOU FORGET THAT!
HMMM... WHY ARE ALL THE LIGHTS OUT?
Ding-Dong
HI, WOODY.
H--? WHAT'S HE DOING HERE?
JENNY, AREN'T WE GOING TO--?
NO, I'M SORRY, WOODY. SOMETHING'S COME UP. I'M GOING TO ZOT'S WORLD FOR THE EVENING.
UH... HI, WOODY.

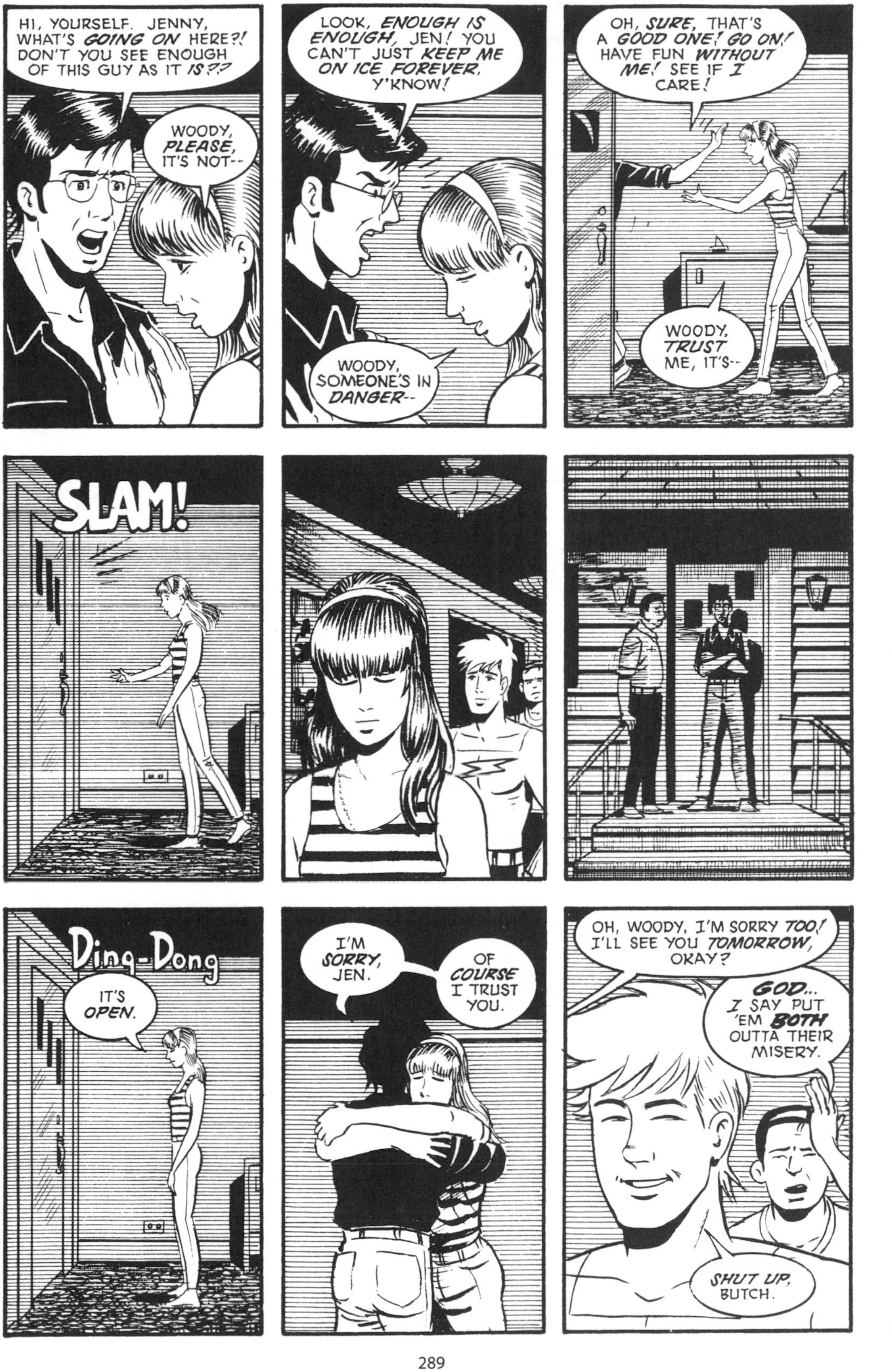
HI, YOURSELF. JENNY, WHAT'S GOING ON HERE?! DON'T YOU SEE ENOUGH OF THIS GUY AS IT IS??
WOODY, PLEASE, IT'S NOT--
LOOK, ENOUGH IS ENOUGH, JEN! YOU CAN'T JUST KEEP ME ON ICE FOREVER, Y'KNOW!
WOODY, SOMEONE'S IN DANGER--
OH, SURE, THAT'S A GOOD ONE! GO ON! HAVE FUN WITHOUT ME! SEE IF I CARE!
WOODY, TRUST ME, IT'S--
SLAM!
Ding-Dong
IT'S OPEN.
I'M SORRY, JEN.
OF COURSE I TRUST YOU.
OH, WOODY, I'M SORRY TOO! I'LL SEE YOU TOMORROW, OKAY?
GOD... I SAY PUT 'EM BOTH OUTTA THEIR MISERY.
SHUT UP, BUTCH.

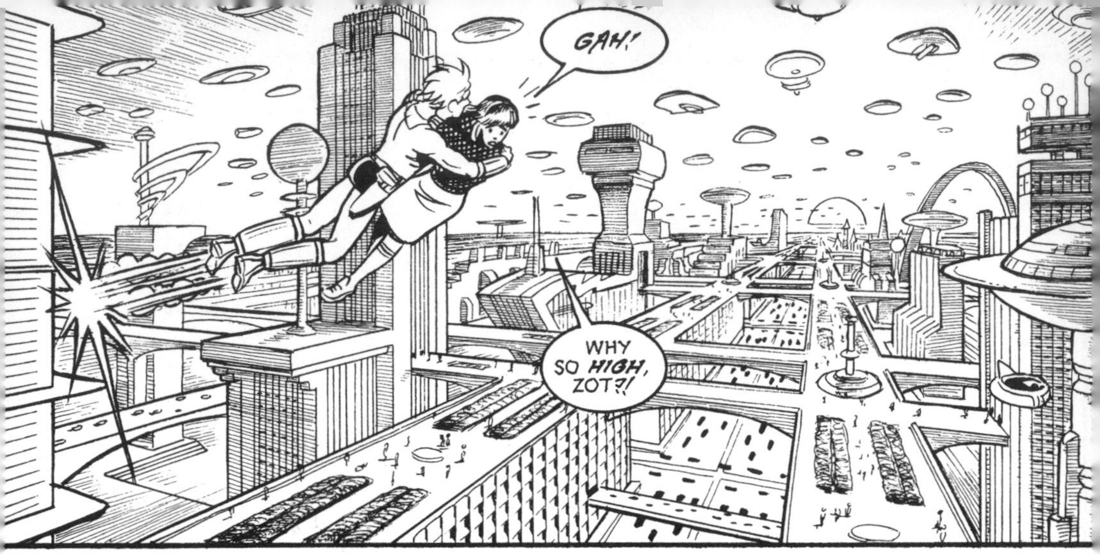
GAH!
WHY SO HIGH, ZOT?!
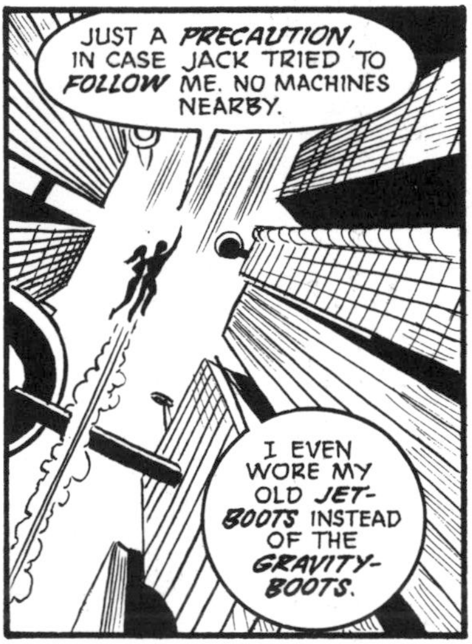
JUST A PRECAUTION, IN CASE JACK TRIED TO FOLLOW ME. NO MACHINES NEARBY.
I EVEN WORE MY OLD JET-BOOTS INSTEAD OF THE GRAVITY-BOOTS.
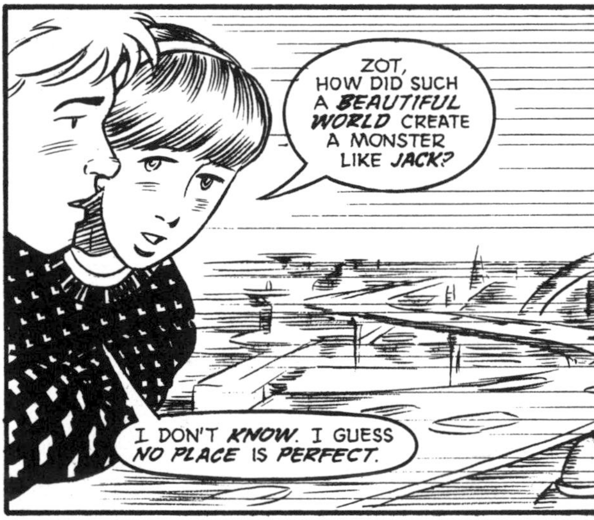
ZOT, HOW DID SUCH A BEAUTIFUL WORLD CREATE A MONSTER LIKE JACK?
I DON'T KNOW. I GUESS NO PLACE IS PERFECT.
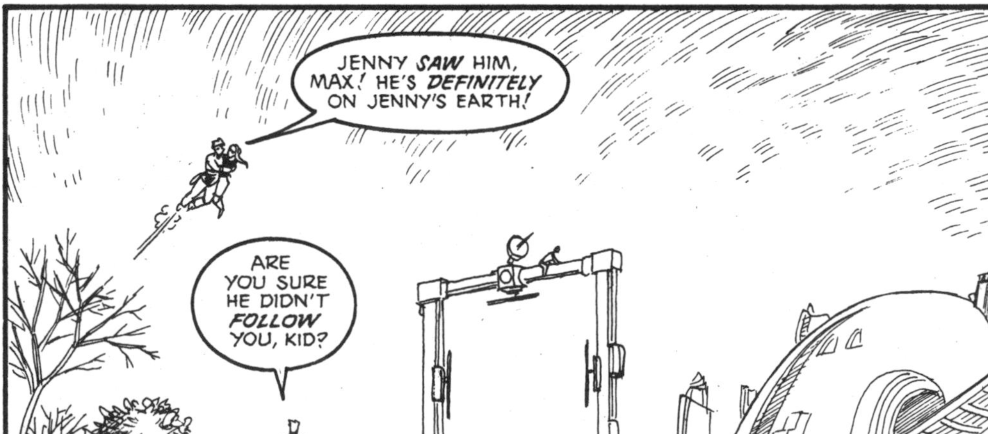
JENNY SAW HIM, MAX! HE'S DEFINITELY ON JENNY'S EARTH!
ARE YOU SURE HE DIDN'T FOLLOW YOU, KID?

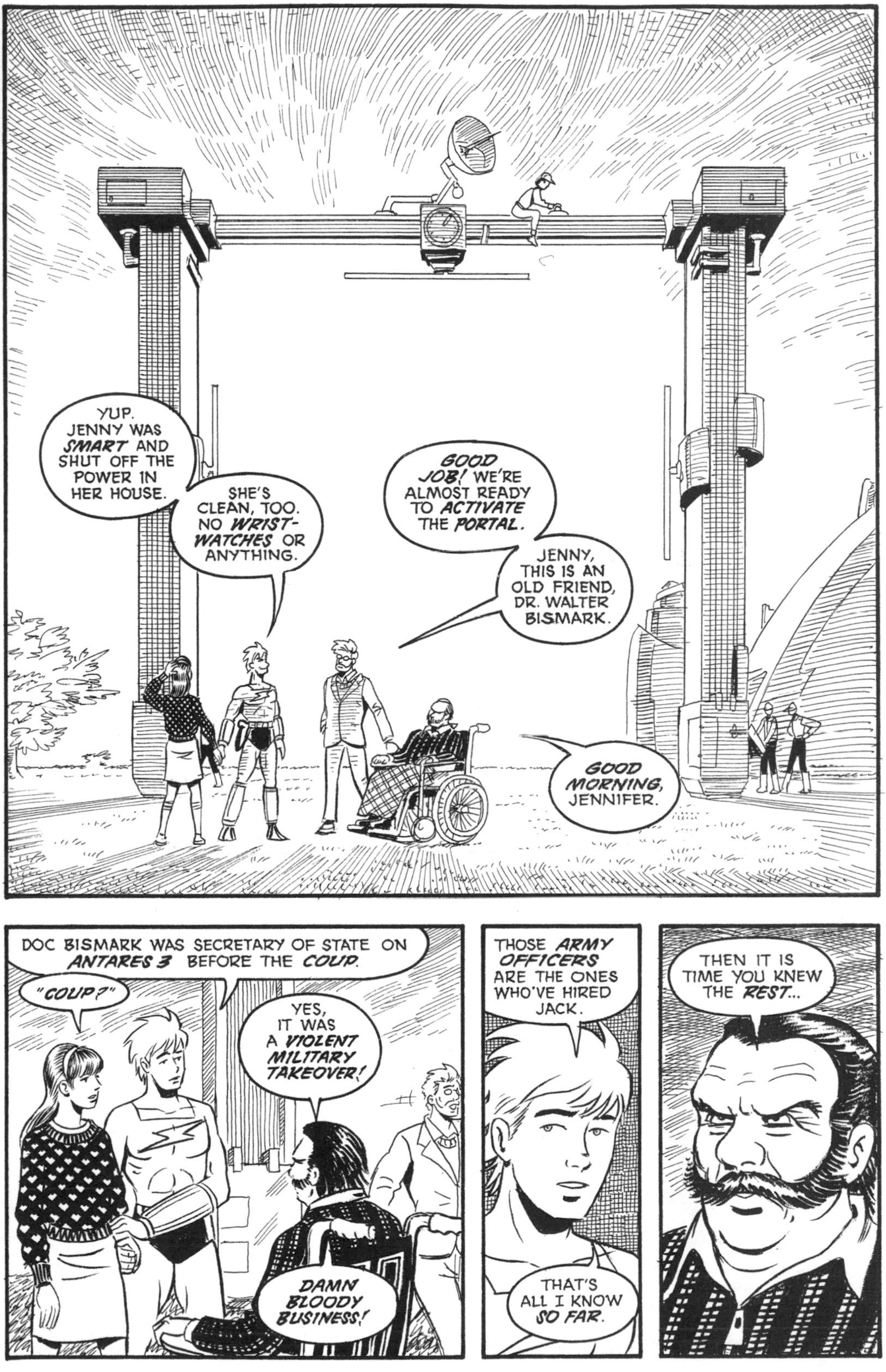
YUP. JENNY WAS SMART AND SHUT OFF THE POWER IN HER HOUSE.
SHE'S CLEAN, TOO. NO WRIST-WATCHES OR ANYTHING.
GOOD JOB! WE'RE ALMOST READY TO ACTIVATE THE PORTAL.
JENNY, THIS IS AN OLD FRIEND, DR. WALTER BISMARK.
GOOD MORNING, JENNIFER.
DOC BISMARK WAS SECRETARY OF STATE ON ANTARES 3 BEFORE THE COUP.
"COUP?"
YES, IT WAS A VIOLENT MILITARY TAKEOVER!
DAMN BLOODY BUSINESS!
THOSE ARMY OFFICERS ARE THE ONES WHO'VE HIRED JACK.
THAT'S ALL I KNOW SO FAR.
THEN IT IS TIME YOU KNEW THE REST...

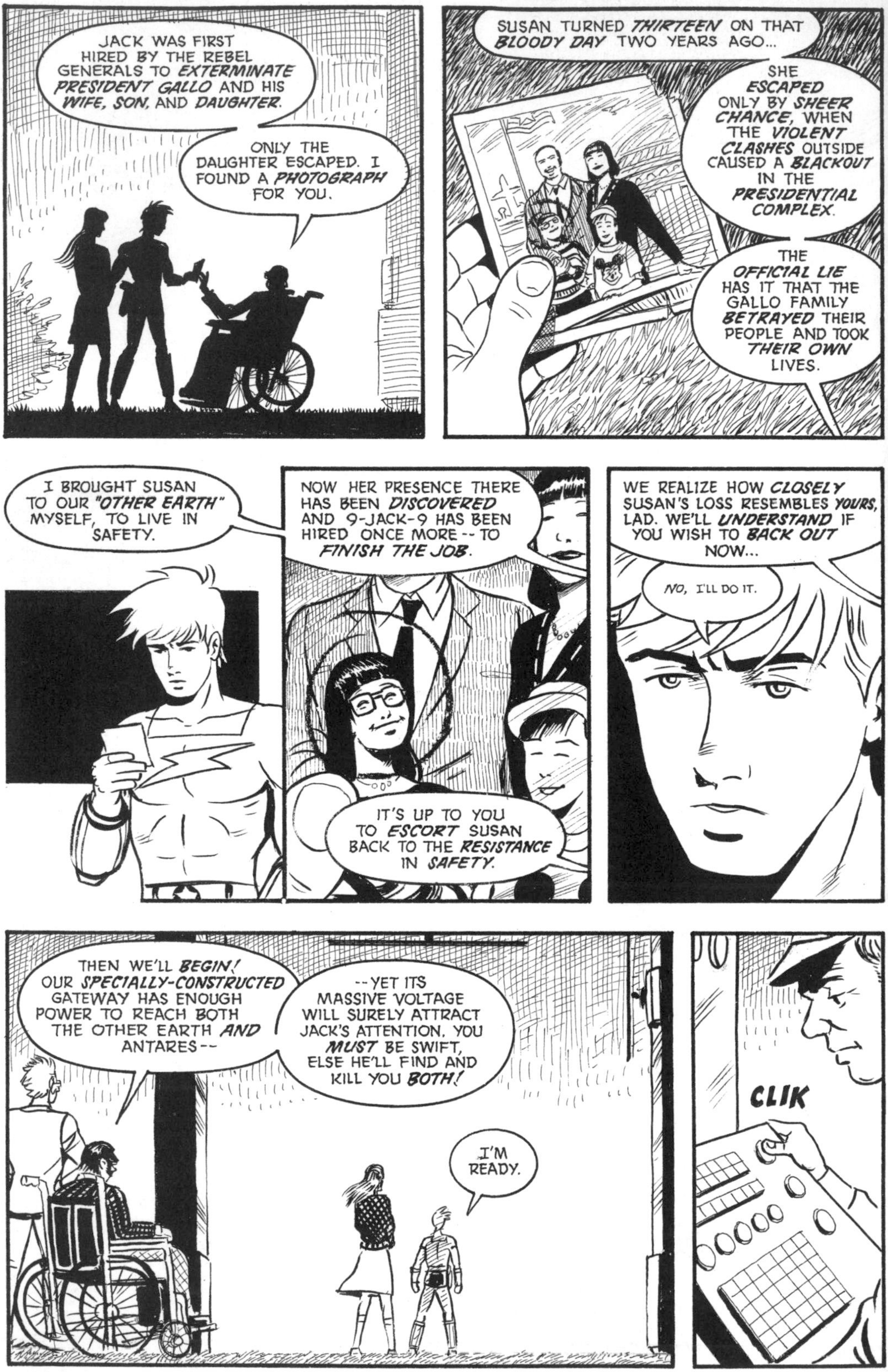
JACK WAS FIRST HIRED BY THE REBEL GENERALS TO EXTERMINATE PRESIDENT GALLO AND HIS WIFE, SON, AND DAUGHTER.
ONLY THE DAUGHTER ESCAPED. I FOUND A PHOTOGRAPH FOR YOU.
SUSAN TURNED THIRTEEN ON THAT BLOODY DAY TWO YEARS AGO...
SHE ESCAPED ONLY BY SHEER CHANCE, WHEN THE VIOLENT CLASHES OUTSIDE CAUSED A BLACKOUT IN THE PRESIDENTIAL COMPLEX.
THE OFFICIAL LIE HAS IT THAT THE GALLO FAMILY BETRAYED THEIR PEOPLE AND TOOK THEIR OWN LIVES.
I BROUGHT SUSAN TO OUR "OTHER EARTH" MYSELF, TO LIVE IN SAFETY.
NOW HER PRESENCE THERE HAS BEEN DISCOVERED AND 9-JACK-9 HAS BEEN HIRED ONCE MORE -- TO FINISH THE JOB.
IT'S UP TO YOU TO ESCORT SUSAN BACK TO THE RESISTANCE IN SAFETY.
WE REALIZE HOW CLOSELY SUSAN'S LOSS RESEMBLES YOURS, LAD. WE'LL UNDERSTAND IF YOU WISH TO BACK OUT NOW...
NO, I'LL DO IT.
THEN WE'LL BEGIN! OUR SPECIALLY-CONSTRUCTED GATEWAY HAS ENOUGH POWER TO REACH BOTH THE OTHER EARTH AND ANTARES--
--YET ITS MASSIVE VOLTAGE WILL SURELY ATTRACT JACK'S ATTENTION. YOU MUST BE SWIFT, ELSE HE'LL FIND AND KILL YOU BOTH!
I'M READY.
CLIK

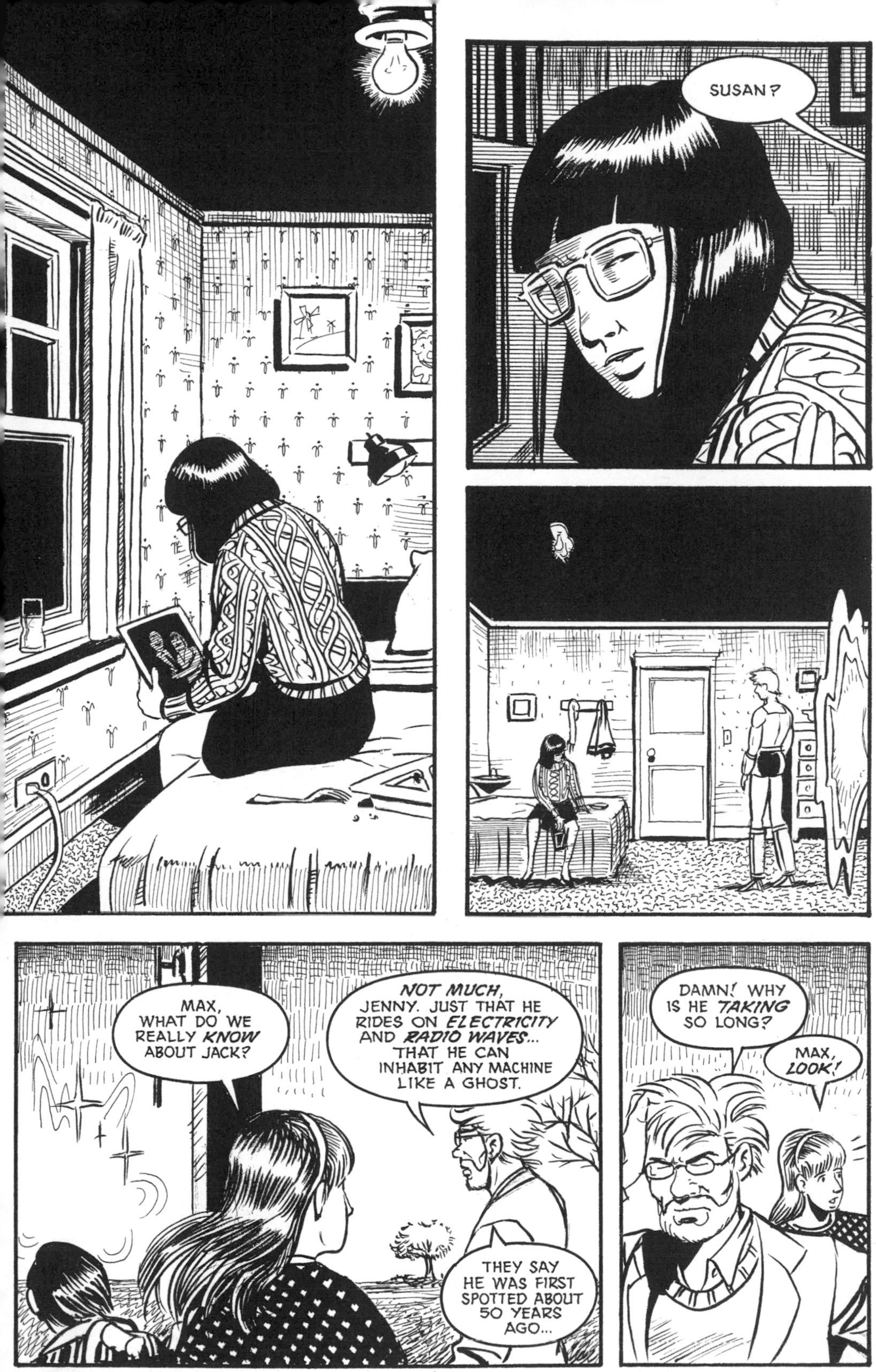
SUSAN?
MAX, WHAT DO WE REALLY KNOW ABOUT JACK?
NOT MUCH, JENNY. JUST THAT HE RIDES ON ELECTRICITY AND RADIO WAVES... THAT HE CAN INHABIT ANY MACHINE LIKE A GHOST.
THEY SAY HE WAS FIRST SPOTTED ABOUT 50 YEARS AGO...
DAMN! WHY IS HE TAKING SO LONG?
MAX, LOOK!

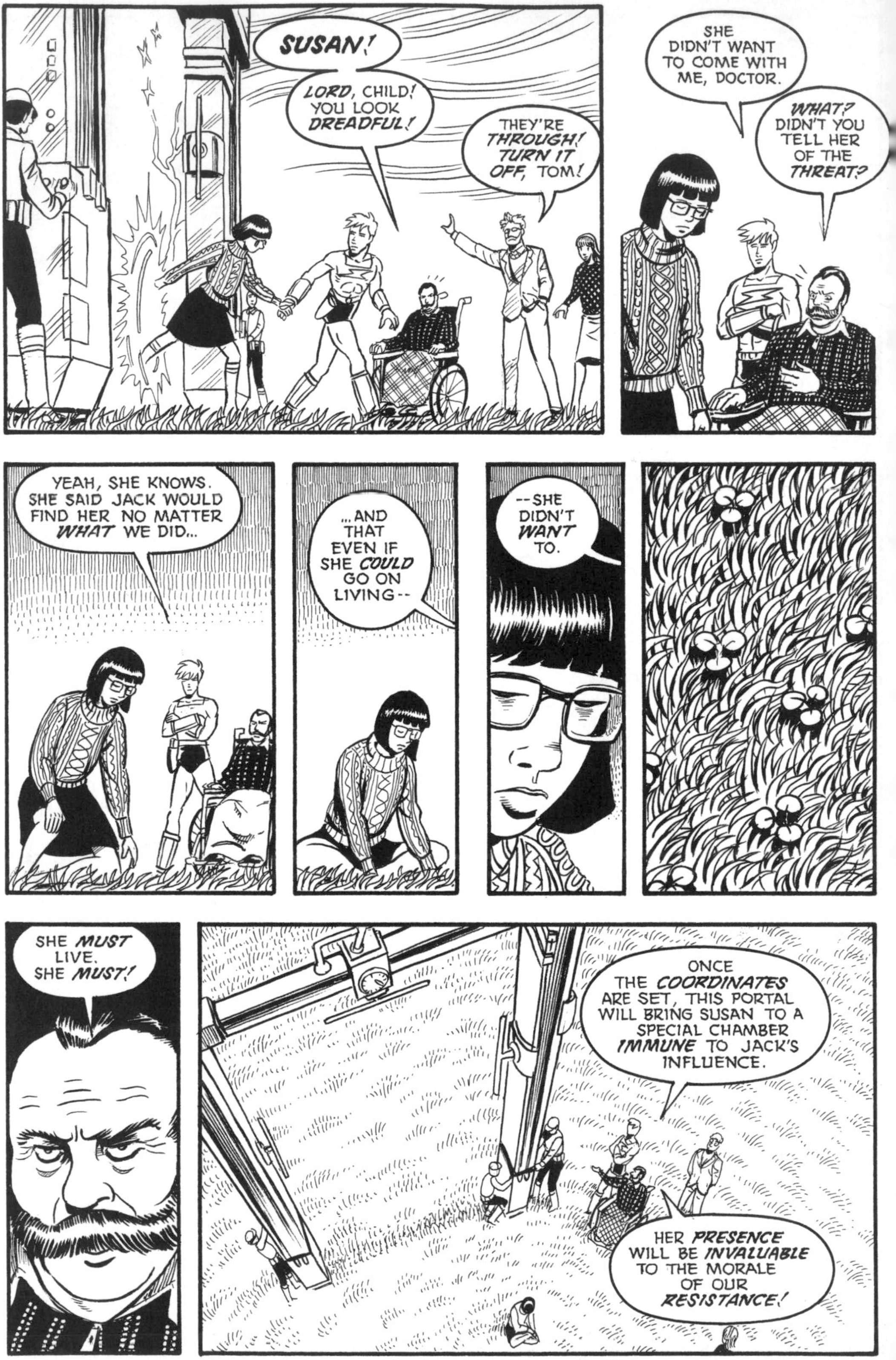
SUSAN!
LORD, CHILD! YOU LOOK DREADFUL!
THEY'RE THROUGH! TURN IT OFF, TOM!
SHE DIDN'T WANT TO COME WITH ME, DOCTOR.
WHAT? DIDN'T YOU TELL HER OF THE THREAT?
YEAH, SHE KNOWS. SHE SAID JACK WOULD FIND HER NO MATTER WHAT WE DID...
...AND THAT EVEN IF SHE COULD GO ON LIVING--
--SHE DIDN'T WANT TO.
SHE MUST LIVE. SHE MUST!
ONCE THE COORDINATES ARE SET, THIS PORTAL WILL BRING SUSAN TO A SPECIAL CHAMBER IMMUNE TO JACK'S INFLUENCE.
HER PRESENCE WILL BE INVALUABLE TO THE MORALE OF OUR RESISTANCE!

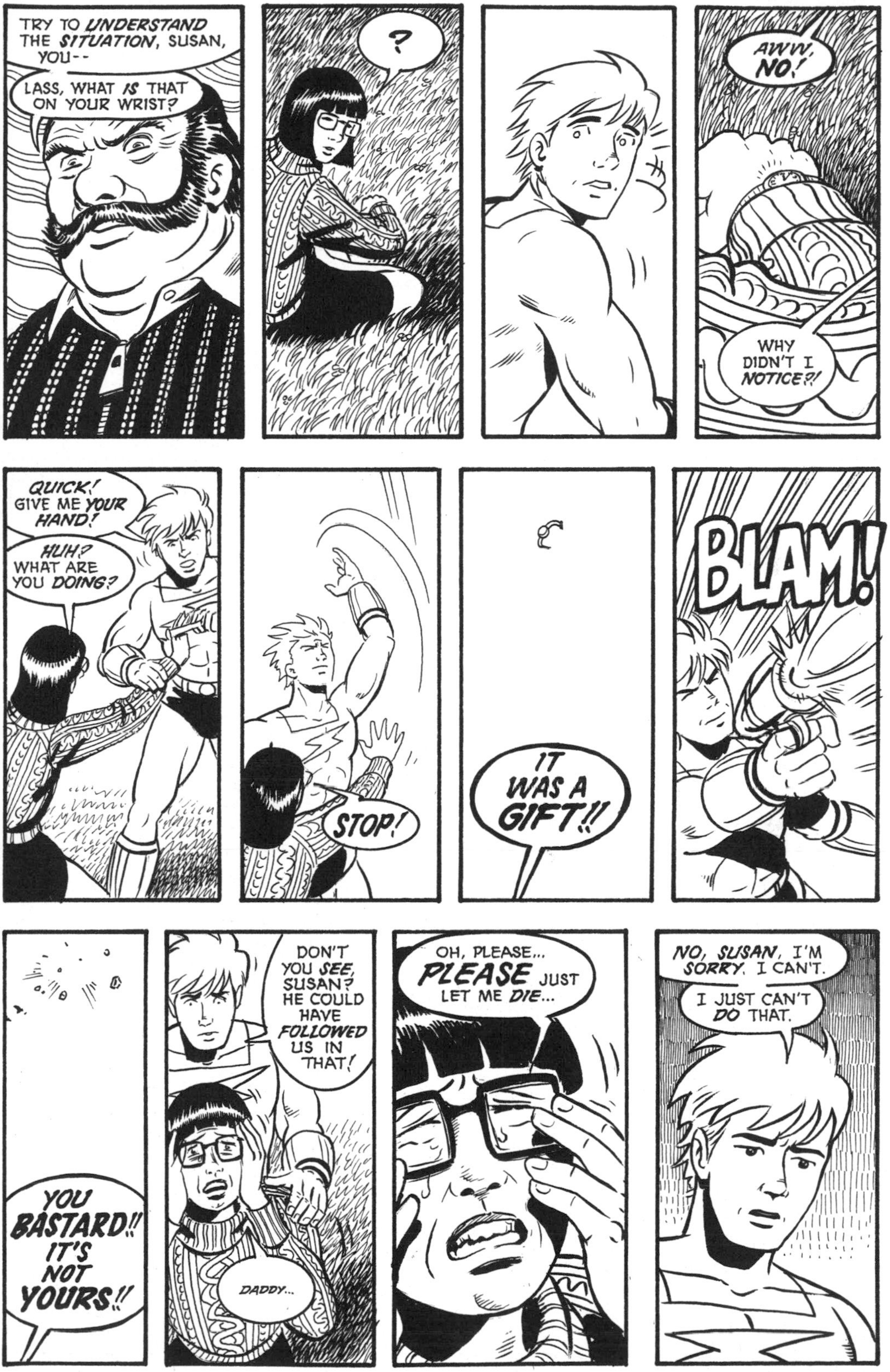
TRY TO UNDERSTAND THE SITUATION, SUSAN, YOU--
LASS, WHAT IS THAT ON YOUR WRIST?
?
AWW, NO!
WHY DIDN'T I NOTICE?!
QUICK! GIVE ME YOUR HAND!
HUH? WHAT ARE YOU DOING?
STOP!
IT WAS A GIFT!!
BLAM!
YOU BASTARD!! IT'S NOT YOURS!!
DON'T YOU SEE, SUSAN? HE COULD HAVE FOLLOWED US IN THAT!
DADDY...
OH, PLEASE... PLEASE JUST LET ME DIE...
NO, SUSAN, I'M SORRY. I CAN'T.
I JUST CAN'T DO THAT.

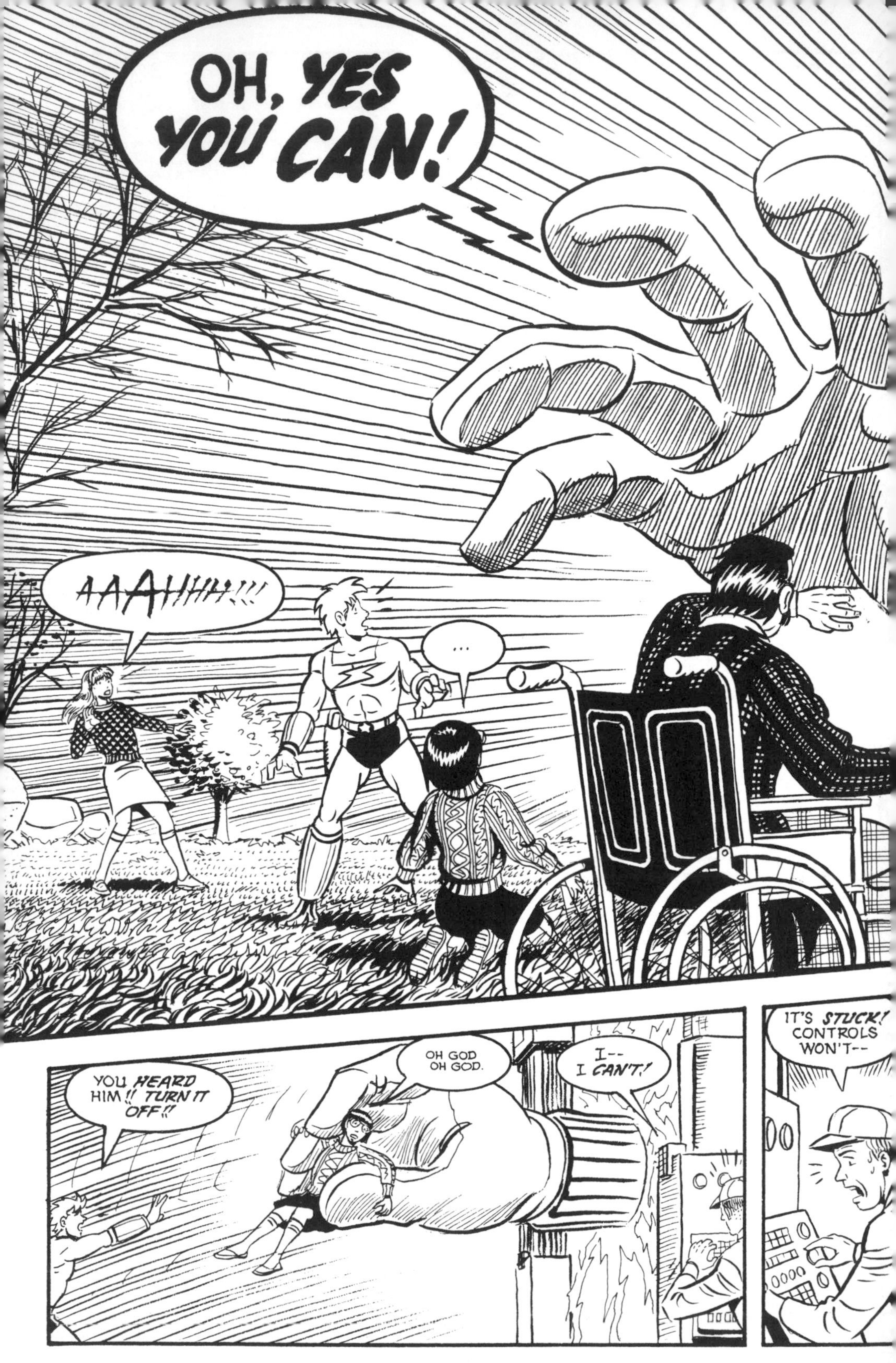
OH, YES YOU CAN!
AAAHHHH!!!
...
YOU HEARD HIM!! TURN IT OFF!!
OH GOD OH GOD.
I-- I CAN'T!
IT'S STUCK! CONTROLS WON'T--

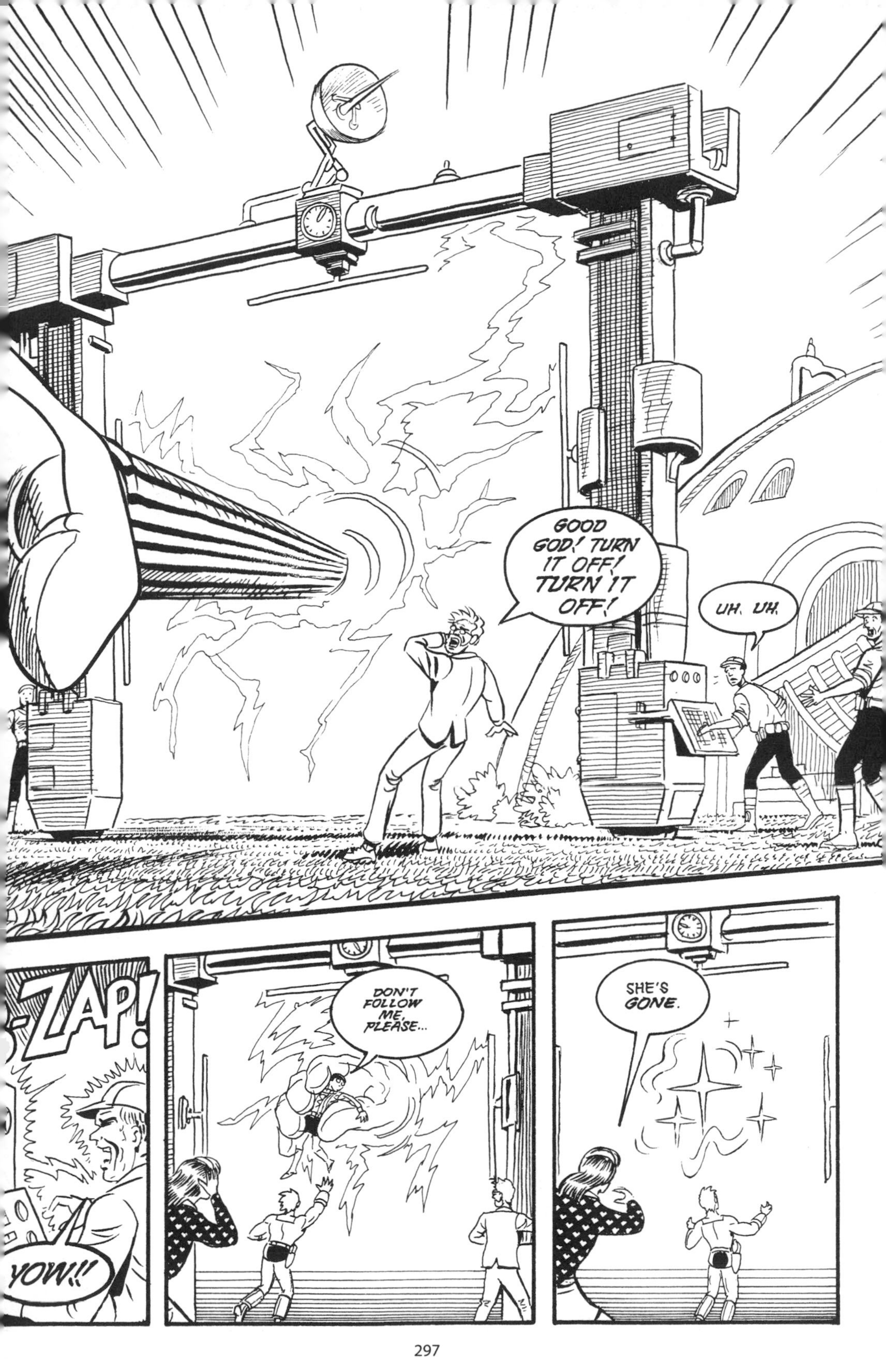
GOOD GOD! TURN IT OFF! TURN IT OFF!
UH. UH.
ZAP!
YOW!!
DON'T FOLLOW ME, PLEASE...
SHE'S GONE.

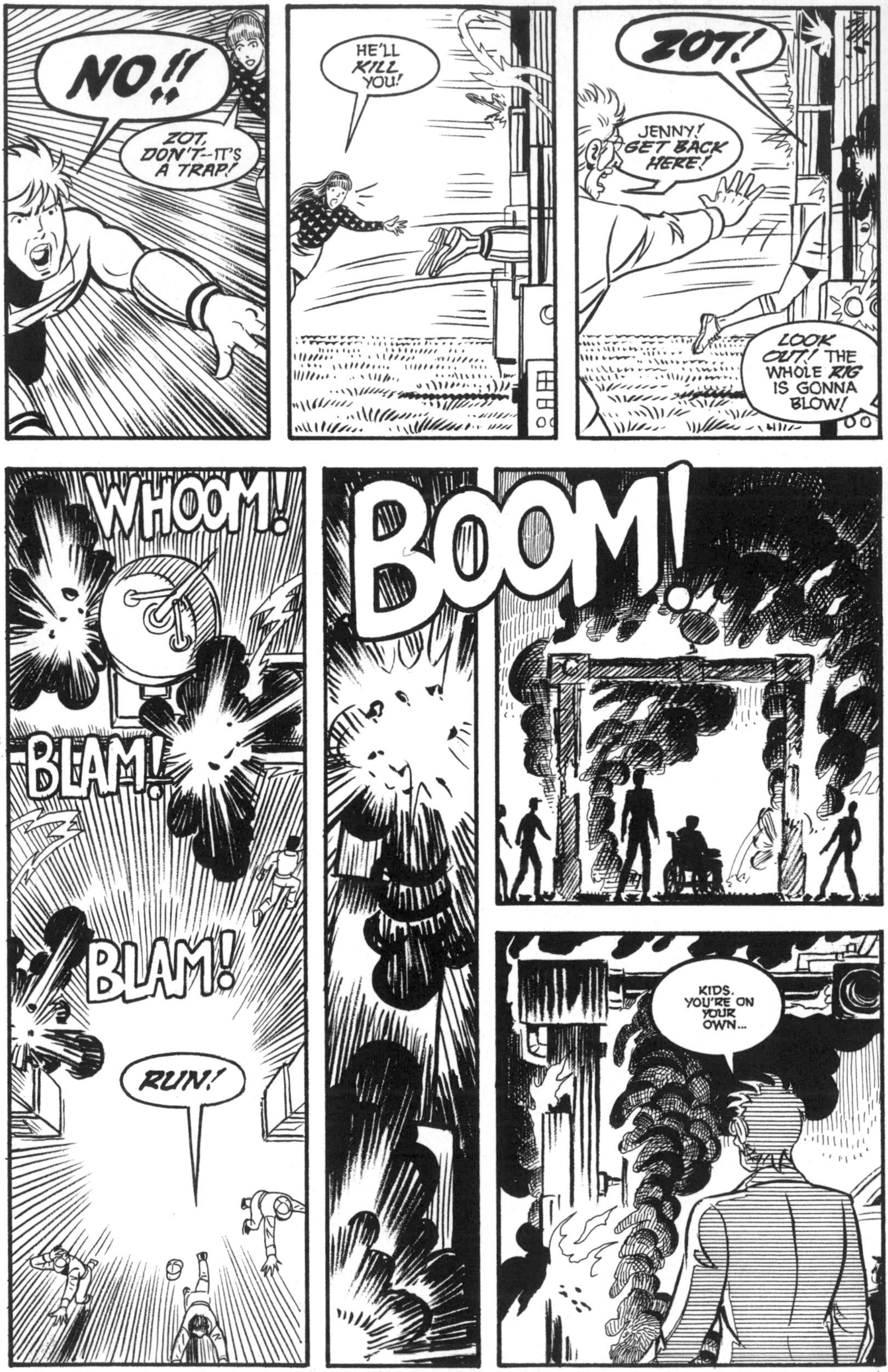
NO!!
ZOT, DON'T--IT'S A TRAP!
HE'LL KILL YOU!
ZOT!
JENNY! GET BACK HERE!
LOOK OUT! THE WHOLE RIG IS GONNA BLOW!
WHOOM!
BLAM!
BLAM!
RUN!
BOOM!
KIDS. YOU'RE ON YOUR OWN...

THE GHOST IN THE MACHINE

PART TWO OF THREE

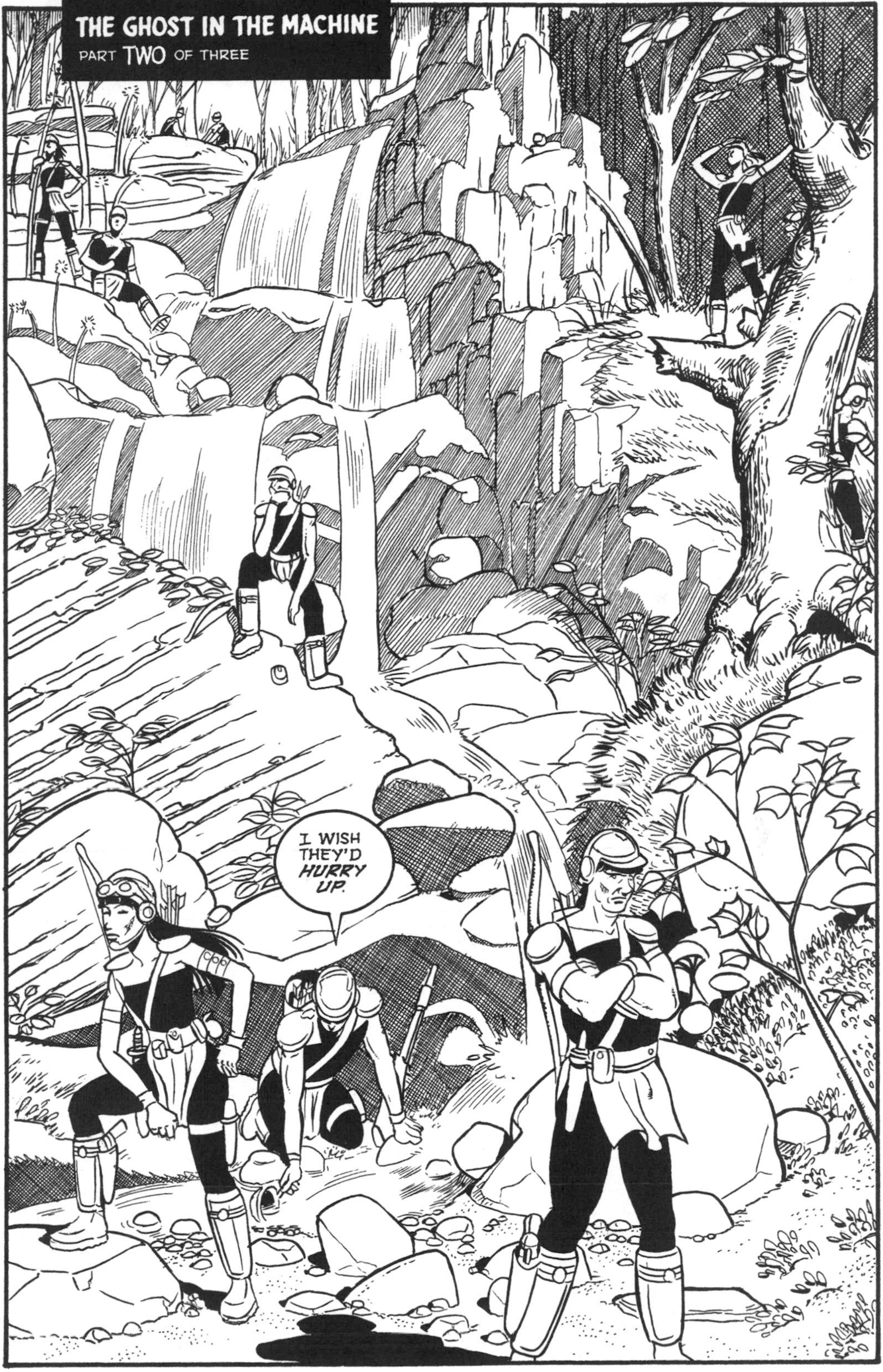
I WISH THEY'D *HURRY UP.*

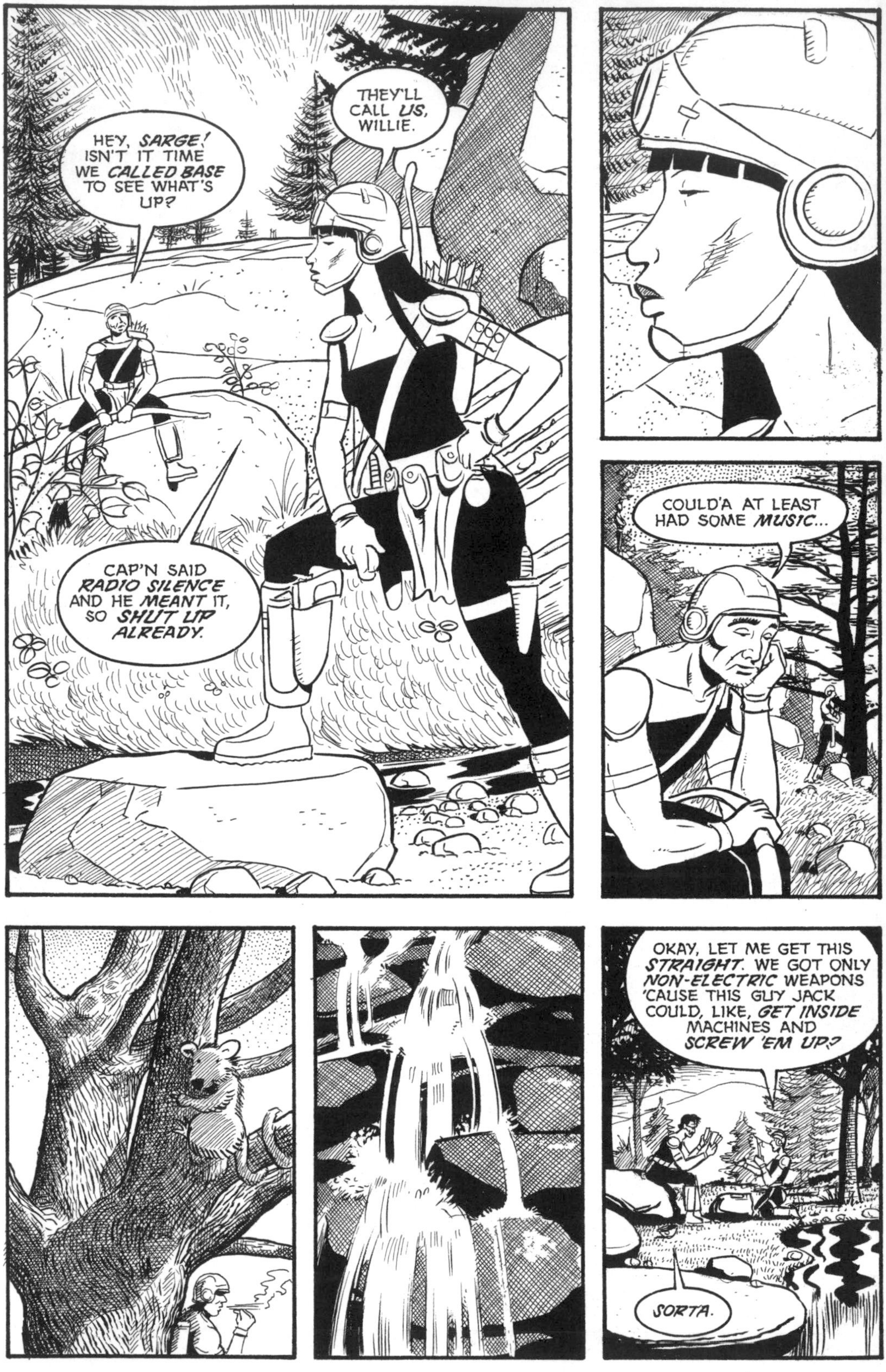
HEY, SARGE! ISN'T IT TIME WE CALLED BASE TO SEE WHAT'S UP?
THEY'LL CALL US, WILLIE.
CAP'N SAID RADIO SILENCE AND HE MEANT IT, SO SHUT UP ALREADY.
COULD'A AT LEAST HAD SOME MUSIC...
OKAY, LET ME GET THIS STRAIGHT. WE GOT ONLY NON-ELECTRIC WEAPONS 'CAUSE THIS GUY JACK COULD, LIKE, GET INSIDE MACHINES AND SCREW 'EM UP?
SORTA.

WHAT HE DOES IS *CONTROL* 'EM, USE 'EM *AGAINST* YOU AND THEN JUMP FROM MACHINE TO MACHINE-- *FAST AS LIGHTNING!*

WOW...

ANYWAY, WE SHOULDN'T HAVE TO *FIGHT* HIM. WE'RE JUST HERE IF THEY NEED HELP GETTING *"GOLDILOCKS"* TO THE *SAFE HOUSE.* THEY WANNA *AVOID* JACK COMPLETELY.

WHO IS *"GOLDILOCKS,"* ANYWAY?

I DUNNO. SOME *DIPLOMAT,* I THINK.

BEEP! BEEP!

KLIK

SERGEANT CHOW.

WE'VE ACTIVATED THE *PORTAL,* SERGEANT. "GOLDILOCKS" IS COMING THROUGH!

WE SHOULDN'T NEED YOU TO... WAIT A MOMENT. WHAT? OH MY GOD, IS THAT--? WHAT IS--?

CRASH

CAPTAIN, WHAT IS IT?!

JACK IS HERE!! HE'S HERE!!

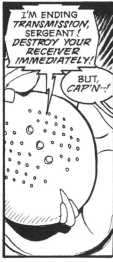

I'M ENDING *TRANSMISSION,* SERGEANT! DESTROY YOUR *RECEIVER* IMMEDIATELY!

BUT, CAP'N--!

DO IT! *NOW!!*
-CLIK-

DAMN!

CRAK!

SERGEANT? WHAT *HAPPENED?*

SARGE?

HE'S *COMING.*

301

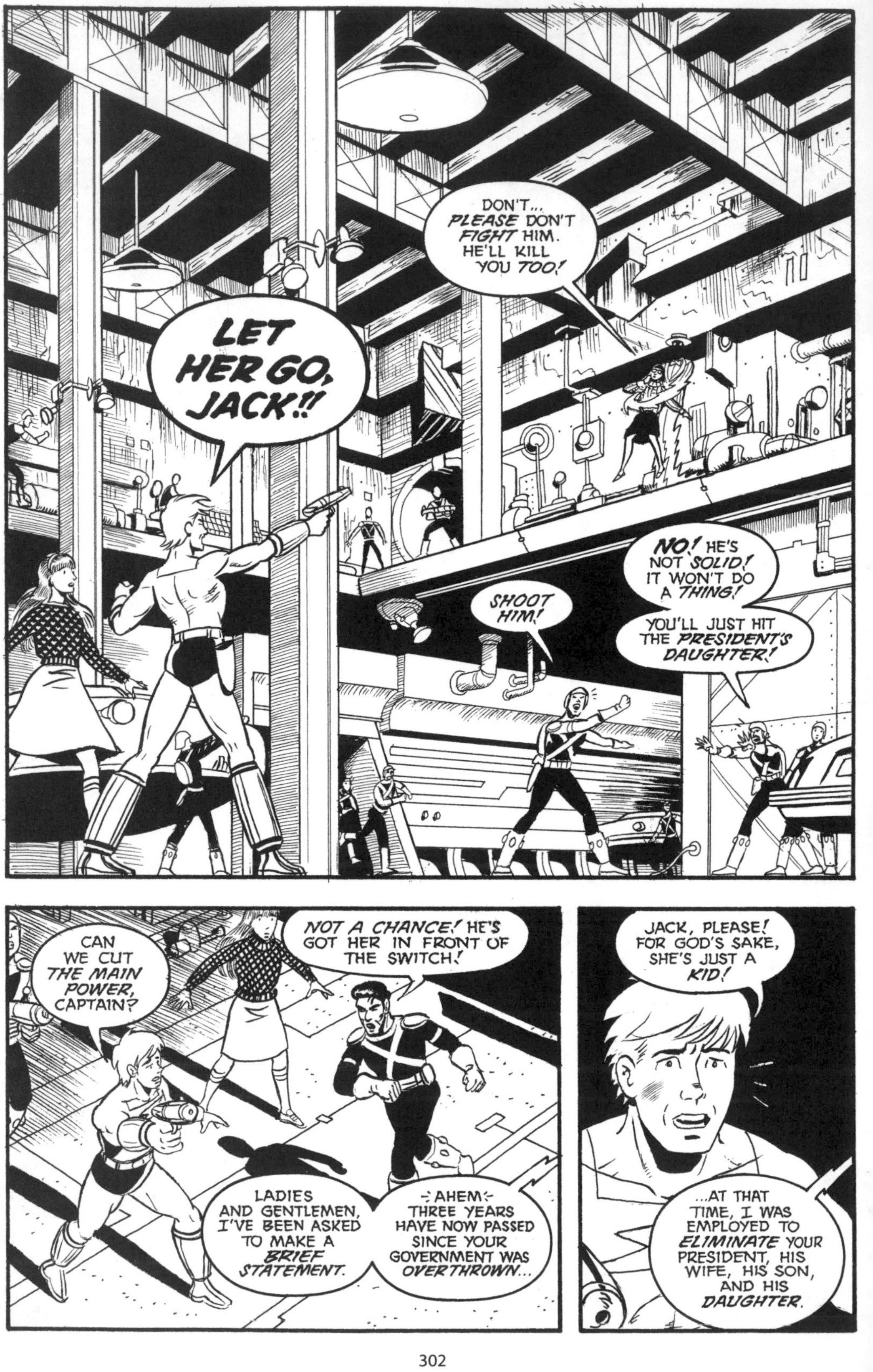
LET HER GO, JACK!!
DON'T... PLEASE DON'T FIGHT HIM. HE'LL KILL YOU TOO!
SHOOT HIM!
NO! HE'S NOT SOLID! IT WON'T DO A THING!
YOU'LL JUST HIT THE PRESIDENT'S DAUGHTER!
CAN WE CUT THE MAIN POWER, CAPTAIN?
NOT A CHANCE! HE'S GOT HER IN FRONT OF THE SWITCH!
LADIES AND GENTLEMEN, I'VE BEEN ASKED TO MAKE A BRIEF STATEMENT.
-AHEM- THREE YEARS HAVE NOW PASSED SINCE YOUR GOVERNMENT WAS OVERTHROWN...
JACK, PLEASE! FOR GOD'S SAKE, SHE'S JUST A KID!
...AT THAT TIME, I WAS EMPLOYED TO ELIMINATE YOUR PRESIDENT, HIS WIFE, HIS SON, AND HIS DAUGHTER.

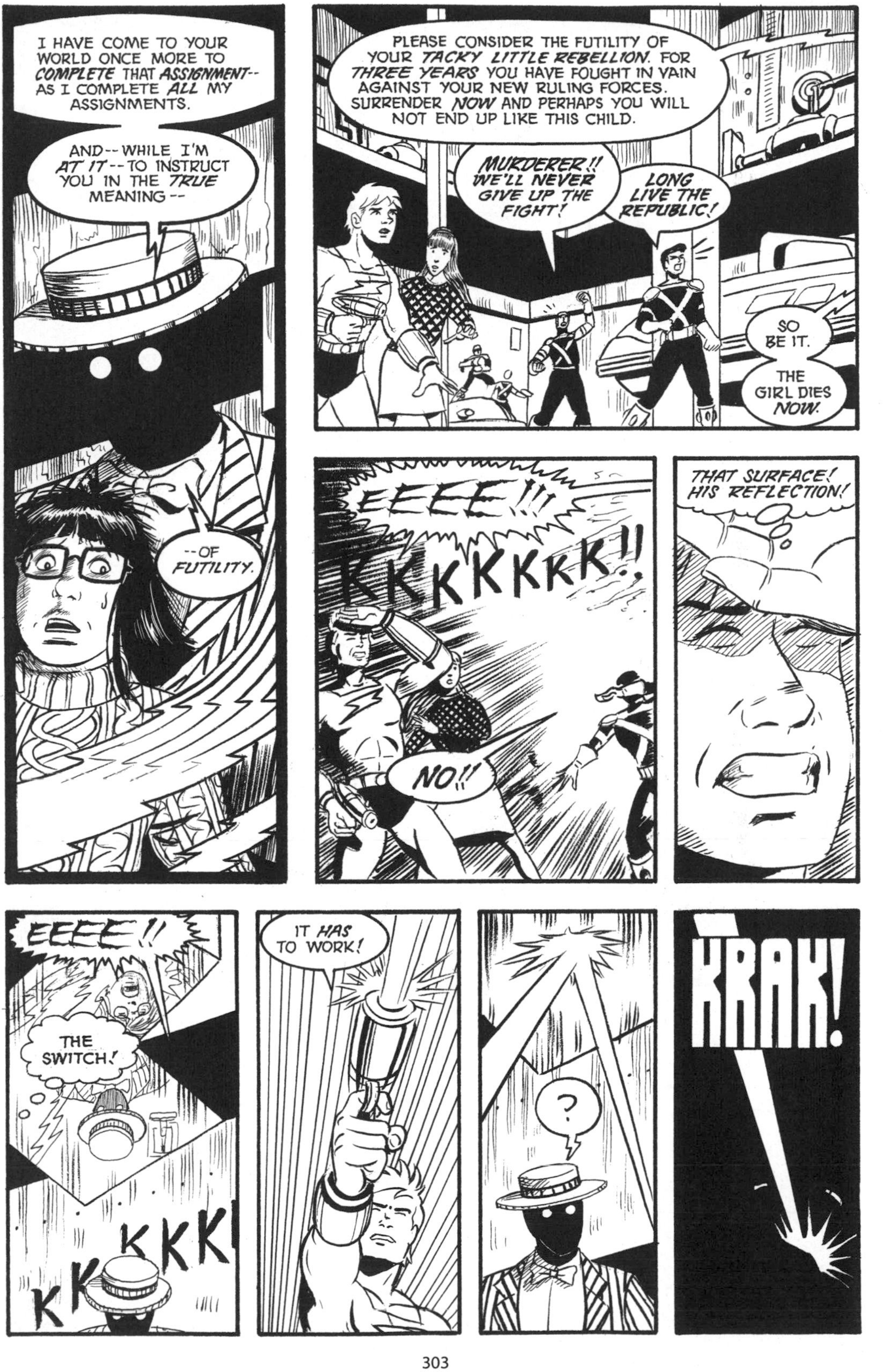
I HAVE COME TO YOUR WORLD ONCE MORE TO COMPLETE THAT ASSIGNMENT-- AS I COMPLETE ALL MY ASSIGNMENTS.
AND--WHILE I'M AT IT--TO INSTRUCT YOU IN THE TRUE MEANING--
--OF FUTILITY.
PLEASE CONSIDER THE FUTILITY OF YOUR TACKY LITTLE REBELLION. FOR THREE YEARS YOU HAVE FOUGHT IN VAIN AGAINST YOUR NEW RULING FORCES. SURRENDER NOW AND PERHAPS YOU WILL NOT END UP LIKE THIS CHILD.
MURDERER!! WE'LL NEVER GIVE UP THE FIGHT!
LONG LIVE THE REPUBLIC!
SO BE IT.
THE GIRL DIES NOW.
EEEE!!!
KKKKKKK!!
NO!!
THAT SURFACE! HIS REFLECTION!
EEEE!!
THE SWITCH!
KKKKK
IT HAS TO WORK!
?
KRAK!

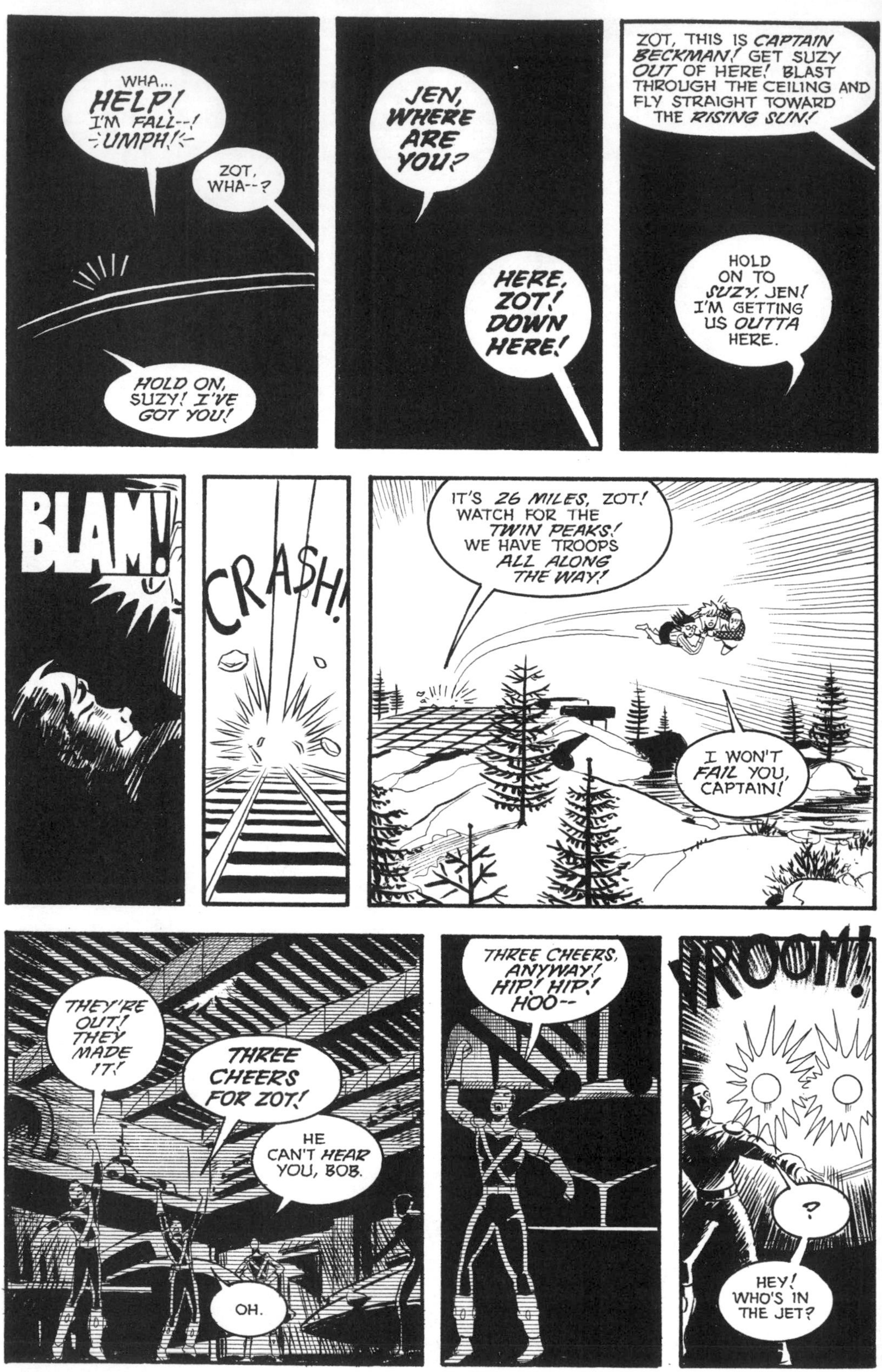
WHA... HELP! I'M FALL--! UMPH!
ZOT, WHA--?
HOLD ON, SUZY! I'VE GOT YOU!
JEN, WHERE ARE YOU?
HERE, ZOT! DOWN HERE!
ZOT, THIS IS CAPTAIN BECKMAN! GET SUZY OUT OF HERE! BLAST THROUGH THE CEILING AND FLY STRAIGHT TOWARD THE RISING SUN!
HOLD ON TO SUZY, JEN! I'M GETTING US OUTTA HERE.
BLAM!
CRASH!
IT'S 26 MILES, ZOT! WATCH FOR THE TWIN PEAKS! WE HAVE TROOPS ALL ALONG THE WAY!
I WON'T FAIL YOU, CAPTAIN!
THEY'RE OUT! THEY MADE IT!
THREE CHEERS FOR ZOT!
HE CAN'T HEAR YOU, BOB.
OH.
THREE CHEERS, ANYWAY! HIP! HIP! HOO--
VROOM!
?
HEY! WHO'S IN THE JET?

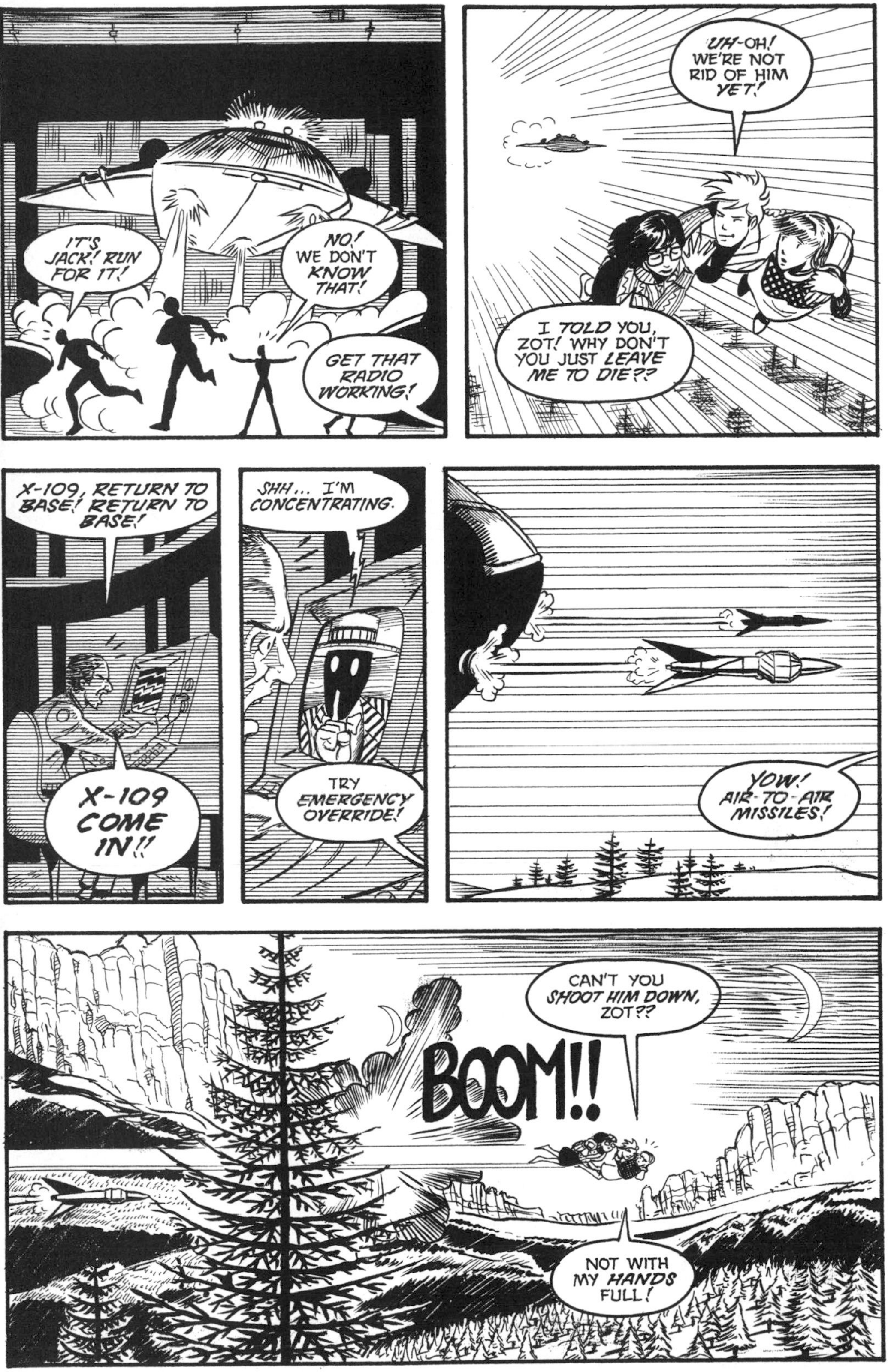
IT'S JACK! RUN FOR IT!
NO! WE DON'T KNOW THAT!
GET THAT RADIO WORKING!
UH-OH! WE'RE NOT RID OF HIM YET!
I TOLD YOU, ZOT! WHY DON'T YOU JUST LEAVE ME TO DIE??
X-109, RETURN TO BASE! RETURN TO BASE!
X-109 COME IN!!
SHH... I'M CONCENTRATING.
TRY EMERGENCY OVERRIDE!
YOW! AIR-TO-AIR MISSILES!
CAN'T YOU SHOOT HIM DOWN, ZOT??
BOOM!!
NOT WITH MY HANDS FULL!

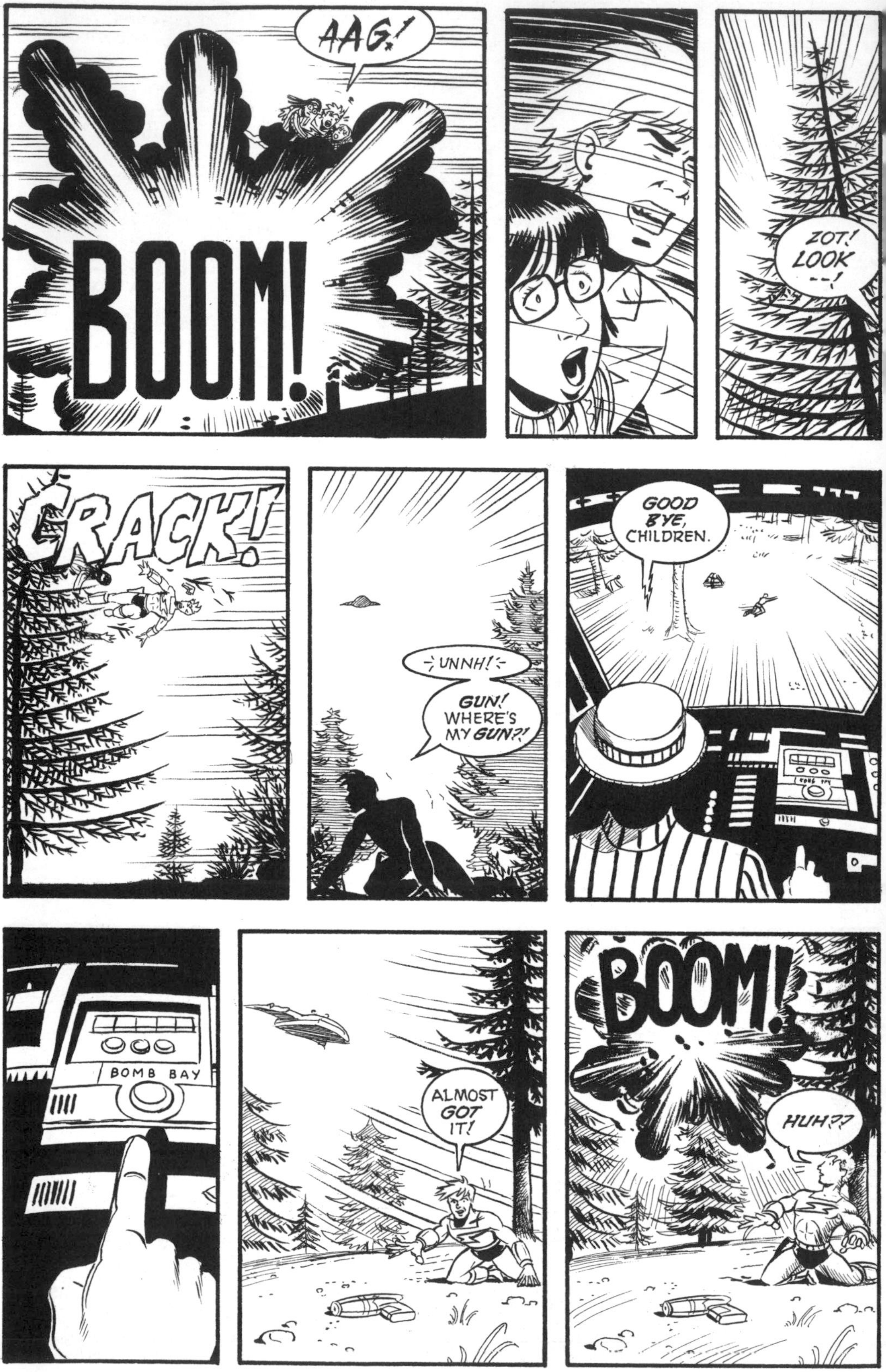
AAG!
BOOM!
ZOT! LOOK --!
CRACK!
UNNH!
GUN! WHERE'S MY GUN?!
GOOD BYE, CHILDREN.
BOMB BAY
ALMOST GOT IT!
BOOM!
HUH??

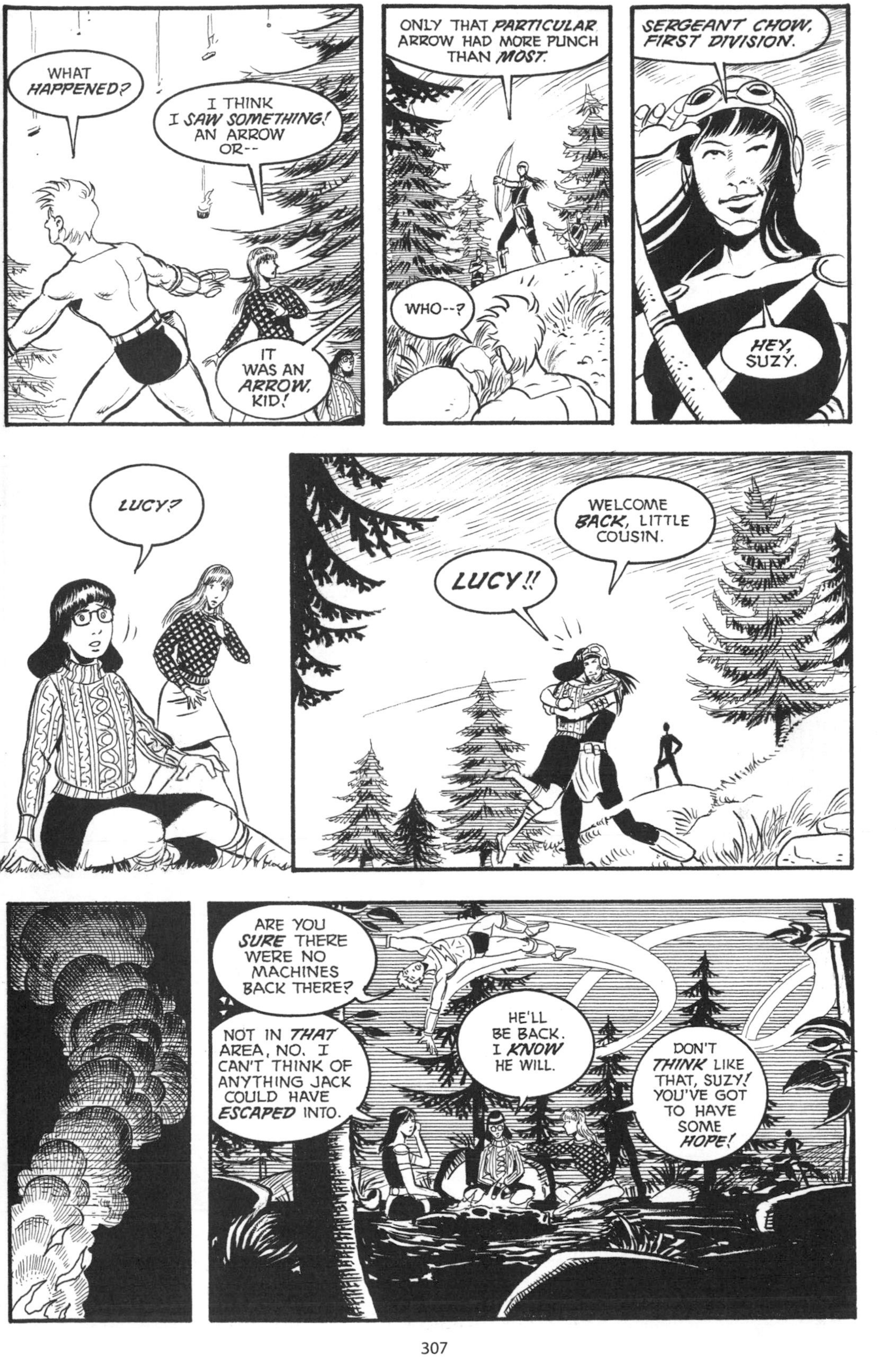
WHAT HAPPENED?
I THINK I SAW SOMETHING! AN ARROW OR--
IT WAS AN ARROW, KID!
ONLY THAT PARTICULAR ARROW HAD MORE PUNCH THAN MOST.
WHO--?
SERGEANT CHOW, FIRST DIVISION.
HEY, SUZY.
LUCY?
WELCOME BACK, LITTLE COUSIN.
LUCY!!
ARE YOU SURE THERE WERE NO MACHINES BACK THERE?
NOT IN THAT AREA, NO. I CAN'T THINK OF ANYTHING JACK COULD HAVE ESCAPED INTO.
HE'LL BE BACK. I KNOW HE WILL.
DON'T THINK LIKE THAT, SUZY! YOU'VE GOT TO HAVE SOME HOPE!

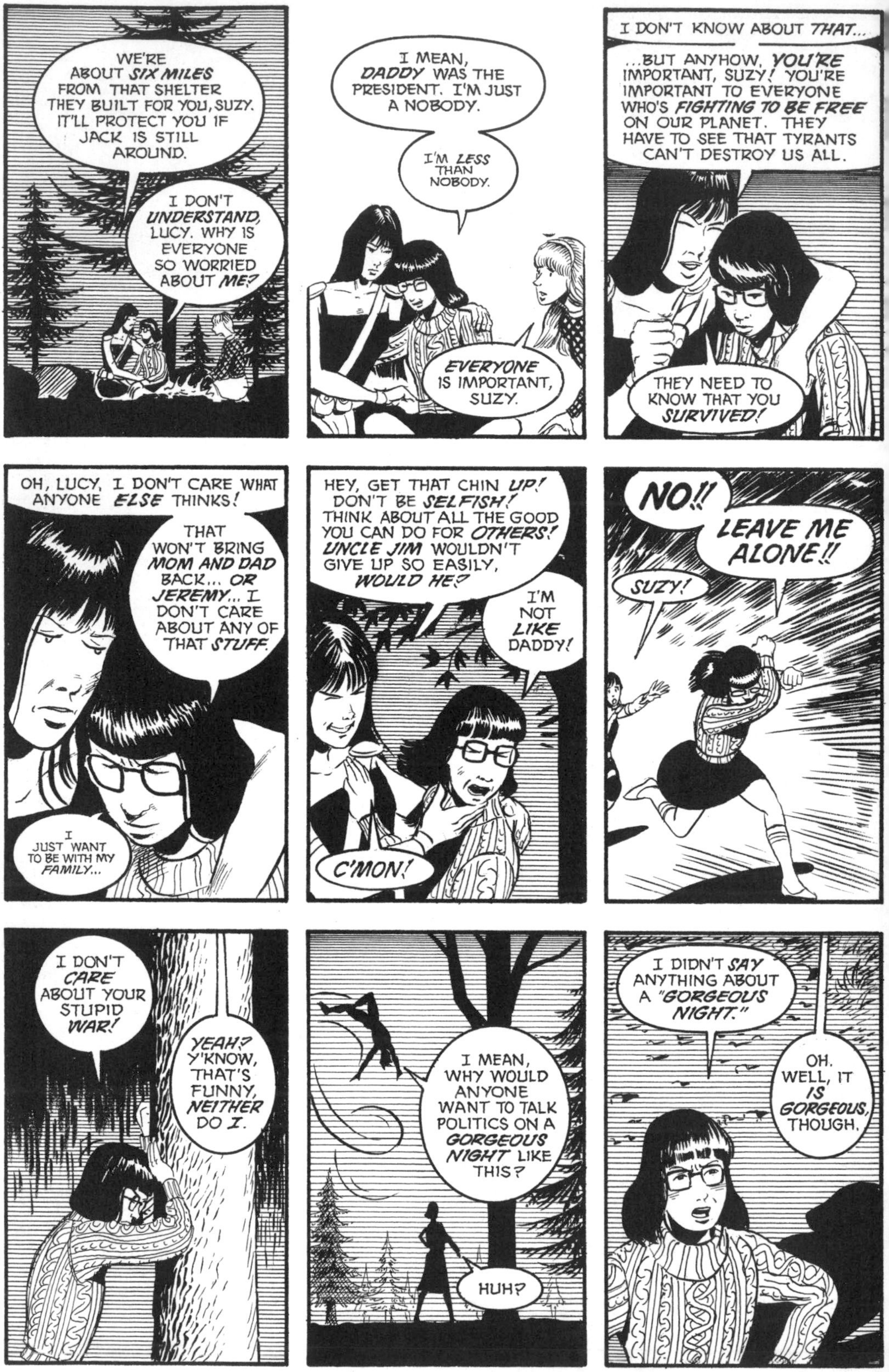
WE'RE ABOUT SIX MILES FROM THAT SHELTER THEY BUILT FOR YOU, SUZY. IT'LL PROTECT YOU IF JACK IS STILL AROUND.
I DON'T UNDERSTAND, LUCY. WHY IS EVERYONE SO WORRIED ABOUT ME?
I MEAN, DADDY WAS THE PRESIDENT. I'M JUST A NOBODY.
I'M LESS THAN NOBODY.
EVERYONE IS IMPORTANT, SUZY.
I DON'T KNOW ABOUT THAT...
...BUT ANYHOW, YOU'RE IMPORTANT, SUZY! YOU'RE IMPORTANT TO EVERYONE WHO'S FIGHTING TO BE FREE ON OUR PLANET. THEY HAVE TO SEE THAT TYRANTS CAN'T DESTROY US ALL.
THEY NEED TO KNOW THAT YOU SURVIVED!
OH, LUCY, I DON'T CARE WHAT ANYONE ELSE THINKS!
THAT WON'T BRING MOM AND DAD BACK... OR JEREMY... I DON'T CARE ABOUT ANY OF THAT STUFF.
I JUST WANT TO BE WITH MY FAMILY...
HEY, GET THAT CHIN UP! DON'T BE SELFISH! THINK ABOUT ALL THE GOOD YOU CAN DO FOR OTHERS! UNCLE JIM WOULDN'T GIVE UP SO EASILY, WOULD HE?
I'M NOT LIKE DADDY!
C'MON!
NO!!
LEAVE ME ALONE!!
SUZY!
I DON'T CARE ABOUT YOUR STUPID WAR!
YEAH? Y'KNOW, THAT'S FUNNY, NEITHER DO I.
I MEAN, WHY WOULD ANYONE WANT TO TALK POLITICS ON A GORGEOUS NIGHT LIKE THIS?
HUH?
I DIDN'T SAY ANYTHING ABOUT A "GORGEOUS NIGHT."
OH. WELL, IT IS GORGEOUS, THOUGH.

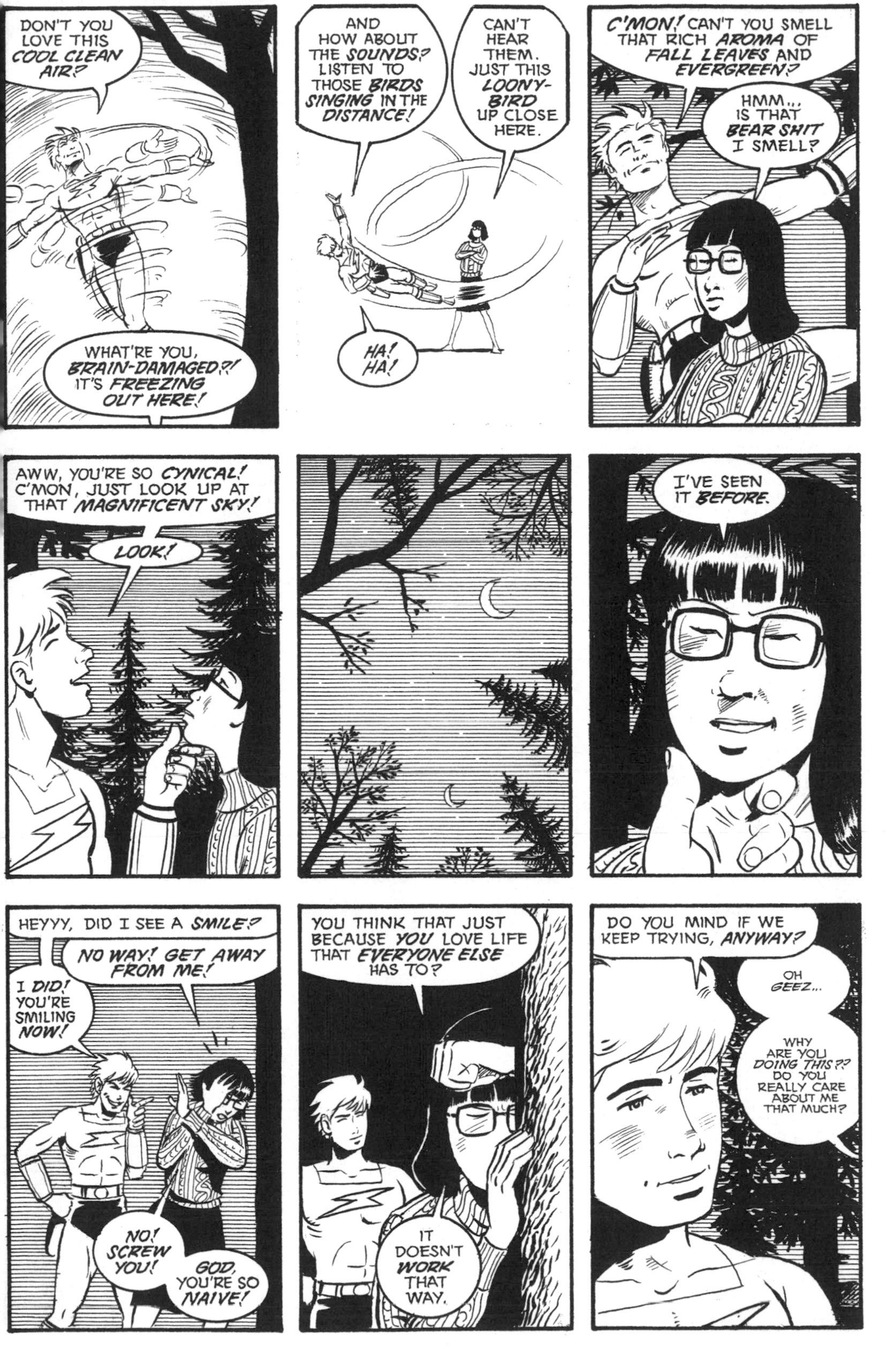
DON'T YOU LOVE THIS COOL CLEAN AIR?
WHAT'RE YOU, BRAIN-DAMAGED?! IT'S FREEZING OUT HERE!
AND HOW ABOUT THE SOUNDS? LISTEN TO THOSE BIRDS SINGING IN THE DISTANCE!
CAN'T HEAR THEM. JUST THIS LOONY-BIRD UP CLOSE HERE.
HA! HA!
C'MON! CAN'T YOU SMELL THAT RICH AROMA OF FALL LEAVES AND EVERGREEN?
HMM.., IS THAT BEAR SHIT I SMELL?
AWW, YOU'RE SO CYNICAL! C'MON, JUST LOOK UP AT THAT MAGNIFICENT SKY!
LOOK!
I'VE SEEN IT BEFORE.
HEYYY, DID I SEE A SMILE?
NO WAY! GET AWAY FROM ME!
I DID! YOU'RE SMILING NOW!
NO! SCREW YOU!
GOD, YOU'RE SO NAIVE!
YOU THINK THAT JUST BECAUSE YOU LOVE LIFE THAT EVERYONE ELSE HAS TO?
IT DOESN'T WORK THAT WAY.
DO YOU MIND IF WE KEEP TRYING, ANYWAY?
OH GEEZ...
WHY ARE YOU DOING THIS?? DO YOU REALLY CARE ABOUT ME THAT MUCH?

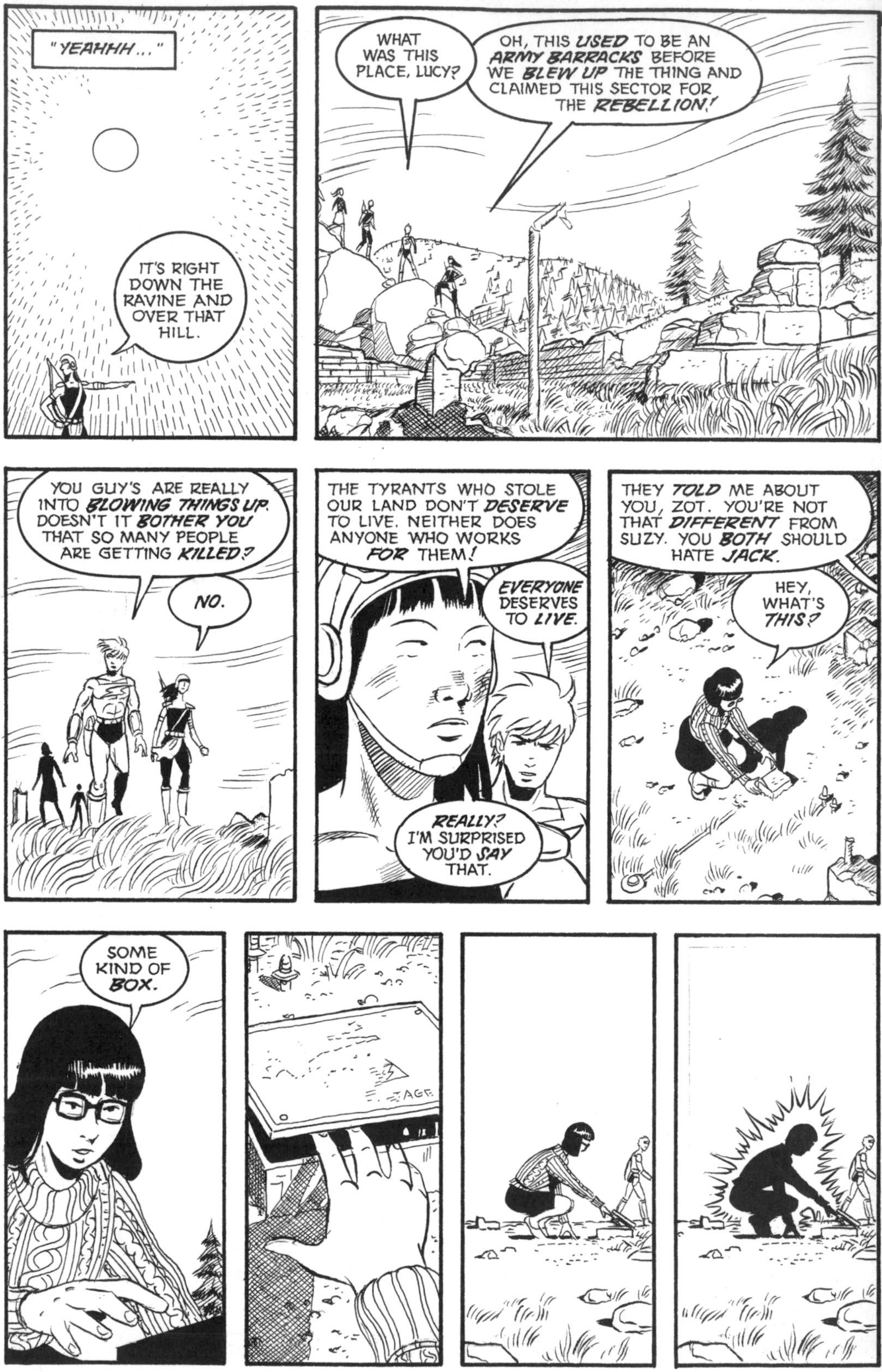
"YEAHHH..."
IT'S RIGHT DOWN THE RAVINE AND OVER THAT HILL.
WHAT WAS THIS PLACE, LUCY?
OH, THIS USED TO BE AN ARMY BARRACKS BEFORE WE BLEW UP THE THING AND CLAIMED THIS SECTOR FOR THE REBELLION!
YOU GUY'S ARE REALLY INTO BLOWING THINGS UP. DOESN'T IT BOTHER YOU THAT SO MANY PEOPLE ARE GETTING KILLED?
NO.
THE TYRANTS WHO STOLE OUR LAND DON'T DESERVE TO LIVE. NEITHER DOES ANYONE WHO WORKS FOR THEM!
EVERYONE DESERVES TO LIVE.
REALLY? I'M SURPRISED YOU'D SAY THAT.
THEY TOLD ME ABOUT YOU, ZOT. YOU'RE NOT THAT DIFFERENT FROM SUZY. YOU BOTH SHOULD HATE JACK.
HEY, WHAT'S THIS?
SOME KIND OF BOX.

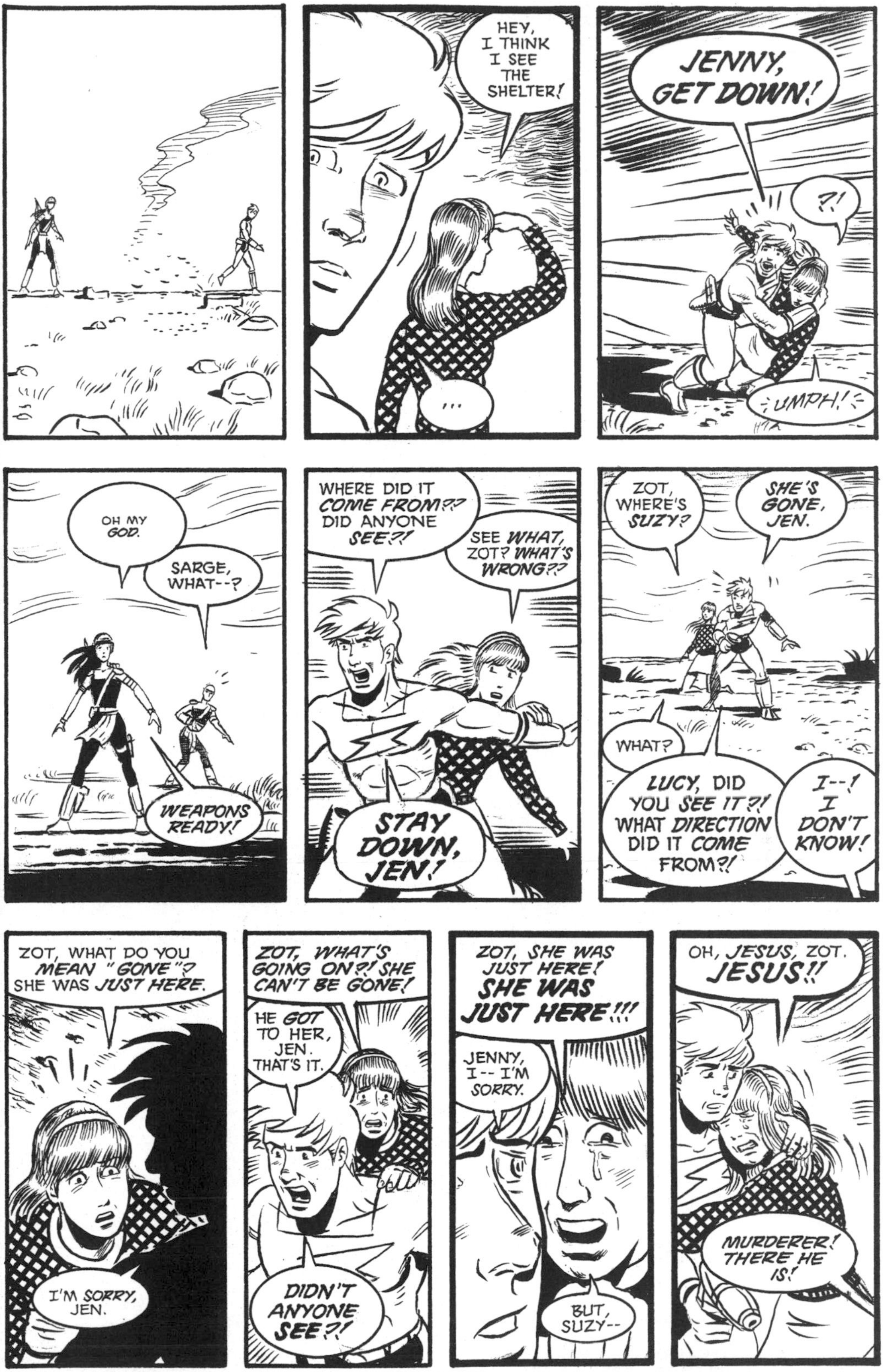
HEY, I THINK I SEE THE SHELTER!
...
JENNY, GET DOWN!
?!
UMPH!
OH MY GOD.
SARGE, WHAT--?
WEAPONS READY!
WHERE DID IT COME FROM?? DID ANYONE SEE?!
SEE WHAT, ZOT? WHAT'S WRONG??
STAY DOWN, JEN!
ZOT, WHERE'S SUZY?
SHE'S GONE, JEN.
WHAT?
LUCY, DID YOU SEE IT?! WHAT DIRECTION DID IT COME FROM?!
I--! I DON'T KNOW!
ZOT, WHAT DO YOU MEAN "GONE"? SHE WAS JUST HERE.
I'M SORRY, JEN.
ZOT, WHAT'S GOING ON?! SHE CAN'T BE GONE!
HE GOT TO HER, JEN. THAT'S IT.
DIDN'T ANYONE SEE?!
ZOT, SHE WAS JUST HERE! SHE WAS JUST HERE!!!
JENNY, I -- I'M SORRY.
BUT, SUZY--
OH, JESUS, ZOT. JESUS!!
MURDERER! THERE HE IS!

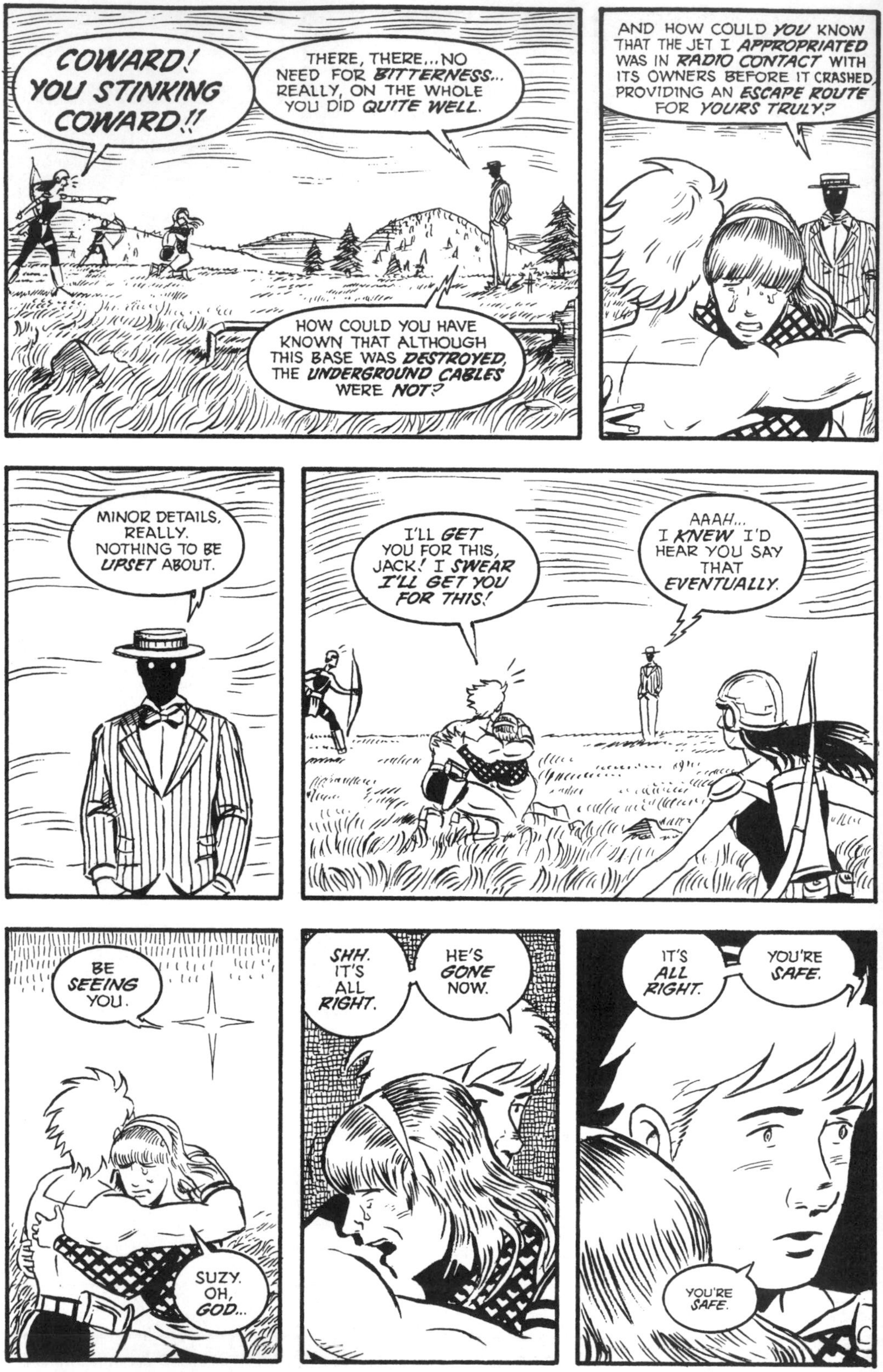
COWARD! YOU STINKING COWARD!!
THERE, THERE... NO NEED FOR BITTERNESS... REALLY, ON THE WHOLE YOU DID QUITE WELL.
HOW COULD YOU HAVE KNOWN THAT ALTHOUGH THIS BASE WAS DESTROYED, THE UNDERGROUND CABLES WERE NOT?
AND HOW COULD YOU KNOW THAT THE JET I APPROPRIATED WAS IN RADIO CONTACT WITH ITS OWNERS BEFORE IT CRASHED, PROVIDING AN ESCAPE ROUTE FOR YOURS TRULY?
MINOR DETAILS, REALLY. NOTHING TO BE UPSET ABOUT.
I'LL GET YOU FOR THIS, JACK! I SWEAR I'LL GET YOU FOR THIS!
AAAH... I KNEW I'D HEAR YOU SAY THAT EVENTUALLY.
BE SEEING YOU.
SUZY. OH, GOD...
SHH. IT'S ALL RIGHT.
HE'S GONE NOW.
IT'S ALL RIGHT.
YOU'RE SAFE.
YOU'RE SAFE.

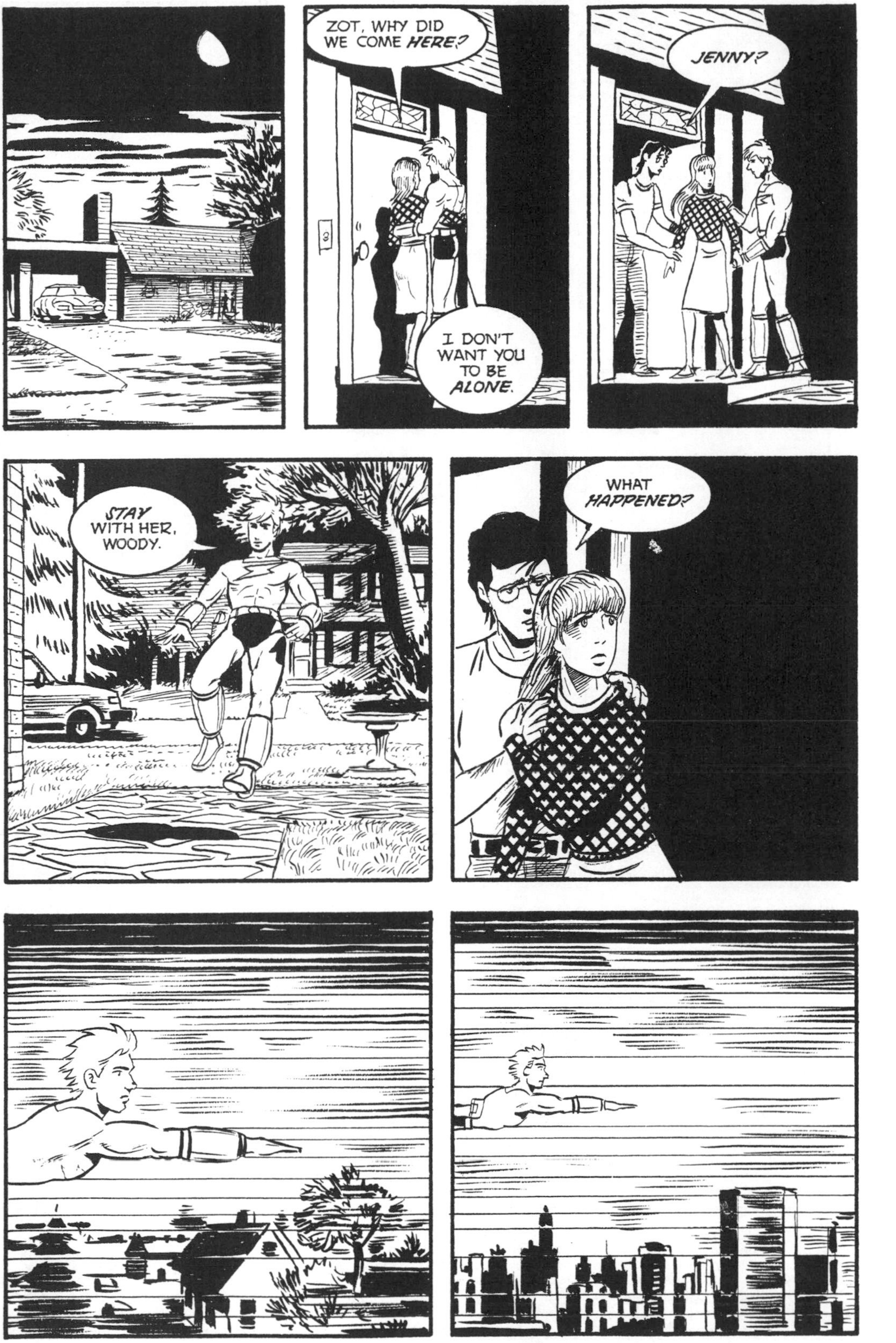
ZOT, WHY DID WE COME *HERE*?
I DON'T WANT YOU TO BE *ALONE*.
JENNY?
STAY WITH HER, WOODY.
WHAT *HAPPENED?*

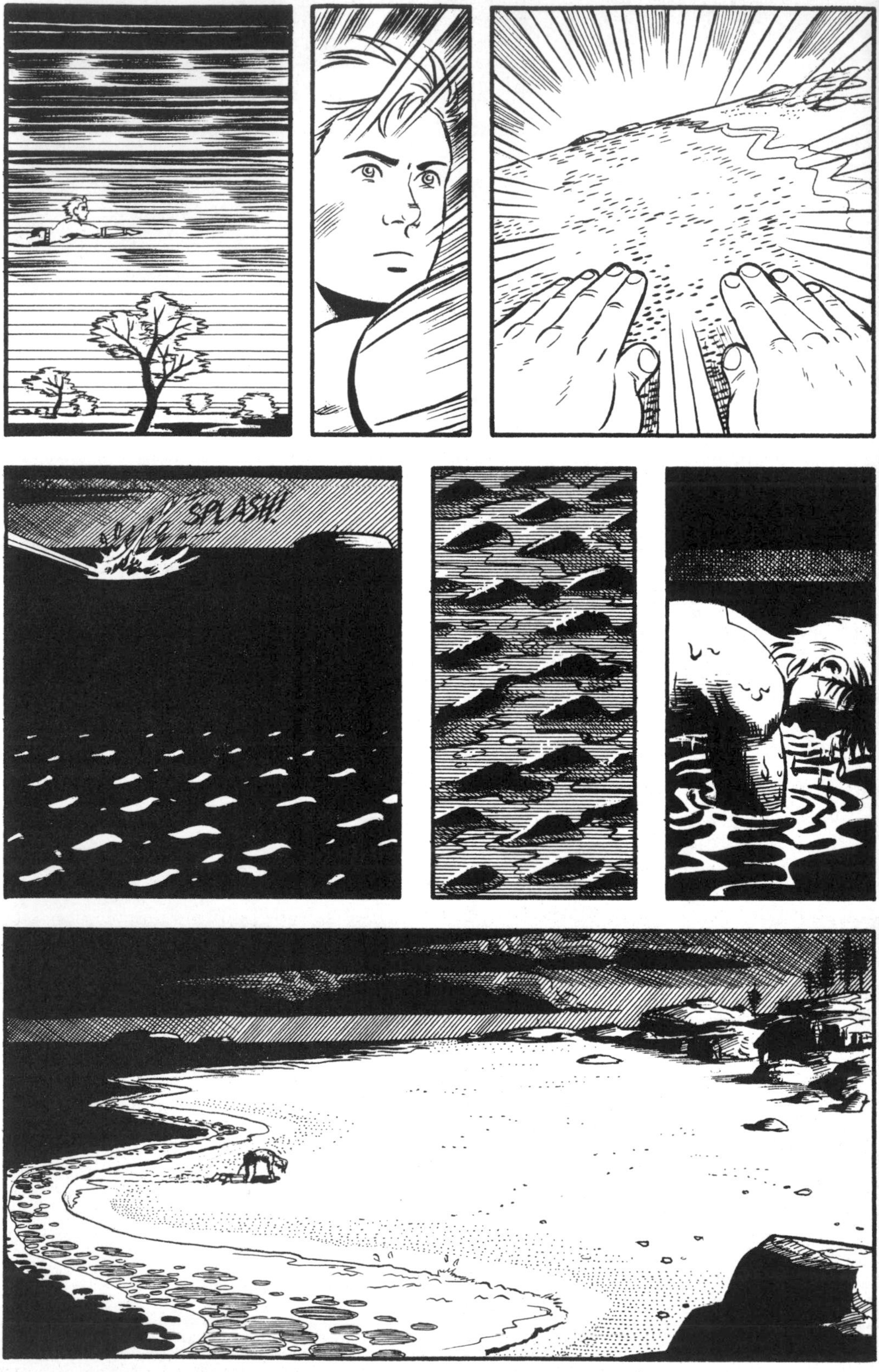
SPLASH!

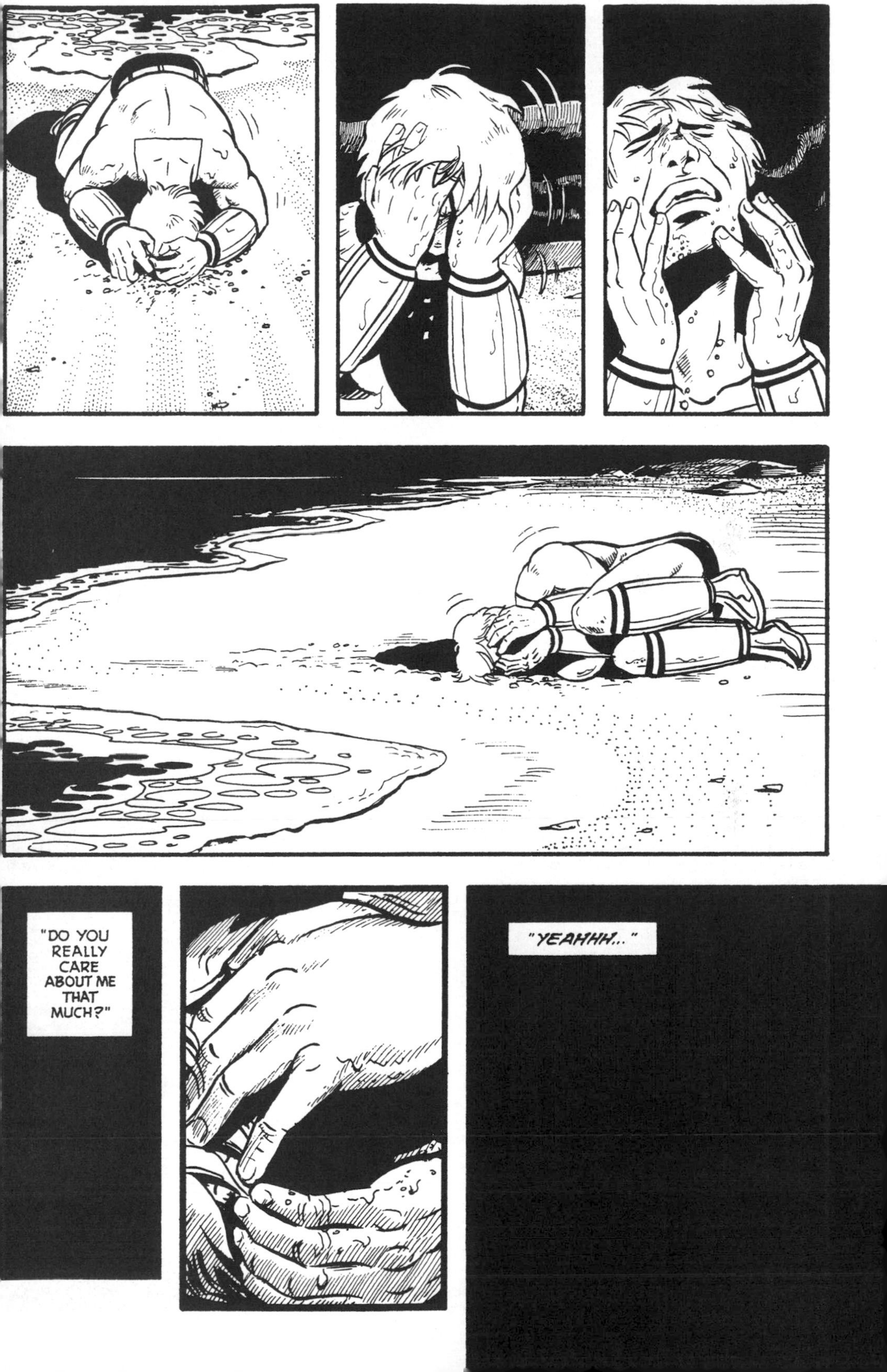
"DO YOU REALLY CARE ABOUT ME THAT MUCH?"
"YEAHHH..."

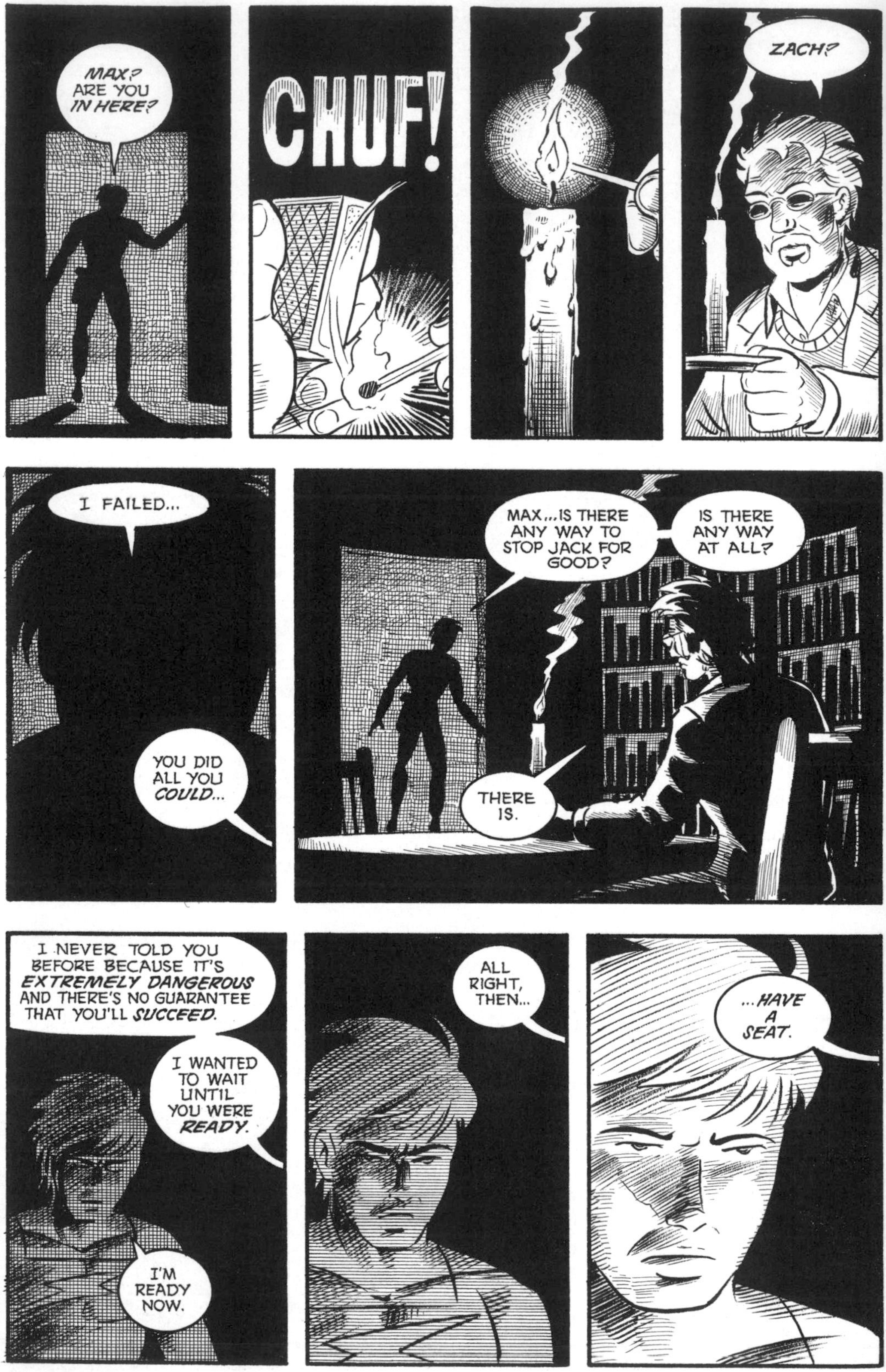
MAX? ARE YOU IN HERE?
CHUF!
ZACH?
I FAILED...
YOU DID ALL YOU COULD...
MAX...IS THERE ANY WAY TO STOP JACK FOR GOOD?
IS THERE ANY WAY AT ALL?
THERE IS.
I NEVER TOLD YOU BEFORE BECAUSE IT'S EXTREMELY DANGEROUS AND THERE'S NO GUARANTEE THAT YOU'LL SUCCEED.
I WANTED TO WAIT UNTIL YOU WERE READY.
I'M READY NOW.
ALL RIGHT, THEN...
...HAVE A SEAT.

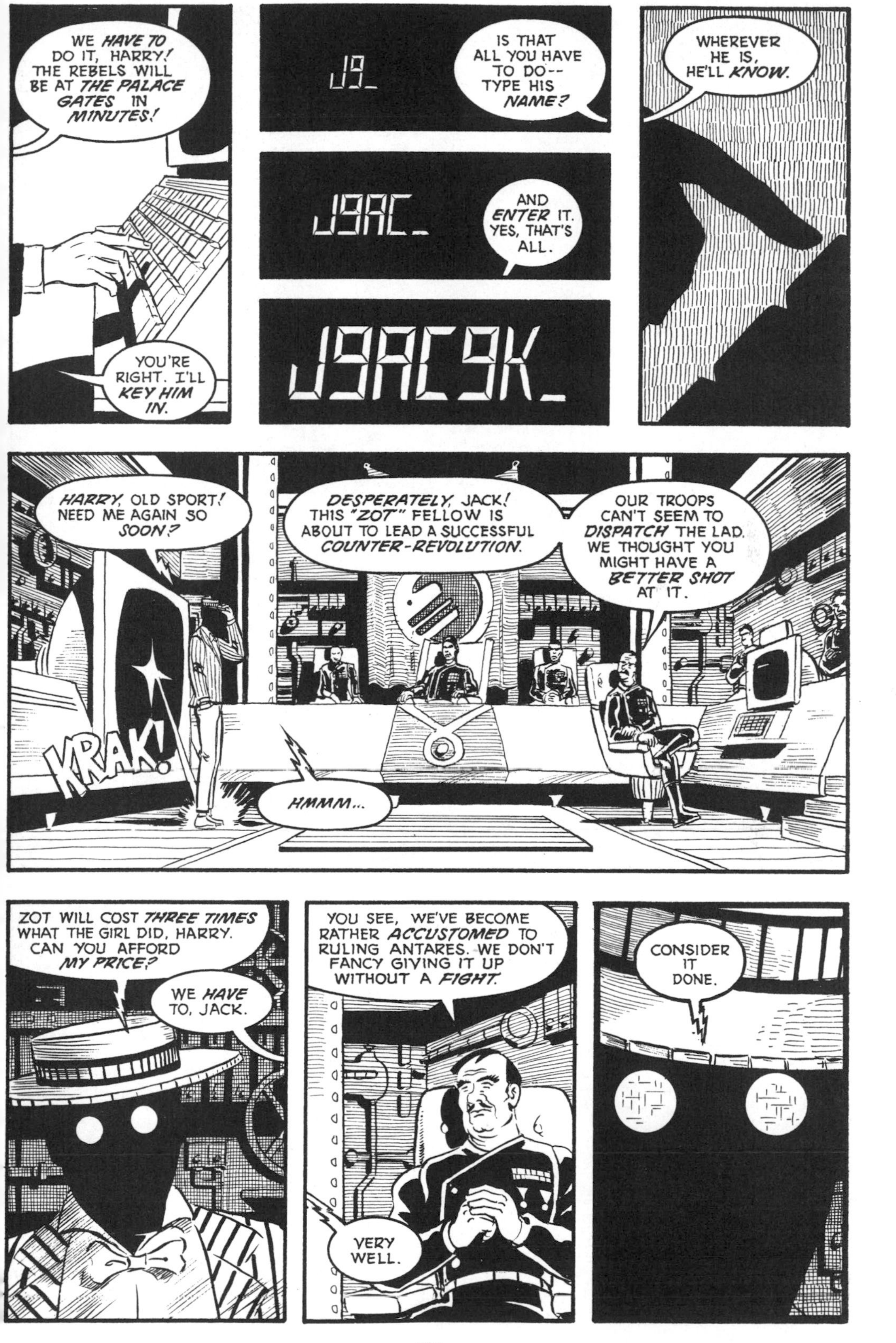
WE HAVE TO DO IT, HARRY! THE REBELS WILL BE AT THE PALACE GATES IN MINUTES!
YOU'RE RIGHT. I'LL KEY HIM IN.
J9_
IS THAT ALL YOU HAVE TO DO-- TYPE HIS NAME?
J9AC_
AND ENTER IT. YES, THAT'S ALL.
J9AC9K_
WHEREVER HE IS, HE'LL KNOW.
HARRY, OLD SPORT! NEED ME AGAIN SO SOON?
KRAK!
DESPERATELY, JACK! THIS "ZOT" FELLOW IS ABOUT TO LEAD A SUCCESSFUL COUNTER-REVOLUTION.
OUR TROOPS CAN'T SEEM TO DISPATCH THE LAD. WE THOUGHT YOU MIGHT HAVE A BETTER SHOT AT IT.
HMMM...
ZOT WILL COST THREE TIMES WHAT THE GIRL DID, HARRY. CAN YOU AFFORD MY PRICE?
WE HAVE TO, JACK.
YOU SEE, WE'VE BECOME RATHER ACCUSTOMED TO RULING ANTARES. WE DON'T FANCY GIVING IT UP WITHOUT A FIGHT.
VERY WELL.
CONSIDER IT DONE.

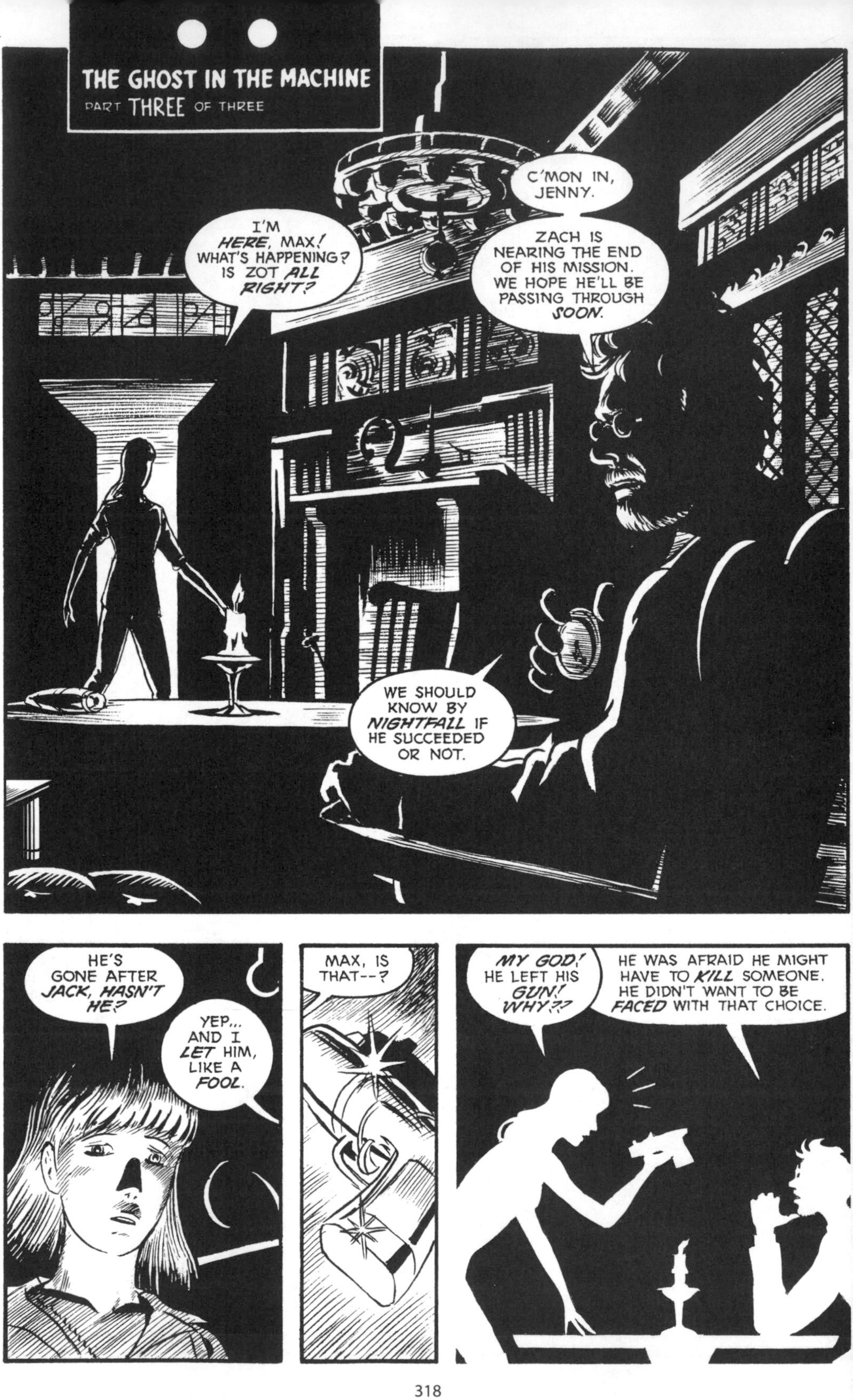
THE GHOST IN THE MACHINE
PART THREE OF THREE
I'M HERE, MAX! WHAT'S HAPPENING? IS ZOT ALL RIGHT?
C'MON IN, JENNY.
ZACH IS NEARING THE END OF HIS MISSION. WE HOPE HE'LL BE PASSING THROUGH SOON.
WE SHOULD KNOW BY NIGHTFALL IF HE SUCCEEDED OR NOT.
HE'S GONE AFTER JACK, HASN'T HE?
YEP... AND I LET HIM, LIKE A FOOL.
MAX, IS THAT--?
MY GOD! HE LEFT HIS GUN! WHY??
HE WAS AFRAID HE MIGHT HAVE TO KILL SOMEONE. HE DIDN'T WANT TO BE FACED WITH THAT CHOICE.

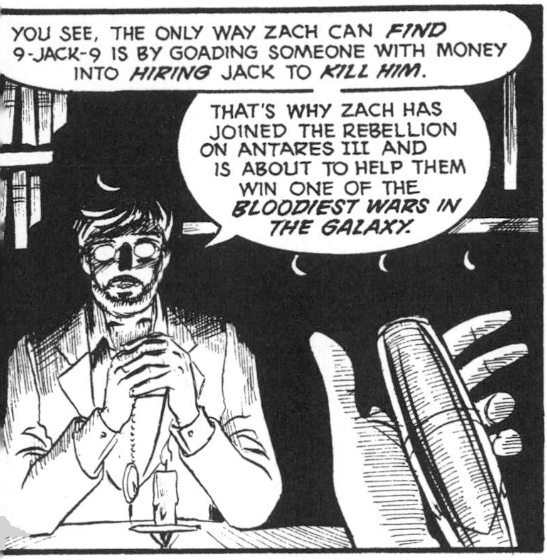
YOU SEE, THE ONLY WAY ZACH CAN *FIND* 9-JACK-9 IS BY GOADING SOMEONE WITH MONEY INTO *HIRING* JACK TO *KILL HIM*.
THAT'S WHY ZACH HAS JOINED THE REBELLION ON ANTARES III AND IS ABOUT TO HELP THEM WIN ONE OF THE *BLOODIEST WARS IN THE GALAXY*.

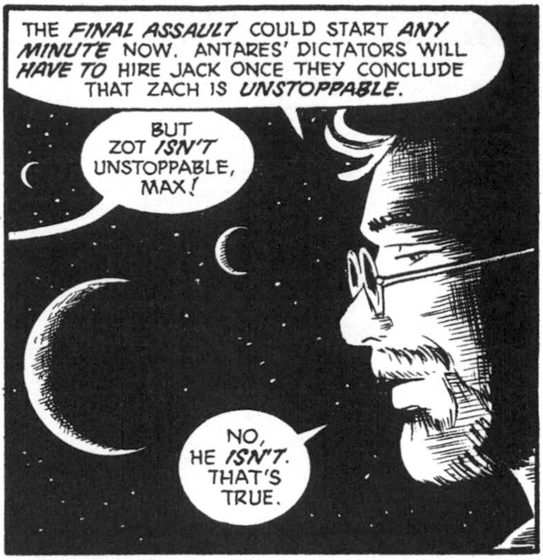
THE *FINAL ASSAULT* COULD START *ANY MINUTE* NOW. ANTARES' DICTATORS WILL *HAVE TO* HIRE JACK ONCE THEY CONCLUDE THAT ZACH IS *UNSTOPPABLE*.
BUT ZOT *ISN'T* UNSTOPPABLE, MAX!
NO, HE *ISN'T*. THAT'S TRUE.

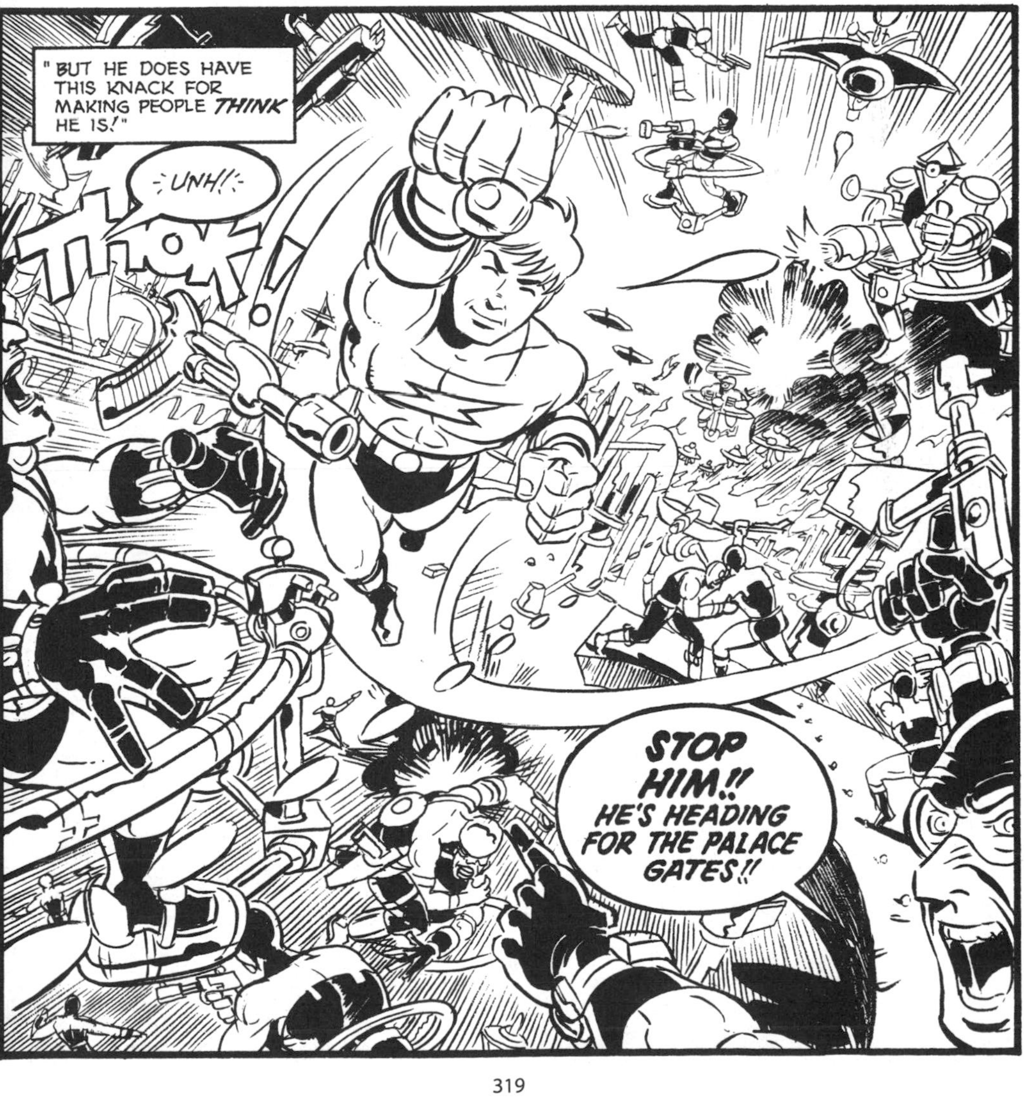
"BUT HE DOES HAVE THIS KNACK FOR MAKING PEOPLE *THINK* HE IS!"
UNH!
THOK!
STOP HIM!! HE'S HEADING FOR THE PALACE GATES!!

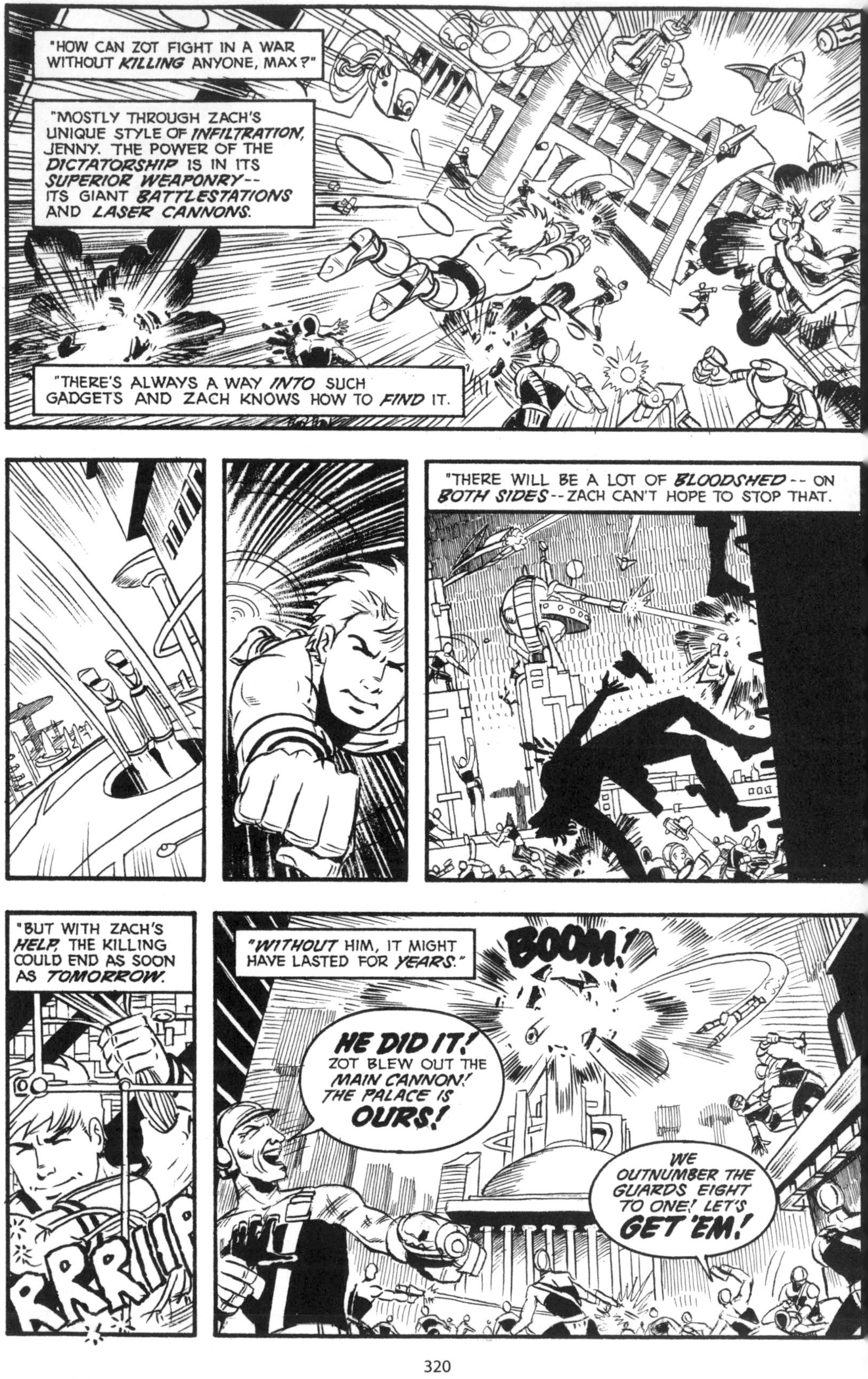
"HOW CAN ZOT FIGHT IN A WAR WITHOUT KILLING ANYONE, MAX?"
"MOSTLY THROUGH ZACH'S UNIQUE STYLE OF INFILTRATION, JENNY. THE POWER OF THE DICTATORSHIP IS IN ITS SUPERIOR WEAPONRY-- ITS GIANT BATTLESTATIONS AND LASER CANNONS.
"THERE'S ALWAYS A WAY INTO SUCH GADGETS AND ZACH KNOWS HOW TO FIND IT.
"THERE WILL BE A LOT OF BLOODSHED -- ON BOTH SIDES--ZACH CAN'T HOPE TO STOP THAT.
"BUT WITH ZACH'S HELP, THE KILLING COULD END AS SOON AS TOMORROW.
"WITHOUT HIM, IT MIGHT HAVE LASTED FOR YEARS."
BOOM!
HE DID IT! ZOT BLEW OUT THE MAIN CANNON! THE PALACE IS OURS!
WE OUTNUMBER THE GUARDS EIGHT TO ONE! LET'S GET 'EM!

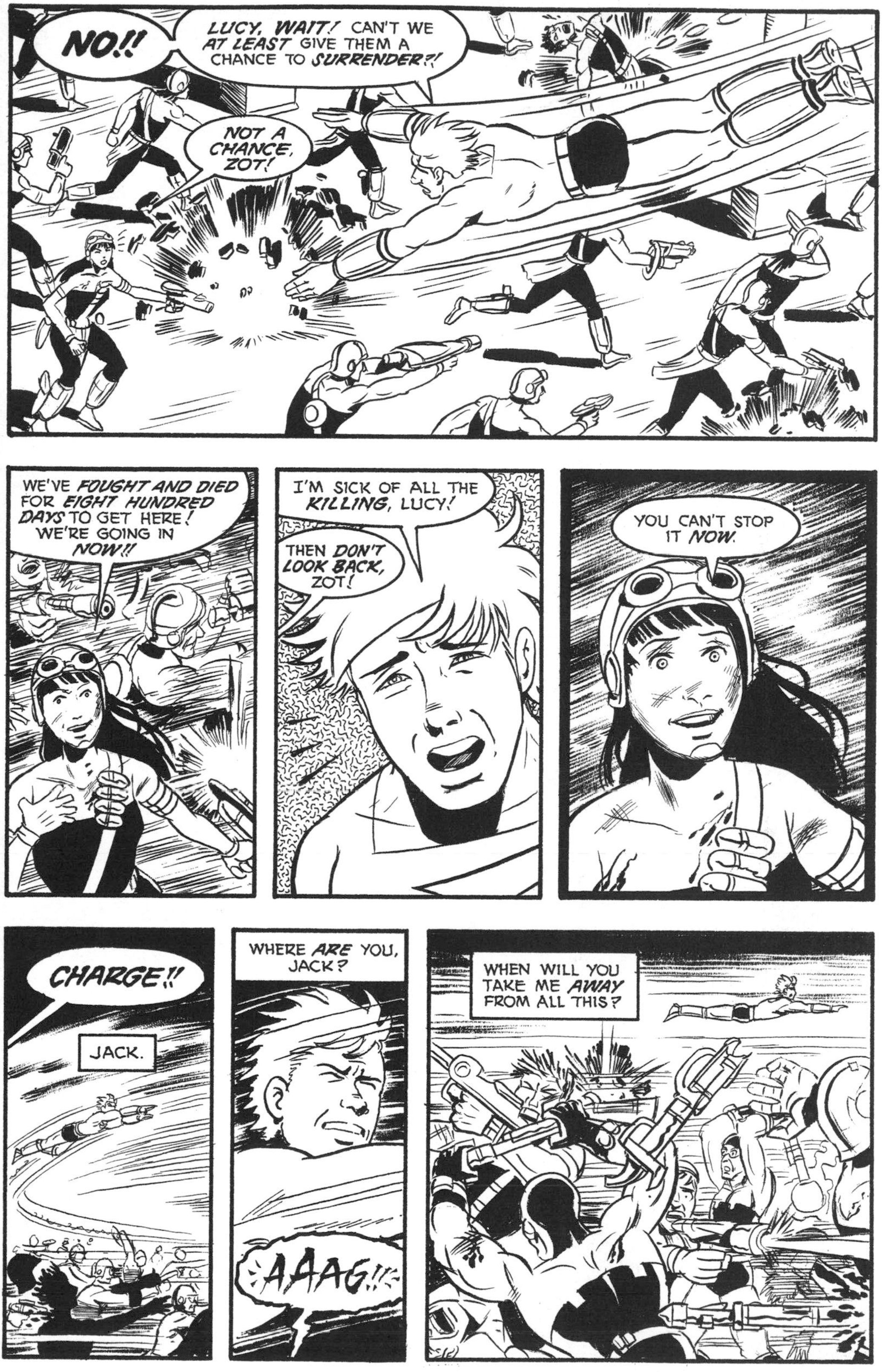
NO!!
LUCY, WAIT! CAN'T WE AT LEAST GIVE THEM A CHANCE TO SURRENDER?!
NOT A CHANCE, ZOT!
WE'VE FOUGHT AND DIED FOR EIGHT HUNDRED DAYS TO GET HERE! WE'RE GOING IN NOW!!
I'M SICK OF ALL THE KILLING, LUCY!
THEN DON'T LOOK BACK, ZOT!
YOU CAN'T STOP IT NOW.
CHARGE!!
JACK.
WHERE ARE YOU, JACK?
AAAG!!
WHEN WILL YOU TAKE ME AWAY FROM ALL THIS?

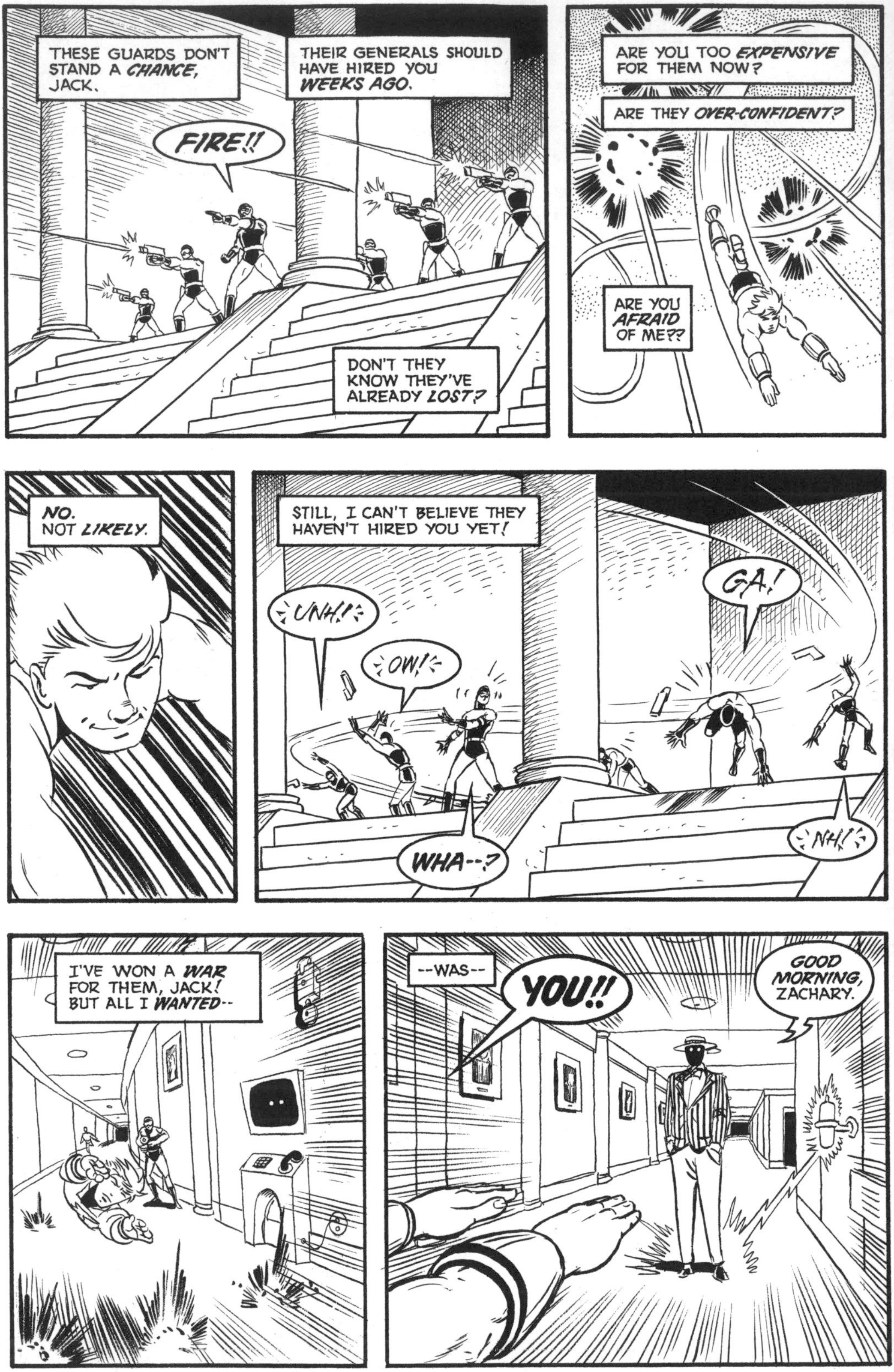
THESE GUARDS DON'T STAND A CHANCE, JACK.
THEIR GENERALS SHOULD HAVE HIRED YOU WEEKS AGO.
FIRE!!
DON'T THEY KNOW THEY'VE ALREADY LOST?
ARE YOU TOO EXPENSIVE FOR THEM NOW?
ARE THEY OVER-CONFIDENT?
ARE YOU AFRAID OF ME??
NO. NOT LIKELY.
STILL, I CAN'T BELIEVE THEY HAVEN'T HIRED YOU YET!
UNH!
OW!
GA!
WHA--?
NH!
I'VE WON A WAR FOR THEM, JACK! BUT ALL I WANTED--
--WAS--
YOU!!
GOOD MORNING, ZACHARY.

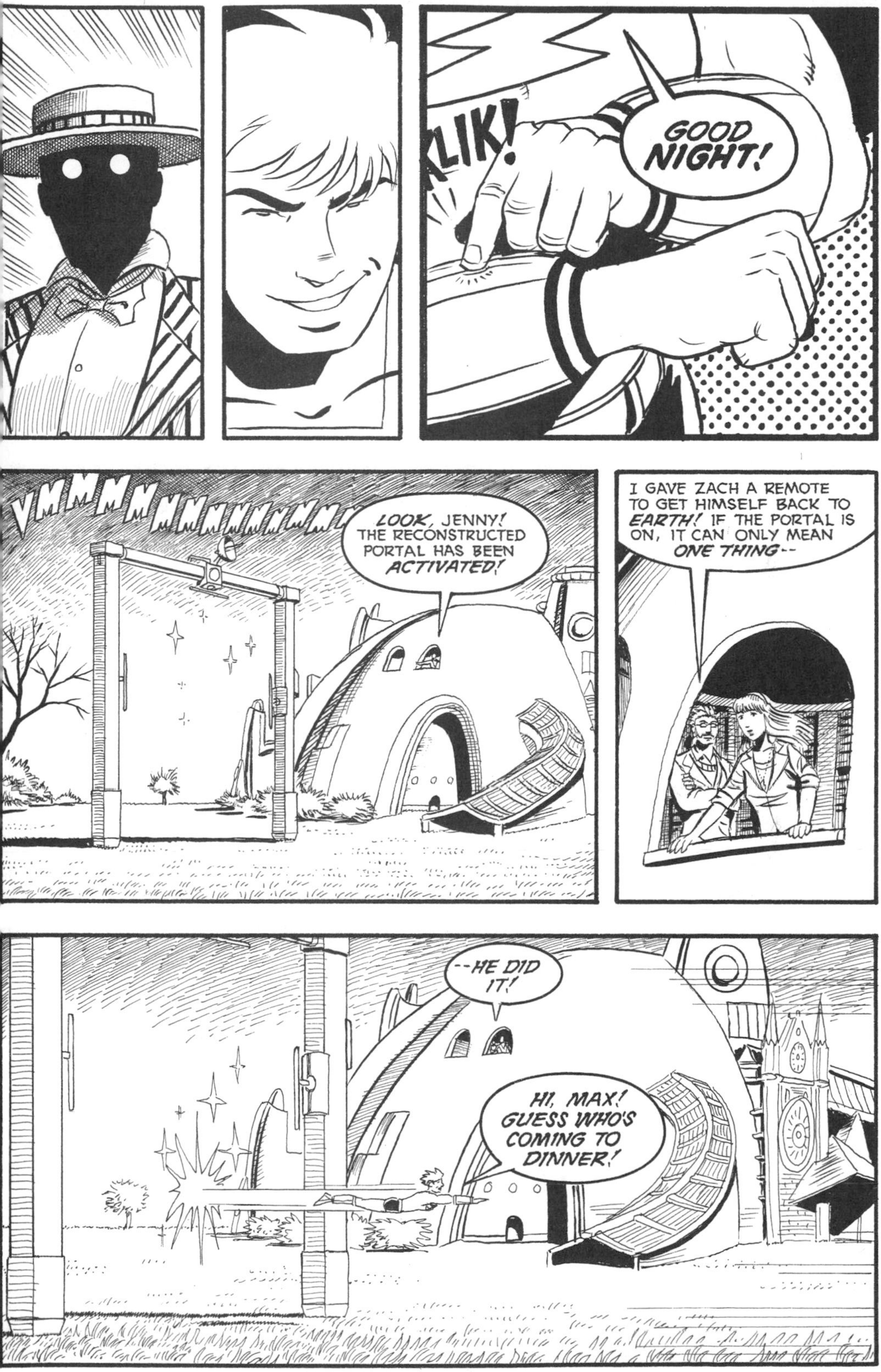
KLIK!
GOOD NIGHT!
VMMMMMMMMMMMMMMMMM
LOOK, JENNY! THE RECONSTRUCTED PORTAL HAS BEEN ACTIVATED!
I GAVE ZACH A REMOTE TO GET HIMSELF BACK TO EARTH! IF THE PORTAL IS ON, IT CAN ONLY MEAN ONE THING--
--HE DID IT!
HI, MAX! GUESS WHO'S COMING TO DINNER!

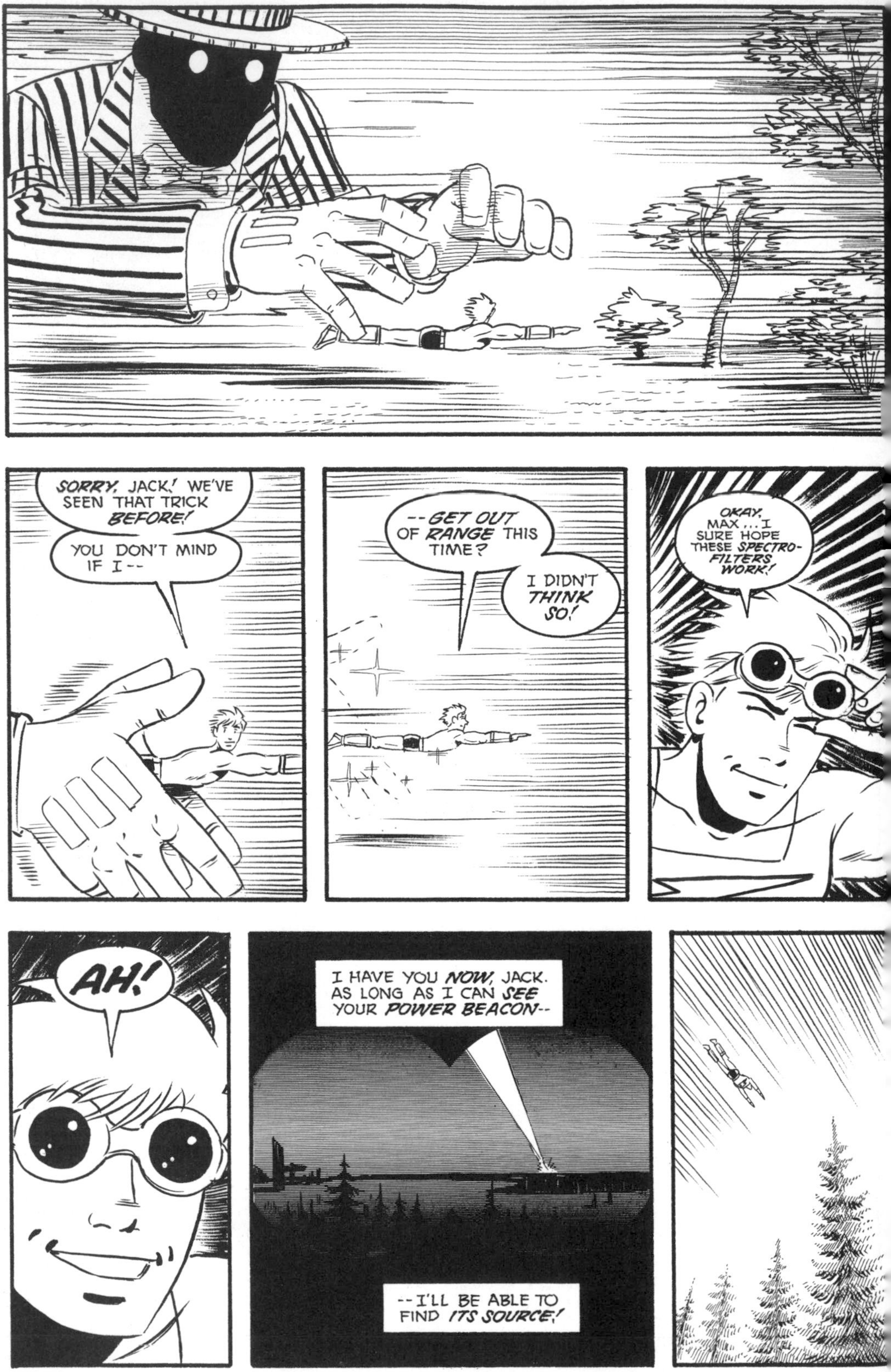
SORRY, JACK! WE'VE SEEN THAT TRICK BEFORE!
YOU DON'T MIND IF I--
--GET OUT OF RANGE THIS TIME?
I DIDN'T THINK SO!
OKAY, MAX... I SURE HOPE THESE SPECTRO-FILTERS WORK!
AH!
I HAVE YOU NOW, JACK. AS LONG AS I CAN SEE YOUR POWER BEACON--
--I'LL BE ABLE TO FIND ITS SOURCE!

HE'S HEADING *DUE EAST.* JUST AS I THOUGHT. HE'S TRACING JACK TO *THE OLD HOUSE!*

WHAT HOUSE, MAX?

THE *BRITISH ESTATE* OF SIR JOHN SHEERS, JENNY, AN *OLD FRIEND* OF MINE. SIR JOHN IS JACK'S *HUMAN OPERATOR,* HIS *"ALTER-EGO,"* YOU MIGHT SAY.

WHAT-- HOLD ON!

MAX, YOU *KNOW* 9-JACK-9??

SURE. YOU'VE *MET* HIM, IN FACT. JOHNNY PLAYS FIDDLE WITH OUR LITTLE *THURSDAY NIGHT QUARTET.* HE'S ACTUALLY A FAIRLY NICE FELLOW...*ALL THINGS CONSIDERED...*

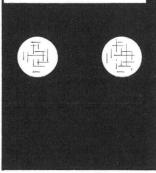

"JACK WASN'T *BORN* JOHN SHEERS... THE *REAL* SIR JOHN DIED *YEARS* AGO. JACK SIMPLY *ASSUMED* HIS IDENTITY THROUGH *PLASTIC SURGERY* AND ALTERED *COMPUTER RECORDS.* "

I DON'T KNOW WHAT JACK'S *TRUE FACE* LOOKED LIKE, OR HIS *TRUE NAME* OR WHO BUILT THE MACHINES. WE MAY *NEVER* KNOW THAT.

MAX, YOU COULD HAVE STOPPED HIM *BEFORE!*

NO.

"ONLY *ZACH* HAD ANY CHANCE OF *SUCCESS,* AND A *SLIM ONE* AT THAT. I COULDN'T SEND HIM UNTIL HE WAS *READY.*

"HE'S READY *NOW.*"

MAX, I'M *SCARED!* I WAS THERE WHEN JACK KILLED SUZY GALLO. I JUST LOOKED AWAY FOR A SECOND AND--

--AND SHE WAS JUST *GONE.*

ZACH WON'T BE QUITE SO *EASY.*

BRILLIANT! BLOODY BRILLIANT! I HAD NO IDEA HOW YOU'D GET TO LONDON WITHOUT ELECTRICITY!
GLAD YOU LIKED IT!
OH, YES! RIDING ON THE FRICTIONLESS' CABOOSE YOU WERE PERFECTLY SAFE!
?
BUT NO MORE!
!!
EH? WHO--?
SAY, WE'RE OUT OF CONTROL!!
LOOK OUT!
EEEK!
HE CAN JUMP FROM CAR TO CAR ALL DAY! GOT TO FLY HIGHER!
HIGHER!
THERE!
I CAN SEE IT AGAIN!
GIVE IT UP, ZACHARY! YOU HAVEN'T A PRAYER!
POLICE CRUISER! IF I GET HIT BY A STUNBOLT AT THIS ALTITUDE, I'M A GONER!
GOT TO KEEP MOVING!

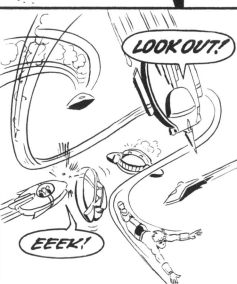

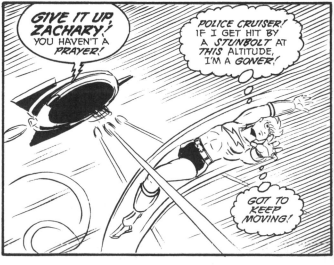

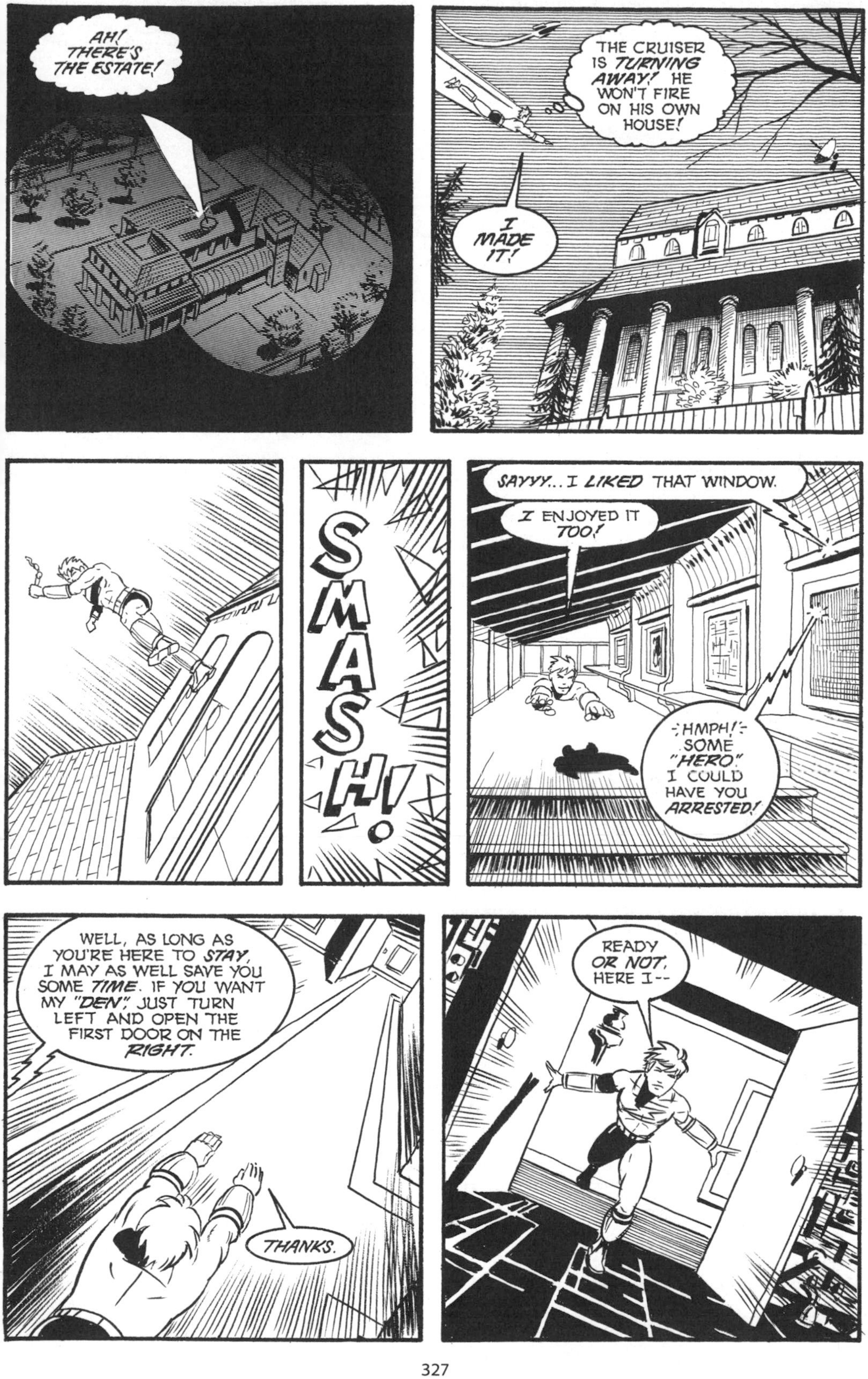
AH! THERE'S THE ESTATE!
THE CRUISER IS TURNING AWAY! HE WON'T FIRE ON HIS OWN HOUSE!
I MADE IT!
SMASH!
SAYYY... I LIKED THAT WINDOW.
I ENJOYED IT TOO!
HMPH! SOME "HERO." I COULD HAVE YOU ARRESTED!
WELL, AS LONG AS YOU'RE HERE TO STAY, I MAY AS WELL SAVE YOU SOME TIME. IF YOU WANT MY "DEN," JUST TURN LEFT AND OPEN THE FIRST DOOR ON THE RIGHT.
THANKS.
READY OR NOT, HERE I--

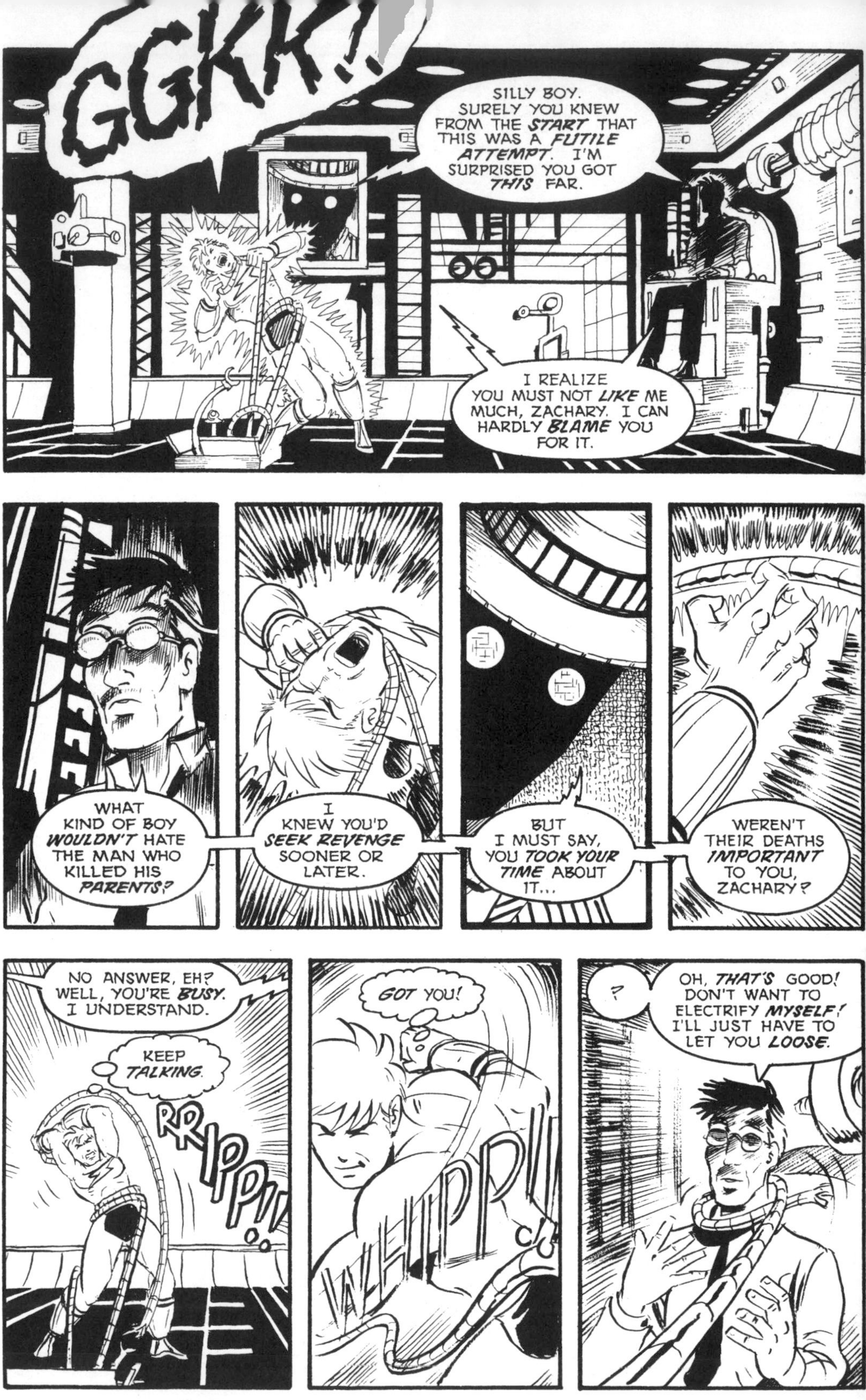
GGKK!!
SILLY BOY. SURELY YOU KNEW FROM THE START THAT THIS WAS A FUTILE ATTEMPT. I'M SURPRISED YOU GOT THIS FAR.
I REALIZE YOU MUST NOT LIKE ME MUCH, ZACHARY. I CAN HARDLY BLAME YOU FOR IT.
WHAT KIND OF BOY WOULDN'T HATE THE MAN WHO KILLED HIS PARENTS?
I KNEW YOU'D SEEK REVENGE SOONER OR LATER.
BUT I MUST SAY, YOU TOOK YOUR TIME ABOUT IT...
WEREN'T THEIR DEATHS IMPORTANT TO YOU, ZACHARY?
NO ANSWER, EH? WELL, YOU'RE BUSY. I UNDERSTAND.
KEEP TALKING.
RRIPPP!!
GOT YOU!
WHIPP!!
?
OH, THAT'S GOOD! DON'T WANT TO ELECTRIFY MYSELF! I'LL JUST HAVE TO LET YOU LOOSE.

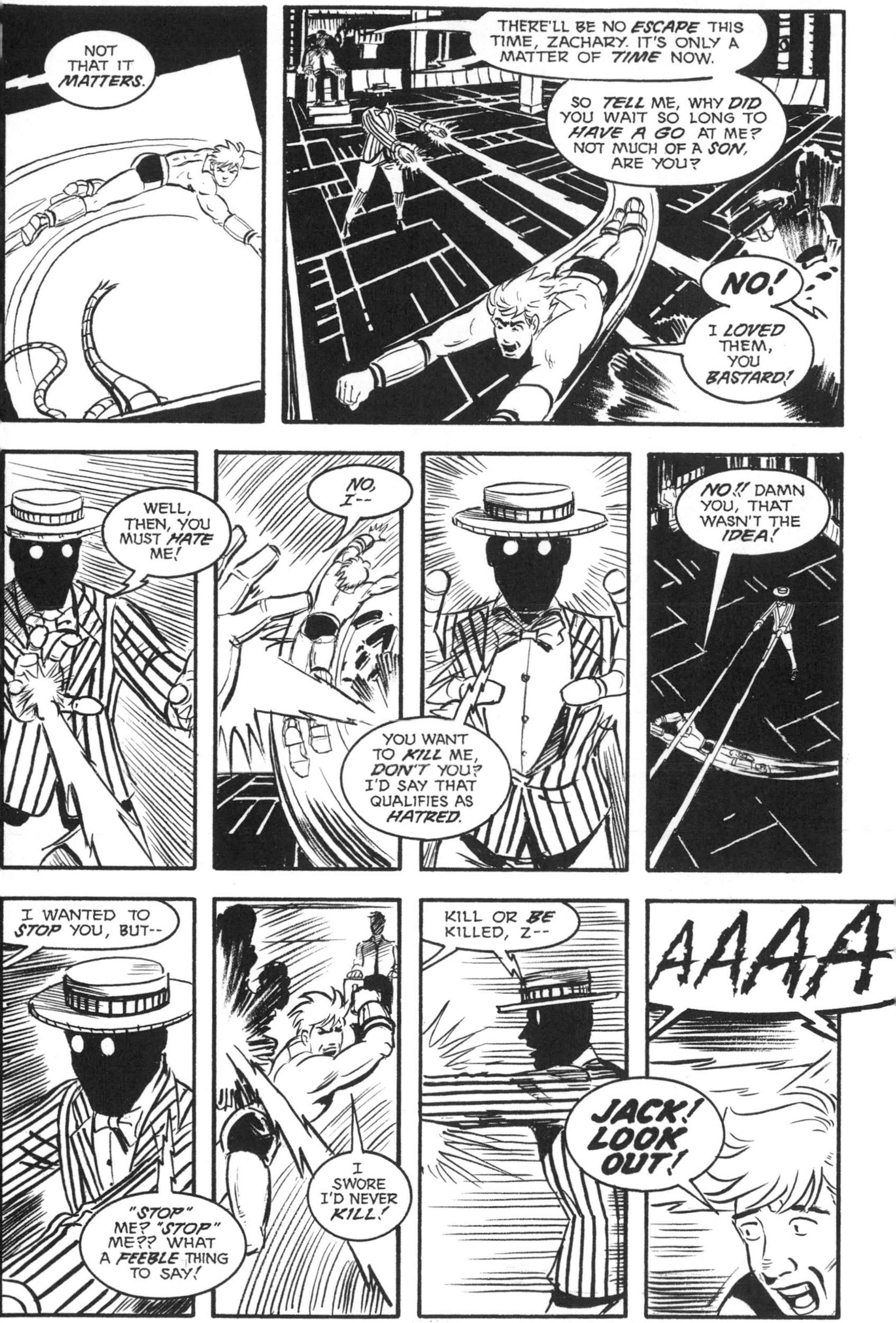
NOT THAT IT MATTERS.
THERE'LL BE NO ESCAPE THIS TIME, ZACHARY. IT'S ONLY A MATTER OF TIME NOW.
SO TELL ME, WHY DID YOU WAIT SO LONG TO HAVE A GO AT ME? NOT MUCH OF A SON, ARE YOU?
NO!
I LOVED THEM, YOU BASTARD!
WELL, THEN, YOU MUST HATE ME!
NO, I--
YOU WANT TO KILL ME, DON'T YOU? I'D SAY THAT QUALIFIES AS HATRED.
NO!! DAMN YOU, THAT WASN'T THE IDEA!
I WANTED TO STOP YOU, BUT--
"STOP" ME? "STOP" ME?? WHAT A FEEBLE THING TO SAY!
I SWORE I'D NEVER KILL!
KILL OR BE KILLED, Z--
AAAA
JACK! LOOK OUT!

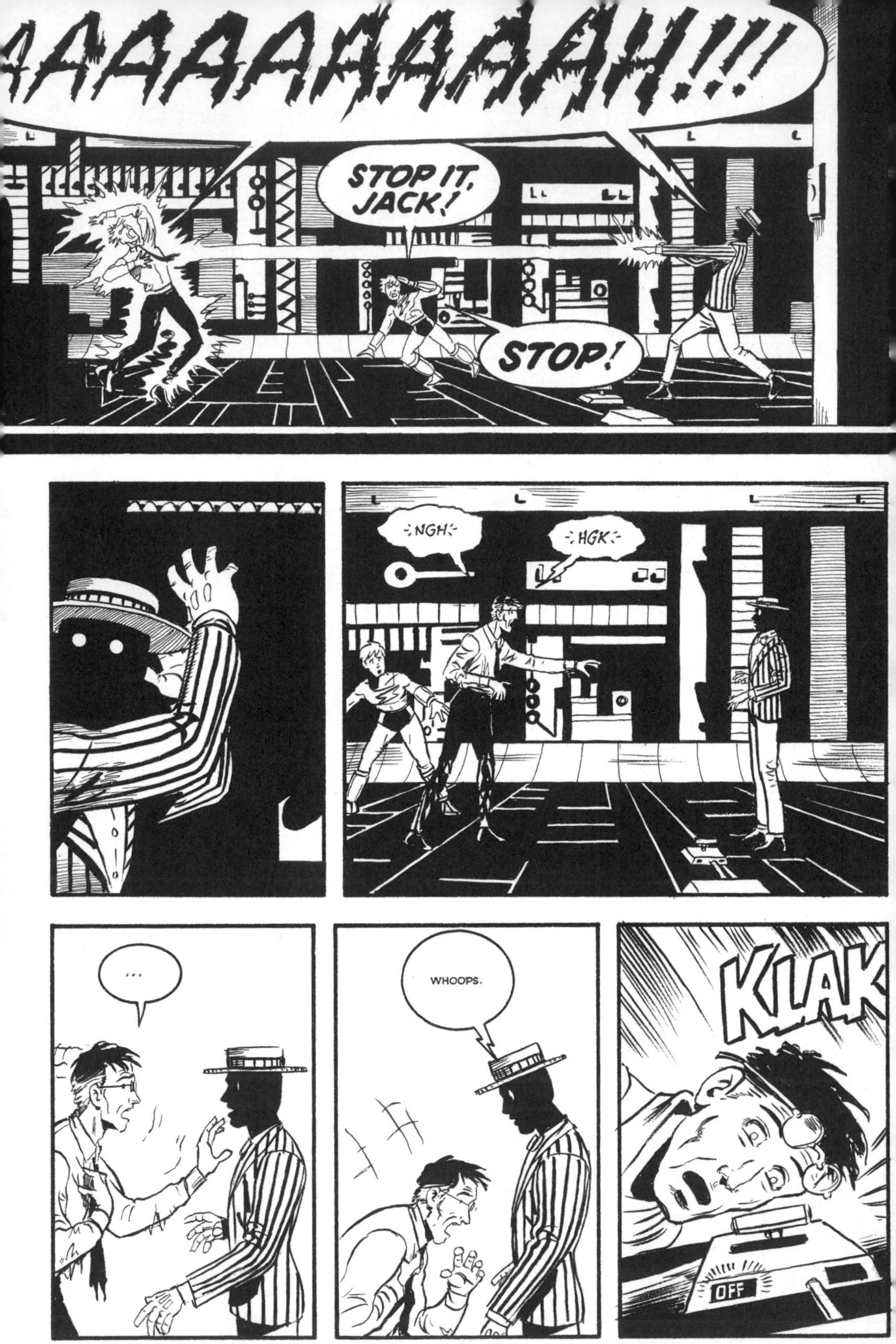
AAAAAAAAAAH!!!
STOP IT, JACK!
STOP!
NGH
HGK
...
WHOOPS.
KLAK
OFF

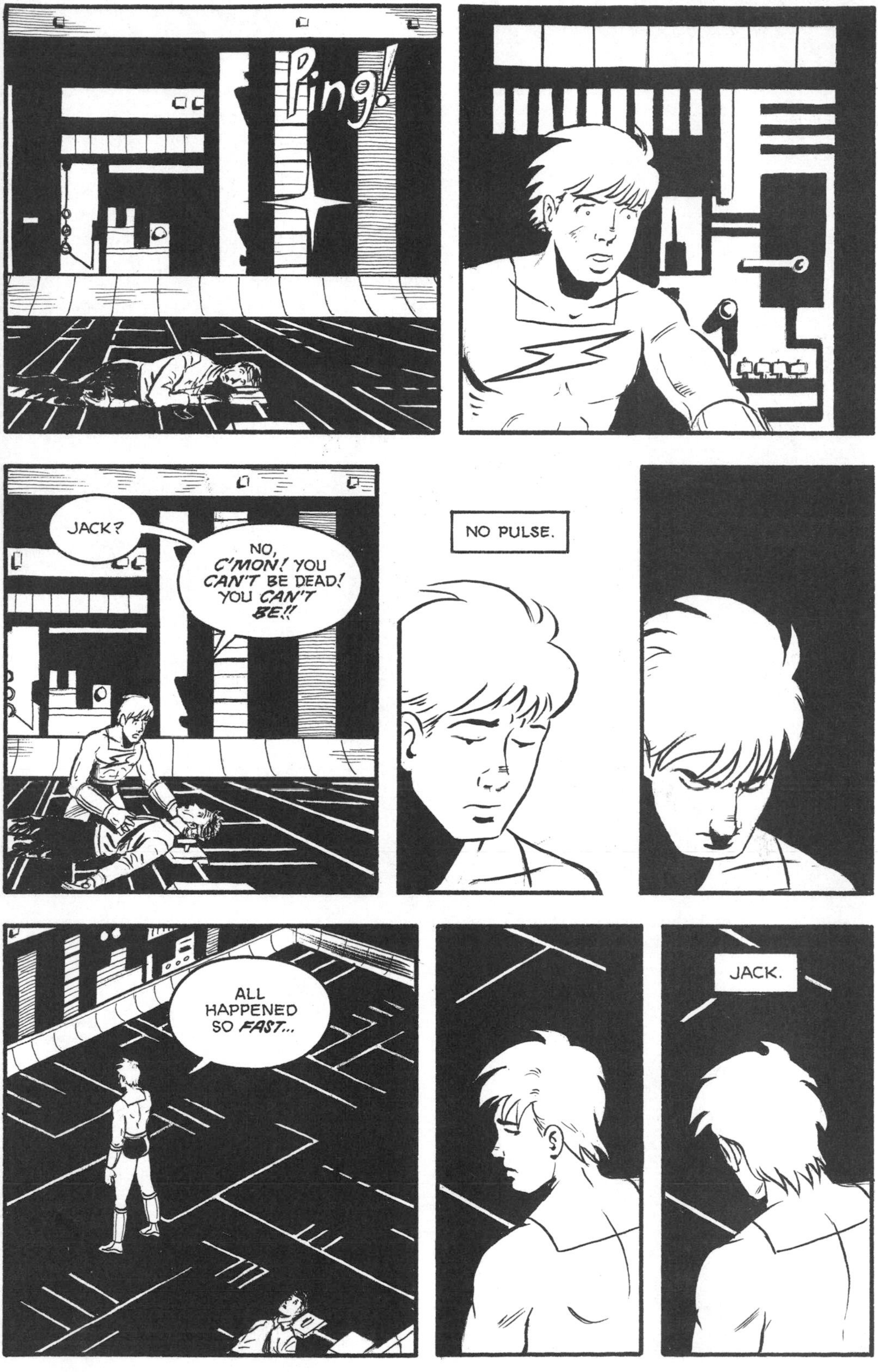
Ping!
JACK?
NO, C'MON! YOU CAN'T BE DEAD! YOU CAN'T BE!!
NO PULSE.
ALL HAPPENED SO FAST...
JACK.

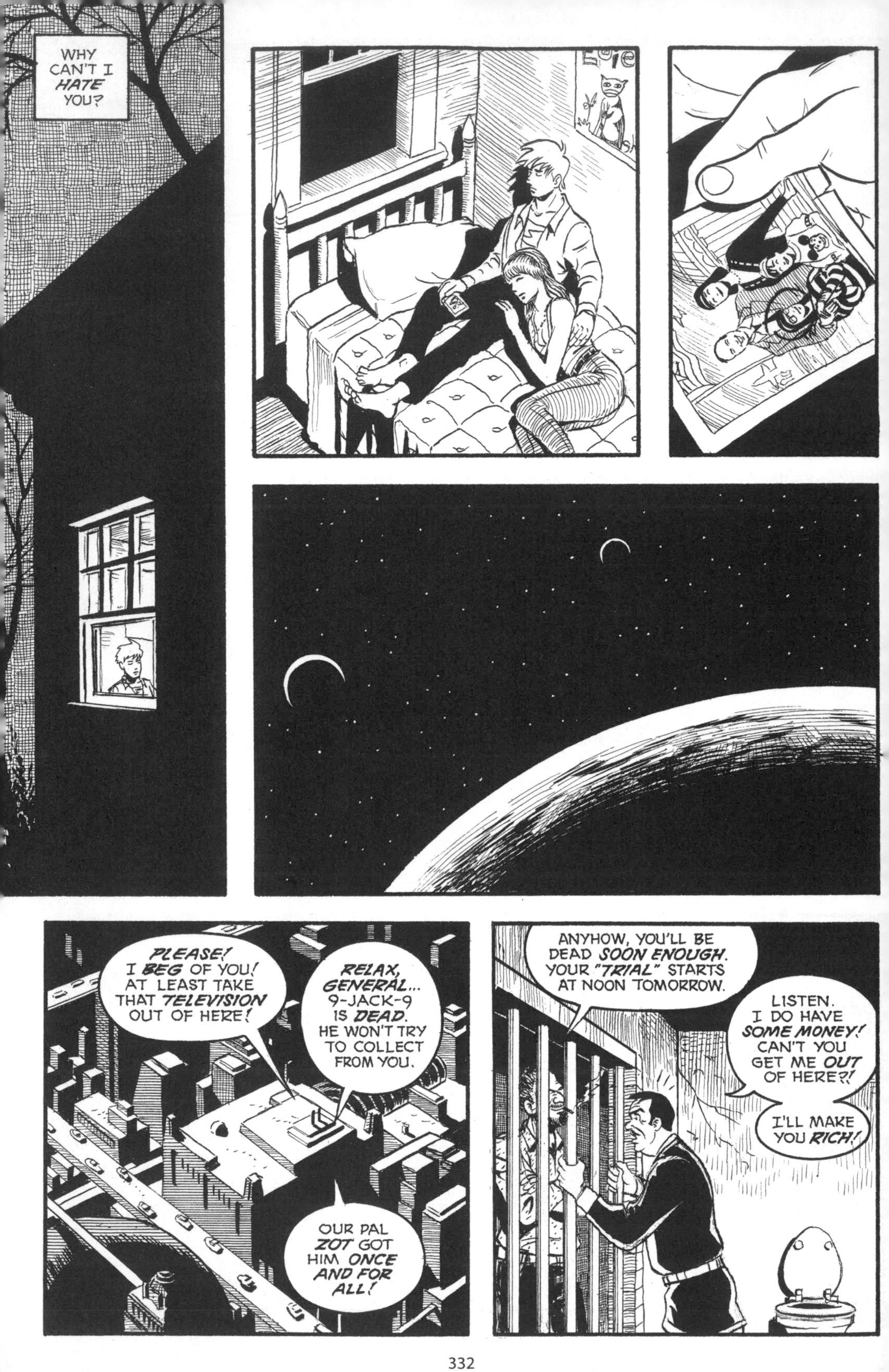
WHY CAN'T I HATE YOU?
PLEASE! I BEG OF YOU! AT LEAST TAKE THAT TELEVISION OUT OF HERE!
RELAX, GENERAL... 9-JACK-9 IS DEAD. HE WON'T TRY TO COLLECT FROM YOU.
OUR PAL ZOT GOT HIM ONCE AND FOR ALL!
ANYHOW, YOU'LL BE DEAD SOON ENOUGH. YOUR "TRIAL" STARTS AT NOON TOMORROW.
LISTEN. I DO HAVE SOME MONEY! CAN'T YOU GET ME OUT OF HERE?!
I'LL MAKE YOU RICH!

BUDDY, YOU DON'T HAVE A *THING.*

HA! HA! HA!

:HMF: *BARBARIANS.*

MIGHT AS WELL GET SOME *SLEEP...* PROBABLY MY *LAST CHANCE...*

DAMN *COT...* WHOLE PLACE STINKS... WORSE THAN A *MEAT PACKING PLANT DURING SUMMER...*

ZZZZZZZ...

HARRY, WAKE UP.

WHW? MRSHMRM!

HARRY, YOU DOLT, IT'S ME! WAKE UP!

HNH?

:Gasp!:

JACK! BUT YOU-- THEY SAID YOU WERE *DEAD!*

I *AM* DEAD, HARRY. DEAD AS A *DOORNAIL,* I'M AFRAID.

EVEN STAYED TO SEE THEM ZIP UP THE *BODY BAG.*

APPARENTLY THIS *ELECTRIC STAMP* UPON THE *ETHER* WAS A BIT MORE *PERMANENT* THAN MY *HUMAN SHELL.*

EVEN WITHOUT ITS *OPERATOR,* THE MATRIX KNOWN AS JACK *REMAINS.*

YOU'VE COME TO BE P-PAID, H-HAVEN'T YOU? JACK, I--I--

OH, *RELAX,* HARRY. I WON'T *HURT* YOU.

I WOULDN'T TRY TO *COLLECT* FOR A JOB I FAILED TO *COMPLETE.*

NO, I JUST CAME TO SAY HELLO.

I...UH...DON'T HAVE A LOT OF *FRIENDS,* HARRY...

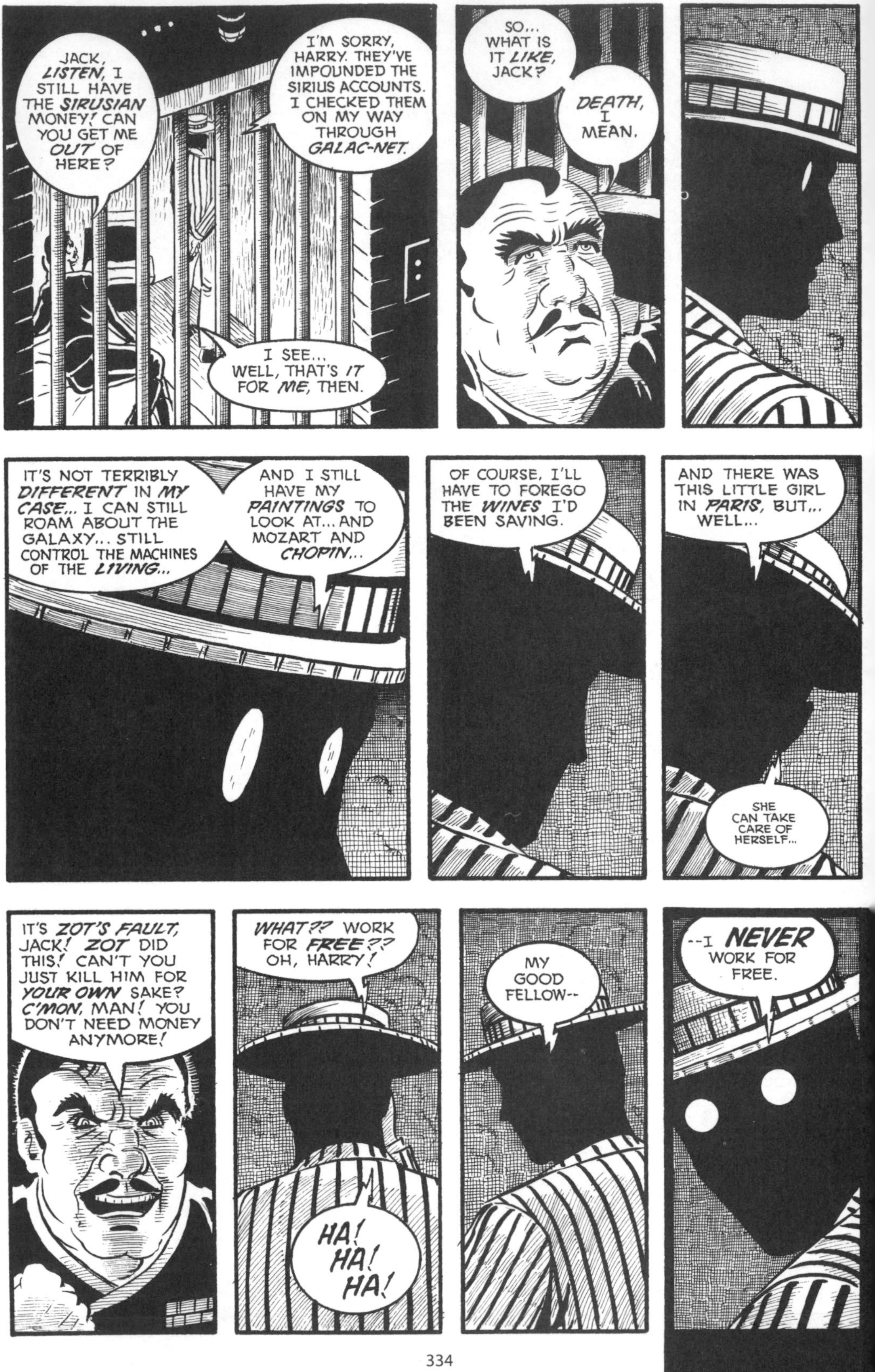
JACK, LISTEN, I STILL HAVE THE SIRUSIAN MONEY! CAN YOU GET ME OUT OF HERE?
I'M SORRY, HARRY. THEY'VE IMPOUNDED THE SIRIUS ACCOUNTS. I CHECKED THEM ON MY WAY THROUGH GALAC-NET.
I SEE... WELL, THAT'S IT FOR ME, THEN.
SO... WHAT IS IT LIKE, JACK?
DEATH, I MEAN.
IT'S NOT TERRIBLY DIFFERENT IN MY CASE... I CAN STILL ROAM ABOUT THE GALAXY... STILL CONTROL THE MACHINES OF THE LIVING...
AND I STILL HAVE MY PAINTINGS TO LOOK AT... AND MOZART AND CHOPIN...
OF COURSE, I'LL HAVE TO FOREGO THE WINES I'D BEEN SAVING.
AND THERE WAS THIS LITTLE GIRL IN PARIS, BUT... WELL...
SHE CAN TAKE CARE OF HERSELF...
IT'S ZOT'S FAULT, JACK! ZOT DID THIS! CAN'T YOU JUST KILL HIM FOR YOUR OWN SAKE? C'MON, MAN! YOU DON'T NEED MONEY ANYMORE!
WHAT?? WORK FOR FREE?? OH, HARRY!
HA! HA! HA!
MY GOOD FELLOW--
--I NEVER WORK FOR FREE.

Of all the *Zot!* stories, this is probably the darkest. Every major villain I created for the series represented a different potential future, and the level of credibility I assigned to that future determined the gravity of the character. 9-Jack-9 represented the most credible of all those futures—the very real possibility that technology, for all its benefits, would eventually do us all in.

Zot's unbeatable optimism referenced in issue #12 falls apart in one catastrophic, irreversible failure—this time on Zot's side of the portal. Unfortunately, to get the effect I was going for, I had to muddle the contrasts between Zot's universe and ours. That "ideal world" would never look quite the same again.

Jack also represented the bland apathy of death: the idea that death is simply going about its business, noticing you briefly when it's your time, forgetting you ever existed a moment later.

When I was a little kid, I used to watch old monster movies in the basement on our old black and white television set. One of them, a little Danish gem called *Reptilicus,* had a scene where the giant reptile tore the roof off a house in which a family had just sat down to dinner and ate one of the family members. Later, the hero sacrifices himself to defeat Reptilicus. It struck me at the time that I felt real compassion for the family, but very little for the hero. The hero's story had meaning, an audience, mourners and friends giving speeches, but that poor family was just sitting down to dinner. It wasn't even their story! Their loved one's death was meaningless and random and thus more disturbing.

When Suzy dies, it may have been less than random (and she certainly didn't go unmourned), but I wanted to capture at least a hint of that creepy feeling I got as a little kid, watching old monster movies in the basement and contemplating a violent, random, morally neutral universe for the first time.

A lot of readers couldn't buy the way Sir John Sheers (Get it? Get it? Mr. Subtlety, that's me!) was allowed to hang out in Max's company for so long, even though Max knew he was really Jack all along. His comment that Sir John was "a fairly nice fellow all things considered" certainly raised a few hackles. It's a weird bit, I'll admit. I think I understand where Max is coming from, but I'm not sure I could explain it to anyone else. Both Max and Zot are nonjudgmental in their dealings with others, but at times, like in this story, that quality may be hard to relate to.

Zot! officially went "monthly" with this story's first issue (#23), but I stumbled over my new deadlines almost immediately, despite cutting the page count from 24 to 18. Deadlines were always a problem for me and a prime source of our money troubles. It didn't help that my pages kept getting denser and more detailed. The splash page for this story took forever!

In Comics History: It was while working on the beginning of this story that I wrote the first draft of the *Bill of Rights for Comics Creators,* which I discuss in greater detail on scottmccloud.com and in my second book, *Reinventing Comics* (2000).

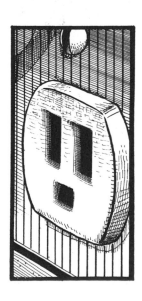

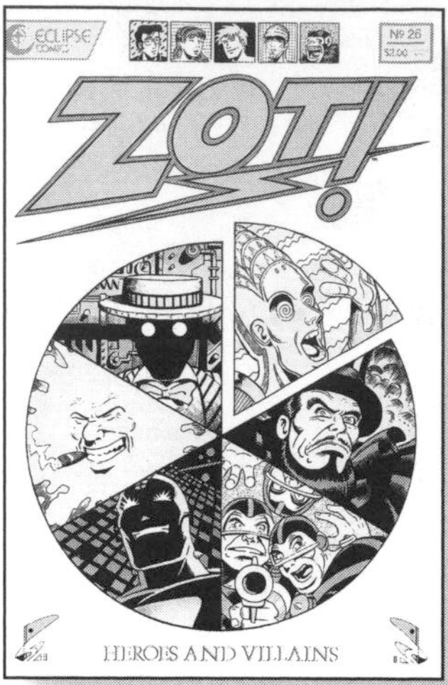
ECLIPSE COMICS
Nº 26
$2.00
ZOT!
HEROES AND VILLAINS

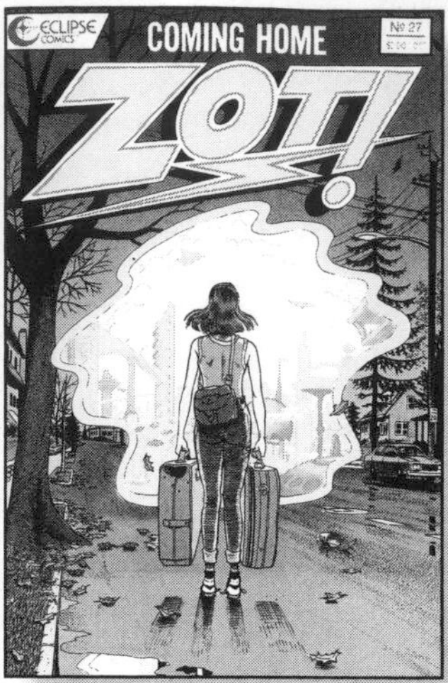
ECLIPSE COMICS
COMING HOME
Nº 27
ZOT!

Ring in the New

First published in *Zot! #26–27*.

Lettering:

Bob Lappan

Original series editor:

cat yronwode

Plot assist:

Ivy Ratafia

Note: For over three years prior to this issue, there'd been a contest in the letters page to see which character readers would most enjoy seeing hit in the face with a pie. This odd little "story" is the result.

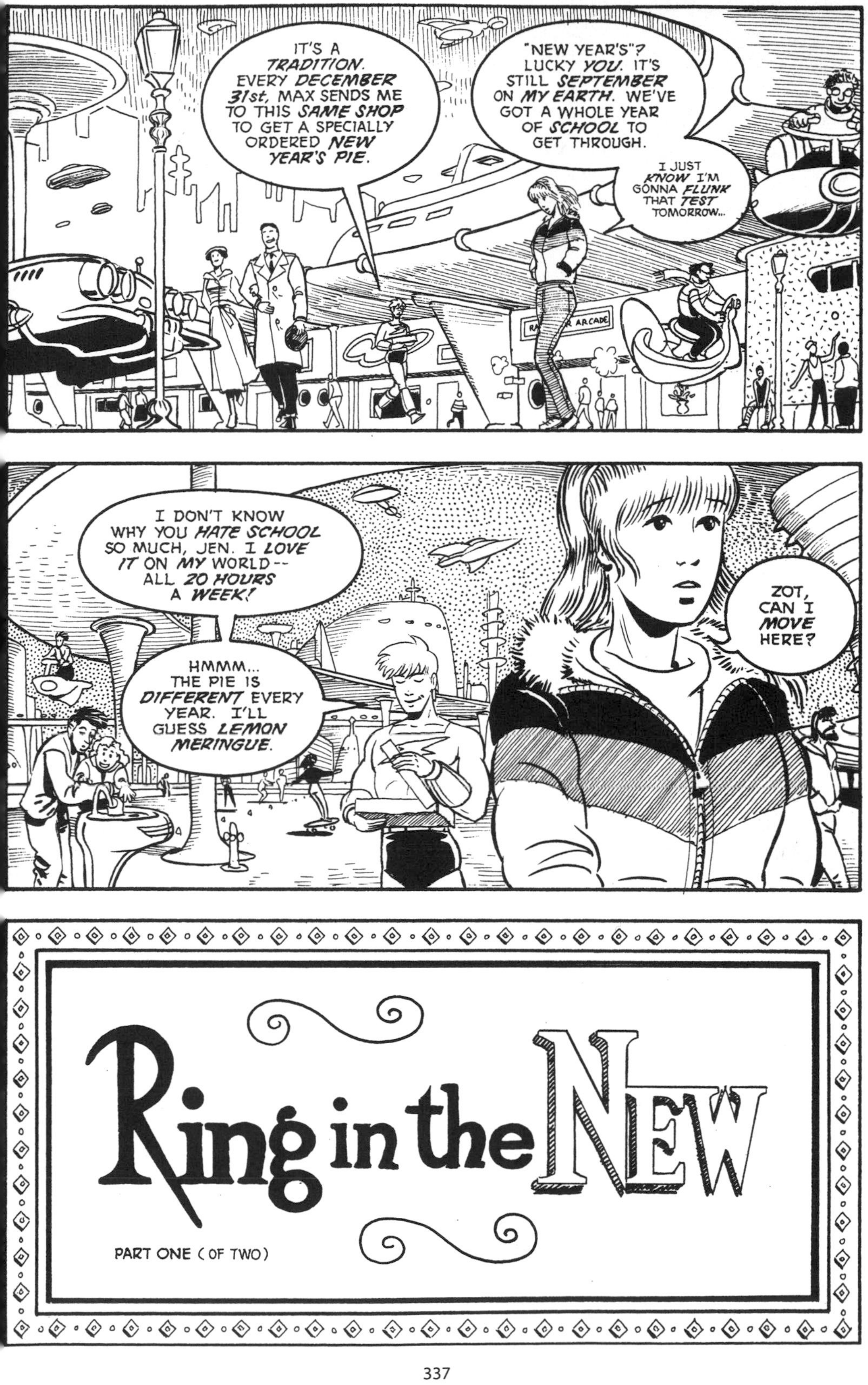
IT'S A TRADITION. EVERY DECEMBER 31st, MAX SENDS ME TO THIS SAME SHOP TO GET A SPECIALLY ORDERED NEW YEAR'S PIE.
"NEW YEAR'S"? LUCKY YOU. IT'S STILL SEPTEMBER ON MY EARTH. WE'VE GOT A WHOLE YEAR OF SCHOOL TO GET THROUGH.
I JUST KNOW I'M GONNA FLUNK THAT TEST TOMORROW...
I DON'T KNOW WHY YOU HATE SCHOOL SO MUCH, JEN. I LOVE IT ON MY WORLD-- ALL 20 HOURS A WEEK!
HMMM... THE PIE IS DIFFERENT EVERY YEAR. I'LL GUESS LEMON MERINGUE.
ZOT, CAN I MOVE HERE?

Ring in the NEW

PART ONE (OF TWO)

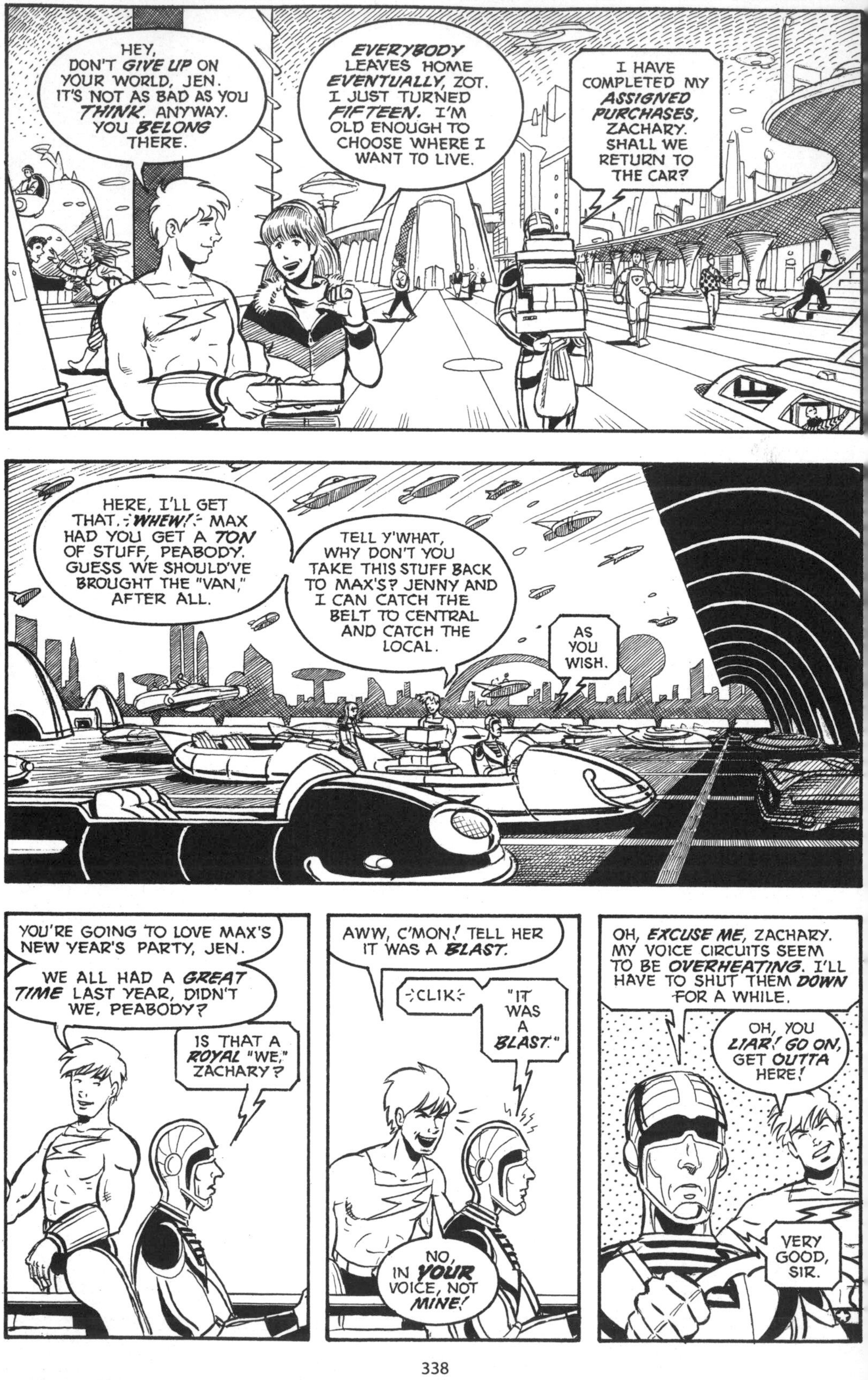
HEY, DON'T GIVE UP ON YOUR WORLD, JEN. IT'S NOT AS BAD AS YOU THINK. ANYWAY. YOU BELONG THERE.
EVERYBODY LEAVES HOME EVENTUALLY, ZOT. I JUST TURNED FIFTEEN. I'M OLD ENOUGH TO CHOOSE WHERE I WANT TO LIVE.
I HAVE COMPLETED MY ASSIGNED PURCHASES, ZACHARY. SHALL WE RETURN TO THE CAR?
HERE, I'LL GET THAT. -WHEW!- MAX HAD YOU GET A TON OF STUFF, PEABODY. GUESS WE SHOULD'VE BROUGHT THE "VAN," AFTER ALL.
TELL Y'WHAT, WHY DON'T YOU TAKE THIS STUFF BACK TO MAX'S? JENNY AND I CAN CATCH THE BELT TO CENTRAL AND CATCH THE LOCAL.
AS YOU WISH.
YOU'RE GOING TO LOVE MAX'S NEW YEAR'S PARTY, JEN.
WE ALL HAD A GREAT TIME LAST YEAR, DIDN'T WE, PEABODY?
IS THAT A ROYAL "WE," ZACHARY?
AWW, C'MON! TELL HER IT WAS A BLAST.
-CLIK-
"IT WAS A BLAST."
NO, IN YOUR VOICE, NOT MINE!
OH, EXCUSE ME, ZACHARY. MY VOICE CIRCUITS SEEM TO BE OVERHEATING. I'LL HAVE TO SHUT THEM DOWN FOR A WHILE.
OH, YOU LIAR! GO ON, GET OUTTA HERE!
VERY GOOD, SIR.

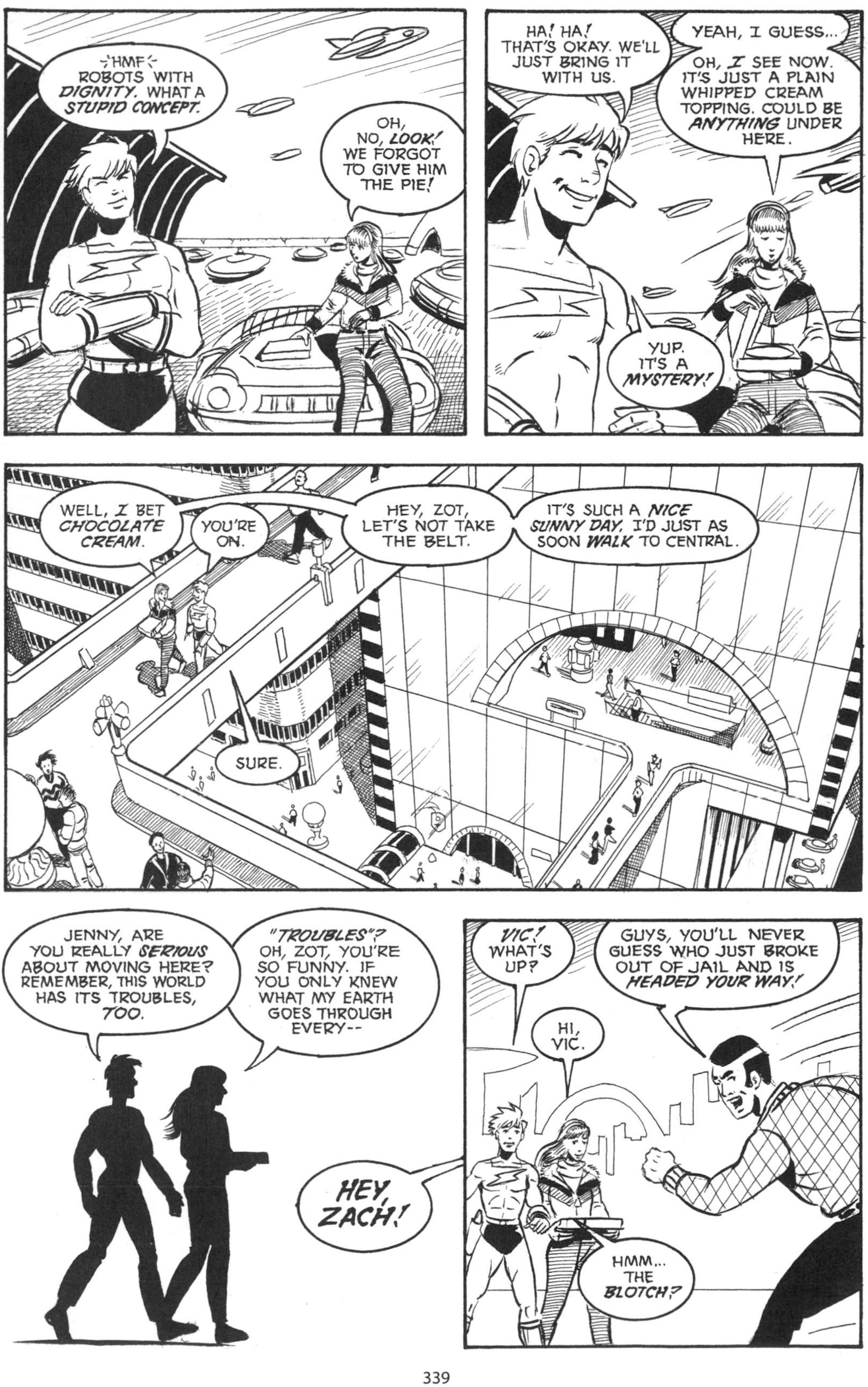

HMF
ROBOTS WITH DIGNITY. WHAT A STUPID CONCEPT.
OH, NO, LOOK! WE FORGOT TO GIVE HIM THE PIE!
HA! HA! THAT'S OKAY. WE'LL JUST BRING IT WITH US.
YEAH, I GUESS...
OH, I SEE NOW. IT'S JUST A PLAIN WHIPPED CREAM TOPPING. COULD BE ANYTHING UNDER HERE.
YUP. IT'S A MYSTERY!
WELL, I BET CHOCOLATE CREAM.
YOU'RE ON.
HEY, ZOT, LET'S NOT TAKE THE BELT.
IT'S SUCH A NICE SUNNY DAY, I'D JUST AS SOON WALK TO CENTRAL.
SURE.
JENNY, ARE YOU REALLY SERIOUS ABOUT MOVING HERE? REMEMBER, THIS WORLD HAS ITS TROUBLES, TOO.
"TROUBLES"? OH, ZOT, YOU'RE SO FUNNY. IF YOU ONLY KNEW WHAT MY EARTH GOES THROUGH EVERY--
HEY, ZACH!
VIC! WHAT'S UP?
HI, VIC.
GUYS, YOU'LL NEVER GUESS WHO JUST BROKE OUT OF JAIL AND IS HEADED YOUR WAY!
HMM... THE BLOTCH?

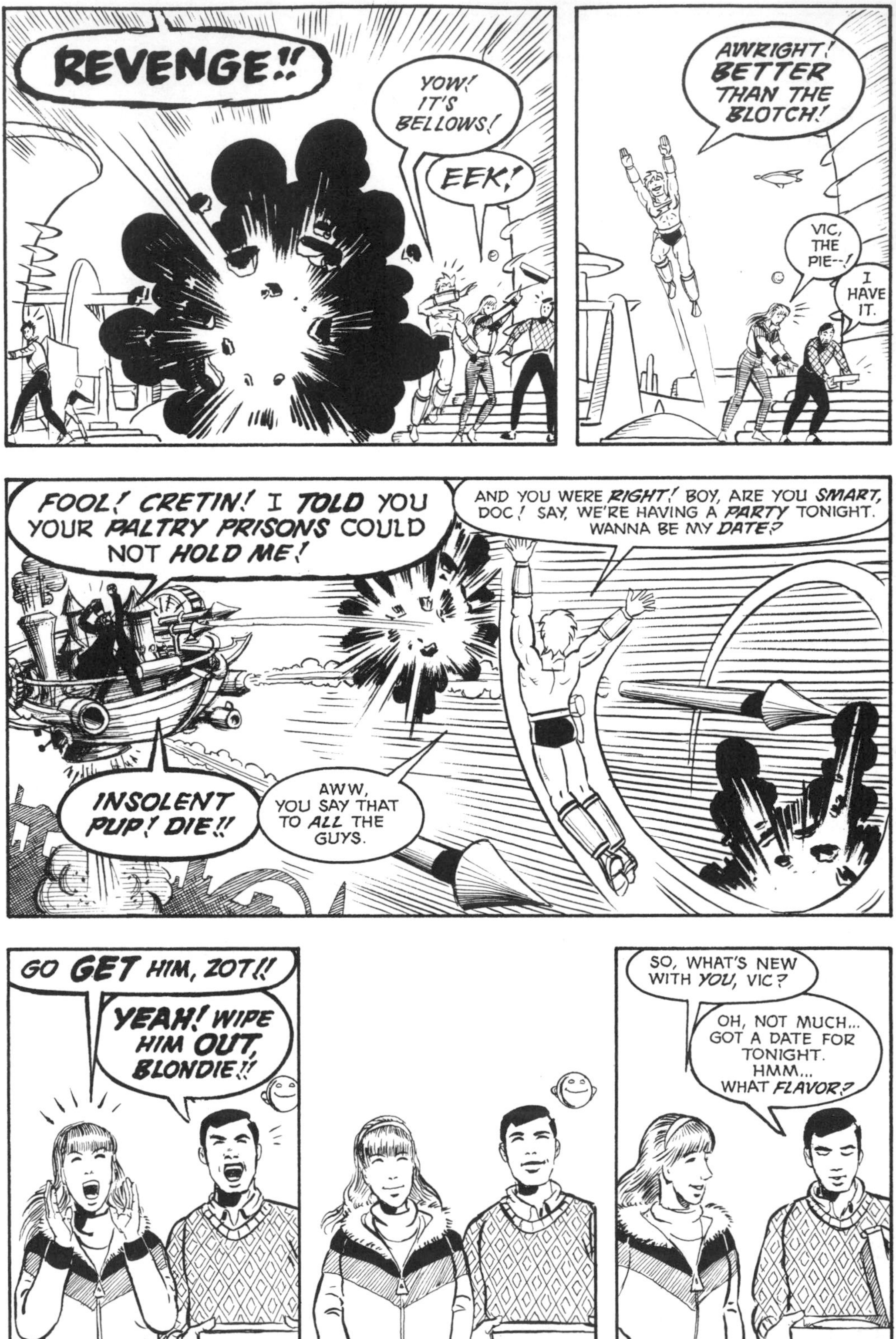
REVENGE!!
YOW! IT'S BELLOWS!
EEK!
AWRIGHT! BETTER THAN THE BLOTCH!
VIC, THE PIE--!
I HAVE IT.
FOOL! CRETIN! I TOLD YOU YOUR PALTRY PRISONS COULD NOT HOLD ME!
AND YOU WERE RIGHT! BOY, ARE YOU SMART, DOC! SAY, WE'RE HAVING A PARTY TONIGHT. WANNA BE MY DATE?
INSOLENT PUP! DIE!!
AWW, YOU SAY THAT TO ALL THE GUYS.
GO GET HIM, ZOT!!
YEAH! WIPE HIM OUT, BLONDIE!!
SO, WHAT'S NEW WITH YOU, VIC?
OH, NOT MUCH... GOT A DATE FOR TONIGHT. HMM... WHAT FLAVOR?

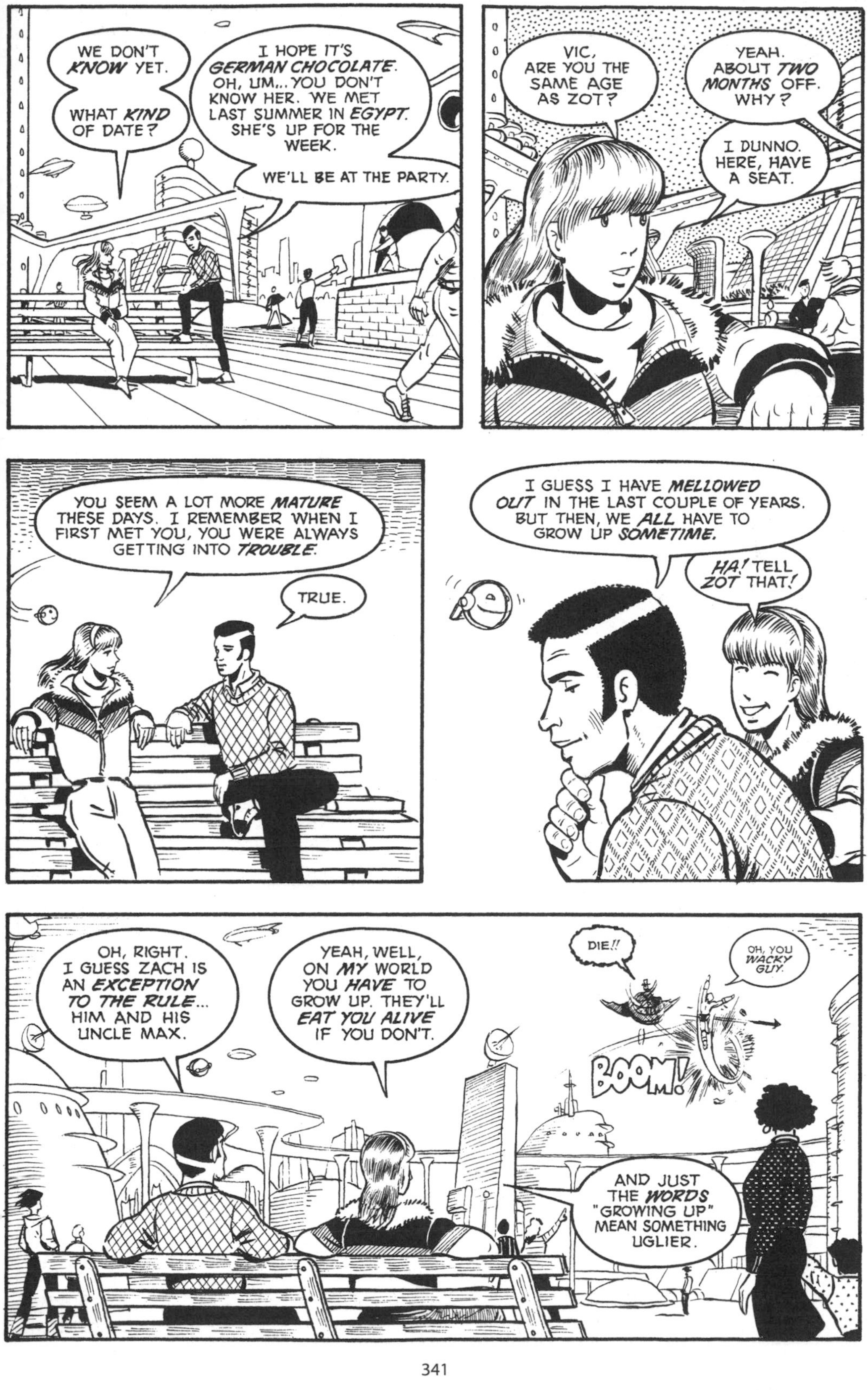
WE DON'T KNOW YET.
WHAT KIND OF DATE?
I HOPE IT'S GERMAN CHOCOLATE. OH, UM... YOU DON'T KNOW HER. WE MET LAST SUMMER IN EGYPT. SHE'S UP FOR THE WEEK.
WE'LL BE AT THE PARTY.
VIC, ARE YOU THE SAME AGE AS ZOT?
YEAH. ABOUT TWO MONTHS OFF. WHY?
I DUNNO. HERE, HAVE A SEAT.
YOU SEEM A LOT MORE MATURE THESE DAYS. I REMEMBER WHEN I FIRST MET YOU, YOU WERE ALWAYS GETTING INTO TROUBLE.
TRUE.
I GUESS I HAVE MELLOWED OUT IN THE LAST COUPLE OF YEARS. BUT THEN, WE ALL HAVE TO GROW UP SOMETIME.
HA! TELL ZOT THAT!
OH, RIGHT. I GUESS ZACH IS AN EXCEPTION TO THE RULE... HIM AND HIS UNCLE MAX.
YEAH, WELL, ON MY WORLD YOU HAVE TO GROW UP. THEY'LL EAT YOU ALIVE IF YOU DON'T.
DIE!!
OH, YOU WACKY GUY.
BOOM!
AND JUST THE WORDS "GROWING UP" MEAN SOMETHING UGLIER.

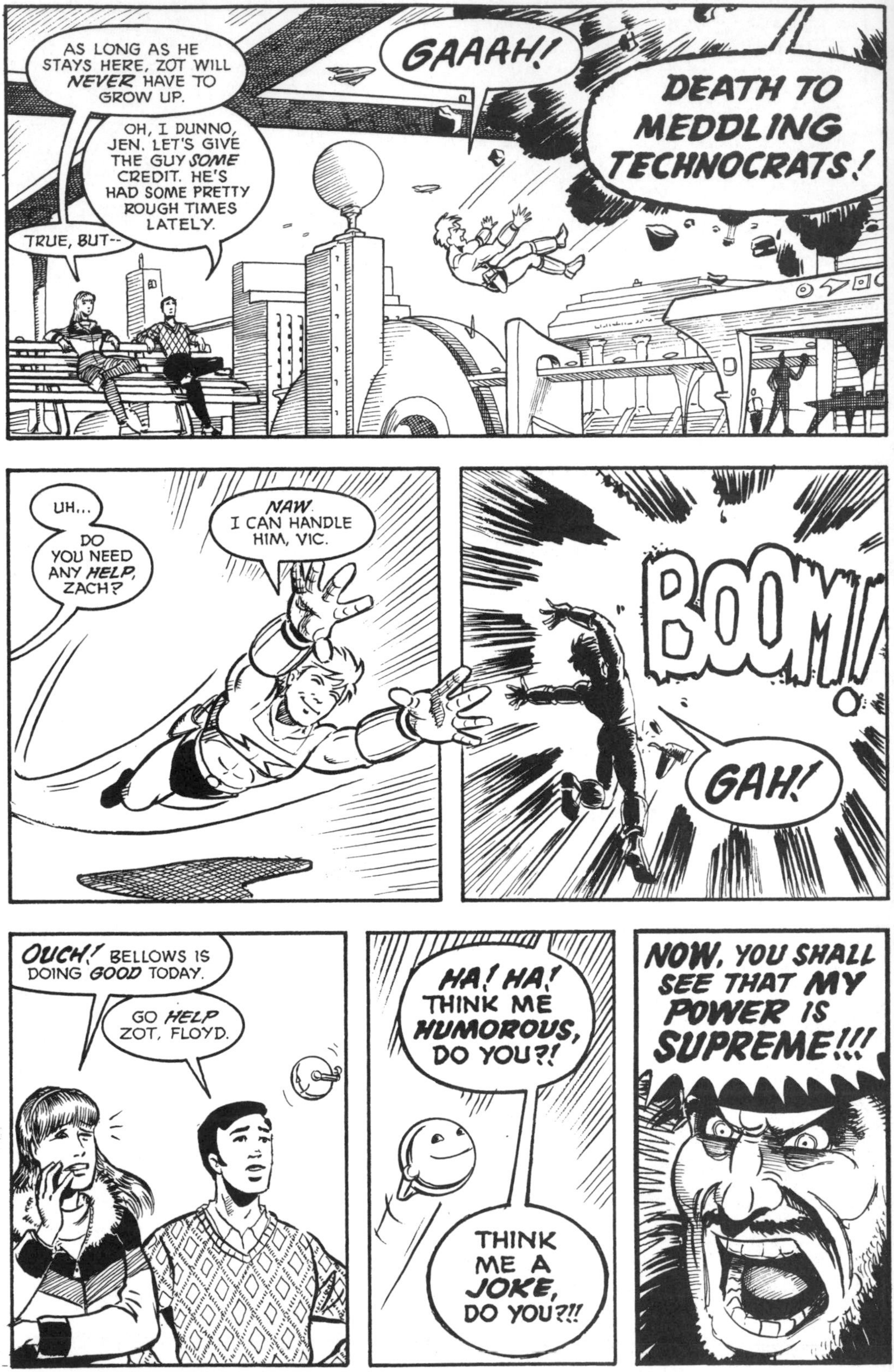

AS LONG AS HE STAYS HERE, ZOT WILL NEVER HAVE TO GROW UP.
OH, I DUNNO, JEN. LET'S GIVE THE GUY SOME CREDIT. HE'S HAD SOME PRETTY ROUGH TIMES LATELY.
TRUE, BUT--
GAAAH!
DEATH TO MEDDLING TECHNOCRATS!
UH...
DO YOU NEED ANY HELP, ZACH?
NAW. I CAN HANDLE HIM, VIC.
BOOM!
GAH!
OUCH! BELLOWS IS DOING GOOD TODAY.
GO HELP ZOT, FLOYD.
HA! HA! THINK ME HUMOROUS, DO YOU?!
THINK ME A JOKE, DO YOU?!!
NOW, YOU SHALL SEE THAT MY POWER IS SUPREME!!!

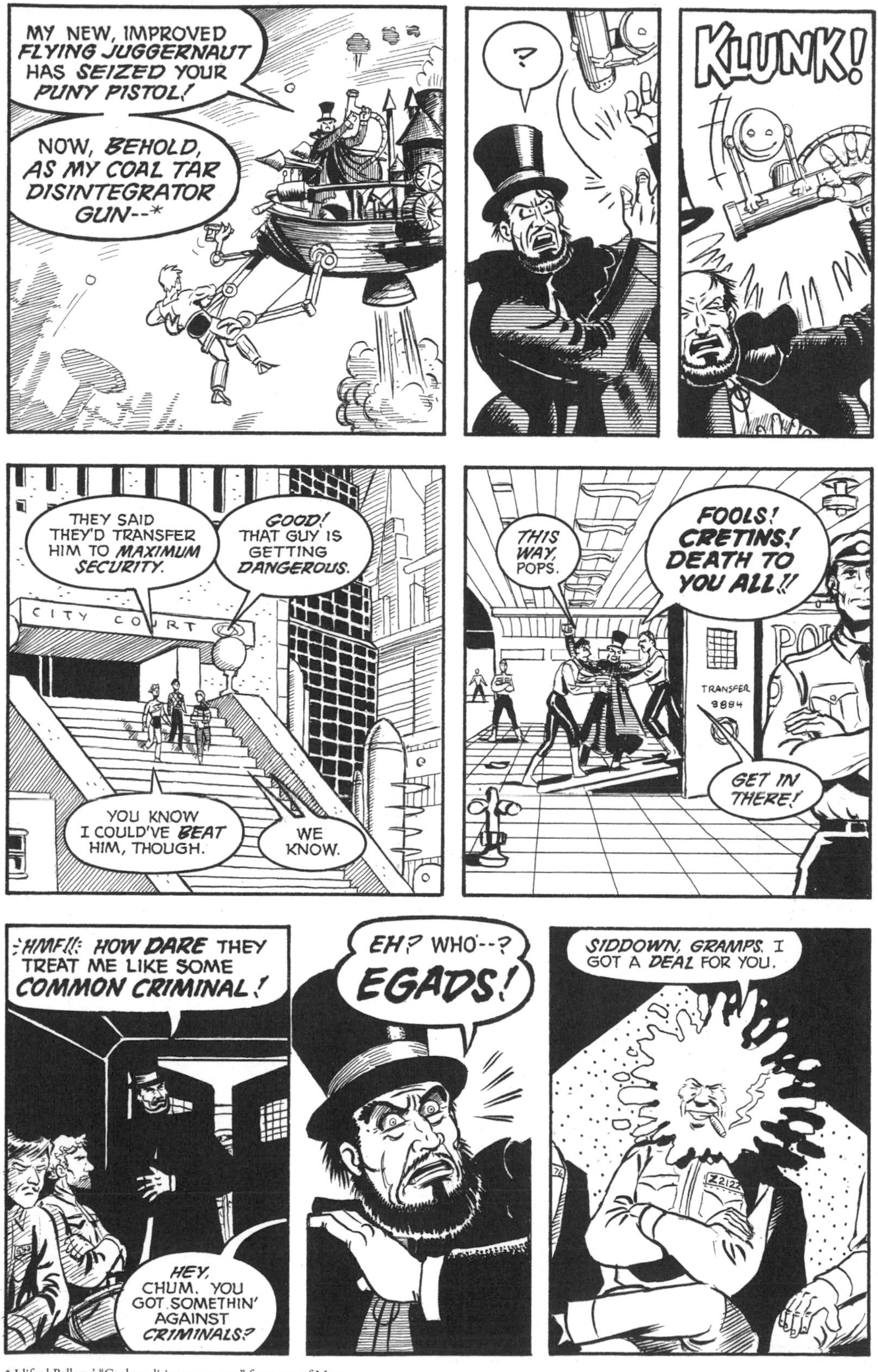
MY NEW, IMPROVED FLYING JUGGERNAUT HAS SEIZED YOUR PUNY PISTOL!
NOW, BEHOLD, AS MY COAL TAR DISINTEGRATOR GUN--*
?
KLUNK!
CITY COURT
THEY SAID THEY'D TRANSFER HIM TO MAXIMUM SECURITY.
GOOD! THAT GUY IS GETTING DANGEROUS.
YOU KNOW I COULD'VE BEAT HIM, THOUGH.
WE KNOW.
THIS WAY, POPS.
FOOLS! CRETINS! DEATH TO YOU ALL!!
TRANSFER 3884
GET IN THERE!
HMF!!! HOW DARE THEY TREAT ME LIKE SOME COMMON CRIMINAL!
HEY, CHUM. YOU GOT SOMETHIN' AGAINST CRIMINALS?
EH? WHO--? EGADS!
SIDDOWN, GRAMPS. I GOT A DEAL FOR YOU.
Z2122

* I lifted Bellows' "Coal tar disintegrator gun" from one of Matt Feazell's hilarious stick figure back-up stories in an earlier issue.

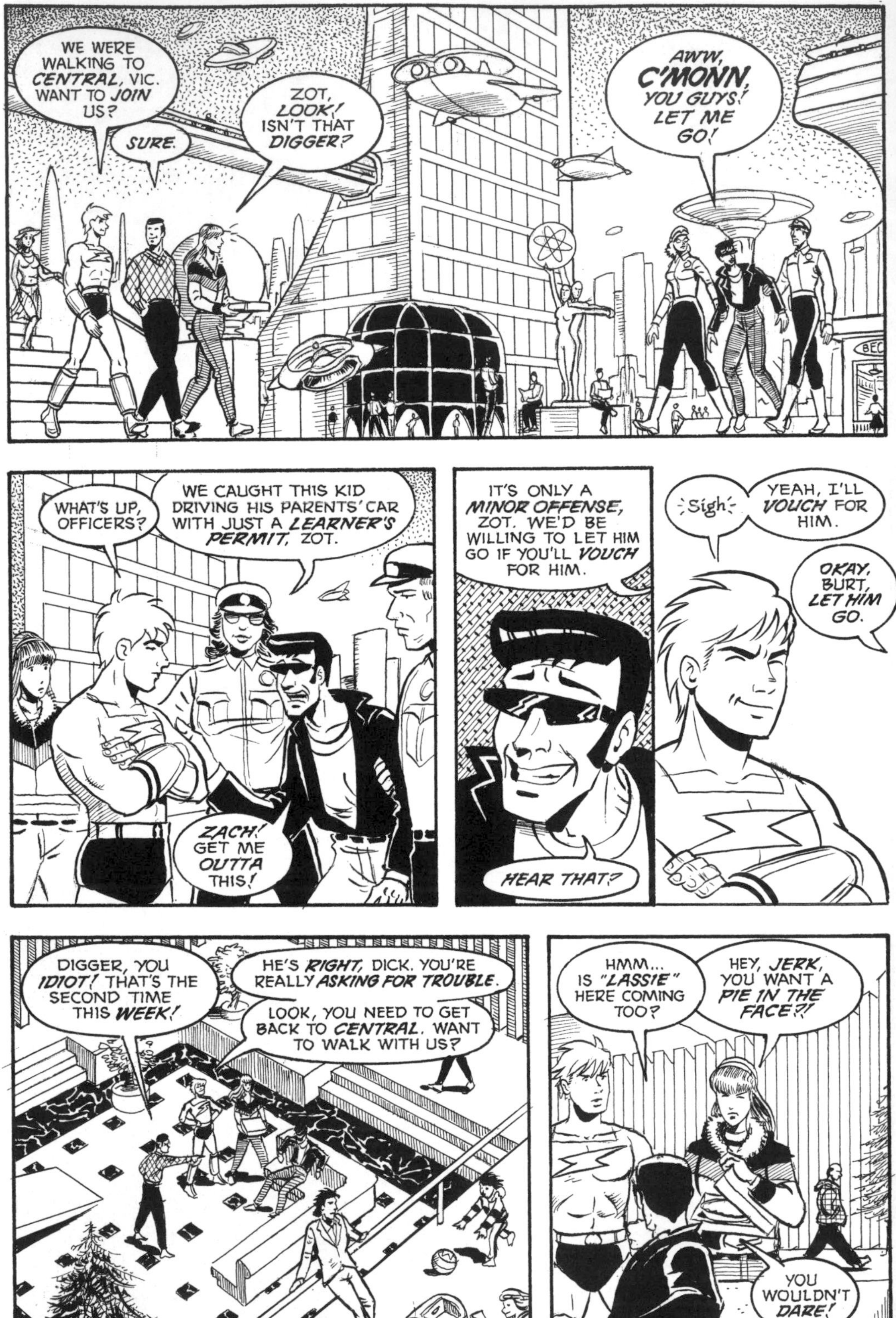
WE WERE WALKING TO CENTRAL, VIC. WANT TO JOIN US?
SURE.
ZOT, LOOK! ISN'T THAT DIGGER?
AWW, C'MONN, YOU GUYS! LET ME GO!
WHAT'S UP, OFFICERS?
WE CAUGHT THIS KID DRIVING HIS PARENTS' CAR WITH JUST A LEARNER'S PERMIT, ZOT.
ZACH! GET ME OUTTA THIS!
IT'S ONLY A MINOR OFFENSE, ZOT. WE'D BE WILLING TO LET HIM GO IF YOU'LL VOUCH FOR HIM.
HEAR THAT?
Sigh
YEAH, I'LL VOUCH FOR HIM.
OKAY, BURT, LET HIM GO.
DIGGER, YOU IDIOT! THAT'S THE SECOND TIME THIS WEEK!
HE'S RIGHT, DICK. YOU'RE REALLY ASKING FOR TROUBLE.
LOOK, YOU NEED TO GET BACK TO CENTRAL. WANT TO WALK WITH US?
HMM... IS "LASSIE" HERE COMING TOO?
HEY, JERK, YOU WANT A PIE IN THE FACE?!
YOU WOULDN'T DARE!

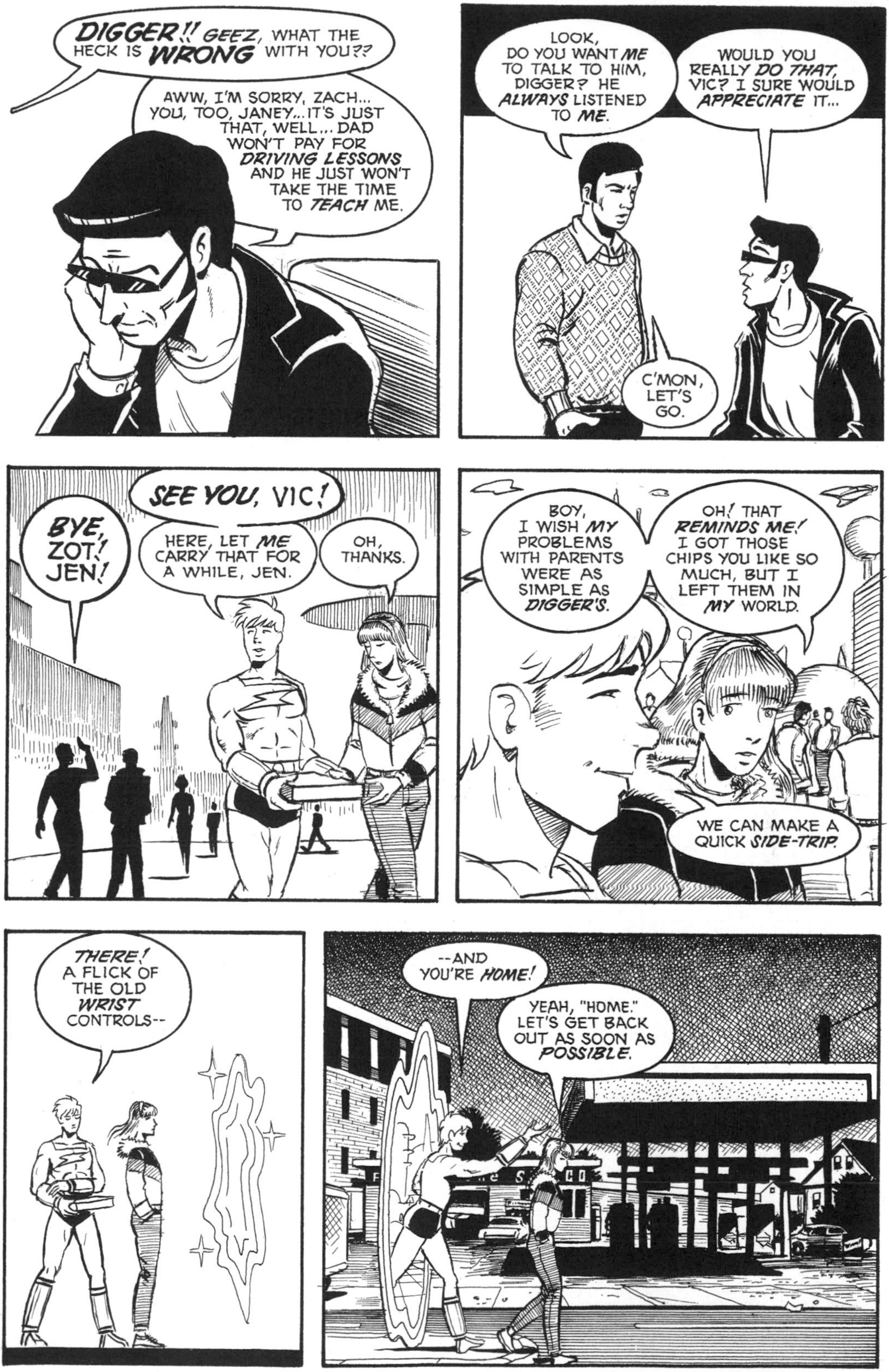
DIGGER!! GEEZ, WHAT THE HECK IS WRONG WITH YOU??
AWW, I'M SORRY, ZACH... YOU, TOO, JANEY... IT'S JUST THAT, WELL... DAD WON'T PAY FOR DRIVING LESSONS AND HE JUST WON'T TAKE THE TIME TO TEACH ME.
LOOK, DO YOU WANT ME TO TALK TO HIM, DIGGER? HE ALWAYS LISTENED TO ME.
WOULD YOU REALLY DO THAT, VIC? I SURE WOULD APPRECIATE IT...
C'MON, LET'S GO.
BYE, ZOT! JEN!
SEE YOU, VIC!
HERE, LET ME CARRY THAT FOR A WHILE, JEN.
OH, THANKS.
BOY, I WISH MY PROBLEMS WITH PARENTS WERE AS SIMPLE AS DIGGER'S.
OH! THAT REMINDS ME! I GOT THOSE CHIPS YOU LIKE SO MUCH, BUT I LEFT THEM IN MY WORLD.
WE CAN MAKE A QUICK SIDE-TRIP.
THERE! A FLICK OF THE OLD WRIST CONTROLS--
--AND YOU'RE HOME!
YEAH, "HOME." LET'S GET BACK OUT AS SOON AS POSSIBLE.

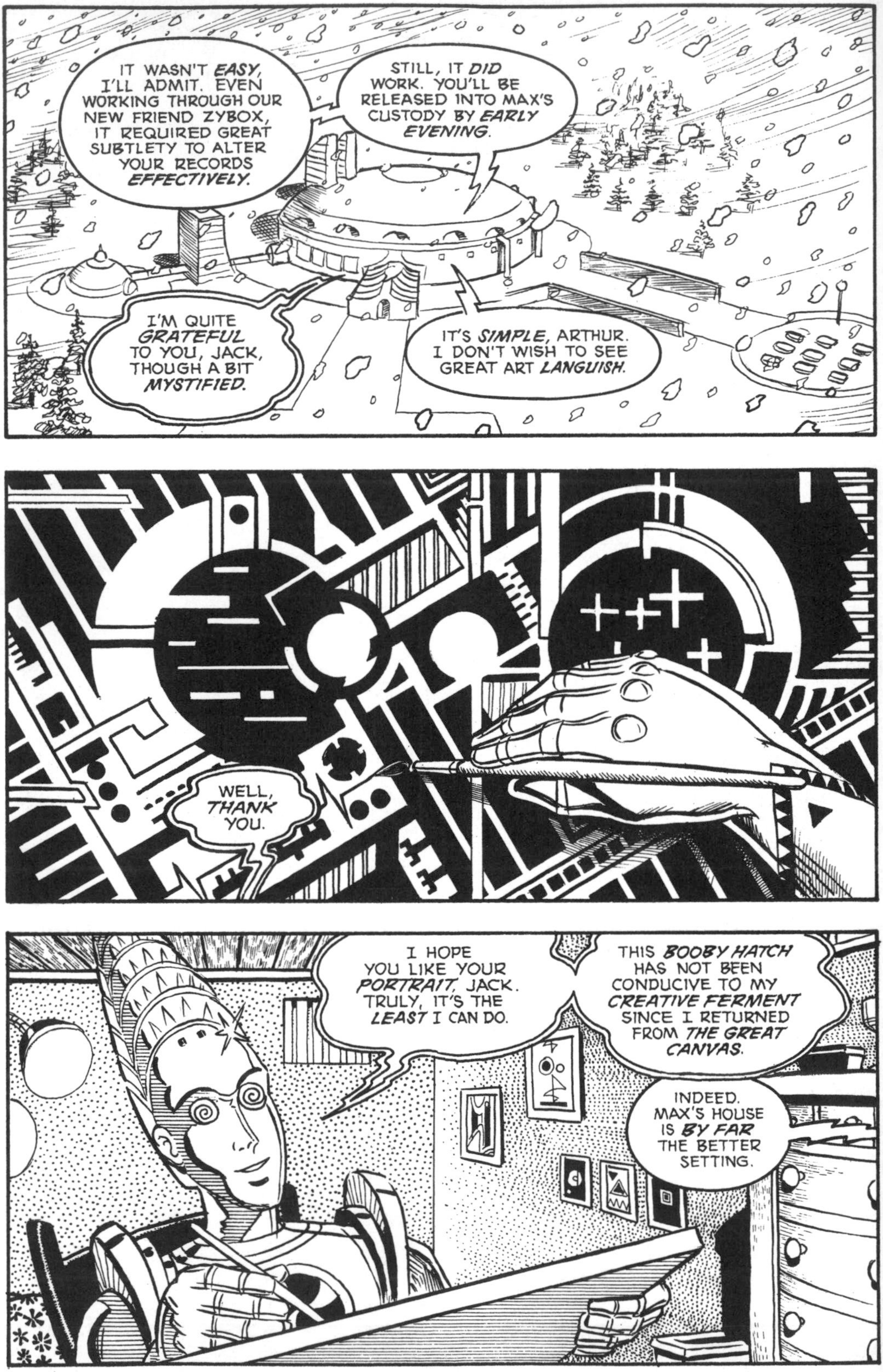
IT WASN'T *EASY*, I'LL ADMIT. EVEN WORKING THROUGH OUR NEW FRIEND ZYBOX, IT REQUIRED GREAT SUBTLETY TO ALTER YOUR RECORDS *EFFECTIVELY*.
STILL, IT *DID* WORK. YOU'LL BE RELEASED INTO MAX'S CUSTODY BY *EARLY EVENING*.
I'M QUITE *GRATEFUL* TO YOU, JACK, THOUGH A BIT *MYSTIFIED*.
IT'S *SIMPLE*, ARTHUR. I DON'T WISH TO SEE GREAT ART *LANGUISH*.
WELL, *THANK* YOU.
I HOPE YOU LIKE YOUR *PORTRAIT*, JACK. TRULY, IT'S THE *LEAST* I CAN DO.
THIS *BOOBY HATCH* HAS NOT BEEN CONDUCIVE TO MY *CREATIVE FERMENT* SINCE I RETURNED FROM *THE GREAT CANVAS*.
INDEED. MAX'S HOUSE IS *BY FAR* THE BETTER SETTING.

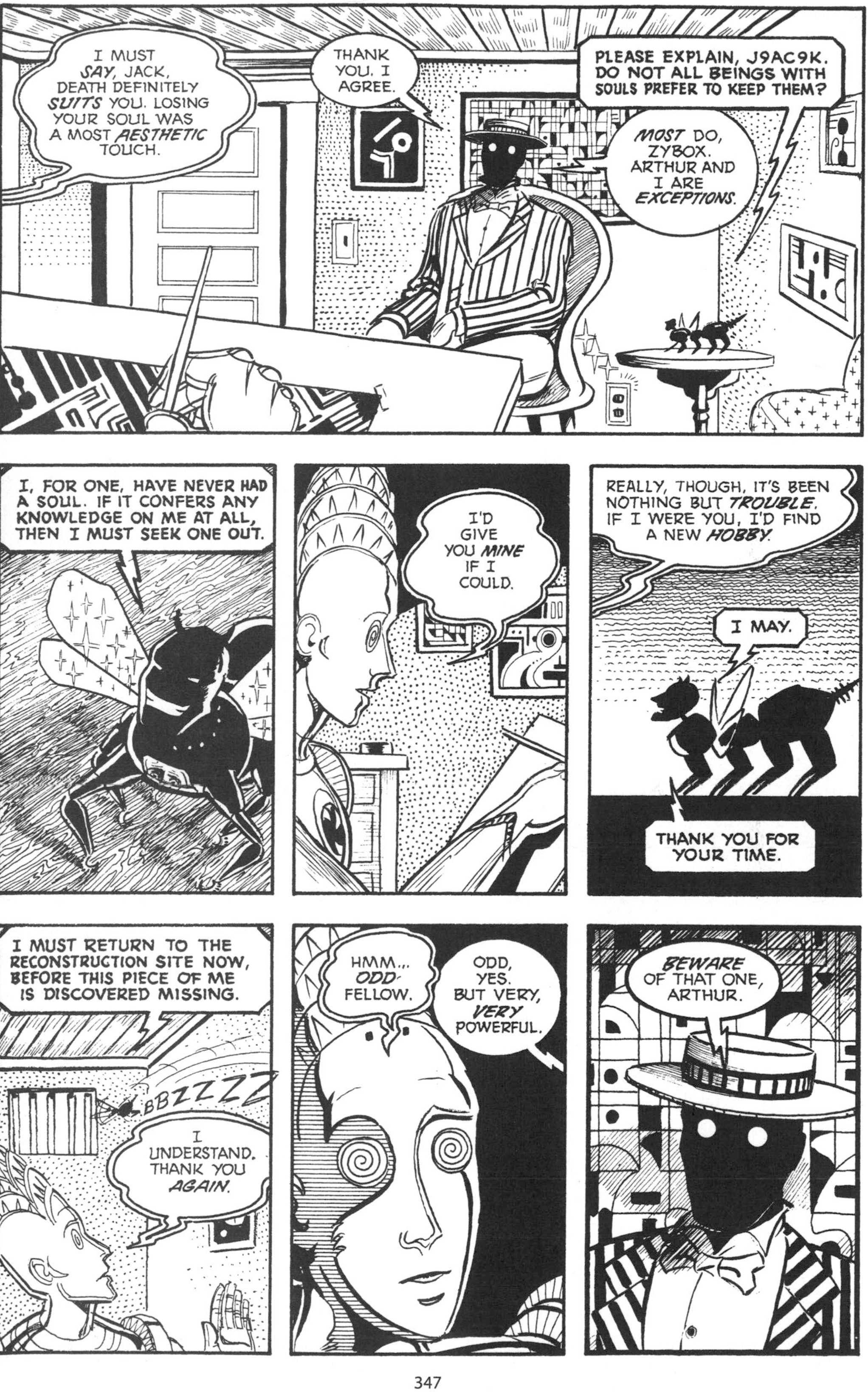
I MUST SAY, JACK, DEATH DEFINITELY SUITS YOU. LOSING YOUR SOUL WAS A MOST AESTHETIC TOUCH.
THANK YOU. I AGREE.
PLEASE EXPLAIN, J9AC9K. DO NOT ALL BEINGS WITH SOULS PREFER TO KEEP THEM?
MOST DO, ZYBOX. ARTHUR AND I ARE EXCEPTIONS.
I, FOR ONE, HAVE NEVER HAD A SOUL. IF IT CONFERS ANY KNOWLEDGE ON ME AT ALL, THEN I MUST SEEK ONE OUT.
I'D GIVE YOU MINE IF I COULD.
REALLY, THOUGH, IT'S BEEN NOTHING BUT TROUBLE. IF I WERE YOU, I'D FIND A NEW HOBBY.
I MAY.
THANK YOU FOR YOUR TIME.
I MUST RETURN TO THE RECONSTRUCTION SITE NOW, BEFORE THIS PIECE OF ME IS DISCOVERED MISSING.
BBZZZZ
I UNDERSTAND. THANK YOU AGAIN.
HMM... ODD FELLOW.
ODD, YES. BUT VERY, VERY POWERFUL.
BEWARE OF THAT ONE, ARTHUR.

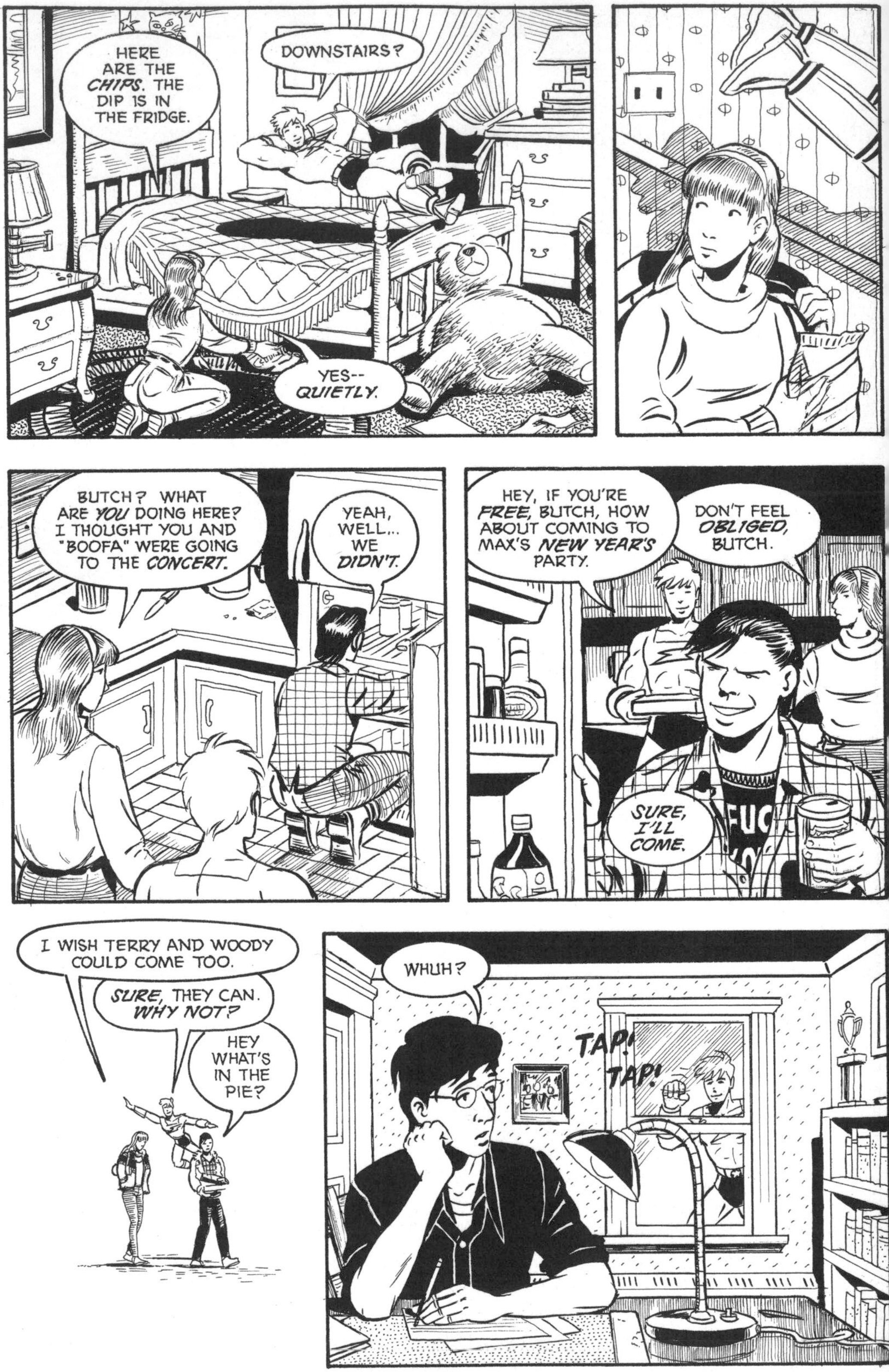
HERE ARE THE CHIPS. THE DIP IS IN THE FRIDGE.
DOWNSTAIRS?
YES-- QUIETLY.
BUTCH? WHAT ARE YOU DOING HERE? I THOUGHT YOU AND "BOOFA" WERE GOING TO THE CONCERT.
YEAH, WELL... WE DIDN'T.
HEY, IF YOU'RE FREE, BUTCH, HOW ABOUT COMING TO MAX'S NEW YEAR'S PARTY.
DON'T FEEL OBLIGED, BUTCH.
SURE, I'LL COME.
I WISH TERRY AND WOODY COULD COME TOO.
SURE, THEY CAN. WHY NOT?
HEY WHAT'S IN THE PIE?
WHUH?
TAP! TAP!

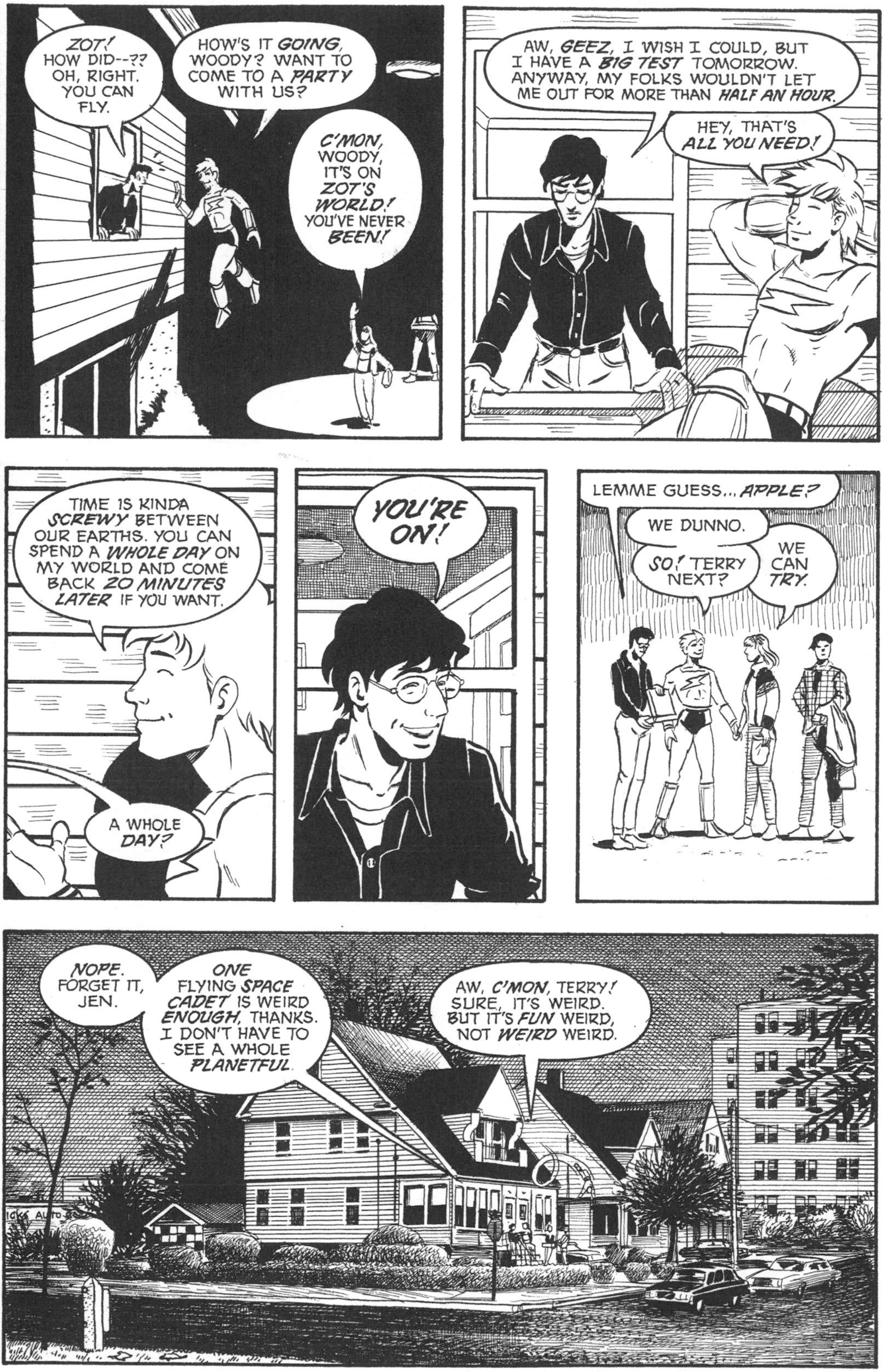
ZOT! HOW DID--?? OH, RIGHT. YOU CAN FLY.
HOW'S IT GOING, WOODY? WANT TO COME TO A PARTY WITH US?
C'MON, WOODY, IT'S ON ZOT'S WORLD! YOU'VE NEVER BEEN!
AW, GEEZ, I WISH I COULD, BUT I HAVE A BIG TEST TOMORROW. ANYWAY, MY FOLKS WOULDN'T LET ME OUT FOR MORE THAN HALF AN HOUR.
HEY, THAT'S ALL YOU NEED!
TIME IS KINDA SCREWY BETWEEN OUR EARTHS. YOU CAN SPEND A WHOLE DAY ON MY WORLD AND COME BACK 20 MINUTES LATER IF YOU WANT.
A WHOLE DAY?
YOU'RE ON!
LEMME GUESS... APPLE?
WE DUNNO.
SO! TERRY NEXT?
WE CAN TRY.
NOPE. FORGET IT, JEN.
ONE FLYING SPACE CADET IS WEIRD ENOUGH, THANKS. I DON'T HAVE TO SEE A WHOLE PLANETFUL.
AW, C'MON, TERRY! SURE, IT'S WEIRD. BUT IT'S FUN WEIRD, NOT WEIRD WEIRD.

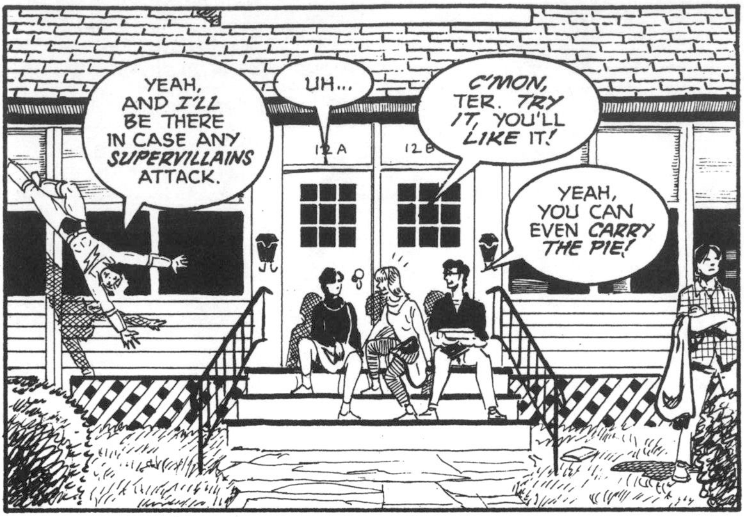
YEAH, AND I'LL BE THERE IN CASE ANY SUPERVILLAINS ATTACK.
UH...
C'MON, TER. TRY IT, YOU'LL LIKE IT!
YEAH, YOU CAN EVEN CARRY THE PIE!
12A
12B

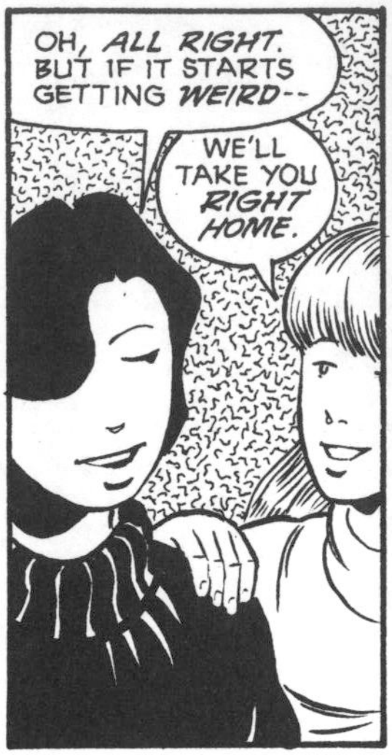
OH, ALL RIGHT. BUT IF IT STARTS GETTING WEIRD--
WE'LL TAKE YOU RIGHT HOME.

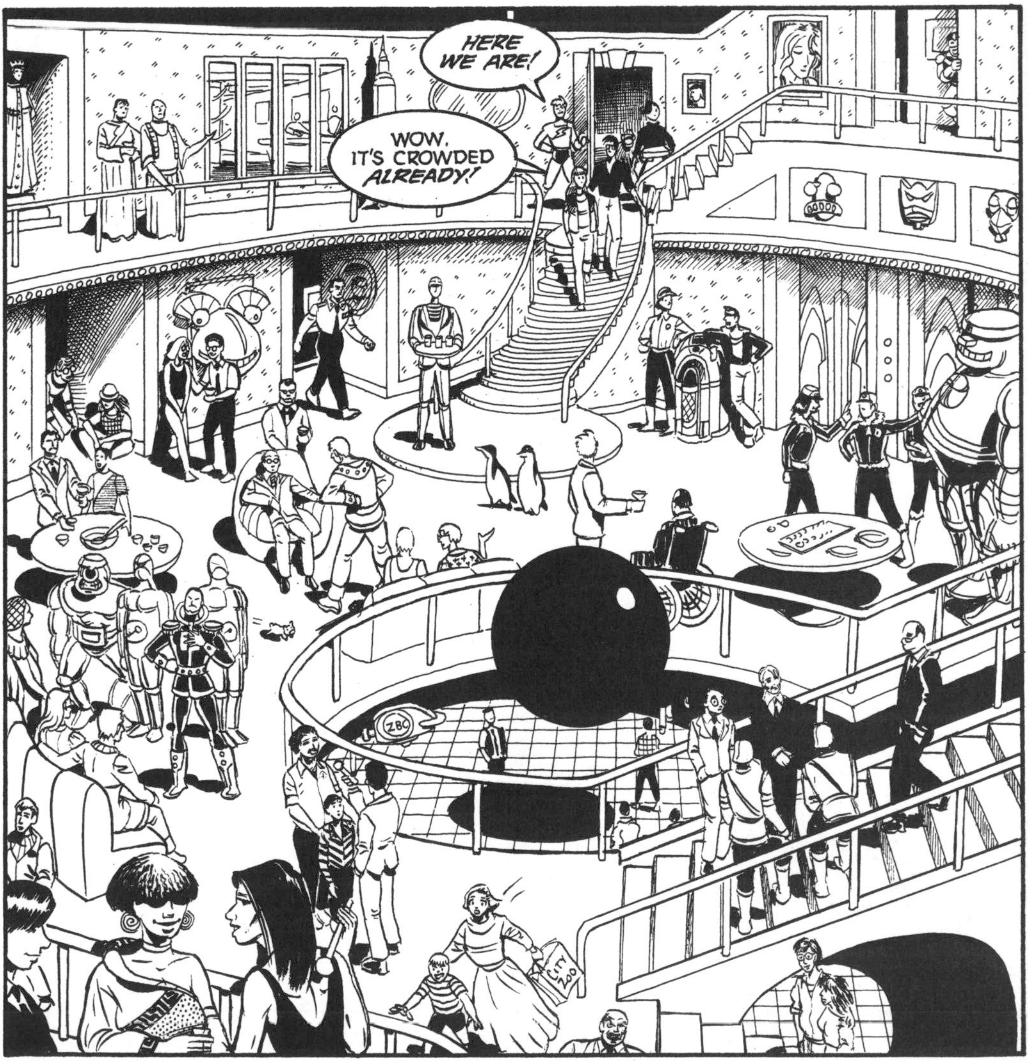
HERE WE ARE!
WOW. IT'S CROWDED ALREADY!
ZBC
CITY ZOO

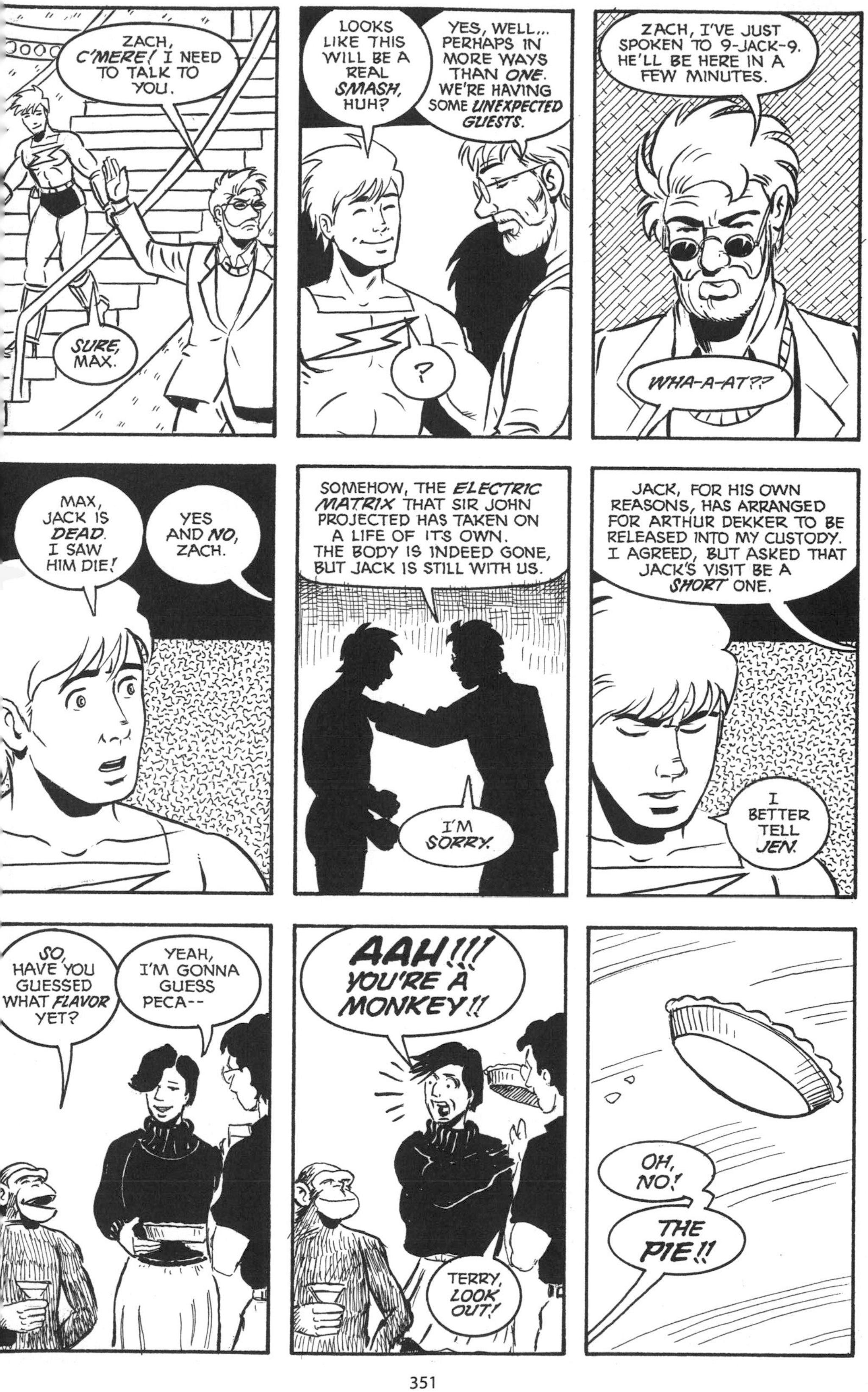
ZACH, C'MERE! I NEED TO TALK TO YOU.
SURE, MAX.
LOOKS LIKE THIS WILL BE A REAL SMASH, HUH?
YES, WELL... PERHAPS IN MORE WAYS THAN ONE. WE'RE HAVING SOME UNEXPECTED GUESTS.
?
ZACH, I'VE JUST SPOKEN TO 9-JACK-9. HE'LL BE HERE IN A FEW MINUTES.
WHA-A-AT??
MAX, JACK IS DEAD. I SAW HIM DIE!
YES AND NO, ZACH.
SOMEHOW, THE ELECTRIC MATRIX THAT SIR JOHN PROJECTED HAS TAKEN ON A LIFE OF ITS OWN. THE BODY IS INDEED GONE, BUT JACK IS STILL WITH US.
I'M SORRY.
JACK, FOR HIS OWN REASONS, HAS ARRANGED FOR ARTHUR DEKKER TO BE RELEASED INTO MY CUSTODY. I AGREED, BUT ASKED THAT JACK'S VISIT BE A SHORT ONE.
I BETTER TELL JEN.
SO, HAVE YOU GUESSED WHAT FLAVOR YET?
YEAH, I'M GONNA GUESS PECA--
AAH!!! YOU'RE A MONKEY!!
TERRY, LOOK OUT!
OH, NO!
THE PIE!!

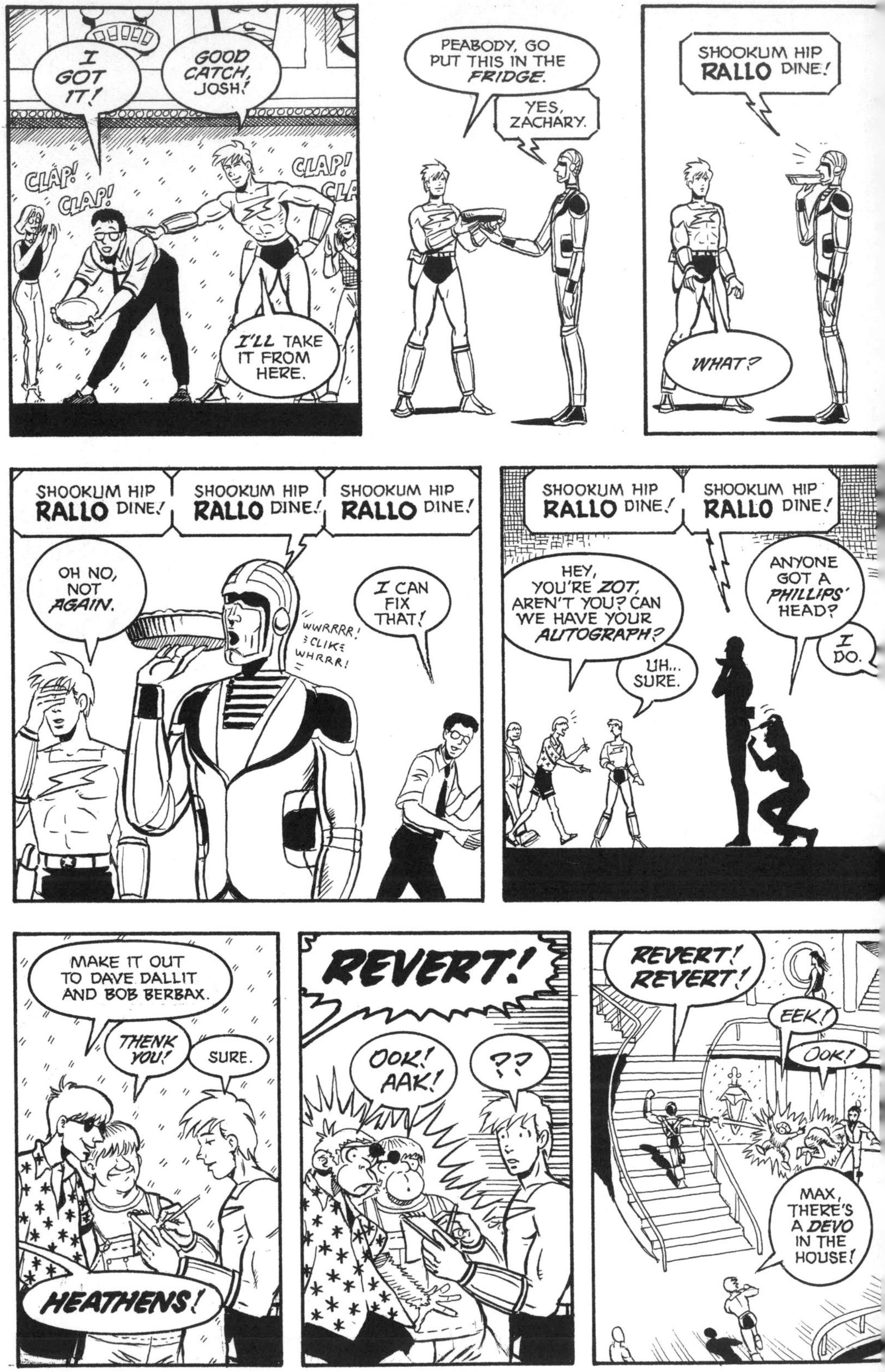
I GOT IT!
GOOD CATCH, JOSH!
CLAP! CLAP!
CLAP!
I'LL TAKE IT FROM HERE.
PEABODY, GO PUT THIS IN THE FRIDGE.
YES, ZACHARY.
SHOOKUM HIP RALLO DINE!
WHAT?
SHOOKUM HIP RALLO DINE!
SHOOKUM HIP RALLO DINE!
SHOOKUM HIP RALLO DINE!
OH NO, NOT AGAIN.
WWRRRR! CLIK WHRRR!
I CAN FIX THAT!
SHOOKUM HIP RALLO DINE!
SHOOKUM HIP RALLO DINE!
HEY, YOU'RE ZOT, AREN'T YOU? CAN WE HAVE YOUR AUTOGRAPH?
UH... SURE.
ANYONE GOT A PHILLIPS' HEAD?
I DO.
MAKE IT OUT TO DAVE DALLIT AND BOB BERBAX.
THENK YOU!
SURE.
HEATHENS!
REVERT!
OOK! AAK!
??
REVERT! REVERT!
EEK!
OOK!
MAX, THERE'S A DEVO IN THE HOUSE!

STOP IT, YOU!!
HI, DEKKO.
REVERT!
DREEP! DREEP!
I SWEAR, THIS HAPPENS EVERY YEAR!
REVERT!
REV--
GAAA!!
CRAK!
IEEEE!!
IT IS THE GREAT SATAN!!
IS THIS CHAP BEING A NUISANCE, MAX?
NO, JACK. LET HIM GO. HE'S HARMLESS WITHOUT THE GUN.
HELLO, JACK.
GOOD EVENING, ZACHARY.
ARTHUR, COME THIS WAY. I'LL SHOW YOU TO YOUR ROOM.
YOU'LL BE IN THE--
BOOM!
??

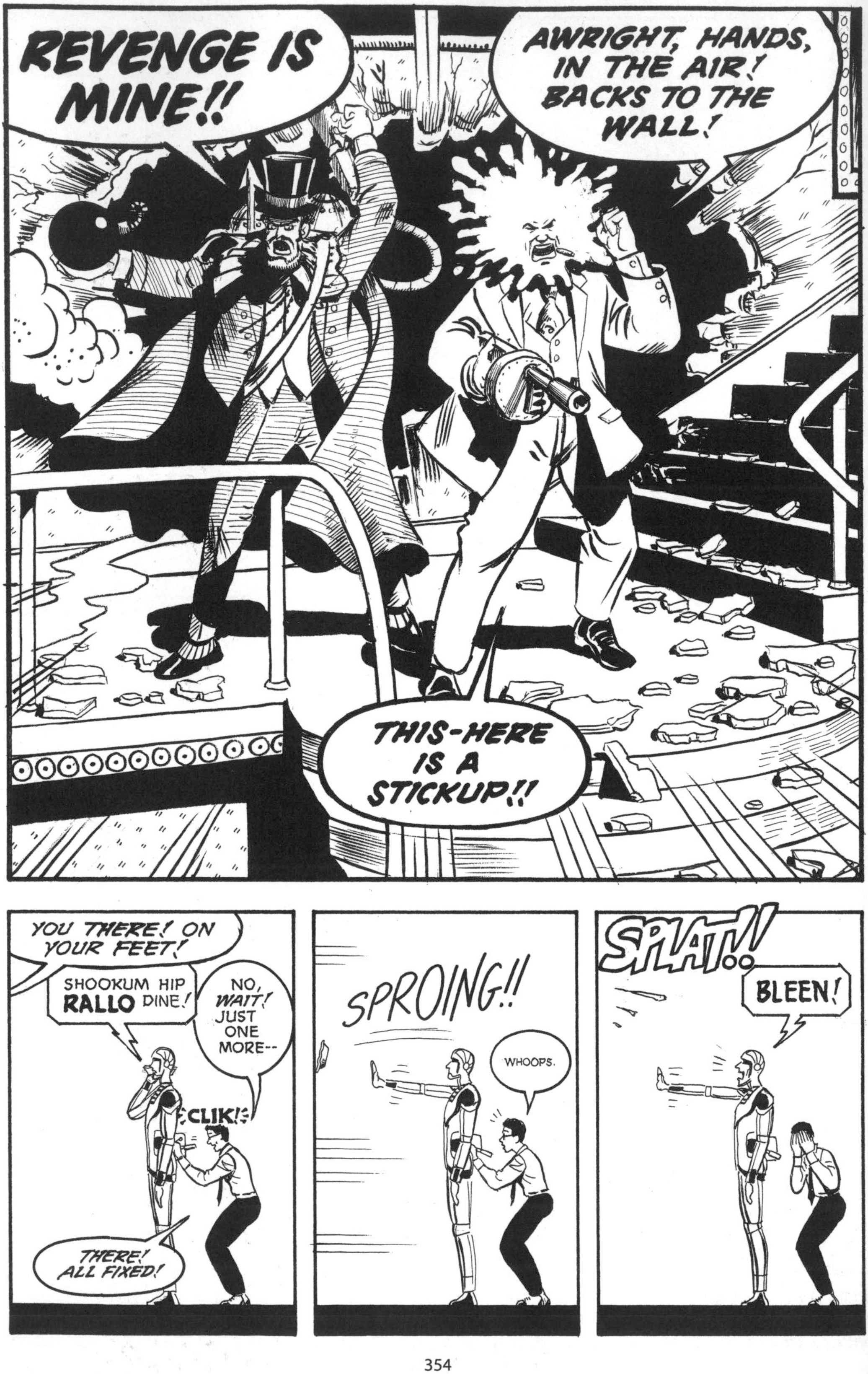
REVENGE IS MINE!!
AWRIGHT, HANDS, IN THE AIR! BACKS TO THE WALL!
THIS-HERE IS A STICKUP!!
YOU THERE! ON YOUR FEET!
SHOOKUM HIP RALLO DINE!
NO, WAIT! JUST ONE MORE--
CLIK!
THERE! ALL FIXED!
SPROING!!
WHOOPS.
SPLAT!!
BLEEN!

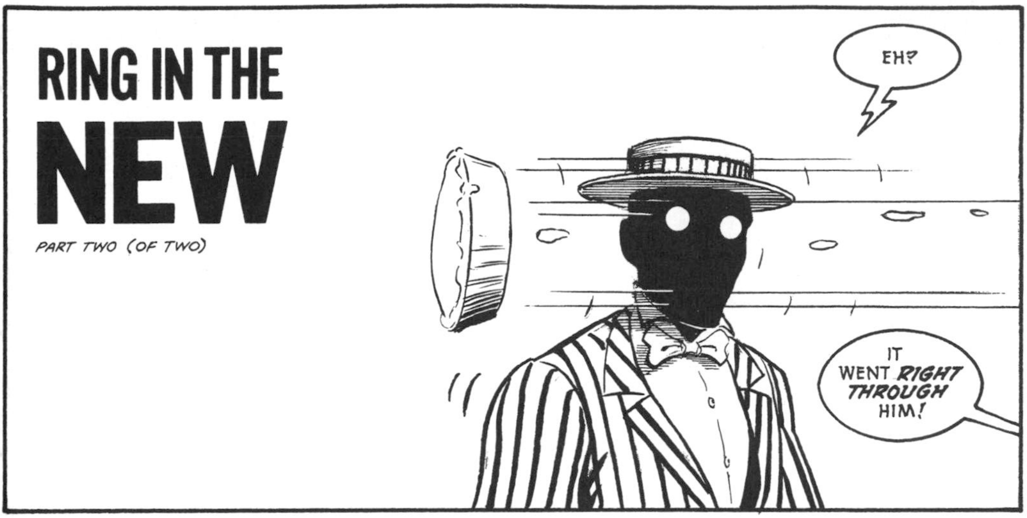
RING IN THE NEW
PART TWO (OF TWO)
EH?
IT WENT RIGHT THROUGH HIM!

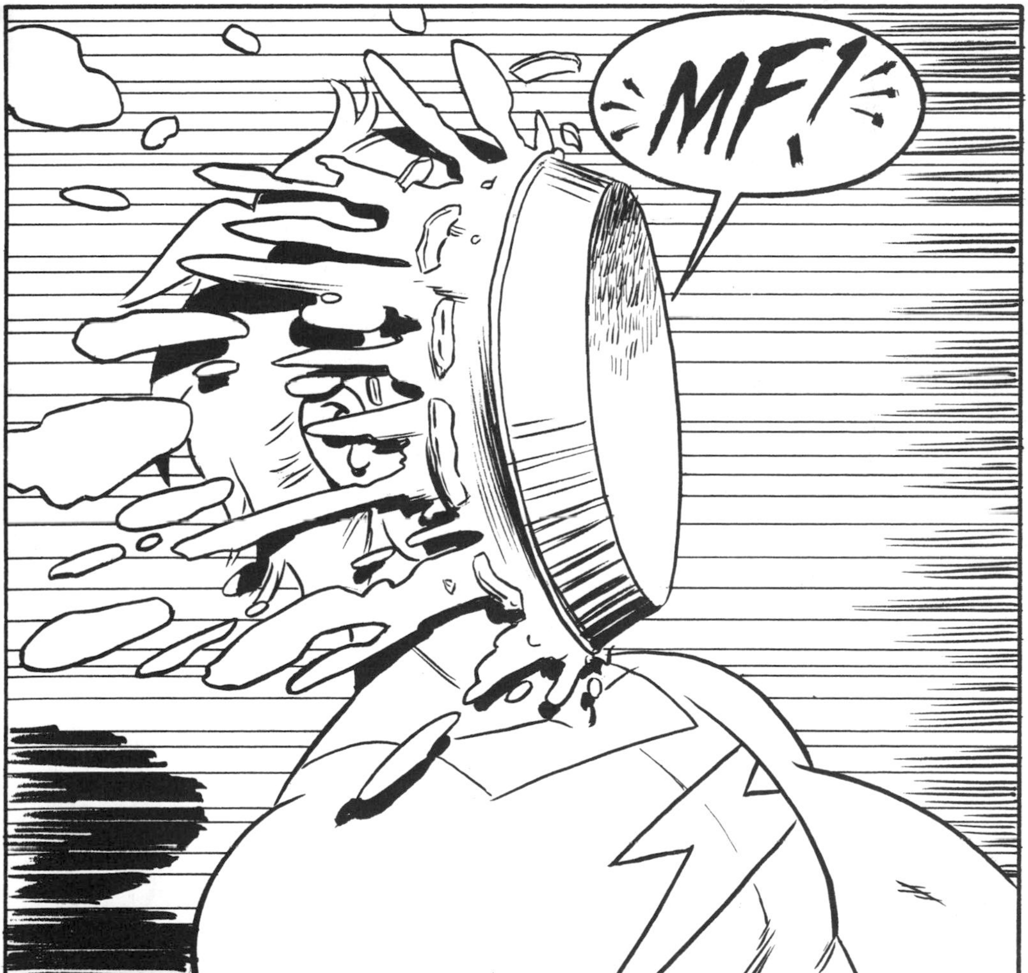
MF!

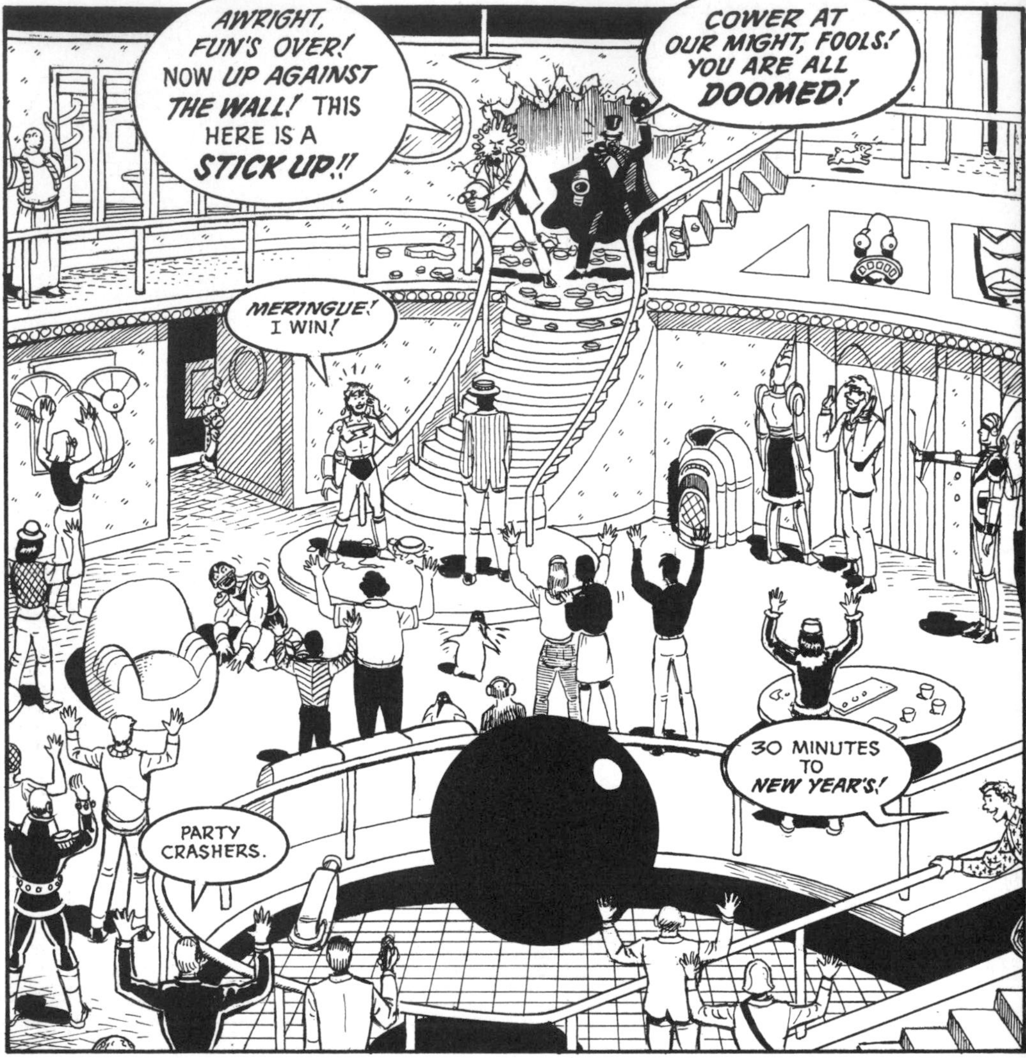
AWRIGHT, FUN'S OVER! NOW UP AGAINST THE WALL! THIS HERE IS A STICK UP!!
COWER AT OUR MIGHT, FOOLS! YOU ARE ALL DOOMED!
MERINGUE! I WIN!
30 MINUTES TO NEW YEAR'S!
PARTY CRASHERS.

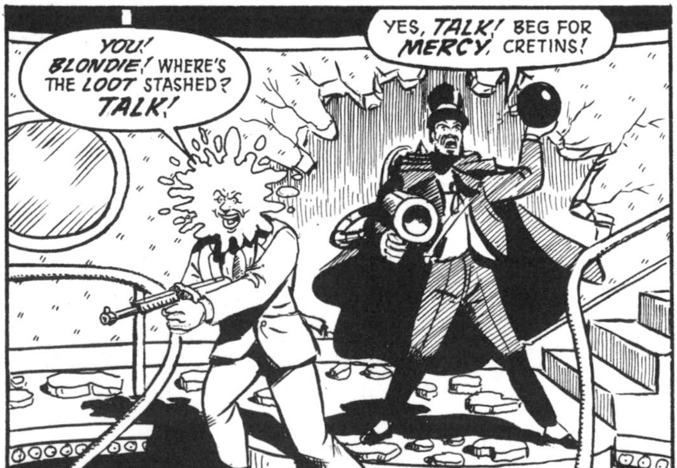
YOU! BLONDIE! WHERE'S THE LOOT STASHED? TALK!
YES, TALK! BEG FOR MERCY, CRETINS!

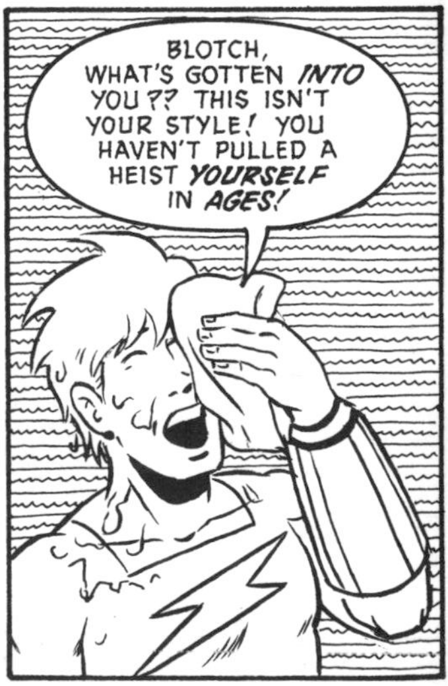
BLOTCH, WHAT'S GOTTEN INTO YOU?? THIS ISN'T YOUR STYLE! YOU HAVEN'T PULLED A HEIST YOURSELF IN AGES!

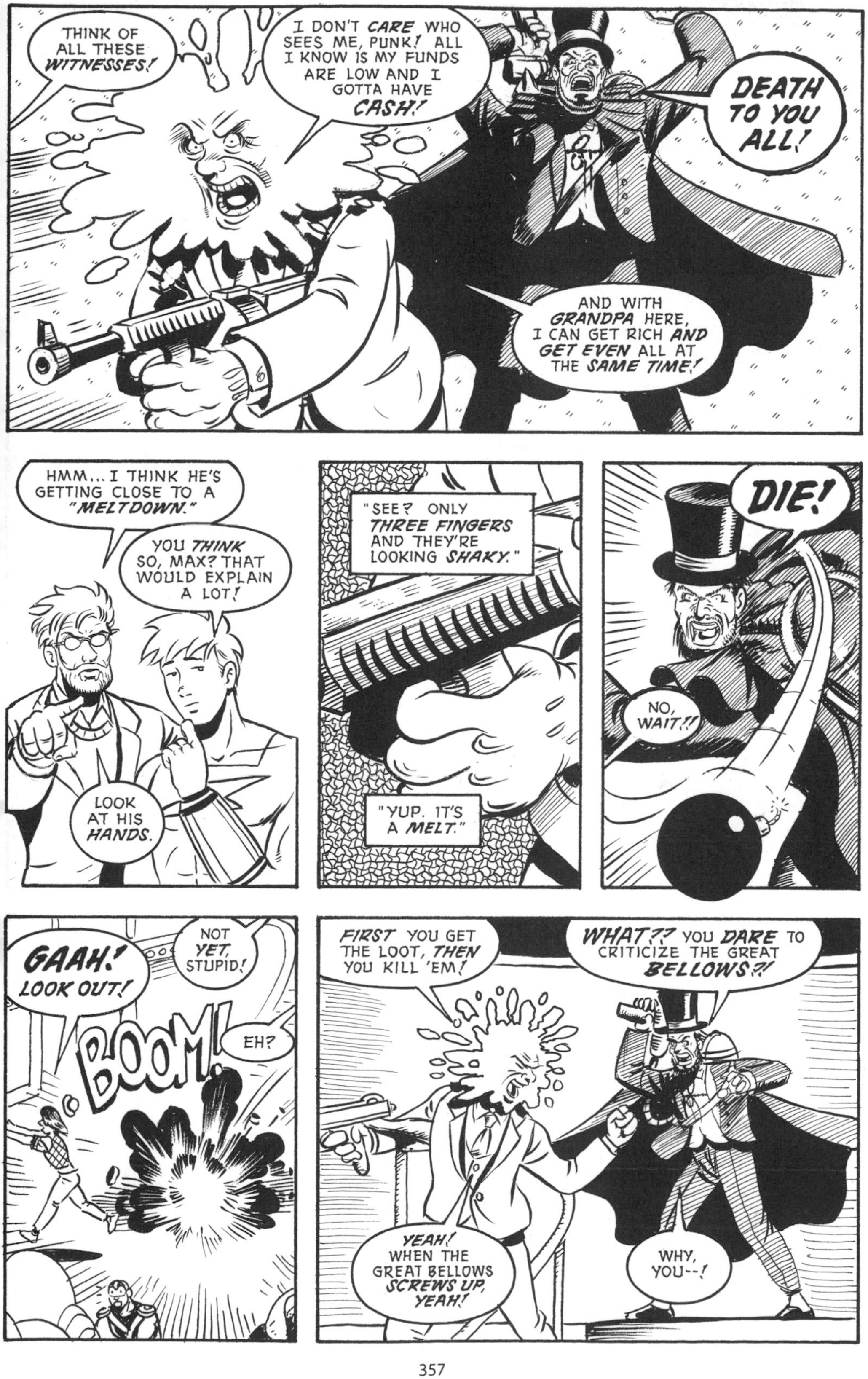
THINK OF ALL THESE WITNESSES!
I DON'T CARE WHO SEES ME, PUNK! ALL I KNOW IS MY FUNDS ARE LOW AND I GOTTA HAVE CASH!
DEATH TO YOU ALL!
AND WITH GRANDPA HERE, I CAN GET RICH AND GET EVEN ALL AT THE SAME TIME!
HMM... I THINK HE'S GETTING CLOSE TO A "MELTDOWN."
YOU THINK SO, MAX? THAT WOULD EXPLAIN A LOT!
LOOK AT HIS HANDS.
"SEE? ONLY THREE FINGERS AND THEY'RE LOOKING SHAKY."
"YUP. IT'S A MELT."
DIE!
NO, WAIT!!
GAAH! LOOK OUT!
NOT YET, STUPID!
BOOM!
EH?
FIRST YOU GET THE LOOT, THEN YOU KILL 'EM!
WHAT?? YOU DARE TO CRITICIZE THE GREAT BELLOWS?!
YEAH! WHEN THE GREAT BELLOWS SCREWS UP, YEAH!
WHY, YOU--!

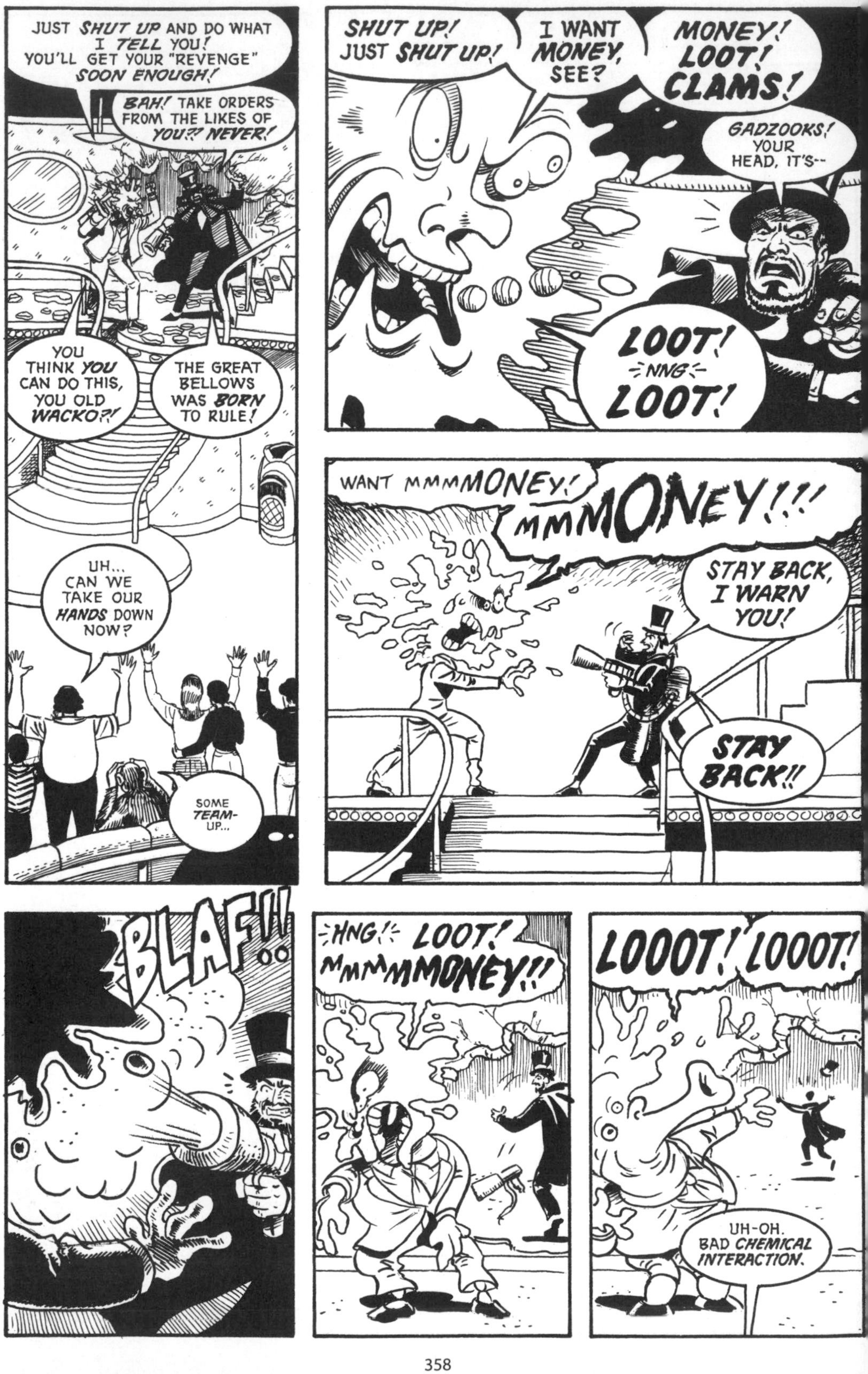
JUST SHUT UP AND DO WHAT I TELL YOU! YOU'LL GET YOUR "REVENGE" SOON ENOUGH!
BAH! TAKE ORDERS FROM THE LIKES OF YOU?!? NEVER!
YOU THINK YOU CAN DO THIS, YOU OLD WACKO?!
THE GREAT BELLOWS WAS BORN TO RULE!
UH... CAN WE TAKE OUR HANDS DOWN NOW?
SOME TEAM-UP...
SHUT UP! JUST SHUT UP!
I WANT MONEY, SEE?
MONEY! LOOT! CLAMS!
GADZOOKS! YOUR HEAD, IT'S--
LOOT! NNG LOOT!
WANT MMMMONEY!
MMMONEY!!!
STAY BACK, I WARN YOU!
STAY BACK!!
BLAF!!
HNG! LOOT! MMMMMONEY!!
LOOOT! LOOOT!
UH-OH. BAD CHEMICAL INTERACTION.

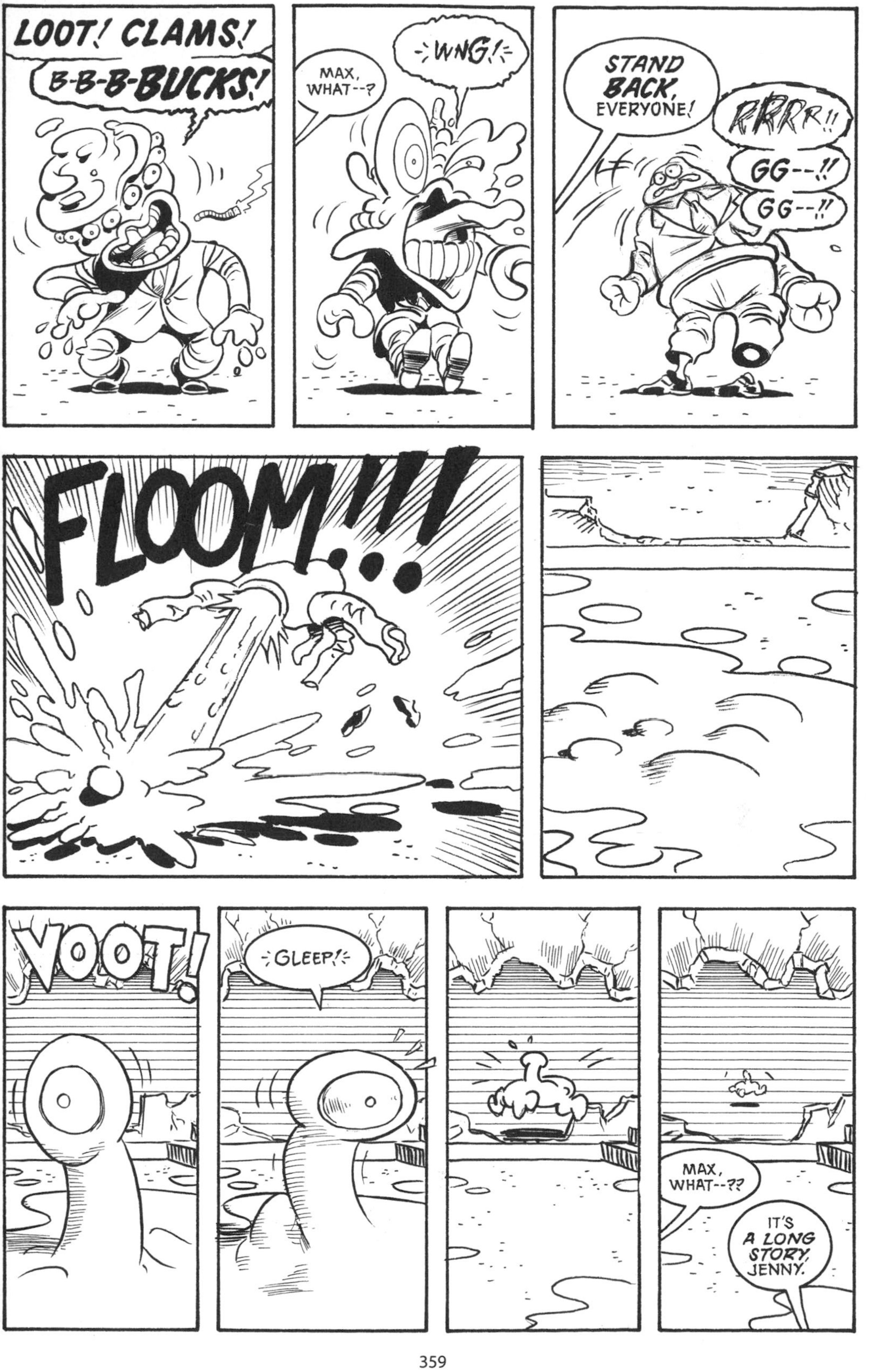
LOOT! CLAMS!
B-B-B-BUCKS!
MAX, WHAT--?
WNG!
STAND BACK, EVERYONE!
RRRR!!
GG--!!
GG--!!
FLOOM!!!
VOOT!
GLEEP!
MAX, WHAT--??
IT'S A LONG STORY, JENNY.

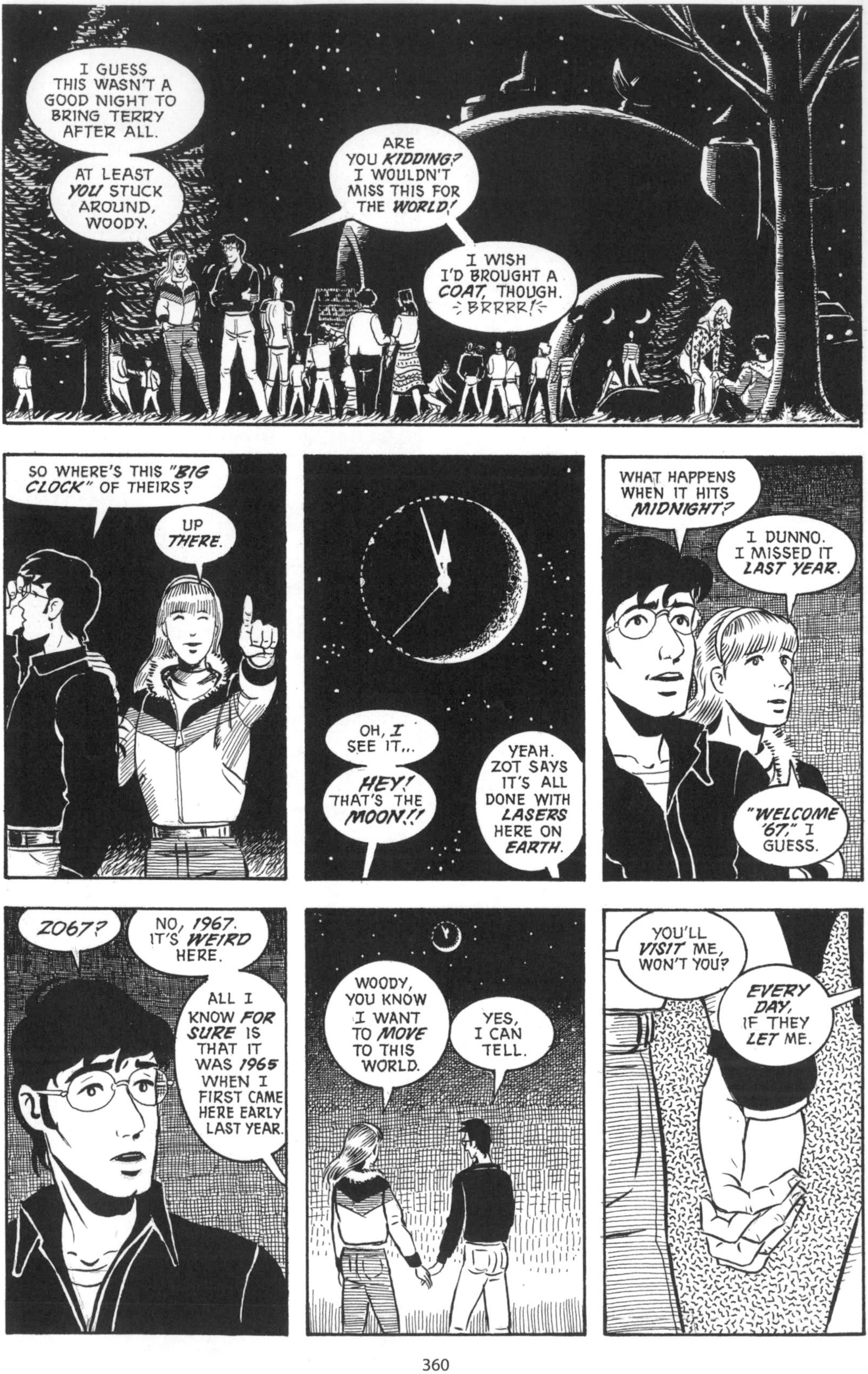
I GUESS THIS WASN'T A GOOD NIGHT TO BRING TERRY AFTER ALL.
AT LEAST *YOU* STUCK AROUND, WOODY.
ARE YOU *KIDDING?* I WOULDN'T MISS THIS FOR THE *WORLD!*
I WISH I'D BROUGHT A *COAT,* THOUGH. BRRRR!
SO WHERE'S THIS "*BIG CLOCK*" OF THEIRS?
UP *THERE*.
OH, *I* SEE IT...
HEY! THAT'S THE *MOON!!*
YEAH. ZOT SAYS IT'S ALL DONE WITH *LASERS* HERE ON *EARTH*.
WHAT HAPPENS WHEN IT HITS *MIDNIGHT?*
I DUNNO. I MISSED IT *LAST YEAR*.
"*WELCOME '67,*" I GUESS.
2067?
NO, *1967*. IT'S *WEIRD* HERE.
ALL I KNOW *FOR SURE* IS THAT IT WAS *1965* WHEN I FIRST CAME HERE EARLY LAST YEAR.
WOODY, YOU KNOW I WANT TO *MOVE* TO THIS WORLD.
YES, I CAN TELL.
YOU'LL *VISIT* ME, WON'T YOU?
EVERY DAY, IF THEY *LET* ME.

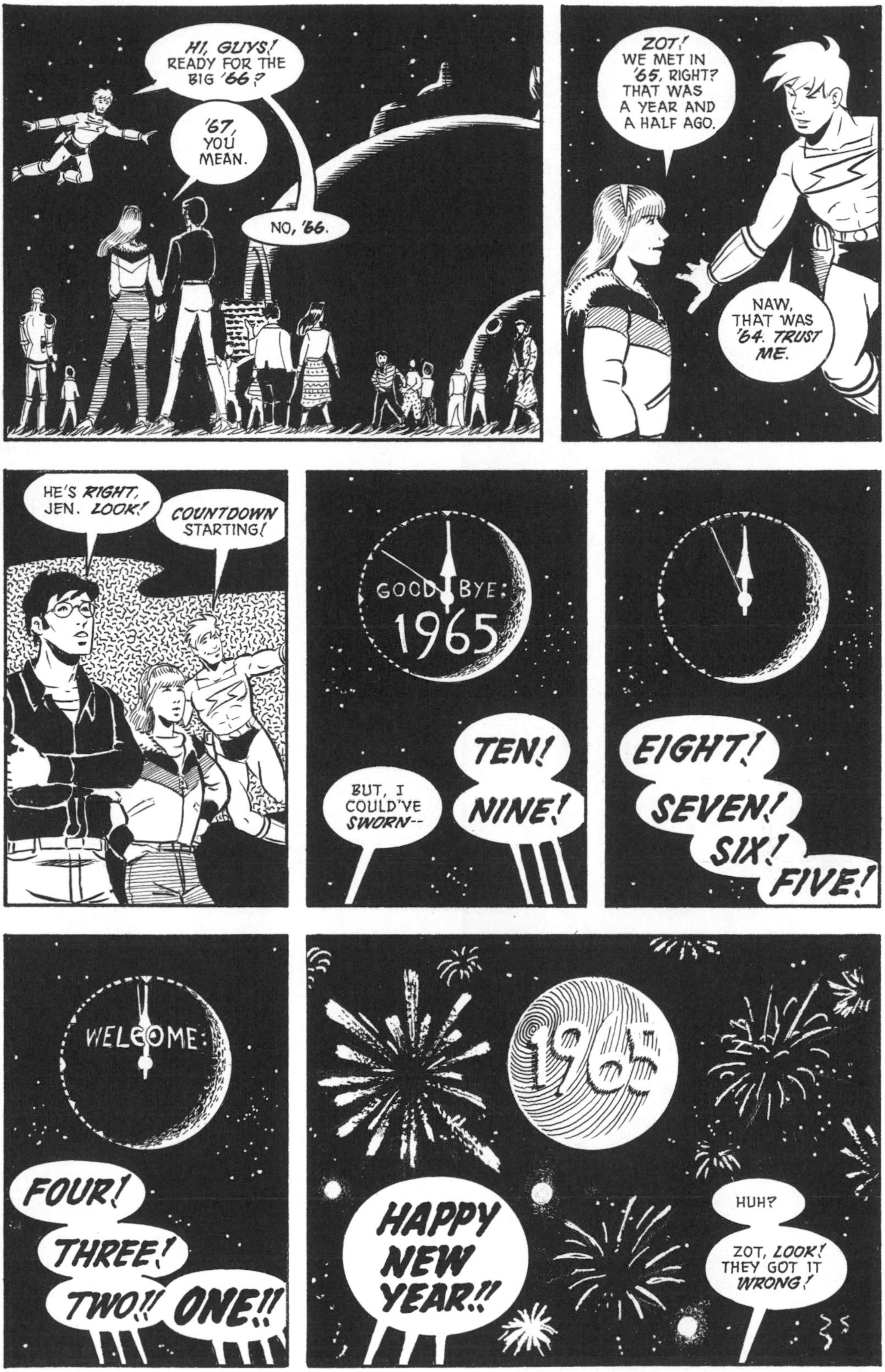
HI, GUYS! READY FOR THE BIG '66?
'67, YOU MEAN.
NO, '66.
ZOT! WE MET IN '65, RIGHT? THAT WAS A YEAR AND A HALF AGO.
NAW, THAT WAS '64. TRUST ME.
HE'S RIGHT, JEN. LOOK!
COUNTDOWN STARTING!
GOOD BYE: 1965
BUT, I COULD'VE SWORN--
TEN!
NINE!
EIGHT!
SEVEN!
SIX!
FIVE!
WELCOME:
FOUR!
THREE!
TWO!!
ONE!!
1965
HAPPY NEW YEAR!!
HUH?
ZOT, LOOK! THEY GOT IT WRONG!

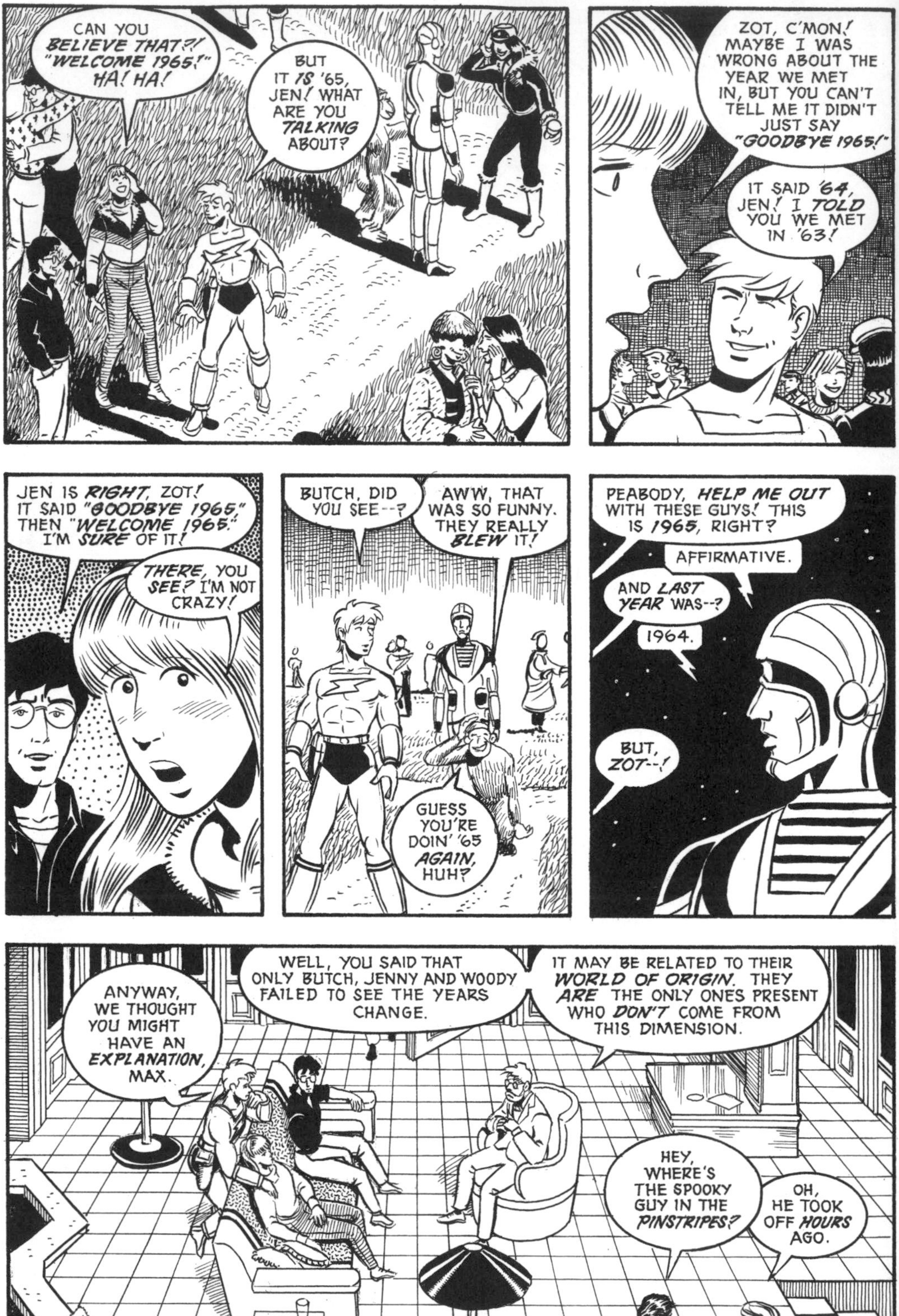
CAN YOU BELIEVE THAT?! "WELCOME 1965!" HA! HA!
BUT IT IS '65, JEN! WHAT ARE YOU TALKING ABOUT?
ZOT, C'MON! MAYBE I WAS WRONG ABOUT THE YEAR WE MET IN, BUT YOU CAN'T TELL ME IT DIDN'T JUST SAY "GOODBYE 1965!"
IT SAID '64, JEN! I TOLD YOU WE MET IN '63!
JEN IS RIGHT, ZOT! IT SAID "GOODBYE 1965," THEN "WELCOME 1965." I'M SURE OF IT!
THERE, YOU SEE? I'M NOT CRAZY!
BUTCH, DID YOU SEE--?
AWW, THAT WAS SO FUNNY. THEY REALLY BLEW IT!
GUESS YOU'RE DOIN' '65 AGAIN, HUH?
PEABODY, HELP ME OUT WITH THESE GUYS! THIS IS 1965, RIGHT?
AFFIRMATIVE.
AND LAST YEAR WAS--?
1964.
BUT, ZOT--!
ANYWAY, WE THOUGHT YOU MIGHT HAVE AN EXPLANATION, MAX.
WELL, YOU SAID THAT ONLY BUTCH, JENNY AND WOODY FAILED TO SEE THE YEARS CHANGE.
IT MAY BE RELATED TO THEIR WORLD OF ORIGIN. THEY ARE THE ONLY ONES PRESENT WHO DON'T COME FROM THIS DIMENSION.
HEY, WHERE'S THE SPOOKY GUY IN THE PINSTRIPES?
OH, HE TOOK OFF HOURS AGO.

I'VE BEEN WORKING ON THE ASSUMPTION THAT *JENNY'S* EARTH IS AN *IMPERFECT REPLICA* OF OUR OWN.

I BELIEVE THAT.

COULD IT BE THE OTHER WAY AROUND, MAX?

POSSIBLY, WOODY.

I'D LIKE TO SEE *MORE* OF THIS WORLD, MAX. MAYBE I COULD HELP FIGURE OUT WHICH CAME *FIRST!*

YOU MIGHT INDEED, WOODY. ALL RIGHT, *TOMORROW,* THEN*!*

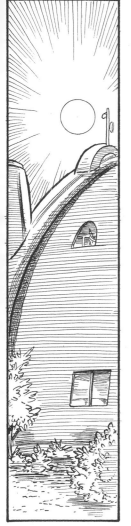

KNOCK! KNOCK!

WAKE UP, JEN! ZOT AND MAX ARE TAKING US ON THE GRAND TOUR.

HUH? OH, YOU GO AHEAD, WOODY.

IS BUTCH STILL HERE?

HE WENT HOME. IT'S JUST *YOU AND ME.* ARE YOU *SURE* YOU DON'T WANT TO COME?

NAW, I'VE SEEN IT *BEFORE...*

YAAAWNNNNN...

...I'LL SEE IT *AGAIN.*

THIS IS MY *NEW HOME.*

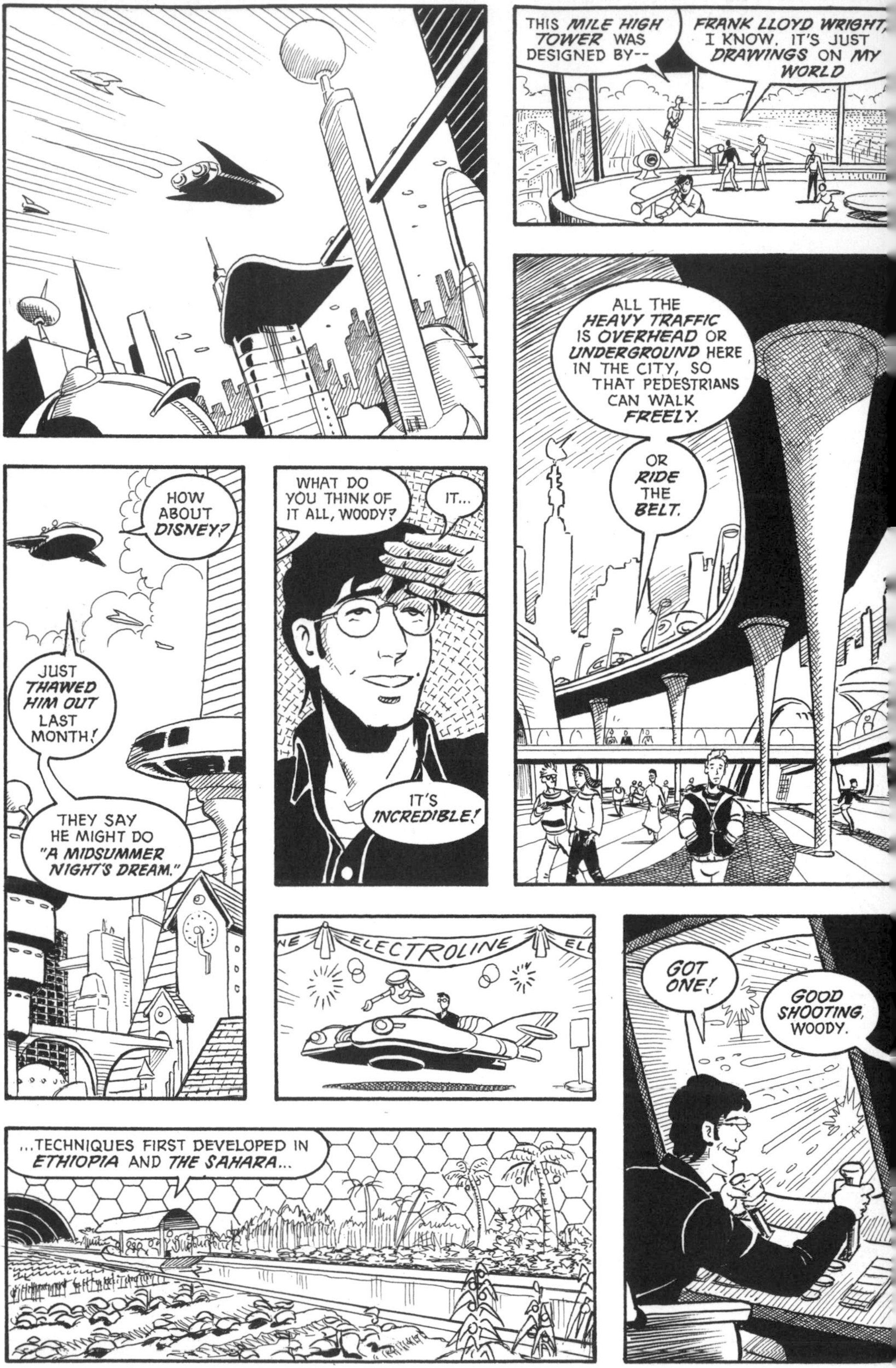
THIS MILE HIGH TOWER WAS DESIGNED BY--
FRANK LLOYD WRIGHT, I KNOW. IT'S JUST DRAWINGS ON MY WORLD
HOW ABOUT DISNEY?
JUST THAWED HIM OUT LAST MONTH!
THEY SAY HE MIGHT DO "A MIDSUMMER NIGHT'S DREAM."
WHAT DO YOU THINK OF IT ALL, WOODY?
IT...
IT'S INCREDIBLE!
ALL THE HEAVY TRAFFIC IS OVERHEAD OR UNDERGROUND HERE IN THE CITY, SO THAT PEDESTRIANS CAN WALK FREELY.
OR RIDE THE BELT.
ELECTROLINE
...TECHNIQUES FIRST DEVELOPED IN ETHIOPIA AND THE SAHARA...
GOT ONE!
GOOD SHOOTING, WOODY.

THIS WING OF THE MUSEUM IS ALL *PARTICIPATORY DIGITAL PAINTINGS* AND *HOLOGRAMS.*

HERE. TRY THE *COLOR WAND.*

...12 *MILLION* PEOPLE.

THAT MANY?

BUT IT SEEMS SO *SPACIOUS!*

YOU DON'T HAVE *C.D.'s?*

OH, THE *DISCS?* SURE! WE USE THOSE IN *JUKEBOXES.* EACH SIDE OF *"THE CUBE"* IS ABOUT A C.D. IN *PLAYING TIME.*

MAYBE MAX WAS RIGHT THE *FIRST* TIME.

MAYBE OUR WORLD IS THE COPY... THE *"IMPERFECT COPY."*

LIKE IT?

DELICIOUS!

IT'S *SEAWEED.*

--STILL *UNEXPLORED TERRITORY*--

--UNDERWATER CITIES NOW HOME TO--

THEN WHY CAN'T I SHAKE THIS FEELING THAT *SOMETHING* HERE IS *WRONG.*

SOMETHING DOESN'T MAKE SENSE.

WHAT *IS* IT??

WE BETTER *HEAD BACK,* WOODY.

WAIT A SEC, ZOT. I WANT TO *CHECK OUT* SOMETHING.

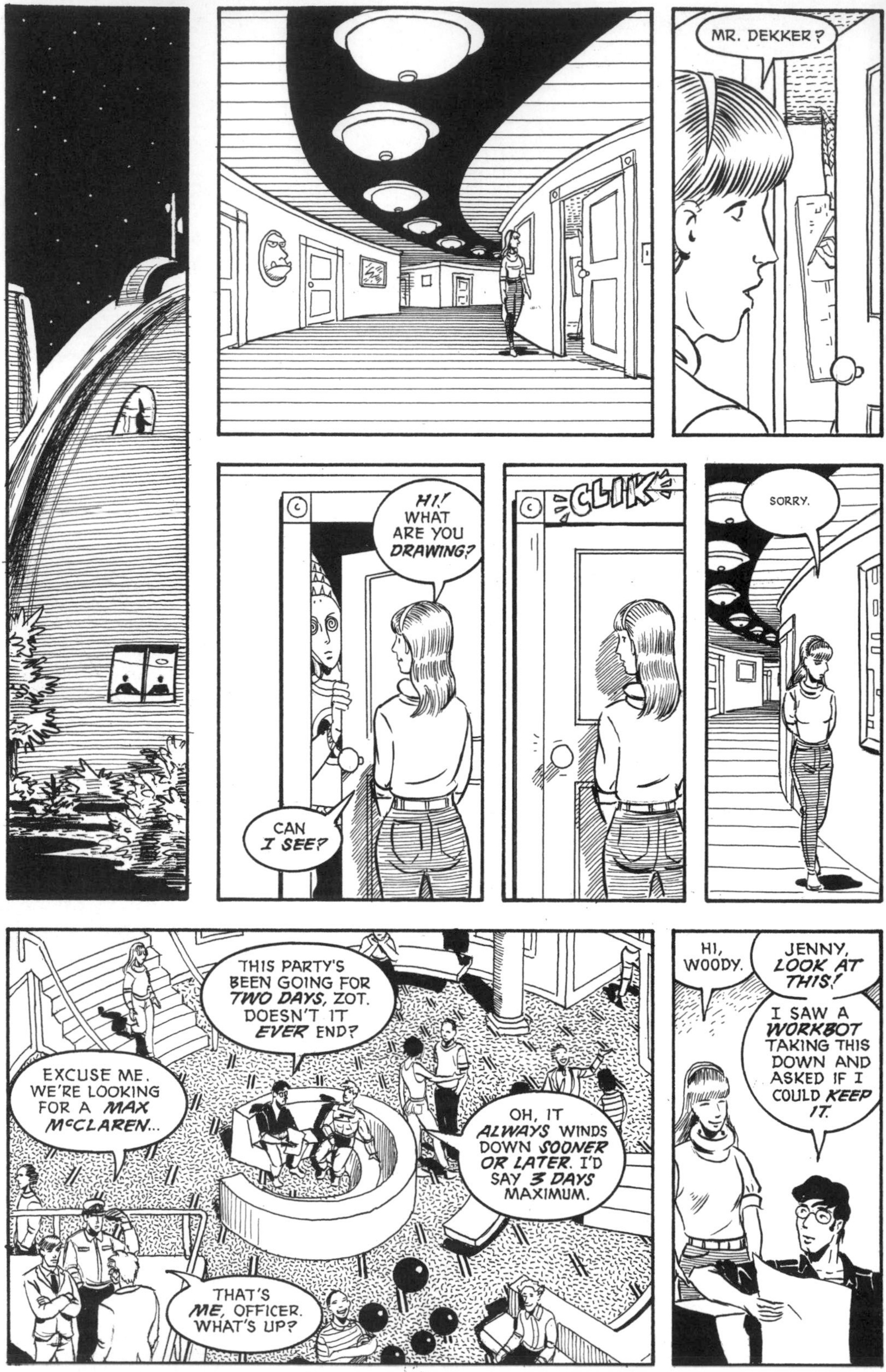

MR. DEKKER?
HI! WHAT ARE YOU DRAWING?
CAN I SEE?
CLIK
SORRY.
THIS PARTY'S BEEN GOING FOR TWO DAYS, ZOT. DOESN'T IT EVER END?
EXCUSE ME. WE'RE LOOKING FOR A MAX McCLAREN...
OH, IT ALWAYS WINDS DOWN SOONER OR LATER. I'D SAY 3 DAYS MAXIMUM.
THAT'S ME, OFFICER. WHAT'S UP?
HI, WOODY.
JENNY, LOOK AT THIS!
I SAW A WORKBOT TAKING THIS DOWN AND ASKED IF I COULD KEEP IT.

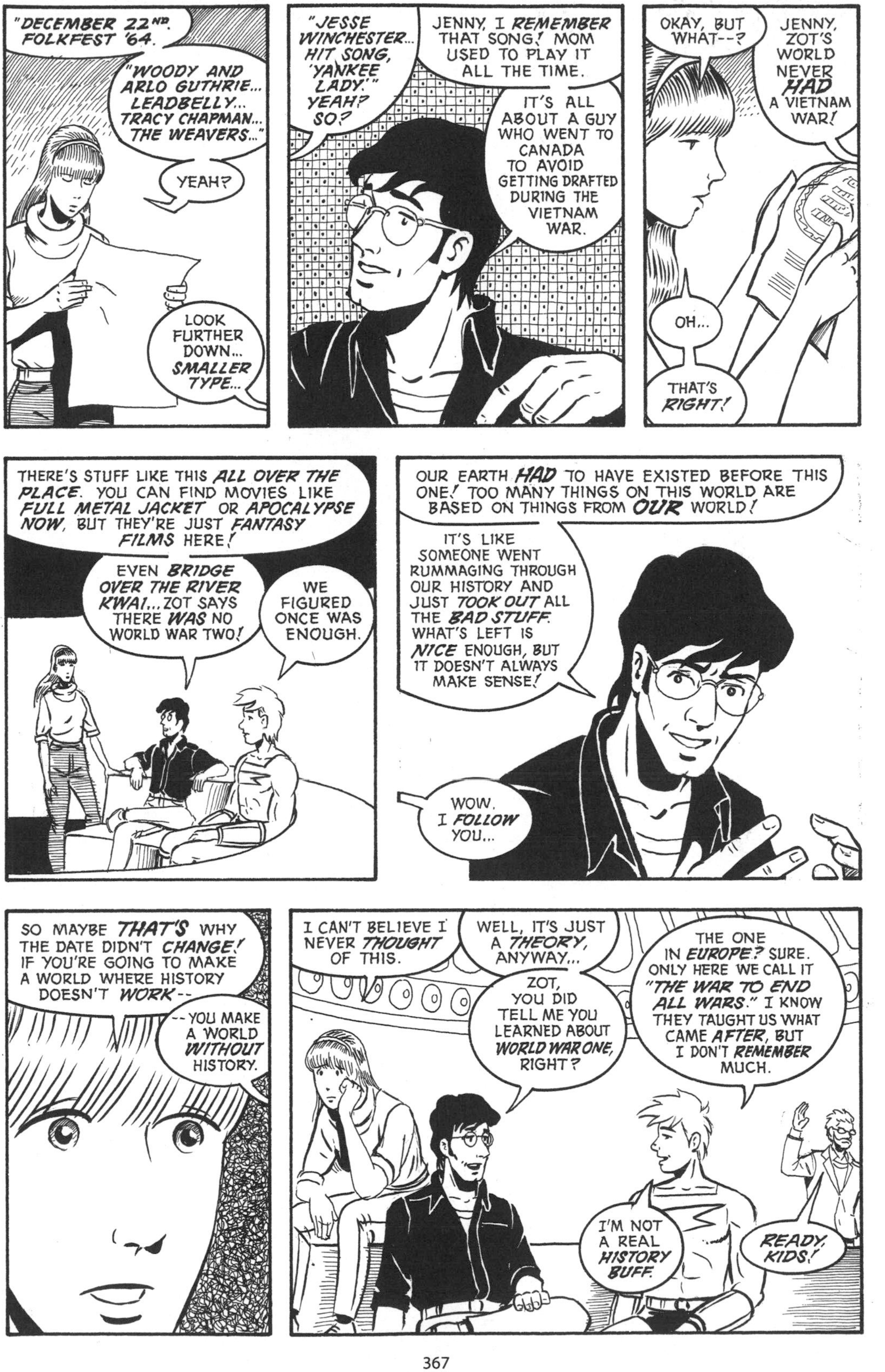
"DECEMBER 22ND. FOLKFEST '64.
"WOODY AND ARLO GUTHRIE... LEADBELLY... TRACY CHAPMAN... THE WEAVERS..."
YEAH?
LOOK FURTHER DOWN... SMALLER TYPE...
"JESSE WINCHESTER... HIT SONG, 'YANKEE LADY.'" YEAH? SO?
JENNY, I REMEMBER THAT SONG! MOM USED TO PLAY IT ALL THE TIME.
IT'S ALL ABOUT A GUY WHO WENT TO CANADA TO AVOID GETTING DRAFTED DURING THE VIETNAM WAR.
OKAY, BUT WHAT--?
JENNY, ZOT'S WORLD NEVER HAD A VIETNAM WAR!
OH...
THAT'S RIGHT!
THERE'S STUFF LIKE THIS ALL OVER THE PLACE. YOU CAN FIND MOVIES LIKE FULL METAL JACKET OR APOCALYPSE NOW, BUT THEY'RE JUST FANTASY FILMS HERE!
EVEN BRIDGE OVER THE RIVER KWAI... ZOT SAYS THERE WAS NO WORLD WAR TWO!
WE FIGURED ONCE WAS ENOUGH.
OUR EARTH HAD TO HAVE EXISTED BEFORE THIS ONE! TOO MANY THINGS ON THIS WORLD ARE BASED ON THINGS FROM OUR WORLD!
IT'S LIKE SOMEONE WENT RUMMAGING THROUGH OUR HISTORY AND JUST TOOK OUT ALL THE BAD STUFF. WHAT'S LEFT IS NICE ENOUGH, BUT IT DOESN'T ALWAYS MAKE SENSE!
WOW. I FOLLOW YOU...
SO MAYBE THAT'S WHY THE DATE DIDN'T CHANGE! IF YOU'RE GOING TO MAKE A WORLD WHERE HISTORY DOESN'T WORK--
--YOU MAKE A WORLD WITHOUT HISTORY.
I CAN'T BELIEVE I NEVER THOUGHT OF THIS.
WELL, IT'S JUST A THEORY, ANYWAY...
ZOT, YOU DID TELL ME YOU LEARNED ABOUT WORLD WAR ONE, RIGHT?
THE ONE IN EUROPE? SURE. ONLY HERE WE CALL IT "THE WAR TO END ALL WARS." I KNOW THEY TAUGHT US WHAT CAME AFTER, BUT I DON'T REMEMBER MUCH.
I'M NOT A REAL HISTORY BUFF.
READY, KIDS!

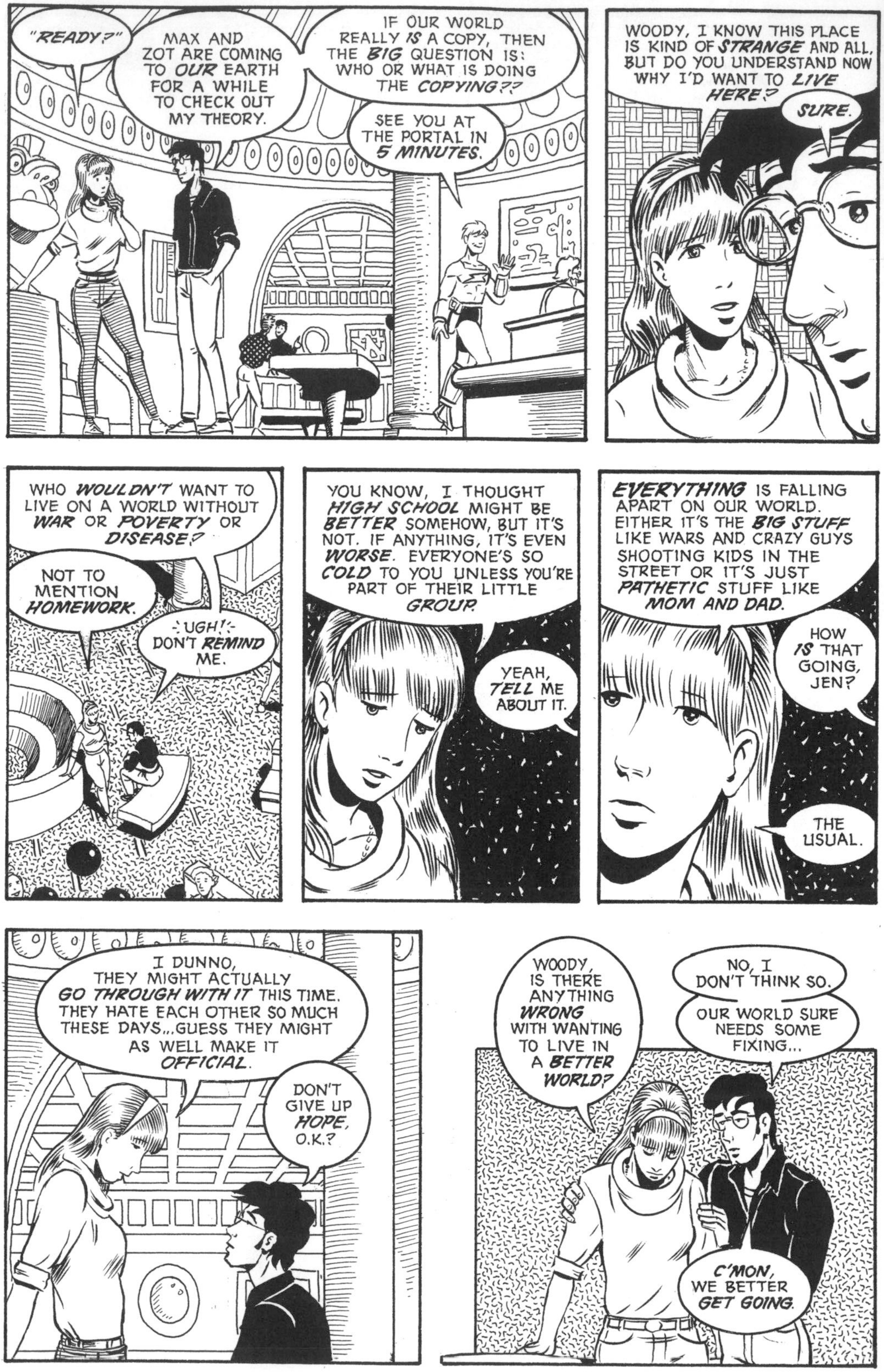
"READY?"
MAX AND ZOT ARE COMING TO OUR EARTH FOR A WHILE TO CHECK OUT MY THEORY.
IF OUR WORLD REALLY IS A COPY, THEN THE BIG QUESTION IS: WHO OR WHAT IS DOING THE COPYING??
SEE YOU AT THE PORTAL IN 5 MINUTES.
WOODY, I KNOW THIS PLACE IS KIND OF STRANGE AND ALL, BUT DO YOU UNDERSTAND NOW WHY I'D WANT TO LIVE HERE?
SURE.
WHO WOULDN'T WANT TO LIVE ON A WORLD WITHOUT WAR OR POVERTY OR DISEASE?
NOT TO MENTION HOMEWORK.
UGH! DON'T REMIND ME.
YOU KNOW, I THOUGHT HIGH SCHOOL MIGHT BE BETTER SOMEHOW, BUT IT'S NOT. IF ANYTHING, IT'S EVEN WORSE. EVERYONE'S SO COLD TO YOU UNLESS YOU'RE PART OF THEIR LITTLE GROUP.
YEAH, TELL ME ABOUT IT.
EVERYTHING IS FALLING APART ON OUR WORLD. EITHER IT'S THE BIG STUFF LIKE WARS AND CRAZY GUYS SHOOTING KIDS IN THE STREET OR IT'S JUST PATHETIC STUFF LIKE MOM AND DAD.
HOW IS THAT GOING, JEN?
THE USUAL.
I DUNNO, THEY MIGHT ACTUALLY GO THROUGH WITH IT THIS TIME. THEY HATE EACH OTHER SO MUCH THESE DAYS...GUESS THEY MIGHT AS WELL MAKE IT OFFICIAL.
DON'T GIVE UP HOPE, O.K.?
WOODY, IS THERE ANYTHING WRONG WITH WANTING TO LIVE IN A BETTER WORLD?
NO, I DON'T THINK SO.
OUR WORLD SURE NEEDS SOME FIXING...
C'MON, WE BETTER GET GOING.

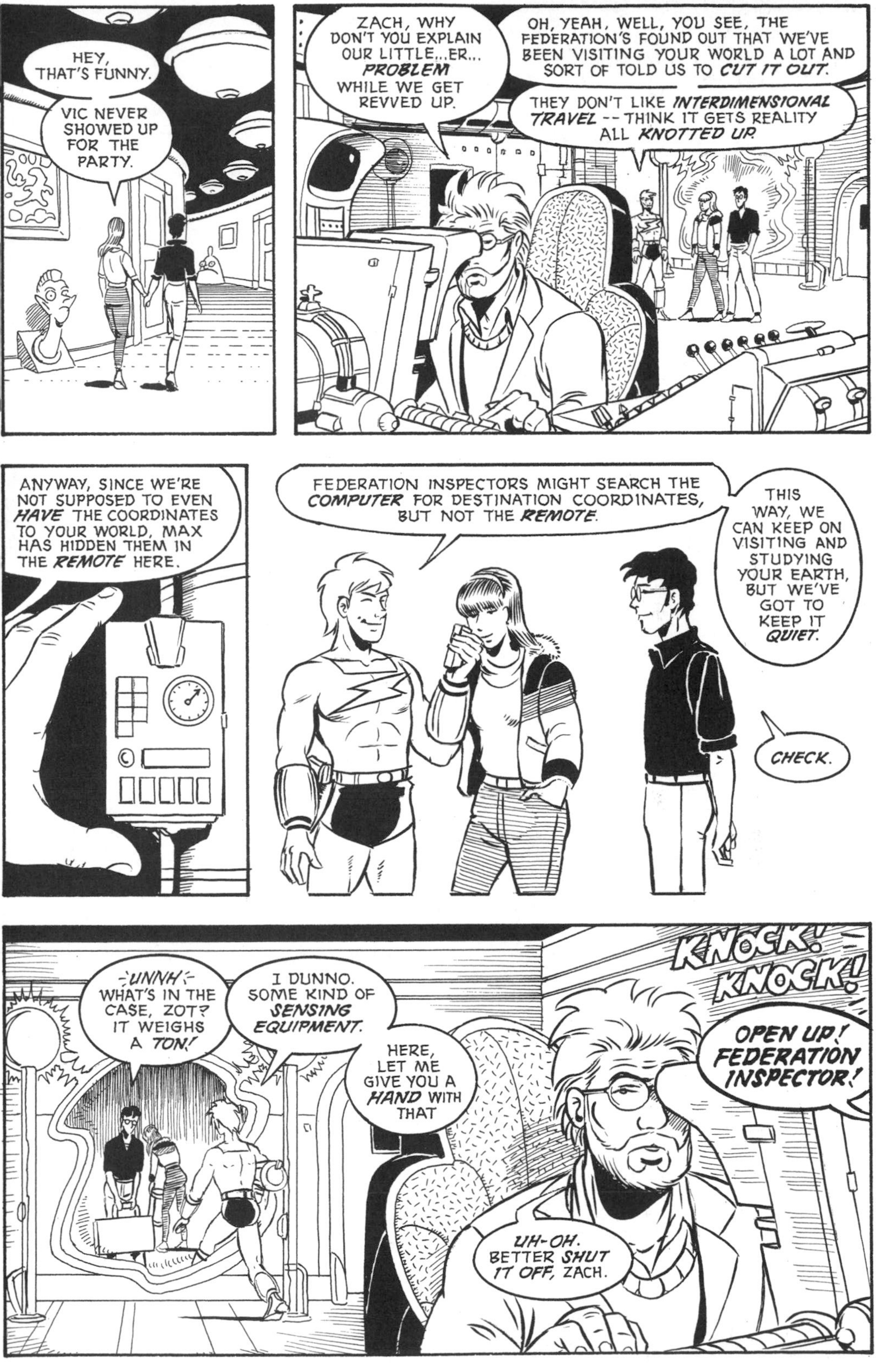
HEY, THAT'S FUNNY.
VIC NEVER SHOWED UP FOR THE PARTY.
ZACH, WHY DON'T YOU EXPLAIN OUR LITTLE...ER... PROBLEM WHILE WE GET REVVED UP.
OH, YEAH, WELL, YOU SEE, THE FEDERATION'S FOUND OUT THAT WE'VE BEEN VISITING YOUR WORLD A LOT AND SORT OF TOLD US TO CUT IT OUT.
THEY DON'T LIKE INTERDIMENSIONAL TRAVEL -- THINK IT GETS REALITY ALL KNOTTED UP.
ANYWAY, SINCE WE'RE NOT SUPPOSED TO EVEN HAVE THE COORDINATES TO YOUR WORLD, MAX HAS HIDDEN THEM IN THE REMOTE HERE.
FEDERATION INSPECTORS MIGHT SEARCH THE COMPUTER FOR DESTINATION COORDINATES, BUT NOT THE REMOTE.
THIS WAY, WE CAN KEEP ON VISITING AND STUDYING YOUR EARTH, BUT WE'VE GOT TO KEEP IT QUIET.
CHECK.
-UNNH- WHAT'S IN THE CASE, ZOT? IT WEIGHS A TON!
I DUNNO. SOME KIND OF SENSING EQUIPMENT.
HERE, LET ME GIVE YOU A HAND WITH THAT
KNOCK! KNOCK!
OPEN UP! FEDERATION INSPECTOR!
UH-OH. BETTER SHUT IT OFF, ZACH.

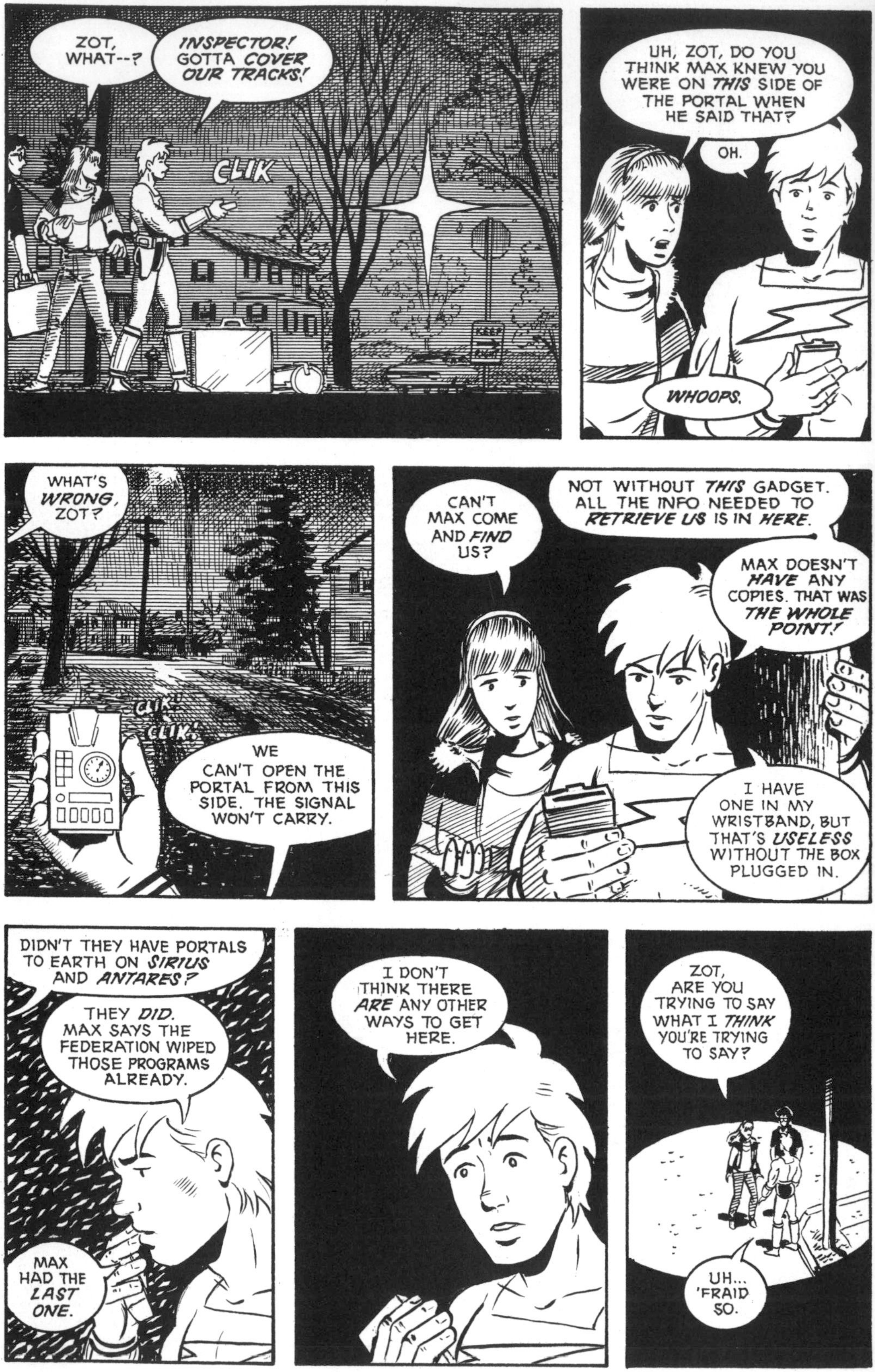
ZOT, WHAT--?
INSPECTOR! GOTTA COVER OUR TRACKS!
CLIK
UH, ZOT, DO YOU THINK MAX KNEW YOU WERE ON THIS SIDE OF THE PORTAL WHEN HE SAID THAT?
OH.
WHOOPS.
WHAT'S WRONG, ZOT?
CLIK! CLIK!
WE CAN'T OPEN THE PORTAL FROM THIS SIDE. THE SIGNAL WON'T CARRY.
CAN'T MAX COME AND FIND US?
NOT WITHOUT THIS GADGET. ALL THE INFO NEEDED TO RETRIEVE US IS IN HERE.
MAX DOESN'T HAVE ANY COPIES. THAT WAS THE WHOLE POINT!
I HAVE ONE IN MY WRISTBAND, BUT THAT'S USELESS WITHOUT THE BOX PLUGGED IN.
DIDN'T THEY HAVE PORTALS TO EARTH ON SIRIUS AND ANTARES?
THEY DID. MAX SAYS THE FEDERATION WIPED THOSE PROGRAMS ALREADY.
MAX HAD THE LAST ONE.
I DON'T THINK THERE ARE ANY OTHER WAYS TO GET HERE.
ZOT, ARE YOU TRYING TO SAY WHAT I THINK YOU'RE TRYING TO SAY?
UH... 'FRAID SO.

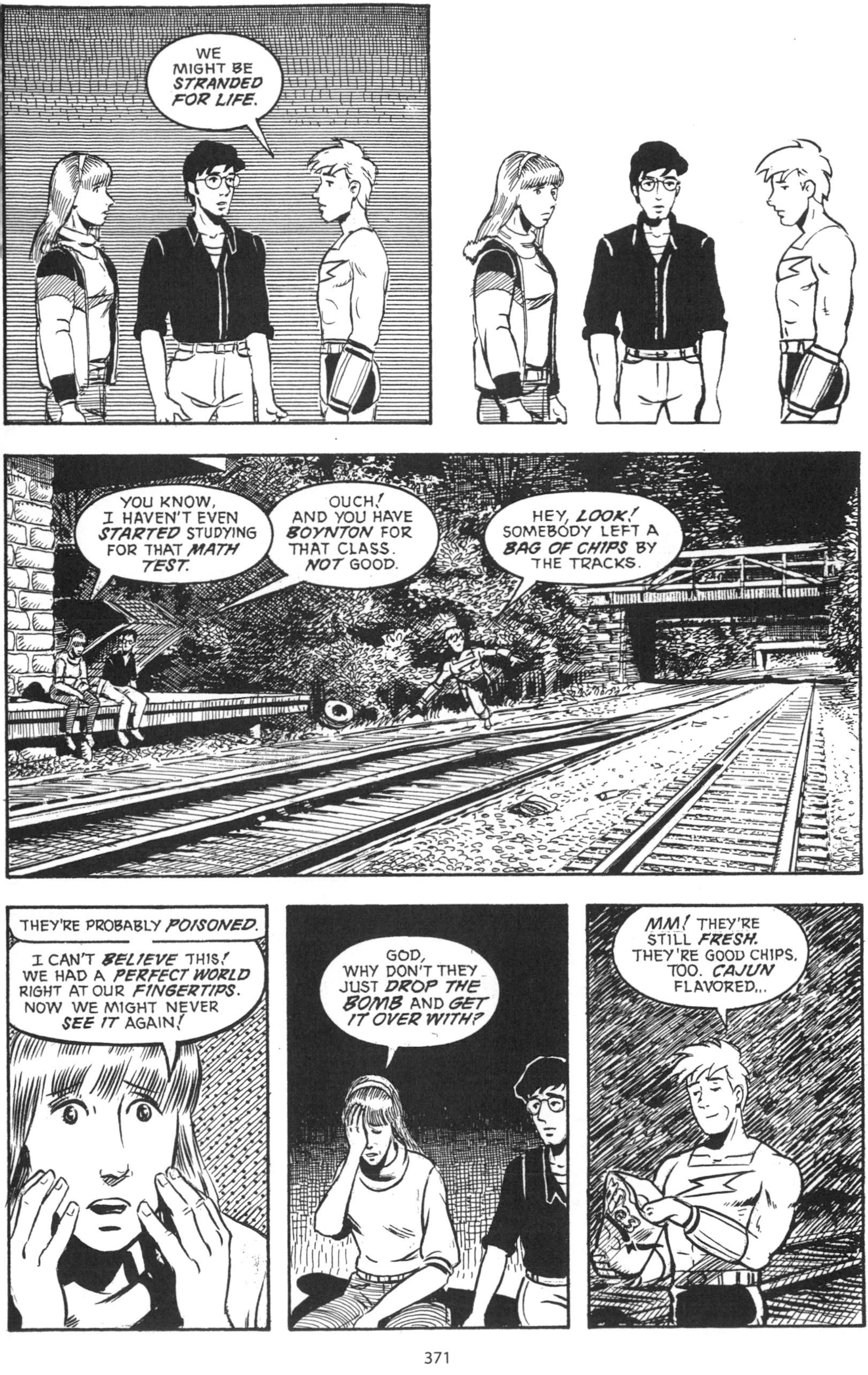
WE MIGHT BE STRANDED FOR LIFE.
YOU KNOW, I HAVEN'T EVEN STARTED STUDYING FOR THAT MATH TEST.
OUCH! AND YOU HAVE BOYNTON FOR THAT CLASS. NOT GOOD.
HEY, LOOK! SOMEBODY LEFT A BAG OF CHIPS BY THE TRACKS.
THEY'RE PROBABLY POISONED.
I CAN'T BELIEVE THIS! WE HAD A PERFECT WORLD RIGHT AT OUR FINGERTIPS. NOW WE MIGHT NEVER SEE IT AGAIN!
GOD, WHY DON'T THEY JUST DROP THE BOMB AND GET IT OVER WITH?
MM! THEY'RE STILL FRESH. THEY'RE GOOD CHIPS, TOO. CAJUN FLAVORED...

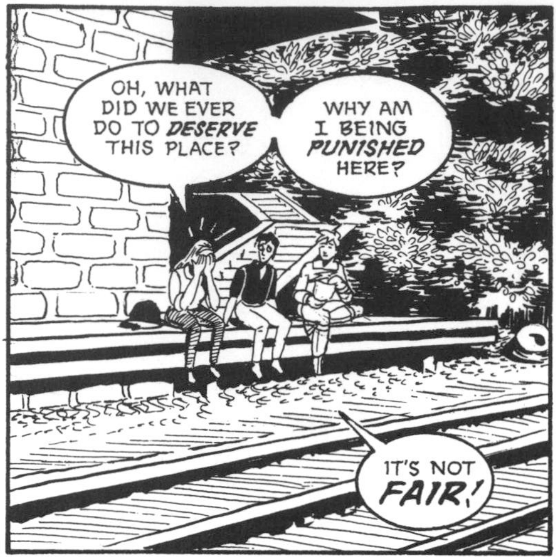
OH, WHAT DID WE EVER DO TO DESERVE THIS PLACE?
WHY AM I BEING PUNISHED HERE?
IT'S NOT FAIR!

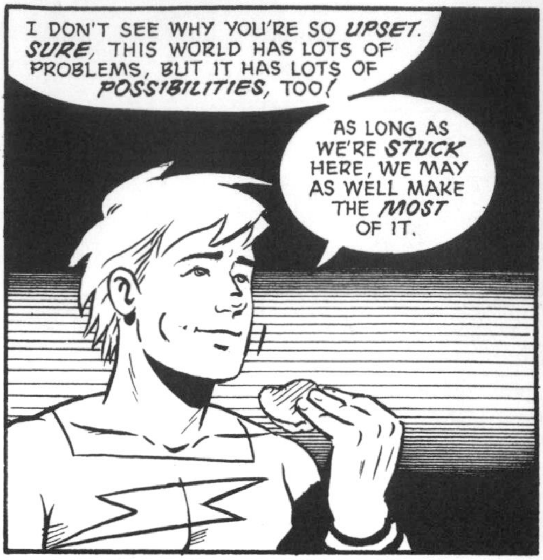
I DON'T SEE WHY YOU'RE SO UPSET. SURE, THIS WORLD HAS LOTS OF PROBLEMS, BUT IT HAS LOTS OF POSSIBILITIES, TOO!
AS LONG AS WE'RE STUCK HERE, WE MAY AS WELL MAKE THE MOST OF IT.

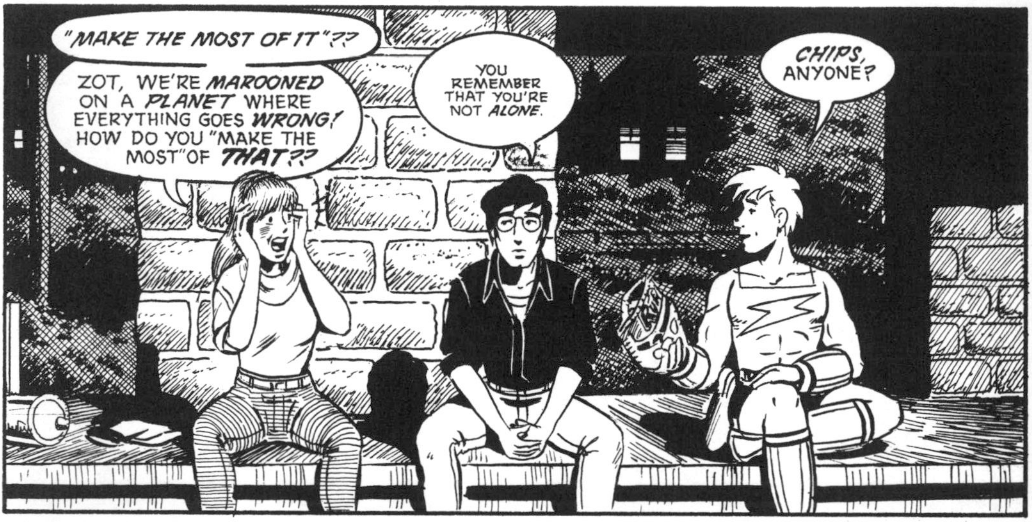
"MAKE THE MOST OF IT"??
ZOT, WE'RE MAROONED ON A PLANET WHERE EVERYTHING GOES WRONG! HOW DO YOU "MAKE THE MOST" OF THAT??
YOU REMEMBER THAT YOU'RE NOT ALONE.
CHIPS, ANYONE?

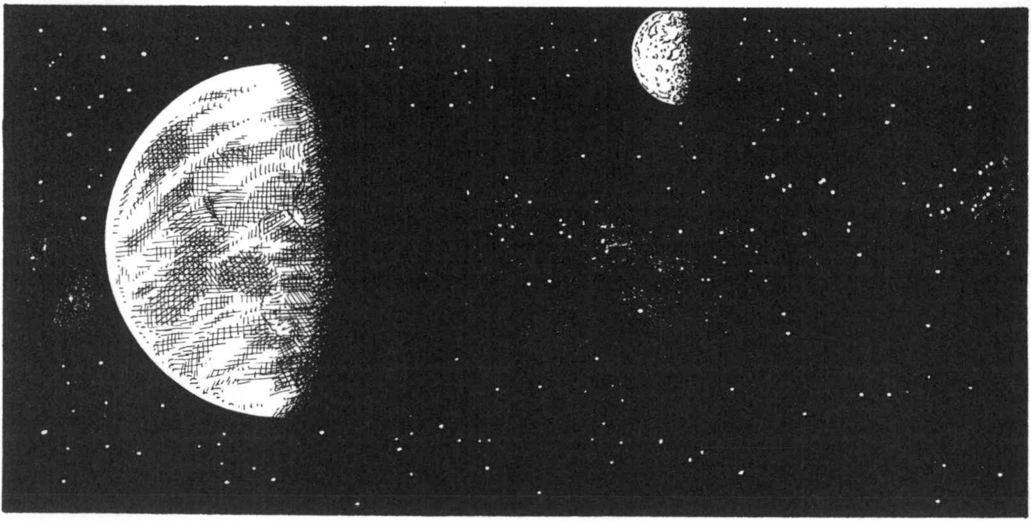

This is the last time you'll see any of my crazy supervillains in this collection. Starting with the next issue, *Zot!* became a very different sort of series, taking place entirely on our Earth, the only science fiction elements being Zot himself and the few gadgets he brought with him. Since all six villains appear in this story, I'd like to offer a bit more information about the hidden significance of the six primary characters in Zot's rogues' gallery.

Ever since Jules Verne, we've had hundreds of compelling visions for the future of technology and society, some good, some bad. In *Zot!,* I took the good ones and mashed them together to make a world. Then I took six of the bad ones and molded each into a character. Those six break down into two groups: the loud villains and the quiet villains.

The three loud villains were Bellows, the Blotch, and the De-Evolutionaries. All three were ultimately impotent, because the chances of their futures coming true seemed remote. Bellows' smoke-belching, clumsy, industrial revolutionary future, and the Blotch's hyper-capitalist nightmare, have both gotten a few new teeth in the intervening years, but at the time, I didn't see society heading full-speed in either direction—at least, not without a whole lot of people dedicating themselves to putting on the brakes. Meanwhile, the Devoes' hopes of putting the technological genie back in the bottle is as futile today as it ever was, hence they're the loudest and least serious of the lot.

The three quiet Villains were Dekko, Zybox, and 9-Jack-9. All three represented potent, credible futures when I created them in the '80s, and nothing has happened in the last twenty years to change my mind. I was particularly interested in the mirrored pair of Dekko and Zybox, the future in which we become our machines and the future in which our machines become us. Anyone following developments in artificial intelligence and the biomedical sciences knows that we may be in for a very weird century in which either of those scenarios could come to pass.

And finally there's Jack, the quietest and most powerful of the lot, the future of no future at all: the prospect that technology will simply wipe us out in the end. I had nuclear war in mind in the '80s, but any Armageddon will do. I wish I was as optimistic as my hero, but as of this writing, Jack still gets my vote for villain most likely to succeed.

As whimsical as it looked, there wasn't anything in Zot's world that technology couldn't eventually bring about. All those quaint old predictions for the future weren't dead ends, they just hadn't happened *yet.* The way I figured it, if our species screwed up in the end, then this was nothing more than a fond look in the rearview mirror. But if there was even a one in three chance of making our collective futures bright, then where better to focus our attention?

QUIET
LOUD
POTENT
IMPOTENT

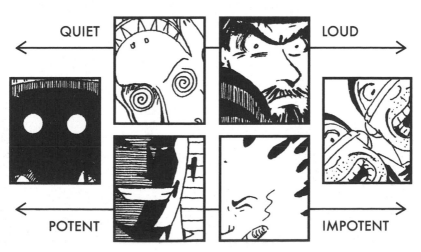

Long before message boards and blogs took over fandom, letters pages provided a sense of shared community for fans and pros alike. *Zot!*'s letters page played host to a lively group of opinionated readers. Only a few issues before this one, we'd printed a letter from the legendary letter hack, the late "T. M. Maple," in which he'd signed his real name, Jim Burke, for the first time. He was celebrating his tenth anniversary of writing letters to comic books. By his count, that letter was number "three thousand one-hundred and twenty-eight."

We loved getting letters. Every time a new batch showed up in my post office box, Ivy would sit in my big green swivel chair and read them out loud while I drew (something she'd also do with trade magazines and the occasional novel). I couldn't listen to talking while writing or laying out a story, but tasks like inking went great with the sound track. We sincerely wished we could have printed them all—even the obnoxious ones—but space was limited. I often skewed in favor of the more critical letters for fear of feeling as if I were suppressing dissent(!), but the vast majority were supportive.

Sometimes we staged contests. One was a running vote tally for favorite character (fun fact: Digger was *nobody's* favorite character), and at the bottom of that chart was an invitation to vote for the character you'd most like to see get hit in the face with a pie. Unfortunately, when 9-Jack-9 won the contest, I had a bit of a quandary: I'd clearly established that Jack didn't really *have* a face. My solution, lame though it is, was to show the pie passing through Jack and hitting second-place "winner" Zot. Then, on the letters page, I included the graphics you see below and at right.

Note that a number of the characters shown in the, um . . . pie chart at right appeared only in the color issues. The contest had been running for a long time! There are also some odd in-jokes. I have no idea after all these years why comics writer Steve Gerber (creator of *Howard the Duck,* a great comic that became a bad movie through no fault of Steve's) received four votes.

I started listing Ivy as "plot assist" with this story since she helped me work out a lot of the pie's close encounters. In truth she'd been helping all along and would continue to give me ideas throughout the run. Maybe this big, fluffy meringue hardly deserves to be called a "story" at all, but at least we both had fun baking it.

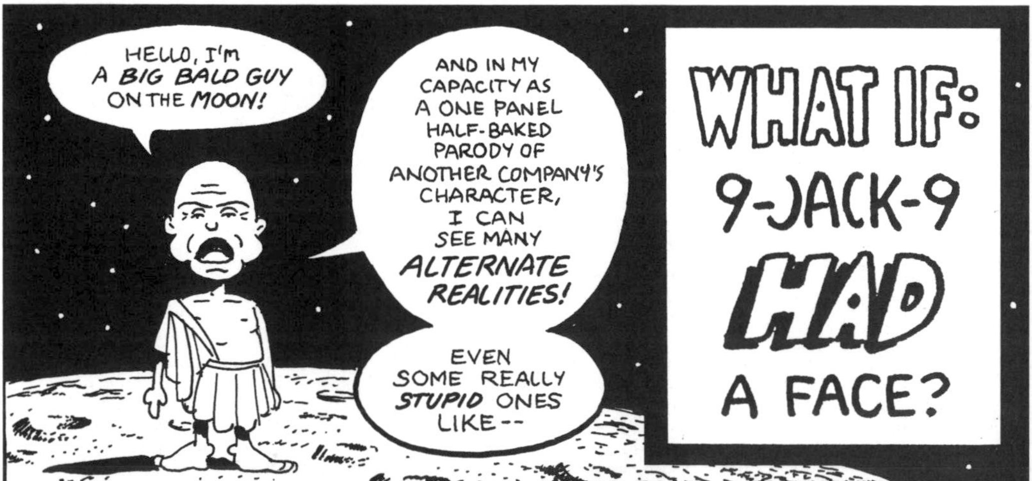
HELLO, I'M A BIG BALD GUY ON THE MOON!
AND IN MY CAPACITY AS A ONE PANEL HALF-BAKED PARODY OF ANOTHER COMPANY'S CHARACTER, I CAN SEE MANY ALTERNATE REALITIES!
EVEN SOME REALLY STUPID ONES LIKE --
WHAT IF:
9-JACK-9
HAD
A FACE?

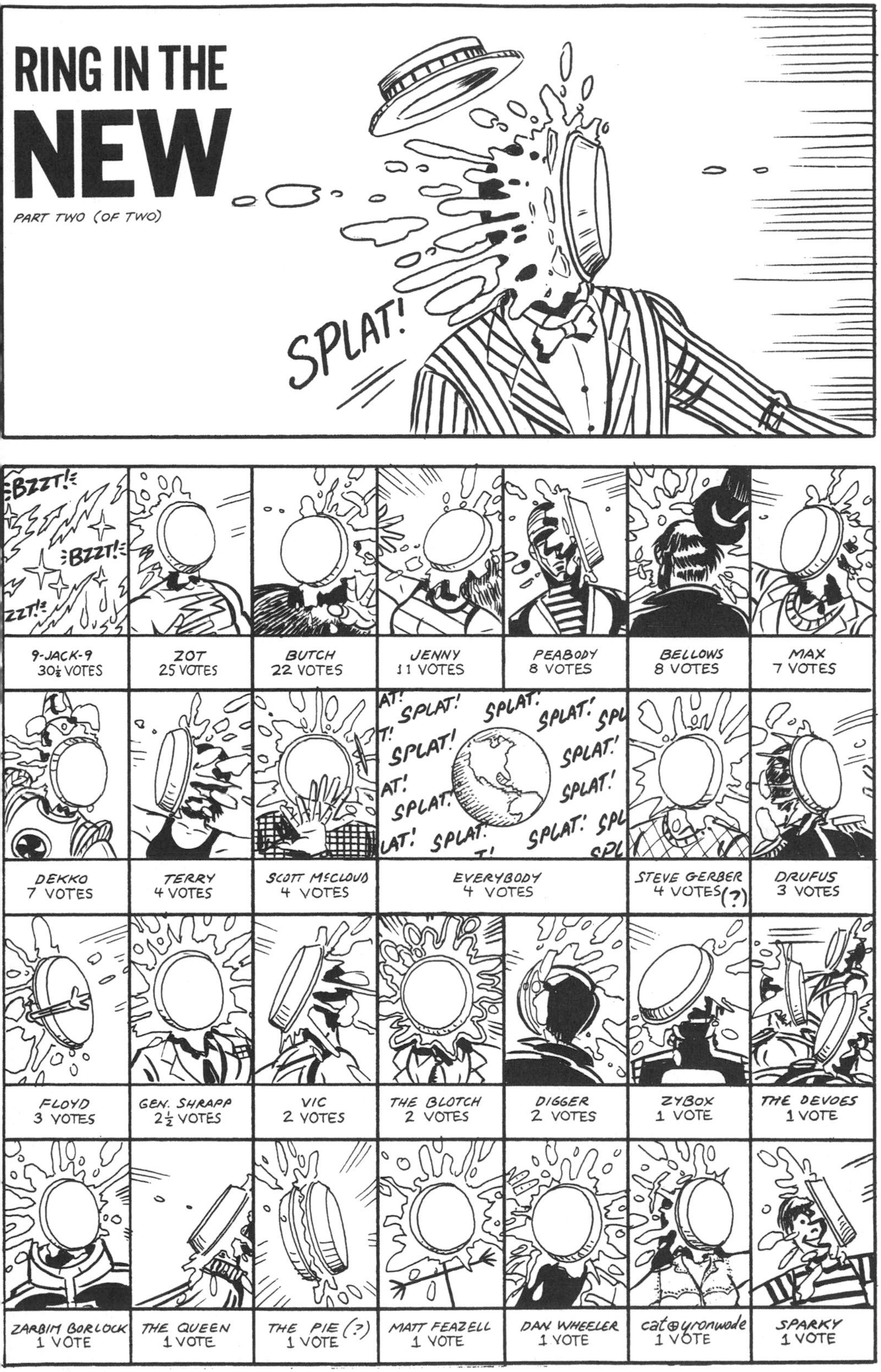
RING IN THE NEW
PART TWO (OF TWO)
SPLAT!
BZZT!
BZZT!
ZZT!
9-JACK-9
30½ VOTES
ZOT
25 VOTES
BUTCH
22 VOTES
JENNY
11 VOTES
PEABODY
8 VOTES
BELLOWS
8 VOTES
MAX
7 VOTES
DEKKO
7 VOTES
TERRY
4 VOTES
SCOTT McCLOUD
4 VOTES
SPLAT! SPLAT! SPLAT! SPLAT! SPLAT! SPLAT! SPLAT! SPLAT! SPLAT! SPLAT!
EVERYBODY
4 VOTES
STEVE GERBER
4 VOTES(?)
DRUFUS
3 VOTES
FLOYD
3 VOTES
GEN. SHRAPP
2½ VOTES
VIC
2 VOTES
THE BLOTCH
2 VOTES
DIGGER
2 VOTES
ZYBOX
1 VOTE
THE DEVOES
1 VOTE
ZARBIM BORLOCK
1 VOTE
THE QUEEN
1 VOTE
THE PIE (?)
1 VOTE
MATT FEAZELL
1 VOTE
DAN WHEELER
1 VOTE
cat⊕yronwode
1 VOTE
SPARKY
1 VOTE

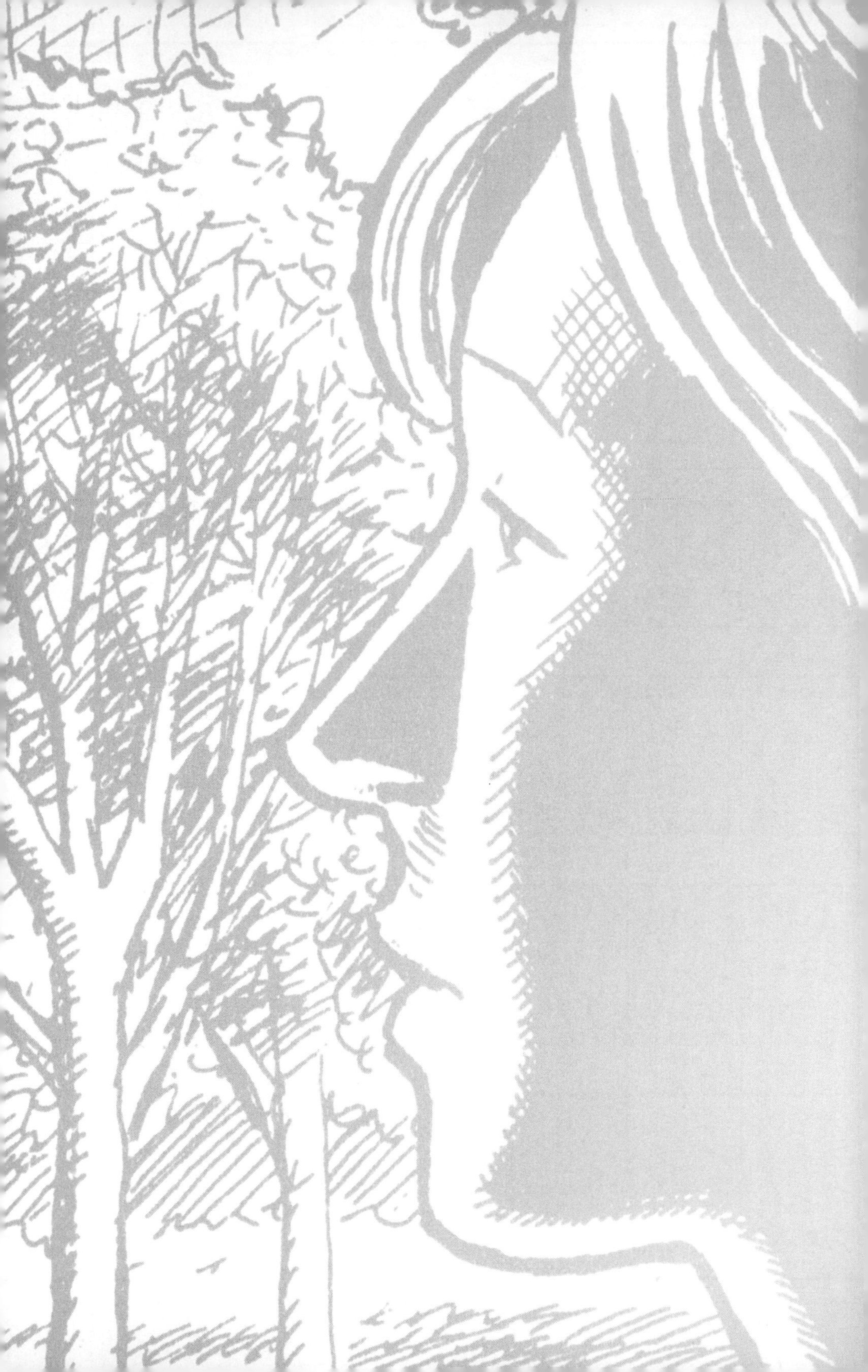

Part Two
The Earth Stories

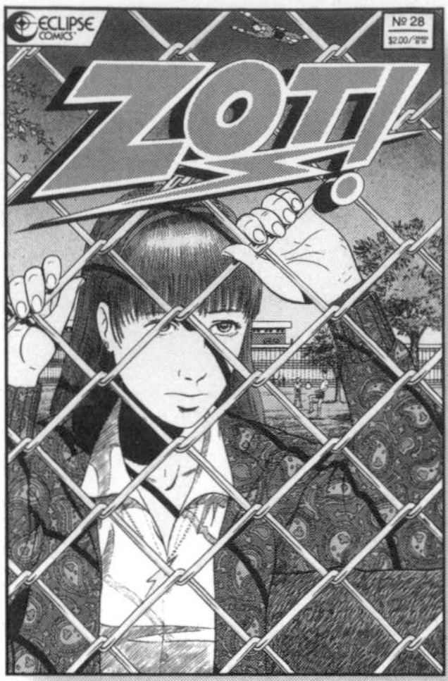
ECLIPSE COMICS
№ 28
ZOT!
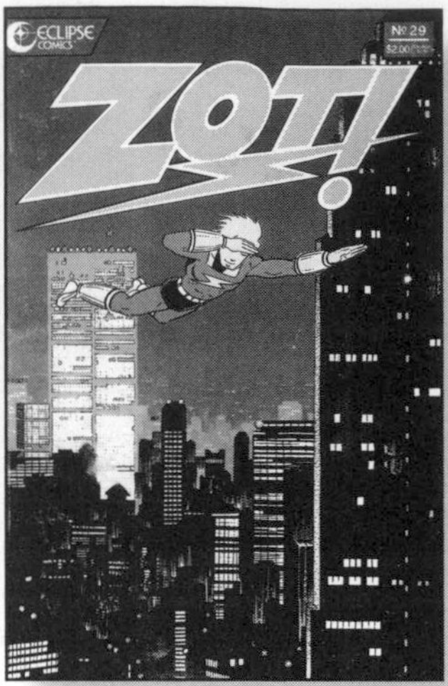
ECLIPSE COMICS
№ 29
ZOT!

Jenny's Day

First published in *Zot! #28*

Looking for Crime

First published in *Zot! #29*

Lettering:

Bob Lappan

Original series editor:

cat yronwode

Plot assist:

Ivy Ratafia

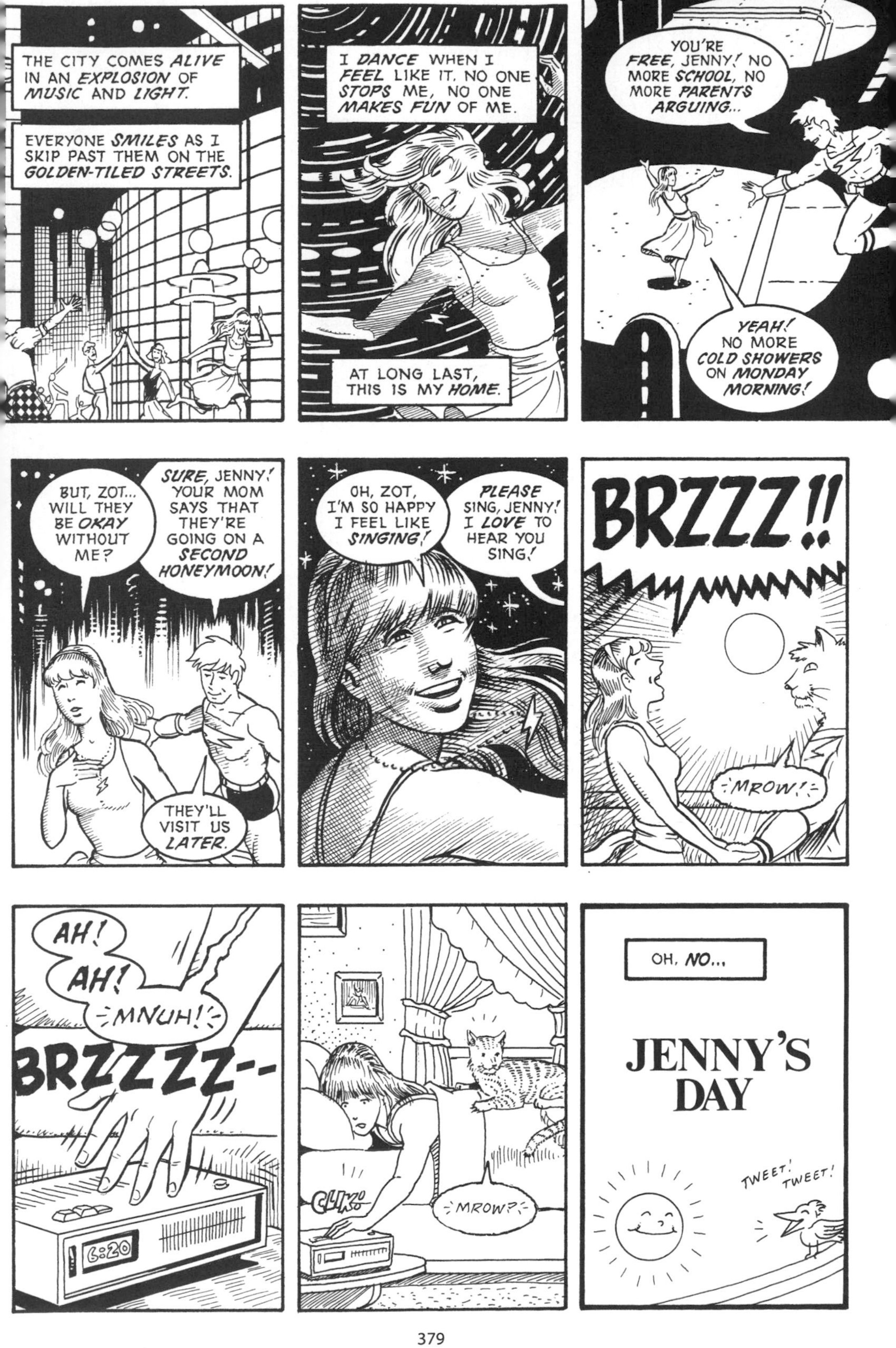

THE CITY COMES ALIVE IN AN EXPLOSION OF MUSIC AND LIGHT.
EVERYONE SMILES AS I SKIP PAST THEM ON THE GOLDEN-TILED STREETS.
I DANCE WHEN I FEEL LIKE IT. NO ONE STOPS ME, NO ONE MAKES FUN OF ME.
AT LONG LAST, THIS IS MY HOME.
YOU'RE FREE, JENNY! NO MORE SCHOOL, NO MORE PARENTS ARGUING...
YEAH! NO MORE COLD SHOWERS ON MONDAY MORNING!
BUT, ZOT... WILL THEY BE OKAY WITHOUT ME?
SURE, JENNY! YOUR MOM SAYS THAT THEY'RE GOING ON A SECOND HONEYMOON!
THEY'LL VISIT US LATER.
OH, ZOT, I'M SO HAPPY I FEEL LIKE SINGING!
PLEASE SING, JENNY! I LOVE TO HEAR YOU SING!
BRZZZ!!
MROW!
AH!
AH!
MNUH!
BRZZZZ--
6:20
CLIK
MROW?
OH, NO...
JENNY'S DAY
TWEET! TWEET!

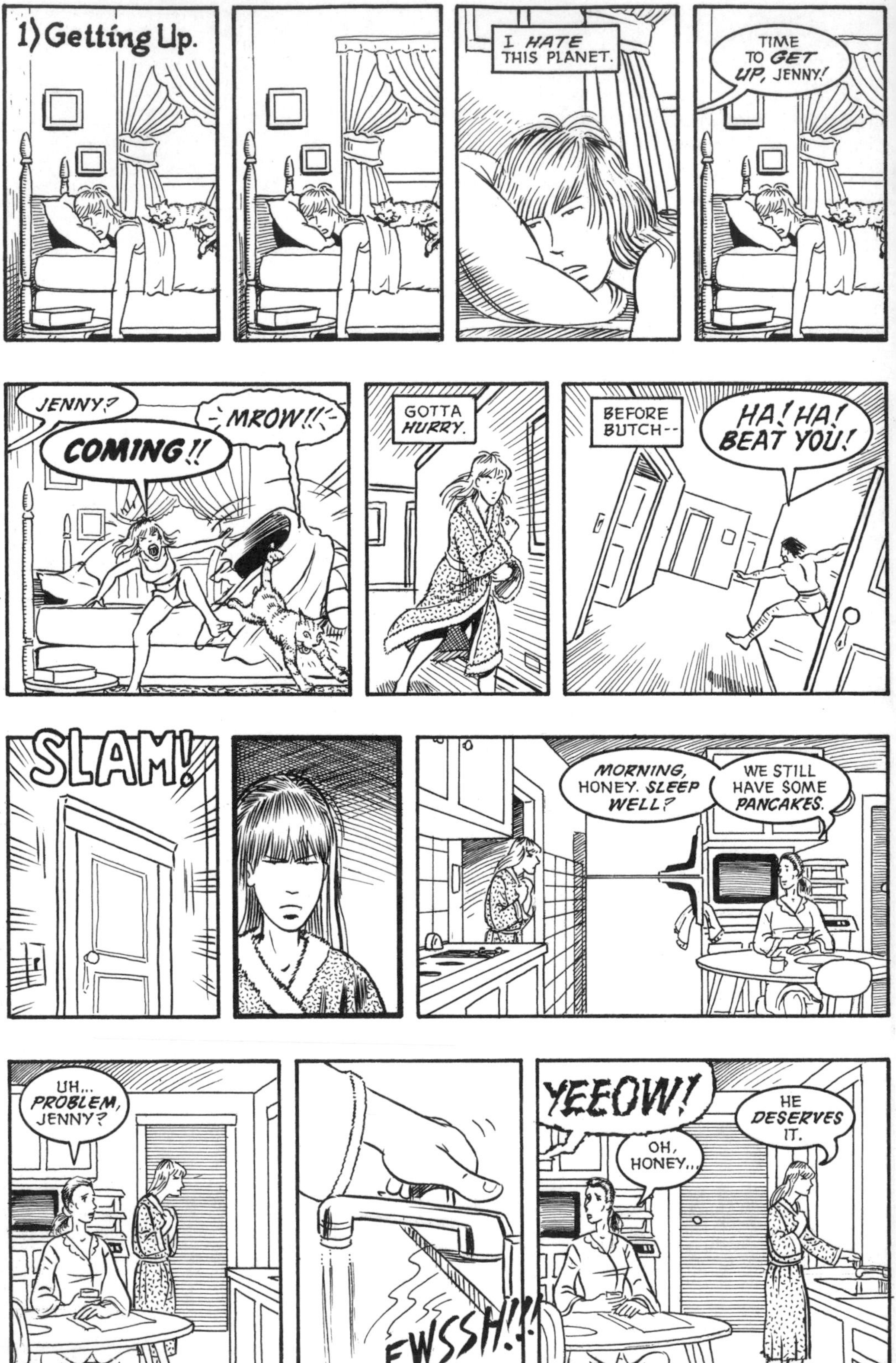
1) Getting Up.
I HATE THIS PLANET.
TIME TO GET UP, JENNY!
JENNY?
COMING!!
MROW!!
GOTTA HURRY.
BEFORE BUTCH--
HA! HA! BEAT YOU!
SLAM!
MORNING, HONEY. SLEEP WELL?
WE STILL HAVE SOME PANCAKES.
UH... PROBLEM, JENNY?
FWSSH!!!
YEEOW!
OH, HONEY...
HE DESERVES IT.

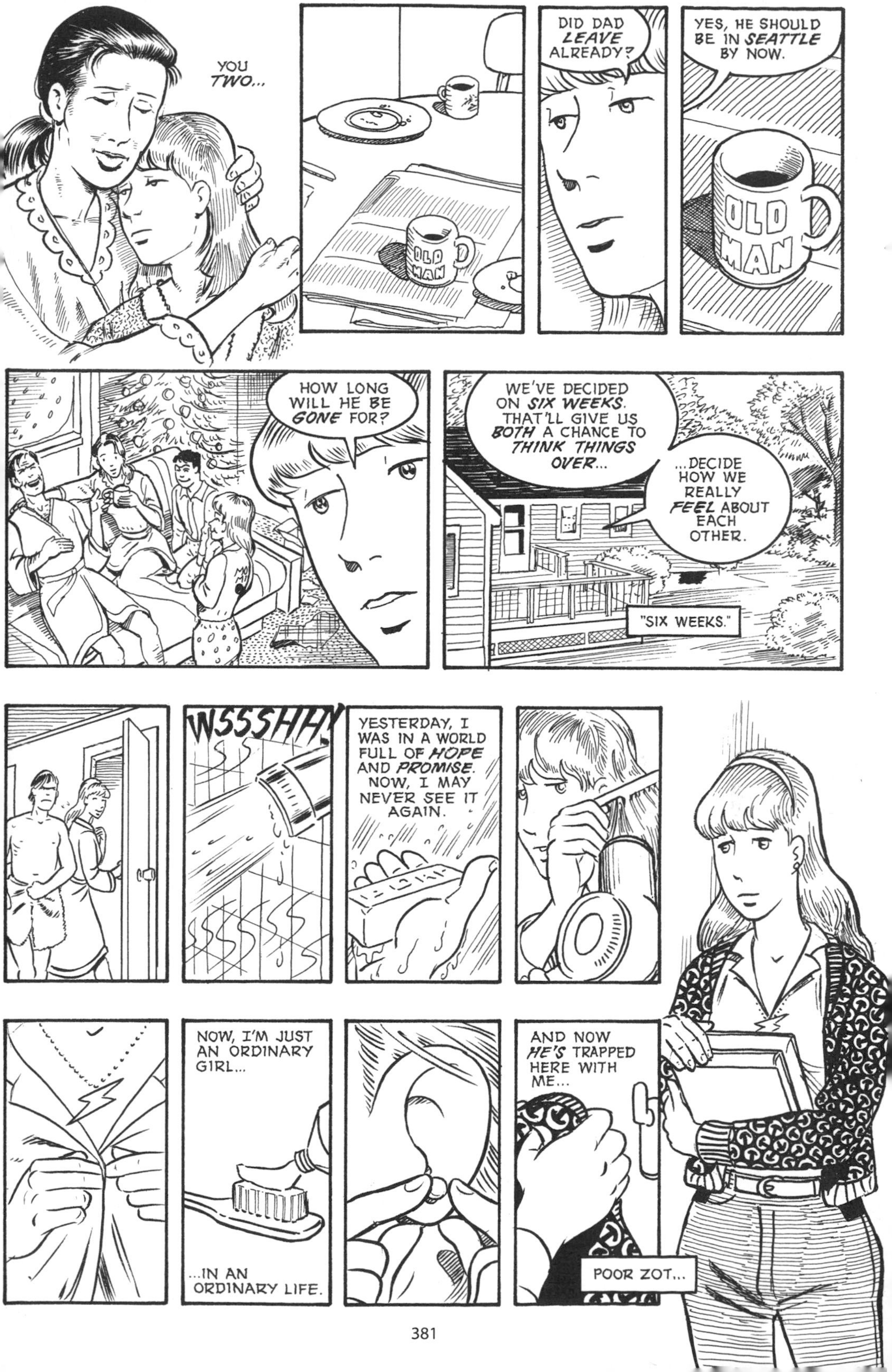

YOU TWO...
DID DAD LEAVE ALREADY?
YES, HE SHOULD BE IN SEATTLE BY NOW.
OLD MAN
HOW LONG WILL HE BE GONE FOR?
WE'VE DECIDED ON SIX WEEKS. THAT'LL GIVE US BOTH A CHANCE TO THINK THINGS OVER...
...DECIDE HOW WE REALLY FEEL ABOUT EACH OTHER.
"SIX WEEKS."
WSSSHH!
YESTERDAY, I WAS IN A WORLD FULL OF HOPE AND PROMISE. NOW, I MAY NEVER SEE IT AGAIN.
NOW, I'M JUST AN ORDINARY GIRL...
...IN AN ORDINARY LIFE.
AND NOW HE'S TRAPPED HERE WITH ME...
POOR ZOT...

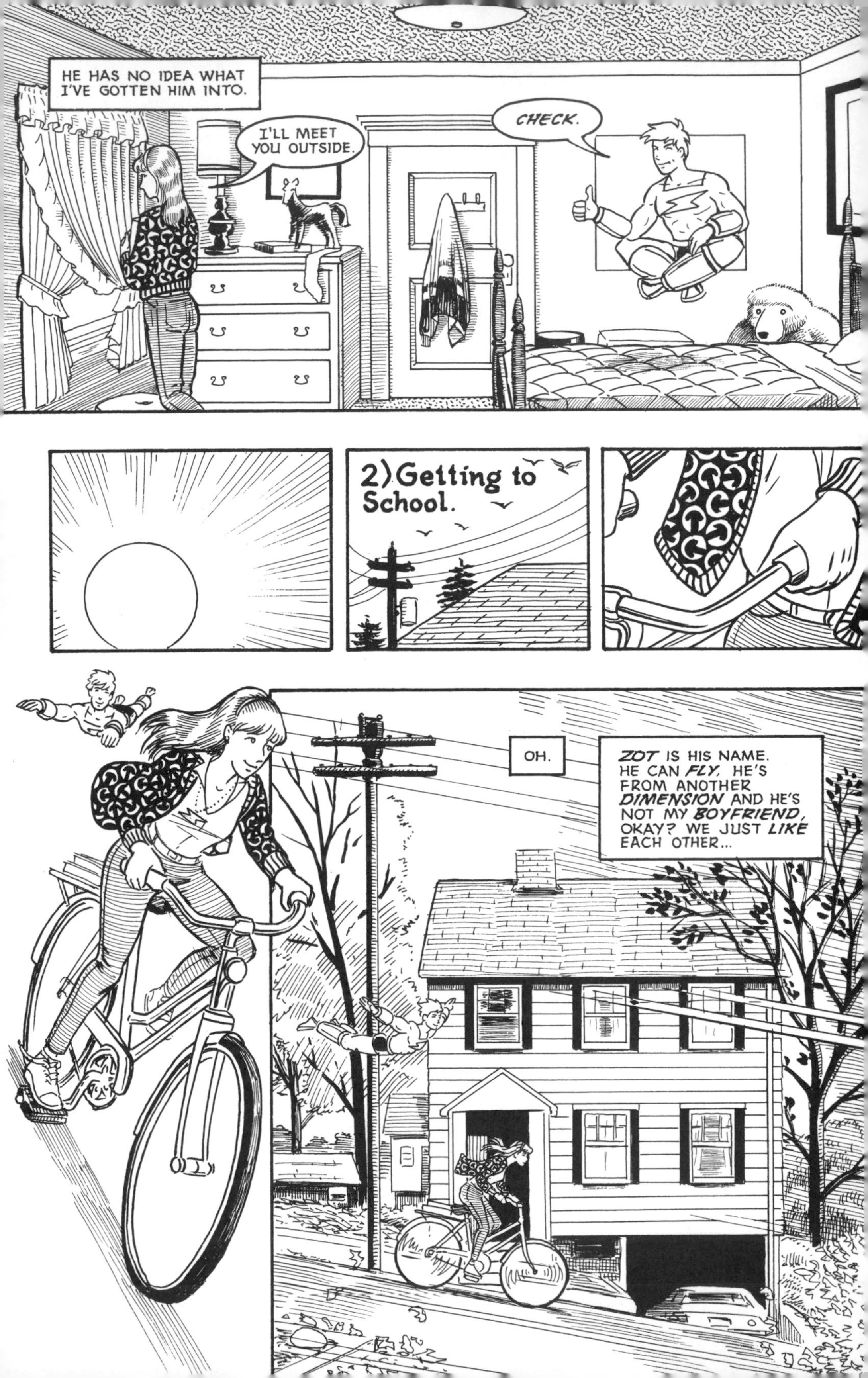
HE HAS NO IDEA WHAT I'VE GOTTEN HIM INTO.
I'LL MEET YOU OUTSIDE.
CHECK.
2) Getting to School.
OH.
ZOT IS HIS NAME. HE CAN FLY, HE'S FROM ANOTHER DIMENSION AND HE'S NOT MY BOYFRIEND, OKAY? WE JUST LIKE EACH OTHER...

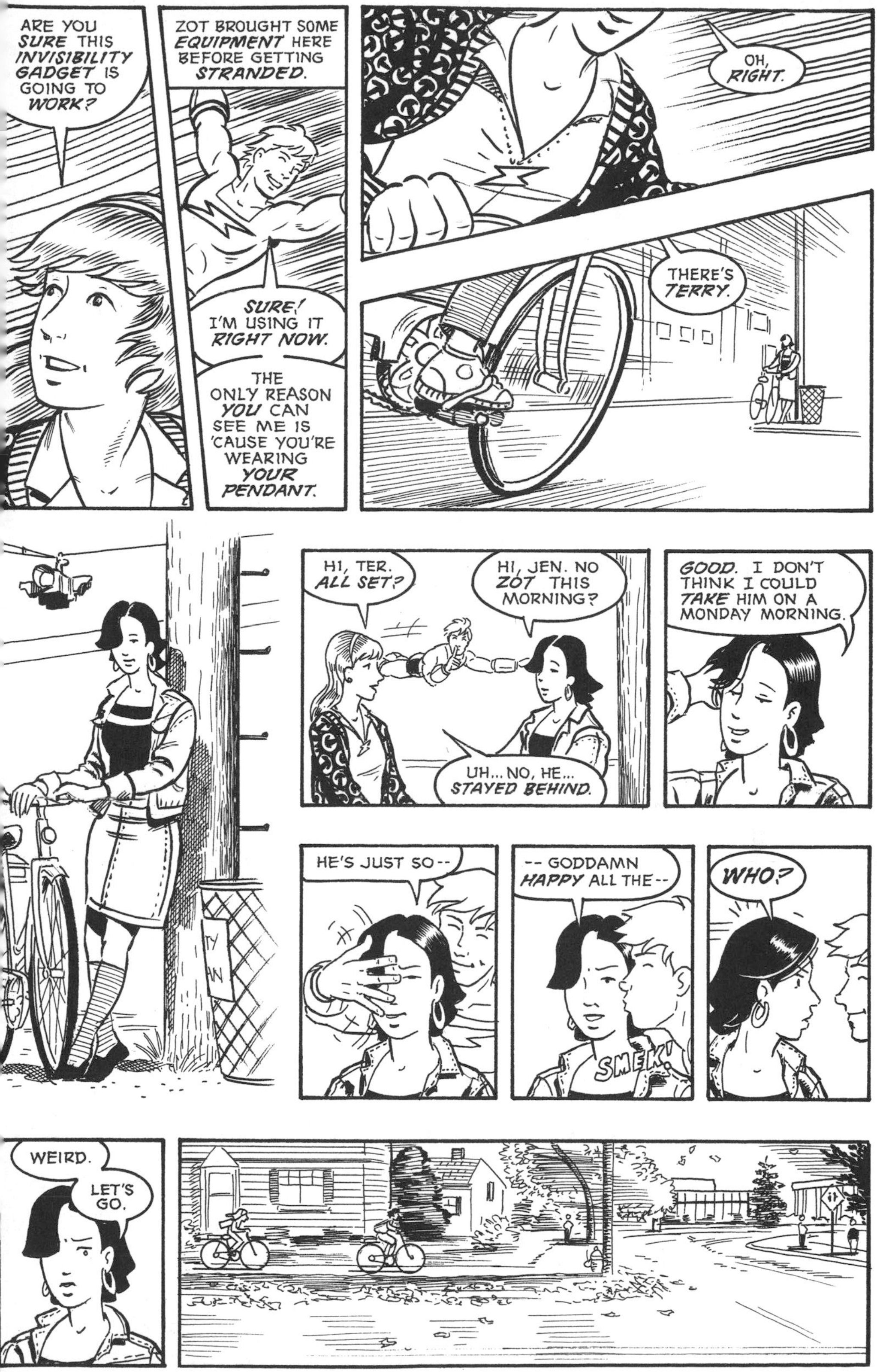
ARE YOU *SURE* THIS *INVISIBILITY GADGET* IS GOING TO *WORK?*
ZOT BROUGHT SOME *EQUIPMENT* HERE BEFORE GETTING *STRANDED.*
SURE! I'M USING IT *RIGHT NOW.*
THE ONLY REASON *YOU* CAN SEE ME IS 'CAUSE YOU'RE WEARING *YOUR PENDANT.*
OH, *RIGHT.*
THERE'S *TERRY.*
HI, TER. *ALL SET?*
HI, JEN. NO *ZOT* THIS MORNING?
UH... NO, HE... *STAYED BEHIND.*
GOOD. I DON'T THINK I COULD *TAKE* HIM ON A MONDAY MORNING.
HE'S JUST SO --
-- GODDAMN *HAPPY* ALL THE --
SMEK!
WHO?
WEIRD.
LET'S GO.

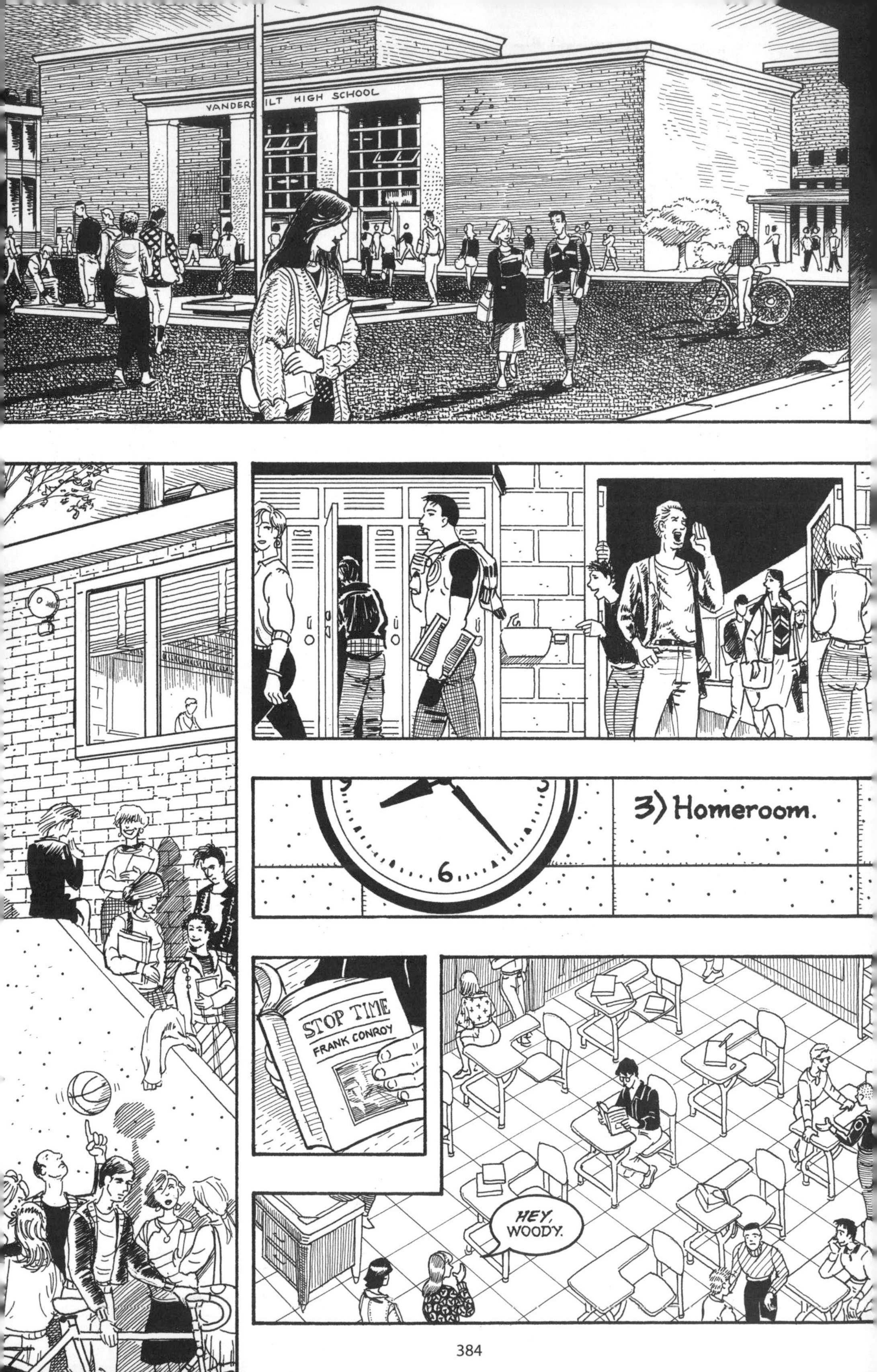
VANDERBILT HIGH SCHOOL
3) Homeroom.
STOP TIME
FRANK CONROY
HEY, WOODY.

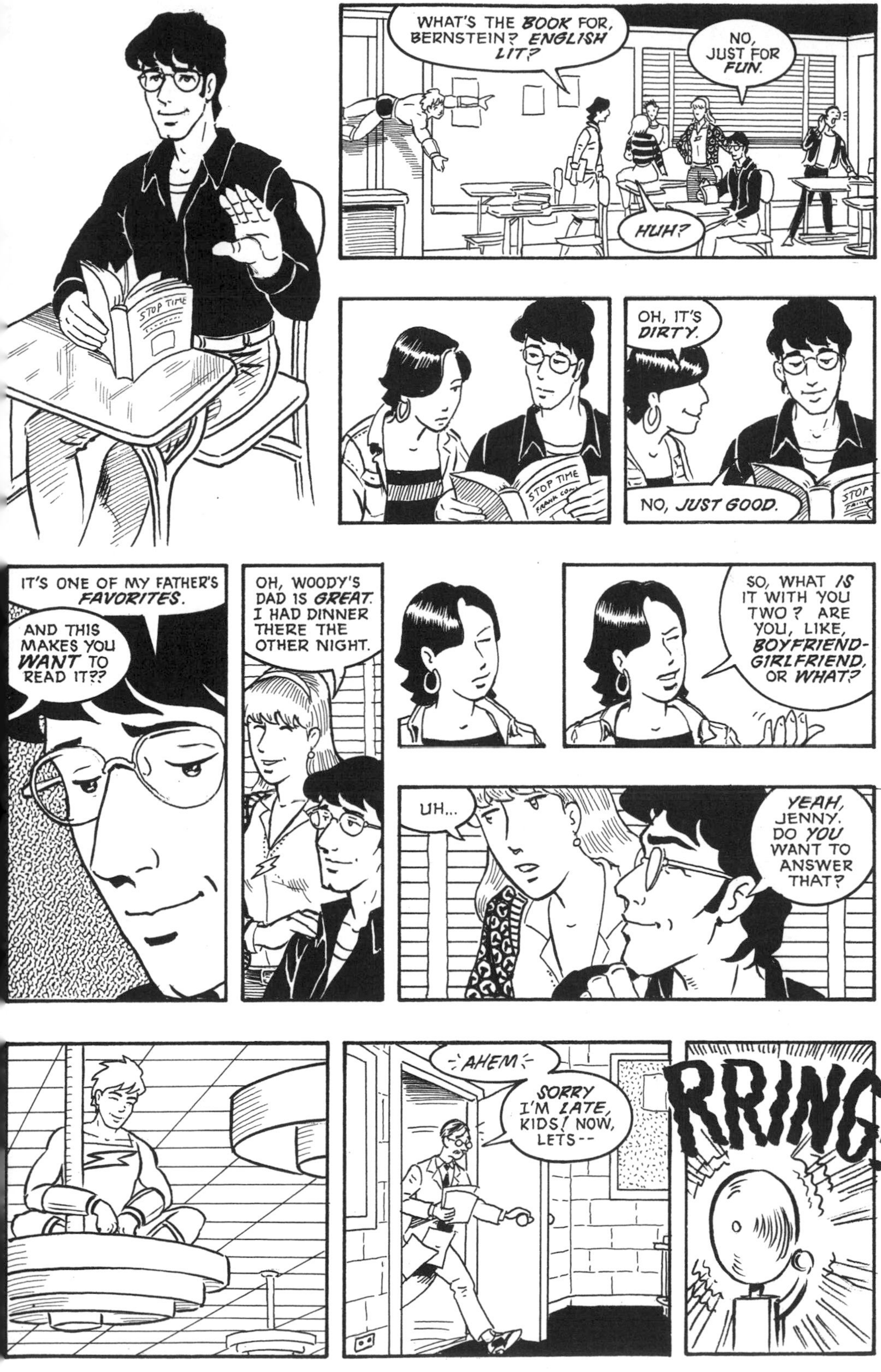

WHAT'S THE BOOK FOR, BERNSTEIN? ENGLISH LIT?
NO, JUST FOR FUN.
HUH?
STOP TIME
STOP TIME
FRANK CON
OH, IT'S DIRTY.
NO, JUST GOOD.
IT'S ONE OF MY FATHER'S FAVORITES.
AND THIS MAKES YOU WANT TO READ IT??
OH, WOODY'S DAD IS GREAT. I HAD DINNER THERE THE OTHER NIGHT.
SO, WHAT IS IT WITH YOU TWO? ARE YOU, LIKE, BOYFRIEND-GIRLFRIEND, OR WHAT?
UH...
YEAH, JENNY. DO YOU WANT TO ANSWER THAT?
AHEM
SORRY I'M LATE, KIDS! NOW, LETS--
RRING!

4) English.

I'M IN LUCK. ALMOST *NO ONE* DID THE ASSIGNMENT.

SURPRISE QUIZ!

-GROAN-

I MAKE IT UP AS I GO ALONG.

① What *is little Peter cryds* rolled out of the room?

"*Oh no!* ②

t does the a

REVIEW:

SO!

HOW *DOES* THE YOUNG BLIND MUSICIAN TRY TO *KILL* HIMSELF?

READINGS:

"ON THE NEXT FLOOR BELOW ARE THE ABDOMINAL AND SPINE CASES, HEAD WOUND AND DOUBLE AMPUTATIONS. ON THE RIGHT SIDE OF THE WING ARE THE JAW WOUNDS, GAS CASES, NOSE, EAR AND NECK WOUNDS."

A BIT *LOUDER*, RICHARD. WE CAN'T HEAR YOU.

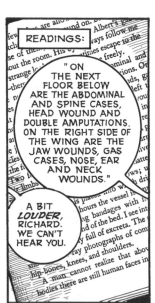

-AHEM- "ON THE LEFT, THE BLIND AND THE LUNG WOUNDS, PELVIS WOUNDS, WOUNDS IN THE JOINTS, WOUNDS IN THE KIDNEYS, WOUNDS IN THE TESTICLES, WOUNDS IN THE INTESTINES."

LOUDER! SPEAK UP!

"TWO FELLOWS DIE OF TETANUS. THEIR SKIN TURNS PALE, THEIR LIMBS STIFFEN, AT LAST ONLY THEIR EYES LIVE..."

NEVER HAVE PANCAKES BEFORE ENGLISH.

"...THEIR SHATTERED LIMBS HANGING FREE IN THE AIR FROM GALLOWS; UNDERNEATH THE WOUND A BASIN IS PLACED INTO WHICH DRIPS THE PUS..."

5) Math.

YOU *STUDY?*

ME *NEITHER.*

YOU *HAVE* TO STUDY FOR *BOYNTON'S* TESTS.

$4x^2 + y$

$-y^2 - 148 - 8y + 3$

$(x = 14x - 49)(y^2 +$

$\dfrac{(x-7)^2}{-4} \div \dfrac{(y+4)^2}{2}$

$\dfrac{(y+4)^{\frac{4}{2}}}{2} - \Big($

WOODY STUDIED. HE *ALWAYS* STUDIES. I WOULDN'T DARE *COPY* HIM, THOUGH.

WOULD I?

Y'KNOW, *FAILING TESTS* WOULDN'T BE SO *BAD* IF YOU COULD ONLY KNOW *AHEAD OF TIME* THAT YOU WERE *GOING* TO FAIL. THEN AT LEAST YOU WOULDN'T HAVE TO *WORK* SO HARD.

}Yawwn}

OH, *LOOK* AT HIM.

I *WARNED* YOU, ZOT. SCHOOL IS *NO PICNIC* ON--

UH- OH.

I WISH HE WOULDN'T STAND SO *CLOSE.*

-}WHEW}- PASSED ME BY!

WHAT?

HEY! I WASN'T COPYING!

=RRRIP=

AWW, *C'MON,* MR. B!

C'MON, I WASN'T *COPYING!*

OUT.

6) French.

I'VE HAD *SIX YEARS* OF FRENCH CLASS SO FAR.

EVERY FRENCH TEACHER I HAVE EVER HAD HAS BEEN *CHEERFUL, KIND, HELPFUL* AND *ENTHUSIASTIC.*

"VIALAT: MON É PAULE ME FAIT MAL..."

MONIQUE!

POLICIER: UN PEU DE PATIENCE. VOUS ALLEZ...

I'VE ALWAYS DONE THE ASSIGNMENTS JUST AS I WAS *TOLD* TO.

BIEN!

BIEN!

AND *I'VE* ALWAYS GOTTEN *A's* AND *B's*

tionaire

e presentent les rt d'em avion ? quoi le policier ce que les chau ours bavards ? travail des pol ulier ?

l'arc de Triumph

I *SWEAR TO GOD,* I DON'T KNOW A *WORD* OF FRENCH.

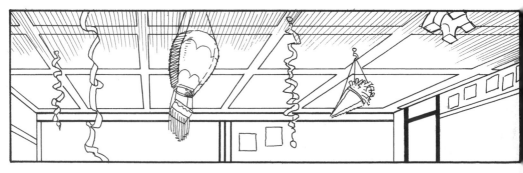

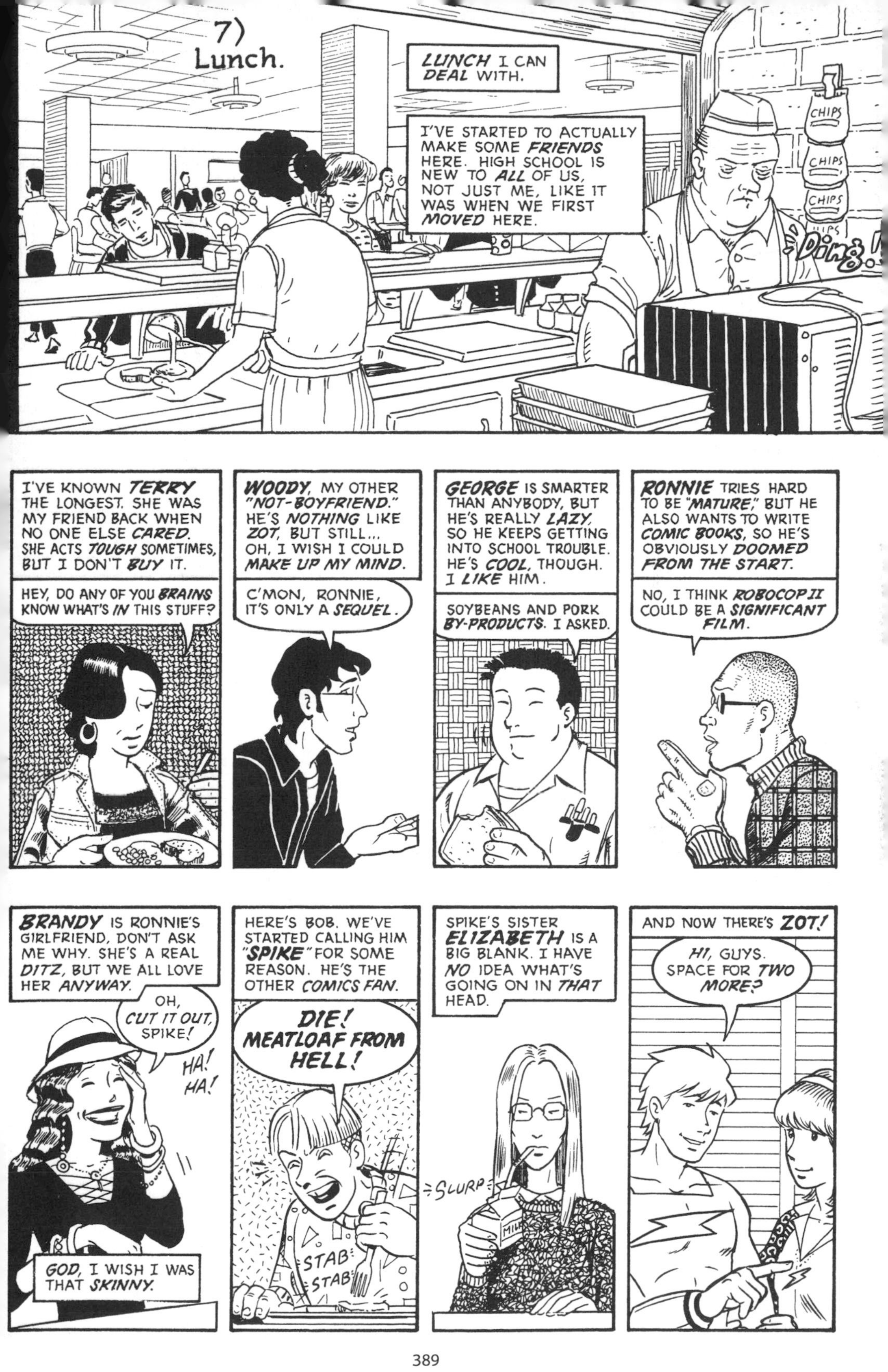
7) Lunch.
LUNCH I CAN DEAL WITH.
I'VE STARTED TO ACTUALLY MAKE SOME FRIENDS HERE. HIGH SCHOOL IS NEW TO ALL OF US, NOT JUST ME, LIKE IT WAS WHEN WE FIRST MOVED HERE.
CHIPS
CHIPS
CHIPS
Ding
I'VE KNOWN TERRY THE LONGEST. SHE WAS MY FRIEND BACK WHEN NO ONE ELSE CARED. SHE ACTS TOUGH SOMETIMES, BUT I DON'T BUY IT.
HEY, DO ANY OF YOU BRAINS KNOW WHAT'S IN THIS STUFF?
WOODY, MY OTHER "NOT-BOYFRIEND." HE'S NOTHING LIKE ZOT, BUT STILL... OH, I WISH I COULD MAKE UP MY MIND.
C'MON, RONNIE, IT'S ONLY A SEQUEL.
GEORGE IS SMARTER THAN ANYBODY, BUT HE'S REALLY LAZY, SO HE KEEPS GETTING INTO SCHOOL TROUBLE. HE'S COOL, THOUGH. I LIKE HIM.
SOYBEANS AND PORK BY-PRODUCTS. I ASKED.
RONNIE TRIES HARD TO BE "MATURE," BUT HE ALSO WANTS TO WRITE COMIC BOOKS, SO HE'S OBVIOUSLY DOOMED FROM THE START.
NO, I THINK ROBOCOP II COULD BE A SIGNIFICANT FILM.
BRANDY IS RONNIE'S GIRLFRIEND, DON'T ASK ME WHY. SHE'S A REAL DITZ, BUT WE ALL LOVE HER ANYWAY.
OH, CUT IT OUT, SPIKE!
HA! HA!
GOD, I WISH I WAS THAT SKINNY.
HERE'S BOB. WE'VE STARTED CALLING HIM "SPIKE" FOR SOME REASON. HE'S THE OTHER COMICS FAN.
DIE! MEATLOAF FROM HELL!
STAB STAB
SLURP
SPIKE'S SISTER ELIZABETH IS A BIG BLANK. I HAVE NO IDEA WHAT'S GOING ON IN THAT HEAD.
MILK
AND NOW THERE'S ZOT!
HI, GUYS. SPACE FOR TWO MORE?

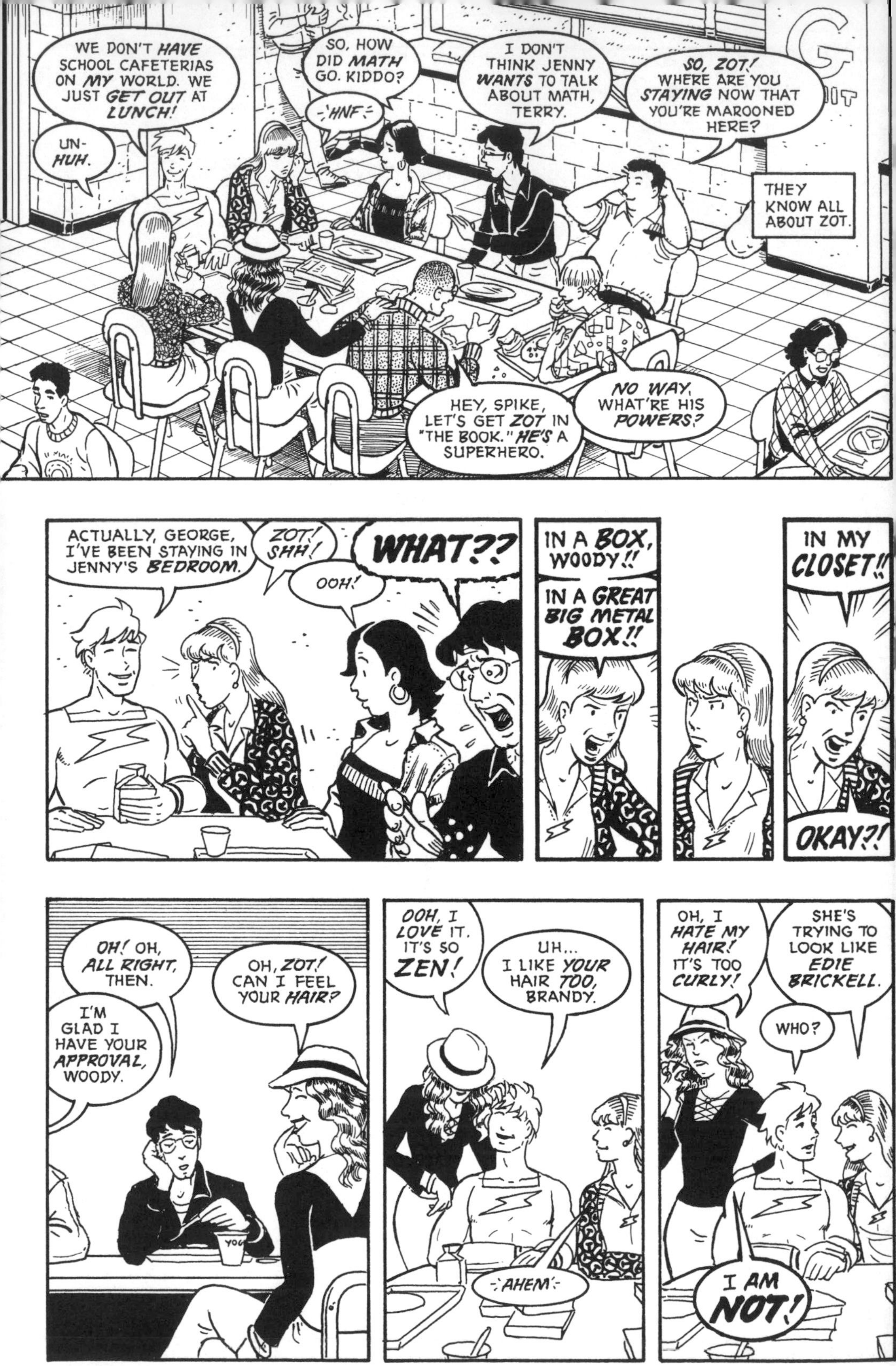
WE DON'T HAVE SCHOOL CAFETERIAS ON MY WORLD. WE JUST GET OUT AT LUNCH!
UN-HUH.
SO, HOW DID MATH GO. KIDDO?
HNF
I DON'T THINK JENNY WANTS TO TALK ABOUT MATH, TERRY.
SO, ZOT! WHERE ARE YOU STAYING NOW THAT YOU'RE MAROONED HERE?
THEY KNOW ALL ABOUT ZOT.
HEY, SPIKE, LET'S GET ZOT IN "THE BOOK." HE'S A SUPERHERO.
NO WAY. WHAT'RE HIS POWERS?
ACTUALLY, GEORGE, I'VE BEEN STAYING IN JENNY'S BEDROOM.
ZOT! SHH!
OOH!
WHAT??
IN A BOX, WOODY!!
IN A GREAT BIG METAL BOX!!
IN MY CLOSET!!
OKAY?!
OH! OH, ALL RIGHT, THEN.
I'M GLAD I HAVE YOUR APPROVAL, WOODY.
OH, ZOT! CAN I FEEL YOUR HAIR?
OOH, I LOVE IT. IT'S SO ZEN!
UH... I LIKE YOUR HAIR TOO, BRANDY.
AHEM
OH, I HATE MY HAIR! IT'S TOO CURLY!
SHE'S TRYING TO LOOK LIKE EDIE BRICKELL.
WHO?
I AM NOT!

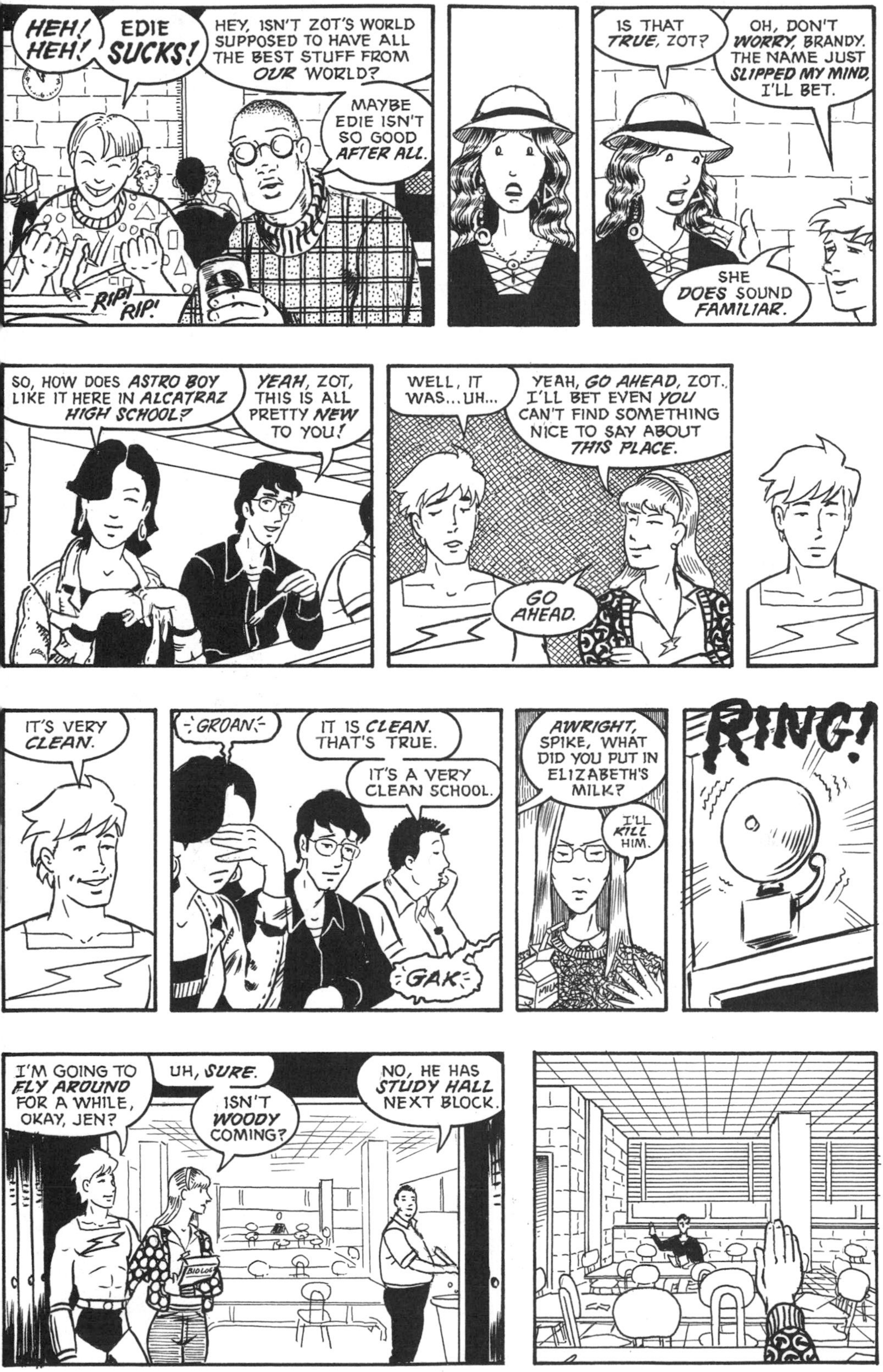
HEH! HEH!
EDIE SUCKS!
HEY, ISN'T ZOT'S WORLD SUPPOSED TO HAVE ALL THE BEST STUFF FROM OUR WORLD?
MAYBE EDIE ISN'T SO GOOD AFTER ALL.
RIP! RIP!
IS THAT TRUE, ZOT?
OH, DON'T WORRY, BRANDY. THE NAME JUST SLIPPED MY MIND, I'LL BET.
SHE DOES SOUND FAMILIAR.
SO, HOW DOES ASTRO BOY LIKE IT HERE IN ALCATRAZ HIGH SCHOOL?
YEAH, ZOT, THIS IS ALL PRETTY NEW TO YOU!
WELL, IT WAS...UH...
YEAH, GO AHEAD, ZOT. I'LL BET EVEN YOU CAN'T FIND SOMETHING NICE TO SAY ABOUT THIS PLACE.
GO AHEAD.
IT'S VERY CLEAN.
GROAN
IT IS CLEAN. THAT'S TRUE.
IT'S A VERY CLEAN SCHOOL.
GAK
AWRIGHT, SPIKE, WHAT DID YOU PUT IN ELIZABETH'S MILK?
I'LL KILL HIM.
RING!
I'M GOING TO FLY AROUND FOR A WHILE, OKAY, JEN?
UH, SURE.
ISN'T WOODY COMING?
NO, HE HAS STUDY HALL NEXT BLOCK.

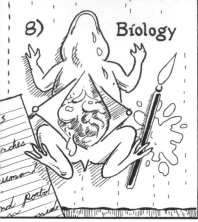

8) Biology

GOD, THIS IS *SO GROSS*... THIS IS *SO* GROSS...

IT'LL BE OVER *SOON,* KIDDO.

HEY, IF *LAST* PERIOD WAS *LUNCH,* DOES THAT MAKE THIS *DESSERT?*

PISS OFF, SPIKE!

AT LEAST *ART* IS NEXT. I ACTUALLY *LIKE* ART CLASS.

ART CLASS
D BLOCK
CANCELLED

AW *RIGHT!*

YEH!

CANCELLED? *GREAT!*

I'M *OUTTA* HERE!

HI, ZOT. I'VE DECIDED TO SKIP *GYM* CLASS.

AW, YOU SHOULDN'T NEGLECT YOUR *PHYSICAL FITTNESS,* JEN!

I *SAID* I'M SKIPPING GYM.

UM... OKAY.

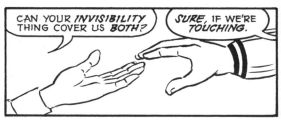

CAN YOUR *INVISIBILITY* THING COVER US *BOTH?*

SURE, IF WE'RE *TOUCHING.*

392

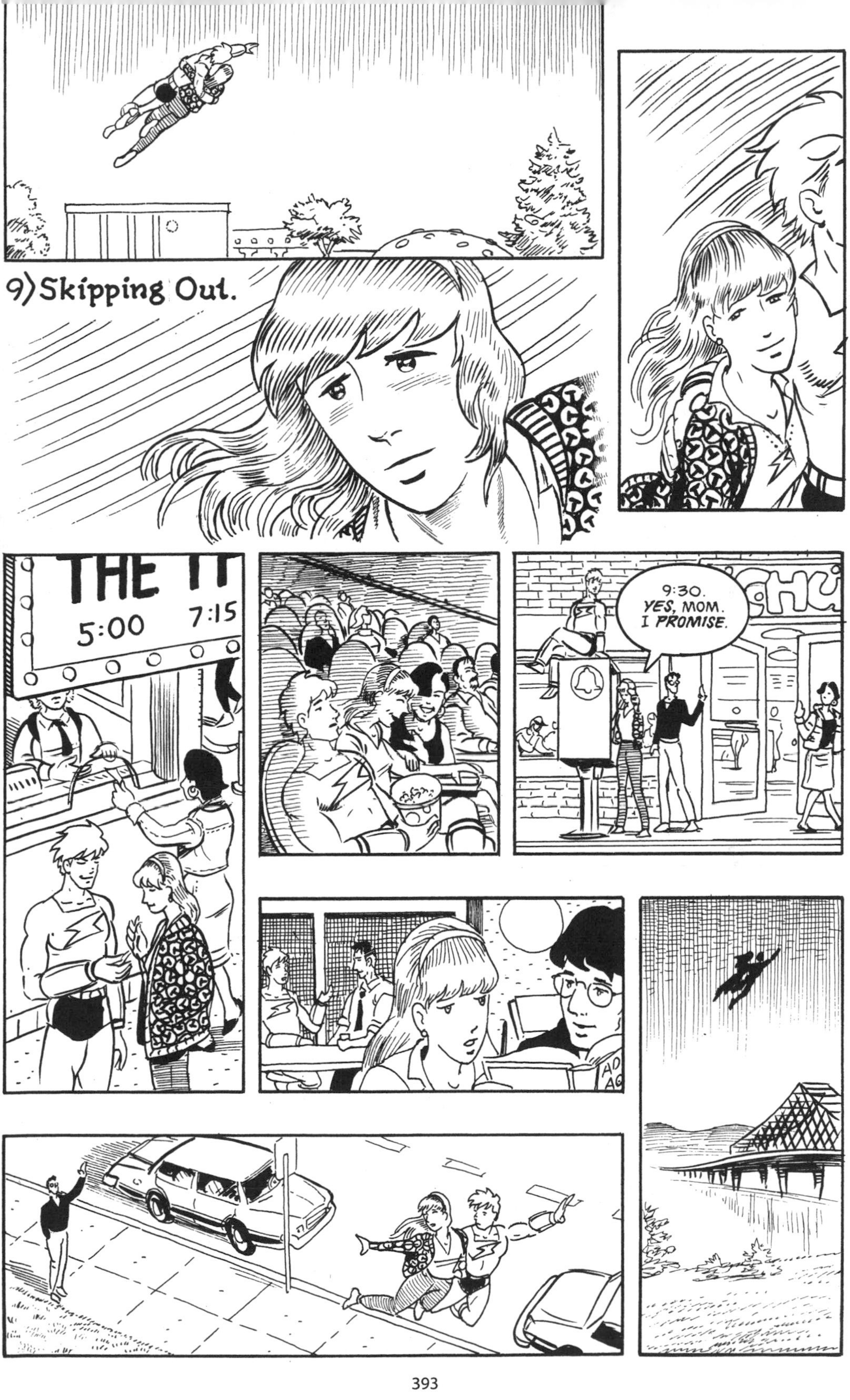
9) Skipping Out.
THE
5:00 7:15
9:30. YES, MOM. I PROMISE.

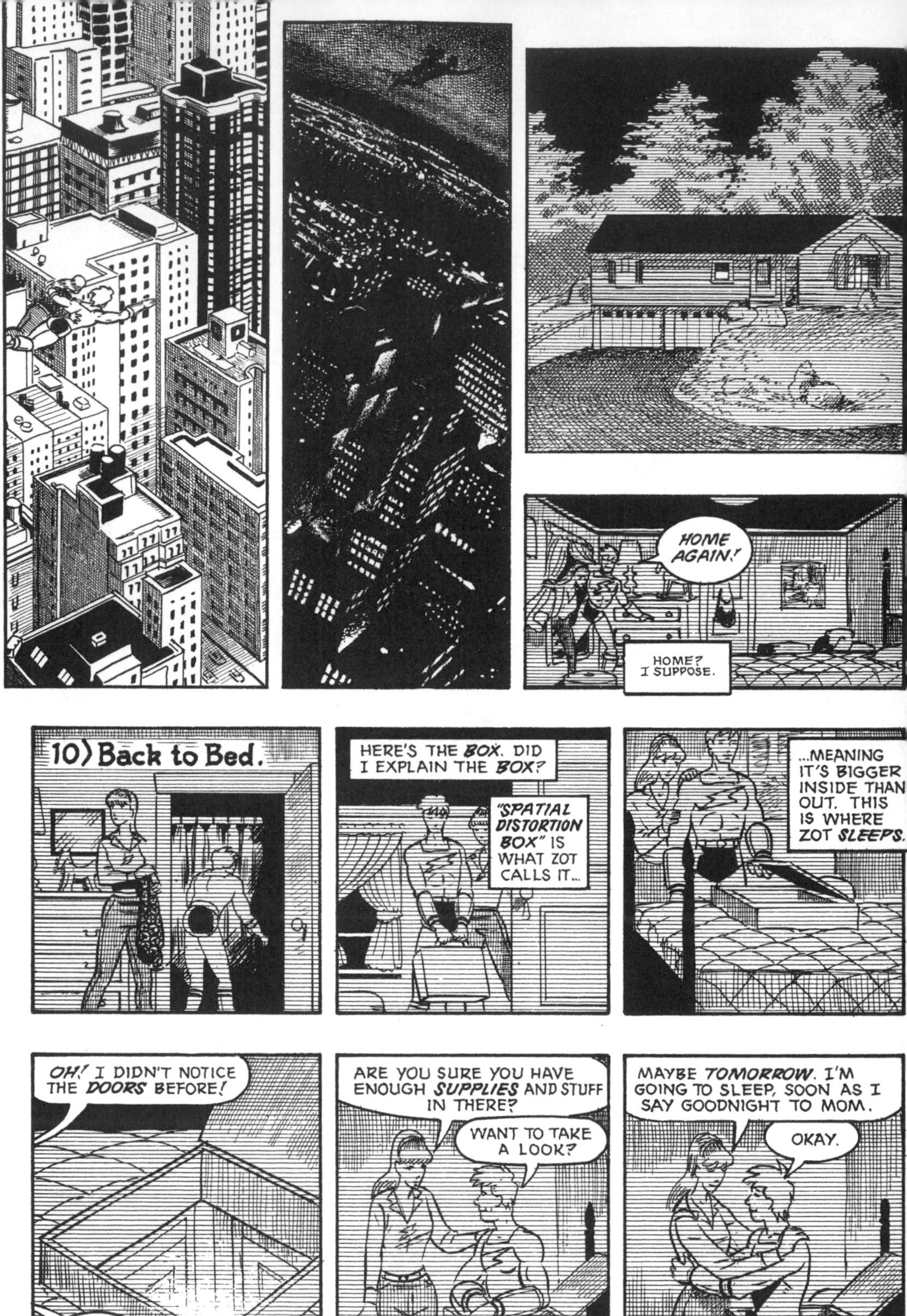
HOME AGAIN!
HOME? I SUPPOSE.
10) Back to Bed.
HERE'S THE BOX. DID I EXPLAIN THE BOX?
"SPATIAL DISTORTION BOX" IS WHAT ZOT CALLS IT...
...MEANING IT'S BIGGER INSIDE THAN OUT. THIS IS WHERE ZOT SLEEPS.
OH! I DIDN'T NOTICE THE DOORS BEFORE!
YEAH, IT'S COMFY.
ARE YOU SURE YOU HAVE ENOUGH SUPPLIES AND STUFF IN THERE?
WANT TO TAKE A LOOK?
MAYBE TOMORROW. I'M GOING TO SLEEP, SOON AS I SAY GOODNIGHT TO MOM.
OKAY.

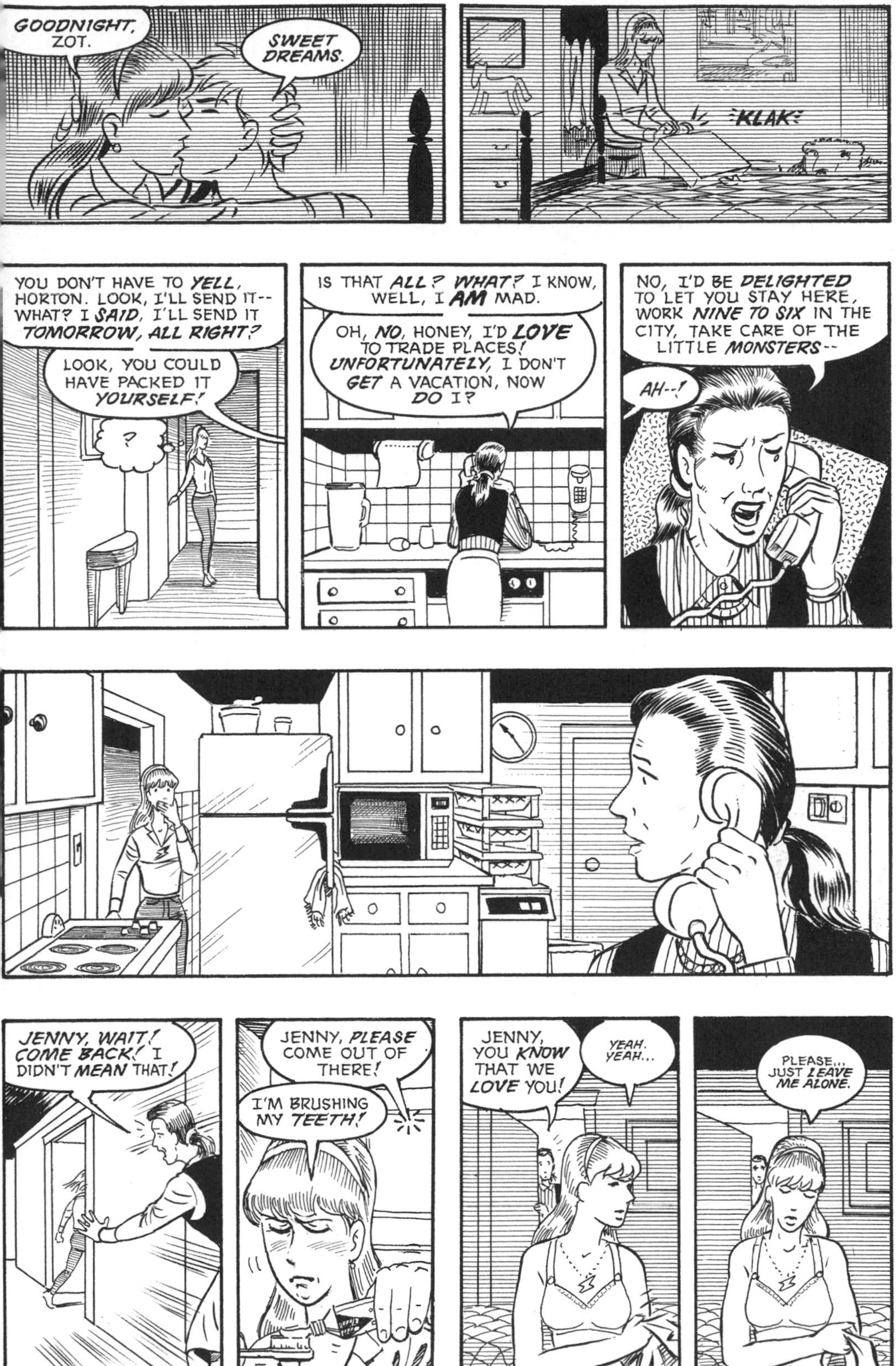
GOODNIGHT, ZOT.
SWEET DREAMS.
KLAK
YOU DON'T HAVE TO YELL, HORTON. LOOK, I'LL SEND IT-- WHAT? I SAID, I'LL SEND IT TOMORROW, ALL RIGHT?
LOOK, YOU COULD HAVE PACKED IT YOURSELF!
?
IS THAT ALL? WHAT? I KNOW, WELL, I AM MAD.
OH, NO, HONEY, I'D LOVE TO TRADE PLACES! UNFORTUNATELY, I DON'T GET A VACATION, NOW DO I?
NO, I'D BE DELIGHTED TO LET YOU STAY HERE, WORK NINE TO SIX IN THE CITY, TAKE CARE OF THE LITTLE MONSTERS--
AH--!
JENNY, WAIT! COME BACK! I DIDN'T MEAN THAT!
JENNY, PLEASE COME OUT OF THERE!
I'M BRUSHING MY TEETH!
JENNY, YOU KNOW THAT WE LOVE YOU!
YEAH. YEAH...
PLEASE... JUST LEAVE ME ALONE.

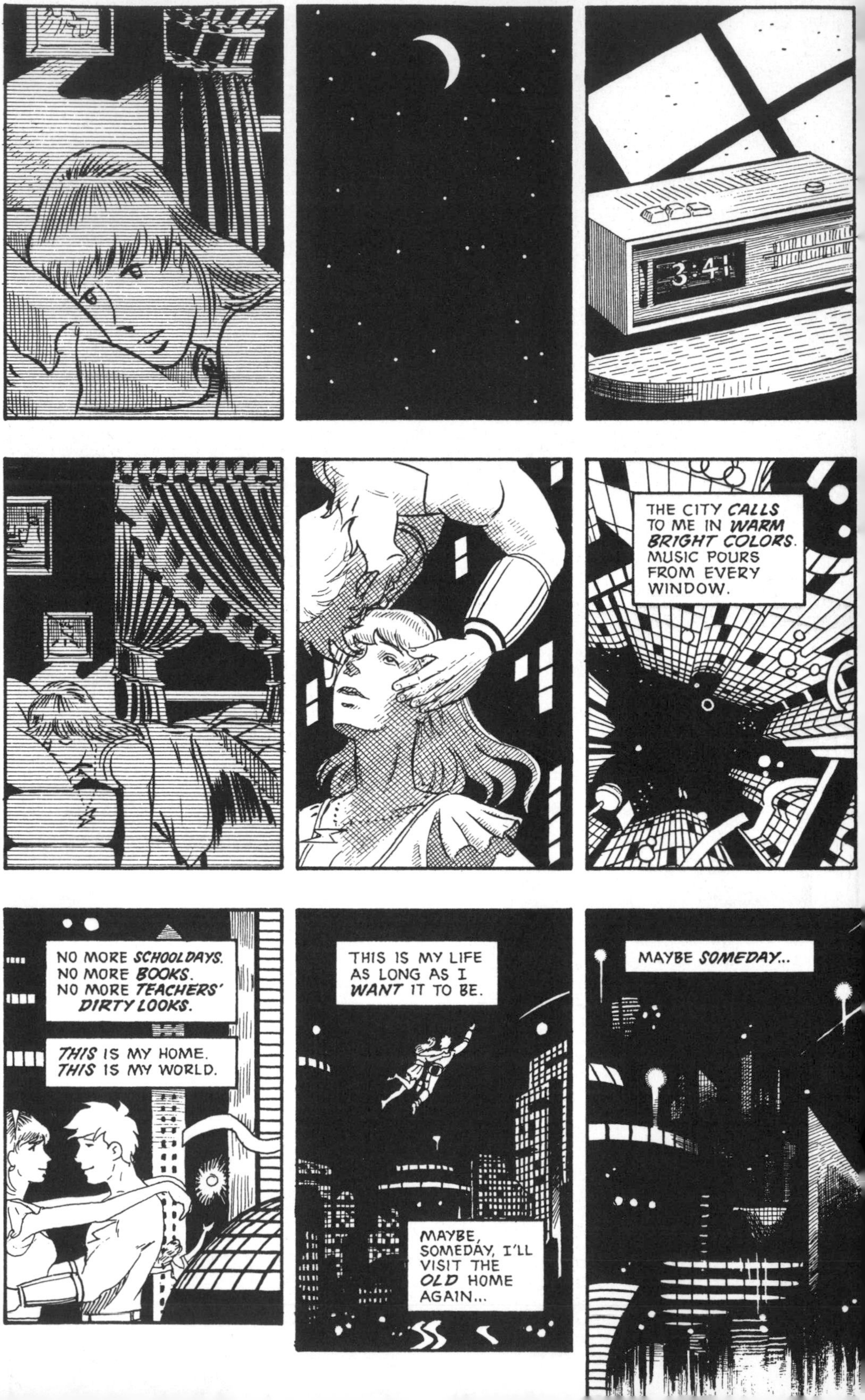
3:41
THE CITY CALLS TO ME IN WARM BRIGHT COLORS. MUSIC POURS FROM EVERY WINDOW.
NO MORE SCHOOLDAYS. NO MORE BOOKS. NO MORE TEACHERS' DIRTY LOOKS.
THIS IS MY HOME. THIS IS MY WORLD.
THIS IS MY LIFE AS LONG AS I WANT IT TO BE.
MAYBE, SOMEDAY, I'LL VISIT THE OLD HOME AGAIN...
MAYBE SOMEDAY...

LOOKING FOR CRIME

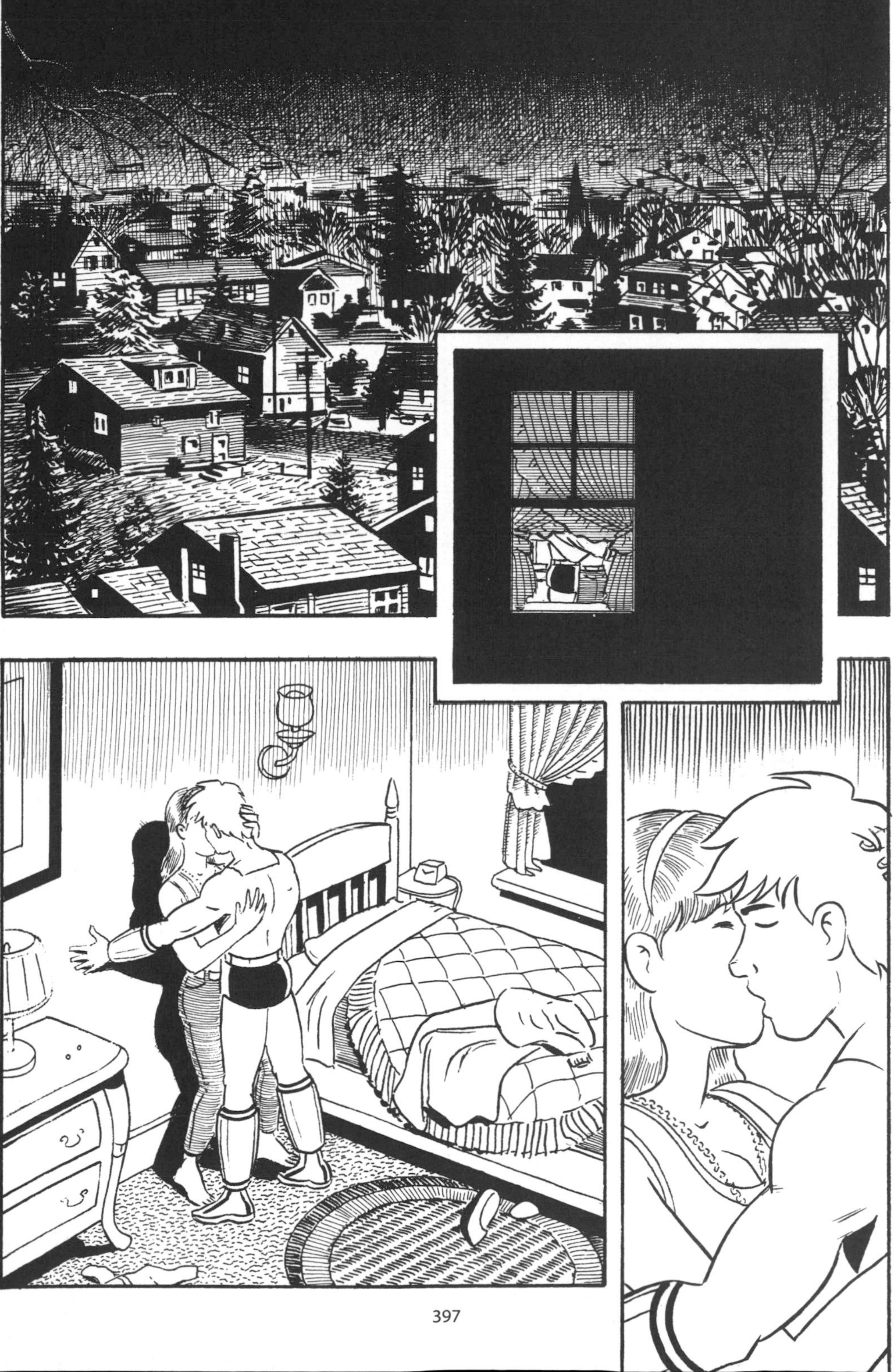

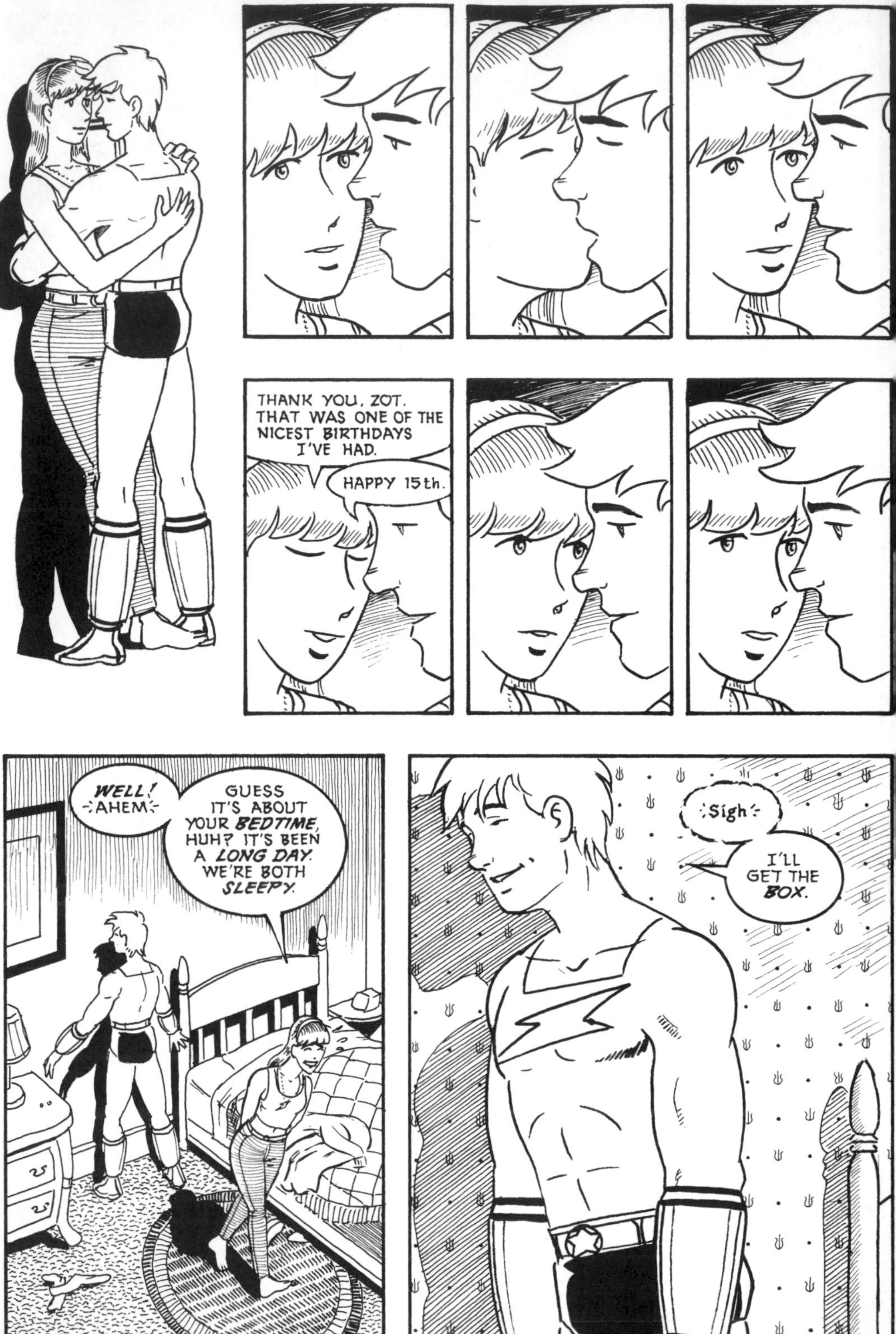
THANK YOU, ZOT. THAT WAS ONE OF THE NICEST BIRTHDAYS I'VE HAD.
HAPPY 15th.
WELL! AHEM
GUESS IT'S ABOUT YOUR BEDTIME, HUH? IT'S BEEN A LONG DAY. WE'RE BOTH SLEEPY.
Sigh
I'LL GET THE BOX.

ARE YOU SURE YOU HAVE ENOUGH *ROOM* IN THIS THING?

YUP!

WANT TO TAKE A LOOK *INSIDE?*

MAYBE *TOMORROW.*

GOOD NIGHT, JEN.

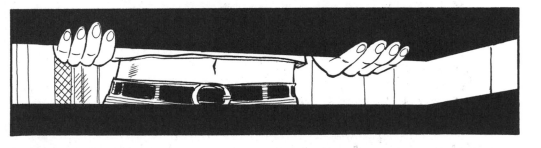

KLAK

CLIK!

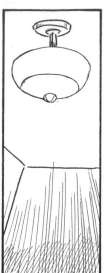

KLAK
KLAK
KLAK
KLAK

DINNER, SIR?

NO THANKS, CHARLIE. I ATE ALREADY.

JUST GOING TO RECORD SOME NOTES FOR *UNCLE MAX* AND GO TO BED.

DAY TWELVE: I'M SORRY I HAVEN'T KEPT TAKING NOTES *EVERY DAY,* MAX. I HAVEN'T FOUND MUCH WORTH REPORTING JUST YET.

I MUST ADMIT, I'M BEGINNING TO WONDER IF I'LL EVER SEE YOU AND OUR WORLD AGAIN, SO I'M LIKEWISE DOUBTFUL THAT THESE TAPES WILL BE OF MUCH USE.

NOT THAT I'M LETTING IT *GET ME DOWN* OR ANYTHING. LIFE IS STILL *FULL OF SURPRISES* AND THE COMPANY IS GOOD.

BEING *STRANDED* HERE HASN'T BEEN *TOO* BAD. EVERYTHING I NEED IS HERE IN THE BOX, AND IT'S SMALL ENOUGH ON THE *OUTSIDE* TO FIT IN JENNY'S *CLOSET.*

I HAD CHARLIE MAKE ME SOME REPLICAS OF THIS EARTH'S *MONEY.* JUST ENOUGH TO *GET AROUND* ON. I PROMISE NOT TO *OVERDO* IT...

400

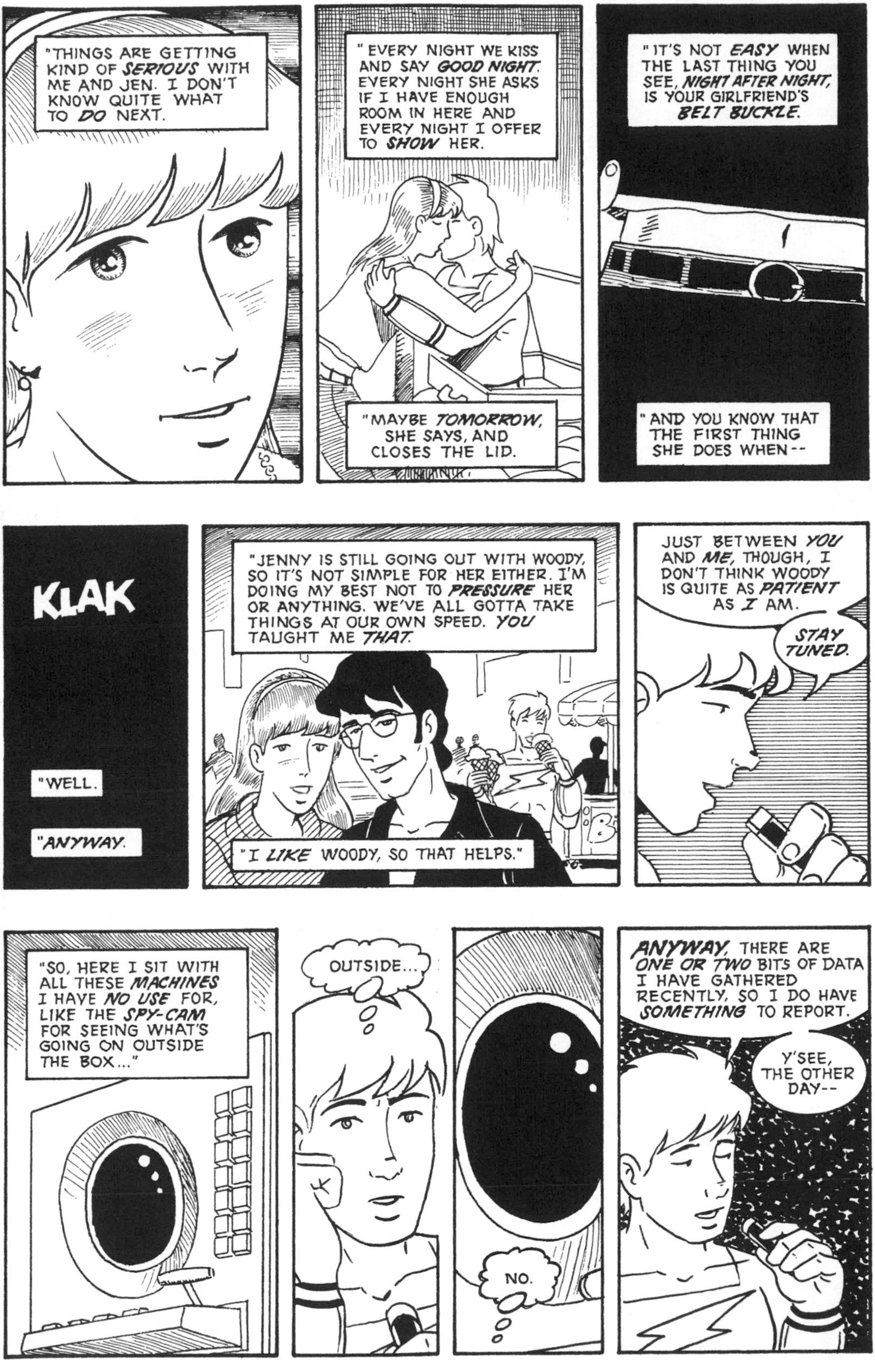
"THINGS ARE GETTING KIND OF SERIOUS WITH ME AND JEN. I DON'T KNOW QUITE WHAT TO DO NEXT.
" EVERY NIGHT WE KISS AND SAY GOOD NIGHT. EVERY NIGHT SHE ASKS IF I HAVE ENOUGH ROOM IN HERE AND EVERY NIGHT I OFFER TO SHOW HER.
"MAYBE TOMORROW, SHE SAYS, AND CLOSES THE LID.
"IT'S NOT EASY WHEN THE LAST THING YOU SEE, NIGHT AFTER NIGHT, IS YOUR GIRLFRIEND'S BELT BUCKLE.
"AND YOU KNOW THAT THE FIRST THING SHE DOES WHEN--
KLAK
"WELL.
"ANYWAY.
"JENNY IS STILL GOING OUT WITH WOODY, SO IT'S NOT SIMPLE FOR HER EITHER. I'M DOING MY BEST NOT TO PRESSURE HER OR ANYTHING. WE'VE ALL GOTTA TAKE THINGS AT OUR OWN SPEED. YOU TAUGHT ME THAT.
"I LIKE WOODY, SO THAT HELPS."
JUST BETWEEN YOU AND ME, THOUGH, I DON'T THINK WOODY IS QUITE AS PATIENT AS I AM.
STAY TUNED.
"SO, HERE I SIT WITH ALL THESE MACHINES I HAVE NO USE FOR, LIKE THE SPY-CAM FOR SEEING WHAT'S GOING ON OUTSIDE THE BOX..."
OUTSIDE...
NO.
ANYWAY, THERE ARE ONE OR TWO BITS OF DATA I HAVE GATHERED RECENTLY, SO I DO HAVE SOMETHING TO REPORT.
Y'SEE, THE OTHER DAY--

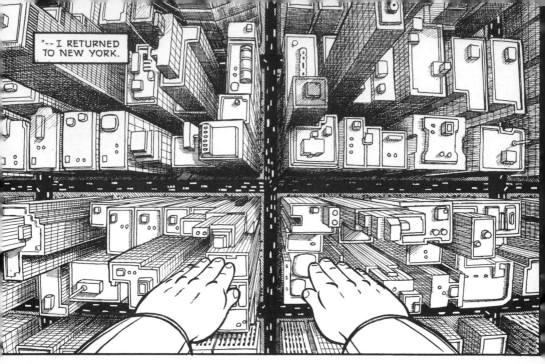

"-- I RETURNED TO NEW YORK.

"*LAST TIME* I VISITED THIS WORLD'S PRIMITIVE REPLICA OF MANHATTAN, ALL I MANAGED TO DO WAS STOP A *PURSE-SNATCHING* AND GET *BEATEN UP.*

"THIS TIME WAS GOING TO BE *DIFFERENT,* THOUGH.

"THIS TIME I WAS *LOOKING* FOR CRIME."

HELLO, NEW YORK!

MY NAME IS ZOT! I'M A CRIMEFIGHTER! ANYONE KNOW WHERE I CAN FIND SOME CRIME?

"A NUMBER OF PEOPLE *STARED,* BUT NO ONE *ANSWERED.*

"IT'S HARD TO GET AN *ANSWER* FROM PEOPLE IN THIS TOWN."

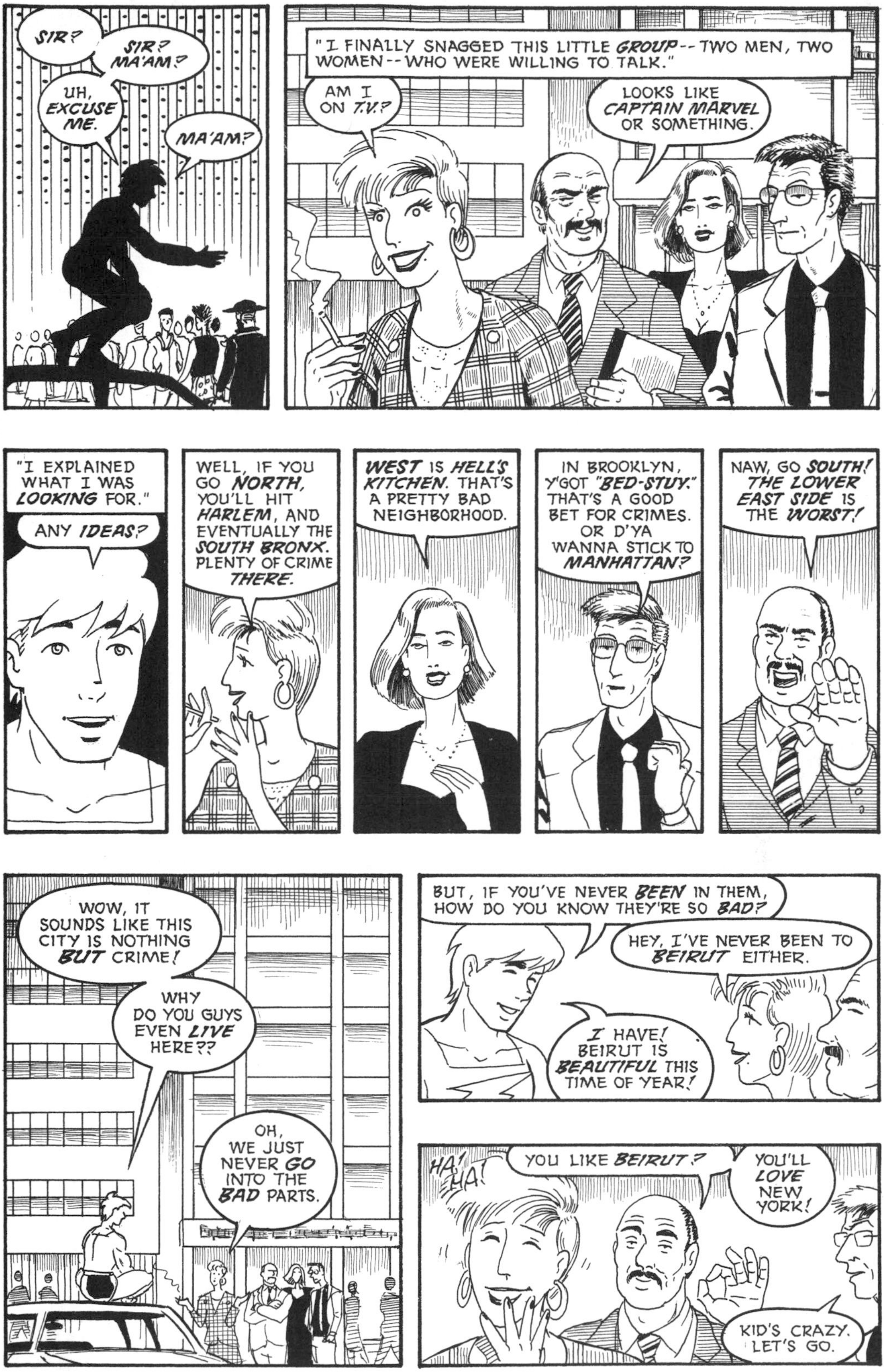
SIR?
SIR? MA'AM?
UH, EXCUSE ME.
MA'AM?
"I FINALLY SNAGGED THIS LITTLE GROUP-- TWO MEN, TWO WOMEN-- WHO WERE WILLING TO TALK."
AM I ON T.V.?
LOOKS LIKE CAPTAIN MARVEL OR SOMETHING.
"I EXPLAINED WHAT I WAS LOOKING FOR."
ANY IDEAS?
WELL, IF YOU GO NORTH, YOU'LL HIT HARLEM, AND EVENTUALLY THE SOUTH BRONX. PLENTY OF CRIME THERE.
WEST IS HELL'S KITCHEN. THAT'S A PRETTY BAD NEIGHBORHOOD.
IN BROOKLYN, Y'GOT "BED-STUY." THAT'S A GOOD BET FOR CRIMES. OR D'YA WANNA STICK TO MANHATTAN?
NAW, GO SOUTH! THE LOWER EAST SIDE IS THE WORST!
WOW, IT SOUNDS LIKE THIS CITY IS NOTHING BUT CRIME!
WHY DO YOU GUYS EVEN LIVE HERE??
OH, WE JUST NEVER GO INTO THE BAD PARTS.
BUT, IF YOU'VE NEVER BEEN IN THEM, HOW DO YOU KNOW THEY'RE SO BAD?
HEY, I'VE NEVER BEEN TO BEIRUT EITHER.
I HAVE! BEIRUT IS BEAUTIFUL THIS TIME OF YEAR!
HA! HA!
YOU LIKE BEIRUT?
YOU'LL LOVE NEW YORK!
KID'S CRAZY. LET'S GO.

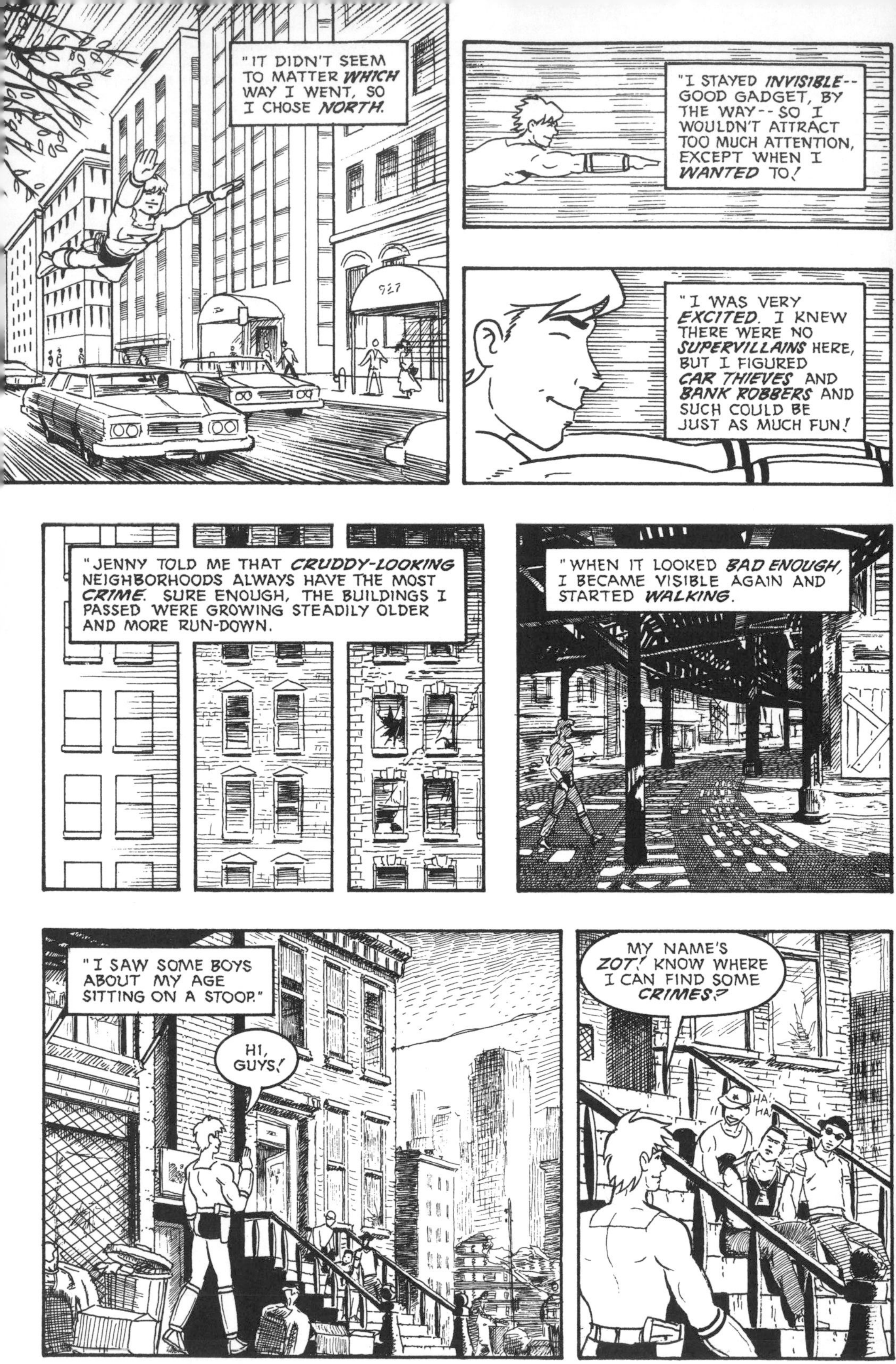
"IT DIDN'T SEEM TO MATTER *WHICH* WAY I WENT, SO I CHOSE *NORTH*.
927
"I STAYED *INVISIBLE*-- GOOD GADGET, BY THE WAY--SO I WOULDN'T ATTRACT TOO MUCH ATTENTION, EXCEPT WHEN I *WANTED* TO!
"I WAS VERY *EXCITED*. I KNEW THERE WERE NO *SUPERVILLAINS* HERE, BUT I FIGURED *CAR THIEVES* AND *BANK ROBBERS* AND SUCH COULD BE JUST AS MUCH FUN!
"JENNY TOLD ME THAT *CRUDDY-LOOKING* NEIGHBORHOODS ALWAYS HAVE THE MOST *CRIME*. SURE ENOUGH, THE BUILDINGS I PASSED WERE GROWING STEADILY OLDER AND MORE RUN-DOWN.
"WHEN IT LOOKED *BAD ENOUGH*, I BECAME VISIBLE AGAIN AND STARTED *WALKING*.
"I SAW SOME BOYS ABOUT MY AGE SITTING ON A STOOP."
HI, GUYS!
MY NAME'S *ZOT!* KNOW WHERE I CAN FIND SOME *CRIMES*?
HA! HA!

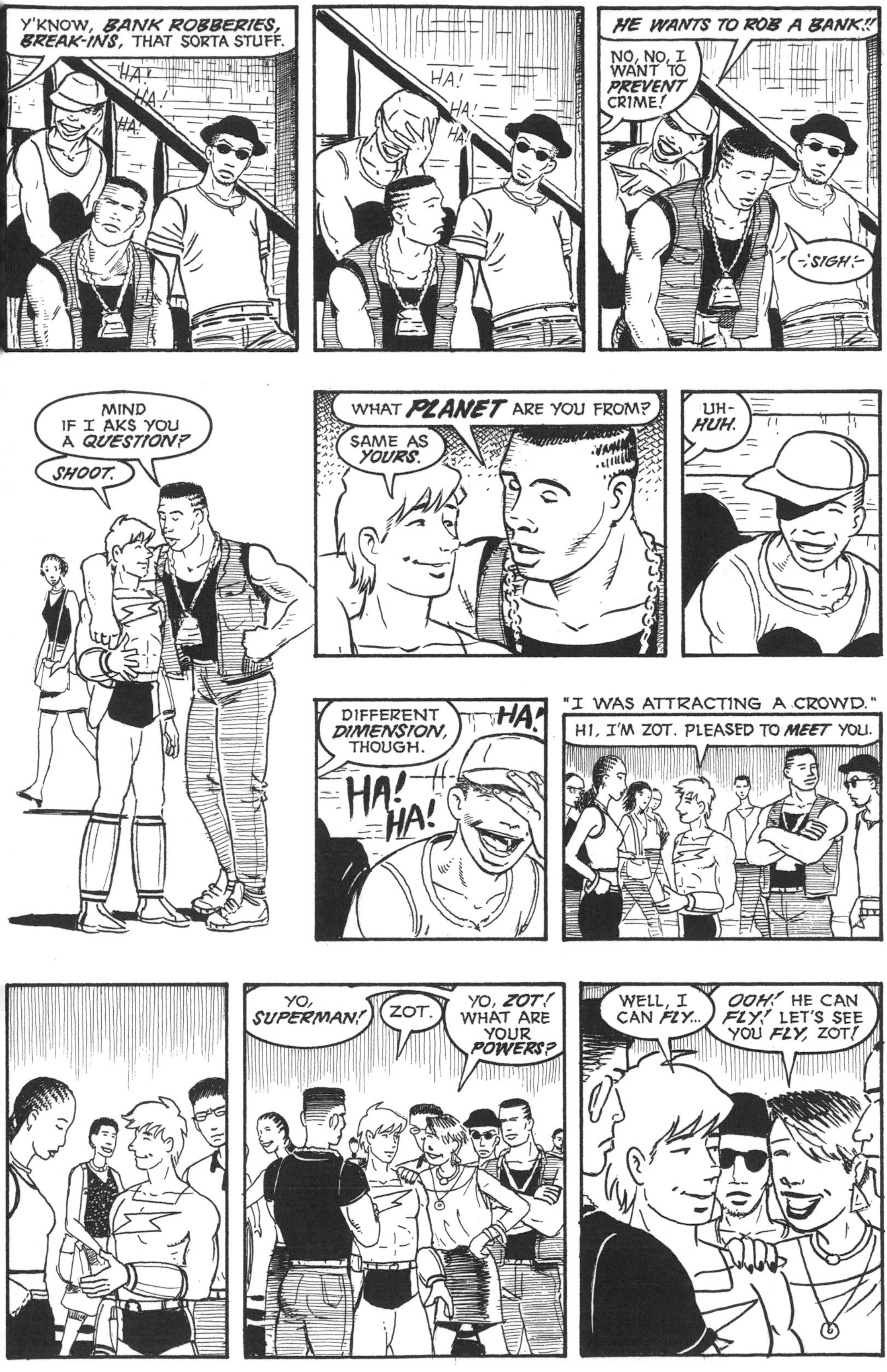

Y'KNOW, BANK ROBBERIES, BREAK-INS, THAT SORTA STUFF.
HA! HA! HA!
HA! HA! HA!
HE WANTS TO ROB A BANK!!
NO, NO, I WANT TO PREVENT CRIME!
-'SIGH'-
MIND IF I AKS YOU A QUESTION?
SHOOT.
WHAT PLANET ARE YOU FROM?
SAME AS YOURS.
UH-HUH.
DIFFERENT DIMENSION, THOUGH.
HA! HA! HA!
"I WAS ATTRACTING A CROWD."
HI, I'M ZOT. PLEASED TO MEET YOU.
YO, SUPERMAN!
ZOT.
YO, ZOT! WHAT ARE YOUR POWERS?
WELL, I CAN FLY...
OOH! HE CAN FLY! LET'S SEE YOU FLY, ZOT!

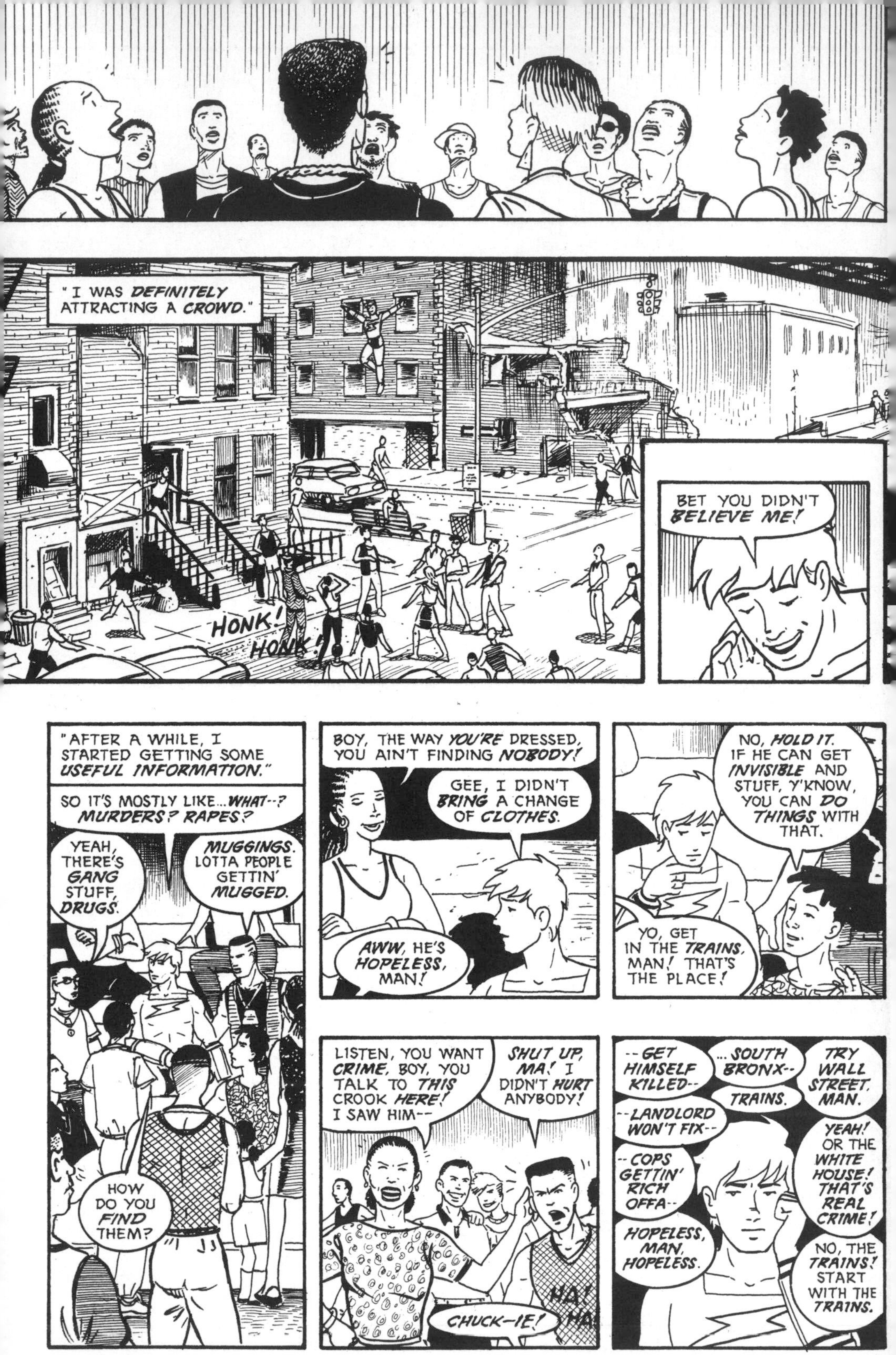
"I WAS DEFINITELY ATTRACTING A CROWD."
HONK!
HONK!
BET YOU DIDN'T BELIEVE ME!
"AFTER A WHILE, I STARTED GETTING SOME USEFUL INFORMATION."
SO IT'S MOSTLY LIKE... WHAT--? MURDERS? RAPES?
YEAH, THERE'S GANG STUFF, DRUGS.
MUGGINGS. LOTTA PEOPLE GETTIN' MUGGED.
HOW DO YOU FIND THEM?
BOY, THE WAY YOU'RE DRESSED, YOU AIN'T FINDING NOBODY!
GEE, I DIDN'T BRING A CHANGE OF CLOTHES.
AWW, HE'S HOPELESS, MAN!
NO, HOLD IT. IF HE CAN GET INVISIBLE AND STUFF, Y'KNOW, YOU CAN DO THINGS WITH THAT.
YO, GET IN THE TRAINS, MAN! THAT'S THE PLACE!
LISTEN, YOU WANT CRIME, BOY, YOU TALK TO THIS CROOK HERE! I SAW HIM--
SHUT UP, MA! I DIDN'T HURT ANYBODY!
HA! HA!
CHUCK-IE!
--GET HIMSELF KILLED--
...SOUTH BRONX--
TRY WALL STREET, MAN.
TRAINS.
--LANDLORD WON'T FIX--
--COPS GETTIN' RICH OFFA--
YEAH! OR THE WHITE HOUSE! THAT'S REAL CRIME!
HOPELESS, MAN, HOPELESS.
NO, THE TRAINS! START WITH THE TRAINS.

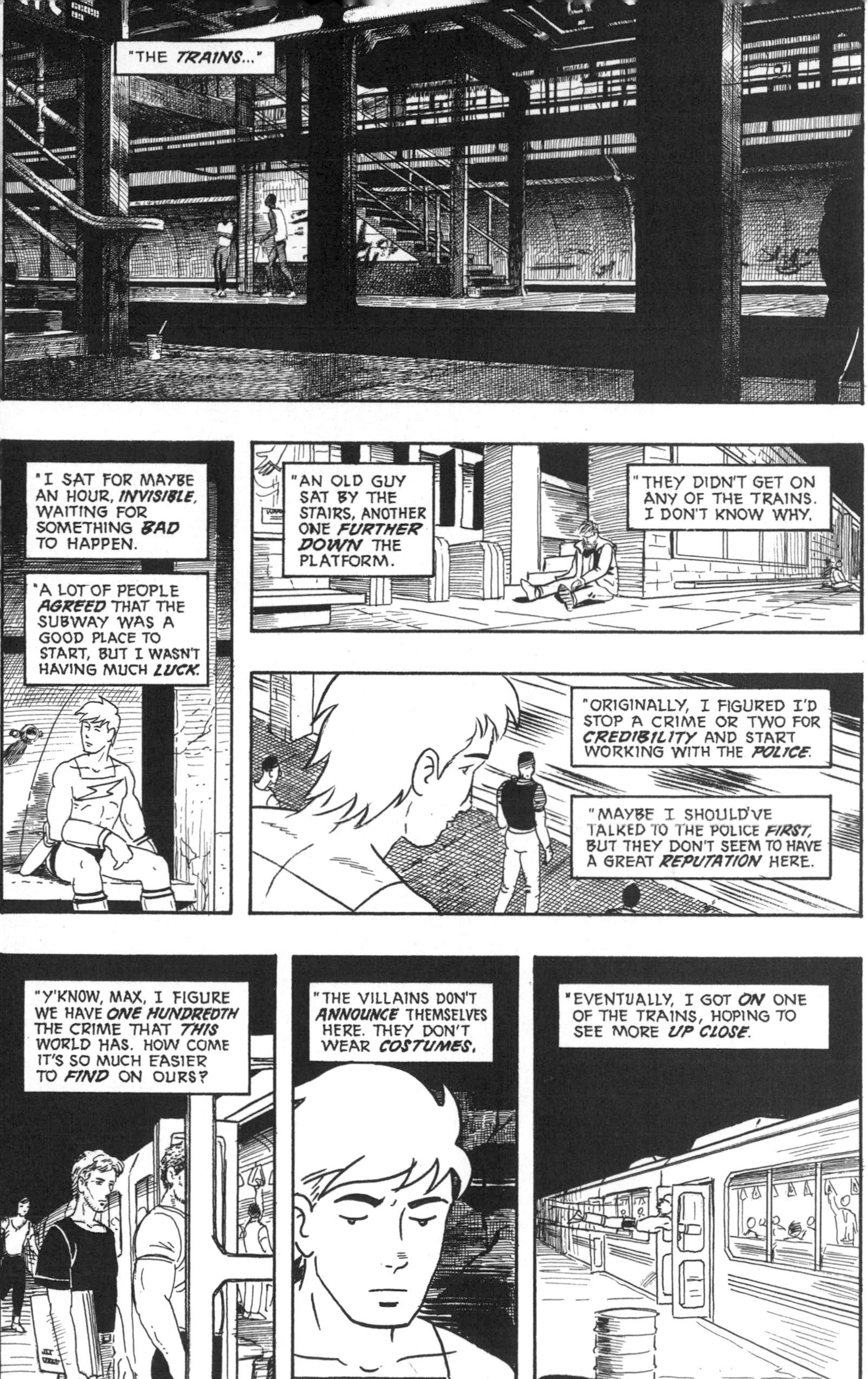
"THE TRAINS..."
"I SAT FOR MAYBE AN HOUR, INVISIBLE, WAITING FOR SOMETHING BAD TO HAPPEN.
"A LOT OF PEOPLE AGREED THAT THE SUBWAY WAS A GOOD PLACE TO START, BUT I WASN'T HAVING MUCH LUCK.
"AN OLD GUY SAT BY THE STAIRS, ANOTHER ONE FURTHER DOWN THE PLATFORM.
"THEY DIDN'T GET ON ANY OF THE TRAINS. I DON'T KNOW WHY.
"ORIGINALLY, I FIGURED I'D STOP A CRIME OR TWO FOR CREDIBILITY AND START WORKING WITH THE POLICE.
"MAYBE I SHOULD'VE TALKED TO THE POLICE FIRST, BUT THEY DON'T SEEM TO HAVE A GREAT REPUTATION HERE.
"Y'KNOW, MAX, I FIGURE WE HAVE ONE HUNDREDTH THE CRIME THAT THIS WORLD HAS. HOW COME IT'S SO MUCH EASIER TO FIND ON OURS?
"THE VILLAINS DON'T ANNOUNCE THEMSELVES HERE. THEY DON'T WEAR COSTUMES.
"EVENTUALLY, I GOT ON ONE OF THE TRAINS, HOPING TO SEE MORE UP CLOSE.

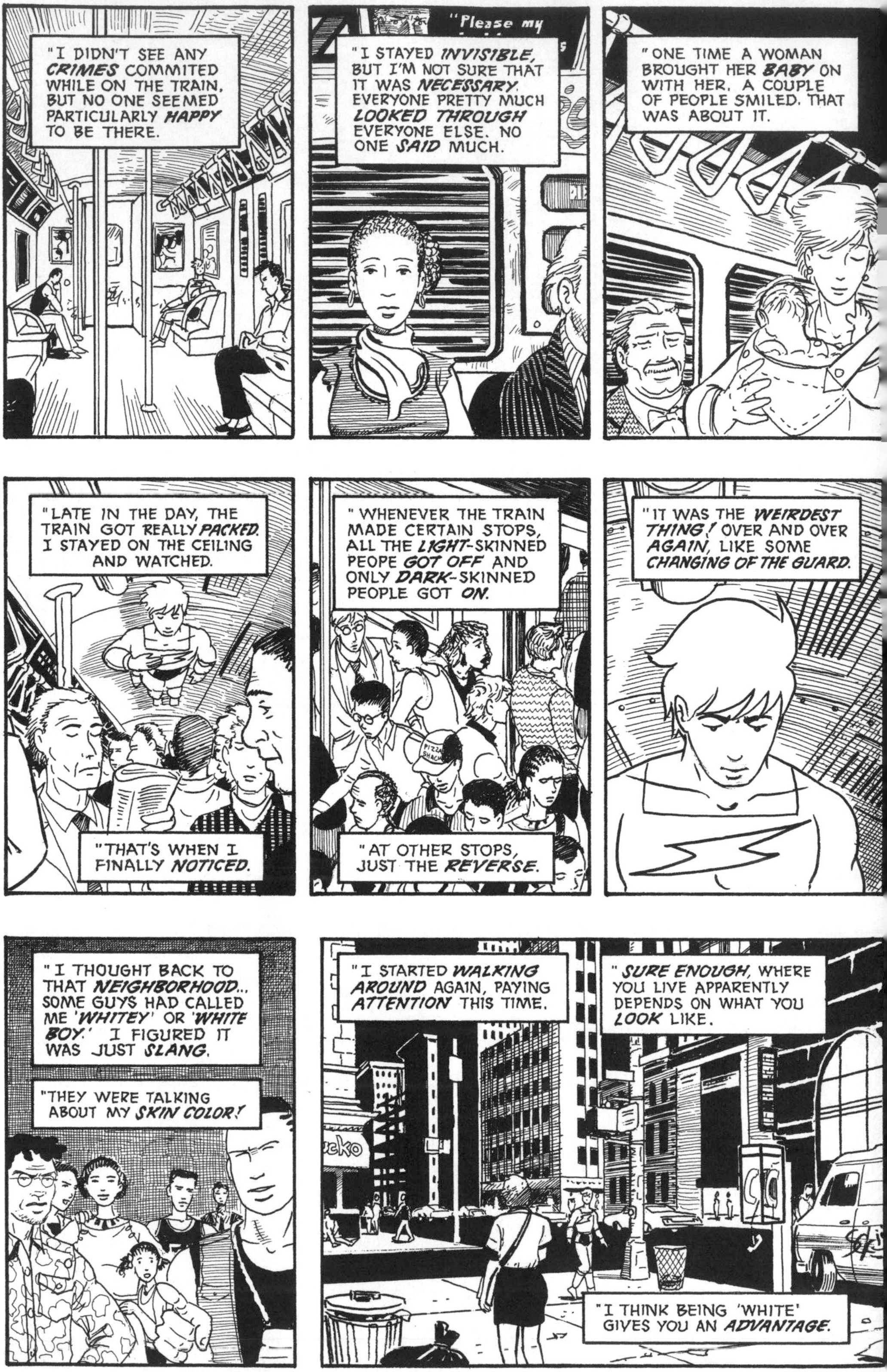
"I DIDN'T SEE ANY CRIMES COMMITED WHILE ON THE TRAIN, BUT NO ONE SEEMED PARTICULARLY HAPPY TO BE THERE.
"Please my
"I STAYED INVISIBLE, BUT I'M NOT SURE THAT IT WAS NECESSARY. EVERYONE PRETTY MUCH LOOKED THROUGH EVERYONE ELSE. NO ONE SAID MUCH.
"ONE TIME A WOMAN BROUGHT HER BABY ON WITH HER. A COUPLE OF PEOPLE SMILED. THAT WAS ABOUT IT.
"LATE IN THE DAY, THE TRAIN GOT REALLY PACKED. I STAYED ON THE CEILING AND WATCHED.
"THAT'S WHEN I FINALLY NOTICED.
"WHENEVER THE TRAIN MADE CERTAIN STOPS, ALL THE LIGHT-SKINNED PEOPE GOT OFF AND ONLY DARK-SKINNED PEOPLE GOT ON.
"AT OTHER STOPS, JUST THE REVERSE.
"IT WAS THE WEIRDEST THING! OVER AND OVER AGAIN, LIKE SOME CHANGING OF THE GUARD.
"I THOUGHT BACK TO THAT NEIGHBORHOOD... SOME GUYS HAD CALLED ME 'WHITEY' OR 'WHITE BOY.' I FIGURED IT WAS JUST SLANG.
"THEY WERE TALKING ABOUT MY SKIN COLOR!
"I STARTED WALKING AROUND AGAIN, PAYING ATTENTION THIS TIME.
"SURE ENOUGH, WHERE YOU LIVE APPARENTLY DEPENDS ON WHAT YOU LOOK LIKE.
"I THINK BEING 'WHITE' GIVES YOU AN ADVANTAGE.

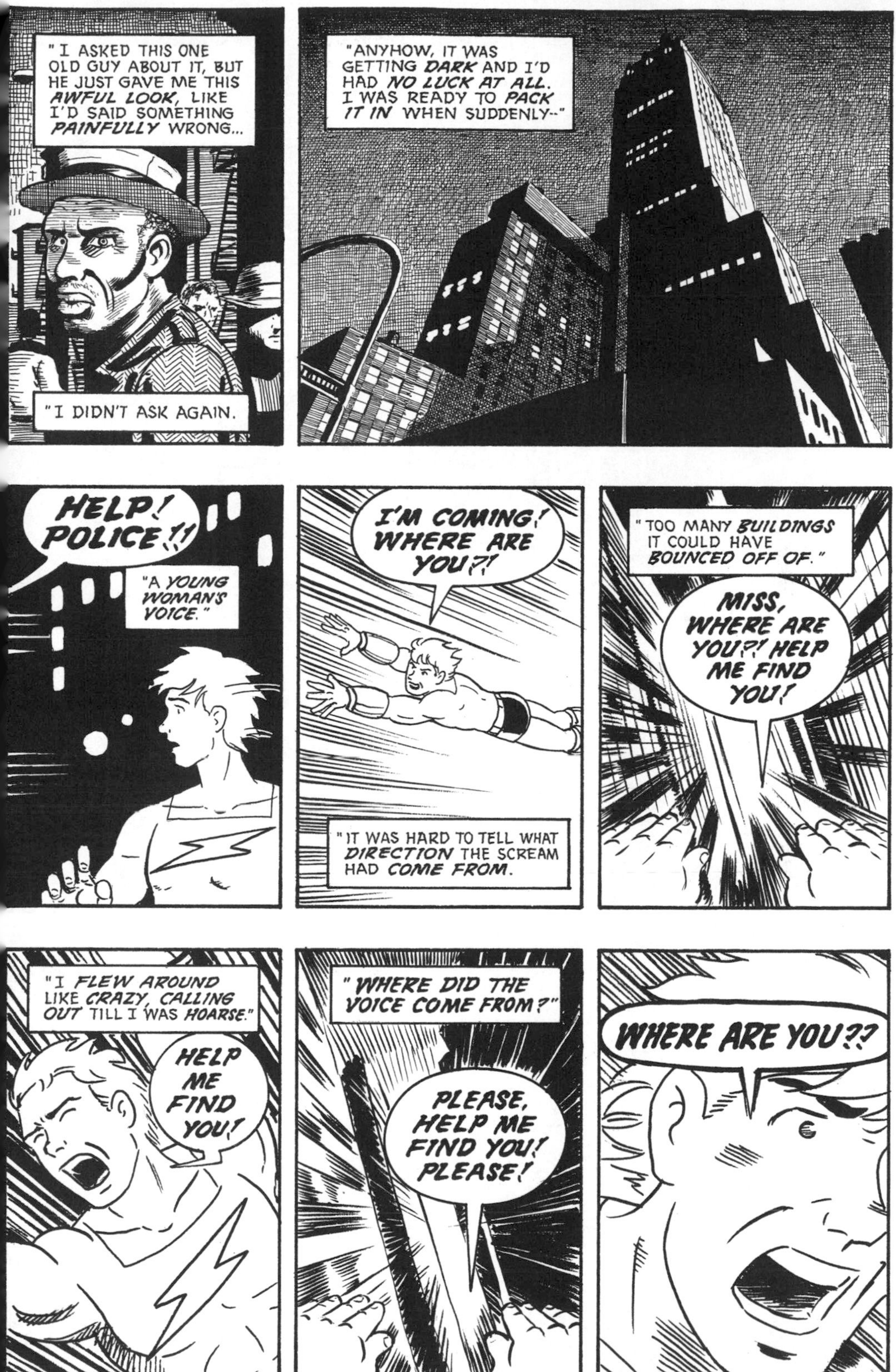
"I ASKED THIS ONE OLD GUY ABOUT IT, BUT HE JUST GAVE ME THIS AWFUL LOOK, LIKE I'D SAID SOMETHING PAINFULLY WRONG...
"I DIDN'T ASK AGAIN.
"ANYHOW, IT WAS GETTING DARK AND I'D HAD NO LUCK AT ALL. I WAS READY TO PACK IT IN WHEN SUDDENLY--"
HELP! POLICE!!!
"A YOUNG WOMAN'S VOICE."
I'M COMING! WHERE ARE YOU?!
"IT WAS HARD TO TELL WHAT DIRECTION THE SCREAM HAD COME FROM.
"TOO MANY BUILDINGS IT COULD HAVE BOUNCED OFF OF."
MISS, WHERE ARE YOU?! HELP ME FIND YOU!
"I FLEW AROUND LIKE CRAZY, CALLING OUT TILL I WAS HOARSE."
HELP ME FIND YOU!
"WHERE DID THE VOICE COME FROM?"
PLEASE, HELP ME FIND YOU! PLEASE!
WHERE ARE YOU??

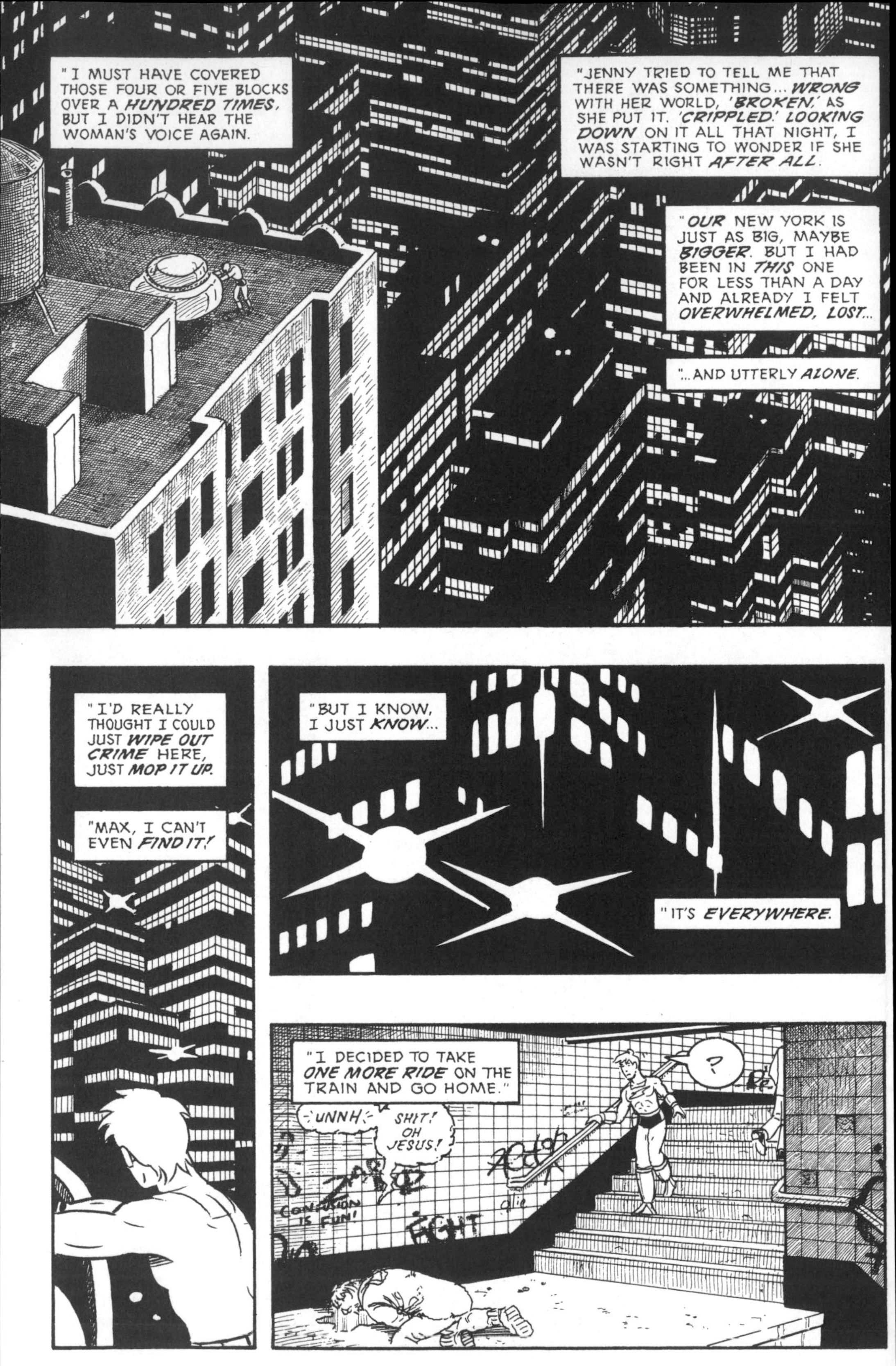
"I MUST HAVE COVERED THOSE FOUR OR FIVE BLOCKS OVER A *HUNDRED TIMES*, BUT I DIDN'T HEAR THE WOMAN'S VOICE AGAIN.
"JENNY TRIED TO TELL ME THAT THERE WAS SOMETHING... *WRONG* WITH HER WORLD, *'BROKEN,'* AS SHE PUT IT. *'CRIPPLED.' LOOKING DOWN* ON IT ALL THAT NIGHT, I WAS STARTING TO WONDER IF SHE WASN'T RIGHT *AFTER ALL*.
"*OUR* NEW YORK IS JUST AS BIG, MAYBE *BIGGER*. BUT I HAD BEEN IN *THIS* ONE FOR LESS THAN A DAY AND ALREADY I FELT *OVERWHELMED, LOST*...
"...AND UTTERLY *ALONE*.
"I'D REALLY THOUGHT I COULD JUST *WIPE OUT CRIME* HERE, JUST *MOP IT UP*.
"MAX, I CAN'T EVEN *FIND IT!*
"BUT I KNOW, I JUST *KNOW*...
"IT'S *EVERYWHERE*.
"I DECIDED TO TAKE *ONE MORE RIDE* ON THE TRAIN AND GO HOME."
UNNH
SHIT! OH JESUS!
?

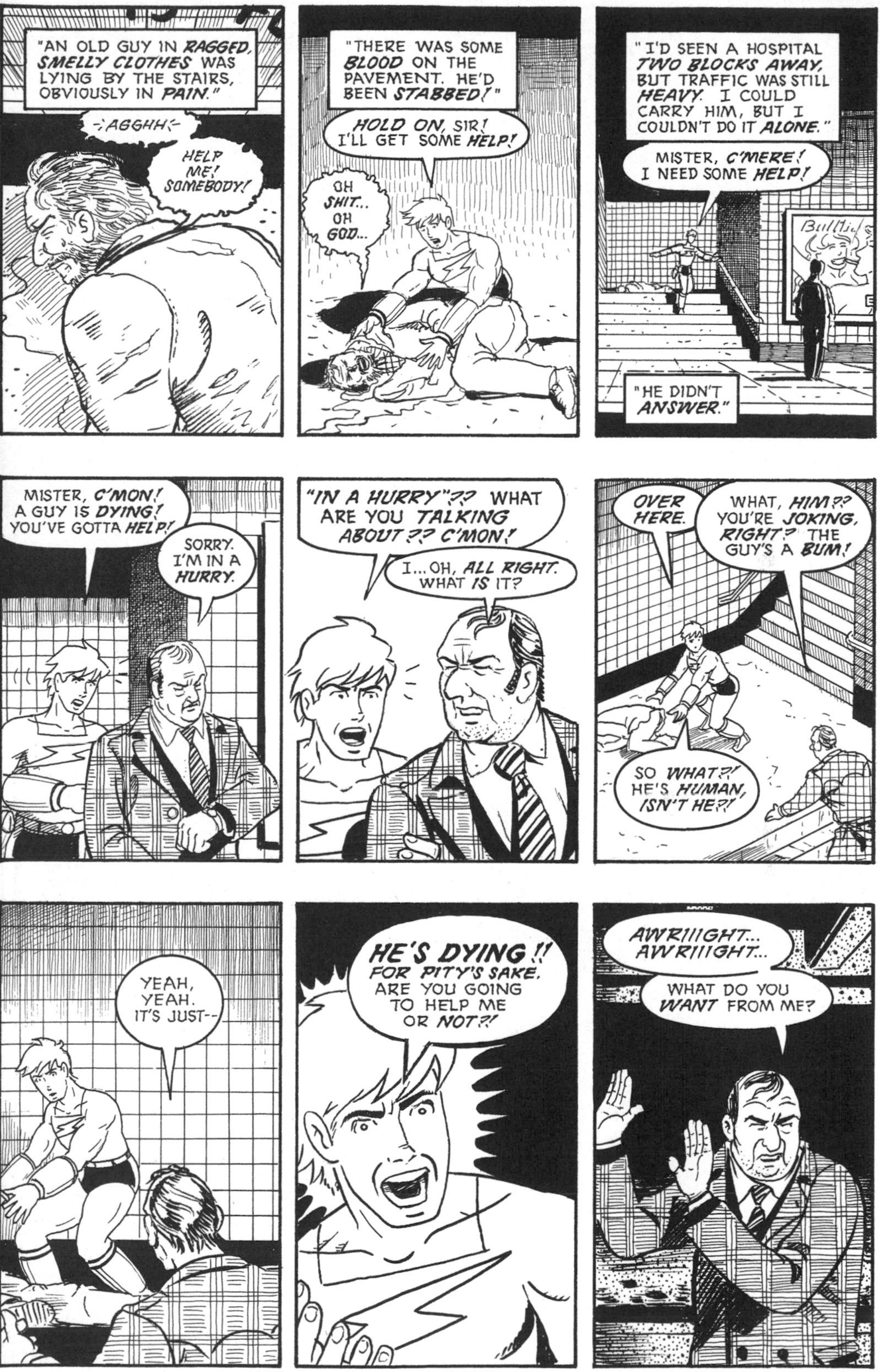
"AN OLD GUY IN RAGGED, SMELLY CLOTHES WAS LYING BY THE STAIRS, OBVIOUSLY IN PAIN."
AGGHH
HELP ME! SOMEBODY!
"THERE WAS SOME BLOOD ON THE PAVEMENT. HE'D BEEN STABBED!"
HOLD ON, SIR! I'LL GET SOME HELP!
OH SHIT... OH GOD...
"I'D SEEN A HOSPITAL TWO BLOCKS AWAY, BUT TRAFFIC WAS STILL HEAVY. I COULD CARRY HIM, BUT I COULDN'T DO IT ALONE."
MISTER, C'MERE! I NEED SOME HELP!
"HE DIDN'T ANSWER."
MISTER, C'MON! A GUY IS DYING! YOU'VE GOTTA HELP!
SORRY. I'M IN A HURRY.
"IN A HURRY"?? WHAT ARE YOU TALKING ABOUT?? C'MON!
I...OH, ALL RIGHT. WHAT IS IT?
OVER HERE.
WHAT, HIM?? YOU'RE JOKING, RIGHT? THE GUY'S A BUM!
SO WHAT?! HE'S HUMAN, ISN'T HE?!
YEAH, YEAH. IT'S JUST--
HE'S DYING!! FOR PITY'S SAKE, ARE YOU GOING TO HELP ME OR NOT?!
AWRIIIGHT... AWRIIIGHT...
WHAT DO YOU WANT FROM ME?

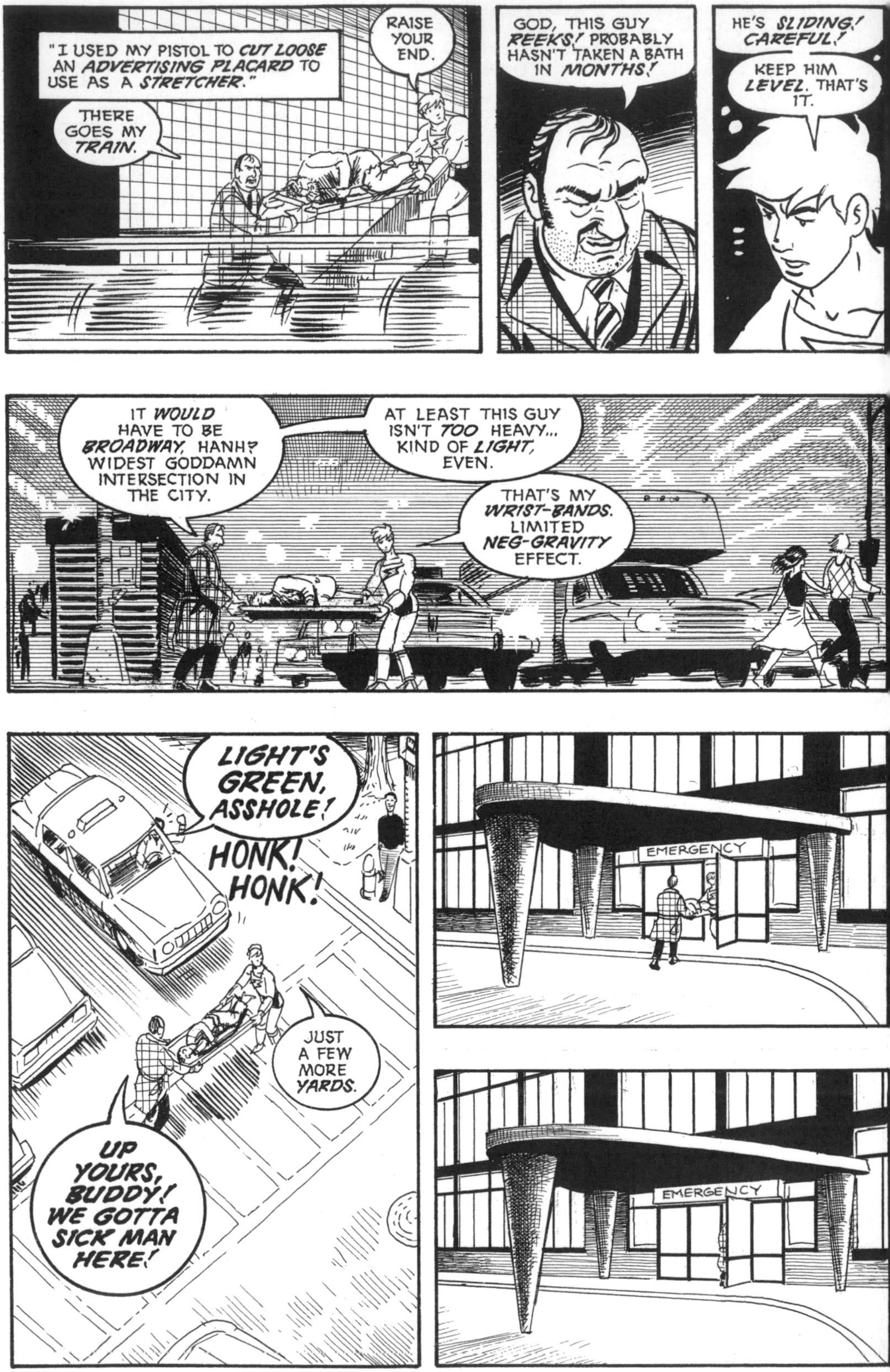

"I USED MY PISTOL TO CUT LOOSE AN ADVERTISING PLACARD TO USE AS A STRETCHER."
RAISE YOUR END.
THERE GOES MY TRAIN.
GOD, THIS GUY REEKS! PROBABLY HASN'T TAKEN A BATH IN MONTHS!
HE'S SLIDING! CAREFUL!
KEEP HIM LEVEL. THAT'S IT.
IT WOULD HAVE TO BE BROADWAY, HANH? WIDEST GODDAMN INTERSECTION IN THE CITY.
AT LEAST THIS GUY ISN'T TOO HEAVY... KIND OF LIGHT, EVEN.
THAT'S MY WRIST-BANDS. LIMITED NEG-GRAVITY EFFECT.
LIGHT'S GREEN, ASSHOLE!
HONK! HONK!
JUST A FEW MORE YARDS.
UP YOURS, BUDDY! WE GOTTA SICK MAN HERE!
EMERGENCY
EMERGENCY

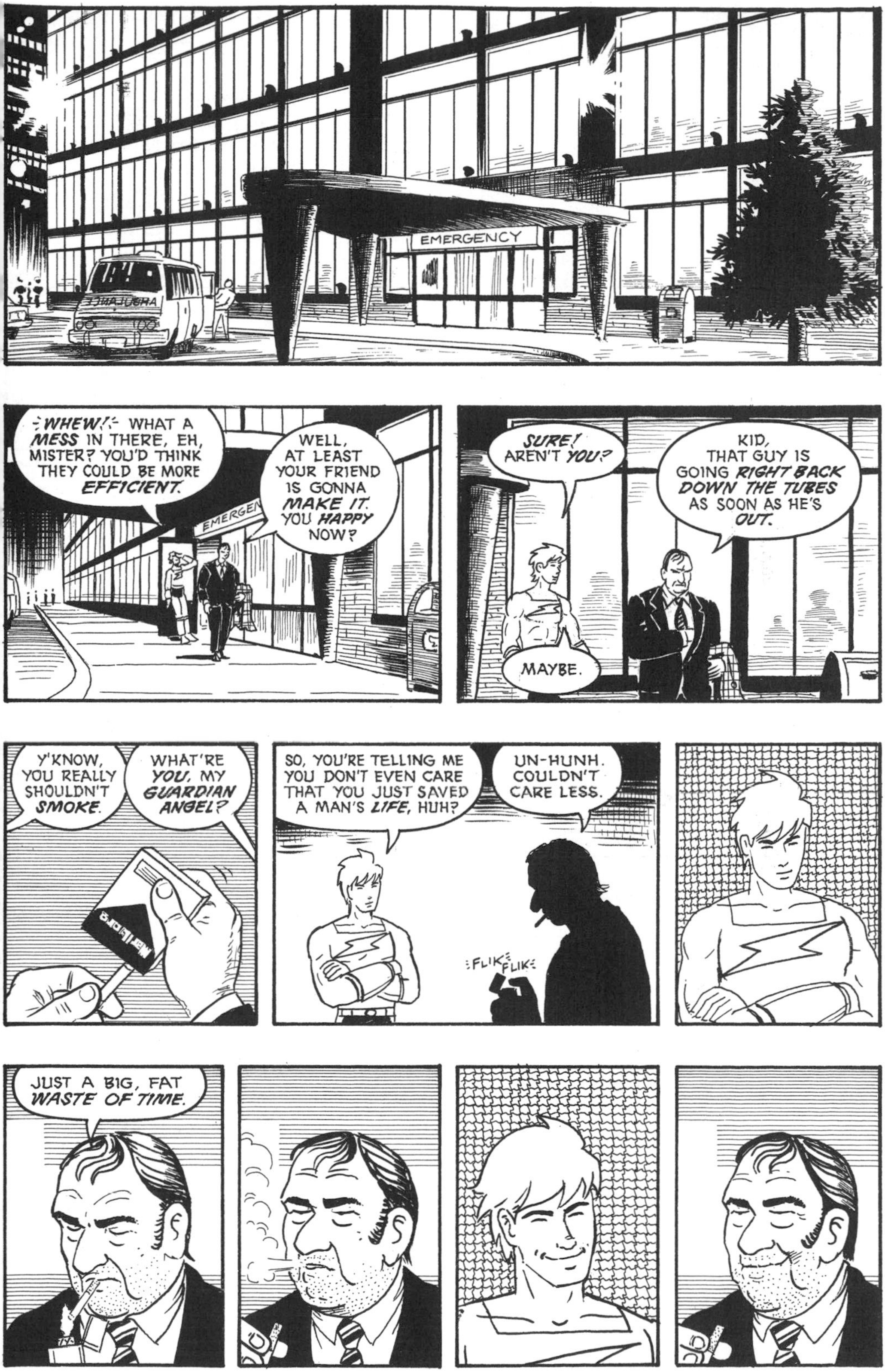
EMERGENCY
AMBULANCE
WHEW! WHAT A MESS IN THERE, EH, MISTER? YOU'D THINK THEY COULD BE MORE EFFICIENT.
EMERGEN
WELL, AT LEAST YOUR FRIEND IS GONNA MAKE IT. YOU HAPPY NOW?
SURE! AREN'T YOU?
KID, THAT GUY IS GOING RIGHT BACK DOWN THE TUBES AS SOON AS HE'S OUT.
MAYBE.
Y'KNOW, YOU REALLY SHOULDN'T SMOKE.
WHAT'RE YOU, MY GUARDIAN ANGEL?
SO, YOU'RE TELLING ME YOU DON'T EVEN CARE THAT YOU JUST SAVED A MAN'S LIFE, HUH?
UN-HUNH. COULDN'T CARE LESS.
FLIK FLIK
JUST A BIG, FAT WASTE OF TIME.

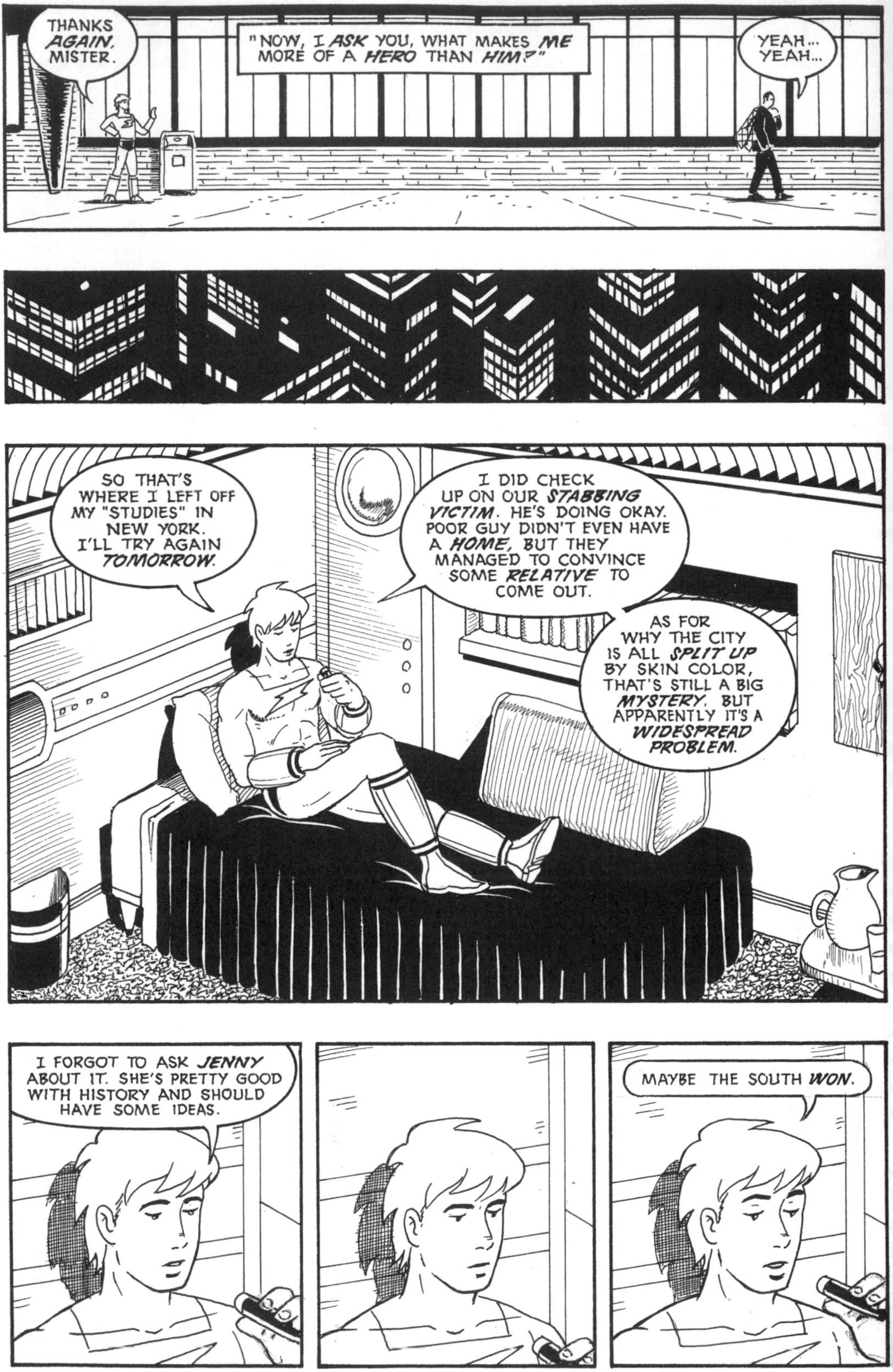
THANKS AGAIN, MISTER.
"NOW, I ASK YOU, WHAT MAKES ME MORE OF A HERO THAN HIM?"
YEAH... YEAH...
SO THAT'S WHERE I LEFT OFF MY "STUDIES" IN NEW YORK. I'LL TRY AGAIN TOMORROW.
I DID CHECK UP ON OUR STABBING VICTIM. HE'S DOING OKAY. POOR GUY DIDN'T EVEN HAVE A HOME, BUT THEY MANAGED TO CONVINCE SOME RELATIVE TO COME OUT.
AS FOR WHY THE CITY IS ALL SPLIT UP BY SKIN COLOR, THAT'S STILL A BIG MYSTERY. BUT APPARENTLY IT'S A WIDESPREAD PROBLEM.
I FORGOT TO ASK JENNY ABOUT IT. SHE'S PRETTY GOOD WITH HISTORY AND SHOULD HAVE SOME IDEAS.
MAYBE THE SOUTH WON.

There are nine Earth Stories altogether, all of them 18 pages long except for the double-sized final issue. "Jenny's Day" isn't much more than introduction and exposition, but it gives a sense of the effects I was reaching for. Barely a decade out of high school myself, I had pretty fresh memories of the place and, if necessary, I could head over to Lexington High School for reference, living as we were by then in nearby Somerville, Massachusetts.

"Looking for Crime" is my attempt to counterbalance the more stereotypical comic book approach to street crime used in issue #11. When I look at it again, all these years later, I want to reach over and pat my younger self on the head and say: "Nice effort, but let's try sticking closer to home from now on, okay?" Fortunately, that's exactly what happened starting with the next issue. When *Zot!* fans tell me the Earth Stories were their favorites, it's almost always one or more of the next several stories they're thinking about. Some forget these first two even existed.

This was a strange, difficult time for us. Ivy and I had decided to start having children, but the process turned out to be a lot more difficult than we'd anticipated, and problems at work were getting Ivy down. Meanwhile, I was going quietly insane with frustration. Only one issue into the Earth Stories, I realized that what I really wanted—no, *needed*—was to be working on my massive, book-length comic book about the comics medium, a project I'd had in mind for years and which I suddenly realized I was finally ready for. I had to finish what I'd begun: I had to follow through on the Earth Stories, but the idea that I'd have to wait over a year even to *begin* a project that would, itself, take over a year to complete was maddening. I often wonder if the Earth Stories became what they did in spite of those external pressures and frustrations, or at least partially *because* of them.

My days at the drawing board were getting longer and longer as my pages were getting more and more detailed and my deadlines more and more battered. And my free hours started to get eaten up by a renewed obsession with chess, an affliction I'll always be grateful to Ivy for tolerating with such grace and understanding. I vividly remember working on "Looking for Crime" sixteen hours a day at the drawing board, while behind me, halfway across the room, a little computerized chess set I'd borrowed from our friend Clarence would ponder over its moves. Every several minutes, I'd hear a beep, turn around to look briefly at the board, make a move, then turn back to the drawing board.

Last minute note: As I'm getting ready to send this book out in 2008, I just heard some songs from a new album by Edie Brickell and Harper Simon (recording as The Heavy Circles). They sounded great! Brickell was a pretty new act when I wrote the bit on pages 390 and 391 way back in 1989. I liked her album but didn't know if she was going to turn out to be a flash in the pan or not. Apparently *not*.

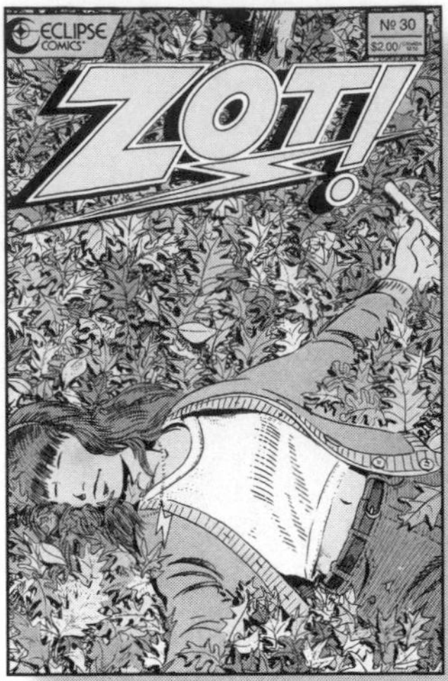
ECLIPSE COMICS
№ 30
$2.00
ZOT!

Autumn

First published in *Zot! #30*.

Lettering:

Bob Lappan

Original series editor:

cat yronwode

Plot assist:

Ivy Ratafia

THIS USED TO BE MY *FAVORITE SEASON*.

THESE DAYS, I DON'T *HAVE* A FAVORITE. THE SEASONS PASS TOO *QUICKLY*.

THE TREES ARE PUTTING ON A NICE SHOW LIKE ALWAYS... BRIGHT *REDS, YELLOWS* AND *ORANGES,* EVERYWHERE YOU LOOK.

YET ALL I CAN THINK OF IS THE *DIRTY LAUNDRY* IN THE BASEMENT.

AND WHETHER TO TELL HARRY PETERSON I WANT TO GO *PART-TIME.*

AND WHEN DO I GET THE *TOYOTA* BACK FROM THE *SUNOCO STATION* SINCE HORTON WAS TOO CHEAP TO TAKE IT TO THE DEALER.

AND SHOULD WE GO AHEAD WITH THE DIVORCE.

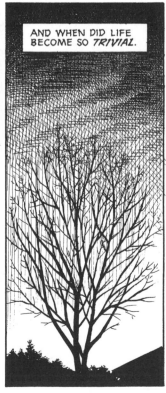

AND WHEN DID LIFE BECOME SO *TRIVIAL.*

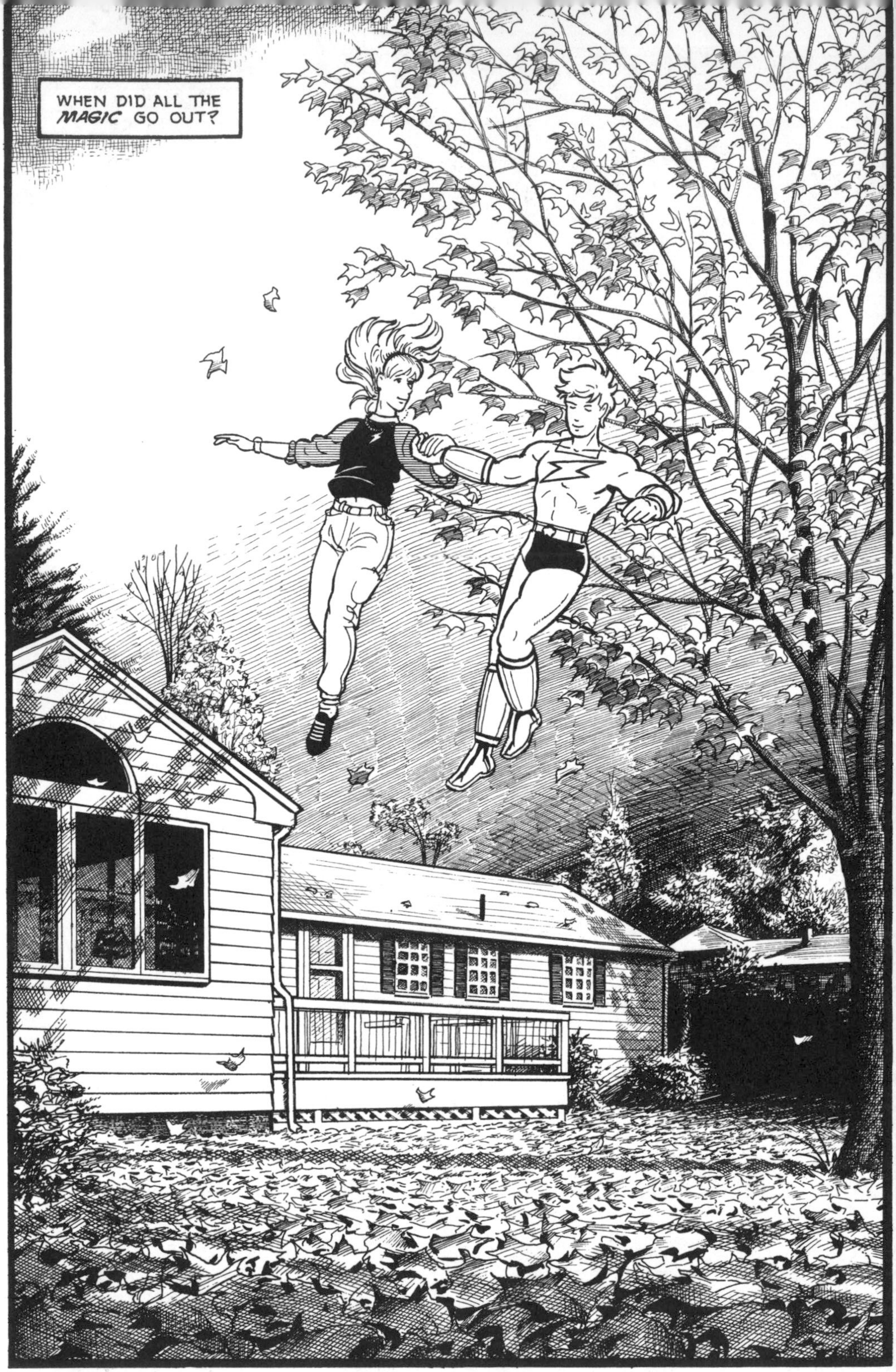
WHEN DID ALL THE *MAGIC* GO OUT?

AUTUMN

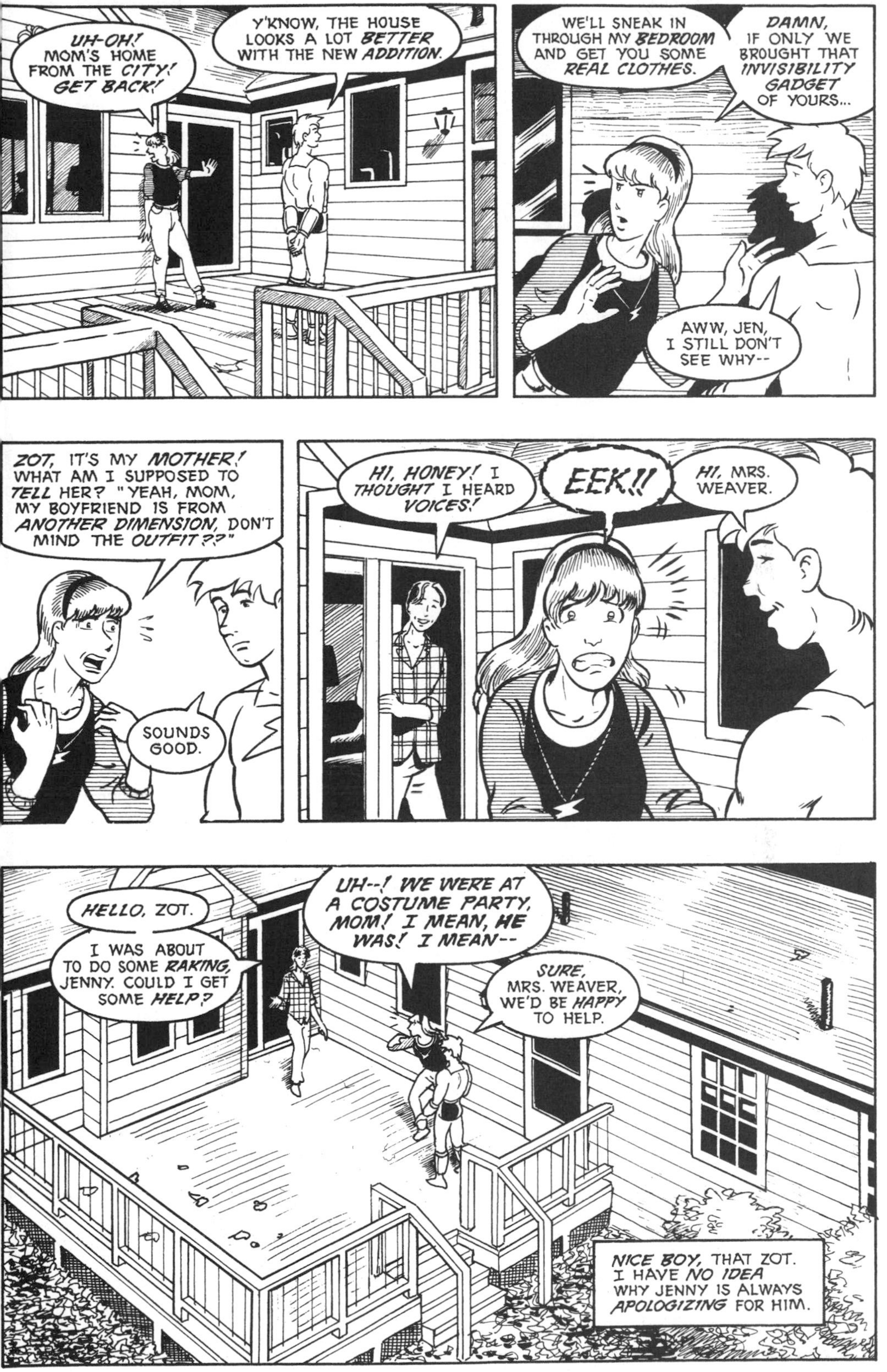
UH-OH! MOM'S HOME FROM THE CITY! GET BACK!
Y'KNOW, THE HOUSE LOOKS A LOT BETTER WITH THE NEW ADDITION.
WE'LL SNEAK IN THROUGH MY BEDROOM AND GET YOU SOME REAL CLOTHES.
DAMN, IF ONLY WE BROUGHT THAT INVISIBILITY GADGET OF YOURS...
AWW, JEN, I STILL DON'T SEE WHY--
ZOT, IT'S MY MOTHER! WHAT AM I SUPPOSED TO TELL HER? "YEAH, MOM, MY BOYFRIEND IS FROM ANOTHER DIMENSION, DON'T MIND THE OUTFIT??"
SOUNDS GOOD.
HI, HONEY! I THOUGHT I HEARD VOICES!
EEK!!
HI, MRS. WEAVER.
HELLO, ZOT.
I WAS ABOUT TO DO SOME RAKING, JENNY. COULD I GET SOME HELP?
UH--! WE WERE AT A COSTUME PARTY, MOM! I MEAN, HE WAS! I MEAN--
SURE, MRS. WEAVER, WE'D BE HAPPY TO HELP.
NICE BOY, THAT ZOT. I HAVE NO IDEA WHY JENNY IS ALWAYS APOLOGIZING FOR HIM.

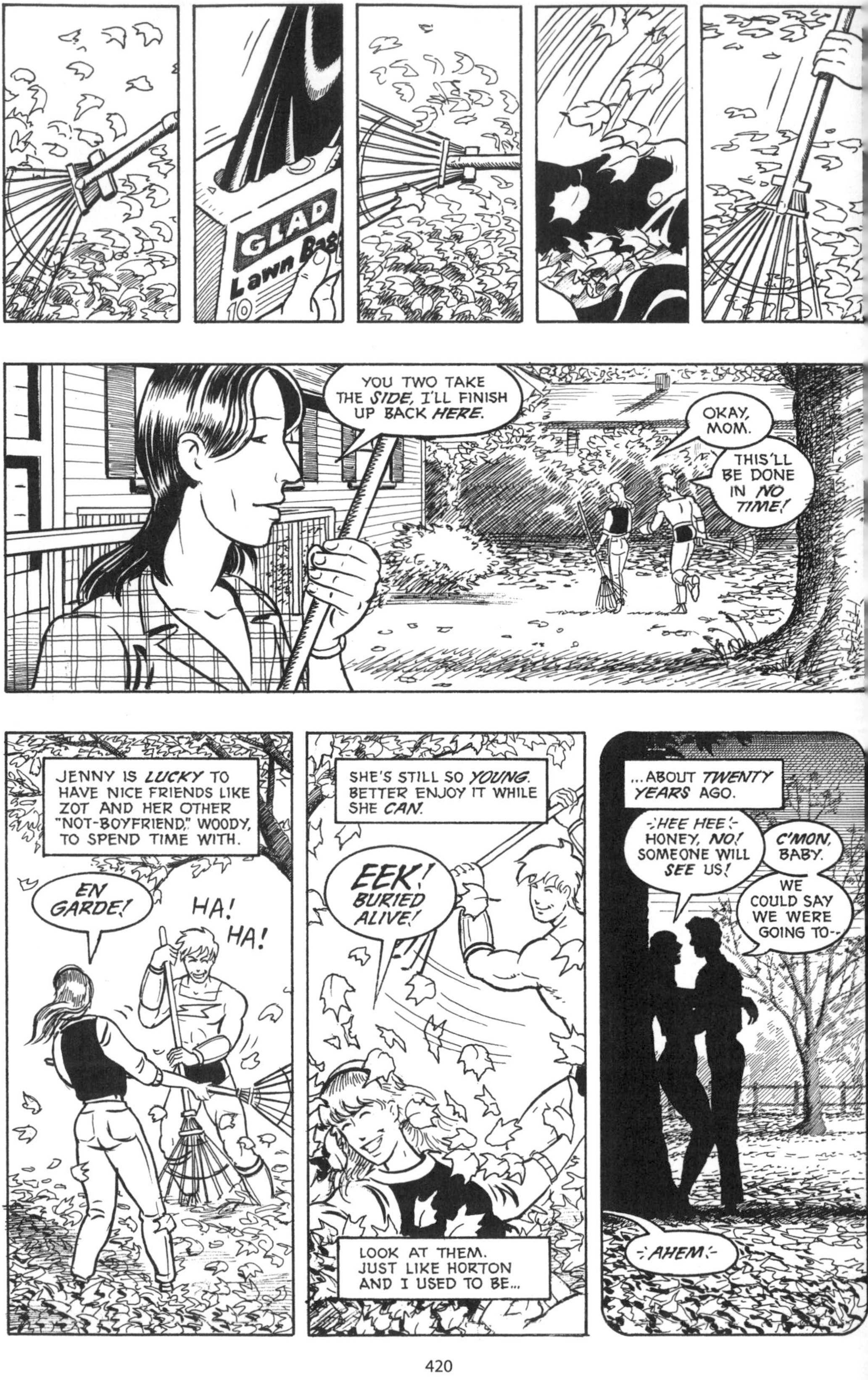
GLAD
Lawn Bag
10
YOU TWO TAKE THE *SIDE*, I'LL FINISH UP BACK *HERE*.
OKAY, MOM.
THIS'LL BE DONE IN *NO TIME!*
JENNY IS *LUCKY* TO HAVE NICE FRIENDS LIKE ZOT AND HER OTHER "NOT-BOYFRIEND," WOODY, TO SPEND TIME WITH.
EN GARDE!
HA! HA!
SHE'S STILL SO *YOUNG*. BETTER ENJOY IT WHILE SHE *CAN*.
EEK! BURIED ALIVE!
LOOK AT THEM. JUST LIKE HORTON AND I USED TO BE...
...ABOUT *TWENTY YEARS* AGO.
HEE HEE HONEY, *NO!* SOMEONE WILL *SEE* US!
C'MON, BABY.
WE COULD SAY WE WERE GOING TO--
AHEM

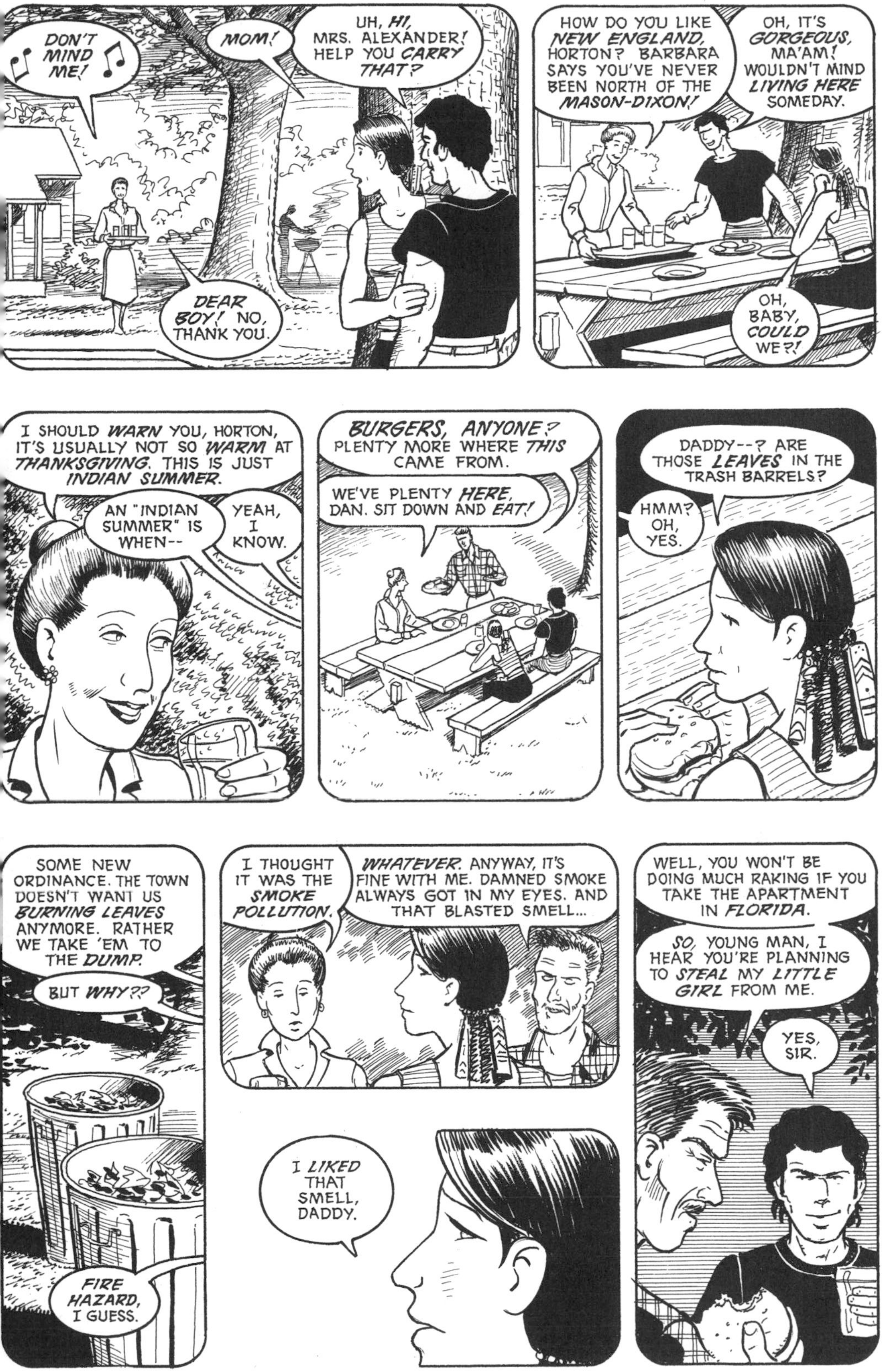
DON'T MIND ME!
MOM!
UH, HI, MRS. ALEXANDER! HELP YOU CARRY THAT?
DEAR BOY! NO, THANK YOU.
HOW DO YOU LIKE NEW ENGLAND, HORTON? BARBARA SAYS YOU'VE NEVER BEEN NORTH OF THE MASON-DIXON!
OH, IT'S GORGEOUS, MA'AM! WOULDN'T MIND LIVING HERE SOMEDAY.
OH, BABY, COULD WE?!
I SHOULD WARN YOU, HORTON, IT'S USUALLY NOT SO WARM AT THANKSGIVING. THIS IS JUST INDIAN SUMMER.
AN "INDIAN SUMMER" IS WHEN--
YEAH, I KNOW.
BURGERS, ANYONE? PLENTY MORE WHERE THIS CAME FROM.
WE'VE PLENTY HERE, DAN. SIT DOWN AND EAT!
DADDY--? ARE THOSE LEAVES IN THE TRASH BARRELS?
HMM? OH, YES.
SOME NEW ORDINANCE. THE TOWN DOESN'T WANT US BURNING LEAVES ANYMORE. RATHER WE TAKE 'EM TO THE DUMP.
BUT WHY??
FIRE HAZARD, I GUESS.
I THOUGHT IT WAS THE SMOKE POLLUTION.
WHATEVER. ANYWAY, IT'S FINE WITH ME. DAMNED SMOKE ALWAYS GOT IN MY EYES. AND THAT BLASTED SMELL...
I LIKED THAT SMELL, DADDY.
WELL, YOU WON'T BE DOING MUCH RAKING IF YOU TAKE THE APARTMENT IN FLORIDA.
SO, YOUNG MAN, I HEAR YOU'RE PLANNING TO STEAL MY LITTLE GIRL FROM ME.
YES, SIR.

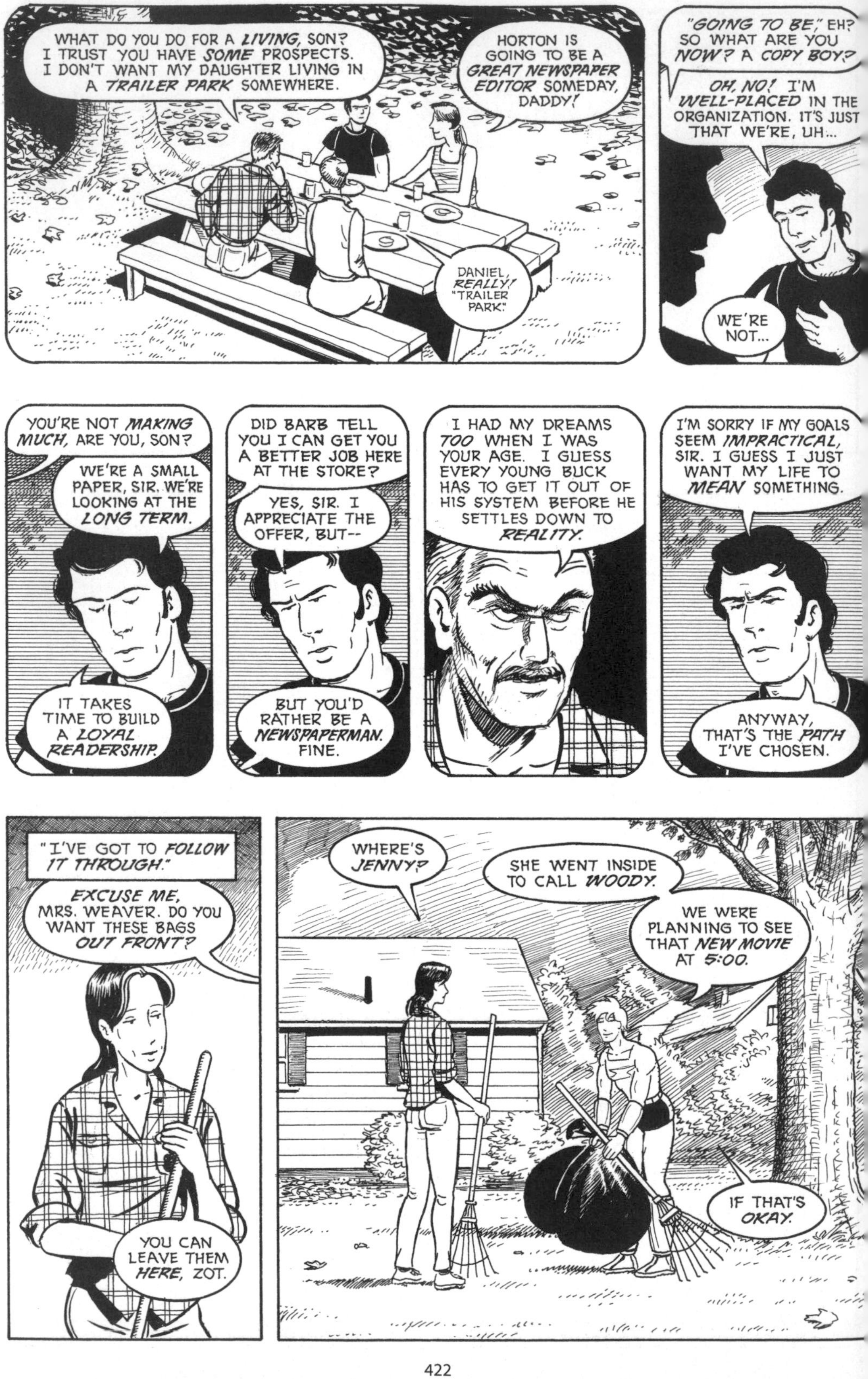
WHAT DO YOU DO FOR A LIVING, SON? I TRUST YOU HAVE SOME PROSPECTS. I DON'T WANT MY DAUGHTER LIVING IN A TRAILER PARK SOMEWHERE.
HORTON IS GOING TO BE A GREAT NEWSPAPER EDITOR SOMEDAY, DADDY!
DANIEL, REALLY! "TRAILER PARK."
"GOING TO BE," EH? SO WHAT ARE YOU NOW? A COPY BOY?
OH, NO! I'M WELL-PLACED IN THE ORGANIZATION. IT'S JUST THAT WE'RE, UH...
WE'RE NOT...
YOU'RE NOT MAKING MUCH, ARE YOU, SON?
WE'RE A SMALL PAPER, SIR. WE'RE LOOKING AT THE LONG TERM.
IT TAKES TIME TO BUILD A LOYAL READERSHIP.
DID BARB TELL YOU I CAN GET YOU A BETTER JOB HERE AT THE STORE?
YES, SIR. I APPRECIATE THE OFFER, BUT--
BUT YOU'D RATHER BE A NEWSPAPERMAN. FINE.
I HAD MY DREAMS TOO WHEN I WAS YOUR AGE. I GUESS EVERY YOUNG BUCK HAS TO GET IT OUT OF HIS SYSTEM BEFORE HE SETTLES DOWN TO REALITY.
I'M SORRY IF MY GOALS SEEM IMPRACTICAL, SIR. I GUESS I JUST WANT MY LIFE TO MEAN SOMETHING.
ANYWAY, THAT'S THE PATH I'VE CHOSEN.
"I'VE GOT TO FOLLOW IT THROUGH."
EXCUSE ME, MRS. WEAVER. DO YOU WANT THESE BAGS OUT FRONT?
YOU CAN LEAVE THEM HERE, ZOT.
WHERE'S JENNY?
SHE WENT INSIDE TO CALL WOODY.
WE WERE PLANNING TO SEE THAT NEW MOVIE AT 5:00.
IF THAT'S OKAY.

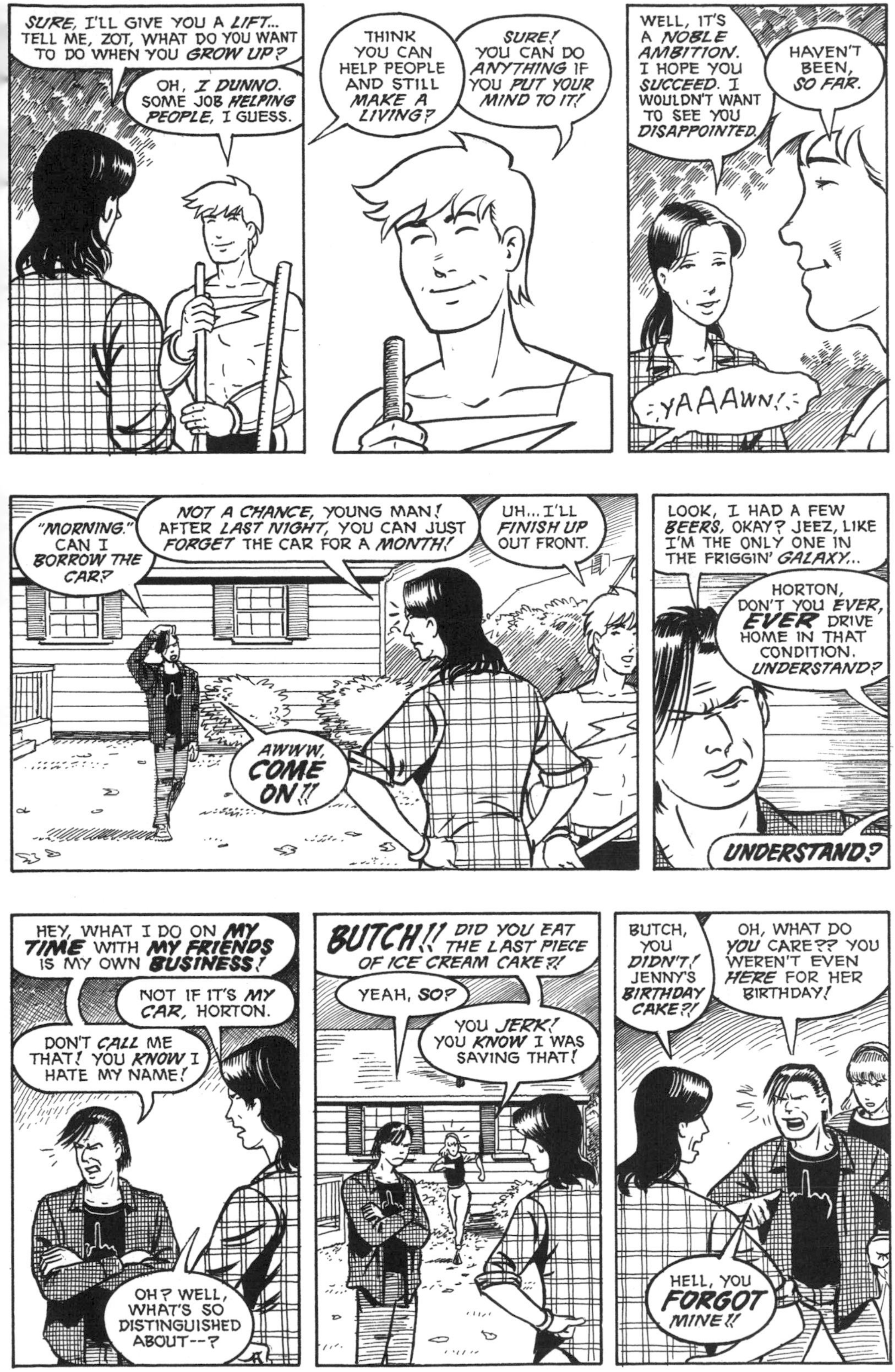
SURE, I'LL GIVE YOU A LIFT... TELL ME, ZOT, WHAT DO YOU WANT TO DO WHEN YOU GROW UP?
OH, I DUNNO. SOME JOB HELPING PEOPLE, I GUESS.
THINK YOU CAN HELP PEOPLE AND STILL MAKE A LIVING?
SURE! YOU CAN DO ANYTHING IF YOU PUT YOUR MIND TO IT!
WELL, IT'S A NOBLE AMBITION. I HOPE YOU SUCCEED. I WOULDN'T WANT TO SEE YOU DISAPPOINTED.
HAVEN'T BEEN, SO FAR.
YAAAWN!
"MORNING." CAN I BORROW THE CAR?
NOT A CHANCE, YOUNG MAN! AFTER LAST NIGHT, YOU CAN JUST FORGET THE CAR FOR A MONTH!
UH... I'LL FINISH UP OUT FRONT.
AWWW, COME ON!!
LOOK, I HAD A FEW BEERS, OKAY? JEEZ, LIKE I'M THE ONLY ONE IN THE FRIGGIN' GALAXY...
HORTON, DON'T YOU EVER, EVER DRIVE HOME IN THAT CONDITION. UNDERSTAND?
UNDERSTAND?
HEY, WHAT I DO ON MY TIME WITH MY FRIENDS IS MY OWN BUSINESS!
NOT IF IT'S MY CAR, HORTON.
DON'T CALL ME THAT! YOU KNOW I HATE MY NAME!
OH? WELL, WHAT'S SO DISTINGUISHED ABOUT--?
BUTCH!! DID YOU EAT THE LAST PIECE OF ICE CREAM CAKE?!
YEAH, SO?
YOU JERK! YOU KNOW I WAS SAVING THAT!
BUTCH, YOU DIDN'T! JENNY'S BIRTHDAY CAKE?!
OH, WHAT DO YOU CARE?? YOU WEREN'T EVEN HERE FOR HER BIRTHDAY!
HELL, YOU FORGOT MINE!!

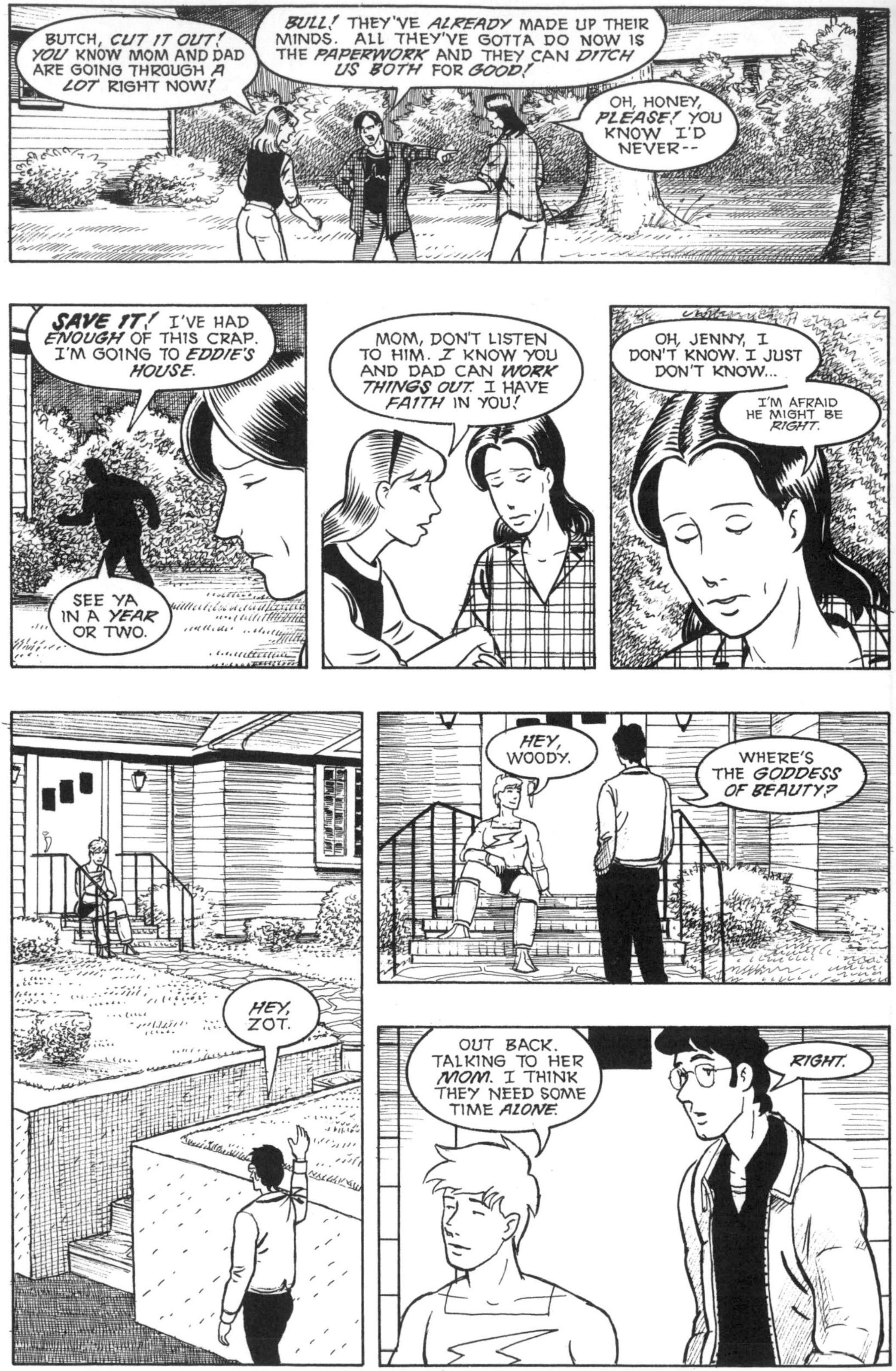
BUTCH, CUT IT OUT! YOU KNOW MOM AND DAD ARE GOING THROUGH A LOT RIGHT NOW!
BULL! THEY'VE ALREADY MADE UP THEIR MINDS. ALL THEY'VE GOTTA DO NOW IS THE PAPERWORK AND THEY CAN DITCH US BOTH FOR GOOD!
OH, HONEY, PLEASE! YOU KNOW I'D NEVER--
SAVE IT! I'VE HAD ENOUGH OF THIS CRAP. I'M GOING TO EDDIE'S HOUSE.
SEE YA IN A YEAR OR TWO.
MOM, DON'T LISTEN TO HIM. I KNOW YOU AND DAD CAN WORK THINGS OUT. I HAVE FAITH IN YOU!
OH, JENNY, I DON'T KNOW. I JUST DON'T KNOW...
I'M AFRAID HE MIGHT BE RIGHT.
HEY, ZOT.
HEY, WOODY.
WHERE'S THE GODDESS OF BEAUTY?
OUT BACK. TALKING TO HER MOM. I THINK THEY NEED SOME TIME ALONE.
RIGHT.

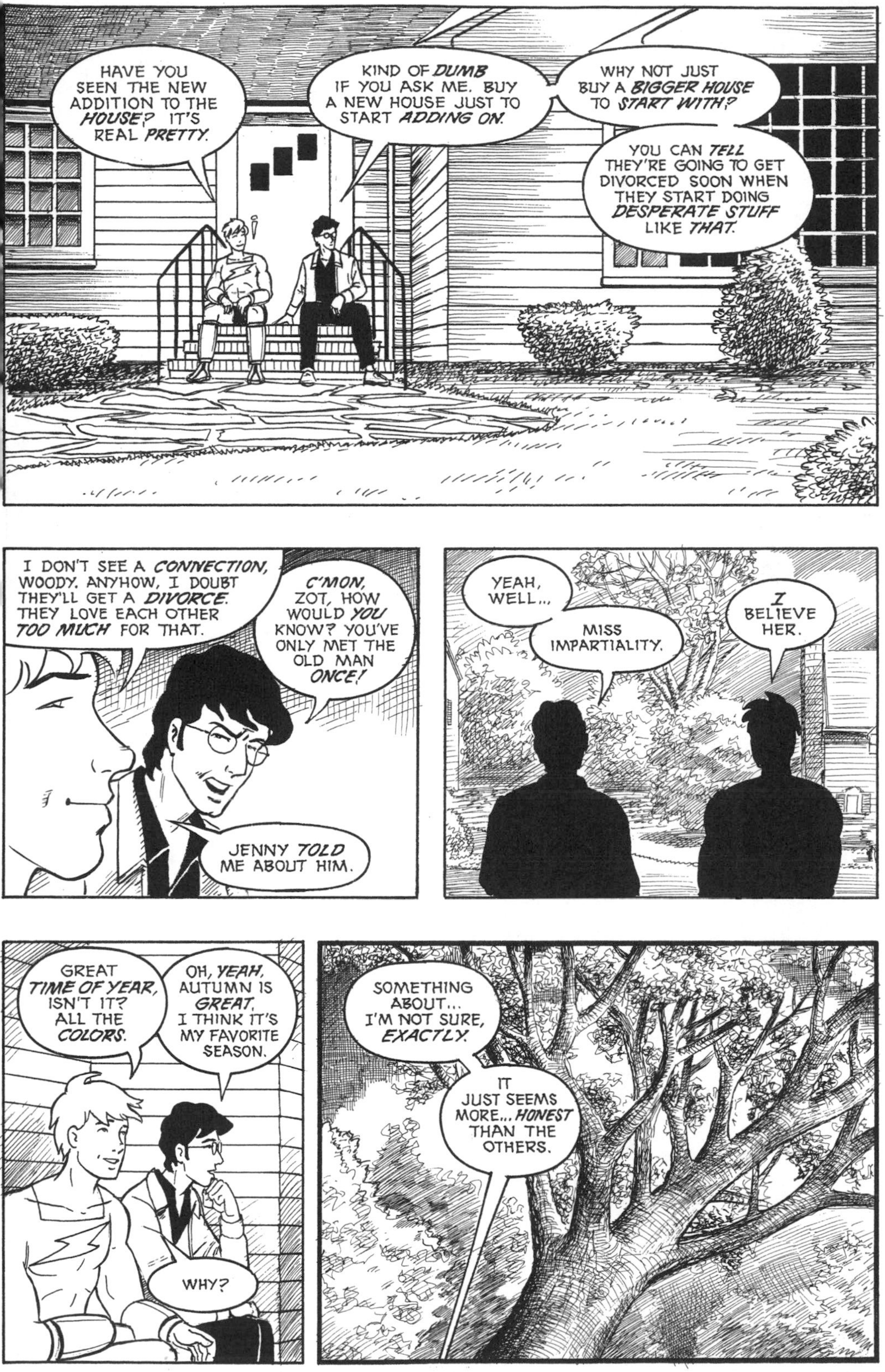
HAVE YOU SEEN THE NEW ADDITION TO THE HOUSE? IT'S REAL PRETTY.
KIND OF DUMB IF YOU ASK ME. BUY A NEW HOUSE JUST TO START ADDING ON.
WHY NOT JUST BUY A BIGGER HOUSE TO START WITH?
YOU CAN TELL THEY'RE GOING TO GET DIVORCED SOON WHEN THEY START DOING DESPERATE STUFF LIKE THAT.
I DON'T SEE A CONNECTION, WOODY. ANYHOW, I DOUBT THEY'LL GET A DIVORCE. THEY LOVE EACH OTHER TOO MUCH FOR THAT.
C'MON, ZOT, HOW WOULD YOU KNOW? YOU'VE ONLY MET THE OLD MAN ONCE!
JENNY TOLD ME ABOUT HIM.
YEAH, WELL...
MISS IMPARTIALITY.
I BELIEVE HER.
GREAT TIME OF YEAR, ISN'T IT? ALL THE COLORS.
OH, YEAH, AUTUMN IS GREAT. I THINK IT'S MY FAVORITE SEASON.
WHY?
SOMETHING ABOUT... I'M NOT SURE, EXACTLY.
IT JUST SEEMS MORE... HONEST THAN THE OTHERS.

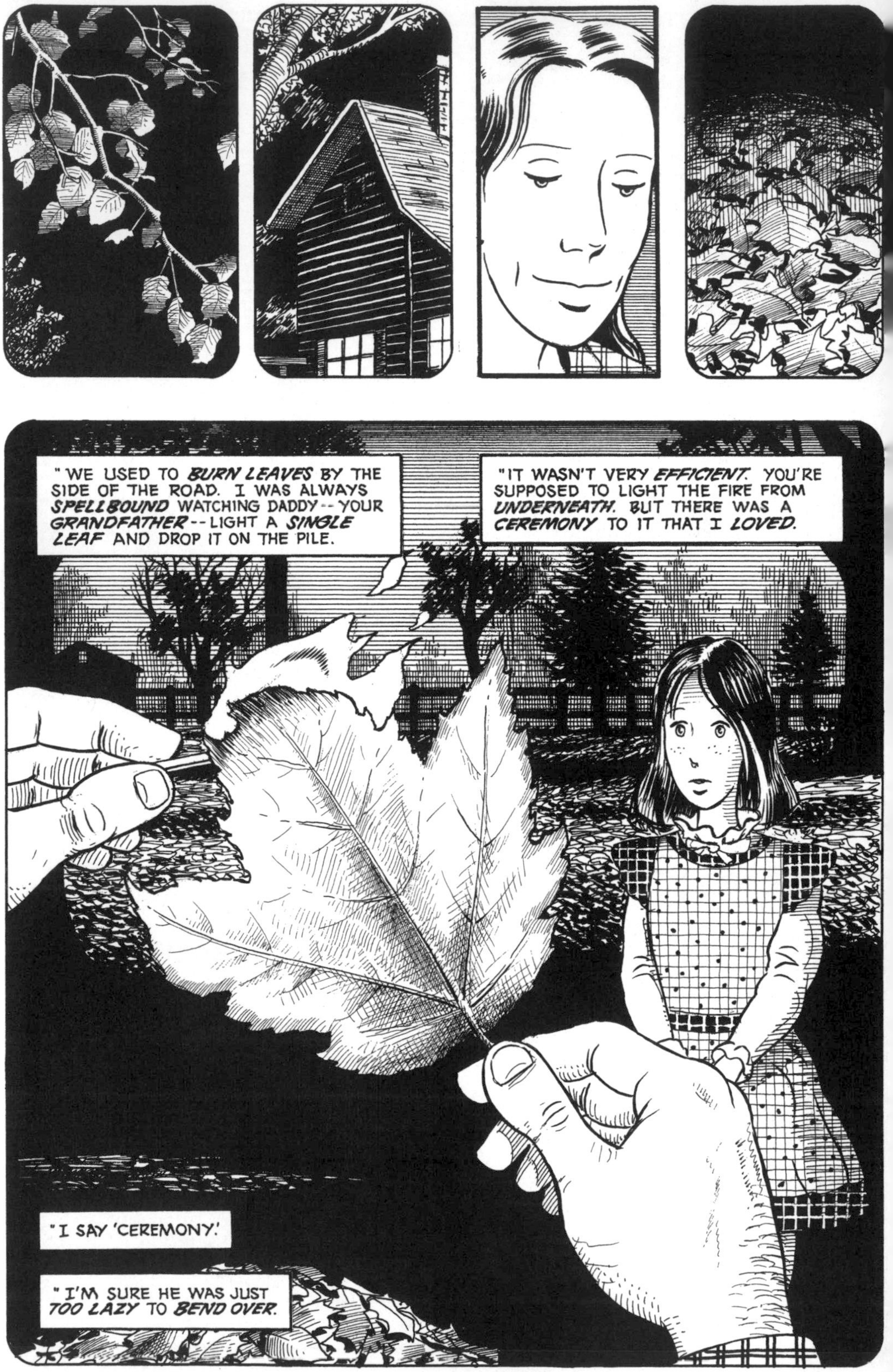
"WE USED TO BURN LEAVES BY THE SIDE OF THE ROAD. I WAS ALWAYS SPELLBOUND WATCHING DADDY--YOUR GRANDFATHER--LIGHT A SINGLE LEAF AND DROP IT ON THE PILE.
"IT WASN'T VERY EFFICIENT. YOU'RE SUPPOSED TO LIGHT THE FIRE FROM UNDERNEATH. BUT THERE WAS A CEREMONY TO IT THAT I LOVED.
"I SAY 'CEREMONY.'
"I'M SURE HE WAS JUST TOO LAZY TO BEND OVER.

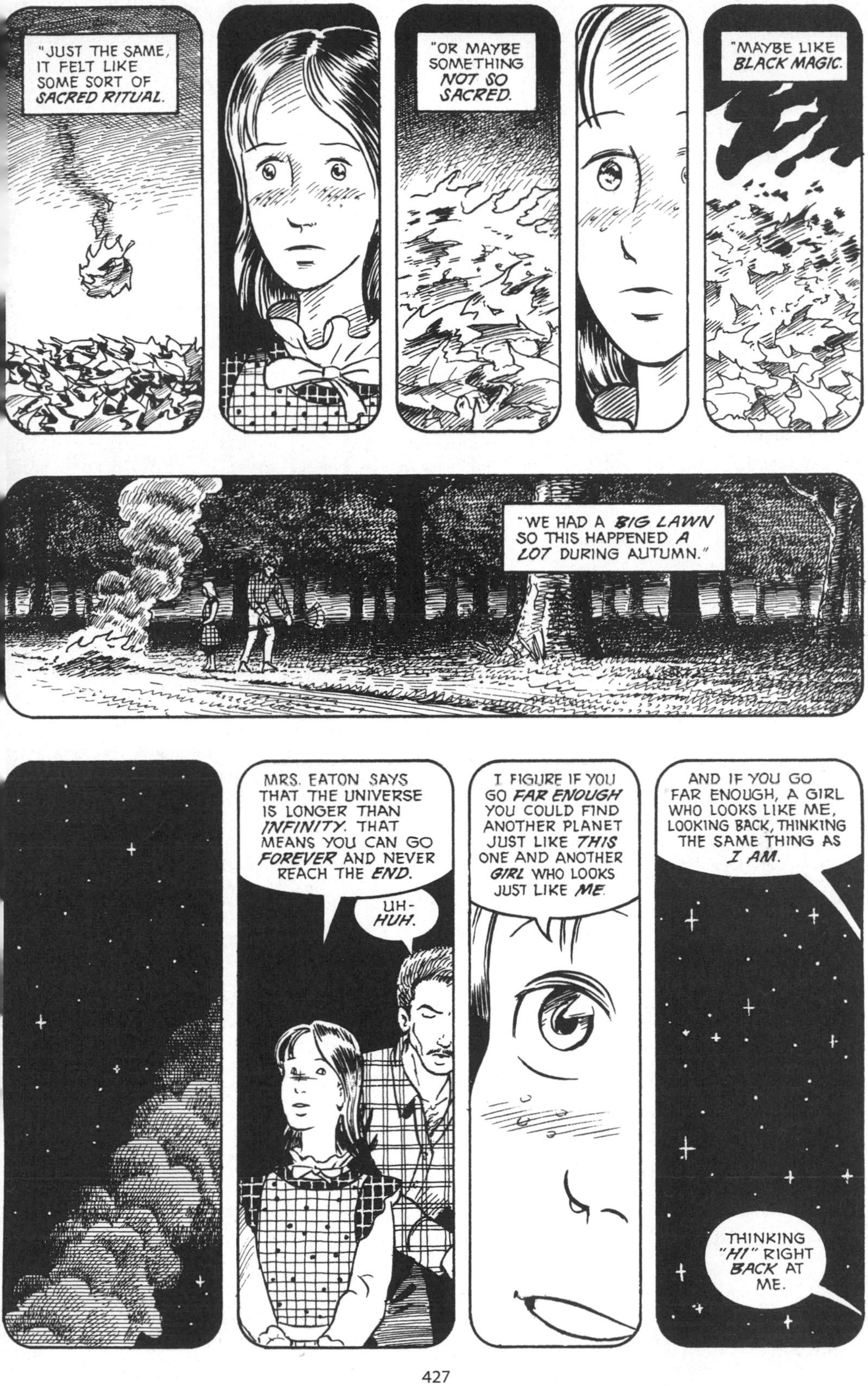
"JUST THE SAME, IT FELT LIKE SOME SORT OF SACRED RITUAL.
"OR MAYBE SOMETHING NOT SO SACRED.
"MAYBE LIKE BLACK MAGIC.
"WE HAD A BIG LAWN SO THIS HAPPENED A LOT DURING AUTUMN."
MRS. EATON SAYS THAT THE UNIVERSE IS LONGER THAN INFINITY. THAT MEANS YOU CAN GO FOREVER AND NEVER REACH THE END.
UH-HUH.
I FIGURE IF YOU GO FAR ENOUGH YOU COULD FIND ANOTHER PLANET JUST LIKE THIS ONE AND ANOTHER GIRL WHO LOOKS JUST LIKE ME.
AND IF YOU GO FAR ENOUGH, A GIRL WHO LOOKS LIKE ME, LOOKING BACK, THINKING THE SAME THING AS I AM.
THINKING "HI" RIGHT BACK AT ME.

DINNERTIME!

C'MON, HONEY.

"AT DINNER, MY FATHER COMPLAINED THAT TEACHERS WERE FILLING HIS KID'S HEAD WITH *NONSENSE.*

"MOM *APPROVED* OF MY IMAGINATIVE THEORIES, HOWEVER, AND TOLD HIM TO STOP BEING SUCH AN OLD *CRAB APPLE.*

"AFTER DINNER, WE BURNED THE LAST TWO PILES. I SAT BY THE *SMOKING ASHES* FOR A WHILE AFTER DAD WENT INSIDE TO WATCH THE NEWS.

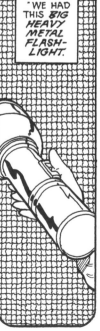

"WE HAD THIS *BIG HEAVY METAL FLASH-LIGHT.*

"THROUGH THE SMOKE YOU COULD SEE ITS BEACON... *STEADY* AND *STRAIGHT* LIKE A *LASER BEAM.*

"*LEAPING INTO THE SKY AT 186,000 MILES PER SECOND.*

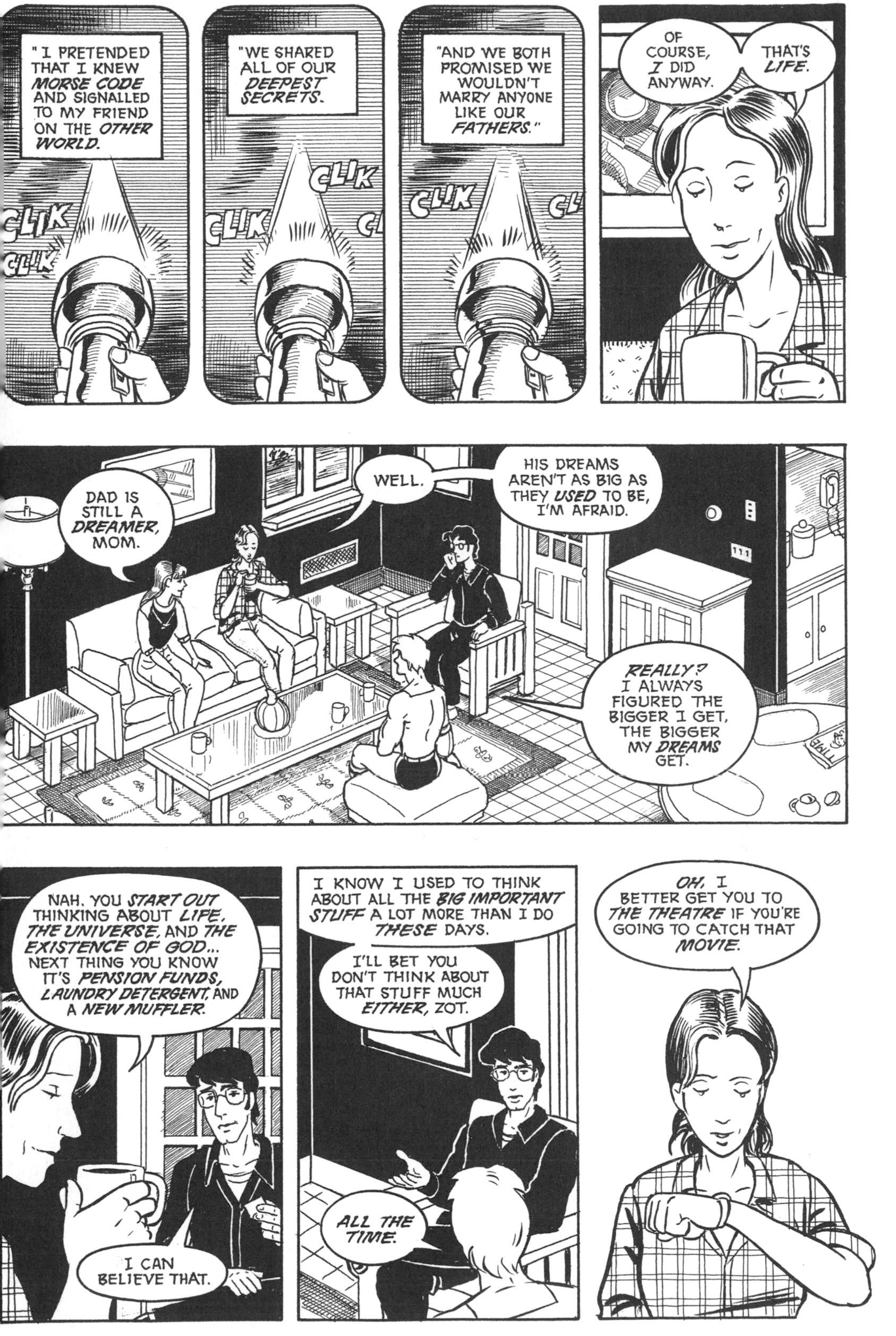
"I PRETENDED THAT I KNEW MORSE CODE AND SIGNALLED TO MY FRIEND ON THE OTHER WORLD.
CLIK
CLIK
"WE SHARED ALL OF OUR DEEPEST SECRETS.
CLIK
CLIK
CL
"AND WE BOTH PROMISED WE WOULDN'T MARRY ANYONE LIKE OUR FATHERS."
CLIK
CL
OF COURSE, I DID ANYWAY.
THAT'S LIFE.
DAD IS STILL A DREAMER, MOM.
WELL.
HIS DREAMS AREN'T AS BIG AS THEY USED TO BE, I'M AFRAID.
REALLY? I ALWAYS FIGURED THE BIGGER I GET, THE BIGGER MY DREAMS GET.
NAH. YOU START OUT THINKING ABOUT LIFE, THE UNIVERSE, AND THE EXISTENCE OF GOD... NEXT THING YOU KNOW IT'S PENSION FUNDS, LAUNDRY DETERGENT, AND A NEW MUFFLER.
I CAN BELIEVE THAT.
I KNOW I USED TO THINK ABOUT ALL THE BIG IMPORTANT STUFF A LOT MORE THAN I DO THESE DAYS.
I'LL BET YOU DON'T THINK ABOUT THAT STUFF MUCH EITHER, ZOT.
ALL THE TIME.
OH, I BETTER GET YOU TO THE THEATRE IF YOU'RE GOING TO CATCH THAT MOVIE.

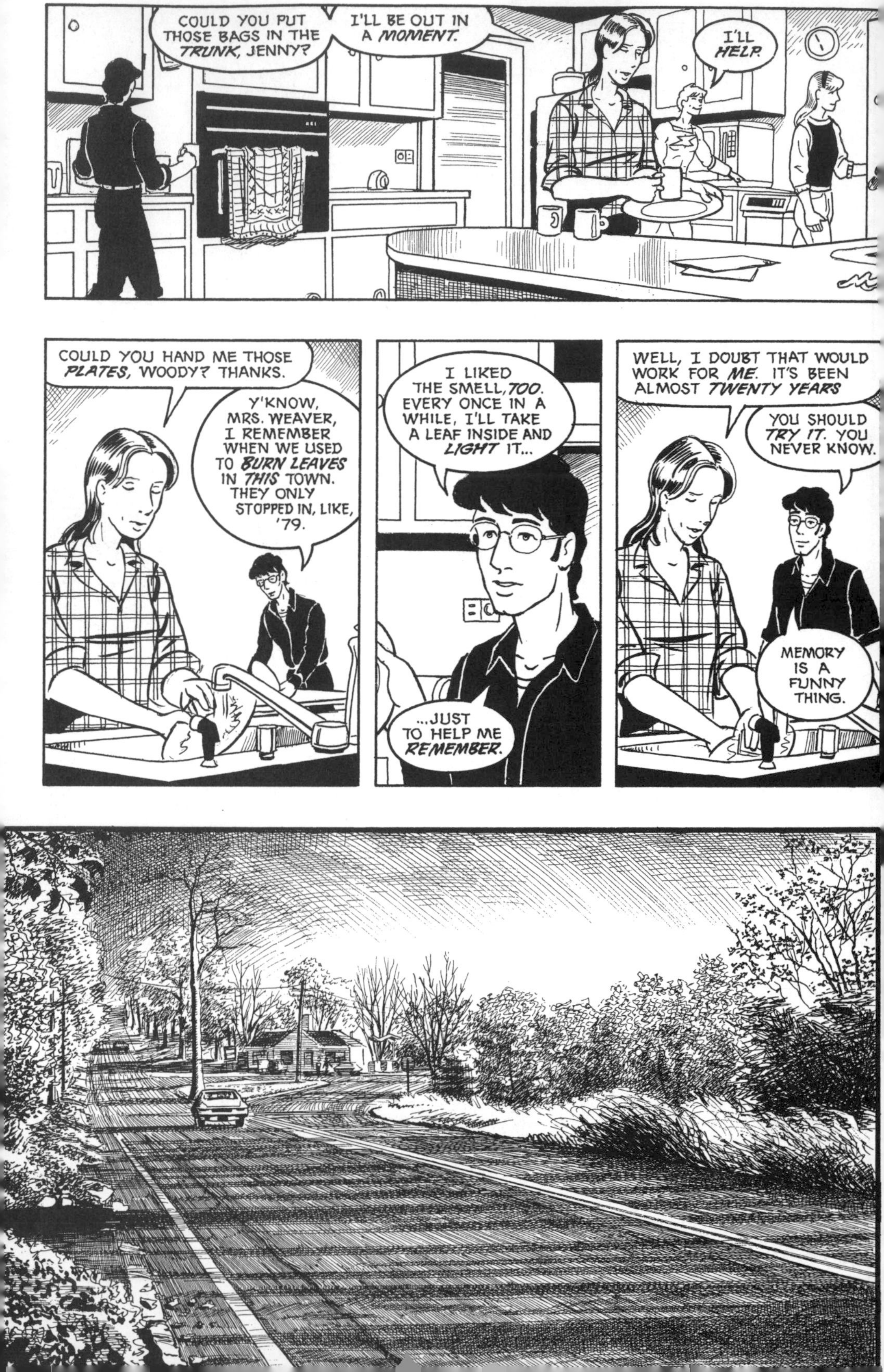
COULD YOU PUT THOSE BAGS IN THE TRUNK, JENNY?
I'LL BE OUT IN A MOMENT.
I'LL HELP.
COULD YOU HAND ME THOSE PLATES, WOODY? THANKS.
Y'KNOW, MRS. WEAVER, I REMEMBER WHEN WE USED TO BURN LEAVES IN THIS TOWN. THEY ONLY STOPPED IN, LIKE, '79.
I LIKED THE SMELL, TOO. EVERY ONCE IN A WHILE, I'LL TAKE A LEAF INSIDE AND LIGHT IT...
...JUST TO HELP ME REMEMBER.
WELL, I DOUBT THAT WOULD WORK FOR ME. IT'S BEEN ALMOST TWENTY YEARS
YOU SHOULD TRY IT. YOU NEVER KNOW.
MEMORY IS A FUNNY THING.

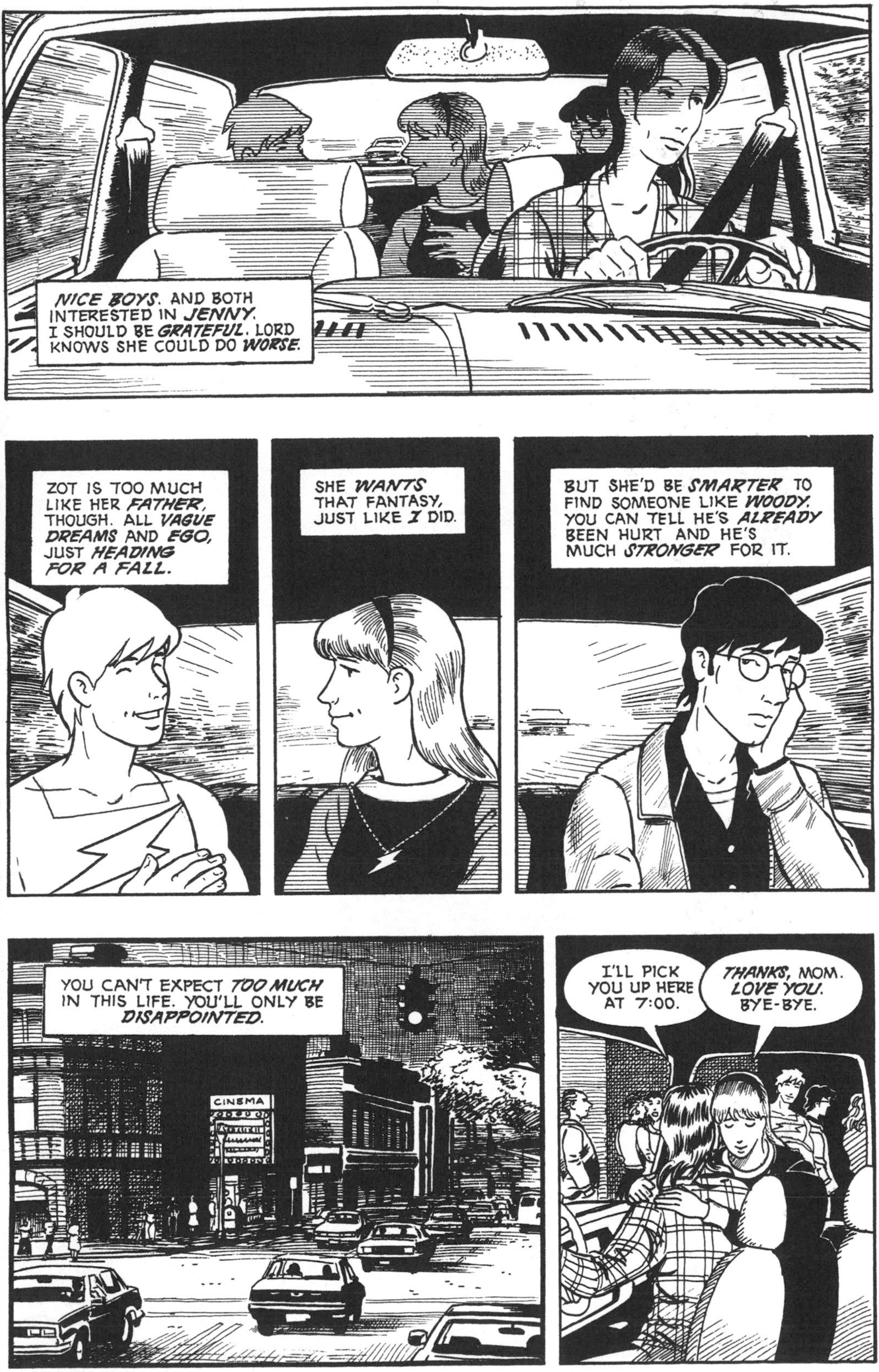

NICE BOYS. AND BOTH INTERESTED IN JENNY. I SHOULD BE GRATEFUL. LORD KNOWS SHE COULD DO WORSE.
ZOT IS TOO MUCH LIKE HER FATHER, THOUGH. ALL VAGUE DREAMS AND EGO, JUST HEADING FOR A FALL.
SHE WANTS THAT FANTASY, JUST LIKE I DID.
BUT SHE'D BE SMARTER TO FIND SOMEONE LIKE WOODY. YOU CAN TELL HE'S ALREADY BEEN HURT AND HE'S MUCH STRONGER FOR IT.
YOU CAN'T EXPECT TOO MUCH IN THIS LIFE. YOU'LL ONLY BE DISAPPOINTED.
CINEMA
I'LL PICK YOU UP HERE AT 7:00.
THANKS, MOM. LOVE YOU. BYE-BYE.

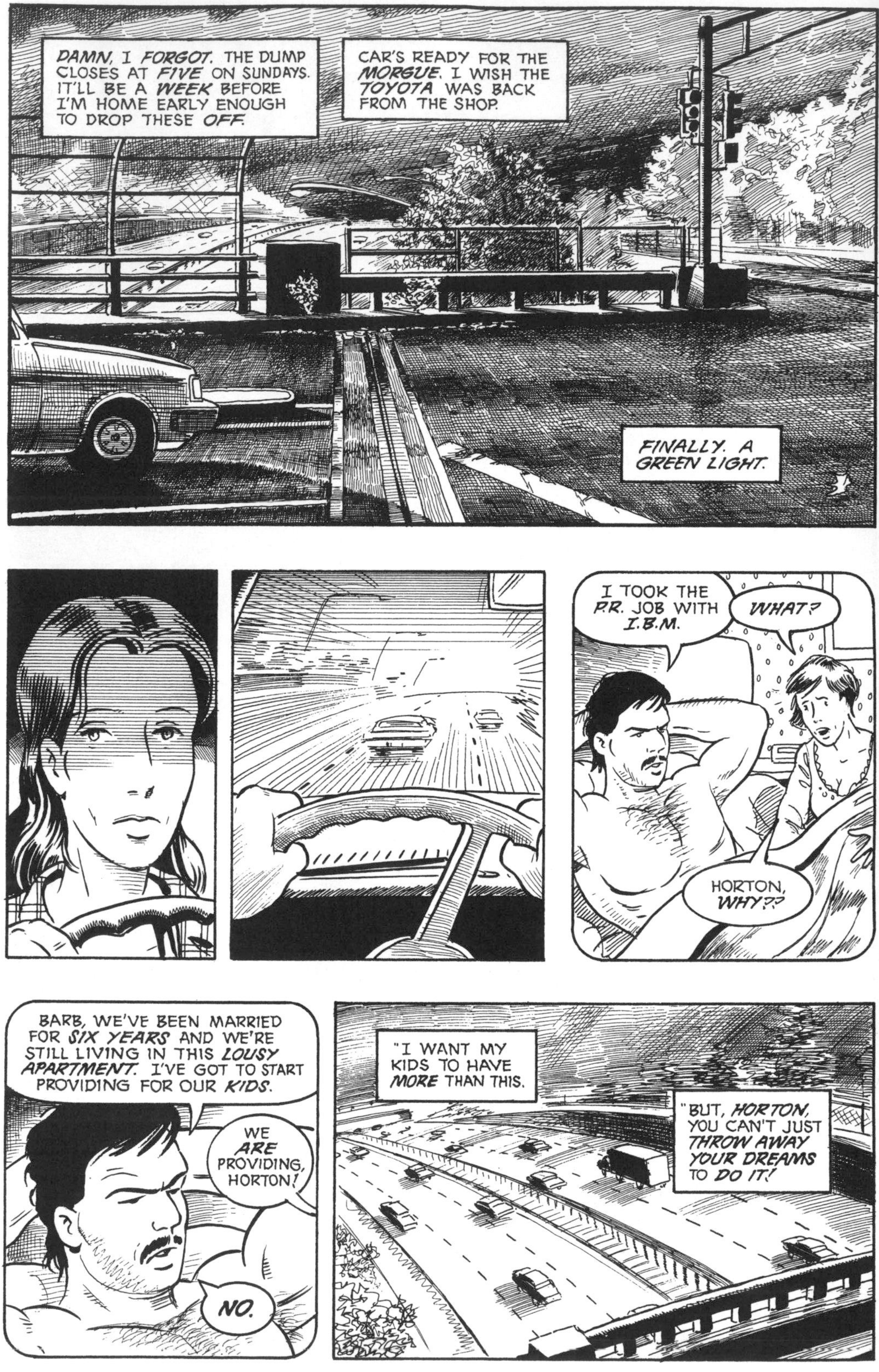
DAMN, I FORGOT. THE DUMP CLOSES AT FIVE ON SUNDAYS. IT'LL BE A WEEK BEFORE I'M HOME EARLY ENOUGH TO DROP THESE OFF.
CAR'S READY FOR THE MORGUE. I WISH THE TOYOTA WAS BACK FROM THE SHOP.
FINALLY. A GREEN LIGHT.
I TOOK THE P.R. JOB WITH I.B.M.
WHAT?
HORTON, WHY??
BARB, WE'VE BEEN MARRIED FOR SIX YEARS AND WE'RE STILL LIVING IN THIS LOUSY APARTMENT. I'VE GOT TO START PROVIDING FOR OUR KIDS.
WE ARE PROVIDING, HORTON!
NO.
"I WANT MY KIDS TO HAVE MORE THAN THIS.
"BUT, HORTON, YOU CAN'T JUST THROW AWAY YOUR DREAMS TO DO IT!

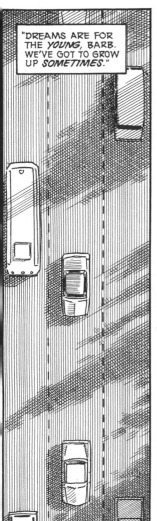

"DREAMS ARE FOR THE *YOUNG*, BARB. WE'VE GOT TO GROW UP *SOMETIMES*."

WELL, HORTON, WE'RE ALL *GROWN UP* NOW, JUST LIKE YOU WANTED.

WE HAVE THE *HOUSE* NOW. THE *TWO CARS*.

THE *INSURANCE POLICY*. THE *PENSIONS*. THE MONEY FOR *COLLEGE*. THE NEW *ADDITION*.

WE DID *GOOD*.

KEYS. HERE THEY ARE. SHOULD HAVE THOSE *FLAGSTONES* REPLACED. MAYBE PUT IN *CERAMIC*.

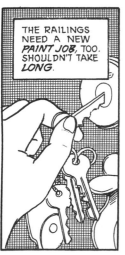

THE RAILINGS NEED A NEW *PAINT JOB*, TOO. SHOULDN'T TAKE *LONG*.

CLIK

HMM...

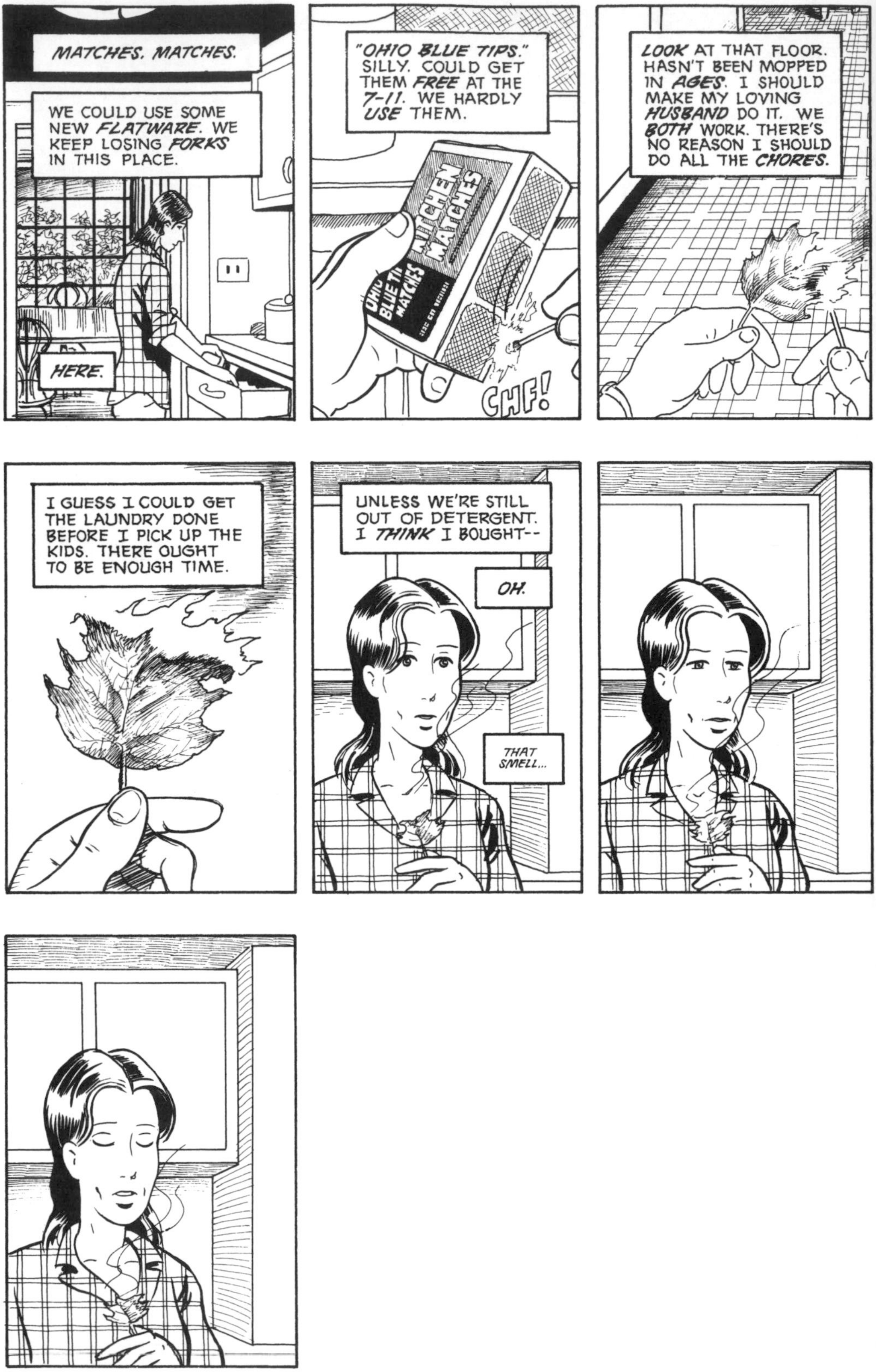
MATCHES. MATCHES.
WE COULD USE SOME NEW *FLATWARE*. WE KEEP LOSING *FORKS* IN THIS PLACE.
HERE.
"OHIO BLUE TIPS." SILLY. COULD GET THEM *FREE* AT THE *7-11*. WE HARDLY *USE* THEM.
CHF!
LOOK AT THAT FLOOR. HASN'T BEEN MOPPED IN *AGES*. I SHOULD MAKE MY LOVING *HUSBAND* DO IT. WE *BOTH* WORK. THERE'S NO REASON I SHOULD DO ALL THE *CHORES*.
I GUESS I COULD GET THE LAUNDRY DONE BEFORE I PICK UP THE KIDS. THERE OUGHT TO BE ENOUGH TIME.
UNLESS WE'RE STILL OUT OF DETERGENT. I *THINK* I BOUGHT--
OH.
THAT SMELL...

"Autumn" was the first of five issues in a row in which I plucked a single supporting character and devoted a whole issue to his or her daily life. More tone poem than story, "Autumn" was about as far from a typical superhero story as anything I'd done to that point (with the exception of some weird little mini-comics). Looking back on it now, it's clearly a self-conscious attempt on a young genre writer's part to step up to "real" writing, while still clinging to his security blanket (the guy in the spandex costume). Somehow, though, the superhero elements don't seem all that out of place. There was always a bit of Peter Pan in Zot, ready to plug into whatever nostalgia metaphors his writer might take a fancy to.

Bill Loebs had recommended Sherwood Anderson's *Winesburg, Ohio* and I'm sure that Anderson's character portraits helped me visualize what I was going for. I also had observations from my own life to draw upon. As I neared thirty, I was a bit more attuned to the daily struggles of adult life, and it wasn't hard to imagine circumstances in which I might have to get a "real" job someday, especially if Ivy and I succeeded in having children while the U.S. comics market failed to enlarge its own family of readers. I could see life through either of Jenny's parents' eyes.

Most importantly, the artist in me rejoiced at the opportunity to draw some of the images I saw all around me. I loved New England, and found suburbia intensely beautiful and strange. One of my reference-taking missions took me on an hours-long walk after the rain through miles and miles of chilly, tree-lined streets in Arlington and Belmont, Massachusetts. Some of those images arrived intact—via about twenty miles of cross-hatching—in the big silent panels that punctuate this issue.

Jenny's house was my own mother's house in nearby Lexington, bought a few years before when our old family home seemed unnecessarily large following my father's death in 1982. The back porch on page 2 didn't exist when I drew it; I added it for visual interest. What I didn't know at the time was that my mother had indeed decided to add a porch to the

house, one that was eerily close to my drawn version. Neither of us had any idea what the other was up to. This was one of a handful of spooky coincidences that occurred around this time where my comics accidentally "predicted" real-life events.

Unfortunately for my long-suffering publisher, my usually slow pace of production became downright glacial as a result of the obsessive detail in this issue. Eclipse had wanted to promote both a collection of the first four issues and this issue together as a special promotion for the San Diego convention, and in the end neither one could ship in time. There had also been a well-meaning but ultimately doomed plan on their part to ship the issue with the scent of autumn leaves added. Pretty much everything that could go wrong did. Just speak the words "*Zot!* Month" to me at a convention if you want to see me cringe.

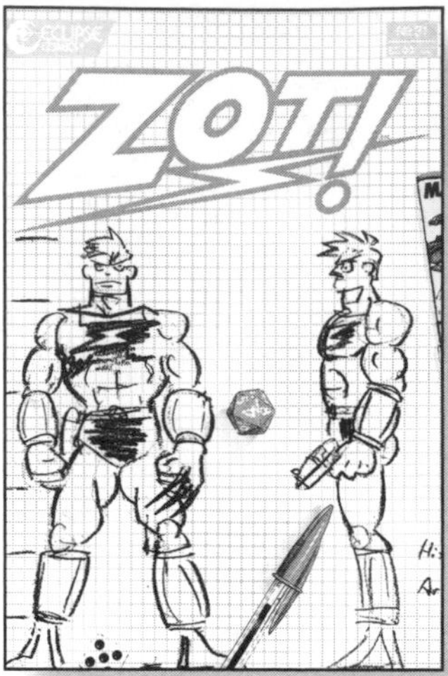
ZOT!
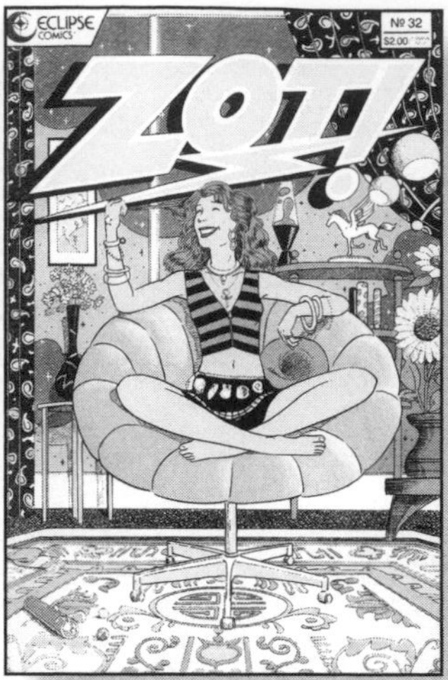
ECLIPSE COMICS
№ 32
$2.00
ZOT!

Clash of Titans

First published in *Zot! #31*.

Invincible

First published in *Zot! #32*.

Lettering:

Bob Lappan

Original series editor:

cat yronwode

Plot assist:

Ivy Ratafia

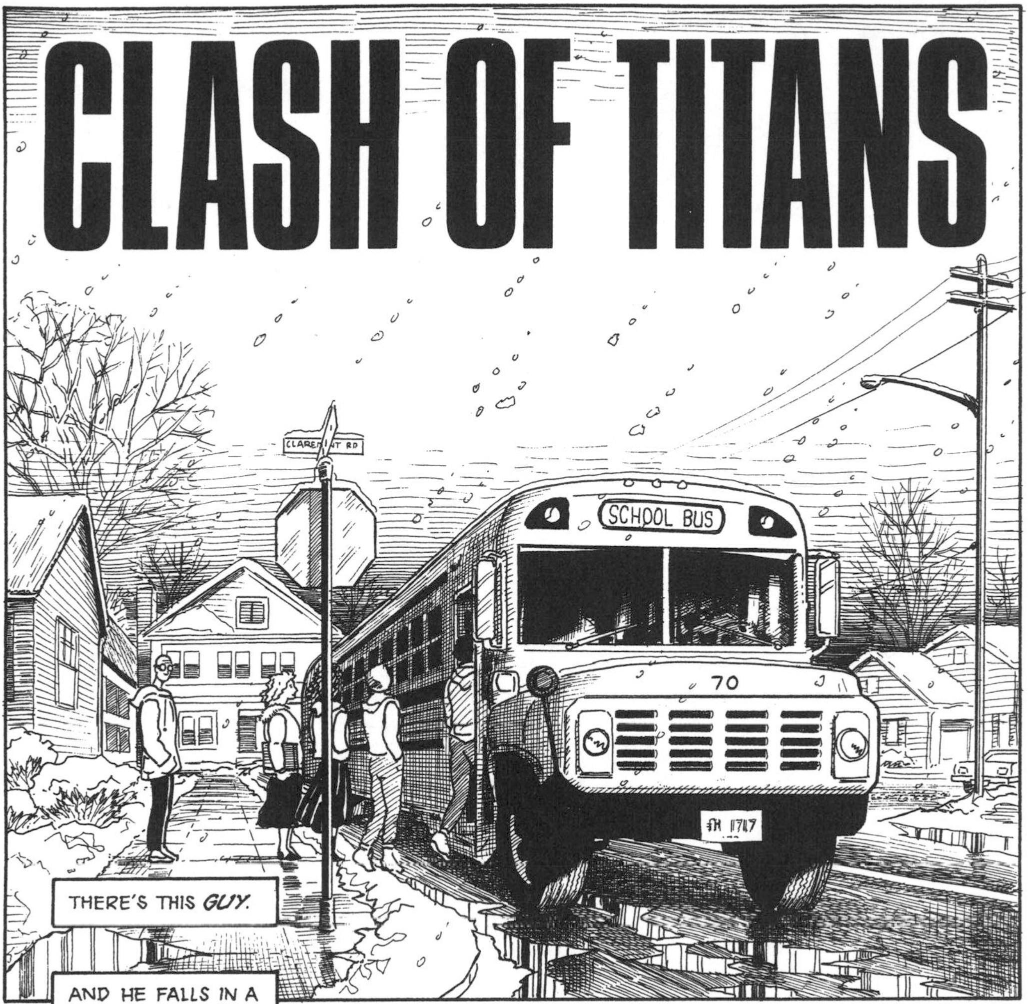
CLASH OF TITANS
SCHOOL BUS
70
THERE'S THIS *GUY.*

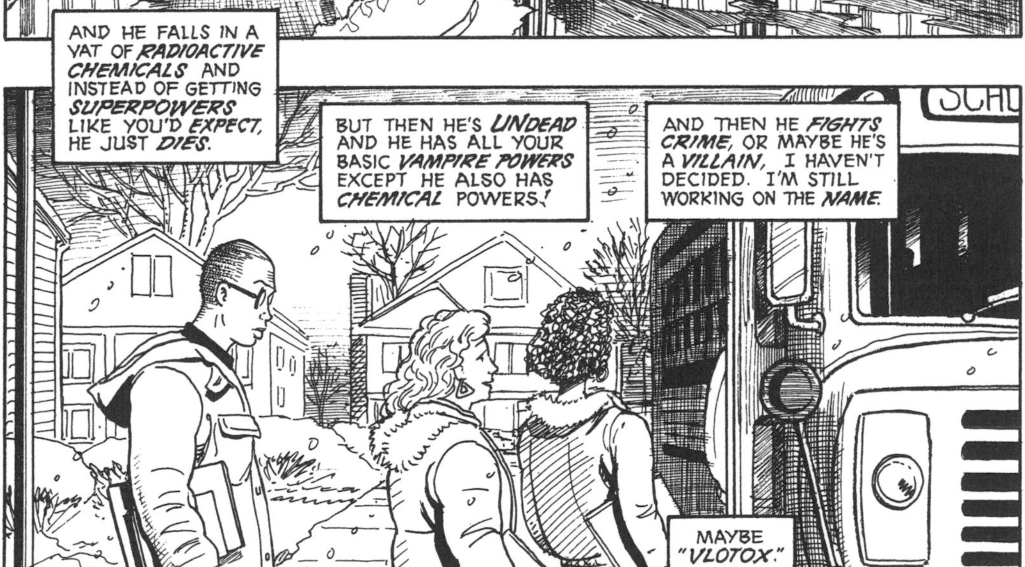
AND HE FALLS IN A VAT OF *RADIOACTIVE CHEMICALS* AND INSTEAD OF GETTING *SUPERPOWERS* LIKE YOU'D *EXPECT,* HE JUST *DIES.*
BUT THEN HE'S *UNDEAD* AND HE HAS ALL YOUR BASIC *VAMPIRE POWERS* EXCEPT HE ALSO HAS *CHEMICAL* POWERS!
AND THEN HE *FIGHTS CRIME,* OR MAYBE HE'S A *VILLAIN,* I HAVEN'T DECIDED. I'M STILL WORKING ON THE *NAME.*
MAYBE *"VLOTOX."*

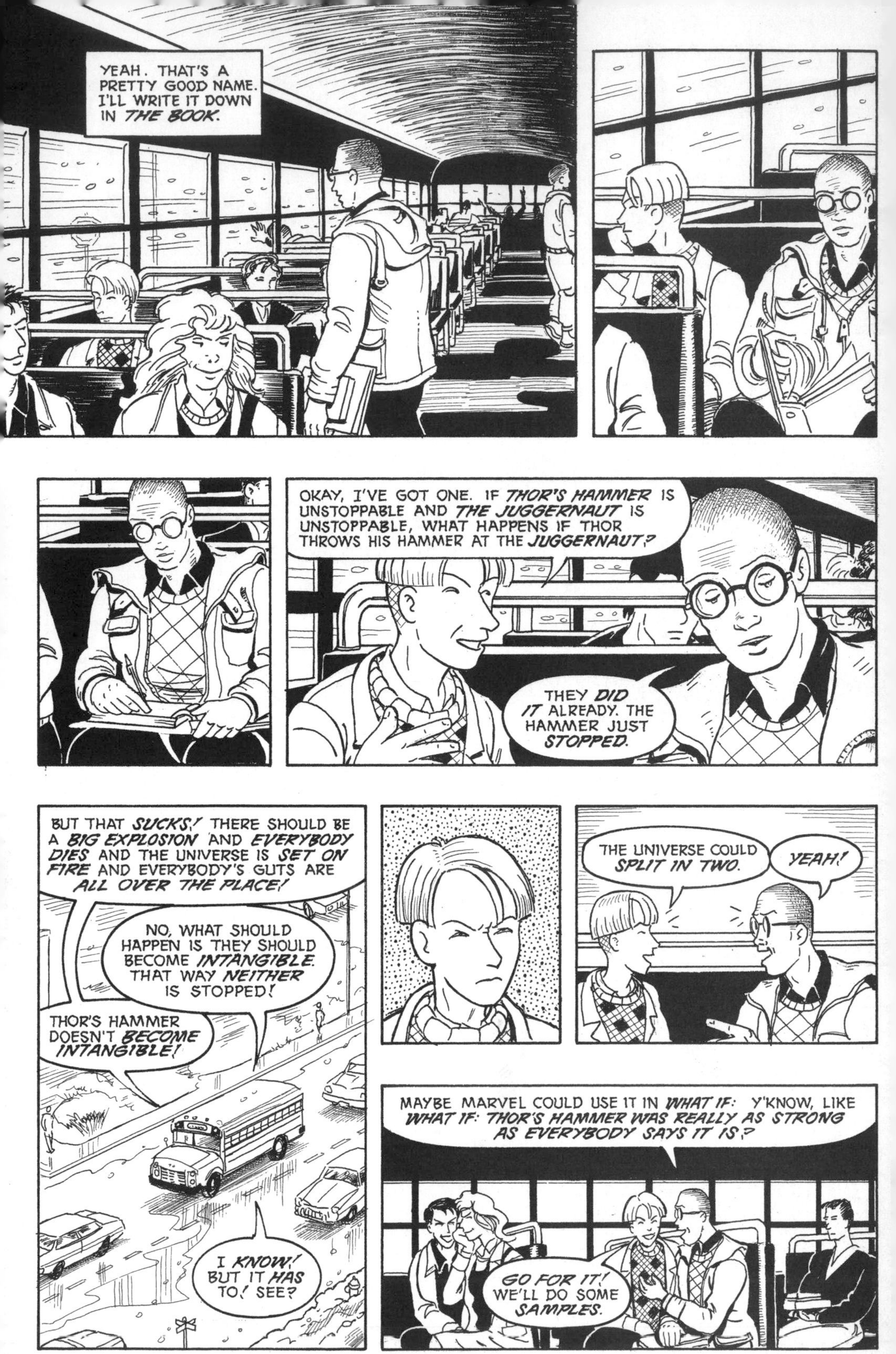
YEAH. THAT'S A PRETTY GOOD NAME. I'LL WRITE IT DOWN IN *THE BOOK*.
OKAY, I'VE GOT ONE. IF *THOR'S HAMMER* IS UNSTOPPABLE AND *THE JUGGERNAUT* IS UNSTOPPABLE, WHAT HAPPENS IF THOR THROWS HIS HAMMER AT THE *JUGGERNAUT*?
THEY *DID IT* ALREADY. THE HAMMER JUST *STOPPED*.
BUT THAT *SUCKS!* THERE SHOULD BE A *BIG EXPLOSION* AND *EVERYBODY DIES* AND THE UNIVERSE IS *SET ON FIRE* AND EVERYBODY'S GUTS ARE *ALL OVER THE PLACE!*
NO, WHAT SHOULD HAPPEN IS THEY SHOULD BECOME *INTANGIBLE*. THAT WAY *NEITHER* IS STOPPED!
THOR'S HAMMER DOESN'T *BECOME INTANGIBLE!*
I *KNOW!* BUT IT *HAS* TO! SEE?
THE UNIVERSE COULD *SPLIT IN TWO*.
YEAH!
MAYBE MARVEL COULD USE IT IN *WHAT IF:* Y'KNOW, LIKE *WHAT IF: THOR'S HAMMER WAS REALLY AS STRONG AS EVERYBODY SAYS IT IS?*
GO FOR IT! WE'LL DO SOME *SAMPLES*.

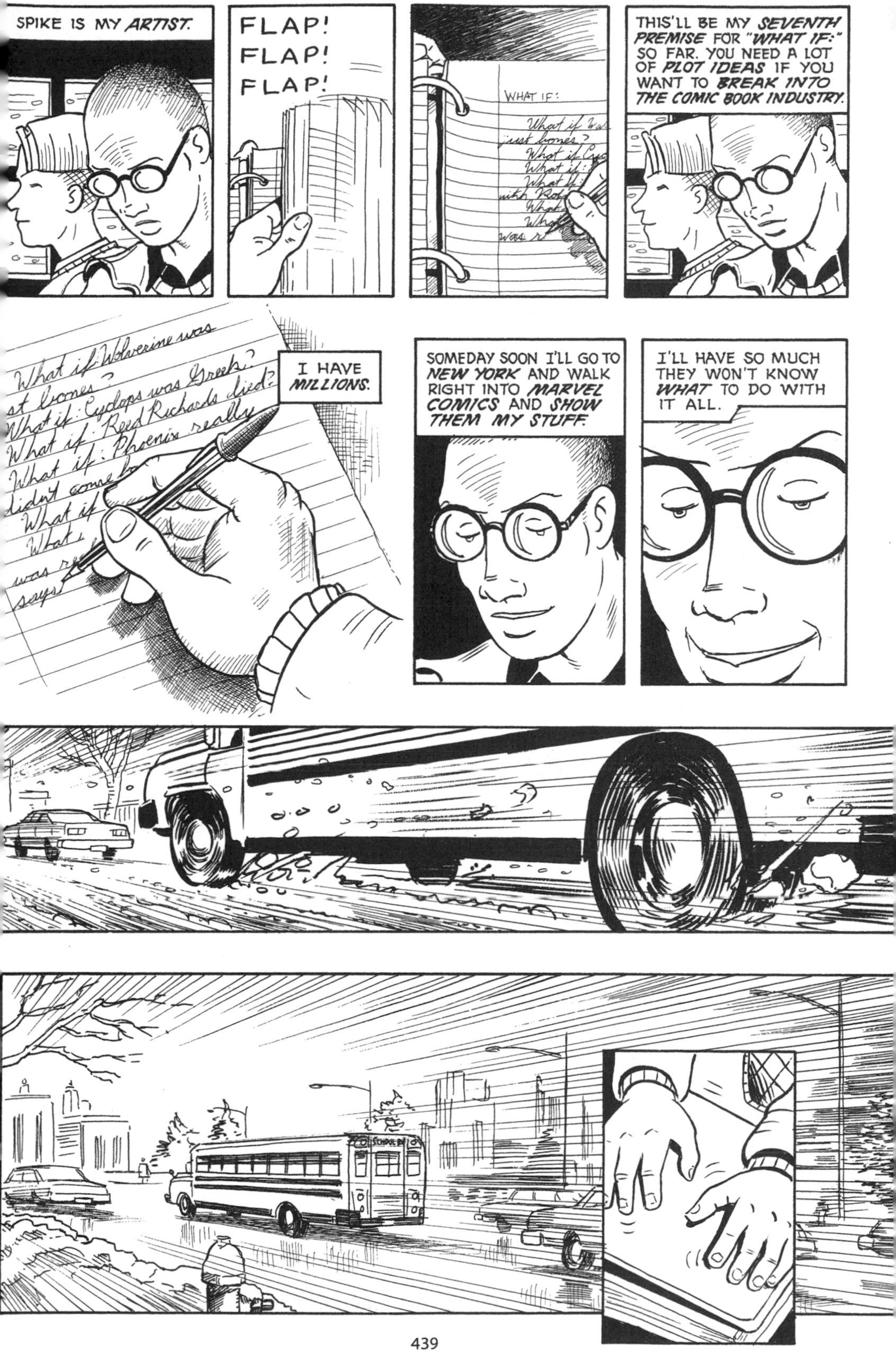
SPIKE IS MY ARTIST.
FLAP! FLAP! FLAP!
WHAT IF:
THIS'LL BE MY SEVENTH PREMISE FOR "WHAT IF:" SO FAR. YOU NEED A LOT OF PLOT IDEAS IF YOU WANT TO BREAK INTO THE COMIC BOOK INDUSTRY.
What if Wolverine was
What if: Reed Richards died?
What if: Phoenix really
I HAVE MILLIONS.
SOMEDAY SOON I'LL GO TO NEW YORK AND WALK RIGHT INTO MARVEL COMICS AND SHOW THEM MY STUFF.
I'LL HAVE SO MUCH THEY WON'T KNOW WHAT TO DO WITH IT ALL.
SCHOOL BUS

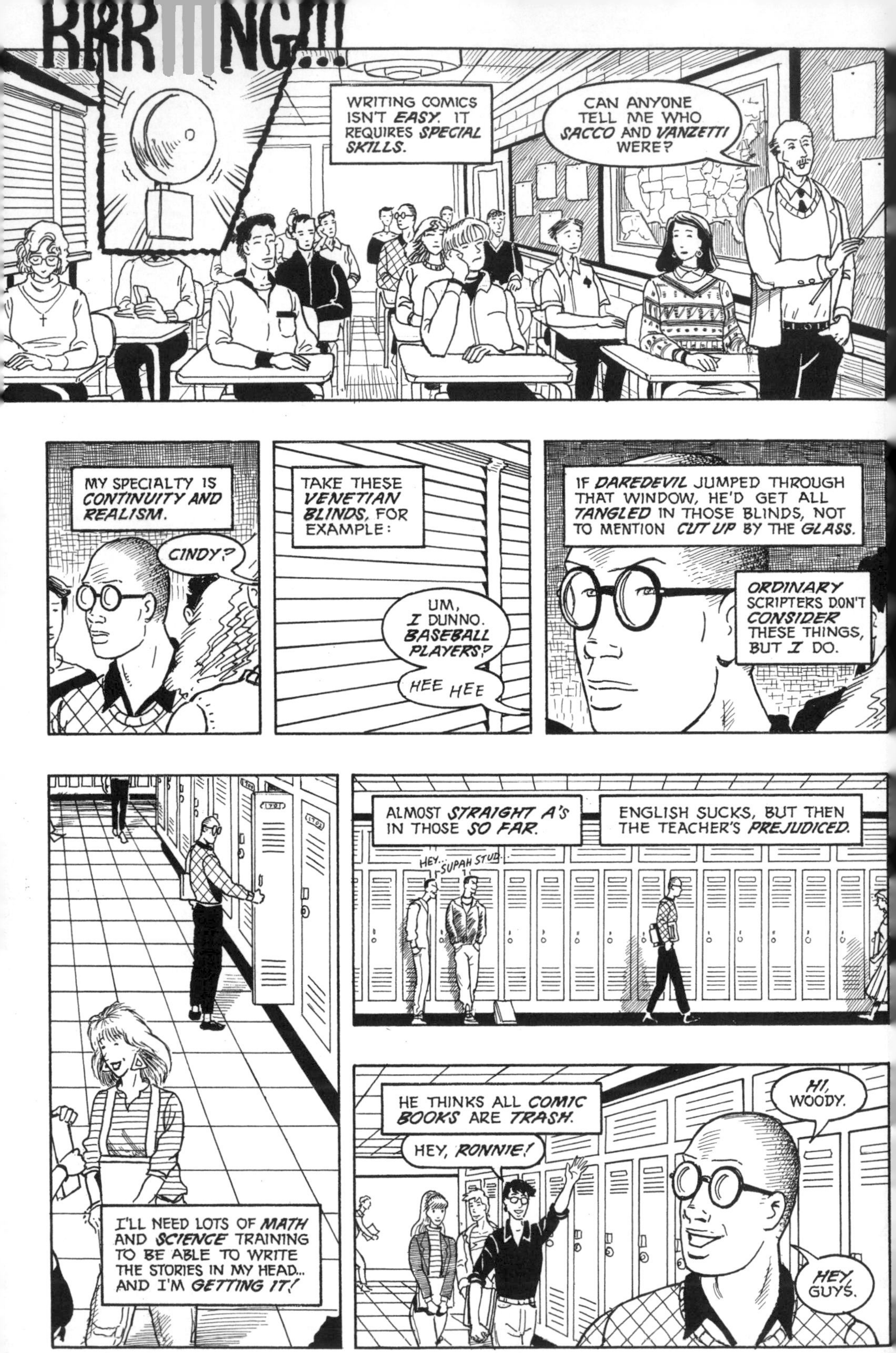

RRRIIING!!!...
WRITING COMICS ISN'T *EASY*. IT REQUIRES *SPECIAL SKILLS*.
CAN ANYONE TELL ME WHO *SACCO* AND *VANZETTI* WERE?
MY SPECIALTY IS *CONTINUITY AND REALISM*.
CINDY?
TAKE THESE *VENETIAN BLINDS*, FOR EXAMPLE:
UM, *I* DUNNO. *BASEBALL PLAYERS?*
HEE HEE
IF *DAREDEVIL* JUMPED THROUGH THAT WINDOW, HE'D GET ALL *TANGLED* IN THOSE BLINDS, NOT TO MENTION *CUT UP* BY THE *GLASS*.
ORDINARY SCRIPTERS DON'T *CONSIDER* THESE THINGS, BUT *I* DO.
I'LL NEED LOTS OF *MATH* AND *SCIENCE* TRAINING TO BE ABLE TO WRITE THE STORIES IN MY HEAD... AND I'M *GETTING IT!*
ALMOST *STRAIGHT A'S* IN THOSE *SO FAR*.
ENGLISH SUCKS, BUT THEN THE TEACHER'S *PREJUDICED*.
HEY.. SUPAH STUD..
HE THINKS ALL *COMIC BOOKS* ARE *TRASH*.
HEY, *RONNIE!*
HI, WOODY.
HEY, GUYS.

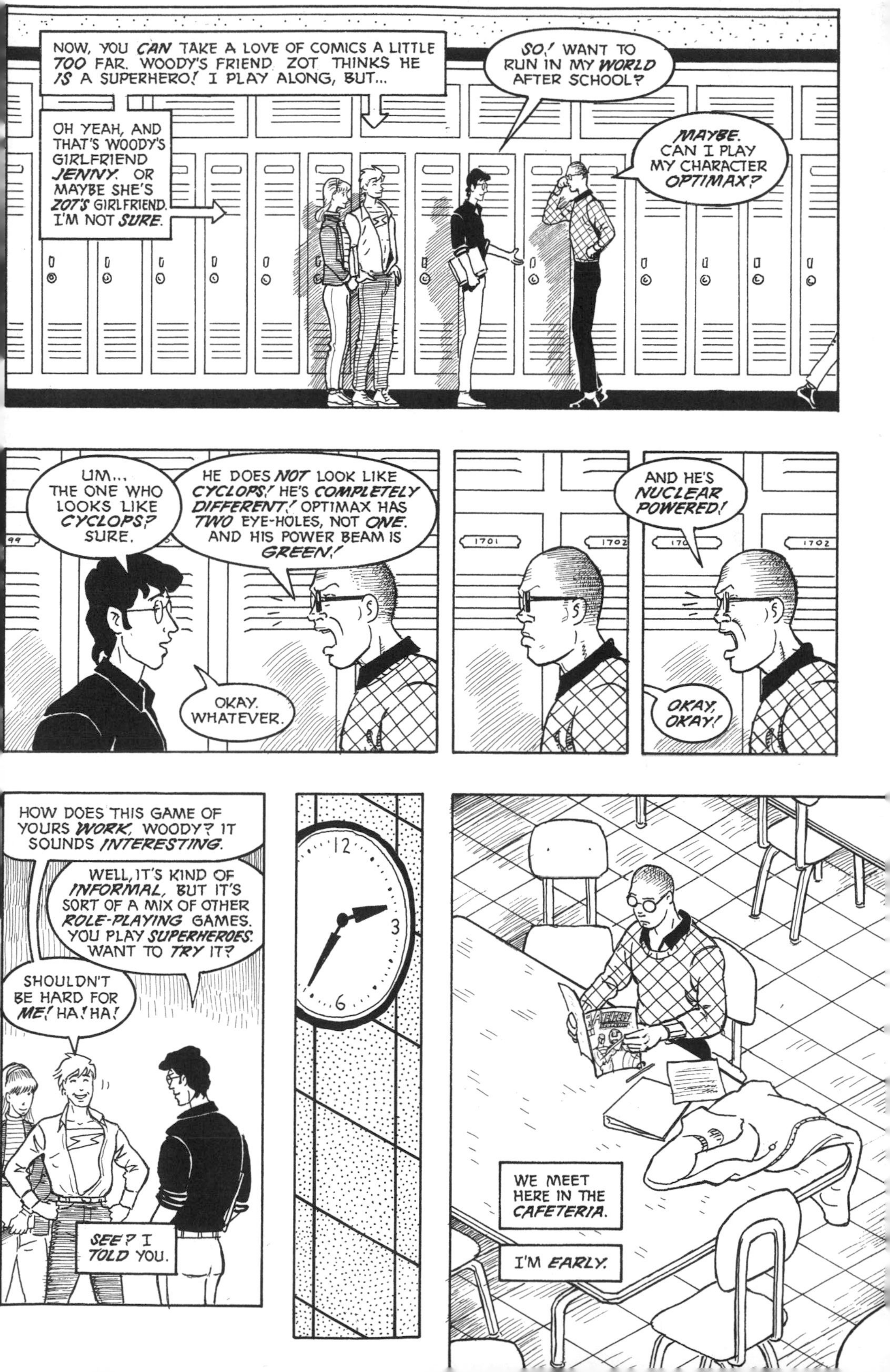
NOW, YOU CAN TAKE A LOVE OF COMICS A LITTLE TOO FAR. WOODY'S FRIEND ZOT THINKS HE IS A SUPERHERO! I PLAY ALONG, BUT...
OH YEAH, AND THAT'S WOODY'S GIRLFRIEND JENNY. OR MAYBE SHE'S ZOT'S GIRLFRIEND. I'M NOT SURE.
SO! WANT TO RUN IN MY WORLD AFTER SCHOOL?
MAYBE. CAN I PLAY MY CHARACTER OPTIMAX?
UM... THE ONE WHO LOOKS LIKE CYCLOPS? SURE.
HE DOES NOT LOOK LIKE CYCLOPS! HE'S COMPLETELY DIFFERENT! OPTIMAX HAS TWO EYE-HOLES, NOT ONE. AND HIS POWER BEAM IS GREEN!
OKAY. WHATEVER.
1701
1702
AND HE'S NUCLEAR POWERED!
OKAY, OKAY!
HOW DOES THIS GAME OF YOURS WORK, WOODY? IT SOUNDS INTERESTING.
WELL, IT'S KIND OF INFORMAL, BUT IT'S SORT OF A MIX OF OTHER ROLE-PLAYING GAMES. YOU PLAY SUPERHEROES. WANT TO TRY IT?
SHOULDN'T BE HARD FOR ME! HA! HA!
SEE? I TOLD YOU.
WE MEET HERE IN THE CAFETERIA.
I'M EARLY.

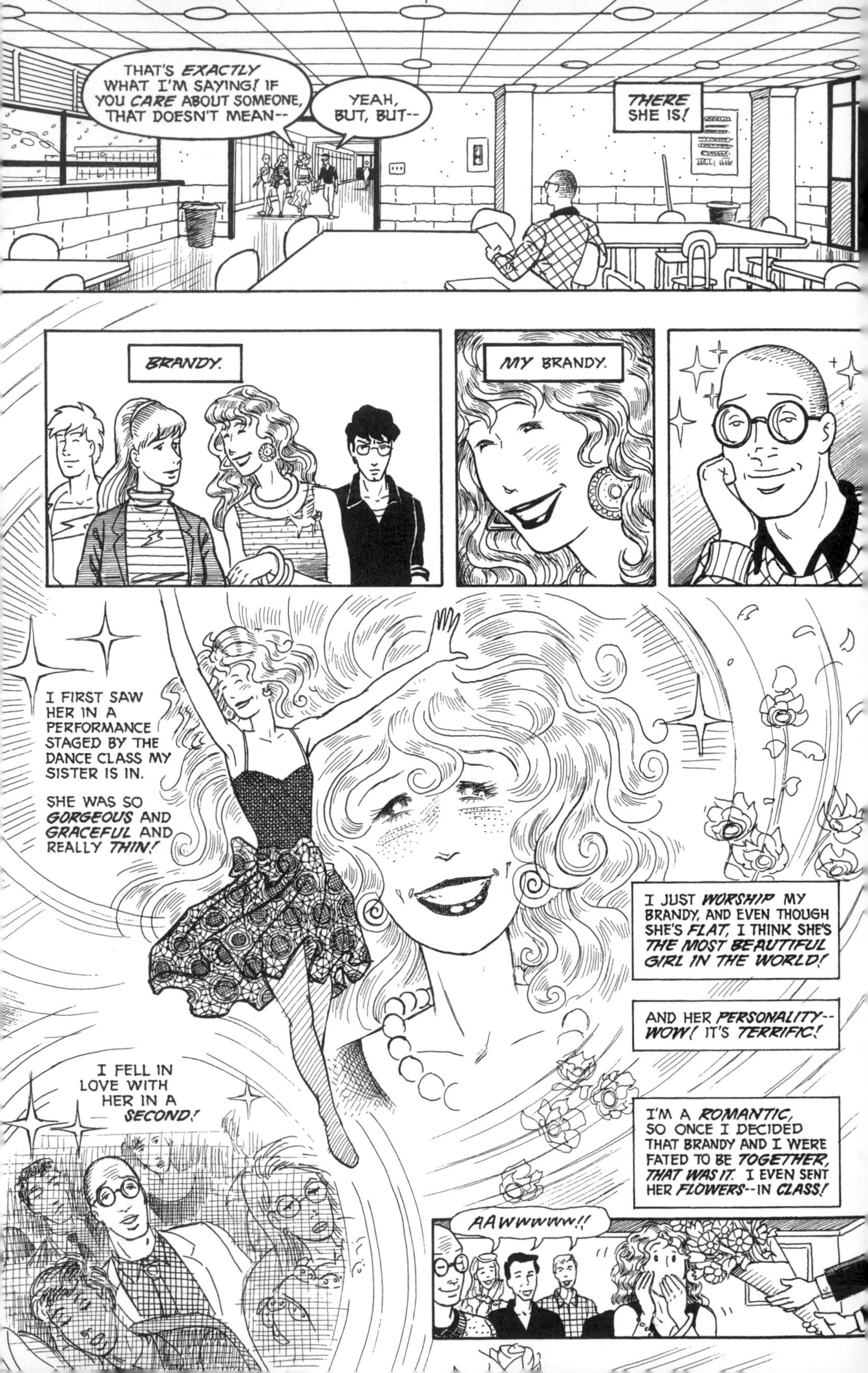

THAT'S EXACTLY WHAT I'M SAYING! IF YOU CARE ABOUT SOMEONE, THAT DOESN'T MEAN--
YEAH, BUT, BUT--
THERE SHE IS!
BRANDY.
MY BRANDY.
I FIRST SAW HER IN A PERFORMANCE STAGED BY THE DANCE CLASS MY SISTER IS IN.
SHE WAS SO GORGEOUS AND GRACEFUL AND REALLY THIN!
I JUST WORSHIP MY BRANDY, AND EVEN THOUGH SHE'S FLAT, I THINK SHE'S THE MOST BEAUTIFUL GIRL IN THE WORLD!
AND HER PERSONALITY-- WOW! IT'S TERRIFIC!
I FELL IN LOVE WITH HER IN A SECOND!
I'M A ROMANTIC, SO ONCE I DECIDED THAT BRANDY AND I WERE FATED TO BE TOGETHER, THAT WAS IT. I EVEN SENT HER FLOWERS--IN CLASS!
AAWWWWWW!!

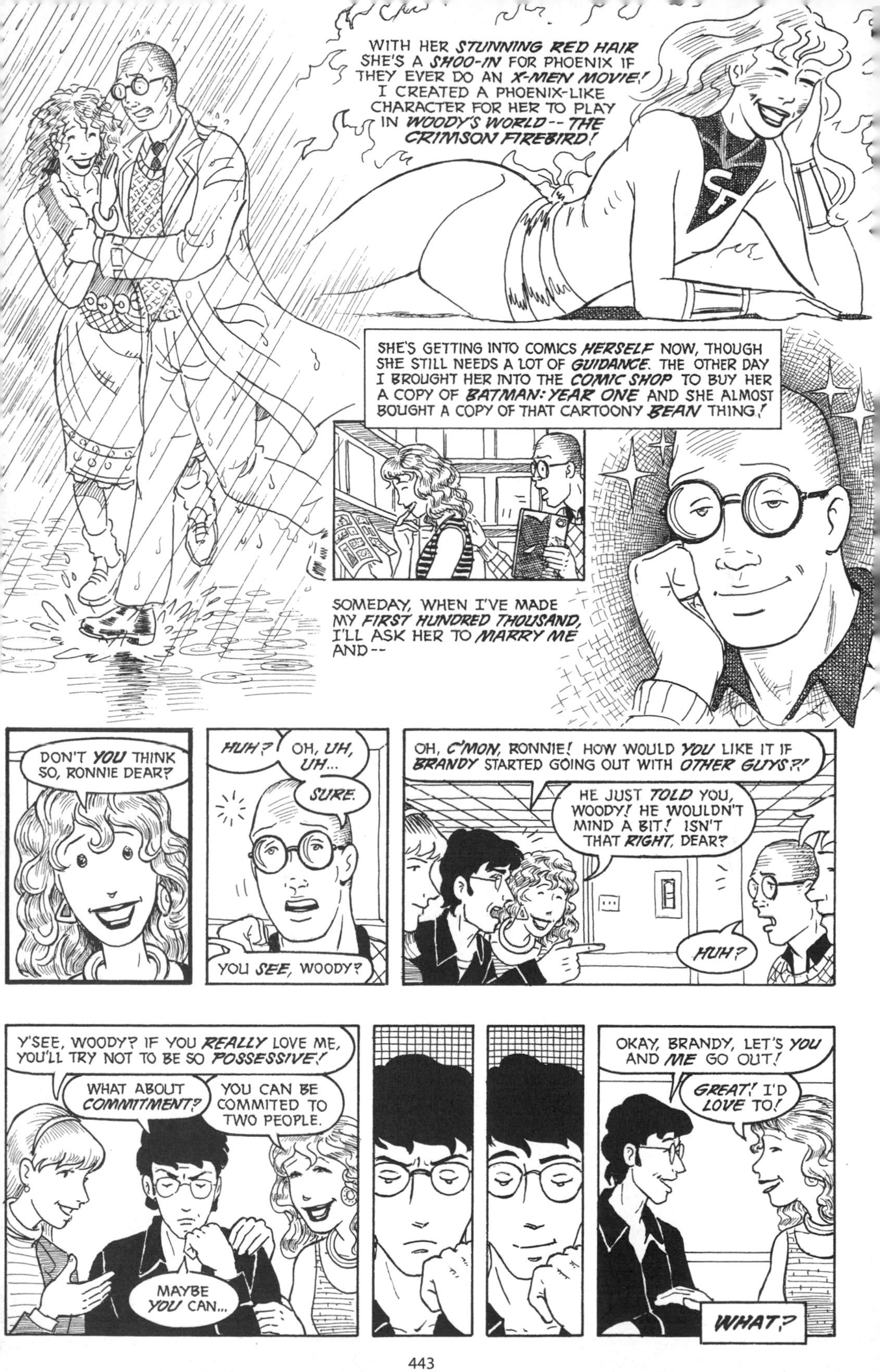
WITH HER STUNNING RED HAIR SHE'S A SHOO-IN FOR PHOENIX IF THEY EVER DO AN X-MEN MOVIE! I CREATED A PHOENIX-LIKE CHARACTER FOR HER TO PLAY IN WOODY'S WORLD -- THE CRIMSON FIREBIRD!
SHE'S GETTING INTO COMICS HERSELF NOW, THOUGH SHE STILL NEEDS A LOT OF GUIDANCE. THE OTHER DAY I BROUGHT HER INTO THE COMIC SHOP TO BUY HER A COPY OF BATMAN: YEAR ONE AND SHE ALMOST BOUGHT A COPY OF THAT CARTOONY BEAN THING!
SOMEDAY, WHEN I'VE MADE MY FIRST HUNDRED THOUSAND, I'LL ASK HER TO MARRY ME AND--
DON'T YOU THINK SO, RONNIE DEAR?
HUH?
OH, UH, UH...
SURE.
YOU SEE, WOODY?
OH, C'MON, RONNIE! HOW WOULD YOU LIKE IT IF BRANDY STARTED GOING OUT WITH OTHER GUYS?!
HE JUST TOLD YOU, WOODY! HE WOULDN'T MIND A BIT! ISN'T THAT RIGHT, DEAR?
HUH?
Y'SEE, WOODY? IF YOU REALLY LOVE ME, YOU'LL TRY NOT TO BE SO POSSESSIVE!
WHAT ABOUT COMMITMENT?
YOU CAN BE COMMITED TO TWO PEOPLE.
MAYBE YOU CAN...
OKAY, BRANDY, LET'S YOU AND ME GO OUT!
GREAT! I'D LOVE TO!
WHAT?

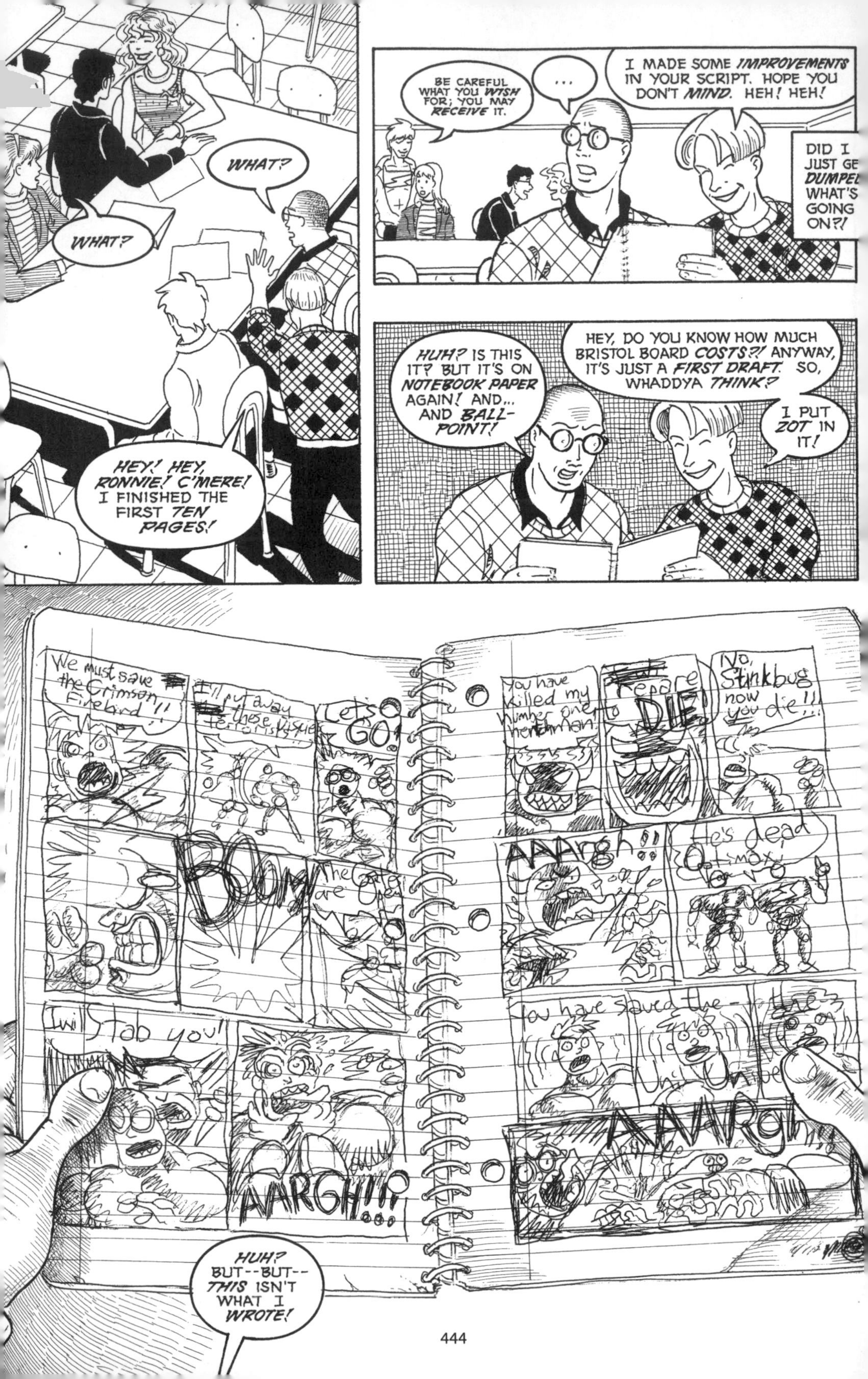

WHAT?
WHAT?
HEY! HEY, RONNIE! C'MERE! I FINISHED THE FIRST TEN PAGES!
BE CAREFUL WHAT YOU WISH FOR; YOU MAY RECEIVE IT.
...
I MADE SOME IMPROVEMENTS IN YOUR SCRIPT. HOPE YOU DON'T MIND. HEH! HEH!
DID I JUST GE DUMPE WHAT'S GOING ON?!
HUH? IS THIS IT? BUT IT'S ON NOTEBOOK PAPER AGAIN! AND... AND BALL-POINT!
HEY, DO YOU KNOW HOW MUCH BRISTOL BOARD COSTS?! ANYWAY, IT'S JUST A FIRST DRAFT. SO, WHADDYA THINK?
I PUT ZOT IN IT!
We must save the Crimson Firebird!!
Let's GO!
BOOM
The Gates are Open
I will Stab you!
AARGH!!!
You have killed my number one henchman
to DIE!
No, Stinkbug now you die!!
AAArgh!!
He's dead Optimax!
You have saved the -
AAARgh!!
HUH? BUT--BUT-- THIS ISN'T WHAT I WROTE!

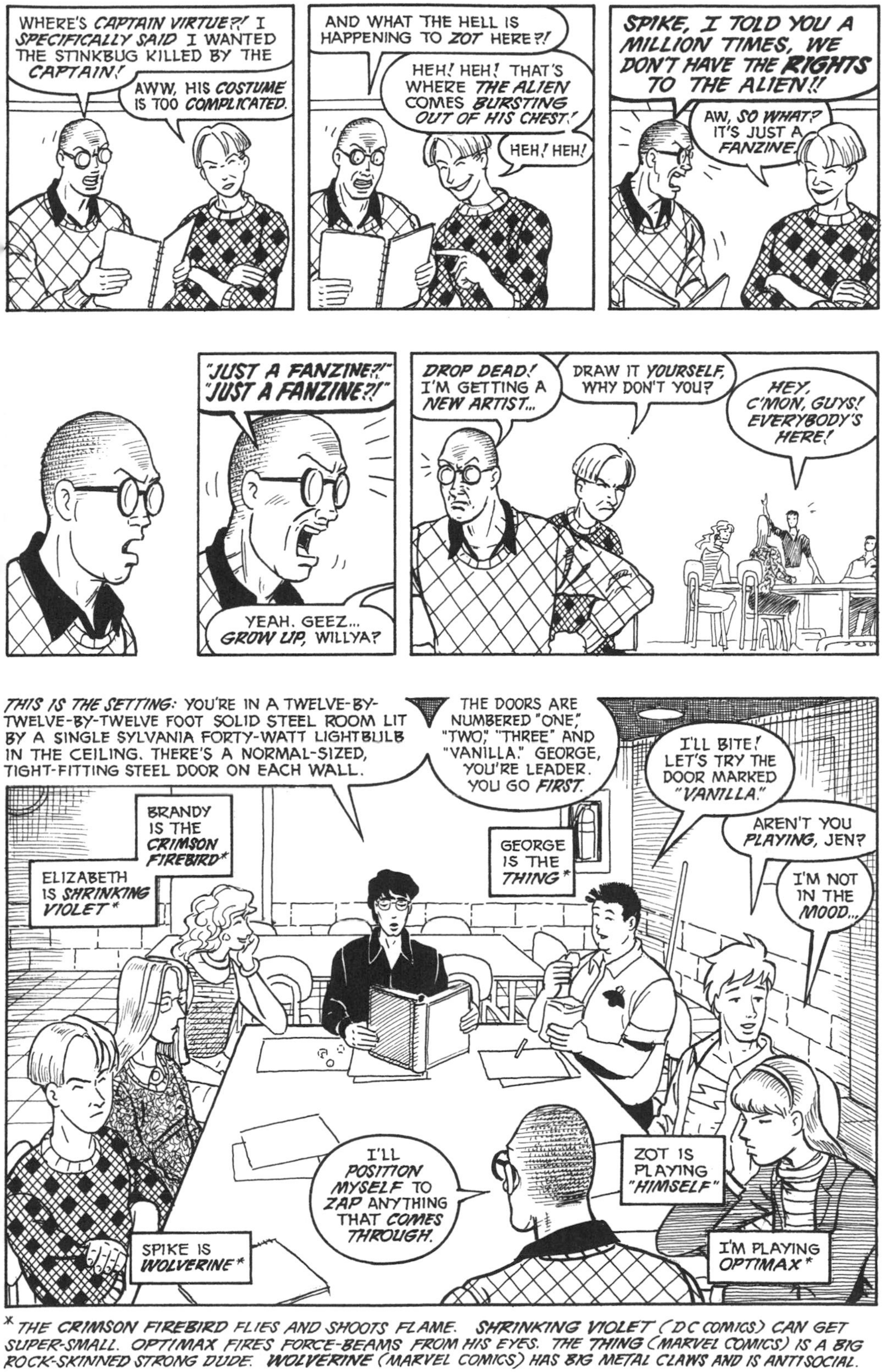
WHERE'S CAPTAIN VIRTUE?! I SPECIFICALLY SAID I WANTED THE STINKBUG KILLED BY THE CAPTAIN!
AWW, HIS COSTUME IS TOO COMPLICATED.
AND WHAT THE HELL IS HAPPENING TO ZOT HERE?!
HEH! HEH! THAT'S WHERE THE ALIEN COMES BURSTING OUT OF HIS CHEST!
HEH! HEH!
SPIKE, I TOLD YOU A MILLION TIMES, WE DON'T HAVE THE RIGHTS TO THE ALIEN!!
AW, SO WHAT? IT'S JUST A FANZINE!
"JUST A FANZINE?!" "JUST A FANZINE?!"
YEAH. GEEZ... GROW UP, WILLYA?
DROP DEAD! I'M GETTING A NEW ARTIST...
DRAW IT YOURSELF, WHY DON'T YOU?
HEY, C'MON, GUYS! EVERYBODY'S HERE!
THIS IS THE SETTING: YOU'RE IN A TWELVE-BY-TWELVE-BY-TWELVE FOOT SOLID STEEL ROOM LIT BY A SINGLE SYLVANIA FORTY-WATT LIGHTBULB IN THE CEILING. THERE'S A NORMAL-SIZED, TIGHT-FITTING STEEL DOOR ON EACH WALL.
THE DOORS ARE NUMBERED "ONE," "TWO," "THREE" AND "VANILLA." GEORGE, YOU'RE LEADER. YOU GO FIRST.
I'LL BITE! LET'S TRY THE DOOR MARKED "VANILLA."
AREN'T YOU PLAYING, JEN?
I'M NOT IN THE MOOD...
BRANDY IS THE CRIMSON FIREBIRD*
ELIZABETH IS SHRINKING VIOLET*
GEORGE IS THE THING*
I'LL POSITION MYSELF TO ZAP ANYTHING THAT COMES THROUGH.
ZOT IS PLAYING "HIMSELF"
SPIKE IS WOLVERINE*
I'M PLAYING OPTIMAX*

* THE CRIMSON FIREBIRD FLIES AND SHOOTS FLAME. SHRINKING VIOLET (DC COMICS) CAN GET SUPER-SMALL. OPTIMAX FIRES FORCE-BEAMS FROM HIS EYES. THE THING (MARVEL COMICS) IS A BIG ROCK-SKINNED STRONG DUDE. WOLVERINE (MARVEL COMICS) HAS BIG METAL CLAWS AND IS ANTISOCIAL.

--SCOTT

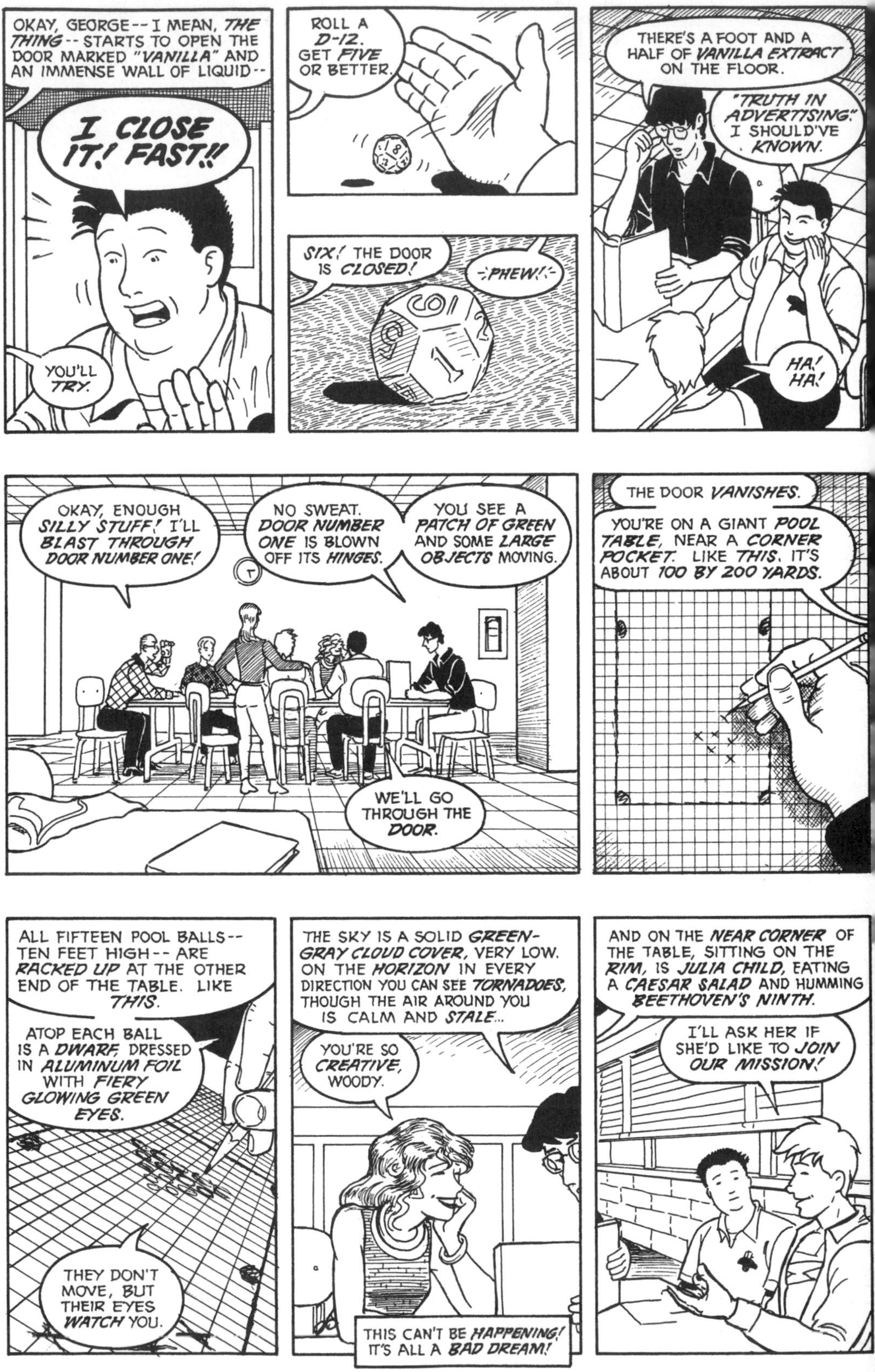
OKAY, GEORGE-- I MEAN, THE THING -- STARTS TO OPEN THE DOOR MARKED "VANILLA" AND AN IMMENSE WALL OF LIQUID--
I CLOSE IT! FAST!!
YOU'LL TRY.
ROLL A D-12. GET FIVE OR BETTER.
SIX! THE DOOR IS CLOSED!
PHEW!
THERE'S A FOOT AND A HALF OF VANILLA EXTRACT ON THE FLOOR.
"TRUTH IN ADVERTISING." I SHOULD'VE KNOWN.
HA! HA!
OKAY, ENOUGH SILLY STUFF! I'LL BLAST THROUGH DOOR NUMBER ONE!
NO SWEAT. DOOR NUMBER ONE IS BLOWN OFF ITS HINGES.
YOU SEE A PATCH OF GREEN AND SOME LARGE OBJECTS MOVING.
WE'LL GO THROUGH THE DOOR.
THE DOOR VANISHES.
YOU'RE ON A GIANT POOL TABLE, NEAR A CORNER POCKET. LIKE THIS. IT'S ABOUT 100 BY 200 YARDS.
ALL FIFTEEN POOL BALLS-- TEN FEET HIGH-- ARE RACKED UP AT THE OTHER END OF THE TABLE. LIKE THIS.
ATOP EACH BALL IS A DWARF, DRESSED IN ALUMINUM FOIL WITH FIERY GLOWING GREEN EYES.
THEY DON'T MOVE, BUT THEIR EYES WATCH YOU.
THE SKY IS A SOLID GREEN-GRAY CLOUD COVER, VERY LOW. ON THE HORIZON IN EVERY DIRECTION YOU CAN SEE TORNADOES, THOUGH THE AIR AROUND YOU IS CALM AND STALE...
YOU'RE SO CREATIVE, WOODY.
THIS CAN'T BE HAPPENING! IT'S ALL A BAD DREAM!
AND ON THE NEAR CORNER OF THE TABLE, SITTING ON THE RIM, IS JULIA CHILD, EATING A CAESAR SALAD AND HUMMING BEETHOVEN'S NINTH.
I'LL ASK HER IF SHE'D LIKE TO JOIN OUR MISSION!

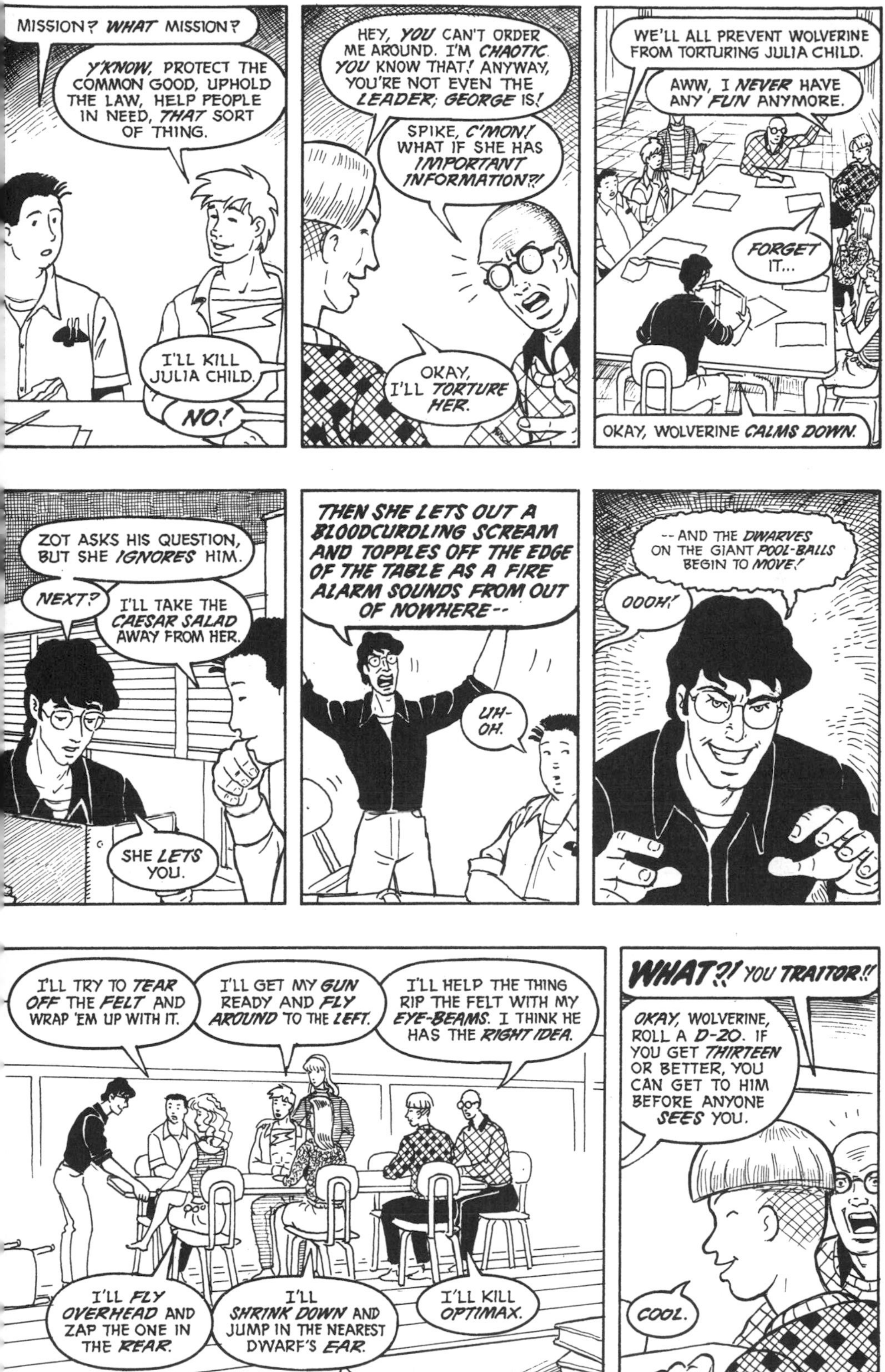
MISSION? WHAT MISSION?
Y'KNOW, PROTECT THE COMMON GOOD, UPHOLD THE LAW, HELP PEOPLE IN NEED, THAT SORT OF THING.
I'LL KILL JULIA CHILD.
NO!
HEY, YOU CAN'T ORDER ME AROUND. I'M CHAOTIC. YOU KNOW THAT! ANYWAY, YOU'RE NOT EVEN THE LEADER; GEORGE IS!
SPIKE, C'MON! WHAT IF SHE HAS IMPORTANT INFORMATION?!
OKAY, I'LL TORTURE HER.
WE'LL ALL PREVENT WOLVERINE FROM TORTURING JULIA CHILD.
AWW, I NEVER HAVE ANY FUN ANYMORE.
FORGET IT...
OKAY, WOLVERINE CALMS DOWN.
ZOT ASKS HIS QUESTION, BUT SHE IGNORES HIM.
NEXT?
I'LL TAKE THE CAESAR SALAD AWAY FROM HER.
SHE LETS YOU.
THEN SHE LETS OUT A BLOODCURDLING SCREAM AND TOPPLES OFF THE EDGE OF THE TABLE AS A FIRE ALARM SOUNDS FROM OUT OF NOWHERE--
UH-OH.
--AND THE DWARVES ON THE GIANT POOL-BALLS BEGIN TO MOVE!
OOOH!
I'LL TRY TO TEAR OFF THE FELT AND WRAP 'EM UP WITH IT.
I'LL GET MY GUN READY AND FLY AROUND TO THE LEFT.
I'LL HELP THE THING RIP THE FELT WITH MY EYE-BEAMS. I THINK HE HAS THE RIGHT IDEA.
I'LL FLY OVERHEAD AND ZAP THE ONE IN THE REAR.
I'LL SHRINK DOWN AND JUMP IN THE NEAREST DWARF'S EAR.
I'LL KILL OPTIMAX.
WHAT?! YOU TRAITOR!!
OKAY, WOLVERINE, ROLL A D-20. IF YOU GET THIRTEEN OR BETTER, YOU CAN GET TO HIM BEFORE ANYONE SEES YOU.
COOL.

I DON'T **BELIEVE** THIS!

NINETEEN!

AWRIGHT! I'LL GO FOR THE *JUGULAR*.

NO!! I QUIT! HE'S JUST PISSED OFF AT ME 'CAUSE I TOLD HIM HE COULDN'T USE THE ALIEN!

AWW, GO *STUFF* YOURSELF.

C'MON, RONNIE! SPIKE *ALWAYS* TRIES TO KILL *SOMEONE*. IT'S HIS *STYLE*.

HA! WHY SHOULD I LISTEN TO *YOU*, WOODY?

YOU-- YOU--

-- GIRLFRIEND STEALER!

WHAT? OH, COME ON!

GOOD RIDDANCE.

RONNIE, *PLEASE* DON'T GO!

RONNIE!

TO HELL WITH *ALL* OF THEM! THEY'LL SEE!

SOMEDAY, I'LL *CHANGE THE WHOLE WORLD* AND *THEN* THEY'LL SEE.

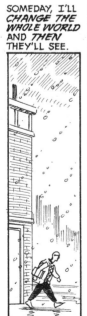

THEN THEY'LL SEE.

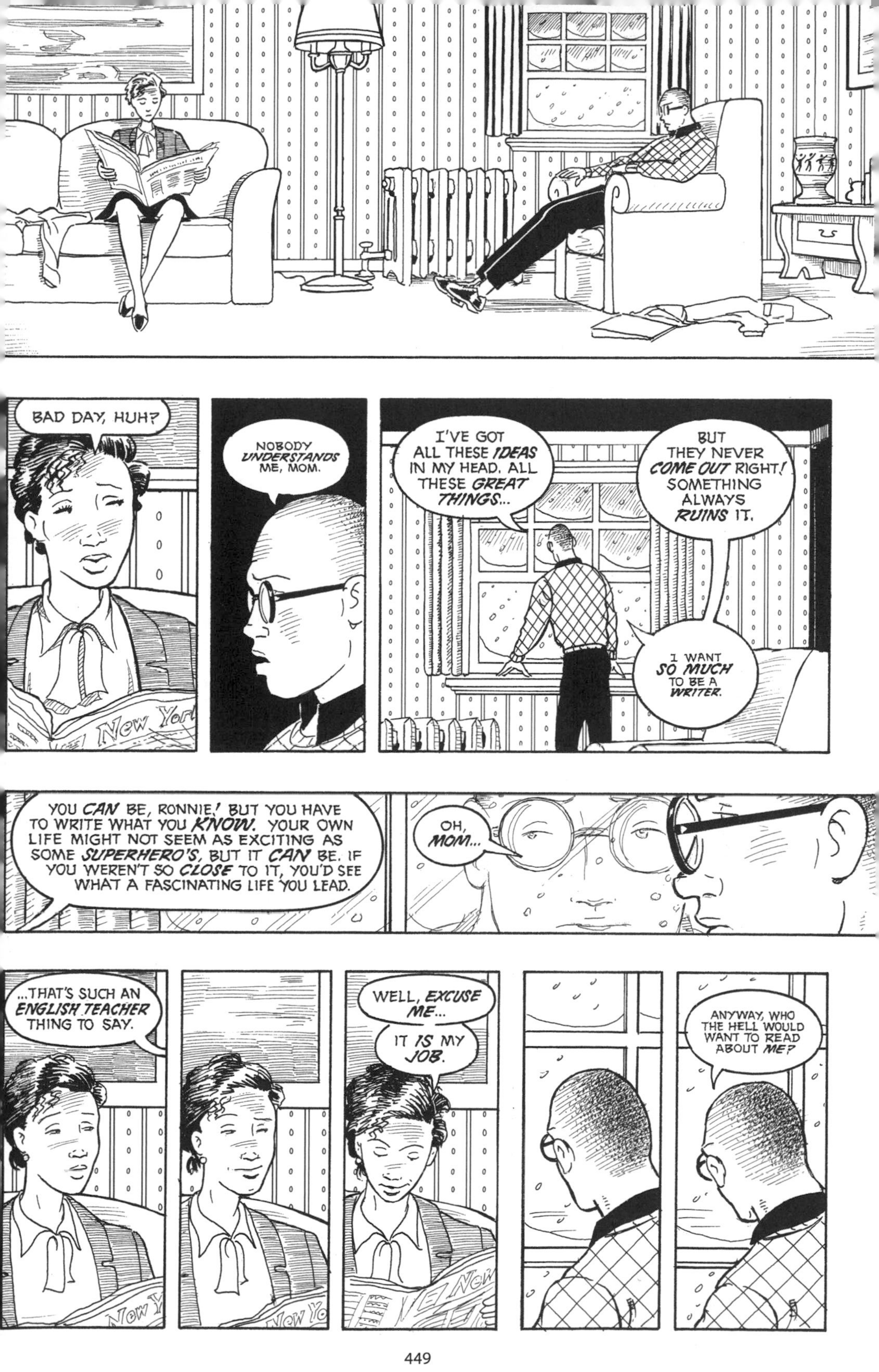
BAD DAY, HUH?
NOBODY UNDERSTANDS ME, MOM.
I'VE GOT ALL THESE IDEAS IN MY HEAD. ALL THESE GREAT THINGS...
BUT THEY NEVER COME OUT RIGHT! SOMETHING ALWAYS RUINS IT.
I WANT SO MUCH TO BE A WRITER.
YOU CAN BE, RONNIE! BUT YOU HAVE TO WRITE WHAT YOU KNOW. YOUR OWN LIFE MIGHT NOT SEEM AS EXCITING AS SOME SUPERHERO'S, BUT IT CAN BE. IF YOU WEREN'T SO CLOSE TO IT, YOU'D SEE WHAT A FASCINATING LIFE YOU LEAD.
OH, MOM...
...THAT'S SUCH AN ENGLISH TEACHER THING TO SAY.
WELL, EXCUSE ME...
IT IS MY JOB.
ANYWAY, WHO THE HELL WOULD WANT TO READ ABOUT ME?

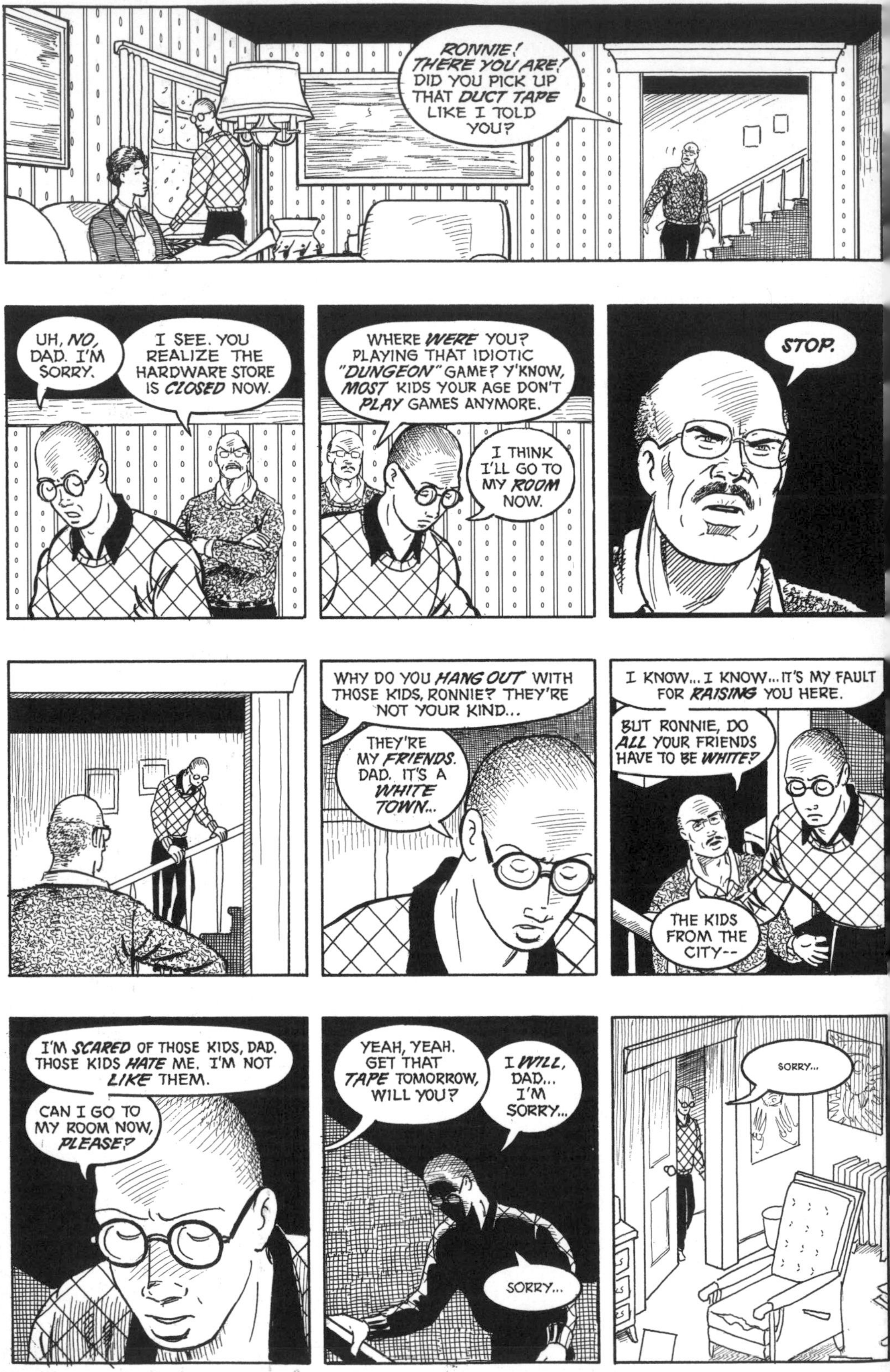
RONNIE! THERE YOU ARE! DID YOU PICK UP THAT DUCT TAPE LIKE I TOLD YOU?
UH, NO, DAD. I'M SORRY.
I SEE. YOU REALIZE THE HARDWARE STORE IS CLOSED NOW.
WHERE WERE YOU? PLAYING THAT IDIOTIC "DUNGEON" GAME? Y'KNOW, MOST KIDS YOUR AGE DON'T PLAY GAMES ANYMORE.
I THINK I'LL GO TO MY ROOM NOW.
STOP.
WHY DO YOU HANG OUT WITH THOSE KIDS, RONNIE? THEY'RE NOT YOUR KIND...
THEY'RE MY FRIENDS. DAD. IT'S A WHITE TOWN...
I KNOW... I KNOW... IT'S MY FAULT FOR RAISING YOU HERE.
BUT RONNIE, DO ALL YOUR FRIENDS HAVE TO BE WHITE?
THE KIDS FROM THE CITY--
I'M SCARED OF THOSE KIDS, DAD. THOSE KIDS HATE ME. I'M NOT LIKE THEM.
CAN I GO TO MY ROOM NOW, PLEASE?
YEAH, YEAH. GET THAT TAPE TOMORROW, WILL YOU?
I WILL, DAD... I'M SORRY...
SORRY...
SORRY...

CLIK

BRANDY BOUGHT ME THIS CHAIR AT A *YARDSALE.* SAID IT COULD BE MY *THINKING CHAIR.*

NEED SOME *MUSIC.*

WAGNER
SELECTED OVERTURES

KLIK

SONY

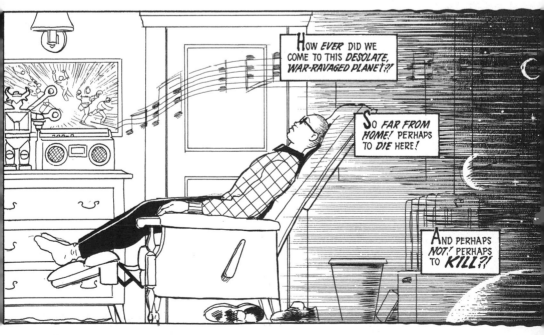

HOW *EVER* DID WE COME TO THIS *DESOLATE, WAR-RAVAGED PLANET?!*

SO *FAR FROM HOME!* PERHAPS TO *DIE* HERE!

AND PERHAPS *NOT!* PERHAPS TO *KILL?!*

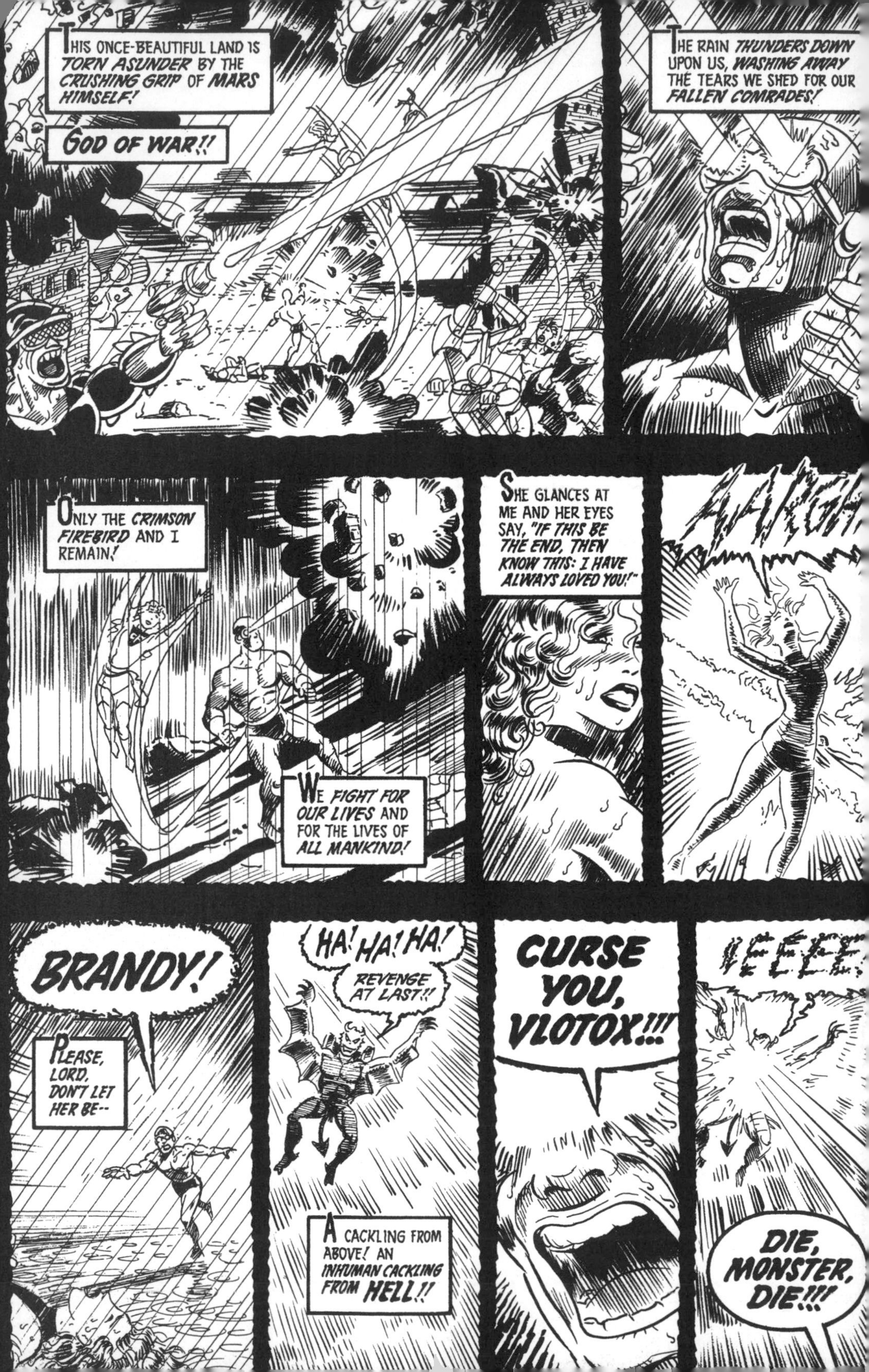
THIS ONCE-BEAUTIFUL LAND IS TORN ASUNDER BY THE CRUSHING GRIP OF MARS HIMSELF!
GOD OF WAR!!
THE RAIN THUNDERS DOWN UPON US, WASHING AWAY THE TEARS WE SHED FOR OUR FALLEN COMRADES!
ONLY THE CRIMSON FIREBIRD AND I REMAIN!
WE FIGHT FOR OUR LIVES AND FOR THE LIVES OF ALL MANKIND!
SHE GLANCES AT ME AND HER EYES SAY, "IF THIS BE THE END, THEN KNOW THIS: I HAVE ALWAYS LOVED YOU!"
AARGH
BRANDY!
PLEASE, LORD, DON'T LET HER BE--
HA! HA! HA!
REVENGE AT LAST!!
A CACKLING FROM ABOVE! AN INHUMAN CACKLING FROM HELL!!
CURSE YOU, VLOTOX!!!
IEEEE
DIE, MONSTER, DIE!!!

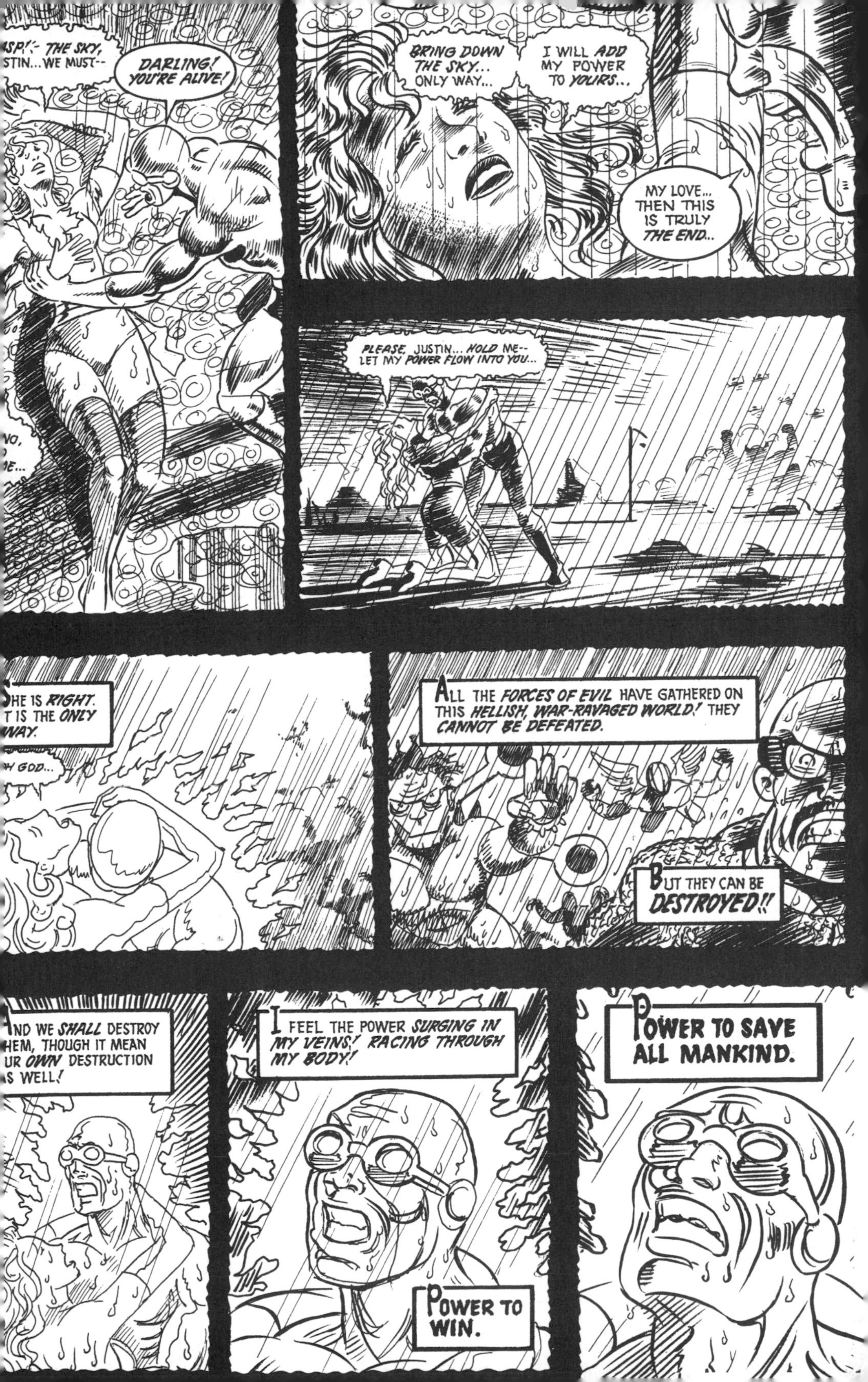

ASP!- THE SKY, STIN... WE MUST--
DARLING! YOU'RE ALIVE!
BRING DOWN THE SKY... ONLY WAY...
I WILL ADD MY POWER TO YOURS...
MY LOVE... THEN THIS IS TRULY THE END...
PLEASE, JUSTIN... HOLD ME-- LET MY POWER FLOW INTO YOU...
HE IS RIGHT. T IS THE ONLY WAY.
H GOD...
ALL THE FORCES OF EVIL HAVE GATHERED ON THIS HELLISH, WAR-RAVAGED WORLD! THEY CANNOT BE DEFEATED.
BUT THEY CAN BE DESTROYED!!
ND WE SHALL DESTROY HEM, THOUGH IT MEAN UR OWN DESTRUCTION S WELL!
I FEEL THE POWER SURGING IN MY VEINS! RACING THROUGH MY BODY!
POWER TO WIN.
POWER TO SAVE ALL MANKIND.

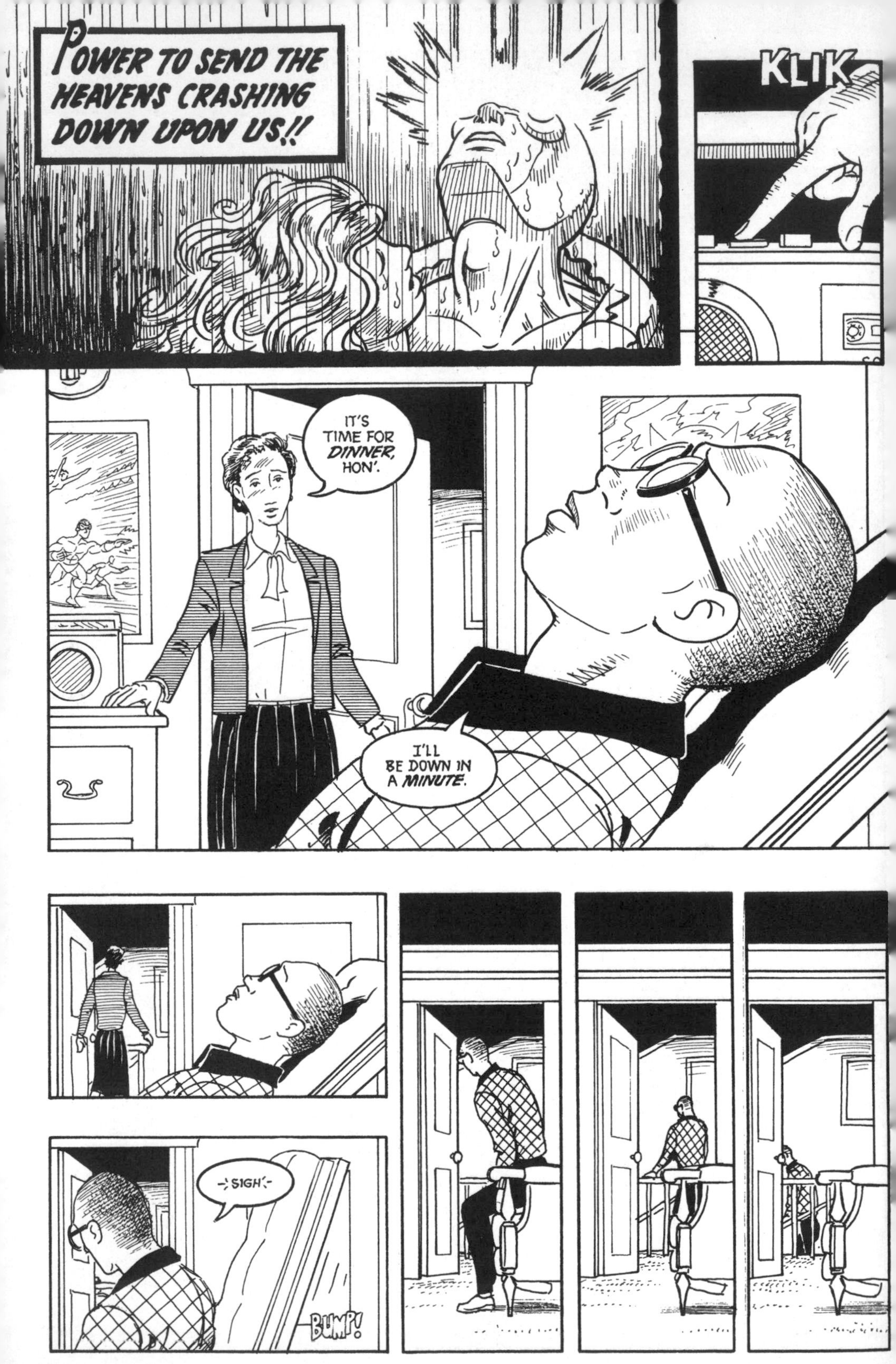
POWER TO SEND THE HEAVENS CRASHING DOWN UPON US!!
KLIK
IT'S TIME FOR DINNER, HON'.
I'LL BE DOWN IN A MINUTE.
-SIGH-
BUMP!

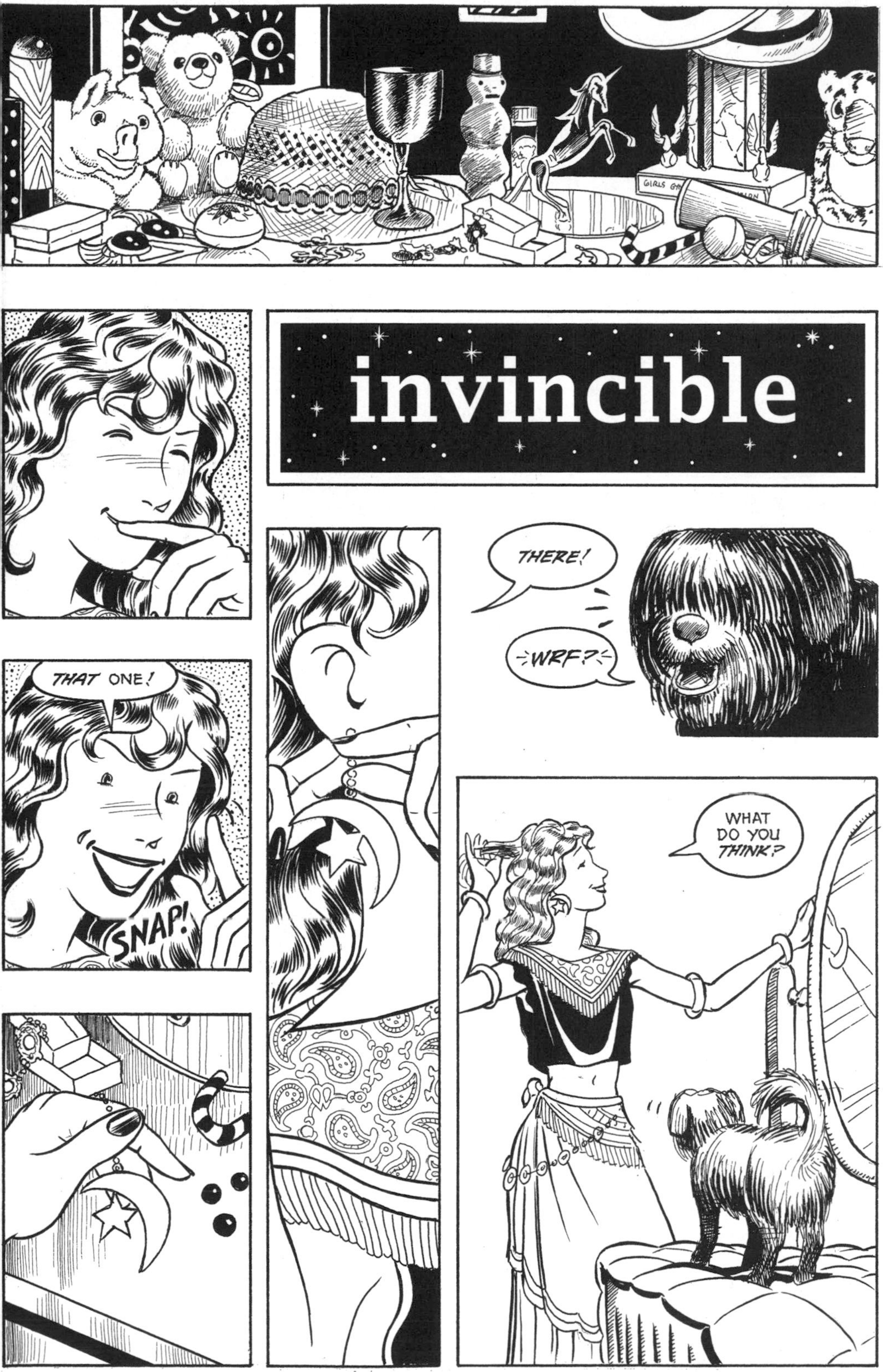
invincible
THAT ONE!
SNAP!
THERE!
WRF?
WHAT DO YOU THINK?

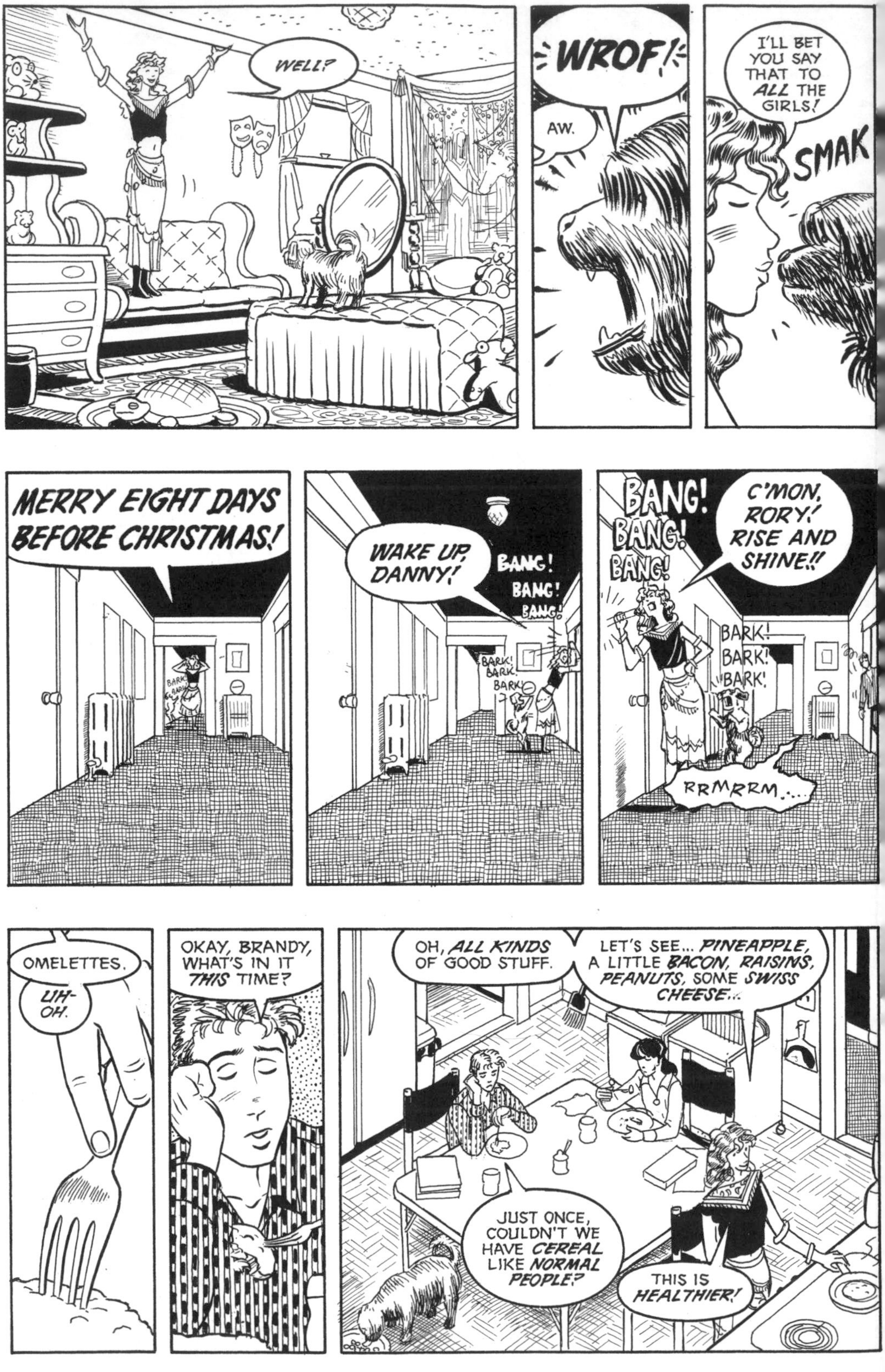

WELL?
WROF!
AW.
I'LL BET YOU SAY THAT TO ALL THE GIRLS!
SMAK
MERRY EIGHT DAYS BEFORE CHRISTMAS!
WAKE UP, DANNY!
BANG! BANG! BANG!
BARK! BARK! BARK!
BANG! BANG! BANG!
C'MON, RORY! RISE AND SHINE!!
BARK! BARK! BARK!
RRMRRM....
OMELETTES.
UH-OH.
OKAY, BRANDY, WHAT'S IN IT THIS TIME?
OH, ALL KINDS OF GOOD STUFF.
LET'S SEE... PINEAPPLE, A LITTLE BACON, RAISINS, PEANUTS, SOME SWISS CHEESE...
JUST ONCE, COULDN'T WE HAVE CEREAL LIKE NORMAL PEOPLE?
THIS IS HEALTHIER!

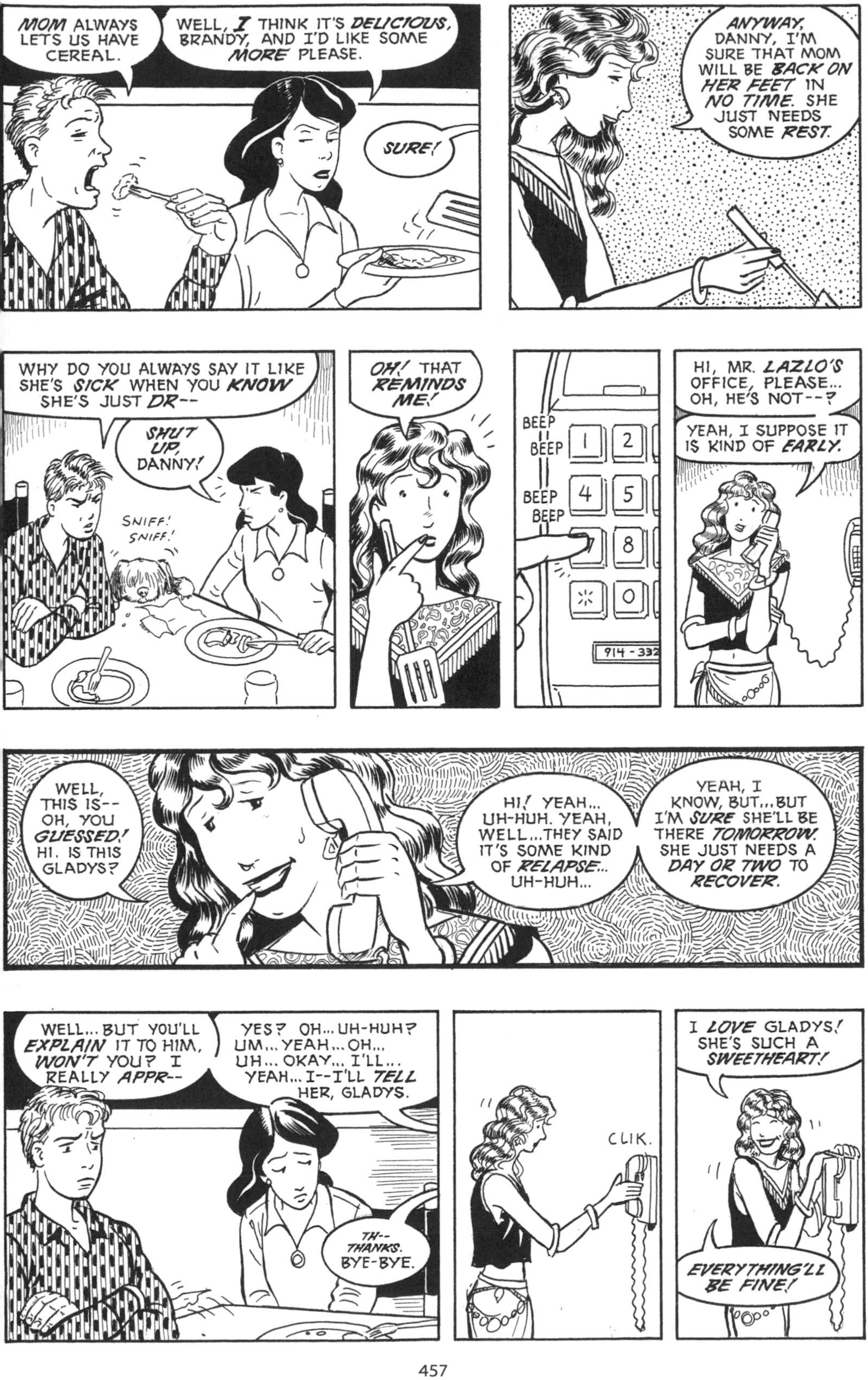
MOM ALWAYS LETS US HAVE CEREAL.
WELL, I THINK IT'S DELICIOUS, BRANDY, AND I'D LIKE SOME MORE PLEASE.
SURE!
ANYWAY, DANNY, I'M SURE THAT MOM WILL BE BACK ON HER FEET IN NO TIME. SHE JUST NEEDS SOME REST.
WHY DO YOU ALWAYS SAY IT LIKE SHE'S SICK WHEN YOU KNOW SHE'S JUST DR--
SHUT UP, DANNY!
SNIFF! SNIFF!
OH! THAT REMINDS ME!
BEEP BEEP
BEEP BEEP
914-332
HI, MR. LAZLO'S OFFICE, PLEASE... OH, HE'S NOT--?
YEAH, I SUPPOSE IT IS KIND OF EARLY.
WELL, THIS IS-- OH, YOU GUESSED! HI. IS THIS GLADYS?
HI! YEAH... UH-HUH. YEAH, WELL...THEY SAID IT'S SOME KIND OF RELAPSE... UH-HUH...
YEAH, I KNOW, BUT...BUT I'M SURE SHE'LL BE THERE TOMORROW. SHE JUST NEEDS A DAY OR TWO TO RECOVER.
WELL... BUT YOU'LL EXPLAIN IT TO HIM, WON'T YOU? I REALLY APPR--
YES? OH...UH-HUH? UM...YEAH...OH... UH...OKAY...I'LL... YEAH...I--I'LL TELL HER, GLADYS.
TH-- THANKS. BYE-BYE.
CLIK.
I LOVE GLADYS! SHE'S SUCH A SWEETHEART!
EVERYTHING'LL BE FINE!

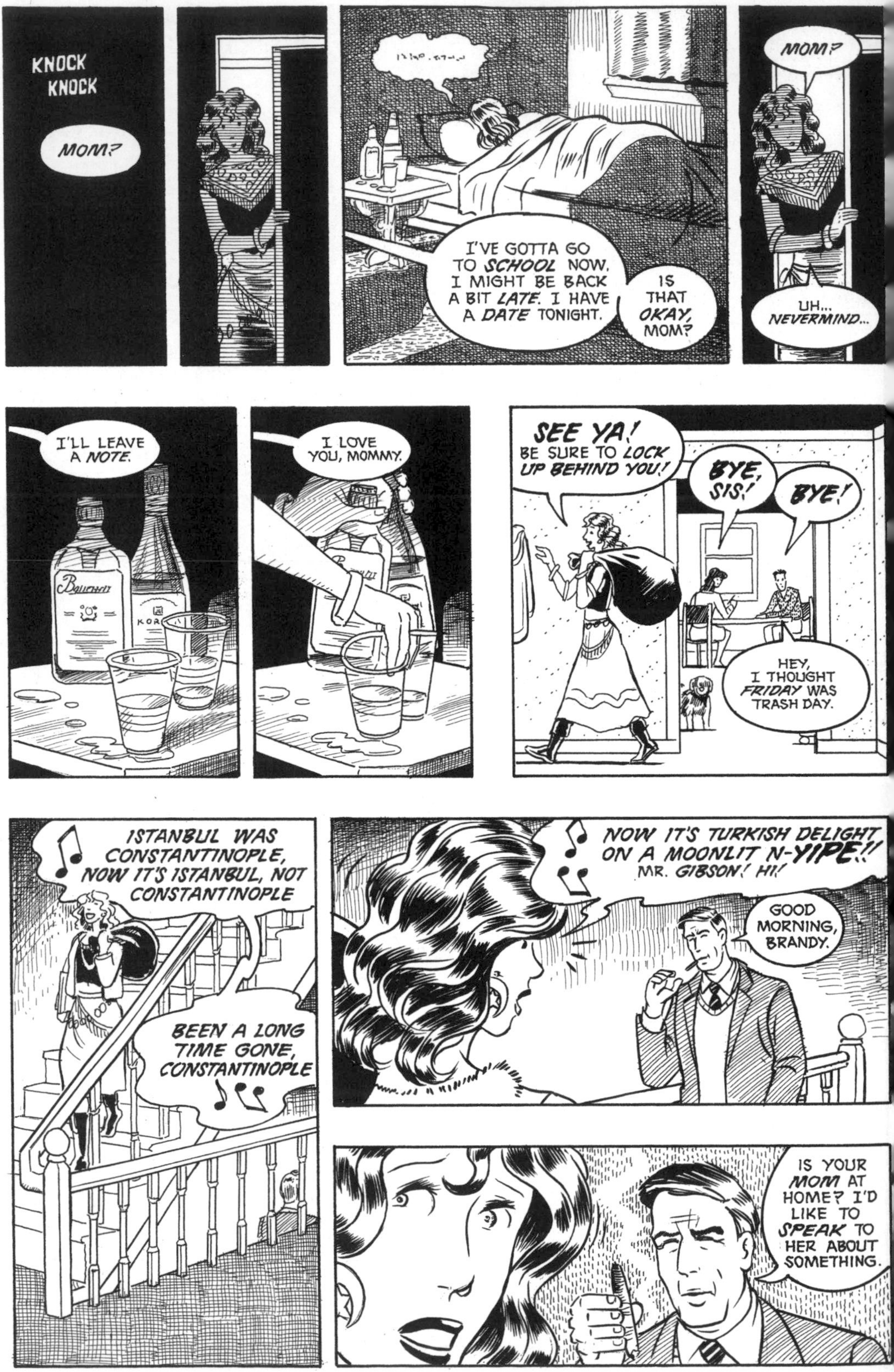
KNOCK KNOCK
MOM?
I'VE GOTTA GO TO SCHOOL NOW. I MIGHT BE BACK A BIT LATE. I HAVE A DATE TONIGHT.
IS THAT OKAY, MOM?
MOM?
UH... NEVERMIND...
I'LL LEAVE A NOTE.
I LOVE YOU, MOMMY.
SEE YA! BE SURE TO LOCK UP BEHIND YOU!
BYE, SIS!
BYE!
HEY, I THOUGHT FRIDAY WAS TRASH DAY.
ISTANBUL WAS CONSTANTINOPLE, NOW IT'S ISTANBUL, NOT CONSTANTINOPLE
BEEN A LONG TIME GONE, CONSTANTINOPLE
NOW IT'S TURKISH DELIGHT ON A MOONLIT N-YIPE!! MR. GIBSON! HI!
GOOD MORNING, BRANDY.
IS YOUR MOM AT HOME? I'D LIKE TO SPEAK TO HER ABOUT SOMETHING.

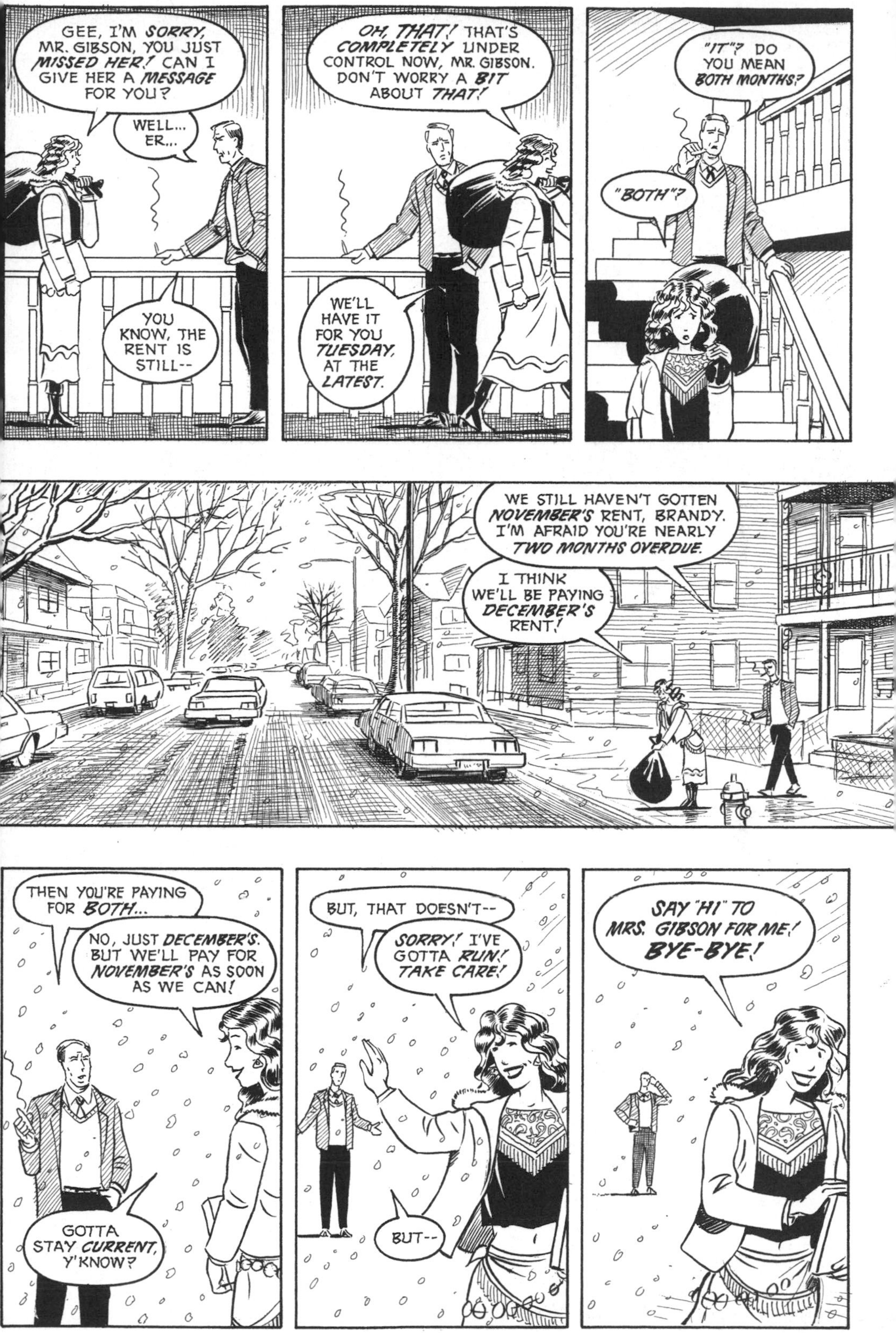
GEE, I'M SORRY, MR. GIBSON, YOU JUST MISSED HER! CAN I GIVE HER A MESSAGE FOR YOU?
WELL... ER...
YOU KNOW, THE RENT IS STILL--
OH, THAT! THAT'S COMPLETELY UNDER CONTROL NOW, MR. GIBSON. DON'T WORRY A BIT ABOUT THAT!
WE'LL HAVE IT FOR YOU TUESDAY, AT THE LATEST.
"IT"? DO YOU MEAN BOTH MONTHS?
"BOTH"?
WE STILL HAVEN'T GOTTEN NOVEMBER'S RENT, BRANDY. I'M AFRAID YOU'RE NEARLY TWO MONTHS OVERDUE.
I THINK WE'LL BE PAYING DECEMBER'S RENT!
THEN YOU'RE PAYING FOR BOTH...
NO, JUST DECEMBER'S. BUT WE'LL PAY FOR NOVEMBER'S AS SOON AS WE CAN!
GOTTA STAY CURRENT, Y'KNOW?
BUT, THAT DOESN'T--
SORRY! I'VE GOTTA RUN! TAKE CARE!
BUT--
SAY "HI" TO MRS. GIBSON FOR ME! BYE-BYE!

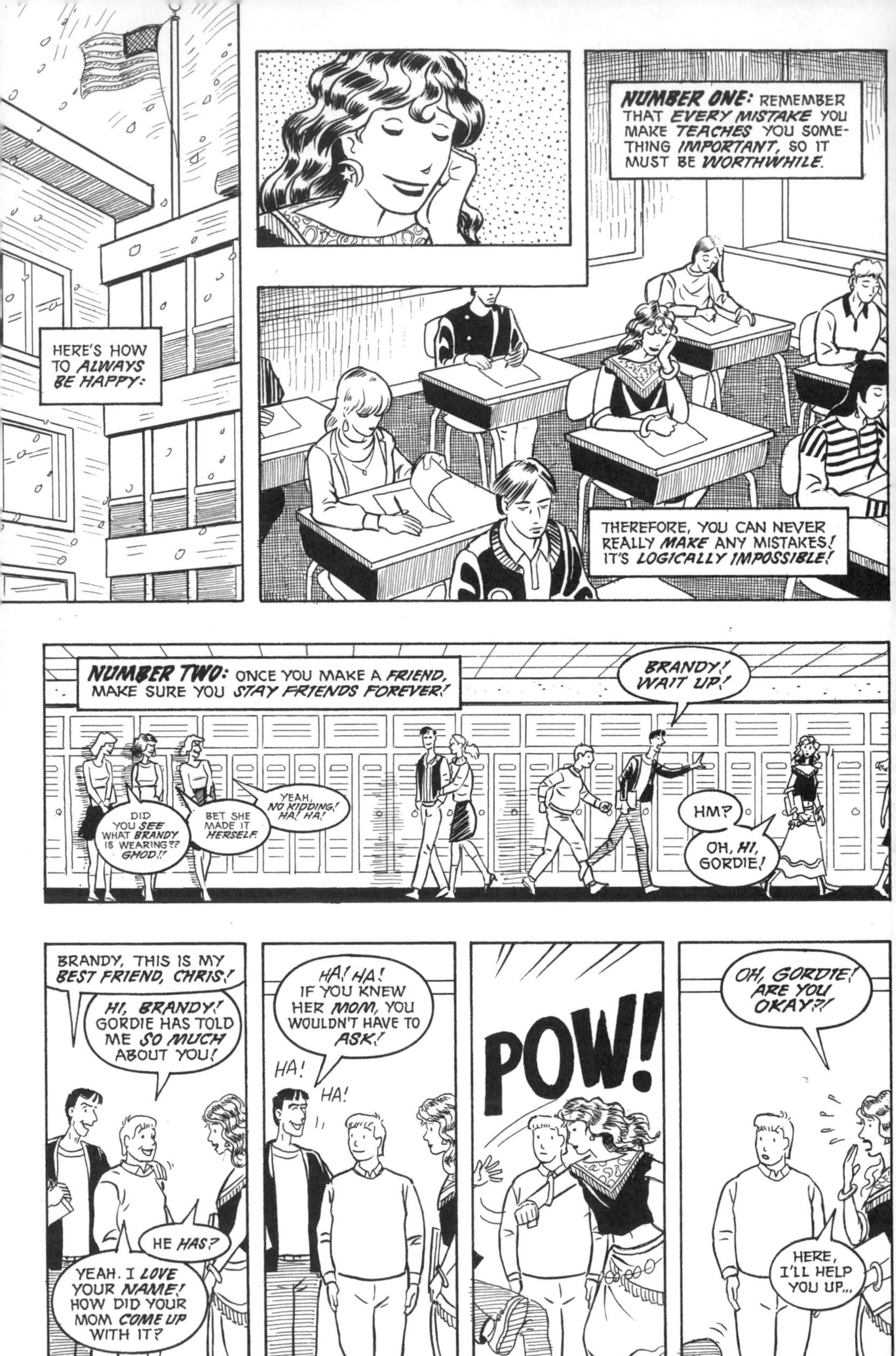
HERE'S HOW TO ALWAYS BE HAPPY:
NUMBER ONE: REMEMBER THAT EVERY MISTAKE YOU MAKE TEACHES YOU SOMETHING IMPORTANT, SO IT MUST BE WORTHWHILE.
THEREFORE, YOU CAN NEVER REALLY MAKE ANY MISTAKES! IT'S LOGICALLY IMPOSSIBLE!
NUMBER TWO: ONCE YOU MAKE A FRIEND, MAKE SURE YOU STAY FRIENDS FOREVER!
DID YOU SEE WHAT BRANDY IS WEARING?? GHOD!!
BET SHE MADE IT HERSELF.
YEAH, NO KIDDING! HA! HA!
BRANDY! WAIT UP!
HM?
OH, HI, GORDIE!
BRANDY, THIS IS MY BEST FRIEND, CHRIS!
HI, BRANDY! GORDIE HAS TOLD ME SO MUCH ABOUT YOU!
HE HAS?
YEAH. I LOVE YOUR NAME! HOW DID YOUR MOM COME UP WITH IT?
HA! HA! IF YOU KNEW HER MOM, YOU WOULDN'T HAVE TO ASK!
HA!
HA!
POW!
OH, GORDIE! ARE YOU OKAY?!
HERE, I'LL HELP YOU UP...

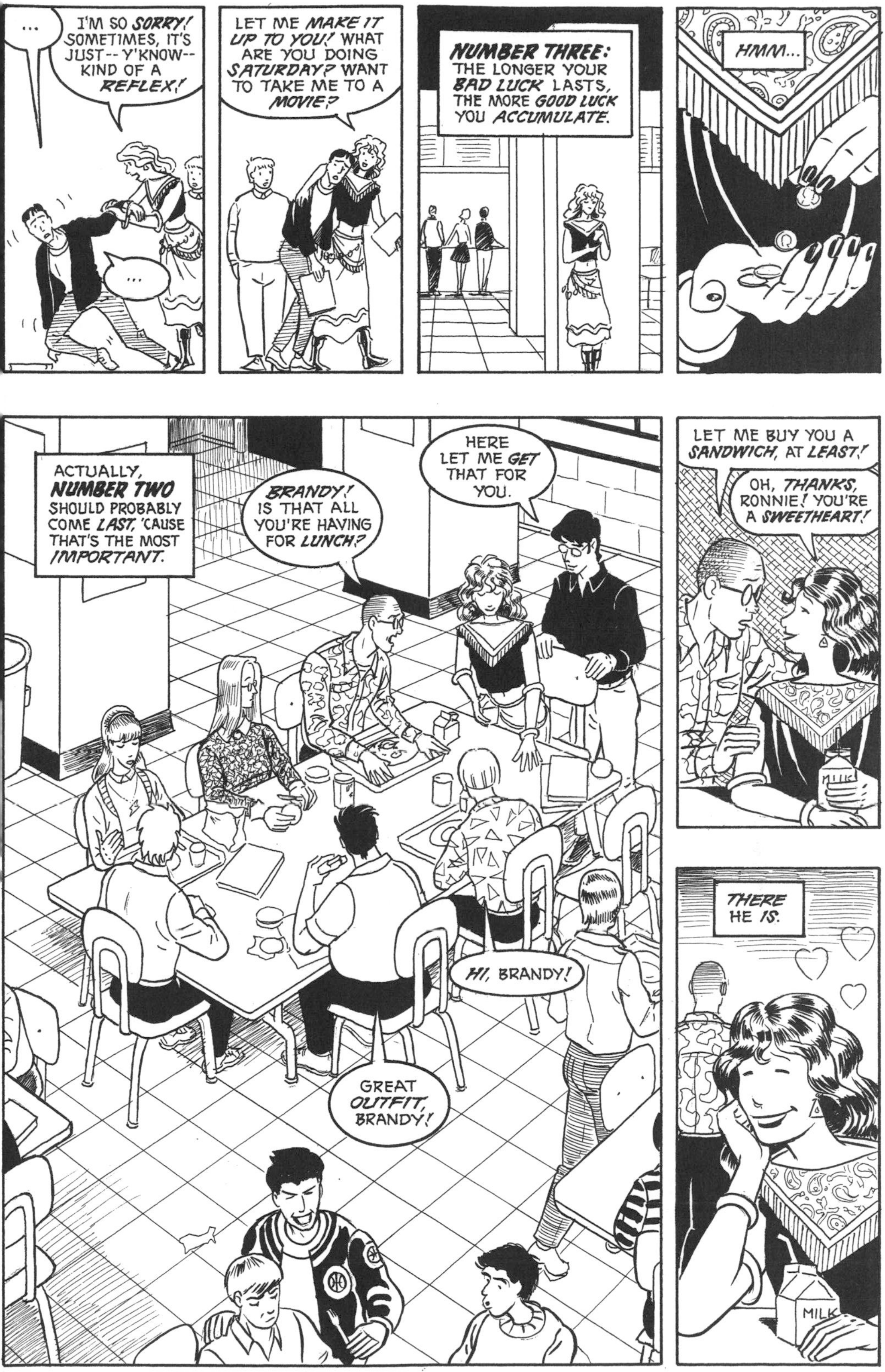
...
I'M SO SORRY! SOMETIMES, IT'S JUST -- Y'KNOW -- KIND OF A REFLEX!
...
LET ME MAKE IT UP TO YOU! WHAT ARE YOU DOING SATURDAY? WANT TO TAKE ME TO A MOVIE?
NUMBER THREE: THE LONGER YOUR BAD LUCK LASTS, THE MORE GOOD LUCK YOU ACCUMULATE.
HMM...
ACTUALLY, NUMBER TWO SHOULD PROBABLY COME LAST, 'CAUSE THAT'S THE MOST IMPORTANT.
BRANDY! IS THAT ALL YOU'RE HAVING FOR LUNCH?
HERE LET ME GET THAT FOR YOU.
HI, BRANDY!
GREAT OUTFIT, BRANDY!
LET ME BUY YOU A SANDWICH, AT LEAST!
OH, THANKS, RONNIE! YOU'RE A SWEETHEART!
MILK
THERE HE IS.
MILK

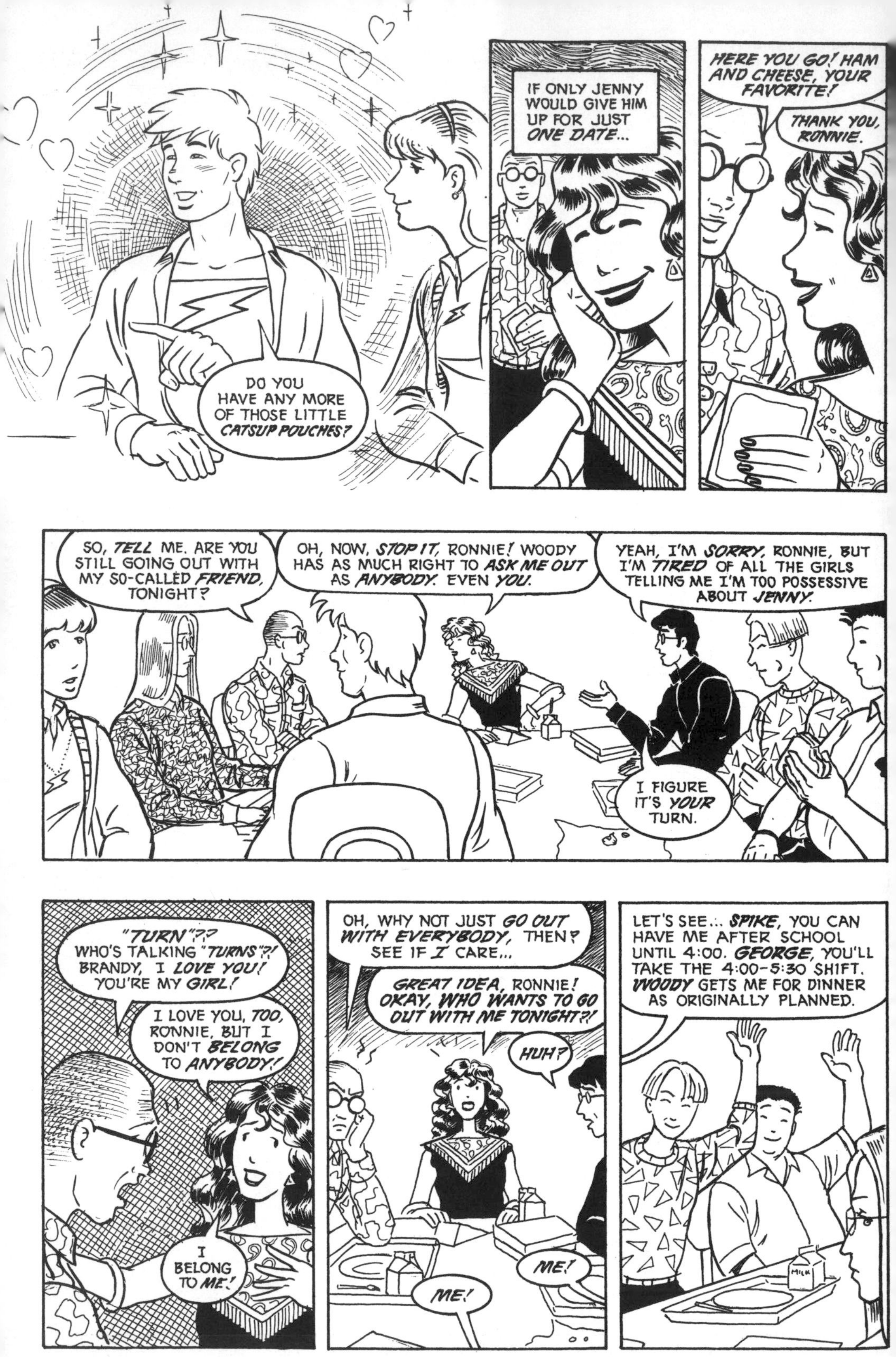
DO YOU HAVE ANY MORE OF THOSE LITTLE CATSUP POUCHES?
IF ONLY JENNY WOULD GIVE HIM UP FOR JUST ONE DATE...
HERE YOU GO! HAM AND CHEESE, YOUR FAVORITE!
THANK YOU, RONNIE.
SO, TELL ME. ARE YOU STILL GOING OUT WITH MY SO-CALLED FRIEND, TONIGHT?
OH, NOW, STOP IT, RONNIE! WOODY HAS AS MUCH RIGHT TO ASK ME OUT AS ANYBODY. EVEN YOU.
YEAH, I'M SORRY, RONNIE, BUT I'M TIRED OF ALL THE GIRLS TELLING ME I'M TOO POSSESSIVE ABOUT JENNY.
I FIGURE IT'S YOUR TURN.
"TURN"?? WHO'S TALKING "TURNS"?! BRANDY, I LOVE YOU! YOU'RE MY GIRL!
I LOVE YOU, TOO, RONNIE, BUT I DON'T BELONG TO ANYBODY!
I BELONG TO ME!
OH, WHY NOT JUST GO OUT WITH EVERYBODY, THEN? SEE IF I CARE...
GREAT IDEA, RONNIE! OKAY, WHO WANTS TO GO OUT WITH ME TONIGHT?!
HUH?
ME!
ME!
LET'S SEE... SPIKE, YOU CAN HAVE ME AFTER SCHOOL UNTIL 4:00. GEORGE, YOU'LL TAKE THE 4:00-5:30 SHIFT. WOODY GETS ME FOR DINNER AS ORIGINALLY PLANNED.
MILK

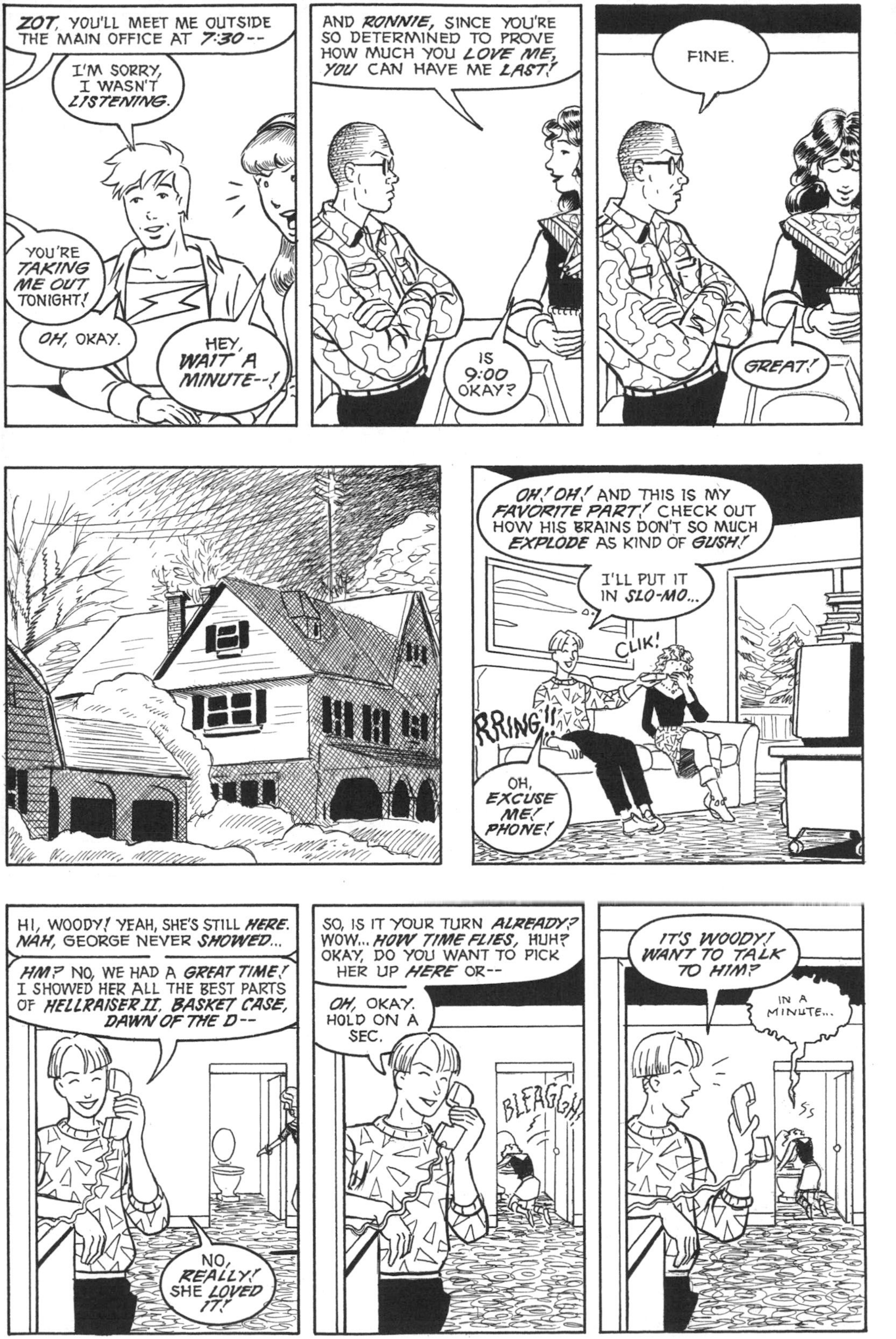
ZOT, YOU'LL MEET ME OUTSIDE THE MAIN OFFICE AT 7:30--
I'M SORRY, I WASN'T LISTENING.
YOU'RE TAKING ME OUT TONIGHT!
OH, OKAY.
HEY, WAIT A MINUTE--!
AND RONNIE, SINCE YOU'RE SO DETERMINED TO PROVE HOW MUCH YOU LOVE ME, YOU CAN HAVE ME LAST!
IS 9:00 OKAY?
FINE.
GREAT!
OH! OH! AND THIS IS MY FAVORITE PART! CHECK OUT HOW HIS BRAINS DON'T SO MUCH EXPLODE AS KIND OF GUSH!
I'LL PUT IT IN SLO-MO...
CLIK!
RRING!!!
OH, EXCUSE ME! PHONE!
HI, WOODY! YEAH, SHE'S STILL HERE. NAH, GEORGE NEVER SHOWED...
HM? NO, WE HAD A GREAT TIME! I SHOWED HER ALL THE BEST PARTS OF HELLRAISER II, BASKET CASE, DAWN OF THE D--
NO, REALLY! SHE LOVED IT!
SO, IS IT YOUR TURN ALREADY? WOW... HOW TIME FLIES, HUH? OKAY, DO YOU WANT TO PICK HER UP HERE OR--
OH, OKAY. HOLD ON A SEC.
BLEAGGH
IT'S WOODY! WANT TO TALK TO HIM?
IN A MINUTE...

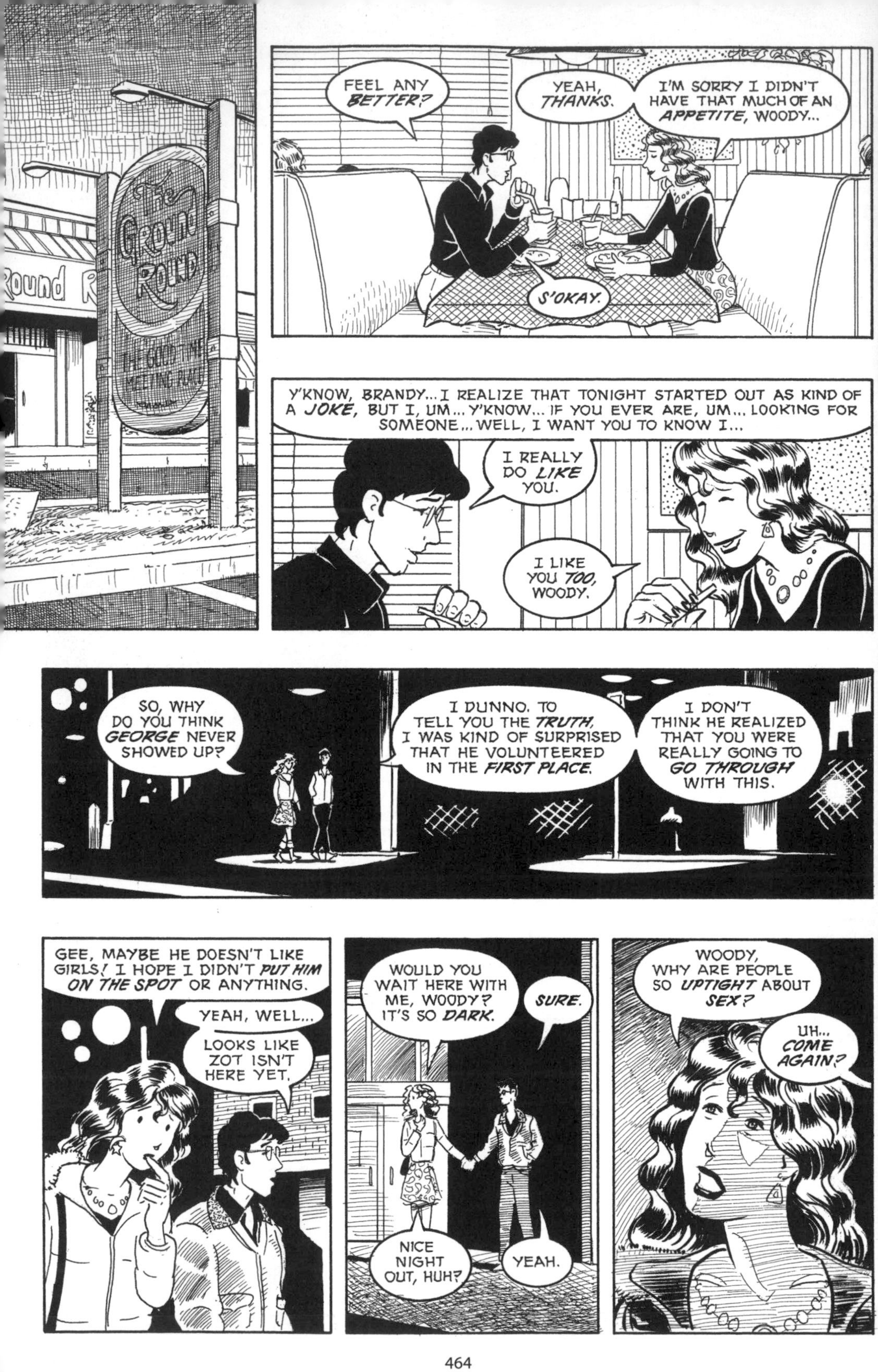
The Ground Round
THE GOOD TIME MEETING PLACE
Round R
FEEL ANY BETTER?
YEAH, THANKS.
I'M SORRY I DIDN'T HAVE THAT MUCH OF AN APPETITE, WOODY...
S'OKAY.
Y'KNOW, BRANDY... I REALIZE THAT TONIGHT STARTED OUT AS KIND OF A JOKE, BUT I, UM... Y'KNOW... IF YOU EVER ARE, UM... LOOKING FOR SOMEONE... WELL, I WANT YOU TO KNOW I...
I REALLY DO LIKE YOU.
I LIKE YOU TOO, WOODY.
SO, WHY DO YOU THINK GEORGE NEVER SHOWED UP?
I DUNNO. TO TELL YOU THE TRUTH, I WAS KIND OF SURPRISED THAT HE VOLUNTEERED IN THE FIRST PLACE.
I DON'T THINK HE REALIZED THAT YOU WERE REALLY GOING TO GO THROUGH WITH THIS.
GEE, MAYBE HE DOESN'T LIKE GIRLS! I HOPE I DIDN'T PUT HIM ON THE SPOT OR ANYTHING.
YEAH, WELL...
LOOKS LIKE ZOT ISN'T HERE YET.
WOULD YOU WAIT HERE WITH ME, WOODY? IT'S SO DARK.
SURE.
NICE NIGHT OUT, HUH?
YEAH.
WOODY, WHY ARE PEOPLE SO UPTIGHT ABOUT SEX?
UH... COME AGAIN?

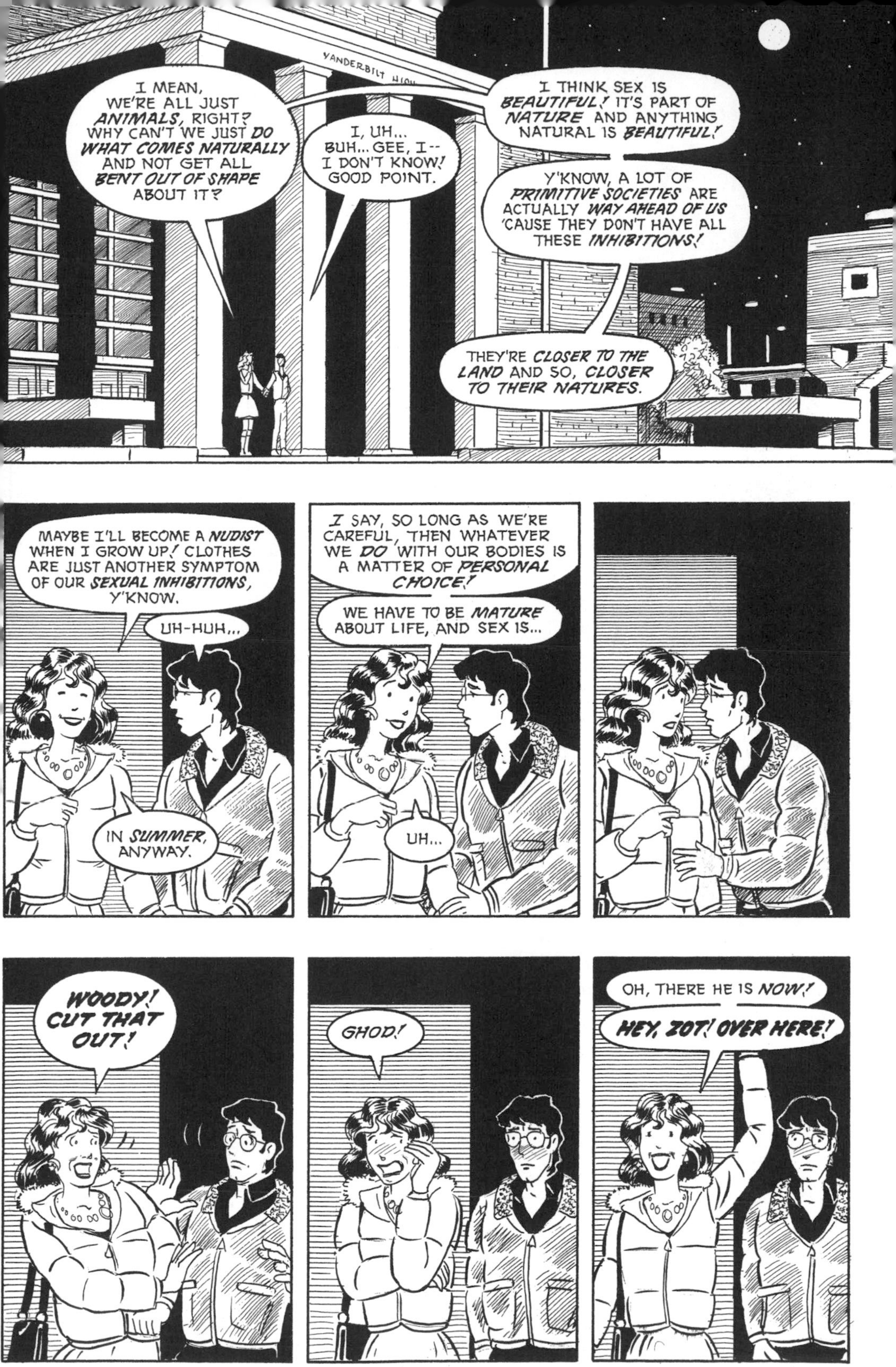
VANDERBILT HIGH
I MEAN, WE'RE ALL JUST ANIMALS, RIGHT? WHY CAN'T WE JUST DO WHAT COMES NATURALLY AND NOT GET ALL BENT OUT OF SHAPE ABOUT IT?
I, UH... BUH... GEE, I-- I DON'T KNOW! GOOD POINT.
I THINK SEX IS BEAUTIFUL! IT'S PART OF NATURE AND ANYTHING NATURAL IS BEAUTIFUL!
Y'KNOW, A LOT OF PRIMITIVE SOCIETIES ARE ACTUALLY WAY AHEAD OF US 'CAUSE THEY DON'T HAVE ALL THESE INHIBITIONS!
THEY'RE CLOSER TO THE LAND AND SO, CLOSER TO THEIR NATURES.
MAYBE I'LL BECOME A NUDIST WHEN I GROW UP! CLOTHES ARE JUST ANOTHER SYMPTOM OF OUR SEXUAL INHIBITIONS, Y'KNOW.
UH-HUH...
IN SUMMER, ANYWAY.
I SAY, SO LONG AS WE'RE CAREFUL, THEN WHATEVER WE DO WITH OUR BODIES IS A MATTER OF PERSONAL CHOICE!
WE HAVE TO BE MATURE ABOUT LIFE, AND SEX IS...
UH...
WOODY! CUT THAT OUT!
GHOD!
OH, THERE HE IS NOW!
HEY, ZOT! OVER HERE!

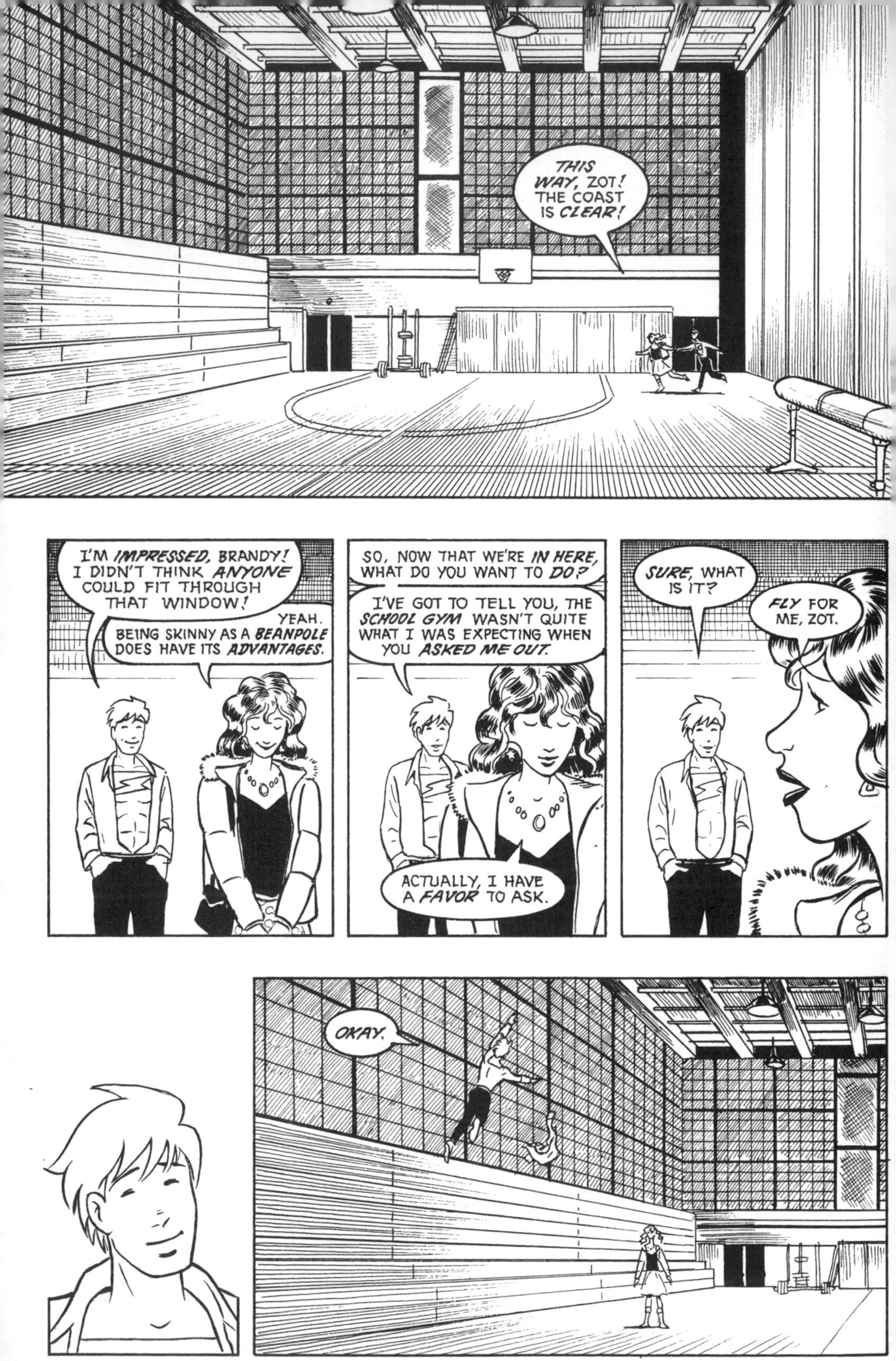
THIS WAY, ZOT! THE COAST IS CLEAR!
I'M IMPRESSED, BRANDY! I DIDN'T THINK ANYONE COULD FIT THROUGH THAT WINDOW!
YEAH. BEING SKINNY AS A BEANPOLE DOES HAVE ITS ADVANTAGES.
SO, NOW THAT WE'RE IN HERE, WHAT DO YOU WANT TO DO?
I'VE GOT TO TELL YOU, THE SCHOOL GYM WASN'T QUITE WHAT I WAS EXPECTING WHEN YOU ASKED ME OUT.
ACTUALLY, I HAVE A FAVOR TO ASK.
SURE, WHAT IS IT?
FLY FOR ME, ZOT.
OKAY.

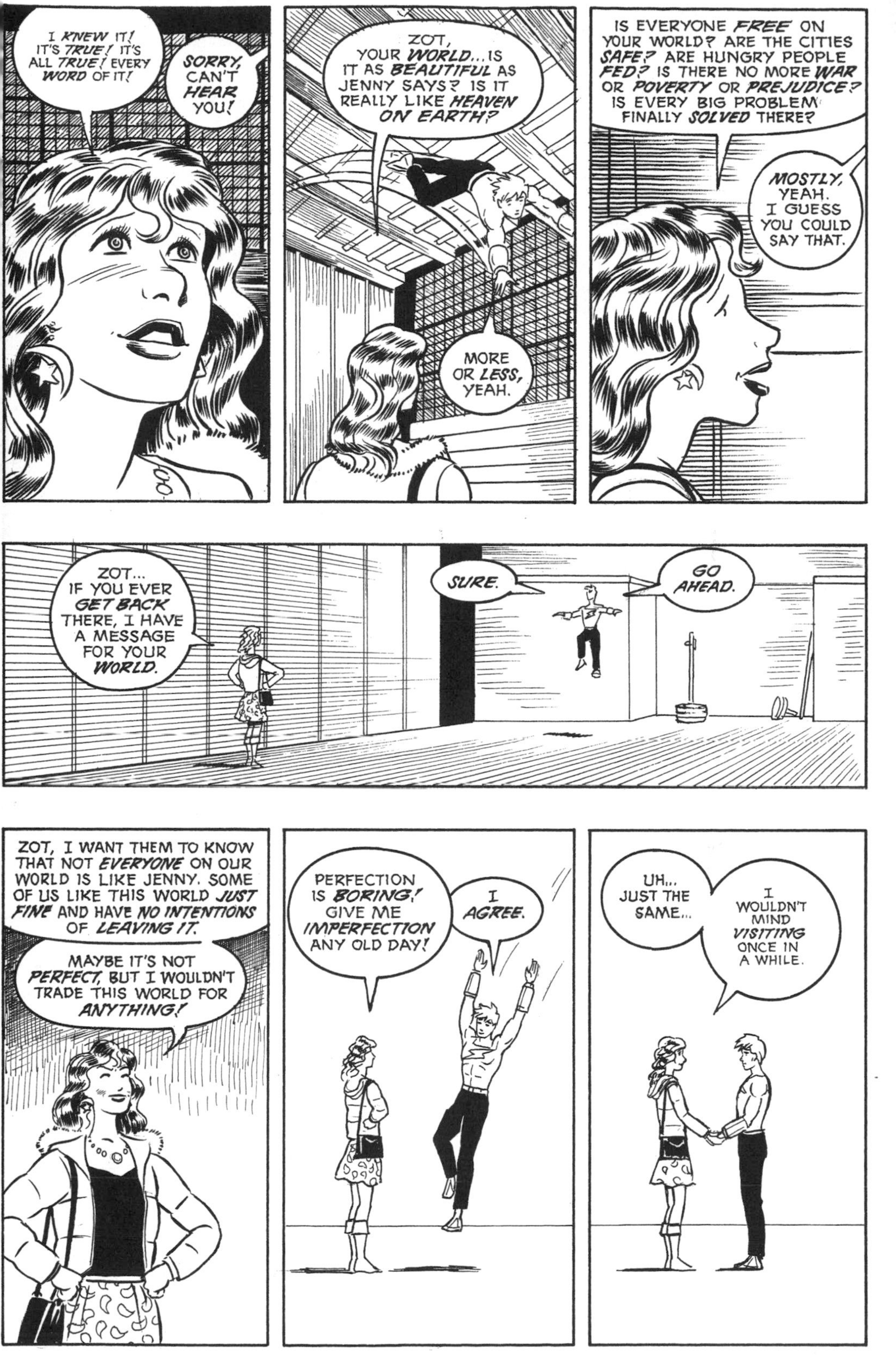
I KNEW IT! IT'S TRUE! IT'S ALL TRUE! EVERY WORD OF IT!
SORRY, CAN'T HEAR YOU!
ZOT, YOUR WORLD... IS IT AS BEAUTIFUL AS JENNY SAYS? IS IT REALLY LIKE HEAVEN ON EARTH?
MORE OR LESS, YEAH.
IS EVERYONE FREE ON YOUR WORLD? ARE THE CITIES SAFE? ARE HUNGRY PEOPLE FED? IS THERE NO MORE WAR OR POVERTY OR PREJUDICE? IS EVERY BIG PROBLEM FINALLY SOLVED THERE?
MOSTLY, YEAH. I GUESS YOU COULD SAY THAT.
ZOT... IF YOU EVER GET BACK THERE, I HAVE A MESSAGE FOR YOUR WORLD.
SURE.
GO AHEAD.
ZOT, I WANT THEM TO KNOW THAT NOT EVERYONE ON OUR WORLD IS LIKE JENNY. SOME OF US LIKE THIS WORLD JUST FINE AND HAVE NO INTENTIONS OF LEAVING IT.
MAYBE IT'S NOT PERFECT, BUT I WOULDN'T TRADE THIS WORLD FOR ANYTHING!
PERFECTION IS BORING! GIVE ME IMPERFECTION ANY OLD DAY!
I AGREE.
UH... JUST THE SAME...
I WOULDN'T MIND VISITING ONCE IN A WHILE.

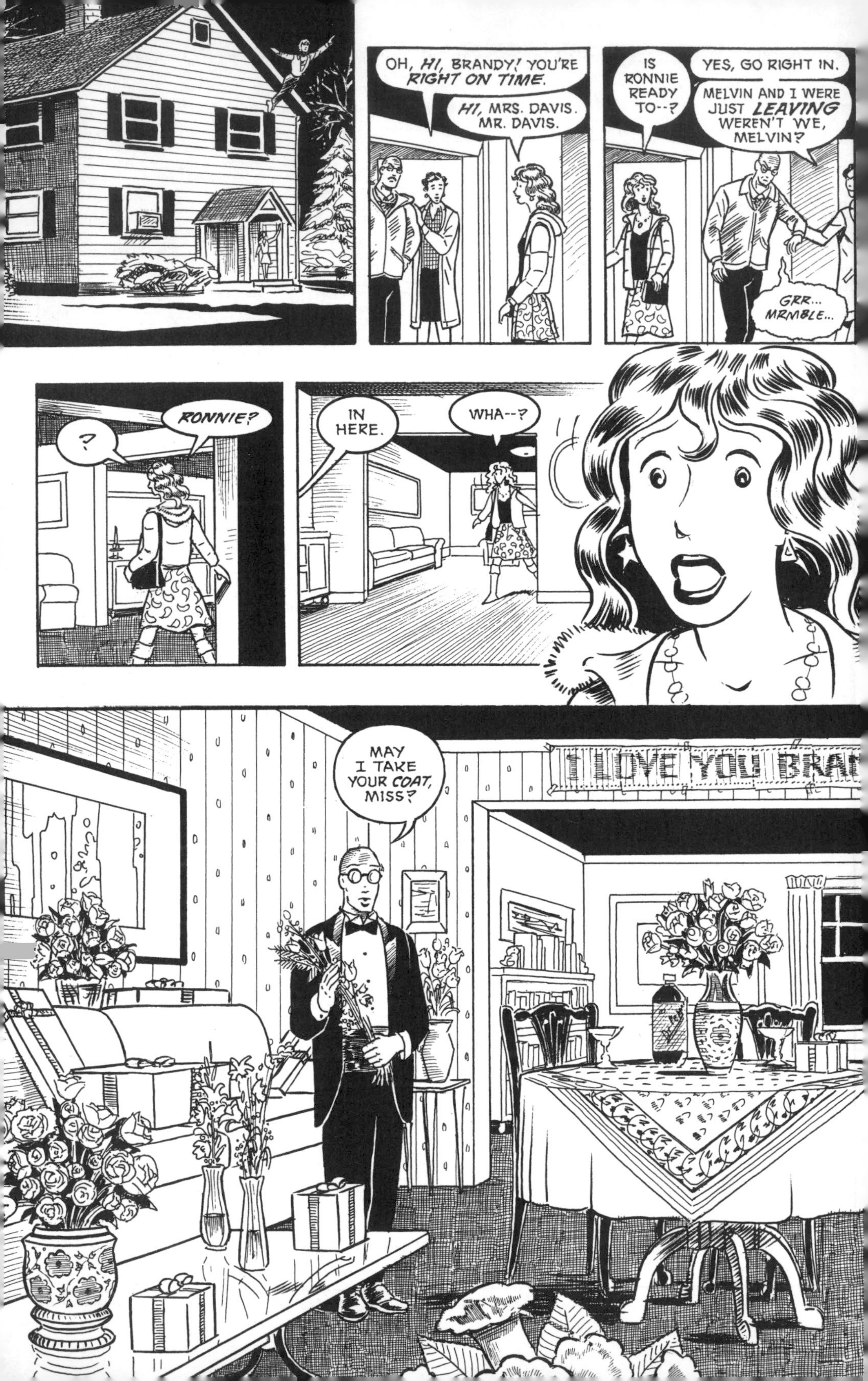
OH, HI, BRANDY! YOU'RE RIGHT ON TIME.
HI, MRS. DAVIS. MR. DAVIS.
IS RONNIE READY TO--?
YES, GO RIGHT IN.
MELVIN AND I WERE JUST LEAVING WEREN'T WE, MELVIN?
GRR... MRMBLE...
?
RONNIE?
IN HERE.
WHA--?
MAY I TAKE YOUR COAT, MISS?
I LOVE YOU BRAN

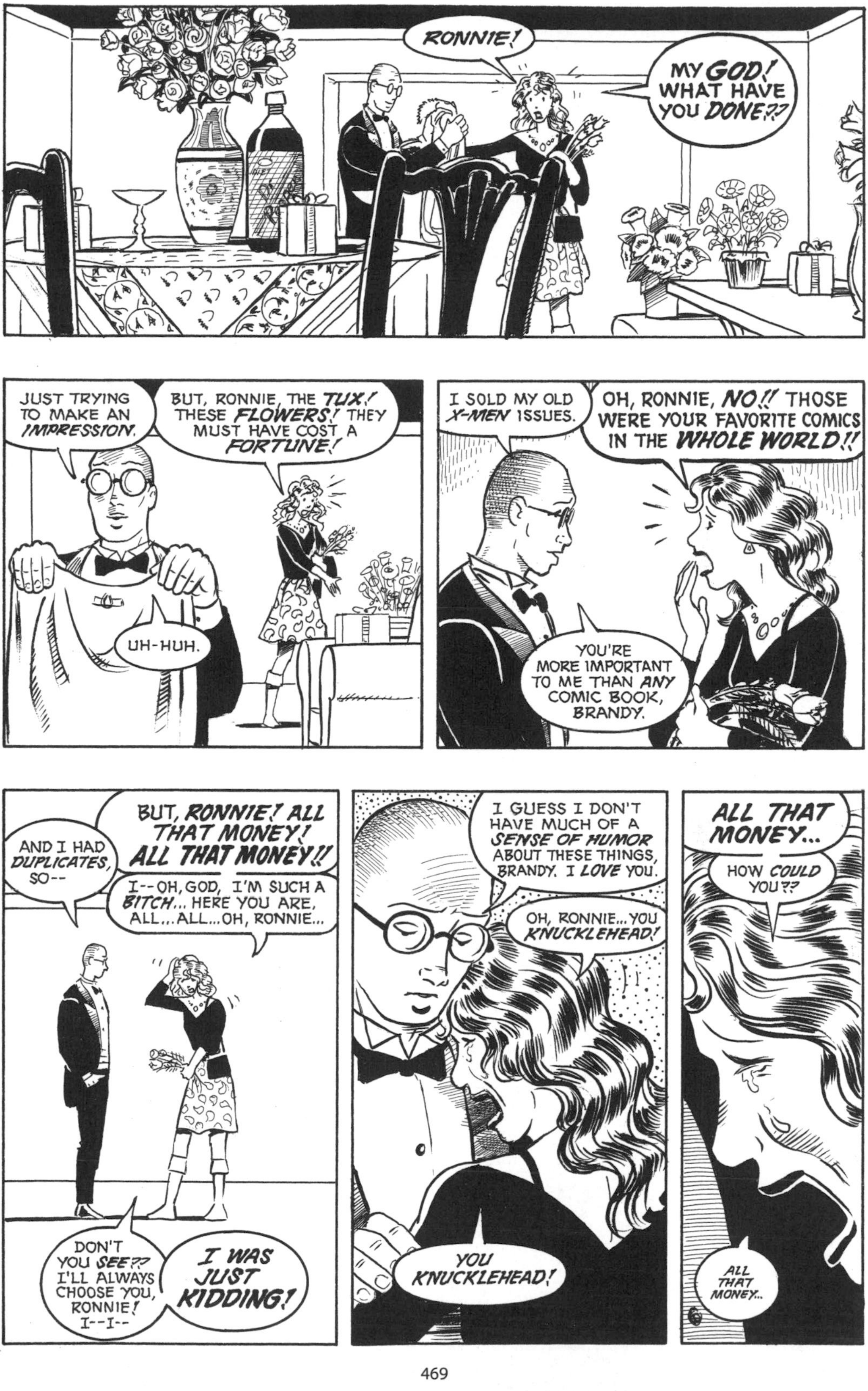
RONNIE!
MY GOD! WHAT HAVE YOU DONE??
JUST TRYING TO MAKE AN IMPRESSION.
BUT, RONNIE, THE TUX! THESE FLOWERS! THEY MUST HAVE COST A FORTUNE!
UH-HUH.
I SOLD MY OLD X-MEN ISSUES.
OH, RONNIE, NO!! THOSE WERE YOUR FAVORITE COMICS IN THE WHOLE WORLD!!
YOU'RE MORE IMPORTANT TO ME THAN ANY COMIC BOOK, BRANDY.
AND I HAD DUPLICATES, SO--
BUT, RONNIE! ALL THAT MONEY! ALL THAT MONEY!!
I--OH, GOD, I'M SUCH A BITCH... HERE YOU ARE, ALL... ALL...OH, RONNIE...
DON'T YOU SEE?? I'LL ALWAYS CHOOSE YOU, RONNIE! I--I--
I WAS JUST KIDDING!
I GUESS I DON'T HAVE MUCH OF A SENSE OF HUMOR ABOUT THESE THINGS, BRANDY. I LOVE YOU.
OH, RONNIE... YOU KNUCKLEHEAD!
YOU KNUCKLEHEAD!
ALL THAT MONEY...
HOW COULD YOU??
ALL THAT MONEY...

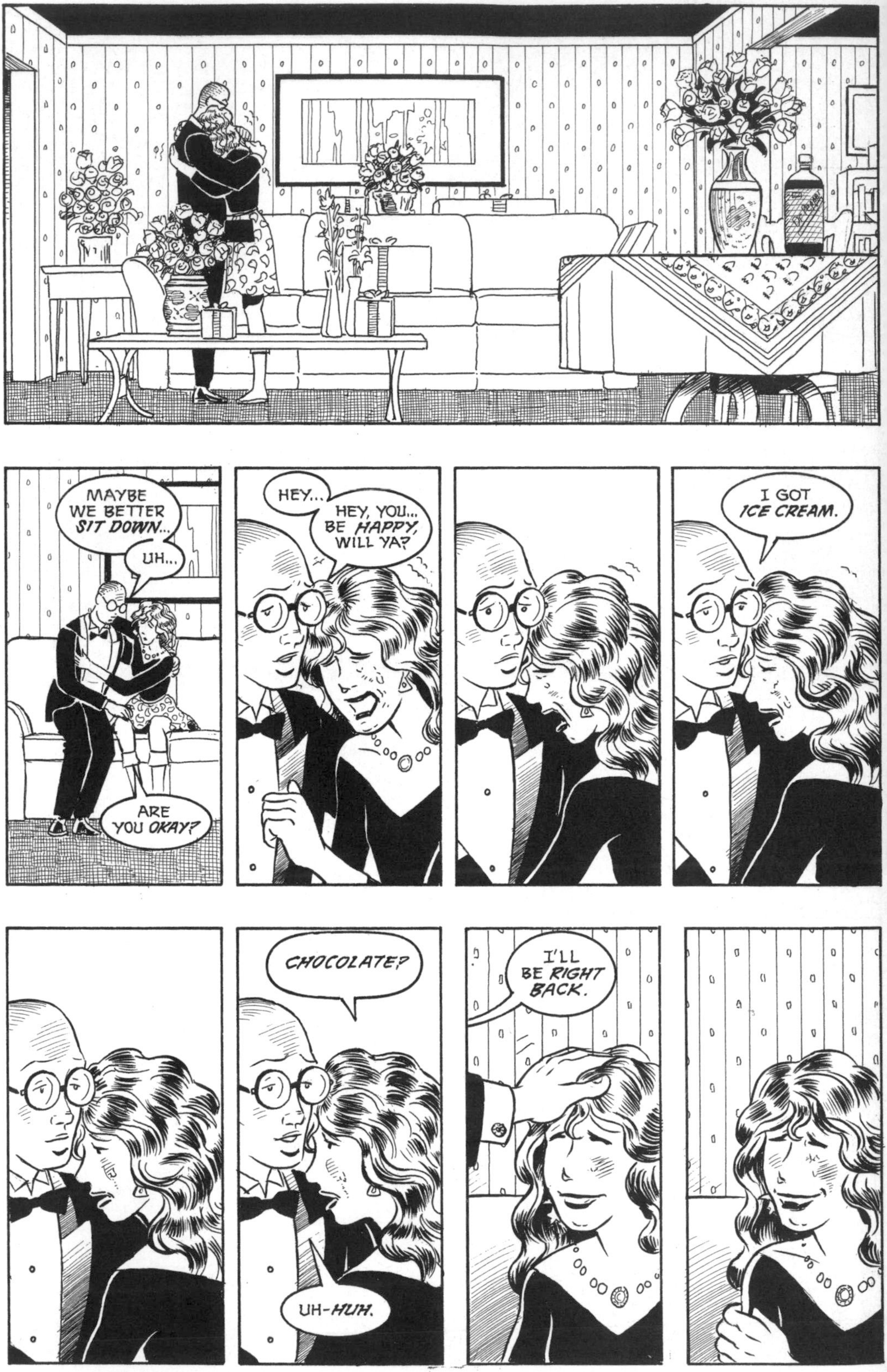
MAYBE WE BETTER SIT DOWN...
UH...
ARE YOU OKAY?
HEY...
HEY, YOU... BE HAPPY, WILL YA?
I GOT ICE CREAM.
CHOCOLATE?
UH-HUH.
I'LL BE RIGHT BACK.

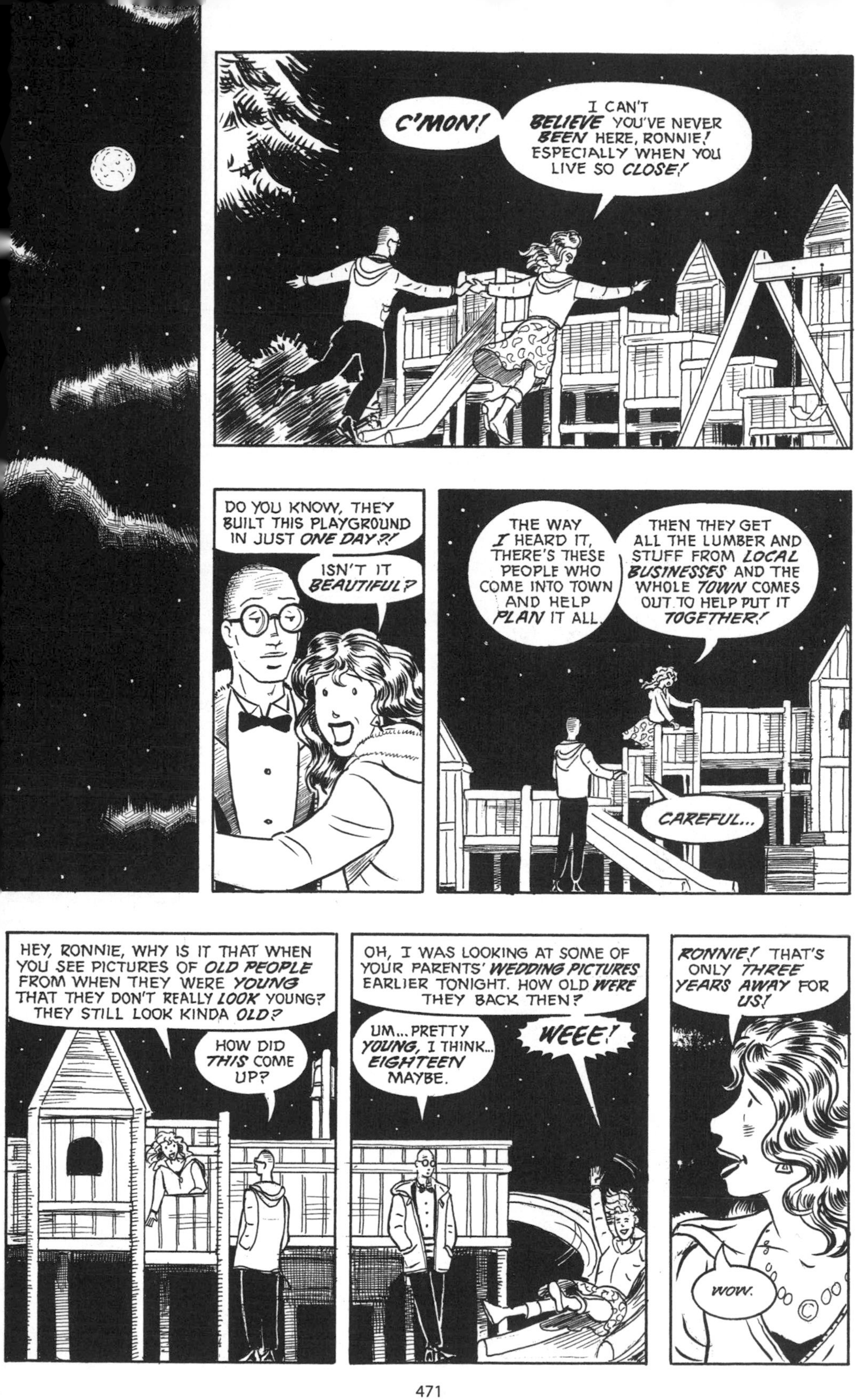
C'MON!
I CAN'T BELIEVE YOU'VE NEVER BEEN HERE, RONNIE! ESPECIALLY WHEN YOU LIVE SO CLOSE!
DO YOU KNOW, THEY BUILT THIS PLAYGROUND IN JUST ONE DAY?!
ISN'T IT BEAUTIFUL?
THE WAY I HEARD IT, THERE'S THESE PEOPLE WHO COME INTO TOWN AND HELP PLAN IT ALL.
THEN THEY GET ALL THE LUMBER AND STUFF FROM LOCAL BUSINESSES AND THE WHOLE TOWN COMES OUT TO HELP PUT IT TOGETHER!
CAREFUL...
HEY, RONNIE, WHY IS IT THAT WHEN YOU SEE PICTURES OF OLD PEOPLE FROM WHEN THEY WERE YOUNG THAT THEY DON'T REALLY LOOK YOUNG? THEY STILL LOOK KINDA OLD?
HOW DID THIS COME UP?
OH, I WAS LOOKING AT SOME OF YOUR PARENTS' WEDDING PICTURES EARLIER TONIGHT. HOW OLD WERE THEY BACK THEN?
UM... PRETTY YOUNG, I THINK... EIGHTEEN MAYBE.
WEEE!
RONNIE! THAT'S ONLY THREE YEARS AWAY FOR US!
WOW.

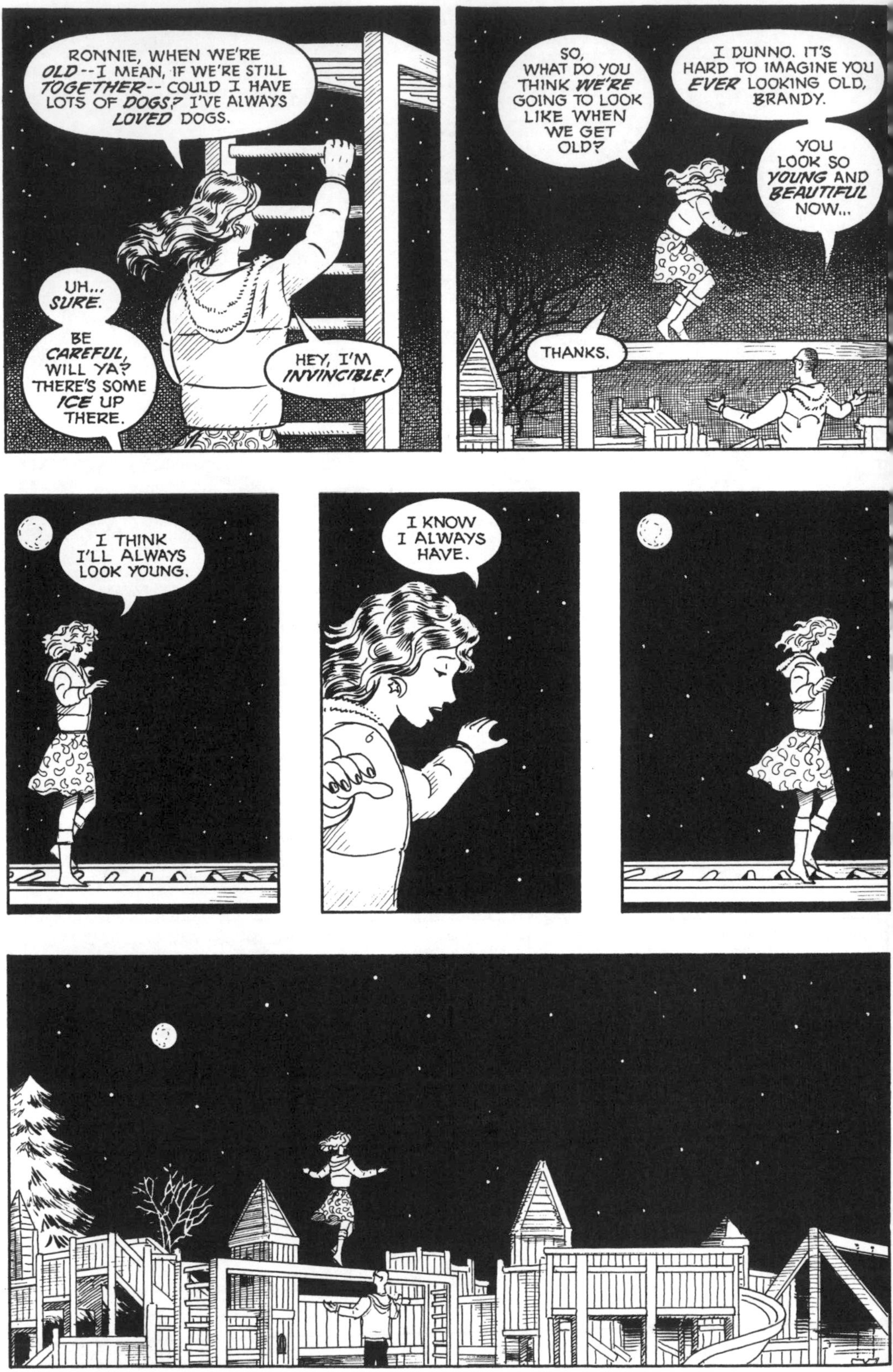

RONNIE, WHEN WE'RE OLD--I MEAN, IF WE'RE STILL TOGETHER-- COULD I HAVE LOTS OF DOGS? I'VE ALWAYS LOVED DOGS.
UH... SURE.
BE CAREFUL, WILL YA? THERE'S SOME ICE UP THERE.
HEY, I'M INVINCIBLE!
SO, WHAT DO YOU THINK WE'RE GOING TO LOOK LIKE WHEN WE GET OLD?
I DUNNO. IT'S HARD TO IMAGINE YOU EVER LOOKING OLD, BRANDY.
YOU LOOK SO YOUNG AND BEAUTIFUL NOW...
THANKS.
I THINK I'LL ALWAYS LOOK YOUNG.
I KNOW I ALWAYS HAVE.

I was riding on a bus to Harvard Square one day when a slightly shifty-looking older man walked past me and asked a girl with a young voice directly behind me if he could take the seat next to her. He began asking her questions, some of which seemed a bit overly probing to me, though she didn't seem to mind. She was chatty and volunteered a lot of information about herself. I dutifully eavesdropped (following the advice of all good writing teachers), and at a certain point the conversation turned to her physical appearance. He said she looked younger than her stated age. "I think I'll always look young," she said, "I know I always have." I stole the line and gave it to Brandy, pulling together a moment I now like as much as anything in the series.

Ronnie and Brandy's stories have aged pretty well, I think. Apart from my usual reservations about the art—and wondering occasionally why there's some guy in a superhero costume hanging around—I can look through these pages without shuddering much. I have real affection for the characters and wish them success on the long, bumpy road ahead of them.

Needless to say, Ronnie and his friends weren't much of a stretch for a card-carrying nerd like me. I still have my own three-ring binder, filled with superhero ideas from high school. (In fact, Kurt Busiek and I may yet collaborate on one idea we worked on together back in the day that's kind of cool.)

Woody's role-playing universe is a lot like the kind I created for our circle of friends. I wasn't interested in the official rule books and such, so my "dungeons" were informal pencil-and-paper creations that included characters from comics, TV, movies, and literature. It wasn't unusual to find a hero like Ultra Boy* fighting Rover (the big white balloon from the classic BBC show *The Prisoner*) while dodging those stilt-legged Apple Bonker guys from *Yellow Submarine*.

Creating Brandy was a mental excursion that took me a bit further from home than Ronnie, but I had many of the parts close at hand, including Ivy's bohemian flourishes and fearless affection for those around her, our daily money struggles, and that same third floor walk-up in Somerville, Massachusetts (complete with an equally reasonable landlord). Happily, Brandy's alcoholic mother was pure invention; neither of us had that kind of addiction in our family.

When I imagine them growing up, I have trouble deciding how life will go for Brandy, but I firmly believe that Ronnie will break into comics someday and that he will grow as a writer over time. I have to believe it about him because I have to believe it about myself.

In Comics History: It was while working on these stories that I took time out to try drawing a complete 24-page comics story in a single day as a challenge to my friend Steve Bissette, and as therapy for my chronic slowness at the drawing board. Steve did likewise a few days later. He sent copies to Dave Sim, Rick Veitch, and Neil Gaiman, each of whom made their own such comics. In the eighteen years since, thousands have taken the 24 Hour Comics Challenge, culminating in the annual international 24 Hour Comics Day (now in its fifth year) and inspiring several spin-offs, including the 24 Hour Plays phenomenon. For more information on the 24 Hour Comics, check out 24hourcomics.com.

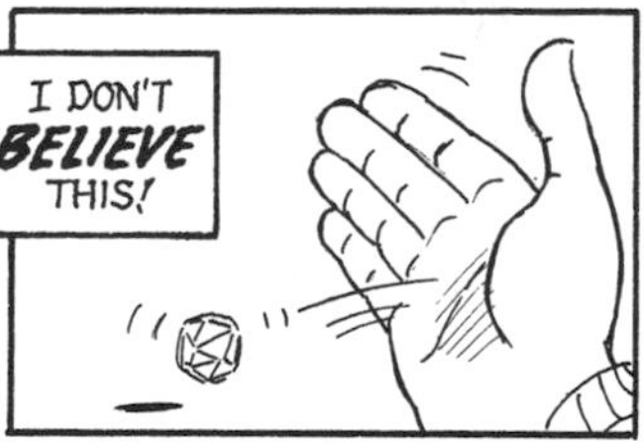
I DON'T BELIEVE THIS!

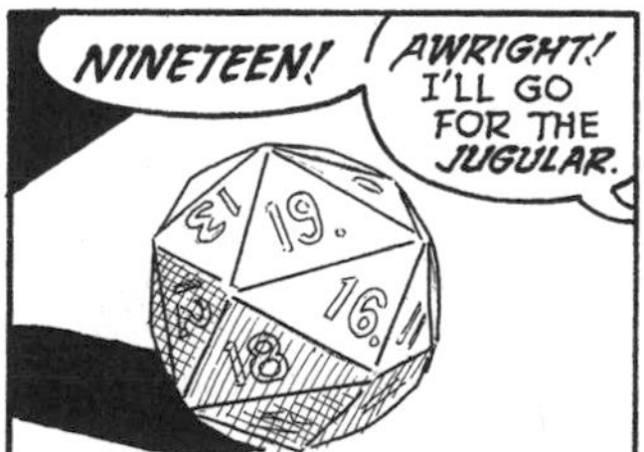
NINETEEN!
AWRIGHT! I'LL GO FOR THE JUGULAR.

*Dude, Ultra Boy has all of Superboy's powers, but can only use them *one at a time*. How cool is that?!

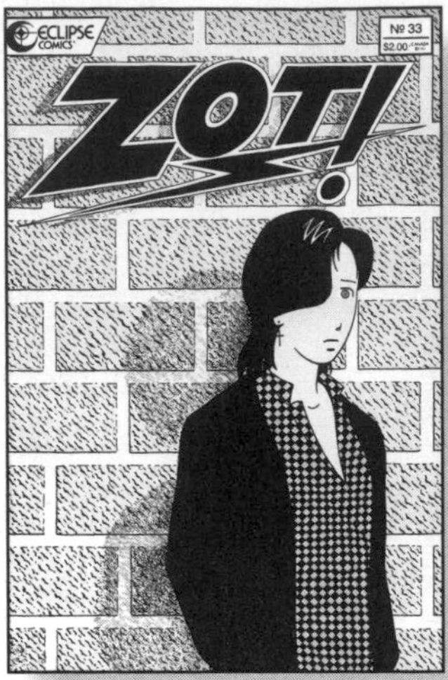
ECLIPSE COMICS
№ 33
$2.00
ZOT!

Normal

First published in *Zot! #33*.

Lettering:

Bob Lappan

Original series editor:

cat yronwode

Plot assist:

Ivy Ratafia

Harvey Award Nominee 1991:

"Best Single Issue"

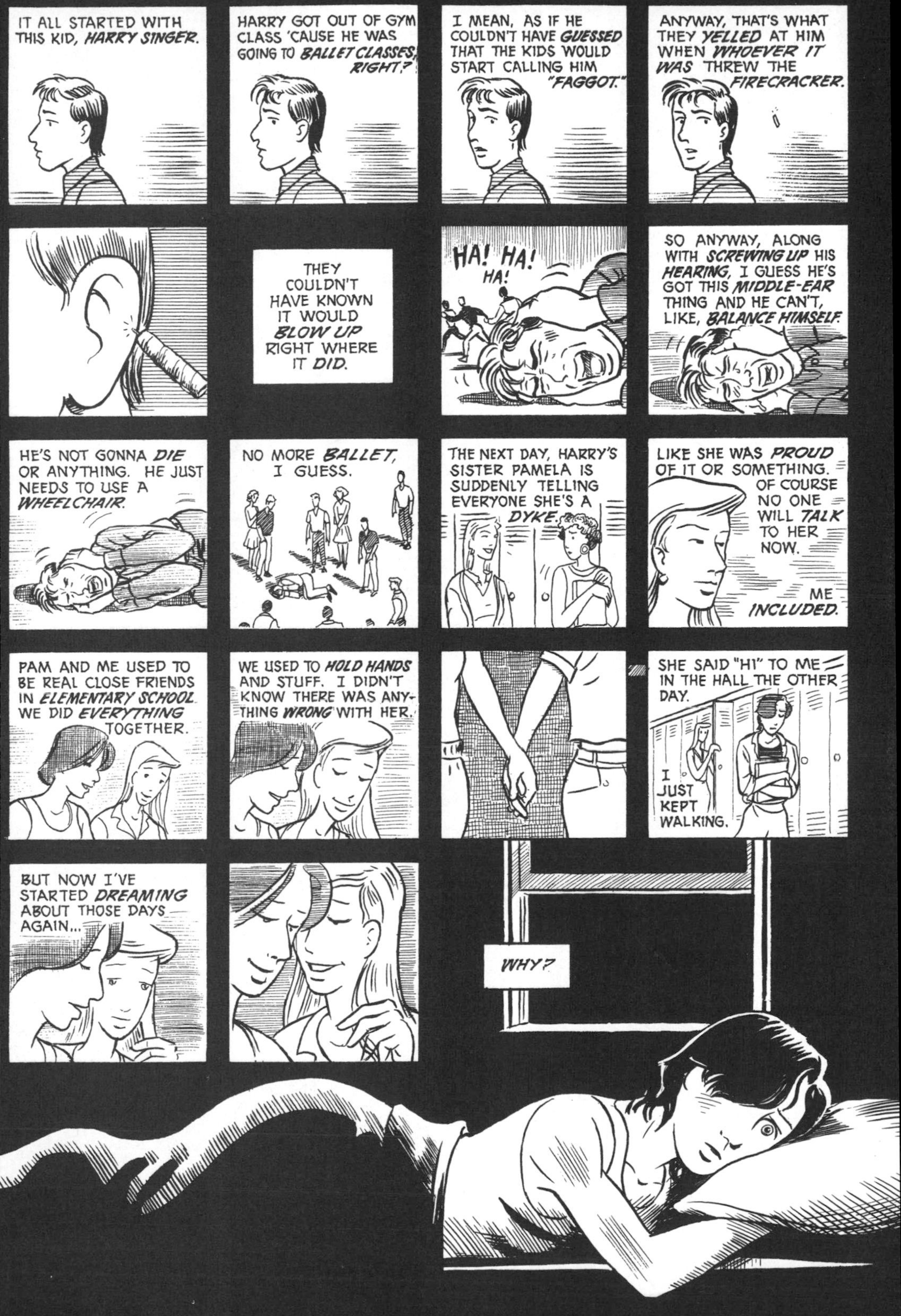
IT ALL STARTED WITH THIS KID, HARRY SINGER.
HARRY GOT OUT OF GYM CLASS 'CAUSE HE WAS GOING TO BALLET CLASSES, RIGHT?
I MEAN, AS IF HE COULDN'T HAVE GUESSED THAT THE KIDS WOULD START CALLING HIM "FAGGOT."
ANYWAY, THAT'S WHAT THEY YELLED AT HIM WHEN WHOEVER IT WAS THREW THE FIRECRACKER.
THEY COULDN'T HAVE KNOWN IT WOULD BLOW UP RIGHT WHERE IT DID.
HA! HA! HA!
SO ANYWAY, ALONG WITH SCREWING UP HIS HEARING, I GUESS HE'S GOT THIS MIDDLE-EAR THING AND HE CAN'T, LIKE, BALANCE HIMSELF.
HE'S NOT GONNA DIE OR ANYTHING. HE JUST NEEDS TO USE A WHEELCHAIR.
NO MORE BALLET, I GUESS.
THE NEXT DAY, HARRY'S SISTER PAMELA IS SUDDENLY TELLING EVERYONE SHE'S A DYKE.
LIKE SHE WAS PROUD OF IT OR SOMETHING.
OF COURSE NO ONE WILL TALK TO HER NOW.
ME INCLUDED.
PAM AND ME USED TO BE REAL CLOSE FRIENDS IN ELEMENTARY SCHOOL. WE DID EVERYTHING TOGETHER.
WE USED TO HOLD HANDS AND STUFF. I DIDN'T KNOW THERE WAS ANYTHING WRONG WITH HER.
SHE SAID "HI" TO ME IN THE HALL THE OTHER DAY.
I JUST KEPT WALKING.
BUT NOW I'VE STARTED DREAMING ABOUT THOSE DAYS AGAIN...
WHY?

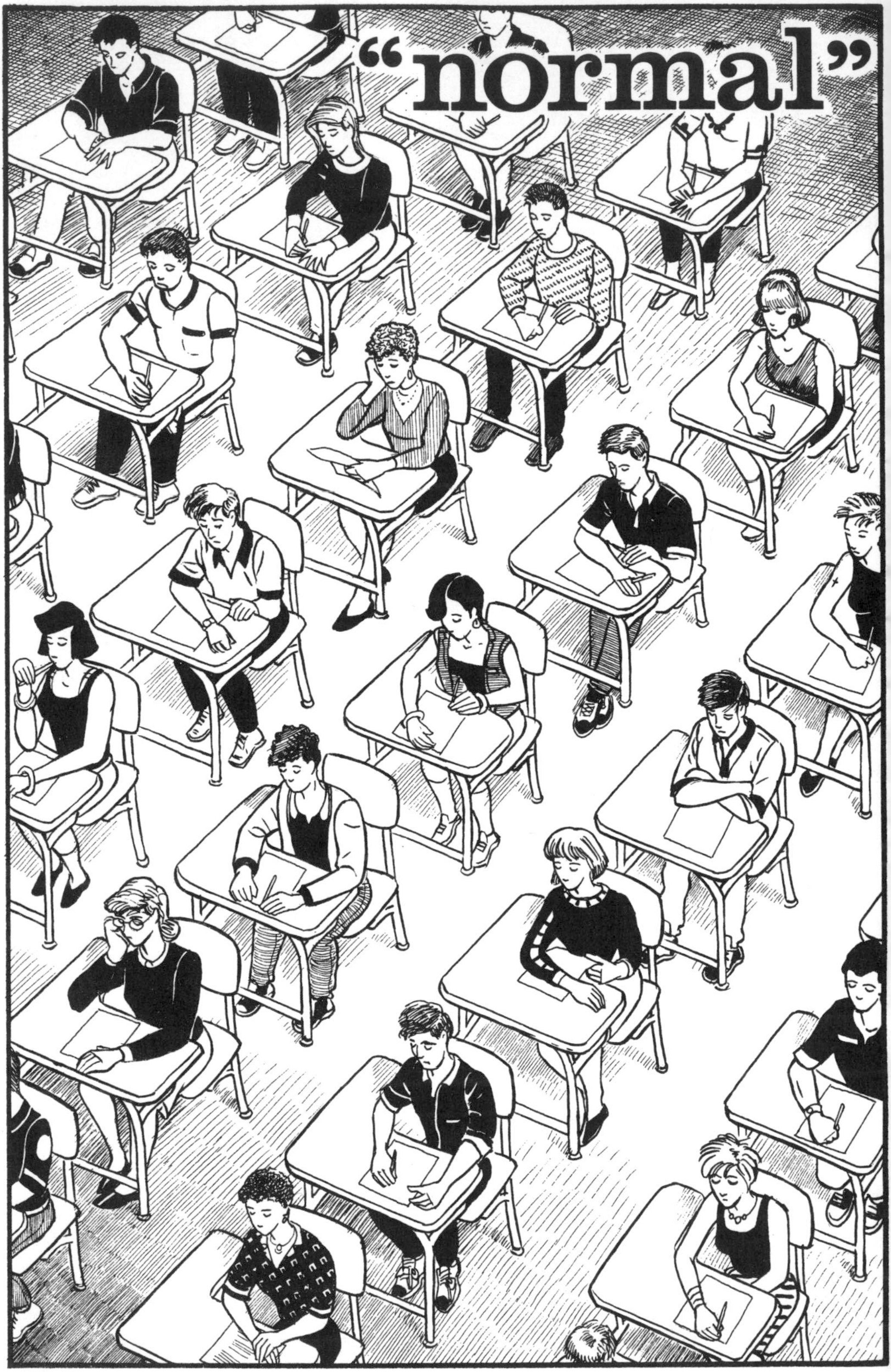
"normal"

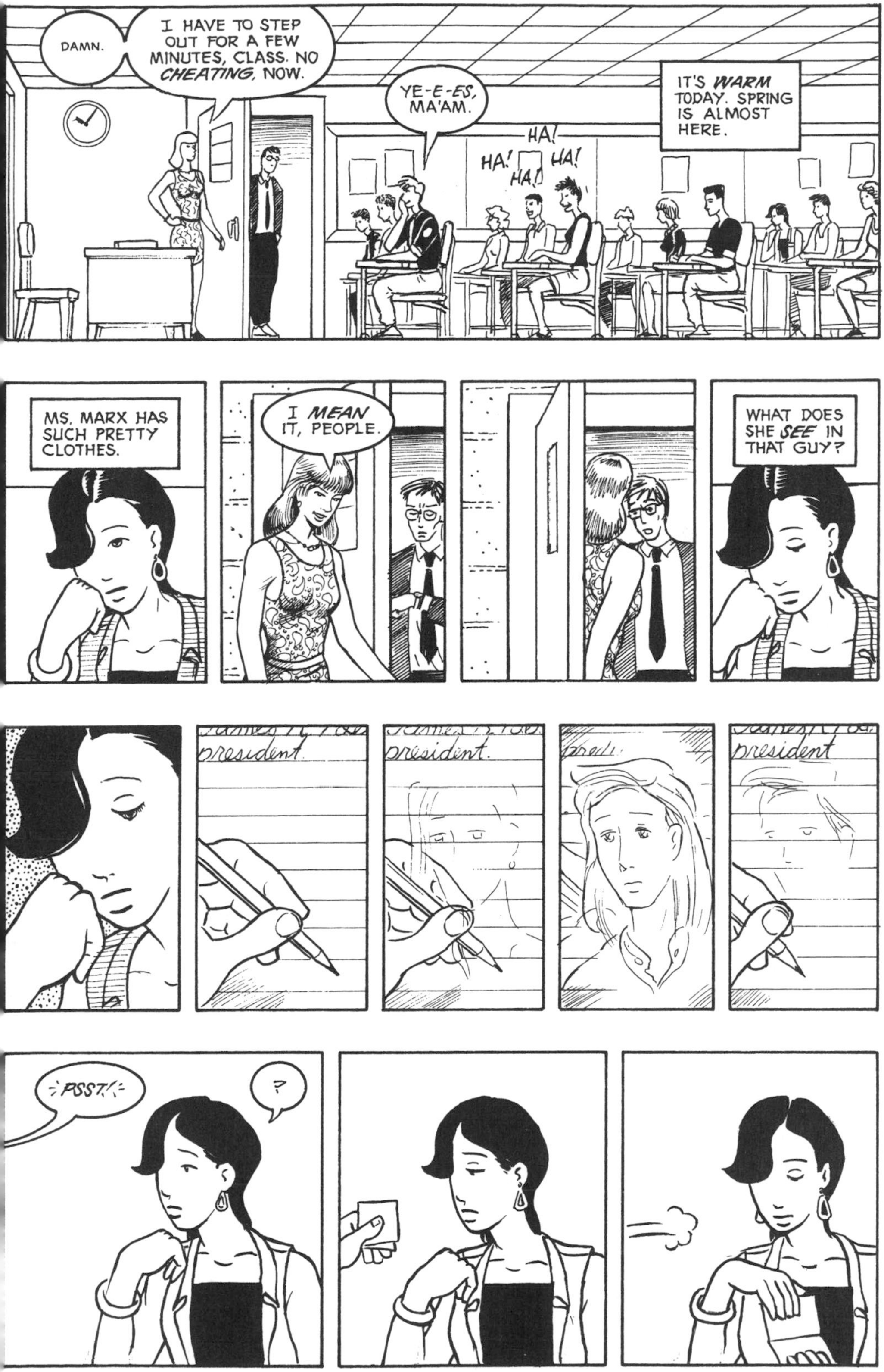
DAMN.
I HAVE TO STEP OUT FOR A FEW MINUTES, CLASS. NO *CHEATING*, NOW.
YE-E-ES, MA'AM.
HA! HA! HA! HA!
IT'S *WARM* TODAY. SPRING IS ALMOST HERE.
MS. MARX HAS SUCH PRETTY CLOTHES.
I *MEAN* IT, PEOPLE.
WHAT DOES SHE *SEE* IN THAT GUY?
president
president
president
PSST!
?

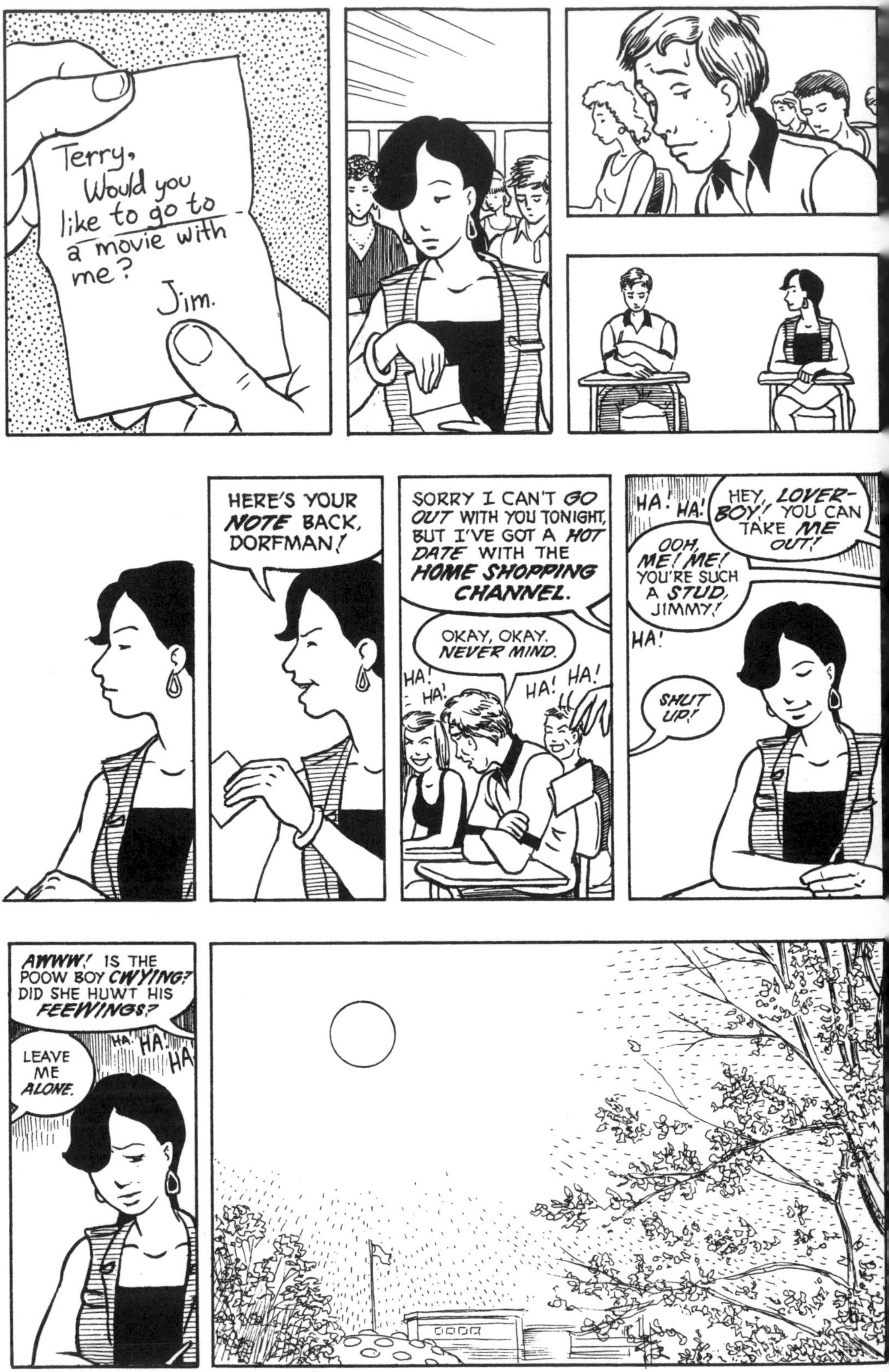
Terry, Would you like to go to a movie with me? Jim.
HERE'S YOUR NOTE BACK, DORFMAN!
SORRY I CAN'T GO OUT WITH YOU TONIGHT, BUT I'VE GOT A HOT DATE WITH THE HOME SHOPPING CHANNEL.
OKAY, OKAY. NEVER MIND.
HA! HA! HA! HA!
HA. HA!
HEY, LOVER-BOY! YOU CAN TAKE ME OUT!
OOH, ME! ME! YOU'RE SUCH A STUD, JIMMY!
HA!
SHUT UP!
AWWW! IS THE POOW BOY CWYING? DID SHE HUWT HIS FEEWINGS?
HA. HA! HA
LEAVE ME ALONE.

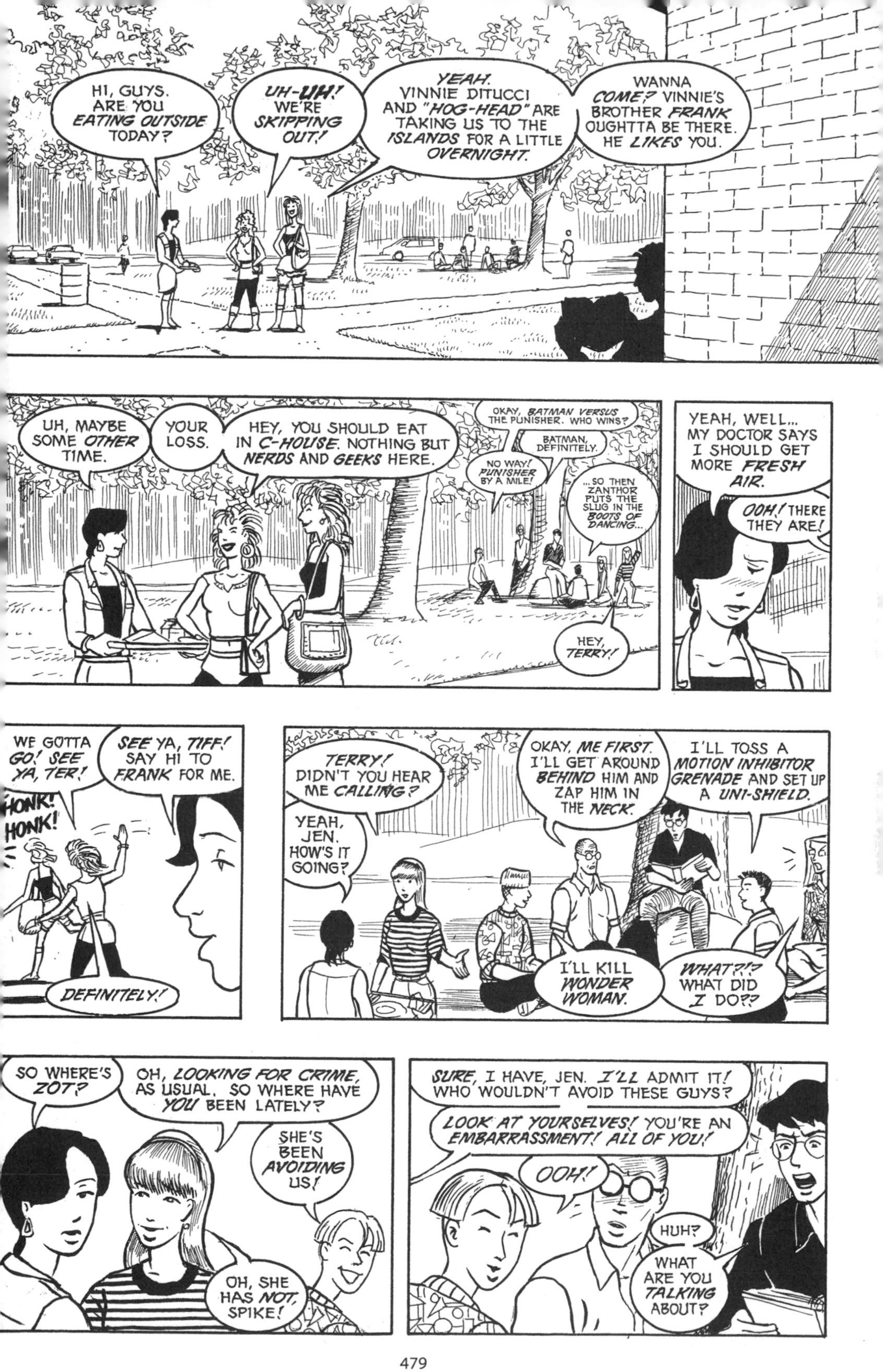
HI, GUYS. ARE YOU EATING OUTSIDE TODAY?
UH-UH! WE'RE SKIPPING OUT!
YEAH. VINNIE DITUCCI AND "HOG-HEAD" ARE TAKING US TO THE ISLANDS FOR A LITTLE OVERNIGHT.
WANNA COME? VINNIE'S BROTHER FRANK OUGHTTA BE THERE. HE LIKES YOU.
UH, MAYBE SOME OTHER TIME.
YOUR LOSS.
HEY, YOU SHOULD EAT IN C-HOUSE. NOTHING BUT NERDS AND GEEKS HERE.
OKAY, BATMAN VERSUS THE PUNISHER. WHO WINS?
BATMAN, DEFINITELY.
NO WAY! PUNISHER BY A MILE!
...SO THEN ZANTHOR PUTS THE SLUG IN THE BOOTS OF DANCING...
HEY, TERRY!
YEAH, WELL... MY DOCTOR SAYS I SHOULD GET MORE FRESH AIR.
OOH! THERE THEY ARE!
WE GOTTA GO! SEE YA, TER!
SEE YA, TIFF! SAY HI TO FRANK FOR ME.
HONK! HONK!
DEFINITELY!
TERRY! DIDN'T YOU HEAR ME CALLING?
YEAH, JEN. HOW'S IT GOING?
OKAY, ME FIRST. I'LL GET AROUND BEHIND HIM AND ZAP HIM IN THE NECK.
I'LL TOSS A MOTION INHIBITOR GRENADE AND SET UP A UNI-SHIELD.
I'LL KILL WONDER WOMAN.
WHAT?!? WHAT DID I DO??
SO WHERE'S ZOT?
OH, LOOKING FOR CRIME, AS USUAL. SO WHERE HAVE YOU BEEN LATELY?
SHE'S BEEN AVOIDING US!
OH, SHE HAS NOT, SPIKE!
SURE, I HAVE, JEN. I'LL ADMIT IT! WHO WOULDN'T AVOID THESE GUYS?
LOOK AT YOURSELVES! YOU'RE AN EMBARRASSMENT! ALL OF YOU!
OOH!
HUH?
WHAT ARE YOU TALKING ABOUT?

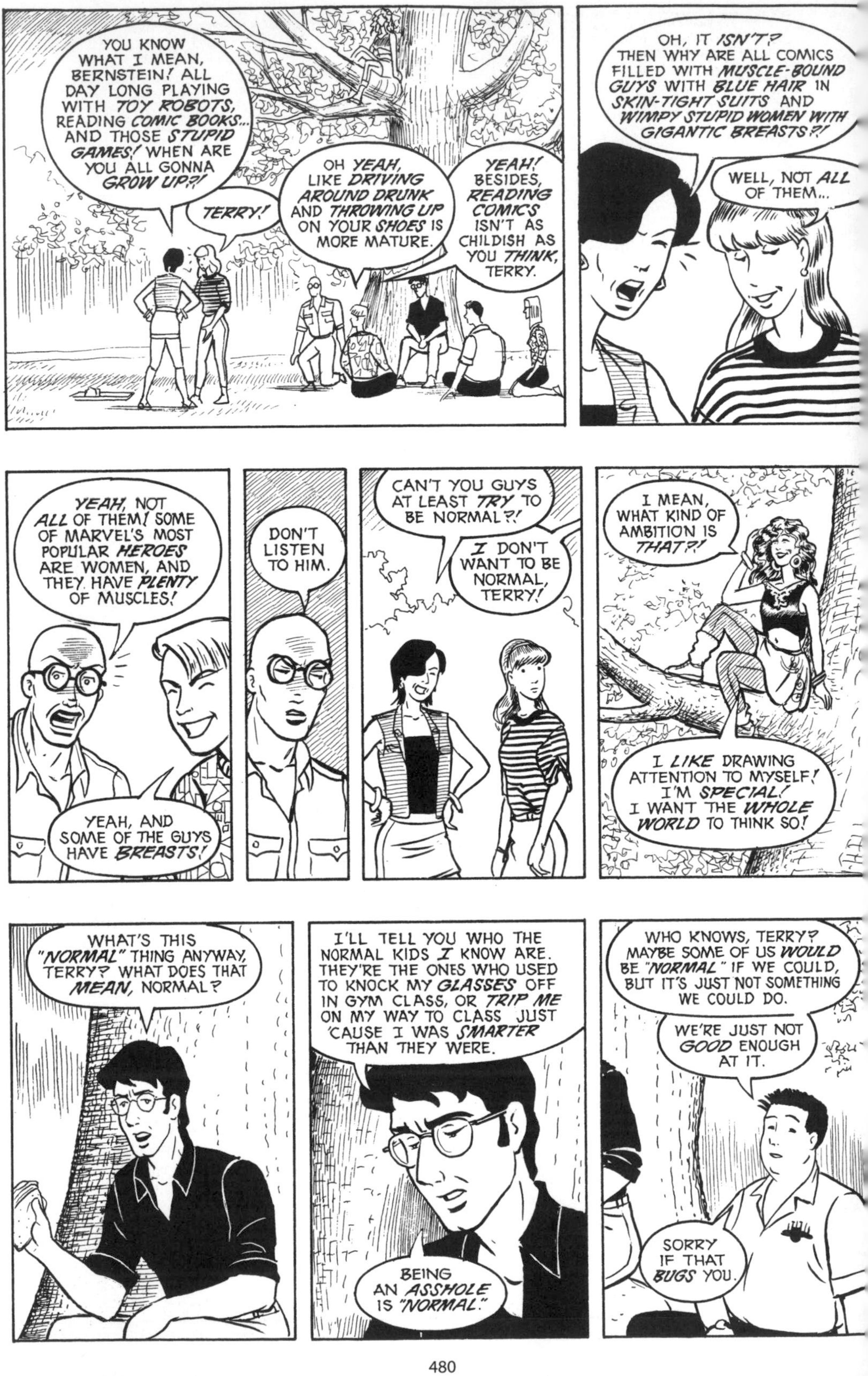
YOU KNOW WHAT I MEAN, BERNSTEIN! ALL DAY LONG PLAYING WITH TOY ROBOTS, READING COMIC BOOKS... AND THOSE STUPID GAMES! WHEN ARE YOU ALL GONNA GROW UP?!
TERRY!
OH YEAH, LIKE DRIVING AROUND DRUNK AND THROWING UP ON YOUR SHOES IS MORE MATURE.
YEAH! BESIDES, READING COMICS ISN'T AS CHILDISH AS YOU THINK, TERRY.
OH, IT ISN'T? THEN WHY ARE ALL COMICS FILLED WITH MUSCLE-BOUND GUYS WITH BLUE HAIR IN SKIN-TIGHT SUITS AND WIMPY STUPID WOMEN WITH GIGANTIC BREASTS?!
WELL, NOT ALL OF THEM...
YEAH, NOT ALL OF THEM! SOME OF MARVEL'S MOST POPULAR HEROES ARE WOMEN, AND THEY HAVE PLENTY OF MUSCLES!
YEAH, AND SOME OF THE GUYS HAVE BREASTS!
DON'T LISTEN TO HIM.
CAN'T YOU GUYS AT LEAST TRY TO BE NORMAL?!
I DON'T WANT TO BE NORMAL, TERRY!
I MEAN, WHAT KIND OF AMBITION IS THAT?!
I LIKE DRAWING ATTENTION TO MYSELF! I'M SPECIAL! I WANT THE WHOLE WORLD TO THINK SO!
WHAT'S THIS "NORMAL" THING ANYWAY, TERRY? WHAT DOES THAT MEAN, NORMAL?
I'LL TELL YOU WHO THE NORMAL KIDS I KNOW ARE. THEY'RE THE ONES WHO USED TO KNOCK MY GLASSES OFF IN GYM CLASS, OR TRIP ME ON MY WAY TO CLASS JUST 'CAUSE I WAS SMARTER THAN THEY WERE.
BEING AN ASSHOLE IS "NORMAL."
WHO KNOWS, TERRY? MAYBE SOME OF US WOULD BE "NORMAL" IF WE COULD, BUT IT'S JUST NOT SOMETHING WE COULD DO.
WE'RE JUST NOT GOOD ENOUGH AT IT.
SORRY IF THAT BUGS YOU.

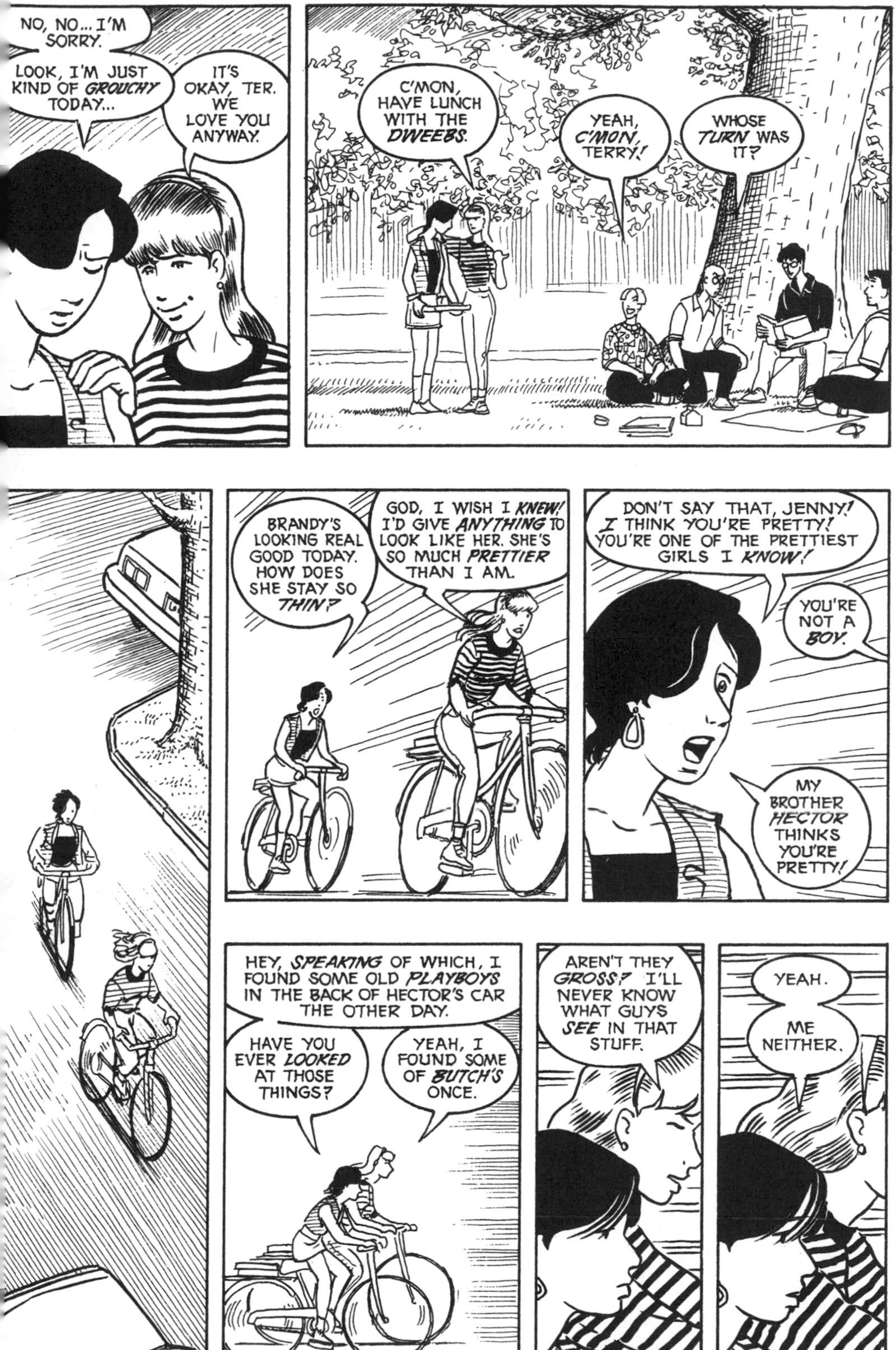
NO, NO... I'M SORRY.
LOOK, I'M JUST KIND OF GROUCHY TODAY...
IT'S OKAY, TER. WE LOVE YOU ANYWAY.
C'MON, HAVE LUNCH WITH THE DWEEBS.
YEAH, C'MON, TERRY!
WHOSE TURN WAS IT?
BRANDY'S LOOKING REAL GOOD TODAY. HOW DOES SHE STAY SO THIN?
GOD, I WISH I KNEW! I'D GIVE ANYTHING TO LOOK LIKE HER. SHE'S SO MUCH PRETTIER THAN I AM.
DON'T SAY THAT, JENNY! I THINK YOU'RE PRETTY! YOU'RE ONE OF THE PRETTIEST GIRLS I KNOW!
YOU'RE NOT A BOY.
MY BROTHER HECTOR THINKS YOU'RE PRETTY!
HEY, SPEAKING OF WHICH, I FOUND SOME OLD PLAYBOYS IN THE BACK OF HECTOR'S CAR THE OTHER DAY.
HAVE YOU EVER LOOKED AT THOSE THINGS?
YEAH, I FOUND SOME OF BUTCH'S ONCE.
AREN'T THEY GROSS? I'LL NEVER KNOW WHAT GUYS SEE IN THAT STUFF.
YEAH.
ME NEITHER.

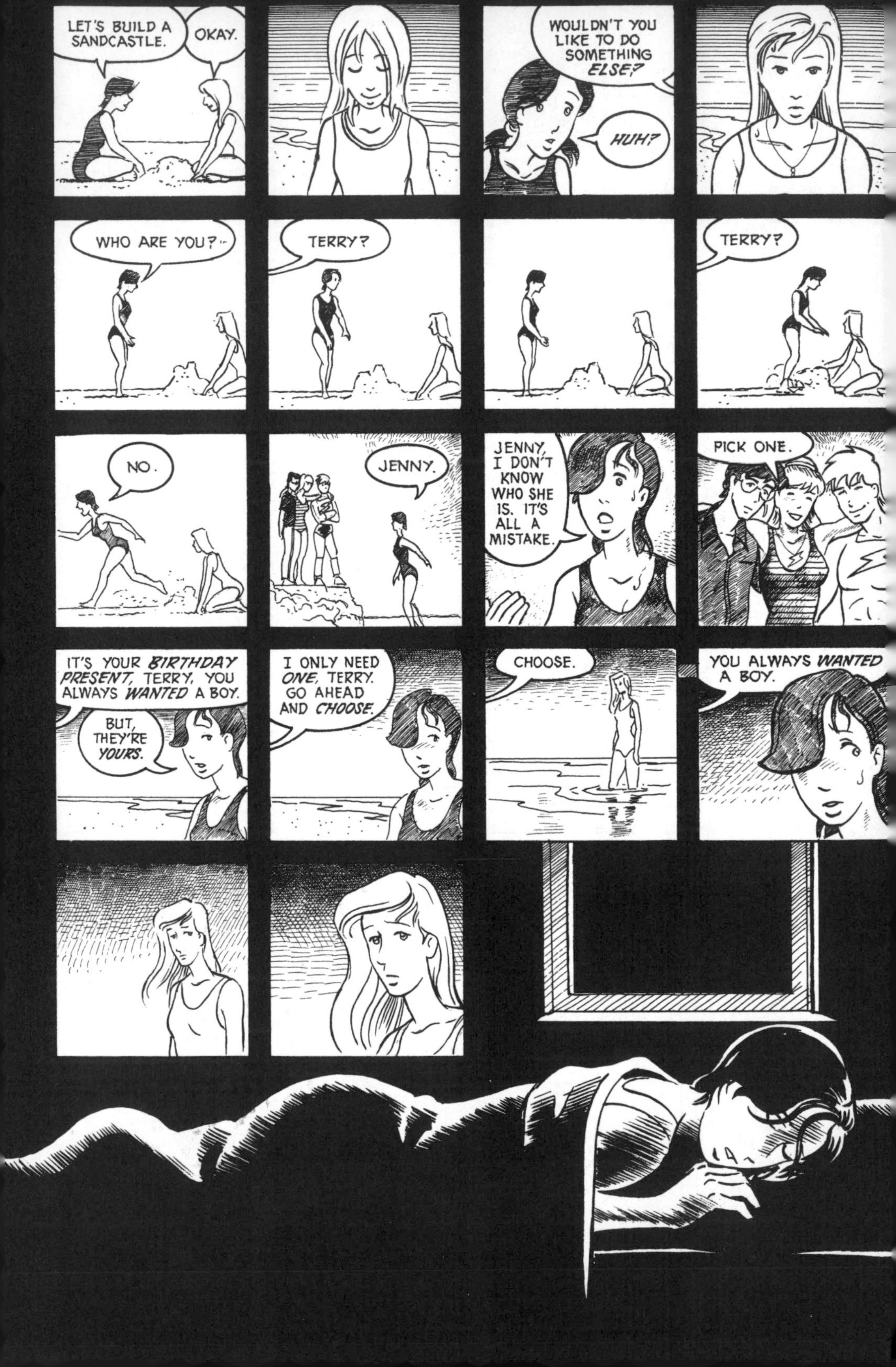
LET'S BUILD A SANDCASTLE.
OKAY.
WOULDN'T YOU LIKE TO DO SOMETHING *ELSE?*
HUH?
WHO ARE YOU?
TERRY?
TERRY?
NO.
JENNY.
JENNY, I DON'T KNOW WHO SHE IS. IT'S ALL A MISTAKE.
PICK ONE.
IT'S YOUR *BIRTHDAY PRESENT,* TERRY. YOU ALWAYS *WANTED* A BOY.
BUT, THEY'RE *YOURS.*
I ONLY NEED *ONE,* TERRY. GO AHEAD AND *CHOOSE.*
CHOOSE.
YOU ALWAYS *WANTED* A BOY.

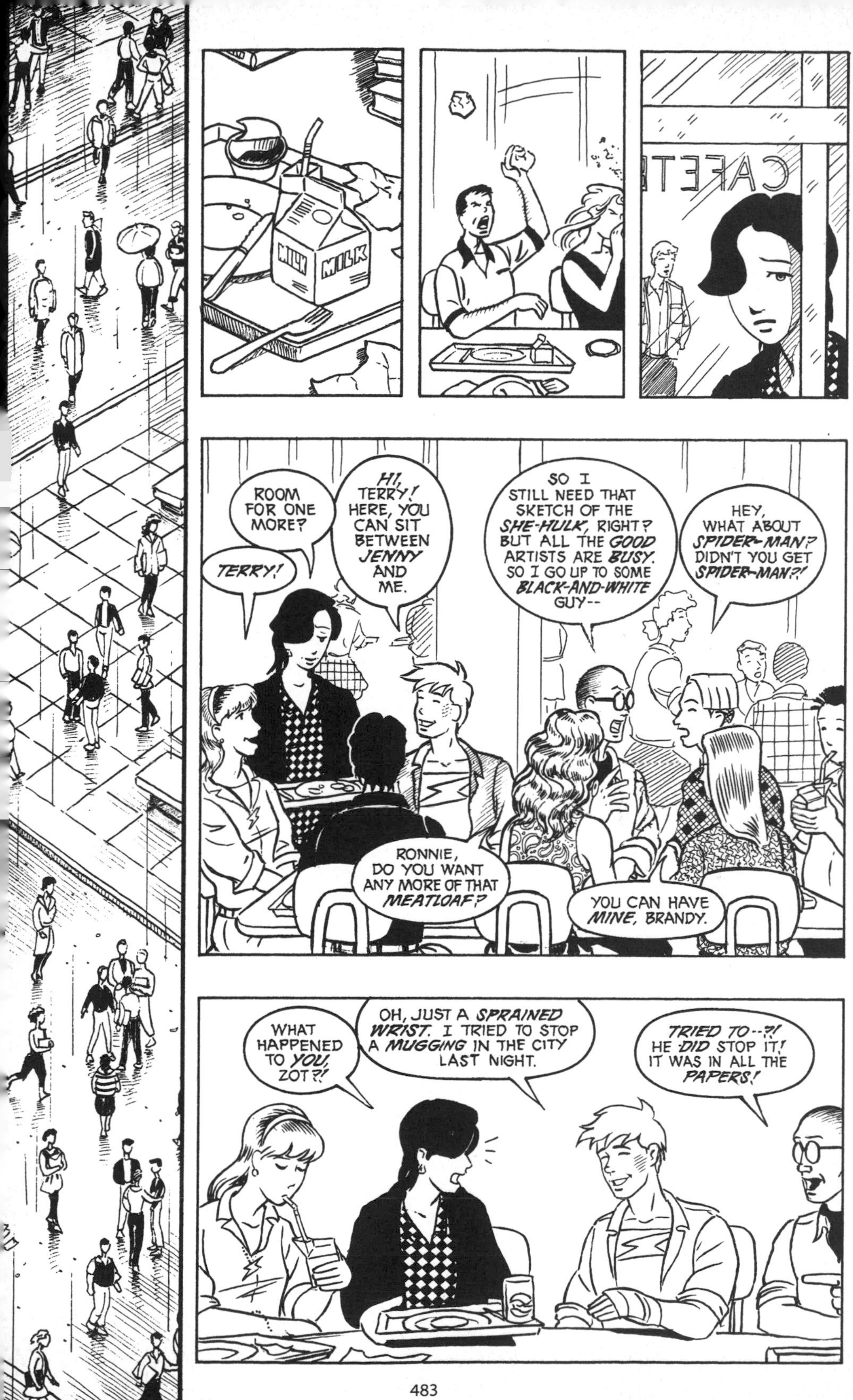
MILK
MILK
ROOM FOR ONE MORE?
TERRY!
HI, TERRY! HERE, YOU CAN SIT BETWEEN JENNY AND ME.
SO I STILL NEED THAT SKETCH OF THE SHE-HULK, RIGHT? BUT ALL THE GOOD ARTISTS ARE BUSY. SO I GO UP TO SOME BLACK-AND-WHITE GUY--
HEY, WHAT ABOUT SPIDER-MAN? DIDN'T YOU GET SPIDER-MAN?!
RONNIE, DO YOU WANT ANY MORE OF THAT MEATLOAF?
YOU CAN HAVE MINE, BRANDY.
WHAT HAPPENED TO YOU, ZOT?!
OH, JUST A SPRAINED WRIST. I TRIED TO STOP A MUGGING IN THE CITY LAST NIGHT.
TRIED TO--?! HE DID STOP IT! IT WAS IN ALL THE PAPERS!

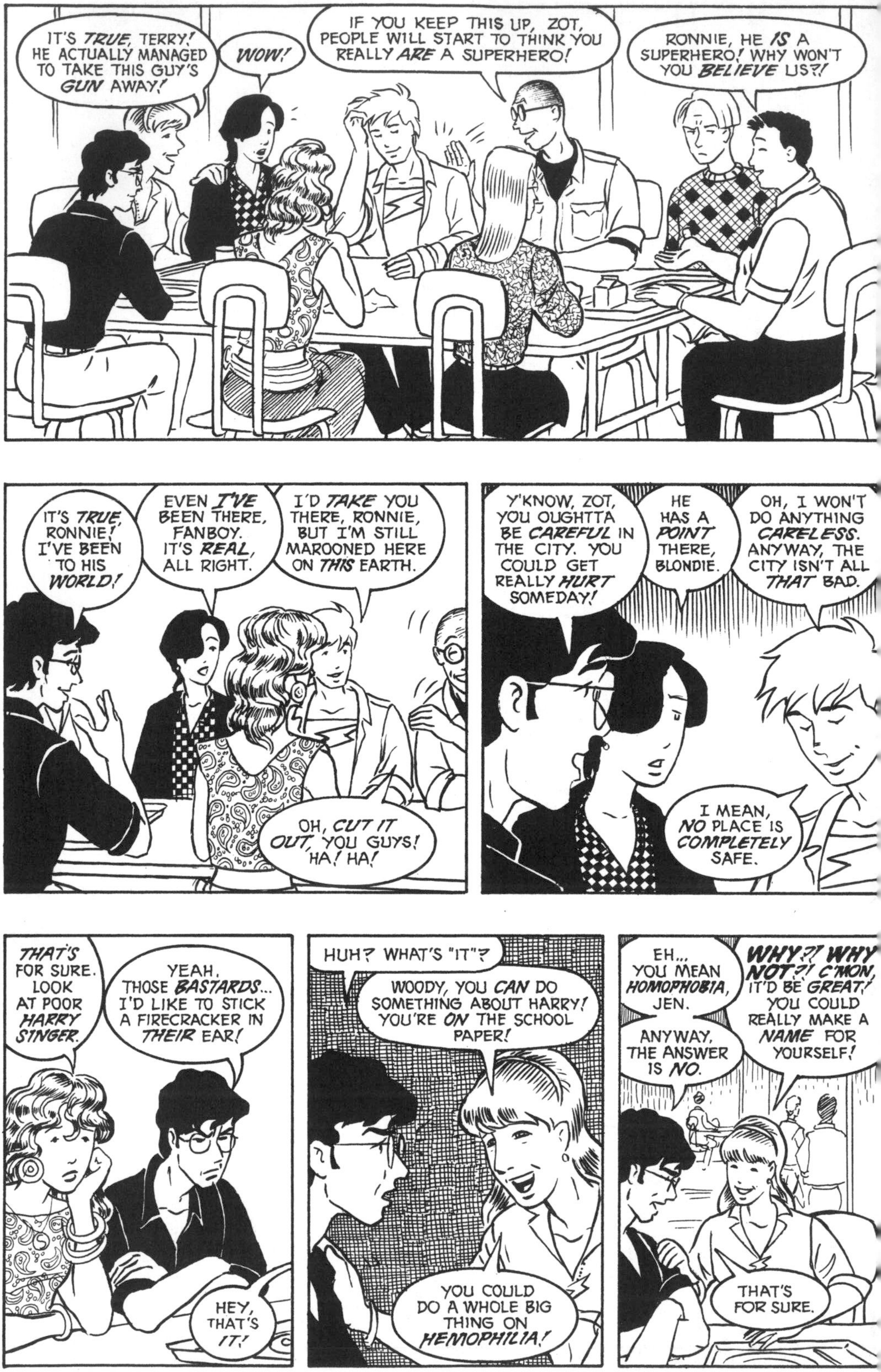
IT'S TRUE, TERRY! HE ACTUALLY MANAGED TO TAKE THIS GUY'S GUN AWAY!
WOW!
IF YOU KEEP THIS UP, ZOT, PEOPLE WILL START TO THINK YOU REALLY ARE A SUPERHERO!
RONNIE, HE IS A SUPERHERO! WHY WON'T YOU BELIEVE US?!
IT'S TRUE, RONNIE! I'VE BEEN TO HIS WORLD!
EVEN I'VE BEEN THERE, FANBOY. IT'S REAL, ALL RIGHT.
I'D TAKE YOU THERE, RONNIE, BUT I'M STILL MAROONED HERE ON THIS EARTH.
OH, CUT IT OUT, YOU GUYS! HA! HA!
Y'KNOW, ZOT, YOU OUGHTTA BE CAREFUL IN THE CITY. YOU COULD GET REALLY HURT SOMEDAY!
HE HAS A POINT THERE, BLONDIE.
OH, I WON'T DO ANYTHING CARELESS. ANYWAY, THE CITY ISN'T ALL THAT BAD.
I MEAN, NO PLACE IS COMPLETELY SAFE.
THAT'S FOR SURE. LOOK AT POOR HARRY SINGER.
YEAH, THOSE BASTARDS... I'D LIKE TO STICK A FIRECRACKER IN THEIR EAR!
HEY, THAT'S IT!
HUH? WHAT'S "IT"?
WOODY, YOU CAN DO SOMETHING ABOUT HARRY! YOU'RE ON THE SCHOOL PAPER!
YOU COULD DO A WHOLE BIG THING ON HEMOPHILIA!
EH... YOU MEAN HOMOPHOBIA, JEN.
ANYWAY, THE ANSWER IS NO.
WHY?! WHY NOT?! C'MON, IT'D BE GREAT! YOU COULD REALLY MAKE A NAME FOR YOURSELF!
THAT'S FOR SURE.

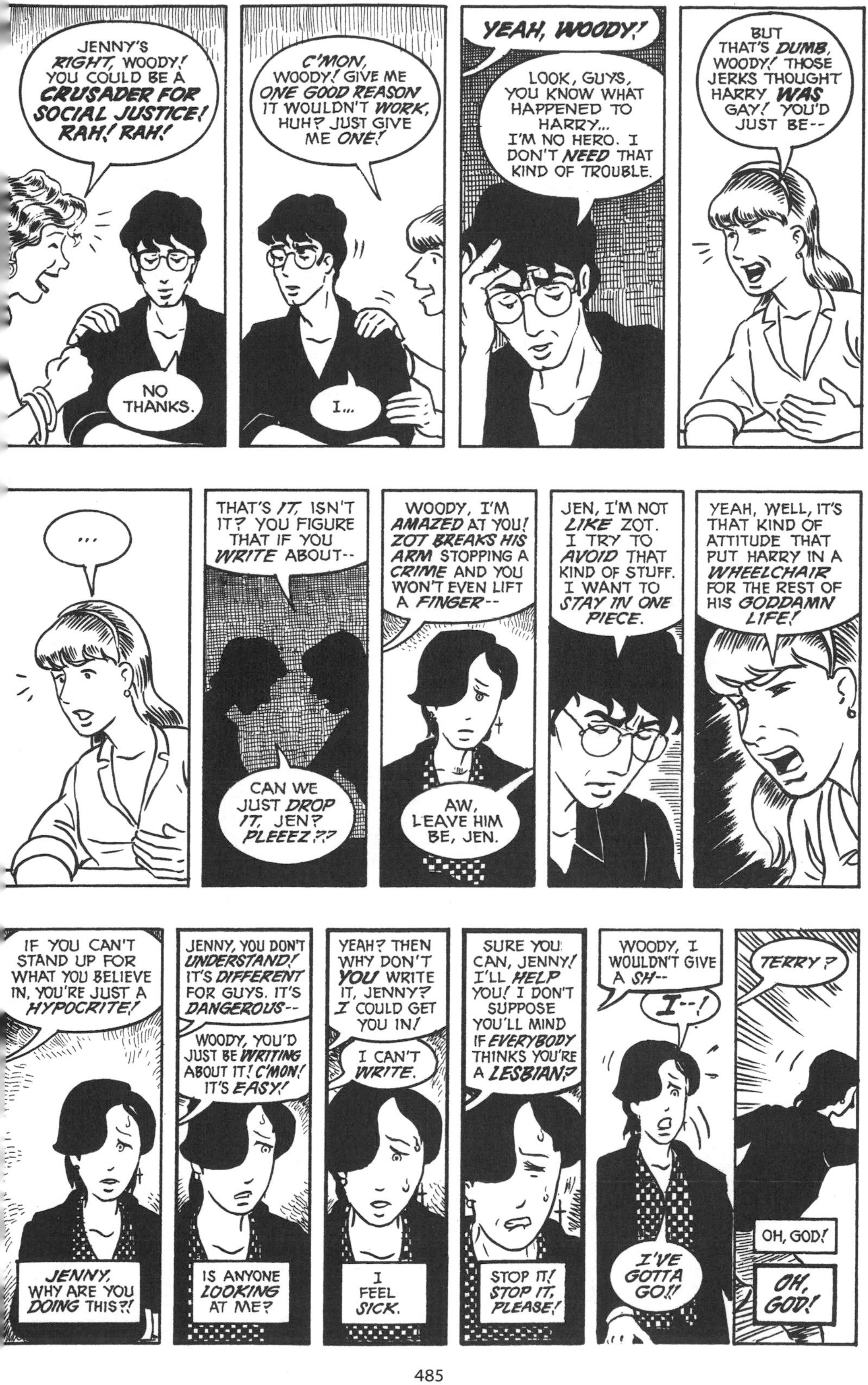
JENNY'S RIGHT, WOODY! YOU COULD BE A CRUSADER FOR SOCIAL JUSTICE! RAH! RAH!
NO THANKS.
C'MON, WOODY! GIVE ME ONE GOOD REASON IT WOULDN'T WORK, HUH? JUST GIVE ME ONE!
I...
YEAH, WOODY!
LOOK, GUYS, YOU KNOW WHAT HAPPENED TO HARRY... I'M NO HERO. I DON'T NEED THAT KIND OF TROUBLE.
BUT THAT'S DUMB, WOODY! THOSE JERKS THOUGHT HARRY WAS GAY! YOU'D JUST BE--
...
THAT'S IT, ISN'T IT? YOU FIGURE THAT IF YOU WRITE ABOUT--
CAN WE JUST DROP IT, JEN? PLEEEZ??
WOODY, I'M AMAZED AT YOU! ZOT BREAKS HIS ARM STOPPING A CRIME AND YOU WON'T EVEN LIFT A FINGER--
AW, LEAVE HIM BE, JEN.
JEN, I'M NOT LIKE ZOT. I TRY TO AVOID THAT KIND OF STUFF. I WANT TO STAY IN ONE PIECE.
YEAH, WELL, IT'S THAT KIND OF ATTITUDE THAT PUT HARRY IN A WHEELCHAIR FOR THE REST OF HIS GODDAMN LIFE!
IF YOU CAN'T STAND UP FOR WHAT YOU BELIEVE IN, YOU'RE JUST A HYPOCRITE!
JENNY, WHY ARE YOU DOING THIS?!
JENNY, YOU DON'T UNDERSTAND! IT'S DIFFERENT FOR GUYS. IT'S DANGEROUS--
WOODY, YOU'D JUST BE WRITING ABOUT IT! C'MON! IT'S EASY!
IS ANYONE LOOKING AT ME?
YEAH? THEN WHY DON'T YOU WRITE IT, JENNY? I COULD GET YOU IN!
I CAN'T WRITE.
I FEEL SICK.
SURE YOU CAN, JENNY! I'LL HELP YOU! I DON'T SUPPOSE YOU'LL MIND IF EVERYBODY THINKS YOU'RE A LESBIAN?
STOP IT! STOP IT, PLEASE!
WOODY, I WOULDN'T GIVE A SH--
I--!
I'VE GOTTA GO!!
TERRY?
OH, GOD!
OH, GOD!

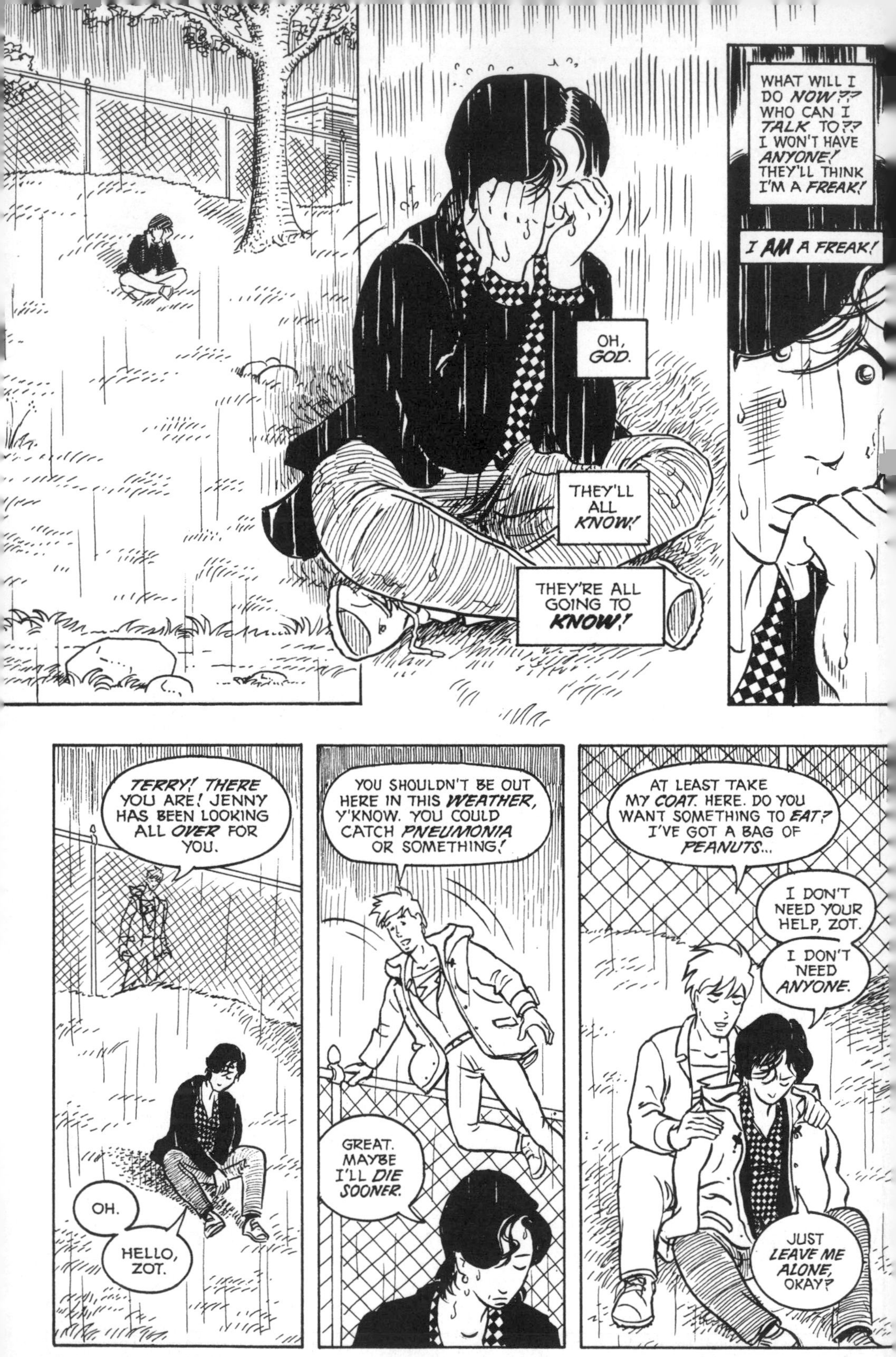
OH, GOD.
THEY'LL ALL KNOW!
THEY'RE ALL GOING TO KNOW!
WHAT WILL I DO NOW?? WHO CAN I TALK TO?? I WON'T HAVE ANYONE! THEY'LL THINK I'M A FREAK!
I AM A FREAK!
TERRY! THERE YOU ARE! JENNY HAS BEEN LOOKING ALL OVER FOR YOU.
OH.
HELLO, ZOT.
YOU SHOULDN'T BE OUT HERE IN THIS WEATHER, Y'KNOW. YOU COULD CATCH PNEUMONIA OR SOMETHING!
GREAT. MAYBE I'LL DIE SOONER.
AT LEAST TAKE MY COAT. HERE. DO YOU WANT SOMETHING TO EAT? I'VE GOT A BAG OF PEANUTS...
I DON'T NEED YOUR HELP, ZOT.
I DON'T NEED ANYONE.
JUST LEAVE ME ALONE, OKAY?

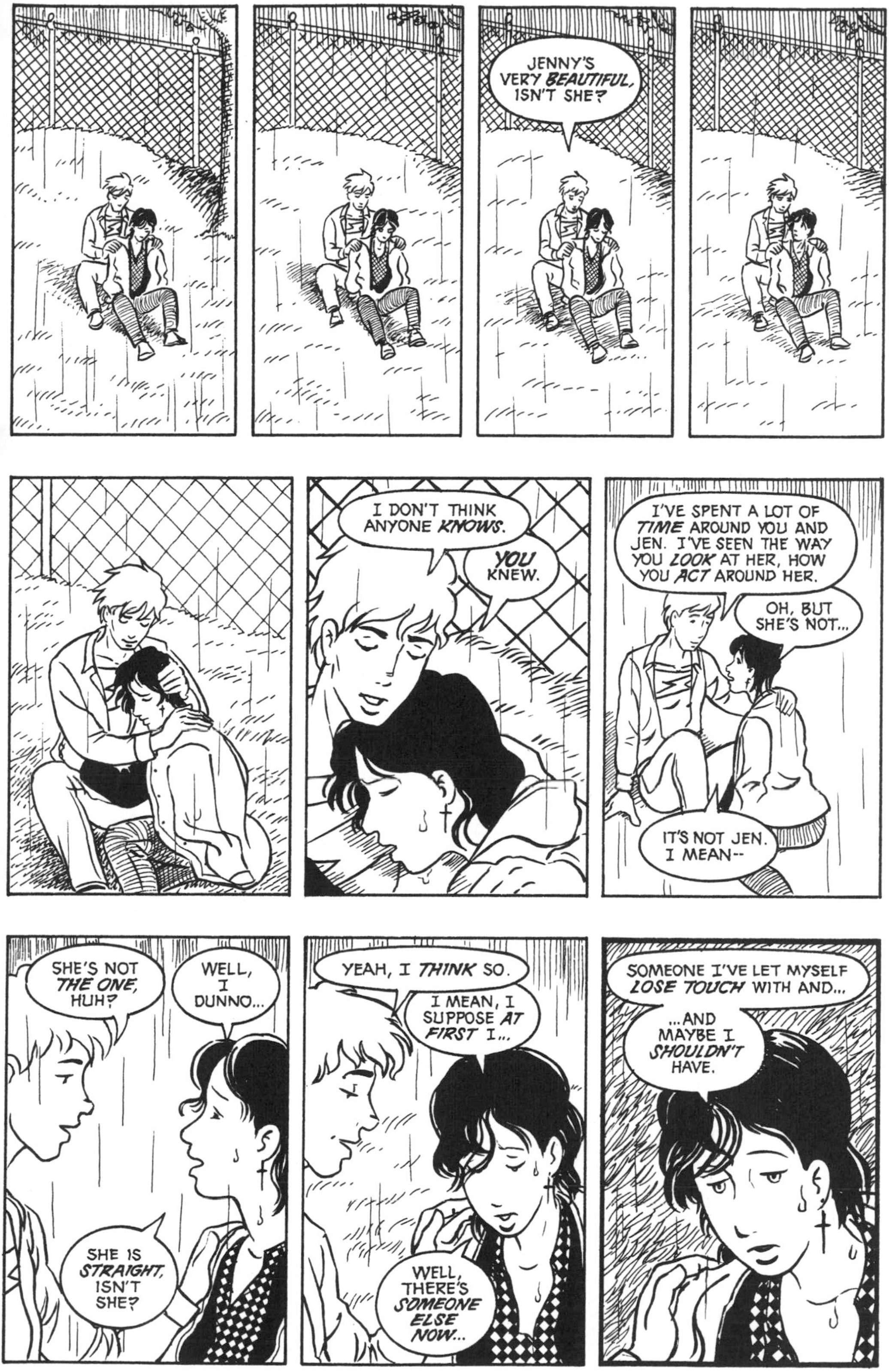
JENNY'S VERY *BEAUTIFUL,* ISN'T SHE?
I DON'T THINK ANYONE *KNOWS.*
YOU KNEW.
I'VE SPENT A LOT OF *TIME* AROUND YOU AND JEN. I'VE SEEN THE WAY YOU *LOOK* AT HER, HOW YOU *ACT* AROUND HER.
OH, BUT SHE'S NOT...
IT'S NOT JEN. I MEAN--
SHE'S NOT *THE ONE,* HUH?
WELL, I DUNNO...
SHE IS *STRAIGHT,* ISN'T SHE?
YEAH, I *THINK* SO.
I MEAN, I SUPPOSE *AT FIRST* I...
WELL, THERE'S *SOMEONE ELSE NOW...*
SOMEONE I'VE LET MYSELF *LOSE TOUCH* WITH AND...
...AND MAYBE I *SHOULDN'T* HAVE.

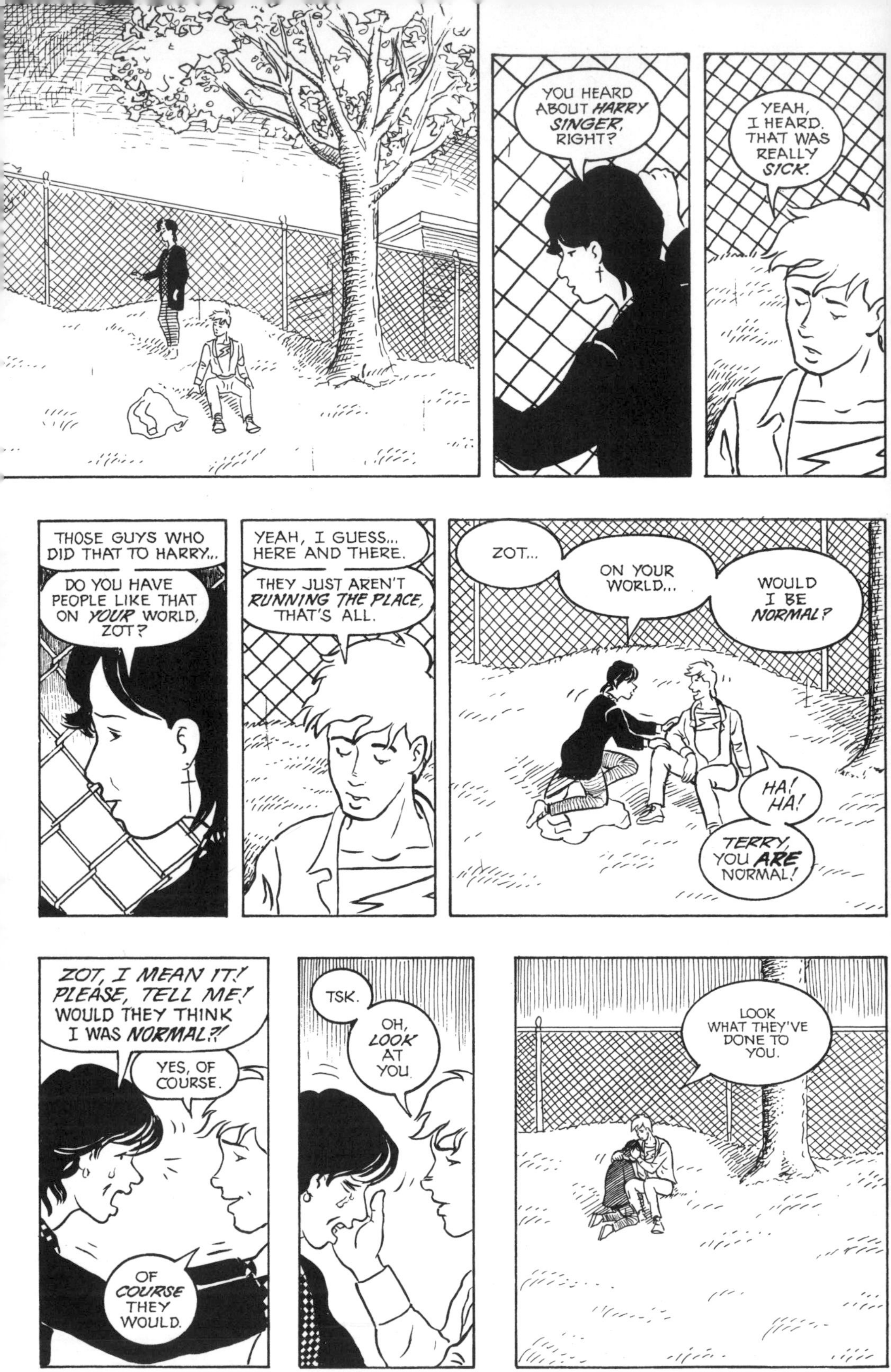
YOU HEARD ABOUT HARRY SINGER, RIGHT?
YEAH, I HEARD. THAT WAS REALLY SICK.
THOSE GUYS WHO DID THAT TO HARRY...
DO YOU HAVE PEOPLE LIKE THAT ON YOUR WORLD, ZOT?
YEAH, I GUESS... HERE AND THERE.
THEY JUST AREN'T RUNNING THE PLACE, THAT'S ALL.
ZOT...
ON YOUR WORLD...
WOULD I BE NORMAL?
HA! HA!
TERRY, YOU ARE NORMAL!
ZOT, I MEAN IT! PLEASE, TELL ME! WOULD THEY THINK I WAS NORMAL?!
YES, OF COURSE.
OF COURSE THEY WOULD.
TSK.
OH, LOOK AT YOU.
LOOK WHAT THEY'VE DONE TO YOU.

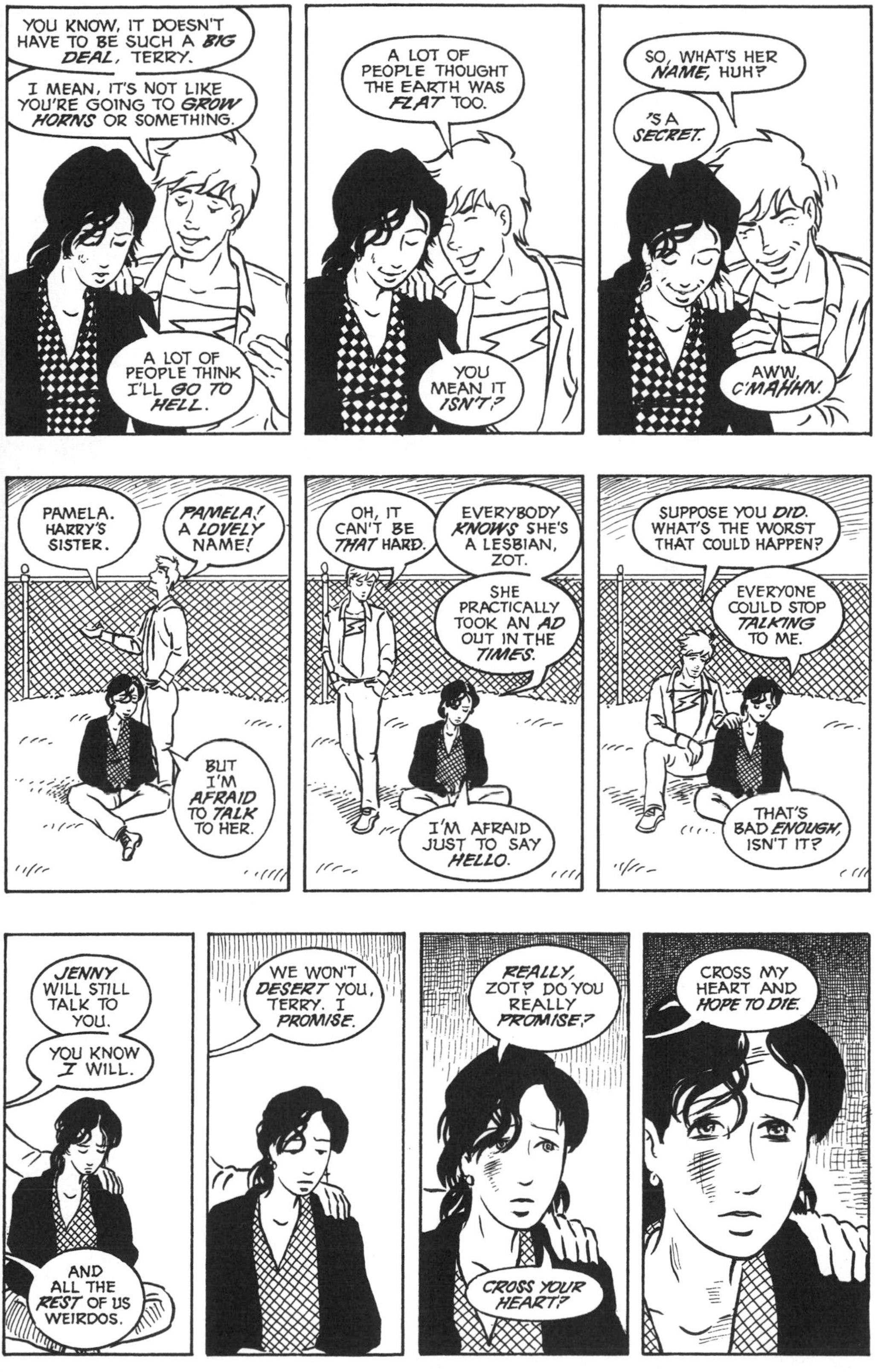
YOU KNOW, IT DOESN'T HAVE TO BE SUCH A BIG DEAL, TERRY.
I MEAN, IT'S NOT LIKE YOU'RE GOING TO GROW HORNS OR SOMETHING.
A LOT OF PEOPLE THINK I'LL GO TO HELL.
A LOT OF PEOPLE THOUGHT THE EARTH WAS FLAT TOO.
YOU MEAN IT ISN'T?
SO, WHAT'S HER NAME, HUH?
'S A SECRET.
AWW, C'MAHHN.
PAMELA. HARRY'S SISTER.
PAMELA! A LOVELY NAME!
BUT I'M AFRAID TO TALK TO HER.
OH, IT CAN'T BE THAT HARD.
EVERYBODY KNOWS SHE'S A LESBIAN, ZOT.
SHE PRACTICALLY TOOK AN AD OUT IN THE TIMES.
I'M AFRAID JUST TO SAY HELLO.
SUPPOSE YOU DID. WHAT'S THE WORST THAT COULD HAPPEN?
EVERYONE COULD STOP TALKING TO ME.
THAT'S BAD ENOUGH, ISN'T IT?
JENNY WILL STILL TALK TO YOU.
YOU KNOW I WILL.
AND ALL THE REST OF US WEIRDOS.
WE WON'T DESERT YOU, TERRY. I PROMISE.
REALLY, ZOT? DO YOU REALLY PROMISE?
CROSS YOUR HEART?
CROSS MY HEART AND HOPE TO DIE.

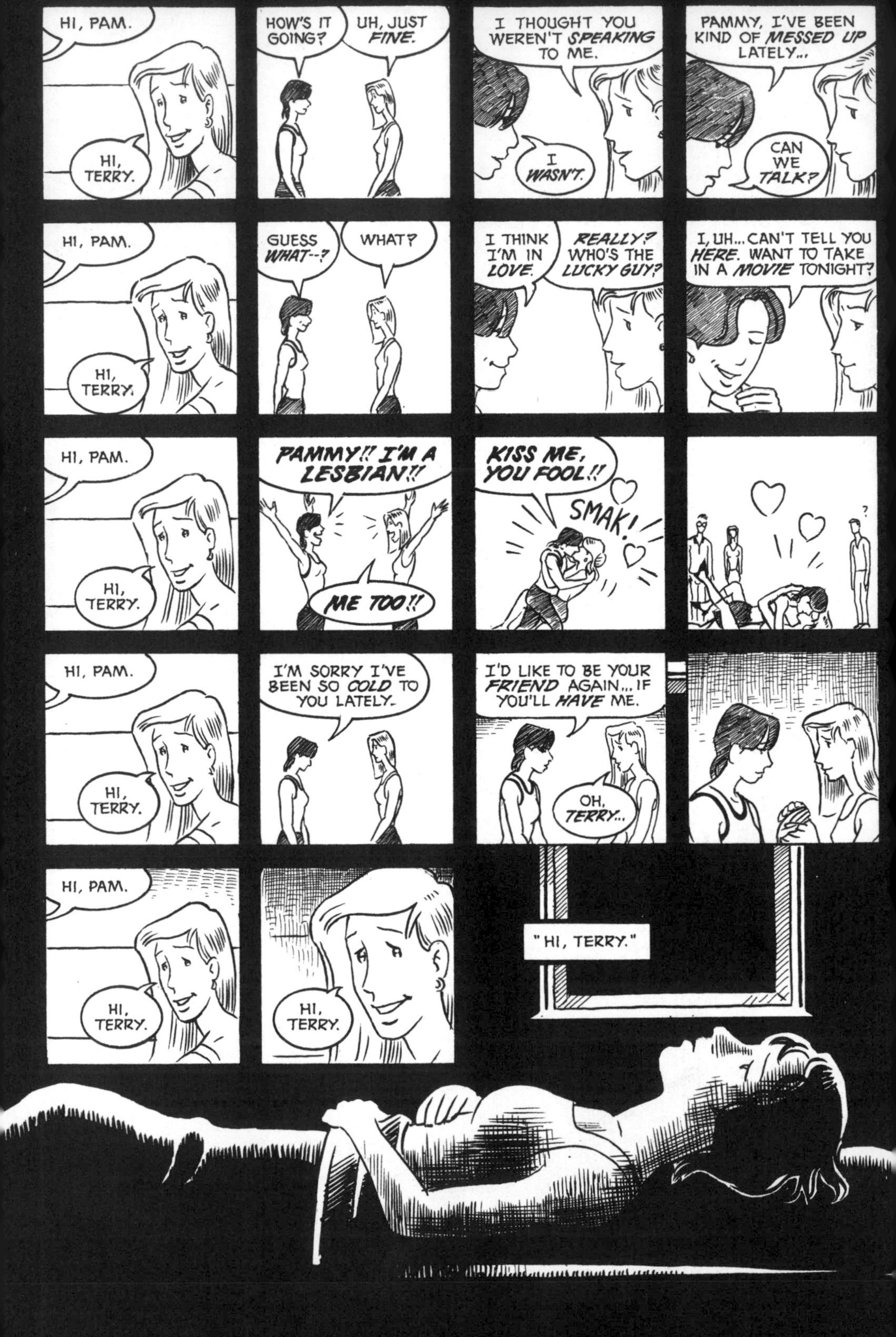
HI, PAM.
HI, TERRY.
HOW'S IT GOING?
UH, JUST *FINE*.
I THOUGHT YOU WEREN'T *SPEAKING* TO ME.
I *WASN'T*.
PAMMY, I'VE BEEN KIND OF *MESSED UP* LATELY...
CAN WE *TALK?*
HI, PAM.
HI, TERRY.
GUESS *WHAT--?*
WHAT?
I THINK I'M IN *LOVE*.
REALLY? WHO'S THE *LUCKY GUY?*
I, UH... CAN'T TELL YOU *HERE*. WANT TO TAKE IN A *MOVIE* TONIGHT?
HI, PAM.
HI, TERRY.
PAMMY!! I'M A LESBIAN!!
ME TOO!!
KISS ME, YOU FOOL!!
SMAK!
?
HI, PAM.
HI, TERRY.
I'M SORRY I'VE BEEN SO *COLD* TO YOU LATELY.
I'D LIKE TO BE YOUR *FRIEND* AGAIN... IF YOU'LL *HAVE* ME.
OH, *TERRY*...
HI, PAM.
HI, TERRY.
HI, TERRY.
"HI, TERRY."

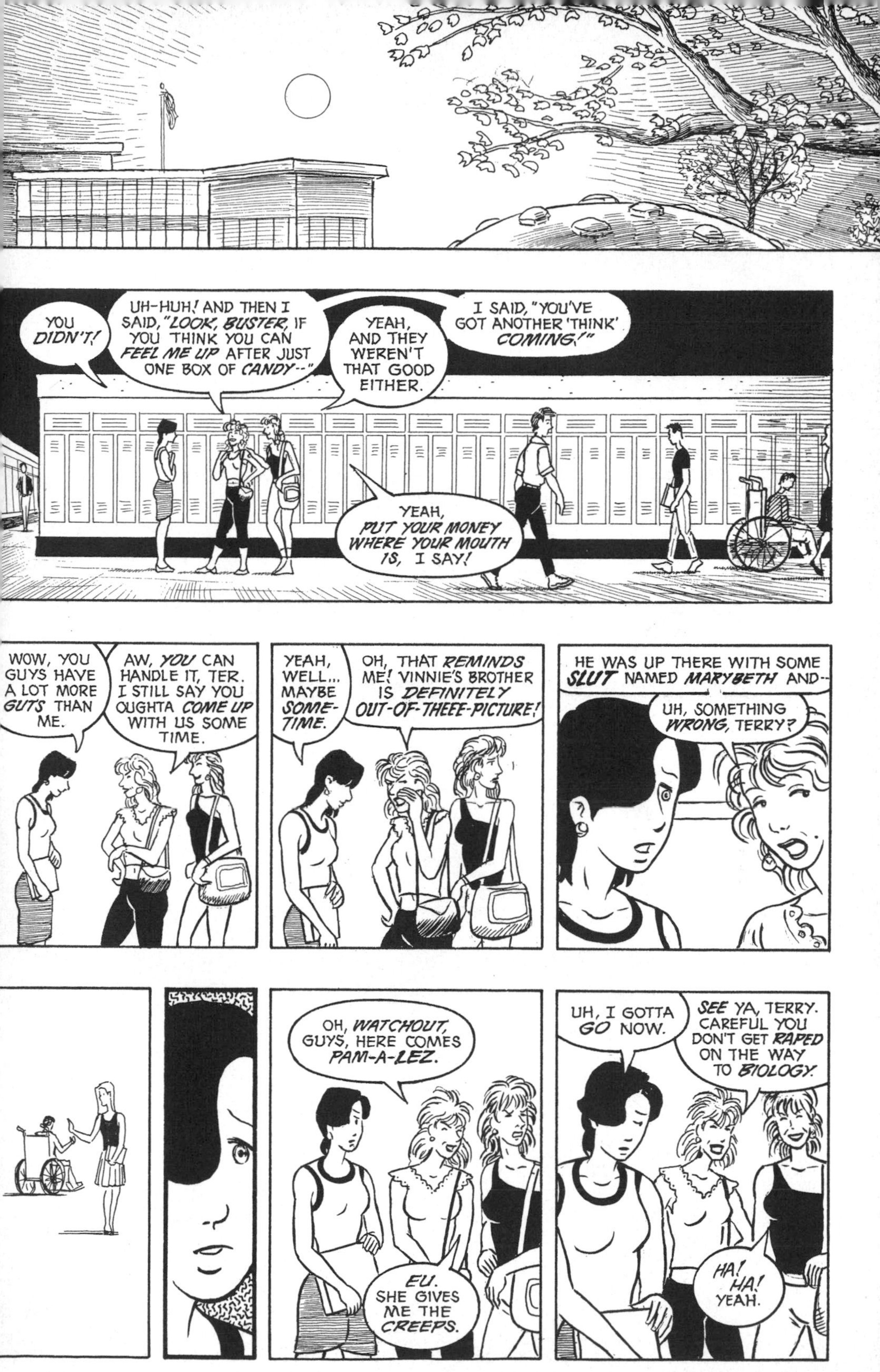
YOU DIDN'T!
UH-HUH! AND THEN I SAID, "LOOK, BUSTER, IF YOU THINK YOU CAN FEEL ME UP AFTER JUST ONE BOX OF CANDY--"
YEAH, AND THEY WEREN'T THAT GOOD EITHER.
I SAID, "YOU'VE GOT ANOTHER 'THINK' COMING!"
YEAH, PUT YOUR MONEY WHERE YOUR MOUTH IS, I SAY!
WOW, YOU GUYS HAVE A LOT MORE GUTS THAN ME.
AW, YOU CAN HANDLE IT, TER. I STILL SAY YOU OUGHTA COME UP WITH US SOME TIME.
YEAH, WELL... MAYBE SOME-TIME.
OH, THAT REMINDS ME! VINNIE'S BROTHER IS DEFINITELY OUT-OF-THEEE-PICTURE!
HE WAS UP THERE WITH SOME SLUT NAMED MARYBETH AND--
UH, SOMETHING WRONG, TERRY?
OH, WATCHOUT, GUYS, HERE COMES PAM-A-LEZ.
EU. SHE GIVES ME THE CREEPS.
UH, I GOTTA GO NOW.
SEE YA, TERRY. CAREFUL YOU DON'T GET RAPED ON THE WAY TO BIOLOGY.
HA! HA! YEAH.

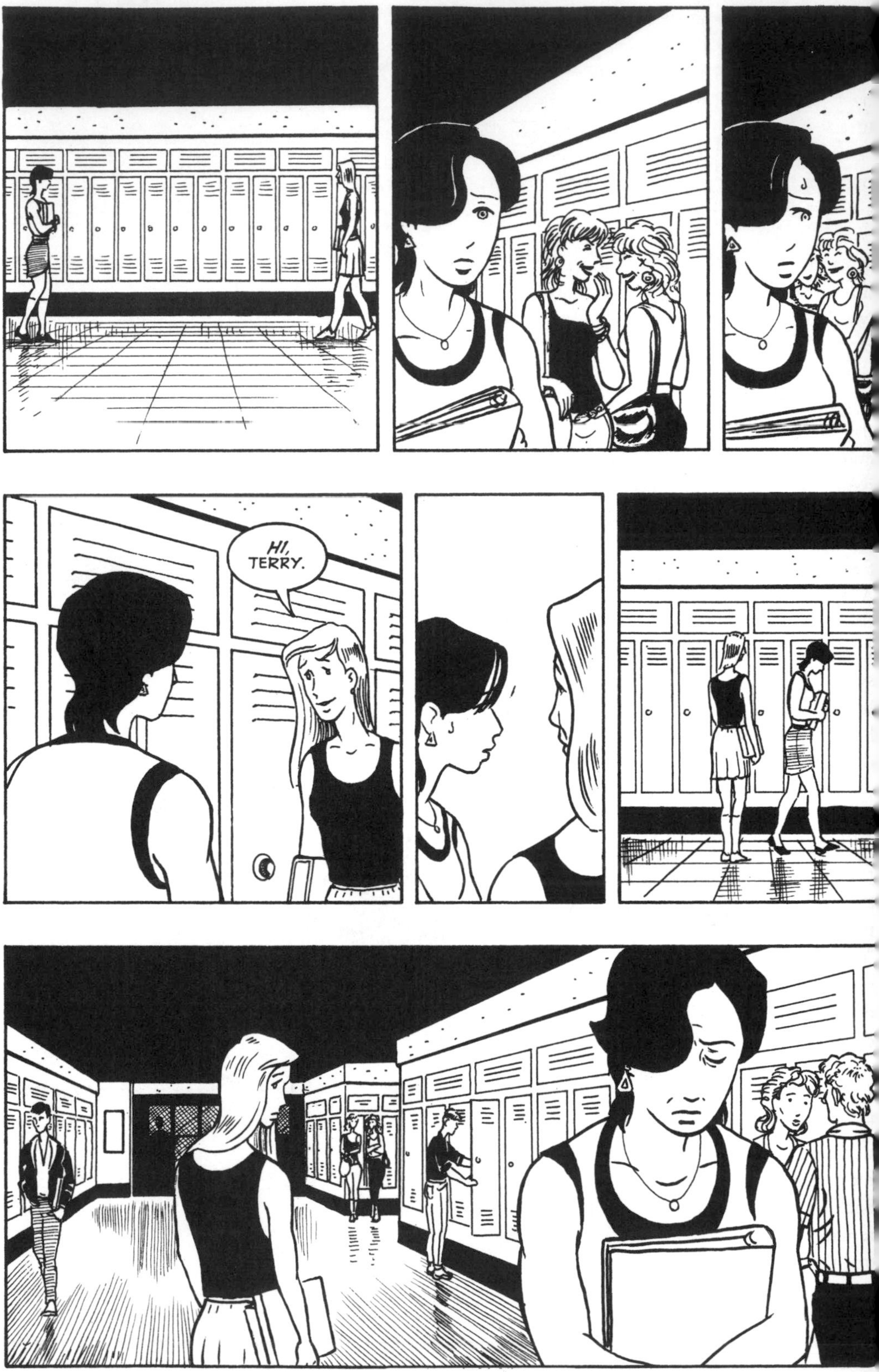
HI, TERRY.

Whatever its virtues or flaws as a story, "Normal" is the issue that left the most lasting impression on *Zot!*'s readers, many of whom have told me their own experiences in the intervening years and the ways in which Terry connected to them. Reaction was mostly positive at the time; I was preaching to the converted in the progressive independent comics scene. One of the exceptions, a longtime reader with religious objections to homosexuality, wrote an earnest, strongly worded objection to the story, but then kept reading the series and commenting, which I thought was awfully charitable of him.

The climate in 1990 for such a story was mixed. On the one hand, underground and erotic comics had dealt with sexual identity issues long before I entered the fray, and magazines and newspaper with gay and lesbian readerships regularly showcased great comics from significant talents like Howard Cruse and Alison Bechdel. On the other hand, the popular mainstream publishers Marvel and DC that dominated comics stores and subscribed to the rigid Comics Code Authority had a zero tolerance policy for openly gay heroes (at least for another two years, though that's another story).

Zot! was a different animal entirely, however—neither fish nor fowl. As part of the ground-level independent comics wing, featuring a superhero in the title role, it was allowed to share the shelves with more mainstream fare and wasn't hidden behind an "over 18" curtain or banished entirely. This meant that for a young reader questioning his or her sexuality in 1990, *Zot!* #33 stood a decent chance of being their earliest encounter with such themes in a comic book. For those readers, I'm grateful for the opportunity to have been there and told them that they had nothing to be ashamed of, and of all the moments from "Normal" I've heard repeated back to me across the years, I think Zot's remark "Look what they've done to you" is the one that readers remember most vividly.

That, and the trick ending.

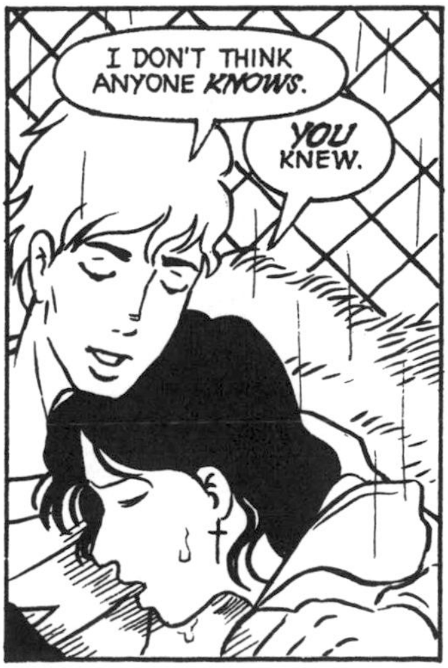
I DON'T THINK ANYONE *KNOWS*.
YOU KNEW.

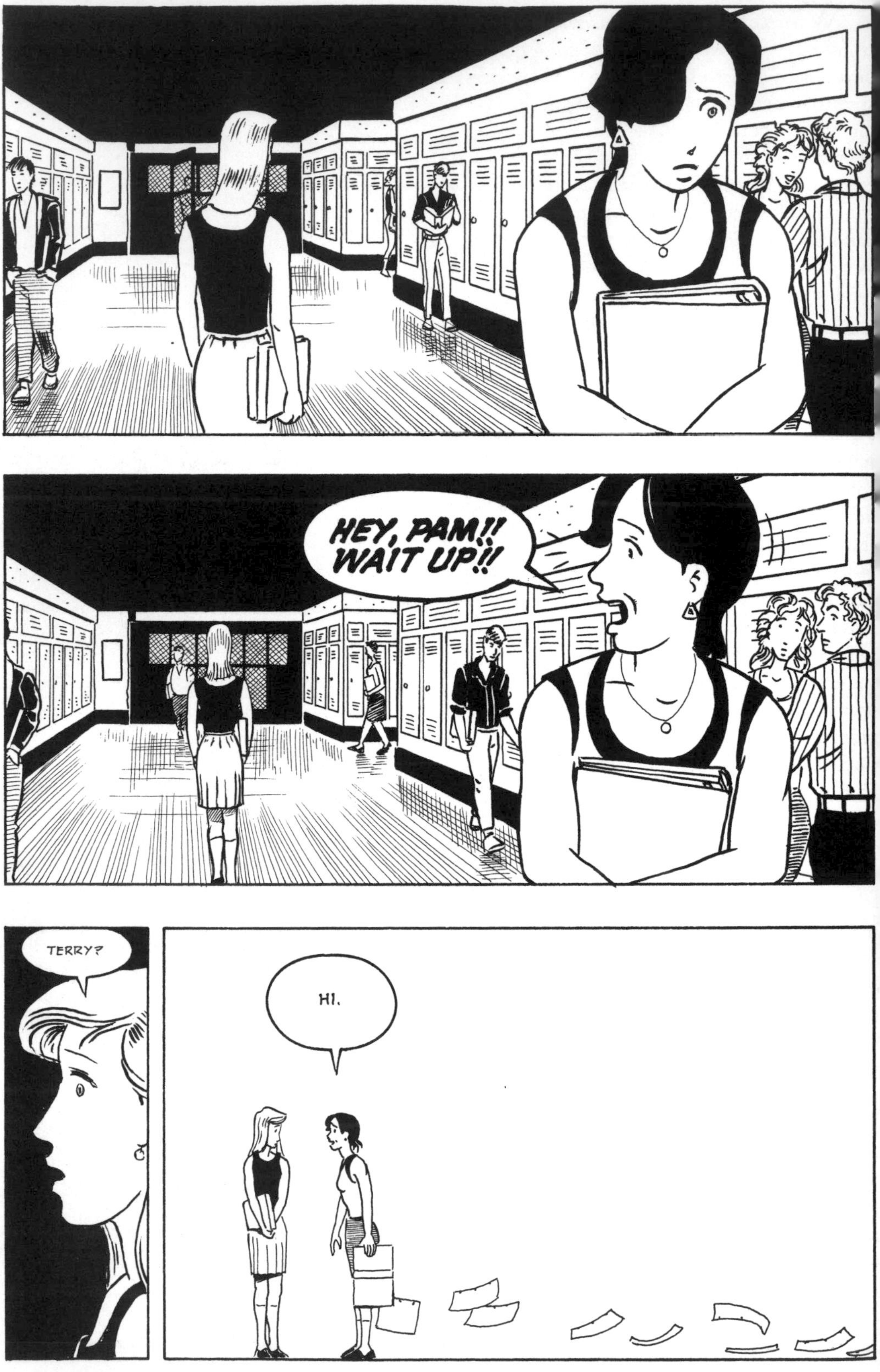
HEY, PAM!! WAIT UP!!
TERRY?
HI.

When originally laying out issue #33, I planned to end Terry's story with the downbeat missed opportunity seen on the previous spread. It seemed the more plausible real-world ending to a situation of that kind, at least in the average American high school. In the end, though, I decided that even though I'd sidelined the guy in the red suit, this was still a *Zot!* story, and that meant that in close contests between hope and disillusionment, hope should at least win the coin toss.

Adding the nineteenth page seen here provided an interesting challenge though. It was customary to end all *Zot!* stories on the left-hand page, allowing the letters pages to start on the facing right hand page. If we had just added the extra page, it would have thrown off that tradition, so I placed the new last page after the first letters page, hiding it from view in much the same way I did here, and providing a welcome surprise for most readers (at least those who hadn't peeked ahead to see if their letter had been printed).

Years later, I discovered that a few readers were so upset by the grim first ending that they put the issue down and wouldn't look at it again, unaware of the second ending for hours or even days. I wonder sometimes if there isn't a disgruntled 32-year-old former *Zot!* fan somewhere out there who gave up with issue #33, page 18, and still has no idea that Terry ever turned around.

Compared to a modern multilayered graphic novel with sexual themes like Bechdel's *Fun Home,* such a short, simple story may seem no more substantial than the comics equivalent of an old CBS after-school special or public service announcement. But even if that's true, I still have no regrets about the story. Even baby steps serve a purpose if they're in the right direction, and I'd like to think that's where I was heading.

As I write this in 2008, our local news in southern California is reporting from a middle school in nearby Oxnard, where an openly gay student named Lawrence King had actually dared to wear feminine clothes to school and apparently ruffled a few feathers in the process.

As Lawrence sat in computer class last Tuesday, one of his classmates walked up to him, pulled out a handgun, and shot the him in the head.

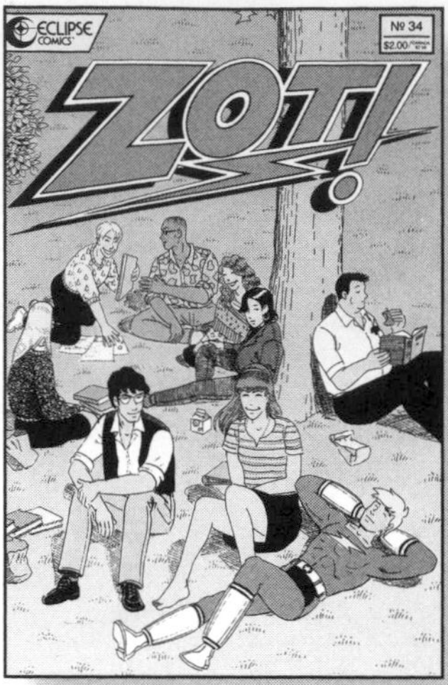
ECLIPSE
COMICS
Nº 34
$2.00
ZOT!

Sometimes, a Direction...

First published in *Zot! #34*.

Lettering:

Bob Lappan

Original series editor:

cat yronwode

Plot assist:

Ivy Ratafia

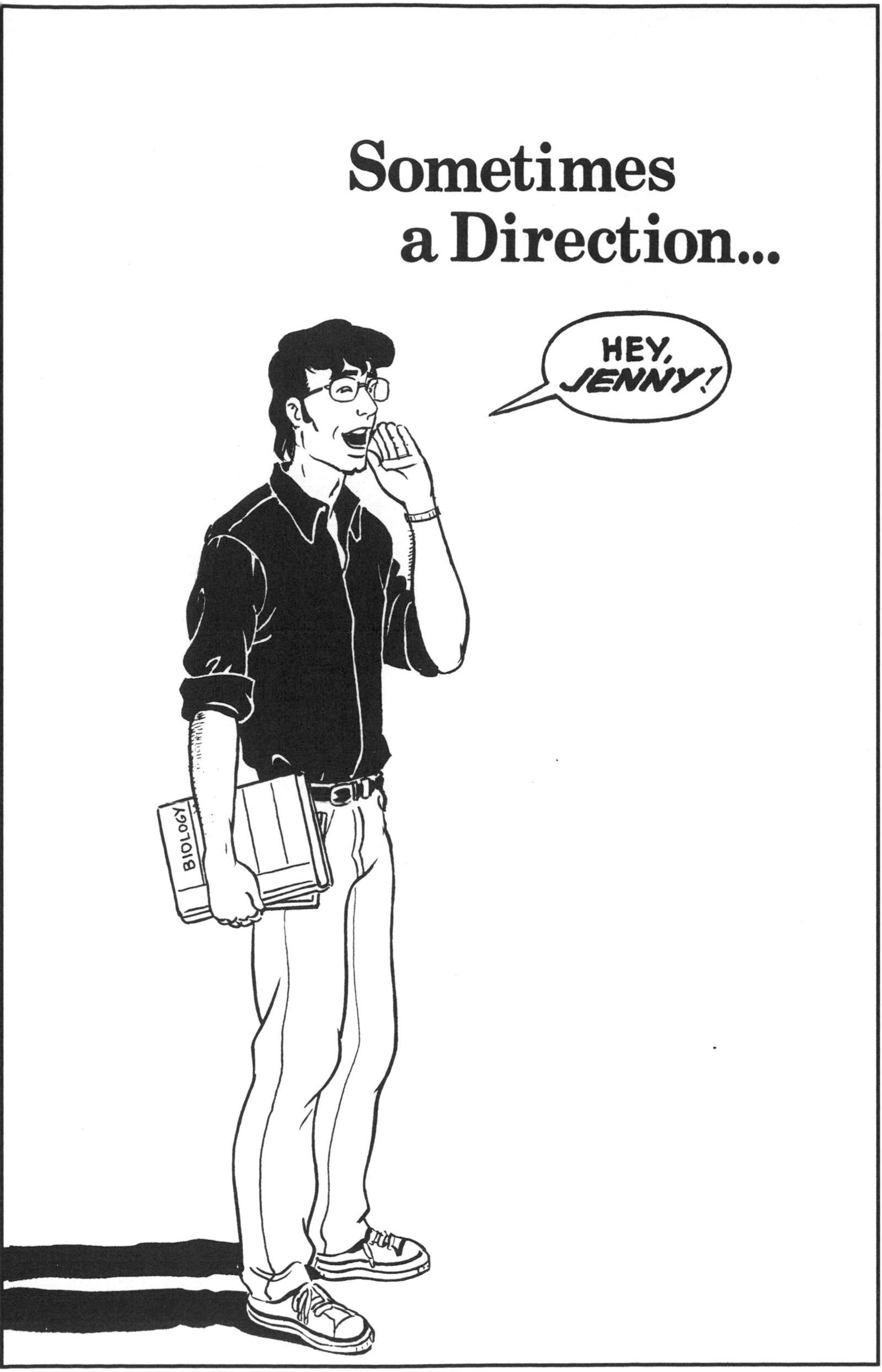
Sometimes a Direction...
HEY, JENNY!
BIOLOGY

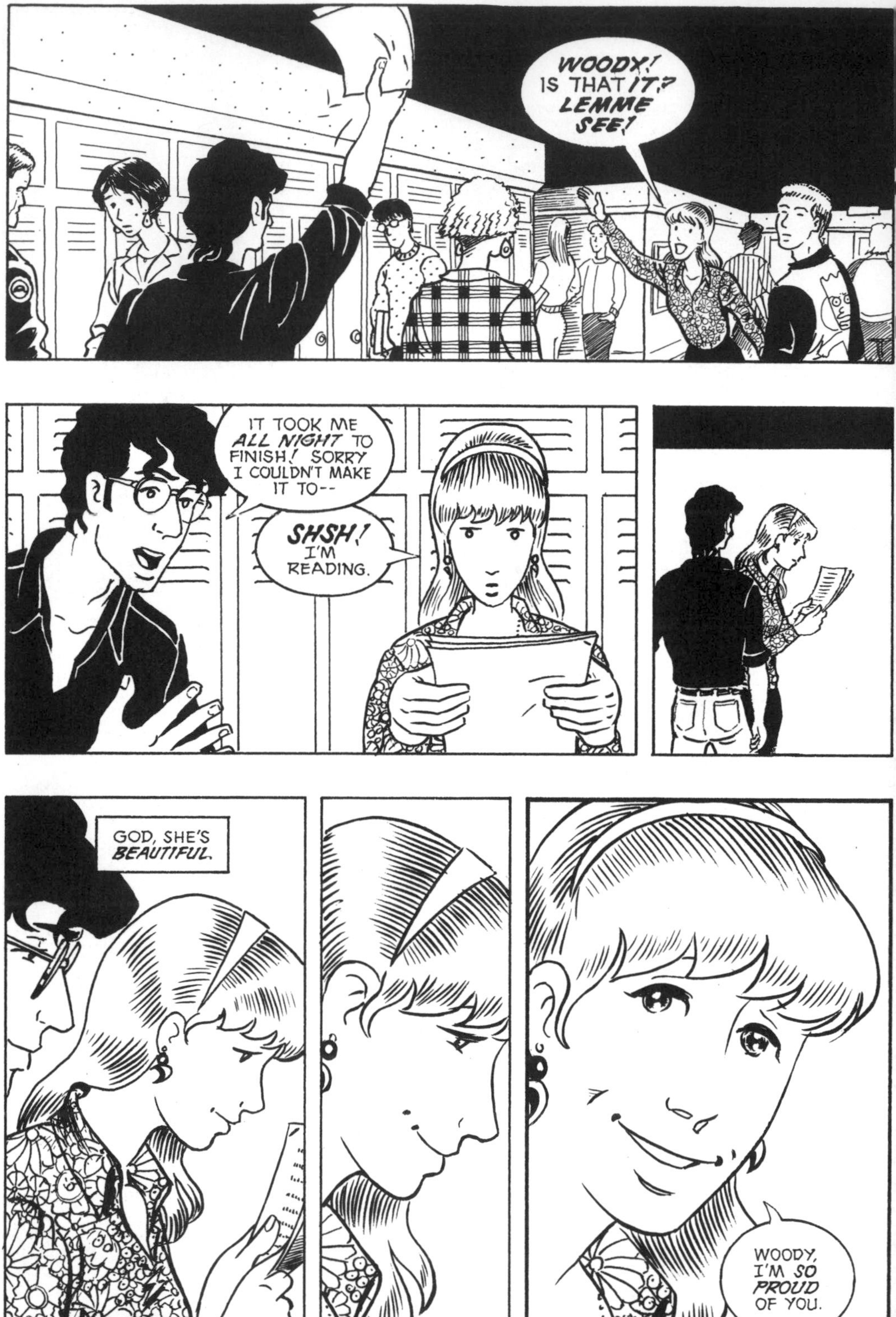
WOODY! IS THAT IT?? LEMME SEE!
IT TOOK ME ALL NIGHT TO FINISH! SORRY I COULDN'T MAKE IT TO--
SHSH! I'M READING.
GOD, SHE'S BEAUTIFUL.
WOODY, I'M SO PROUD OF YOU.

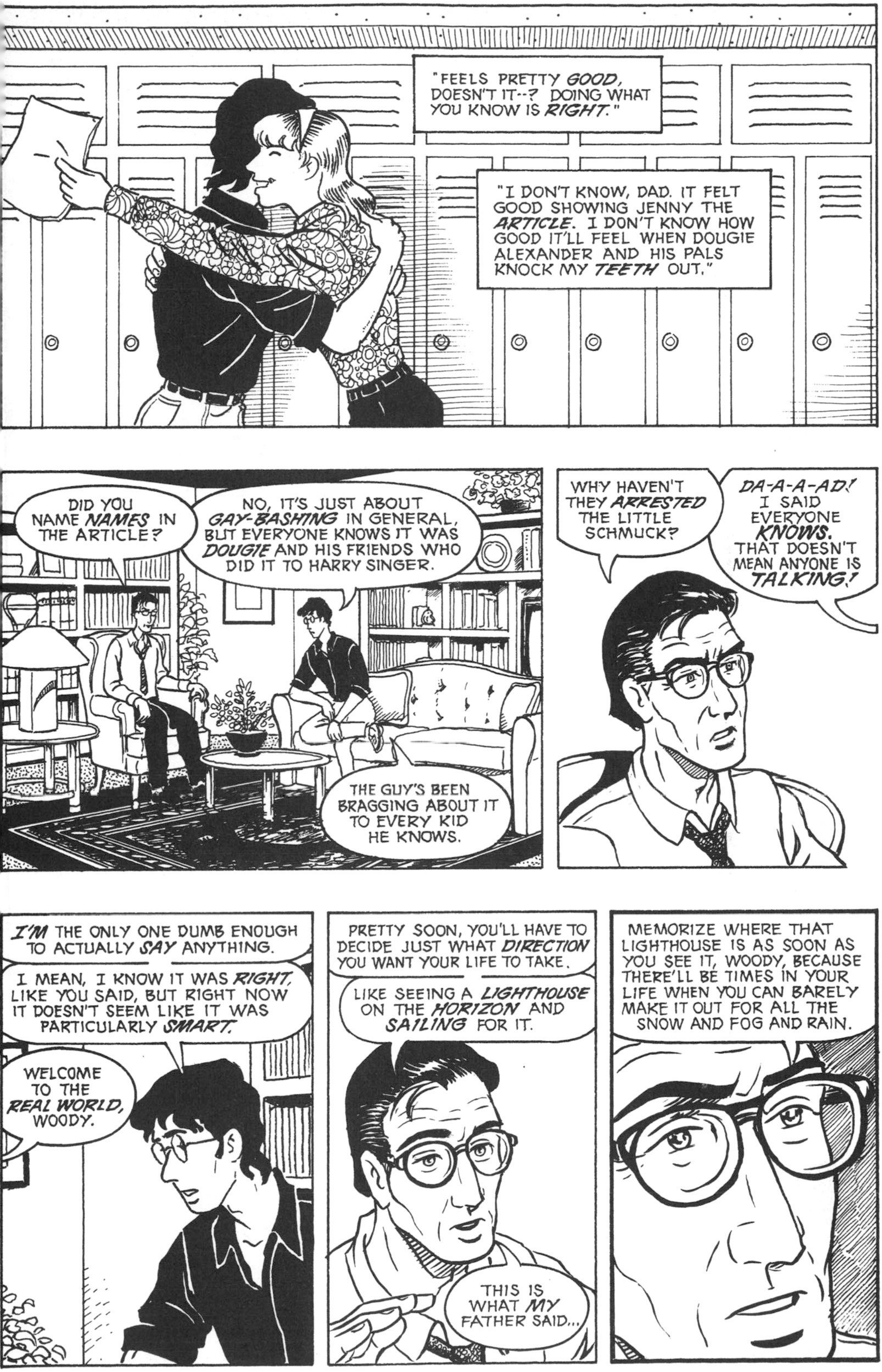
"FEELS PRETTY GOOD, DOESN'T IT--? DOING WHAT YOU KNOW IS RIGHT."
"I DON'T KNOW, DAD. IT FELT GOOD SHOWING JENNY THE ARTICLE. I DON'T KNOW HOW GOOD IT'LL FEEL WHEN DOUGIE ALEXANDER AND HIS PALS KNOCK MY TEETH OUT."
DID YOU NAME NAMES IN THE ARTICLE?
NO, IT'S JUST ABOUT GAY-BASHING IN GENERAL, BUT EVERYONE KNOWS IT WAS DOUGIE AND HIS FRIENDS WHO DID IT TO HARRY SINGER.
THE GUY'S BEEN BRAGGING ABOUT IT TO EVERY KID HE KNOWS.
WHY HAVEN'T THEY ARRESTED THE LITTLE SCHMUCK?
DA-A-A-AD! I SAID EVERYONE KNOWS. THAT DOESN'T MEAN ANYONE IS TALKING!
I'M THE ONLY ONE DUMB ENOUGH TO ACTUALLY SAY ANYTHING.
I MEAN, I KNOW IT WAS RIGHT, LIKE YOU SAID, BUT RIGHT NOW IT DOESN'T SEEM LIKE IT WAS PARTICULARLY SMART.
WELCOME TO THE REAL WORLD, WOODY.
PRETTY SOON, YOU'LL HAVE TO DECIDE JUST WHAT DIRECTION YOU WANT YOUR LIFE TO TAKE.
LIKE SEEING A LIGHTHOUSE ON THE HORIZON AND SAILING FOR IT.
THIS IS WHAT MY FATHER SAID...
MEMORIZE WHERE THAT LIGHTHOUSE IS AS SOON AS YOU SEE IT, WOODY, BECAUSE THERE'LL BE TIMES IN YOUR LIFE WHEN YOU CAN BARELY MAKE IT OUT FOR ALL THE SNOW AND FOG AND RAIN.

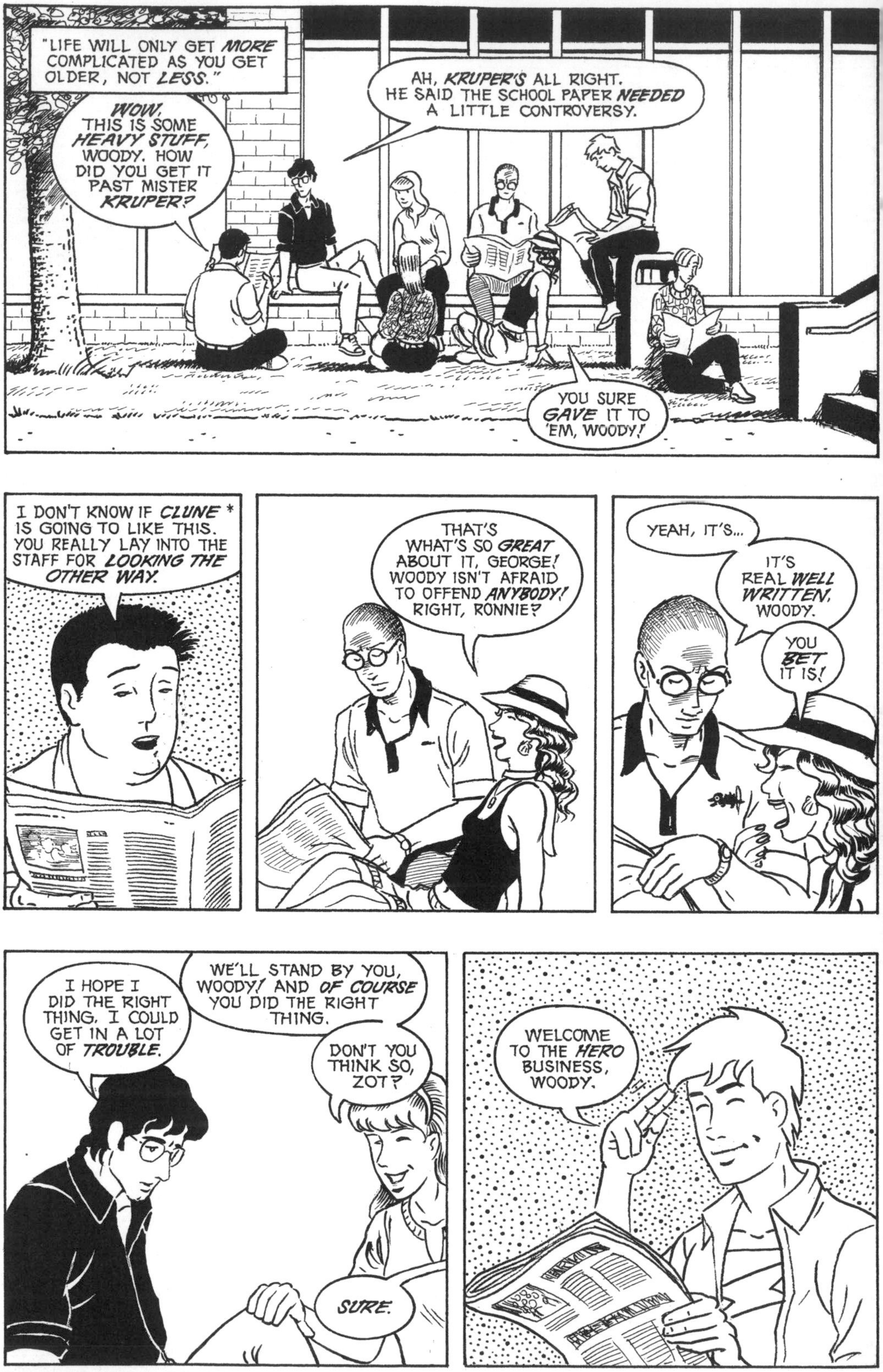
"LIFE WILL ONLY GET *MORE* COMPLICATED AS YOU GET OLDER, NOT *LESS*."
WOW. THIS IS SOME *HEAVY STUFF,* WOODY. HOW DID YOU GET IT PAST MISTER *KRUPER?*
AH, *KRUPER'S* ALL RIGHT. HE SAID THE SCHOOL PAPER *NEEDED* A LITTLE CONTROVERSY.
YOU SURE *GAVE* IT TO 'EM, WOODY!
I DON'T KNOW IF *CLUNE* * IS GOING TO LIKE THIS. YOU REALLY LAY INTO THE STAFF FOR *LOOKING THE OTHER WAY.*
THAT'S WHAT'S SO *GREAT* ABOUT IT, GEORGE! WOODY ISN'T AFRAID TO OFFEND *ANYBODY!* RIGHT, RONNIE?
YEAH, IT'S...
IT'S REAL *WELL WRITTEN,* WOODY.
YOU *BET* IT IS!
I HOPE I DID THE RIGHT THING. I COULD GET IN A LOT OF *TROUBLE.*
WE'LL STAND BY YOU, WOODY! AND *OF COURSE* YOU DID THE RIGHT THING.
DON'T YOU THINK SO, ZOT?
SURE.
WELCOME TO THE *HERO* BUSINESS, WOODY.

*DR. BERNARD F. CLUNE, PRINCIPAL.

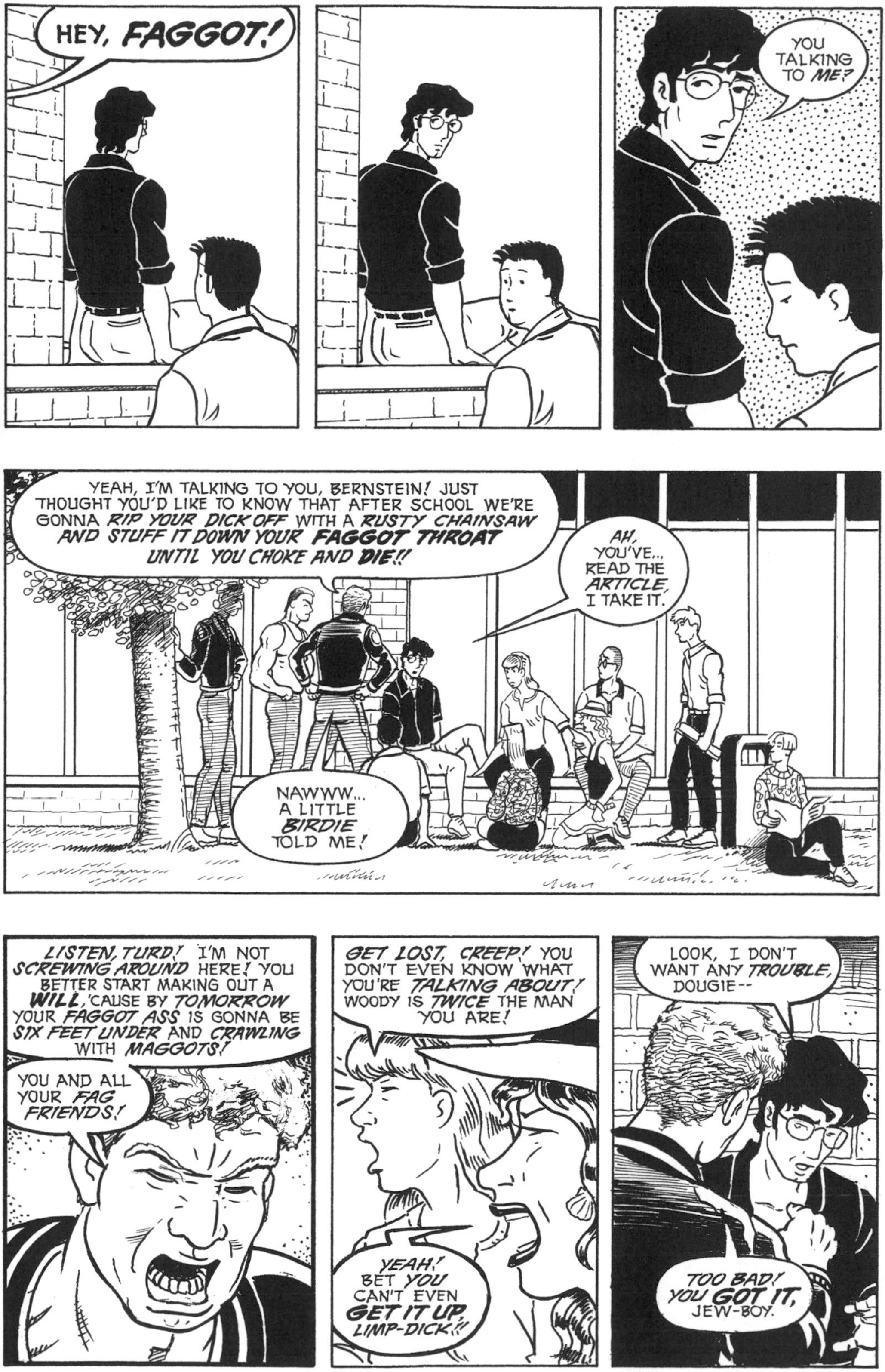
HEY, FAGGOT!
YOU TALKING TO ME?
YEAH, I'M TALKING TO YOU, BERNSTEIN! JUST THOUGHT YOU'D LIKE TO KNOW THAT AFTER SCHOOL WE'RE GONNA RIP YOUR DICK OFF WITH A RUSTY CHAINSAW AND STUFF IT DOWN YOUR FAGGOT THROAT UNTIL YOU CHOKE AND DIE!!
AH, YOU'VE... READ THE ARTICLE, I TAKE IT.
NAWWW... A LITTLE BIRDIE TOLD ME!
LISTEN, TURD! I'M NOT SCREWING AROUND HERE! YOU BETTER START MAKING OUT A WILL, 'CAUSE BY TOMORROW YOUR FAGGOT ASS IS GONNA BE SIX FEET UNDER AND CRAWLING WITH MAGGOTS!
YOU AND ALL YOUR FAG FRIENDS!
GET LOST, CREEP! YOU DON'T EVEN KNOW WHAT YOU'RE TALKING ABOUT! WOODY IS TWICE THE MAN YOU ARE!
YEAH! BET YOU CAN'T EVEN GET IT UP, LIMP-DICK!!
LOOK, I DON'T WANT ANY TROUBLE, DOUGIE--
TOO BAD! YOU GOT IT, JEW-BOY.

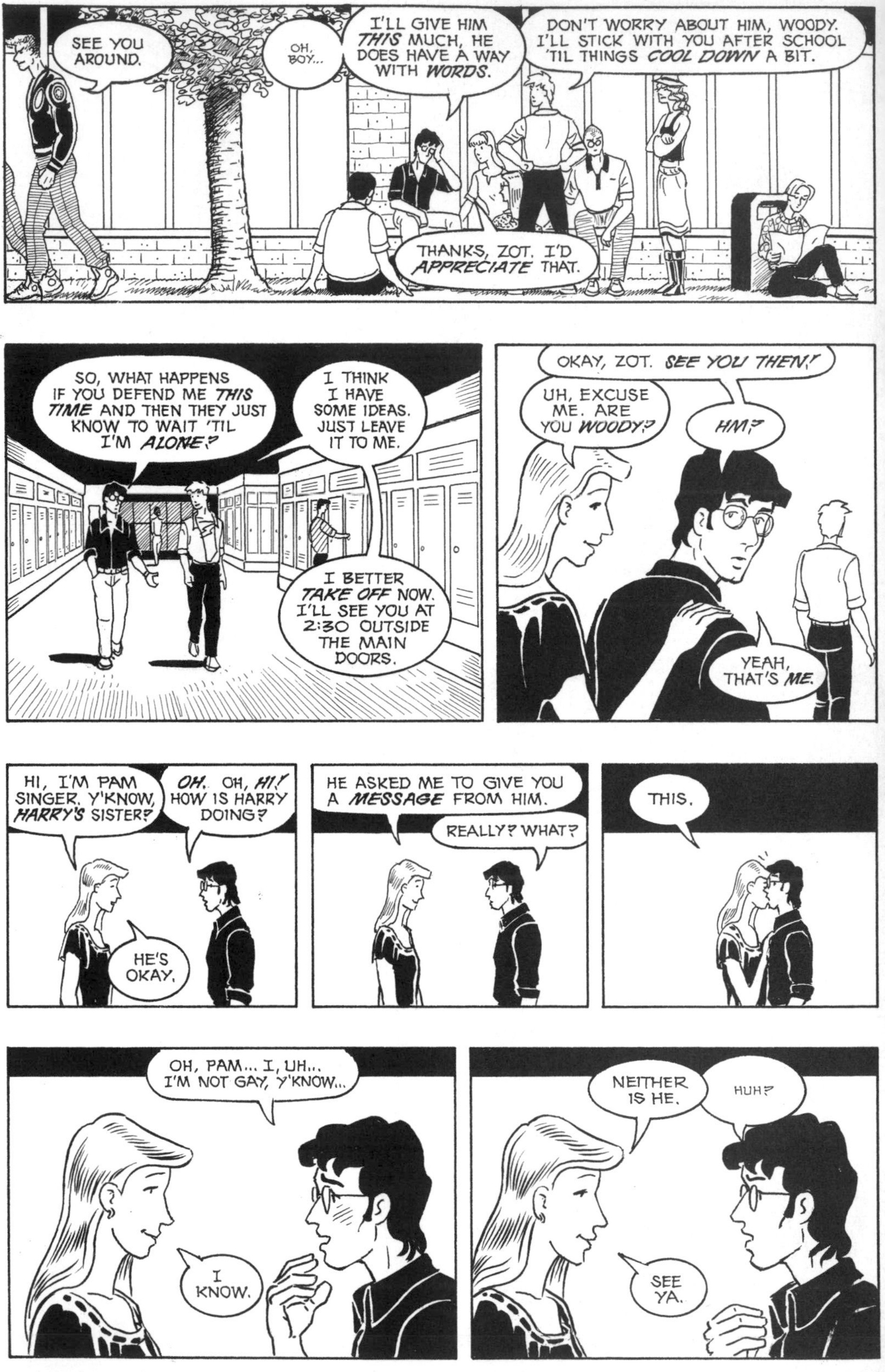
SEE YOU AROUND.
OH, BOY...
I'LL GIVE HIM THIS MUCH, HE DOES HAVE A WAY WITH WORDS.
DON'T WORRY ABOUT HIM, WOODY. I'LL STICK WITH YOU AFTER SCHOOL 'TIL THINGS COOL DOWN A BIT.
THANKS, ZOT. I'D APPRECIATE THAT.
SO, WHAT HAPPENS IF YOU DEFEND ME THIS TIME AND THEN THEY JUST KNOW TO WAIT 'TIL I'M ALONE?
I THINK I HAVE SOME IDEAS. JUST LEAVE IT TO ME.
I BETTER TAKE OFF NOW. I'LL SEE YOU AT 2:30 OUTSIDE THE MAIN DOORS.
OKAY, ZOT. SEE YOU THEN!
UH, EXCUSE ME. ARE YOU WOODY?
HM?
YEAH, THAT'S ME.
HI, I'M PAM SINGER. Y'KNOW, HARRY'S SISTER?
OH. OH, HI! HOW IS HARRY DOING?
HE'S OKAY.
HE ASKED ME TO GIVE YOU A MESSAGE FROM HIM.
REALLY? WHAT?
THIS.
OH, PAM... I, UH... I'M NOT GAY, Y'KNOW...
I KNOW.
NEITHER IS HE.
HUH?
SEE YA.

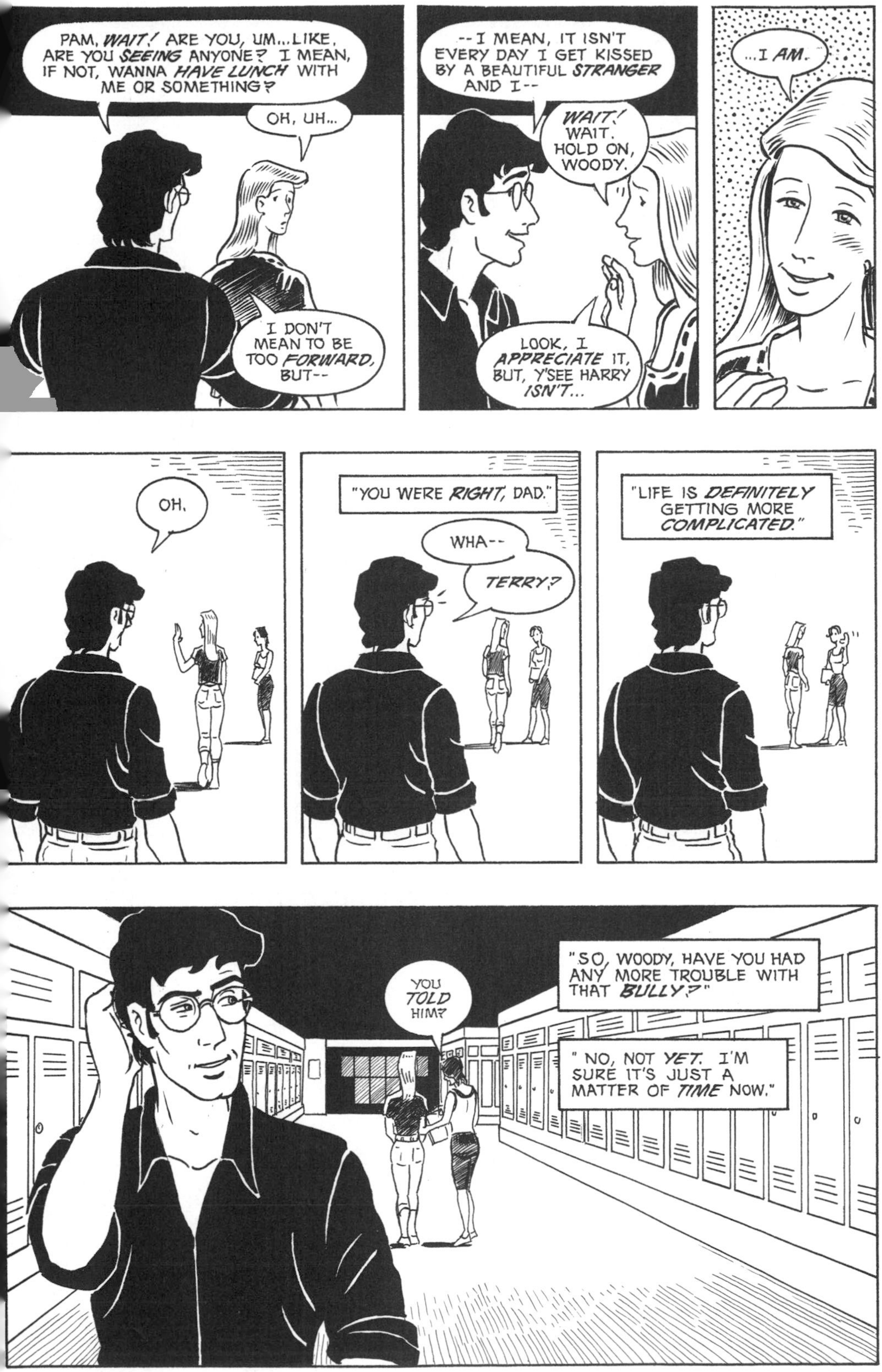
PAM, *WAIT!* ARE YOU, UM...LIKE, ARE YOU *SEEING* ANYONE? I MEAN, IF NOT, WANNA *HAVE LUNCH* WITH ME OR SOMETHING?
OH, UH...
I DON'T MEAN TO BE TOO *FORWARD*, BUT--
--I MEAN, IT ISN'T EVERY DAY I GET KISSED BY A BEAUTIFUL *STRANGER* AND I--
WAIT! WAIT. HOLD ON, WOODY.
LOOK, I *APPRECIATE* IT, BUT, Y'SEE HARRY *ISN'T*...
...I *AM*.
OH.
"YOU WERE *RIGHT*, DAD."
WHA--
TERRY?
"LIFE IS *DEFINITELY* GETTING MORE *COMPLICATED*."
YOU *TOLD* HIM?
"SO, WOODY, HAVE YOU HAD ANY MORE TROUBLE WITH THAT *BULLY*?"
"NO, NOT *YET*. I'M SURE IT'S JUST A MATTER OF *TIME* NOW."

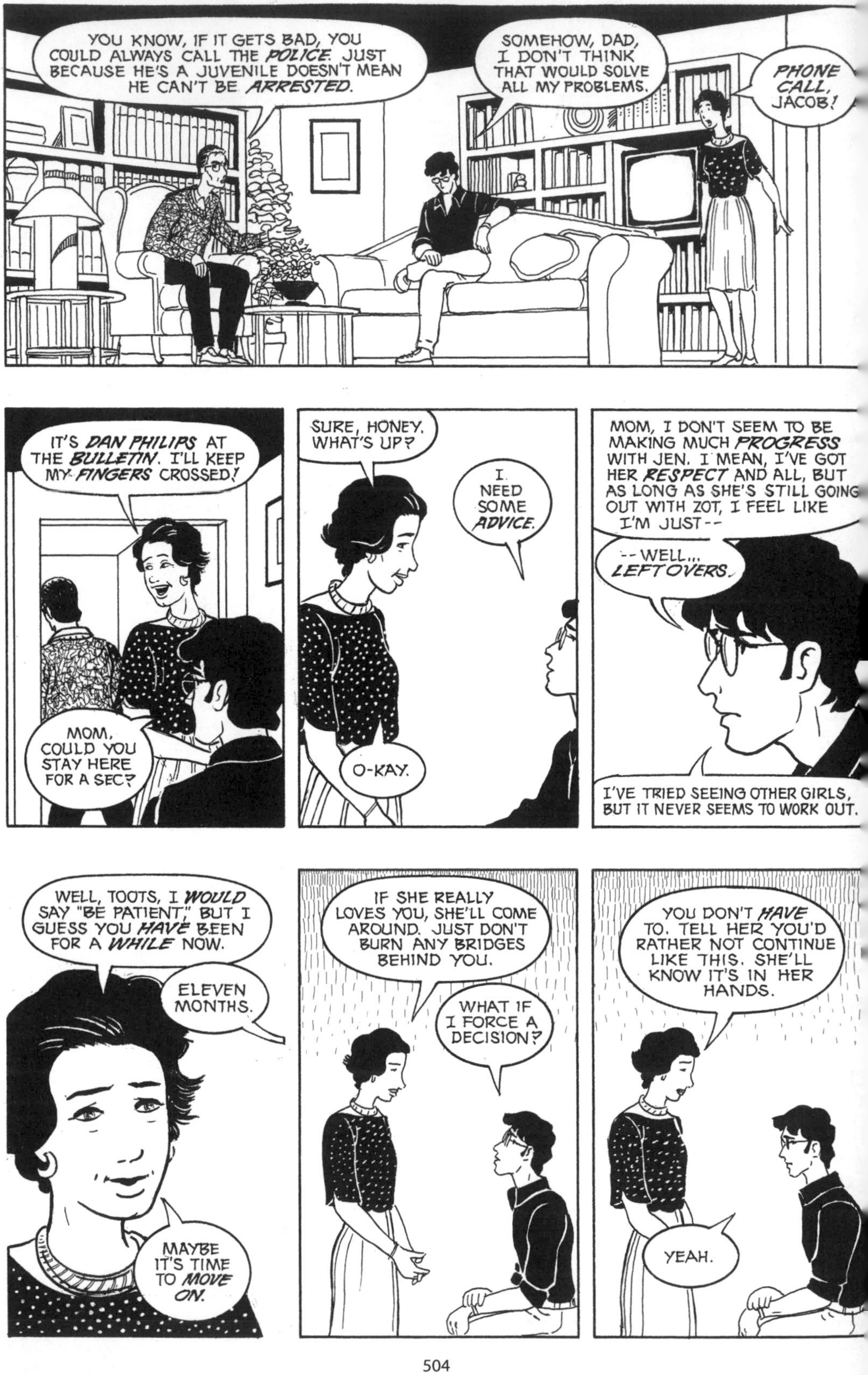
YOU KNOW, IF IT GETS BAD, YOU COULD ALWAYS CALL THE POLICE. JUST BECAUSE HE'S A JUVENILE DOESN'T MEAN HE CAN'T BE ARRESTED.
SOMEHOW, DAD, I DON'T THINK THAT WOULD SOLVE ALL MY PROBLEMS.
PHONE CALL, JACOB!
IT'S DAN PHILIPS AT THE BULLETIN. I'LL KEEP MY FINGERS CROSSED!
MOM, COULD YOU STAY HERE FOR A SEC?
SURE, HONEY. WHAT'S UP?
I NEED SOME ADVICE.
O-KAY.
MOM, I DON'T SEEM TO BE MAKING MUCH PROGRESS WITH JEN. I MEAN, I'VE GOT HER RESPECT AND ALL, BUT AS LONG AS SHE'S STILL GOING OUT WITH ZOT, I FEEL LIKE I'M JUST --
-- WELL... LEFTOVERS.
I'VE TRIED SEEING OTHER GIRLS, BUT IT NEVER SEEMS TO WORK OUT.
WELL, TOOTS, I WOULD SAY "BE PATIENT," BUT I GUESS YOU HAVE BEEN FOR A WHILE NOW.
ELEVEN MONTHS.
MAYBE IT'S TIME TO MOVE ON.
IF SHE REALLY LOVES YOU, SHE'LL COME AROUND. JUST DON'T BURN ANY BRIDGES BEHIND YOU.
WHAT IF I FORCE A DECISION?
YOU DON'T HAVE TO. TELL HER YOU'D RATHER NOT CONTINUE LIKE THIS. SHE'LL KNOW IT'S IN HER HANDS.
YEAH.

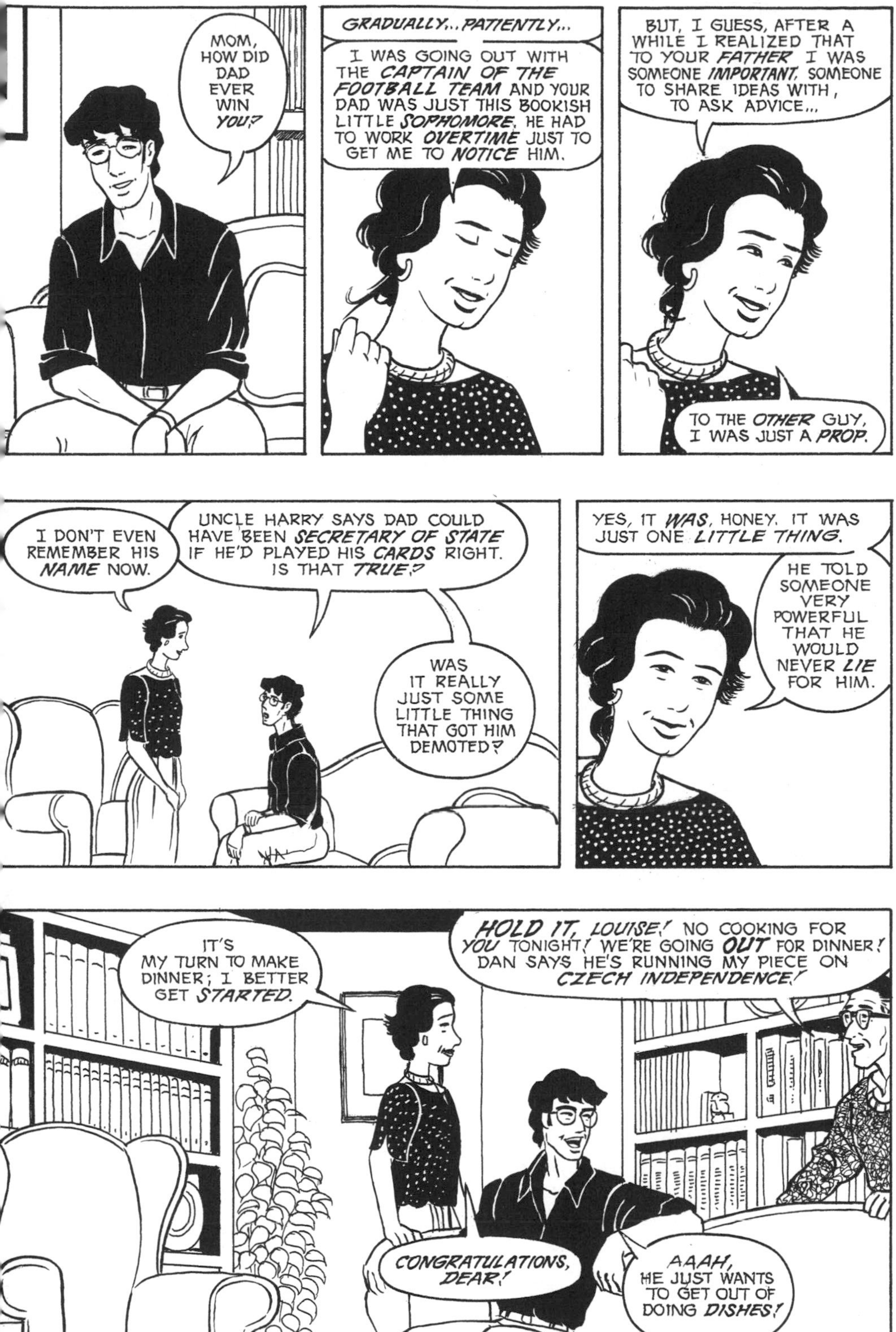
MOM, HOW DID DAD EVER WIN YOU?
GRADUALLY... PATIENTLY...
I WAS GOING OUT WITH THE CAPTAIN OF THE FOOTBALL TEAM AND YOUR DAD WAS JUST THIS BOOKISH LITTLE SOPHOMORE. HE HAD TO WORK OVERTIME JUST TO GET ME TO NOTICE HIM.
BUT, I GUESS, AFTER A WHILE I REALIZED THAT TO YOUR FATHER I WAS SOMEONE IMPORTANT, SOMEONE TO SHARE IDEAS WITH, TO ASK ADVICE...
TO THE OTHER GUY, I WAS JUST A PROP.
I DON'T EVEN REMEMBER HIS NAME NOW.
UNCLE HARRY SAYS DAD COULD HAVE BEEN SECRETARY OF STATE IF HE'D PLAYED HIS CARDS RIGHT. IS THAT TRUE?
WAS IT REALLY JUST SOME LITTLE THING THAT GOT HIM DEMOTED?
YES, IT WAS, HONEY. IT WAS JUST ONE LITTLE THING.
HE TOLD SOMEONE VERY POWERFUL THAT HE WOULD NEVER LIE FOR HIM.
IT'S MY TURN TO MAKE DINNER; I BETTER GET STARTED.
HOLD IT, LOUISE! NO COOKING FOR YOU TONIGHT! WE'RE GOING OUT FOR DINNER! DAN SAYS HE'S RUNNING MY PIECE ON CZECH INDEPENDENCE!
CONGRATULATIONS, DEAR!
AAAH, HE JUST WANTS TO GET OUT OF DOING DISHES!

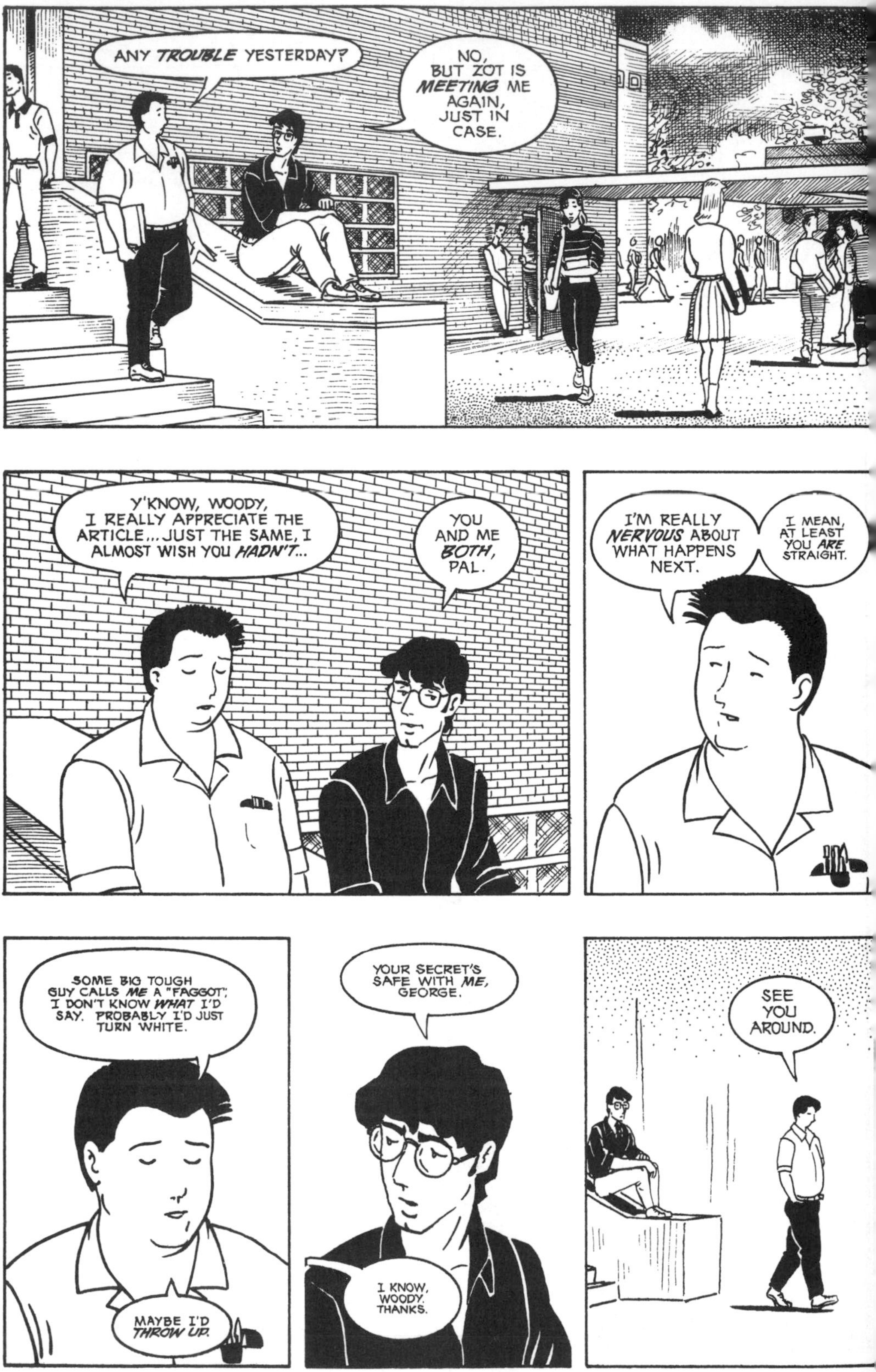
ANY TROUBLE YESTERDAY?
NO, BUT ZOT IS MEETING ME AGAIN, JUST IN CASE.
Y'KNOW, WOODY, I REALLY APPRECIATE THE ARTICLE... JUST THE SAME, I ALMOST WISH YOU HADN'T...
YOU AND ME BOTH, PAL.
I'M REALLY NERVOUS ABOUT WHAT HAPPENS NEXT.
I MEAN, AT LEAST YOU ARE STRAIGHT.
SOME BIG TOUGH GUY CALLS ME A "FAGGOT", I DON'T KNOW WHAT I'D SAY. PROBABLY I'D JUST TURN WHITE.
MAYBE I'D THROW UP.
YOUR SECRET'S SAFE WITH ME, GEORGE.
I KNOW, WOODY. THANKS.
SEE YOU AROUND.

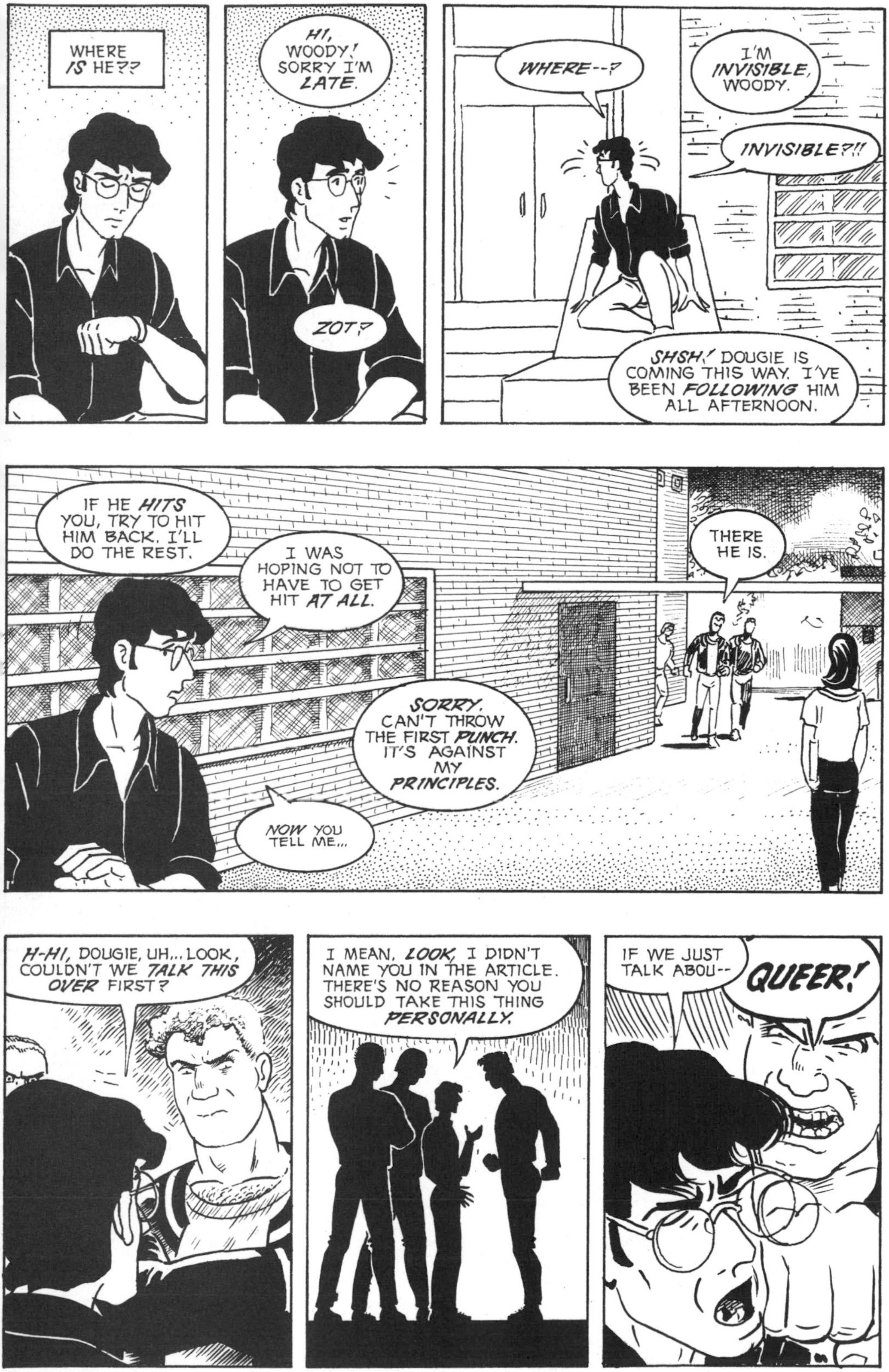
WHERE IS HE??
HI, WOODY! SORRY I'M LATE.
ZOT?
WHERE--?
I'M INVISIBLE, WOODY.
INVISIBLE?!!
SHSH! DOUGIE IS COMING THIS WAY. I'VE BEEN FOLLOWING HIM ALL AFTERNOON.
IF HE HITS YOU, TRY TO HIT HIM BACK. I'LL DO THE REST.
I WAS HOPING NOT TO HAVE TO GET HIT AT ALL.
SORRY. CAN'T THROW THE FIRST PUNCH. IT'S AGAINST MY PRINCIPLES.
NOW YOU TELL ME...
THERE HE IS.
H-HI, DOUGIE, UH... LOOK, COULDN'T WE TALK THIS OVER FIRST?
I MEAN, LOOK, I DIDN'T NAME YOU IN THE ARTICLE. THERE'S NO REASON YOU SHOULD TAKE THIS THING PERSONALLY.
IF WE JUST TALK ABOU--
QUEER!

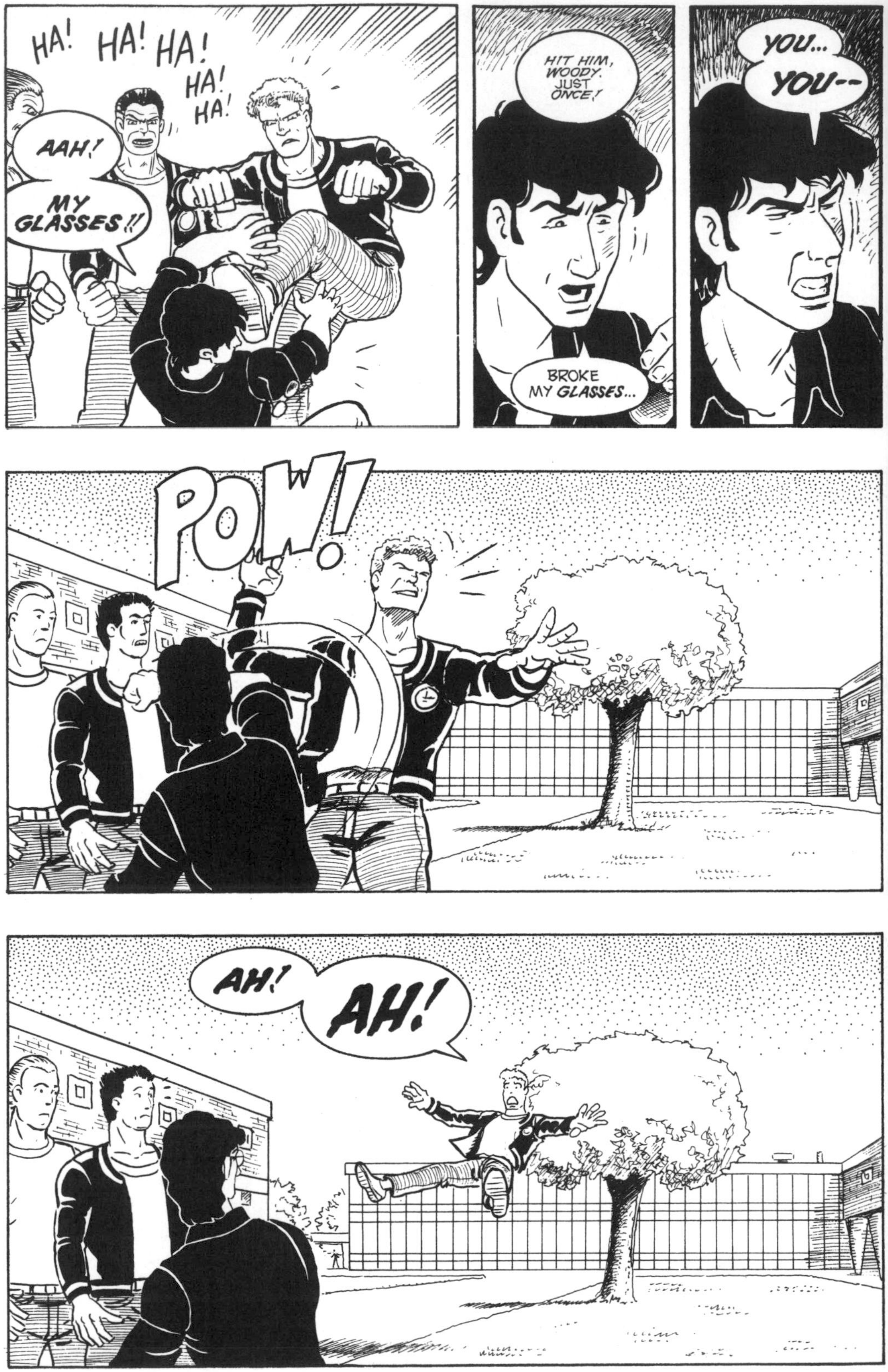
HA! HA! HA! HA! HA!
AAH!
MY GLASSES!!
HIT HIM, WOODY. JUST ONCE!
BROKE MY GLASSES...
YOU...
YOU--
POW!
AH!
AH!

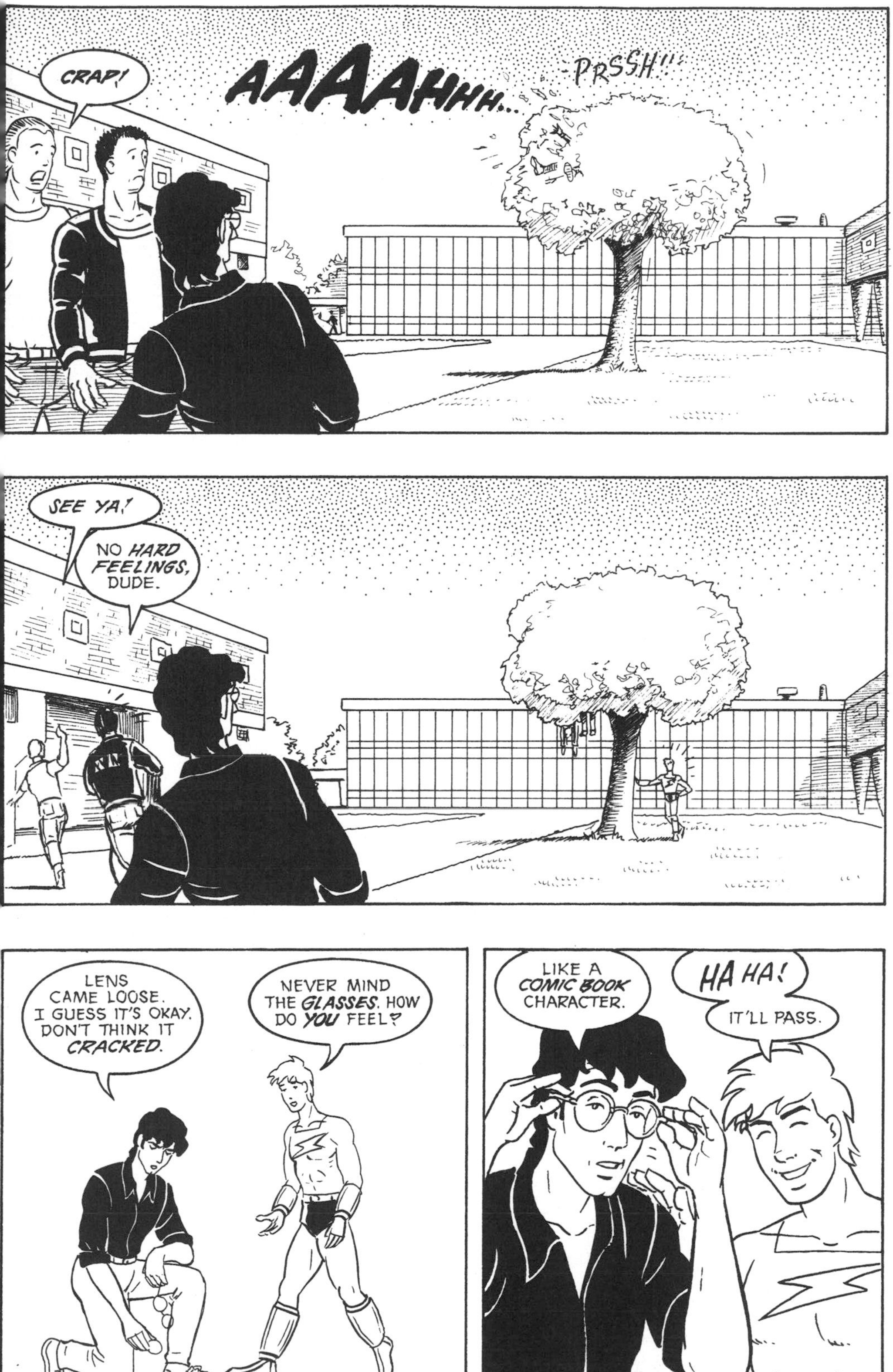
CRAP!
AAAAAHHH...
PRSSH!!
SEE YA!
NO HARD FEELINGS, DUDE.
LENS CAME LOOSE. I GUESS IT'S OKAY. DON'T THINK IT CRACKED.
NEVER MIND THE GLASSES. HOW DO YOU FEEL?
LIKE A COMIC BOOK CHARACTER.
HA HA!
IT'LL PASS.

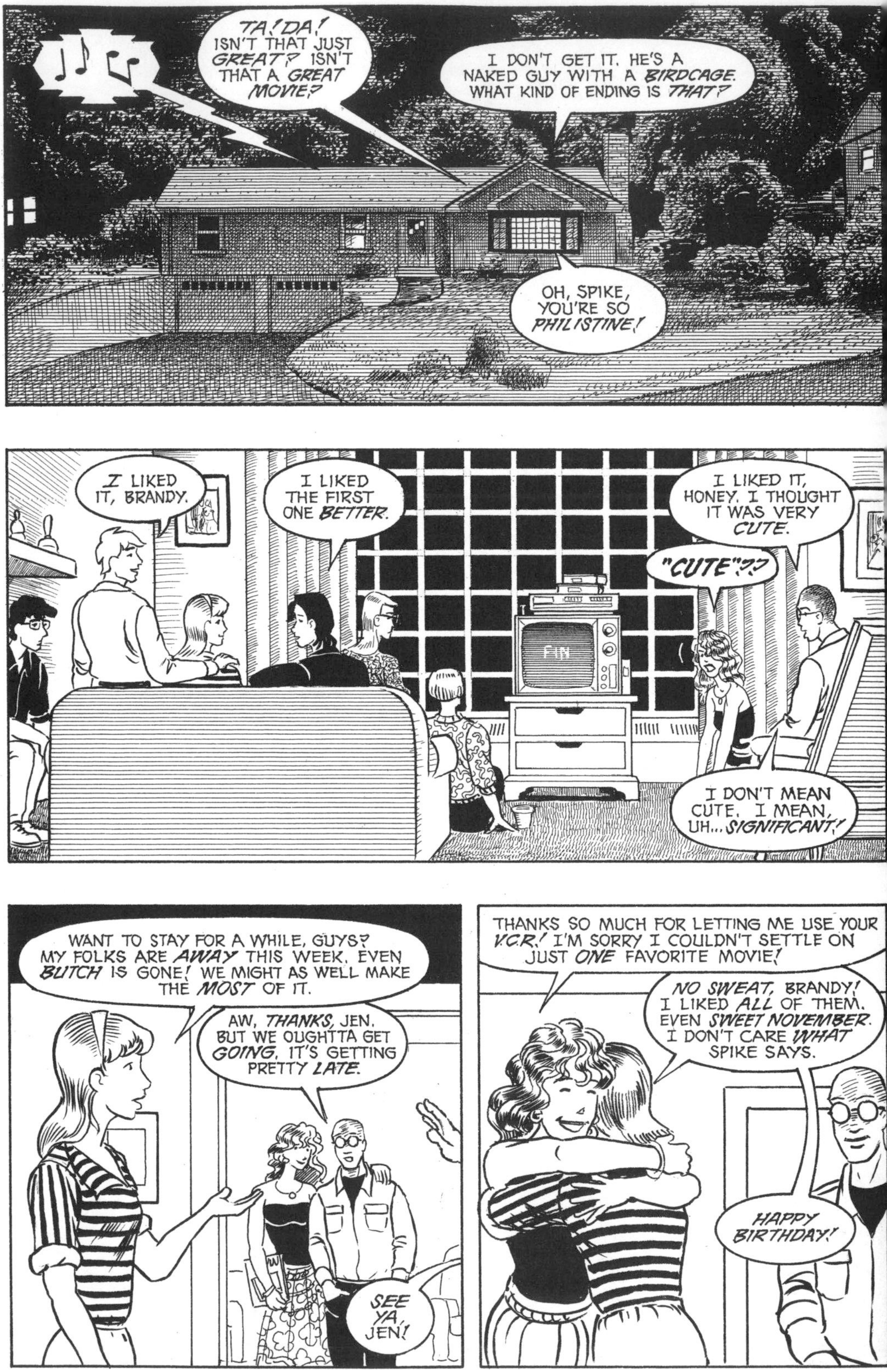
TA! DA! ISN'T THAT JUST GREAT? ISN'T THAT A GREAT MOVIE?
I DON'T GET IT. HE'S A NAKED GUY WITH A BIRDCAGE. WHAT KIND OF ENDING IS THAT?
OH, SPIKE, YOU'RE SO PHILISTINE!
I LIKED IT, BRANDY.
I LIKED THE FIRST ONE BETTER.
I LIKED IT, HONEY. I THOUGHT IT WAS VERY CUTE.
"CUTE"??
I DON'T MEAN CUTE. I MEAN, UH... SIGNIFICANT!
WANT TO STAY FOR A WHILE, GUYS? MY FOLKS ARE AWAY THIS WEEK. EVEN BUTCH IS GONE! WE MIGHT AS WELL MAKE THE MOST OF IT.
AW, THANKS, JEN. BUT WE OUGHTTA GET GOING. IT'S GETTING PRETTY LATE.
SEE YA, JEN!
THANKS SO MUCH FOR LETTING ME USE YOUR V.C.R.! I'M SORRY I COULDN'T SETTLE ON JUST ONE FAVORITE MOVIE!
NO SWEAT, BRANDY! I LIKED ALL OF THEM. EVEN SWEET NOVEMBER. I DON'T CARE WHAT SPIKE SAYS.
HAPPY BIRTHDAY!

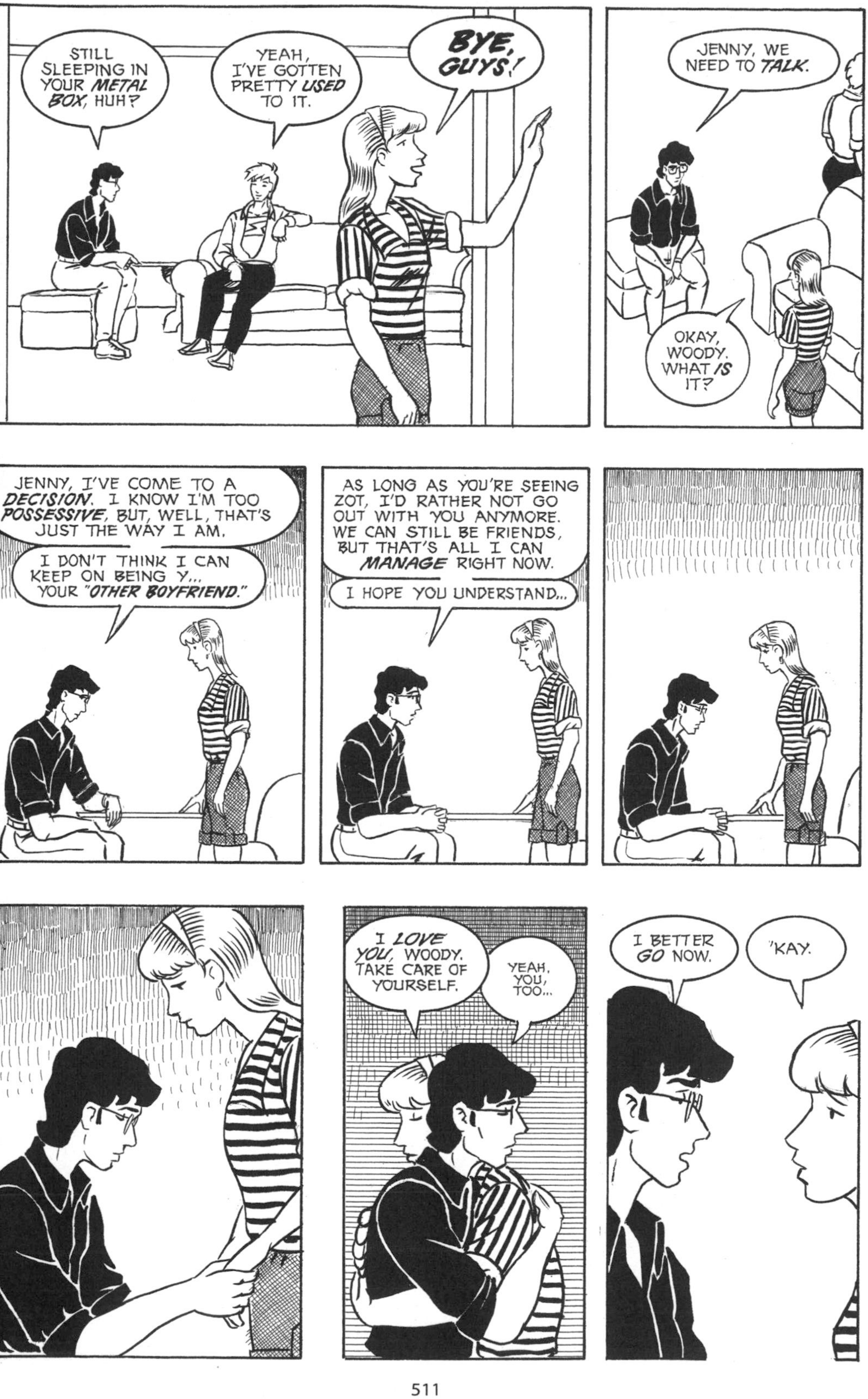
STILL SLEEPING IN YOUR *METAL BOX*, HUH?
YEAH, I'VE GOTTEN PRETTY *USED* TO IT.
BYE, GUYS!
JENNY, WE NEED TO *TALK*.
OKAY, WOODY. WHAT *IS* IT?
JENNY, I'VE COME TO A *DECISION*. I KNOW I'M TOO *POSSESSIVE*, BUT, WELL, THAT'S JUST THE WAY I AM.
I DON'T THINK I CAN KEEP ON BEING Y... YOUR *"OTHER BOYFRIEND."*
AS LONG AS YOU'RE SEEING ZOT, I'D RATHER NOT GO OUT WITH YOU ANYMORE. WE CAN STILL BE FRIENDS, BUT THAT'S ALL I CAN *MANAGE* RIGHT NOW.
I HOPE YOU UNDERSTAND...
I *LOVE YOU*, WOODY. TAKE CARE OF YOURSELF.
YEAH, YOU, TOO...
I BETTER *GO* NOW.
'KAY.

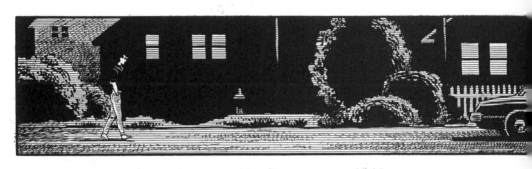

HEY, *MISTER!* COULD YOU HELP ME? MY BROTHER THREW MY *BASEBALL CAP* ON THE ROOF AND I CAN'T *REACH* IT!

SURE, I'LL GET IT.

WE HAVE A *RAKE* IN THE GARAGE.

NO, I CAN JUST *CLIMB UP.*

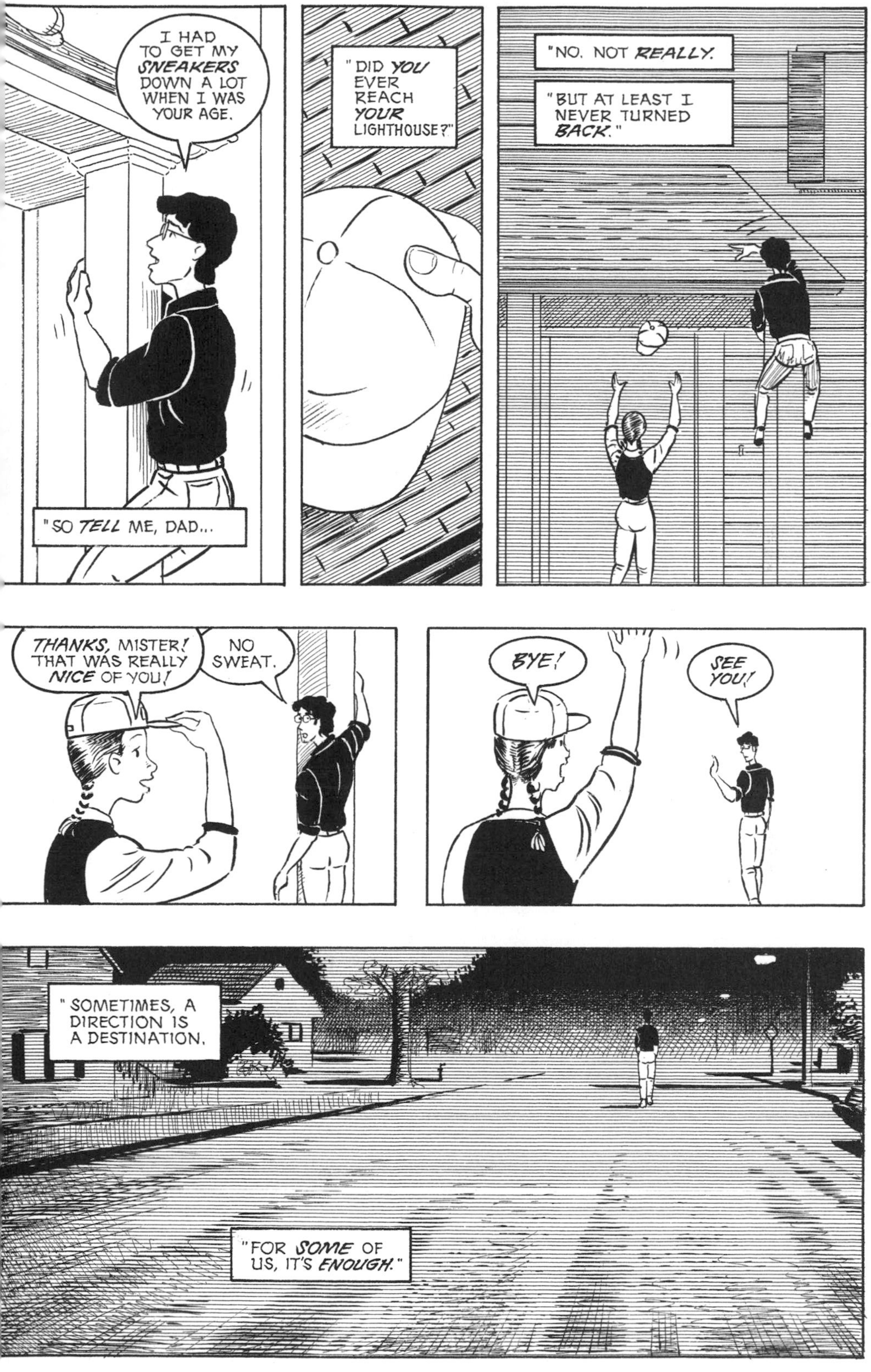
I HAD TO GET MY SNEAKERS DOWN A LOT WHEN I WAS YOUR AGE.
"SO TELL ME, DAD...
"DID YOU EVER REACH YOUR LIGHTHOUSE?"
"NO. NOT REALLY.
"BUT AT LEAST I NEVER TURNED BACK."
THANKS, MISTER! THAT WAS REALLY NICE OF YOU!
NO SWEAT.
BYE!
SEE YOU!
"SOMETIMES, A DIRECTION IS A DESTINATION.
"FOR SOME OF US, IT'S ENOUGH."

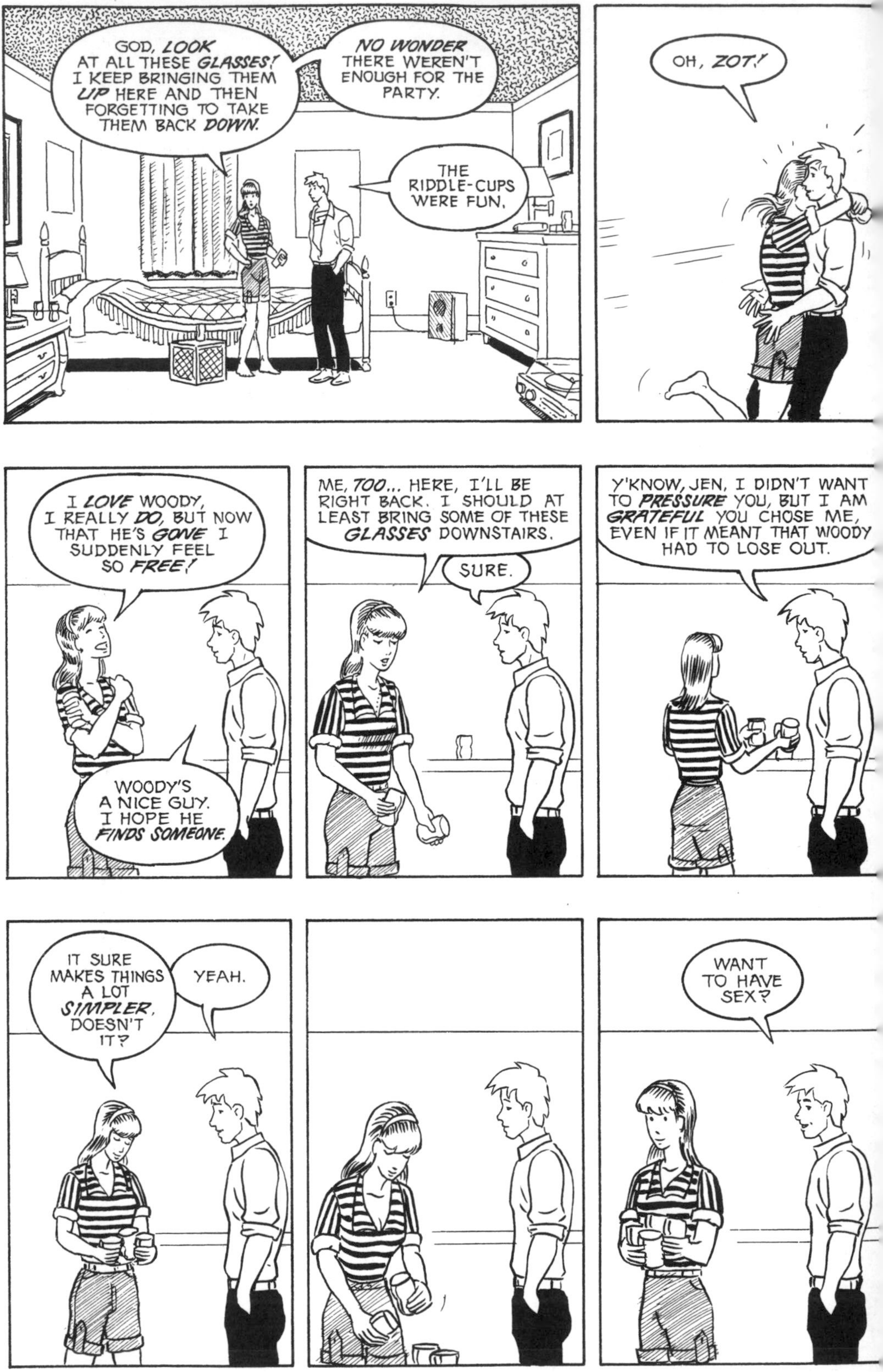
GOD, LOOK AT ALL THESE GLASSES! I KEEP BRINGING THEM UP HERE AND THEN FORGETTING TO TAKE THEM BACK DOWN.
NO WONDER THERE WEREN'T ENOUGH FOR THE PARTY.
THE RIDDLE-CUPS WERE FUN.
OH, ZOT!
I LOVE WOODY, I REALLY DO, BUT NOW THAT HE'S GONE I SUDDENLY FEEL SO FREE!
WOODY'S A NICE GUY. I HOPE HE FINDS SOMEONE.
ME, TOO... HERE, I'LL BE RIGHT BACK. I SHOULD AT LEAST BRING SOME OF THESE GLASSES DOWNSTAIRS.
SURE.
Y'KNOW, JEN, I DIDN'T WANT TO PRESSURE YOU, BUT I AM GRATEFUL YOU CHOSE ME, EVEN IF IT MEANT THAT WOODY HAD TO LOSE OUT.
IT SURE MAKES THINGS A LOT SIMPLER, DOESN'T IT?
YEAH.
WANT TO HAVE SEX?

As noted up front, I made changes to the bully Dougie's dialogue in this story. In the original version, his language was so strong that even regular readers were taken aback and yanked out of the story to some degree. Many of us who grew up on mainstream superhero comics where strong language of any sort was prohibited were still exercising our new freedom, seeing how far we could take it. Terry's story had been a successful bit of limit-testing, I think, but looking back on Woody's issue a few years after the fact I found myself agreeing with readers who'd written in to complain that Dougie's over-the-top swearing didn't fit the tone of the series ("a turd in the punch bowl" as one reader put it). When we were planning the collection, I volunteered without prompting to trim back some of Dougie's excesses. It's still some pretty menacing stuff as it stands, but hopefully more in keeping with the stories that surround it.

A related problem that's too late to fix was the fact that I'd demonized this fictionalized real-world bully more than the assassins, crooks, megalomaniacs, and dictators that populated the rest of the series. I remember thinking myself justified (and maybe a bit clever) to have made my worst villain an ordinary school yard bully. Now I realize, looking back, that I was simply getting my own symbolic revenge on a handful of aggressive kids I had to deal with in my own grade school years, particularly elementary school. I had an emotional agenda, and it distorted what, up until then, had been an underlying current of understanding and acceptance of the fact that everyone is a hero in their own mind.

Real-world parallels abound during these issues. Spike's comics in Ronnie's story were inspired the lunchroom doodles of our friend Rob Morrison, and Clune was indeed the last name of our principal at Lexington High School during the years 1978–1982. Kurt and I thought "Clune!" made a great sound effect and put it into a comic we were working on at the time. I also did a short silent comic where "Dr. Clune"—a giant plastic levitating version of our principal—battled Brian Dewan's

character "The Incredible Indestructible Floating Fool." Yeah … It's a wonder I ever got a date before college.

Some readers guessed that Woody was a thinly fictionalized version of me, and there's plenty of evidence to support the theory. Looking at my old high school peers though, I saw Woody as a bit more like the kids in my class whose families were more politically engaged: the ones writing for the school newspaper or running for class president; nerds to a degree, perhaps, but more adult somehow, more engaged with the outside world. These were the children of journalists and Harvard law professors rather than my crowd, the geeky kids of engineers and computer scientists.

The art was unraveling even more than usual in these pages. An odd tendency to draw my characters as long, stiff shampoo bottles was starting to creep in here and there, and you can tell I was rushed in places. Figure drawing was always my Achilles' heel, but as the stories focused more on ordinary teenagers having ordinary conversations, my artistic limitations were increasingly getting in the way of the intended effects.

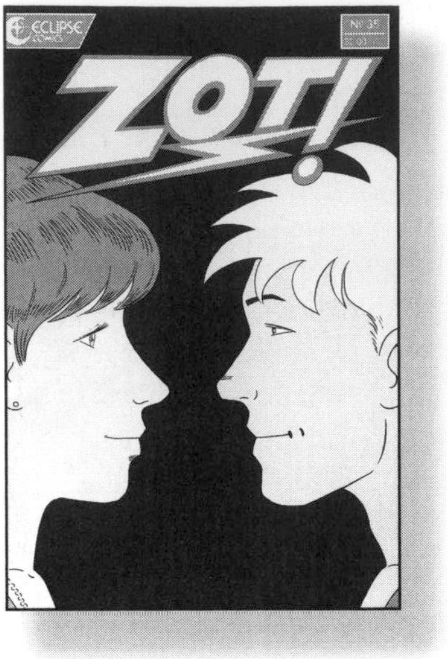
ECLIPSE
ZOT!

The Conversation

First published in *Zot! #35.*

Lettering:

Bob Lappan

Original series editor:

cat yronwode

Plot assist:

Ivy Ratafia

Eisner Award Nominee 1991:

"Best Single Issue"

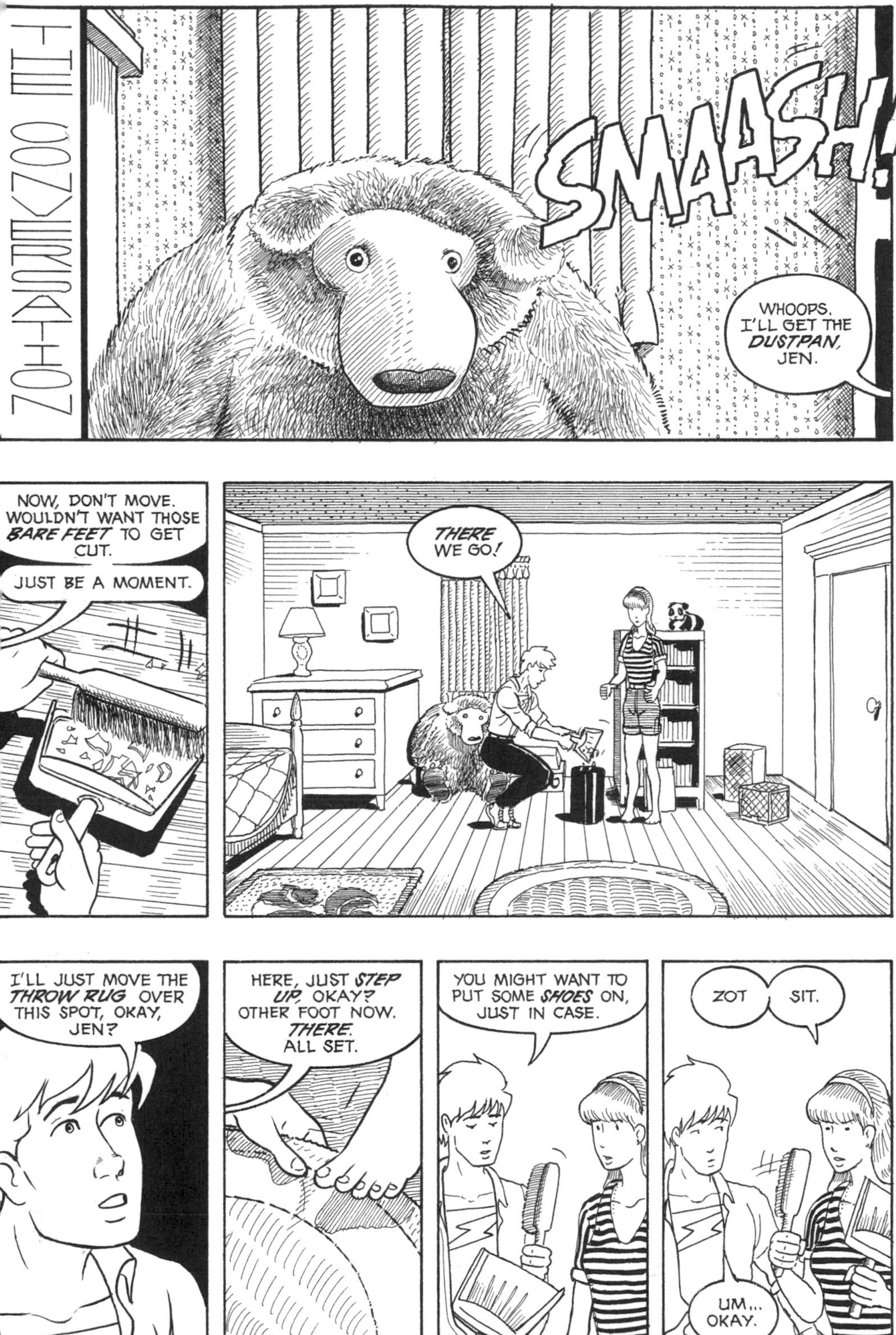
SMAASH!
WHOOPS. I'LL GET THE DUSTPAN, JEN.
NOW, DON'T MOVE. WOULDN'T WANT THOSE BARE FEET TO GET CUT.
JUST BE A MOMENT.
THERE WE GO!
I'LL JUST MOVE THE THROW RUG OVER THIS SPOT, OKAY, JEN?
HERE, JUST STEP UP, OKAY? OTHER FOOT NOW. THERE. ALL SET.
YOU MIGHT WANT TO PUT SOME SHOES ON, JUST IN CASE.
ZOT
SIT.
UM... OKAY.

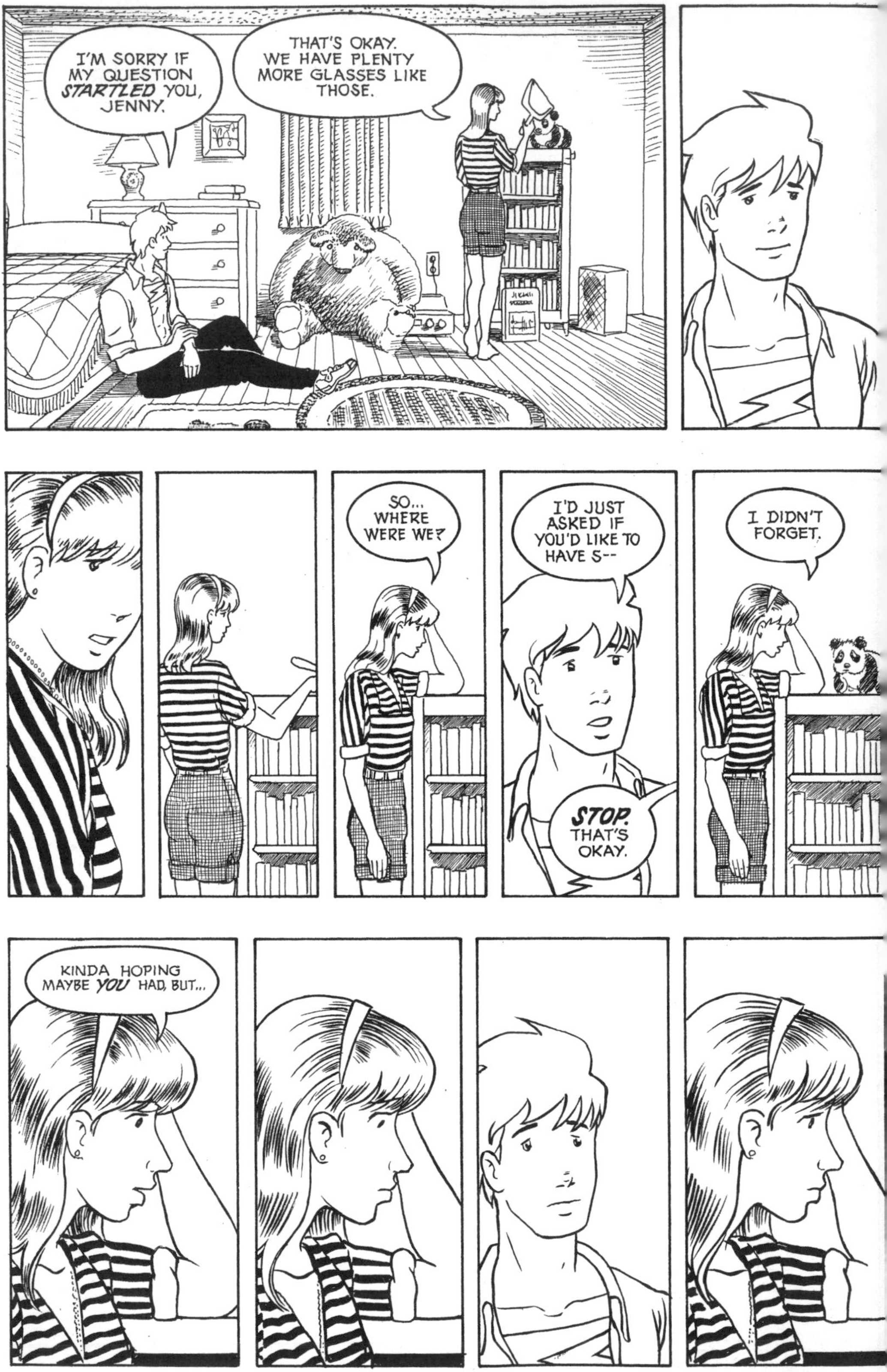
I'M SORRY IF MY QUESTION STARTLED YOU, JENNY.
THAT'S OKAY. WE HAVE PLENTY MORE GLASSES LIKE THOSE.
SO... WHERE WERE WE?
I'D JUST ASKED IF YOU'D LIKE TO HAVE S--
STOP. THAT'S OKAY.
I DIDN'T FORGET.
KINDA HOPING MAYBE YOU HAD, BUT...

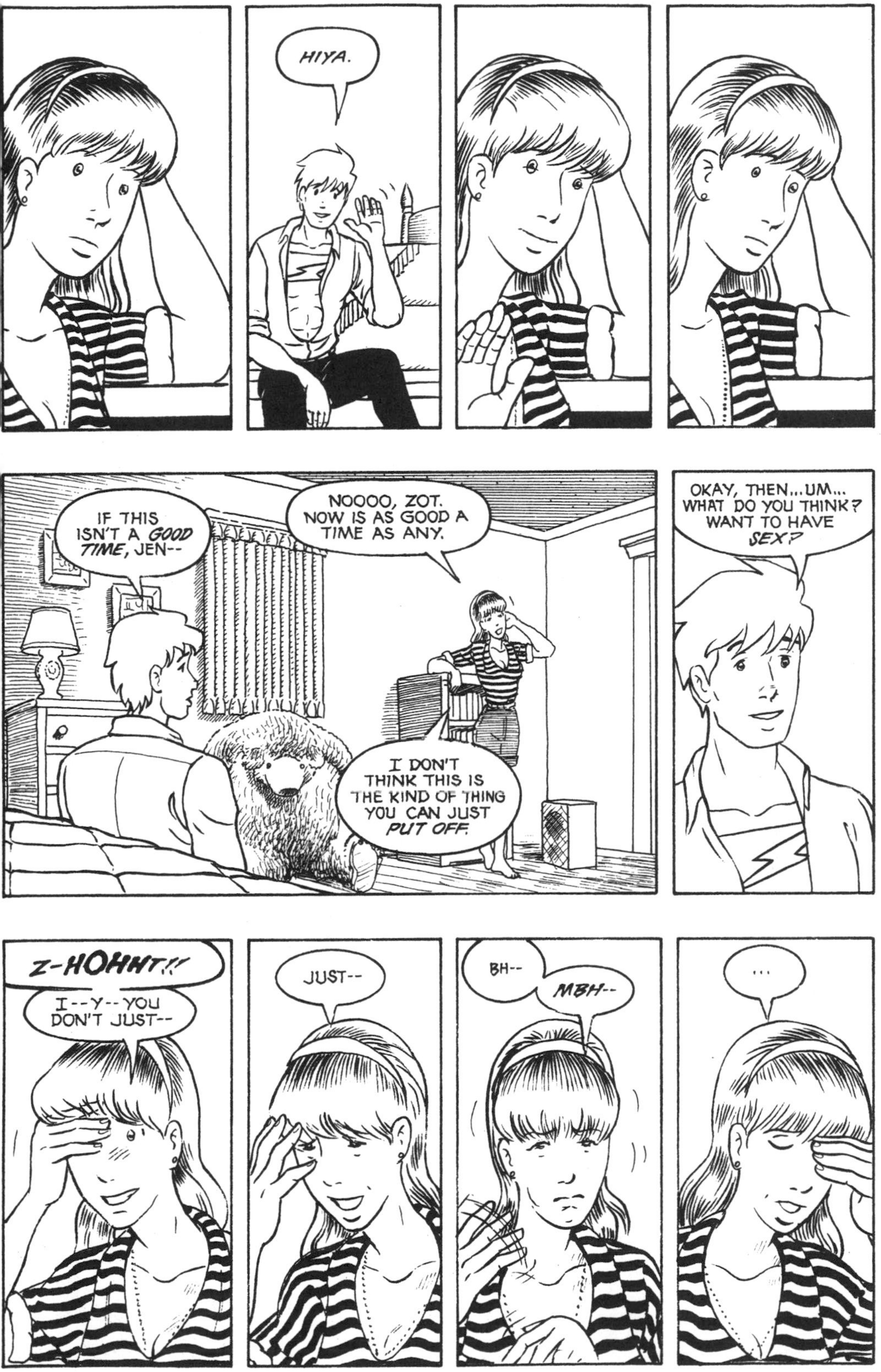
HIYA.
IF THIS ISN'T A GOOD TIME, JEN--
NOOOO, ZOT. NOW IS AS GOOD A TIME AS ANY.
I DON'T THINK THIS IS THE KIND OF THING YOU CAN JUST PUT OFF.
OKAY, THEN...UM... WHAT DO YOU THINK? WANT TO HAVE SEX?
Z-HOHNT!!
I--Y--YOU DON'T JUST--
JUST--
BH--
MBH--
...

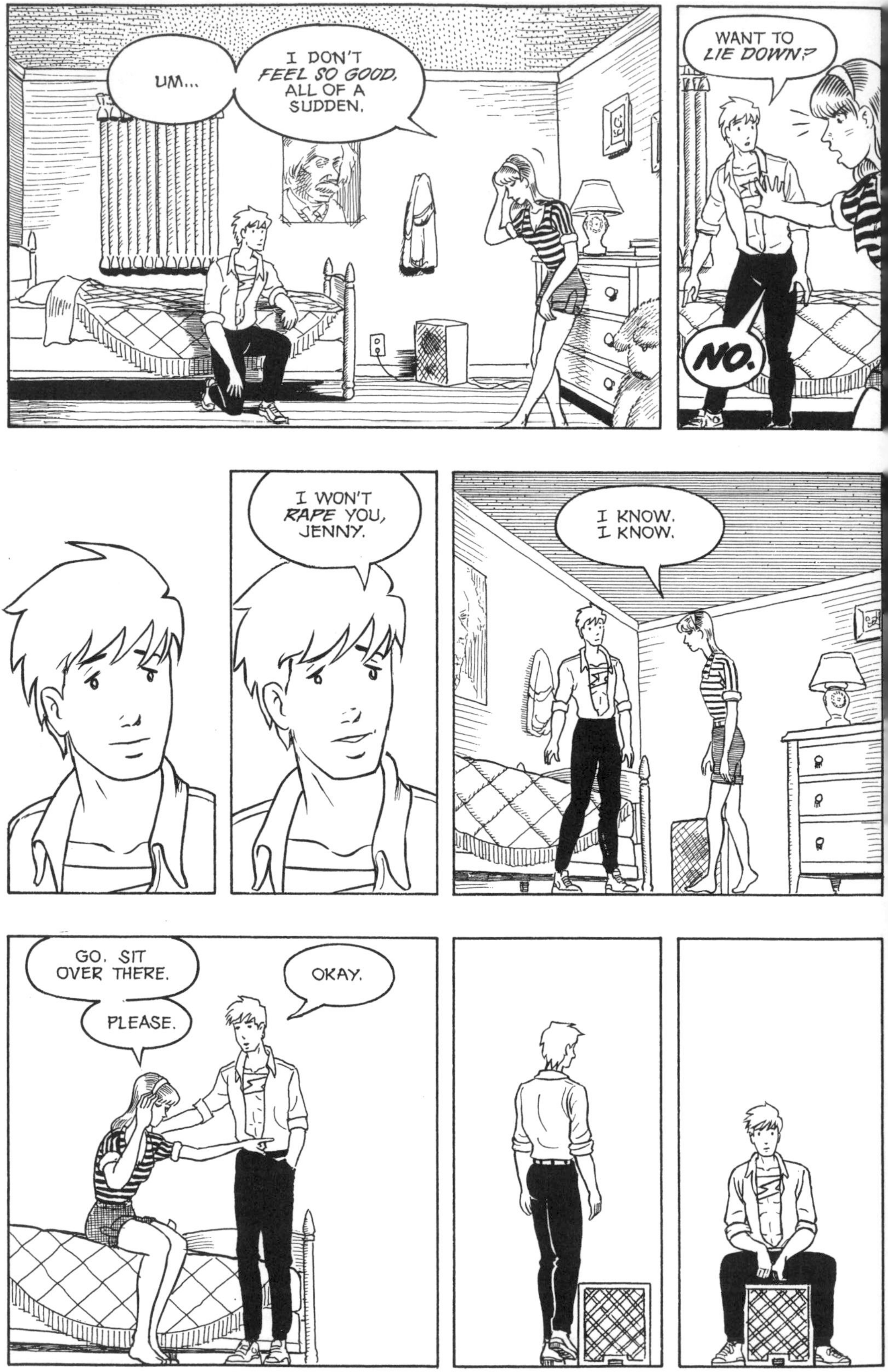
UM...
I DON'T FEEL SO GOOD, ALL OF A SUDDEN.
WANT TO LIE DOWN?
NO.
I WON'T RAPE YOU, JENNY.
I KNOW. I KNOW.
GO. SIT OVER THERE.
PLEASE.
OKAY.

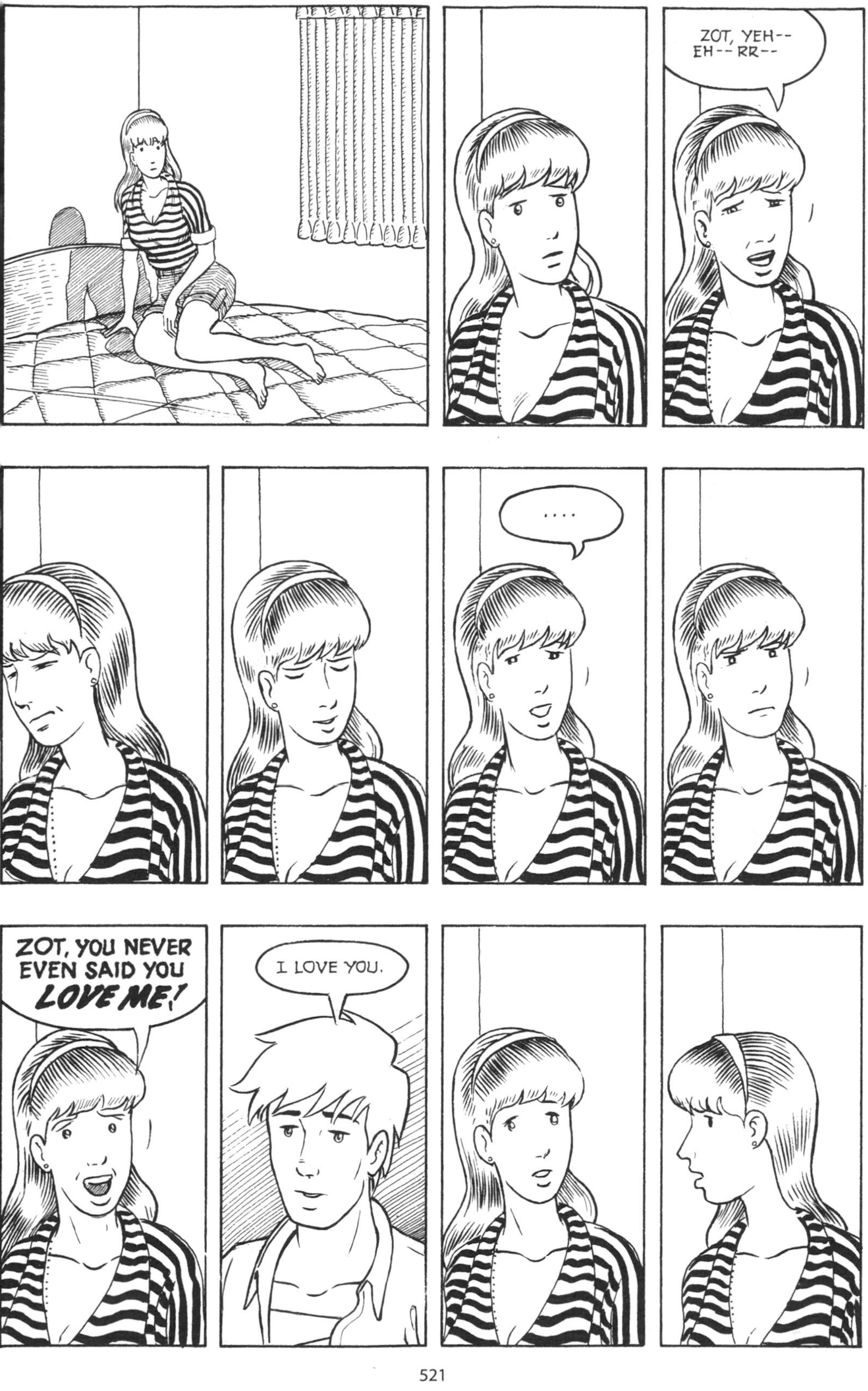
ZOT, YEH--
EH--RR--
....
ZOT, YOU NEVER EVEN SAID YOU *LOVE ME*!
I LOVE YOU.

WELL, IT'S THE WRONG ORDER.

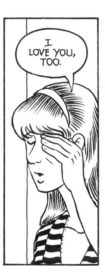

I LOVE YOU, TOO.

MR. PERFECT TIMING.

SO YOU WANT US TO M-MAKE LOVE, HUH?

IF YOU'D LIKE TO, YEAH.

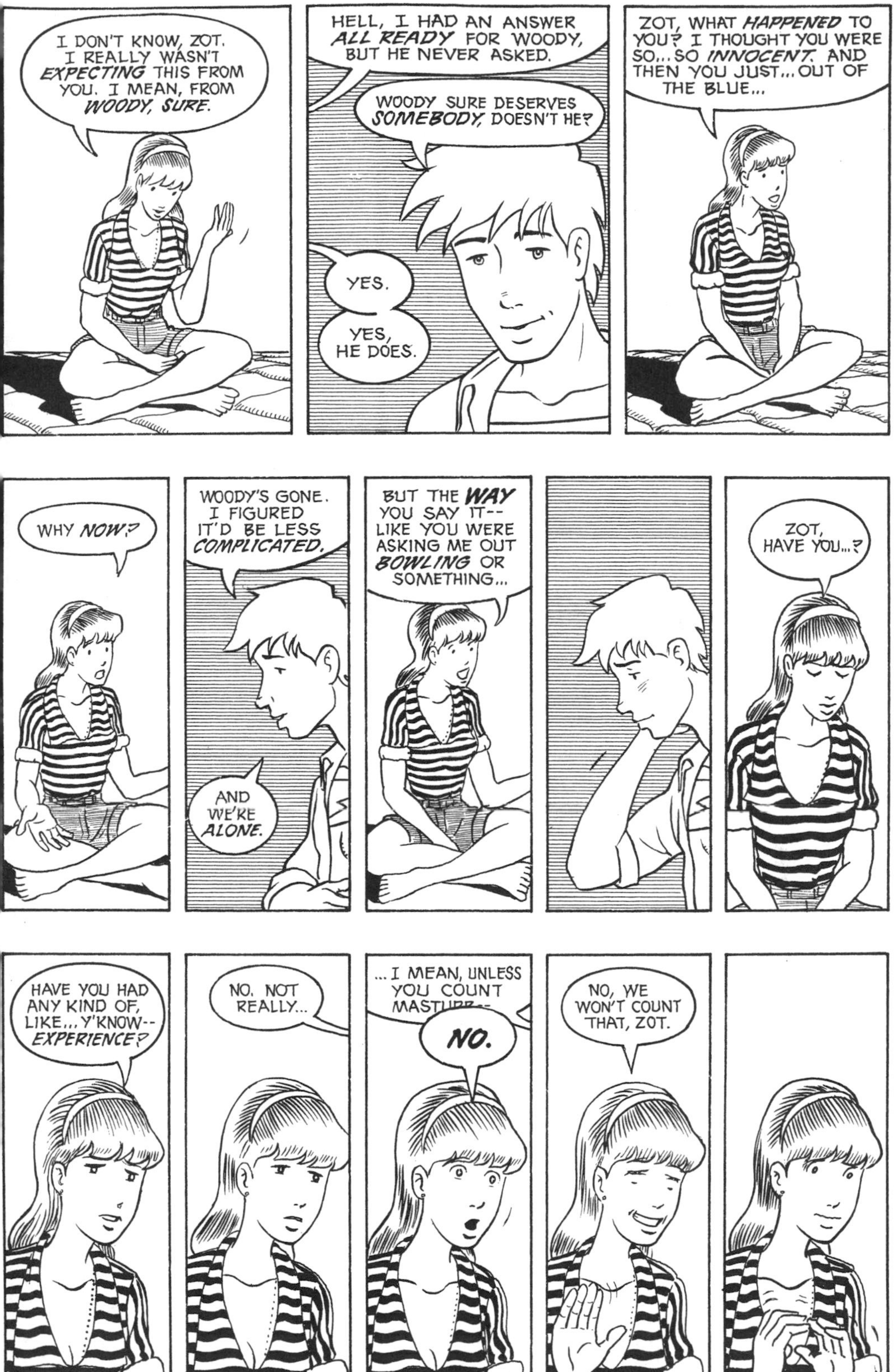
I DON'T KNOW, ZOT. I REALLY WASN'T *EXPECTING* THIS FROM YOU. I MEAN, FROM *WOODY, SURE.*
HELL, I HAD AN ANSWER *ALL READY* FOR WOODY, BUT HE NEVER ASKED.
WOODY SURE DESERVES *SOMEBODY,* DOESN'T HE?
YES.
YES, HE DOES.
ZOT, WHAT *HAPPENED* TO YOU? I THOUGHT YOU WERE SO... SO *INNOCENT.* AND THEN YOU JUST... OUT OF THE BLUE...
WHY *NOW?*
WOODY'S GONE. I FIGURED IT'D BE LESS *COMPLICATED.*
AND WE'RE *ALONE.*
BUT THE *WAY* YOU SAY IT-- LIKE YOU WERE ASKING ME OUT *BOWLING* OR SOMETHING...
ZOT, HAVE YOU...?
HAVE YOU HAD ANY KIND OF, LIKE... Y'KNOW-- *EXPERIENCE?*
NO. NOT REALLY...
...I MEAN, UNLESS YOU COUNT MASTURB--
NO.
NO, WE WON'T COUNT THAT, ZOT.

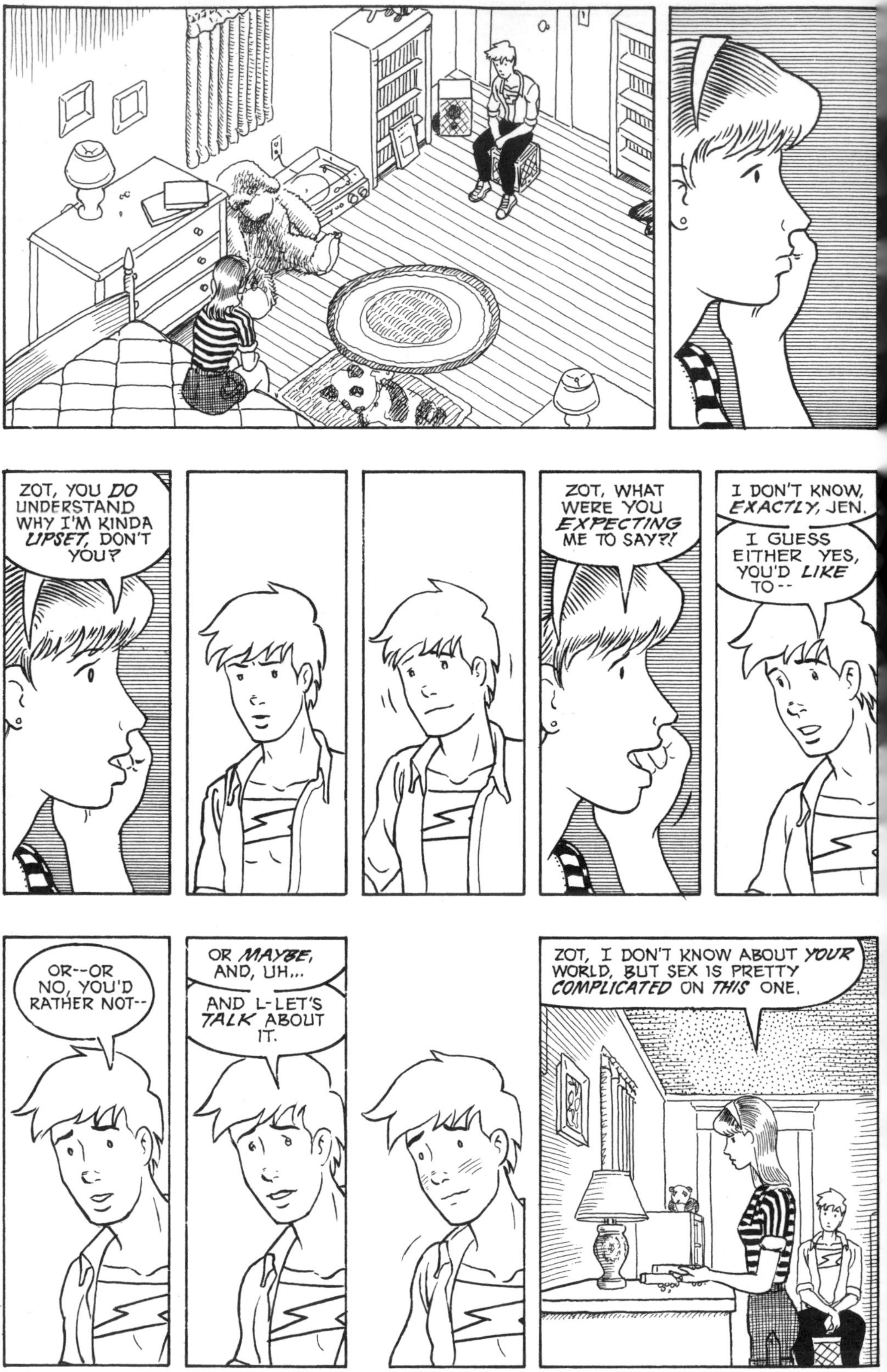
ZOT, YOU *DO* UNDERSTAND WHY I'M KINDA *UPSET*, DON'T YOU?
ZOT, WHAT WERE YOU *EXPECTING* ME TO SAY?!
I DON'T KNOW, *EXACTLY*, JEN.
I GUESS EITHER YES, YOU'D *LIKE* TO--
OR--OR NO, YOU'D RATHER NOT--
OR *MAYBE*, AND, UH...
AND L-LET'S *TALK* ABOUT IT.
ZOT, I DON'T KNOW ABOUT *YOUR* WORLD, BUT SEX IS PRETTY *COMPLICATED* ON *THIS* ONE.

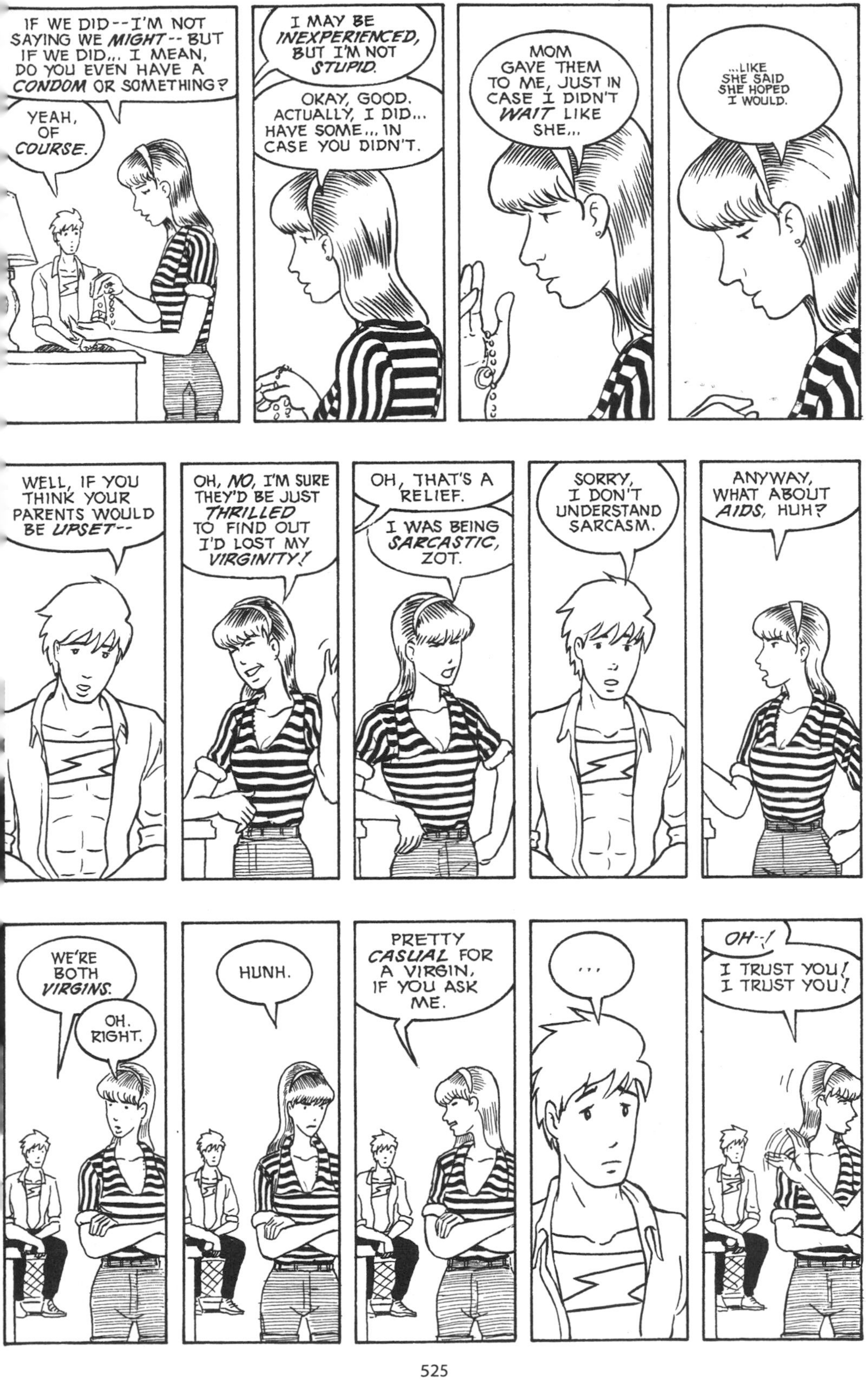

IF WE DID--I'M NOT SAYING WE MIGHT-- BUT IF WE DID... I MEAN, DO YOU EVEN HAVE A CONDOM OR SOMETHING?
YEAH, OF COURSE.
I MAY BE INEXPERIENCED, BUT I'M NOT STUPID.
OKAY, GOOD. ACTUALLY, I DID... HAVE SOME... IN CASE YOU DIDN'T.
MOM GAVE THEM TO ME, JUST IN CASE I DIDN'T WAIT LIKE SHE...
...LIKE SHE SAID SHE HOPED I WOULD.
WELL, IF YOU THINK YOUR PARENTS WOULD BE UPSET--
OH, NO, I'M SURE THEY'D BE JUST THRILLED TO FIND OUT I'D LOST MY VIRGINITY!
OH, THAT'S A RELIEF.
I WAS BEING SARCASTIC, ZOT.
SORRY, I DON'T UNDERSTAND SARCASM.
ANYWAY, WHAT ABOUT AIDS, HUH?
WE'RE BOTH VIRGINS.
OH. RIGHT.
HUNH.
PRETTY CASUAL FOR A VIRGIN, IF YOU ASK ME.
...
OH--!
I TRUST YOU! I TRUST YOU!

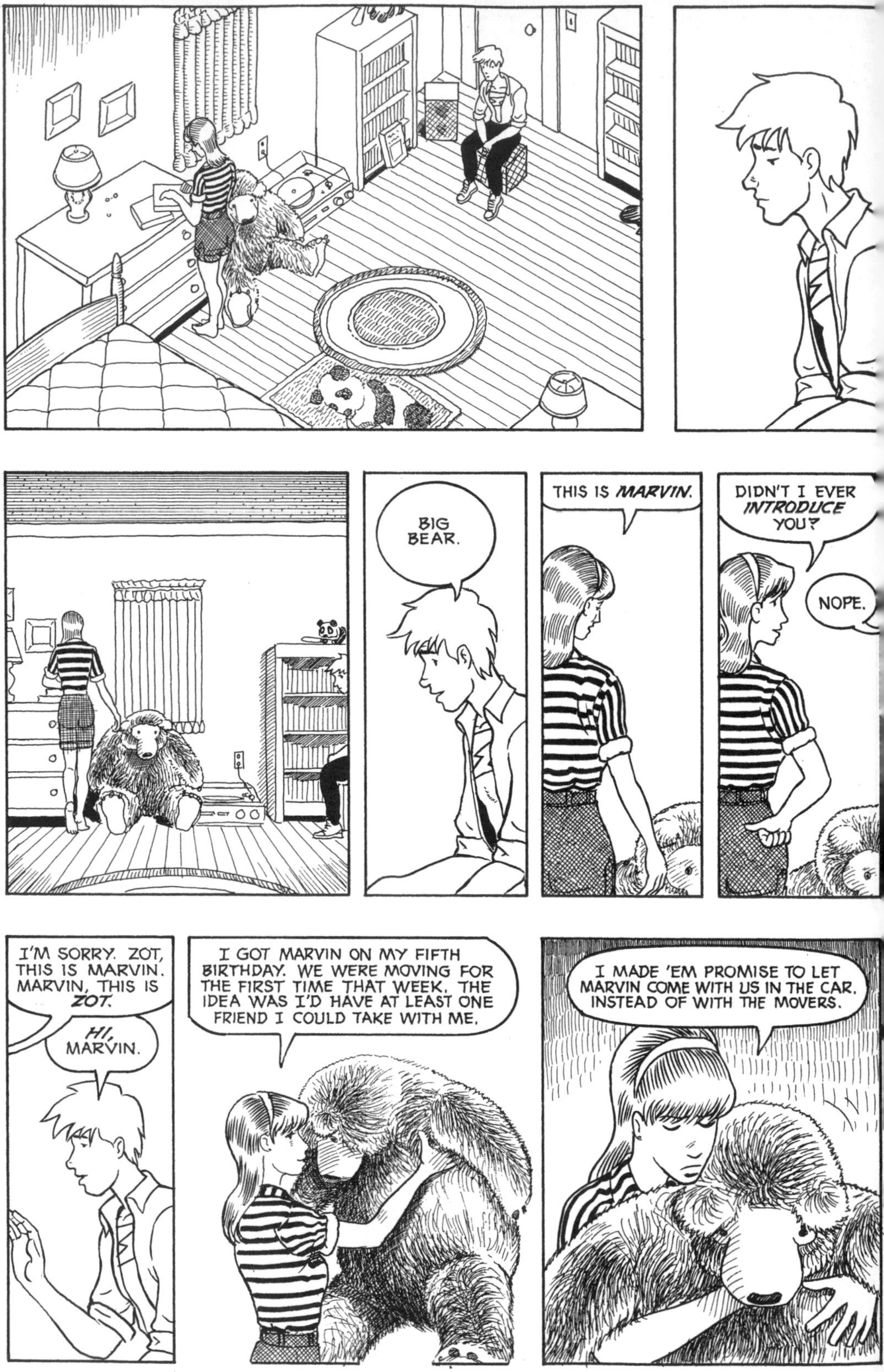
BIG BEAR.
THIS IS MARVIN.
DIDN'T I EVER INTRODUCE YOU?
NOPE.
I'M SORRY. ZOT, THIS IS MARVIN. MARVIN, THIS IS ZOT.
HI, MARVIN.
I GOT MARVIN ON MY FIFTH BIRTHDAY. WE WERE MOVING FOR THE FIRST TIME THAT WEEK. THE IDEA WAS I'D HAVE AT LEAST ONE FRIEND I COULD TAKE WITH ME.
I MADE 'EM PROMISE TO LET MARVIN COME WITH US IN THE CAR, INSTEAD OF WITH THE MOVERS.

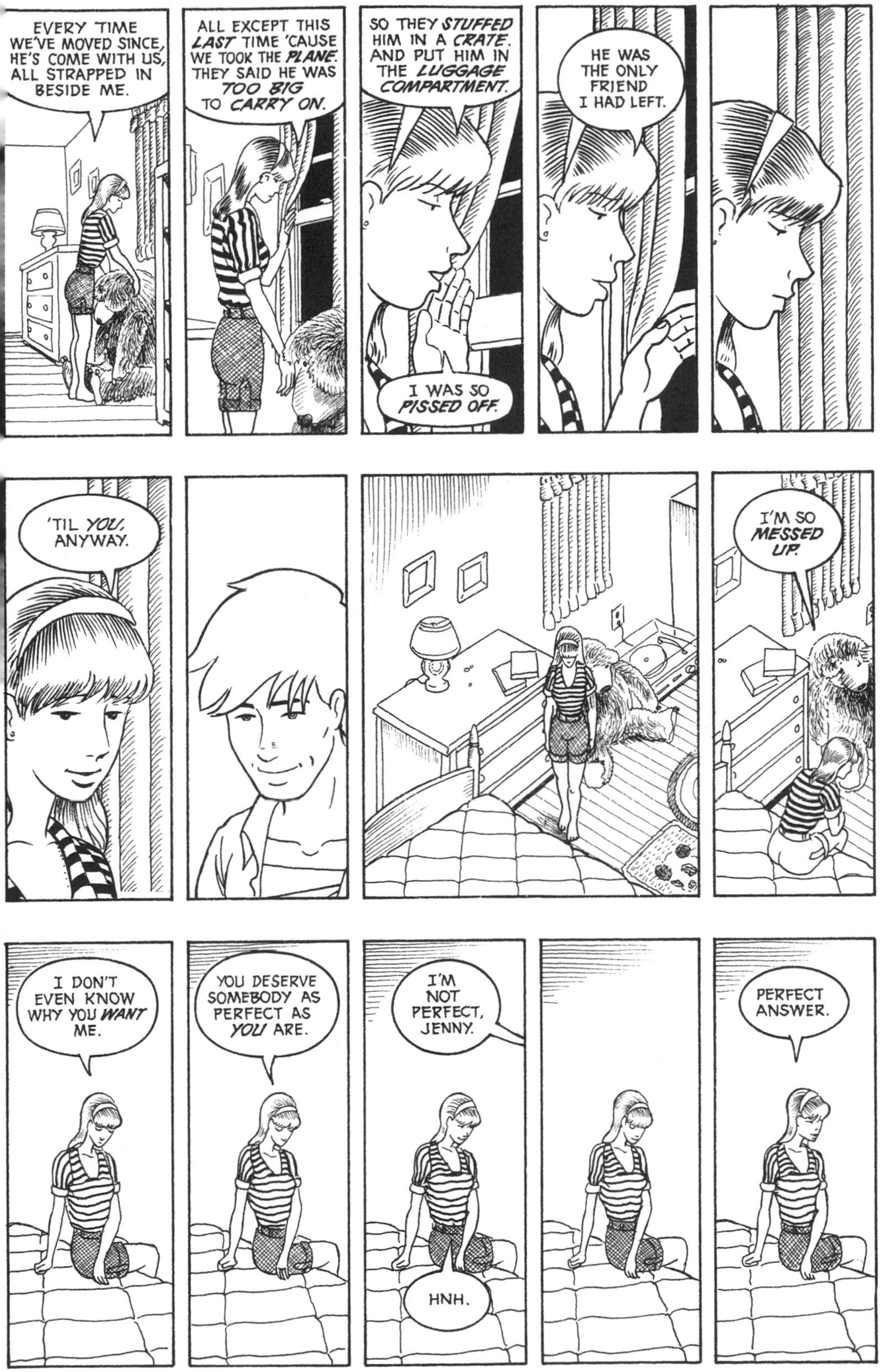

EVERY TIME WE'VE MOVED SINCE, HE'S COME WITH US, ALL STRAPPED IN BESIDE ME.
ALL EXCEPT THIS *LAST* TIME 'CAUSE WE TOOK THE *PLANE*. THEY SAID HE WAS *TOO BIG* TO *CARRY ON*.
SO THEY *STUFFED* HIM IN A *CRATE*. AND PUT HIM IN THE *LUGGAGE COMPARTMENT*.
I WAS SO *PISSED OFF*.
HE WAS THE ONLY FRIEND I HAD LEFT.
'TIL *YOU*, ANYWAY.
I'M SO *MESSED UP*.
I DON'T EVEN KNOW WHY YOU *WANT* ME.
YOU DESERVE SOMEBODY AS PERFECT AS *YOU* ARE.
I'M NOT PERFECT, JENNY.
HNH.
PERFECT ANSWER.

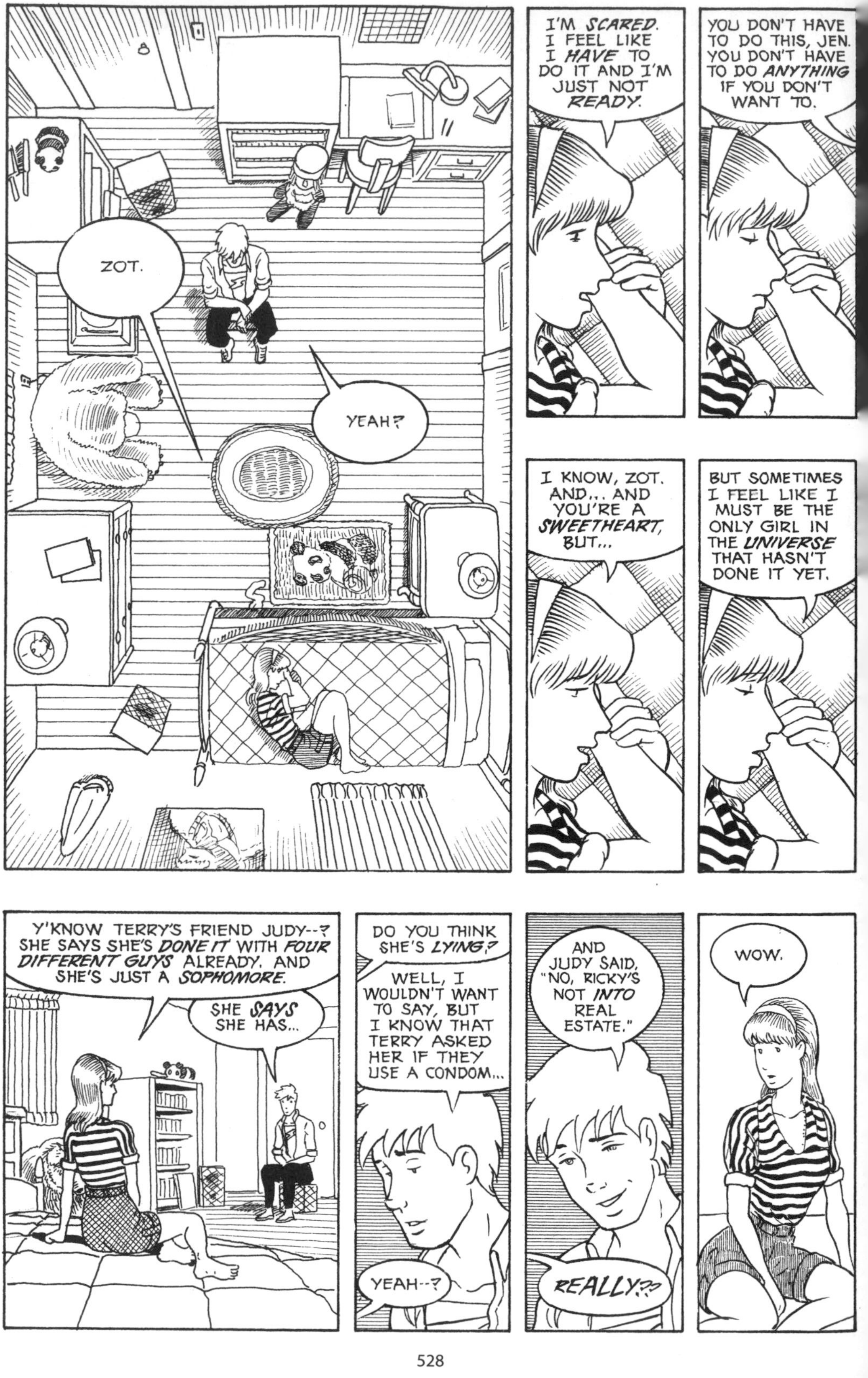
ZOT.
YEAH?
I'M SCARED. I FEEL LIKE I HAVE TO DO IT AND I'M JUST NOT READY.
YOU DON'T HAVE TO DO THIS, JEN. YOU DON'T HAVE TO DO ANYTHING IF YOU DON'T WANT TO.
I KNOW, ZOT. AND... AND YOU'RE A SWEETHEART, BUT...
BUT SOMETIMES I FEEL LIKE I MUST BE THE ONLY GIRL IN THE UNIVERSE THAT HASN'T DONE IT YET.
Y'KNOW TERRY'S FRIEND JUDY--? SHE SAYS SHE'S DONE IT WITH FOUR DIFFERENT GUYS ALREADY. AND SHE'S JUST A SOPHOMORE.
SHE SAYS SHE HAS...
DO YOU THINK SHE'S LYING?
WELL, I WOULDN'T WANT TO SAY, BUT I KNOW THAT TERRY ASKED HER IF THEY USE A CONDOM...
YEAH--?
AND JUDY SAID, "NO, RICKY'S NOT INTO REAL ESTATE."
REALLY??
WOW.

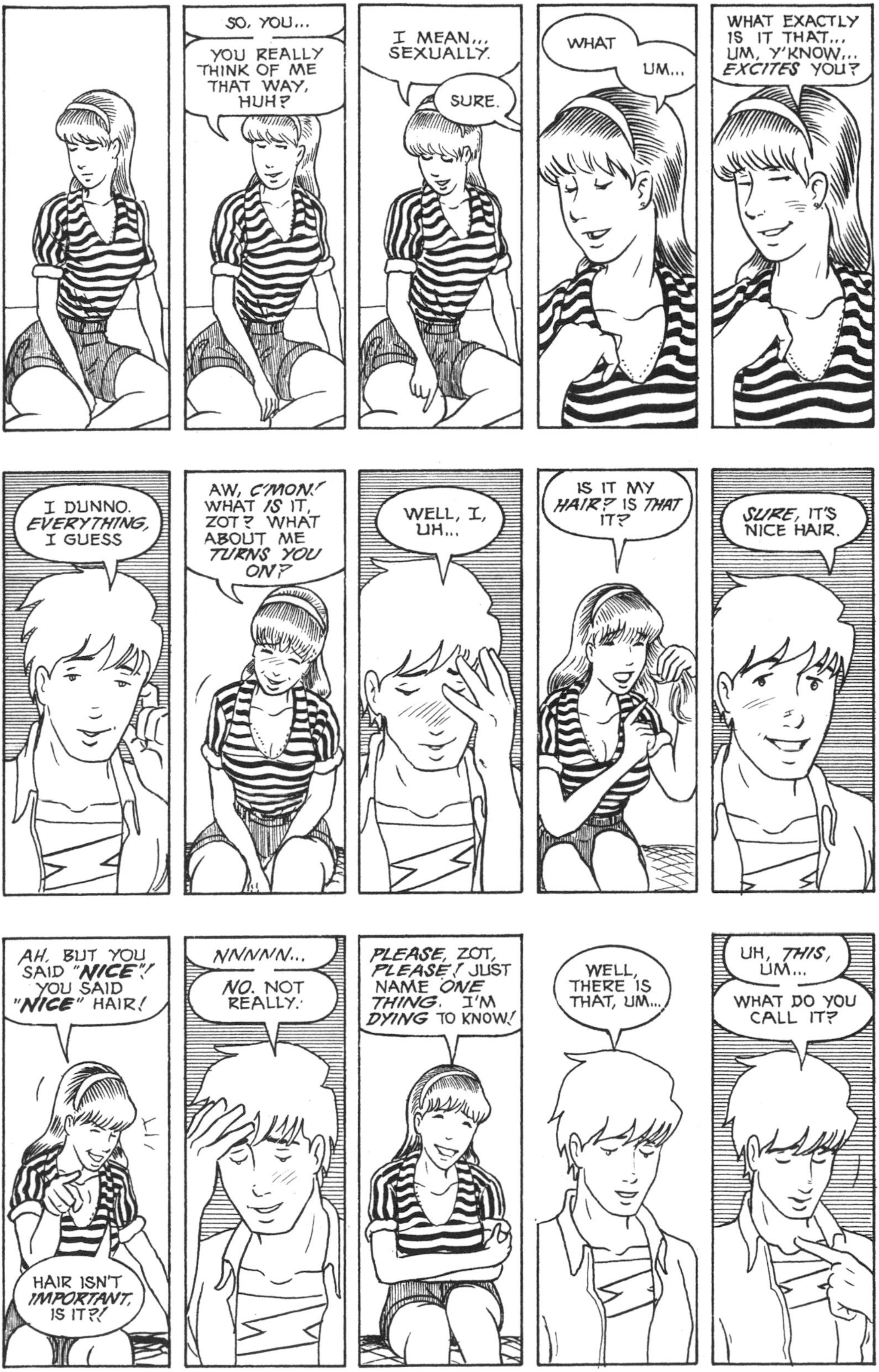
SO, YOU...
YOU REALLY THINK OF ME THAT WAY, HUH?
I MEAN... SEXUALLY.
SURE.
WHAT
UM...
WHAT EXACTLY IS IT THAT... UM, Y'KNOW... EXCITES YOU?
I DUNNO. EVERYTHING, I GUESS
AW, C'MON! WHAT IS IT, ZOT? WHAT ABOUT ME TURNS YOU ON?
WELL, I, UH...
IS IT MY HAIR? IS THAT IT?
SURE, IT'S NICE HAIR.
AH, BUT YOU SAID "NICE"! YOU SAID "NICE" HAIR!
HAIR ISN'T IMPORTANT, IS IT?!
NNNNN...
NO. NOT REALLY.
PLEASE, ZOT, PLEASE! JUST NAME ONE THING. I'M DYING TO KNOW!
WELL, THERE IS THAT, UM...
UH, THIS, UM...
WHAT DO YOU CALL IT?

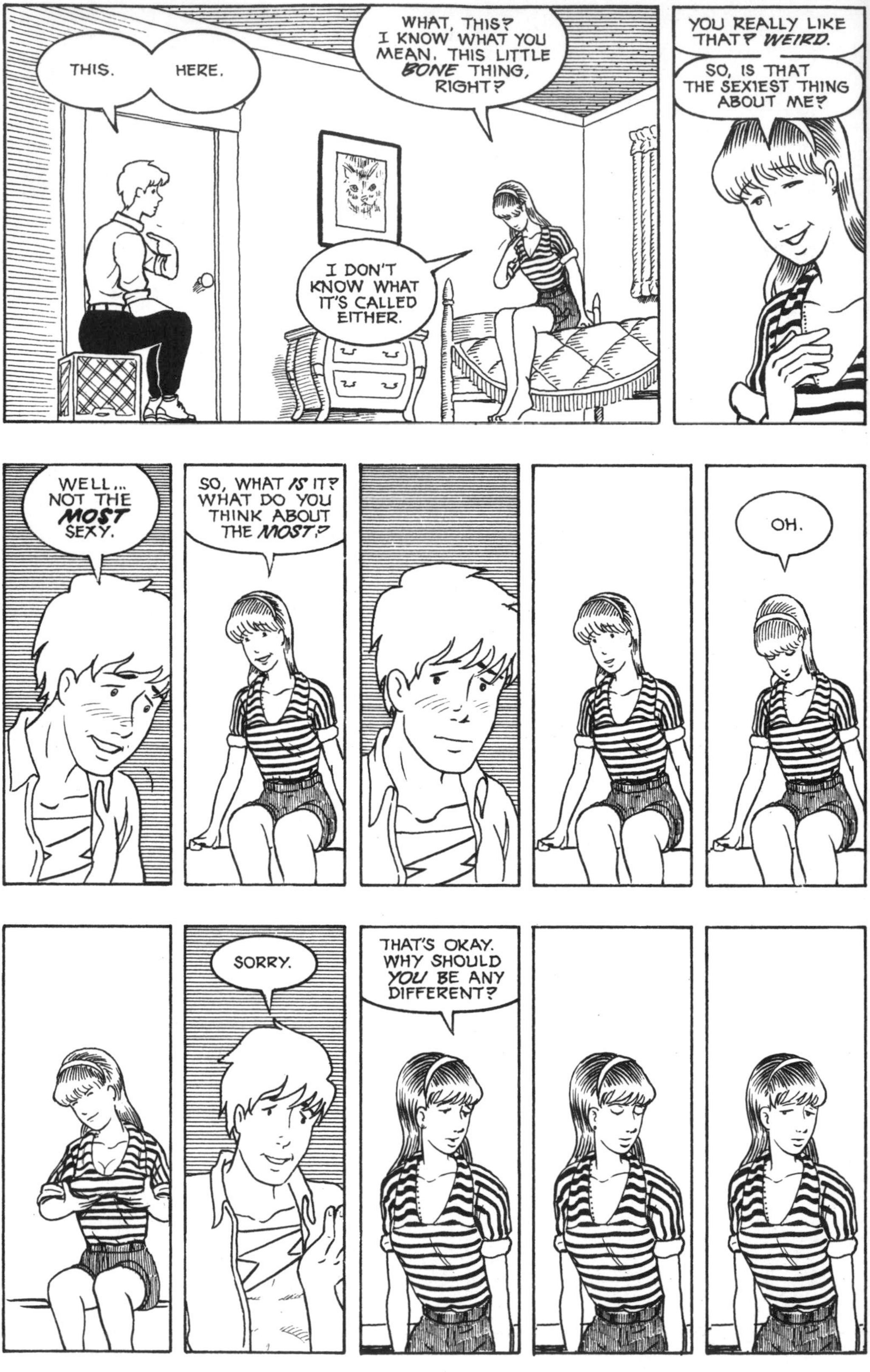
THIS.
HERE.
WHAT, THIS? I KNOW WHAT YOU MEAN. THIS LITTLE BONE THING, RIGHT?
I DON'T KNOW WHAT IT'S CALLED EITHER.
YOU REALLY LIKE THAT? WEIRD.
SO, IS THAT THE SEXIEST THING ABOUT ME?
WELL... NOT THE MOST SEXY.
SO, WHAT IS IT? WHAT DO YOU THINK ABOUT THE MOST?
OH.
SORRY.
THAT'S OKAY. WHY SHOULD YOU BE ANY DIFFERENT?

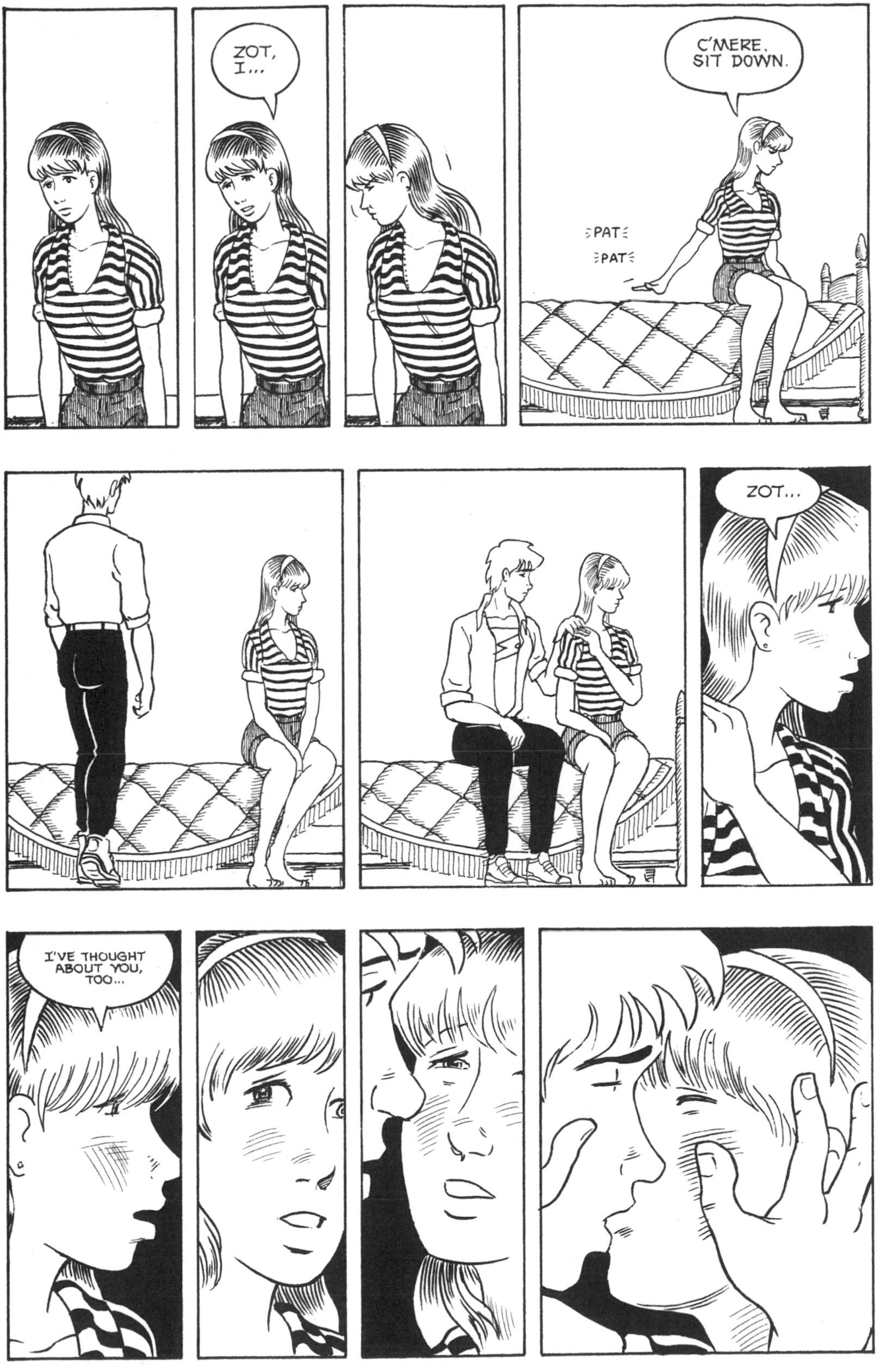
ZOT, I...
C'MERE. SIT DOWN.
PAT
PAT
ZOT...
I'VE THOUGHT ABOUT YOU, TOO...

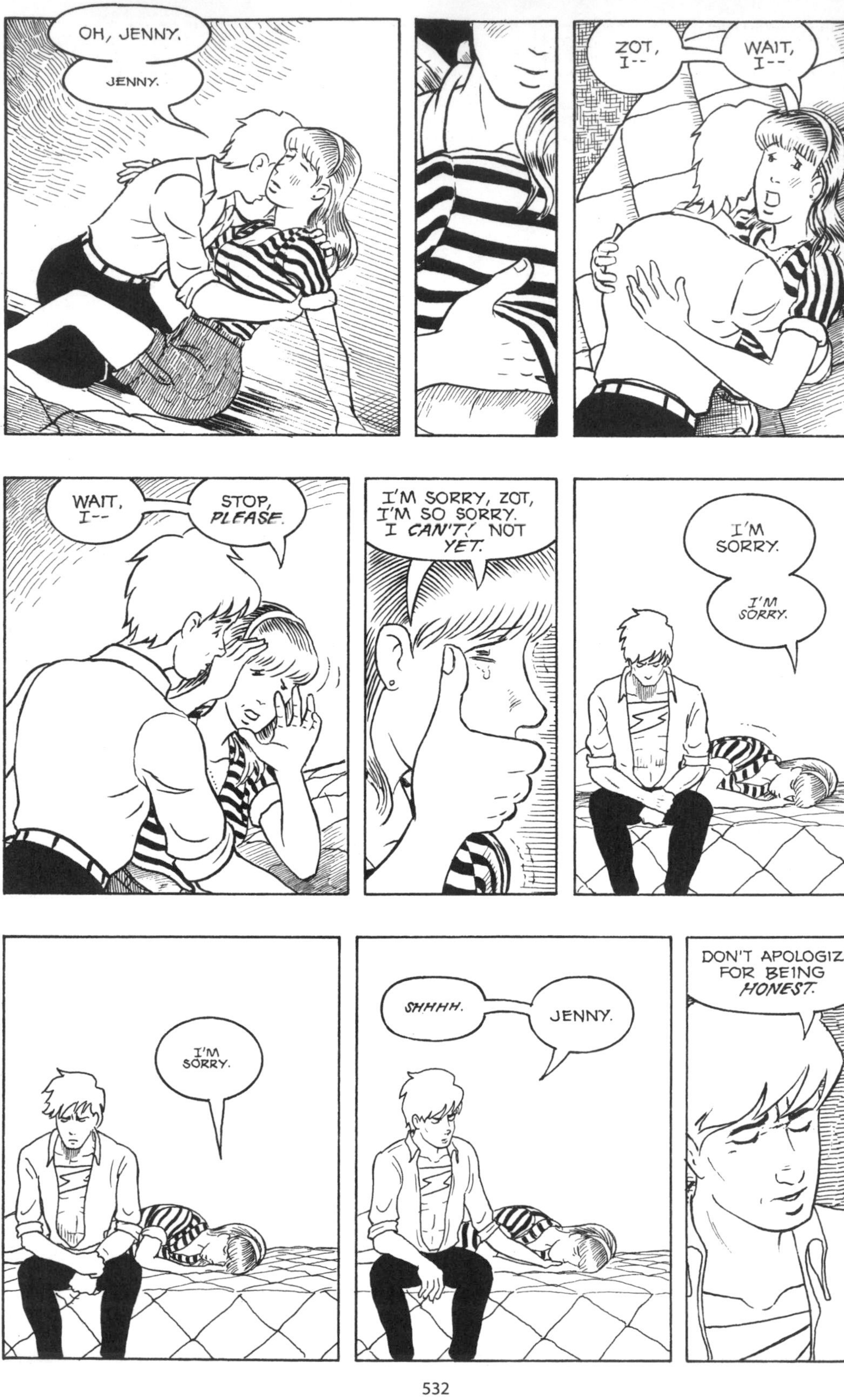
OH, JENNY.
JENNY.
ZOT, I--
WAIT, I--
WAIT, I--
STOP, PLEASE.
I'M SORRY, ZOT, I'M SO SORRY. I CAN'T! NOT YET.
I'M SORRY.
I'M SORRY.
I'M SORRY.
SHHHH.
JENNY.
DON'T APOLOGIZE FOR BEING HONEST.

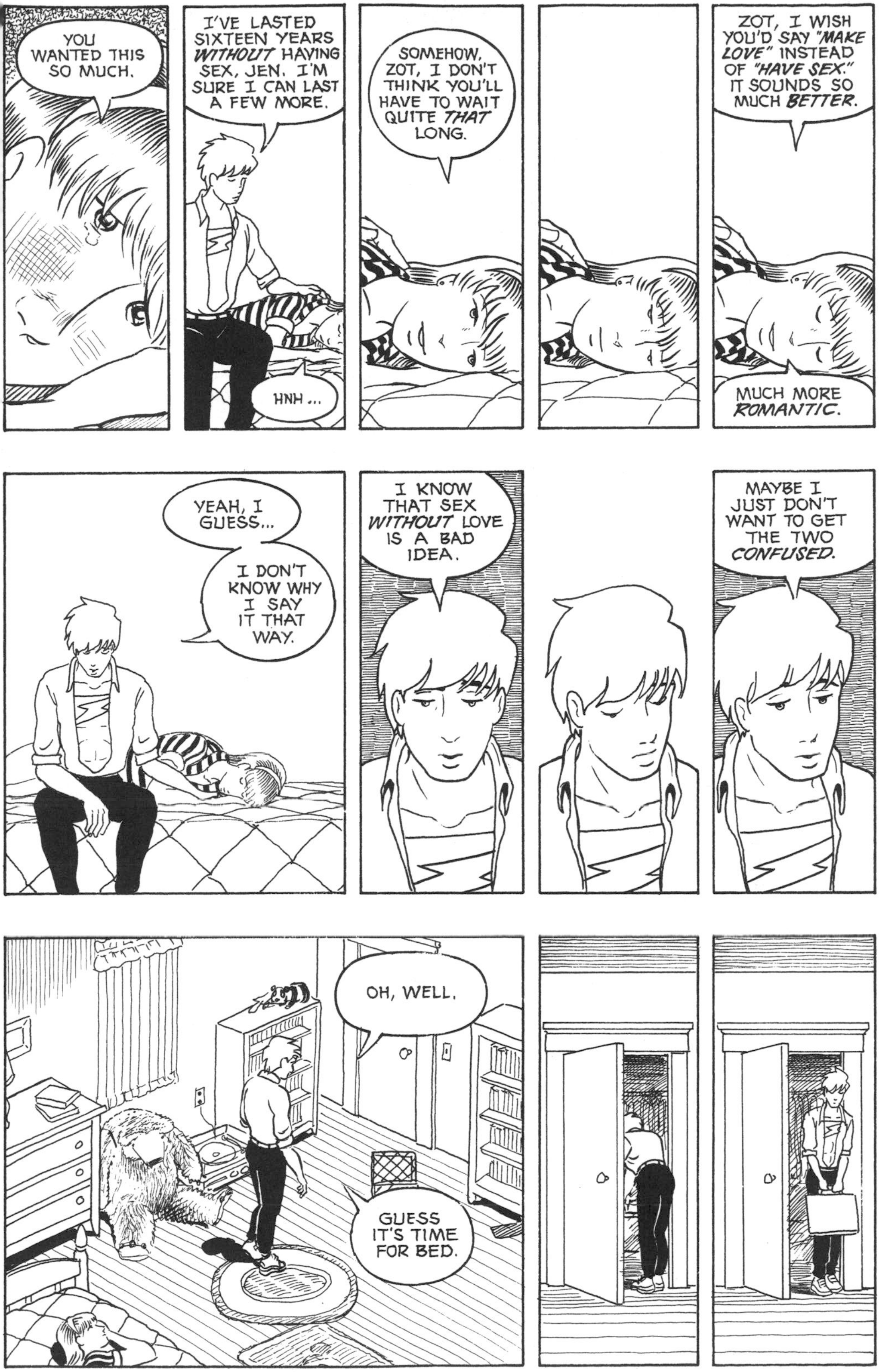
YOU WANTED THIS SO MUCH.
I'VE LASTED SIXTEEN YEARS *WITHOUT* HAVING SEX, JEN. I'M SURE I CAN LAST A FEW MORE.
HNH ...
SOMEHOW, ZOT, I DON'T THINK YOU'LL HAVE TO WAIT QUITE *THAT* LONG.
ZOT, I WISH YOU'D SAY *"MAKE LOVE"* INSTEAD OF *"HAVE SEX."* IT SOUNDS SO MUCH *BETTER*.
MUCH MORE *ROMANTIC*.
YEAH, I GUESS...
I DON'T KNOW WHY I SAY IT THAT WAY.
I KNOW THAT SEX *WITHOUT* LOVE IS A BAD IDEA.
MAYBE I JUST DON'T WANT TO GET THE TWO *CONFUSED*.
OH, WELL.
GUESS IT'S TIME FOR BED.

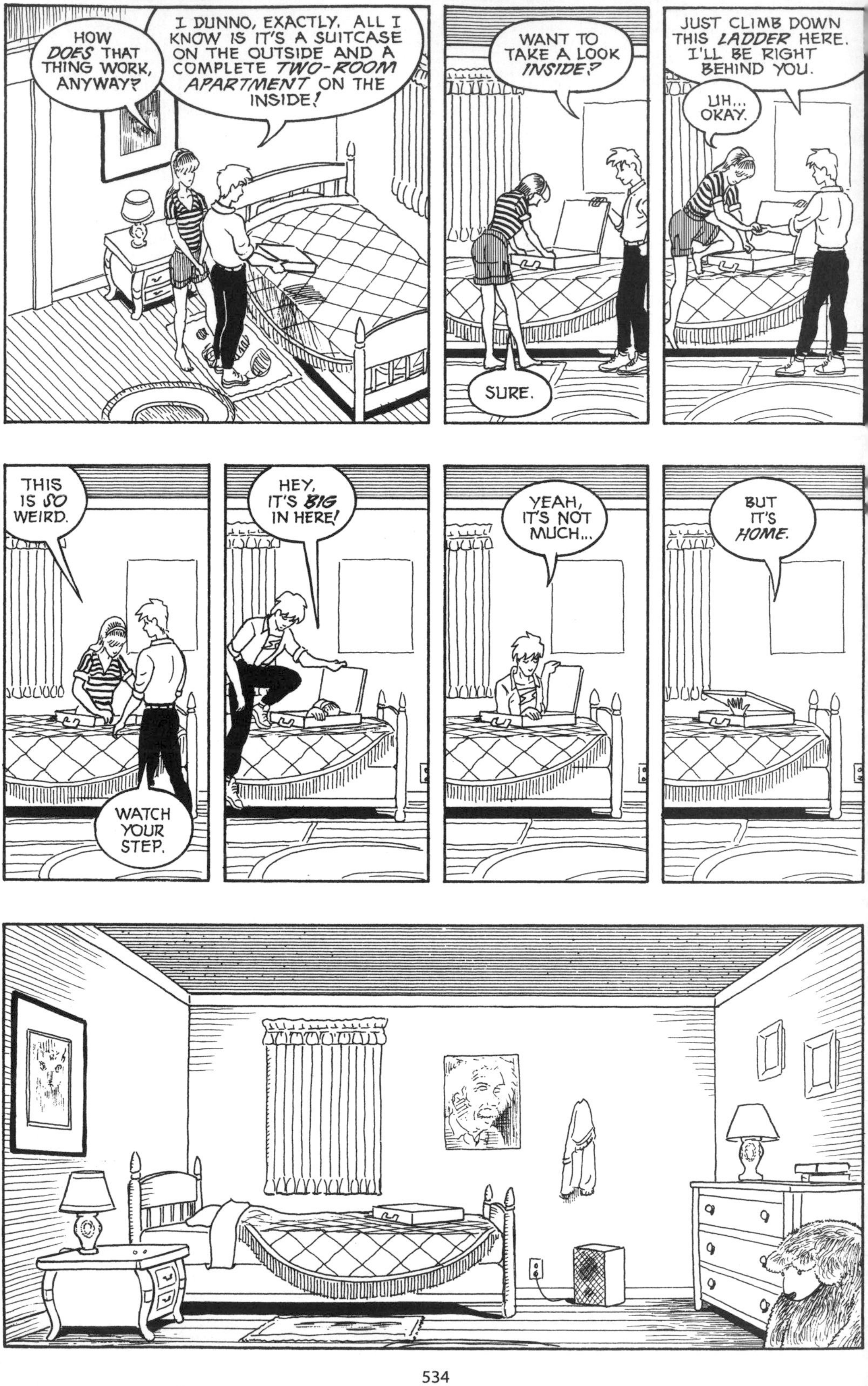
HOW *DOES* THAT THING WORK, ANYWAY?
I DUNNO, EXACTLY. ALL I KNOW IS IT'S A SUITCASE ON THE OUTSIDE AND A COMPLETE *TWO-ROOM APARTMENT* ON THE INSIDE!
WANT TO TAKE A LOOK *INSIDE?*
SURE.
JUST CLIMB DOWN THIS *LADDER* HERE. I'LL BE RIGHT BEHIND YOU.
UH... OKAY.
THIS IS *SO* WEIRD.
WATCH YOUR STEP.
HEY, IT'S *BIG* IN HERE!
YEAH, IT'S NOT MUCH...
BUT IT'S *HOME*.

What a strange artifact this story is! It was nominated for an Eisner Award, so *someone* must have liked it. It was an unusual exercise for its day and it was worth trying in principle. I can even live with the script; the dialogue may induce cringes, but they're mostly in the right places. No, all that's fine.

The *art,* however, has always bugged me. Somehow, I managed to create the perfect showcase for everything awkward and embarrassing about my drawing style. Worst of all, I remember how earnestly I was trying to get it right, even as I could see it slipping through my fingers. Throughout this collection, I've made a few adjustments where possible, but the only way I could truly fix this one eighteen years later is by drawing it over from scratch, and in that way lies madness.

A big problem in this particular instance was the need not only to create natural, convincing poses and expressions for Zot and Jenny (hard enough for me on a good day) but then to repeat them with only minimal variations throughout dozens of subsequent panels. In my attempt to keep those rows rigidly consistent, any life I might have been able to breathe into a single image was choked out of its various clones.

Consistency is a big problem for cartoonists with formalist tendencies like me. We get bored easily and want to change gears and try new things constantly. Character designs waver, inking styles shift. But consistency is indispensable for creating the illusion of life from panel to panel and issue to issue. Without it, the fact that the reader is just looking at lines on paper reasserts itself.

I'm not always so negative about my art. I like the varied visual designs of most of my characters. I like the crazy abstractions of Dekko. I like the compositions and effects I found in ordinary objects like school desks and buses. And my perspective and environments were solid for the most part.

I just couldn't draw *people* yet. And people have a way of turning up.

As for the ending, yes, I deliberately left it open to interpretation. It was important to assert Zot's basic decency in the way he accepted Jenny's wish to wait, but I didn't have a lot of strong opinions about what teenagers should do with each other in interdimensional suitcases, provided they took appropriate precautions.

Again, now I'm the parent of a teenager myself, so *ha ha,* the joke's on me. (Jenny is, for the record, a couple of years older by this issue.)

I won't tell you what I think happened next, but I will tell you that my editor thinks they did and Ivy thinks they didn't. Readers were similarly split.

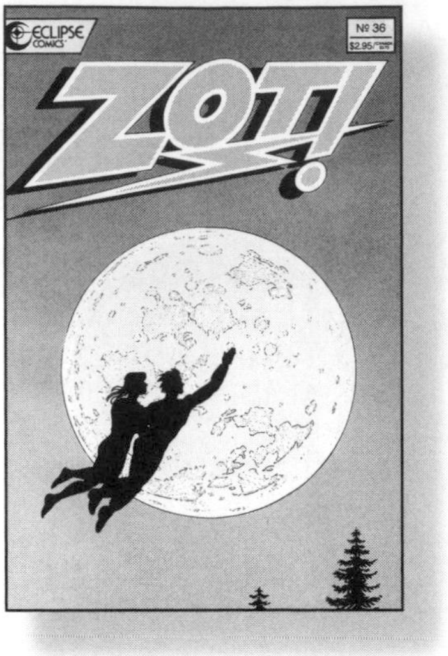
ECLIPSE
COMICS
№ 36
$2.95
ZOT!

The Great Escape

First published in *Zot! #36*.

Lettering:

Bob Lappan

Original series editor:

cat yronwode

Plot assist:

Ivy Ratafia

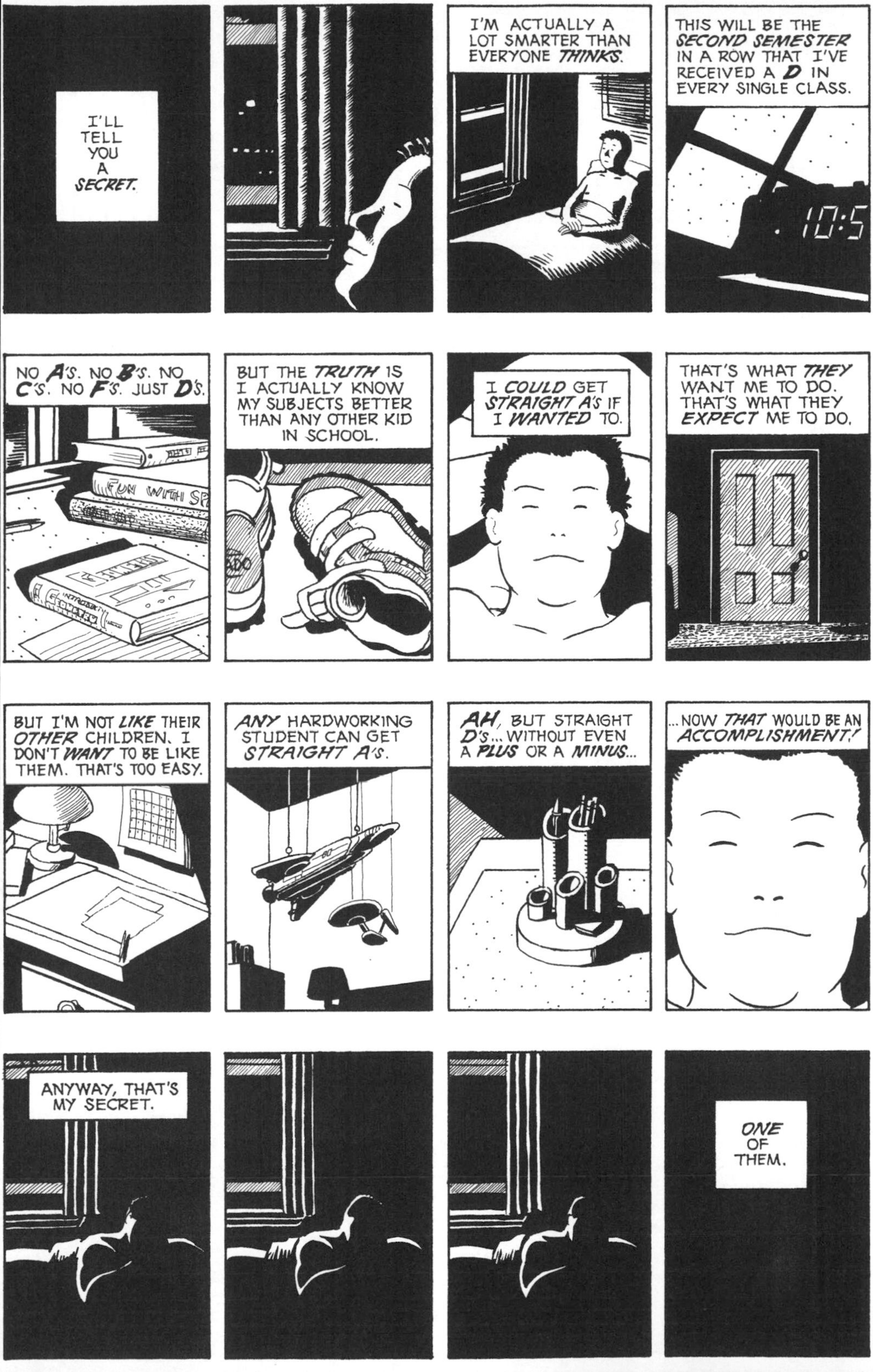
I'LL TELL YOU A SECRET.
I'M ACTUALLY A LOT SMARTER THAN EVERYONE THINKS.
THIS WILL BE THE SECOND SEMESTER IN A ROW THAT I'VE RECEIVED A D IN EVERY SINGLE CLASS.
10:5
NO A'S. NO B'S. NO C'S. NO F'S. JUST D'S.
FUN WITH SP
BUT THE TRUTH IS I ACTUALLY KNOW MY SUBJECTS BETTER THAN ANY OTHER KID IN SCHOOL.
I COULD GET STRAIGHT A'S IF I WANTED TO.
THAT'S WHAT THEY WANT ME TO DO. THAT'S WHAT THEY EXPECT ME TO DO.
BUT I'M NOT LIKE THEIR OTHER CHILDREN. I DON'T WANT TO BE LIKE THEM. THAT'S TOO EASY.
ANY HARDWORKING STUDENT CAN GET STRAIGHT A'S.
AH, BUT STRAIGHT D'S... WITHOUT EVEN A PLUS OR A MINUS...
...NOW THAT WOULD BE AN ACCOMPLISHMENT!
ANYWAY, THAT'S MY SECRET.
ONE OF THEM.

THE GREAT ESCAPE

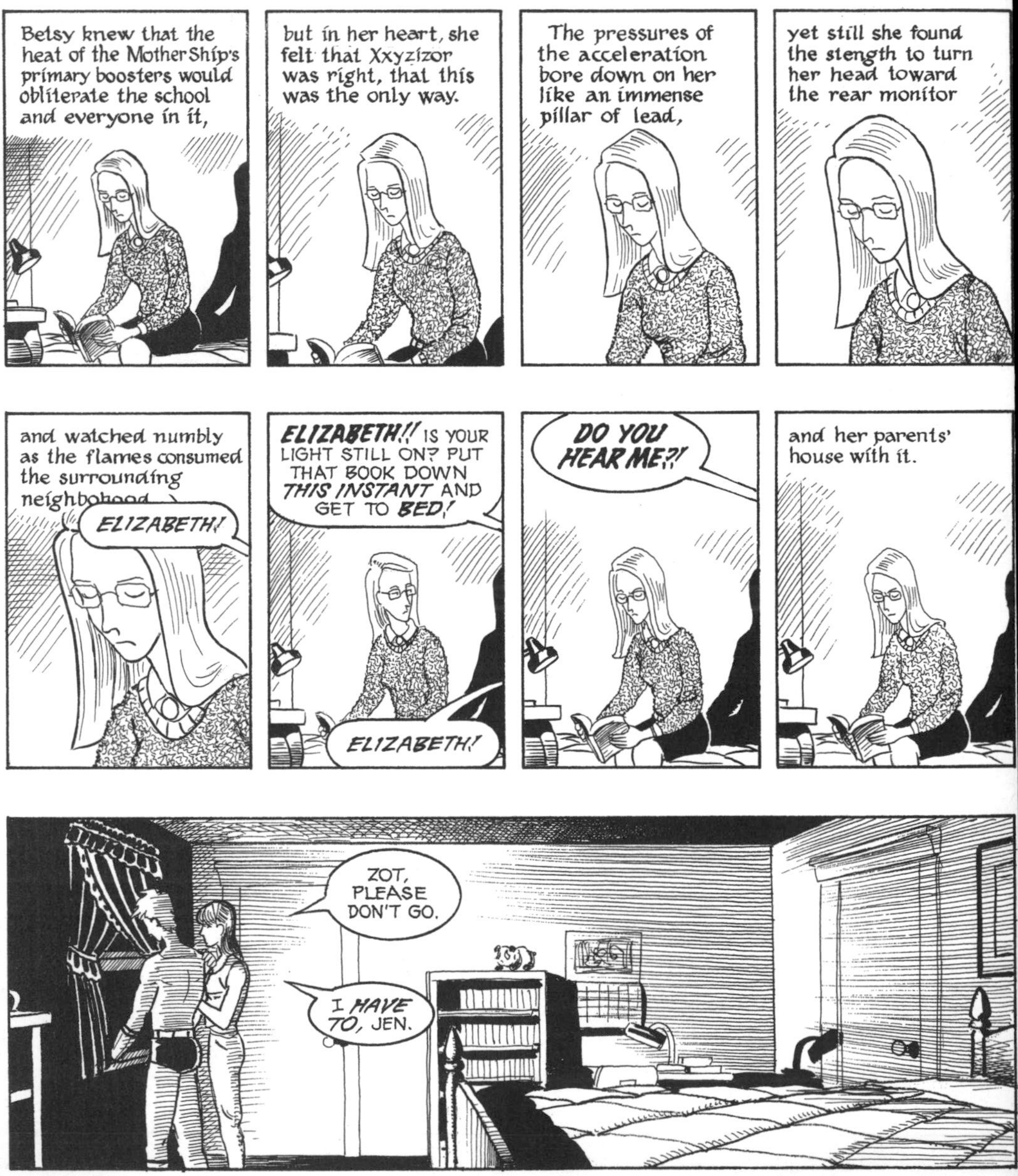
Betsy knew that the heat of the MotherShip's primary boosters would obliterate the school and everyone in it,
but in her heart, she felt that Xxyzizor was right, that this was the only way.
The pressures of the acceleration bore down on her like an immense pillar of lead,
yet still she found the stength to turn her head toward the rear monitor
and watched numbly as the flames consumed the surrounding neighbo
ELIZABETH!
ELIZABETH!! IS YOUR LIGHT STILL ON? PUT THAT BOOK DOWN THIS INSTANT AND GET TO BED!
ELIZABETH!
DO YOU HEAR ME?!
and her parents' house with it.
ZOT, PLEASE DON'T GO.
I HAVE TO, JEN.

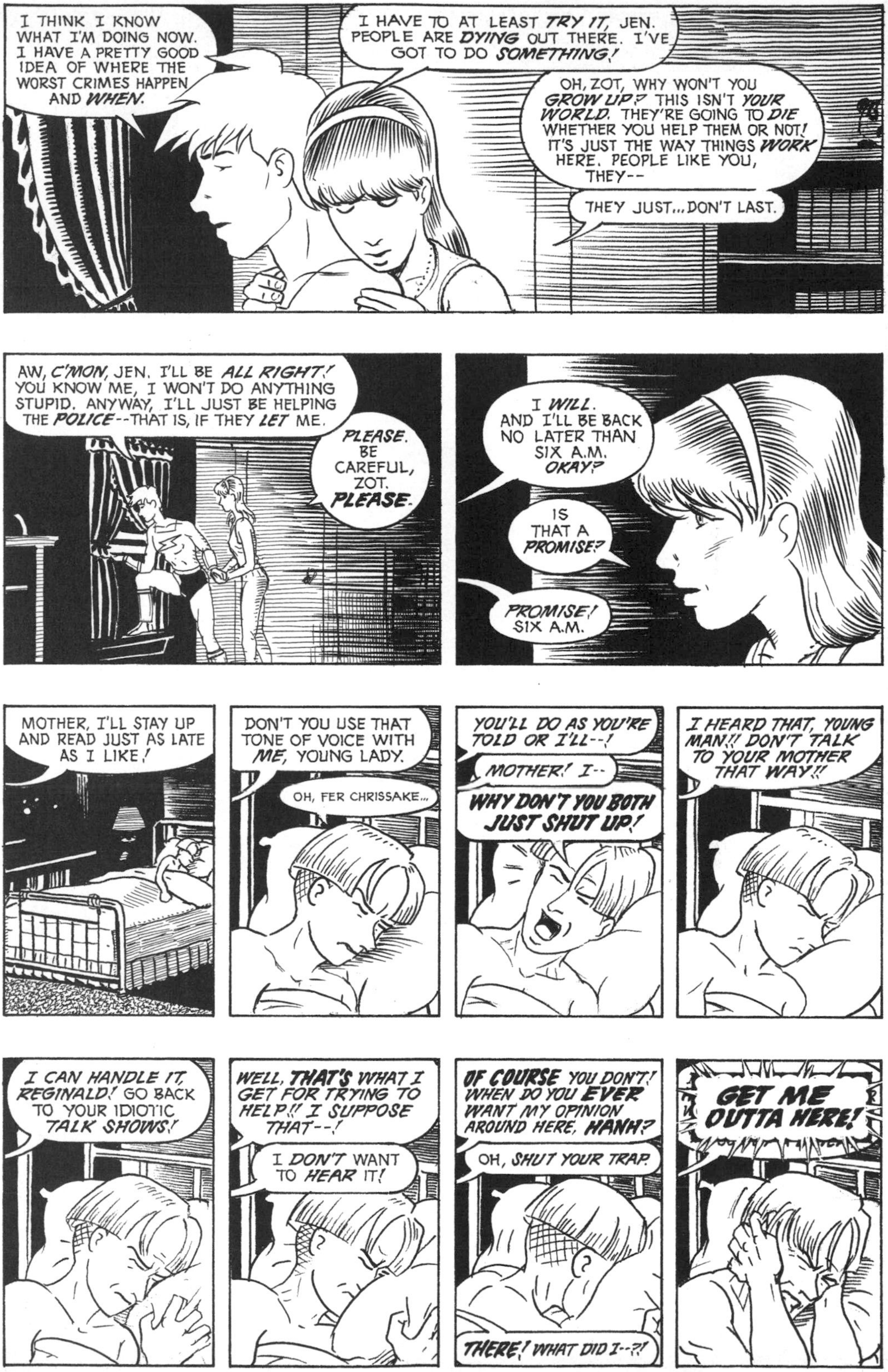

I THINK I KNOW WHAT I'M DOING NOW. I HAVE A PRETTY GOOD IDEA OF WHERE THE WORST CRIMES HAPPEN AND *WHEN*.
I HAVE TO AT LEAST *TRY IT*, JEN. PEOPLE ARE *DYING* OUT THERE. I'VE GOT TO DO *SOMETHING*!
OH, ZOT, WHY WON'T YOU *GROW UP*? THIS ISN'T *YOUR WORLD*. THEY'RE GOING TO *DIE* WHETHER YOU HELP THEM OR NOT! IT'S JUST THE WAY THINGS *WORK* HERE. PEOPLE LIKE YOU, THEY--
THEY JUST... DON'T LAST.
AW, *C'MON*, JEN. I'LL BE *ALL RIGHT*! YOU KNOW ME, I WON'T DO ANYTHING STUPID. ANYWAY, I'LL JUST BE HELPING THE *POLICE*--THAT IS, IF THEY *LET* ME.
PLEASE. BE CAREFUL, ZOT. ***PLEASE***.
I *WILL*. AND I'LL BE BACK NO LATER THAN SIX A.M. *OKAY*?
IS THAT A *PROMISE*?
PROMISE! SIX A.M.
MOTHER, I'LL STAY UP AND READ JUST AS LATE AS I LIKE!
DON'T YOU USE THAT TONE OF VOICE WITH *ME*, YOUNG LADY.
OH, FER CHRISSAKE...
YOU'LL DO AS YOU'RE TOLD OR I'LL--!
MOTHER! I--
WHY DON'T YOU BOTH JUST SHUT UP!
I HEARD THAT, YOUNG MAN!! DON'T TALK TO YOUR MOTHER THAT WAY!!
I CAN HANDLE IT, REGINALD! GO BACK TO YOUR IDIOTIC *TALK SHOWS!*
*WELL, **THAT'S** WHAT I GET FOR TRYING TO HELP!! I SUPPOSE THAT--!*
I *DON'T* WANT TO *HEAR* IT!
***OF COURSE** YOU DON'T! WHEN DO YOU **EVER** WANT MY OPINION AROUND HERE, **HANH**?*
OH, *SHUT YOUR TRAP.*
***THERE!** WHAT DID I--?!*
GET ME OUTTA HERE!

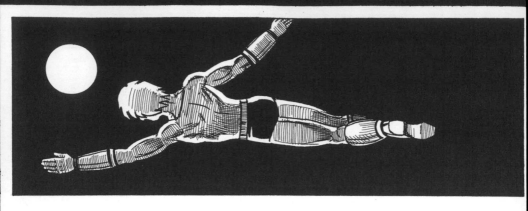

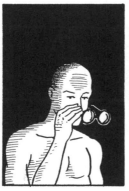

THERE'S THIS GUY.

AND HE HAS THE POWER TO ESCAPE FROM *ANYTHING.*

HE *TELEPORTS...*

OR NO, HE HAS A *CAPE* OR SOMETHING.

AND HE CAN JUST *STEP THROUGH* THE *CAPE* AND BE *ANYWHERE ELSE.*

IF HE DOESN'T LIKE WHERE HE IS, HE CAN JUST STEP THROUGH THE CAPE.

AND BE *FAR, FAR AWAY*...

THAT'S A *GOOD* ONE. I SHOULD WRITE THAT DOWN IN *THE BOOK.*

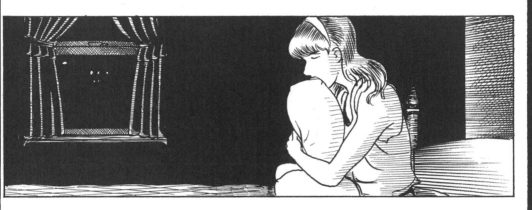

IT'S OKAY, ZOE, MY MOMMY DIDN'T MEAN TO HIT YOU.

-*WRUF!*-

YE-ES, DEAR. I KNOW. I KNOW.

MOMMY WILL BE OKAY, ZOE, JUST YOU *WAIT AND SEE.*

HEY, DO YOU KNOW HOW TO MAKE EVERYTHING GET BETTER?

YOU JUST *CLOSE YOUR EYES* AND THINK OF EXACTLY HOW YOU WANT LIFE TO BE.

IF YOU DO THIS *OFTEN ENOUGH,* YOU'LL JUST *WAKE UP* ONE DAY AND *THERE YOU'LL BE.*

NO ONE HAD TO *TELL ME* THIS! I KNEW IT *INSTINCTIVELY!*

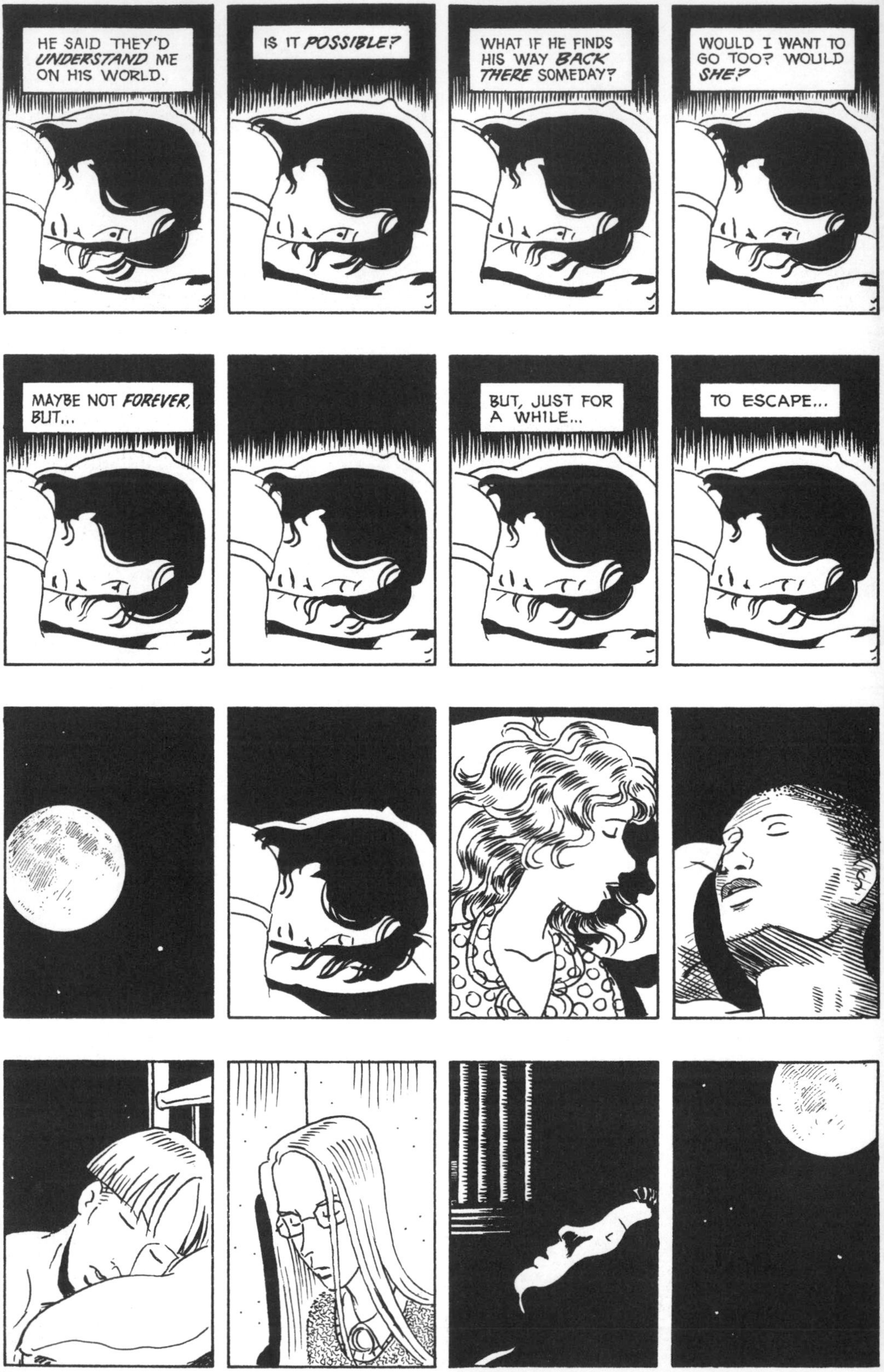
HE SAID THEY'D *UNDERSTAND* ME ON HIS WORLD.
IS IT *POSSIBLE?*
WHAT IF HE FINDS HIS WAY *BACK THERE* SOMEDAY?
WOULD I WANT TO GO TOO? WOULD *SHE?*
MAYBE NOT *FOREVER*, BUT...
BUT, JUST FOR A WHILE...
TO ESCAPE...

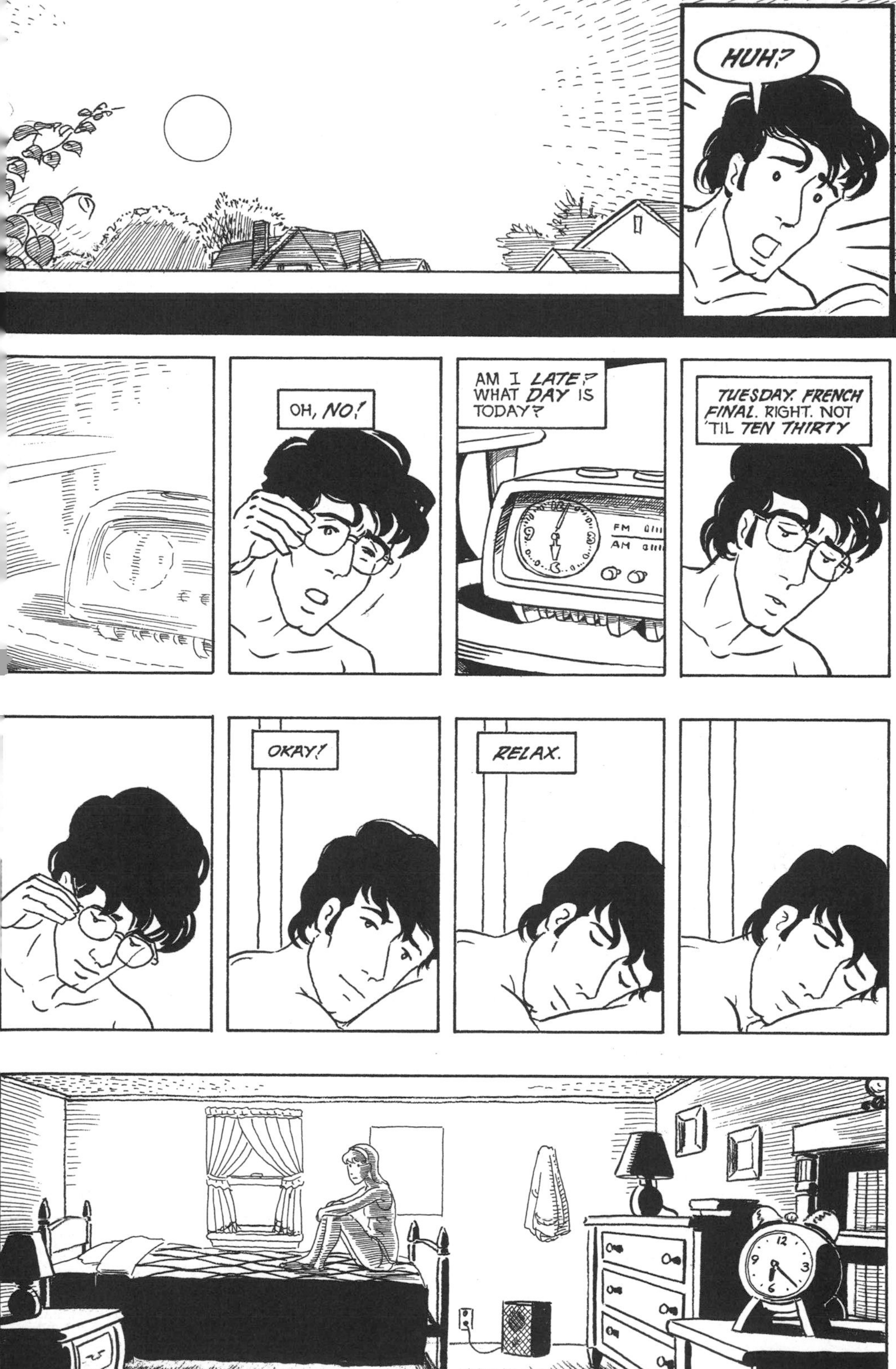
HUH?
OH, NO!
AM I LATE? WHAT DAY IS TODAY?
TUESDAY. FRENCH FINAL. RIGHT. NOT 'TIL TEN THIRTY
OKAY!
RELAX.

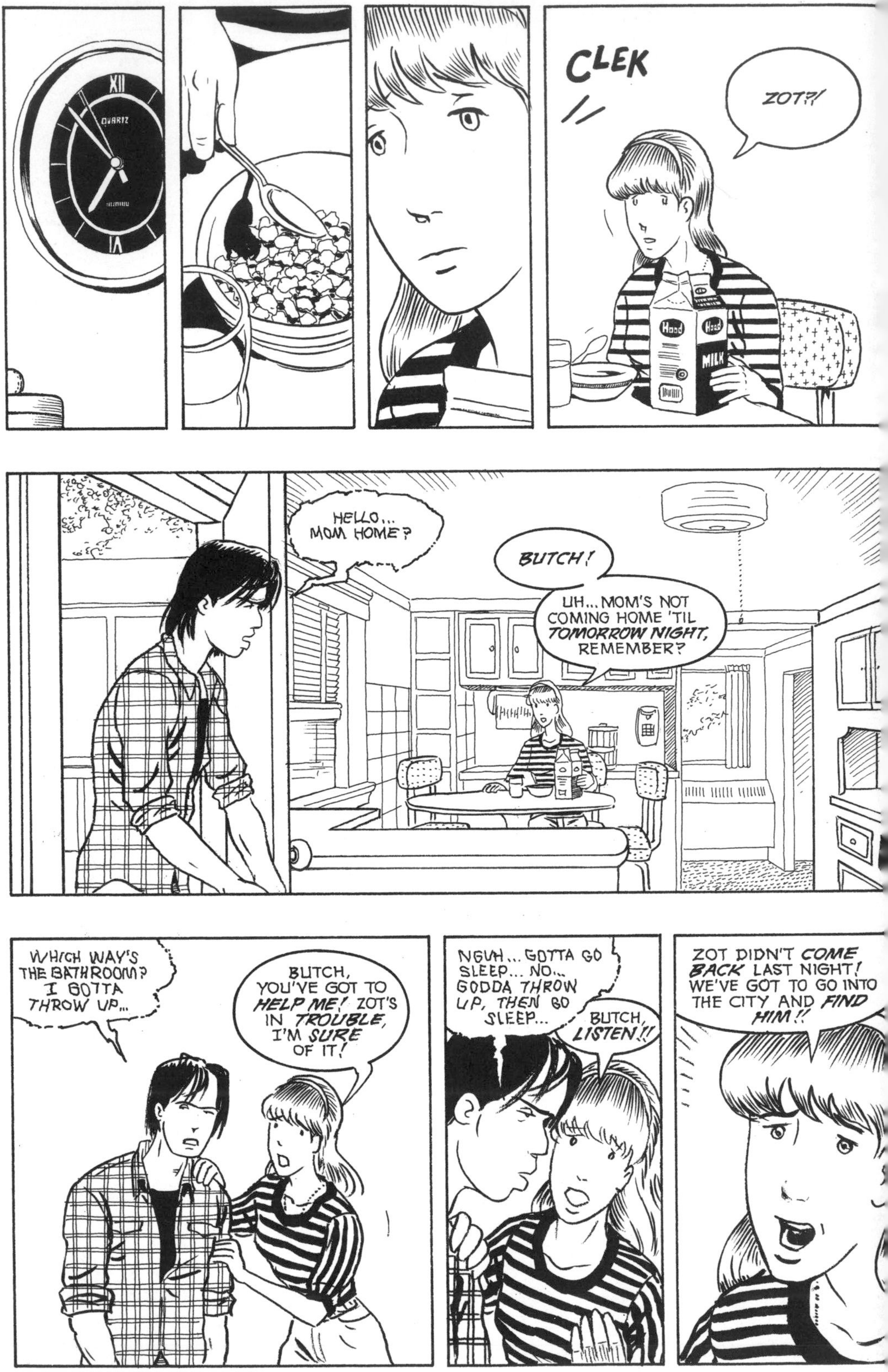
CLEK
ZOT?!
HELLO... MOM HOME?
BUTCH!
UH... MOM'S NOT COMING HOME 'TIL TOMORROW NIGHT, REMEMBER?
WHICH WAY'S THE BATHROOM? I GOTTA THROW UP...
BUTCH, YOU'VE GOT TO HELP ME! ZOT'S IN TROUBLE, I'M SURE OF IT!
NGUH... GOTTA GO SLEEP... NO... GODDA THROW UP, THEN GO SLEEP...
BUTCH, LISTEN!!
ZOT DIDN'T COME BACK LAST NIGHT! WE'VE GOT TO GO INTO THE CITY AND FIND HIM!!

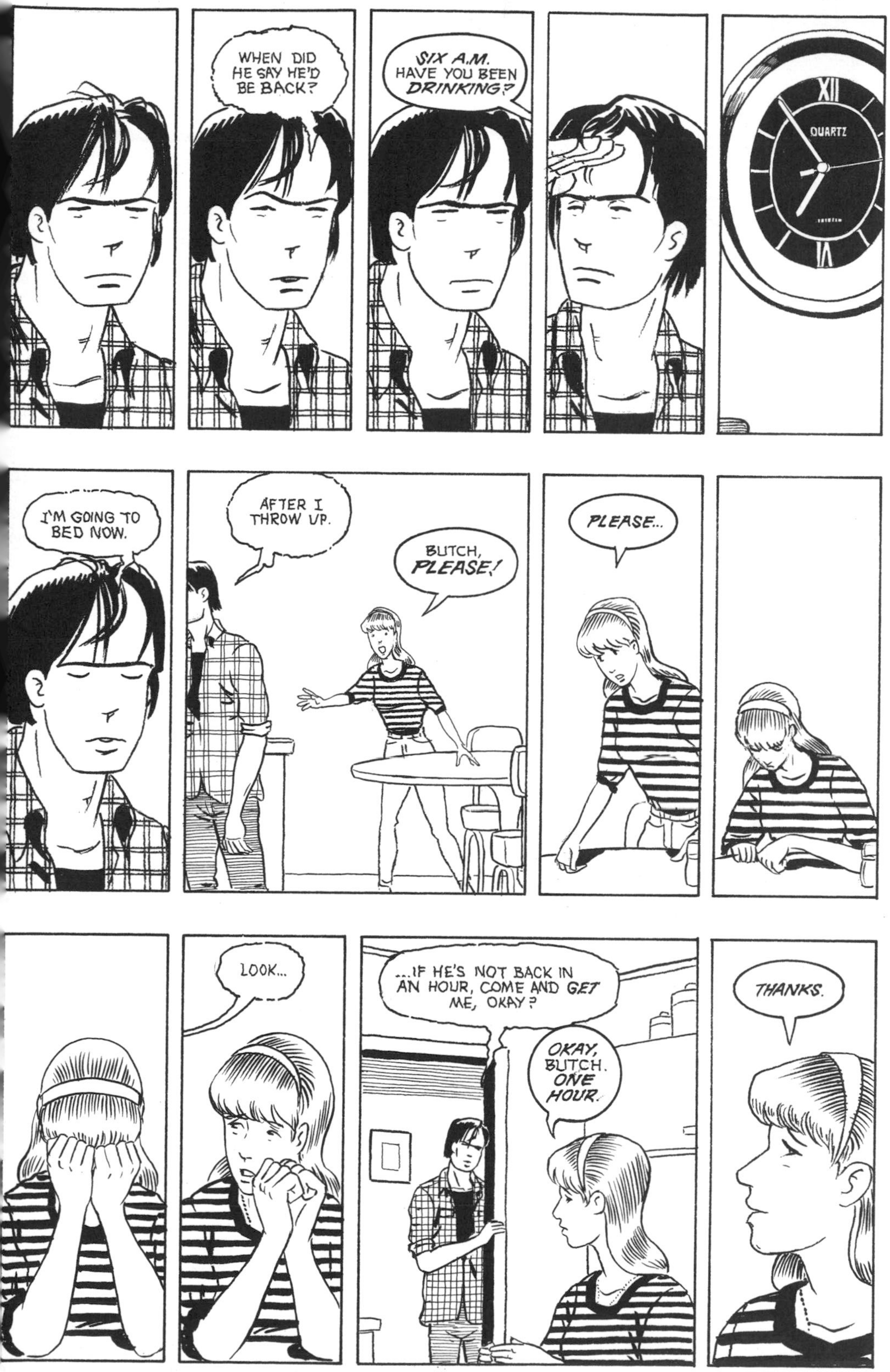
WHEN DID HE SAY HE'D BE BACK?
SIX A.M. HAVE YOU BEEN DRINKING?
QUARTZ
I'M GOING TO BED NOW.
AFTER I THROW UP.
BUTCH, PLEASE!
PLEASE...
LOOK...
...IF HE'S NOT BACK IN AN HOUR, COME AND GET ME, OKAY?
OKAY, BUTCH. ONE HOUR.
THANKS.

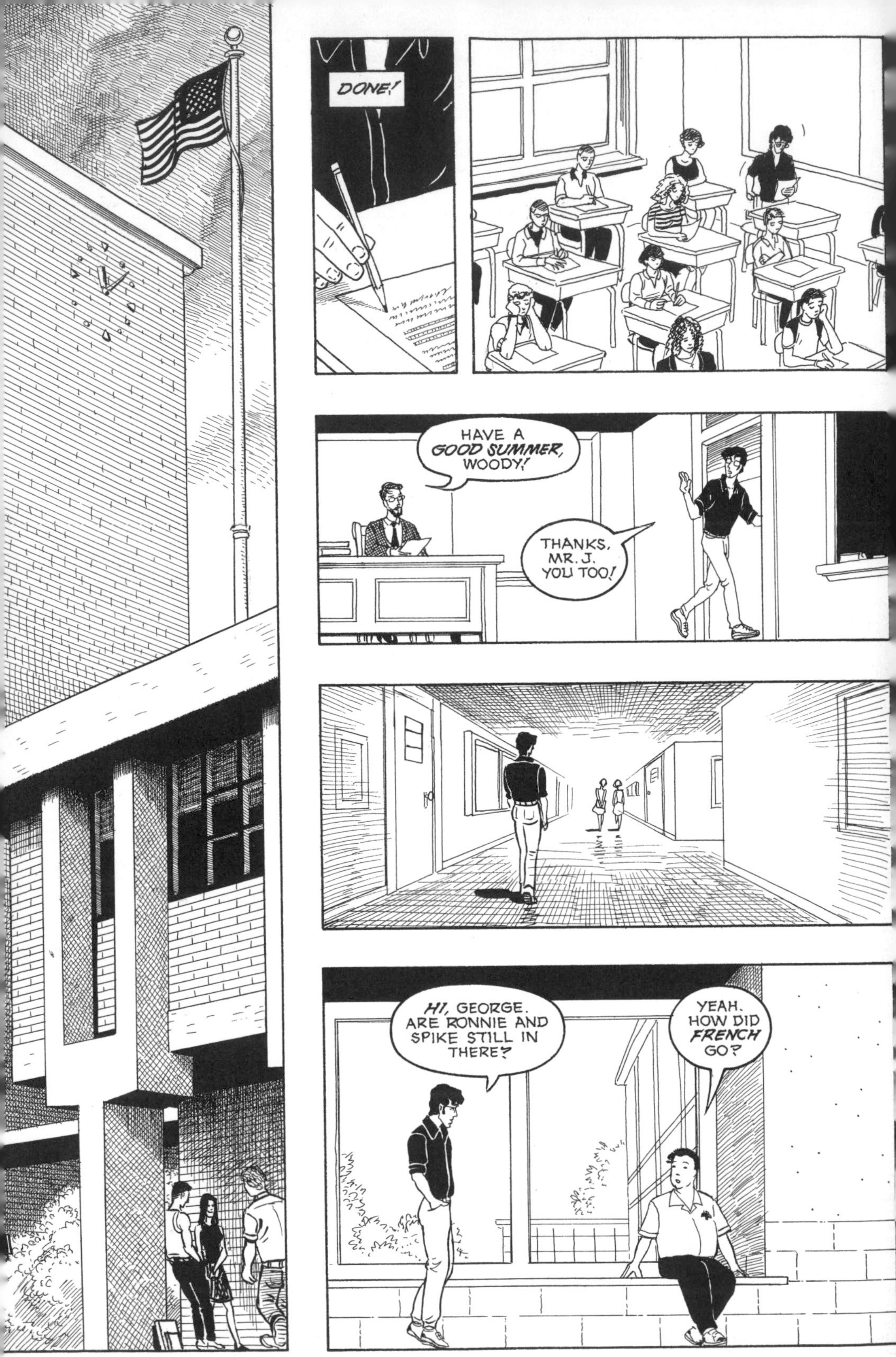
DONE!
HAVE A GOOD SUMMER, WOODY!
THANKS, MR. J. YOU TOO!
HI, GEORGE. ARE RONNIE AND SPIKE STILL IN THERE?
YEAH. HOW DID FRENCH GO?

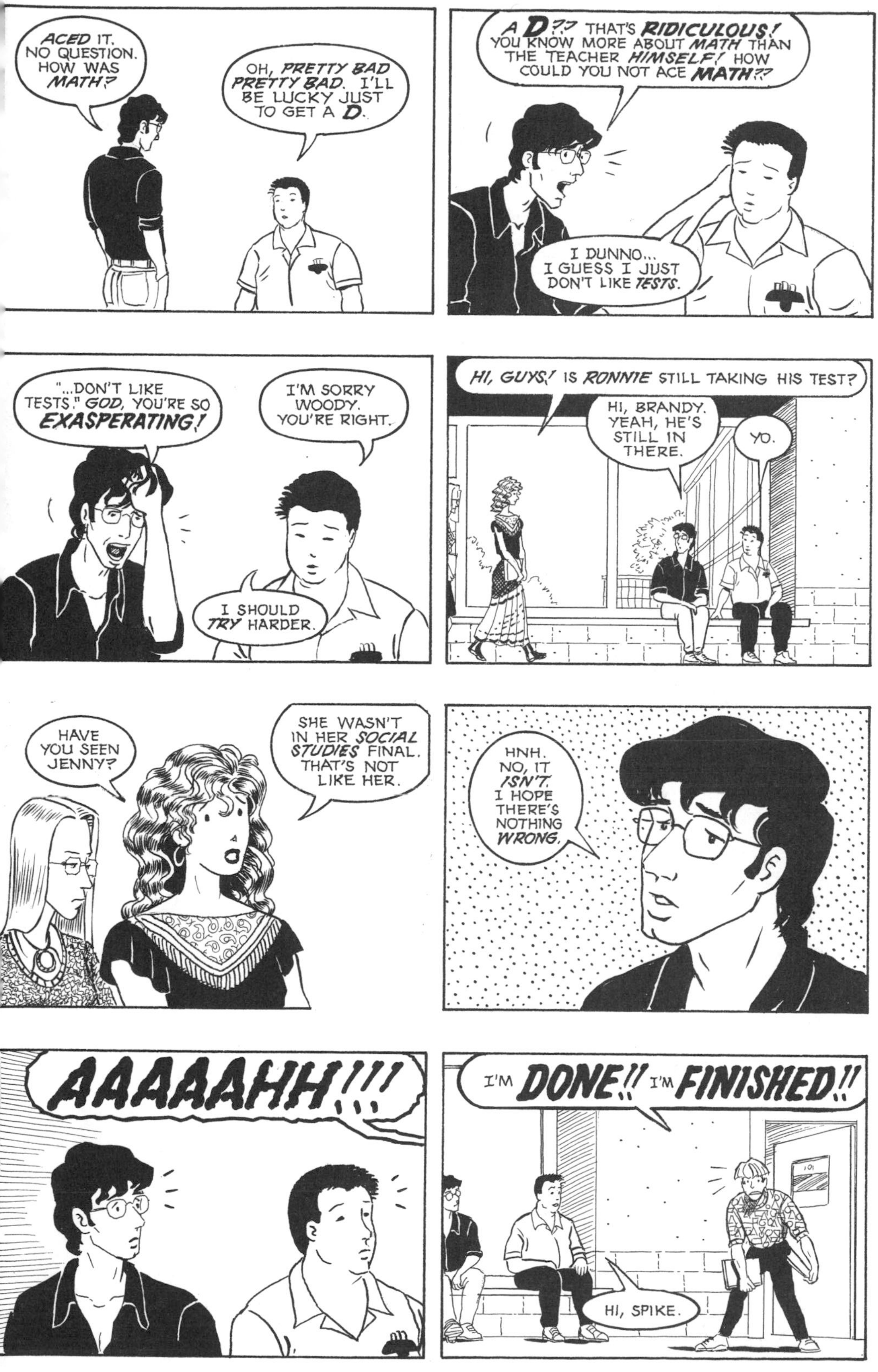
ACED IT. NO QUESTION. HOW WAS MATH?
OH, PRETTY BAD PRETTY BAD. I'LL BE LUCKY JUST TO GET A D.
A D?? THAT'S RIDICULOUS! YOU KNOW MORE ABOUT MATH THAN THE TEACHER HIMSELF! HOW COULD YOU NOT ACE MATH??
I DUNNO... I GUESS I JUST DON'T LIKE TESTS.
"...DON'T LIKE TESTS." GOD, YOU'RE SO EXASPERATING!
I'M SORRY WOODY. YOU'RE RIGHT.
I SHOULD TRY HARDER.
HI, GUYS! IS RONNIE STILL TAKING HIS TEST?
HI, BRANDY. YEAH, HE'S STILL IN THERE.
YO.
HAVE YOU SEEN JENNY?
SHE WASN'T IN HER SOCIAL STUDIES FINAL. THAT'S NOT LIKE HER.
HNH. NO, IT ISN'T. I HOPE THERE'S NOTHING WRONG.
AAAAAHH!!!
I'M DONE!! I'M FINISHED!!
HI, SPIKE.

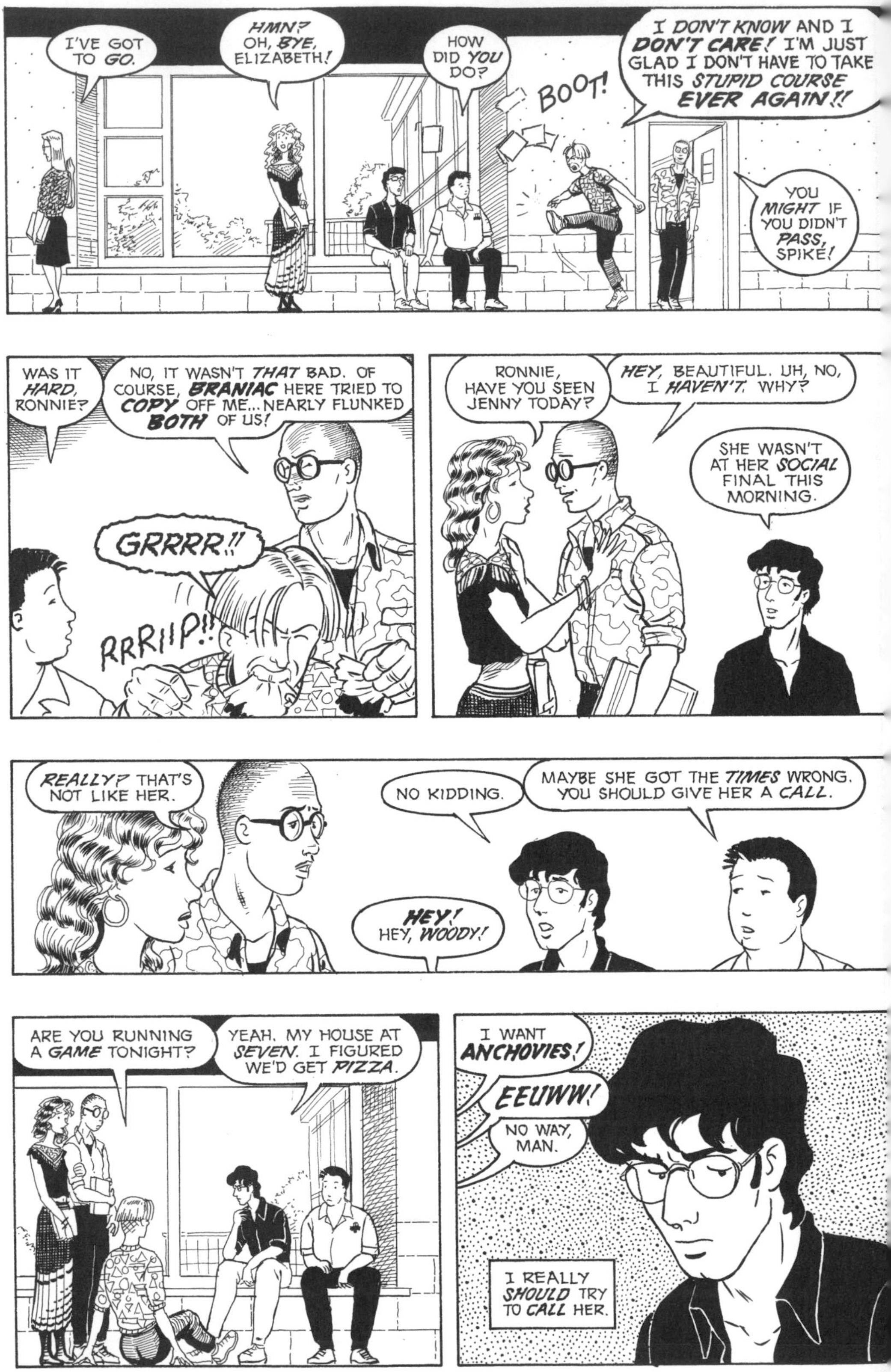
I'VE GOT TO GO.
HMN? OH, BYE, ELIZABETH!
HOW DID YOU DO?
BOOT!
I DON'T KNOW AND I DON'T CARE! I'M JUST GLAD I DON'T HAVE TO TAKE THIS STUPID COURSE EVER AGAIN!!
YOU MIGHT IF YOU DIDN'T PASS, SPIKE!
WAS IT HARD, RONNIE?
NO, IT WASN'T THAT BAD. OF COURSE, BRANIAC HERE TRIED TO COPY OFF ME... NEARLY FLUNKED BOTH OF US!
GRRRR!!
RRRIIP!!
RONNIE, HAVE YOU SEEN JENNY TODAY?
HEY, BEAUTIFUL. UH, NO, I HAVEN'T. WHY?
SHE WASN'T AT HER SOCIAL FINAL THIS MORNING.
REALLY? THAT'S NOT LIKE HER.
NO KIDDING.
MAYBE SHE GOT THE TIMES WRONG. YOU SHOULD GIVE HER A CALL.
HEY! HEY, WOODY!
ARE YOU RUNNING A GAME TONIGHT?
YEAH. MY HOUSE AT SEVEN. I FIGURED WE'D GET PIZZA.
I WANT ANCHOVIES!
EEUWW!
NO WAY, MAN.
I REALLY SHOULD TRY TO CALL HER.

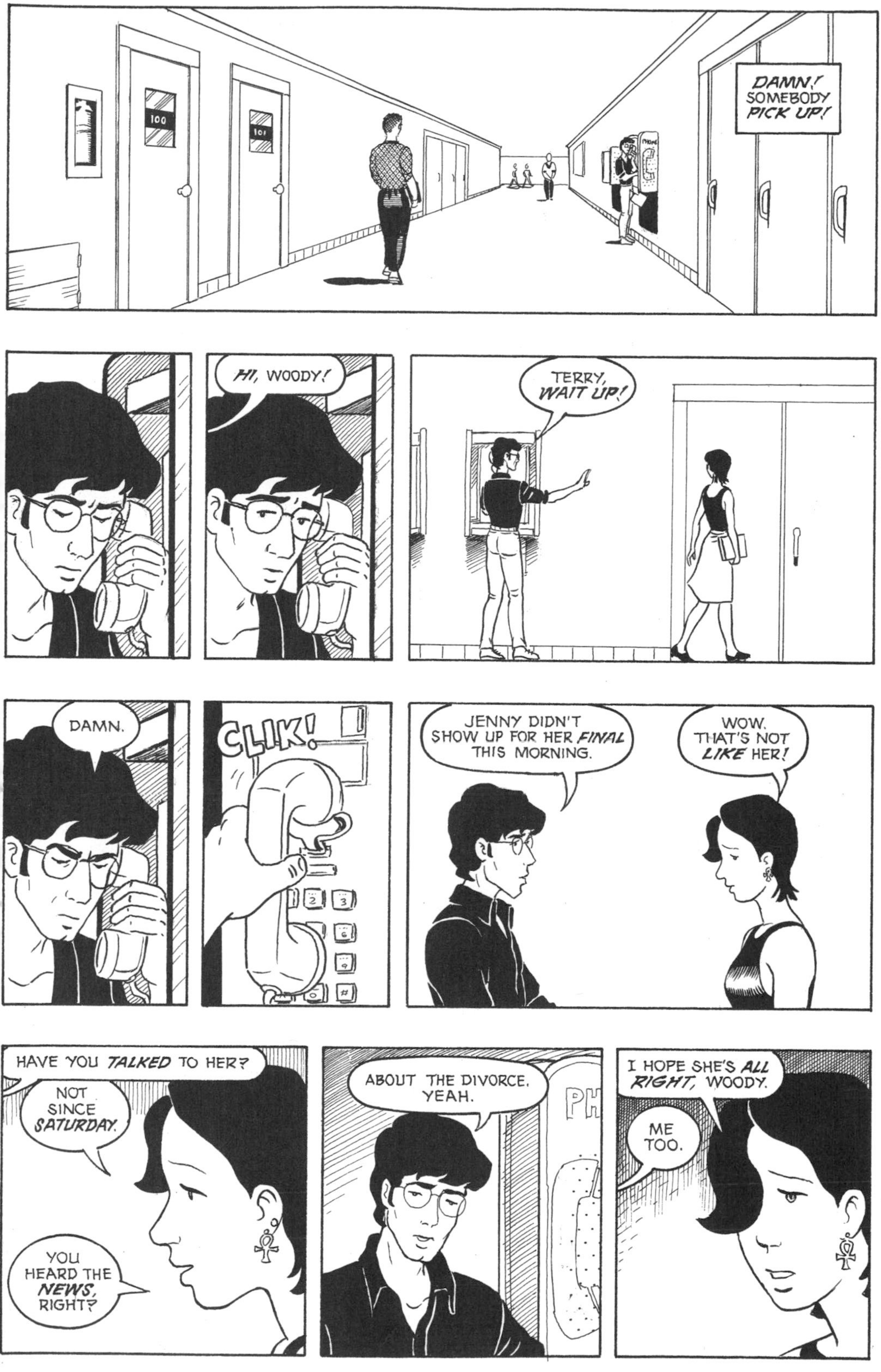

DAMN! SOMEBODY PICK UP!
HI, WOODY!
TERRY, WAIT UP!
DAMN.
CLIK!
JENNY DIDN'T SHOW UP FOR HER FINAL THIS MORNING.
WOW. THAT'S NOT LIKE HER!
HAVE YOU TALKED TO HER?
NOT SINCE SATURDAY.
YOU HEARD THE NEWS, RIGHT?
ABOUT THE DIVORCE. YEAH.
I HOPE SHE'S ALL RIGHT, WOODY.
ME TOO.

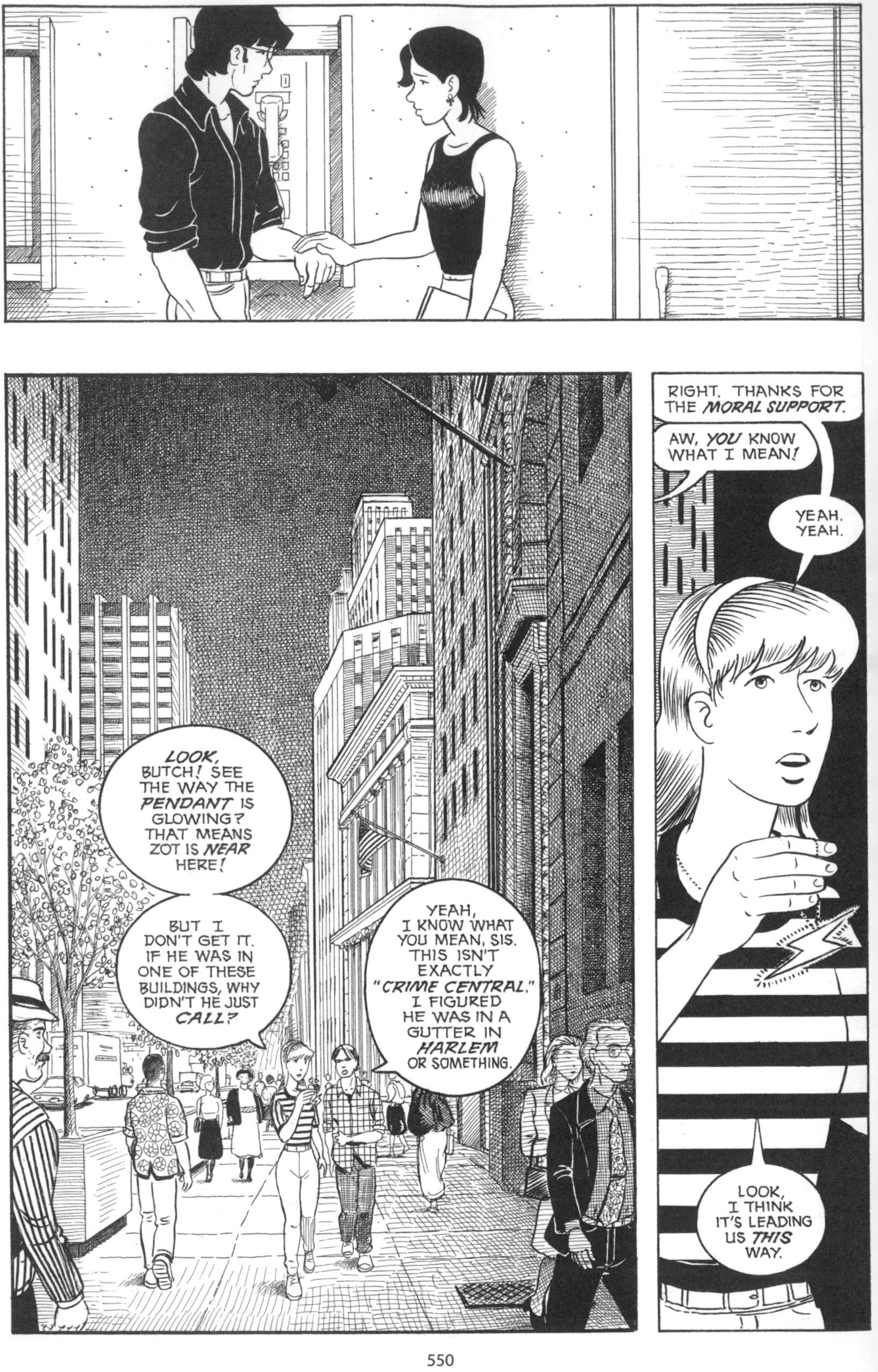
LOOK, BUTCH! SEE THE WAY THE PENDANT IS GLOWING? THAT MEANS ZOT IS NEAR HERE!
BUT I DON'T GET IT. IF HE WAS IN ONE OF THESE BUILDINGS, WHY DIDN'T HE JUST CALL?
YEAH, I KNOW WHAT YOU MEAN, SIS. THIS ISN'T EXACTLY "CRIME CENTRAL." I FIGURED HE WAS IN A GUTTER IN HARLEM OR SOMETHING.
RIGHT. THANKS FOR THE MORAL SUPPORT.
AW, YOU KNOW WHAT I MEAN!
YEAH. YEAH.
LOOK, I THINK IT'S LEADING US THIS WAY.

AROUND THIS *CORNER*.
HERE. I THINK...
TO THE LEFT. YEAH.
OKAY. DON'T PANIC.
GAVIN MILES MEMORIAL
HOSPITAL
ERGENCY ENTRANCE
501

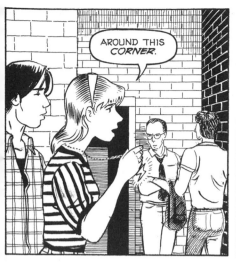

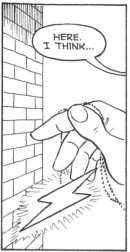

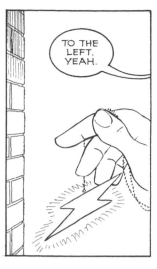

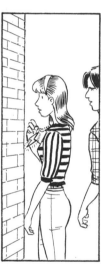

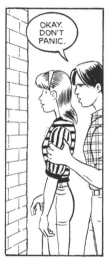

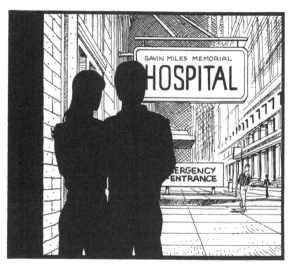

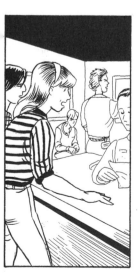

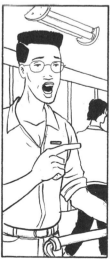

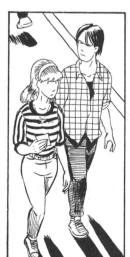

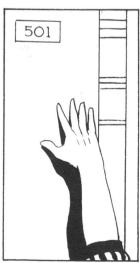

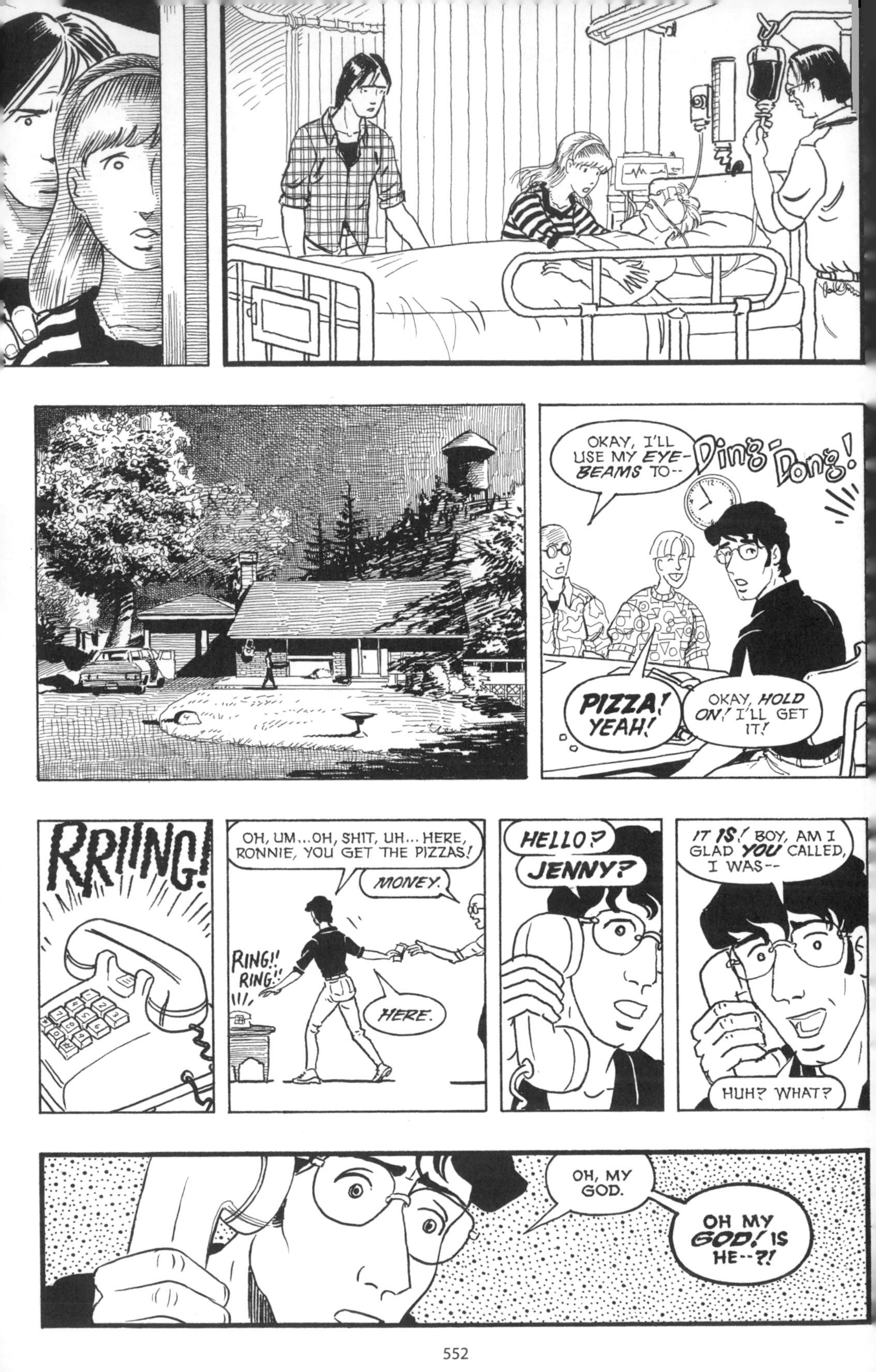
OKAY, I'LL USE MY EYE-BEAMS TO--
Ding-Dong!
PIZZA! YEAH!
OKAY, HOLD ON! I'LL GET IT!
RRIING!
OH, UM...OH, SHIT, UH... HERE, RONNIE, YOU GET THE PIZZAS!
MONEY.
RING!! RING!!
HERE.
HELLO?
JENNY?
IT IS! BOY, AM I GLAD YOU CALLED, I WAS--
HUH? WHAT?
OH, MY GOD.
OH MY GOD! IS HE--?!

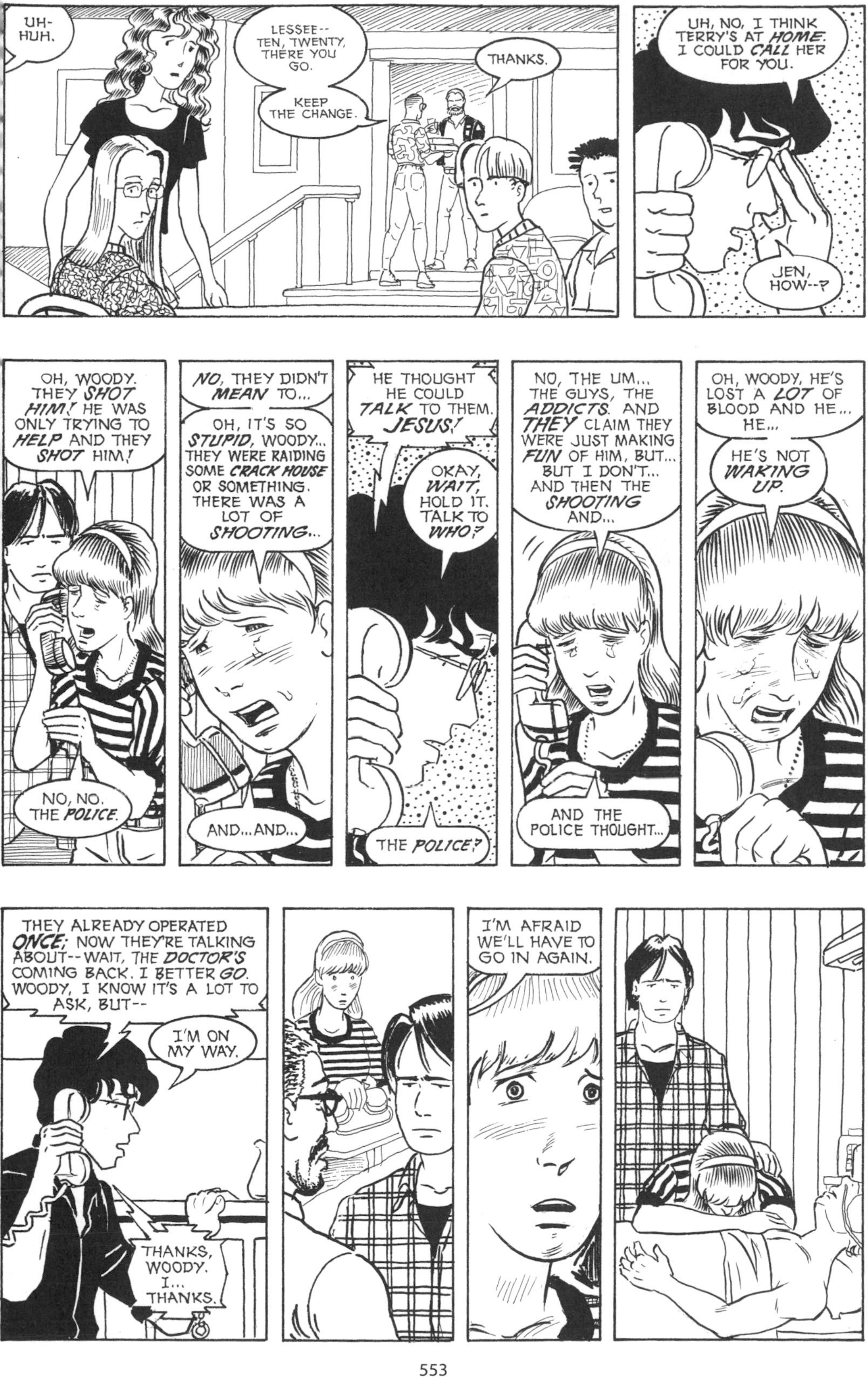
UH-HUH.
LESSEE-- TEN, TWENTY, THERE YOU GO.
KEEP THE CHANGE.
THANKS.
UH, NO, I THINK TERRY'S AT HOME. I COULD CALL HER FOR YOU.
JEN, HOW--?
OH, WOODY. THEY SHOT HIM! HE WAS ONLY TRYING TO HELP AND THEY SHOT HIM!
NO, NO. THE POLICE.
NO, THEY DIDN'T MEAN TO...
OH, IT'S SO STUPID, WOODY... THEY WERE RAIDING SOME CRACK HOUSE OR SOMETHING. THERE WAS A LOT OF SHOOTING...
AND...AND...
HE THOUGHT HE COULD TALK TO THEM. JESUS!
OKAY, WAIT, HOLD IT. TALK TO WHO?
THE POLICE?
NO, THE UM... THE GUYS, THE ADDICTS. AND THEY CLAIM THEY WERE JUST MAKING FUN OF HIM, BUT... BUT I DON'T... AND THEN THE SHOOTING AND...
AND THE POLICE THOUGHT...
OH, WOODY, HE'S LOST A LOT OF BLOOD AND HE... HE...
HE'S NOT WAKING UP.
THEY ALREADY OPERATED ONCE; NOW THEY'RE TALKING ABOUT--WAIT, THE DOCTOR'S COMING BACK. I BETTER GO. WOODY, I KNOW IT'S A LOT TO ASK, BUT--
I'M ON MY WAY.
THANKS, WOODY. I... THANKS.
I'M AFRAID WE'LL HAVE TO GO IN AGAIN.

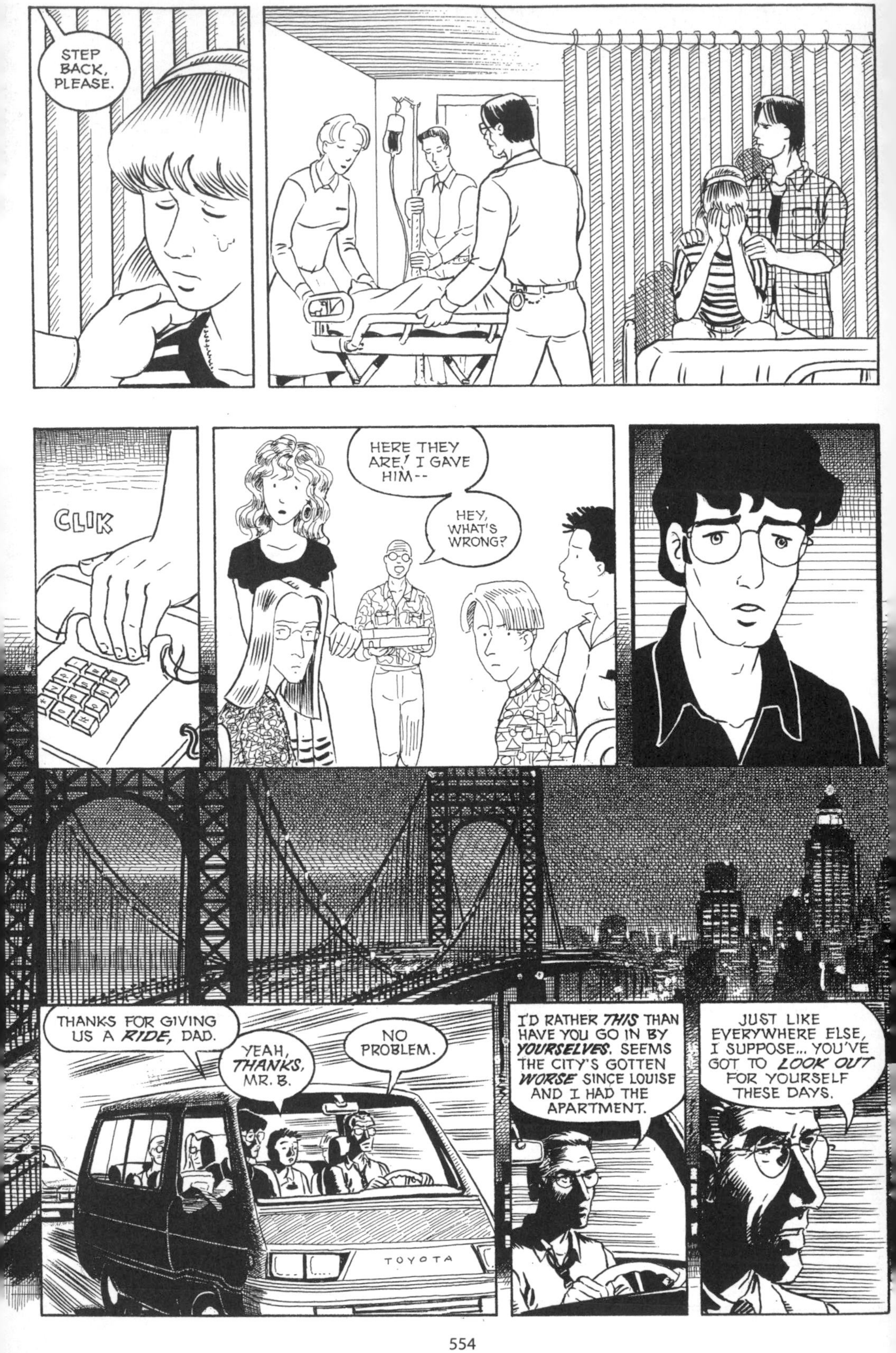
STEP BACK, PLEASE.
CLIK
HERE THEY ARE! I GAVE HIM--
HEY, WHAT'S WRONG?
THANKS FOR GIVING US A RIDE, DAD.
YEAH, THANKS, MR. B.
NO PROBLEM.
TOYOTA
I'D RATHER THIS THAN HAVE YOU GO IN BY YOURSELVES. SEEMS THE CITY'S GOTTEN WORSE SINCE LOUISE AND I HAD THE APARTMENT.
JUST LIKE EVERYWHERE ELSE, I SUPPOSE... YOU'VE GOT TO LOOK OUT FOR YOURSELF THESE DAYS.

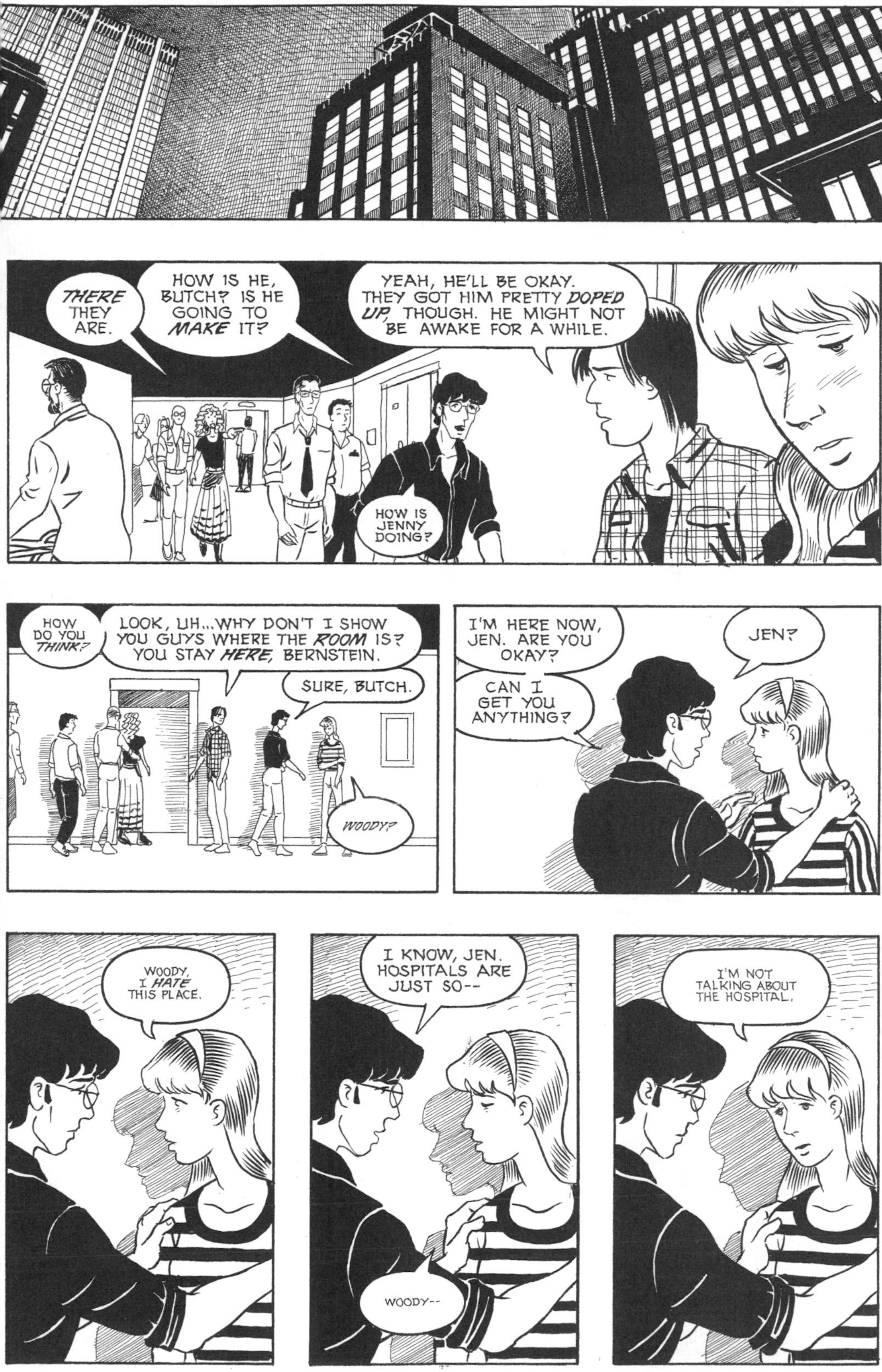
THERE THEY ARE.
HOW IS HE, BUTCH? IS HE GOING TO MAKE IT?
YEAH, HE'LL BE OKAY. THEY GOT HIM PRETTY DOPED UP, THOUGH. HE MIGHT NOT BE AWAKE FOR A WHILE.
HOW IS JENNY DOING?
HOW DO YOU THINK?
LOOK, UH...WHY DON'T I SHOW YOU GUYS WHERE THE ROOM IS? YOU STAY HERE, BERNSTEIN.
SURE, BUTCH.
WOODY?
I'M HERE NOW, JEN. ARE YOU OKAY?
JEN?
CAN I GET YOU ANYTHING?
WOODY, I HATE THIS PLACE.
I KNOW, JEN. HOSPITALS ARE JUST SO--
WOODY--
I'M NOT TALKING ABOUT THE HOSPITAL.

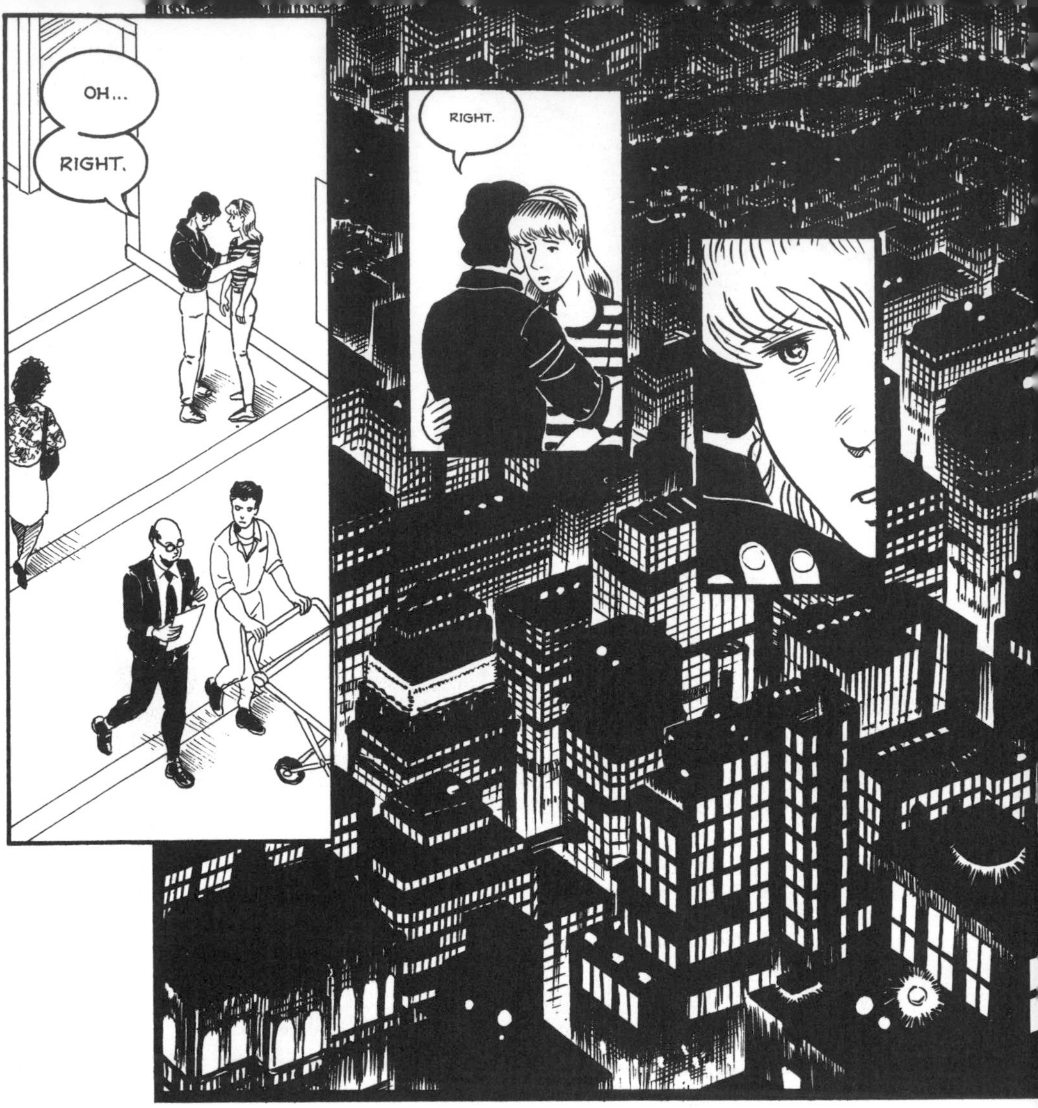
OH...
RIGHT.
RIGHT.

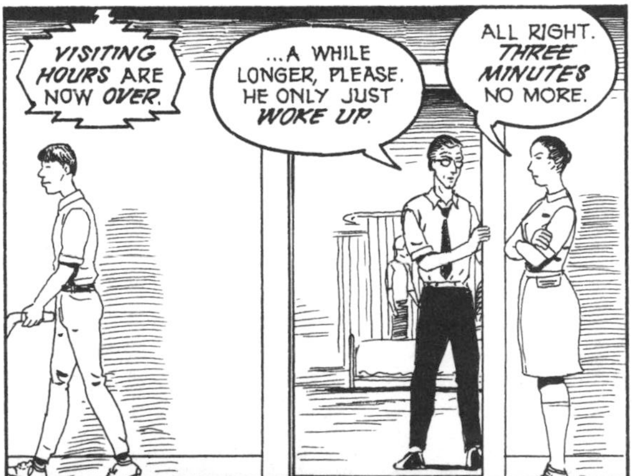
VISITING HOURS ARE NOW *OVER*.
...A WHILE LONGER, PLEASE. HE ONLY JUST *WOKE UP*.
ALL RIGHT. *THREE MINUTES* NO MORE.

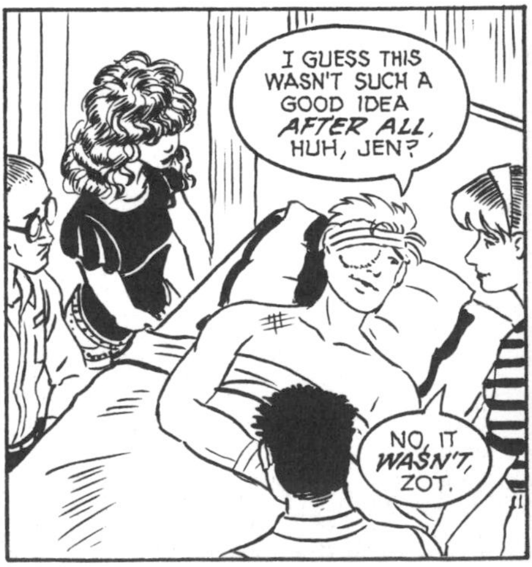
I GUESS THIS WASN'T SUCH A GOOD IDEA *AFTER ALL*, HUH, JEN?
NO, IT *WASN'T*, ZOT.

STILL KINDA SLEEPY... ARE YOU GOING TO VISIT ME *TOMORROW*, JEN?

ZOT, I DON'T WANT TO LEAVE YOU, *EVER AGAIN*.

MMM... SOUNDS NICE.

C'MON, KIDS.

TIME TO GO *HOME*.

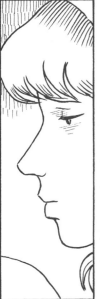

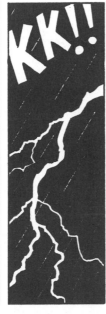

KK!!

ARE YOU GONNA BE *OKAY*, SIS?

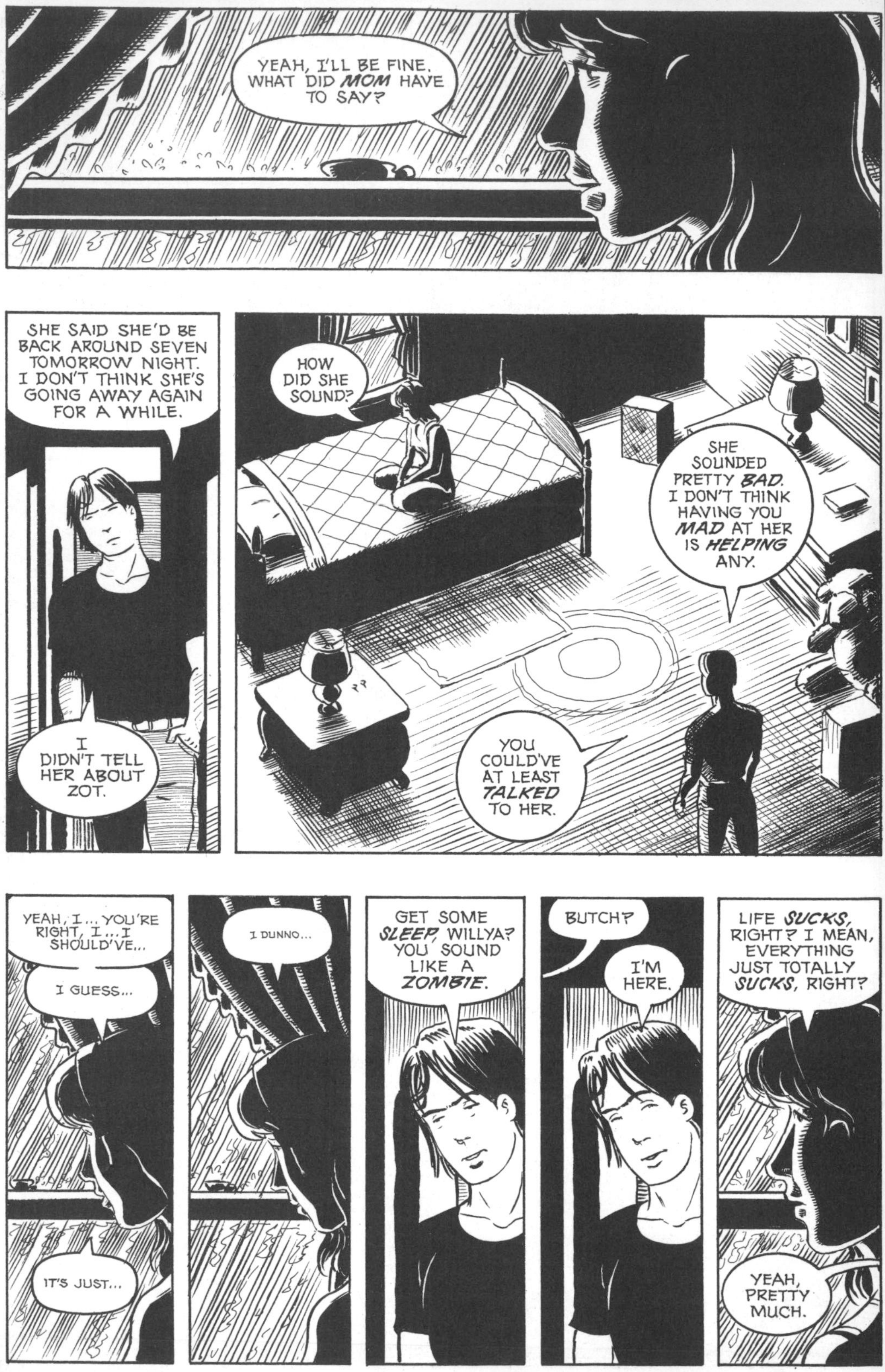

YEAH, I'LL BE FINE. WHAT DID MOM HAVE TO SAY?
SHE SAID SHE'D BE BACK AROUND SEVEN TOMORROW NIGHT. I DON'T THINK SHE'S GOING AWAY AGAIN FOR A WHILE.
I DIDN'T TELL HER ABOUT ZOT.
HOW DID SHE SOUND?
SHE SOUNDED PRETTY BAD. I DON'T THINK HAVING YOU MAD AT HER IS HELPING ANY.
YOU COULD'VE AT LEAST TALKED TO HER.
YEAH, I... YOU'RE RIGHT, I... I SHOULD'VE...
I GUESS...
IT'S JUST...
I DUNNO...
GET SOME SLEEP, WILLYA? YOU SOUND LIKE A ZOMBIE.
BUTCH?
I'M HERE.
LIFE SUCKS, RIGHT? I MEAN, EVERYTHING JUST TOTALLY SUCKS, RIGHT?
YEAH, PRETTY MUCH.

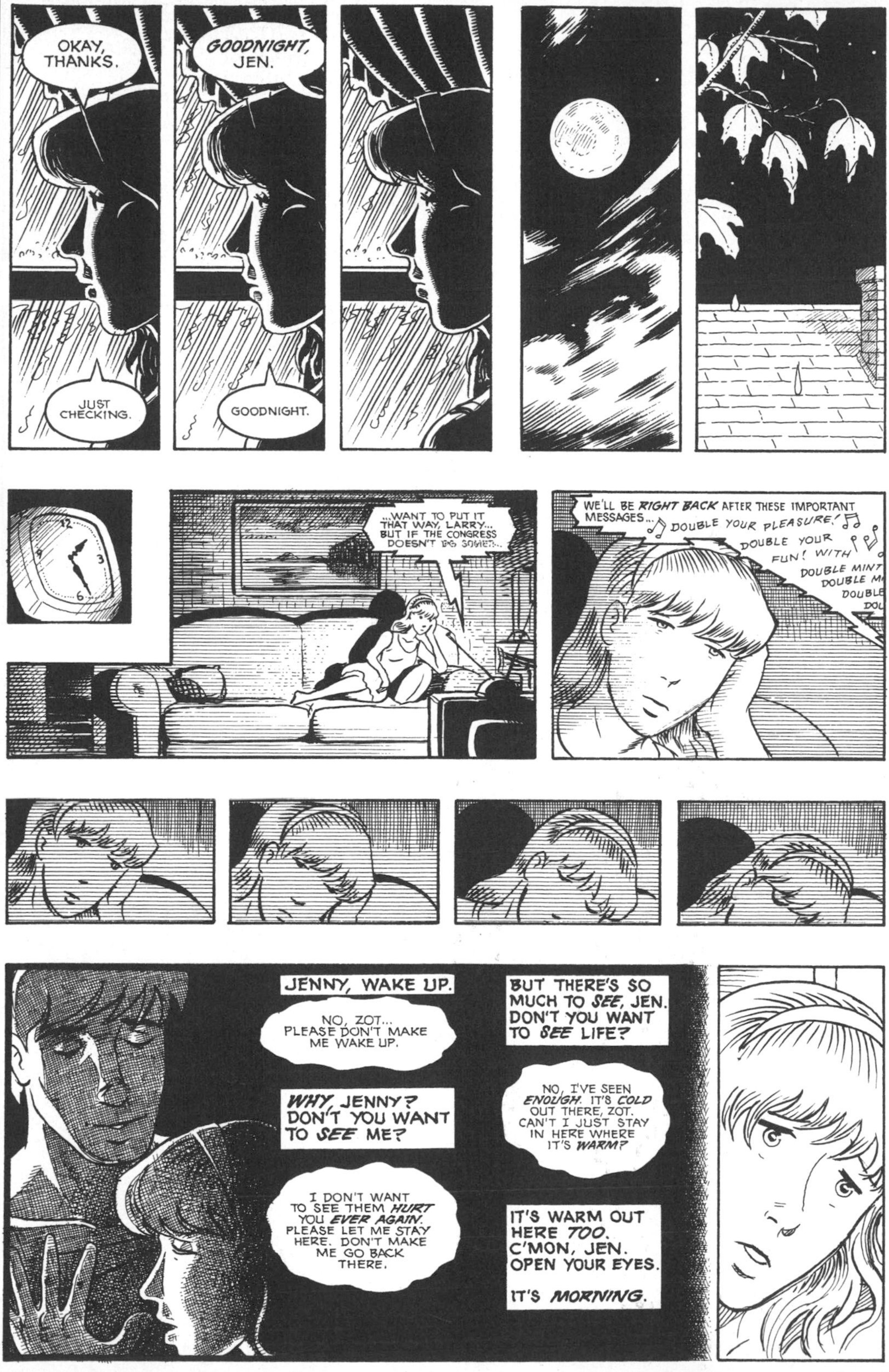

OKAY, THANKS.
JUST CHECKING.
GOODNIGHT, JEN.
GOODNIGHT.
...WANT TO PUT IT THAT WAY, LARRY... BUT IF THE CONGRESS DOESN'T DO SOMET...
WE'LL BE RIGHT BACK AFTER THESE IMPORTANT MESSAGES...
DOUBLE YOUR PLEASURE! DOUBLE YOUR FUN! WITH DOUBLE MINT DOUBLE M DOUBLE DOU
JENNY, WAKE UP.
NO, ZOT... PLEASE DON'T MAKE ME WAKE UP.
WHY, JENNY? DON'T YOU WANT TO SEE ME?
I DON'T WANT TO SEE THEM HURT YOU EVER AGAIN. PLEASE LET ME STAY HERE. DON'T MAKE ME GO BACK THERE.
BUT THERE'S SO MUCH TO SEE, JEN. DON'T YOU WANT TO SEE LIFE?
NO, I'VE SEEN ENOUGH. IT'S COLD OUT THERE, ZOT. CAN'T I JUST STAY IN HERE WHERE IT'S WARM?
IT'S WARM OUT HERE TOO. C'MON, JEN. OPEN YOUR EYES.
IT'S MORNING.

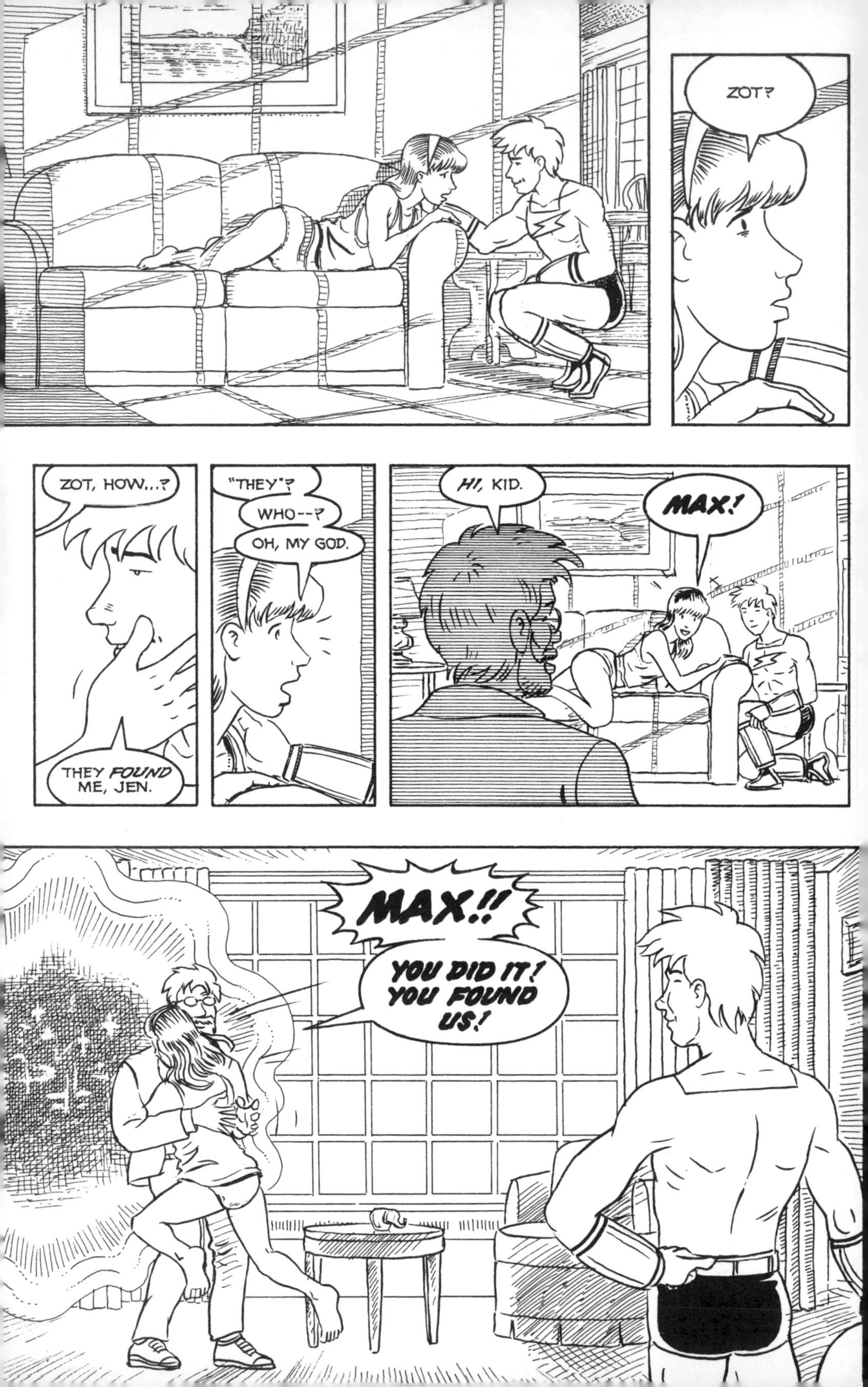
ZOT?
ZOT, HOW...?
THEY *FOUND* ME, JEN.
"THEY"?
WHO--?
OH, MY GOD.
HI, KID.
MAX!
MAX!!
YOU DID IT! YOU FOUND US!

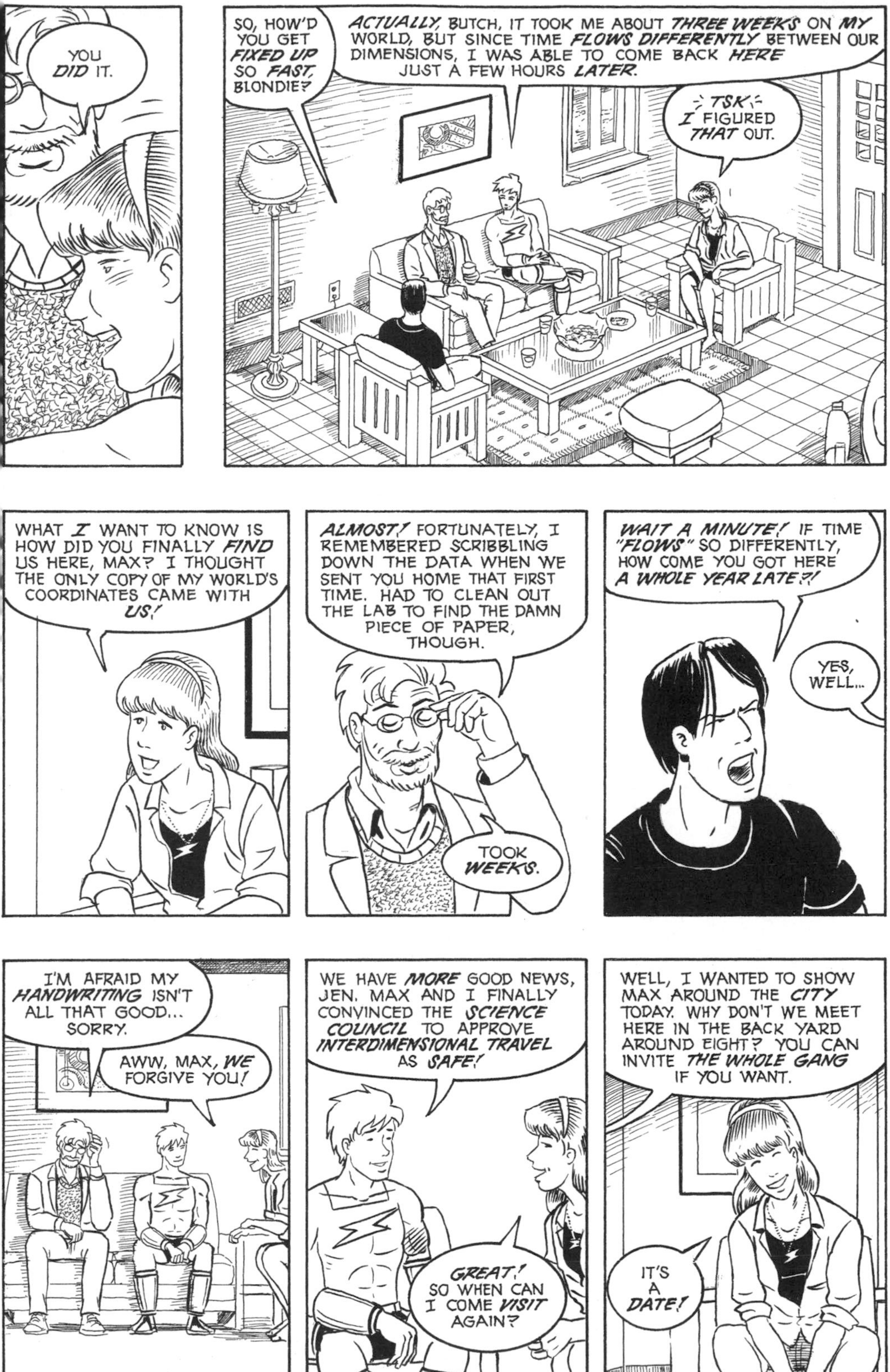
YOU DID IT.
SO, HOW'D YOU GET FIXED UP SO FAST, BLONDIE?
ACTUALLY, BUTCH, IT TOOK ME ABOUT THREE WEEKS ON MY WORLD, BUT SINCE TIME FLOWS DIFFERENTLY BETWEEN OUR DIMENSIONS, I WAS ABLE TO COME BACK HERE JUST A FEW HOURS LATER.
TSK I FIGURED THAT OUT.
WHAT I WANT TO KNOW IS HOW DID YOU FINALLY FIND US HERE, MAX? I THOUGHT THE ONLY COPY OF MY WORLD'S COORDINATES CAME WITH US!
ALMOST! FORTUNATELY, I REMEMBERED SCRIBBLING DOWN THE DATA WHEN WE SENT YOU HOME THAT FIRST TIME. HAD TO CLEAN OUT THE LAB TO FIND THE DAMN PIECE OF PAPER, THOUGH.
TOOK WEEKS.
WAIT A MINUTE! IF TIME "FLOWS" SO DIFFERENTLY, HOW COME YOU GOT HERE A WHOLE YEAR LATE?!
YES, WELL...
I'M AFRAID MY HANDWRITING ISN'T ALL THAT GOOD... SORRY.
AWW, MAX, WE FORGIVE YOU!
WE HAVE MORE GOOD NEWS, JEN. MAX AND I FINALLY CONVINCED THE SCIENCE COUNCIL TO APPROVE INTERDIMENSIONAL TRAVEL AS SAFE!
GREAT! SO WHEN CAN I COME VISIT AGAIN?
WELL, I WANTED TO SHOW MAX AROUND THE CITY TODAY. WHY DON'T WE MEET HERE IN THE BACK YARD AROUND EIGHT? YOU CAN INVITE THE WHOLE GANG IF YOU WANT.
IT'S A DATE!

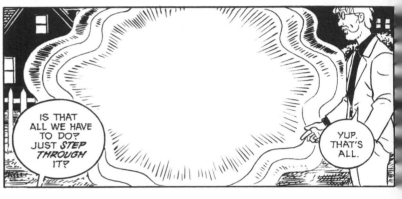

IS THAT ALL WE HAVE TO DO? JUST *STEP THROUGH* IT?

YUP. THAT'S ALL.

WILL IT *HURT?*

IT'LL *TINGLE* A LITTLE. NOTHING *SERIOUS.*

WILL WE BE...*WELCOME* HERE, MAX?

EVERYONE IS *WELCOME* HERE. C'MON IN.

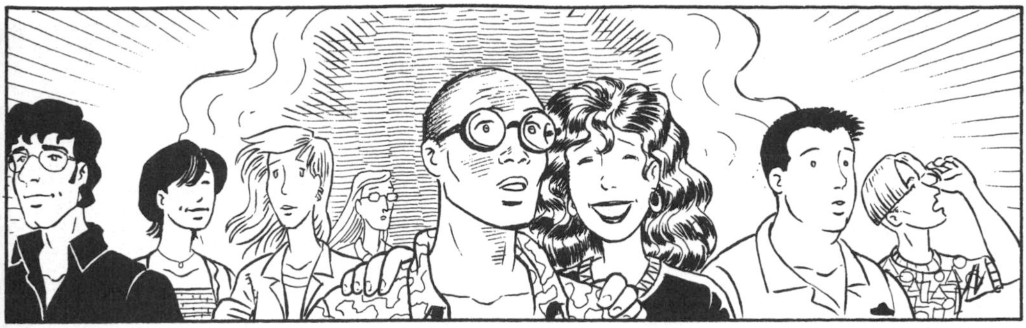

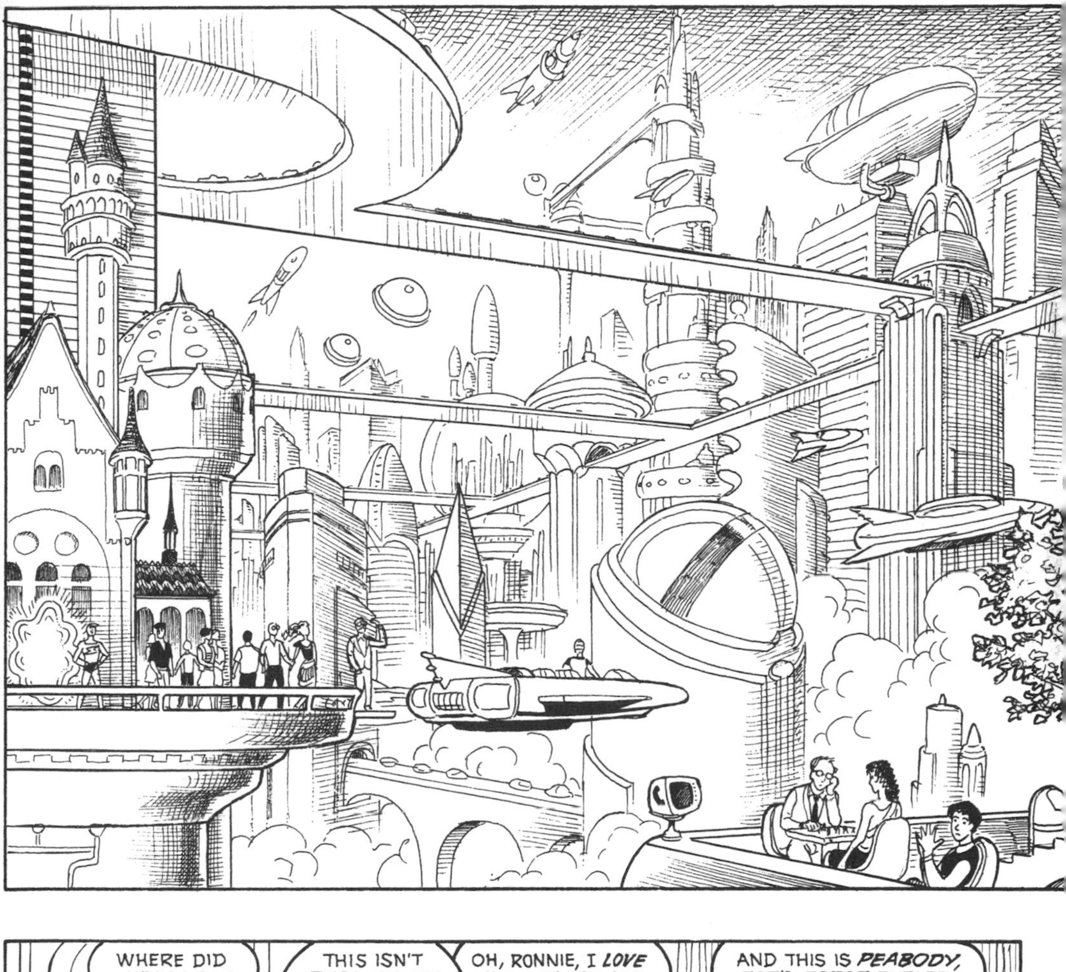

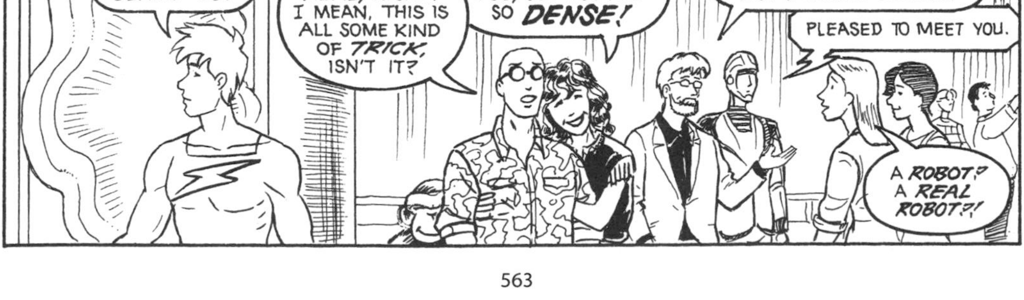
WHERE DID *JENNY* GO?
THIS ISN'T *REAL*, RIGHT? I MEAN, THIS IS ALL SOME KIND OF *TRICK*, ISN'T IT?
OH, RONNIE, I *LOVE* YOU, BUT YOU ARE SO ***DENSE!***
AND THIS IS *PEABODY*, ZOT'S ROBOT BUTLER.
PLEASED TO MEET YOU.
A *ROBOT*?! A *REAL ROBOT*?!

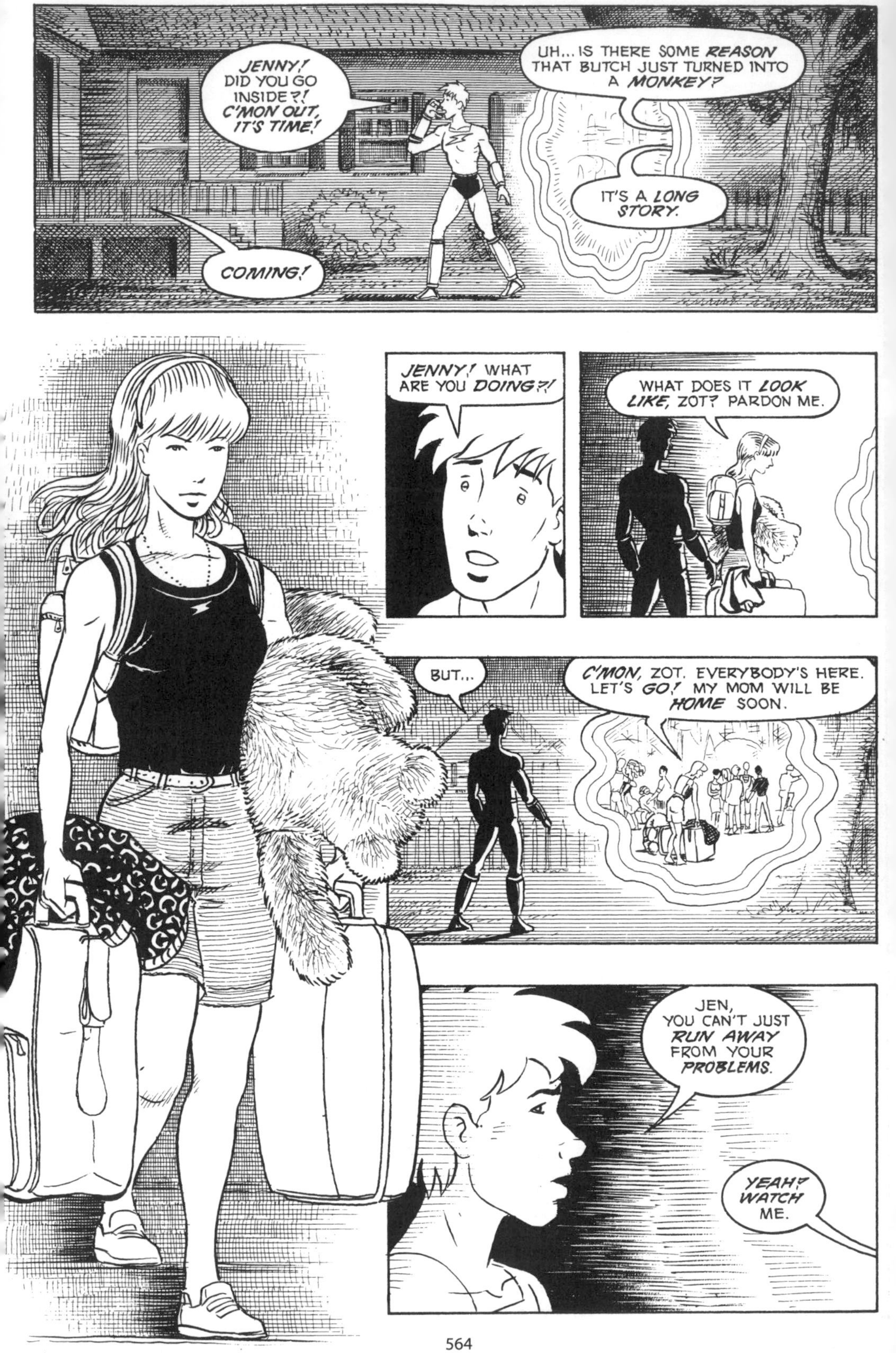
JENNY! DID YOU GO INSIDE?! C'MON OUT, IT'S TIME!
UH... IS THERE SOME REASON THAT BUTCH JUST TURNED INTO A MONKEY?
IT'S A LONG STORY.
COMING!
JENNY! WHAT ARE YOU DOING?!
WHAT DOES IT LOOK LIKE, ZOT? PARDON ME.
BUT...
C'MON, ZOT. EVERYBODY'S HERE. LET'S GO! MY MOM WILL BE HOME SOON.
JEN, YOU CAN'T JUST RUN AWAY FROM YOUR PROBLEMS.
YEAH? WATCH ME.

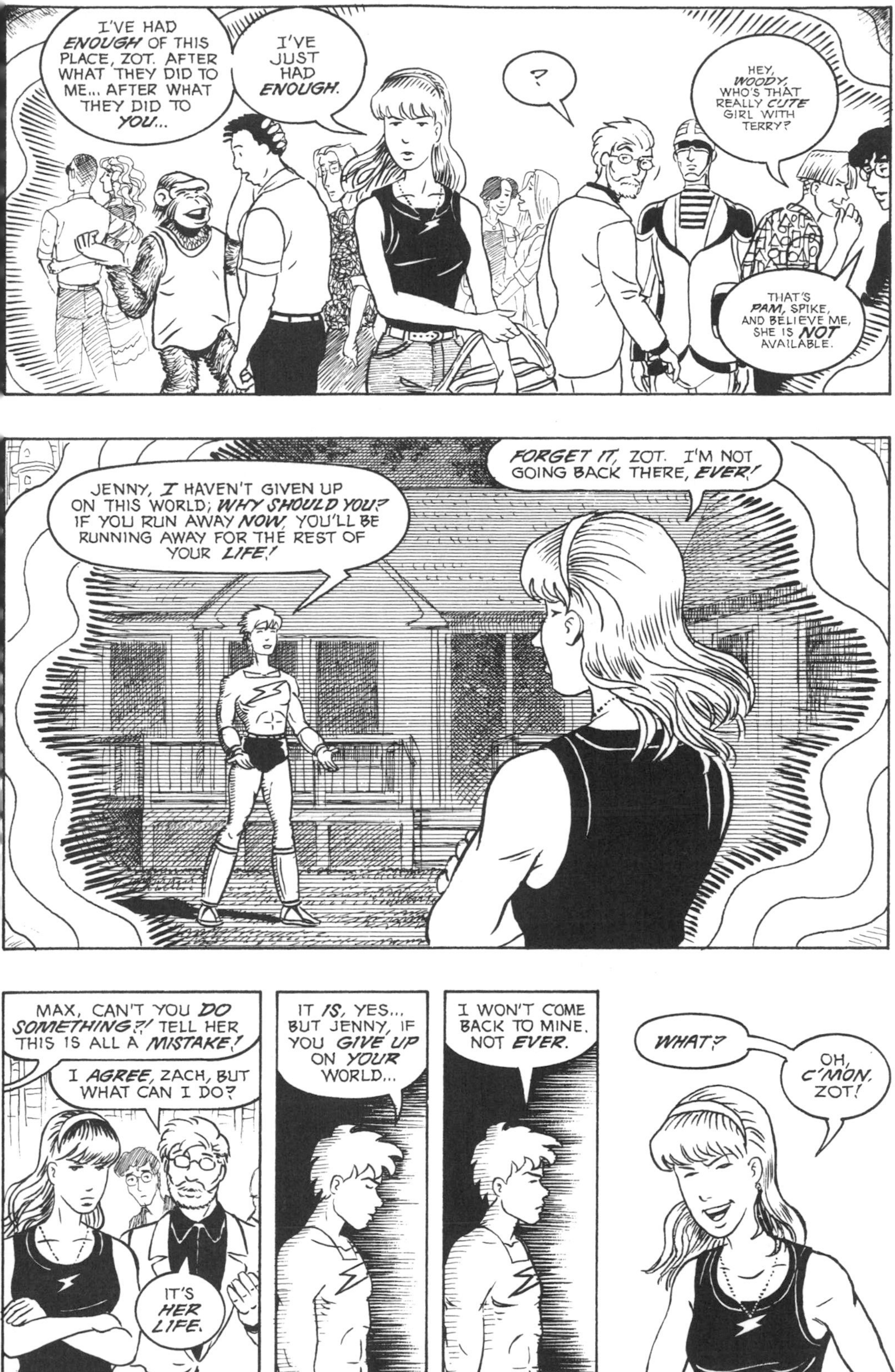
I'VE HAD ENOUGH OF THIS PLACE, ZOT. AFTER WHAT THEY DID TO ME... AFTER WHAT THEY DID TO YOU...
I'VE JUST HAD ENOUGH.
?
HEY, WOODY, WHO'S THAT REALLY CUTE GIRL WITH TERRY?
THAT'S PAM, SPIKE, AND BELIEVE ME, SHE IS NOT AVAILABLE.
JENNY, I HAVEN'T GIVEN UP ON THIS WORLD; WHY SHOULD YOU? IF YOU RUN AWAY NOW, YOU'LL BE RUNNING AWAY FOR THE REST OF YOUR LIFE!
FORGET IT, ZOT. I'M NOT GOING BACK THERE, EVER!
MAX, CAN'T YOU DO SOMETHING?! TELL HER THIS IS ALL A MISTAKE!
I AGREE, ZACH, BUT WHAT CAN I DO?
IT'S HER LIFE.
IT IS, YES... BUT JENNY, IF YOU GIVE UP ON YOUR WORLD...
I WON'T COME BACK TO MINE. NOT EVER.
WHAT?
OH, C'MON, ZOT!

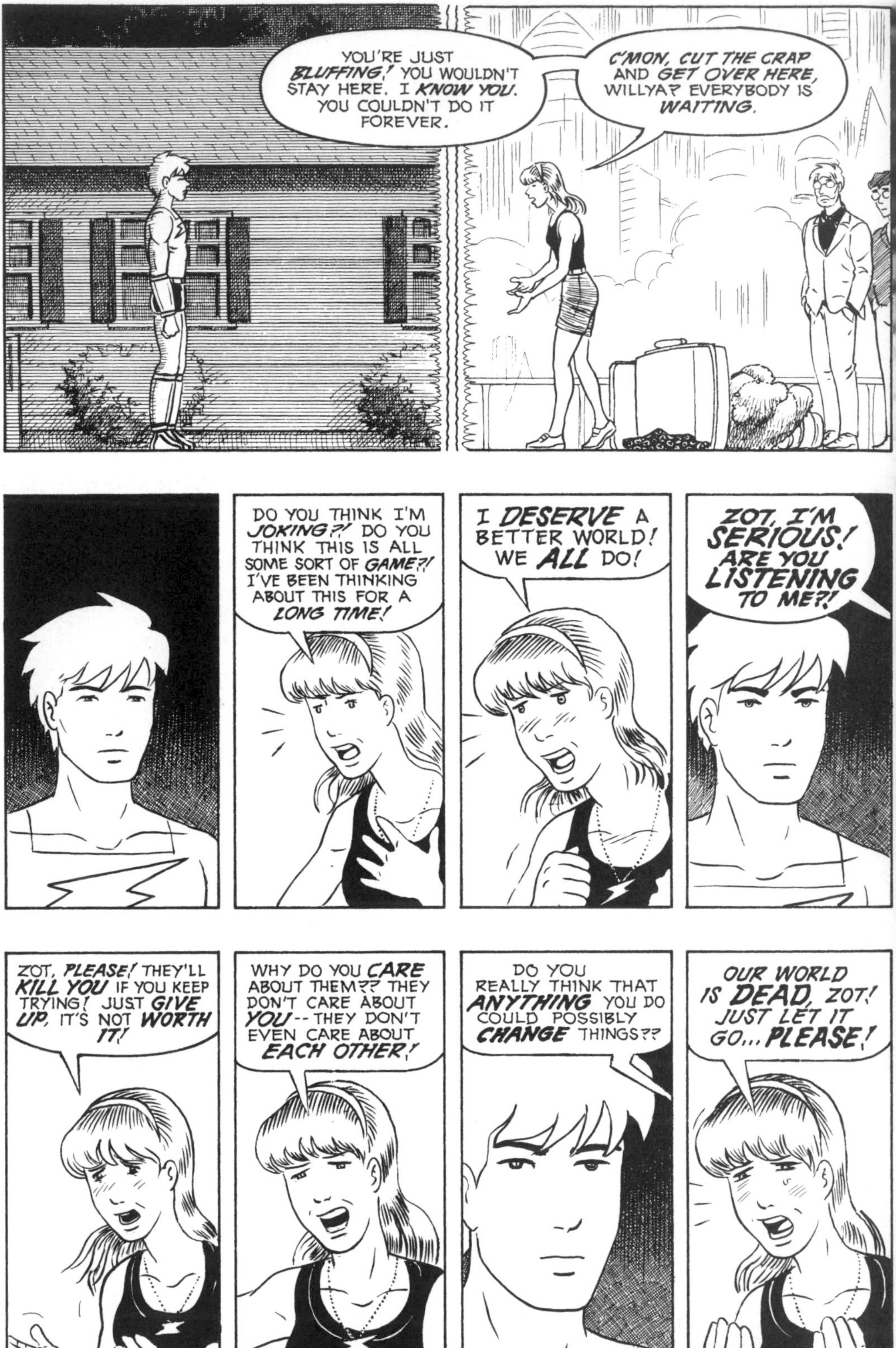
YOU'RE JUST BLUFFING! YOU WOULDN'T STAY HERE. I KNOW YOU. YOU COULDN'T DO IT FOREVER.
C'MON, CUT THE CRAP AND GET OVER HERE, WILLYA? EVERYBODY IS WAITING.
DO YOU THINK I'M JOKING?! DO YOU THINK THIS IS ALL SOME SORT OF GAME?! I'VE BEEN THINKING ABOUT THIS FOR A LONG TIME!
I DESERVE A BETTER WORLD! WE ALL DO!
ZOT, I'M SERIOUS! ARE YOU LISTENING TO ME?!
ZOT, PLEASE! THEY'LL KILL YOU IF YOU KEEP TRYING! JUST GIVE UP, IT'S NOT WORTH IT!
WHY DO YOU CARE ABOUT THEM?? THEY DON'T CARE ABOUT YOU -- THEY DON'T EVEN CARE ABOUT EACH OTHER!
DO YOU REALLY THINK THAT ANYTHING YOU DO COULD POSSIBLY CHANGE THINGS??
OUR WORLD IS DEAD, ZOT! JUST LET IT GO... PLEASE!

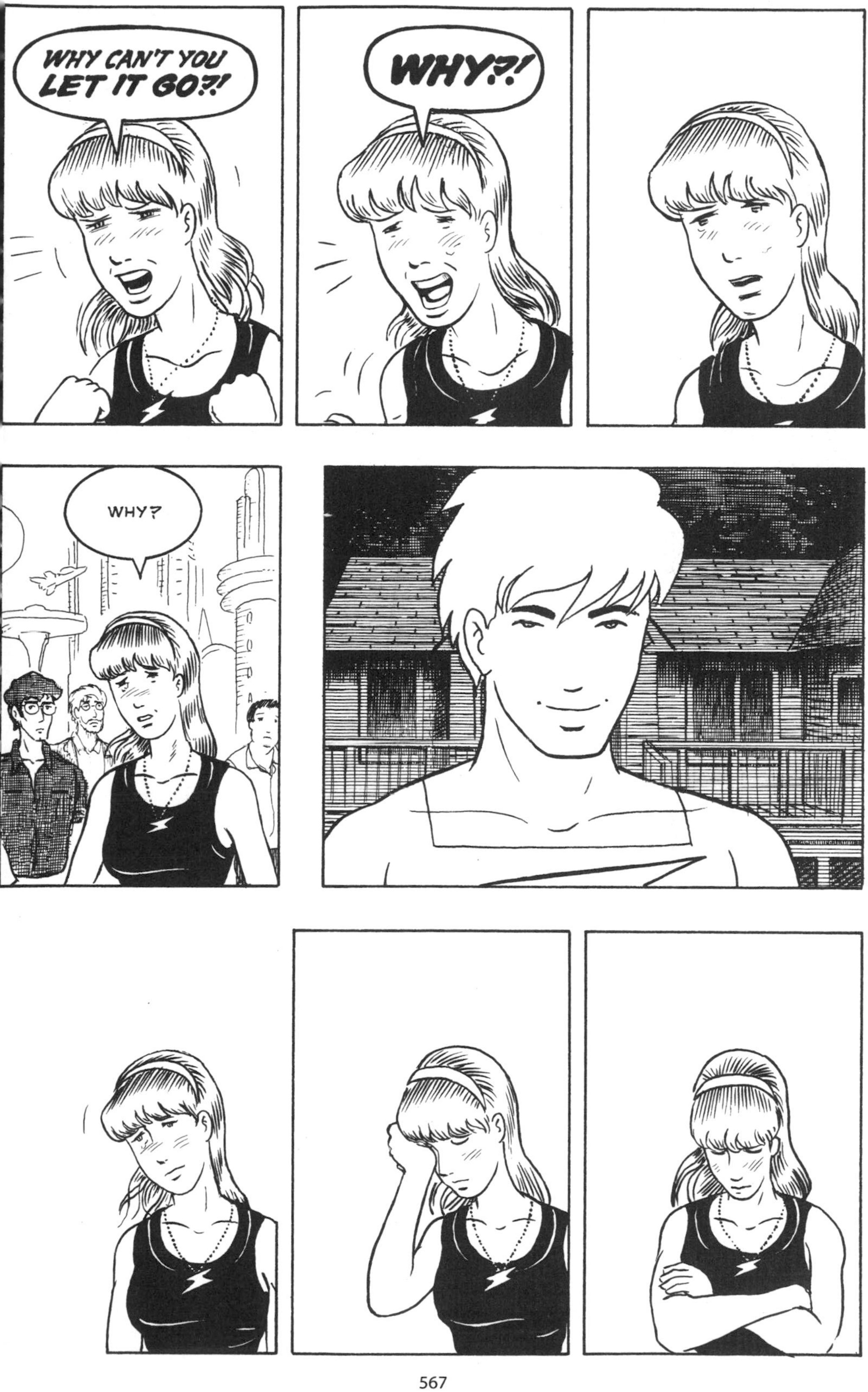
WHY CAN'T YOU LET IT GO?!
WHY?!
WHY?

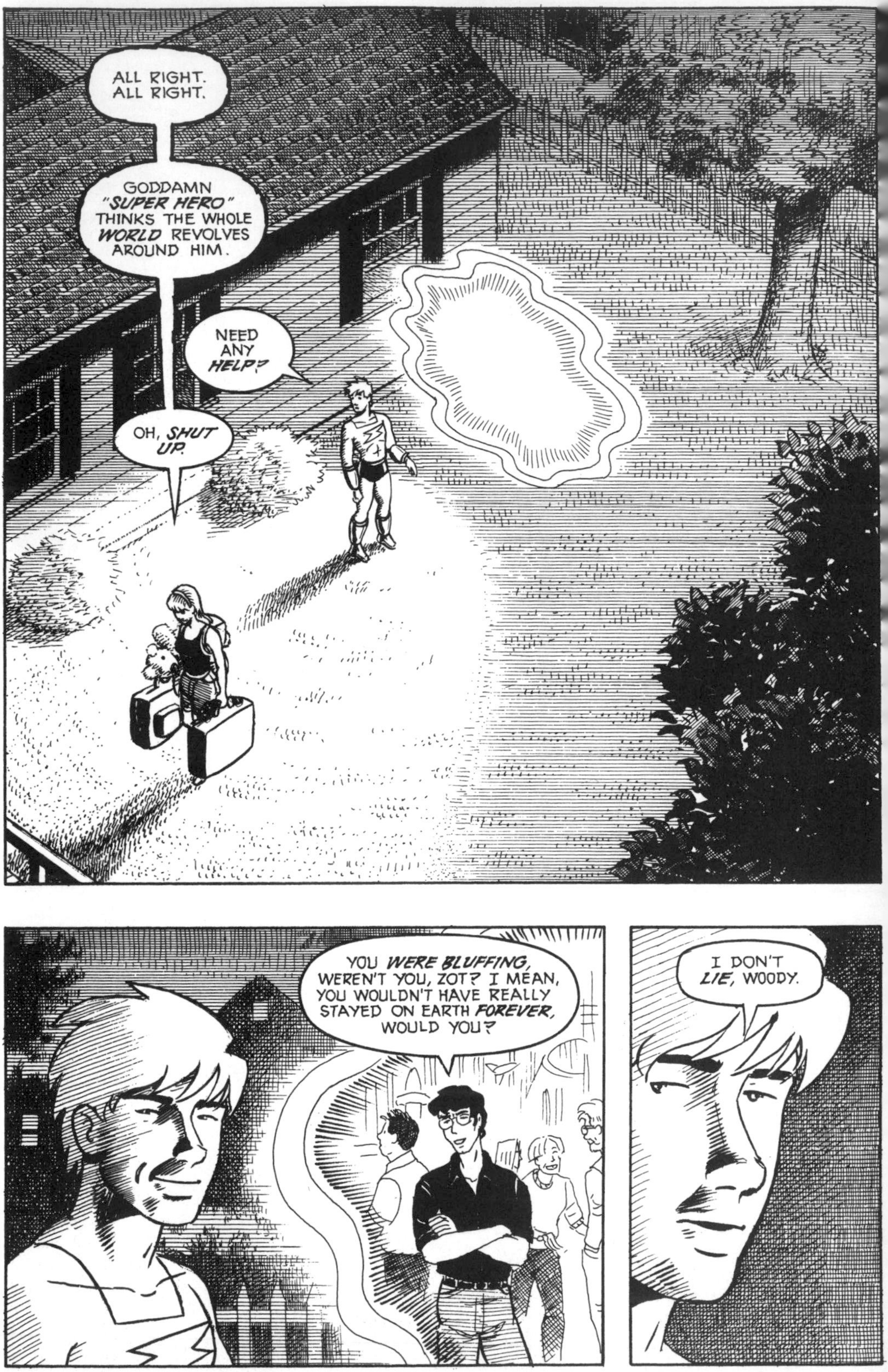
ALL RIGHT. ALL RIGHT.
GODDAMN *"SUPER HERO"* THINKS THE WHOLE *WORLD* REVOLVES AROUND HIM.
NEED ANY *HELP?*
OH, *SHUT UP.*
YOU *WERE BLUFFING,* WEREN'T YOU, ZOT? I MEAN, YOU WOULDN'T HAVE REALLY STAYED ON EARTH *FOREVER,* WOULD YOU?
I DON'T *LIE,* WOODY.

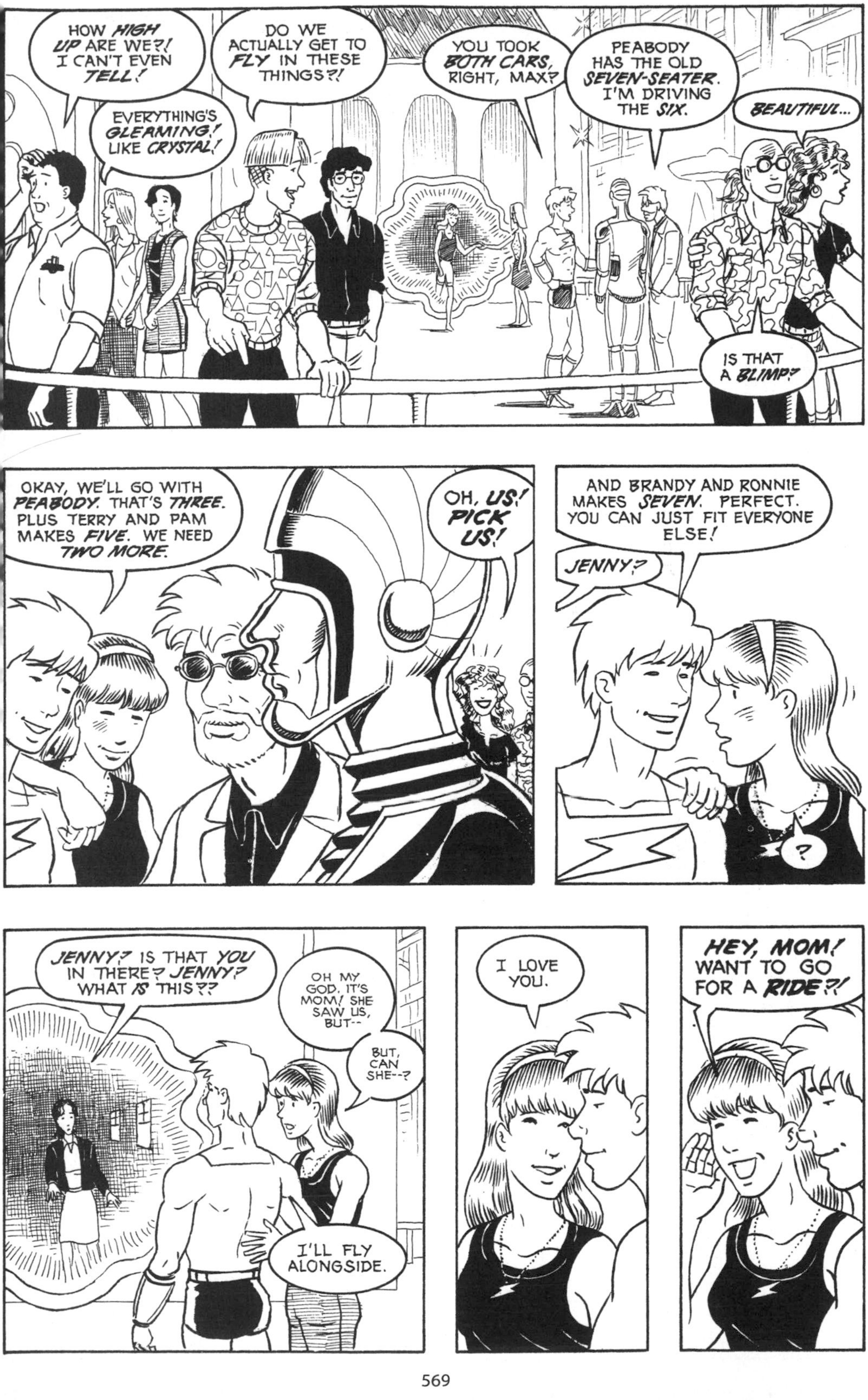
HOW HIGH UP ARE WE?! I CAN'T EVEN TELL!
EVERYTHING'S GLEAMING! LIKE CRYSTAL!
DO WE ACTUALLY GET TO FLY IN THESE THINGS?!
YOU TOOK BOTH CARS, RIGHT, MAX?
PEABODY HAS THE OLD SEVEN-SEATER. I'M DRIVING THE SIX.
BEAUTIFUL...
IS THAT A BLIMP?
OKAY, WE'LL GO WITH PEABODY. THAT'S THREE. PLUS TERRY AND PAM MAKES FIVE. WE NEED TWO MORE.
OH, US! PICK US!
AND BRANDY AND RONNIE MAKES SEVEN. PERFECT. YOU CAN JUST FIT EVERYONE ELSE!
JENNY?
?
JENNY? IS THAT YOU IN THERE? JENNY? WHAT IS THIS??
OH MY GOD. IT'S MOM! SHE SAW US, BUT--
BUT, CAN SHE--?
I'LL FLY ALONGSIDE.
I LOVE YOU.
HEY, MOM! WANT TO GO FOR A RIDE?!

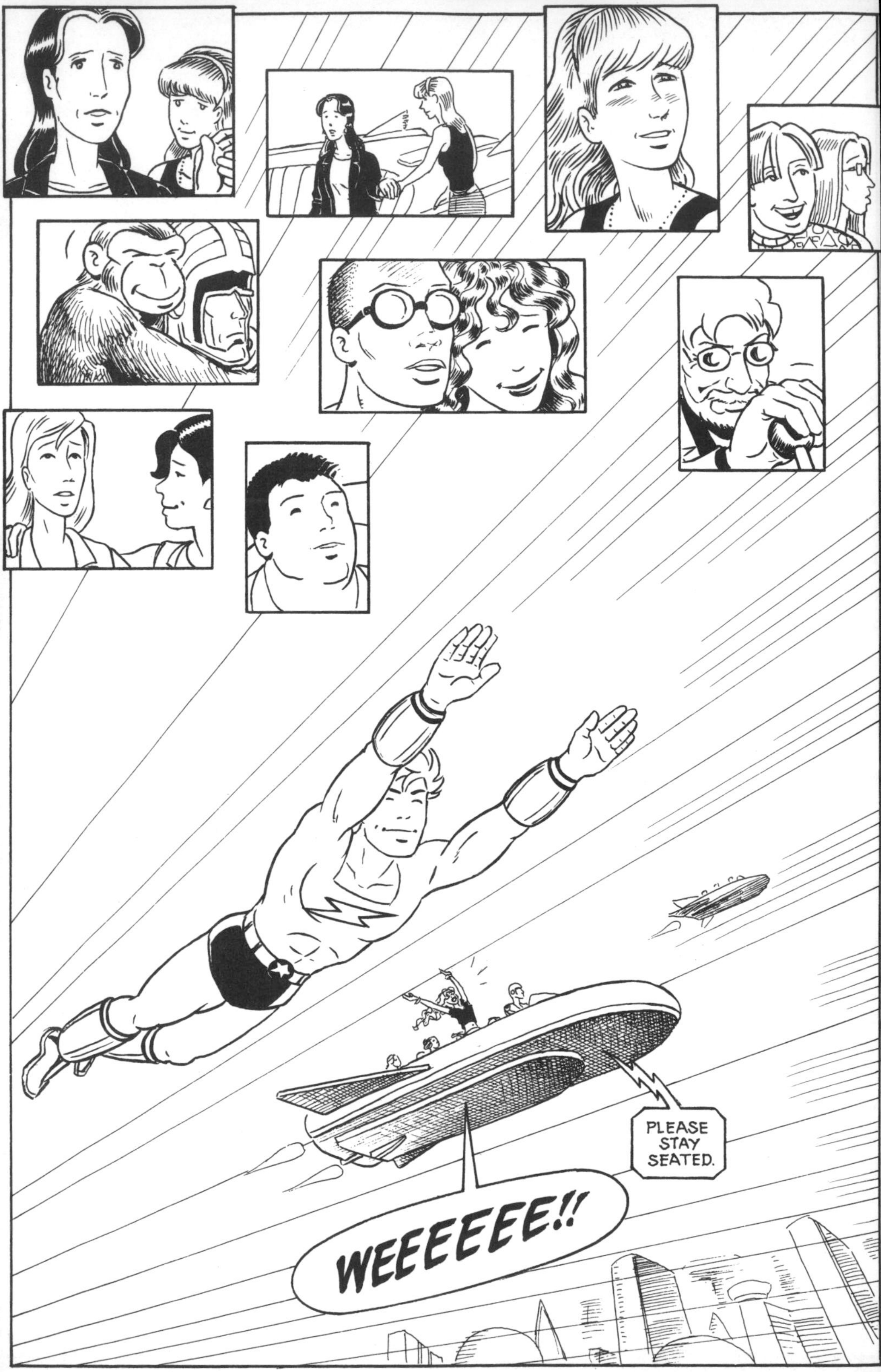
PLEASE STAY SEATED.
WEEEEEEE!!

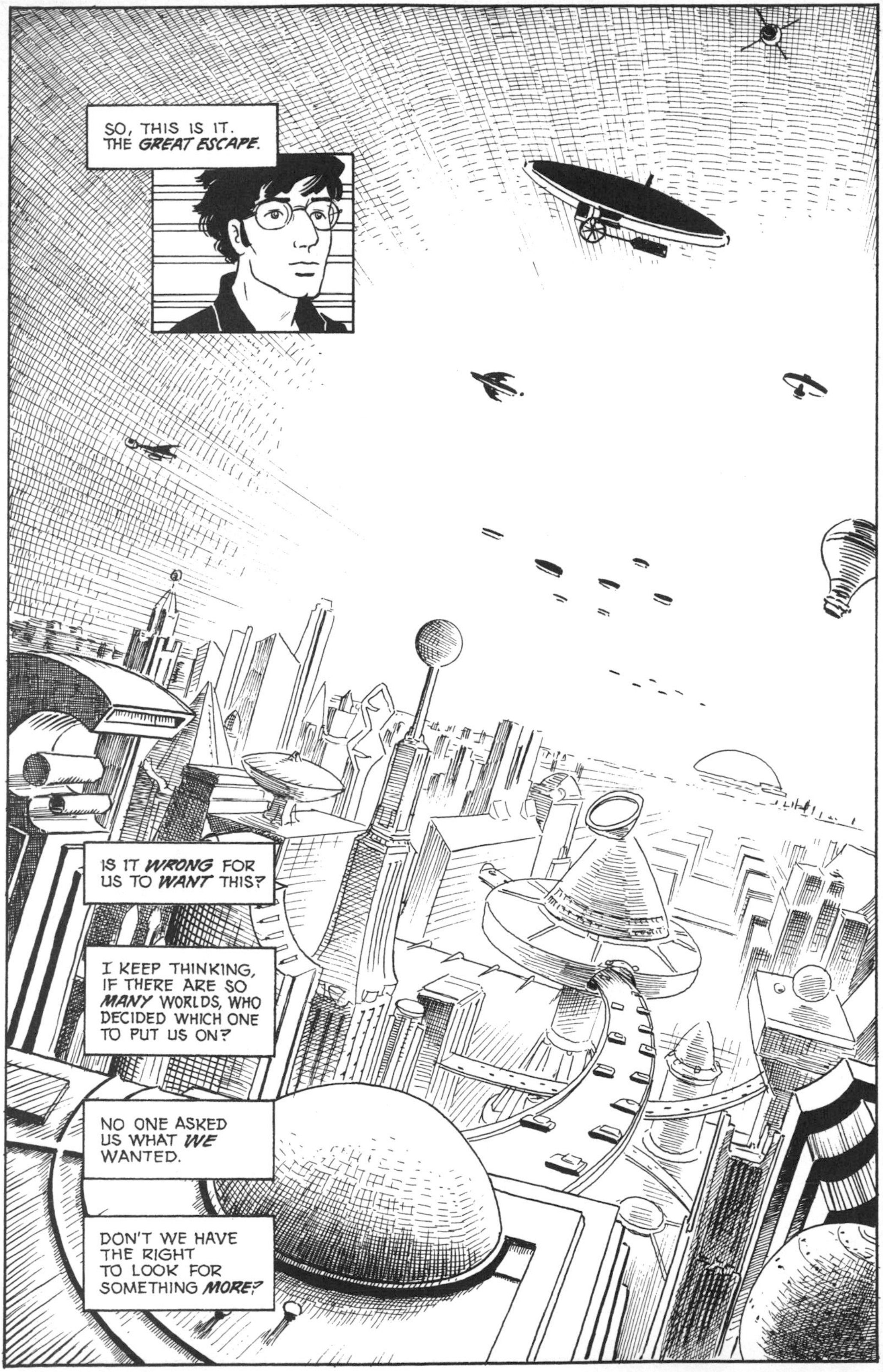
SO, THIS IS IT. THE *GREAT ESCAPE.*
IS IT *WRONG* FOR US TO *WANT* THIS?
I KEEP THINKING, IF THERE ARE SO *MANY* WORLDS, WHO DECIDED WHICH ONE TO PUT US ON?
NO ONE ASKED US WHAT *WE* WANTED.
DON'T WE HAVE THE RIGHT TO LOOK FOR SOMETHING *MORE?*

WE'LL BE BACK; WE KNOW WE CAN'T STAY AWAY FOREVER.
BUT JUST FOR A WHILE...
JUST FOR A WHILE...

I think it was my editor at Eclipse, cat yronwode, who described the ending of this story as my attempt at a defense of fiction, or at least the escapist variety that *Zot!* grew out of. A cartoonist I know said it came across more like a case for taking drugs (whoops!). If I had to hazard a guess, I think that on some level, I may have been trying to justify the very existence of comics like *Zot!* to myself.

Understanding Comics was already taking shape on my drawing board by the time this issue hit the stands. I was on fire with the conviction that comics were a medium, not a genre. I saw comics as a blank slate, capable of accommodating any style, any technique, any subject matter. I was inspired by the depth and beauty of the great European masters, by the dizzying variety of the huge manga industry (long before it conquered the U.S. market), and by the aggressive experimentation of Art Spiegelman and his allies. I knew that making better comics was about so much more than just making better superhero comics, even though the spandex set still comprised the vast majority of the comics market in America despite all our advances to that point.

What then was I to make of that first six years of my career? Was I part of the problem? Was the entire superhero genre just one big dead horse I'd been trying to find new ways to beat?

As it turns out, I wasn't so much struggling to correct an imbalance in the marketplace as I was trying to correct an imbalance in myself. Creating a book like *Understanding Comics* satisfied that need perfectly as I plunged into a prolonged formalist adventure, but it led eventually to a different kind of imbalance that I'm only now beginning to correct after seventeen years as I prepare to head back into fiction.

Revisiting these stories, rediscovering what I loved about comics in those early days, and the ways in which my own skills served or hampered my goals, has been enormously valuable for me. Other work by talented writers and artists from this period is still sadly out of print, so I'm grateful for the opportunity.

When we announced this collection, one online journalist familiar with my later career remarked that it was unusual to see me turning my attention to the past after such a consistent focus on the future of comics. He had a point. Looking back was never my strong point.

But this is *Zot!*, after all, a world where looking back and looking forward are one and the same. The far-flung future, the distant past, and every moment in between.

Life After Zot

As soon as the final pages of *Zot!* were sent off, I dove head-long into writing and drawing the 215 pages of *Understanding Comics.* During the fifteen months it took to complete the book, we finally succeeded at conceiving, with a little help from Boston IVF, and our first daughter was born only a few weeks before the book was published. We had been trying to have a baby for four years by that point. Those nine months of Ivy reading to me in the green swivel chair while both our little "projects" grew was one of the most gratifying periods of our lives.

When *Understanding Comics* hit the stands in May 1993, fans saw it as a book about comics by the guy who did *Zot!,* but within a few months, *Zot!* was demoted to "that series McCloud did before *Understanding Comics.*" *U.C.* has since been translated into sixteen languages and presumably read by twenty times as many people as ever read *Zot!* in its original incarnation. Many readers who have come to recognize me for my little cartoon avatar had no idea why the little guy was wearing a T-shirt with a lightning bolt on it.

Still, a loyal group of fans at conventions would frequently ask me when *Zot!* was coming back. I always told them that I wanted to bring *Zot!* back "in a year or two," but that I had a few projects to get out of the way first. I always meant it, but somehow the date kept getting pushed back and the list of projects kept growing. There were too many other possibilities to pursue.

My avatar, complete with Zot! *T-shirt.*

For the rest of the '90s and the early part of this decade, computers and the Web became a full-time obsession. Unlike my earlier obsession with chess, comics and digital media didn't have to compete for my attention, since they combined quite naturally. I became closely associated with the webcomics movement, though a lot of my aesthetic and economic theories about where we could go got me in hot water with others in the fast-growing field, especially when many of those ideas saw print in my second, more controversial book, *Reinventing Comics,* in 2000.

That same year, *Zot!* did return briefly in the form of an experimental webcomic. It was a Dekko story in sixteen "chapters," each of which were laid out in long rows of panels, connected by the linking lines I call "trails." The art is a bit raw, drawn clumsily on a small Wacom tablet at 72 dots per inch to make it impossible for me to "repurpose" it for print (yes the Dekko in me won over the Max in that instance). Still, it has some nice moments. If 559 story pages of *Zot!* aren't enough for you, feel free to check it out.

The future was no longer some abstract fictional concept as it was in *Zot!* Talking about strategies for the future of comics became a daily concern. I found myself lecturing at computer

companies, conferences, and universities with increasing frequency (a good thing too, since I was giving away the webcomics for the most part, and my royalties on the books, as good as they were, were hardly enough to live on exclusively all these years). I also took on the occasional interesting side job, doing comics features for magazines like *Wired, Computer Gaming World,* and *Nickelodeon,* as well as writing some *Superman* titles for DC Comics.

Graphic novel at-a-glance: A "long shot" of Zot! *Online's 440 panels, available at scottmccloud.com.*

Some of my hopes for webcomics have yet to pan out, but I'm optimistic that the thousands of creators making them and the hundreds of thousands of readers who enjoy them will continue searching for new ways improve the experience on both sides of the monitor. Meanwhile, I get to take a few years off from rolling that particular boulder up the hill, because as of now, I have a *new* obsession.

Since 2002, I've been teaching seminars in the art of making comics, starting at the Minneapolis College of Art and Design, then moving on to destinations as diverse as M.I.T., a Boston arts high school, and a Barcelona getaway for the writers of Danish Disney duck comics. Teaching how to tell stories in comics form awakened my desire to tell one of my own; an idea I'd had since the *Zot!* days that I realized could make a great graphic novel.

In 2006, my third book, *Making Comics,* gave me the opportunity to sharpen my ideas on storytelling and teach myself enough about the subject that I could do my new story justice. If all goes well, I hope to start work on that graphic novel shortly.

I feel like Halley's Comet, returning to fiction after all these years. The pull of its gravity gets stronger every day. Now that I've passed back through *Zot!*'s old orbit, I'm more at peace with all the mistakes the younger me made, and better able to appreciate the spots where I got it right. I'm also more at peace with the role that genre fiction, including superhero fiction, plays in the greater ecology of the narrative arts.

I think that at the heart of most genres is the desire to escape to a new world every bit as convincing as this one, yet safely removed from this one's daily pain, while at the heart of most progressive narrative movements is the desire to meaningfully reconnect with that pain, or to strip away the illusion entirely and rethink the nature of the creative act itself.

I jumped to that third option in 1993 and have rarely looked back since, but I've also continued to enjoy genre fiction in other media. I've seen what a powerful effect it's had on my family and I can appreciate the deeper truths such stories can unearth while still entertaining us. Meanwhile, though, that middle option has tantalized me from afar as modern masters like Ware, Bechdel, and Spiegelman have given us a much more honest document of the world we live in than anything comics in America could offer in its first hundred years—a revolution in content to offset the revolution in form that's kept me excited all these years.

I don't know exactly where I'll next land on that expanding creative landscape, but I can't wait to find out.

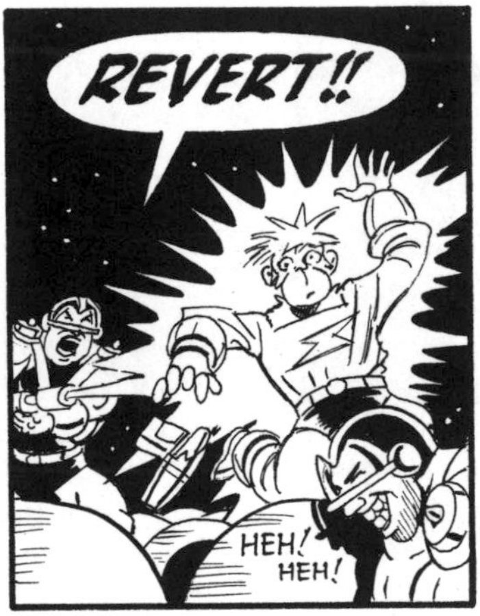
REVERT!!
HEH!
HEH!

www.scottmccloud.com